GONE WITH THE WIND

MARGARET MITCHELL

GONE WITH THE WIND

MACMILLAN
LONDON

First published 1936 by
MACMILLAN LONDON LIMITED
a division of Pan Macmillan Publishers Limited
Cavaye Place London SW10 9PG
and Basingstoke

Associated companies throughout the world

This paperback edition published 1993

ISBN 0-333-58518-6

9 8 7 6 5 4 3 2 1

A CIP catalogue record for this book is available
from the British Library

Typeset by Pan Macmillan Limited
Printed by Clays Ltd., St Ives plc

To
J. R. M.

Part One

Chapter I

Scarlett O'Hara was not beautiful, but men seldom realized it when caught by her charm as the Tarleton twins were. In her face were too sharply blended the delicate features of her mother, a Coast aristocrat of French descent, and the heavy ones of her florid Irish father. But it was an arresting face, pointed of chin, square of jaw. Her eyes were pale green without a touch of hazel, starred with bristly black lashes and slightly tilted at the ends. Above them, her thick black brows slanted upward, cutting a startling oblique line in her magnolia-white skin – that skin so prized by Southern women and so carefully guarded with bonnets, veils and mittens against hot Georgia suns.

Seated with Stuart and Brent Tarleton in the cool shade of the porch of Tara, her father's plantation, that bright April afternoon of 1861, she made a pretty picture. Her new green flowered-muslin dress spread its twelve yards of billowing material over her hoops and exactly matched the flat-heeled green morocco slippers her father had recently brought her from Atlanta. The dress set off to perfection the seventeen-inch waist, the smallest in three counties, and the tightly fitting basque showed breasts well matured for her sixteen years. But for all the modesty of her spreading skirts, the demureness of hair netted smoothly into a chignon and the quietness of small white hands folded in her lap, her true self was poorly concealed. The green eyes in the carefully sweet face were turbulent, wilful, lusty with life, distinctly at variance with her decorous demeanour. Her manners had been imposed upon her by her mother's gentle admonitions and the sterner discipline of her mammy; her eyes were her own.

On either side of her, the twins lounged easily in their chairs, squinting at the sunlight through tall mint-garnished glasses as they laughed and talked, their long legs, booted to the knee and thick with saddle muscles, crossed negligently. Nineteen years old, six feet two inches tall, long of bone and hard of muscle, with sunburned faces and deep auburn hair, their eyes merry and arrogant, their bodies clothed in identical blue coats and mustard-coloured breeches, they were as much alike as two bolls of cotton.

Outside, the late afternoon sun slanted down in the yard, throwing into gleaming brightness the dogwood trees that were solid masses of white blossoms against the background of new green. The twins' horses were hitched in the driveway, big animals, red as their masters' hair; and around the horses' legs quarrelled the pack of lean, nervous possum hounds that accompanied Stuart and Brent wherever they went. A little aloof, as became an aristocrat, lay a black-spotted carriage dog, muzzle on paws, patiently waiting for the boys to go home to supper.

Between the hounds and the horses and the twins there was a kinship deeper than that of their constant companionship. They were all healthy, thoughtless young animals, sleek, graceful, high-spirited, the boys as mettlesome as the horses they rode, mettlesome and dangerous but, withal, sweet-tempered to those who knew how to handle them.

Although born to the ease of plantation life, waited on hand and foot since infancy, the faces of the three on the porch were neither slack nor soft. They had the vigour and alertness of country people who have spent all their lives in the open and troubled their heads very little with dull things in books. Life in the north Georgia county of Clayton was still new and, according to the standards of Augusta, Savannah and Charleston, a little crude. The more sedate and older sections of the South looked down their noses at the up-country Georgians, but here in north Georgia, a lack of the niceties of classical education carried no shame, provided a man was smart in the things that mattered. And raising good cotton, riding well, shooting straight, dancing lightly, squiring the ladies with elegance and carrying one's liquor like a gentleman were the things that mattered.

In these accomplishments the twins excelled, and they were equally outstanding in their notorious inability to learn anything contained between the covers of books. Their family had more money, more horses, more slaves than anyone else in the County, but the boys had less grammar than most of their poor Cracker neighbours.

It was for this precise reason that Stuart and Brent were idling on the porch of Tara this April afternoon. They had just been expelled from the University of Georgia, the fourth university that had thrown them out in two years; and their older brothers, Tom and Boyd, had come home with them, because they refused to remain at an institution where the twins were not welcome. Stuart and Brent considered their latest expulsion a fine joke, and Scarlett, who had not willingly opened a book since leaving the Fayetteville Female Academy the year before, thought it just as amusing as they did.

'I know you two don't care about being expelled, or Tom either,' she said. 'But what about Boyd? He's kind of set on getting an education, and you two have pulled him out of the University of Virginia and Alabama and South Carolina and now Georgia. He'll never get finished at this rate.'

'Oh, he can read law in Judge Parmalee's office over in Fayetteville,' answered Brent carelessly. 'Besides, it don't matter much. We'd have had to come home before the term was out anyway.'

'Why?'

'The war, goose! The war's going to start any day, and you don't suppose any of us would stay in college with a war going on, do you?'

'You know there isn't going to be any war,' said Scarlett, bored. 'It's all just talk. Why, Ashley Wilkes and his father told Pa just last week that our commissioners in Washington would come to – to – an – amicable agreement with Mr Lincoln about the Confederacy. And anyway, the Yankees are too scared of us to fight. There won't be any war, and I'm tired of hearing about it.'

'Not going to be any war!' cried the twins indignantly, as though they had been defrauded.

'Why, honey, of course there's going to be a war,' said Stuart. 'The Yankees may be scared of us, but after the way General Beauregard shelled them out of Fort Sumter day before yesterday, they'll have to fight or stand branded as cowards before the whole world. Why, the Confederacy—'

Scarlett made a mouth of bored impatience.

'If you say "war" just once more, I'll go in the house and shut the door. I've never gotten so tired of any one word in my life as "war", unless it's "secession". Pa talks war morning, noon and night, and all the gentlemen who come to see him shout about Fort Sumter and States' Rights and Abe Lincoln till I get so bored I could scream! And that's all the boys talk about, too, that and their old Troop. There hasn't been any fun at any party this spring because the boys can't talk about anything else. I'm mighty glad Georgia waited till after Christmas before it seceded or it would have ruined the Christmas parties, too. If you say "war" again, I'll go in the house.'

She meant what she said, for she could never long endure any conversation of which she was not the chief subject. But she smiled when she spoke, consciously deepening her dimple and fluttering her bristly black lashes as swiftly as butterflies' wings. The boys were enchanted, as she had intended them to be, and they hastened to apologize for boring her. They thought none the less of her for her lack of interest. Indeed, they thought more. War was men's business, not ladies', and they took her attitude as evidence of her femininity.

Having manoeuvred them away from the boring subject of war, she went back with interest to their immediate situation.

'What did your mother say about you two being expelled again?'

The boys looked uncomfortable, recalling their mother's conduct three months ago when they had come home, by request, from the University of Virginia.

'Well,' said Stuart, 'she hasn't had a chance to say anything yet. Tom and us left home early this morning before she got up, and Tom's laying out over at the Fontaines' while we came over here.'

'Didn't she say anything when you got home last night?'

'We were in luck last night. Just before we got home that new stallion Ma got in Kentucky last month was brought in, and the place was in a stew. The big brute – he's a grand horse, Scarlett; you must tell your pa to come over and see him right away – he'd already bitten a hunk out of his groom on the way down here and he'd trampled two of Ma's darkies who met the train at Jonesboro. And just before we got home, he'd about kicked the stable down and half-killed Strawberry, Ma's old stallion. When we got home, Ma was out in the stable with a sackful of sugar smoothing

him down and doing it mighty well, too. The darkies were hanging from
the rafters, pop-eyed, they were so scared, but Ma was talking to the horse
like he was folks and he was eating out of her hand. There ain't nobody like
Ma with a horse. And when she saw us she said: "In Heaven's name, what
are you four doing home again? You're worse than the plagues of Egypt!"
And then the horse began snorting and rearing and she said: "Get out of
here! Can't you see he's nervous, the big darling? I'll tend to you four in
the morning!" So we went to bed, and this morning we got away before
she could catch us and left Boyd to handle her.'

'Do you suppose she'll hit Boyd?' Scarlett, like the rest of the County, could
never get used to the way small Mrs Tarleton bullied her grown sons and laid
her riding-crop on their backs if the occasion seemed to warrant it.

Beatrice Tarleton was a busy woman, having on her hands not only a large
cotton plantation, a hundred negroes and eight children, but the largest
horse-breeding farm in the state as well. She was hot-tempered and easily
plagued by the frequent scrapes of her four sons, and while no one was
permitted to whip a horse or a slave, she felt that a lick now and then
didn't do the boys any harm.

'Of course she won't hit Boyd. She never did beat Boyd much because
he's the oldest and besides he's the runt of the litter,' said Stuart, proud
of his six feet two. 'That's why we left him at home to explain things to
her. God'lmighty, Ma ought to stop licking us! We're nineteen and Tom's
twenty-one, and she acts like we're six years old.'

'Will your mother ride the new horse to the Wilkes barbecue tomorrow?'

'She wants to, but Pa says he's too dangerous. And, anyway, the girls won't
let her. They said they were going to have her go to one party at least like a
lady, riding in the carriage.'

'I hope it doesn't rain tomorrow,' said Scarlett. 'It's rained nearly every
day for a week. There's nothing worse than a barbecue turned into an indoor
picnic.'

'Oh, it'll be clear tomorrow and hot as June,' said Stuart. 'Look at that
sunset. I never saw one redder. You can always tell weather by sunsets.'

They looked out across the endless acres of Gerald O'Hara's newly
ploughed cotton fields toward the red horizon. Now that the sun was
setting in a welter of crimson behind the hills across the Flint River, the
warmth of the April day was ebbing into a faint but balmy chill.

Spring had come early that year, with warm quick rains and sudden frothing
of pink peach blossoms and dogwood dappling with white stars the dark river
swamp and far-off hills. Already the ploughing was nearly finished, and the
bloody glory of the sunset coloured the fresh-cut furrows of red Georgia
clay to even redder hues. The moist hungry earth, waiting upturned for the
cotton seeds, showed pinkish on the sandy tops of furrows, vermilion and
scarlet and maroon where shadows lay along the sides of the trenches. The
whitewashed brick plantation house seemed an island set in a wild red sea, a

sea of spiralling, curving, crescent billows petrified suddenly at the moment when the pink-tipped waves were breaking into surf. For here were no long, straight furrows, such as could be seen in the yellow clay fields of the flat middle Georgia country or in the lush black earth of the coastal plantations. The rolling foothill country of north Georgia was ploughed in a million curves to keep the rich earth from washing down into the river bottoms.

It was savagely red land, blood-coloured after rains, brick-dust in droughts, the best cotton land in the world. It was a pleasant land of white houses, peaceful ploughed fields and sluggish yellow rivers, but a land of contrasts, of brightest sun-glare and densest shade. The plantation clearings and miles of cotton fields smiled up to a warm sun, placid, complacent. At their edges rose the virgin forests, dark and cool even in the hottest noons, mysterious, a little sinister, the soughing pines seeming to wait with an age-old patience, to threaten with soft sighs: 'Be careful! Be careful! We had you once. We can take you back again.'

To the ears of the three on the porch came the sounds of hooves, the jingling of harness chains and the shrill careless laughter of negro voices, as the field hands and mules came in from the fields. From within the house floated the soft voice of Scarlett's mother, Ellen O'Hara, as she called to the little black girl who carried her basket of keys. The high-pitched childish voice answered 'Yas'm,' and there were sounds of footsteps going out the back way toward the smoke-house where Ellen would ration out the food to the home-coming hands. There was the click of china and the rattle of silver as Pork, the valet-butler of Tara, laid the table for supper.

At these last sounds, the twins realized it was time they were starting home. But they were loath to face their mother and they lingered on the porch of Tara, momentarily expecting Scarlett to give them an invitation to supper.

'Look, Scarlett. About tomorrow,' said Brent. 'Just because we've been away and didn't know about the barbecue and ball, that's no reason why we shouldn't get plenty of dances tomorrow night. You haven't promised them all, have you?'

'Well, I have! How did I know you all would be home? I couldn't risk being a wallflower just waiting on you two.'

'You a wallflower!' The boys laughed uproariously.

'Look, honey. You've got to give me the first waltz and Stu the last one and you've got to eat supper with us. We'll sit on the stair landing like we did at the last ball and get Mammy Jincy to come tell our fortunes again.'

'I don't like Mammy Jincy's fortunes. You know she said I was going to marry a gentleman with jet-black hair and a long black moustache, and I don't like black-haired gentlemen.'

'You like 'em red-headed, don't you, honey?' grinned Brent. 'Now, come on, promise us all the waltzes and the supper.'

'If you'll promise, we'll tell you a secret,' said Stuart.

'What?' cried Scarlett, alert as a child at the word.

'Is it what we heard yesterday in Atlanta, Stu? If it is, you know we promised not to tell.'

'Well, Miss Pitty told us.'

'Miss Who?'

'You know, Ashley Wilkes' cousin who lives in Atlanta, Miss Pittypat Hamilton – Charles and Melanie Hamilton's aunt.'

'I do, and a sillier old lady I never met in all my life.'

'Well, when we were in Atlanta yesterday, waiting for the home train, her carriage went by the depot and she stopped and talked to us, and she told us there was going to be an engagement announced tomorrow night at the Wilkes ball.'

'Oh, I know about that,' said Scarlett in disappointment. 'That silly nephew of hers, Charlie Hamilton, and Honey Wilkes. Everybody's known for years that they'd get married some time, even if he did seem kind of lukewarm about it.'

'Do you think he's silly?' questioned Brent. 'Last Christmas you sure let him buzz round you plenty.'

'I couldn't help him buzzing,' Scarlett shrugged negligently. 'I think he's an awful sissy.'

'Besides, it isn't his engagement that's going to be announced,' said Stuart triumphantly. 'It's Ashley's to Charlie's sister, Miss Melanie!'

Scarlett's face did not change but her lips went white – like a person who has received a stunning blow without warning and who, in the first moments of shock, does not realize what has happened. So still was her face as she stared at Stuart that he, never analytic, took it for granted that she was merely surprised and very interested.

'Miss Pitty told us they hadn't intended announcing it till next year, because Miss Melly hasn't been very well; but with all the war talk going around, everybody in both families thought it would be better to get married real soon. So it's to be announced tomorrow night at the supper intermission. Now, Scarlett, we've told you the secret, so you've got to promise to eat supper with us.'

'Of course I will,' Scarlett said automatically.

'And all the waltzes?'

'All.'

'You're sweet! I'll bet the other boys will be hopping mad.'

'Let 'em be mad,' said Brent. 'We two can handle 'em. Look, Scarlett. Sit with us at the barbecue in the morning.'

'What?'

Stuart repeated his request.

'Of course.'

The twins looked at each other jubilantly but with some surprise. Although they considered themselves Scarlett's favoured suitors, they had never before gained tokens of this favour so easily. Usually she made them beg and plead, while she put them off, refusing to give a Yes or No answer, laughing if they sulked, growing cool if they became angry. And here she had practically promised them the whole of tomorrow – seats by her at the barbecue, all the waltzes (and they'd see to it that the dances were all waltzes!) and the supper intermission. That was worth getting expelled from the university.

Filled with new enthusiasm by their success, they lingered on, talking about the barbecue and the ball and Ashley Wilkes and Melanie Hamilton, interrupting each other, making jokes and laughing at them, hinting broadly for invitations to supper. Some time had passed before they realized that Scarlett was having very little to say. The atmosphere had somehow changed. Just how, the twins did not know, but the fine glow had gone out of the afternoon. Scarlett seemed to be paying little attention to what they said, although she made the correct answers. Sensing something they could not understand, baffled and annoyed by it, the twins struggled along for a while, and then rose reluctantly, looking at their watches.

The sun was low across the new-ploughed fields and the tall woods across the river were looming blackly in silhouette. Chimney swallows were darting swiftly across the yard, and chickens, ducks and turkeys were waddling and strutting and straggling in from the fields.

Stuart bellowed: 'Jeems!' And after an interval a tall black boy of their own age ran breathlessly around the house and out toward the tethered horses. Jeems was their body-servant and, like the dogs, accompanied them everywhere. He had been their childhood playmate and had been given to the twins for their own on their tenth birthday. At the sight of him, the Tarleton hounds rose up out of the red dust and stood waiting expectantly for their masters. The boys bowed, shook hands and told Scarlett they'd be over at the Wilkeses' early in the morning, waiting for her. Then they were off down the walk at a rush, mounted their horses and, followed by Jeems, went down the avenue of cedars at a gallop, waving their hats and yelling back to her.

When they had rounded the curve of the dusty road that hid them from Tara, Brent drew his horse to a stop under a clump of dogwood. Stuart halted, too, and the darky boy pulled up a few paces behind them. The horses, feeling slack reins, stretched down their necks to crop the tender spring grass, and the patient hounds lay down again in the soft red dust and looked up longingly at the chimney swallows circling in the gathering dusk. Brent's wide ingenuous face was puzzled and mildly indignant.

'Look,' he said. 'Don't it look to you like she would of asked us to stay for supper?'

'I thought she would,' said Stuart. 'I kept waiting for her to do it, but she didn't. What do you make of it?'

'I don't make anything of it. But it just looks to me like she might of.

After all, it's our first day home and she hasn't seen us in quite a spell. And we had lots more things to tell her.'

'It looked to me like she was mighty glad to see us when we came.'

'I thought so, too.'

'And then, about a half-hour ago, she got kind of quiet, like she had a headache.'

'I noticed that but I didn't pay it any mind then. What do you suppose ailed her?'

'I dunno. Do you suppose we said something that made her mad?'

They both thought for a minute.

'I can't think of anything. Besides, when Scarlett gets mad, everybody knows it. She don't hold herself in like some girls do.'

'Yes, that's what I like about her. She don't go around being cold and hateful when she's mad – she tells you about it. But it was something we did or said that made her shut up talking and look sort of sick. I could swear she was glad to see us when we came and was aiming to ask us to supper.'

'You don't suppose it's because we got expelled?'

'Hell, no! Don't be a fool. She laughed like everything when we told her about it. And besides Scarlett don't set any more store by book learning than we do.'

Brent turned in the saddle and called to the negro groom.

'Jeems!'

'Suh?'

'You heard what we were talking to Miss Scarlett about?'

'Nawsuh, Mist' Brent! Huccome you think Ah be spyin' on w'ite folks?'

'Spying, my God! You darkies know everything that goes on. Why, you liar, I saw you with my own eyes sidle round the corner of the porch and squat in the cape jessamine bush by the wall. Now, did you hear us say anything that might have made Miss Scarlett mad – or hurt her feelings?'

Thus appealed to, Jeems gave up further pretence of not having overheard the conversation and furrowed his black brow.

'Nawsuh, Ah din' notice y'all say anything ter mek her mad. Look ter me lak she sho glad ter see you an' sho had missed you, an' she cheep along happy as a bird, tell 'bout de time y'all got ter talkin' 'bout Mist' Ashley an' Miss Melly Hamilton gittin' mah'ied. Den she quiet down lak a bird w'en de hawk fly ober.'

The twins looked at each other and nodded, but without comprehension.

'Jeems is right. But I don't see why,' said Stuart. 'My Lord! Ashley don't mean anything to her, 'cept a friend. She's not crazy about him. It's us she's crazy about.'

Brent nodded an agreement.

'But do you suppose,' he said, 'that maybe Ashley hadn't told her he was going to announce it tomorrow night and she was mad at him for not telling her, an old friend, before he told everybody else? Girls set a big store on knowing such things first.'

'Well, maybe. But what if he hadn't told her it was tomorrow? It was supposed to be a secret and a surprise, and a man's got a right to keep his own engagement quiet, hasn't he? We wouldn't have known it if Miss Melly's aunt hadn't let it out. But Scarlett must have known he was going to marry Miss Melly some time. Why, we've known it for years. The Wilkes and Hamiltons always marry their own cousins. Everybody knew he'd probably marry her some day, just like Honey Wilkes is going to marry Miss Melly's brother, Charles.'

'Well, I give it up. But I'm sorry she didn't ask us to supper. I swear I don't want to go home and listen to Ma take on about us being expelled. It isn't as if this was the first time.'

'Maybe Boyd will have smoothed her down by now. You know what a slick talker that little varmint is. You know he always can smooth her down.'

'Yes, he can do it, but it takes Boyd time. He has to talk around in circles till Ma gets so confused that she gives up and tells him to save his voice for his law practice. But he ain't had time to get good started yet. Why, I'll bet you Ma is still so excited about the new horse that she'll never realize we're home again till she sits down to supper tonight and sees Boyd. And before supper is over she'll be going strong and breathing fire. And it'll be ten o'clock before Boyd gets a chance to tell her that it wouldn't have been honourable for any of us to stay in college after the way the Chancellor talked to you and me. And it'll be midnight before he gets her turned around to where she's so mad at the Chancellor she'll be asking Boyd why he didn't shoot him. No, we can't go home till after midnight.'

The twins looked at each other glumly. They were completely fearless of wild horses, shooting affrays and the indignation of their neighbours, but they had a wholesome fear of their red-haired mother's outspoken remarks and the riding-crop that she did not scruple to lay across their breeches.

'Well, look,' said Brent. 'Let's go over to the Wilkes. Ashley and the girls'll be glad to have us for supper.'

Stuart looked a little discomforted.

'No, don't let's go there. They'll be in a stew getting ready for the barbecue tomorrow and besides—'

'Oh, I forgot about that,' said Brent hastily. 'No, don't let's go there.'

They clucked to their horses and rode along in silence for a while, a flush of embarrassment on Stuart's brown cheeks. Until the previous summer, Stuart had courted India Wilkes with the approbation of both families and the entire County. The County felt that perhaps the cool and contained India Wilkes would have a quieting effect on him. They fervently hoped so, at any rate. And Stuart might have made the match, but Brent had not been satisfied. Brent liked India but he thought her mighty plain and tame, and he simply could not fall in love with her himself to keep Stuart company. That was the first time the twins' interests had ever diverged, and Brent was resentful of his brother's attentions to a girl who seemed to him not at all remarkable.

Then, last summer at a political speaking in a grove of oak trees at Jonesboro, they both suddenly became aware of Scarlett O'Hara. They had known her for years, and, since their childhood, she had been a favourite playmate, for she could ride horses and climb trees almost as well as they. But now to their amazement she had become a grown-up young lady and quite the most charming one in all the world.

They noticed for the first time how her green eyes danced, how deep her dimples were when she laughed, how tiny her hands and feet and what a small waist she had. Their clever remarks sent her into merry peals of laughter and, inspired by the thought that she considered them a remarkable pair, they fairly outdid themselves.

It was a memorable day in the life of the twins. Thereafter, when they talked it over, they always wondered just why they had failed to notice Scarlett's charms before. They never arrived at the correct answer, which was that Scarlett on that day had decided to make them notice. She was constitutionally unable to endure any man being in love with any woman not herself, and the sight of India Wilkes and Stuart at the speaking had been too much for her predatory nature. Not content with Stuart alone, she had set her cap for Brent as well, and with a thoroughness that overwhelmed the two of them.

Now they were both in love with her, and India Wilkes and Letty Munroe, from Lovejoy, whom Brent had been half-heartedly courting, were far in the back of their minds. Just what the loser would do, should Scarlett accept either one of them, the twins did not ask. They would cross that bridge when they came to it. For the present they were quite satisfied to be in accord again about one girl, for they had no jealousies between them. It was a situation which interested the neighbours and annoyed their mother, who had no liking for Scarlett.

'It will serve you right if that sly piece does accept one of you,' she said. 'Or maybe she'll accept both of you, and then you'll have to move to Utah, if the Mormons'll have you – which I doubt . . . All that bothers me is that some one of these days you're both going to get lickered up and jealous of each other about that two-faced, little, green-eyed baggage, and you'll shoot each other. But that might not be a bad idea either.'

Since the day of the speaking, Stuart had been uncomfortable in India's presence. Not that India ever reproached him or even indicated by look or gesture that she was aware of his abruptly changed allegiance. She was too much of a lady. But Stuart felt guilty and ill at ease with her. He knew he had made India love him and he knew that she still loved him and, deep in his heart, he had the feeling that he had not played the gentleman. He still liked her tremendously and respected her for her cool good breeding, her book learning and all the sterling qualities she possessed. But, damn it, she was just so pallid and uninteresting and always the same, beside Scarlett's bright and changeable charm. You always knew where you stood with India and you never had the slightest notion with Scarlett. That was enough to drive a man to distraction, but it had its charm.

'Well, let's go over to Cade Calvert's and have supper. Scarlett said Cathleen was home from Charleston. Maybe she'll have some news about Fort Sumter that we haven't heard.'

'Not Cathleen. I'll lay you two to one she didn't even know the fort was out there in the harbour, much less that it was full of Yankees until we shelled them out. All she'll know about is the balls she went to and the beaux she collected.'

'Well, it's fun to hear her gabble. And it'll be somewhere to hide out till Ma has gone to bed.'

'Well, hell! I like Cathleen and she is fun and I'd like to hear about Caro Rhett and the rest of the Charleston folks; but I'm damned if I can stand sitting through another meal with that Yankee stepmother of hers.'

'Don't be too hard on her, Stuart. She means well.'

'I'm not being hard on her. I feel sorry for her, but I don't like people I've got to feel sorry for. And she fusses around so much, trying to do the right thing and make you feel at home, that she always manages to say and do just exactly the wrong thing. She gives me the fidgets! And she thinks Southerners are wild barbarians. She even told Ma so. She's afraid of Southerners. Whenever we're there she always looks scared to death. She reminds me of a skinny hen perched on a chair, her eyes kind of bright and blank and scared, all ready to flap and squawk at the slightest move anybody makes.'

'Well, you can't blame her. You did shoot Cade in the leg.'

'Well, I was lickered up or I wouldn't have done it,' said Stuart. 'And Cade never had any hard feelings. Neither did Cathleen or Raiford or Mr Calvert. It was just that Yankee stepmother who squalled and said I was a wild barbarian and decent people weren't safe around uncivilized Southerners.'

'Well, you can't blame her. She's a Yankee and ain't got very good manners; and, after all, you did shoot him and he is her stepson.'

'Well, hell! That's no excuse for insulting me! You are Ma's own blood son, but did she take on that time Tony Fontaine shot you in the leg? No, she just sent for old Doc Fontaine to dress it and asked the doctor what ailed Tony's aim. Said she guessed licker was spoiling his marksmanship. Remember how mad that made Tony?'

Both boys yelled with laughter.

'Ma's a card!' said Brent with loving approval. 'You can always count on her to do the right thing and not embarrass you in front of folks.'

'Yes, but she's mighty liable to talk embarrassing in front of Father and the girls when we get home tonight,' said Stuart gloomily. 'Look, Brent, I guess this means we don't go to Europe. You know Mother said if we got expelled from another college we couldn't have our Grand Tour.'

'Well, hell! We don't care, do we? What is there to see in Europe? I'll bet those foreigners can't show us a thing we haven't got right here in Georgia. I'll bet their horses aren't as fast or their girls as pretty, and I know damn well they haven't got any rye whisky that can touch Father's.'

'Ashley Wilkes said they had an awful lot of scenery and music. Ashley liked Europe. He's always talking about it.'

'Well – you know how the Wilkes are. They are kind of queer about music and books and scenery. Mother says it's because their grandfather came from Virginia. She says Virginians set quite a store by such things.'

'They can have 'em. Give me a good horse to ride and some good licker to drink and a good girl to court and a bad girl to have fun with and anybody can have their Europe . . . What do we care about missing the Tour? Suppose we were in Europe now, with the war coming on? We couldn't get home soon enough. I'd heap rather go to a war than go to Europe.'

'So would I, any day . . . Look, Brent! I know where we can go for supper. Let's ride across the swamp to Able Wynder's place and tell him we're all four home again and ready for drill.'

'That's an idea!' cried Brent with enthusiasm. 'And we can hear all the news of the Troop and find out what colour they finally decided on for the uniforms.'

'If it's Zouave, I'm damned if I'll go in the Troop. I'd feel like a sissy in those baggy red pants. They look like ladies' red flannel drawers to me.'

'Is y'all aimin' ter go ter Mist' Wynder's? 'Cause ef you is, you ain' gwine git much supper,' said Jeems. 'Dey cook done died, an' dey ain' bought a new one. Dey got a fe'el han' cookin', an' de niggers tells me she is de wustest cook in de state.'

'Good God! Why don't they buy another cook?'

'Huccome po' w'ite trash buy any niggers? Dey ain't never owned mo'n fo' at de mostes'.'

There was frank contempt in Jeems' voice. His own social status was assured because the Tarletons owned a hundred negroes and, like all slaves of large planters, he looked down on small farmers whose slaves were few.

'I'm going to beat your hide off for that,' cried Stuart fiercely. 'Don't you call Able Wynder "po' white". Sure he's poor, but he ain't trash; and I'm damned if I'll have any man, darky or white, throwing off on him. There ain't a better man in this County, or why else did the Troop elect him lieutenant?'

'Ah ain' never figgered dat out, mahseff,' replied Jeems, undisturbed by his master's scowl. 'Look ter me lak dey'd 'lect all de awficers frum rich gempmum, 'stead of swamp trash.'

'He ain't trash! Do you mean to compare him with real white trash like the Slatterys? Able just ain't rich. He's a small farmer, not a big planter, and if the boys thought enough of him to elect him lieutenant, then it's not for any darky to talk impudent about him. The Troop knows what it's doing.'

The troop of cavalry had been organized three months before, the very day that Georgia seceded from the Union, and since then the recruits had been whistling for war. The outfit was as yet unnamed, though not for want of suggestions. Everyone had his own idea on that subject and was loath to relinquish it, just as everyone had ideas about the colour and cut of the uniforms. 'Clayton Wild Cats', 'Fire Eaters',' North Georgia Hussars', 'Zouaves', 'The Inland Rifles' (although the Troop was to be armed with pistols, sabres and bowie knives, and not with rifles), 'The Clayton Grays', The Blood and Thunderers', 'The Rough and Readys', all had their adherents. Until matters were settled, everyone referred to the organization as the Troop and, despite the high-sounding name finally adopted, they were known to the end of their usefulness simply as 'The Troop'.

The officers were elected by the members, for no one in the County had had any military experience except a few veterans of the Mexican and Seminole wars and, besides, the Troop would have scorned a veteran as a leader if they had not personally liked him and trusted him. Everyone liked the four Tarleton boys and the three Fontaines, but regretfully refused to elect them, because the Tarletons got lickered up too quickly and liked to skylark, and the Fontaines had such quick, murderous tempers. Ashley Wilkes was elected captain, because he was the best rider in the County and because his cool head was counted on to keep some semblance of order. Raiford Calvert was made first lieutenant, because everybody liked Raif, and Able Wynder, son of a swamp trapper, himself a small farmer, was elected second lieutenant.

Able was a shrewd, grave giant, illiterate, kind of heart, older than the other boys and with as good or better manners in the presence of ladies. There was little snobbery in the Troop. Too many of their fathers and grandfathers had come up to wealth from the small farmer class for that. Moreover, Able was the best shot in the Troop, a real sharpshooter who could pick out the eye of a squirrel at seventy-five yards, and, too, he knew all about living outdoors, building fires in the rain, tracking animals and finding water. The Troop bowed to real worth and moreover, because they liked him, they made him an officer. He bore the honour gravely and with no untoward conceit, as though it were only his due. But the planters' ladies and the planters' slaves could not overlook the fact that he was not born a gentleman, even if their men folks could.

In the beginning, the Troop had been recruited exclusively from the sons of planters, a gentleman's outfit, each man supplying his own horse, arms, equipment, uniform and body-servant. But rich planters were few in the young county of Clayton, and, in order to muster a full-strength troop, it had been necessary to raise more recruits among the sons of small farmers, hunters in the backwoods, swamp trappers, Crackers and, in a very few cases, even poor whites, if they were above the average of their class.

These latter young men were as anxious to fight the Yankees, should war come, as were their richer neighbours; but the delicate question of money arose. Few small farmers owned horses. They carried on their farm operations with mules and they had no surplus of these, seldom more than four. The mules could not be spared to go off to war, even if they had been acceptable for the Troop, which they emphatically were not. As for the poor whites, they considered themselves well off if they owned one mule. The backwoods folks and the swamp dwellers owned neither horses nor mules. They lived entirely off the produce of their lands and the game in the swamp, conducting their business generally by the barter system and seldom seeing five dollars in cash a year, and horses and uniforms were out of their reach. But they were as fiercely proud in their poverty as the planters were in their wealth, and they would accept nothing that smacked of charity from their rich neighbours. So, to save the feelings of all and to bring the Troop up to full strength, Scarlett's father, John Wilkes, Buck Munroe, Jim Tarleton, Hugh Calvert, in fact every large planter in the County with the one exception of Angus MacIntosh, had contributed money to completely outfit the Troop, horse and man. The upshot of the matter was that every planter agreed to pay for equipping his own sons and a certain number of the others, but the manner of handling the arrangements was such that the less wealthy members of the outfit could accept horses and uniforms without offence to their honour.

The Troop met twice a week in Jonesboro to drill and to pray for the war to begin. Arrangements had not yet been completed for obtaining the full quota of horses, but those who had horses performed what they imagined to be cavalry manoeuvres in the field behind the courthouse, kicked up a great deal of dust, yelled themselves hoarse and waved the Revolutionary-war swords that had been taken down from parlour walls. Those who, as yet, had no horses sat on the kerb in front of Bullard's store and watched their mounted comrades, chewed tobacco and told yarns. Or else engaged in shooting matches. There was no need to teach any of the men to shoot. Most Southerners were born with guns in their hands, and lives spent in hunting had made marksmen of them all.

From planters' homes and swamp cabins, a varied array of firearms came to each muster. There were long squirrel guns that had been new when first the Alleghenies were crossed, old muzzle-loaders that had claimed many an Indian when Georgia was new, horse pistols that had seen service in 1812, in the Seminole wars and in Mexico, silver-mounted duelling pistols, pocket derringers, double-barrelled hunting pieces and handsome new rifles of English make with shining stocks of fine wood.

Drill always ended in the saloons of Jonesboro, and by nightfall so many fights had broken out that the officers were hard put to ward off casualties until the Yankees could inflict them. It was during one of these brawls that Stuart Tarleton had shot Cade Calvert and Tony Fontaine had shot Brent. The twins had been at home, freshly expelled from the University of Virginia, at the time the Troop was organized and they had joined enthusiastically; but after the shooting episode, two months ago, their mother had packed them off to the state university, with orders to stay there. They had sorely missed the excitement of the drills while away, and they counted education well lost if only they could ride and yell and shoot rifles in the company of their friends.

'Well, let's cut across country to Able's,' suggested Brent. 'We can go through Mr O'Hara's river bottom and the Fontaines' pasture and get there in no time.'

'We ain' gwine git nothin' ter eat 'cept possum an' greens,' argued Jeems.

'You ain't going to get anything,' grinned Stuart. 'Because you are going home and tell Ma that we won't be home for supper.'

'No, Ah ain'!' cried Jeems in alarm. 'No, Ah ain'! Ah doan git no mo' fun outer havin' Miss Beetriss lay me out dan y'all does. Fust place she'll ast me huccome Ah let y'all git expelled agin. An' nex' thing, huccome Ah din' bring y'all home ternight so she could lay you out. An' den she'll light on me lak a duck on a June bug, an' fust thing Ah know Ah'll be ter blame fer it all. Ef y'all doan tek me ter Mist' Wynder's, Ah'll lay out in de woods all night an' maybe de patterollers git me, 'cause Ah heap ruther de patterollers git me dan Miss Beetriss when she in a state.'

The twins looked at the determined black boy in perplexity and indignation.

'He'd be just fool enough to let the patterollers get him and that would give Ma something else to talk about for weeks. I swear, darkies are more trouble. Sometimes I think the Abolitionists have got the right idea.'

'Well, it wouldn't be right to make Jeems face what we don't want to face. We'll have to take him. But, look, you impudent black fool, if you put on any airs in front of the Wynder darkies and hint that we all the time have fried chicken and ham, while they don't have nothing but rabbit and possum, I'll – I'll tell Ma. And we won't let you go to the war with us, either.'

'Airs? Me put on airs fo' dem cheap niggers? Nawsuh, Ah got better manners. Ain' Miss Beetriss taught me manners same as she taught y'all?'

'She didn't do a very good job on any of the three of us,' said Stuart. 'Come on, let's get going.'

He backed his big red horse and then, putting spurs to his side, lifted him easily over the split-rail fence into the soft field of Gerald O'Hara's plantation. Brent's horse followed and then Jeems', with Jeems clinging to pommel and mane. Jeems did not like to jump fences, but he had jumped higher ones than this in order to keep up with his masters.

As they picked their way across the red furrows and down the hill to the river bottom in the deepening dusk, Brent yelled to his brother:

'Look, Stu! Don't it seem like to you that Scarlett *would* have asked us to supper?'

'I kept thinking she would,' yelled Stuart. 'Why do you suppose . . .'

Chapter II

When the twins left Scarlett standing on the porch of Tara and the last sound of flying hooves had died away, she went back to her chair like a sleepwalker. Her face felt stiff as from pain and her mouth actually hurt from having stretched it, unwillingly, in smiles to prevent the twins from learning her secret. She sat down wearily, tucking one foot under her, and her heart swelled up with misery, until it felt too large for her bosom. It beat with odd little jerks; her hands were cold, and a feeling of disaster oppressed her. There were pain and bewilderment in her face, the bewilderment of a pampered child who has always had her own way for the asking and who now, for the first time, was in contact with the unpleasantness of life.

Ashley to marry Melanie Hamilton!

Oh, it couldn't be true! The twins were mistaken. They were playing one of their jokes on her. Ashley couldn't, couldn't be in love with her. Nobody could, not with a mousy little person like Melanie. Scarlett recalled with contempt Melanie's thin childish figure, her serious heart-shaped face that was plain almost to homeliness. And Ashley couldn't have seen her in months. He hadn't been in Atlanta more than twice since the house party he gave last year at Twelve Oaks. No, Ashley couldn't be in love with Melanie, because – oh, she couldn't be mistaken! – because he was in love with her! She, Scarlett, was the one he loved – she knew it!

Scarlett heard Mammy's lumbering tread shaking the floor of the hall and she hastily untucked her foot and tried to rearrange her face in more placid lines. It would never do for Mammy to suspect that anything was wrong. Mammy felt that she owned the O'Haras, body and soul, that their secrets were her secrets; and even a hint of a mystery was enough to set her upon the trail as relentlessly as a bloodhound. Scarlett knew from experience that, if Mammy's curiosity were not immediately satisfied, she would take up the matter with Ellen, and then Scarlett would be forced to reveal everything to her mother, or think up some plausible lie.

Mammy emerged from the hall, a huge old woman with the small, shrewd eyes of an elephant. She was shining black, pure African, devoted to her last drop of blood to the O'Haras, Ellen's mainstay, the despair of her three daughters, the terror of the other house servants. Mammy was black, but her code of conduct and her sense of pride were as high as or higher than those of her owners. She had been raised in the bedroom of Solange Robillard, Ellen O'Hara's mother, a dainty, cold, high-nosed Frenchwoman, who spared neither her children nor her servants their just punishment for any infringement of decorum. She had been Ellen's mammy and had come with her from Savannah to the up-country when she married. Whom Mammy loved, she chastened. And, as her love for Scarlett and her pride in her were enormous, the chastening process was practically continuous.

'Is de gempmum gone? Huccome you din' ast dem ter stay fer supper, Miss Scarlett? Ah done tole Poke ter lay two extry plates fer dem. Whar's yo' manners?'

'Oh, I was so tired of hearing them talk about the war that I couldn't have endured it through supper, especially with Pa joining in and shouting about Mr Lincoln.'

'You ain' got no mo' manners dan a fe'el han', an' affer Miss Ellen an' me done laboured wid you. An' hyah you is widout yo' shawl! An' de night air fixin' ter set in! Ah done tole you an' tole you 'bout gittin' fever frum settin' in de night air wid nuthin' on yo' shoulders. Come on in de house, Miss Scarlett.'

Scarlett turned away from Mammy with studied nonchalance, thankful that her face had been unnoticed in Mammy's preoccupation with the matter of the shawl.

'No, I want to sit here and watch the sunset. It's so pretty. You run get my shawl. Please, Mammy, and I'll sit here till Pa comes home.'

'Yo' voice soun' lak you catchin' a cole,' said Mammy suspiciously.

'Well, I'm not,' said Scarlett impatiently. 'You fetch me my shawl.'

Mammy waddled back into the hall and Scarlett heard her call softly up the stairwell to the upstairs maid.

'You, Rosa! Drap me Miss Scarlett's shawl.' Then, more loudly: 'Wuthless nigger! She ain' never whar she does nobody no good. Now, Ah got ter climb up an' git it mahseff.'

Scarlett heard the stairs groan and she got softly to her feet. When Mammy returned she would resume her lecture on Scarlett's breach of hospitality, and Scarlett felt that she could not endure prating about such a trivial matter when her heart was breaking. As she stood, hesitant, wondering where she could hide until the ache in her breast subsided a little, a thought came to her, bringing a small ray of hope. Her father had ridden over to Twelve Oaks, the Wilkes plantation, that afternoon to offer to buy Dilcey, the broad wife of his valet, Pork. Dilcey was head woman and midwife at Twelve Oaks, and, since the marriage six months ago, Pork had devilled his master night and day to buy Dilcey, so the two could live on the same plantation. That afternoon, Gerald, his resistance worn thin, had set out to make an offer for Dilcey.

'Surely,' thought Scarlett, 'Pa will know whether this awful story is true.

Even if he hasn't actually heard anything this afternoon, perhaps he's noticed something, sensed some excitement in the Wilkes family. If I can just see him privately before supper, perhaps I'll find out the truth – that it's just one of the twins' nasty practical jokes.'

It was time for Gerald's return and, if she expected to see him alone, there was nothing for her to do except meet him where the driveway entered the road. She went quietly down the front steps, looking carefully over her shoulder to make sure Mammy was not observing her from the upstairs windows. Seeing no broad black face, turbaned in snowy white, peering disapprovingly from between fluttering curtains, she boldly snatched up her green flowered skirts and sped down the path toward the driveway as fast as her small ribbon-laced slippers would carry her.

The dark cedars on either side of the gravelled drive met in an arch overhead, turning the long avenue into a dim tunnel. As soon as she was beneath the gnarled arms of the cedars, she knew she was safe from observation from the house and she slowed her swift pace. She was panting, for her stays were laced too tightly to permit much running, but she walked on as rapidly as she could. Soon she was at the end of the driveway and out on the main road, but she did not stop until she had rounded a curve that put a large clump of trees between her and the house.

Flushed and breathing hard, she sat down on a stump to wait for her father. It was past time for him to come home, but she was glad that he was late. The delay would give her time to quiet her breathing and calm her face so that his suspicions would not be aroused. Every moment she expected to hear the pounding of his horse's hooves and see him come charging up the hill at his usual breakneck speed. But the minutes slipped by and Gerald did not come. She looked down the road for him, the pain in her heart swelling up again.

'Oh, it can't be true!' she thought. 'Why doesn't he come?'

Her eyes followed the winding road, blood-red now after the morning rain. In her thought she traced its course as it ran down the hill to the sluggish Flint River, through the tangled swampy bottoms and up the next hill to Twelve Oaks where Ashley lived. That was all the road meant now – a road to Ashley and the beautiful white-columned house that crowned the hill like a Greek temple.

'Oh, Ashley! Ashley!' she thought, and her heart beat faster.

Some of the cold sense of bewilderment and disaster that had weighted her down since the Tarleton boys told her their gossip was pushed into the background of her mind, and in its place crept the fever that had possessed her for two years.

It seemed strange now that when she was growing up Ashley had never seemed so very attractive to her. In childhood days, she had seen him come and go and never given him a thought. But since that day two years ago when Ashley, newly home from his three years' Grand Tour in Europe, had called to pay his respects, she had loved him. It was as simple as that.

She had been on the front porch and he had ridden up the long avenue, dressed in grey broadcloth with a wide black cravat setting off his frilled shirt to perfection. Even now, she could recall each detail of his dress, how brightly his boots shone, the head of a Medusa in cameo on his cravat pin, the wide Panama hat that was instantly in his hand when he saw her. He had alighted and tossed his bridle reins to a piccaninny and stood looking up at her, his drowsy grey eyes wide with a smile and the sun so bright on his blond hair that it seemed like a cap of shining silver. And he said, 'So you've grown up, Scarlett.' And, coming lightly up the steps, he had kissed her hand. And his voice! She would never forget the leap of her heart as she heard it, as if for the first time, drawling, resonant, musical.

She had wanted him, in that first instant, wanted him as simply and unreasoningly as she wanted food to eat, horses to ride and a soft bed on which to lay herself.

For two years he had squired her about the County, to balls, fish-fries, picnics and court days, never so often as the Tarleton twins or Cade Calvert, never so importunate as the younger Fontaine boys, but, still, never the week went by that Ashley did not come calling at Tara.

True, he never made love to her, nor did the clear grey eyes ever glow with that hot light Scarlett knew so well in other men. And yet – and yet – she knew he loved her. She could not be mistaken about it. Instinct stronger than reason and knowledge born of experience told her that he loved her. Too often she had surprised him when his eyes were neither drowsy nor remote, when he looked at her with a yearning and a sadness which puzzled her. She *knew* he loved her. Why did he not tell her so? That she could not understand. But there were so many things about him that she did not understand.

He was courteous always, but aloof, remote. No one could ever tell what he was thinking about, Scarlett least of all. In a neighbourhood where everyone said exactly what he thought as soon as he thought it, Ashley's quality of reserve was exasperating. He was as proficient as any of the other young men in the usual County diversions, hunting, gambling, dancing and politics, and was the best rider of them all; but he differed from all the rest in that these pleasant activities were not the end and aim of life to him. And he stood alone in his interest in books and music and his fondness for writing poetry.

Oh, why was he so handsomely blond, so courteously aloof, so maddeningly boring with his talk of Europe and books and music and poetry and things that interested her not at all – and yet so desirable? Night after night, when Scarlett went to bed after sitting on the front porch in the semi-darkness with him, she tossed restlessly for hours and comforted herself only with the thought that the very next time he saw her he certainly would propose. But the next time came and went, and the result was nothing – nothing except that the fever possessing her rose higher and hotter.

She loved him and she wanted him and she did not understand him. She was as forthright and simple as the winds that blew over Tara and the yellow river that wound about it, and to the end of her days she would never be able to understand a complexity. And now, for the first time in her life, she was facing a complex nature.

For Ashley was born of a line of men who used their leisure for thinking, not doing, for spinning brightly coloured dreams that had in them no touch of reality. He moved in an inner world that was more beautiful than Georgia and came back to reality with reluctance. He looked on people, and he neither liked nor disliked them. He looked on life and was neither heartened nor saddened. He accepted the universe and his place in it for what they were and, shrugging, turned to his music and books and his better world.

Why he should have captivated Scarlett when his mind was a stranger to hers she did not know. The very mystery of him excited her curiosity like a door that had neither lock nor key. The things about him which she could not understand only made her love him more, and his odd, restrained courtship only served to increase her determination to have him for her own. That he would propose some day she had never doubted, for she was too young and too spoiled ever to have known defeat. And now, like a thunderclap, had come this horrible news. Ashley to marry Melanie! It couldn't be true!

Why, only last week, when they were riding home at twilight from Fairhill, he had said: 'Scarlett, I have something so important to tell you that I hardly know how to say it.'

She had cast down her eyes demurely, her heart beating with wild pleasure, thinking the happy moment had come. Then he had said: 'Not now! We're nearly home and there isn't time. Oh, Scarlett, what a coward I am!' And putting spurs to his horse, he had raced her up the hill to Tara.

Scarlett, sitting on the stump, thought of those words which had made her so happy, and suddenly they took on another meaning, a hideous meaning. Suppose it was the news of his engagement he had intended to tell her!

Oh, if Pa would only come home! She could not endure the suspense another moment. She looked impatiently down the road again, and again she was disappointed.

The sun was now below the horizon and the red glow at the rim of the world faded into pink. The sky above turned slowly from azure to the delicate blue-green of a robin's egg, and the unearthly stillness of rural twilight came stealthily down about her. Shadowy dimness crept over the countryside. The red furrows and the gashed red road lost their magical blood colour and became plain brown earth. Across the road, in the pasture, the horses, mules and cows stood quietly with heads over the split-rail fence, waiting to be driven to the stables and supper. They did not like the dark shade of the thickets hedging the pasture creek, and they twitched their ears at Scarlett as if appreciative of human companionship.

In the strange half-light, the tall pines of the river swamp, so warmly green in the sunshine, were black against the pastel sky, an impenetrable row of black giants hiding the slow yellow water at their feet. On the hill across the river, the tall white chimneys of the Wilkes home faded gradually into the darkness of the thick oaks surrounding them, and only far-off pin points of supper lamps showed that a house was here. The warm damp balminess of spring encompassed her sweetly with the moist smells of new-ploughed earth and all the fresh green things pushing up to the air.

Sunset and spring and new-fledged greenery were no miracle to Scarlett. Their beauty she accepted as casually as the air she breathed and the water she drank, for she had never consciously seen beauty in anything but women's faces, horses, silk dresses and like tangible things. Yet the serene half-light over Tara's well-kept acres brought a measure of quiet to her disturbed mind. She loved this land so much, without even knowing she loved it, loved it as she loved her mother's face under the lamp at prayer time.

Still there was no sign of Gerald on the quiet winding road. If she had to wait much longer, Mammy would certainly come in search of her and bully her into the house. But even as she strained her eyes down the darkening road, she heard a pounding of hooves at the bottom of the pasture hill and saw the horses and cows scatter in fright. Gerald O'Hara was coming home across country and at top speed.

He came up the hill at a gallop on his thick-barrelled, long-legged hunter, appearing in the distance like a boy on a too large horse. His long white hair standing out behind him, he urged the horse forward with crop and loud cries.

Filled with her own anxieties, she nevertheless watched him with affectionate pride, for Gerald was an excellent horseman.

'I wonder why he always wants to jump fences when he's had a few drinks,' she thought. 'And after that fall he had right here last year when he broke his knee. You'd think he'd learn. Especially when he promised Mother on oath he'd never jump again.'

Scarlett had no awe of her father and felt him more her contemporary than her sisters, for jumping fences and keeping it a secret from his wife gave him a boyish pride and guilty glee that matched her own pleasure in outwitting Mammy. She rose from her seat to watch him.

The big horse reached the fence, gathered himself and soared over as effortlessly as a bird, his rider yelling enthusiastically, his crop beating the air, his white curls jerking out behind him. Gerald did not see his daughter in the shadow of the trees, and he drew rein in the road, patting his horse's neck with approbation.

'There's none in the County can touch you, nor in the state,' he informed his mount, with pride, the brogue of County Meath still heavy on his tongue in spite of thirty-nine years in America. Then he hastily set about smoothing his hair and settling his ruffled shirt and his cravat which had slipped awry behind one ear. Scarlett knew these hurried preenings were being made with an eye toward meeting his wife with the appearance of a gentleman who had ridden sedately home from a call on a neighbour. She knew also that he was presenting her with just the opportunity she wanted for opening the conversation without revealing her true purpose.

She laughed aloud. As she had intended, Gerald was startled by the sound; then he recognized her, and a look both sheepish and defiant came over his florid face. He dismounted with difficulty, because his knee was stiff, and, slipping the reins over his arm, stumped toward her.

'Well, Missy,' he said, pinching her cheek, 'so, you've been spying on me and, like your sister Suellen last week, you'll be telling your mother on me?'

There was indignation in his hoarse bass voice but also a wheedling note, and Scarlett teasingly clicked her tongue against her teeth as she reached out to pull his cravat into place. His breath in her face was strong with Bourbon whisky mingled with a faint fragrance of mint. Accompanying him also were the smells of chewing tobacco, well-oiled leather and horses – a combination of odours that she always associated with her father and instinctively liked in other men.

'No, Pa, I'm no tattletale like Suellen,' she assured him, standing off to view his rearranged attire with a judicious air.

Gerald was a small man, little more than five feet tall, but so heavy of barrel and thick of neck that his appearance, when seated, led strangers to think him a larger man. His thickset torso was supported by short sturdy legs, always encased in the finest leather boots procurable and always planted wide apart like a swaggering small boy's. Most small people who take themselves seriously are a little ridiculous; but the bantam cock is respected in the barnyard, and so it was with Gerald. No one would ever have the temerity to think of Gerald O'Hara as a ridiculous little figure.

He was sixty years old and his crisp curly hair was silver-white, but his shrewd face was unlined and his hard little blue eyes were young with the unworried youthfulness of one who has never taxed his brain with problems more abstract than how many cards to draw in a poker game. His was as Irish a face as could be found in the length and breadth of the homeland he had left so long ago – round, high-coloured, short-nosed, wide-mouthed and belligerent.

Beneath his choleric exterior Gerald O'Hara had the tenderest of hearts. He could not bear to see a slave pouting under a reprimand, no matter how well deserved, or hear a kitten mewing or a child crying; but he had a horror of having this weakness discovered. That everyone who met him did discover his kindly heart within five minutes was unknown to him; and his vanity would have suffered tremendously if he had found it out, for he liked to think that when he bawled orders at the top of his voice everyone trembled and obeyed. It had never occurred to him that only one voice was obeyed on the plantation – the soft voice of his wife Ellen. It was a secret he would never learn, for everyone from Ellen down to the stupidest field hand was in a tacit and kindly conspiracy to keep him believing that his word was law.

Scarlett was impressed less than anyone else by his tempers and his roarings. She was his oldest child and, now that Gerald knew there would be no more sons to follow the three who lay in the family burying-ground, he had drifted into a habit of treating her in a man-to-man manner which she found most pleasant. She was more like her father than her younger sisters, for Carreen, who had been born Caroline Irene, was delicate and dreamy, and Suellen, christened Susan Elinor, prided herself on her elegance and lady-like deportment.

Moreover, Scarlett and her father were bound together by a mutual suppression agreement. If Gerald caught her climbing a fence instead of walking half a mile to a gate, or sitting too late on the front steps with a beau, he castigated her personally and with vehemence, but he did not mention the fact to Ellen or to Mammy. And when Scarlett discovered him jumping fences after his solemn promise to his wife, or learned the exact amount of his losses at poker, as she always did from County gossip, she refrained from mentioning the fact at the supper table in the artfully artless manner Suellen had. Scarlett and her father each assured the other solemnly that to bring such matters to the ears of Ellen would only hurt her, and nothing would induce them to wound her gentleness.

Scarlett looked at her father in the fading light, and, without knowing why, she found it comforting to be in his presence. There was something vital and earthy and coarse about him that appealed to her. Being the least analytic of people, she did not realize that this was because she possessed in some degree these same qualities, despite sixteen years of effort on the part of Ellen and Mammy to obliterate them.

'You look very presentable now,' she said, 'and I don't think anyone will suspect you've been up to your tricks unless you brag about them. But it does seem to me that after you broke your knee last year, jumping that same fence—'

'Well, may I be damned if I'll have me own daughter telling me what I shall jump and not jump,' he shouted, giving her cheek another pinch. 'It's me own neck, so it is. And besides, Missy, what are you doing out here without your shawl?'

Seeing that he was employing familiar manoeuvres to extricate himself from unpleasant conversation, she slipped her arm through his and said: 'I was waiting for you. I didn't know you would be so late. I just wondered if you had bought Dilcey.'

'Bought her I did, and the price has ruined me. Bought her and her little wench, Prissy. John Wilkes was for almost giving them away, but never will I have it said that Gerald O'Hara used friendship in a trade. I made him take three thousand for the two of them.'

'In the name of Heaven, Pa, three thousand! And you didn't need to buy Prissy!'

'Has the time come when me own daughters sit in judgment on me?' shouted Gerald rhetorically. 'Prissy is a likely little wench and so—'

'I know her. She's a sly, stupid creature,' Scarlett rejoined calmly, unimpressed by his uproar. 'And the only reason you bought her was because Dilcey asked you to buy her.'

Gerald looked crestfallen and embarrassed, as always when caught out in a kind deed, and Scarlett laughed outright at his transparency.

'Well, what if I did? Was there any use buying Dilcey if she was going to mope about the child? Well, never again will I let a darky on this place marry off it. It's too expensive. Well, come on, Puss, let's go in to supper.'

The shadows were falling thicker now, the last greenish tinge had left the sky and a slight chill was displacing the balminess of spring. But Scarlett loitered, wondering how to bring up the subject of Ashley without permitting Gerald to suspect her motive. This was difficult, for Scarlett had not a subtle bone in her body; and Gerald was so much like her he never failed to penetrate her weak subterfuges, even as she penetrated his. And he was seldom tactful in doing it.

'How are they all over at Twelve Oaks?'

'About as usual. Cade Calvert was there and, after I settled about Dilcey, we all set on the gallery and had several toddies. Cade has just come from Atlanta, and it's all upset they are there and talking war and—'

Scarlett sighed. If Gerald once got on the subject of war and secession, it would be hours before he relinquished it. She broke in with another line.

'Did they say anything about the barbecue tomorrow?'

'Now that I think of it they did. Miss – what's-her-name – the sweet little thing who was here last year, you know, Ashley's cousin – oh, yes, Miss Melanie Hamilton, that's the name – she and her brother Charles have already come from Atlanta and—'

'Oh, so she did come?'

'She did, and a sweet quiet thing she is, with never a word to say for herself, like a woman should be. Come now, daughter, don't lag. Your mother will be hunting for us.'

Scarlett's heart sank at the news. She had hoped against hope that something would keep Melanie Hamilton in Atlanta where she belonged, and the knowledge that even her father approved of her sweet quiet nature, so different from her own, forced her into the open.

'Was Ashley there, too?'

'He was,' Gerald let go of his daughter's arm and turned, peering sharply into her face. 'And if that's why you came out here to wait for me, why didn't you say so without beating around the bush?'

Scarlett could think of nothing to say, and she felt her face growing red with annoyance.

'Well, speak up.'

Still she said nothing, wishing that it was permissible to shake one's father and tell him to hush his mouth.

'He was there and he asked most kindly after you, as did his sisters, and said they hoped nothing would keep you from the barbecue tomorrow. I'll warrant nothing will,' he said shrewdly. 'And now, daughter, what's all this about you and Ashley?'

'There is nothing,' she said shortly, tugging at his arm. 'Let's go in, Pa.'

'So now 'tis you wanting to go in,' he observed. 'But here I'm going to stand till I'm understanding you. Now that I think of it, 'tis strange you've been recently. Has he been trifling with you? Has he asked to marry you?'

'No,' she said shortly.

'Nor will he,' said Gerald.

Fury flamed in her, but Gerald waved her quiet with a hand.

'Hold your tongue, Miss! I had it from John Wilkes this afternoon in the strictest confidence that Ashley's to marry Miss Melanie. It's to be announced tomorrow.'

Scarlett's hand fell from his arm. So it was true!

A pain slashed at her heart as savagely as a wild animal's fangs. Through it all, she felt her father's eyes on her, a little pitying, a little annoyed at being faced with a problem for which he knew no answer. He loved Scarlett, but it made him uncomfortable to have her forcing her childish problems on him for a solution. Ellen knew all the answers. Scarlett should have taken her troubles to her.

'Is it a spectacle you've been making of yourself – of all of us?' he bawled, his voice rising as always in moments of excitement. 'Have you been running after a man who's not in love with you, when you could have any of the bucks in the County?'

Anger and hurt pride drove out some of the pain.

'I haven't been running after him. It – it just surprised me.'

'It's lying you are!' said Gerald, and then, peering at her stricken face, he added in a burst of kindliness: 'I'm sorry, daughter. But after all, you are nothing but a child and there's lots of other beaux.'

'Mother was only fifteen when she married you, and I'm sixteen,' said Scarlett, her voice muffled.

'Your mother was different,' said Gerald. 'She was never flighty like you. Now come, daughter, cheer up, and I'll take you to Charleston next week to visit your Aunt Eulalie and, what with all the hullabaloo they are having over there about Fort Sumter, you'll be forgetting about Ashley in a week.'

'He thinks I'm a child,' thought Scarlett, grief and rage choking utterance, 'and he's only got to dangle a new toy and I'll forget my bumps.'

'Now, don't be jerking your chin at me,' warned Gerald. 'If you had any sense you'd have married Stuart or Brent Tarleton long ago. Think it over, daughter. Marry one of the twins and then the plantations will run together and Jim Tarleton and I will build you a fine house, right where they join, in that big pine grove and—'

'Will you stop treating me like a child!' cried Scarlett. 'I don't want to go to Charleston or have a house or marry the twins. I only want—' She caught herself but not in time.

Gerald's voice was strangely quiet and he spoke slowly as if drawing his words from a store of thought seldom used.

'It's only Ashley you're wanting, and you'll not be having him. And if he wanted to marry you, 'twould be with misgivings that I'd say Yes, for all the fine friendship that's between me and John Wilkes.' And, seeing her startled look, he continued: 'I want my girl to be happy and you wouldn't be happy with him.'

'Oh, I would! I would!'

'That you would not, daughter. Only when like marries like can there be any happiness.'

Scarlett had a sudden treacherous desire to cry out, 'But you've been happy, and you and Mother aren't alike,' but she repressed it, fearing that he would box her ears for her impertinence.

'Our people and the Wilkes are different,' he went on slowly, fumbling for words. 'The Wilkes are different from any of our neighbours – different from any family I ever knew. They are queer folk, and it's best that they marry their cousins and keep their queerness to themselves.'

'Why, Pa, Ashley is not—'

'Hold your whist, Puss! I said nothing against the lad, for I like him. And when I say queer, it's not crazy I'm meaning. He's not queer like the Calverts who'd gamble everything they have on a horse, or the Tarletons who turn out a drunkard or two in every litter, or the Fontaines who are hot-headed little brutes and after murdering a man for a fancied slight. That kind of queerness is easy to understand, for sure, and but for the grace of God Gerald O'Hara would be having all those faults! And I don't mean that Ashley would run off with another woman, if you were his wife, or beat you. You'd be happier if he did, for at least you'd be understanding that. But he's queer in other ways, and there's no understanding him at all. I like him, but it's neither heads nor tails I can make of most he says. Now, Puss, tell me true, do you understand his folderol about books and poetry and music and oil paintings and such foolishness?'

'Oh, Pa,' cried Scarlett impatiently, 'if I married him, I'd change all that!'

'Oh, you would, would you now?' said Gerald testily, shooting a sharp look at her. 'Then it's little enough you are knowing of any man living, let alone Ashley. No wife has ever changed a husband one whit, and don't you be forgetting that. And as for changing a Wilkes – God's nightgown, daughter! The whole family is that way, and they've always been that way. And probably always will. I tell you they're born queer. Look at the way they go tearing up to New York and Boston to hear operas and see oil paintings. And ordering French and German books by the crate from the Yankees! And there they sit reading and dreaming the dear God knows what, when they'd be better spending their time hunting and playing poker as proper men should.'

'There's nobody in the County sits a horse better than Ashley,' said Scarlett, furious at the slur of effeminacy flung on Ashley, 'nobody except maybe his father. And as for poker, didn't Ashley take two hundred dollars away from you just last week in Jonesboro?'

'The Calvert boys have been blabbing again,' Gerald said resignedly, 'else you'd not be knowing the amount. Ashley can ride with the best and play poker with the best – that's me, Puss! And I'm not denying that when he sets out to drink he can put even the Tarletons under the table. He can do all those things, but his heart's not in it. That's why I say he's queer.'

Scarlett was silent and her heart sank. She could think of no defence for this last, for she knew Gerald was right. Ashley's heart was in none of the pleasant things he did so well. He was never more than politely interested in any of the things that vitally interested everyone else.

Rightly interpreting her silence, Gerald patted her arm and said triumphantly: 'There now, Scarlett! You admit 'tis true. What would you be doing with a husband like Ashley? 'Tis moonstruck they all are, all the Wilkes.' And then, in a wheedling tone: 'When I was mentioning the Tarletons the while ago, I wasn't pushing them. They're fine lads, but if it's Cade Calvert you're setting your cap after, why, 'tis the same with me. The Calverts are good folk, all of them, for all the old man marrying a Yankee. And when I'm gone— Whist, darlin', listen to me! I'll leave Tara to you and Cade—'

'I wouldn't have Cade on a silver tray,' cried Scarlett in fury. 'And I wish you'd quit pushing him at me! I don't want Tara or any old plantation. Plantations don't amount to anything when—'

She was going to say 'when you haven't the man you want', but Gerald, incensed by the cavalier way in which she treated his proffered gift, the thing which, next to Ellen, he loved best in the whole world, uttered a roar.

'Do you stand there, Scarlett O'Hara, and tell me that Tara – that land – doesn't amount to anything?'

Scarlett nodded obstinately. Her heart was too sore to care whether or not she put her father in a temper.

'Land is the only thing in the world that amounts to anything,' he shouted, his thick, short arms making wide gestures of indignation, 'for 'tis the only thing in this world that lasts, and don't you be forgetting it! 'Tis the only thing worth working for, worth fighting for – worth dying for.'

'Oh, Pa,' she said disgustedly, 'you talk like an Irishman!'

'Have I ever been ashamed of it? No, 'tis proud I am. And don't be forgetting that you are half Irish, Miss! And to anyone with a drop of Irish blood in them the land they live on is like their mother. 'Tis ashamed of you

I am this minute. I offer you the most beautiful land in the world – saving County Meath in the Old Country – and what do you do? You sniff!'

Gerald had begun to work himself up into a pleasurable shouting rage when something in Scarlett's woebegone face stopped him.

'But there, you're young. 'Twill come to you, this love of land. There's no getting away from it, if you're Irish. You're just a child and bothered about your beaux. When you're older, you'll be seeing how 'tis . . . Now, do you be making up your mind about Cade or the twins or one of Evan Munroe's young bucks, and see how fine I turn you out!'

'Oh, Pa!'

By this time, Gerald was thoroughly tired of the conversation and thoroughly annoyed that the problem should be upon his shoulders. He felt aggrieved, moreover, that Scarlett should still look so desolate after being offered the best of the County boys and Tara, too. Gerald liked his gifts to be received with clapping of hands and kisses.

'Now, none of your pouts, Miss. It doesn't matter who you marry, as long as he thinks like you and is a gentleman and a Southerner and prideful. For a woman, love comes after marriage.'

'Oh, Pa, that's such an Old Country notion!'

'And a good notion it is! All this American business of running around marrying for love, like servants, like Yankees! The best marriages are when the parents choose for the girl. For how can a silly piece like yourself tell a good man from a scoundrel? Now, look at the Wilkes. What's kept them prideful and strong all these generations? Why, marrying the likes of themselves, marrying the cousins their family always expects them to marry.'

'Oh,' cried Scarlett, fresh pain striking her as Gerald's words brought home the terrible inevitability of the truth. Gerald looked at her bowed head and shuffled his feet uneasily.

'It's not crying you are?' he questioned, fumbling clumsily at her chin, trying to turn her face upward, his own face furrowed with pity.

'No,' she cried vehemently, jerking away.

'It's lying you are, and I'm proud of it. I'm glad there's pride in you, Puss. And I want to see pride in you tomorrow at the barbecue. I'll not be having the County gossiping and laughing at you for mooning your heart out about a man who never gave you a thought beyond friendship.'

'He did give me a thought,' thought Scarlett, sorrowfully in her heart. 'Oh, a lot of thoughts! I know he did. I could tell. If I'd just had a little longer, I know I could have made him say – Oh, if only it wasn't that the Wilkes always feel that they have to marry their cousins!'

Gerald took her arm and passed it through his.

'We'll be going in to supper now, and all this is between us. I'll not be worrying your mother with this – nor do you do it, either. Blow your nose, daughter.'

Scarlett blew her nose on her torn handkerchief, and they started up the dark drive arm in arm, the horse following slowly. Near the house, Scarlett was at the point of speaking again when she saw her mother in the dim shadows of the porch. She had on her bonnet, shawl and mittens, and behind her was Mammy, her face like a thundercloud, holding in her hand the black leather bag in which Ellen O'Hara always carried the bandages and medicines she used in doctoring the slaves. Mammy's lips were large and pendulous and, when indignant, she could push out her lower one to twice its normal length. It was pushed out now, and Scarlett knew that Mammy was seething over something of which she did not approve.

'Mr O'Hara,' called Ellen as she saw the two coming up the driveway – Ellen belonged to a generation that was formal even after seventeen years of wedlock and the bearing of six children – 'Mr O'Hara, there is illness at the Slattery house. Emmie's baby has been born and is dying and must be baptized. I am going there with Mammy to see what I can do.'

Her voice was raised questioningly, as though she hung on Gerald's assent to her plan, a mere formality but one dear to the heart of Gerald.

'In the name of God!' blustered Gerald. 'Why should those white trash take you away just at your supper hour and just when I'm wanting to tell you about the war talk that's going on in Atlanta! Go, Mrs O'Hara. You'd not rest easy on your pillow the night if there was trouble abroad and you not there to help.'

'She doan never git no res' on her piller fer hoppin' up at night time nursin' niggers an' po' w'ite trash dat could ten' to deyseff,' grumbled Mammy in a monotone as she went down the stairs toward the carriage which was waiting in the side drive.

'Take my place at the table, dear,' said Ellen, patting Scarlett's cheek softly with a mittened hand.

In spite of her choked-back tears, Scarlett thrilled to the never-failing magic of her mother's touch, to the faint fragrance of lemon verbena sachet that came from her rustling silk dress. To Scarlett, there was something breath-taking about Ellen O'Hara, a miracle that lived in the house with her and awed her and charmed and soothed her.

Gerald helped his wife into the carriage and gave orders to the coachman to drive carefully. Toby, who had handled Gerald's horses for twenty years, pushed out his lips in mute indignation at being told how to conduct his own business. Driving off, with Mammy beside him, each was a perfect picture of pouting African disapproval.

'If I didn't do so much for those trashy Slatterys that they'd have to pay money for elsewhere,' fumed Gerald, 'they'd be willing to sell me their miserable few acres of swamp bottom, and the County would be well rid of them.' Then, brightening, in anticipation of one of his practical jokes: 'Come, daughter, let's go tell Pork that instead of buying Dilcey, I've sold him to John Wilkes.'

He tossed the reins of his horse to a small piccaninny standing near and started up the steps. He had already forgotten Scarlett's heartbreak and his mind was only on plaguing his valet. Scarlett slowly climbed the steps after him, her feet leaden. She thought that, after all, a mating between herself and Ashley could be no queerer than that of her father and Ellen Robillard O'Hara. As always, she wondered how her loud, insensitive father had managed to marry a woman like her mother, for never were two people farther apart in birth, breeding and habits of mind.

Chapter III

Ellen O'Hara was thirty-two years old, and, according to the standards of her day, she was a middle-aged woman, one who had borne six children and buried three. She was a tall woman, standing a head higher than her fiery little husband, but she moved with such quiet grace in her swaying hoops that her height attracted no attention to itself. Her neck, rising from the black taffeta sheath of her basque, was creamy-skinned, rounded and slender, and it seemed always tilted slightly backward by the weight of her luxuriant hair in its net at the back of her head. From her French mother, whose parents had fled Haiti in the Revolution of 1791, had come her slanting dark eyes, shadowed by inky lashes, and her black hair; and from her father, a soldier of Napoleon, she had her long straight nose and her square-cut jaw that was softened by the gentle curving of her cheeks. But only from life could Ellen's face have acquired its look of pride that had no haughtiness, its graciousness, its melancholy and its utter lack of humour.

She would have been a strikingly beautiful woman had there been any glow in her eyes, any responsive warmth in her smile or any spontaneity in her voice that fell with gentle melody on the ears of her family and her servants. She spoke in the soft slurring voice of the coastal Georgian, liquid of vowels, kind to consonants and with the barest trace of French accent. It was a voice never raised in command to a servant or reproof to a child but a voice that was obeyed instantly at Tara, where her husband's blustering and roaring were quietly disregarded.

As far back as Scarlett could remember, her mother had always been the same, her voice soft and sweet whether in praising or in reproving, her manner efficient and unruffled despite the daily emergencies of Gerald's turbulent household, her spirit always calm and her back unbowed, even in the deaths of her three baby sons. Scarlett had never seen her mother's back touch the back of any chair on which she sat. Nor had she ever seen her sit down without a bit of needlework in her hands, except at mealtime, while attending the sick or while working at the bookkeeping of the plantation. It was delicate embroidery if company were present, but at other times her hands were occupied with Gerald's ruffled shirts, the girls' dresses or garments for the slaves. Scarlett could not imagine her mother's hands without her gold thimble or her rustling figure unaccompanied by the small negro girl whose sole function in life was to remove basting threads and carry the rosewood sewing-box from room to room, as Ellen moved about the house superintending the cooking, the cleaning and the wholesale clothes-making for the plantation.

She had never seen her mother stirred from her austere placidity, nor her personal appointments anything but perfect, no matter what the hour of day or night. When Ellen was dressing for a ball or for guests or even to go to Jonesboro for Court Day, it frequently required two hours, two maids and Mammy to turn her out to her own satisfaction; but her swift toilets in times of emergency were amazing.

Scarlett, whose room lay across the hall from her mother's, knew from babyhood the soft sound of scurrying bare black feet on the hardwood floor in the hours of dawn, the urgent tappings on her mother's door, and the muffled, frightened negro voices that whispered of sickness and birth and death in the long row of whitewashed cabins in the quarters. As a child, she often had crept to the door and, peeping through the tiniest crack, had seen Ellen emerge from the dark room, where Gerald's snores were rhythmic and untroubled, into the flickering light of an upheld candle, her medicine-case under her arm, her hair smoothed neatly into place, and no button on her basque unlooped.

It had always been so soothing to Scarlett to hear her mother whisper, firmly but compassionately, as she tiptoed down the hall: 'Hush, not so loudly. You will wake Mr O'Hara. They are not sick enough to die.'

Yes, it was good to creep back into bed and know that Ellen was abroad in the night and everything was right.

In the mornings, after all-night sessions at births and deaths, when old Dr Fontaine and young Dr Fontaine were both out on calls and could not be found to help her, Ellen presided at the breakfast table as usual, her dark eyes circled with weariness but her voice and manner revealing none of the strain. There was a steely quality under her stately gentleness that awed the whole household, Gerald as well as the girls, though he would have died rather than admit it.

Sometimes when Scarlett tiptoed at night to kiss her tall mother's cheek, she looked up at the mouth with its too short, too tender upper lip, a mouth too easily hurt by the world, and wondered if it had ever curved in silly girlish giggling or whispered secrets through long nights to intimate girl friends. But no, that wasn't possible. Mother had always been just as she was, a pillar of strength, a fount of wisdom, the one person who knew the answers to everything.

But Scarlett was wrong, for, years before, Ellen Robillard of Savannah had giggled as inexplicably as any fifteen-year-old in the charming coastal city and whispered the long nights through with friends, exchanging confidences, telling all secrets but one. That was the year when Gerald O'Hara, twenty-eight years older than she, came into her life – the year, too, when youth and her black-eyed cousin, Philippe Robillard, went out of it. For when Philippe, with his snapping eyes and his wild ways, left Savannah forever, he took with him all the glow that was in Ellen's heart and left for the bandy-legged little Irishman who married her only a gentle shell.

But that was enough for Gerald, overwhelmed at his unbelievable luck in actually marrying her. And if anything was gone from her, he never missed it. Shrewd man that he was, he knew that it was no less than a miracle that he, an Irishman with nothing of family and wealth to recommend him, should win the daughter of one of the wealthiest and proudest families on the Coast. For Gerald was a self-made man.

Gerald had come to America from Ireland when he was twenty-one. He had come hastily, as many a better and worse Irishman before and since, with the clothes he had on his back, two shillings above his passage money and a price on his head that he felt was larger than his misdeed warranted. There was no Orangeman this side of hell worth a hundred pounds to the British government or to the devil himself; but if the government felt so strongly about the death of an English absentee landlord's rent agent, it was time for Gerald O'Hara to be leaving and leaving suddenly. True, he had called the rent agent 'a bastard of an Orangeman', but that, according to Gerald's way of looking at it, did not give the man any right to insult him by whistling the opening bars of 'The Boyne Water'.

The Battle of the Boyne had been fought more than a hundred years before, but, to the O'Haras and their neighbours, it might have been yesterday when their hopes and their dreams, as well as their lands and wealth, went off in the same cloud of dust that enveloped a frightened and fleeing Stuart prince, leaving William of Orange and his hated troops with their orange cockades to cut down the Irish adherents of the Stuarts.

For this and other reasons, Gerald's family was not inclined to view the fatal outcome of his quarrel as anything very serious, except for the fact that it was charged with serious consequences. For years, the O'Haras had been in bad odour with the English constabulary on account of suspected activities against the government, and Gerald was not the first O'Hara to take his foot in his hand and quit Ireland between dawn and morning. His two oldest brothers, James and Andrew, he hardly remembered, save as close-lipped youths who came and went at odd hours of the night on mysterious errands or disappeared for weeks at a time, to their mother's gnawing anxiety. They had come to America years before, after the discovery of a small arsenal of rifles buried under the O'Hara pigsty. Now they were successful merchants in Savannah, 'though the dear God alone knows where that may be,' as their mother always interpolated when mentioning the two oldest of her male brood, and it was to them that young Gerald was sent.

He left home with his mother's hasty kiss on his cheek and her fervent Catholic blessing in his ears, and his father's parting admonition, 'Remember who ye are and don't be taking nothing off no man.' His five tall brothers gave him good-bye with admiring but slightly patronizing smiles, for Gerald was the baby and the little one of a brawny family.

His five brothers and their father stood six feet and over and broad in proportion, but little Gerald, at twenty-one, knew that five feet four and a half inches was as much as the Lord in His wisdom was going to allow him. It was like Gerald that he never wasted regrets on his lack of height and never found it an obstacle to his acquisition of anything he wanted. Rather, it was Gerald's compact smallness that made him what he was, for he had learned early that little people must be hardy to survive among large ones. And Gerald was hardy.

His tall brothers were a grim, quiet lot, in whom the family tradition of past glories, lost forever, rankled in unspoken hate and crackled out in bitter humour. Had Gerald been brawny he would have gone the way of the other O'Haras and moved quietly and darkly among the rebels against the government. But Gerald was 'loud-mouthed and bullheaded', as his mother fondly phrased it, hair-trigger of temper, quick with his fists and possessed of a chip on his shoulder so large as to be almost visible to the naked eye. He swaggered among the tall O'Haras like a strutting bantam in a barnyard of giant Cochin roosters, and they loved him, baited him affectionately to hear him roar and hammered on him with their large fists no more than was necessary to keep a baby brother in his proper place.

If the educational equipment which Gerald brought to America was scant, he did not even know it. Nor would he have cared if he had been told. His mother had taught him to read and to write a clear hand. He was adept at ciphering. And there his book knowledge stopped. The only Latin he knew was the responses of the Mass and the only history the manifold wrongs of Ireland. He knew no poetry save that of Moore and no music except the songs of Ireland that had come down through the years. While he entertained the liveliest respect for those who had more book learning than he, he never felt his own lack. And what need had he of these things in a new country where the most ignorant of bogtrotters had made great fortunes? in this country which asked only that a man be strong and unafraid of work?

Nor did James and Andrew, who took him into their store in Savannah, regret his lack of education. His clear hand, his accurate figures and his shrewd ability in bargaining won their respect, where a knowledge of literature and a fine appreciation of music, had young Gerald possessed them, would have moved them to snorts of contempt. America, in the early days of the century, had been kind to the Irish. James and Andrew, who had begun by hauling goods in covered wagons from Savannah to Georgia's inland towns, had prospered into a store of their own, and Gerald prospered with them.

He liked the South, and he soon became, in his opinion, a Southerner. There was much about the South – and Southerners – that he would never comprehend; but, with the whole-heartedness that was his nature, he adopted its ideas and customs, as he understood them, for his own – poker and horse racing, red-hot politics and the code duello, States' Rights and damnation to all Yankees, slavery and King Cotton, contempt for white trash and exaggerated courtesy to women. He even learned to chew tobacco. There was no need for him to acquire a good head for whisky, he had been born with one.

But Gerald remained Gerald. His habits of living and his ideas changed, but his manners he would not change, even had he been able to change them. He admired the drawling elegance of the wealthy rice and cotton planters, who rode into Savannah from their moss-hung kingdoms, mounted on thoroughbred horses and followed by the carriages of their equally elegant ladies and the wagons of their slaves. But Gerald could never attain elegance. Their lazy, blurred voices fell pleasantly on his ears, but his own brisk brogue clung to his tongue. He liked the casual grace with which they conducted affairs of importance, risking a fortune, a plantation or a slave on the turn of a card and writing off their losses with careless good humour and no more ado than when they scattered pennies to piccaninnies. But Gerald had known poverty, and he could never learn to lose money with good humour or good grace. They were a pleasant race, these coastal Georgians, with their soft-voiced, quick rages and their charming inconsistencies, and Gerald liked them. But there was a brisk and restless vitality about the young Irishman, fresh from a country where winds blew wet and chill, where misty swamps held no fevers, that set him apart from these indolent gentlefolk of semi-tropical weather and malarial marshes.

From them he learned what he found useful, and the rest he dismissed. He found poker the most useful of all Southern customs, poker and a steady head for whisky; and it was his natural aptitude for cards and amber liquor that brought to Gerald two of his most prized possessions, his valet and his plantation. The other was his wife, and he could only attribute her to the mysterious kindness of God.

The valet, Pork by name, shining black, dignified and trained in all the arts of sartorial elegance, was the result of an all-night poker game with a planter from St. Simon's Island, whose courage in a bluff equalled Gerald's but whose head for New Orleans rum did not. Though Pork's former owner later offered to buy him back at twice his value, Gerald obstinately refused, for the possession of his first slave, and that slave the 'best damned valet on the Coast', was the first step upward toward his heart's desire. Gerald wanted to be a slave-owner and a landed gentleman.

His mind was made up that he was not going to spend all of his days, like

James and Andrew, in bargaining, or all his nights, by candlelight, over long columns of figures. He felt keenly, as his brothers did not, the social stigma attached to those 'in trade'. Gerald wanted to be a planter. With the deep hunger of an Irishman who has been a tenant on the lands his people once had owned and hunted, he wanted to see his own acres stretching green before his eyes. With a ruthless singleness of purpose, he desired his own house, his own plantation, his own horses, his own slaves. And here in this new country, safe from the twin perils of the land he had left – taxation that ate up crops and barns and the ever-present threat of sudden confiscation – he intended to have them. But having that ambition and bringing it to realization were two different matters, he discovered as time went by. Coastal Georgia was too firmly held by an entrenched aristocracy for him ever to hope to win the place he intended to have.

Then the hand of Fate and a hand of poker combined to give him the plantation which he afterwards called Tara, and at the same time moved him out of the Coast into the upland country of north Georgia.

It was in a saloon in Savannah, on a hot night in spring, when the chance conversation of a stranger sitting near-by made Gerald prick up his ears. The stranger, a native of Savannah, had just returned after twelve years in the inland country. He had been one of the winners in the land lottery conducted by the State to divide up the vast area in middle Georgia, ceded by the Indians the year before Gerald came to America. He had gone up there and established a plantation; but, now the house had burned down, he was tired of the 'accursed place' and would be most happy to get it off his hands.

Gerald, his mind never free of the thought of owning a plantation of his own, arranged an introduction, and his interest grew as the stranger told how the northern section of the state was filling up with newcomers from the Carolinas and Virginia. Gerald had lived in Savannah long enough to acquire the viewpoint of the Coast – that all the rest of the state was backwoods, with an Indian lurking in every thicket. In transacting business for O'Hara Brothers, he had visited Augusta, a hundred miles up the Savannah River, and he had travelled inland far enough to visit the old towns westward from that city. He knew that section to be as well settled as the Coast, but from the stranger's description, his plantation was more than two hundred and fifty miles inland from Savannah to the north and west, and not many miles south of the Chattahoochee River. Gerald knew that northward beyond that stream the land was still held by the Cherokees, so it was with amazement that he heard the stranger jeer at suggestions of trouble with the Indians and narrate how thriving towns were growing up and plantations prospering in the new country.

An hour later when the conversation began to lag, Gerald, with a guile that belied the wide innocence of his bright blue eyes, proposed a game. As the night wore on and the drinks went round, there came a time when all the others in the game laid down their hands and Gerald and the stranger were battling alone. The stranger shoved in all his chips and followed with the deed to his plantation. Gerald shoved in all his chips and laid on top of them his wallet. If the money it contained happened to belong to the firm of O'Hara Brothers, Gerald's conscience was not sufficiently troubled to confess it before Mass the following morning. He knew what he wanted, and when Gerald wanted something he gained it by taking the most direct route. Moreover, such was his faith in his destiny and four deuces that he never for a moment wondered just how the money would be paid back should a higher hand be laid down across the table.

'It's no bargain you're getting and I am glad not to have to pay more taxes on the place,' sighed the possessor of an 'ace full', as he called for pen and ink. 'The big house burned a year ago and the fields are growing up in brush and seedling pine. But it's yours.'

'Never mix cards and whisky unless you were weaned on Irish poteen,' Gerald told Pork gravely the same evening, as Pork assisted him to bed. And the valet, who had begun to attempt a brogue out of admiration for his new master, made requisite answer in a combination of Geechee and County Meath that would have puzzled anyone except those two alone.

The muddy Flint River, running silently between walls of pine and water oak covered with tangled vines, wrapped about Gerald's new land like a curving arm and embraced it on two sides. To Gerald, standing on the small knoll where the house had been, this tall barrier of green was as visible and pleasing an evidence of ownership as though it were a fence that he himself had built to mark his own. He stood on the blackened foundation stones of the burned building, looked down the long avenue of trees leading toward the road and swore lustily, with a joy too deep for thankful prayer. These twin lines of sombre trees were his, his the abandoned lawn, waist-high in weeds under white-starred young magnolia trees. The uncultivated fields, studded with tiny pines and underbrush, that stretched their rolling red-clay surface away into the distance on four sides belonged to Gerald O'Hara – were all his because he had an unbefuddled Irish head and the courage to stake everything on a hand of cards.

Gerald closed his eyes and, in the stillness of the unworked acres, he felt that he had come home. Here under his feet would rise a house of whitewashed brick. Across the road would be new rail fences, enclosing fat cattle and blooded horses, and the red earth that rolled down the hillside to the rich river bottom land would gleam white as eiderdown in the sun – cotton, acres and acres of cotton! The fortunes of the O'Haras would rise again.

With his own small stake, what he could borrow from his unenthusiastic brothers and a neat sum from mortgaging the land, Gerald bought his first field hands and came to Tara to live in bachelor solitude in the four-room overseer's house, till such a time as the white walls of Tara should rise.

He cleared the fields and planted cotton and borrowed more money from

James and Andrew to buy more slaves. The O'Haras were a clannish tribe, clinging to one another in prosperity as well as in adversity, not for any overweening family affection but because they had learned through grim years that to survive a family must present an unbroken front to the world. They lent Gerald the money and, in the years that followed, the money came back to them with interest. Gradually the plantation widened out, as Gerald bought more acres lying near him, and in time the white house became a reality instead of a dream.

It was built by slave labour, a clumsy sprawling building that crowned the rise of ground overlooking the green incline of pasture land running down to the river; and it pleased Gerald greatly, for, even when new, it wore a look of mellowed years. The old oaks, which had seen Indians pass under their limbs, hugged the house closely with their great trunks and towered their branches over the roof in dense shade. The lawn, reclaimed from weeds, grew thick with clover and Bermuda grass, and Gerald saw to it that it was well kept. From the avenue of cedars to the row of white cabins in the slave quarters, there was an air of solidness, of stability and permanence about Tara; and whenever Gerald galloped around the bend in the road and saw his own roof rising through green branches, his heart swelled with pride as though each sight of it were the first sight.

He had done it all, little, hard-headed, blustering Gerald.

Gerald was on excellent terms with all his neighbours in the County, except the MacIntoshes whose land adjoined his on the left and the Slatterys whose meagre three acres stretched on his right along the swamp bottoms between the river and John Wilkes' plantation.

The MacIntoshes were Scotch-Irish and Orangemen and, had they possessed all the saintly qualities of the Catholic calendar, this ancestry would have damned them forever in Gerald's eyes. True, they had lived in Georgia for seventy years and, before that, had spent a generation in the Carolinas; but the first of the family who set foot on American shores had come from Ulster, and that was enough for Gerald.

They were a close-mouthed and stiff-necked family, who kept strictly to themselves and intermarried with their Carolina relatives, and Gerald was not alone in disliking them, for the County people were neighbourly and sociable and none too tolerant of anyone lacking in those same qualities. Rumours of Abolitionist sympathies did not enhance the popularity of the MacIntoshes. Old Angus had never manumitted a single slave and had committed the unpardonable social breach of selling some of his negroes to passing slave-traders en route to the cane fields of Louisiana, but the rumours persisted.

'He's an Abolitionist, no doubt,' observed Gerald to John Wilkes. 'But, in an Orangeman, when a principle comes up against Scotch tightness, the principle fares ill.'

The Slatterys were another affair. Being poor white, they were not even accorded the grudging respect that Angus MacIntosh's dour independence wrung from neighbouring families. Old Slattery, who clung persistently to his few acres, in spite of repeated offers from Gerald and John Wilkes, was shiftless and whining. His wife was a snarly-haired woman, sickly and washed-out of appearance, the mother of a brood of sullen and rabbity-looking children – a brood which was increased regularly every year. Tom Slattery owned no slaves, and he and his two oldest boys spasmodically worked their few acres of cotton, while the wife and younger children tended what was supposed to be a vegetable garden. But, somehow, the cotton always failed, and the garden, due to Mrs Slattery's constant childbearing, seldom furnished enough to feed her flock.

The sight of Tom Slattery dawdling on his neighbours' porches, begging cotton seed for planting or a side of bacon to 'tide him over', was a familiar one. Slattery hated his neighbours with what little energy he possessed, sensing their contempt beneath their courtesy, and especially did he hate 'rich folks' uppity niggers'. The house negroes of the County considered themselves superior to white trash, and their unconcealed scorn stung him, while their more secure position in life stirred his envy. By contrast with his own miserable existence, they were well fed, well clothed and looked after in sickness and old age. They were proud of the good names of their owners and, for the most part, proud to belong to people who were quality, while he was despised by all.

Tom Slattery could have sold his farm for three times its value to any of the planters in the County. They would have considered it money well spent to rid the community of an eyesore, but he was well satisfied to remain and to subsist miserably on the proceeds of a bale of cotton a year and the charity of his neighbours.

With all the rest of the County, Gerald was on terms of amity and some intimacy. The Wilkeses, the Calverts, the Tarletons, the Fontaines, all smiled when the small figure on the big white horse galloped up their driveways, smiled and signalled for tall glasses in which a pony of Bourbon had been poured over a teaspoon of sugar and a sprig of crushed mint. Gerald was likeable, and the neighbours learned in time what the children, negroes and dogs discovered at first sight, that a kind heart, a ready and sympathetic ear and an open pocketbook lurked just behind his bawling voice and his truculent manner.

His arrival was always amid a bedlam of hounds and barking and small black children shouting as they raced to meet him, quarrelling for the privilege of holding his horse and squirming and grinning under his good-natured insults. The white children clamoured to sit on his knee and be trotted, while he denounced to their elders the infamy of Yankee politicians; the daughters of his friends took him into their confidence about their love affairs; and the youths of the neighbourhood, fearful of confessing debts of honour upon the carpets of their fathers, found him a friend in need.

'So, you've been owing this for a month, you young rascal!' he would shout. 'And, in God's name, why haven't you been asking me for the money before this?'

His rough manner of speech was too well known to give offence, and it only made the young men grin sheepishly and reply: 'Well, sir, I hated to trouble you, and my father—'

'Your father's a good man, and no denying it, but strict, and so take this and let's be hearing no more of it.'

The planters' ladies were the last to capitulate. But, when Mrs Wilkes, 'a great lady and with a rare gift for silence', as Gerald characterized her, told her husband one evening, after Gerald's horse had pounded down the driveway, 'He has a rough tongue, but he is a gentleman,' Gerald had definitely arrived.

He did not know that he had taken nearly ten years to arrive, for it never occured to him that his neighbours had eyed him askance at first. In his own mind, there had never been any doubt that he belonged, from the moment he first set foot on Tara.

When Gerald was forty-three, so thickset of body and florid of face that he looked like a hunting squire out of a sporting print, it came to him that Tara, dear though it was, and the County folk, with their open hearts and open houses, were not enough. He wanted a wife.

Tara cried out for a mistress. The fat cook, a yard negro elevated by necessity to the kitchen, never had the meals on time, and the chamber-maid, formerly a field hand, let dust accumulate on the furniture and never seemed to have clean linen on hand, so that the arrival of guests was always the occasion of much stirring and to-do. Pork, the only trained house negro on the place, had general supervision over the other servants, but even he had grown slack and careless after several years of exposure to Gerald's happy-go-lucky mode of living. As valet, he kept Gerald's bedroom in order, and, as butler, he served the meals with dignity and style but otherwise he pretty well let matters follow their own course.

With unerring African instinct, the negroes had all discovered that Gerald had a loud bark and no bite at all, and they took shameless advantage of him. The air was always thick with threats of selling slaves south and of direful whippings, but there never had been a slave sold from Tara and only one whipping, and that administered for not grooming down Gerald's pet horse after a long day's hunting.

Gerald's sharp blue eyes noticed how efficiently his neighbours' houses were run and with what ease the smooth-haired wives in rustling skirts managed their servants. He had no knowledge of the dawn-till-midnight activities of these women, chained to supervision of cooking, nursing, sewing and laundering. He only saw the outward results, and those results impressed him.

The urgent need of a wife became clear to him one morning when he was dressing to ride to town for Court Day. Pork brought forth his favourite ruffled shirt, so inexpertly mended by the chambermaid as to be unwearable by anyone except his valet.

'Mist' Gerald,' said Pork, gratefully rolling up the shirt as Gerald fumed, 'whut you needs is a wife, and a wife whut has got plen'y of house niggers.'

Gerald upbraided Pork for his impertinence, but he knew that he was right. He wanted a wife and he wanted children and, if he did not acquire them soon, it would be too late. But he was not going to marry just anyone, as Mr Calvert had done, taking to wife the Yankee governess of his motherless children. His wife must be a lady and a lady of blood, with as many airs and graces as Mrs Wilkes and the ability to manage Tara as well as Mrs Wilkes ordered her own domain.

But there were two difficulties in the way of marriage into the County families. The first was the scarcity of girls of marriageable age. The second, and more serious one, was that Gerald was a 'new man', despite his nearly ten years' residence, and a foreigner. No one knew anything about his family. While the society of up-country Georgia was not so impregnable as that of the Coast aristocrats, no family wanted a daughter to wed a man about whose grandfather nothing was known.

Gerald knew that despite the genuine liking of the County men with whom he hunted, drank and talked politics there was hardly one whose daughter he could marry. And he did not intend to have it gossiped about over supper tables that this, that or the other father had regretfully refused to let Gerald O'Hara pay court to his daughter. This knowledge did not make Gerald feel inferior to his neighbours. Nothing could ever make Gerald feel that he was inferior in any way to anyone. It was merely a quaint custom of the County that daughters only married into families who had lived in the South much longer than twenty-two years, had owned land and slaves and been addicted only to the fashionable vices during that time.

'Pack up. We're going to Savannah,' he told Pork. 'And if I hear you say "Whist!" or "Faith!" but once, it's selling you I'll be doing, for they are words I seldom say meself.'

James and Andrew might have some advice to offer on this subject of marriage, and there might be daughters among their old friends who would both meet his requirements and find him acceptable as a husband. James and Andrew listened to his story patiently but they gave him little encouragement. They had no Savannah relatives to whom they might look for assistance, for they had been married when they came to America. And the daughters of their old friends had long since married and were raising small children of their own.

'You're not a rich man and you haven't a great family,' said James.

'I've made me money and I can make a great family. And I won't be marrying just anyone.'

'You fly high,' observed Andrew, dryly.

But they did their best for Gerald. James and Andrew were old men and they stood well in Savannah. They had many friends, and for a month they carried Gerald from home to home, to suppers, dances and picnics.

'There's only one who takes me eye,' Gerald said finally. 'And she not even born when I landed here.'

'And who is it takes your eye?'

'Miss Ellen Robillard,' said Gerald, trying to speak casually, for the slightly tilting dark eyes of Ellen Robillard had taken more than his eye. Despite a mystifying listlessness of manner, so strange in a girl of fifteen, she charmed him. Moreover, there was a haunting look of despair about her that went to his heart and made him more gentle with her than he had ever been with any person in all the world.

'And you old enough to be her father!'

'And me in me prime!' cried Gerald, stung.

James spoke quietly.

'Jerry, there's no girl in Savannah you'd have less chance of marrying. Her father is a Robillard, and those French are proud as Lucifer. And her mother – God rest her soul – was a very great lady.'

'I care not,' said Gerald heatedly. 'Besides, her mother is dead, and old man Robillard likes me.'

'As a man, yes, but as a son-in-law, no.'

'The girl wouldn't have you anyway,' interposed Andrew. 'She's been in love with that wild buck of a cousin of hers, Philippe Robillard, for a year now, despite her family being at her morning and night to give him up.'

'He's been gone to Louisiana this month now,' said Gerald.

'And how do you know?'

'I know,' answered Gerald, who did not care to disclose that Pork had supplied this valuable bit of information, or that Philippe had departed for the West at the express desire of his family. 'And I do not think she's been so much in love with him that she won't forget him. Fifteen is too young to know much about love.'

'They'd rather have that breakneck cousin for her than you.'

So, James and Andrew were as startled as anyone when the news came out that the daughter of Pierre Robillard was to marry the little Irishman from up the country. Savannah buzzed behind its doors and speculated about Philippe Robillard, who had gone West, but the gossiping brought no answer. Why the loveliest of the Robillard daughters should marry a loud-voiced, red-faced little man who came hardly up to her ears remained a mystery to all.

Gerald himself never quite knew how it all came about. He only knew that a miracle had happened. And, for once in his life, he was utterly humble when Ellen, very white but very calm, put a light hand on his arm and said: 'I will marry you, Mr O'Hara.'

The thunderstruck Robillards knew the answer in part, but only Ellen and her mammy ever knew the whole story of the night when the girl sobbed till the dawn like a broken-hearted child and rose up in the morning a woman with her mind made up.

With foreboding, Mammy had brought her young mistress a small package, addressed in a strange hand from New Orleans, a package containing a miniature of Ellen, which she flung to the floor with a cry, four letters in her own handwriting to Philippe Robillard, and a brief letter from a New Orleans priest, announcing the death of her cousin in a bar-room brawl.

'They drove him away, Father and Pauline and Eulalie. They drove him away. I hate them. I hate them all. I never want to see them again. I want to get away. I will go away where I'll never see them again, or this town, or anyone who reminds me of – of – him.'

And when the night was nearly spent, Mammy, who had cried herself out over her mistress' dark head, protested, 'But, honey, you kain do dat!'

'I will do it. He is a kind man. I will do it or go into the convent at Charleston.'

It was the threat of the convent that finally won the assent of bewildered and heartstricken Pierre Robillard. He was staunchly Presbyterian, even though his family were Catholic, and the thought of his daughter becoming a nun was even worse than that of her marrying Gerald O'Hara. After all, the man had nothing against him but a lack of family.

So, Ellen, no longer Robillard, turned her back on Savannah, never to see it again, and with a middle-aged husband, Mammy, and twenty 'house niggers' journeyed toward Tara.

The next year, their first child was born and they named her Katie Scarlett, after Gerald's mother. Gerald was disappointed, for he had wanted a son, but he nevertheless was pleased enough over his small black-haired daughter to serve rum to every slave at Tara and to get roaringly, happily drunk himself.

If Ellen had ever regretted her sudden decision to marry him, no one ever knew it, certainly not Gerald, who almost burst with pride whenever he looked at her. She had put Savannah and its memories behind her when she left that gently mannered city by the sea, and, from the moment of her arrival in the County, north Georgia was her home.

When she departed from her father's house forever, she had left a home whose lines were as beautiful and flowing as a woman's body, as a ship in full sail; a pale-pink stucco house built in the French colonial style, set high from the ground in a dainty manner, approached by swirling stairs, banistered with wrought iron as delicate as lace; a dim, rich house, gracious but aloof.

She had left not only that graceful dwelling but also the entire civilization that was behind the building of it, and she found herself in a world that was as strange and different as if she had crossed a continent.

Here in north Georgia was a rugged section held by a hardy people. High up on the plateau at the foot of the Blue Ridge Mountains, she saw rolling red hills wherever she looked, with huge outcroppings of the underlying granite and gaunt pines towering sombrely everywhere. It all seemed wild and untamed to her coast-bred eyes accustomed to the quiet jungle beauty of the sea islands draped in their grey moss and tangled green, the white stretches of beach hot beneath a semi-tropic sun, the long flat vistas of sandy land studded with palmetto and palm.

This was a section that knew the chill of winter, as well as the heat of summer, and there was a vigour and energy in the people that was strange to her. They were a kindly people, courteous, generous, filled with abounding good nature, but sturdy, virile, easy to anger. The people of the Coast which she had left might pride themselves on taking all of their affairs, even their duels and their feuds, with a careless air; but these north Georgia people had a streak of violence in them. On the Coast, life had mellowed – here it was young and lusty and new.

All the people Ellen had known in Savannah might have been cast from the same mould, so similar were their viewpoints and traditions, but here was a variety of people. North Georgia's settlers were coming in from many different places, from other parts of Georgia, from the Carolinas and Virginia, from Europe and the North. Some of them, like Gerald, were new people seeking their fortunes. Some, like Ellen, were members of old families who had found life intolerable in their former homes and sought haven in a distant land. Many had moved for no reason at all, except that the restless blood of pioneering fathers quickened in their veins.

These people, drawn from many different places and with many different backgrounds, gave the whole life of the County an informality that was new to Ellen, an informality to which she never quite accustomed herself. She instinctively knew how Coast people would act in any circumstance. There was never any telling what north Georgians would do.

And, quickening all of the affairs of the section, was the high tide of prosperity then rolling over the South. All of the world was crying out for cotton, and the new land of the County, unworn and fertile, produced it abundantly. Cotton was the heartbeat of the section, the planting and the picking were the diastole and systole of the red earth. Wealth came out of the curving furrows, and arrogance came too – arrogance built on green bushes and the acres of fleecy white. If cotton could make them rich in one generation, how much richer they would be in the next!

This certainty of the morrow gave zest and enthusiasm to life, and the County people enjoyed life with a heartiness that Ellen could never understand. They had money enough and slaves enough to give them time to play, and they liked to play. They seemed never too busy to drop work for a fish-fry, a hunt or a horse race, and scarcely a week went by without its barbecue or ball.

Ellen never would, or could, quite become one of them – she had left too much of herself in Savannah – but she respected them and, in time, learned to admire the frankness and forthrightness of these people, who had few reticences and who valued a man for what he was.

She became the best-loved neighbour in the County. She was a thrifty and kind mistress, a good mother and a devoted wife. The heartbreak and selflessness that she would have dedicated to the Church were devoted instead to the service of her child, her household and the man who had taken her out of Savannah and its memories and had never asked any questions.

When Scarlett was a year old, and more healthy and vigorous than a girl baby had any right to be, in Mammy's opinion, Ellen's second child, named Susan Elinor, but always called Suellen, was born, and in due time came Carreen, listed in the family Bible as Caroline Irene. Then followed three little boys, each of whom died before he had learned to walk – three little boys who now lay under the twisted cedars in the burying-ground a hundred yards from the house, beneath three stones, each bearing the name of 'Gerald O'Hara, Jr'.

From the day when Ellen first came to Tara, the place had been transformed. If she was only fifteen years old, she was nevertheless ready for the responsibilities of the mistress of a plantation. Before marriage, young girls must be, above all other things, sweet, gentle, beautiful and ornamental, but, after marriage, they were expected to manage households that numbered a hundred people or more, white and black, and they were trained with that in view.

Ellen had been given this preparation for marriage which any well-brought-up young lady received, and she also had Mammy, who could galvanize the most shiftless negro into energy. She quickly brought order, dignity and grace into Gerald's household, and she gave to Tara a beauty it had never had before.

The house had been built according to no architectural plan whatever, with extra rooms added where and when it seemed convenient, but, with Ellen's care and attention, it gained a charm that made up for its lack of design. The avenue of cedars leading from the main road to the house – that avenue of cedars without which no Georgia planter's home could be complete – had a cool dark shadiness that gave a brighter tinge, by contrast, to the green of the other trees. The wisteria tumbling over the verandas showed bright against the whitewashed brick, and it joined with the pink crêpe myrtle bushes by the door and the white-blossomed magnolias in the yard to disguise some of the awkward lines of the house.

In springtime and summer, the Bermuda grass and clover on the lawn became emerald, so enticing an emerald that it presented an irresistible temptation to the flocks of turkeys and white geese that were supposed to roam only the regions in the rear of the house. The elders of the flocks continually led stealthy advances into the front yard, lured on by the green of the grass and the luscious promise of the cape jessamine buds and the zinnia beds. Against their depredations, a small black sentinel was stationed on the front porch. Armed with a ragged towel, the little negro boy sitting on the steps was part of the picture of Tara – and an unhappy one, for he was forbidden to chunk the fowls and could only flap the towel at them and shoo them.

Ellen set dozens of little black boys to this task, the first position of responsibility a male slave had at Tara. After they had passed their tenth year, they were sent to old Daddy the plantation cobbler to learn his trade, or to Amos the wheelwright and carpenter, or Phillip the cow man, or Cuffee the mule boy. If they showed no aptitude for any of these trades, they became field hands and, in the opinion of the negroes, they had lost their claim to any social standing at all.

Ellen's life was not easy, nor was it happy, but she did not expect life to be easy, and, if it was not happy, that was woman's lot. It was a man's world, and she accepted it as such. The man owned the property, and the woman managed it. The man took the credit for the management, and the woman praised his cleverness. The man roared like a bull when a splinter was in his finger, and the woman muffled the moans of childbirth, lest she disturb him. Men were rough of speech and often drunk. Women ignored the lapses of speech and put the drunkards to bed without bitter words. Men were rude and outspoken; women were always kind, gracious and forgiving.

She had been reared in the tradition of great ladies, which had taught her how to carry her burden and still retain her charm, and she intended that her three daughters should be great ladies also. With her younger daughters, she had success, for Suellen was so anxious to be attractive she lent an attentive and obedient ear to her mother's teachings, and Carreen was shy and easily led. But Scarlett, child of Gerald, found the road to ladyhood hard.

To Mammy's indignation, her preferred playmates were not her demure sisters or the well-brought-up Wilkes girls but the negro children on the plantation and the boys of the neighbourhood, and she could climb a tree or throw a rock as well as any of them. Mammy was greatly perturbed that Ellen's daughter should display such traits and frequently adjured her to 'ack lak a lil lady'. But Ellen took a more tolerant and long-sighted view of the matter. She knew that from childhood playmates grew beaux in later years, and the first duty of a girl was to get married. She told herself that the child was merely full of life and there was still time in which to teach her the arts and graces of being attractive to men.

To this end, Ellen and Mammy bent their efforts, and as Scarlett grew older she became an apt pupil in this subject, even though she learned little else. Despite a succession of governesses and two years at the near-by Fayetteville Female Academy, her education was sketchy, but no girl in the County danced more gracefully than she. She knew how to smile so that her dimples leaped, how to walk pigeon-toed so that her wide hoop skirts swayed entrancingly, how to look up into a man's face and then drop her eyes and bat the lids rapidly so that she seemed a-tremble with gentle emotion. Most of all she learned how to conceal from men a sharp intelligence beneath a face as sweet and bland as a baby's.

Ellen, by soft-voiced admonition, and Mammy, by constant carping, laboured to inculcate in her the qualities that would make her truly desirable as a wife.

'You must be more gentle, dear, more sedate,' Ellen told her daughter. 'You must not interrupt gentlemen when they are speaking, even if you do know more about matters than they do. Gentlemen do not like forward girls.'

'Young misses whut frowns an' pushes out dey chins an' says "Ah will" an' "Ah woan" mos' gener'ly doan ketch husbands,' prophesied Mammy gloomily. 'Young misses should cas' down dey eyes an' say, "Well, suh, Ah mout" an' "Jes' as you say, suh".'

Between them, they taught her all that a gentlewoman should know, but she learned only the outward signs of gentility. The inner grace from which these signs should spring, she never learned nor did she see any reason for learning it. Appearances were enough, for the appearances of ladyhood won her popularity and that was all she wanted. Gerald bragged that she was the belle of five counties, and with some truth, for she had received proposals from nearly all the young men in the neighbourhood and many from places as far away as Atlanta and Savannah.

At sixteen, thanks to Mammy and Ellen, she looked sweet, charming and giddy, but she was, in reality, self-willed, vain and obstinate. She had the easily stirred passions of her Irish father and nothing except the thinnest veneer of her mother's unselfish and forbearing nature. Ellen never fully realized that it was only a veneer, for Scarlett always showed her best face to her mother, concealing her escapades, curbing her temper and appearing as sweet-natured as she could in Ellen's presence, for her mother could shame her to tears with a reproachful glance.

But Mammy was under no illusions about her and was constantly alert for breaks in the veneer. Mammy's eyes were sharper than Ellen's, and Scarlett could never recall in all her life having fooled Mammy for long.

It was not that these two loving mentors deplored Scarlett's high spirits, vivacity and charm. These were traits of which Southern women were proud. It was Gerald's headstrong and impetuous nature in her that gave them concern, and they sometimes feared they would not be able to conceal her damaging qualities until she had made a good match. But Scarlett intended to marry – and marry Ashley – and she was willing to appear demure, pliable and scatterbrained, if those were the qualities that attracted men. Just why men should be this way, she did not know. She only knew that such methods worked. It never interested her enough to try to think out the reason for it, for she knew nothing of the inner workings of any human being's mind, not even her own. She knew only that if she did or said thus-and-so, men would unerringly respond with the complementary thus-and-so. It was like a mathematical formula and no more difficult, for mathematics was the one subject that had come easy to Scarlett in her schooldays.

If she knew little about men's minds, she knew even less about the minds of women, for they interested her less. She had never had a girl friend, and she never felt any lack on that account. To her, all women, including her two sisters, were natural enemies in pursuit of the same prey – man.

All women with the one exception of her mother.

Ellen O'Hara was different, and Scarlett regarded her as something holy and apart from all the rest of humankind. When Scarlett was a child, she had confused her mother with the Virgin Mary, and now that she was older she saw no reason for changing her opinion. To her, Ellen represented the utter security that only Heaven or a mother can give. She knew that her mother was the embodiment of justice, truth, loving tenderness and profound wisdom – a great lady.

Scarlett wanted very much to be like her mother. The only difficulty was that by being just and truthful and tender and unselfish, one missed most of the joys of life, and certainly many beaux. And life was too short to miss such pleasant things. Some day when she was married to Ashley and old, some day when she had time for it, she intended to be like Ellen. But, until then . . .

Chapter IV

That night at supper, Scarlett went through the motions of presiding over the table in her mother's absence, but her mind was in a ferment over the dreadful news she had heard about Ashley and Melanie. Desperately she longed for her mother's return from the Slatterys', for, without her, she felt lost and alone. What right had the Slatterys and their everlasting sickness to take Ellen away from home just at this time when she, Scarlett, needed her so much?

Throughout the dismal meal, Gerald's booming voice battered against her ears until she thought she could endure it no longer. He had forgotten completely about his conversation with her that afternoon and was carrying on a monologue about the latest news from Fort Sumter, which he punctuated by hammering his fist on the table and waving his arms in the air. Gerald made a habit of dominating the conversation at mealtimes, and usually Scarlett, occupied with her own thoughts, scarcely heard him; but tonight she could not shut out his voice, no matter how much she strained to listen for the sound of carriage wheels that would herald Ellen's return.

Of course, she did not intend to tell her mother what was so heavy on her heart, for Ellen would be shocked and grieved to know that a daughter of hers wanted a man who was engaged to another girl. But, in the depths of the first tragedy she had ever known, she wanted the very comfort of her mother's presence. She always felt secure when Ellen was by her, for there was nothing so bad that Ellen could not better it, simply by being there.

She rose suddenly from her chair at the sound of creaking wheels in the driveway and then sank down again as they went on around the house to the back yard. It could not be Ellen, for she would alight at the front steps. Then there was an excited babble of negro voices in the darkness of the yard and high-pitched negro laughter. Looking out of the window, Scarlett saw Pork, who had left the room a moment before, holding high a flaring pine knot, while indistinguishable figures descended from a wagon. The laughter and talking rose and fell in the dark night air, pleasant, homely, carefree sounds, gutturally soft, musically shrill. Then feet shuffled up the back-porch stairs and into the passageway leading to the main house, stopping in the hall just outside the dining-room. There was a brief interval of whispering, and Pork entered, his usual dignity gone, his eyes rolling and his white teeth a-gleam.

'Mist' Gerald,' he announced, breathing hard, the pride of a bridegroom all over his shining face, 'yo' new 'oman done come.'

'New woman? I didn't buy any new woman,' declared Gerald, pretending to glare.

'Yassah, you did, Mist' Gerald! Yassah! An' she out hyah now wantin' ter speak wid you,' answered Pork, giggling and twisting his hands in excitement.

'Well, bring in the bride,' said Gerald, and Pork, turning, beckoned into the hall to his wife, newly arrived from the Wilkes plantation to become a part of the household of Tara. She entered, and behind her, almost hidden by her voluminous calico skirts, came her twelve-year-old daughter, squirming against her mother's legs.

Dilcey was tall and bore herself erectly. She might have been any age from thirty to sixty, so unlined was her immobile bronze face. Indian blood was plain in her features, overbalancing the negroid characteristics. The red colour of her skin, narrow high forehead, prominent cheek-bones and the hawk-bridged nose which flattened at the end above thick negro lips, all showed the mixture of two races. She was self-possessed and walked with a dignity that surpassed even Mammy's, for Mammy had acquired her dignity and Dilcey's was in her blood.

When she spoke, her voice was not so slurred as most negroes' and she chose her words more carefully.

'Good evenin', young Misses. Mist' Gerald, I is sorry to 'sturb you, but I wanted to come here and thank you agin fo' buyin' me and my chile. Lots of gentlemens might a' bought me but they wouldn't a' bought my Prissy, too, jes' to keep me frum grievin' and I thanks you. I'm gwine do my bes' fo' you and show you I ain't forgettin'.'

'Hum – hurrump,' said Gerald, clearing his throat in embarrassment at being caught openly in an act of kindness.

Dilcey turned to Scarlett and something like a smile wrinkled the corners of her eyes. 'Miss Scarlett, Poke done tole me how you ast Mist' Gerald to buy me. And so I'm gwine give you my Prissy fo' yo' own maid.'

She reached behind her and jerked the little girl forward. She was a brown little creature, with skinny legs like a bird and a myriad of pigtails carefully wrapped with twine sticking stiffly out from her head. She had sharp, knowing eyes that missed nothing and a studiedly stupid look on her face.

'Thank you, Dilcey,' Scarlett replied, 'but I'm afraid Mammy will have something to say about that. She's been my maid ever since I was born.'

'Mammy gettin' ole,' said Dilcey, with a calmness that would have enraged Mammy. 'She a good mammy, but you a young lady now and needs a good maid, and my Prissy been maidin' fo' Miss India fo' a year now. She kin sew and fix hair good as a grown pusson.'

Prodded by her mother, Prissy bobbed a sudden curtsy and grinned at Scarlett, who could not help grinning back.

'A sharp little wench,' she thought, and said aloud: 'Thank you, Dilcey, we'll see about it when Mother comes home.'

'Thank'ee, Ma'm. I gives you good night,' said Dilcey, and, turning, left the room with her child, Pork dancing attendance.

The supper things cleared away, Gerald resumed his oration, but with little satisfaction to himself and none at all to his audience. His thunderous predictions of immediate war and his rhetorical questions as to whether the South would stand for further insults from the Yankees only produced faintly bored, 'Yes, Papas' and 'No, Pas'. Carreen, sitting on a hassock under the big lamp, was deep in the romance of a girl who had taken the veil after her lover's death and, with silent tears of enjoyment oozing from her eyes, was pleasurably picturing herself in a white coif. Suellen, embroidering on what she gigglingly called her 'hope chest', was wondering if she could possibly detach Stuart Tarleton from her sister's side at the barbecue tomorrow and fascinate him with the sweet womanly qualities which she possessed and Scarlett did not. And Scarlett was in a tumult about Ashley.

How could Pa talk on and on about Fort Sumter and the Yankees when he knew her heart was breaking? As usual in the very young, she marvelled that people could be so selfishly oblivious to her pain and the world rock along just the same, in spite of her heartbreak.

Her mind was as if a cyclone had gone through it, and it seemed strange that the dining-room where they sat should be so placid, so unchanged from what it had always been. The heavy mahogany table and sideboards, the massive silver, the bright rag rugs on the shining floor were all in their accustomed places, just as if nothing had happened. It was a friendly and comfortable room and, ordinarily, Scarlett loved the quiet hours which the family spent there after supper; but tonight she hated the sight of it and, if she had not feared her father's loudly bawled questions, she would have slipped away, down the dark hall to Ellen's little office and cried out her sorrow on the old sofa.

That was the room that Scarlett liked best in all the house. There, Ellen sat before her tall secretary each morning, keeping the accounts of the plantation and listening to the reports of Jonas Wilkerson, the overseer. There also the family idled while Ellen's quill scratched across her ledgers, Gerald in the old rocker, the girls on the sagging cushions of the sofa that was too battered and worn for the front of the house. Scarlett longed to be there now, alone with Ellen, so she could put her head in her mother's lap and cry in peace. Wouldn't Mother ever come home?

Then, wheels ground sharply on the gravelled driveway, and the soft murmur of Ellen's voice dismissing the coachman floated into the room. The whole group looked up eagerly as she entered rapidly, her hoops swaying, her face tired and sad. There entered with her the faint fragrance of lemon verbena sachet, which seemed always to creep from the folds of her dresses, a fragrance that was always linked in Scarlett's mind with her mother. Mammy followed at a few paces, the leather bag in her hand, her underlip pushed out and her brow lowering. Mammy muttered darkly to herself as she waddled, taking care that her remarks were pitched too low to be understood but loud enough to register her unqualified disapproval.

'I am sorry I am so late,' said Ellen, slipping her plaid shawl from drooping shoulders and handing it to Scarlett, whose cheek she patted in passing.

Gerald's face had brightened as if by magic at her entrance.

'Is the brat baptized?' he questioned.

'Yes, and dead, poor thing,' said Ellen. 'I feared Emmie would die too, but I think she will live.'

The girls' faces turned to her, startled and questioning, and Gerald wagged his head philosophically.

'Well, 'tis better so that the brat is dead, no doubt, poor fatherle—'

'It is late. We had better have prayers now,' interrupted Ellen so smoothly that, if Scarlett had not known her mother well, the interruption would have passed unnoticed.

It would be interesting to know who was the father of Emmie Slattery's baby, but Scarlett knew she would never learn the truth of the matter if she waited to hear it from her mother. Scarlett suspected Jonas Wilkerson, for she had frequently seen him walking down the road with Emmie at nightfall. Jonas was a Yankee and a bachelor, and the fact that he was an overseer forever barred him from any contact with the County social life. There was no family of any standing into which he could marry, no people with whom he could associate except the Slatterys and riff-raff like them. As he was several cuts above the Slatterys in education, it was only natural that he should not want to marry Emmie, no matter how often he might walk with her in the twilight.

Scarlett sighed, for her curiosity was sharp. Things were always happening under her mother's eyes which she noticed no more than if they had not happened at all. Ellen ignored all things contrary to her ideas of propriety and tried to teach Scarlett to do the same, but with poor success.

Ellen had stepped to the mantel to take her rosary beads from the small inlaid casket in which they always reposed when Mammy spoke up with firmness.

'Miss Ellen, you gwine eat some supper befo' you does any prayin'.'

'Thank you, Mammy, but I am not hungry.'

'Ah gwine fix yo' supper mahseff an' you eats it,' said Mammy, her brow furrowed with indignation as she started down the hall for the kitchen. 'Poke!' she called, 'tell Cookie stir up de fiah. Miss Ellen home.'

As the boards shuddered under her weight, the soliloquy she had been muttering in the front hall grew louder and louder, coming clearly to the ears of the family in the dining-room.

'Ah has said time an' agin, it doan do no good doin' nuthin' fer w'ite trash. Dey is de shiflesses', mos' ungrateful passel of no-counts livin'. An' Miss Ellen got no bizness weahin' herseff out waitin' on folks dat did dey be wuth shootin' dey'd have niggers ter wait on dem. An' Ah has said—'

Her voice trailed off as she went down the long open passageway, covered only by a roof, that led into the kitchen. Mammy had her own method of letting her owners know exactly where she stood on all matters. She knew it was beneath the dignity of quality white folks to pay the slightest attention to what a darky said when she was just grumbling to herself. She knew that to uphold this dignity, they must ignore what she said, even if she stood in the next room and almost shouted. It protected her from reproof, and it left no doubt in anyone's mind as to her exact views on any subject.

Pork entered the room, bearing a plate, silver and a napkin. He was followed closely by Jack, a black little boy of ten, hastily buttoning a white linen jacket with one hand and bearing in the other a fly-swisher, made of thin strips of newspaper tied to a reed longer than he was. Ellen had a beautiful peacock-feather fly-brusher, but it was used only on very special occasions and then only after domestic struggle, due to the obstinate conviction of Pork, Cookie and Mammy that peacock feathers were bad luck.

Ellen sat down in the chair which Gerald pulled out for her and four voices attacked her.

'Mother, the lace is loose on my new ball dress and I want to wear it tomorrow night at Twelve Oaks. Won't you please fix it?'

'Mother, Scarlett's new dress is prettier than mine and I look like a fright in pink. Why can't she wear my pink and let me wear her green? She looks all right in pink.'

'Mother, can I stay up for the ball tomorrow night? I'm thirteen now—'

'Mrs O'Hara, would you believe it— Hush, you girls, before I take me crop to you! Cade Calvert was in Atlanta this morning and he says – Will you be quiet and let me be hearing me own voice? – and he says it's all upset they are there and talking nothing but war, militia drilling, troops forming. And he says the news from Charleston is that they will be putting up with no more Yankee insults.'

Ellen's tired mouth smiled into the tumult as she addressed herself first to her husband, as a wife should.

'If the nice people of Charleston feel that way, I'm sure we will all feel the same way soon,' she said, for she had a deeply rooted belief that, excepting only Savannah, most of the gentle blood of the whole continent could be found in that small seaport city, a belief shared largely by Charlestonians.

'No, Carreen, next year, dear. Then you can stay up for balls and wear grown-up dresses, and what a good time my little pink cheeks will have! Don't pout, dear. You can go to the barbecue, remember that, and stay up through supper, but no balls till you are fourteen.

'Give me your gown, Scarlett. I will whip the lace for you after prayers.

'Suellen, I do not like your tone, dear. Your pink gown is lovely and suitable to your complexion, as Scarlett's is to hers. But you may wear my garnet necklace tomorrow night.'

Suellen, behind her mother's back, wrinkled her nose triumphantly at Scarlett, who had been planning to beg the necklace for herself. Scarlett put out her tongue at her. Suellen was an annoying sister with her whining and selfishness, and had it not been for Ellen's restraining hand, Scarlett would frequently have boxed her ears.

'Now, Mr O'Hara, tell me more about what Mr Calvert said about Charleston,' said Ellen.

Scarlett knew her mother cared nothing at all about war and politics and thought them masculine matters about which no lady could intelligently concern herself. But it gave Gerald pleasure to air his views, and Ellen was unfailingly thoughtful of her husband's pleasure.

While Gerald launched forth on his news, Mammy set the plates before her mistress, golden-topped biscuits, breast of fried chicken and a yellow yam open and steaming, with melted butter dripping from it. Mammy pinched small Jack, and he hastened to his business of slowly swishing the paper ribbons back and forth behind Ellen. Mammy stood beside the table, watching every forkful that travelled from plate to mouth, as though she intended to force the food down Ellen's throat should she see signs of flagging. Ellen ate diligently, but Scarlett could see that she was too tired to know what she was eating. Only Mammy's implacable face forced her to it.

When the dish was empty and Gerald only midway in his remarks on the thievishness of Yankees who wanted to free darkies and yet offered no penny to pay for their freedom, Ellen rose.

'We'll be having prayers?' he questioned, reluctantly.

'Yes. It is so late – why, it is actually ten o'clock,' as the clock with coughing and tinny thumps marked the hour. 'Carreen should have been asleep long ago. The lamp, please, Pork, and my prayer-book, Mammy.'

Prompted by Mammy's hoarse whisper, Jack set his fly-brush in the corner and removed the dishes, while Mammy fumbled in the sideboard drawer for Ellen's worn prayer-book. Pork, tiptoeing, reached the ring in the chain and drew the lamp slowly down until the table top was brightly bathed in light and the ceiling receded into shadows. Ellen arranged her skirts and sank to the floor on her knees, laying the open prayer-book on the table before her and clasping her hands upon it. Gerald knelt beside her, and Scarlett and Suellen took their accustomed places on the opposite side of the table, folding their voluminous petticoats in pads under their knees, so they would ache less from contact with the hard floor. Carreen, who was small for her age, could not kneel comfortably at the table and so knelt facing a chair, her elbows on the seat. She liked this position, for she seldom failed to go to sleep during prayers and, in this posture, it escaped her mother's notice.

The house servants shuffled and rustled in the hall to kneel by the doorway, Mammy groaning aloud as she sank down, Pork straight as a ramrod, Rosa and Teena, the maids, graceful in their spreading bright calicoes, Cookie gaunt and yellow beneath her snowy head-rag, and Jack, stupid with sleep, as far away from Mammy's pinching fingers as possible. Their dark eyes gleamed expectantly, for praying with their white folks was one of the events of the day. The old and colourful phrases of the litany with its Oriental imagery meant little to them but it satisfied something in their hearts, and they always swayed when they chanted the responses: 'Lord, have mercy on us,' 'Christ, have mercy on us.'

Ellen closed her eyes and began praying, her voice rising and falling, lulling and soothing. Heads bowed in the circle of yellow light as Ellen thanked God for the health and happiness of her home, her family and her negroes.

When she had finished her prayers for those beneath the roof of Tara, her father, mother, sister, three dead babies and 'all the poor souls in Purgatory', she clasped her white beads between long fingers and began the Rosary. Like the rushing of a soft wind, the responses from black throats and white throats rolled back:

'Holy Mary, Mother of God, pray for us sinners, now, and at the hour of our death.'

Despite her heartache and the pain of unshed tears, a deep sense of quiet and peace fell upon Scarlett as it always did at this hour. Some of the disappointment of the day and the dread of the morrow departed from her, leaving a feeling of hope. It was not the lifting up of her heart to God which brought this balm, for religion went no more than lip-deep with her. It was the sight of her mother's serene face upturned to the throne of God and His saints and angels, praying for blessings on those whom she loved. When Ellen intervened with Heaven, Scarlett felt certain that Heaven heard.

Ellen finished and Gerald, who could never find his beads at prayer time, began furtively counting his decade on his fingers. As his voice droned on, Scarlett's thoughts strayed, in spite of herself. She knew she should be examining her conscience. Ellen had taught her that at the end of each day it was her duty to examine her conscience thoroughly, to admit her numerous faults and pray to God for forgiveness and strength never to repeat them. But Scarlett was examining her heart.

She dropped her head upon her folded hands so that her mother could not see her face, and her thoughts went sadly back to Ashley. How could he be planning to marry Melanie when he really loved her, Scarlett? And when he knew how much she loved him? How could he deliberately break her heart?

Then, suddenly, an idea, shining and new, flashed like a comet through her brain.

'Why, Ashley hasn't an idea that I'm in love with him!'

She almost gasped aloud in the shock of its unexpectedness. Her mind stood still as if paralysed for a long, breathless instant, and then raced forward.

'How could he know? I've always acted so prissy and ladylike and touch-me-not around him he probably thinks I don't care a thing about him except as a friend. Yes, that's why he's never spoken! He thinks his love is hopeless. And that's why he's looked so—'

Her mind went swiftly back to those times when she had caught him looking at her in that strange manner, when the grey eyes that were such perfect curtains for his thoughts had been wide and naked and had in them a look of torment and despair.

'He's been broken-hearted because he thinks I'm in love with Brent or Stuart or Cade. And probably he thinks that if he can't have me, he might as well please his family and marry Melanie. But if he knew I did love him—'

Her volatile spirits shot up from the deepest depression to excited happiness. This was the answer to Ashley's reticence, to his strange conduct. He didn't know! Her vanity leaped to the aid of her desire to believe, making belief a certainty. If he knew she loved him, he would hasten to her side. She had only to—

'Oh!' she thought rapturously, digging her fingers into her lowered brow. 'What a fool I've been not to think of this till now! I must think of some way to let him know. He wouldn't marry her if he knew I loved him! How could he?'

With a start, she realized that Gerald had finished and her mother's eyes were on her. Hastily she began her decade, telling off the beads automatically but with a depth of emotion in her voice that caused Mammy to open her eyes and shoot a searching glance at her. As she finished her prayers and Suellen, then Carreen, began their decades, her mind was still speeding onward with her entrancing new thought.

Even now, it wasn't too late! Too often the County had been scandalized by elopements when one or the other of the participating parties was practically at the altar with a third. And Ashley's engagement had not even been announced yet! Yes, there was plenty of time!

If no love lay between Ashley and Melanie but only a promise given long ago, then why wasn't it possible for him to break that promise and marry her? Surely he would do it, if he knew that she, Scarlett, loved him. She must find some way to let him know. She would find some way! And then—

Scarlett came abruptly out of her dream of delight, for she had neglected to make the responses and her mother was looking at her reprovingly. As she resumed the ritual, she opened her eyes briefly and cast a quick glance around the room. The kneeling figures, the soft glow of the lamp, the dim shadows where the negroes swayed, even the familiar objects that had been so hateful to her sight an hour ago, in an instant took on the colour of her own emotions, and the room seemed once more a lovely place. She would never forget this moment or this scene!

'Virgin most faithful!' her mother intoned. The Litany of the Virgin was beginning, and obediently Scarlett responded: 'Pray for us,' as Ellen praised in soft contralto the attributes of the Mother of God.

As always since childhood, this was, for Scarlett, a moment for adoration of Ellen, rather than the Virgin. Sacrilegious though it might be, Scarlett always saw, through her closed eyes, the upturned face of Ellen and not the Blessed Virgin, as the ancient phrases were repeated. 'Health of the Sick', 'Seat of Wisdom', 'Refuge of Sinners', 'Mystical Rose' – they were beautiful words because they were the attributes of Ellen. But tonight, because of the exaltation of her own spirit, Scarlett found in the whole ceremonial, the softly spoken words, the murmur of the responses, a surpassing beauty beyond any that she had ever experienced before. And her heart went up to God in sincere thankfulness that a pathway for her feet had been opened – out of her misery and straight to the arms of Ashley.

When the last 'Amen' sounded, they all rose, somewhat stiffly, Mammy being hauled to her feet by the combined efforts of Teena and Rosa. Pork took a long spiller from the mantelpiece, lit it from the lamp-flame and went into the hall. Opposite the winding stair stood a walnut sideboard, too large for use in the dining-room, bearing on its wide top several lamps and a long row of candles in candlesticks. Pork lit one lamp and three candles and, with the pompous dignity of a first chamberlain of the royal bedchamber lighting a king and queen to their rooms, he led the procession up the stairs, holding the light high above his head. Ellen, on Gerald's arm, followed him, and the girls, each taking her own candlestick, mounted after them.

Scarlett entered her room, set the candle on the tall chest of drawers and fumbled in the dark closet for the dancing dress that needed stitching. Throwing it across her arm, she crossed the hall quietly. The door of her parents' bedroom was slightly ajar and, before she could knock, Ellen's voice, low but stern, came to her ears.

'Mr O'Hara, you must dismiss Jonas Wilkerson.'

Gerald exploded, 'And where will I be getting another overseer who wouldn't be cheating me out of my eyeteeth?'

'He must be dismissed, immediately, tomorrow morning. Big Sam is a good foreman and he can take over the duties until you can hire another overseer.'

'Ah, ha!' came Gerald's voice. 'So, I understand! Then the worthy Jonas sired the—'

'He must be dismissed.'

'So, he is the father of Emmie Slattery's baby,' thought Scarlett. 'Oh, well. What else can you expect from a Yankee man and a white-trash girl?'

Then, after a discreet pause which gave Gerald's splutterings time to die away, she knocked on the door and handed the dress to her mother.

By the time Scarlett had undressed and blown out the candle, her plan for tomorrow had worked itself out in every detail. It was a simple plan, for, with Gerald's single-mindedness of purpose, her eyes were centred on the goal and she thought only of the most direct steps by which to reach it.

First, she would be 'prideful', as Gerald had commanded. From the moment she arrived at Twelve Oaks, she would be her gayest, most spirited self. No one would suspect that she had ever been downhearted because of Ashley and Melanie. And she would flirt with every man there. That would be cruel to Ashley, but it would make him yearn for her all the more. She wouldn't overlook a man of marriageable age, from ginger-whiskered old Frank Kennedy, who was Suellen's beau, on down to shy, quiet, blushing Charles Hamilton, Melanie's brother. They would swarm around her like bees around a hive, and certainly Ashley would be drawn from Melanie to join the circle of her admirers. Then somehow she would manoeuvre to get a few minutes alone with him, away from the crowd. She hoped everything would work out that way, because it would be more difficult otherwise. But if Ashley didn't make the first move, she would simply have to do it herself.

When they were finally alone, he would have fresh in his mind the picture of the other men thronging about her, he would be newly impressed with the fact that every one of them wanted her, and that look of sadness and despair would be in his eyes. Then she would make him happy again by letting him discover that, popular though she was, she preferred him above any other man in all the world. And when she admitted it, modestly and sweetly, she would look a thousand things more. Of course, she would do it all in a ladylike way. She wouldn't even dream of saying to him boldly that she loved him – that would never do. But the manner of telling him was a detail that troubled her not at all. She had managed such situations before and she could do it again.

Lying in the bed with the moonlight streaming dimly over her, she pictured the whole scene in her mind. She saw the look of surprise and happiness that would come over his face when he realized that she really loved him, and she heard the words he would say asking her to be his wife.

Naturally, she would have to say then that she simply couldn't think of marrying a man when he was engaged to another girl, but he would insist and finally she would let herself be persuaded. Then they would decide to run off to Jonesboro that very afternoon and—

Why, by this time tomorrow night, she might be Mrs Ashley Wilkes!

She sat up in bed, hugging her knees, and for a long happy moment she *was* Mrs Ashley Wilkes – Ashley's bride! Then a slight chill entered her heart. Suppose it didn't work out this way? Suppose Ashley didn't beg her to run away with him? Resolutely she pushed the thought from her mind.

'I won't think of that now,' she said firmly. 'If I think of it now, it will upset me. There's no reason why things won't come out the way I want them – if he loves me. And I know he does!'

She raised her chin and her pale, black-fringed eyes sparkled in the moon-light. Ellen had never told her that desire and attainment were two different matters; life had not taught her that the race was not to the swift. She lay in the silvery shadows with courage rising and made the plans that a sixteen-year-old makes when life has been so pleasant that defeat is an impossibility and a pretty dress and a clear complexion are weapons to vanquish fate.

Chapter V

It was ten o'clock in the morning. The day was warm for April and the golden sunlight streamed brilliantly into Scarlett's room through the blue curtains of the wide windows. The cream-coloured walls glowed with light and the depths of the mahogany furniture gleamed deep red like wine, while the floor glistened as if it were glass, except where the rag rugs covered it and they were spots of gay colour.

Already summer was in the air, the first hint of Georgia summer when the high tide of spring gives way reluctantly before a fiercer heat. A balmy, soft warmth poured into the room, heavy with velvety smells, redolent of many blossoms, of newly fledged trees and of the moist, freshly turned red earth. Through the window Scarlett could see the bright riot of the twin lines of daffodils bordering the gravelled driveway and the golden masses of yellow jessamine spreading flowery spangles modestly to the earth like crinolines. The mocking-birds and the jays, engaged in their old feud for possession of the magnolia tree beneath her window, were bickering, the jays strident, acrimonious, the mockers sweet-voiced and plaintive.

Such a glowing morning usually called Scarlett to the window, to lean arms on the broad sill and drink in the scents and sounds of Tara. But today she had no eye for sun or azure sky beyond a hasty thought, 'Thank God, it isn't raining.' On the bed lay the apple-green, watered-silk ball dress with its festoons of ecru lace, neatly packed in a large cardboard box. It was ready to be carried to Twelve Oaks to be donned before the dancing began, but Scarlett shrugged at the sight of it. If her plans were successful, she would not wear that dress tonight. Long before the ball began, she and Ashley would be on their way to Jonesboro to be married. The troublesome question was – what dress should she wear to the barbecue?

What dress would best set off her charms and make her most irresistible to Ashley? Since eight o'clock she had been trying on and rejecting dresses, and now she stood dejected and irritable in lace pantalets, linen corset cover and three billowing lace and linen petticoats. Discarded garments lay about her on the floor, the bed, the chairs, in bright heaps of colour and straying ribbons.

The rose organdie with long pink sash was becoming, but she had worn it last summer when Melanie visited Twelve Oaks and she'd be sure to remember it. And might be catty enough to mention it. The black bombazine, with its puffed sleeves and princess lace collar, set off her white skin superbly, but it did make her look a trifle elderly. Scarlett peered anxiously in the mirror at her sixteen-year-old face as if expecting to see wrinkles and sagging chin muscles. It would never do to appear sedate and elderly before Melanie's sweet youthfulness. The lavender-barred muslin was beautiful with those wide insets of lace and net about the hem, but it had never suited her type. It would suit Carreen's delicate profile and wishy-washy expression perfectly, but Scarlett felt that it made her look like a schoolgirl. It would never do to appear schoolgirlish beside Melanie's poised self. The green plaid taffeta, frothing with flounces and each flounce edged in green velvet ribbon, was most becoming, in fact her favourite dress, for it darkened her eyes to emerald. But there was unmistakably a grease spot on the front of the basque. Of course, her brooch could be pinned over the spot, but perhaps Melanie had sharp eyes. There remained varicoloured cotton dresses which Scarlett felt were not festive enough for the occasion, ball dresses and the green sprigged muslin she had worn yesterday. But it was an afternoon dress. It was not suitable for a barbecue, for it had only tiny puffed sleeves and the neck was low enough for a dancing dress. But there was nothing else to do but wear it. After all, she was not ashamed of her neck and arms and bosom, even if it was not correct to show them in the morning.

As she stood before the mirror and twisted herself about to get a side view, she thought that there was absolutely nothing about her figure to cause her shame. Her neck was short but rounded and her arms plump and enticing. Her breasts, pushed high by her stays, were very nice breasts. She had never had to sew tiny rows of silk ruffles in the lining of her basques, as most sixteen-year-old girls did, to give their figures the desired curves and fullness. She was glad she had inherited Ellen's slender white hands and tiny feet, and she wished she had Ellen's height, too, but her own height pleased her very well. What a pity legs could not be shown, she thought, pulling up her petticoats and regretfully viewing them, plump and neat under pantalets. She had such nice legs. Even the girls at the Fayetteville Academy had admitted as much. And as for her waist – there was no one in Fayetteville, Jonesboro or in three counties, for that matter, who had so small a waist.

The thought of her waist brought her back to practical matters. The green muslin measured seventeen inches about the waist, and Mammy had laced her for the eighteen-inch bombazine. Mammy would have to lace her tighter. She pushed open the door, listened and heard Mammy's heavy tread in the downstairs hall. She shouted for her impatiently, knowing she could raise her voice with impunity, as Ellen was in the smokehouse, measuring out the day's food to Cookie.

'Some folks thinks as how Ah kin fly,' grumbled Mammy, shuffling up the stairs. She entered puffing, with the expression of one who expects battle and welcomes it. In her large black hands was a tray upon which food smoked, two large yams covered with butter, a pile of buckwheat cakes dripping syrup, and a large slice of ham swimming in gravy. Catching sight of Mammy's burden, Scarlett's expression changed from one of minor irritation to obstinate belligerency. In the excitement of trying on dresses she had forgotten Mammy's ironclad rule that, before going to any party, the O'Hara girls must be crammed so full of food at home they would be unable to eat any refreshments at the party.

'It's no use. I won't eat it. You can just take it back to the kitchen.'

Mammy set the tray on the table and squared herself, hands on hips.

'Yas'm, you is! Ah ain' figgerin' on havin' happen whut happen at dat las' barbecue w'en Ah wuz too sick frum dem chittlins Ah et ter fetch you no tray befo' you went. You is gwine eat eve'y bite of dis.'

'I am not! Now, come here and lace me tighter because we are late already. I heard the carriage come round to the front of the house.'

Mammy's tone became wheedling.

'Now, Miss Scarlett, you be good an' come eat jes' a lil. Miss Carreen an' Miss Suellen done eat all dey'n.'

'They would,' said Scarlett contemptuously. 'They haven't any more spirit than a rabbit. But I won't! I'm through with trays. I'm not forgetting the time I ate a whole tray and went to the Calverts' and they had ice-cream out of ice they'd brought all the way from Savannah, and I couldn't eat but a spoonful. I'm going to have a good time today and eat as much as I please.'

At this defiant heresy, Mammy's brow lowered with indignation. What a young miss could do and what she could not do were as different as black and white in Mammy's mind; there was no middle ground of deportment between. Suellen and Carreen were clay in her powerful hands and harkened respectfully to her warnings. But it had always been a struggle to teach Scarlett that most of her natural impulses were unladylike. Mammy's victories over Scarlett were hard-won and represented guile unknown to the white mind.

'Ef you doan care 'bout how folks talks 'bout dis fambly, Ah does,' she rumbled. 'Ah ain' gwine stand by an' have eve'ybody at de pahty sayin' how you ain' fotched up right. Ah has tole you an' tole you dat you kin allus tell a lady by dat she eat lak a bird. An' Ah ain' aimin' ter have you go ter Mist' Wilkes' an' eat lak a fe'el han' an' gobble lak a hawg.'

'Mother is a lady and she eats,' countered Scarlett.

'W'en you is mahied, you kin eat, too,' retorted Mammy. 'W'en Miss Ellen yo' age, she never et nuthin' w'en she went out, an' needer yo' Aunt Pauline nor yo' Aunt Eulalie. An' dey all done mahied. Young misses whut eats heavy mos' gener'ly doan never ketch husbands.'

'I don't believe it. At that barbecue when you were sick and I didn't eat beforehand, Ashley Wilkes told me he *liked* to see a girl with a healthy appetite.'

Mammy shook her head ominously.

'Whut gempmums says an' whut dey thinks is two diffunt things. An' Ah ain' noticed Mist' Ashley axing fer ter mahy you.'

Scarlett scowled, started to speak sharply and then caught herself. Mammy had her there and there was no argument. Seeing the obdurate look on Scarlett's face, Mammy picked up the tray and, with the bland guile of her race, changed her tactics. As she started for the door, she sighed.

'Well'm, awright. Ah wuz tellin' Cookie w'ile she wuz a-fixin' dis tray "You kin sho tell a lady by whut she *doan* eat," an' Ah say ter Cookie, "Ah ain' never seed no w'ite lady who et less'n Miss Melly Hamilton did las' time she wuz visitin' Mist' Ashley" – Ah means, visitin' Miss India.'

Scarlett shot a look of sharp suspicion at her, but Mammy's broad face carried only a look of innocence and of regret that Scarlett was not the lady Melanie Hamilton was.

'Put down that tray and come lace me tighter,' said Scarlett irritably. 'And I'll try to eat a little afterwards. If I ate now I couldn't lace tight enough.'

Cloaking her triumph, Mammy set down the tray.

'Whut mah lamb gwine wear?'

'That,' answered Scarlett, pointing at the fluffy mass of green flowered muslin. Instantly Mammy was in arms.

'No, you ain'. It ain' fittin' fer mawnin'. You kain show yo' buzzum befo' three o'clock an' dat dress ain' got no neck an' no sleeves. An' you'll git freckled sho as you born, an' Ah ain' figgerin' on you gittin' freckled affer all de buttermilk Ah been puttin' on you all dis winter, bleachin' dem freckles you got at Savannah settin' on de beach. Ah sho gwine speak ter yo' Ma 'bout you.'

'If you say one word to her before I'm dressed I won't eat a bite,' said

Scarlett coolly. 'Mother won't have time to send me back to change once I'm dressed.'

Mammy sighed resignedly, beholding herself outguessed. Between the two evils, it was better to have Scarlett wear an afternoon dress at a morning barbecue than to have her gobble like a hog.

'Hole onter sumpin' an' suck in yo' breaf,' she commanded.

Scarlett obeyed, bracing herself and catching firm hold of one of the bedposts. Mammy pulled and jerked vigorously and, as the tiny circumference of whalebone-girdled waist grew smaller, a proud, fond look came into her eyes.

'Ain' nobody got a wais' lak mah lamb,' she said approvingly. 'Eve'y time Ah pulls Miss Suellen littler dan twenty inches, she up an' faint!'

'Pooh!' gasped Scarlett, speaking with difficulty. 'I never fainted in my life.'

'Well, 'twouldn' do no hahm ef you wuz ter faint now an' den,' advised Mammy. 'You is so brash sometimes, Miss Scarlett. Ah been aimin' ter tell you, it jes' doan look good de way you doan faint 'bout snakes an' mouses an' sech. Ah doan mean round home but w'en you is out in comp'ny. An' Ah has tole you an'—'

'Oh, hurry! Don't talk so much. I'll catch a husband. See if I don't, even if I don't scream and faint. Goodness, but my stays are tight! Put on the dress.'

Mammy carefully dropped the twelve yards of green sprigged muslin over the mountainous petticoats and hooked up the back of the tight, low-cut basque.

'You keep yo' shawl on yo' shoulders w'en you is in de sun, an' doan you go takin' off yo' hat w'en you is wahm,' she commanded. 'Elsewise you be comin' home lookin' brown lak Ole Miz Slattery. Now, you come eat, honey, but doan eat too fas'. No use havin' it come right back up agin.'

Scarlett obediently sat down before the tray, wondering if she would be able to get any food into her stomach and still have room to breathe. Mammy plucked a large towel from the washstand and carefully tied it around Scarlett's neck, spreading the white folds over her lap. Scarlett began on the ham, because she liked ham, and forced it down.

'I wish to Heaven I was married,' she said resentfully as she attacked the yams with loathing. 'I'm tired of everlastingly being unnatural and never doing anything I want to do. I'm tired of acting like I don't eat more than a bird, and walking when I want to run and saying I feel faint after a waltz, when I could dance for two days and never get tired. I'm tired of saying, "How wonderful you are!" to fool men who haven't got one-half the sense I've got, and I'm tired of pretending I don't know anything, so men can tell me things and feel important while they're doing it . . . I can't eat another bite.'

'Try a hot cake,' said Mammy inexorably.

'Why is it a girl has to be so silly to catch a husband?'

'Ah specs it's kase gempmums doan know whut dey wants. Dey jes' knows whut dey thinks dey wants. An' givin' dem whut dey thinks dey wants saves a pile of mizry an' bein' a ole maid. An' dey thinks dey wants mousy lil gals wid bird's tastes an' no sense at all. It doan make a gempmum feel lak mahyin' a lady ef he suspicions she got mo' sense dan he has.'

'Don't you suppose men get surprised after they're married to find that their wives do have sense?'

'Well, it's too late den. Dey's already mahied. 'Sides, gempmums specs dey wives ter have sense.'

'Some day I'm going to do and say everything I want to do and say, and if people don't like it I don't care.'

'No, you ain',' said Mammy grimly. 'Not while Ah got breaf. You eat dem cakes. Sop dem in de gravy, honey.'

'I don't think Yankee girls have to act like such fools. When we were at Saratoga last year, I noticed plenty of them acting like they had right good sense and in front of men, too.'

Mammy snorted.

'Yankee gals! Yas'm, Ah guess dey speaks dey minds awright, but Ah ain' noticed many of dem gittin' proposed ter at Saratoga.'

'But Yankees must get married,' argued Scarlett. 'They don't just grow. They must get married and have children. There's too many of them.'

'Men mahys dem fer dey money,' said Mammy firmly.

Scarlett sopped the wheat cake in the gravy and put it in her mouth. Perhaps there was something in what Mammy said. There must be something in it, for Ellen said the same things, in different and more delicate words. In fact, the mothers of all her girl friends impressed on their daughters the necessity of being helpless, clinging, doe-eyed creatures. Really, it took a lot of sense to cultivate and hold such a pose. Perhaps she had been too brash. Occasionally she had argued with Ashley and frankly aired her opinions. Perhaps this and her healthy enjoyment of walking and riding had turned him from her to the frail Melanie. Perhaps if she changed her tactics— But she felt that if Ashley succumbed to premeditated feminine tricks, she could never respect him as she now did. Any man who was fool enough to fall for a simper, a faint and an 'Oh, how wonderful you are!' wasn't worth having. But they all seemed to like it.

If she had used the wrong tactics with Ashley in the past – well, that was the past and done with. Today she would use different ones, the right ones. She wanted him and she had only a few hours in which to get him. If fainting, or pretending to faint, would do the trick, then she would faint. If simpering, coquetry or empty-headedness would attract him, she would gladly play the flirt and be more empty-headed than even Cathleen Calvert. And if bolder measures were necessary, she would take them. Today was the day!

There was no one to tell Scarlett that her own personality, frighteningly vital though it was, was more attractive than any masquerade she might adopt. Had she been told, she would have been pleased but unbelieving. And the civilization of which she was a part would have been unbelieving too, for at no time, before or since, had so low a premium been placed on feminine naturalness.

As the carriage bore her down the red road toward the Wilkes plantation, Scarlett had a feeling of guilty pleasure that neither her mother nor Mammy was with the party. There would be no one at the barbecue who, by delicately lifted brows or out-thrust underlip, could interfere with her plan of action. Of course, Suellen would be certain to tell tales tomorrow, but if all went as Scarlett hoped, the excitement of the family over her engagement to Ashley or her elopement would more than overbalance their displeasure. Yes, she was very glad Ellen had been forced to stay at home.

Gerald, primed with brandy, had given Jonas Wilkerson his dismissal that morning, and Ellen had remained at Tara to go over the accounts of the plantation before he took his departure. Scarlett had kissed her mother good-bye in the little office where she sat before the tall secretary with its paper-stuffed pigeonholes. Jonas Wilkerson, hat in hand, stood beside her, his sallow tight-skinned face hardly concealing the fury of hate that possessed him at being so unceremoniously turned out of the best overseer's job in the County. And all because of a bit of minor philandering. He had told Gerald over and over that Emmie Slattery's baby might have been fathered by any one of a dozen men as easily as himself – an idea in which Gerald concurred – but that had not altered his case so far as Ellen was concerned. Jonas hated all Southerners. He hated their cool courtesy to him and their contempt for his social status, so inadequately covered by their courtesy. He hated Ellen O'Hara above anyone else, for she was the epitome of all that he hated in Southerners.

Mammy, as head woman of the plantation, had remained to help Ellen, and it was Dilcey who rode on the driver's seat beside Toby, the girls' dancing dresses in a long box across her lap. Gerald rode beside the carriage on his big hunter, warm with brandy and pleased with himself for having gotten through with the unpleasant business of Wilkerson so speedily. He had shoved the responsibility on to Ellen, and her disappointment at missing the barbecue and the gathering of her friends did not enter his mind; for it was a fine spring day and his fields were beautiful and the birds were singing and he felt too young and frolicsome to think of anyone else. Occasionally he burst out with 'Peg in a Low-backed Car' and other Irish ditties or the more lugubrious lament for Robert Emmet, 'She is far from the land where her young hero sleeps.'

He was happy, pleasantly excited over the prospect of spending the day shouting about the Yankees and the war, and proud of his three pretty daughters in their bright spreading hoop skirts beneath foolish little lace parasols. He gave no thought to his conversation of the day before with Scarlett, for it had completely slipped his mind. He only thought that she was pretty and a great credit to him and that, today, her eyes were as green as the hills of Ireland. The last thought made him think better of himself, for it had a certain poetic ring to it, and so he favoured the girls with a loud and slightly off-key rendition of 'The Wearin' o' the Green'.

Scarlett, looking at him with the affectionate contempt that mothers feel for small swaggering sons, knew that he would try, as usual, to jump every fence between Twelve Oaks and Tara and, she hoped, by the mercy of Providence and the good sense of his horse, would escape breaking his neck. He would disdain the bridge and swim his horse through the river and come home roaring, to be put to bed on the sofa in the office by Pork, who always waited up with a lamp in the front hall on such occasions.

He would ruin his new grey broadcloth suit, which would cause him to swear horribly in the morning and tell Ellen at great length how his horse fell off the bridge in the darkness – a palpable lie which would fool no one but which would be accepted by all and make him feel very clever.

'Pa is a sweet, selfish, irresponsible darling,' Scarlett thought, with a surge of affection for him. She felt so excited and happy this morning that she included the whole world, as well as Gerald, in her affection. She was pretty and she knew it; she would have Ashley for her own before the day was over; the sun was warm and tender and the glory of the Georgia spring was spread before her eyes. Along the roadside the blackberry brambles were concealing with softest green the savage red gulches cut by the winter's rains, and the bare granite boulders pushing up through the red earth were being draped with sprangles of Cherokee roses and compassed about by wild violets of palest purple hue. Upon the wooded hills above the river, the dogwood blossoms lay glistening and white, as if snow still lingered among the greenery. The flowering crab trees were bursting their buds and rioting from delicate white to deepest pink and, beneath the trees where the sunshine dappled the pine straw, the wild honeysuckle made a varicoloured carpet of scarlet and orange and rose. There was a faint wild fragrance of sweet shrub on the breeze and the world smelled good enough to eat.

'I'll remember how beautiful this day is till I die,' thought Scarlett. 'Perhaps it will be my wedding day!'

And she thought with a tingling in her heart how she and Ashley might ride swiftly through this beauty of blossom and greenery this very afternoon, or tonight by moonlight, toward Jonesboro and a preacher. Of course, she would have to be remarried by a priest from Atlanta, but that would be something for Ellen and Gerald to worry about. She quailed a little as she thought how white with mortification Ellen would be at hearing that her daughter had eloped with another girl's fiancé, but she knew Ellen would forgive her when she saw her happiness. And Gerald would scold and bawl but, for all his remarks of yesterday about not wanting her to marry Ashley, he would be pleased beyond words at an alliance between his family and the Wilkeses.

'But that'll be something to worry about after I'm married,' she thought, tossing the worry from her.

It was impossible to feel anything but palpitating joy in this warm sun, in this spring, with the chimneys of Twelve Oaks just beginning to show on the hill across the river.

'I'll live there all my life and I'll see fifty springs like this and maybe more, and I'll tell my children and grandchildren how beautiful this spring was, lovelier than any they'll ever see.' She was so happy at this last thought that she joined in the last chorus of 'The Wearin' o' the Green' and won Gerald's shouted approval.

'I don't know why you're so happy this morning,' said Suellen crossly, for the thought still rankled in her mind that she would look far better in Scarlett's green silk dancing frock than its rightful owner would. And why was Scarlett always so selfish about lending her clothes and bonnets? And why did Mother always back her up, declaring green was not Suellen's colour? 'You know as well as I do that Ashley's engagement is going to be announced tonight. Pa said so this morning. And I know you've been sweet on him for months.'

'That's all you know,' said Scarlett, putting out her tongue and refusing to lose her good humour. How surprised Miss Sue would be by this time tomorrow morning!

'Susie, you know that's not so,' protested Carreen, shocked. 'It's Brent that Scarlett cares about.'

Scarlett turned smiling green eyes upon her younger sister, wondering how anyone could be so sweet. The whole family knew that Carreen's thirteen-year-old heart was set upon Brent Tarleton, who never gave her a thought except as Scarlett's baby sister. When Ellen was not present, the O'Haras teased her to tears about him.

'Darling, I don't care a thing about Brent,' declared Scarlett, happy enough to be generous. 'And he doesn't care a thing about me. Why, he's waiting for you to grow up!'

Carreen's round little face became pink, as pleasure struggled with incredulity.

'Oh, Scarlett, really?'

'Scarlett, you know Mother said Carreen was too young to think about beaux yet, and there you go putting ideas in her head.'

'Well, go and tattle and see if I care,' replied Scarlett. 'You want to hold Sissy back, because you know she's going to be prettier than you in a year or so.'

'You'll be keeping civil tongues in your heads this day, or I'll be taking me crop to you,' warned Gerald. 'Now whist! Is it wheels I'm hearing? That'll be the Tarletons or the Fontaines.'

As they neared the intersecting road that came down the thickly wooded hill from Mimosa and Fairhill, the sound of hooves and carriage wheels became plainer and clamorous feminine voices raised in pleasant dispute sounded from behind the screen of trees. Gerald, riding ahead, pulled up his horse and signed to Toby to stop the carriage where the two roads met.

''Tis the Tarleton ladies,' he announced to his daughters, his florid face abeam, for excepting Ellen there was no lady in the County he liked more than the red-haired Mrs Tarleton. 'And 'tis herself at the reins. Ah, there's a woman with fine hands for a horse! Feather light and strong as rawhide, and pretty enough to kiss for all that. More's the pity none of you have such hands,' he added, casting fond but reproving glances at his girls. 'With Carreen afraid of the poor beasts and Sue with hands like sad-irons when it comes to reins and you, Puss—'

'Well, at any rate I've never been thrown,' cried Scarlett indignantly. 'And Mrs Tarleton takes a toss at every hunt.'

'And breaks a collar-bone like a man,' said Gerald. 'No fainting, no fussing. Now, no more of it, for here she comes.'

He stood up in his stirrups and took off his hat with a sweep, as the Tarleton carriage, overflowing with girls in bright dresses and parasols and fluttering veils, came into view, with Mrs Tarleton on the box as Gerald had said. With her four daughters, their mammy and their ball dresses in long cardboard boxes crowding the carriage, there was no room for the coachman. And, besides, Beatrice Tarleton never willingly permitted anyone, black or white, to hold reins when her arms were out of slings. Frail, fine-boned, so white of skin that her flaming hair seemed to have drawn all the colour from her face into its vital burnished mass, she was nevertheless possessed of exuberant health and untiring energy. She had borne eight children, as red of hair and as full of life as she, and had raised them most successfully, so the County said, because she gave them all the loving neglect and the stern discipline she gave the colts she bred. 'Curb them but don't break their spirits,' was Mrs Tarleton's motto.

She loved horses and talked horses constantly. She understood them and handled them better than any man in the County. Colts overflowed the paddocks on to the front lawn, even as her eight children overflowed the rambling house on the hill, and colts and sons and daughters and hunting dogs tagged after her as she went about the plantation. She credited her horses, especially her red mare, Nellie, with human intelligence; and if the cares of the house kept her busy beyond the time when she expected to take her daily ride, she put the sugar-bowl in the hands of some small piccaninny and said: 'Give Nellie a handful and tell her I'll be out terrectly.'

Except on rare occasions she always wore her riding habit, for whether she rode or not she always expected to ride and in that expectation put on her habit upon arising. Each morning, rain or shine, Nellie was saddled and walked up and down in front of the house, waiting for the time when Mrs

Tarleton could spare an hour away from her duties. But Fairhill was a difficult plantation to manage and spare time hard to get, and more often than not Nellie walked up and down riderless hour after hour, while Beatrice Tarleton went through the day with the skirt of her habit absently looped up over her arm and six inches of shining boot showing below it.

Today, dressed in dull black silk over unfashionably narrow hoops, she still looked as though in her habit, for the dress was as severely tailored as her riding costume and the small black hat with its long black plume perched over one warm, twinkling, brown eye was a replica of the battered old hat she used for hunting.

She waved her whip when she saw Gerald and drew her dancing pair of red horses to a halt, and the four girls in the back of the carriage leaned out and gave such vociferous cries of greeting that the team pranced in alarm. To a casual observer it would seem that years had passed since the Tarletons had seen the O'Haras, instead of only two days. But they were a sociable family and liked their neighbours, especially the O'Hara girls. That is, they liked Suellen and Carreen. No girl in the County, with the possible exception of the empty-headed Cathleen Calvert, really liked Scarlett.

In summers, the County averaged a barbecue and ball nearly every week, but to the red-haired Tarletons with their enormous capacity for enjoying themselves, each barbecue and each ball was as exciting as if it were the first they had ever attended. They were a pretty, buxom quartette, so crammed into the carriage that their hoops and flounces overlapped and their parasols nudged and bumped together above their wide leghorn sun hats, crowned with roses and dangling with black velvet chin ribbons. All shades of red hair were represented beneath these hats, Hetty's plain red hair, Camilla's strawberry blonde, Randa's coppery auburn and small Betsy's carrot top.

'That's a fine bevy, Ma'm,' said Gerald gallantly, reining his horse alongside the carriage. 'But it's far they'll go to beat their mother.'

Mrs Tarleton rolled her red-brown eyes and sucked in her lower lip in burlesqued appreciation, and the girls cried, 'Ma, stop making eyes or we'll tell Pa!' 'I vow, Mr O'Hara, she never gives us a chance when there's a handsome man like you around!'

Scarlett laughed with the rest at these sallies but, as always, the freedom with which the Tarletons treated their mother came as a shock. They acted as if she were one of themselves and not a day over sixteen. To Scarlett, the very idea of saying such things to her own mother was almost sacrilegious. And yet – and yet – there was something very pleasant about the Tarleton girls' relations with their mother, and they adored her for all that they criticized and scolded and teased her. Not, Scarlett loyally hastened to tell herself, that she would prefer a mother like Mrs Tarleton to Ellen, but still it would be fun to romp with a mother. She knew that even that thought was disrespectful to Ellen and felt ashamed of it. She knew no such troublesome thoughts ever disturbed the brains under the four flaming thatches in the carriage and, as always when she felt herself different from her neighbours, an irritated confusion fell upon her.

Quick though her brain was, it was not made for analysis, but she half-consciously realized that, for all the Tarleton girls were as unruly as colts and wild as March hares, there was an unworried single-mindedness about them that was part of their inheritance. On both their mother's and their father's side they were Georgians, north Georgians, only a generation away from pioneers. They were sure of themselves and of their environment. They knew instinctively what they were about, as did the Wilkeses, though in widely divergent ways, and in them there was no such conflict as frequently raged in Scarlett's bosom where the blood of a soft-voiced, overbred Coast aristocrat mingled with the shrewd, earthy blood of an Irish peasant. Scarlett wanted to respect and adore her mother like an idol and to rumple her hair and tease her too. And she knew she should be altogether one way or the other. It was the same conflicting emotion that made her desire to appear a delicate and high-bred lady with boys and to be, as well, a hoyden who was not above a few kisses.

'Where's Ellen this morning?' asked Mrs Tarleton.

'She's after discharging our overseer and stayed home to go over the accounts with him. Where's himself and the lads?'

'Oh, they rode over to Twelve Oaks hours ago – to sample the punch and see if it was strong enough, I dare say, as if they wouldn't have from now till tomorrow morning to do it! I'm going to ask John Wilkes to keep them overnight, even if he has to bed them down in the stable. Five men in their cups are just too much for me. Up to three, I do very well but—'

Gerald hastily interrupted to change the subject. He could feel his own daughters snickering behind his back as they remembered in what condition he had come home from the Wilkeses' last barbecue the autumn before.

'And why aren't you riding today, Mrs Tarleton? Sure, you don't look yourself at all without Nellie. It's a stentor, you are.'

'A stentor, me ignorant broth of a boy!' cried Mrs Tarleton, aping his brogue. 'You mean a centaur. Stentor was a man with a voice like a brass gong.'

'Stentor or centaur, 'tis no matter,' answered Gerald, unruffled by his error. 'And 'tis a voice like brass you have, M'am, when you're urging on the hounds, so it is.'

'That's one on you, Ma,' said Hetty. 'I told you you yelled like a Comanche whenever you saw a fox.'

'But not as loud as you yell when Mammy washes your ears,' returned Mrs Tarleton. 'And you sixteen! Well, as to why I'm not riding today, Nellie foaled early this morning.'

'Did she now!' cried Gerald with real interest, his Irishman's passion for horses shining in his eyes, and Scarlett again felt the sense of shock in comparing her mother with Mrs Tarleton. To Ellen, mares never foaled nor cows calved. In fact, hens almost didn't lay eggs. Ellen ignored these matters completely. But Mrs Tarleton had no such reticences.

'A little filly, was it?'

'No, a fine little stallion with legs two yards long. You must ride over and see him, Mr O'Hara. He's a real Tarleton horse. He's as red as Hetty's curls.'

'And looks a lot like Hetty, too,' said Camilla, and then disappeared shrieking amid a welter of skirts and pantalets and bobbing hats, as Hetty, who did have a long face, began pinching her.

'My fillies are feeling their oats this morning,' said Mrs Tarleton. 'They've been kicking up their heels ever since we heard the news this morning about Ashley and that little cousin of his from Atlanta. What's her name? Melanie? Bless the child, she's a sweet little thing, but I can never remember either her name or her face. Our cook is the broad wife of the Wilkes butler, and he was over last night with the news that the engagement would be announced tonight and Cookie told us this morning. The girls are all excited about it, though I can't see why. Everybody's known for years that Ashley would marry her, that is, if he didn't marry one of his Burr cousins from Macon. Just like Honey Wilkes is going to marry Melanie's brother, Charles. Now, tell me, Mr O'Hara, is it illegal for the Wilkes to marry outside of their family? Because if—'

Scarlett did not hear the rest of the laughing words. For one short instant, it was as though the sun had ducked behind a cool cloud, leaving the world in shadow, taking the colour out of things. The freshly green foliage looked sickly, the dogwood pallid, and the flowering crab, so beautifully pink a moment ago, faded and dreary. Scarlett dug her fingers into the upholstery of the carriage and for a moment her parasol wavered. It was one thing to know that Ashley was engaged but it was another to hear people talk about it so casually. Then her courage flowed strongly back and the sun came out again and the landscape glowed anew. She knew Ashley loved her. That was certain. And she smiled as she thought how surprised Mrs Tarleton would be when no engagement was announced that night – how surprised if there were an elopement. And she'd tell neighbours what a slyboots Scarlett was to sit there and listen to her talk about Melanie when all the time she and Ashley— She dimpled at her own thoughts and Hetty, who had been watching sharply the effect of her mother's words, sank back with a small puzzled frown.

'I don't care what you say, Mr O'Hara,' Mrs Tarleton was saying emphatically. 'It's all wrong, this marrying of cousins. It's bad enough for Ashley to be marrying the Hamilton child, but for Honey to be marrying that pale-looking Charles Hamilton—'

'Honey'll never catch anybody else if she doesn't marry Charlie,' said Randa, cruel and secure in her own popularity. 'She's never had another beau except him. And he's never acted very sweet on her, for all that they're engaged. Scarlett, you remember how he ran after you last Christmas—'

'Don't be a cat, Miss,' said her mother. 'Cousins shouldn't marry, even second cousins. It weakens the strain. It isn't like horses. You can breed a mare to a brother or a sire to a daughter and get good results if you know your blood strains, but in people it just doesn't work. You get good lines, perhaps, but no stamina. You—'

'Now, Ma'm, I'm taking issue with you on that! Can you name me better people than the Wilkes? And they've been intermarrying since Brian Boru was a boy.'

'And high time they stopped it, for it's beginning to show. Oh, not Ashley so much, for he's a good-looking devil, though even he— But look at those two washed-out-looking Wilkes girls, poor things! Nice girls, of course, but washed out. And look at little Miss Melanie. Thin as a rail and delicate enough for the wind to blow away and no spirit at all. Not a notion of her own. "No, Ma'm!" "Yes, Ma'm!" That's all she has to say. You see what I mean? That family needs new blood, fine vigorous blood like my red-heads or your Scarlett. Now, don't misunderstand me. The Wilkes are fine folks in their way, and you know I'm fond of them all, but be frank! They are overbred and inbred too, aren't they? They'll do fine on a dry track, a fast track, but mark my words, I don't believe the Wilkes can run on a mud track. I believe the stamina has been bred out of them, and when the emergency arises I don't believe they can run against odds. Dry-weather stock. Give me a big horse who can run in any weather! And their intermarrying has made them different from other folks around here. Always fiddling with the piano or sticking their heads in a book. I do believe Ashley would rather read than hunt! Yes, I honestly believe that, Mr O'Hara! And just look at the bones, of them. Too slender. They need dams and sires with strength—'

'Ah-ah-hum,' said Gerald, suddenly and guiltily aware that the conversation, a most interesting and entirely proper one to him, would seem quite otherwise to Ellen. In fact, he knew she would never recover should she learn that her daughters had been exposed to so frank a conversation. But Mrs Tarleton was, as usual, deaf to all other ideas when pursuing her favourite topic, breeding, whether it be horses or humans.

'I know what I'm talking about because I had some cousins who married each other and I give you my word their children all turned out as popeyed as bullfrogs, poor things. And when my family wanted me to marry a second cousin, I bucked like a colt. I said, "No, Ma. Not for me. My children will all have spavins and heaves." Well, Ma fainted when I said that about spavins, but I stood firm and Grandma backed me up. She knew a lot about horse breeding too, you see, and said I was right. And she helped me run away with Mr Tarleton. And look at my children! Big and healthy and not a sickly one or a runt among them, though Boyd is only five feet ten. Now, the Wilkes—'

'Not meaning to change the subject, Ma'm,' broke in Gerald hurriedly, for he had noticed Carreen's bewildered look and the avid curiosity on

Suellen's face and feared lest they might ask Ellen embarrassing questions which would reveal how inadequate a chaperon he was. Puss, he was glad to notice, appeared to be thinking of other matters as a lady should.

Hetty Tarleton rescued him from his predicament.

'Good Heavens, Ma, do let's get on!' she cried impatiently. 'This sun is broiling me and I can just hear freckles popping out on my neck.'

'Just a minute, Ma'm, before you go,' said Gerald. 'But what have you decided to do about selling us the horses for the Troop? War may break any day now and the boys want the matter settled. It's a Clayton County troop and it's Clayton County horses we want for them. But you, obstinate creature that you are, are still refusing to sell us your fine beasts.'

'Maybe there won't be any war,' Mrs Tarleton temporized, her mind diverted completely from the Wilkeses' odd marriage habits.

'Why, Ma'm, you can't—'

'Ma,' Hetty interrupted again, 'can't you and Mr O'Hara talk about the horses at Twelve Oaks as well as here?'

'That's just it, Miss Hetty,' said Gerald, 'and I won't be keeping you but one minute by the clock. We'll be getting to Twelve Oaks in a little bit, and every man there, old and young, wanting to know about the horses. Ah, but it's breaking me heart to see such a fine pretty lady as your mother so stingy with her beasts! Now, where's your patriotism, Mrs Tarleton? Does the Confederacy mean nothing to you at all?'

'Ma,' cried small Betsy, 'Randa's sitting on my dress and I'm getting all wrinkled.'

'Well, push Randa off you, Betsy, and hush. Now, listen to me, Gerald O'Hara,' she retorted, her eyes beginning to snap. 'Don't you go throwing the Confederacy in my face! I reckon the Confederacy means as much to me as it does to you, me with four boys in the Troop and you with none. But my boys can take care of themselves and my horses can't. I'd gladly give the horses free of charge if I knew they were going to be ridden by boys I know, gentlemen used to thoroughbreds. No, I wouldn't hesitate a minute. But let my beauties be at the mercy of backwoodsmen and Crackers who are used to riding mules! No, sir! I'd have nightmares thinking they were being ridden with saddle-galls and not groomed properly. Do you think I'd let ignorant fools ride my tender-mouthed darlings and saw their mouths to pieces and beat them till their spirits were broken? Why, I've got gooseflesh this minute, just thinking about it! No, Mr O'Hara, you're mighty nice to want my horses, but you'd better go to Atlanta and buy some old plugs for your clodhoppers. They'll never know the difference.'

'Ma, can't we please go on?' asked Camilla, joining the impatient chorus. 'You know mighty well you're going to end up giving them your darlings anyhow. When Pa and the boys get through talking about the Confederacy needing them and so on, you'll cry and let them go.'

Mrs Tarleton grinned and shook the lines.

'I'll do no such thing,' she said, touching the horses lightly with the whip. The carriage went off swiftly.

'That's a fine woman,' said Gerald, putting on his hat and taking his place beside his own carriage. 'Drive on, Toby. We'll wear her down and get the horses yet. Of course, she's right. She's right. If a man's not a gentleman, he's no business on a horse. The infantry is the place for him. But more's the pity, there's not enough planters' sons in this County to make up a full troop. What did you say, Puss?'

'Pa, please ride behind us or in front of us. You kick up such a heap of dust that we're choking,' said Scarlett, who felt that she could endure conversation no longer. It distracted her from her thoughts and she was very anxious to arrange both her thoughts and her face in attractive lines before reaching Twelve Oaks. Gerald obediently put spurs to his horse and was off in a red cloud after the Tarleton carriage where he could continue his horsy conversation.

Chapter VI

They crossed the river and the carriage mounted the hill. Even before Twelve Oaks came into view Scarlett saw a haze of smoke hanging lazily in the tops of the tall trees and smelled the mingled savoury odours of burning hickory logs and roasting pork and mutton.

The barbecue pits, which had been slowly burning since last night, would now be long troughs of rose-red embers, with the meats turning on spits above them and the juices trickling down and hissing into the coals. Scarlett knew that the fragrance carried on the faint breeze came from the grove of great oaks in the rear of the big house. John Wilkes always held his barbecues there, on the gentle slope leading down to the rose garden, a pleasant shady place and a far pleasanter place, for instance, than that used by the Calverts. Mrs Calvert did not like barbecue food and declared that the smells remained in the house for days, so her guests always sweltered on a flat unshaded spot a quarter of a mile from the house. But John Wilkes, famed throughout the state for his hospitality, really knew how to give a barbecue.

The long trestled picnic tables, covered with the finest of the Wilkes' linen, always stood under the thickest shade, with backless benches on either side; and chairs, hassocks and cushions from the house were scattered about the glade for those who did not fancy the benches. At a distance great enough to keep the smoke away from the guests were the long pits where the meats cooked and the huge iron wash-pots from which the succulent odours of barbecue sauce and Brunswick stew floated. Mr Wilkes always had at least a dozen darkies busy running back and forth with trays to serve the guests.

Over behind the barns there was always another barbecue pit, where the house servants and the coachmen and maids of the guests had their own feast of hoecakes and yams and chitterlings, that dish of hog entrails so dear to negro hearts, and, in season, watermelons enough to satiate.

As the smell of crisp fresh pork came to her, Scarlett wrinkled her nose appreciatively, hoping that by the time it was cooked she would feel some appetite. As it was, she was so full of food and so tightly laced that she feared every moment she was going to belch. That would be fatal, as only old men and very old ladies could belch without fear of social disapproval.

They topped the rise and the white house reared its perfect symmetry before her, tall of columns, wide of verandas, flat of roof, beautiful as a woman is beautiful who is so sure of her charm that she can be generous and gracious to all. Scarlett loved Twelve Oaks even more than Tara, for it had a stately beauty, a mellowed dignity that Gerald's house did not possess.

The wide curving driveway was full of saddle horses and carriages and guests alighting and calling greetings to friends. Grinning negroes, excited as always at a party, were leading the animals to the barnyard to be unharnessed and unsaddled for the day. Swarms of children, black and white, ran yelling about the newly green lawn, playing hopscotch and tag and boasting how much they were going to eat. The wide hall which ran from front to back of the house was swarming with people, and as the O'Hara carriage drew up at the front steps, Scarlett saw girls in crinolines, bright as butterflies, going up and coming down the stairs from the second floor, arms about each other's waists, stopping to lean over the delicate handrail of the banisters, laughing and calling to young men in the hall below them.

Through the open french windows, she caught glimpses of the older women seated in the drawing-room, sedate in dark silks as they sat fanning themselves and talking of babies and sicknesses and who had married whom and why. The Wilkes butler, Tom, was hurrying through the halls, a silver tray in his hands, bowing and grinning, as he offered tall glasses to young men in fawn and grey trousers and fine ruffled linen shirts.

The sunny front veranda was thronged with guests. Yes, the whole County was here, thought Scarlett. The four Tarleton boys and their father leaned against the tall columns, the twins, Stuart and Brent, side by side, inseparable as usual, Boyd and Tom with their father, James Tarleton. Mr Calvert was standing close by the side of his Yankee wife, who even after fifteen years in Georgia never seemed to quite belong anywhere. Everyone was very polite and kind to her because they felt sorry for her, but no one could forget that she had compounded her initial error of birth by being the governess of Mr Calvert's children. The two Calvert boys, Raiford and Cade, were there with their dashing blonde sister, Cathleen, teasing the dark-faced Joe Fontaine and Sally Munroe, his pretty bride-to-be. Alex and Tony Fontaine were whispering in the ears of Dimity Munroe and sending her into gales of giggles. There were families from as far as Lovejoy, ten miles away, and from Fayetteville and Jonesboro, a few even from Atlanta and Macon. The house seemed bursting with the crowd, and a ceaseless babble of talking and laughter and giggles and shrill feminine squeaks and screams rose and fell.

On the porch steps stood John Wilkes, silver-haired, erect, radiating the quiet charm and hospitality that was as warm and never-failing as the sun of Georgia summer. Beside him Honey Wilkes, so called because she indiscriminately addressed everyone from her father to the field hands by that endearment, fidgeted and giggled as she called greetings to the arriving guests.

Honey's nervously obvious desire to be attractive to every man in sight contrasted sharply with her father's poise, and Scarlett had the thought that perhaps there was something in what Mrs Tarleton said, after all. Certainly the Wilkes men got the family looks. The thick deep-gold lashes that set off the grey eyes of John Wilkes and Ashley were sparse and colourless in the faces of Honey and her sister India. Honey had the odd lashless look of a rabbit, and India could be described by no other word than plain.

India was nowhere to be seen, but Scarlett knew she probably was in the kitchen giving final instructions to the servants. 'Poor India,' thought Scarlett, 'she's had so much trouble keeping house since her mother died that she's never had the chance to catch any beau except Stuart Tarleton, and it certainly wasn't my fault if he thought I was prettier than she.'

John Wilkes came down the steps to offer his arm to Scarlett. As she descended from the carriage, she saw Suellen smirk and knew that she must have picked out Frank Kennedy in the crowd.

'If I couldn't catch a better beau than that old maid in britches!' she thought contemptuously, as she stepped to the ground and smiled her thanks to John Wilkes.

Frank Kennedy was hurrying to the carriage to assist Suellen, and Suellen was bridling in a way that made Scarlett want to slap her. Frank Kennedy might own more land than anyone in the County and he might have a very kind heart, but these things counted for nothing against the fact that he was forty, slight and nervous, and had a thin ginger-coloured beard and an old-maidish, fussy way about him. However, remembering her plan, Scarlett smothered her contempt and cast such a flashing smile of greeting at him that he stopped short, his arm outheld to Suellen, and goggled at Scarlett in pleased bewilderment.

Scarlett's eyes searched the crowd for Ashley, even while she made pleasant small talk with John Wilkes, but he was not on the porch. There were cries of greeting from a dozen voices and Stuart and Brent Tarleton moved toward her. The Munroe girls rushed up to exclaim over her dress, and she was speedily the centre of a circle of voices that rose higher and higher in efforts to be heard above the din. But where was Ashley? And Melanie and Charles? She tried not to be obvious as she looked about and peered down the hall into the laughing group inside.

As she chattered and laughed and cast quick glances into the house and yard, her eyes fell on a stranger, standing alone in the hall, staring at her in a cool impertinent way that brought her up sharply with a mingled feeling of feminine pleasure that she had attracted a man and an embarrassed sensation that her dress was too low in the bosom. He looked quite old, at least thirty-five. He was a tall man and powerfully built. Scarlett thought she had never seen a man with such wide shoulders, so heavy with muscles, almost too heavy for gentility. When her eye caught his, he smiled, showing animal-white teeth below a close-clipped black moustache. He was dark of face, swarthy as a pirate, and his eyes were as bold and black as any pirate's appraising a galleon to be scuttled or a maiden to be ravished. There was a cool recklessness in his face and a cynical humour in his mouth as he smiled at her, and Scarlett caught her breath. She felt that she should be insulted by such a look and was annoyed with herself because she did not feel insulted. She did not know who he could be, but there was undeniably a look of good blood in his dark face. It showed in the thin hawk nose over the full red lips, the high forehead and the wide-set eyes.

She dragged her eyes away from his without smiling back, and he turned as someone called: 'Rhett! Rhett Butler! Come here! I want you to meet the most hard-hearted girl in Georgia.'

Rhett Butler? The name had a familiar sound, somehow connected with something pleasantly scandalous, but her mind was on Ashley and she dismissed the thought.

'I must run upstairs and smooth my hair,' she told Stuart and Brent, who were trying to get her cornered from the crowd. 'You boys wait for me and don't run off with any other girl or I'll be furious.'

She could see that Stuart was going to be difficult to handle today if she flirted with anyone else. He had been drinking and wore the arrogant looking-for-a-fight expression that she knew from experience meant trouble. She paused in the hall to speak to friends and to greet India who was emerging from the back of the house, her hair untidy and tiny beads of perspiration on her forehead. Poor India! It would be bad enough to have pale hair and eyelashes and a jutting chin that meant a stubborn disposition, without being twenty years old and an old maid in the bargain. She wondered if India resented very much her taking Stuart away from her. Lots of people said she was still in love with him, but then you could never tell what a Wilkes was thinking about. If she did resent it, she never gave any sign of it, treating Scarlett with the same slightly aloof, kindly courtesy she had always shown her.

Scarlett spoke pleasantly to her and started up the wide stairs. As she did, a shy voice behind her called her name and, turning, she saw Charles Hamilton. He was a nice-looking boy with a riot of soft brown curls on his white forehead and eyes as deep brown, as clean and as gentle as a collie dog's. He was well turned out in mustard-coloured trousers and black coat and his pleated shirt was topped by the widest and most fashionable of black cravats. A faint blush was creeping over his face as she turned, for he was timid with girls. Like most shy men he greatly admired airy, vivacious, always-at-ease girls like Scarlett. She had never given him more than perfunctory courtesy before, and so the beaming smile of pleasure with which she greeted him and the two hands outstretched to his almost took his breath away.

'Why, Charles Hamilton, you handsome old thing, you! I'll bet you came all the way down here from Atlanta just to break my poor heart!'

Charles almost stuttered with excitement, holding her warm little hands in his and looking into the dancing green eyes. This was the way girls talked to other boys but never to him. He never knew why, but girls always treated him like a younger brother and were very kind, but never bothered to tease him. He had always wanted girls to flirt and frolic with him as they did with boys much less handsome and less endowed with this world's goods than he. But on the few occasions when this had happened he could never think of anything to say and he suffered agonies of embarrassment at his dumbness. Then he lay awake at night thinking of all the charming gallantries he might have employed; but he rarely got a second chance, for the girls left him alone after a trial or two.

Even with Honey, with whom he had an unspoken understanding of marriage when he came into his property next fall, he was diffident and silent. At times, he had an ungallant feeling that Honey's coquetries and proprietary airs were no credit to him, for she was so boy-crazy he imagined she would use them on any man who gave her the opportunity. Charles was not excited over the prospect of marrying her, for she stirred in him none of the emotions of wild romance that his beloved books had assured him were proper for a lover. He had always yearned to be loved by some beautiful, dashing creature full of fire and mischief.

And here was Scarlett O'Hara teasing him about breaking her heart!

He tried to think of something to say and couldn't and silently he blessed her because she kept up a steady chatter which relieved him of any necessity for conversation. It was too good to be true.

'Now, you wait right here till I come back, for I want to eat barbecue with you. And don't you go off philandering with those other girls, because I'm mighty jealous,' came the incredible words from red lips with a dimple on each side; and bristly black lashes swept demurely over green eyes.

'I won't,' he finally managed to breathe, never dreaming that she was thinking he looked like a calf waiting for the butcher.

Tapping him lightly on the arm with her folded fan, she turned to start up the stairs and her eyes again fell on the man called Rhett Butler, who stood alone a few feet away from Charles. Evidently he had overheard the whole conversation, for he grinned up at her as maliciously as a tomcat, and again his eyes went over her, in a gaze totally devoid of the deference she was accustomed to.

'God's nightgown!' said Scarlett to herself in indignation, using Gerald's favourite oath. 'He looks as if – as if he knew what I looked like without my shimmy,' and, tossing her head, she went up the steps.

In the bedroom where the wraps were laid, she found Cathleen Calvert preening before the mirror and biting her lips to make them look redder. There were fresh roses in her sash that matched her cheeks, and her cornflower-blue eyes were dancing with excitement.

'Cathleen,' said Scarlett, trying to pull the corsage of her dress higher, 'who is that nasty man downstairs named Butler?'

'My dear, don't you know?' whispered Cathleen excitedly, a weather eye on the next room where Dilcey and the Wilkes girls' mammy were gossiping. 'I can't imagine how Mr Wilkes must feel having him here, but he was visiting Mr Kennedy in Jonesboro – something about buying cotton – and, of course, Mr Kennedy had to bring him along with him. He couldn't just go off and leave him.'

'What is the matter with him?'

'My dear, he isn't received!'

'Not really!'

'No.'

Scarlett digested this in silence, for she had never before been under the same roof with anyone who was not received. It was very exciting.

'What did he do?'

'Oh, Scarlett, he has the most terrible reputation. His name is Rhett Butler and he's from Charleston and his folks are some of the nicest people there, but they won't even speak to him. Caro Rhett told me about him last summer. He isn't any kin to her family, but she knows all about him, everybody does. He was expelled from West Point. Imagine! And for things too bad for Caro to know. And then there was that business about the girl he didn't marry.'

'Do tell me!'

'Darling, don't you know anything? Caro told me all about it last summer and her mamma would die if she thought Caro even knew about it. Well, this Mr Butler took a Charleston girl out buggy riding. I never did know who she was, but I've got my suspicions. She couldn't have been very nice or she wouldn't have gone out with him in the late afternoon without a chaperon. And, my dear, they stayed out nearly all night and walked home finally, saying the horse had run away and smashed the buggy and they had gotten lost in the woods. And guess what—'

'I can't guess. Tell me,' said Scarlett enthusiastically, hoping for the worst.

'He refused to marry her the next day!'

'Oh,' said Scarlett, her hopes dashed.

'He said he hadn't – er – done anything to her and he didn't see why he should marry her. And, of course, her brother called him out, and Mr Butler said he'd rather be shot than marry a stupid fool. And so they fought a duel and Mr Butler shot the girl's brother and he died, and Mr Butler had to leave Charleston and now nobody receives him,' finished Cathleen triumphantly, and just in time, for Dilcey came back into the room to oversee the toilet of her charge.

'Did she have a baby?' whispered Scarlett in Cathleen's ear.

Cathleen shook her head violently. 'But she was ruined just the same,' she hissed back.

'I wish I had gotten Ashley to compromise me,' thought Scarlett suddenly. 'He'd be too much of a gentleman not to marry me.' But somehow, unbidden, she had a feeling of respect for Rhett Butler for refusing to marry a girl who was a fool.

Scarlett sat on a high rosewood ottoman, under the shade of a huge oak in the rear of the house, her flounces and ruffles billowing about her and two inches of green morocco slippers – all that a lady could show and still remain a lady – peeping from beneath them. She had a scarcely touched plate in her hands and seven cavaliers about her. The barbecue had reached its peak and the warm air was full of laughter and talk, the click of silver on porcelain and the rich heavy smells of roasting meats and redolent gravies. Occasionally when the slight breeze veered, puffs of smoke from the long barbecue pits floated over the crowd and were greeted with squeals of mock dismay from the ladies and violent flappings of palmetto fans.

Most of the young ladies were seated with partners on the long benches that faced the tables, but Scarlett, realizing that a girl has only two sides and only one man can sit on each of these sides, had elected to sit apart so she could gather about her as many men as possible.

Under the arbour sat the married women, their dark dresses decorous notes in the surrounding colour and gaiety. Matrons, regardless of their ages, always grouped together apart from the bright-eyed girls, beaux and laughter, for there were no married belles in the South. From Grandma Fontaine, who was belching frankly with the privilege of her age, to seventeen-year-old Alice Munroe, struggling against the nausea of a first pregnancy, they had their heads together in the endless genealogical and obstetrical discussions that made such gatherings very pleasant and instructive affairs.

Casting contemptuous glances at them, Scarlett thought that they looked like a clump of fat crows. Married women never had any fun. It did not occur to her that if she married Ashley she would automatically be relegated to arbours and front parlours with staid matrons in dull silks, as staid and dull as they and not a part of the fun and frolicking. Like most girls, her imagination carried her just as far as the altar and no further. Besides, she was too unhappy now to pursue an abstraction.

She dropped her eyes to her plate and nibbled daintily on a beaten biscuit with an elegance and an utter lack of appetite that would have won Mammy's approval. For all that she had a superfluity of beaux, she had never been more miserable in her life. In some way that she could not understand, her plans of last night had failed utterly so far as Ashley was concerned. She had attracted other beaux by the dozens, but not Ashley, and all the fears of yesterday afternoon were sweeping back upon her, making her heart beat fast and then slow, and colour flame and whiten in her cheeks.

Ashley had made no attempt to join the circle about her, in fact she had not had a word alone with him since arriving, or even spoken to him since their first greeting. He had come forward to welcome her when she came into the back garden, but Melanie had been on his arm then, Melanie who hardly came up to his shoulder.

She was a tiny, frailly built girl, who gave the appearance of a child masquerading in her mother's enormous hoop skirts -an illusion that was heightened by the shy, almost frightened look in her too large brown eyes. She had a cloud of curly dark hair which was so sternly repressed beneath its net that no vagrant tendrils escaped, and this dark mass, with its long widow's peak, accentuated the heart shape of her face. Too wide across the cheek-bones, too pointed at the chin, it was a sweet, timid face but a plain face, and she had no feminine tricks of allure to make observers forget its plainness. She looked – and was – as simple as earth, as good as bread, as transparent as spring water. But for all her plainness of feature and smallness of stature, there was a sedate dignity about her movements that was oddly touching and far older than her seventeen years.

Her grey organdie dress, with its cherry-coloured satin sash, disguised with its billows and ruffles how childishly underdeveloped her body was, and the yellow hat with long cherry streamers made her creamy skin glow. Her heavy earbobs with their long gold fringe hung down from loops of tidily netted hair, swinging close to her brown eyes, eyes that had the still gleam of a forest pool in winter when brown leaves shine up through quiet water.

She had smiled with timid liking when she greeted Scarlett and told her how pretty her green dress was, and Scarlett had been hard put to be even civil in reply, so violently did she want to speak alone with Ashley. Since then, Ashley had sat on a stool at Melanie's feet, apart from the other guests, and talked quietly with her, smiling that slow drowsy smile that Scarlett loved. What made matters worse was that under his smile a little sparkle had come into Melanie's eyes, so that even Scarlett had to admit that she looked almost pretty. As Melanie looked at Ashley, her plain face lit up as with an inner fire, for if ever a loving heart showed itself upon a face, it was showing now on Melanie Hamilton's.

Scarlett tried to keep her eyes from these two but could not, and after each glance she redoubled her gaiety with her cavaliers, laughing, saying daring things, teasing, tossing her head at their compliments until her earrings danced. She said 'Fiddle-dee-dee!' many times, declared that the truth wasn't in any of them, and vowed that she'd never believe anything any man told her. But Ashley did not seem to notice her at all. He only looked up at Melanie and talked on, and Melanie looked down at him with an expression that radiated the fact that she belonged to him.

So, Scarlett was miserable.

To the outward eye, never had a girl less cause to be miserable. She was undoubtedly the belle of the barbecue, the centre of attention. The furore she was causing among the men, coupled with the heart-burnings of the other girls, would have pleased her enormously at any other time.

Charles Hamilton, emboldened by her notice, was firmly planted on her right, refusing to be dislodged by the combined efforts of the Tarleton twins. He held her fan in one hand and his untouched plate of barbecue in the other and stubbornly refused to meet the eyes of Honey, who seemed on the verge of an outburst of tears. Cade lounged gracefully on her left, plucking at her skirt to attract her attention and staring up with smouldering eyes at Stuart. Already the air was electric between him and the twins and rude words had passed. Frank Kennedy fussed about like a hen with one chick, running back and forth from the shade of the oak to the tables to fetch dainties to tempt Scarlett, as if there were not a dozen servants there for that purpose. As a result, Suellen's sullen resentment had passed beyond the point of ladylike concealment and she glowered at Scarlett. Small Carreen could have cried because, for all Scarlett's encouraging words that morning, Brent had done no more than say 'Hello, Sis' and jerk her hair-ribbon before turning his full attention to Scarlett. Usually he was so kind and treated her with a careless deference that made her feel grown up, and Carreen secretly dreamed of the day when she would put her hair up and her skirts down and receive him as a real beau. And now it seemed that Scarlett had him. The Munroe girls were concealing their chagrin at the defection of the swarthy Fontaine boys, but they were annoyed at the way Tony and Alex stood about the circle, jockeying for a position near Scarlett should any of the others arise from their places.

They telegraphed their disapproval of Scarlett's conduct to Hetty Tarleton by delicately raised eyebrows. 'Fast' was the only word for Scarlett. Simultaneously, the three young ladies raised lacy parasols, said they had had quite enough to eat, thank you, and, laying light fingers on the arms of the men nearest them, clamoured sweetly to see the rose garden, the spring and the summerhouse. This strategic retreat in good order was not lost on a woman present or observed by a man.

Scarlett giggled as she saw three men dragged out of the line of her charms to investigate landmarks familiar to the girls from childhood, and cut her eye sharply to see if Ashley had taken note. But he was playing with the ends of Melanie's sash and smiling up at her. Pain twisted Scarlett's heart. She felt that she could claw Melanie's ivory skin till the blood ran and take pleasure in doing it.

As her eyes wandered from Melanie, she caught the gaze of Rhett Butler, who was not mixing with the crowd but standing apart talking to John

Wilkes. He had been watching her and when she looked at him he laughed outright. Scarlett had an uneasy feeling that this man who was not received was the only one present who knew what lay behind her wild gaiety and that it was affording him sardonic amusement. She could have clawed him with pleasure too.

'If I can just live through this barbecue till this afternoon,' she thought, 'all the girls will go upstairs to take naps to be fresh for tonight and I'll stay downstairs and get to talk to Ashley. Surely he must have noticed how popular I am.' She soothed her heart with another hope: 'Of course, he has to be attentive to Melanie because, after all, she is his cousin and she isn't popular at all, and if he didn't look out for her she'd just be a wallflower.'

She took new courage at this thought and redoubled her efforts in the direction of Charles, whose brown eyes glowed down eagerly at her. It was a wonderful day for Charles, a dream day, and he had fallen in love with Scarlett with no effort at all. Before this new emotion, Honey receded into a dim haze. Honey was a shrill-voiced sparrow and Scarlett a gleaming humming-bird. She teased him and favoured him and asked him questions and answered them herself, so that he appeared very clever without having to say a word. The other boys were puzzled and annoyed by her obvious interest in him, for they knew Charles was too shy to hitch two consecutive words together, and politeness was being severely strained to conceal their growing rage. Everyone was smouldering, and it would have been a positive triumph for Scarlett, except for Ashley.

When the last forkful of pork and chicken and mutton had been eaten, Scarlett hoped the time had come when India would rise and suggest that the ladies retire to the house. It was two o'clock and the sun was warm overhead, but India, wearied with the three-day preparations for the barbecue, was only too glad to remain sitting beneath the arbour, shouting remarks to a deaf old gentleman from Fayetteville.

A lazy somnolence descended on the crowd. The negroes idled about, clearing the long tables on which the food had been laid. The laughter and talking became less animated and groups here and there fell silent. All were waiting for their hostess to signal the end of the morning festivities. Palmetto fans were wagging more slowly, and several old gentlemen were nodding from the heat and overloaded stomachs. The barbecue was over and all were content to take their ease while the sun was at its height.

In this interval between the morning party and the evening's ball, they seemed a placid, peaceful lot. Only the young men retained the restless energy which had filled the whole throng a short while before. Moving from group to group, drawling in their soft voices, they were as handsome as blooded stallions and as dangerous. The languor of midday had taken hold of the gathering, but underneath lurked tempers that could rise to killing heights in a second and flare out as quickly. Men and women, they were beautiful and wild, all a little violent under their pleasant ways and only a little tamed.

Some time dragged by while the sun grew hotter, and Scarlett and others looked again toward India. Conversation was dying out when, in the lull, everyone in the grove heard Gerald's voice raised in furious accents. Standing some little distance away from the barbecue tables, he was at the peak of an argument with John Wilkes.

'God's nightgown, man! Pray for a peaceable settlement with the Yankees? After we've fired on the rascals at Fort Sumter? Peaceable? The South should show by arms that she cannot be insulted and that she is not leaving the Union by the Union's kindness but by her own strength!'

'Oh, my God!' thought Scarlett. 'He's done it! Now, we'll all sit here till midnight.'

In an instant, the somnolence had fled from the lounging throng and something electric went snapping through the air. The men sprang from benches and chairs, arms in wide gestures, voices clashing for the right to be heard above other voices. There had been no talk of politics or impending war all during the morning, because of Mr Wilkes' request that the ladies should not be bored. But now Gerald had bawled the words 'Fort Sumter', and every man present forgot his host's admonition.

'Of course we'll fight—' 'Yankee thieves—' 'We could lick them in a month—' 'Why, one Southerner can lick twenty Yankees—' 'Teach them a lesson they won't soon forget—' 'Peaceably? They won't let us go in peace—' 'No, look how Mr Lincoln insulted our Commissioners!' 'Yes, kept them hanging around for weeks – swearing he'd have Sumter evacuated!' 'They want war; we'll make them sick of war—' And above all the voices, Gerald's boomed. All Scarlett could hear was 'States' rights, by God!' shouted over and over. Gerald was having an excellent time, but not his daughter.

Secession, war – these words long since had become acutely boring to Scarlett from much repetition, but now she hated the sound of them, for they meant that the men would stand there for hours haranguing one another and she would have no chance to corner Ashley. Of course there would be no war and the men all knew it. They just loved to talk and hear themselves talk.

Charles Hamilton had not risen with the others and, finding himself comparatively alone with Scarlett, he leaned closer and, with the daring born of new love, whispered a confession.

'Miss O'Hara – I – I had already decided that if we did fight, I'd go over to South Carolina and join a troop there. It's said that Mr Wade Hampton is organizing a cavalry troop, and of course I would want to go with him. He's a splendid person and was my father's best friend.'

Scarlett thought, 'What am I supposed to do – give three cheers?' for Charles' expression showed that he was baring his heart's secrets to her. She could think of nothing to say and so merely looked at him wondering why men were such fools as to think women interested in such matters. He took her expression to mean stunned approbation and went on rapidly, daringly—

'If I went – would – would you be sorry, Miss O'Hara?'

'I should cry into my pillow every night,' said Scarlett, meaning to be flippant, but he took the statement at face value and went red with pleasure. Her hand was concealed in the folds of her dress and he cautiously wormed his hand to it and squeezed it, overwhelmed at his own boldness and at her acquiescence.

'Would you pray for me?'

'What a fool!' thought Scarlett bitterly, casting a surreptitious glance about her in the hope of being rescued from the conversation.

'Would you?'

'Oh – yes, indeed, Mr Hamilton. Three Rosaries a night, at least!'

Charles gave a swift look about him, drew in his breath, stiffened the muscles of his stomach. They were practically alone and he might never get another such opportunity. And, even given another such Godsent occasion, his courage might fail him.

'Miss O'Hara – I must tell you something. I – I love you!'

'Um?' said Scarlett absently, trying to peer through the crowd of arguing men to where Ashley still sat talking at Melanie's feet.

'Yes!' whispered Charles, in a rapture that she had neither laughed, screamed nor fainted, as he had always imagined young girls did under such circumstances. 'I love you! You are the most – the most—' and he found his tongue for the first time in his life. 'The most beautiful girl I've ever known and the sweetest and the kindest, and you have the dearest ways and I love you with all my heart. I cannot hope that you could love anyone like me but, my dear Miss O'Hara, if you can give me any encouragement, I will do anything in the world to make you love me. I will—'

Charles stopped, for he couldn't think of anything difficult enough of accomplishment to really prove to Scarlett the depth of his feeling, so he said simply: 'I want to marry you.'

Scarlett came back to earth with a jerk, at the sound of the word 'marry'. She had been thinking of marriage and of Ashley, and she looked at Charles with poorly concealed irritation. Why must this calf-like fool intrude his feelings on this particular day when she was so worried she was about to lose her mind? She looked into the pleading brown eyes and she saw none of the beauty of a shy boy's first love, of the adoration of an ideal come true or the wild happiness and tenderness that were sweeping through him like a flame. Scarlett was used to men asking her to marry them, men much more attractive than Charles Hamilton, and men who had more finesse than to propose at a barbecue when she had more important matters on her mind. She only saw a boy of twenty, red as a beet and looking very silly. She wished that she could tell him how silly he looked. But automatically, the words Ellen had taught her to say in such emergencies rose to her lips and, casting down her eyes, from force of long habit, she murmured: 'Mr Hamilton, I am not unaware of the honour you have bestowed on me in wanting me to become your wife, but this is all so sudden that I do not know what to say.'

That was a neat way of smoothing a man's vanity and yet keeping him on the string, and Charles rose to it as though such bait were new and he the first to swallow it.

'I would wait forever! I wouldn't want you unless you were quite sure. Please, Miss O'Hara, tell me that I may hope?'

'Um,' said Scarlett, her sharp eyes noting that Ashley, who had not risen to take part in the war talk, was smiling up at Melanie. If this fool who was grappling for her hand would only keep quiet for a moment, perhaps she could hear what they were saying. She must hear what they said. What did Melanie say to him that brought that look of interest to his eyes?

Charles' words blurred the voices she strained to hear.

'Oh, hush!' she hissed at him, pinching his hand and not even looking at him.

Startled, at first abashed, Charles blushed at the rebuff and then, seeing how her eyes were fastened on his sister, he smiled. Scarlett was afraid someone might hear his words. She was naturally embarrassed and shy, and in agony lest they be overheard. Charles felt a surge of masculinity such as he had never experienced, for this was the first time in his life that he had ever embarrassed any girl. The thrill was intoxicating. He arranged his face in what he fancied was an expression of careless unconcern and cautiously returned Scarlett's pinch to show that he was man of the world enough to understand and accept her reproof.

She did not even feel his pinch, for she could hear clearly the sweet voice that was Melanie's chief charm: 'I fear I cannot agree with you about Mr Thackeray's works. He is a cynic. I fear he is not the gentleman Mr Dickens is.'

What a silly thing to say to a man, thought Scarlett, ready to giggle with relief. Why, she's no more than a bluestocking and everyone knows what men think of bluestockings . . . The way to get a man interested and to hold his interest was to talk about him, and then gradually lead the conversation around to yourself – and keep it there. Scarlett would have felt some cause for alarm if Melanie had been saying: 'How wonderful you are!' or 'How do you ever think of such things? My little ole brain would bust if I even tried to think about them!' But here she was, with a man at her feet, talking as seriously as if she were in church. The prospect looked brighter to Scarlett, so bright in fact that she turned beaming eyes on Charles and smiled from pure joy. Enraptured at this evidence of her affection, he grabbed up her fan and plied it so enthusiastically her hair began to blow about untidily.

'Ashley, you have not favoured us with your opinion,' said Jim Tarleton, turning from the group of shouting men, and with an apology Ashley excused himself and rose. There was no one there so handsome, thought Scarlett, as she marked how graceful was his negligent pose and how the sun gleamed on his gold hair and moustache. Even the older men stopped to listen to his words.

'Why, gentlemen, if Georgia fights, I'll go with her. Why else would I have joined the Troop?' he said. His grey eyes opened wide and their drowsiness disappeared in an intensity that Scarlett had never seen before. 'But, like Father, I hope the Yankees will let us go in peace and that there will be no fighting—' He held up his hand with a smile, as a babel of voices from the Fontaine and Tarleton boys began. 'Yes, yes, I know we've been insulted and lied to – but if we'd been in the Yankees' shoes and they were trying to leave the Union, how would we have acted? Pretty much the same. We wouldn't have liked it.'

'There he goes again,' thought Scarlett. 'Always putting himself in the other fellow's shoes.' To her, there was never but one fair side to an argument. Sometimes, there was no understanding Ashley.

'Let's don't be too hot-headed and let's don't have any war. Most of the misery of the world has been caused by wars. And when the wars were over, no one ever knew what they were all about.'

Scarlett sniffed. Lucky for Ashley that he had an unassailable reputation for courage, or else there'd be trouble. As she thought this, the clamour of dissenting voices rose up about Ashley, indignant, fiery.

Under the arbour, the deaf old gentleman from Fayetteville punched India.

'What's it all about? What are they saying?'

'War!' shouted India, cupping her hand to his ear. 'They want to fight the Yankees!'

'War, is it?' he cried, fumbling about him for his cane and heaving himself out of his chair with more energy than he had shown in years. 'I'll tell 'um about war. I've been there.' It was not often that Mr McRae had the opportunity to talk about war, the way his women folks shushed him.

He stumped rapidly to the group, waving his cane and shouting and, because he could not hear the voices about him, he soon had undisputed possession of the field.

'You fire-eating young bucks, listen to me. You don't want to fight. I fought and I know. Went out in the Seminole War and was a big enough fool to go to the Mexico War, too. You all don't know what war is. You think it's riding a pretty horse and having the girls throw flowers at you and coming home a hero. Well, it ain't. No, sir! It's going hungry, and getting the measles and pneumonia from sleeping in the wet. And if it ain't measles and pneumonia, it's your bowels. Yes, sir, what war does to a man's bowels – dysentery and things like that—'

The ladies were pink with blushes. Mr McRae was a reminder of a cruder era, like Grandma Fontaine and her embarrassingly loud belches, an era everyone would like to forget.

'Run get your grandpa,' hissed one of the old gentleman's daughters to a young girl standing near by. 'I declare,' she whispered to the fluttering matrons about her, 'he gets worse every day. Would you believe it, this very morning he said to Mary – and she's only sixteen: "Now, Missy . . ." ' and the voice went off into a whisper as the granddaughter slipped out to try to induce Mr McRae to return to his seat in the shade.

Of all the group that milled about under the trees, girls smiling excitedly, men talking impassionedly, there was only one who seemed calm. Scarlett's eyes turned to Rhett Butler, who leaned against a tree, his hands shoved deep in his trouser pockets. He stood alone, since Mr Wilkes had left his side, and had uttered no word as the conversation grew hotter. The red lips under the close-clipped black moustache curled down and there was a glint of amused contempt in his black eyes – contempt, as if he listened to the braggings of children. A very disagreeable smile, Scarlett thought. He listened quietly until Stuart Tarleton, his red hair tousled and his eyes gleaming, repeated: 'Why, we could lick them in a month! Gentlemen always fight better than rabble. A month – why, one battle—'

'Gentlemen,' said Rhett Butler, in a flat drawl that bespoke his Charleston birth, not moving from his position against the tree or taking his hands from his pockets, 'may I say a word?'

There was contempt in his manner as in his eyes, contempt overlaid with an air of courtesy that somehow burlesqued their own manners.

The group turned toward him and accorded him the politeness always due an outsider.

'Has any one of you gentlemen ever thought that there's not a cannon factory south of the Mason-Dixon Line? Or how few iron foundries there are in the South? Or woollen mills or cotton factories or tanneries? Have you thought that we would not have a single warship and that the Yankee fleet could bottle up our harbours in a week, so that we could not sell our cotton abroad? But – of course – you gentlemen have thought of all these things.'

'Why, he means the boys are a passel of fools!' thought Scarlett indignantly, the hot blood coming to her cheeks.

Evidently, she was not the only one to whom this idea occurred, for several of the boys were beginning to stick out their chins. John Wilkes casually but swiftly came back to his place beside the speaker, as if to impress on all present that this man was his guest and that, moreover, there were ladies present.

'The trouble with most of us Southerners,' continued Rhett Butler, 'is that we either don't travel enough or we don't profit enough by our travels. Now, of course, all you gentlemen are well travelled. But what have you seen? Europe and New York and Philadelphia and, of course, the ladies have been to Saratoga' (he bowed slightly to the group under the arbour). 'You've seen the hotels and the museums and the balls and the gambling houses. And you've come home believing that there's no place like the South. As for me, I was

Charleston born, but I have spent the last few years in the North.' His white teeth showed in a grin, as though he realized that everyone present knew just why he no longer lived in Charleston, and cared not at all if they did know. 'I have seen many things that you all have not seen. The thousands of immigrants who'd be glad to fight for the Yankees for food and a few dollars, the factories, the foundries, the shipyards, the iron and coal mines – all the things we haven't got. Why, all we have is cotton and slaves and arrogance. They'd lick us in a month.'

For a tense moment, there was silence. Rhett Butler removed a fine linen handkerchief from his coat pocket and idly flicked dust from his sleeve. Then an ominous murmuring arose in the crowd and from under the arbour came a humming as unmistakable as that of a hive of newly disturbed bees. Even while she felt the hot blood of wrath still in her cheeks, something in Scarlett's practical mind prompted the thought that what this man said was right, and it sounded like common sense. Why, she'd never even seen a factory, or known anyone who had seen a factory. But, even if it were true, he was no gentleman to make such a statement – and at a party, too, where everyone was having a good time.

Stuart Tarleton, brows lowering, came forward with Brent close at his heels. Of course, the Tarleton twins had nice manners and they wouldn't make a scene at a barbecue, even though tremendously provoked. Just the same, all the ladies felt pleasantly excited, for it was so seldom that they actually saw a scene or a quarrel. Usually they had to hear of it third-hand.

'Sir,' said Stuart heavily, 'what do you mean?'

Rhett looked at him with polite but mocking eyes.

'I mean,' he answered, 'what Napoleon – perhaps you've heard of him? – remarked once, "God is on the side of the strongest battalion!" ' and, turning to John Wilkes, he said with courtesy that was unfeigned: 'You promised to show me your library, sir. Would it be too great a favour to ask to see it now? I fear I must go back to Jonesboro early this afternoon where a bit of business calls me.'

He swung about, facing the crowd, clicked his heels together and bowed like a dancing master, a bow that was graceful for so powerful a man, and as full of impertinence as a slap in the face. Then he walked across the lawn with John Wilkes, his black head in the air, and the sound of his discomforting laughter floated back to the group about the tables.

There was a startled silence and then the buzzing broke out again. India rose tiredly from her seat beneath the arbour and went toward the angry Stuart Tarleton. Scarlett could not hear what she said, but the look in her eyes as she gazed up into his lowering face gave Scarlett something like a twinge of conscience. It was the same look of belonging that Melanie wore when she looked at Ashley, only Stuart did not see it. So India did love him. Scarlett thought for an instant that if she had not flirted so blatantly with

Stuart at that political speaking a year ago, he might have married India long ere this. But then the twinge passed with the comforting thought that it wasn't her fault if other girls couldn't keep their men.

Finally Stuart smiled down at India, an unwilling smile, and nodded his head. Probably India had been pleading with him not to follow Mr Butler and make trouble. A polite tumult broke out under the trees as the guests arose, shaking crumbs from their laps. The married women called to nurses and small children and gathered their broods together to take their departure, and groups of girls started off, laughing and talking, toward the house to exchange gossip in the upstairs bedrooms and to take their naps.

All the ladies except Mrs Tarleton moved out of the back yard, leaving the shade of oaks and arbour to the men. She was detained by Gerald, Mr Calvert and the others who wanted an answer from her about the horses for the Troop.

Ashley strolled over to where Scarlett and Charles sat, a thoughtful and amused smile on his face.

'Arrogant devil, isn't he?' he observed, looking after Butler. 'He looks like one of the Borgias.'

Scarlett thought quickly but could remember no family in the County or Atlanta or Savannah by that name.

'I don't know them. Is he kin to them? Who are they?'

An odd look came over Charles' face, incredulity and shame struggling with love. Love triumphed as he realized that it was enough for a girl to be sweet and gentle and beautiful, without having an education to hamper her charms, and he made swift answer: 'The Borgias were Italians.'

'Oh,' said Scarlett, losing interest, 'foreigners.'

She turned her prettiest smile on Ashley, but for some reason he was not looking at her. He was looking at Charles, and there was understanding in his face and a little pity.

Scarlett stood on the landing and peered cautiously over the banisters into the hall below. It was empty. From the bedrooms on the floor above came an unending hum of low voices, rising and falling, punctuated with squeaks of laughter and, 'Now, you didn't, really!' and 'What did he say then?' On the beds and couches of the six great bedrooms, the girls were resting, their dresses off, their stays loosed, their hair flowing down their backs. Afternoon naps were a custom of the country and never were they so necessary as on the all-day parties, beginning early in the morning and culminating in a ball. For half an hour, the girls would chatter and laugh, and then servants would pull in the shutters, and in the warm half-gloom the talk would die to whispers and finally expire in silence broken only by soft regular breathing.

Scarlett had made certain that Melanie was lying down on the bed with Honey and Hetty Tarleton before she slipped into the hall and started down the stairs. From the window on the landing, she could see the group of men sitting under the arbour, drinking from tall glasses, and she knew they would remain there until late afternoon. Her eyes searched the group but Ashley was not among them. Then she listened and she heard his voice. As she had hoped, he was still in the front driveway bidding good-bye to the departing matrons and children.

Her heart in her throat, she went swiftly down the stairs. What if she should meet Mr Wilkes? What excuse could she give for prowling about the house when all the other girls were getting their beauty naps? Well, that had to be risked.

As she reached the bottom step, she heard the servants moving about in the dining-room under the butler's orders, lifting out the table and chairs in preparation for the dancing. Across the wide hall was the open door of the library and she sped into it noiselessly. She could wait there until Ashley finished his adieux and then call to him when he came into the house.

The library was in semi-darkness, for the blinds had been drawn against the sun. The dim room with towering walls completely filled with dark books depressed her. It was not the place which she would have chosen for a tryst such as she hoped this one would be. Large numbers of books always depressed her, as did people who liked to read large numbers of books. That is – all people except Ashley. The heavy furniture rose up at her in the half-light: high-backed chairs with deep seats and wide arms, made for the tall Wilkes men, squatty soft chairs of velvet with velvet hassocks before them for the girls. Far across the long room before the hearth, the seven-foot sofa, Ashley's favourite seat, reared its high back, like some huge sleeping animal.

She closed the door except for a crack and tried to make her heart beat more slowly. She tried to remember just exactly what she had planned last night to say to Ashley, but she couldn't recall anything. Had she thought up something and forgotten it – or had she only planned that Ashley should say something to her? She couldn't remember, and a sudden cold fright fell upon her. If her heart would only stop pounding in her ears, perhaps she could think of what to say. But the quick thudding only increased as she heard him call a final farewell and walk into the front hall.

All she could think of was that she loved him – everything about him, from the proud lift of his gold head to his slender dark boots, loved his laughter even when it mystified her, loved his bewildering silences. Oh, if only he would walk in on her now and take her in his arms, so she would be spared the need of saying anything. He must love her – 'Perhaps if I prayed—' She squeezed her eyes tightly and began gabbling to herself, 'Hail Mary, fullofgrace—'

'Why, Scarlett!' said Ashley's voice, breaking in through the roaring in her ears and throwing her into utter confusion. He stood in the hall peering at her through the partly opened door, a quizzical smile on his face.

'Who are you hiding from – Charles or the Tarletons?'

She gulped. So he had noticed how the men had swarmed about her! How unutterably dear he was standing there with his eyes twinkling, all unaware of her excitement. She could not speak, but she put out a hand and drew him into the room. He entered, puzzled but interested. There was a tenseness about her, a glow in her eyes that he had never seen before, and even in the dim light he could see the rosy flush on her cheeks. Automatically he closed the door behind him and took her hand.

'What is it?' he said, almost in a whisper.

At the touch of his hand, she began to tremble. It was going to happen now, just as she had dreamed it. A thousand incoherent thoughts shot through her mind, and she could not catch a single one to mould into a word. She could only shake and look up into his face. Why didn't he speak?

'What is it?' he repeated. 'A secret to tell me?'

Suddenly she found her tongue and just as suddenly all the years of Ellen's teachings fell away, and the forthright Irish blood of Gerald spoke from his daughter's lips.

'Yes – a secret. I love you.'

For an instant there was a silence so acute it seemed that neither of them even breathed. Then the trembling fell away from her, as happiness and pride surged through her. Why hadn't she done this before? How much simpler than all the ladylike manoeuvrings she had been taught. And then her eyes sought his.

There was a look of consternation in them, of incredulity and something more – what was it? Yes, Gerald had looked that way the day his pet hunter had broken his leg and he had had to shoot him. Why did she have to think of that now? Such a silly thought. And why did Ashley look so oddly and say nothing? Then something like a well-trained mask came down over his face and he smiled gallantly.

'Isn't it enough that you've collected every other man's heart here today?' he said, with the old, teasing, caressing note in his voice. 'Do you want to make it unanimous? Well, you've always had my heart, you know. You cut your teeth on it.'

Something was wrong – all wrong! This was not the way she had planned it. Through the mad tearing of ideas round and round in her brain, one was beginning to take form. Somehow – for some reason – Ashley was acting as if he thought she was just flirting with him. But he knew differently. She knew he did.

'Ashley – Ashley – tell me – you must – oh, don't tease me now! Have I your heart? Oh, my dear, I lo—'

His hand went across her lips, swiftly. The mask was gone.

'You must not say these things, Scarlett! You mustn't. You don't mean them. You'll hate yourself for saying them, and you'll hate me for hearing them!'

She jerked her head away. A hot swift current was running through her.

'I couldn't ever hate you. I tell you I love you and I know you must care about me because—' She stopped. Never before had she seen so much misery in anyone's face. 'Ashley, do you care – you do, don't you?'

'Yes,' he said dully. 'I care.'

If he had said he loathed her, she could not have been more frightened. She plucked at his sleeve, speechless.

'Scarlett,' he said, 'can't we go away and forget that we have ever said these things?'

'No,' she whispered. 'I can't. What do you mean? Don't you want to – to marry me?'

He replied, 'I'm going to marry Melanie.'

Somehow she found that she was sitting on the low velvet chair and Ashley, on the hassock at her feet, was holding both her hands in his, in a hard grip. He was saying things – things that made no sense. Her mind was quite blank, quite empty of all the thoughts that had surged through it only a moment before, and his words made no more impression than rain on glass. They fell on unhearing ears, words that were swift and tender and full of pity, like a father speaking to a hurt child.

The sound of Melanie's name caught her consciousness and she looked into his crystal-grey eyes. She saw in them the old remoteness that had always baffled her – and a look of self-hatred.

'Father is to announce the engagement tonight. We are to be married soon. I should have told you, but I thought you knew. I thought everyone knew – had known for years. I never dreamed that you— You've so many beaux. I thought Stuart—'

Life and feeling and comprehension were beginning to flow back into her.

'But you just said you cared for me.'

His warm hands hurt hers.

'My dear, must you make me say things that will hurt you?'

Her silence pressed him on.

'How can I make you see these things, my dear? You who are so young and unthinking that you do not know what marriage means.'

'I know I love you.'

'Love isn't enough to make a successful marriage when two people are as different as we are. You would want all of a man, Scarlett, his body, his heart, his soul, his thoughts. And if you did not have them, you would be miserable. And I couldn't give you all of me. I couldn't give all of me to anyone. And I would not want all of your mind and soul. And you would be hurt, and then you would come to hate me – how bitterly! You would hate the books I read and the music I loved, because they took me away from you even for a moment. And I – perhaps I—'

'Do you love her?'

'She is like me, part of my blood, and we understand each other. Scarlett!

Scarlett! Can't I make you see that a marriage can't go on in any sort of peace unless the two people are alike?'

Someone else had said that: 'Like must marry like or there'll be no happiness.' Who was it? It seemed a million years since she had heard that, but it still did not make sense.

'But you said you cared.'

'I shouldn't have said it.'

Somewhere in her brain, a slow fire rose and rage began to blot out everything else.

'Well, having been cad enough to say it—'

His face went white.

'I was a cad to say it, as I'm going to marry Melanie. I did you a wrong and Melanie a greater one. I should not have said it, for I knew you wouldn't understand. How could I help caring for you – you who have all the passion for life that I have not? You who can love and hate with a violence impossible to me? Why, you are as elemental as fire and wind and wild things and I—'

She thought of Melanie and saw suddenly her quiet brown eyes with their far-off look, her placid little hands in their black lace mitts, her gentle silences. And then her rage broke, the same rage that drove Gerald to murder and other Irish ancestors to misdeeds that cost them their necks. There was nothing in her now of the well-bred Robillards who could bear with white silence anything the world might cast.

'Why don't you say it, you coward! You're afraid to marry me! You'd rather live with that stupid little fool who can't open her mouth except to say "Yes" or "No" and raise a passel of mealy-mouthed brats just like her! Why—'

'You must not say these things about Melanie!'

' "I mustn't" be damned to you! Who are you to tell me I mustn't? You coward, you cad, you— You made me believe you were going to marry me—'

'Be fair,' his voice pleaded. 'Did I ever—'

She did not want to be fair, although she knew what he said was true. He had never once crossed the borders of friendliness with her and, when she thought of this, fresh anger rose, the anger of hurt pride and feminine vanity. She had run after him and he would have none of her. He preferred a whey-faced little fool like Melanie to her. Oh, far better that she had followed Ellen and Mammy's precepts and never, never revealed that she even liked him – better anything than to be faced with this scorching shame!

She sprang to her feet, her hands clenched, and he rose towering over her, his face full of the mute misery of one forced to face realities when realities are agonies.

'I shall hate you till I die, you cad – you lowdown – lowdown—' What was the word she wanted? She could not think of any word bad enough.

'Scarlett – please—'

He put out his hand toward her and, as he did, she slapped him across the face with all the strength she had. The noise cracked like a whip in the still room and suddenly her rage was gone, and there was desolation in her heart.

The red mark of her hand showed plainly on his white tired face. He said nothing, but lifted her limp hand to his lips and kissed it. Then he was gone before she could speak again, closing the door softly behind him.

She sat down again very suddenly, the reaction from her rage making her knees feel weak. He was gone and the memory of his stricken face would haunt her till she died.

She heard the soft muffled sound of his footsteps dying away down the long hall, and the complete enormity of her actions came over her. She had lost him forever. Now he would hate her and every time he looked at her he would remember how she threw herself at him when he had given her no encouragement at all.

'I'm as bad as Honey Wilkes,' she thought suddenly, and remembered how everyone, and she more than anyone else, had laughed contemptuously at Honey's forward conduct. She saw Honey's awkward wigglings and heard her silly titters as she hung on to boys' arms, and the thought stung her to new rage, rage at herself, at Ashley, at the world. Because she hated herself, she hated them all with the fury of the thwarted and humiliated love of sixteen. Only a little true tenderness had been mixed into her love. Mostly it had been compounded out of vanity and complacent confidence in her own charms. Now she had lost, and greater than her sense of loss was the fear that she had made a public spectacle of herself. Had she been as obvious as Honey? Was everyone laughing at her? She began to shake at the thought.

Her hand dropped to a little table beside her, fingering a tiny china rose-bowl on which two china cherubs smirked. The room was so still she almost screamed to break the silence. She must do something or go mad. She picked up the bowl and hurled it viciously across the room toward the fireplace. It barely cleared the tall back of the sofa and splintered with a little crash against the marble mantelpiece.

'This,' said a voice from the depths of the sofa, 'is too much.'

Nothing had ever startled or frightened her so much, and her mouth went too dry for her to utter a sound. She caught hold of the back of the chair, her knees going weak under her, as Rhett Butler rose from the sofa where he had been lying and made her a bow of exaggerated politeness.

'It is bad enough to have an afternoon nap disturbed by such a passage as I've been forced to hear, but why should my life be endangered?'

He was real. He wasn't a ghost. But, saints preserve us, he had heard everything! She rallied her forces into a semblance of dignity.

'Sir, you should have made known your presence.'

'Indeed?' His white teeth gleamed and his bold dark eyes laughed at her.

'But you were the intruder. I was forced to wait for Mr Kennedy, and feeling that I was perhaps persona non grata in the back yard, I was thoughtful enough to remove my unwelcome presence here where I thought I would be undisturbed. But, alas!' He shrugged and laughed softly.

Her temper was beginning to rise again at the thought that this rude and impertinent man had heard everything – heard things she now wished she had died before she ever uttered.

'Eavesdroppers—' she began furiously.

'Eavesdroppers often hear highly entertaining and instructive things,' he grinned. 'From a long experience in eavesdropping, I—'

'Sir,' she said, 'you are no gentleman!'

'An apt observation,' he answered airily. 'And you, Miss, are no lady.' He seemed to find her very amusing, for he laughed softly again. 'No one can remain a lady after saying and doing what I have just overheard. However, ladies have seldom held any charms for me. I know what they are thinking, but they never have the courage or lack of breeding to say what they think. And that, in time, becomes a bore. But you, my dear Miss O'Hara, are a girl of rare spirit, very admirable spirit, and I take off my hat to you. I fail to understand what charms the elegant Mr Wilkes can hold for a girl of your tempestuous nature. He should thank God on bended knee for a girl with your – how did he put it? – "passion for living", but being a poor-spirited wretch—'

'You aren't fit to wipe his boots!' she shouted in rage.

'And you were going to hate him all your life!' He sank down on the sofa and she heard him laughing.

If she could have killed him, she would have done it. Instead, she walked out of the room with such dignity as she could summon and banged the heavy door behind her.

She went up the stairs so swiftly that, when she reached the landing, she thought she was going to faint. She stopped, clutching the banisters, her heart hammering so hard from anger, insult and exertion that it seemed about to burst through her basque. She tried to draw deep breaths but Mammy's lacings were too tight. If she should faint and they should find her here on the landing, what would they think? Oh, they'd think everything, Ashley and that vile Butler man and those nasty girls who were so jealous! For once in her life, she wished that she carried smelling salts, like the other girls, but she had never owned a vinaigrette. She had always been so proud of never feeling giddy. She simply could not let herself faint now!

Gradually the sickening feeling began to depart. In a minute, she'd feel all right and then she'd slip quietly into the little dressing-room adjoining India's room, unloose her stays and creep in and lay herself on one of the beds beside the sleeping girls. She tried to quiet her heart and fix her face into more composed lines, for she knew she must look like a crazy woman.

If any of the girls were awake, they'd know something was wrong. And no one must ever, ever know that anything had happened.

Through the wide bay window on the landing, she could see the men still lounging in their chairs under the trees and in the shade of the arbour. How she envied them! How wonderful to be a man and never have to undergo miseries such as she had just passed through! As she stood watching them, hot-eyed and dizzy, she heard the rapid pounding of a horse's hooves on the front drive, the scattering of gravel and the sound of an excited voice calling a question to one of the negroes. The gravel flew again and across her vision a man on horseback galloped over the green lawn toward the lazy group under the trees.

Some late-come guest; but why did he ride his horse across the turf that was India's pride? She could not recognize him, but as he flung himself from the saddle and clutched John Wilkes' arm, she could see that there was excitement in every line of him. The crowd swarmed about him, tall glasses and palmetto fans abandoned on tables and on the ground. In spite of the distance, she could hear the hubbub of voices, questioning, calling, feel the fever-pitch tenseness of the men. Then above the confused sounds Stuart Tarleton's voice rose, in an exultant shout, 'Yee-aay-ee!' as if he were on the hunting field. And she heard for the first time, without knowing it, the Rebel yell.

As she watched, the four Tarletons followed by the Fontaine boys broke from the group and began hurrying toward the stable, yelling as they ran, 'Jeems! You, Jeems! Saddle the horses!'

'Somebody's house must have caught fire,' Scarlett thought. But fire or no fire, her job was to get herself back into the bedroom before she was discovered.

Her heart was quieter now and she tiptoed up the steps into the silent hall. A heavy warm somnolence lay over the house, as if it slept at ease like the girls, until night when it would burst into its full beauty with music and candle-flames. Carefully, she eased open the door of the dressing-room and slipped in. Her hand was behind her, still holding the knob, when Honey Wilkes' voice, low pitched, almost in a whisper, came to her through the crack of the opposite door leading into the bedroom.

'I think Scarlett acted as fast as a girl could act today.'

Scarlett felt her heart begin its mad racing again and she clutched her hand against it unconsciously, as if she would squeeze it into submission. 'Eavesdroppers often hear highly instructive things,' jibed a memory. Should she slip out again? Or make herself known and embarrass Honey as she deserved? But the next voice made her pause. A team of mules could not have dragged her away when she heard Melanie's voice.

'Oh, Honey, no! Don't be unkind. She's just high-spirited and vivacious. I thought her most charming.'

'Oh,' thought Scarlett, clawing her nails into her basque. 'To have that mealy-mouthed little mess take up for me!'

It was harder to hear than Honey's out-and-out cattiness. Scarlett had never trusted any woman and had never credited any woman except her mother with motives other than selfish ones. Melanie knew she had Ashley securely, so she could well afford to show such a Christian spirit. Scarlett felt it was just Melanie's way of parading her conquest and getting credit for being sweet at the same time. Scarlett had frequently used the same trick herself when discussing other girls with men, and it had never failed to convince foolish males of her sweetness and unselfishness.

'Well, Miss,' said Honey tartly, her voice rising, 'you must be blind.'

'Hush, Honey,' hissed the voice of Sally Munroe. 'They'll hear you all over the house!'

Honey lowered her voice, but went on.

'Well, you saw how she was carrying on with every man she could get hold of – even Mr Kennedy and he's her own sister's beau. I never saw the like! And she certainly was going after Charles.' Honey giggled self-consciously. 'And you know, Charles and I—'

'Are you really?' whispered voices excitedly.

'Well, don't tell anybody, girls – not yet!'

There were more gigglings and the bed-springs creaked as someone squeezed Honey. Melanie murmured something about how happy she was that Honey would be her sister.

'Well, I won't be happy to have Scarlett for my sister, because she's a fast piece if ever I saw one,' came the aggrieved voice of Hetty Tarleton. 'But she's as good as engaged to Stuart. Brent says she doesn't give a rap about him, but, of course, Brent's crazy about her, too.'

'If you should ask me,' said Honey with mysterious importance, 'there's only one person she does give a rap about. And that's Ashley!'

As the whisperings merged together violently, questioning, interrupting, Scarlett felt herself go cold with fear and humiliation. Honey was a fool, a silly, a simpleton about men, but she had a feminine instinct about other women that Scarlett had under-estimated. The mortification and hurt pride that she had suffered in the library with Ashley and with Rhett Butler were pin-pricks to this. Men could be trusted to keep their mouths shut, even men like Mr Butler, but with Honey Wilkes giving tongue like a hound in the field, the entire County would know about it before six o'clock. And Gerald had said only last night that he wouldn't be having the County laughing at his daughter. And how they would all laugh now! Clammy perspiration, starting under her armpits, began to creep down her ribs.

Melanie's voice, measured and peaceful, a little reproving, rose above the others.

'Honey, you know that isn't so. And it's so unkind.'

'It is too, Melly, and if you weren't always so busy looking for the good in people that haven't got any good in them, you'd see it. And I'm glad it's so. It serves her right. All Scarlett O'Hara has ever done has been to stir up trouble and try to get other girls' beaux. You know mighty well she took Stuart from India and she didn't want him. And today she tried to take Mr Kennedy and Ashley and Charles—'

'I must get home!' thought Scarlett. 'I must get home!'

If she could only be transferred by magic to Tara and to safety. If she could only be with Ellen, just to see her, to hold on to her skirt, to cry and pour out the whole story in her lap. If she had to listen to another word, she'd rush in and pull out Honey's straggly pale hair in big handfuls and spit on Melanie Hamilton to show her just what she thought of her charity. But she'd already acted common enough today, enough like white trash – that was where all her trouble lay.

She pressed her hands hard against her skirts, so they would not rustle, and backed out as stealthily as an animal. 'Home,' she thought, as she sped down the hall, past the closed doors and still rooms, 'I must go home.'

She was already on the front porch when a new thought brought her up sharply – she couldn't go home! She couldn't run away! She would have to see it through, bear all the malice of the girls and her own humiliation and heartbreak. To run away would only give them more ammunition.

She pounded her clenched fist against the tall white pillar beside her, and she wished that she were Samson, so that she could pull down all of Twelve Oaks and destroy every person in it. She'd make them sorry. She'd show them. She didn't quite see how she'd show them, but she'd do it all the same. She'd hurt them worse than they hurt her.

For the moment, Ashley as Ashley was forgotten. He was not the tall drowsy boy she loved but part and parcel of the Wilkeses, Twelve Oaks, the County – and she hated them all because they laughed. Vanity was stronger than love at sixteen and there was no room in her hot heart now for anything but hate.

'I won't go home,' she thought. 'I'll stay here and I'll make them sorry. And I'll never tell Mother. No, I'll never tell anybody.' She braced herself to go back into the house, to reclimb the stairs and go into another bedroom.

As she turned, she saw Charles coming into the house from the other end of the long hall. When he saw her, he hurried toward her. His hair was tousled and his face near geranium with excitement.

'Do you know what's happened?' he cried, even before he reached her. 'Have you heard? Paul Wilson just rode over from Jonesboro with the news!'

He paused, breathless, as he came up to her. She said nothing and only stared at him.

'Mr Lincoln has called for men, soldiers – I mean volunteers – seventy-five thousand of them!'

Mr Lincoln again! Didn't men ever think about anything that really mattered? Here was this fool expecting her to be excited about Mr Lincoln's didoes when her heart was broken and her reputation as good as ruined.

Charles stared at her. Her face was paper white and her narrow eyes blazing like emeralds. He had never seen such fire in any girl's face, such a glow in anyone's eyes.

'I'm so clumsy,' he said. 'I should have told you more gently. I forgot how delicate ladies are. I'm sorry I've upset you so. You don't feel faint, do you? Can I get you a glass of water?'

'No,' she said, and managed a crooked smile.

'Shall we go sit on the bench?' he asked, taking her arm.

She nodded and he carefully handed her down the front steps and led her across the grass to the iron bench beneath the largest oak in the front yard. 'How fragile and tender women are,' he thought; 'the mere mention of war and harshness makes them faint.' The idea made him feel very masculine and he was doubly gentle as he seated her. She looked so strangely, and there was a wild beauty about her white face that set his heart leaping. Could it be that she was distressed by the thought that he might go to the war? No, that was too conceited for belief. But why did she look at him so oddly? And why did her hands shake as they fingered her lace handkerchief? And her thick sooty lashes – they were fluttering just like the eyes of girls in romances he had read, fluttering with timidity and love.

He cleared his throat three times to speak and failed each time. He dropped his eyes because her own green ones met his so piercingly, almost as if she were not seeing him.

'He has a lot of money,' she was thinking swiftly, as a thought and a plan went through her brain. 'And he hasn't any parents to bother me and he lives in Atlanta. And if I married him right away, it would show Ashley that I didn't care a rap – that I was only flirting with him. And it would just kill Honey. She'd never, never catch another beau and everybody'd laugh fit to die at her. And it would hurt Melanie, because she loves Charles so much. And it would hurt Stu and Brent—' She didn't quite know why she wanted to hurt them, except that they had catty sisters. 'And they'd all be sorry when I came back here to visit in a fine carriage and with lots of pretty clothes and a house of my own. And they would never, never laugh at me.'

'Of course, it will mean fighting,' said Charles, after several more embarrassed attempts. 'But don't you fret, Miss Scarlett, it'll be over in a month and we'll have them howling. Yes, sir! Howling! I wouldn't miss it for anything. I'm afraid there won't be much of a ball tonight, because the Troop is going to meet at Jonesboro. The Tarleton boys have gone to spread the news. I know the ladies will be sorry.'

She said, 'Oh,' for want of anything better, but it sufficed.

Coolness was beginning to come back to her and her mind was collecting itself. A frost lay over all her emotions and she thought that she would never feel anything warmly again. Why not take this pretty, flushed boy? He was as good as anyone else and she didn't care. No, she could never care about anything again, not if she lived to be ninety.

'I can't decide now whether to go with Mr Wade Hampton's South Carolina Legion or with the Atlanta Gate City Guard.'

She said, 'Oh,' again and their eyes met and the fluttering lashes were his undoing.

'Will you wait for me, Miss Scarlett? It – it would be Heaven just knowing that you were waiting for me until after we licked them!' He hung breathless on her words, watching the way her lips curled up at the corners, noting for the first time the shadows about these corners and thinking what it would mean to kiss them. Her hand, with palm clammy with perspiration, slid into his.

'I wouldn't want to wait,' she said, and her eyes were veiled.

He sat clutching her hand, his mouth wide open. Watching him from under her lashes, Scarlett thought detachedly that he looked like a gigged frog. He stuttered several times, closed his mouth and opened it again, and again became geranium-coloured.

'Can you possibly love me?'

She said nothing but looked down into her lap, and Charles was thrown into new states of ecstasy and embarrassment. Perhaps a man should not ask a girl such a question. Perhaps it would be unmaidenly for her to answer it. Having never possessed the courage to get himself into such a situation before, Charles was at a loss as to how to act. He wanted to shout and to sing and to kiss her and to caper about the lawn and then run tell everyone, black and white, that she loved him. But he only squeezed her hand until he drove her rings into the flesh.

'You will marry me soon, Miss Scarlett?'

'Um,' she said, fingering a fold of her dress.

'Shall we make it a double wedding with Mel—'

'No,' she said quickly, her eyes glinting up at him ominously. Charles knew again that he had made an error. Of course, a girl wanted her own wedding – not shared glory. How kind she was to overlook his blunderings! If it were only dark and he had the courage of shadows and could kiss her hand and say the things he longed to say.

'When may I speak to your father?'

'The sooner the better,' she said, hoping that perhaps he would release the crushing pressure on her rings before she had to ask him to do it.

He leaped up and for a moment she thought he was going to cut a caper, before dignity claimed him. He looked down at her radiantly, his whole clean simple heart in his eyes. She had never had anyone look at her thus before and would never have it from any other man, but in her queer detachment she only thought that he looked like a calf.

'I'll go now and find your father,' he said, smiling all over his face. 'I can't wait. Will you excuse me – dear?' The endearment came hard but having said it once, he repeated it again with pleasure.

'Yes,' she said, 'I'll wait here. It's so cool and nice here.'

He went off across the lawn and disappeared around the house, and she was alone under the rustling oak. From the stables, men were streaming out on horseback, negro servants riding hard behind their master. The Munroe boys tore past waving their hats, and the Fontaines and Calverts went down the road yelling. The four Tarletons charged across the lawn by her and Brent shouted: 'Mother's going to give us the horses! Yee-aay-ee!' Turf flew and they were gone, leaving her alone again.

The white house reared its tall columns before her, seeming to withdraw with dignified aloofness from her. It would never be her house now. Ashley would never carry her over the threshold as his bride. Oh, Ashley, Ashley! What have I done? Deep in her, under layers of hurt pride and cold practicality, something stirred hurtingly. An adult emotion was being born, stronger than her vanity or her wilful selfishness. She loved Ashley and she knew she loved him, and she had never cared so much as in that instant when she saw Charles disappearing around the curved gravelled walk.

Chapter VII

Within two weeks Scarlett had become a wife, and within two months more she was a widow. She was soon released from the bonds she had assumed with so much haste and so little thought, but she was never again to know the careless freedom of her unmarried days. Widowhood had crowded closely on the heels of marriage but, to her dismay, motherhood soon followed.

In after years when she thought of those last days of April, 1861, Scarlett could never quite remember details. Time and events were telescoped, jumbled together like a nightmare that had no reality or reason. Till the day she died there would be blank spots in her memories of those days. Especially vague were her recollections of the time between her acceptance of Charles and her wedding. Two weeks! So short an engagement would have been impossible in times of peace. Then there would have been a decorous interval of a year or at least six months. But the South was aflame with war, events roared along as swiftly as if carried by a mighty wind and the slow tempo of the old days was gone. Ellen had wrung her hands and counselled delay, in order that Scarlett might think the matter over at greater length. But to her pleadings, Scarlett turned a sullen face and a deaf ear. Marry she would! And quickly too. Within two weeks.

Learning that Ashley's wedding had been moved up from the autumn to the first of May, so he could leave with the Troop as soon as it was called into service, Scarlett set the date of her wedding for the day before his. Ellen protested but Charles pleaded with new-found eloquence, for he was impatient to be off to South Carolina to join Wade Hampton's Legion, and Gerald sided with the two young people. He was excited by the war fever and pleased that Scarlett had made so good a match, and who was he to stand in the way of young love when there was a war? Ellen, distracted, finally gave in as other mothers throughout the South were doing. Their leisured world had been turned topsy-turvy, and their pleadings, prayers and advice availed nothing against the powerful forces sweeping them along.

The South was intoxicated with enthusiasm and excitement. Everyone knew that one battle would end the war and every young man hastened to enlist before the war should end – hastened to marry his sweetheart before he rushed off to Virginia to strike a blow at the Yankees. There were dozens of war weddings in the County and there was little time for the sorrow of parting, for everyone was too busy and excited for either solemn thoughts or tears. The ladies were making uniforms, knitting socks and rolling bandages, and the men were drilling and shooting. Train-loads of troops passed through Jonesboro daily on their way north to Atlanta and Virginia. Some detachments were gaily uniformed in the scarlets and light blues and greens of select social-militia companies; some small groups were in homespun and coonskin caps; others, ununiformed, were in broadcloth and fine linen; all were half-drilled, half-armed, wild with excitement and shouting as though en route to a picnic. The sight of these men threw the County boys into a panic for fear the war would be over before they could reach Virginia, and preparations for the Troop's departure were speeded.

In the midst of the turmoil, preparations went forward for Scarlett's wedding and, almost before she knew it, she was clad in Ellen's wedding dress and veil, coming down the wide stairs of Tara on her father's arm, to face a house packed full with guests. Afterward she remembered, as from a dream, the hundreds of candles flaring on the walls, her mother's face, loving, a little bewildered, her lips moving in a silent prayer for her daughter's happiness, Gerald flushed with brandy and pride that his daughter was marrying both money, a fine name and an old one – and Ashley, standing at the bottom of the steps with Melanie's arm through his.

When she saw the look on his face, she thought: 'This can't be real. It can't be. It's a nightmare. I'll wake up and find it's all been a nightmare. I mustn't think of it now, or I'll begin screaming in front of all these people. I can't think now. I'll think later, when I can stand it – when I can't see his eyes.'

It was all very dreamlike, the passage through the aisle of smiling people, Charles' scarlet face and stammering voice and her own replies, so startlingly clear, so cold. And the congratulations afterward and the kissing and the toasts and the dancing – all, all like a dream. Even the feel of Ashley's kiss upon her cheek, even Melanie's soft whisper, 'Now, we're really and truly sisters,' were unreal. Even the excitement caused by the swooning spell that overtook Charles' plump emotional aunt, Miss Pittypat Hamilton, had the quality of a nightmare.

But when the dancing and toasting were finally ended and the dawn was coming, when all the Atlanta guests who could be crowded into Tara and the overseer's house had gone to sleep on beds, sofas and pallets on the floor, and all the neighbours had gone home to rest in preparation for the wedding at Twelve Oaks the next day, then the dreamlike trance shattered like crystal before reality. The reality was the blushing Charles, emerging from her dressing-room in his nightshirt, avoiding the startled look she gave him over the high-pulled sheet.

Of course, she knew that married people occupied the same bed but she had never given the matter a thought before. It seemed very natural in the case of her mother and father, but she had never applied it to herself. Now for the first time since the barbecue she realized just what she had brought on herself. The thought of this strange boy whom she hadn't really wanted to marry getting into bed with her, when her heart was breaking with an agony of regret at her hasty action and the anguish of losing Ashley forever, was too much to be borne. As he hesitatingly approached the bed she spoke in a hoarse whisper.

'I'll scream out loud if you come near me. I will! I will – at the top of my voice! Get away from me! Don't you dare touch me!'

So Charles Hamilton spent his wedding night in an armchair in the corner, not too unhappily, for he understood, or thought he understood, the modesty and delicacy of his bride. He was willing to wait until her fears subsided, only – only— He sighed as he twisted about seeking a comfortable position, for he was going away to the war so very soon.

Nightmarish as her own wedding had been, Ashley's wedding was even worse. Scarlett stood in her apple-green 'second-day' dress in the parlour of Twelve Oaks amid the blaze of hundreds of candles, jostled by the same throng as the night before, and saw the plain little face of Melanie Hamilton glow into beauty as she became Melanie Wilkes. Now, Ashley was gone forever. Her Ashley. No, not her Ashley now. Had he ever been hers? It was all so mixed up in her mind and her mind was so tired, so bewildered. He had said he loved her, but what was it that had separated them? If she could only remember. She had stilled the County's gossiping tongue by marrying Charles, but what did that matter now? It had seemed so important once, but now it didn't seem important at all. All that mattered was Ashley. Now he was gone and she was married to a man she not only did not love but for whom she had an active contempt.

Oh, how she regretted it all. She had often heard of people cutting off their noses to spite their faces but heretofore it had been only a figure of speech. Now she knew just what it meant. And mingled with her frenzied desire to be free of Charles and safely back at Tara, an unmarried girl again, ran the knowledge that she had only herself to blame. Ellen had tried to stop her and she would not listen.

So she danced through the night of Ashley's wedding in a daze and said things mechanically and smiled and irrelevantly wondered at the stupidity of people who thought her a happy bride and could not see that her heart was broken. Well, thank God, they couldn't see!

That night after Mammy had helped her undress and had departed and Charles had emerged shyly from the dressing-room, wondering if he was to spend a second night in the horsehair chair, she burst into tears. She cried until Charles climbed into bed beside her and tried to comfort her, cried without words until no more tears would come and at last she lay sobbing quietly on his shoulder.

If there had not been a war, there would have been a week of visiting about the County, with balls and barbecues in honour of the two newly married couples before they set off to Saratoga or White Sulphur for wedding trips. If there had not been a war, Scarlett would have had third-day and fourth-day and fifth-day dresses to wear to the Fontaine and Calvert and Tarleton parties in her honour. But there were no parties now and no wedding trips. A week after the wedding Charles left to join Colonel Wade Hampton, and two weeks later Ashley and the Troop departed, leaving the whole County bereft.

In those two weeks, Scarlett never saw Ashley alone, never had a private word with him. Not even at the terrible moment of parting, when he stopped by Tara on his way to the train, did she have a private talk. Melanie, bonneted and shawled, sedate in newly acquired matronly dignity, hung on his arm and the entire personnel of Tara, black and white, turned out to see Ashley off to the war.

Melanie said: 'You must kiss Scarlett, Ashley. She's my sister now,' and Ashley bent and touched her cheek with cold lips, his face drawn and taut. Scarlett could hardly take any joy from that kiss, so sullen was her heart at Melly's prompting it. Melanie smothered her with an embrace at parting.

'You will come to Atlanta and visit me and Aunt Pittypat, won't you? Oh, darling, we want to have you so much! We want to know Charlie's wife better.'

Five weeks passed during which letters, shy, ecstatic, loving, came from Charles in South Carolina telling of his love, his plans for the future when the war was over, his desire to become a hero for her sake and his worship of his commander, Wade Hampton. In the seventh week, there came a telegram from Colonel Hampton himself, and then a letter, a kind, dignified letter of condolence. Charles was dead. The colonel would have wired earlier, but Charles, thinking his illness a trifling one, did not wish to have his family worried. The unfortunate boy had not only been cheated of the love he thought he had won but also of his high hopes of honour and glory on the field of battle. He had died ignominiously and swiftly of pneumonia, following measles, without ever having gotten any closer to the Yankees than the camp in South Carolina.

In due time, Charles' son was born and, because it was fashionable to name boys after their fathers' commanding officers, he was called Wade Hampton Hamilton. Scarlett had wept with despair at the knowledge that she was pregnant and wished that she were dead. But she carried the child through its time with minimum of discomfort, bore him with little distress and recovered so quickly that Mammy told her privately it was downright common – ladies should suffer more. She felt little affection for the child, hide the fact though she might. She had not wanted him and she resented his coming and, now that he was here, it did not seem possible that he was hers, a part of her.

Though she recovered physically from Wade's birth in a disgracefully short time, mentally she was dazed and sick. Her spirits drooped, despite the efforts of the whole plantation to revive them. Ellen went about with a puckered, worried forehead and Gerald swore more frequently than usual and brought her useless gifts from Jonesboro. Even old Dr Fontaine admitted that he was puzzled, after his tonic of sulphur, molasses and herbs failed to perk her up. He told Ellen privately that it was a broken heart that made Scarlett so irritable and listless by turns. But Scarlett, had she wished to speak, could have told them that it was a far different and more complex trouble. She did not tell them that it was utter boredom, bewilderment at actually being a mother and, most of all, the absence of Ashley that made her look so woebegone.

Her boredom was acute and ever-present. The County had been devoid of any entertainment or social life ever since the Troop had gone away to war. All of the interesting young men were gone – the four Tarletons, the two Calverts, the Fontaines, the Munroes and everyone from Jonesboro, Fayetteville and Lovejoy who was young and attractive. Only the older men, the cripples and the women were left, and they spent their time knitting and sewing, growing more cotton and corn, raising more hogs and sheep and cows for the army. There was never a sight of a real man except when the commissary troop under Suellen's middle-aged beau, Frank Kennedy, rode by every month to collect supplies. The men in the commissary were not very exciting, and the sight of Frank's timid courting annoyed her until she found it difficult to be polite to him. If he and Suellen would only get it over with!

Even if the commissary troop had been more interesting, it would not have helped her situation any. She was a widow and her heart was in the grave. At least, everyone thought it was in the grave and expected her to act accordingly. This irritated her for, try as she could, she could recall nothing about Charles except the dying-calf look on his face when she told him she would marry him. And even that picture was fading. But she was a widow and she had to watch her behaviour. Not for her the pleasures of unmarried girls. She had to be grave and aloof. Ellen had stressed this at great length after catching Frank's lieutenant swinging Scarlett in the garden swing and making her squeal with laughter. Deeply distressed, Ellen had told her how easily a widow might get herself talked about. The conduct of a widow must be twice as circumspect as that of a matron.

'And God only knows,' thought Scarlett, listening obediently to her mother's soft voice, 'matrons never have any fun at all. So widows might as well be dead.'

A widow had to wear hideous black dresses without even a touch of braid to enliven them, no flower or ribbon or lace or even jewellery, except onyx mourning brooches or necklaces made from the deceased's hair. And the black crêpe veil on her bonnet had to reach to her knees, and only after three years of widowhood could it be shortened to shoulder length. Widows could never chatter vivaciously or laugh aloud. Even when they smiled, it must be a sad, tragic smile. And, most dreadful of all, they could in no way indicate an interest in the company of gentlemen. And should a gentleman be so ill-bred as to indicate an interest in her, she must freeze him with a dignified but well-chosen reference to her dead husband. 'Oh, yes,' thought Scarlett, drearily, 'some widows do remarry eventually, when they are old and stringy. Though Heaven knows how they manage it, with their neighbours watching. And then it's generally to some desperate old widower with a large plantation and a dozen children.'

Marriage was bad enough, but to be widowed – oh, then life was over forever! How stupid people were when they talked about what a comfort little Wade Hampton must be to her, now that Charles was gone! How stupid of them to say that now she had something to live for! Everyone talked about how sweet it was that she had this posthumous token of her love and she naturally did not disabuse their minds. But that thought was farthest from her mind. She had very little interest in Wade and sometimes it was difficult to remember that he was actually hers.

Every morning she woke up and for a drowsy moment she was Scarlett O'Hara again and the sun was bright in the magnolia outside her window and the mockers were singing and the sweet smell of frying bacon was stealing to her nostrils. She was carefree and young again. Then she heard the fretful hungry wail and always – always there was a startled moment when she thought: 'Why, there's a baby in the house!' Then she remembered that it was her baby. It was all very bewildering.

And Ashley! Oh, most of all Ashley! For the first time in her life, she hated Tara, hated the long red road that led down the hill to the river, hated the red fields with springing green cotton. Every foot of ground, every tree and brook, every lane and bridle path reminded her of him. He belonged to another woman and he had gone to the war, but his ghost still haunted the roads in the twilight, still smiled at her from drowsy grey eyes in the shadows of the porch. She never heard the sound of hooves coming up the river road from Twelve Oaks that for a sweet moment she did not think – Ashley!

She hated Twelve Oaks now and once she had loved it. She hated it but she was drawn there, so she could hear John Wilkes and the girls talk about him – hear them read his letters from Virginia. They hurt her but she had to hear them. She disliked the stiff-necked India and the foolish prattling Honey and knew they disliked her equally, but she could not stay away from them. And every time she came home from Twelve Oaks, she lay down on her bed morosely and refused to get up for supper.

It was this refusal of food that worried Ellen and Mammy more than anything else. Mammy brought up tempting trays, insinuating that now she was a widow she might eat as much as she pleased, but Scarlett had no appetite.

When Dr Fontaine told Ellen gravely that heartbreak frequently led to a decline and women pined away into the grave, Ellen went white, for that fear was what she had carried in her heart.

'Isn't there anything to be done, Doctor?'

'A change of scene will be the best thing in the world for her,' said the doctor, only too anxious to be rid of an unsatisfactory patient.

So Scarlett, unenthusiastic, went off with her child, first to visit her O'Hara and Robillard relatives in Savannah and then to Ellen's sisters, Pauline and Eulalie, in Charleston. But she was back at Tara a month before Ellen expected her, with no explanation of her return. They had been kind in Savannah, but James and Andrew and their wives were old and content to sit quietly and talk of a past in which Scarlett had no interest. It was the same with the Robillards, and Charleston was terrible, Scarlett thought.

Aunt Pauline and her husband, a little old man, with a formal, brittle courtesy and the absent air of one living in an older age, lived on a plantation on the river, far more isolated than Tara. Their nearest neighbour was twenty miles away by dark roads through still jungles of cypress swamp and oak. The live oaks with their waving curtains of grey moss gave Scarlett the creeps and always brought to her mind Gerald's stories of Irish ghosts roaming in shimmering grey mists. There was nothing to do but knit all day and at night listen to Uncle Carey read aloud from the improving works of Mr Bulwer-Lytton.

Eulalie, hidden behind a high-walled garden in a great house on the Battery in Charleston, was no more entertaining. Scarlett, accustomed to wide vistas of rolling red hills, felt that she was in prison. There was more social life here than at Aunt Pauline's, but Scarlett did not like the people who called, with their airs and their traditions and their emphasis on family. She knew very well they all thought she was a child of a mésalliance and wondered how a Robillard ever married a newly come Irishman. Scarlett felt that Aunt Eulalie apologized for her behind her back. This aroused her temper, for she cared no more about family than her father. She was proud of Gerald and what he had accomplished unaided except by his shrewd Irish brain.

And the Charlestonians took so much upon themselves about Fort Sumter! Good Heavens, didn't they realize that if they hadn't been silly enough to fire the shot that started the war some other fools would have done it? Accustomed to the brisk voices of upland Georgia, the drawling flat voices of the low country seemed affected to her. She thought if she ever again heard voices that said 'paams' for 'palms' and 'hoose' for 'house' and 'woon't' for 'won't' and 'Maa and Paa' for 'Ma and Pa', she would scream. It irritated her so much that during one formal call she aped Gerald's brogue to her aunt's distress. Then she went back to Tara. Better to be tormented with memories of Ashley than Charleston accents.

Ellen, busy night and day, doubling the productiveness of Tara to aid the Confederacy, was terrified when her eldest daughter came home from Charleston thin, white and sharp-tongued. She had known heartbreak herself, and night after night she lay beside the snoring Gerald trying to think of some way to lessen Scarlett's distress. Charles' aunt, Miss Pittypat Hamilton, had written her several times, urging her to permit Scarlett to come to Atlanta for a long visit, and now for the first time Ellen considered it seriously.

She and Melanie were alone in a big house 'and without male protection,' wrote Miss Pittypat, 'now that dear Charlie has gone. Of course, there is my brother Henry but he does not make his home with us. But perhaps Scarlett has told you of Henry. Delicacy forbids my putting more concerning him on paper. Melly and I would feel so much easier and safer if Scarlett were with us. Three lonely women are better than two. And perhaps dear Scarlett could find some ease for her sorrow, as Melly is doing, by nursing our brave boys in the hospitals here – and, of course, Melly and I are longing to see the dear baby . . . '

So Scarlett's trunk was packed again with her mourning clothes and off she went to Atlanta with Wade Hampton and his nurse Prissy, a headful of admonitions as to her conduct from Ellen and Mammy and a hundred dollars in Confederate bills from Gerald. She did not especially want to go to Atlanta. She thought Aunt Pitty the silliest of old ladies and the very idea of living under the same roof with Ashley's wife was abhorrent. But the County with its memories was impossible now, and any change was welcome.

Part Two

Chapter VIII

As the train carried Scarlett northward that May morning in 1862, she thought that Atlanta couldn't possibly be so boring as Charleston and Savannah had been, and, in spite of her distaste for Miss Pittypat and Melanie, she looked forward with some curiosity toward seeing how the town had fared since her last visit, in the winter before the war began.

Atlanta had always interested her more than any other town because when she was a child Gerald had told her that she and Atlanta were exactly the same age. She discovered when she grew older that Gerald had stretched the truth somewhat, as was his habit when a little stretching would improve a story; but Atlanta was only nine years older than she was, and that still left the place amazingly young by comparison with any other town she had ever heard of. Savannah and Charleston had the dignity of their years, one being well along in its second century and the other entering its third, and in her young eyes they had always seemed like aged grandmothers fanning themselves placidly in the sun. But Atlanta was of her own generation, crude with the crudities of youth and as headstrong and impetuous as herself.

The story Gerald had told her was based on the fact that she and Atlanta were christened in the same year. In the nine years before Scarlett was born, the town had been called, first, Terminus and then Marthasville, and not until the year of Scarlett's birth had it become Atlanta.

When Gerald first moved to north Georgia, there had been no Atlanta at all, not even the semblance of a village, and the wilderness rolled over the site. But the next year, in 1836, the State had authorized the building of a railroad north-westward through the territory which the Cherokees had recently ceded. The destination of the proposed railroad, Tennessee and the West, was clear and definite, but its beginning point in Georgia was somewhat uncertain until, a year later, an engineer drove a stake in the red clay to mark the southern end of the line, and Atlanta, born Terminus, had begun.

There were no railroads then in north Georgia, and very few anywhere else. But during the years before Gerald married Ellen, the tiny settlement, twenty-five miles north of Tara, slowly grew into a village and the tracks slowly pushed northward. Then the railroad-building era really began. From the old city of Augusta, a second railroad was extended westward across the state to connect with the new road to Tennessee. From the old city of Savannah, a third railroad was built first to Macon, in the heart of Georgia, and then north through Gerald's own county to Atlanta, to link up with the other two roads and give Savannah's harbour a highway to the West. From the same junction point, the young Atlanta, a fourth railroad was constructed south-westward to Montgomery and Mobile.

Born of a railroad, Atlanta grew as its railroads grew. With the completion of the four lines, Atlanta was now connected with the West, with the South, with the Coast and, through Augusta, with the North and East. It had become the crossroads of travel north and south and east and west, and the little village leaped to life.

In a space of time but little longer than Scarlett's seventeen years, Atlanta had grown from a single stake driven in the ground into a thriving small city of ten thousand that was the centre of attention for the whole state. The older, quieter cities were wont to look upon the bustling new town with the sensations of a hen which has hatched a duckling. Why was the place so different from the other Georgia towns? Why did it grow so fast? After all, they thought, it had nothing whatever to recommend it – only its railroads and a bunch of mighty pushy people.

The people who settled the town called successively Terminus, Marthasville and Atlanta were a pushy people. Restless, energetic people from the older sections of Georgia and from more distant states were drawn to this town that sprawled itself around the junction of the railroads in its centre. They came with enthusiasm. They built their stores around the five muddy red roads that crossed near the depot. They built their fine homes on Whitehall and Washington streets and along the high ridge of land on which countless generations of moccasined Indian feet had beaten a path called the Peachtree Trail. They were proud of the place, proud of its growth, proud of themselves for making it grow. Let the older towns call Atlanta anything they pleased. Atlanta did not care.

Scarlett had always liked Atlanta for the very same reasons that made Savannah, Augusta and Macon condemn it. Like herself, the town was a mixture of the old and new in Georgia, in which the old often came off second best in its conflicts with the self-willed and vigorous new. Moreover, there was something personal, exciting about a town that was born – or at least christened – the same year she was christened.

The night before had been wild and wet with rain, but when Scarlett arrived in Atlanta a warm sun was at work, bravely attempting to dry the streets that were winding rivers of red mud. In the open space around the depot, the soft ground had been cut and churned by the constant flow of traffic in and out until it resembled an enormous hog wallow, and here and there vehicles were mired to the hubs in the ruts. A never-ceasing line of army wagons and ambulances, loading and unloading supplies and wounded from the trains, made the mud and confusion worse as they toiled in and struggled out, drivers swearing, mules plunging and mud spattering for yards.

Scarlett stood on the lower step of the train, a pale pretty figure in her black mourning dress, her crêpe veil fluttering almost to her heels. She hesitated, unwilling to soil her slippers and hems, and looked about in the shouting tangle of wagons, buggies and carriages for Miss Pittypat. There was no sign of that chubby pink-cheeked lady, but as Scarlett searched anxiously a spare old negro, with grizzled kinks and an air of dignified authority, came toward her through the mud, his hat in his hand.

'Dis Miss Scarlett, ain' it? Dis hyah Peter, Miss Pitty's coachman. Doan step down in dat mud,' he ordered severely, as Scarlett gathered up her skirts preparatory to descending. 'You is as bad as Miss Pitty an' she lak a chile 'bout gittin' her feets wet. Lemme cahy you.'

He picked Scarlett up with ease despite his apparent frailness and age and, observing Prissy standing on the platform of the train, the baby in her arms, he paused: 'Is dat air chile yo' nuss? Miss Scarlett, she too young ter be handlin' Mist' Charles' onlies' baby! But we ten' to dat later. You gal, foller me, an' doan you go drappin' dat baby.'

Scarlett submitted meekly to being carried toward the carriage and also to the peremptory manner in which Uncle Peter criticized her and Prissy. As they went through the mud with Prissy sloshing, pouting, after them, she recalled what Charles had said about Uncle Peter.

'He went through all the Mexican campaigns with Father, nursed him when he was wounded – in fact, he saved his life. Uncle Peter practically raised Melanie and me, for we were very young when Father and Mother died. Aunt Pitty had a falling-out with her brother, Uncle Henry, about that time, so she came to live with us and take care of us. She is the most helpless soul – just like a sweet grown-up child, and Uncle Peter treats her that way. To save her life, she couldn't make up her mind about anything, so Peter makes it up for her. He was the one who decided I should have a larger allowance when I was fifteen, and he insisted that I should go to Harvard for my senior year, when Uncle Henry wanted me to take my degree at the University. And he decided when Melly was old enough to put up her hair and go to parties. He tells Aunt Pitty when it's too cold or too wet for her to go calling and when she should wear a shawl . . . He's the smartest old darky I've ever seen and about the most devoted. The only trouble with him is that he owns the three of us, body and soul, and he knows it.'

Charles' words were confirmed as Peter climbed on to the box and took the whip.

'Miss Pitty in a state bekase she din' come ter meet you. She's feared you mout not unnerstan' but Ah tole her she an' Miss Melly jes' git splashed wid mud an' ruin dey new dresses an' Ah'd 'splain ter you. Miss Scarlett, you better tek dat chile. Dat lil piccaninny gwine let it drap.'

Scarlett looked at Prissy and sighed. Prissy was not the most adequate of nurses. Her recent graduation from a skinny piccaninny with brief skirts and stiffly wrapped braids into the dignity of a long calico dress and starched white turban was an intoxicating affair. She would never have arrived at this eminence so early in life had not the exigencies of war and the demands of the commissary department on Tara made it impossible for Ellen to spare Mammy or Dilcey or even Rosa or Teena. Prissy had never been more than a mile away from Twelve Oaks or Tara before, and the trip on the train plus her elevation to nurse was almost more than the brain in her little black skull could bear. The twenty-mile journey from Jonesboro to Atlanta had so excited her that Scarlett had been forced to hold the baby all the way. Now, the sight of so many buildings and people completed Prissy's demoralization. She twisted from side to side, pointed, bounced about and so jounced the baby that he wailed miserably.

Scarlett longed for the fat old arms of Mammy. Mammy had only to lay hands on a child and it hushed crying. But Mammy was at Tara and there was nothing Scarlett could do. It was useless for her to take little Wade from Prissy. He yelled just as loudly when she held him as when Prissy did. Besides, he would tug at the ribbons of her bonnet and, no doubt, rumple her dress. So she pretended she had not heard Uncle Peter's suggestion.

'Maybe I'll learn about babies some time,' she thought irritably, as the carriage jolted and swayed out of the morass surrounding the station, 'but I'm never going to like fooling with them.' And as Wade's face went purple with his squalling, she snapped crossly: 'Give him that sugar-tit in your pocket, Priss. Anything to make him hush. I know he's hungry, but I can't do anything about that now.'

Prissy produced the sugar-tit, given her that morning by Mammy, and the baby's wails subsided. With quiet restored and with the new sights that met her eyes, Scarlett's spirits began to rise a little. When Uncle Peter finally manoeuvred the carriage out of the mudholes and on to Peachtree Street, she felt the first surge of interest she had known in months. How the town had grown! It was not much more than a year since she had last been here, and it did not seem possible that the little Atlanta she knew could have changed so much.

For the past year, she had been so engrossed in her own woes, so bored by any mention of war, she did not know that from the minute the fighting first began, Atlanta had been transformed. The same railroads which had made the town the crossroads of commerce in time of peace were now of vital strategic importance in time of war. Far from the battle-lines, the town and its railroads provided the connecting link between the two armies of the Confederacy, the army in Virginia and the army in Tennessee and the West. And Atlanta likewise linked both of the armies with the deeper South from which they drew their supplies. Now, in response to the needs of war, Atlanta had become a manufacturing centre, a hospital base and one of the South's chief depots for the collecting of food and supplies for the armies in the field.

Scarlett looked about her for the little town she remembered so well. It was gone. The town she was now seeing was like a baby grown overnight into a busy, sprawling giant.

Atlanta was humming like a beehive, proudly conscious of its importance to the Confederacy, and work was going forward night and day toward turning an agricultural section into an industrial one. Before the war there had been few cotton factories, woollen mills, arsenals and machine shops south of Maryland – a fact of which all Southerners were proud. The South produced statesmen and soldiers, planters and doctors, lawyers and poets, but certainly not engineers or mechanics. Let the Yankees adopt such low callings. But now the Confederate ports were stoppered with Yankee gunboats, only a trickle of blockade-run goods was slipping in from Europe, and the South was desperately trying to manufacture her own war materials. The North could call on the whole world for supplies and for soldiers, and thousands of Irish and Germans were pouring into the Union Army, lured by the bounty money offered by the North. The South could only turn in upon itself.

In Atlanta, there were machine factories tediously turning out machinery to manufacture war materials – tediously, because there were few machines in the South from which they could model and nearly every wheel and cog had to be made from drawings that came through the blockade from England. There were strange faces on the streets of Atlanta now, and citizens who a year ago would have pricked up their ears at the sound of even a Western accent paid no heed to the foreign tongues of Europeans who had run the blockade to build machines and turn out Confederate munitions. Skilled men these, without whom the Confederacy would have been hard put to make pistols, rifles, cannon and powder.

Almost the pulsing of the town's heart could be felt as the work went forward night and day, pumping the materials of war up the railway arteries to the two battle fronts. Trains roared in and out of the town at all hours. Soot from the newly erected factories fell in showers on the white houses. By night, the furnaces glowed and the hammers clanged long after townsfolk were abed. Where vacant lots had been a year before, there were now factories turning out harness, saddles and shoes, ordnance-supply plants making rifles and cannon, rolling mills and foundries producing iron rails and freight cars to replace those destroyed by the Yankees, and a variety of industries manufacturing spurs, bridle bits, buckles, tents, buttons, pistols and swords. Already the foundries were beginning to feel the lack of iron, for little or none came through the blockade, and the mines in Alabama were standing almost idle while the miners were at the front. There were no iron picket fences, iron summerhouses, iron gates or even iron statuary on the lawns of Atlanta now, for they had early found their way into the melting-pots of the rolling mills.

Here along Peachtree Street and near-by streets were the headquarters of the various army departments, each office swarming with uniformed men, the commissary, the signal corps, the mail service, the railway transport, the provost marshal. On the outskirts of town were the remount depots where horses and mules milled about in large corrals, and along side streets were the hospitals. As Uncle Peter told her about them, Scarlett felt that Atlanta must be a city of the wounded, for there were general hospitals, contagious hospitals, convalescent hospitals without number. And every day the trains just below Five Points disgorged more sick and more wounded.

The little town was gone and the face of the rapidly growing city was animated with never-ceasing energy and bustle. The sight of so much hurrying made Scarlett, fresh from rural leisure and quiet, almost breathless, but she liked it. There was an exciting atmosphere about the place that uplifted her. It was as if she could actually feel the accelerated steady pulse of the town's heart beating in time with her own.

As they slowly made their way through the mudholes of the town's chief street, she noted with interest all the new buildings and the new faces. The sidewalks were crowded with men in uniform, bearing the insignia of all ranks and all service branches; the narrow street was jammed with vehicles – carriages, buggies, ambulances, covered army wagons with profane drivers swearing as the mules struggled through the ruts; grey-clad couriers dashed spattering through the streets from one headquarters to another, bearing orders and telegraphic dispatches; convalescents limped about on crutches, usually with a solicitous lady at either elbow; bugle and drum and barked orders sounded from the drill fields where the recruits were being turned into soldiers; and with her heart in her throat, Scarlett had her first sight of Yankee uniforms, as Uncle Peter pointed with his whip to a detachment of dejected-looking bluecoats being shepherded toward the depot by a squad of Confederates with fixed bayonets, to entrain for the prison camp.

'Oh,' thought Scarlett, with the first feeling of real pleasure she had experienced since the day of the barbecue, 'I'm going to like it here! It's so alive and exciting!'

The town was even more alive than she realized, for there were new bar-rooms by the dozens; prostitutes, following the army, swarmed the town and bawdy houses were blossoming with women to the consternation of the Church people. Every hotel, boarding house and private residence was crammed with visitors who had come to be near wounded relatives in the big Atlanta hospitals. There were parties and balls and bazaars every week and war weddings without number, with the grooms on furlough in bright grey and gold braid and the brides in blockade-run finery, aisles of crossed swords, toasts drunk in blockaded champagne and tearful farewells. Nightly the dark tree-lined streets resounded with dancing feet, and from parlours tinkled pianos where soprano voices blended with those of soldier guests in the pleasing melancholy of 'The Bugles Sang Truce' and 'Your Letter Came, but Came Too Late' – plaintive ballads that brought exciting tears to soft eyes which had never known the tears of real grief.

As they progressed down the street, through the sucking mud, Scarlett bubbled over with questions and Peter answered them, pointing here and there with his whip, proud to display his knowledge.

'Dat air de arsenal. Yas'm, dey keeps guns an' sech lak dar. No'm, dem air ain' sto's, dey's blockade awfisses. Law, Miss Scarlett, doan you know whut blockade awfisses is? Dey's awfisses whar furriners stays dat buys us Confedruts' cotton an' ship it outer Cha'ston and Wilmin'ton an' ship us back gunpowder. No'm, Ah ain' sho whut kine of furriners dey is. Miss Pitty, she say dey is Inlish but kain nobody unnerstan' a wud dey says. Yas'm, 'tis pow'ful smoky an' de soot jes' ruinin' Miss Pitty's silk cuttins. It's frum de foun'ry an' de rollin' mills. An' de noise dey meks at night! Kain nobody sleep. No'm, Ah kain stop fer you ter look around. Ah done promise Miss Pitty Ah bring you straight home . . . Miss Scarlett, mek yo' cu'tsy. Dar's Miss Merriwether an' Miss Elsing a-bowin' to you.'

Scarlett vaguely remembered two ladies of those names who came from Atlanta to Tara to attend her wedding and she remembered that they were Miss Pittypat's best friends. So she turned quickly where Uncle Peter pointed and bowed. The two were sitting in a carriage outside a drygoods store. The proprietor and two clerks stood on the sidewalk with armfuls of bolts of cotton cloth they had been displaying. Mrs Merriwether was a tall, stout woman and so tightly corseted that her bust jutted forward like the prow of a ship. Her iron-grey hair was eked out by a curled false fringe that was proudly brown and disdained to match the rest of her hair. She had a round, highly coloured face in which were combined good-natured shrewdness and the habit of command. Mrs Elsing was younger, a thin frail woman, who had been a beauty, and about her there still clung a faded freshness, a dainty imperious air.

These two ladies with a third, Mrs Whiting, were the pillars of Atlanta. They ran the three churches to which they belonged, the clergy, the choirs and the parishioners. They organized bazaars and presided over sewing circles, they chaperoned balls and picnics, they knew who made good matches and who did not, who drank secretly, who were to have babies and when. They were authorities on the genealogies of everyone who was anyone in Georgia, South Carolina and Virginia and did not bother their heads about the other states, because they believed that no one who was anybody ever came from states other than these three. They knew what was decorous behaviour and what was not and they never failed to make their opinions known – Mrs Merriwether at the top of her voice, Mrs Elsing in an elegant die-away drawl and Mrs Whiting in a distressed whisper which showed how much she hated to speak of such things. These three ladies disliked and distrusted one another as heartily as the First Triumvirate of Rome, and their close alliance was probably for the same reason.

'I told Pitty I had to have you in my hospital,' called Mrs Merriwether, smiling. 'Don't you go promising Mrs Meade or Mrs Whiting!'

'I won't,' said Scarlett, having no idea what Mrs Merriwether was talking about but feeling a glow of warmth at being welcomed and wanted. 'I hope to see you again soon.'

The carriage ploughed its way farther and halted for a moment to permit two ladies with baskets of bandages on their arms to pick precarious passages across the sloppy street on stepping-stones. At the same moment, Scarlett's eye was caught by a figure on the sidewalk in a brightly coloured dress – too bright for street wear – covered by a Paisley shawl with fringes to the heels. Turning, she saw a tall handsome woman with a bold face and a mass of red hair, too red to be true. It was the first time she had ever seen any woman who she knew for certain had 'done something to her hair' and she watched her, fascinated.

'Uncle Peter, who is that?' she whispered.

'Ah doan know.'

'You do, too. I can tell. Who is she?'

'Her name Belle Watling,' said Uncle Peter, his lower lip beginning to protrude.

Scarlett was quick to catch the fact that he had not preceded the name with 'Miss' or 'Mrs'.

'Who is she?'

'Miss Scarlett,' said Peter darkly, laying the whip on the startled horse, 'Miss Pitty ain' gwine ter lak it you astin' questions dat ain' none of yo' bizness. Dey's a passel of no-count folks in dis town now dat it ain' no use talkin' about.'

'Good Heavens!' thought Scarlett, reproved into silence. 'That must be a bad woman!'

She had never seen a bad woman before and she twisted her head and stared after her until she was lost in the crowd.

The stores and the new war buildings were farther apart now, with vacant lots between. Finally the business section fell behind and the residences came into view. Scarlett picked them out as old friends: the Leyden house, dignified and stately; the Bonnells', with little white columns and green blinds; the close-lipped red-brick Georgian home of the McLure family, behind its low box hedges. Their progress was slower now, for from porches and gardens and sidewalks ladies called to her. Some she knew slightly, others she vaguely remembered, but most of them she knew not at all. Pittypat had certainly broadcast her arrival. Little Wade had to be held up time and again, so that ladies who ventured as far through the ooze as their carriage blocks could exclaim over him. They all cried to her that she must join their knitting and sewing circles and their hospital committees, and no one else's, and she promised recklessly to right and left.

As they passed a rambling green clapboard house, a little black girl posted on the front steps cried, 'Hyah she come,' and Dr Meade and his wife and little thirteen-year-old Phil emerged, calling greetings. Scarlett recalled that they too had been at her wedding. Mrs Meade mounted her carriage block and craned her neck for a view of the baby, but the doctor, disregarding the mud, ploughed through to the side of the carriage. He was tall and gaunt and wore a pointed beard of iron grey, and his clothes hung on his spare figure as though blown there by a hurricane. Atlanta considered him the root of all strength and all wisdom and it was not strange that he had absorbed something of their belief. But for all his habit of making oracular statements and his slightly pompous manner, he was as kindly a man as the town possessed.

After shaking her hand and prodding Wade in the stomach and complimenting him, the doctor announced that Aunt Pittypat had promised on oath that Scarlett should be on no other hospital and bandage-rolling committee save Mrs Meade's.

'Oh, dear, but I've promised a thousand ladies already!' said Scarlett.

'Mrs Merriwether, I'll be bound!' cried Mrs Meade indignantly. 'Drat the woman! I believe she meets every train!'

'I promised because I hadn't a notion what it was all about,' Scarlett confessed. 'What are hospital committees anyway?'

Both the doctor and his wife looked slightly shocked at her ignorance.

'But, of course, you've been buried in the country and couldn't know,' Mrs Meade apologized for her. 'We have nursing committees for different hospitals and for different days. We nurse the men and help the doctors and make bandages and clothes and when the men are well enough to leave the hospitals we take them into our homes to convalesce till they are able to go back in the army. And we look after the wives and families of some of the wounded who are destitute – yes, worse than destitute. Dr Meade is at the Institute hospital where my committee works, and everyone says he is marvellous and—'

'There, there, Mrs Meade,' said the doctor fondly. 'Don't go bragging on me in front of folks. It's little enough I can do, since you wouldn't let me go in the army.'

' "Wouldn't let!" she cried indignantly. 'Me? The town wouldn't let you and you know it. Why, Scarlett, when folks heard he was intending to go to Virginia as an army surgeon, all the ladies signed a petition begging him to stay here. Of course, the town couldn't do without you.'

'There, there, Mrs Meade,' said the doctor, basking obviously in the praise. 'Perhaps with one boy at the front, that's enough for the time being.'

'And I'm going next year!' cried little Phil, hopping about excitedly. 'As a drummer boy. I'm learning how to drum now. Do you want to hear me? I'll run get my drum.'

'No, not now,' said Mrs Meade, drawing him closer to her, a sudden look of strain coming over her face. 'Not next year, darling. Maybe the year after.'

'But the war will be over then!' he cried petulantly, pulling away from her. 'And you promised!'

Over his head the eyes of the parents met and Scarlett saw the look. Darcy Meade was in Virginia and they were clinging closer to the little boy that was left.

Uncle Peter cleared his throat.

'Miss Pitty were in a state when Ah lef' home an' ef Ah doan git dar soon, she'll done swooned.'

'Good-bye. I'll be over this afternoon,' called Mrs Meade. 'And you tell Pitty for me that if you aren't on my committee, she's going to be in a worse state.'

The carriage slipped and slid down the muddy road and Scarlett leaned back on the cushions and smiled. She felt better now than she had felt in months. Atlanta, with its crowds and its hurry and its undercurrent of driving excitement, was very pleasant, very exhilarating, so very much nicer than the lonely plantation out from Charleston, where the bellow of alligators broke the night stillness; better than Charleston itself, dreaming of its gardens behind its high walls; better than Savannah with its wide streets lined with palmetto and the muddy river beside it. Yes, and temporarily even better than Tara, dear though Tara was.

There was something exciting about this town with its narrow muddy streets, lying among rolling red hills, something raw and crude that appealed to the rawness and crudeness underlying the fine veneer that Ellen and Mammy had given her. She suddenly felt that this was where she belonged, not in serene and quiet old cities, flat beside yellow waters.

The houses were farther and farther apart now, and leaning out Scarlett saw the red-brick and slate roof of Miss Pittypat's house. It was almost the last house on the north side of town. Beyond it, Peachtree road narrowed and twisted under great trees out of sight into thick quiet woods. The neat wooden-panelled fence had been newly painted white and the front yard it enclosed was yellow-starred with the last jonquils of the season. On the front steps stood two women in black and behind them a large yellow woman with her hands under her apron and her white teeth showing in a wide smile. Plump Miss Pittypat was teetering excitedly on tiny feet, one hand pressed to her copious bosom to still her fluttering heart. Scarlett saw Melanie standing by her and, with a surge of dislike, she realized that the fly in the ointment of Atlanta would be this slight little person in black mourning dress, her riotous dark curls subdued to matronly smoothness and a loving smile of welcome and happiness on her heart-shaped face.

When a Southerner took the trouble to pack a trunk and travel twenty miles for a visit, the visit was seldom of shorter duration than a month, usually much longer. Southerners were as enthusiastic visitors as they were hosts, and there was nothing unusual in relatives coming to spend the Christmas holidays and remaining until July. Often when newly married couples went on the usual round of honeymoon visits, they lingered in some pleasant home until the birth of their second child. Frequently elderly aunts and uncles came to Sunday dinner and remained until they were buried years later. Visitors presented no problem, for houses were large, servants numerous and the feeding of several extra mouths a minor matter in that land of plenty. All ages and sexes went visiting: honeymooners, young mothers showing off new babies, convalescents, the bereaved, girls whose parents were anxious to remove them from the dangers of unwise matches, girls who had reached the danger age without becoming engaged and who, it was hoped, would make suitable matches under the guidance of relatives in other places. Visitors added excitement and variety to the slow-moving Southern life and they were always welcome.

So Scarlett had come to Atlanta with no idea as to how long she would remain. If her visit proved as dull as those in Savannah and Charleston, she would return home in a month. If her stay was pleasant, she would remain indefinitely. But no sooner had she arrived than Aunt Pitty and Melanie began a campaign to induce her to make her home permanently with them. They brought up every possible argument. They wanted her for her own self because they loved her. They were lonely and often frightened at night in the big house, and she was so brave she gave them courage. She was so charming that she cheered them in their sorrow. Now that Charles was dead, her place and her son's place were with his kindred. Besides, half the house now belonged to her, through Charles' will. Last, the Confederacy needed every pair of hands for sewing, knitting, bandage rolling and nursing the wounded.

Charles' Uncle Henry Hamilton, who lived in bachelor state at the Atlanta Hotel near the depot, also talked seriously to her on this subject. Uncle Henry was a short, pot-bellied, irascible old gentleman with a pink face, a shock of long silver hair and an utter lack of patience with feminine timidities and vapourings. It was for the latter reason that he was barely on speaking terms with his sister, Miss Pittypat. From childhood, they had been exact opposites in temperament and they had been further estranged by his objections to the manner in which she had reared Charles – 'Making a damn sissy out of a soldier's son!' Years before, he had so insulted her that now Miss Pitty never spoke of him except in guarded whispers and with so great reticence that a stranger would have thought the honest old lawyer a murderer, at the least. The insult had occurred on a day when Pitty wished to draw five hundred dollars from her estate, of which he was trustee, to invest in a non-existent gold mine. He had refused to permit it and stated heatedly that she had no more sense than a June bug and furthermore it gave him the fidgets to be around her longer than five minutes. Since that day, she only saw him formally, once a month, when Uncle Peter drove her to his office to get the housekeeping money. After these brief visits, Pitty always took to her bed for the rest of the day with tears and smelling salts. Melanie and Charles, who were on excellent terms with their uncle, had frequently offered to relieve her of this ordeal, but Pitty always set her babyish mouth firmly and refused. Henry was her cross and she must bear him. From this, Charles and Melanie could only infer that she took a profound pleasure in this occasional excitement, the only excitement in her sheltered life.

Uncle Henry liked Scarlett immediately because, he said, he could see that for all her silly affectations she had a few grains of sense. He was trustee, not only of Pitty's and Melanie's estates, but also of that left Scarlett by Charles. It came to Scarlett as a pleasant surprise that she was now a well-to-do young woman, for Charles had not only left her half of Aunt Pitty's house but farm lands and town property as well. And the stores and warehouses along the railroad track near the depot, which were part of her inheritance, had tripled in value since the war began. It was when Uncle Henry was giving her an account of her property that he broached the matter of her permanent residence in Atlanta.

'When Wade Hampton comes of age, he's going to be a rich young man,' he said. 'The way Atlanta is growing his property will be ten times more valuable in twenty years, and it's only right that the boy should be raised where his property is, so he can learn to take care of it – yes, and of Pitty's and Melanie's too. He'll be the only man of the Hamilton name left before long, for I won't be here forever.'

As for Uncle Peter, he took it for granted that Scarlett had come to stay. It was inconceivable to him that Charles' only son should be reared where he could not supervise the rearing. To all these arguments, Scarlett smiled but said nothing, unwilling to commit herself before learning how she would like Atlanta and constant association with her in-laws. She knew, too, that Gerald and Ellen would have to be won over. Moreover, now that she was away from Tara, she missed it dreadfully, missed the red fields and the springing green cotton and the sweet twilight silences. For the first time, she realized dimly what Gerald had meant when he said that the love of the land was in her blood.

So she gracefully evaded, for the time being, a definite answer as to the duration of her visit and slipped easily into the life of the red-brick house at the quiet end of Peachtree Street.

Living with Charles' blood kin, seeing the home from which he came, Scarlett could now understand a little better the boy who had made her wife, widow and mother in such rapid succession. It was easy to see why he had been so shy, so unsophisticated, so idealistic. If Charles had inherited any of the qualities of the stern, fearless, hot-tempered soldier who had been his father, they had been obliterated in childhood by the ladylike atmosphere in which he had been reared. He had been devoted to the childlike Pitty and closer than brothers usually are to Melanie, and two more sweet, unworldly women could not be found.

Aunt Pittypat had been christened Sarah Jane Hamilton sixty years before, but since the long-past day when her doting father had fastened this nickname upon her, because of her airy, restless, pattering little feet, no one had called her anything else. In the years that followed that second christening, many changes had taken place in her that made the pet name incongruous. Of the swiftly scampering child, all that now remained were two tiny feet, inadequate to her weight, and a tendency to prattle happily and aimlessly. She was stout, pink-cheeked and silver-haired and always a little breathless from too tightly laced stays. She was unable to walk more than a block on the tiny feet which she crammed into too small slippers. She had a heart which fluttered at any excitement and she pampered it shamelessly, fainting at any provocation. Everyone knew that her swoons were generally mere ladylike pretences but they loved her enough to refrain from saying so. Everyone loved her, spoiled her like a child and refused to take her seriously – everyone except her brother Henry.

She liked gossip better than anything else in the world, even more than she liked the pleasures of the table, and she prattled on for hours about other people's affairs in a harmless kindly way. She had no memory for names, dates or places and frequently confused the actors in one Atlanta drama with the actors in another, which misled no one for no one was foolish enough to take seriously anything she said. No one ever told her anything really shocking or scandalous, for her spinster state must be protected even if she was sixty years old, and her friends were in a kindly conspiracy to keep her a sheltered and petted old child.

Melanie was like her aunt in many ways. She had her shyness, her sudden blushes, her modesty, but she did have common sense – 'Of a sort, I'll admit that,' Scarlett thought grudgingly. Like Aunt Pitty, Melanie had the face of a sheltered child who had never known anything but simplicity and kindness, truth and love, a child who had never looked upon harshness or evil and would not recognize them if she saw them. Because she had always been happy, she wanted everyone about her to be happy or, at least, pleased with themselves. To this end, she always saw the best in everyone and remarked kindly upon it. There was no servant so stupid that she did not find some redeeming trait of loyalty and kind-heartedness, no girl so ugly and disagreeable that she could not discover grace of form or nobility of character in her, and no man so worthless or so boring that she did not view him in the light of his possibilities rather than his actualities.

Because of these qualities that came sincerely and spontaneously from a generous heart, everyone flocked about her, for who can resist the charm of one who discovers in others admirable qualities undreamed of even by themselves? She had more girl friends than anyone in town and more men friends too, though she had few beaux for she lacked the wilfulness and selfishness that go far toward trapping men's hearts.

What Melanie did was no more than all Southern girls were taught to do – to make those about them feel at ease and pleased with themselves. It was this happy feminine conspiracy which made Southern society so pleasant. Women knew that a land where men were contented, uncontradicted and safe in possession of unpunctured vanity was likely to be a very pleasant place for women to live. So, from the cradle to the grave, women strove to make men pleased with themselves, and the satisfied men repaid lavishly with gallantry and adoration. In fact, men willingly gave the ladies everything in the world except credit for having intelligence. Scarlett exercised the same charms as Melanie but with a studied artistry and consummate skill. The difference between the two girls lay in the fact that Melanie spoke kind and flattering words from a desire to make people happy, if only temporarily, and Scarlett never did it except to further her own aims.

From the two he loved best, Charles had received no toughening influences, learned nothing of harshness or reality, and the home in which he grew to manhood was as soft as a bird's nest. It was such a quiet, old-fashioned, gentle home compared with Tara. To Scarlett, this house cried out for the masculine smells of brandy, tobacco and Macassar oil, for hoarse voices and occasional curses, for guns, for whiskers, for saddles and bridles and for hounds underfoot. She missed the sounds of quarrelling voices that were always heard at Tara when Ellen's back was turned – Mammy quarrelling with Pork, Rosa and Teena bickering, her own acrimonious arguments with Suellen, Gerald's bawled threats. No wonder Charles had been a sissy, coming from a home like this. Here, excitement never entered in, voices were never raised, everyone deferred gently to the opinions of others, and, in the end, the black grizzled autocrat in the kitchen had his way. Scarlett, who had hoped for a freer rein when she escaped Mammy's supervision, discovered to her sorrow that Uncle Peter's standards of ladylike conduct, especially for Mist' Charles' widow, were even stricter than Mammy's.

In such a household, Scarlett came back to herself, and almost before she realized it her spirits rose to normal. She was only seventeen, she had superb health and energy, and Charles' people did their best to make her happy. If they fell a little short of this, it was not their fault, for no one could take out of her heart the ache that throbbed whenever Ashley's name was mentioned. And Melanie mentioned it so often! But Melanie and Pitty were tireless in planning ways to soothe the sorrow under which they thought she laboured. They put their own grief into the background in order to divert her. They fussed about her food and her hours for taking afternoon naps and for taking carriage rides. They not only admired her extravagantly, her high-spiritedness, her figure, her tiny hands and feet, her white skin, but they said so frequently, petting, hugging and kissing her to emphasize their loving words.

Scarlett did not care for the caresses, but she basked in the compliments. No one at Tara had ever said so many charming things about her. In fact, Mammy had spent her time deflating her conceit. Little Wade was no longer an annoyance, for the family, black and white, and the neighbours idolized him and there was a never-ceasing rivalry as to whose lap he should occupy. Melanie especially doted on him. Even in his worst screaming spells, Melanie thought him adorable and said so, adding, 'Oh, you precious darling! I just wish you were mine!'

Sometimes Scarlett found it hard to dissemble her feelings, for she still thought Aunt Pitty the silliest of old ladies and her vagueness and vapourings irritated her unendurably. She disliked Melanie with a jealous dislike that grew as the days went by, and sometimes she had to leave the room abruptly when Melanie, beaming with loving pride, spoke of Ashley or read his letter aloud. But, all in all, life went on as happily as was possible under the circumstances. Atlanta was more interesting than Savannah or Charleston or Tara and it offered so many strange war-time occupations she had little time to think or mope. But, sometimes, when she blew out the candle and burrowed her head in the pillow, she sighed and thought: 'If only Ashley wasn't married! If only I didn't have to nurse in that plagued hospital! Oh, if only I could have some beaux!'

She had immediately loathed nursing but she could not escape this duty because she was on both Mrs Meade's and Mrs Merriwether's committees. That meant four mornings a week in the sweltering, stinking hospital with her hair tied up in a towel and a hot apron covering her from neck to feet. Every matron, old or young, in Atlanta nursed and did it with an enthusiasm that seemed to Scarlett little short of fanatic. They took it for granted that she was imbued with their own patriotic fervour and would have been shocked to know how slight an interest in the war she had. Except for the ever-present torment that Ashley might be killed, the war interested her not at all, and nursing was something she did simply because she didn't know how to get out of it.

Certainly there was nothing romantic about nursing. To her, it meant groans, delirium, death and smells. The hospitals were filled with dirty, bewhiskered, verminous men who smelled terribly and bore on their bodies wounds hideous enough to turn a Christian's stomach. The hospitals stank of gangrene, the odour assaulting her nostrils long before the doors were reached, a sickish sweet smell that clung to her hands and hair and haunted her in her dreams. Flies, mosquitoes and gnats hovered in droning, singing swarms over the wards, tormenting the men to curses and weak sobs; and Scarlett, scratching her own mosquito bites, swung palmetto fans until her shoulders ached and she wished that all the men were dead.

Melanie, however, did not seem to mind the smells, the wounds or the nakedness, which Scarlett thought strange in one who was the most timorous and modest of women. Sometimes when holding basins and instruments while Dr Meade cut out gangrened flesh, Melanie looked very white. And once, after such an operation, Scarlett found her in the linen closet vomiting quietly into a towel. But as long as she was where the wounded could see her, she was gentle, sympathetic and cheerful, and the men in the hospitals called her an angel of mercy. Scarlett would have liked that title too, but it involved touching men crawling with lice, running fingers down throats of unconscious patients to see if they were choking on swallowed tobacco quids, bandaging stumps and picking maggots out of festering flesh. No, she did not like nursing!

Perhaps it might have been endurable if she had been permitted to use her charms on the convalescent men, for many of them were attractive and well born, but this she could not do in her widowed state. The young ladies of the town, who were not permitted to nurse for fear they would see sights unfit for virgin eyes, had the convalescent wards in their charge. Unhampered by matrimony or widowhood, they made vast inroads on the convalescents, and even the least attractive girls, Scarlett observed gloomily, had no difficulty in getting engaged.

With the exception of desperately ill and severely wounded men, Scarlett's was a completely feminized world and this irked her, for she neither liked nor trusted her own sex and, worse still, was always bored by it. But on three afternoons a week she had to attend sewing circles and bandage-rolling committees of Melanie's friends. The girls, who had all known Charles, were very kind and attentive to her at these gatherings, especially Fanny Elsing and Maybelle Merriwether, the daughters of the town dowagers. But they treated her deferentially, as if she were old and finished, and their constant chatter of dances and beaux made her both envious of their pleasures and resentful that her widowhood barred her from such activities. Why, she was three times as attractive as Fanny and Maybelle! Oh, how unfair life was! How unfair that everyone should think her heart was in the grave when it wasn't at all! It was in Virginia with Ashley!

But in spite of these discomforts, Atlanta pleased her very well. And her visit lengthened as the weeks slipped by.

Chapter IX

Scarlett sat in the window of her bedroom that midsummer morning and disconsolately watched the wagons and carriages full of girls, soldiers and chaperons ride gaily out Peachtree road in search of woodland decorations for the bazaar which was to be held that evening for the benefit of the hospitals. The red road lay chequered in shade and sun-glare beneath the over-arching trees and the many hooves kicked up little red clouds of dust. One wagon, ahead of the others, bore four stout negroes with axes to cut evergreens and drag down the vines, and the back of this wagon was piled high with napkin-covered hampers, split-oak baskets of lunch and a dozen watermelons. Two of the black bucks were equipped with banjo and harmonica and they were rendering a spirited version of 'If You Want to Have a Good Time, Jine the Cavalry'. Behind them streamed the merry cavalcade: girls cool in flowered cotton dresses, with light shawls, bonnets and mitts to protect their skins and little parasols held over their heads; elderly ladies placid and smiling amid the laughter and carriage-to-carriage calls and jokes; convalescents from the hospitals wedged in between stout chaperons and slender girls who made great fuss and to-do over them; officers on horseback idling at snail's pace beside the carriages – wheels creaking, spurs jingling, gold braid gleaming, parasols bobbing, fans swishing, negroes singing. Everybody was riding out Peachtree road to gather greenery and have a picnic and melon cutting. 'Everybody,' thought Scarlett, morosely, 'except me.'

They all waved and called to her as they went by and she tried to respond with a good grace, but it was difficult. A hard little pain had started in her heart and was travelling slowly up toward her throat where it would become a lump and the lump would soon become tears. Everybody was going to the picnic except her. And everybody was going to the bazaar and the ball tonight except her. That is everybody except her and Pittypat and Melly and the other unfortunates in town who were in mourning. But Melly and Pittypat did not seem to mind. It had not even occurred to them to want to go. It had occurred to Scarlett. And she did want to go, tremendously.

It simply wasn't fair. She had worked twice as hard as any girl in town, getting things ready for the bazaar. She had knitted socks and baby caps and afghans and mufflers and tatted yards of lace and painted china hair-receivers and moustache cups. And she had embroidered half a dozen sofa-pillow cases with the Confederate flag on them. (The stars were a bit lopsided, to be sure, some of them being almost round and the others having six or even seven points, but the effect was good.) Yesterday she had worked until she was worn out in the dusty old barn of an Armoury draping yellow and pink and green cheesecloth on the booths that lined the walls. Under the supervision of the Ladies' Hospital Committee, this was plain hard work and no fun at all. It was never fun to be around Mrs Merriwether and Mrs Elsing and Mrs Whiting and have them boss you like you were one of the darkies. And have to listen to them brag about how popular their daughters were. And, worst of all, she had burned two blisters on her fingers helping Pittypat and Cookie make layer cakes for raffling.

And now, having worked like a field hand, she had to retire decorously when the fun was just beginning. Oh, it wasn't fair that she should have a dead husband and a baby yelling in the next room and be out of everything that was pleasant. Just a little over a year ago, she was dancing and wearing bright clothes instead of this dark mourning and was practically engaged to three boys. She was only seventeen now and there was still a lot of dancing left in her feet. Oh, it wasn't fair! Life was going past her, down a hot shady summer road – life with grey uniforms and jingling spurs and flowered organdie dresses and banjo playing. She tried not to smile and wave too enthusiastically to the men she knew best, the ones she'd nursed in the hospital, but it was hard to subdue her dimples, hard to look as though her heart were in the grave – when it wasn't.

Her bowing and waving were abruptly halted when Pittypat entered the room, panting as usual from climbing the stairs, and jerked her away from the window unceremoniously.

'Have you lost your mind, honey, waving at men out of your bedroom window? I declare, Scarlett, I'm shocked! What would your mother say?'

'Well, they didn't know it was my bedroom.'

'But they'd suspect it was your bedroom and that's just as bad. Honey, you mustn't do things like that. Everybody will be talking about you and saying you are fast – and anyway, Mrs Merriwether knew it was your bedroom.'

'And I suppose she'll tell all the boys, the old cat.'

'Honey, hush! Dolly Merriwether's my best friend.'

'Well, she's a cat just the same – oh, I'm sorry, Auntie, don't cry! I forgot it was my bedroom window. I won't do it again – I – I just wanted to see them go by. I wish I was going.'

'Honey!'

'Well, I do. I'm so tired of sitting at home.'

'Scarlett, promise me you won't say things like that. People would talk so. They'd say you didn't have the proper respect for poor Charlie—'

'Oh, Auntie, don't cry!'

'Oh, now I've made you cry, too,' sobbed Pittypat, in a pleased way, fumbling in her skirt pocket for her handkerchief.

The hard little pain had at last reached Scarlett's throat and she wailed out loud – not, as Pittypat thought, for poor Charlie but because the last sounds of the wheels and the laughter were dying away. Melanie rustled in from her room, a worried frown puckering her forehead, a brush in her hands, her usually tidy black hair, freed of its net, fluffing about her face in a mass of tiny curls and waves.

'Darlings! What is the matter?'

'Charlie!' sobbed Pittypat, surrendering utterly to the pleasure of her grief and burying her head on Melly's shoulder.

'Oh,' said Melly, her lip quivering at the mention of her brother's name. 'Be brave, dear. Don't cry. Oh, Scarlett!'

Scarlett had thrown herself on the bed and was sobbing at the top of her voice, sobbing for her lost youth and the pleasures of youth that were denied her, sobbing with the indignation and despair of a child who once could get anything she wanted by sobbing and now knows that sobbing can no longer help her. She burrowed her head in the pillow and cried and kicked with her feet at the tufted counterpane.

'I might as well be dead!' she sobbed passionately. Before such an exhibition of grief, Pittypat's easy tears ceased and Melly flew to the bedside to comfort her sister-in-law.

'Dear, don't cry! Try to think how much Charlie loved you and let that comfort you! Try to think of your darling baby.'

Indignation at being misunderstood mingled with Scarlett's forlorn feeling of being out of everything and strangled all utterance. That was fortunate, for if she could have spoken she would have cried out truths couched in

Gerald's forthright words. Melanie patted her shoulder and Pittypat tiptoed heavily about the room pulling down the shades.

'Don't do that!' shouted Scarlett, raising a red and swollen face from the pillow. 'I'm not dead enough for you to pull down the shades – though I might as well be. Oh, do go away and leave me alone!'

She sank her face into the pillow again and, after a whispered conference, the two standing over her tiptoed out. She heard Melanie say to Pittypat in a low voice as they went down the stairs:

'Aunt Pitty, I wish you wouldn't speak of Charles to her. You know how it always affects her. Poor thing, she gets that queer look and I know she's trying not to cry. We mustn't make it harder for her.'

Scarlett kicked the coverlet in impotent rage, trying to think of something bad enough to say.

'God's nightgown!' she cried at last, and felt somewhat relieved. How could Melanie be content to stay at home and never have any fun and wear crêpe for her brother when she was only eighteen years old? Melanie did not seem to know, or care, that life was riding by with jingling spurs.

'But she's such a stick,' thought Scarlett, pounding the pillow. 'And she never was popular like me, so she doesn't miss the things I miss. And – and besides she's got Ashley and I – I haven't got anybody!' And at this fresh woe, she broke into renewed outcries.

She remained gloomily in her room until the afternoon and then the sight of the returning picnickers with wagons piled high with pine boughs, vines and ferns did not cheer her. Everyone looked happily tired as they waved to her again and she returned their greetings drearily. Life was a hopeless affair and certainly not worth living.

Deliverance came in the form she least expected when, during the after-dinner-nap period, Mrs Merriwether and Mrs Elsing drove up. Startled at having callers at such an hour, Melanie, Scarlett and Aunt Pittypat roused themselves, hastily hooked their basques, smoothed their hair and descended to the parlour.

'Mrs Bonnell's children have the measles,' said Mrs Merriwether abruptly, showing plainly that she held Mrs Bonnell personally responsible for permitting such a thing to happen.

'And the McLure girls have been called to Virginia,' said Mrs Elsing in her die-away voice, fanning herself languidly as if neither this nor anything else mattered very much. 'Dallas McLure is wounded.'

'How dreadful!' chorused their hostesses. 'Is poor Dallas—'

'No. Just through the shoulder,' said Mrs Merriwether briskly. 'But it couldn't possibly have happened at a worse time. The girls are going North to bring him home. But, skies above, we haven't time to sit here talking. We must hurry back to the Armoury and get the decorating done. Pitty, we need you and Melly tonight to take Mrs Bonnell's and the McLure girls' places.'

'Oh, but Dolly, we can't go.'

'Don't say "can't" to me, Pittypat Hamilton,' said Mrs Merriwether vigorously. 'We need you to watch the darkies with the refreshments. That was what Mrs Bonnell was to do. And Melly, you must take the McLure girls' booth.'

'Oh, we just couldn't – with poor Charlie dead only a—'

'I know how you feel but there isn't any sacrifice too great for the Cause,' broke in Mrs Elsing in a soft voice that settled matters.

'Oh, we'd love to help but – why can't you get some sweet pretty girls to take the booths?'

Mrs Merriwether snorted a trumpeting snort.

'I don't know what's come over the young people these days. They have no sense of responsibility. All the girls who haven't already taken booths have more excuses than you could shake a stick at. Oh, they don't fool me! They just don't want to be hampered in making up to the officers, that's all. And they're afraid their new dresses won't show off behind booth counters. I wish to goodness that blockade runner – what's his name?'

'Captain Butler,' supplied Mrs Elsing.

'I wish he'd bring in more hospital supplies and less hoop skirts and lace. If I've had to look at one dress today I've had to look at twenty dresses that he ran in. Captain Butler – I'm sick of the name. Now, Pitty, I haven't got time to argue. You must come. Everybody will understand. Nobody will see you in the back room anyway, and Melly won't be conspicuous. The poor McLure girls' booth is way down at the end and not very pretty so nobody will notice you.'

'I think we should go,' said Scarlett, trying to curb her eagerness and to keep her face earnest and simple. 'It is the least we can do for the hospital.'

Neither of the visiting ladies had even mentioned her name, and they turned and looked sharply at her. Even in their extremity, they had not considered asking a widow of scarcely a year to appear at a social function. Scarlett bore their gaze with a wide-eyed childlike expression.

'I think we should go and help to make it a success, all of us. I think I should go in the booth with Melly because – well, I think it would look better for us both to be there instead of just one. Don't you think so, Melly?'

'Well,' began Melly helplessly. The idea of appearing publicly at a social gathering while in mourning was so unheard-of she was bewildered.

'Scarlett's right,' said Mrs Merriwether, observing signs of weakening. She rose and jerked her hoops into place. 'Both of you – all of you must come. Now, Pitty, don't start your excuses again. Just think how much the hospital needs money for new beds and drugs. And I know Charlie would like you to help the Cause he died for.'

'Well,' said Pittypat, helpless as always in the presence of a stronger personality, 'if you think people will understand.'

*

'Too good to be true! Too good to be true!' sang Scarlett's joyful heart as she slipped unobtrusively into the pink- and yellow-draped booth that was to have been the McLure girls'. Actually she was at a party! After a year's seclusion, after crêpe and hushed voices and nearly going crazy with boredom, she was actually at a party, the biggest party Atlanta had ever seen. And she could see people and many lights and hear music and view for herself the lovely laces and frocks and frills that the famous Captain Butler had run through the blockade on his last trip.

She sank down on one of the little stools behind the counter of the booth and looked up and down the long hall which, until this afternoon, had been a bare and ugly drill-room. How the ladies must have worked today to bring it to its present beauty! It looked lovely. Every candle and candlestick in Atlanta must be in this hall tonight, she thought, silver ones with a dozen sprangling arms, china ones with charming figurines clustering their bases, old brass stands, erect and dignified, laden with candles of all sizes and colours, smelling fragrantly of bayberries, standing on the gun-racks that ran the length of the hall, on the long flower-decked tables, on booth counters, even on the sills of the open windows where the draughts of warm summer air were just strong enough to make them flare.

In the centre of the hall the huge ugly lamp, hanging from the ceiling by rusty chains, was completely transformed by twining ivy and wild grapevines that were already withering from the heat. The walls were banked with pine branches that gave out a spicy smell, making the corners of the room into pretty bowers where the chaperons and old ladies would sit. Long graceful ropes of ivy and grapevine and smilax were hung everywhere, in looping festoons on the walls, draped above the windows, twined in scallops all over the brightly coloured cheesecloth booths. And everywhere amid the greenery, on flags and bunting, blazed the bright stars of the Confederacy on their background of red and blue.

The raised platform for the musicians was especially artistic. It was completely hidden from view by the banked greenery and starry bunting, and Scarlett knew that every potted and tubbed plant in town was there: coleus, geranium, hydrangea, oleander, elephant ear – even Mrs Elsing's four treasured rubber plants, which were given posts of honour at the four corners.

At the other end of the hall from the platform, the ladies had eclipsed themselves. On this wall hung large pictures of President Davis and Georgia's own 'Little Alec' Stephens, Vice-President of the Confederacy. Above them was an enormous flag and, beneath, on long tables was the loot of the gardens of the town: ferns, banks of roses, crimson and yellow and white, proud sheaths of golden gladioli, masses of varicoloured nasturtiums, tall stiff hollyhocks rearing deep maroon and creamy heads above the other flowers. Among them, candles burned serenely like altar fires. The two faces looked down on the scene, two faces as different as could be possible in two men at the helm of so momentous an undertaking: Davis with the flat cheeks and cold eyes of an ascetic, his thin proud lips set firmly; Stephens with dark burning eyes deep-socketed in a face that had known nothing but sickness and pain and had triumphed over them with humour and with fire – two faces that were greatly loved.

The elderly ladies of the committee in whose hands rested the responsibility for the whole bazaar rustled in as importantly as full-rigged ships, hurried the belated young matrons and giggling girls into their booths, and then swept through the doors into the back rooms where the refreshments were being laid out. Aunty Pitty panted after them.

The musicians clambered upon their platform, black, grinning, their fat cheeks already shining with perspiration, and began tuning their fiddles and sawing and whanging with their bows in anticipatory importance. Old Levi, Mrs Merriwether's coachman, who had led the orchestras for every bazaar, ball and wedding since Atlanta was named Marthasville, rapped with his bow for attention. Few except the ladies who were conducting the bazaar had arrived yet, but all eyes turned towards him. Then the fiddles, bull fiddles, accordions, banjos and knuckle-bones broke into a slow rendition of 'Lorena' – too slow for dancing, the dancing would come later when the booths were emptied of their wares. Scarlett felt her heart beat faster as the sweet melancholy of the waltz came to her:

> *The years creep slowly by, Lorena!*
> *The snow is on the grass again.*
> *The sun's far down the sky, Lorena . . .*

One-two-three, one-two-three, dip-sway – three, turn – two-three. What a beautiful waltz! She extended her hands slightly, closed her eyes and swayed with the sad haunting rhythm. There was something about the tragic melody and Lorena's lost love that mingled with her own excitement and brought a lump into her throat.

Then, as if brought into being by the waltz music, sounds floated in from the shadowy moonlit street below, the trample of horses' hooves and the sound of carriage wheels, laughter on the warm sweet air and the soft acrimony of negro voices raised in argument over hitching-places for the horses. There was confusion on the stairs and light-hearted merriment, the mingling of girls' fresh voices with the bass notes of their escorts, airy cries of greeting and squeals of joy as girls recognized friends from whom they had parted only that afternoon.

Suddenly the hall burst into life. It was full of girls – girls who floated in butterfly bright dresses, hooped out enormously, laced pantalets peeping from beneath; round little white shoulders bare, and faintest traces of soft little bosoms showing above lace flounces; lace shawls carelessly hanging from arms; fans spangled and painted, fans of swansdown and peacock feathers, dangling at wrists by tiny velvet ribbons; girls with dark hair smoothed sleekly from ears into chignons so heavy that their heads were tilted back with saucy pride; girls with masses of golden curls about their necks and fringed gold earbobs that tossed and danced with their dancing curls. Laces and silks and braid and ribbons, all blockade-run, all the more precious and more proudly worn because of it, finery flaunted with an added pride as an extra affront to the Yankees.

Not all the flowers of the town were standing in tribute to the leaders of the Confederacy. The smallest, the most fragrant blossoms bedecked the girls. Tea roses tucked behind pink ears, cape jessamine and bud roses in round little garlands over cascades of side-curls, blossoms thrust demurely into satin sashes, flowers that before the night was over would find their way into the breast pockets of grey uniforms as treasured souvenirs.

There were so many uniforms in the crowd – so many uniforms on so many men whom Scarlett knew, men she had met on hospital cots, on the streets, at the drill-ground. They were resplendent uniforms, brave with shining buttons and dazzling with twined gold braid on cuffs and collars, the red and yellow and blue stripes on the trousers, for the different branches of the service, setting off the grey to perfection. Scarlet and gold sashes swung to and fro, sabres glittered and banged against shining boots, spurs rattled and jingled.

Such handsome men, thought Scarlett, with a swell of pride in her heart, as the men called greetings, waved to friends, bent low over the hands of elderly ladies. All of them were so young-looking, even with their sweeping yellow moustaches and full black and brown beards, so handsome, so reckless, with their arms in slings, with head bandages startlingly white across sun-browned faces. Some of them were on crutches, and how proud were the girls who solicitously slowed their steps to their escorts' hopping pace! There was one gaudy splash of colour among the uniforms that put the girls' bright finery to shame and stood out in the crowd like a tropical bird – a Louisiana Zouave, with baggy blue and white striped pants, cream gaiters and tight little red jacket, a dark, grinning little monkey of a man, with his arm in a black silk sling. He was Maybelle Merriwether's especial beau, René Picard. The whole hospital must have turned out, at least everybody who could walk, and all the men on furlough and sick leave and all the railroad and mail service and hospital and commissary departments between here and Macon. How pleased the ladies would be! The hospital should make a mint of money tonight.

There was a ruffle of drums from the street below, the tramp of feet, the admiring cries of coachmen. A bugle blared and a bass voice shouted the command to break ranks. In a moment, the Home Guard and the militia unit in their bright uniforms shook the narrow stairs and crowded into the room, bowing, saluting, shaking hands. There were boys in the Home Guard, proud to be playing at war, promising themselves they would be in

Virginia this time next year, if the war would just last that long; old men with white beards, wishing they were younger, proud to march in uniform in the reflected glory of sons at the front. In the militia, there were many middle-aged men and some older men but there was a fair sprinkling of men of military age who did not carry themselves quite so jauntily as their elders or their juniors. Already people were beginning to whisper, asking why they were not with Lee.

How would they all get into the hall! It had seemed such a large place a few minutes before, and now it was packed, warm with summer-night odours of sachet and cologne water and hair pomade and burning bayberry candles, fragrant with flowers, faintly dusty as many feet trod the old drill floors. The din and hubbub of voices made it almost impossible to hear anything and, as if feeling the joy and excitement of the occasion, old Levi choked off 'Lorena' in mid-bar, rapped sharply with his bow and, sawing away for dear life, the orchestra burst into 'Bonnie Blue Flag'.

A hundred voices took it up, sang it, shouted it like a cheer. The Home Guard bugler, climbing on to the platform, caught up with the music just as the chorus began, and the high silver notes soared out thrillingly above the massed singing, causing goose-bumps to break out on bare arms and cold chills of deeply felt emotion to fly down spines:

> *Hurrah! Hurrah! For the Southern Rights, hurrah!*
> *Hurrah for the Bonnie Blue Flag*
> *That bears a single star!*

They crashed into the second verse and Scarlett, singing with the rest, heard the high sweet soprano of Melanie mounting behind her, clear and true and thrilling as the bugle notes. Turning, she saw that Melly was standing with her hands clasped to her breast, her eyes closed, and tiny tears oozing from the corners. She smiled at Scarlett, whimsically, as the music ended, making a little moue of apology as she dabbed with her handkerchief.

'I'm so happy,' she whispered, 'and so proud of the soldiers that I just can't help crying about it.'

There was a deep, almost fanatic glow in her eyes that for a moment lit up her plain little face and made it beautiful.

The same look was on the faces of all the women as the song ended, tears of pride on cheeks, pink or wrinkled, smiles on lips, a deep hot glow in eyes, as they turned to their men, sweetheart to lover, mother to son, wife to husband. They were all beautiful with the blinding beauty that transfigures even the plainest woman when she is utterly protected and utterly loved and is giving back that love a thousandfold.

They loved their men, they believed in them, they trusted them to the last breaths in their bodies. How could disaster ever come to women such as they when their stalwart grey line stood between them and the Yankees? Had there ever been such men as these since the first dawn of the world, so heroic, so reckless, so gallant, so tender? How could anything but overwhelming victory come to a Cause as just and right as theirs? A Cause they loved as much as they loved their men, a Cause they served with their hands and their hearts, a Cause they talked about, thought about, dreamed about – a Cause to which they would sacrifice these men if need be, and bear their loss as proudly as the men bore their battle flags.

It was high tide of devotion and pride in their hearts, high tide of the Confederacy, for final victory was at hand. Stonewall Jackson's triumphs in the Valley and the defeat of the Yankees in the Seven Days' Battle around Richmond showed that clearly. How could it be otherwise with such leaders as Lee and Jackson? One more victory and the Yankees would be on their knees yelling for peace and the men would be riding home and there would be kissing and laughter. One more victory and the war was over!

Of course, there were empty chairs and babies who would never see their fathers' faces and unmarked graves by lonely Virginia creeks and in the still mountains of Tennessee, but was that too great a price to pay for such a Cause? Silks for the ladies and tea and sugar were hard to get, but that was something to joke about. Besides, the dashing blockade runners were bringing in these very things under the Yankee's disgruntled noses, and that made the possession of them many times more thrilling. Soon Raphael Semmes and the Confederate Navy would tend to those Yankee gunboats and the ports would be wide open. And England was coming to help the Confederacy win the war, because the English mills were standing idle for want of Southern cotton. And naturally the British aristocracy sympathized with the Confederacy, as one aristocrat with another, against a race of dollar-lovers like the Yankees.

So the women swished their silks and laughed and, looking on their men with hearts bursting with pride, they knew that love snatched in the face of danger and death was doubly sweet for the strange excitement that went with it.

When first she looked at the crowd, Scarlett's heart had thump-thumped with the unaccustomed excitement of being at a party, but as she half-comprehendingly saw the high-hearted look on the faces about her, her joy began to evaporate. Every woman present was blazing with an emotion she did not feel. It bewildered and depressed her. Somehow, the hall did not seem so pretty nor the girls so dashing, and the white heat of devotion to the Cause that was still shining on every face seemed – why, it just seemed silly!

In a sudden flash of self-knowledge that made her mouth pop open with astonishment, she realized that she did not share with these women their fierce pride, their desire to sacrifice themselves and everything they had for the Cause. Before horror made her think, 'No – no! I mustn't think such things! They're wrong – sinful,' she knew the Cause meant nothing at all to her and that she was bored with hearing other people talk about it with that fanatic look in their eyes. The Cause didn't seem sacred to her. The war didn't seem to be a holy affair, but a nuisance that killed men senselessly and cost money and made luxuries hard to get. She saw that she was tired of the endless knitting and the endless bandage-rolling and lint-picking that roughened the cuticle of her nails. And oh, she was so tired of the hospital! Tired and bored and nauseated with the sickening gangrene smells and the endless moaning, frightened by the look that coming death gave to sunken faces.

She looked furtively around her, as the treacherous, blasphemous thoughts rushed through her mind, fearful that someone might find them written clearly upon her face. Oh, why couldn't she feel like these other women! They were whole-hearted and sincere in their devotion to the Cause. They really meant everything they said and did. And if anyone should ever suspect that she— No, no one must ever know! She must go on making a pretence of enthusiasm and pride in the Cause which she could not feel, acting out her part of the widow of a Confederate officer who bears her grief bravely, whose heart is in the grave, who feels that her husband's death meant nothing if it aided the Cause to triumph.

Oh, why was she different, apart from these loving women? She could never love anything or anyone so selflessly as they did. What a lonely feeling it was – and she had never been lonely either in body or spirit before. At first she tried to stifle the thoughts, but the hard self-honesty that lay at the base of her nature would not permit it. And so, while the bazaar went on, while she and Melanie waited on the customers who came to their booth, her mind was busily working, trying to justify herself to herself – a task which she seldom found difficult.

The other women were simply silly and hysterical with their talk of patriotism and the Cause, and the men were almost as bad with their talk of vital issues and States' Rights. She, Scarlett O'Hara Hamilton, alone had good hard-headed Irish sense. She wasn't going to make a fool out of herself about the Cause, but neither was she going to make a fool out of herself by admitting her true feelings. She was hard-headed enough to be practical about the situation, and no one would ever know how she felt. How surprised the bazaar would be if they knew what she was really thinking! How shocked if she suddenly climbed on the bandstand and declared that she thought the war ought to stop, so everybody could go home and tend to their cotton and there could be parties and beaux again and plenty of pale-green dresses!

For a moment, her self-justification buoyed her up but still she looked about the hall with distaste. The McLure girls' booth was inconspicuous, as Mrs Merriwether had said, and there were long intervals when no one came to their corner and Scarlett had nothing to do but look enviously on the happy throng. Melanie sensed her moodiness but, crediting it to longing for Charlie, did not try to engage her in conversation. She busied herself arranging the articles in the booth in more attractive display, while

Scarlett sat and looked glumly around the room. Even the banked flowers below the pictures of Mr Davis and Mr Stephens displeased her.

'It looks like an altar,' she sniffed. 'And the way they all carry on about those two, they might as well be the Father and the Son!' Then smitten with sudden fright at her irreverence she began hastily to cross herself by way of apology but caught herself in time.

'Well, it's true,' she argued with her conscience. 'Everybody carries on like they were holy and they aren't anything but men, and mighty unattractive-looking ones at that.'

Of course, Mr Stephens couldn't help how he looked for he had been an invalid all his life, but Mr Davis— She looked up at the cameo-clean, proud face. It was his goatee that annoyed her the most. Men should either be clean-shaven, moustached or wear full beards.

'That little wisp looks like it was just the best he could do,' she thought, not seeing in his face the cold hard intelligence that was carrying the weight of a new nation.

No, she was not happy now, and at first she had been radiant with the pleasure of being in a crowd. Now just being present was not enough. She was at the bazaar but not a part of it. No one paid her any attention and she was the only young unmarried woman present who did not have a beau. And all her life she had enjoyed the centre of the stage. It wasn't fair! She was seventeen years old and her feet were patting the floor, wanting to skip and dance. She was seventeen years old and she had a husband lying at Oakland Cemetery and a baby in his cradle at Aunt Pittypat's, and everyone thought she should be content with her lot. She had a whiter bosom and a smaller waist and a tinier foot than any girl present, but for all they mattered she might just as well be lying beside Charles with 'Beloved Wife of' carved over her.

She wasn't a girl who could dance and flirt and she wasn't a wife who could sit with other wives and criticize the dancing and flirting girls. And she wasn't old enough to be a widow. Widows should be old – so terribly old they didn't want to dance and flirt and be admired. Oh, it wasn't fair that she should have to sit here primly and be the acme of widowed dignity and propriety when she was only seventeen. It wasn't fair that she must keep her voice low and her eyes cast modestly down when men, attractive ones, too, came to their booth.

Every girl in Atlanta was three deep in men. Even the plainest girls were carrying on like belles – and, oh, worst of all, they were carrying on in such lovely, lovely dresses!

Here she sat like a crow with hot black taffeta to her wrists and buttoned up to her chin, with not even a hint of lace or braid, not a jewel except Ellen's onyx mourning brooch, watching tacky-looking girls hanging on the arms of good-looking men. All because Charles Hamilton had had the measles. He didn't even die in a fine glow of gallantry in battle, so she could brag about him.

Rebelliously she leaned her elbows on the counter and looked at the crowd, flouting Mammy's oft-repeated admonition against leaning on elbows and making them ugly and wrinkled. What did it matter if they did get ugly? She'd probably never get a chance to show them again. She looked hungrily at the frocks floating by: butter-yellow watered silks with garlands of rosebuds; pink satins with eighteen flounces edged with tiny black velvet ribbons; baby-blue taffeta, ten yards in the skirt and foamy with cascading lace; exposed bosoms; seductive flowers. Maybelle Merriwether went toward the next booth on the arm of the Zouave, in an apple-green tarlatan so wide that it reduced her waist to nothingness. It was showered and flounced with cream-coloured Chantilly lace that had come from Charleston on the last blockader, and Maybelle was flaunting it as saucily as if she and not the famous Captain Butler had run the blockade.

'How sweet I'd look in that dress!' thought Scarlett, a savage envy in her heart. 'Her waist is as big as a cow's. That green is just my colour and it would make my eyes look— Why will blondes try to wear that colour? Her skin looks as green as an old cheese. And to think I'll never wear that colour again, not even when I do get out of mourning. No, not even if I do manage to get married again. Then I'll have to wear tacky old greys and tans and lilacs.'

For a brief moment she considered the unfairness of it all. How short was the time for fun, for pretty clothes, for dancing, for coquetting! Only a few, too few years! Then you married and wore dull-coloured dresses and had babies that ruined your waist-line and sat in corners at dances with other sober matrons and only emerged to dance with your husband or with old gentlemen who stepped on your feet. If you didn't do these things, the other matrons talked about you and then your reputation was ruined and your family disgraced. It seemed such a terrible waste to spend all your little girlhood learning how to be attractive and how to catch men and then only use the knowledge for a year or two. When she considered her training at the hands of Ellen and Mammy, she knew it had been thorough and good because it always reaped results. There were set rules to be followed, and if you followed them success crowned your efforts.

With old ladies you were sweet and guileless and appeared as simple-minded as possible, for old ladies were sharp and they watched girls as jealously as cats, ready to pounce on any indiscretion of tongue or eye. With old gentlemen, a girl was pert and saucy and almost, but not quite, flirtatious, so that the old fools' vanities would be tickled. It made them feel devilish and young and they pinched your cheek and declared you were a minx. And, of course, you always blushed on such occasions, otherwise they would pinch you with more pleasure than was proper and then tell their sons that you were fast.

With young girls and young married women, you slopped over with sugar and kissed them every time you met them, even if it was ten times a day. And you put your arms about their waists and suffered them to do the same to you, no matter how much you disliked it. You admired their frocks or their babies indiscriminately and teased about beaux and complimented husbands and giggled modestly and denied that you had any charms at all compared with theirs. And, above all, you never said what you really thought about anything, any more than they said what they really thought.

Other women's husbands you let severely alone, even if they were your own discarded beaux, and no matter how temptingly attractive they were. If you were too nice to young husbands, their wives said you were fast and you got a bad reputation and never caught any beaux of your own.

But with young bachelors – ah, that was a different matter! You could laugh softly at them and when they came flying to see why you laughed, you could refuse to tell them and laugh harder and keep them around indefinitely trying to find out. You could promise, with your eyes, any number of exciting things that would make a man manoeuvre to get you alone. And, having gotten you alone, you could be very, very hurt or very, very angry when he tried to kiss you. You could make him apologize for being a cur and forgive him so sweetly that he would hang around trying to kiss you a second time. Sometimes, but not often, you did let him kiss you. (Ellen and Mammy had not taught her that but she learned it was effective.) Then you cried and declared you didn't know what had come over you and that he couldn't ever respect you again. Then he had to dry your eyes and usually he proposed to show just how much he did respect you. And then there were— Oh, there were so many things to do to bachelors and she knew them all, the nuance of the sidelong glance, the half-smile behind the fan, the swaying of the hips so that skirts swung like a bell, the tears, the laughter, the flattery, the sweet sympathy. Oh, all the tricks that never failed to work – except with Ashley.

No, it didn't seem right to learn all these smart tricks, use them so briefly and then put them away forever. How wonderful it would be never to marry but to go on being lovely in pale-green dresses and forever courted by handsome men! But, if you went on too long, you got to be an old maid like India Wilkes and everyone said 'poor thing' in that smug hateful way. No, after all it was better to marry and keep your self-respect even if you never had any more fun.

Oh, what a mess life was! Why had she been such an idiot as to marry Charles of all people and have her life end at sixteen?

Her indignant and hopeless reverie was broken when the crowd began pushing back against the walls, the ladies carefully holding their hoops so that no careless contact should turn them up against their bodies and show more pantalets than was proper. Scarlett tiptoed above the crowd and saw the captain of the militia mounting the orchestra platform. He shouted orders and half of the Company fell into line. For a few minutes they went through a brisk drill that brought perspiration to their foreheads and cheers and applause from the audience. Scarlett clapped her hands dutifully with the rest and, as the soldiers pushed forward toward the punch and lemonade booths after they were dismissed, she turned to Melanie, feeling that she had better begin her deception about the Cause as soon as possible.

'They looked fine, didn't they?' she said.

Melanie was fussing about with the knitted things on the counter.

'Most of them would look a lot finer in grey uniforms and in Virginia,' she said, and she did not trouble to lower her voice.

Several of the proud mothers of members of the militia were standing close by and overheard the remark. Mrs Guinan turned scarlet and then white, for her twenty-five-year-old Willie was in the Company.

Scarlett was aghast at such words coming from Melly of all people.

'Why, Melly!'

'You know it's true, Scarlett. I don't mean the little boys and the old gentlemen. But a lot of the militia are perfectly able to tote a rifle and that's what they ought to be doing this minute.'

'But – but—' began Scarlett, who had never considered the matter before. 'Somebody's got to stay home to—' What was it Willie Guinan had told her by way of excusing his presence in Atlanta? 'Somebody's got to stay home to protect the state from invasion.'

'Nobody's invading us and nobody's going to,' said Melly coolly, looking toward a group of the militia. 'And the best way to keep out invaders is to go to Virginia and beat the Yankees there. And as for all this talk about the militia staying here to keep the darkies from rising – why, it's the silliest thing I ever heard of. Why should our people rise? It's just a good excuse for cowards. I'll bet we could lick the Yankees in a month if all the militia of all the states went to Virginia. So there!'

'Why, Melly!' cried Scarlett again, staring.

Melly's soft dark eyes were flashing angrily. 'My husband wasn't afraid to go and neither was yours. And I'd rather they'd both be dead than here at home— Oh, darling, I'm sorry. How thoughtless and cruel of me!'

She stroked Scarlett's arm appealingly and Scarlett stared at her. But it was not of dead Charles she was thinking. It was of Ashley. Suppose he too were to die? She turned quickly and smiled automatically as Dr Meade walked up to their booth.

'Well, girls,' he greeted them, 'it was nice of you to come. I know what a sacrifice it must have been for you to come out tonight. But it's all for the Cause. And I'm going to tell you a secret. I've a surprise way for making some more money tonight for the hospital, but I'm afraid some of the ladies are going to be shocked about it.'

He stopped and chuckled as he tugged at his grey goatee.

'Oh, what? Do tell!'

'On second thought I believe I'll keep you guessing, too. But you girls must stand up for me if the Church members want to run me out of town for doing it. However, it's for the hospital. You'll see. Nothing like this has ever been done before.'

He went off pompously toward a group of chaperons in one corner, and just as the two girls had turned to each other to discuss the possibilities of the secret, two old gentlemen bore down on the booth, declaring in loud voices that they wanted ten miles of tatting. Well, after all, old gentlemen were better than no gentlemen at all, thought Scarlett, measuring out the tatting and submitting demurely to being chucked under the chin. The old blades charged off toward the lemonade booth and others took their places at the counter. Their booth did not have so many customers as did the other booths where the tootling laugh of Maybelle Merriwether sounded and Fanny Elsing's giggles and the Whiting girls' repartee made merriment. Melly sold useless stuff to men who could have no possible use for it as quietly and serenely as a shopkeeper, and Scarlett patterned her conduct on Melly's.

There were crowds in front of every other counter but theirs, girls chattering, men buying. The few who came to them talked about how they went to the university with Ashley and what a fine soldier he was or spoke in respectful tones of Charles and how great a loss to Atlanta his death had been.

Then the music broke into the rollicking strains of 'Johnny Booker, he'p dis Nigger!' and Scarlett thought she would scream. She wanted to dance. She wanted to dance. She looked across the floor and tapped her foot to the music and her green eyes blazed so eagerly that they fairly snapped. All the way across the floor, a man, newly come and standing in the doorway, saw them, started in recognition and watched closely the slanting eyes in the sulky, rebellious face. Then he grinned to himself as he recognized the invitation that any male could read.

He was dressed in black broadcloth, a tall man, towering over the officers who stood near him, bulky in the shoulders but tapering to a small waist and absurdly small feet in varnished boots. His severe black suit, with fine ruffled shirt and trousers smartly strapped beneath high insteps, was oddly at variance with his physique and face, for he was foppishly groomed, the clothes of a dandy on a body that was powerful and latently dangerous in its lazy grace. His hair was jet black, and his black moustache was small and closely clipped, almost foreign-looking compared with the dashing, swooping moustaches of the cavalrymen near by. He looked, and was, a man of lusty and unashamed appetites. He had an air of utter assurance, of displeasing insolence about him, and there was a twinkle of malice in his bold eyes as he stared at Scarlett, until finally, feeling his gaze, she looked toward him.

Somewhere in her mind, the bell of recognition rang, but for the moment she could not recall who he was. But he was the first man in months who had displayed any interest in her, and she threw him a gay smile. She made a little curtsy as he bowed, and then, as he straightened and started toward her with a peculiarly lithe Indian-like gait, her hand went to her mouth in horror, for she knew who he was.

Thunderstruck, she stood as if paralysed while he made his way through the crowd. Then she turned blindly, bent on flight into the refreshment rooms, but her skirt caught on a nail of the booth. She jerked furiously at it, tearing it and, in an instant, he was beside her.

'Permit me,' he said, bending over and disentangling the flounce. 'I hardly hoped that you would recall me, Miss O'Hara.'

His voice was oddly pleasant to the ear, the well-modulated voice of a gentleman, resonant and overlaid with the flat slow drawl of the Charlestonian.

She looked up at him imploringly, her face crimson with the shame of their last meeting, and met two of the blackest eyes she had ever seen, dancing in merciless merriment. Of all the people in the world to turn up here, this terrible person who had witnessed that scene with Ashley which still gave her nightmares; this odious wretch who ruined girls and was not received by nice people; this despicable man who had said, and with good cause, that she was not a lady.

At the sound of his voice, Melanie turned and for the first time in her life Scarlett thanked God for the existence of her sister-in-law.

'Why – it's – it's Mr Rhett Butler, isn't it?' said Melanie with a little smile, putting out her hand. 'I met you—'

'On the happy occasion of the announcement of your betrothal,' he finished, bending over her hand. 'It is kind of you to recall me.'

'And what are you doing so far from Charleston, Mr Butler?'

'A boring matter of business, Mrs Wilkes. I will be in and out of your town from now on. I find I must not only bring in goods but see to the disposal of them.'

'Bring in—' began Melly, her brow wrinkling, and then she broke into a delighted smile. 'Why, you – you must be the famous Captain Butler we've been hearing so much about – the blockade runner. Why, every girl here is wearing dresses you brought in. Scarlett, aren't you thrilled – what's the matter, dear? Are you faint? Do sit down.'

Scarlett sank to the stool, her breath coming so rapidly she feared the lacings of her stays would burst. Oh, what a terrible thing to happen! She had never thought to meet this man again. He picked up her black fan from the counter and began fanning her solicitously, too solicitously, his face grave but his eyes still dancing.

'It is quite warm in here,' he said. 'No wonder Miss O'Hara is faint. May I lead you to a window?'

'No,' said Scarlett, so rudely that Melly stared.

'She is not Miss O'Hara any longer,' said Melly. 'She is Mrs Hamilton. She is my sister now,' and Melly bestowed one of her fond little glances on her. Scarlett felt that she would strangle at the expression on Captain Butler's swarthy piratical face.

'I am sure that is a great gain to two charming ladies,' said he, making a slight bow. That was the kind of remark all men made, but when he said it it seemed to her that he meant just the opposite.

'Your husbands are here tonight, I trust, on this happy occasion? It would be a pleasure to renew acquaintances.'

'My husband is in Virginia,' said Melly with a proud lift of her head. 'But Charles—' Her voice broke.

'He died in camp,' said Scarlett flatly. She almost snapped the words. Would this creature never go away? Melly looked at her, startled, and the Captain made a gesture of self-reproach.

'My dear ladies – how could I! You must forgive me. But permit a stranger to offer the comfort of saying that to die for one's country is to live forever.'

Melanie smiled at him through sparkling tears while Scarlett felt the fox of wrath and impotent hate gnaw at her vitals. Again he had made a graceful remark, the kind of compliment any gentleman would pay under such circumstances, but he did not mean a word of it. He was jeering at her. He knew she hadn't loved Charles. And Melly was just a big fool not to see through him. Oh, please God, don't let anybody else see through him, she thought with a start of terror. Would he tell what he knew? Of course he wasn't a gentleman and there was no telling what men would do when they weren't gentlemen. There was no standard to judge them by. She looked up at him and saw that his mouth was pulled down at the corners in mock sympathy, even while he swished the fan. Something in his look challenged her spirit and brought her strength back in a surge of dislike. Abruptly she snatched the fan from his hand.

'I'm quite all right,' she said tartly. 'There's no need to blow my hair out of place.'

'Scarlett, darling! Captain Butler, you must forgive her. She – she isn't herself when she hears poor Charlie's name spoken – and perhaps, after all, we shouldn't have come here tonight. We're still in mourning, you see, and it's quite a strain on her – all this gaiety and music, poor child.'

'I quite understand,' he said with elaborate gravity, but as he turned and gave Melanie a searching look that went to the bottom of her sweet worried eyes, his expression changed, reluctant respect and gentleness coming over his dark face. 'I think you're a courageous little lady, Mrs Wilkes.'

'Not a word about me!' thought Scarlett indignantly, as Melly smiled in confusion and answered:

'Dear me, no, Captain Butler! The hospital committee just had to have us for this booth because at the last minute— A pillow-case? Here's a lovely one with a flag on it.'

She turned to three cavalrymen who appeared at her counter. For a moment, Melanie thought how nice Captain Butler was. Then she wished that something more substantial than cheesecloth was between her skirt and the spittoon that stood just outside the booth, for the aim of the horsemen with amber streams of tobacco juice was not so unerring as with their long horse pistols. Then she forgot about the Captain, Scarlett and the spittoons as more customers crowded to her.

Scarlett sat quietly on the stool fanning herself, not daring to look up, wishing Captain Butler back on the deck of his ship where he belonged.

'Your husband has been dead long?'

'Oh, yes, a long time. Almost a year.'

'An aeon, I'm sure.'

Scarlett was not sure what an aeon was, but there was no mistaking the baiting quality of his voice, so she said nothing.

'Had you been married long? Forgive my questions but I have been away from this section for so long.'

'Two months,' said Scarlett, unwillingly.

'A tragedy, no less,' his easy voice continued.

'Oh, damn him,' she thought violently. 'If he was any other man in the world I could simply freeze up and order him off. But he knows about Ashley and he knows I didn't love Charlie. And my hands are tied.' She said nothing, still looking down at her fan.

'And this is your first social appearance?'

'I know it looks quite odd,' she explained rapidly. 'But the McLure girls who were to take this booth were called away and there was no one else, so Melanie and I—'

'No sacrifice is too great for the Cause.'

Why, that was what Mrs Elsing had said, but when she said it it didn't sound the same way. Hot words started to her lips but she choked them back. After all, she was here, not for the Cause, but because she was tired of sitting at home.

'I have always thought,' he said reflectively, 'that the system of mourning, of immuring women in crêpe for the rest of their lives and forbidding them normal enjoyment, is just as barbarous as the Hindu suttee.'

'Settee?'

He laughed and she blushed for her ignorance. She hated people who used words unknown to her.

'In India, when a man dies he is burned, instead of buried, and his wife always climbs on the funeral pyre and is burned with him.'

'How dreadful! Why do they do it? Don't the police do anything about it?'

'Of course not. A wife who didn't burn herself would be a social outcast. All the worthy Hindu matrons would talk about her for not behaving as a well-bred lady should – precisely as those worthy matrons in the corner would talk about you, should you appear tonight in a red dress and lead a reel. Personally, I think suttee much more merciful than our charming Southern custom of burying widows alive.'

'How dare you say I'm buried alive!'

'How closely women clutch the very chains that bind them! You think the Hindu custom barbarous – but would you have had the courage to appear here tonight if the Confederacy hadn't needed you?'

Arguments of this character were always confusing to Scarlett. His were doubly confusing because she had a vague idea there was truth in them. But now was the time to squelch him.

'Of course, I wouldn't have come. It would have been – well, disrespectful to – it would have seemed as if I hadn't lov—'

His eyes waited on her words, cynical amusement in them, and she could not go on. He knew she hadn't loved Charlie and he wouldn't let her pretend to the nice polite sentiments that she should express. What a terrible, terrible thing it was to have to do with a man who wasn't a gentleman. A gentleman always appeared to believe a lady even when he knew she was lying. That was Southern chivalry. A gentleman always obeyed the rules and said the correct things and made life easier for a lady. But this man seemed not to care for rules and evidently enjoyed talking of things no one ever talked about.

'I am waiting breathlessly.'

'I think you are horrid,' she said, helplessly, dropping her eyes.

He leaned down across the counter until his mouth was near her ear and hissed, in a very creditable imitation of the stage villains who appeared infrequently at the Athenaeum Hall: 'Fear not, fair lady! Your guilty secret is safe with me!'

'Oh,' she whispered, feverishly, 'how can you say such things!'

'I only thought to ease your mind. What would you have me say? "Be mine, beautiful female, or I will reveal all"?'

She met his eyes unwillingly and saw they were as teasing as a small boy's. Suddenly she laughed. It was such a silly situation, after all. He laughed too, and so loudly that several of the chaperons in the corner looked their way. Observing how good a time Charles Hamilton's widow appeared to be having with a perfect stranger, they put their heads together disapprovingly.

There was a roll of drums and many voices cried 'Sh!' as Dr Meade mounted the platform and spread out his arms for quiet.

'We must all give grateful thanks to the charming ladies whose indefatigable and patriotic efforts have made this bazaar not only a pecuniary success,' he began, 'but have transformed this rough hall into a bower of loveliness, a fit garden for the charming rosebuds I see about me.'

Everyone clapped approvingly.

'The ladies have given their best, not only of their time but of the labour of their hands, and these beautiful objects in the booths are doubly beautiful, made as they are by the fair hands of our charming Southern women.'

There were shouts of approval, and Rhett Butler, who had been lounging negligently against the counter at Scarlett's side, whispered: 'Pompous goat, isn't he?'

Startled, at first horrified, at this lèse-majesty toward Atlanta's most beloved citizen, she stared reprovingly at him. But the doctor did look like a goat with his grey chin-whiskers wagging away at a great rate, and with difficulty she stifled a giggle.

'But these things are not enough. The good ladies of the hospital committee, whose cool hands have soothed many a suffering brow and brought back from the jaws of death our brave men wounded in the bravest of all Causes, know our needs. I will not enumerate them. We must have more money to buy medical supplies from England, and we have with us tonight the intrepid captain who has so successfully run the blockade for a year and who will run it again to bring us the drugs we need. Captain Rhett Butler!'

Though caught unawares, the blockader made a graceful bow – too graceful, thought Scarlett, trying to analyse it. It was almost as if he overdid his courtesy because his contempt for everybody present was so great. There was a loud burst of applause as he bowed and a craning of necks from the ladies in the corner. So that was who poor Charles Hamilton's widow was carrying on with! And Charlie hardly dead a year!

'We need more gold and I am asking you for it,' the doctor continued. 'I am asking a sacrifice but a sacrifice so small compared with the sacrifices our gallant men in grey are making that it will seem laughably small. Ladies, I want your jewellery. *I* want your jewellery? No, the Confederacy wants your jewellery, the Confederacy calls for it and I know no one will hold back. How fair a gem gleams on a lovely wrist! How beautifully gold brooches glitter on the bosoms of our patriotic women! But how much more beautiful is sacrifice than all the gold and gems of the Ind! The gold will be melted and the stones sold and the money used to buy drugs and other medical supplies. Ladies, there will pass among you two of our gallant wounded, with baskets and—' But the rest of his speech was lost in the storm and tumult of clapping hands and cheering voices.

Scarlett's first thought was one of deep thankfulness that mourning forbade her wearing her precious earbobs and the heavy gold chain that had been Grandma Robillard's and the gold and black enamelled bracelets and the garnet brooch. She saw the little Zouave, a split-oak basket over his unwounded arm, making the rounds of the crowd on her side of the hall and saw women, old and young, laughing, eager, tugging at bracelets, squealing in pretended pain as earrings came from pierced flesh, helping each other undo stiff necklace clasps, unpinning brooches from bosoms. There was a steady little clink-clink of metal on metal and cries of 'Wait – wait! I've got it unfastened now. There!' Maybelle Merriwether was pulling off her lovely twin bracelets from above and below her elbows. Fanny Elsing, crying 'Mamma, may I?' was tearing from her curls the seed-pearl ornament set in heavy gold which had been in the family for generations. As each offering went into the basket, there was applause and cheering.

The grinning little man was coming to their booth now, his basket heavy on his arm, and as he passed Rhett Butler a handsome gold cigar-case was thrown carelessly into the basket. When he came to Scarlett and rested his basket on the counter, she shook her head, throwing wide her hands to show that she had nothing to give. It was embarrassing to be the only person present who was giving nothing. And then she saw the bright gleam of her wide gold wedding ring.

For a confused moment she tried to remember Charles' face – how he had looked when he slipped it on her finger. But the memory was blurred, blurred by the sudden feeling of irritation that memory of him always brought to her. Charles – he was the reason why life was over for her, why she was an old woman.

With a sudden wrench she seized the ring but it stuck. The Zouave was moving toward Melanie.

'Wait!' cried Scarlett. 'I have something for you!' The ring came off and, as she started to throw it into the basket, heaped up with chains, watches, rings, pins and bracelets, she caught Rhett Butler's eye. His lips were twisted in a slight smile. Defiantly, she tossed the ring on to the top of the pile.

'Oh, my darling!' whispered Melly, clutching her arm, her eyes blazing with love and pride. 'You brave, brave girl! Wait – please, wait, Lieutenant Picard! I have something for you, too!'

She was tugging at her own wedding ring, the ring Scarlett knew had never once left that finger since Ashley put it there. Scarlett knew, as no one did, how much it meant to her. It came off with difficulty and for a brief instant was clutched tightly in the small palm. Then it was laid gently on the pile of jewellery. The two girls stood looking after the Zouave who was moving toward the group of elderly ladies in the corner, Scarlett defiant, Melanie with a look more pitiful than tears. And neither expression was lost on the man who stood beside them.

'If you hadn't been brave enough to do it, I would never have been, either,' said Melly, putting her arm about Scarlett's waist and giving her a gentle squeeze. For a moment Scarlett wanted to shake her off and cry 'Name of God!' at the top of her lungs, as Gerald did when he was irritated, but she caught Rhett Butler's eye and managed a very sour smile. It was annoying the way Melly always misconstrued her motives – but perhaps that was far preferable to having her suspect the truth.

'What a beautiful gesture!' said Rhett Butler softly. 'It is such sacrifices as yours that hearten our brave lads in grey.'

Hot words bubbled to her lips and it was with difficulty that she checked them. There was mockery in everything he said. She disliked him heartily, lounging there against the booth. But there was something stimulating about him, something warm and vital and electric. All that was Irish in her rose to the challenge of his black eyes. She decided she was going to take this man down a notch or two. His knowledge of her secret gave him an advantage over her that was exasperating, so she would have to change that by putting him at a disadvantage somehow. She stifled her impulse to tell him exactly what she thought of him. Sugar always caught more flies than vinegar, as Mammy often said, and she was going to catch and subdue this fly, so he could never again have her at his mercy.

'Thank you,' she said sweetly, deliberately misunderstanding his jibe. 'A compliment like that coming from so famous a man as Captain Butler is appreciated.'

He threw back his head and laughed freely – yelped, was what Scarlett thought fiercely, her face becoming pink again.

'Why don't you say what you really think?' he demanded, lowering his voice so that in the clatter and excitement of the collection it came only to her ears. 'Why don't you say I'm a damned rascal and no gentleman and that I must take myself off or you'll have one of these gallant boys in grey call me out?'

It was on the tip of her tongue to answer tartly, but she managed by heroic control to say: 'Why, Captain Butler! How you do run on! As if everybody didn't know how famous you are and how brave and what a – what a—'

'I am disappointed in you,' he said.

'Disappointed?'

'Yes. On the occasion of our first eventful meeting I thought to myself that I had at last met a girl who was not only beautiful but who had courage. And now I see that you are only beautiful.'

'Do you mean to call me a coward?' She was ruffling like a hen.

'Exactly. You lack the courage to say what you really think. When I first met you, I thought : there is a girl in a million. She isn't like these other silly little fools who believe everything their mammas tell them and act on it, no matter how they feel. And conceal all their feelings and desires and little heartbreaks behind a lot of sweet words. I thought: Miss O'Hara is a girl of rare spirit. She knows what she wants and she doesn't mind speaking her mind – or throwing vases.'

'Oh,' she said, rage breaking through. 'Then I'll speak my mind right this minute. If you'd had any raising at all you'd never have come over here and talked to me. You'd have known I never wanted to lay eyes on you again! But you aren't a gentleman! You are just a nasty ill-bred little creature! And you think that because your rotten little boats can outrun the Yankees, you've the right to come here and jeer at men who are brave and women who are sacrificing everything for the Cause—'

'Stop, stop—' he begged with a grin. 'You started off very nicely and said what you thought, but don't begin talking to me about the Cause. I'm tired of hearing about it and I'll bet you are, too—'

'Why, how did—' she began, caught off her balance, and then checked herself hastily, boiling with anger at herself for falling into his trap.

'I stood there in the doorway before you saw me and I watched you,' he said. 'And I watched the other girls. And they all looked as though their faces came out of one mould. Yours didn't. You have an easy face to read. You didn't have your mind on your business and I'll wager you weren't thinking about our Cause or the hospital. It was all over your face that you wanted to dance and have a good time and you couldn't. So you were mad clean through. Tell the truth. Am I not right?'

'I have nothing more to say to you, Captain Butler,' she said as formally as she could, trying to draw the rags of her dignity about her. 'Just because you're conceited at being the "great blockader" doesn't give you the right to insult women.'

'The great blockader! That's a joke. Pray give me only one moment more of your precious time before you cast me into darkness. I wouldn't want so charming a little patriot to be left under a misapprehension about my contribution to the Confederate Cause.'

'I don't care to listen to your brags.'

'Blockading is a business with me and I'm making money out of it. When I stop making money out of it, I'll quit. What do you think of that?'

'I think you're a mercenary rascal – just like the Yankees.'

'Exactly,' he grinned. 'And the Yankees help me make my money. Why, last month I sailed my boat right into New York harbour and took on a cargo.'

'What!' cried Scarlett, interested and excited in spite of herself. 'Didn't they shell you?'

'My poor innocent! Of course not. There are plenty of sturdy Union patriots who are not averse to picking up money selling goods to the Confederacy. I run my boat into New York, buy from Yankee firms, sub rosa, of course, and away I go. And when that gets a bit dangerous, I go to Nassau where these same Union patriots have brought powder and shells and hoop skirts for me. It's more convenient than going to England. Sometimes it's a bit difficult running it into Charleston or Wilmington – but you'd be surprised how far a little gold goes.'

'Oh, I knew Yankees were vile but I didn't know—'

'Why quibble about the Yankees earning an honest penny selling out the Union? It won't matter in a hundred years. The result will be the same. They know the Confederacy will be licked eventually, so why shouldn't they cash in on it?'

'Licked – us?'

'Of course.'

'Will you please leave me – or will it be necessary for me to call my carriage and go home to get rid of you?'

'A red-hot little Rebel,' he said, with another sudden grin. He bowed and sauntered off, leaving her with her bosom heaving with impotent rage and indignation. There was disappointment burning in her that she could not quite analyse, the disappointment of a child seeing illusions crumble. How dared he take the glamour from the blockaders! And how dared he say the Confederacy would be licked! He should be shot for that – shot like a traitor. She looked about the hall at the familiar faces, so assured of success, so brave, so devoted, and somehow a cold little chill set in at her heart. Licked? These people – why, of course not! The very idea was impossible, disloyal.

'What were you two whispering about?' asked Melanie, turning to Scarlett as her customers drifted off. 'I couldn't help seeing that Mrs Merriwether had her eye on you all the time and, dear, you know how she talks.'

'Oh, the man's impossible – an ill-bred boor,' said Scarlett. 'And as for old lady Merriwether, let her talk. I'm sick of acting like a ninny, just for her benefit.'

'Why, Scarlett!' cried Melanie, scandalized.

'Sh-sh,' said Scarlett. 'Dr Meade is going to make another announcement.'

The gathering quieted again as the doctor raised his voice, at first in thanks to the ladies who had so willingly given their jewellery.

'And now, ladies and gentlemen, I am going to propose a surprise – an innovation that may shock some of you, but I ask you to remember that all this is done for the hospital and for the benefit of our boys lying there.'

Everyone edged forward, in anticipation, trying to imagine what the sedate doctor could propose that would be shocking.

'The dancing is about to begin and the first number will, of course, be a reel, followed by a waltz. The dances following, the polkas, the schottisches, the mazurkas, will be preceded by short reels. I know the gentle rivalry to lead the reels very well and so—' The doctor mopped his brow and cast a quizzical glance at the corner, where his wife sat among the chaperons. 'Gentlemen, if you wish to lead a reel with the lady of your choice, you must bargain for her. I will be auctioneer and the proceeds will go to the hospital.'

Fans stopped in mid-swish and a ripple of excited murmuring ran through the hall. The chaperons' corner was in tumult and Mrs Meade, anxious to support her husband in an action of which she heartily disapproved, was at a disadvantage. Mrs Elsing, Mrs Merriwether and Mrs Whiting were red with indignation. But suddenly the Home Guard gave a cheer and it was taken up by the other uniformed guests. The young girls clapped their hands and jumped excitedly.

'Don't you think it's – it's just – just a little like a slave auction?' whispered Melanie, staring uncertainly at the embattled doctor who heretofore had been perfect in her eyes.

Scarlett said nothing but her eyes glittered and her heart contracted with a little pain. If only she were not a widow. If only she were Scarlett O'Hara again, out there on the floor in an apple-green dress with dark-green velvet ribbons dangling from her bosom and tuberoses in her black hair – she'd lead that reel. Yes, indeed. There'd be a dozen men battling for her and paying over money to the doctor. Oh, to have to sit here, a wallflower against her will, and see Fanny or Maybelle lead the first reel as the belle of Atlanta!

Above the tumult sounded the voice of the little Zouave, his Creole accent very obvious: 'Eef I may – twenty dollars for Mees Maybelle Merriwether.'

Maybelle collapsed with blushes against Fanny's shoulder and the two girls hid their faces in each other's necks and giggled, as other voices began calling other names, other amounts of money. Dr Meade had begun to smile again, ignoring completely the indignant whispers that came from the Ladies' Hospital Committee in the corner.

At first, Mrs Merriwether had stated flatly and loudly that her Maybelle would never take part in such a proceeding; but as Maybelle's name was called most often and the amount went up to seventy-five dollars, her protests began to dwindle. Scarlett leaned her elbows on the counter and almost glared at the excited laughing crowd surging about the platform, their hands full of Confederate paper money.

Now they would all dance – except her and the old ladies. Now everyone would have a good time, except her. She saw Rhett Butler standing just below the doctor and, before she could change the expression of her face, he saw her and one corner of his mouth went down and one eyebrow went up. She jerked her chin up and turned away from him and suddenly she heard her own name called – called in an unmistakable Charleston voice that rang out above the hubbub of other names.

'Mrs Charles Hamilton – one hundred and fifty dollars – in gold.'

A sudden hush fell on the crowd at the mention of the sum and at the name. Scarlett was so startled she could not even move. She remained sitting with her chin in her hands, her eyes wide with astonishment. Everybody turned to look at her. She saw the doctor lean down from the platform and whisper something to Rhett Butler. Probably telling him she was in mourning and it was impossible for her to appear on the floor. She saw Rhett's shoulders shrug lazily.

'Another one of our belles, perhaps?' questioned the doctor.

'No,' said Rhett clearly, his eye sweeping the crowd carelessly, 'Mrs Hamilton.'

'I tell you it is impossible,' said the doctor testily. 'Mrs Hamilton will not—'

Scarlett heard a voice which, at first, she did not recognize as her own.

'Yes, I will!'

She leaped to her feet, her heart hammering so wildly she feared she could not stand, hammering with the thrill of being the centre of attention again, of being the most highly desired girl present and oh, best of all, at the prospect of dancing again.

'Oh, I don't care! I don't care what they say!' she whispered, as a sweet madness swept over her. She tossed her head and sped out of the booth, tapping her heels like castanets, snapping open her black silk fan to its widest. For a fleeting instant she saw Melanie's incredulous face, the look on the chaperons' faces, the petulant girls, the enthusiastic approval of the soldiers.

Then she was on the floor and Rhett Butler was advancing toward her through the aisle of the crowd, that nasty mocking smile on his face. But she didn't care – didn't care if he were Abe Lincoln himself! She was going to dance again. She was going to lead the reel. She swept him a low curtsy and a dazzling smile and he bowed, one hand on his frilled bosom. Levi, horrified, was quick to cover the situation and bawled: 'Choose yo' padners fo' de Ferginny reel!'

And the orchestra crashed into that best of all reel tunes, 'Dixie'.

'How dare you make me so conspicuous, Captain Butler?'

'But, my dear Mrs Hamilton, you so obviously wanted to be conspicuous!'

'How could you call my name out in front of everybody?'

'You could have refused.'

'But – I owe it to the Cause – I – I couldn't think of myself when you were offering so much in gold. Stop laughing, everyone is looking at us.'

'They will look at us anyway. Don't try to palm off that twaddle about the Cause to me. You wanted to dance and I gave you the opportunity. This march is the last figure of the reel, isn't it?'

'Yes – really, I must stop and sit down now.'

'Why? Have I stepped on your feet?'

'No – but they'll talk about me.'

'Do you really care – down in your heart?'

'Well—'

'You aren't committing any crime, are you? Why not dance the waltz with me?'

'But if Mother ever—'

'Still tied to mamma's apron-strings.'

'Oh, you have the nastiest way of making virtues sound so stupid.'

'But virtues are stupid. Do you care if people talk?'

'No – but – well, let's don't talk about it. Thank goodness the waltz is beginning. Reels always leave me breathless.'

'Don't dodge my questions. Has what other women said ever mattered to you?'

'Oh, if you're going to pin me down – no! But a girl is supposed to mind. Tonight, though, I don't care.'

'Bravo! Now you are beginning to think for yourself instead of letting others think for you. That's the beginning of wisdom.'

'Oh, but—'

'When you've been talked about as much as I have, you'll realize how little it matters. Just think, there's not a home in Charleston where I am received. Not even my contribution to our just and holy Cause lifts the ban.'

'How dreadful!'

'Oh, not at all. Until you've lost your reputation, you never realize what a burden it was or what freedom really is.'

'You do talk scandalous!'

'Scandalously and truly. Always providing you have enough courage – or money – you can do without a reputation.'

'Money can't buy everything.'

'Someone must have told you that. You'd never think of such a platitude all by yourself. What can't it buy?'

'Oh, well, I don't know – not happiness or love, anyway.'

'Generally it can. And when it can't, it can buy some of the most remarkable substitutes.'

'And have you so much money, Captain Butler?'

'What an ill-bred question, Mrs Hamilton! I'm surprised. But, yes. For a young man cut off without a shilling in early youth, I've done very well. And I'm sure I'll clean up a million on the blockade.'

'Oh, no!'

'Oh, yes! What most people don't seem to realize is that there is just as much money to be made out of the wreckage of a civilization as from the upbuilding of one.'

'And what does all that mean?'

'Your family and my family and everyone here tonight made their money out of changing a wilderness into a civilization. That's empire building. There's good money in empire building. But, there's more in empire wrecking.'

'What empire are you talking about?'

'This empire we're living in – the South – the Confederacy – the Cotton Kingdom – it's breaking up right under our feet. Only most fools won't see it and take advantage of the situation created by the collapse. I'm making a fortune out of the wreckage.'

'Then you really think we're going to get licked?'

'Yes. Why be an ostrich?'

'Oh, dear, it bores me to talk about such like. Don't you ever say pretty things, Captain Butler?'

'Would it please you if I said your eyes were twin goldfish bowls filled to the brim with the clearest green water and that when the fish swim to the top, as they are doing now, you are devilishly charming?'

'Oh, I don't like that... Isn't the music gorgeous? Oh, I could waltz forever! I didn't know I had missed it so!'

'You are the most beautiful dancer I've ever held in my arms.'

'Captain Butler, you must not hold me so tightly. Everybody is looking.'

'If no one were looking, would you care?'

'Captain Butler, you forget yourself.'

'Not for a minute. How could I, with you in my arms? . . . What is that tune? Isn't it new?'

'Yes. Isn't it divine? It's something we captured from the Yankees.'

'What's the name of it?'

' "When This Cruel War Is Over".'

'What are the words? Sing them to me.'

> *Dearest one, do you remember*
> *When we last did meet?*
> *When you told me how you loved me,*
> *Kneeling at my feet?*
> *Oh, how proud you stood before me*
> *In your suit of grey,*
> *When you vowed from me and country*
> *Ne'er to go astray.*
> *Weeping sad and lonely,*
> *Sighs and tears how vain!*
> *When this cruel war is over*
> *Pray that we meet again!*

'Of course, it was "suit of blue" but we changed it to "grey" . . . Oh, you waltz so well, Captain Butler. Most big men don't, you know. And to think it will be years and years before I'll dance again.'

'It will only be a few minutes. I'm going to bid you in for the next reel – and the next and the next.'

'Oh, no, I couldn't! You mustn't! My reputation will be ruined.'

'It's in shreds already, so what does another dance matter? Maybe I'll give the other boys a chance after I've had five or six, but I must have the last one.'

'Oh, all right. I know I'm crazy but I don't care. I don't care a bit what anybody says. I'm so tired of sitting at home. I'm going to dance and dance . . .'

'And not wear black? I loathe funeral crêpe.'

'Oh, I couldn't take off mourning— Captain Butler, you must not hold me so tightly. I'll be mad at you if you do.'

'And you look gorgeous when you are mad. I'll squeeze you again – there – just to see if you will really get mad. You have no idea how charming you were that day at Twelve Oaks when you were mad and throwing things.'

'Oh, please – won't you forget that?'

'No, it is one of my most priceless memories – a delicately nurtured Southern belle with her Irish up— You are very Irish, you know.'

'Oh, dear, there's the end of the music and there's Aunt Pittypat coming out of the back room. I know Mrs Merriwether must have told her. Oh, for goodness' sake, let's walk over and look out the window. I don't want her to catch me now. Her eyes are as big as saucers.'

Chapter X

Over the waffles next morning, Pittypat was lachrymose, Melanie was silent and Scarlett defiant.

'I don't care if they do talk. I'll bet I made more money for the hospital than any girl there – more than all the messy old stuff we sold, too.'

'Oh, dear, what does the money matter?' wailed Pittypat, wringing her hands. 'I just couldn't believe my eyes, and poor Charlie hardly dead a year . . . And that awful Captain Butler, making you so conspicuous, and he's a terrible, terrible person, Scarlett. Mrs Whiting's cousin, Mrs Coleman, whose husband came from Charleston, told me about him. He's the black sheep of a lovely family – oh, how could any of the Butlers ever turn out anything like him? He isn't received in Charleston and he has the fastest reputation and there was something about a girl – something so bad Mrs Coleman didn't even know what it was—'

'Oh, I can't believe he's that bad,' said Melly gently. 'He seemed a perfect gentleman and when you think how brave he's been, running the blockade—'

'He isn't brave,' said Scarlett perversely, pouring half a pitcher of syrup over her waffles. 'He just does it for money. He told me so. He doesn't care anything about the Confederacy and he says we're going to get licked. But he dances divinely.'

Her audience was speechless with horror.

'I'm tired of sitting at home and I'm not going to do it any longer. If they all talked about me about last night, then my reputation is already gone and it won't matter what else they say.'

It did not occur to her that the idea was Rhett Butler's. It came so patly and fitted so well with what she was thinking.

'Oh! What will your mother say when she hears? What will she think of me?'

A cold qualm of guilt assailed Scarlett at the thought of Ellen's consternation, should she ever learn of her daughter's scandalous conduct. But she took heart at the thought of the twenty-five miles between Atlanta and Tara. Miss Pitty certainly wouldn't tell Ellen. It would put her in such a bad light as a chaperon. And if Pitty didn't tattle, she was safe.

'I think—' said Pitty, 'yes, I think I'd better write Henry a letter about it – much as I hate it – but he's our only male relative, and make him go speak reprovingly to Captain Butler— Oh, dear, if Charlie were only alive— You must never, never speak to that man again, Scarlett.'

Melanie had been sitting quietly, her hands in her lap, her waffles cooling on her plate. She arose and, coming behind Scarlett, put her arms about her neck.

'Darling,' she said, 'don't you get upset. I understand and it was a brave thing you did last night and it's going to help the hospital a lot. And if anybody dares say one little word about you, I'll tend to them . . . Aunt Pitty, don't cry. It has been hard on Scarlett, not going anywhere. She's just a baby.' Her fingers played in Scarlett's black hair. 'And maybe we'd all be better off if we went out occasionally to parties. Maybe we've been very selfish, staying here with our grief. War times aren't like other times. When I think of all the soldiers in town who are far from home and haven't any friends to call on at night – and the ones in the hospital who are well enough to be out of bed and not well enough to go back in the army— Why, we have been selfish. We ought to have three convalescents in our house this minute, like everybody else, and some of the soldiers out to dinner every Sunday. There, Scarlett, don't you fret. People won't talk when they understand. We know you loved Charlie.'

Scarlett was far from fretting and Melanie's soft hands in her hair were irritating. She wanted to jerk her head away and say 'Oh, fiddle-dee-dee!' for the warming memory was still on her of how the Home Guard and the militia and the soldiers from the hospital had fought for her dances last night. Of all the people in the world, she didn't want Melly for a defender. She could defend herself, thank you, and if the old cats wanted to squall – well, she could get along without the old cats. There were too many nice officers in the world for her to bother about what old women said.

Pittypat was dabbing at her eyes under Melanie's soothing words when Prissy entered with a bulky letter.

'Fer you, Miss Melly. A lil nigger boy brung it.'

'For me?' said Melly, wondering, as she ripped open the envelope.

Scarlett was making headway with her waffles and so noticed nothing until she heard a burst of tears from Melly and, looking up, saw Aunt Pittypat's hand go to her heart.

'Ashley's dead!' screamed Pittypat, throwing her head back and letting her arms go limp.

'Oh, my God!' cried Scarlett, her blood turning to ice water.

'No! No!' cried Melanie. 'Quick! Her smelling salts, Scarlett! There, there, honey, do you feel better? Breathe deep. No, it's not Ashley. I'm so sorry I scared you. I was crying because I'm so happy,' and suddenly she opened her clenched palm and pressed some object that was in it to her lips. 'I'm so happy,' and burst into tears again.

Scarlett caught a fleeting glimpse and saw that it was a broad gold ring.

'Read it,' said Melly, pointing to the letter on the floor. 'Oh, how sweet, how kind he is!'

Scarlett, bewildered, picked up the single sheet and saw written in a black, bold hand: 'The Confederacy may need the lifeblood of its men but not yet does it demand the heart's blood of its women. Accept, dear Madam, this token of my reverence for your courage and do not think that your sacrifice has been in vain, for this ring has been redeemed at ten times its value. Captain Rhett Butler.'

Melanie slipped the ring on her finger and looked at it lovingly.

'I told you he was a gentleman, didn't I?' she said, turning to Pittypat, her smile bright through the teardrops on her face. 'No one but a gentleman of refinement and thoughtfulness would ever have thought how it broke my heart to— I'll send my gold chain instead. Aunt Pittypat, you must write him a note and invite him to Sunday dinner so I can thank him.'

In the excitement, neither of the others seemed to have thought that Captain Butler had not returned Scarlett's ring, too. But she thought of it, annoyed. And she knew it had not been Captain Butler's refinement that had prompted so gallant a gesture. It was that he intended to be asked into Pittypat's house and knew unerringly how to get the invitation.

'I was greatly disturbed to hear of your recent conduct,' ran Ellen's letter, and Scarlett, who was reading it at the table, scowled. Bad news certainly travelled swiftly. She had often heard in Charleston and Savannah that Atlanta people gossiped more and meddled in other people's business more than any other people in the South, and now she believed it. The bazaar had taken place Monday night and today was only Thursday. Which of the old cats had taken it upon herself to write Ellen? For a moment she suspected Pittypat but immediately abandoned that thought. Poor Pittypat had been quaking in her number-three shoes for fear of being blamed for Scarlett's forward conduct and would be the last to notify Ellen of her own inadequate chaperonage. Probably it was Mrs Merriwether.

'It is difficult for me to believe that you could so forget yourself and your rearing. I will pass over the impropriety of your appearing publicly while in mourning, realizing your warm desire to be of assistance to the hospital. But to dance, and with such a man as Captain Butler! I have heard so much of him (as who has not?) and Pauline wrote me only last week that he is a man of bad repute and not even received by his own family in Charleston, except of course by his heartbroken mother. He is a thoroughly bad character who would take advantage of your youth and innocence to make you conspicuous and publicly disgrace you and your family. How could Miss Pittypat have so neglected her duty to you?'

Scarlett looked across the table at her aunt. The old lady had recognized Ellen's handwriting and her fat little mouth was pursed in a frightened way, like a baby who fears a scolding and hopes to ward it off by tears.

'I am heartbroken to think that you could so soon forget your rearing. I have thought of calling you home immediately but will leave that to your father's discretion. He will be in Atlanta Friday to speak with Captain Butler and to escort you home. I fear he will be severe with you despite my pleadings. I hope and pray it was only youth and thoughtlessness that prompted such forward conduct. No one can wish to serve our Cause more than I, and I wish my daughters to feel the same way, but to disgrace—'

There was more in the same vein but Scarlett did not finish it. For once, she was thoroughly frightened. She did not feel reckless and defiant now. She felt as young and guilty as when she was ten and had thrown a buttered biscuit at Suellen at the table. To think of her gentle mother reproving her so harshly and her father coming to town to talk to Captain Butler. The real seriousness of the matter grew on her. Gerald was going to be severe. This was one time when she knew she couldn't wriggle out of her punishment by sitting on his knee and being sweet and pert.

'Not – not bad news?' quavered Pittypat.

'Pa is coming tomorrow and he's going to land on me like a duck on a June bug,' answered Scarlett dolorously.

'Prissy, find my salts,' fluttered Pittypat, pushing back her chair from her half-eaten meal. 'I – I feel faint.'

'Dey's in yo' skirt pocket,' said Prissy, who had been hovering behind Scarlett, enjoying the sensational drama. Mist' Gerald in a temper was always exciting, providing his temper was not directed at her kinky head. Pitty fumbled at her skirt and held the vial to her nose.

'You all must stand by me and not leave me alone with him for one minute,' cried Scarlett. 'He's so fond of you both, and if you are with me he can't fuss at me.'

'I couldn't,' said Pittypat weakly, rising to her feet. 'I – I feel ill. I must go lie down. I shall lie down all day tomorrow. You must give him my excuses.'

'Coward!' thought Scarlett, glowering at her.

Melly rallied to the defence, though white and frightened at the prospect of facing the fire-eating Mr O'Hara. 'I'll – I'll help you explain how you did it for the hospital. Surely he'll understand.'

'No, he won't,' said Scarlett. 'And oh, I shall die if I have to go back to Tara in disgrace, like Mother threatens!'

'Oh, you can't go home,' cried Pittypat, bursting into tears. 'If you did I should be forced – yes, forced to ask Henry to come live with us, and you know I just couldn't live with Henry. I'm so nervous with just Melly in the house at night, with so many strange men in town. You're so brave I don't mind being here without a man!'

'Oh, he couldn't take you to Tara!' said Melly, looking as if she too would cry in a moment. 'This is your home now. What would we ever do without you?'

'You'd be glad to do without me if you knew what I really think of you,' thought Scarlett sourly, wishing there were some other person than Melanie to help ward off Gerald's wrath. It was sickening to be defended by someone you disliked so much.

'Perhaps we should recall our invitation to Captain Butler—' began Pittypat.

'Oh, we couldn't! It would be the height of rudeness!' cried Melly, distressed.

'Help me to bed. I'm going to be ill,' moaned Pittypat. 'Oh, Scarlett, how could you have brought this on me?'

Pittypat was ill and in her bed when Gerald arrived the next afternoon. She sent many messages of regret to him from behind her closed door and left the two frightened girls to preside over the supper table. Gerald was ominously silent although he kissed Scarlett and pinched Melanie's cheek approvingly and called her 'Cousin Melly'. Scarlett would have infinitely preferred bellowing oaths and accusations. True to her promise, Melanie clung to Scarlett's skirts like a small rustling shadow and Gerald was too much of a gentleman to upbraid his daughter in front of her. Scarlett had to admit that Melanie carried off things very well, acting as if she knew nothing was amiss, and she actually succeeded in engaging Gerald in conversation, once the supper had been served.

'I want to know all about the County,' she said, beaming upon him. 'India and Honey are such poor correspondents, and I know you know everything that goes on down there. Do tell us about Joe Fontaine's wedding.'

Gerald warmed to the flattery and said that the wedding had been a quiet affair, 'not like you girls had,' for Joe had only a few days' furlough. Sally, the little Munroe chit, looked very pretty. No, he couldn't recall what she wore but he did hear that she didn't have 'second-day' dress.

'She didn't!' exclaimed the girls, scandalized.

'Sure, because she didn't have a second day,' Gerald explained and bawled with laughter before recalling that perhaps such remarks were not fit for female ears. Scarlett's spirits soared at his laugh and she blessed Melanie's tact.

'Back Joe went to Virginia the next day,' Gerald added hastily. 'There was no visiting about and dancing afterwards. The Tarleton twins are home.'

'We heard that. Have they recovered?'

'They weren't badly wounded. Stuart had it in the knee and a minie ball went through Brent's shoulder. You had it, too, that they were mentioned in dispatches for bravery?'

'No! Tell us!'

'Hare-brained – both of them. I'm believing there's Irish in them,' said Gerald complacently. 'I forget what they did, but Brent is a lieutenant now.'

Scarlett felt pleased at hearing of their exploits, pleased in a proprietary

manner. Once a man had been her beau, she never lost the conviction that
he belonged to her, and all his good deeds redounded to her credit.

'And I've news that'll be holding the both of you,' said Gerald. 'They're
saying Stu is courting at Twelve Oaks again.'

'Honey or India?' questioned Melly excitedly, while Scarlett stared almost
indignantly.

'Oh, Miss India, to be sure. Didn't she have him fast till this baggage of
mine winked at him?'

'Oh,' said Melly, somewhat embarrassed at Gerald's outspokenness.

'And more than that, young Brent has taken to hanging about Tara.
Now!'

Scarlett could not speak. The defection of her beaux was almost insulting.
Especially when she recalled how wildly both the twins had acted when she
told them she was going to marry Charles. Stuart had even threatened
to shoot Charles, or Scarlett, or himself, or all three. It had been most
exciting.

'Suellen?' questioned Melly, breaking into a pleased smile. 'But I thought
Mr Kennedy—'

'Oh, him?' said Gerald. 'Frank Kennedy still pussyfoots about, afraid of
his shadow, and I'll be asking him his intentions soon if he doesn't speak
up. No, 'tis me baby.'

'Carreen?'

'She's nothing but a child!' said Scarlett sharply, finding her tongue.

'She's little more than a year younger than you were, Miss, when
you married,' retorted Gerald. 'Is it you're grudging your old beau to
your sister?'

Melly blushed, unaccustomed to such frankness, and signalled Peter to
bring in the sweet potato pie. Frantically she cast about in her mind for
some other topic of conversation which would not be so personal but
which would divert Mr O'Hara from the purpose of his trip. She could
think of nothing but, once started, Gerald needed no stimulus other than
an audience. He talked on about the thievery of the commissary department
which every month increased its demands, the knavish stupidity of Jefferson
Davis and the black-guardery of the Irish who were being enticed into the
Yankee army by bounty money.

When the wine was on the table and the two girls rose to leave him,
Gerald cocked a severe eye at his daughter from under frowning brows and
commanded her presence alone for a few minutes. Scarlett cast a despairing glance at Melly, who twisted her handkerchief helplessly and went out,
softly pulling the sliding doors together.

'How now, Missy!' bawled Gerald, pouring himself a glass of port. ''Tis
a fine way to act! Is it another husband you're trying to catch and you so
fresh a widow?'

'Not so loud, Pa, the servants—'

'They know already, to be sure, and everybody knows of our disgrace. And your poor mother taking to her bed with it and me not able to hold up me head. 'Tis shameful. No, Puss, you need not think to get around me with tears this time,' he said hastily and with some panic in his voice as Scarlett's lids began to bat and her mouth to screw up. 'I know you. You'd be flirting at the wake of your own husband. Don't cry. There, I'll be saying no more tonight, for I'm going to see this fine Captain Butler who makes so light of me daughter's reputation. But in the morning— There now, don't cry. 'Twill do you no good at all, at all. 'Tis firm that I am and back to Tara you'll be going tomorrow before you're disgracing the lot of us again. Don't cry, pet. Look what I've brought you! Isn't that a pretty present? See, look! How could you be putting so much trouble on me, bringing me all the way up here when 'tis a busy man I am? Don't cry!'

Melanie and Pittypat had gone to sleep hours before, but Scarlett lay awake in the warm darkness, her heart heavy and frightened in her breast. To leave Atlanta when life had just begun again and go home and face Ellen! She would rather die than face her mother. She wished she were dead, this very minute, then everyone would be sorry they had been so hateful. She turned and tossed on the hot pillow until a noise far up the quiet street reached her ears. It was an oddly familiar noise, blurred and indistinct though it was. She slipped out of bed and went to the window. The street with its over-arching trees was softly, deeply black under a dim star-studded sky. The noise came closer, the sound of wheels, the plod of a horse's hooves and voices. And suddenly she grinned for, as a voice thick with brogue and whisky came to her, raised in 'Peg in a Low-backed Car', she knew. This might not be Jonesboro on Court Day, but Gerald was coming home in the same condition.

She saw the dark bulk of a buggy stop in front of the house and indistinct figures alight. Someone was with him. Two figures paused at the gate and she heard the click of the latch and Gerald's voice came plain.

'Now I'll be giving you the "Lament for Robert Emmet". 'Tis a song you should be knowing, me lad. I'll teach it to you.'

'I'd like to learn it,' replied his companion, a hint of buried laughter in his flat drawling voice. 'But not now, Mr O'Hara.'

'Oh, my God, it's that hateful Butler man!' thought Scarlett, at first annoyed. Then she took heart. At least they hadn't shot each other. And they must be on amicable terms to be coming home together at this hour and in this condition.

'Sing it I will and listen you will or I'll be shooting you for the Orangeman you are.'

'Not Orangeman – Charlestonian.'

''Tis no better. 'Tis worse. I have two sister-in-laws in Charleston and I know.'

'Is he going to tell the whole neighbourhood?' thought Scarlett, panic-stricken, reaching for her wrapper. But what could she do? She couldn't go downstairs at this hour of the night and drag her father in from the street.

With no further warning, Gerald, who was hanging on to the gate, threw back his head and began the 'Lament', in a roaring bass. Scarlett rested her elbows on the window-sill and listened, grinning unwillingly. It would be a beautiful song, if only her father could carry a tune. It was one of her favourite songs and, for a moment, she followed the fine melancholy of those verses beginning:

She is far from the land where her young hero sleeps
And lovers are round her sighing.

The song went on and she heard stirrings in Pittypat's and Melly's rooms. Poor things, they'd certainly be upset. They were not used to full-blooded males like Gerald. When the song had finished, two forms merged into one, came up the walk and mounted the steps. A discreet knock sounded at the door.

'I suppose I must go down,' thought Scarlett. 'After all he's my father and poor Pitty would die before she'd go.' Besides, she didn't want the servants to see Gerald in his present condition. And if Peter tried to put him to bed, he might get unruly. Pork was the only one who knew how to handle him.

She pinned the wrapper close about her throat, lit her bedside candle and hurried down the dark stairs into the front hall. Setting the candle on the stand, she unlocked the door and in the wavering light she saw Rhett Butler, not a ruffle disarranged, supporting her small, thickset father. The 'Lament' had evidently been Gerald's swan-song, for he was frankly hanging on to his companion's arm. His hat was gone, his crisp long hair was tumbled in a white mane, his cravat was under one ear, and there were liquor stains down his shirt bosom.

'Your father, I believe?' said Captain Butler, his eyes amused in his swarthy face. He took in her dishabille in one glance that seemed to penetrate through her wrapper.

'Bring him in,' she said shortly, embarrassed at her attire, infuriated at Gerald for putting her in a position where this man could laugh at her.

Rhett propelled Gerald forward. 'Shall I help you take him upstairs? You cannot manage him. He's quite heavy.'

Her mouth fell open with horror at the audacity of his proposal. Just imagine what Pittypat and Melly cowering in their beds would think, should Captain Butler come upstairs!

'Mother of God, no! In here, in the parlour on that settee.'

'The suttee, did you say?'

'I'll thank you to keep a civil tongue in your head. Here. Now lay him down.'

'Shall I take off his boots?'

'No. He's slept in them before.'

She could have bitten off her tongue for that slip, for he laughed softly as he crossed Gerald's legs.

'Please go, now.'

He walked out into the dim hall and picked up the hat he had dropped on the doorsill.

'I will be seeing you Sunday at dinner,' he said and went out, closing the door noiselessly behind him.

Scarlett arose at five-thirty, before the servants had come in from the back yard to start breakfast, and slipped down the steps to the quiet lower floor. Gerald was awake, sitting on the sofa, his hands gripping his bullet head as if he wished to crush it between his palms. He looked up furtively as she entered. The pain of moving his eyes was too excruciating to be borne and he groaned.

'Wurra the day!'

'It's a fine way you've acted, Pa,' she began in a furious whisper. 'Coming home at such an hour and waking all the neighbours with your singing.'

'I sang?'

'Sang! You woke the echoes singing the "Lament".'

''Tis nothing I'm remembering.'

'The neighbours will remember it till their dying day and so will Miss Pittypat and Melanie.'

'Mother of Sorrows,' moaned Gerald, moving a thickly furred tongue around parched lips. ''Tis little I'm remembering after the game started.'

'Game?'

'That laddybuck Butler bragged that he was the best poker player in—'

'How much did you lose?'

'Why, I won, naturally. A drink or two helps me game.'

'Look in your wallet.'

As if every movement was agony, Gerald removed his wallet from his coat and opened it. It was empty and he looked at it in forlorn bewilderment.

'Five hundred dollars,' he said. 'And 'twas to buy things from the blockaders for Mrs O'Hara, and now not even fare left to Tara.'

As she looked indignantly at the empty purse, an idea took form in Scarlett's mind and grew swiftly.

'I'll not be holding up my head in this town,' she began. 'You've disgraced us all.'

'Hold your tongue, Puss. Can you not see me head is bursting?'

'Coming home drunk with a man like Captain Butler, and singing at the top of your lungs for everyone to hear and losing all that money.'

'The man is too clever with cards to be a gentleman. He—'

'What will Mother say when she hears?'

He looked up in sudden anguished apprehension.

'You wouldn't be telling your mother a word and upsetting her, now would you?'

Scarlett said nothing but pursed her lips.

'Think now how 'twould hurt her and her so gentle.'

'And to think, Pa, that you said only last night I had disgraced the family! Me, with my poor little dance to make money for the soldiers. Oh, I could cry.'

'Well, don't,' pleaded Gerald. ''Twould be more than me poor head could stand and sure 'tis bursting now.'

'And you said that I—'

'Now, Puss, now, Puss, don't you be hurt at what your poor old father said and him not meaning a thing and not understanding a thing! Sure, you're a fine well-meaning girl, I'm sure.'

'And wanting to take me home in disgrace.'

'Ah, darling, I wouldn't be doing that. 'Twas to tease you. You won't be mentioning the money to your mother and her in a flutter about expenses already?'

'No,' said Scarlett frankly, 'I won't, if you'll let me stay here and if you'll tell Mother that 'twas nothing but a lot of gossip from old cats.'

Gerald looked mournfully at his daughter.

''Tis blackmail, no less.'

'And last night was a scandal, no less.'

'Well,' he began wheedlingly, 'we'll be forgetting all that. And do you think a fine pretty lady like Miss Pittypat would be having any brandy in the house? The hair of the dog—'

Scarlett turned and tiptoed through the silent hall into the dining-room to get the brandy bottle that she and Melly privately called the 'swoon bottle' because Pittypat always took a sip from it when her fluttering heart made her faint – or seem to faint. Triumph was written on her face and no trace of shame for her unfilial treatment of Gerald. Now Ellen would be soothed with lies if any other busybody wrote her. Now she could stay in Atlanta. Now she could do almost as she pleased, Pittypat being the weak vessel that she was. She unlocked the cellaret and stood for a moment with the bottle and glass pressed to her bosom.

She saw a long vista of picnics by the bubbling waters of Peachtree Creek and barbecues at Stone Mountain, receptions and balls, afternoon danceables, buggy rides and Sunday-night buffet suppers. She would be there, right in the heart of things, right in the centre of a crowd of men. And men fell in love so easily, after you did little things for them at the hospital. She wouldn't mind the hospital so much now. Men were so easily stirred when they had been ill. They fell into a clever girl's hand, just like the ripe peaches at Tara when the trees were gently shaken.

She went back toward her father with the reviving liquor, thanking Heaven that the famous O'Hara head had not been able to survive last night's bout and wondering suddenly if Rhett Butler had had anything to do with that.

Chapter XI

On an afternoon of the following week, Scarlett came home from the hospital weary and indignant. She was tired from standing on her feet all morning and irritable because Mrs Merriwether had scolded her sharply for sitting on a soldier's bed while she dressed his wounded arm. Aunt Pitty and Melanie, bonneted in their best, were on the porch with Wade and Prissy, ready for their weekly round of calls. Scarlett asked to be excused from accompanying them and went upstairs to her room.

When the last sound of carriage wheels had died away and she knew the family was safely out of sight, she slipped quietly into Melanie's room and turned the key in the lock. It was a prim, virginal little room and it lay still and warm in the slanting rays of the four-o'clock sun. The floors were glistening and bare except for a few bright rag rugs, and the white walls unornamented save for one corner which Melanie had fitted up as a shrine.

Here, under a draped Confederate flag, hung the gold-hilted sabre that Melanie's father had carried in the Mexican War, the same sabre Charles had worn away to war. Charles' sash and pistol-belt hung there too, with his revolver in the holster. Between the sabre and the pistol was a daguerreotype of Charles himself, very stiff and proud in his grey uniform, his great brown eyes shining out of the frame and a shy smile on his lips.

Scarlett did not even glance at the picture but went unhesitatingly across the room to the square rosewood writing-box that stood on the table beside the narrow bed. From it she took a pack of letters tied together with a blue ribbon, addressed in Ashley's hand to Melanie. On top was the letter which had come that morning and this one she opened.

When Scarlett first began secretly reading these letters, she had been so stricken of conscience and so fearful of discovery she could hardly open the envelopes for trembling. Now, her never-too-scrupulous sense of honour was dulled by repetition of the offence and even fear of discovery had subsided. Occasionally, she thought with a sinking heart, 'What would Mother say if she knew?' She knew Ellen would rather see her dead than know her guilty of such dishonour. This had worried Scarlett at first, for she still wanted to be like her mother in every respect. But the temptation to read the letters was too great and she put the thought of Ellen out of her mind. She had become adept at putting unpleasant thoughts out of her mind these days.

She had learned to say, 'I won't think of this or that bothersome thought now. I'll think about it tomorrow.' Generally when tomorrow came, the thought either did not occur at all or it was so attenuated by the delay it was not very troublesome. So the matter of Ashley's letters did not lie very heavily on her conscience.

Melanie was always generous with the letters, reading parts of them aloud to Aunt Pitty and Scarlett. But it was the part she did not read that tormented Scarlett, that drove her to surreptitious reading of her sister-in-law's mail. She had to know if Ashley had come to love his wife since marrying her. She had to know if he even pretended to love her. Did he address tender endearments to her? What sentiments did he express and with what warmth?

She carefully smoothed out the letter.

Ashley's small even writing leaped up at her as she read, 'My dear wife,' and she breathed in relief. He wasn't calling Melanie 'Darling' or 'Sweetheart' yet.

'My dear wife: You write me saying you are alarmed lest I be concealing my real thoughts from you and you ask me what is occupying my mind these days—'

'Mother of God!' thought Scarlett, in a panic of guilt. ' "Concealing his real thoughts". Can Melly have read his mind? Or my mind? Does she suspect that he and I—'

Her hands trembled with fright as she held the letter closer, but as she read the next paragraph she relaxed.

'Dear Wife, if I have concealed aught from you it is because I did not wish to lay a burden on your shoulders, to add to your worries for my physical safety with those of my mental turmoil. But I can keep nothing from you, for you know me too well. Do not be alarmed. I have no wound. I have not been ill. I have enough to eat and occasionally a bed to sleep in. A soldier can ask for no more. But, Melanie, heavy thoughts lie on my heart and I will open my heart to you.

'These summer nights I lie awake, long after the camp is sleeping, and I look up at the stars and, over and over, I wonder, "Why are you here, Ashley Wilkes? What are you fighting for?"

'Not for honour and glory, certainly. War is a dirty business and I do not like dirt. I am not a soldier and I have no desire to seek the bubble reputation even in the cannon's mouth. Yet, here I am at the wars – whom God never intended to be other than a studious country gentleman. For, Melanie, bugles do not stir my blood nor drums entice my feet and I see too clearly that we have been betrayed, betrayed by our arrogant Southern selves, believing that one of us could whip a dozen Yankees, believing that King Cotton could rule the world. Betrayed, too, by words and catch-phrases, prejudices and hatreds coming from the mouths of those highly placed, those men whom we respected and revered – "King Cotton, Slavery, States' Rights, Damn Yankees".

'And so when I lie on my blanket and look up at the stars and say "What are you fighting for?" I think of States' Rights and cotton and the darkies and the Yankees whom we have been bred up to hate, and I know that none of these is the reason why I am fighting. Instead, I see Twelve Oaks and remember how the moonlight slants across the white columns, and the unearthly way the magnolias look, opening under the moon, and how the climbing roses make the side porch shady even at hottest noon. And I see Mother, sewing there, as she did when I was a little boy. And I hear the darkies coming home across the fields at dusk, tired and singing and ready for supper, and the sound of the windlass as the bucket goes down into the cool well. And there's the long view down the road to the river, across the cotton fields, and the mist rising from the bottom lands in the twilight. And that is why I'm here who have no love of death or misery or glory and no hatred for anyone. Perhaps that is what is called patriotism, love of home and country. But, Melanie, it goes deeper than that. For, Melanie, these things I have named are but the symbols of the thing for which I risk my life, symbols of the kind of life I love. For I am fighting for the old days, the old ways I love so much but which, I fear, are now gone for ever, no matter how the die may fall. For, win or lose, we lose just the same.

'If we win this war and have the Cotton Kingdom of our dreams, we still have lost, for we will become a different people and the old quiet ways will go. The world will be at our doors clamouring for cotton and we can command our own price. Then, I fear, we will become like the Yankees, at whose money-making activities, acquisitiveness and commercialism we now sneer. And if we lose, Melanie, if we lose!

'I am not afraid of danger or capture or wounds or even death, if death must come, but I do fear that once this war is over, we will never get back to the old times. And I belong in those old times. I do not belong in this mad present of killing and I fear I will not fit into any future, try though I may. Nor will you, my dear, for you and I are of the same blood. I do not know what the future will bring, but it cannot be as beautiful or as satisfying as the past.

'I lie and look at the boys sleeping near me and I wonder if the twins or Alex or Cade think these same thoughts. I wonder if they know they are fighting for a Cause that was lost the minute the first shot was fired, for our Cause is really our own way of living and that is gone already. But I do not think they think these things and they are lucky.

'I had not thought of this for us when I asked you to marry me. I had thought of life going on at Twelve Oaks as it had always done, peacefully, easily, unchanging. We are alike, Melanie, loving the same quiet things, and I saw before us a long stretch of uneventful years in which to read, hear music and dream. But not this! Never this! That this could happen to us all, this wrecking of old ways, this bloody slaughter and hate! Melanie, nothing is worth it – States' Rights, nor slaves, nor cotton. Nothing is worth what is happening to us now and what may happen, for if the Yankees whip us the future will be one of incredible horror. And, my dear, they may yet whip us.

'I should not write those words. I should not even think them. But you have asked me what was in my heart, and the fear of defeat is there. Do you remember at the barbecue, the day our engagement was announced, that a man named Butler, a Charlestonian by his accent, nearly caused a fight by his remarks about the ignorance of Southerners? Do you recall how the twins wanted to shoot him because he said we had few foundries and factories, mills and ships, arsenals and machine shops? Do you recall how he said the Yankee fleet could bottle us up so tightly we could not ship out our cotton? He was right. We are fighting the Yankees' new rifles with Revolutionary War muskets, and soon the blockade will be too tight for even medical supplies to slip in. We should have paid heed to cynics like Butler who knew, instead of statesmen who felt – and talked. He said, in effect, that the South had nothing with which to wage war but cotton and arrogance. Our cotton is worthless and what he called arrogance is all that is left. But I call that arrogance matchless courage. If—'

But Scarlett folded up the letter without finishing it and thrust it back into the envelope, too bored to read farther. Besides, the tone of the letter vaguely depressed her with its foolish talk of defeat. After all, she wasn't reading Melanie's mail to learn Ashley's puzzling and uninteresting ideas. She had had to listen to enough of them when he sat on the porch at Tara in days gone by.

All she wanted to know was whether he wrote impassioned letters to his wife. So far he had not. She had read every letter in the writing-box and there was nothing in any one of them that a brother might not have written to his sister. They were affectionate, humorous, discursive, but not the letters of a lover. Scarlett had received too many ardent love letters herself not to recognize the authentic note of passion when she saw it. And that note was missing. As always after her secret readings, a feeling of smug satisfaction enveloped her, for she felt certain that Ashley still loved her. And always she wondered sneeringly why Melanie did not realize that Ashley only loved her as a friend. Melanie evidently found nothing lacking in her husband's messages, but Melanie had had no other man's love letters with which to compare Ashley's.

'He writes such crazy letters,' Scarlett thought. 'If ever any husband of mine wrote me such twaddle-twaddle, he'd certainly hear from me! Why, even Charlie wrote better letters than these.'

She flipped back the edges of the letters, looking at the dates, remembering their contents. In them there were no fine descriptive passages of bivouacs and charges such as Darcy Meade wrote his parents or poor Dallas McLure had written his old-maid sisters, Misses Faith and Hope. The Meades and the McLures proudly read these letters all over the neighbourhood, and

Scarlett had frequently felt a secret shame that Melanie had no such letters from Ashley to read aloud at sewing circles.

It was as though when writing Melanie, Ashley tried to ignore the war altogether, and sought to draw about the two of them a magic circle of timelessness, shutting out everything that had happened since Fort Sumter was the news of the day. It was almost as if he were trying to believe there wasn't any war. He wrote of books which he and Melanie had read and songs they had sung, of old friends they knew and places he had visited on his Grand Tour. Through the letters ran a wistful yearning to be back home at Twelve Oaks, and for pages he wrote of the hunting and the long rides through the still forest paths under frosty autumn stars, the barbecues, the fish-fries, the quiet of moonlight nights and the serene charm of the old house.

She thought of his words in the letter she had just read: 'Not this! Never this!' and they seemed the cry of a tormented soul facing something he could not face, yet must face. It puzzled her for, if he was not afraid of wounds and death, what was it he feared? Unanalytical, she struggled with the complex thought.

'The war disturbs him and he – he doesn't like things that disturb him . . . Me, for instance . . . He loved me but he was afraid to marry me because – for fear I'd upset his way of thinking and living. No, it wasn't exactly that he was afraid. Ashley isn't a coward. He couldn't be when he's been mentioned in dispatches and when Colonel Sloan wrote that letter to Melly all about his gallant conduct in leading the charge. Once he's made up his mind to something, no one could be braver or more determined but— He lives inside his head instead of outside in the world and he hates to come out into the world and— Oh, I don't know what it is! If I'd just understood this one thing about him years ago, I know he'd have married me.'

She stood for a moment holding the letters to her breast, thinking longingly of Ashley. Her emotions toward him had not changed since the day when she first fell in love with him. They were the same emotions that struck her speechless that day when she was fourteen years old and she had stood on the porch of Tara and seen Ashley ride up smiling, his hair shining silver in the morning sun. Her love was still a young girl's adoration for a man she could not understand, a man who possessed all the qualities she did not own but which she admired. He was still a young girl's dream of the Perfect Knight and her dream asked no more than acknowledgement of his love, went no further than hopes of a kiss.

After reading the letters, she felt certain he did love her, Scarlett, even though he had married Melanie, and that certainty was almost all that she desired. She was still that young and untouched. Had Charles with his fumbling awkwardness and his embarrassed intimacies tapped any of the deep vein of passionate feeling within her, her dreams of Ashley would not be ending with a kiss. But those few moonlight nights alone with Charles had not touched her emotions or ripened her to maturity. Charles had awakened no idea of what passion might be or tenderness or true intimacy of body and spirit.

All that passion meant to her was servitude to inexplicable male madness, unshared by females, a painful and embarrassing process that led inevitably to the still more painful process of childbirth. That marriage should be like this was no surprise to her. Ellen had hinted before the wedding that marriage was something women must bear with dignity and fortitude, and the whispered comments of other matrons since her widowhood had confirmed this. Scarlett was glad to be done with passion and marriage.

She was done with marriage but not with love, for her love for Ashley was something different, having nothing to do with passion or marriage, something sacred and breath-takingly beautiful, an emotion that grew stealthily through the long days of her enforced silence, feeding on oft-thumbed memories and hopes.

She sighed as she carefully tied the ribbon about the packet, wondering for the thousandth time just what it was in Ashley that eluded her understanding. She tried to think the matter to some satisfactory conclusion, but, as always, the conclusion evaded her uncomplex mind. She put the letters back in the lap secretary and closed the lid. Then she frowned, for her mind went back to the last part of the letter she had just read, to his mention of Captain Butler. How strange that Ashley should be impressed by something that scamp had said a year ago! Undeniably Captain Butler was a scamp, for all that he danced divinely. No one but a scamp would say the things about the Confederacy that he had said at the bazaar.

She crossed the room to the mirror and patted her smooth hair approvingly. Her spirits rose, as always at the sight of her white skin and slanting green eyes, and she smiled to bring out her dimples. Then she dismissed Captain Butler from her mind as she happily viewed her reflection, remembering how Ashley had always liked her dimples. No pang of conscience at loving another woman's husband or reading that woman's mail disturbed her pleasure in her youth and charm and her renewed assurance of Ashley's love.

She unlocked the door and went down the dim winding stair with a light heart. Half-way down she began singing 'When This Cruel War Is Over'.

Chapter XII

The war went on, successfully for the most part, but people had stopped saying 'One more victory and the war is over,' just as they had stopped saying the Yankees were cowards. It was obvious to all now that the Yankees were far from cowardly and that it would take more than one victory to conquer them. However, there were the Confederate victories in Tennessee scored by General Morgan and General Forrest and the triumph at the Second Battle of Bull Run hung up like visible Yankee scalps to gloat over. But there was a heavy price on these scalps. The hospitals and homes of Atlanta were overflowing with sick and wounded, and more and more women were appearing in black. The monotonous rows of soldiers' graves at Oakland Cemetery stretched longer every day.

Confederate money had dropped alarmingly and the price of food and clothing had risen accordingly. The commissary was laying such heavy levies on foodstuffs that the tables of Atlanta were beginning to suffer. White flour was scarce and so expensive that corn bread was universal instead of biscuits, rolls and waffles. The butcher shops carried almost no beef and very little mutton, and that mutton cost so much only the rich could afford it. However, there was still plenty of hog meat, as well as chickens and vegetables.

The Yankee blockade about the Confederate ports had tightened, and luxuries such as tea, coffee, silks, whalebone stays, colognes, fashion magazines and books were scarce and dear. Even the cheapest cotton goods had skyrocketed in price and ladies were regretfully making their old dresses do another season. Looms that had gathered dust for years had been brought down from attics, and there were webs of homespun to be found in nearly every parlour. Everyone, soldiers, civilians, women, children and negroes, began to wear homespun. Grey, as the colour of the Confederate uniform, practically disappeared and homespun of a butternut shade took its place.

Already the hospitals were worrying about the scarcity of quinine, calomel, opium, chloroform and iodine. Linen and cotton bandages were too precious now to be thrown away when used, and every lady who nursed at the hospitals brought home baskets of bloody strips to be washed and ironed and returned for use on other sufferers.

But to Scarlett, newly emerged from the chrysalis of widowhood, all the war meant was a time of gaiety and excitement. Even the small privations of clothing and food did not annoy her, so happy was she to be in the world again.

When she thought of the dull times of the past year, with the days going by one very much like another, life seemed to have quickened to an incredible speed. Every day dawned as an exciting adventure, a day in which she would meet new men who would ask to call on her, tell her how pretty she was, and how it was a privilege to fight and, perhaps, to die for her. She could and did love Ashley with the last breath in her body, but that did not prevent her from inveigling other men into asking to marry her.

The ever-present war in the background lent a pleasant informality to social relations, an informality which older people viewed with alarm. Mothers found strange men calling on their daughters, men who came without letters of introduction and whose antecedents were unknown. To their horror, mothers found their daughters holding hands with these men. Mrs Merriwether, who had never kissed her husband until after the wedding ceremony, could scarcely believe her eyes when she caught Maybelle kissing the little Zouave, René Picard, and her consternation was even greater when Maybelle refused to be ashamed. Even the fact that René immediately asked for her hand did not improve matters. Mrs Merriwether felt that the South was heading for a complete moral collapse and frequently said so. Other mothers concurred heartily with her and blamed it on the war.

But men who expected to die within a week or a month could not wait a year before they begged to call a girl by her first name, with 'Miss' of course, preceding it. Nor would they go through the formal and protracted courtships which good manners had prescribed before the war. They were likely to propose in three or four months. And girls who knew very well that a lady always refused a gentleman the first three times he proposed rushed headlong to accept the first time.

This informality made the war a lot of fun for Scarlett. Except for the messy business of nursing and the bore of bandage rolling, she did not care if the war lasted forever. In fact, she could endure the hospital with equanimity now because it was a perfect happy hunting-ground. The helpless wounded succumbed to her charms without a struggle. Renew their bandages, wash their faces, pat up their pillows and fan them, and they fell in love. Oh, it was Heaven after the last dreary year!

Scarlett was back again where she had been before she married Charles and it was as if she had never married him, never felt the shock of his death, never borne Wade. War and marriage and childbirth had passed over her without touching any deep chord within her and she was unchanged. She had a child but he was cared for so well by the others in the red-brick house she could almost forget him. In her mind and heart, she was Scarlett O'Hara again, the belle of the County. Her thoughts and activities were the same as they had been in the old days, but the field of her activities had widened immensely. Careless of the disapproval of Aunt Pitty's friends, she behaved as she had behaved before her marriage – went to parties, danced, went riding with soldiers, flirted, did everything she had done as a girl, except stop wearing mourning. This she knew would be a straw that would break the backs of Pittypat and Melanie. She was as charming a widow as she had been a girl, pleasant when she had her own way, obliging as long as it did not discommode her, vain of her looks and her popularity.

She was happy now where a few weeks before she had been miserable, happy with her beaux and their reassurances of her charm, as happy as she could be with Ashley married to Melanie and in danger. But somehow it was easier to bear the thought of Ashley belonging to someone else when he was far away. With the hundreds of miles stretching between Atlanta and Virginia, he sometimes seemed as much hers as Melanie's.

So the autumn months of 1862 went swiftly by with nursing, dancing, driving and bandage rolling taking up all the time she did not spend on brief visits to Tara. These visits were disappointing, for she had little opportunity for the long quiet talks with her mother to which she looked forward while in Atlanta, no time to sit by Ellen while she sewed, smelling the faint fragrance of lemon verbena sachet as her skirts rustled, feeling her soft hands on her cheek in a gentle caress.

Ellen was thin and preoccupied now and on her feet from morning until long after the plantation was asleep. The demands of the Confederate commissary were growing heavier by the month, and hers was the task of making Tara produce. Even Gerald was busy, for the first time in many years, for he could get no overseer to take Jonas Wilkerson's place and he was riding his own acres. With Ellen too busy for more than a good-night kiss and Gerald in the fields all day, Scarlett found Tara boring. Even her sisters were taken up with their own concerns. Suellen had now come to an 'understanding' with Frank Kennedy and sang 'When This Cruel War Is Over' with an arch meaning that Scarlett found wellnigh unendurable, and Carreen was too wrapped up in dreams of Brent Tarleton to be interesting company.

Though Scarlett always went home to Tara with a happy heart, she was never sorry when the inevitable letters came from Pitty and Melanie, begging her to return. Ellen always sighed at these times, saddened by the thought of her oldest daughter and her only grandchild leaving her.

'But I mustn't be selfish and keep you here when you are needed to nurse in Atlanta,' she said. 'Only – only, my darling, it seems that I never get the time to talk to you and to feel that you are my own little girl again before you are gone from me.'

'I'm always your little girl,' Scarlett would say and bury her head upon Ellen's breast, her guilt rising up to accuse her. She did not tell her mother that it was the dancing and the beaux which drew her back to Atlanta and not the service of the Confederacy. There were many things she kept from her mother these days. But, most of all, she kept secret the fact that Rhett Butler called frequently at Aunt Pittypat's house.

During the months that followed the bazaar, Rhett called whenever he was in town, taking Scarlett riding in his carriage, escorting her to danceables and bazaars and waiting outside the hospital to drive her home. She lost her fear of his betraying her secret, but there always lurked in the back of her mind the disquieting memory that he had seen her at her worst and knew the truth about Ashley. It was this knowledge that checked her tongue when he annoyed her. And he annoyed her frequently.

He was in his mid-thirties, older than any beau she had ever had, and she was as helpless as a child to control and handle him as she had handled beaux nearer her own age. He always looked as if nothing had ever surprised him and much had amused him and, when he had gotten her into a speechless temper, she felt that she amused him more than anything in the world. Frequently she flared into open wrath under his expert baiting, for she had Gerald's Irish temper along with the deceptive sweetness of face she had inherited from Ellen. Heretofore she had never bothered to control her temper except in Ellen's presence. Now it was painful to have to choke back words for fear of his amused grin. If only he would ever lose his temper too, then she would not feel at such a disadvantage.

After tilts with him from which she seldom emerged the victor, she vowed he was impossible, ill-bred and no gentleman and she would have nothing more to do with him. But sooner or later, he returned to Atlanta, called, presumably on Aunt Pitty, and presented Scarlett, with overdone gallantry, a box of bonbons he had brought her from Nassau. Or pre-empted a seat by her at a musicale or claimed her at a dance, and she was usually so amused by his bland impudence that she laughed and overlooked his past misdeeds until the next occurred.

For all his exasperating qualities, she grew to look forward to his calls. There was something exciting about him that she could not analyse, something different from any man she had ever known. There was something breath-taking in the grace of his big body which made his very entrance into a room like an abrupt physical impact, something in the impertinence and bland mockery of his dark eyes that challenged her spirit to subdue him.

'It's almost like I was in love with him!' she thought, bewildered. 'But I'm not and I just can't understand it.'

But the exciting feeling persisted. When he came to call, his complete masculinity made Aunt Pitty's well-bred and ladylike house seem small, pale and a trifle fusty. Scarlett was not the only member of the household who reacted strangely and unwillingly to his presence, for he kept Aunt Pitty in a flutter and a ferment.

While Pitty knew Ellen would disapprove of his calls on her daughter, and knew also that the edict of Charleston banning him from polite society was not one to be lightly disregarded, she could no more resist his elaborate compliments and hand-kissing than a fly can resist a honey-pot. Moreover, he usually brought her some little gift from Nassau which he assured her he had purchased especially for her and blockaded in at risk of his life – papers of pins and needles, buttons, spools of silk thread and hairpins. It was almost impossible to obtain these small luxuries now – ladies were wearing hand-whittled wooden hairpins and covering acorns with cloth for buttons – and Pitty lacked the moral stamina to refuse them. Besides, she had a childish love of surprise packages and could not resist opening his gifts. And, having once opened them, she did not feel that she could refuse them. Then, having accepted his gifts, she could not summon courage enough to tell him his reputation made it improper for him to call on three lone women who had no male protector. Aunt Pitty always felt that she needed a male protector when Rhett Butler was in the house.

'I don't know what it is about him,' she would sigh helplessly. 'But – well,

I do think he'd be a nice, attractive man if I could just feel that – well, that deep down in his heart he respected women.'

Since the return of her wedding ring, Melanie had felt that Rhett was a gentleman of rare refinement and delicacy and she was shocked at this remark. He was unfailingly courteous to her, but she was a little timid with him, largely because she was shy with any man she had not known from childhood. Secretly she was very sorry for him, a feeling which would have amused him had he been aware of it. She was certain that some romantic sorrow had blighted his life and made him hard and bitter, and she felt that what he needed was the love of a good woman. In all her sheltered life she had never seen evil and could scarcely credit its existence, and when gossip whispered things about Rhett and the girl in Charleston she was shocked and unbelieving. And, instead of turning her against him, it only made her more timidly gracious toward him because of her indignation at what she fancied was a gross injustice done him.

Scarlett silently agreed with Aunt Pitty. She, too, felt that he had no respect for any woman, unless perhaps for Melanie. She still felt unclothed every time his eyes ran up and down her figure. It was not that he ever said anything. Then she could have scorched him with hot words. It was the bold way his eyes looked out of his swarthy face with a displeasing air of insolence, as if all women were his property to be enjoyed in his own good time. Only with Melanie was this look absent. There was never that cool look of appraisal, never mockery in his eyes, when he looked at Melanie; and there was an especial note in his voice when he spoke to her, courteous, respectful, anxious to be of service.

'I don't see why you're so much nicer to her than to me,' said Scarlett petulantly, one afternoon when Melanie and Pitty had retired to take their naps and she was alone with him.

For an hour she had watched Rhett hold the yarn Melanie was winding for knitting, had noted the blank inscrutable expression when Melanie talked at length and with pride of Ashley and his promotion. Scarlett knew Rhett had no exalted opinion of Ashley and cared nothing at all about the fact that he had been made a major. Yet he made polite replies and murmured the correct things about Ashley's gallantry.

'And if I so much as mention Ashley's name,' she had thought irritably, 'he cocks his eyebrow up and smiles that nasty, knowing smile!'

'I'm much prettier than she is,' she continued, 'and I don't see why you're nicer to her.'

'Dare I hope that you are jealous?'

'Oh, don't presume!'

'Another hope crushed. If I am "nicer" to Mrs Wilkes, it is because she deserves it. She is one of the very few kind, sincere and unselfish persons I have ever known. But perhaps you have failed to note these qualities. And moreover, for all her youth, she is one of the few great ladies I have ever been privileged to know.'

'Do you mean to say you don't think I'm a great lady, too?'

'I think we agreed on the occasion of our first meeting that you were no lady at all.'

'Oh, if you are going to be hateful and rude enough to bring that up again! How can you hold that bit of childish temper against me? That was so long ago and I've grown up since then and I'd forget all about it if you weren't always harping and hinting about it.'

'I don't think it was childish temper and I don't believe you've changed. You are just as capable now as then of throwing vases if you don't get your own way. But you usually get your own way now. And so there's no necessity for broken bric-à-brac.'

'Oh, you are— I wish I was a man! I'd call you out and—'

'And get killed for your pains. I can drill a dime at fifty yards. Better stick to your own weapons – dimples, vases and the like.'

'You are just a rascal.'

'Do you expect me to fly into a rage at that? I am sorry to disappoint you. You can't make me mad by calling me names that are true. Certainly I'm a rascal, and why not? It's a free country and a man may be a rascal if he chooses. It's only hypocrites like you, my dear lady, just as black at heart but trying to hide it, who become enraged when called by their right names.'

She was helpless before his calm smile and his drawling remarks, for she had never before met anyone who was so completely impregnable. Her weapons of scorn, coldness and abuse blunted in her hands, for nothing she could say would shame him. It had been her experience that the liar was the hottest to defend his veracity, the coward his courage, the ill-bred his gentlemanliness, and the cad his honour. But not Rhett. He admitted everything and laughed and dared her to say more.

He came and went during these months, arriving unheralded and leaving without saying good-bye. Scarlett never discovered just what business brought him to Atlanta, for few other blockaders found it necessary to come so far away from the coast. They landed their cargoes at Wilmington or Charleston, where they were met by swarms of merchants and speculators from all over the South who assembled to buy blockaded goods at auction. It would have pleased her to think that he made these trips to see her, but even her abnormal vanity refused to believe this. If he had ever once made love to her, seemed jealous of the other men who crowded about her, even tried to hold her hand or begged for a picture or a handkerchief to cherish, she would have thought triumphantly he had been caught by her charms. But he remained annoyingly unloverlike and, worst of all, seemed to see through all her manoeuvrings to bring him to his knees.

Whenever he came to town, there was a feminine fluttering. Not only did the romantic aura of the dashing blockader hang about him but there was also the titillating element of the wicked and the forbidden. He had such a bad reputation! And every time the matrons of Atlanta gathered to gossip, his reputation grew worse, which only made him all the more glamorous to the young girls. As most of them were quite innocent, they had heard little more than that he was 'quite loose with women' – and exactly how a man went about the business of being 'loose' they did not know. They also heard whispers that no girl was safe with him. With such a reputation, it was strange that he had never so much as kissed the hand of an unmarried girl since he first appeared in Atlanta. But that only served to make him more mysterious and more exciting.

Outside of the army heroes, he was the most talked-about man in Atlanta. Everyone knew in detail how he had been expelled from West Point for drunkenness and 'something about women'. That terrific scandal concerning the Charleston girl he had compromised and the brother he had killed was public property. Correspondence with Charleston friends elicited the further information that his father, a charming old gentleman with an iron will and a ramrod for a backbone, had cast him out without a penny when he was twenty and even stricken his name from the family Bible. After that he had wandered to California in the gold rush of 1849 and thence to South America and Cuba, and the reports of his activities in these parts were none too savoury. Scrapes about women, several shootings, gun running to the revolutionists in Central America and, worst of all, professional gambling were included in his career, as Atlanta heard it.

There was hardly a family in Georgia who could not own to their sorrow at least one male member or relative who gambled, losing money, houses, land and slaves. But that was different. A man could gamble himself to poverty and still be a gentleman, but a professional gambler could never be anything but an outcast.

Had it not been for the upset conditions due to the war and his own services to the Confederate government, Rhett Butler would never have been received in Atlanta. But now, even the most strait-laced felt that patriotism called upon them to be more broad-minded. The more sentimental were inclined to the view that the black sheep of the Butler family had repented of his evil ways and was making an attempt to atone for his sins. So the ladies felt in duty bound to stretch a point, especially in the case of so intrepid a blockader. Everyone knew now that the fate of the Confederacy rested as much upon the skill of the blockade boats in eluding the Yankee fleet as it did upon the soldiers at the front.

Rumour had it that Captain Butler was one of the best pilots in the South and that he was reckless and utterly without nerves. Reared in Charleston, he knew every inlet, creek, shoal and rock of the Carolina coast near that port, and he was equally at home in the waters around Wilmington. He had never lost a boat or even been forced to dump a cargo. At the onset of the war, he had emerged from obscurity with enough money to buy a small swift boat and now, when blockaded goods realized two thousand per cent on each cargo, he owned four boats. He had good pilots and paid them well, and they slid out of Charleston and Wilmington on dark nights, bearing cotton for Nassau, England and Canada. The cotton mills of England were standing idle and the workers were starving, and any blockader who could outwit the Yankee fleet could command his own price in Liverpool. Rhett's boats were singularly lucky both in taking out cotton for the Confederacy and bringing in the war materials for which the South was desperate. Yes, the ladies felt they could forgive and forget a great many things for such a brave man.

He was a dashing figure and one that people turned to look at. He spent money freely, rode a wild black stallion, and wore clothes which were always the height of style and tailoring. The latter in itself was enough to attract attention to him, for the uniforms of the soldiers were dingy and worn now and the civilians, even when turned out in their best, showed skilful patching and darning. Scarlett thought she had never seen such elegant pants as he wore, fawn-coloured, shepherd's plaid, and checked. As for his waistcoats, they were indescribably handsome, especially the white watered-silk one with tiny pink rosebuds embroidered on it. And he wore these garments with a still more elegant air as though unaware of their glory.

There were few ladies who could resist his charms when he chose to exert them, and finally even Mrs Merriwether unbent and invited him to Sunday dinner.

Maybelle Merriwether was to marry her little Zouave when he got his next furlough, and she cried every time she thought of it, for she had set her heart on marrying in a white satin dress and there was no white satin in the Confederacy. Nor could she borrow a dress, for the satin wedding dresses of years past had all gone into the making of battle flags. Useless for the patriotic Mrs Merriwether to upbraid her daughter and point out that homespun was the proper bridal attire for a Confederate bride. Maybelle wanted satin. She was willing, even proud, to go without hairpins and buttons and nice shoes and candy and tea for the sake of the Cause, but she wanted a satin wedding dress.

Rhett, hearing of this from Melanie, brought in from England yards and yards of gleaming white satin and a lace veil and presented them to her as a wedding gift. He did it in such a way that it was unthinkable to even mention paying him for them, and Maybelle was so delighted she almost kissed him. Mrs Merriwether knew that so expensive a gift – and a gift of clothing at that – was highly improper, but she could think of no way of refusing when Rhett told her in the most florid language that nothing was too good to deck the bride of one of our brave heroes. So Mrs Merriwether invited him to dinner, feeling that this concession more than paid for the gift.

He not only brought Maybelle the satin but he was able to give excellent hints on the making of the wedding dress. Hoops in Paris were wider this season and skirts were shorter. They were no longer ruffled but were gathered up in scalloped festoons, showing braided petticoats beneath. He said, too, that he had seen no pantalets on the streets, so he imagined they were 'out'. Afterwards, Mrs Merriwether told Mrs Elsing she feared that if she had given him any encouragement at all, he would have told her exactly what kind of drawers were being worn by Parisiennes.

Had he been less obviously masculine, his ability to recall details of dresses, bonnets and coiffures would have been put down as the rankest effeminacy. The ladies always felt a little odd when they besieged him with questions about styles, but they did it nevertheless. They were as isolated from the world of fashion as shipwrecked mariners, for few books of fashion came through the blockade. For all they knew the ladies of France might be shaving their heads and wearing coonskin caps, so Rhett's memory for furbelows was an excellent substitute for *Godey's Lady's Book*. He could and did notice details so dear to feminine hearts, and after each trip abroad he could be found in the centre of a group of ladies, telling that bonnets were smaller this year and perched higher, covering most of the top of the head, that plumes and not flowers were being used to trim them, that the Empress of France had abandoned the chignon for evening wear and had her hair piled almost on the top of her head, showing all of her ears, and that evening frocks were shockingly low again.

For some months, he was the most popular and romantic figure the town knew, despite his previous reputation, despite the faint rumours that he was engaged not only in blockading but in speculating on foodstuffs, too. People who did not like him said that after every trip he made to Atlanta, prices jumped five dollars. But even with this under-cover gossip seeping about, he could have retained his popularity had he considered it worth retaining. Instead, it seemed as though, after trying the company of the staid and patriotic citizens and winning their respect and grudging liking, something perverse in him made him go out of his way to affront them and show them that his conduct had been only a masquerade and one which no longer amused him.

It was as though he bore an impersonal contempt for everyone and everything in the South, the Confederacy in particular, and took no pains to conceal it. It was his remarks about the Confederacy that made Atlanta look at him first in bewilderment, then coolly and then with hot rage. Even before 1862 passed into 1863, men were bowing to him with studied frigidity and women beginning to draw their daughters to their sides when he appeared at a gathering.

He seemed to take pleasure not only in affronting the sincere and red-hot loyalties of Atlanta but in presenting himself in the worst possible light. When well-meaning people complimented him on his bravery in running the blockade, he blandly replied that he was always frightened when in danger, as frightened as were the brave boys at the front. Everyone knew there had never been a cowardly Confederate soldier and they found this statement peculiarly irritating. He always referred to the soldiers as 'our brave boys' or 'our heroes in grey' and did it in such a way as to convey the utmost in insult. When daring young ladies, hoping for a flirtation, thanked him for being one of the heroes who fought for them, he bowed and declared that such was not the case, for he would do the same thing for Yankee women if the same amount of money were involved.

Since Scarlett's first meeting with him in Atlanta on the night of the bazaar, he had talked with her in this manner, but now there was a thinly veiled note of mockery in his conversations with everyone. When praised for his services to the Confederacy, he unfailingly replied that blockading was a business with him. If he could make as much money out of government contracts, he would say, picking out with his eyes those who had government contracts, then he would certainly abandon the hazards of blockading and take to selling shoddy cloth, sanded sugar, spoiled flour and rotten leather to the Confederacy.

Most of his remarks were unanswerable, which made them all the worse. There had already been minor scandals about those holding government contracts. Letters from men at the front complained constantly of shoes that wore out in a week, gunpowder that would not ignite, harness that snapped at any strain, meat that was rotten and flour that was full of weevils. Atlanta people tried to think that the men who sold such stuff to the government must be contract-holders from Alabama or Virginia or Tennessee, and not Georgians. For did not the Georgia contract-holders include men from the very best families? Were they not the first to contribute to hospital funds and to the aid of soldiers' orphans? Were they not the first to cheer at 'Dixie' and the most rampant seekers, in oratory at least, for Yankee blood? The full tide of fury against those profiteering on government contracts had not yet risen, and Rhett's words were taken merely as evidence of his own bad breeding.

He not only affronted the town with insinuations of venality on the part of men in high places and slurs on the courage of the men in the field, but he took pleasure in tricking the dignified citizenry into embarrassing situations. He could no more resist pricking the conceits, the hypocrisies and the flamboyant patriotism of those about him than a small boy can resist putting a pin into a balloon. He neatly deflated the pompous and exposed the ignorant and the bigoted, and he did it in such subtle ways, drawing his victims out by his seemingly courteous interest, that they never were quite certain what had happened until they stood exposed as windy, high-flown and slightly ridiculous.

During the months when the town accepted him, Scarlett had been under no illusions about him. She knew that his elaborate gallantries and his florid speeches were all done with his tongue in his cheek. She knew that he was acting the part of the dashing and patriotic blockade runner simply because it amused him. Sometimes he seemed to her like the County boys with whom she had grown up: the wild Tarleton twins with their obsession for practical jokes; the devil-inspired Fontaines, teasing, mischievous; the Calverts who would sit up all night planning hoaxes. But there was a difference, for beneath Rhett's seeming lightness there was something malicious, almost sinister in its suave brutality.

Though she was thoroughly aware of his insincerity, she much preferred him in the rôle of the romantic blockader. For one thing, it made her own situation in associating with him so much easier than it had been at first. So, she was intensely annoyed when he dropped his masquerade and set out apparently upon a deliberate campaign to alienate Atlanta's good will. It annoyed her because it seemed foolish and also because some of the harsh criticism directed at him fell on her.

It was at Mrs Elsing's silver musicale for the benefit of the convalescents that Rhett signed his final warrant of ostracism. That afternoon the Elsing home was crowded with soldiers on leave and men from the hospitals, members of the Home Guard and the militia unit, and matrons, widows and young girls. Every chair in the house was occupied, and even the long winding stair was packed with guests. The large cut-glass bowl held at the door by the Elsings' butler had been emptied twice of its burden of silver coins. That in itself was enough to make the affair a success, for now a dollar in silver was worth sixty dollars in Confederate paper money.

Every girl with any pretence to accomplishments had sung or played the piano, and the tableaux vivants had been greeted with flattering applause. Scarlett was much pleased with herself, for not only had she and Melanie rendered a touching duet, 'When the Dew Is on the Blossom', followed as an encore by the more sprightly 'Oh, Lawd, Ladies, Don't Mind Stephen!' but she had also been chosen to represent the Spirit of the Confederacy in the last tableau.

She had looked most fetching, wearing a modestly draped Greek robe of white cheesecloth girdled with red and blue and holding the Stars and Bars in one hand, while with the other she stretched out to the kneeling Captain Carey Ashburn, of Alabama, the gold-hilted sabre which had belonged to Charles and his father.

When her tableau was over, she could not help seeking Rhett's eyes to see if he had appreciated the pretty picture she made. With a feeling of exasperation, she saw that he was in an argument and probably had not even noticed her. Scarlett could see by the faces of the group surrounding him that they were infuriated by what he was saying.

She made her way toward them and, in one of those odd silences which sometimes fall on a gathering, she heard Willie Guinan, of the militia outfit, say plainly: 'Do I understand, sir, that you mean the Cause for which our heroes have died is not sacred?'

'If you were run over by a railroad train, your death wouldn't sanctify the railroad company, would it?' asked Rhett, and his voice sounded as if he were humbly seeking information.

'Sir,' said Willie, his voice shaking, 'if we were not under this roof—'

'I tremble to think what would happen,' said Rhett. 'For, of course, your bravery is too well known.'

Willie went scarlet and all conversation ceased. Everyone was embarrassed. Willie was strong and healthy and of military age and yet he wasn't at the front. Of course, he was the only boy his mother had and, after all, somebody had to be in the militia to protect the state. But there were a few irreverent snickers from convalescent officers when Rhett spoke of bravery.

'Oh, why doesn't he keep his mouth shut!' thought Scarlett indignantly. 'He's simply spoiling the whole party!'

Dr Meade's brows were thunderous.

'Nothing may be sacred to you, young man,' he said, in the voice he always used when making speeches. 'But there are many things sacred to the patriotic men and ladies of the South. And the freedom of our land from the usurper is one and States' Rights is another and—'

Rhett looked lazy and his voice had a silky, almost bored, note.

'All wars are sacred,' he said. 'To those who have to fight them. If the people who started wars didn't make them sacred, who would be foolish enough to fight? But, no matter what rallying cries the orators give to the idiots who fight, no matter what noble purposes they assign to wars, there is never but one reason for a war. And that is money. All wars are in reality money squabbles. But so few people ever realize it. Their ears are too full of bugles and drums and fine words from stay-at-home orators. Sometimes the rallying cry is "Save the Tomb of Christ from the Heathen!" Sometimes it's "Down With Popery!" and sometimes "Liberty!" and sometimes "Cotton, Slavery and States' Rights!" '

'What on earth has the Pope to do with it?' thought Scarlett. 'Or Christ's tomb, either?'

But as she hurried toward the incensed group, she saw Rhett bow jauntily and start toward the doorway through the crowd. She started after him but Mrs Elsing caught her skirt and held her.

'Let him go,' she said in a clear voice that carried throughout the tensely quiet room. 'Let him go. He is a traitor, a speculator! He is a viper that we have nursed to our bosoms!'

Rhett, standing in the hall, his hat in his hand, heard as he was intended to hear and, turning, surveyed the room for a moment. He looked pointedly at Mrs Elsing's flat bosom, grinned suddenly and, bowing, made his exit.

Mrs Merriwether rode home in Aunt Pitty's carriage, and scarcely had the four ladies seated themselves when she exploded.

'There now, Pittypat Hamilton! I hope you are satisfied!'

'With what?' cried Pitty, apprehensively.

'With the conduct of that wretched Butler man you've been harbouring.'

Pittypat fluttered, too upset by the accusation to recall that Mrs Merriwether had also been Rhett Butler's hostess on several occasions. Scarlett and Melanie thought of this, but bred to politeness to their elders, refrained from remarking on the matter. Instead they studiously looked down at their mittened hands.

'He insulted us all and the Confederacy too,' said Mrs Merriwether, and her stout bust heaved violently beneath its glittering passementerie trimmings. 'Saying that we were fighting for money! Saying that our leaders had lied to us! He should be put in jail. Yes, he should. I shall speak to Dr Meade about it. If Mr Merriwether were only alive, he'd tend to him! Now, Pitty Hamilton, you listen to me. You mustn't ever let that scamp come into your house again!'

'Oh,' mumbled Pitty, helplessly, looking as if she wished she were dead. She looked appealingly at the two girls who kept their eyes cast down and then hopefully toward Uncle Peter's erect back. She knew he was listening attentively to every word and she hoped he would turn and take a hand in the conversation, as he frequently did. She hoped he would say, 'Now, Miss Dolly, you let Miss Pitty be,' but Peter made no move. He disapproved heartily of Rhett Butler and poor Pitty knew it. She sighed and said: 'Well, Dolly, if you think—'

'I do think,' returned Mrs Merriwether firmly. 'I can't imagine what possessed you to receive him in the first place. After this afternoon, there won't be a decent home in town that he'll be welcome in. Do get up some gumption and forbid him your house.'

She turned a sharp eye on the girls. 'I hope you two are marking my words,' she continued, 'for it's partly your fault, being so pleasant to him. Just tell him politely but firmly that his presence and his disloyal talk are distinctly unwelcome at your house.'

By this time Scarlett was boiling, ready to rear like a horse at the touch of a strange rough hand on its bridle. But she was afraid to speak. She could not risk Mrs Merriwether writing another letter to her mother.

'You old buffalo!' she thought, her face crimson with suppressed fury. 'How heavenly it would be to tell you just what I think of you and your bossy ways!'

'I never thought to live long enough to hear such disloyal words spoken of our Cause,' went on Mrs Merriwether, by this time in a ferment of righteous anger. 'Any man who does not think our Cause is just and holy should be hanged! I don't want to hear of you two girls ever even speaking to him again— For Heaven's sake, Melly, what ails you?'

Melanie was white and her eyes were enormous.

'I will speak to him again,' she said in a low voice. 'I will not be rude to him. I will not forbid him the house.'

Mrs Merriwether's breath went out of her lungs as explosively as though she had been punched. Aunt Pitty's fat mouth popped open and Uncle Peter turned to stare.

'Now, why didn't I have the gumption to say that?' thought Scarlett, jealousy mixing with admiration. 'How did that little rabbit ever get up spunk enough to stand up to old lady Merriwether?'

Melanie's hands were shaking but she went on hurriedly, as though fearing her courage would fail her if she delayed.

'I won't be rude to him because of what he said, because— It was rude of him to say it out loud – most ill-advised – but it's – it's what Ashley thinks. And I can't forbid the house to a man who thinks what my husband thinks. It would be unjust.'

Mrs Merriwether's breath had come back and she charged.

'Melly Hamilton, I never heard such a lie in all my life! There was never a Wilkes who was a coward—'

'I never said Ashley was a coward,' said Melanie, her eyes beginning to flash. 'I said he thinks what Captain Butler thinks, only he expresses it in different words. And he doesn't go around saying it at musicales, I hope. But he has written it to me.'

Scarlett's guilty conscience stirred as she tried to recall what Ashley might have written that would lead Melanie to make such a statement, but most of the letters she had read had gone out of her head as soon as she finished reading them. She believed Melanie had simply taken leave of her senses.

'Ashley wrote me that we should not be fighting the Yankees. And that we have been betrayed into it by statesmen and orators mouthing catchwords and prejudices,' said Melly rapidly. 'He said nothing in the world was worth what this war was going to do to us. He said there wasn't anything at all to glory – it was just misery and dirt.'

'Oh! That letter,' thought Scarlett. 'Was that what he meant?'

'I don't believe it,' said Mrs Merriwether firmly. 'You misunderstood his meaning.'

'I never misunderstand Ashley,' Melanie replied quietly, though her lips were trembling. 'I understand him perfectly. He meant exactly what Captain Butler meant, only he didn't say it in a rude way.'

'You should be ashamed of yourself, comparing a fine man like Ashley Wilkes to a scoundrel like Captain Butler! I suppose you, too, think the Cause is nothing!'

'I – I don't know what I think,' Melanie began uncertainly, her fire deserting her and panic at her outspokenness taking hold of her. 'I – I'd die for the Cause, like Ashley would. But – I mean – I mean, I'll let the men folks do the thinking, because they are so much smarter.'

'I never heard the like,' snorted Mrs Merriwether. 'Stop, Uncle Peter, you're driving past my house!'

Uncle Peter, preoccupied with the conversation behind him, had driven past the Merriwether carriage block and he backed up the horse. Mrs Merriwether alighted, her bonnet ribbons shaking like sails in a storm.

'You'll be sorry,' she said.

Uncle Peter whipped up the horse.

'You young misses ought ter tek shame, gittin' Miss Pitty in a state,' he scolded.

'I'm not in a state,' replied Pitty, surprisingly, for less strain than this had frequently brought on fainting fits. 'Melly, honey, I knew you were doing it just to take up for me and, really, I was glad to see somebody take Dolly down a peg. She's so bossy. How did you have the courage? But do you think you should have said that about Ashley?'

'But it's true,' answered Melanie, and she began to cry softly. 'And I'm not ashamed that he thinks that way. He thinks the war is all wrong but he's willing to fight and die anyway, and that takes lots more courage than fighting for something you think is right.'

'Lawd, Miss Melly, doan cry hyah on Peachtree Street,' groaned Uncle Peter, hastening his horse's pace. 'Folks'll talk sumpin' scan'lous. Wait till us gits home.'

Scarlett said nothing. She did not even squeeze the hand that Melanie had inserted into her palm for comfort. She had read Ashley's letters for only one purpose – to assure herself that he still loved her. Now Melanie had given a new meaning to passages in the letters which Scarlett's eyes had barely seen. It shocked her to realize that anyone as absolutely perfect as Ashley could have any thought in common with such a reprobate as Rhett Butler. She thought: 'They both see the truth of this war, but Ashley is willing to die about it and Rhett isn't. I think that shows Rhett's good sense.' She paused a moment, horror-struck that she could have such a thought about Ashley. 'They both see the same unpleasant truth, but Rhett likes to look it in the face and enrage people by talking about it – and Ashley can hardly bear to face it.'

It was very bewildering.

Chapter XIII

Under Mrs Merriwether's goading, Dr Meade took action, in the form of a letter to the newspaper wherein he did not mention Rhett by name, though his meaning was obvious. The editor, sensing the social drama of the letter, put it on the second page of the paper, in itself a startling innovation, as the first two pages of the paper were always devoted to advertisements of slaves, mules, ploughs, coffins, houses for sale or rent, cures for private diseases, abortifacients and restoratives for lost manhood.

The doctor's letter was the first of a chorus of indignation that was beginning to be heard all over the South against speculators, profiteers and holders of government contracts. Conditions in Wilmington, the chief blockade port, now that Charleston's port was practically sealed by the Yankee gunboats, had reached the proportions of an open scandal. Speculators swarmed Wilmington and, having the ready cash, bought up boatloads of goods and held them for a rise in prices. The rise always came, for with the increasing scarcity of necessities, prices leaped higher by the month. The civilian population had either to do without or buy at the speculators' prices, and the poor and those in moderate circumstances were suffering increasing hardships. With the rise in prices, Confederate money sank, and with its rapid fall there rose a wild passion for luxuries. Blockaders were commissioned to bring in necessities and were permitted to trade in luxuries only as a side line, but now it was the higher-priced luxuries that filled their boats to the exclusion of the things the Confederacy vitally needed. People frenziedly bought these luxuries with the money they had today, fearing that tomorrow's prices would be higher and the money worth less.

To make matters worse, there was only one railroad line from Wilmington to Richmond and, while thousands of barrels of flour and boxes of bacon spoiled and rotted in wayside stations for want of transportation, speculators with wines, taffetas and coffee to sell seemed always able to get their goods to Richmond two days after they were landed at Wilmington.

The rumour which had been creeping about underground was now being openly discussed, that Rhett Butler not only ran his own four boats and sold the cargoes at unheard-of prices, but bought up the cargoes of other boats and held them for rises in prices. It was said that he was at the head of a combine worth more than a million dollars, with Wilmington as its headquarters for the purpose of buying blockade goods on the docks. They had dozens of warehouses in that city and in Richmond, so the story ran, and the warehouses were crammed with food and clothing that were being held for higher prices. Already soldiers and civilians alike were feeling the pinch, and the muttering against him and his fellow speculators was bitter.

'There are many brave and patriotic men in the blockade arm of the Confederacy's naval service,' ran the last of the doctor's letter, 'unselfish men who are risking their lives and all their wealth that the Confederacy may survive. They are enshrined in the hearts of all loyal Southerners, and no one begrudges them the scant monetary returns they make for their risks. They are unselfish gentlemen, and we honour them. Of these men, I do not speak.

'But there are others, scoundrels, who masquerade under the cloak of the blockader for their own selfish gains, and I call down the just wrath and vengeance of an embattled people, fighting in the justest of Causes, on these human vultures who bring in satins and laces when our men are dying for want of quinine, who load their boats with tea and wines when our heroes are writhing for lack of morphia. I execrate these vampires who are sucking the lifeblood of the men who follow Robert Lee – these men who are making the very name of blockader a stench in the nostrils of all patriotic men. How can we endure these scavengers in our midst with their varnished boots when our boys are tramping barefoot into battle? How can we tolerate them with their champagnes and their pâtés of Strasbourg when our soldiers are shivering about their camp-fires and gnawing mouldy bacon? I call upon every loyal Confederate to cast them out.'

Atlanta read, knew the oracle had spoken, and, as loyal Confederates, they hastened to cast Rhett out.

Of all the homes which had received him in the fall of 1862, Miss Pittypat's was almost the only one into which he could enter in 1863. And, except for Melanie, he probably would not have been received there. Aunt Pitty was in a state whenever he was in town. She knew very well what her friends were saying when she permitted him to call but she still lacked the courage to tell him he was unwelcome. Each time he arrived in Atlanta, she set her fat mouth and told the girls that she would meet him at the door and forbid him to enter. And each time he came, a little package in his hand and a compliment for her charm and beauty on his lips, she wilted.

'I just don't know what to do,' she would moan. 'He just looks at me and I – I'm scared to death of what he would do if I told him. He's got such a bad reputation. Do you suppose he would strike me – or – or— Oh, dear, if Charlie were only alive! Scarlett, *you* must tell him not to call again – tell him in a nice way. Oh, me! I do believe you encourage him, and the whole town is talking and, if your mother ever finds out, what will she say to me? Melly, you must not be so nice to him. Be cool and distant and he will understand. Oh, Melly, do you think I'd better write Henry a note and ask him to speak to Captain Butler?'

'No, I don't,' said Melanie. 'And I won't be rude to him, either. I think people are acting like chickens with their heads off about Captain Butler. I'm sure he can't be all the bad things Dr Meade and Mrs Merriwether say he is. He wouldn't hold food from starving people. Why, he even gave me a hundred dollars for the orphans. I'm sure he's just as loyal and patriotic as any of us and he's just too proud to defend himself. You know how obstinate men are when they get their backs up.'

Aunt Pitty knew nothing about men, either with their backs up or otherwise, and she could only wave her fat little hands helplessly. As for Scarlett, she had long ago become resigned to Melanie's habit of seeing good in everyone. Melanie was a fool, but there was nothing anybody could do about it.

Scarlett knew that Rhett was not being patriotic and, though she would have died rather than confess it, she did not care. The little presents he brought her from Nassau, little oddments that a lady could accept with propriety, were what mattered most to her. With prices as high as they were, where on earth could she get needles and bonbons and hairpins, if she forbade the house to him? No, it was easier to shift the responsibility to Aunt Pitty, who after all was the head of the house, the chaperon and the arbiter of morals. Scarlett knew the town gossiped about Rhett's calls, and about her too; but she also knew that in the eyes of Atlanta Melanie Wilkes could do no wrong, and if Melanie defended Rhett his calls were still tinged with respectability.

However, life would be pleasanter if Rhett would recant his heresies. She wouldn't have to suffer the embarrassment of seeing him cut openly when she walked down Peachtree Street with him.

'Even if you think such things, why do you say them?' she scolded. 'If you'd just think what you please but keep your mouth shut, everything would be so much nicer.'

'That's your system, isn't it, my green-eyed hypocrite? Scarlett, Scarlett! I hoped for more courageous conduct from you. I thought the Irish said what they thought and the Divvil take the hindermost. Tell me truthfully, don't you sometimes almost burst from keeping your mouth shut?'

'Well – yes,' Scarlett confessed reluctantly. 'I do get awfully bored when they talk about the Cause, morning, noon and night. But goodness, Rhett Butler, if I admitted it nobody would speak to me and none of the boys would dance with me!'

'Ah, yes, and one must be danced with, at all costs. Well, I admire your self-control but I do not find myself equal to it. Nor can I masquerade in a cloak of romance and patriotism, no matter how convenient it might be. There are enough stupid patriots who are risking every cent they have in the blockade and who are going to come out of this war paupers. They don't need me among their number, either to brighten the record of patriotism or to increase the roll of paupers. Let them have the haloes. They deserve them – for once I am being sincere – and, besides, haloes will be about all they will have in a year or so.'

'I think you are very nasty to even hint such things when you know very well that England and France are coming in on our side in no time and—'

'Why, Scarlett! You must have been reading a newspaper! I'm surprised at you. Don't do it again. It addles women's brains. For your information, I was in England, not a month ago, and I'll tell you this. England will never help the Confederacy. England never bets on the underdog. That's why she's England. Besides, the fat Dutch woman who is sitting on the throne is a God-fearing soul and she doesn't approve of slavery. Let the English mill workers starve because they can't get our cotton but never, never strike a blow for slavery. And as for France, that weak imitation of Napoleon is far too busy establishing the French in Mexico to be bothered with us. In fact, he welcomes this war, because it keeps us too busy to run his troops out of Mexico . . . No, Scarlett, the idea of assistance from abroad is just a newspaper invention to keep up the morale of the South. The Confederacy is doomed. It's living on its hump now, like the camel, and even the largest of humps aren't inexhaustible. I give myself about six months more of blockading and then I'm through. After that, it will be too risky. And I'll sell my boats to some foolish Englishman who thinks he can slip them through. But one way or the other, it's not bothering me. I've made money enough, and it's in English banks and in gold. None of this worthless paper for me.'

As always when he spoke, he sounded so plausible. Other people might call his utterances treachery but, to Scarlett, they always rang with common sense and truth. And she knew that this was utterly wrong, knew she should be shocked and infuriated. Actually she was neither, but she could pretend to be. It made her feel more respectable and ladylike.

'I think what Dr Meade wrote about you was right, Captain Butler. The only way to redeem yourself is to enlist after you sell your boats. You're a West Pointer and—'

'You talk like a Baptist preacher making a recruiting speech. Suppose I don't want to redeem myself? Why should I fight to uphold the system that cast me out? I shall take pleasure in seeing it smashed.'

'I never heard of any system,' she said crossly.

'No? And yet you are a part of it, like I was, and I'll wager you don't like it any more than I did. Well, why am I the black sheep of the Butler family? For this reason and no other – I didn't conform to Charleston and I couldn't. And Charleston is the South, only intensified. I wonder if you realize yet what a bore it is? So many things that one must do because they've always been done. So many things, quite harmless, that one must do for the same reason. So many things that annoyed me by their senselessness. Not marrying the young lady, of whom you have probably heard, was merely the last straw. Why should I marry a boring fool, simply because an accident prevented me from getting her home before dark? And why permit her wild-eyed brother to shoot and kill me, when I could shoot straighter? If I had been a gentleman, of course, I would have let him kill me and that would have wiped the blot from the Butler escutcheon. But – I like to live. And so I've lived and I've had a good time . . . When I think of my brother, living among the sacred cows of Charleston, and most reverent toward them, and remember his stodgy wife and his Saint Cecilia Balls and his everlasting rice fields – then I know the compensation for breaking with the system. Scarlett, our Southern way of living is as antiquated as the feudal system of the Middle Ages. The wonder is that it's lasted as long as it has. It had to go and it's going now. And yet you expect me to listen to orators like Dr Meade who tell me our Cause is just and holy? And get so excited by the roll of drums that I'll grab a musket and rush off to Virginia to shed my blood for Marse Robert? What kind of a fool do you think I am? Kissing the rod that chastised me is not in my line. The South and I are even now. The South threw me out to starve once. I haven't starved, and I am making enough money out of the South's death-throes to compensate me for my lost birthright.'

'I think you are vile and mercenary,' said Scarlett, but her remark was automatic. Most of what he was saying went over her head, as did any conversation that was not personal. But part of it made sense. There were such a lot of foolish things about life among nice people. Having to pretend that her heart was in the grave when it wasn't. And how shocked everybody had been when she danced at the bazaar. And the infuriating way people lifted their eyebrows every time she did or said anything the least bit different from what every other young woman did and said. But still, she was jarred at hearing him attack the very traditions that irked her most. She had lived too long among people who dissembled politely not to feel disturbed at hearing her own thoughts put into words.

'Mercenary? No, I'm only farsighted. Though perhaps that is merely a synonym for mercenary. At least, people who were not as farsighted as I will call it that. Any loyal Confederate who had a thousand dollars in cash in 1861 could have done what I did, but how few were mercenary enough to take advantage of their opportunities! As for instance, right after Fort Sumter fell and before the blockade was established, I bought up several thousand bales of cotton at dirt-cheap prices and ran them to England. They are still there in warehouses in Liverpool. I've never sold them. I'm holding them until the English mills have to have cotton and will give me any price I ask. I wouldn't be surprised if I got a dollar a pound.'

'You'll get a dollar a pound when elephants roost in trees!'

'I believe I'll get it. Cotton is at seventy-two cents a pound already. I'm going to be a rich man when this war is over, Scarlett, because I was farsighted – pardon me, mercenary. I told you once before that there were two times for making big money, one in the upbuilding of a country and the other in its destruction. Slow money on the upbuilding, fast money in the crack-up. Remember my words. Perhaps they may be of use to you some day.'

'I do appreciate good advice so much,' said Scarlett, with all the sarcasm she could muster. 'But I don't need your advice. Do you think Pa is a pauper? He's got all the money I'll ever need and then I have Charles' property besides.'

'I imagine the French aristocrats thought practically the same thing until the very moment when they climbed into the tumbrils.'

Frequently Rhett pointed out to Scarlett the inconsistency of her wearing black mourning clothes when she was participating in all social activities. He liked bright colours and Scarlett's funereal dresses and the crêpe veil that hung from her bonnet to her heels both amused and offended him. But she clung to her dull black dresses and her veil, knowing that if she changed them for colours without waiting several more years, the town would buzz even more than it was already buzzing. And besides, how would she ever explain to her mother?

Rhett said frankly that the crêpe veil made her look like a crow and the black dresses added ten years to her age. This ungallant statement sent her flying to the mirror to see if she really did look twenty-eight instead of eighteen.

'I should think you'd have more pride than to try to look like Mrs

Merriwether,' he taunted. 'And better taste than to wear that veil to advertise a grief I'm sure you never felt. I'll lay a wager with you. I'll have that bonnet and veil off your head and a Paris creation on it within two months.'

'Indeed, no, and don't let's discuss it any further,' said Scarlett, annoyed by his reference to Charles. Rhett, who was preparing to leave for Wilmington for another trip abroad, departed with a grin on his face.

One bright summer morning some weeks later, he reappeared with a brightly trimmed hatbox in his hand and, after finding that Scarlett was alone in the house, he opened it. Wrapped in layers of tissue was a bonnet, a creation that made her cry, 'Oh, the darling thing!' as she reached for it. Starved for the sight, much less the touch, of new clothes, it seemed the loveliest bonnet she had ever seen. It was of dark-green taffeta, lined with watered silk of pale-jade colour. The ribbons that tied under the chin were as wide as her hand and they, too, were pale green And curled about the brim of this confection was the perkiest of green ostrich plumes.

'Put it on,' said Rhett, smiling.

She flew across the room to the mirror and popped it on her head, pushing back her hair to show her earrings and tying the ribbon under her chin.

'How do I look?' she cried, pirouetting for his benefit and tossing her head so that the plume danced. But she knew she looked pretty even before she saw confirmation in his eyes. She looked attractively saucy and the green of the lining made her eyes dark emerald and sparkling.

'Oh, Rhett, whose bonnet is it? I'll buy it. I'll give you every cent I've got for it.'

'It's your bonnet,' he said. 'Who else could wear that shade of green? Don't you think I carried the colour of your eyes well in my mind?'

'Did you really have it trimmed just for me?'

'Yes, and there's "Rue de la Paix" on the box, if that means anything to you.'

It meant nothing to her, smiling at her reflection in the mirror. Just at this moment, nothing mattered to her except that she looked utterly charming in the first pretty hat she had put on her head in two years. What she couldn't do with this hat! And then her smile faded.

'Don't you like it?'

'Oh, it's a dream but— Oh, I do hate to have to cover this lovely green with crêpe and dye the feather black.'

He was beside her quickly and his deft fingers untied the wide bow under her chin. In a moment the hat was back in the box.

'What are you doing? You said it was mine.'

'But not to change to a mourning bonnet. I shall find some other charming lady with green eyes who appreciates my taste.'

'Oh, you shan't! I'll die if I don't have it! Oh, please, Rhett, don't be mean! Let me have it.'

'And turn it into a fright like your other hats? No.'

She clutched at the box. That sweet thing that made her look so young and enchanting to be given to some other girl? Oh, never! For a moment she thought of the horror of Pitty and Melanie. She thought of Ellen and what she would say, and she shivered. But vanity was stronger.

'I won't change it. I promise. Now, do let me have it.'

He gave her the box with a slightly sardonic smile and watched her while she put it on again and preened herself.

'How much is it?' she asked suddenly, her face falling. 'I have only fifty dollars but next month—'

'It would cost about two thousand dollars, Confederate money,' he said with a grin at her woebegone expression.

'Oh, dear— Well, suppose I give you the fifty now and then when I get—'

'I don't want any money for it,' he said. 'It's a gift.'

Scarlett's mouth dropped open. The line was so closely, so carefully drawn where gifts from men were concerned.

'Candy and flowers, dear,' Ellen had said time and time again, 'and perhaps a book of poetry or an album or a small bottle of Florida water are the only things a lady may accept from a gentleman. Never, never any expensive gift, even from your fiancé. And never any gift of jewellery or wearing apparel, not even gloves or handkerchiefs. Should you accept such gifts, men would know you were no lady and would try to take liberties.'

'Oh, dear,' thought Scarlett, looking first at herself in the mirror and then at Rhett's unreadable face. 'I simply can't tell him I won't accept it. It's too darling. I'd – I'd almost rather he took a liberty, if it was a very small one.' Then she was horrified at herself for having such a thought and she turned pink.

'I'll – I'll give you the fifty dollars—'

'If you do I will throw it in the gutter. Or, better still, buy masses for your soul. I'm sure your soul could do with a few masses.'

She laughed unwillingly, and the laughing reflection under the green brim decided her instantly.

'Whatever are you trying to do to me?'

'I'm tempting you with fine gifts until your girlish ideals are quite worn away and you are at my mercy,' he said. ' "Accept only candy and flowers from gentlemen, dearie," ' he mimicked, and she burst into a giggle.

'You are a clever, black-hearted wretch, Rhett Butler, and you know very well this bonnet's too pretty to be refused.'

His eyes mocked her, even while they complimented her beauty.

'Of course, you can tell Miss Pitty that you gave me a sample of taffeta and green silk and drew picture of the bonnet and I extorted fifty dollars from you for it.'

'No. I shall say one hundred dollars and she'll tell everybody in town and everybody will be green with envy and talk about my extravagance. But, Rhett, you mustn't bring me anything else so expensive. It's awfully kind of you, but I really couldn't accept anything else.'

'Indeed? Well, I shall bring you presents so long as it pleases me and so long as I see things that will enhance your charms. I shall bring you dark-green watered silk for a frock to match the bonnet. And I warn you that I am not kind. I am tempting you with bonnets and bangles and leading you into a pit. Always remember I never do anything without reason and I never give anything without expecting something in return. I always get paid.'

His black eyes sought her face and travelled to her lips. Scarlett cast down her eyes, excitement filling her. Now, he was going to try to take liberties, just as Ellen predicted. He was going to kiss her, or try to kiss her, and she couldn't quite make up her flurried mind which it should be. If she refused, he might jerk the bonnet right off her head and give it to some other girl. On the other hand, if she permitted one chaste peck, he might bring her other lovely presents in the hope of getting another kiss. Men set such store by kisses, though Heaven alone knew why. And lots of times, after one kiss they fell completely in love with a girl and made most entertaining spectacles of themselves, provided the girl was clever and withheld her kisses after the first one. It would be so exciting to have Rhett Butler in love with her and admitting it and begging for a kiss or a smile. Yes, she would let him kiss her.

But he made no move to kiss her. She gave him a sidelong glance from under her lashes and murmured encouragingly.

'So you always get paid, do you? And what do you expect to get from me?'

'That remains to be seen.'

'Well, if you think I'll marry you to pay for the bonnet, I won't,' she said daringly and gave her head a saucy flirt that set the plume to bobbing.

His white teeth gleamed under his little moustache.

'Madam, you flatter yourself. I do not want to marry you or anyone else. I am not a marrying man.'

'Indeed!' she cried, taken aback and now determined that he should take some liberty. 'I don't even intend to kiss you, either.'

'Then why is your mouth all pursed up in that ridiculous way?'

'Oh!' she cried as she caught a glimpse of herself and saw that her red lips were indeed in the proper pose for a kiss. 'Oh!' she cried again, losing her temper and stamping her foot. 'You are the horridest man I have ever seen and I don't care if I never see you again!'

'If you really felt that way, you'd stamp on the bonnet. My, what a passion you are in and it's quite becoming, as you probably know. Come, Scarlett, stamp on the bonnet to show me what you think of me and my presents.'

'Don't you dare touch this bonnet,' she said, clutching it by the bow and retreating. He came after her, laughing softly, and took her hand in his.

'Oh, Scarlett, you are so young you wring my heart,' he said. 'And I shall kiss you, as you seem to expect it,' and leaning down carelessly, his moustache just grazed her cheek. 'Now, do you feel that you must slap me to preserve the proprieties?'

Her lips mutinous, she looked up into his eyes and saw so much amusement in their dark depths that she burst into laughter. What a tease he was and how exasperating! If he didn't want to marry her and didn't even want to kiss her, what did he want? If he wasn't in love with her, why did he call so often and bring her presents?

'That's better,' he said. 'Scarlett, I'm a bad influence on you and if you have any sense you will send me packing – if you can. I'm very hard to get rid of. But I'm bad for you.'

'Are you?'

'Can't you see it? Ever since I met you at the bazaar, your career has been most shocking and I'm to blame for most of it. Who encouraged you to dance? Who forced you to admit that you thought our glorious Cause was neither glorious nor sacred? Who goaded you into admitting that you thought men were fools to die for high-sounding principles? Who has aided you in giving the old ladies plenty to gossip about? Who is getting you out of mourning several years too soon? And who, to end all this, has lured you into accepting a gift which no lady can accept and still remain a lady?'

'You flatter yourself, Captain Butler. I haven't done anything so scandalous and I'd have done everything you mentioned without your aid anyway.'

'I doubt that,' he said, and his face was suddenly quiet and sombre. 'You'd still be the broken-hearted widow of Charles Hamilton and famed for your good deeds among the wounded. Eventually, however—'

But she was not listening, for she was regarding herself pleasedly in the mirror again, thinking she would wear the bonnet to the hospital this very afternoon and take flowers to the convalescent officers.

That there was truth in his words did not occur to her. She did not see that Rhett had pried open the prison of her widowhood and set her free to queen it over unmarried girls when her days as a belle should have been long past. Nor did she see that under his influence she had come a long way from Ellen's teachings. The change had been so gradual, the flouting of one small convention seeming to have no connection with the flouting of another, and none of them any connection with Rhett. She did not realize that, with his encouragement, she had disregarded many of the sternest injunctions of her mother concerning the proprieties, forgotten the difficult lessons in being a lady.

She only saw that the bonnet was the most becoming one she ever had, that it had not cost her a penny and that Rhett must be in love with her, whether he admitted it or not. And she certainly intended to find a way to make him admit it.

The next day, Scarlett was standing in front of the mirror with a comb in her hand and her mouth full of hairpins, attempting a new coiffure which Maybelle, fresh from a visit to her husband in Richmond, had said was the rage at the Capital. It was called 'Cats, Rats and Mice' and presented many difficulties. The hair was parted in the middle and arranged in three rolls of graduating size on each side of the head, the largest, nearest the part, being the 'cat'. The 'cat' and the 'rat' were easy to fix but the 'mice' kept slipping out of her hairpins in an exasperating manner. However, she was determined to accomplish it, for Rhett was coming to supper and he always noticed and commented upon any innovation of dress or hair.

As she struggled with her bushy, obstinate locks, perspiration beading her forehead, she heard light running feet in the downstairs hall and knew that Melanie was home from the hospital. As she heard her fly up the stairs, two at a time, she paused, hairpin in mid-air, realizing that something must be wrong, for Melanie always moved as decorously as a dowager. She went to the door and threw it open, and Melanie ran in, her face flushed and frightened, looking like a guilty child.

There were tears on her cheeks, her bonnet was hanging on her neck by the ribbons and her hoops swaying violently. She was clutching something in her hand, and the reek of heavy cheap perfume came into the room with her.

'Oh, Scarlett!' she cried, shutting the door and sinking on the bed. 'Is Auntie home yet? She isn't? Oh, thank the Lord! Scarlett, I'm so mortified I could die! I nearly swooned and, Scarlett, Uncle Peter is threatening to tell Aunt Pitty!'

'Tell what?'

'That I was talking to that – to Miss – Mrs—' Melanie fanned her hot face with her handkerchief. 'That woman with red hair, named Belle Watling!'

'Why, Melly!' cried Scarlett, so shocked she could only stare.

Belle Watling was the red-haired woman she had seen on the street the first day she came to Atlanta and, by now, she was easily the most notorious woman in town. Many prostitutes had flocked into Atlanta, following the soldiers, but Belle stood out above the rest, due to her flaming hair and the gaudy, overly fashionable dresses she wore. She was seldom seen on Peachtree Street or in any nice neighbourhood, but when she did appear respectable women made haste to cross the street to remove themselves from her vicinity. And Melanie had been talking with her. No wonder Uncle Peter was outraged.

'I shall die if Aunt Pitty finds out! You know she'll cry and tell everybody in town and I'll be disgraced,' sobbed Melanie. 'And it wasn't my fault. I – I couldn't run away from her. It would have been so rude. Scarlett, I – I felt sorry for her. Do you think I'm bad for feeling that way?'

But Scarlett was not concerned with the ethics of the matter. Like most innocent and well-bred young women, she had a devouring curiosity about prostitutes.

'What did she want? What does she talk like?'

'Oh, she used awful grammar but I could see she was trying so hard to be elegant, poor thing. I came out of the hospital and Uncle Peter and the carriage weren't waiting, so I thought I'd walk home. And when I went by the Emersons' yard, there she was hiding behind the hedge! Oh, thank Heaven the Emersons are in Macon! And she said, "Please, Mrs Wilkes, do speak a minute with me." I don't know how she knew my name. I knew I ought to run as hard as I could but – well, Scarlett, she looked so sad and – well, sort of pleading. And she had on a black dress and black bonnet and no paint and really looked decent but for that red hair. And before I could answer she said, "I know I shouldn't speak to you but I tried to talk to that old peahen, Mrs Elsing, and she ran me away from the hospital." '

'Did she really call her a peahen?' said Scarlett pleasedly and laughed.

'Oh, don't laugh. It isn't funny. It seems that Miss – this woman, wanted to do something for the hospital – can you imagine it? She offered to nurse every morning and, of course, Mrs Elsing must have nearly died at the idea and ordered her out of the hospital. And then she said, "I want to do something, too. Ain't I a Confedrut, good as you?" And, Scarlett, I was right touched at her wanting to help. You know, she can't be all bad if she wants to help the Cause. Do you think I'm bad to feel that way?'

'For Heaven's sake, Melly, who cares if you're bad? What else did she say?'

'She said she'd been watching the ladies go by to the hospital and thought I had – a – a kind face and so she stopped me. She had some money and she wanted me to take it and use it for the hospital and not tell a soul where it came from. She said Mrs Elsing wouldn't let it be used if she knew what kind of money it was. What kind of money! That's when I thought I'd swoon! And I was so upset and anxious to get away, I just said: "Oh, yes, indeed, how sweet of you," or something idiotic, and she smiled and said: "That's right Christian of you," and shoved this dirty handkerchief into my hand. Ugh, can you smell the perfume?'

Melanie held out a man's handkerchief, soiled and highly perfumed, in which some coins were knotted.

'She was saying thank you and something about bringing me some money every week and just then Uncle Peter drove up and saw me!' Melly collapsed into tears and laid her head on the pillow. 'And when he saw who was with me, he— Scarlett, he *hollered* at me! Nobody has ever hollered at me before in my whole life. And he said, "You git in dis hyah cah'ige dis minute!" Of course, I did, and all the way home he blessed me out and wouldn't let me explain and said he was going to tell Aunt Pitty. Scarlett, do go down and beg him not to tell her. Perhaps he will listen to you. It will kill Auntie if she knows I ever even looked that woman in the face. Will you?'

'Yes, I will. But let's see how much money is in here. It feels heavy.'

She untied the knot and a handful of gold coins rolled out on the bed.

'Scarlett, there's fifty dollars here! And in gold!' cried Melanie, awed, as she counted the bright pieces. 'Tell me, do you think it's all right to use this kind – well, money made – er – this way for the boys? Don't you think that maybe God will understand that she wanted to help and won't care if it is tainted? When I think of how many things the hospital needs—'

But Scarlett was not listening. She was looking at the dirty handkerchief, and humiliation and fury were filling her. There was a monogram in the corner in which were the initials 'R. K. B.'. In her top drawer was a handkerchief just like this, one that Rhett Butler had lent her only yesterday to wrap about the stems of wild flowers they had picked. She had planned to return it to him when he came to supper tonight.

So Rhett consorted with that vile Watling creature and gave her money. That was where the contribution to the hospital came from. Blockade gold. And to think that Rhett would have the gall to look a decent woman in the face after being with that creature! And to think that she could have believed he was in love with her! This proved he couldn't be.

Bad women and all they involved were mysterious and revolting matters to her. She knew that men patronized these women for purposes which no lady should mention – or, if she did mention them, in whispers and by indirection and euphemism. She had always thought that only common vulgar men visited such women. Before this moment, it had never occurred to her that nice men – that is, men she met at nice homes and with whom she danced – could possibly do such things. It opened up an entirely new field of thought and one that was horrifying. Perhaps all men did this! It was bad enough that they forced their wives to go through such indecent performances, but to actually seek out low women and pay them for such accommodation! Oh, men were all so vile, and Rhett Butler was the worst of them all!

She would take this handkerchief and fling it in his face and show him the door and never, never speak to him again. But no, of course she couldn't do that. She could never, never let him know she even realized that bad women existed, much less that he visited them. A lady could never do that.

'Oh,' she thought in fury. 'If I just wasn't a lady, what wouldn't I tell that varmint!'

And, crumpling the handkerchief in her hand, she went down the stairs to the kitchen in search of Uncle Peter. As she passed the stove, she shoved the handkerchief into the flames and with impotent anger watched it burn.

Chapter XIV

Hope was rolling high in every Southern heart as the summer of 1863 came in. Despite privation and hardship, despite food speculators and kindred scourges, despite death and sickness and suffering which had now left their mark on nearly every family, the South was again saying, 'One more victory and the war is over,' saying it with even more happy assurance than in the summer before. The Yankees were proving a hard nut to crack but they were cracking at last.

Christmas of 1862 had been a happy one for Atlanta, for the whole South. The Confederacy had scored a smashing victory at Fredericksburg and the Yankee dead and wounded were counted in the thousands. There was universal rejoicing in that holiday season, rejoicing and thankfulness that the tide was turning. The army in butternut were now seasoned fighters, their generals had proven their mettle, and everyone knew that when the campaign reopened in the spring, the Yankees would be crushed for good and all.

Spring came and the fighting recommenced. May came and the Confederacy won another great victory at Chancellorsville. The South roared with elation.

Closer to home, a Union cavalry dash into Georgia had been turned into a Confederate triumph. Folks were still laughing and slapping each other on the back and saying: 'Yes, sir! When old Nathan Bedford Forrest gets after them, they better git!' Late in April, Colonel Streight and eighteen hundred Yankee cavalry had made a surprise raid into Georgia, aiming at Rome, only a little more than sixty miles north of Atlanta. They had ambitious plans to cut the vitally important railroad between Atlanta and Tennessee and then swing southward into Atlanta to destroy the factories and the war supplies concentrated there in that key city of the Confederacy.

It was a bold stroke and it would have cost the South dearly, except for Forrest. With only one-third as many men – but what men and what riders! – he had started after them, engaged them before they even reached Rome, harassed them day and night and finally captured the entire force!

The news reached Atlanta almost simultaneously with the news of the victory at Chancellorsville, and the town fairly rocked with exultation and with laughter. Chancellorsville might be a more important victory but the capture of Streight's raiders made the Yankees positively ridiculous.

'No, sir, they'd better not fool with old Forrest,' Atlanta said gleefully as the story was told over and over.

The tide of the Confederacy's fortune was running strong and full now, sweeping the people jubilantly along on its flood. True, the Yankees under Grant had been besieging Vicksburg since the middle of May. True, the South had suffered a sickening loss when Stonewall Jackson had been fatally wounded at Chancellorsville. True, Georgia had lost one of her bravest and most brilliant sons when General T. R. R. Cobb had been killed at

Fredericksburg. But the Yankees just couldn't stand any more defeats like Fredericksburg and Chancellorsville. They'd have to give in, and then this cruel war would be over.

The first days of July came and with them the rumour, later confirmed by dispatches, that Lee was marching into Pennsylvania. Lee in the enemy's territory! Lee forcing battle! This was the last fight of the war!

Atlanta was wild with excitement, pleasure and a hot thirst for vengeance. Now the Yankees would know what it meant to have the war carried into their own country. Now they'd know what it meant to have fertile fields stripped, horses and cattle stolen, houses burned, old men and boys dragged off to prison and women and children turned out to starve.

Everyone knew what the Yankees had done in Missouri, Kentucky, Tennessee and Virginia. Even small children could recite with hate and fear the horrors the Yankees had inflicted upon the conquered territory. Already Atlanta was full of refugees from east Tennessee, and the town had heard first-hand stories from them of what suffering they had gone through. In that section, the Confederate sympathizers were in the minority and the hand of war fell heavily upon them, as it did on all the border states, neighbour informing against neighbour and brother killing brother. These refugees cried out to see Pennsylvania one solid sheet of flame, and even the gentlest of old ladies wore expressions of grim pleasure.

But when the news trickled back that Lee had issued orders that no private property in Pennsylvania should be touched, that looting would be punished by death and that the army would pay for every article it requisitioned – then it needed all the reverence the General had earned to save his popularity. Not turn the men loose in the rich storehouses of that prosperous state? What was General Lee thinking of? And our boys so hungry and needing shoes and clothes and horses!

A hasty note from Darcy Meade to the doctor, the only first-hand information Atlanta received during those first days of July, was passed from hand to hand with mounting indignation.

'Pa, could you manage to get me a pair of boots? I've been barefooted for two weeks now and I don't see any prospects of getting another pair. If I didn't have such big feet I could get them off dead Yankees like the other boys, but I've never yet found a Yankee whose feet were near as big as mine. If you can get me some, don't mail them. Somebody would steal them on the way and I wouldn't blame them. Put Phil on the train and send him up with them. I'll write you soon, where we'll be. Right now I don't know, except that we're marching north. We're in Maryland now and everybody says we're going on into Pennsylvania . . .

'Pa, I thought that we'd give the Yanks a taste of their own medicine but the General says No, and personally I don't care to get shot just for the pleasure of burning some Yank's house. Pa, today we marched through the grandest cornfields you ever saw. We don't have corn like this down home.

Well, I must admit we did a bit of private looting in that corn, for we were all pretty hungry and what the General don't know won't hurt him. But that green corn didn't do us a bit of good. All the boys have got dysentery anyway, and that corn made it worse. It's easier to walk with a leg wound than with dysentery. Pa, do try to manage some boots for me. I'm a captain now, and a captain ought to have boots, even if he hasn't got a new uniform or epaulets.'

But the army was in Pennsylvania – that was all that mattered. One more victory and the war would be over, and then Darcy Meade could have all the boots he wanted, and the boys would come marching home and everybody would be happy again. Mrs Meade's eyes grew wet as she pictured her soldier son home at last, home to stay.

On the third of July, a sudden silence fell on the wires from the North, a silence that lasted till midday of the fourth when fragmentary and garbled reports began to trickle into headquarters in Atlanta. There had been hard fighting in Pennsylvania, near a little town named Gettysburg, a great battle with all Lee's army massed. The news was uncertain, slow in coming, for the battle had been fought in the enemy's territory and the reports came first through Maryland, were relayed to Richmond and then to Atlanta.

Suspense grew and the beginnings of dread slowly crawled over the town. Nothing was so bad as not knowing what was happening. Families with sons at the front prayed fervently that their boys were not in Pennsylvania, but those who knew their relatives were in the same regiment with Darcy Meade clamped their teeth and said it was an honour for them to be in the big fight that would lick the Yankees for good and all.

In Aunt Pitty's house, the three women looked into one another's eyes with fear they could not conceal. Ashley was in Darcy's regiment.

On the fifth came evil tidings, not from the North but from the West. Vicksburg had fallen, fallen after a long and bitter siege, and practically all the Mississippi River, from St. Louis to New Orleans, was in the hands of the Yankees. The Confederacy had been cut in two. At any other time, the news of this disaster would have brought fear and lamentation to Atlanta. But now they could give little thought to Vicksburg. They were thinking of Lee in Pennsylvania, forcing battle. Vicksburg's loss would be no catastrophe if Lee won in the East. There lay Philadelphia, New York, Washington. Their capture would paralyse the North and more than cancel off the defeat on the Mississippi.

The hours dragged by and the black shadow of calamity brooded over the town, obscuring the hot sun until people looked up startled into the sky as if incredulous that it was clear and blue instead of murky and heavy with scudding clouds. Everywhere, women gathered in knots, huddled in groups on front porches, on sidewalks, even in the middle of the streets, telling each other that no news is good news, trying to comfort each other, trying to present a brave appearance. But hideous rumours that Lee was killed, the battle lost, and enormous casualty lists coming in, fled up and down the quiet streets like darting bats. Though they tried not to believe, whole neighbourhoods, swayed by panic, rushed to town, to the newspapers, to headquarters, pleading for news, any news, even bad news.

Crowds formed at the depot, hoping for news from incoming trains, at the telegraph office, in front of the harried headquarters, before the locked doors of the newspapers. They were oddly still crowds, crowds that quietly grew larger and larger. There was no talking. Occasionally an old man's treble voice begged for news, and instead of inciting the crowd to babbling it only intensified the hush as they heard the oft-repeated: 'Nothing on the wires yet from the North except that there's been fighting.' The fringe of women on foot and in carriages grew greater and greater, and the heat of close-packed bodies and dust rising from restless feet were suffocating. The women did not speak, but their pale set faces pleaded with a mute eloquence that was louder than wailing.

There was hardly a house in the town that had not sent away a son, a brother, a father, a lover, a husband, to this battle. They all waited to hear the news that death had come to their homes. They expected death. They did not expect defeat. That thought they dismissed. Their men might be dying, even now, on the sun-parched grass of the Pennsylvania hills. Even now the Southern ranks might be falling like grain before a hailstorm, but the Cause for which they fought could never fall. They might be dying in thousands but, like the fruit of the dragon's teeth, thousands of fresh men in grey and butternut with the Rebel yell on their lips would spring up from the earth to take their places. Where all these men would come from, no one knew. They only knew, as surely as they knew there was a just and jealous God in Heaven, that Lee was miraculous and the Army of Virginia invincible.

Scarlett, Melanie and Miss Pittypat sat in front of the *Daily Examiner* office in the carriage with the top back, sheltered beneath their parasols. Scarlett's hands shook so that her parasol wobbled above her head, Pitty was so excited her nose quivered in her round face like a rabbit's, but Melanie sat as though carved of stone, her dark eyes growing larger and larger as time went by. She made only one remark in two hours, as she took a vial of smelling salts from her reticule and handed it to her aunt, the only time she had ever spoken to her, in her whole life, with anything but tenderest affection.

'Take this, Auntie, and use it if you feel faint. I warn you if you do faint you'll just have to faint and let Uncle Peter take you home, for I'm not going to leave this place till I hear about – till I hear. And I'm not going to let Scarlett leave me, either.'

Scarlett had no intention of leaving, no intention of placing herself where she could not have the first news of Ashley. No, even if Miss Pitty died, she wouldn't leave this spot. Somewhere, Ashley was fighting, perhaps dying, and the newspaper office was the only place where she could learn the truth.

She looked about the crowd, picking out friends and neighbours: Mrs Meade with her bonnet askew and her arm through that of fifteen-year-old Phil; the Misses McLure trying to make their trembling upper lips cover their buck teeth; Mrs Elsing, erect as a Spartan mother, betraying her inner turmoil only by the straggling grey locks that hung from her chignon; and Fanny Elsing white as a ghost. (Surely Fanny wouldn't be so worried about her brother Hugh. Had she a real beau at the front that no one suspected?) Mrs Merriwether sat in her carriage patting Maybelle's hand. Maybelle looked so very pregnant it was a disgrace for her to be out in public, even if she did have her shawl carefully draped over her. Why should she be so worried? Nobody had heard that the Louisiana troops were in Pennsylvania. Probably her hairy little Zouave was safe in Richmond this very minute.

There was a movement on the outskirts of the crowd and those on foot gave way as Rhett Butler carefully edged his horse toward Aunt Pitty's carriage. Scarlett thought: 'He's got courage, coming here at this time when it wouldn't take anything to make this mob tear him to pieces because he isn't in uniform.' As he came nearer, she thought she might be the first to rend him. How dared he sit there on that fine horse, in shining boots and handsome white linen suit, so sleek and well fed, smoking an expensive cigar, when Ashley and all the other boys were fighting the Yankees, barefooted, sweltering in the heat, hungry, their bellies rotten with disease?

Bitter looks were thrown at him as he came slowly through the press. Old men growled in their beards, and Mrs Merriwether, who feared nothing, rose slightly in her carriage and said clearly, 'Speculator!' in a tone that made the word the foulest and most venomous of epithets. He paid no heed to anyone but raised his hat to Melly and Aunt Pitty and, riding to Scarlett's side, leaned down and whispered: 'Don't you think this would be the time for Dr Meade to give us his familiar speech about victory perching like a screaming eagle on our banners?'

Her nerves taut with suspense, she turned on him as swiftly as an angry cat, hot words bubbling to her lips, but he stopped them with a gesture.

'I came to tell you ladies,' he said loudly, 'that I have been to headquarters and the first casualty lists are coming in.'

At these words a hum rose among those near enough to hear his remark, and the crowd surged, ready to turn and run down Whitehall Street toward headquarters.

'Don't go,' he called, rising in his saddle and holding up his hand. 'The lists have been sent to both newspapers and are now being printed. Stay where you are!'

'Oh, Captain Butler,' cried Melly, turning to him with tears in her eyes. 'How kind of you to come and tell us! When will they be posted?'

'They should be out any minute, Madam. The reports have been in the offices for half an hour now. The major in charge didn't want to let that out until the printing was done, for fear the crowd would wreck the offices trying to get news. Ah! Look!'

The side window of the newspaper office opened and a hand was extended, bearing a sheaf of long narrow galley proofs, smeared with fresh ink and thick with names closely printed. The crowd fought for them, tearing the slips in half, those obtaining them trying to back out through the crowd to read, those behind pushing forward, crying: 'Let me through!'

'Hold the reins,' said Rhett shortly, swinging to the ground and tossing the bridle to Uncle Peter. They saw his heavy shoulders towering above the crowd as he went through, brutally pushing and shoving. In a while he was back, with half a dozen in his hands. He tossed one to Melanie and distributed the others among the ladies in the nearest carriages, the Misses McLure, Mrs Meade, Mrs Merriwether, Mrs Elsing.

'Quick, Melly,' cried Scarlett, her heart in her throat, exasperation sweeping her as she saw that Melly's hands were shaking so that it was impossible for her to read.

'Take it,' whispered Melly, and Scarlett snatched it from her. The Ws. Where were the Ws? Oh, there they were at the bottom and all smeared up. 'White,' she read and her voice shook, 'Wilkins . . . Winn . . . Zebulon . . . Oh, Melly, he's not on it! He's not on it! Oh, for God's sake, Auntie! Melly, pick up the salts! Hold her up, Melly.'

Melly, weeping openly with happiness, steadied Miss Pitty's rolling head and held the smelling salts under her nose. Scarlett braced the fat old lady on the other side, her heart singing with joy. Ashley was alive. He wasn't even wounded. How good God was to pass him by! How—

She heard a low moan and, turning, saw Fanny Elsing lay her head on her mother's bosom, saw the casualty list flutter to the floor of the carriage, saw Mrs Elsing's thin lips quiver as she gathered her daughter in her arms and said quietly to the coachman: 'Home. Quickly.' Scarlett took a quick glance at the lists. Hugh Elsing was not listed. Fanny must have had a beau and now he was dead. The crowd made way in sympathetic silence for the Elsings' carriage, and after them followed the little wicker pony cart of the McLure girls. Miss Faith was driving, her face like a rock, and, for once, her teeth were covered by her lips. Miss Hope, death in her face, sat erect beside her, holding her sister's skirt in a tight grasp. They looked like very old women. Their young brother Dallas was their darling and the only relative the maiden ladies had in the world. Dallas was gone.

'Melly! Melly!' cried Maybelle, joy in her voice, 'René is safe! And Ashley, too! Oh, thank God!' The shawl had slipped from her shoulders and her condition was most obvious but, for once, neither she nor Mrs Merriwether cared. 'Oh, Mrs Meade! René—' Her voice changed, swiftly. 'Melly, look! – Mrs Meade, please! Darcy isn't—?'

Mrs Meade was looking down into her lap and she did not raise her head when her name was called, but the face of little Phil beside her was an open book that all might read.

'There, there, Mother,' he said helplessly. Mrs Meade looked up, meeting Melanie's eyes.

'He won't need those boots now,' she said.

'Oh, darling!' cried Melly, beginning to sob, as she shoved Aunt Pitty on to Scarlett's shoulder and scrambled out of the carriage and toward that of the doctor's wife.

'Mother, you've still got me,' said Phil, in a forlorn effort at comforting the white-faced woman beside him. 'And if you'll just let me, I'll go kill all the Yank—'

Mrs Meade clutched his arm as if she would never let it go, said 'No!' in a strangled voice and seemed to choke.

'Phil Meade, you hush your mouth!' hissed Melanie, climbing in beside Mrs Meade and taking her in her arms. 'Do you think it'll help your mother to have you off getting shot too? I never heard anything so silly. Drive us home, quick!'

She turned to Scarlett as Phil picked up the reins.

'As soon as you take Auntie home, come over to Mrs Meade's. Captain Butler, can you get word to the doctor? He's at the hospital.'

The carriage moved off through the dispersing crowd. Some of the women were weeping with joy, but most looked too stunned to realize the heavy blows that had fallen upon them. Scarlett bent her head over the blurred lists, reading rapidly, to find names of friends. Now that Ashley was safe she could think of other people. Oh, how long the list was! How heavy the toll from Atlanta, from all of Georgia!

Good Heavens! 'Calvert – Raiford, Lieutenant.' Raif! Suddenly she remembered the day, so long ago, when they had run away together but decided to come home at nightfall because they were hungry and afraid of the dark.

'Fontaine – Joseph K., private.' Little bad-tempered Joe! And Sally hardly over having her baby!

'Munroe – LaFayette, Captain.' And Lafe had been engaged to Cathleen Calvert. Poor Cathleen! Hers had been a double loss, a brother and a sweetheart. But Sally's loss was greater – a brother and a husband.

Oh, this was too terrible. She was almost afraid to read further. Aunt Pitty was heaving and sighing on her shoulder and, with small ceremony, Scarlett pushed her over into a corner of the carriage and continued her reading.

Surely, surely – there couldn't be three 'Tarleton' names on that list. Perhaps – perhaps the hurried printer had repeated the name by error. But no. There they were. 'Tarleton – Brenton, Lieutenant.' 'Tarleton – Stuart, Corporal.' 'Tarleton – Thomas, private.' And Boyd, dead the first year of the war, was buried God knew where in Virginia. All the Tarleton boys gone. Tom and the lazy long-legged twins with their love of gossip and their absurd practical jokes and Boyd who had the grace of a dancing master and the tongue of a wasp.

She could not read any more. She could not know if any other of those boys with whom she had grown up, danced, flirted, kissed were on that list. She wished that she could cry, do something to ease the iron fingers that were digging into her throat.

'I'm sorry, Scarlett,' said Rhett. She looked up at him. She had forgotten he was still there. 'Many of your friends?'

She nodded and struggled to speak: 'About every family in the County – and all – all three of the Tarleton boys.'

His face was quiet, almost sombre, and there was no mockery in his eyes.

'And the end is not yet,' he said. 'These are just the first lists and they're incomplete. There'll be a longer list tomorrow.' He lowered his voice so that those in the near-by carriages could not hear. 'Scarlett, General Lee must have lost the battle. I heard at headquarters that he had retreated back into Maryland.'

She raised frightened eyes to his, but her fear did not spring from Lee's defeat. Longer casualty lists tomorrow! Tomorrow. She had not thought of tomorrow, so happy was she at first that Ashley's name was not on that list. Tomorrow. Why, right this minute he might be dead and she would not know until tomorrow, or perhaps a week from tomorrow.

'Oh, Rhett, why do there have to be wars? It would have been so much better for the Yankees to pay for the darkies – or even for us to give them the darkies free of charge than to have this happen.'

'It isn't the darkies, Scarlett. They're just the excuse. There'll always be wars because men love wars. Women don't, but men do – yea, passing the love of women.'

His mouth twisted in his old smile and the seriousness was gone from his face. He lifted his wide Panama hat.

'Good-bye. I'm going to find Dr Meade. I imagine the irony of me being the one to tell him of his son's death will be lost on him, just now. But later, he'll probably hate to think that a speculator brought the news of a hero's death.'

Scarlett put Miss Pitty to bed with a toddy, left Prissy and Cookie in attendance and went down the street to the Meade house. Mrs Meade was upstairs with Phil, waiting her husband's return, and Melanie sat in the parlour, talking in a low voice to a group of sympathetic neighbours. She was busy with needle and scissors, altering a mourning dress that Mrs Elsing had lent to Mrs Meade. Already the house was full of the acrid smell of clothes boiling in home-made black dye for, in the kitchen, the sobbing cook was stirring all of Mrs Meade's dresses in the huge wash-pot.

'How is she?' questioned Scarlett softly.

'Not a tear,' said Melanie. 'It's terrible when women can't cry. I don't know how men stand things without crying. I guess it's because they're stronger and braver than women. She says she's going to Pennsylvania by herself to bring him home. The doctor can't leave the hospital.'

'It will be dreadful for her! Why can't Phil go?'

'She's afraid he'll join the army if he gets out of her sight. You know he's so big for his age and they're taking them at sixteen now.'

One by one the neighbours slipped away, reluctant to be present when the doctor came home, and Scarlett and Melanie were left alone, sewing in the parlour. Melanie looked sad but tranquil, though tears dropped down on the cloth she held in her hands. Evidently she had not thought that the battle might still be going on and Ashley perhaps dead at this very moment. With panic in her heart, Scarlett did not know whether to tell Melanie of Rhett's words and have the dubious comfort of her misery or keep it to herself. Finally she decided to remain quiet. It would never do for Melanie to think her too worried about Ashley. She thanked God that everyone, Melly and Pitty included, had been too engrossed in their own worries that morning to notice her conduct.

After an interval of silent sewing, they heard sounds outside and, peering through the curtains, they saw Dr Meade alighting from his horse. His shoulders were sagging and his head bowed until his grey beard spread out fanlike on his chest. He came slowly into the house and, laying down his hat and bag, kissed both the girls silently. Then he went tiredly up the stairs. In a moment Phil came down, all long legs and arms and awkwardness. The two girls looked an invitation to join them, but he went on to the front porch and, seating himself on the top step, dropped his head on his cupped palm.

Melly sighed.

'He's mad because they won't let him go fight the Yankees. Fifteen years old! Oh, Scarlett, it would be Heaven to have a son like that!'

'And have him get killed?' said Scarlett shortly, thinking of Darcy.

'It would be better to have a son even if he did get killed than to never have one,' said Melanie and gulped. 'You can't understand, Scarlett, because you've got little Wade, but I— Oh, Scarlett, I want a baby so bad! I know you think I'm horrid to say it right out, but it's true and only what every woman wants and you know it.'

Scarlett restrained herself from sniffing.

'If God should will that Ashley should be – taken, I suppose I could bear it, though I'd rather die if he died. But God would give me strength to bear it. But I could not bear having him dead and not having – not having a child of his to comfort me. Oh, Scarlett, how lucky you are! Though you lost Charlie, you have his son. And if Ashley goes, I'll have nothing. Scarlett, forgive me, but sometimes I've been so jealous of you—'

'Jealous – of me?' cried Scarlett, stricken with guilt.

'Because you have a son and I haven't. I've even pretended sometimes that Wade was mine because it's so awful not to have a child.'

'Fiddle-dee-dee!' said Scarlett in relief. She cast a quick glance at the slight figure with blushing face bent over the sewing. Melanie might want children but she certainly did not have the figure for bearing them. She was hardly taller than a twelve-year-old child, her hips were as narrow as a child's and her breasts were very flat. The very thought of Melanie having a child was repellent to Scarlett. It brought up too many thoughts she couldn't bear thinking. If Melanie should have a child of Ashley's, it would be as though something were taken from Scarlett that was her own.

'Do forgive me for saying that about Wade. You know I love him so. You aren't mad at me, are you?'

'Don't be silly,' said Scarlett shortly. 'And go out on the porch and do something for Phil. He's crying.'

Chapter XV

The army, driven back into Virginia, went into winter quarters on the Rapidan – a tired, depleted army since the defeat at Gettysburg – and as the Christmas season approached, Ashley came home on furlough. Scarlett, seeing him for the first time in more than two years, was frightened by the violence of her feelings. When she had stood in the parlour at Twelve Oaks and seen him married to Melanie, she had thought she could never love him with a more heartbreaking intensity than she did at that moment. But now she knew her feelings of that long-past night were those of a spoiled child thwarted of a toy. Now, her emotions were sharpened by her long dreams of him, heightened by the repression she had been forced to put on her tongue.

This Ashley Wilkes in his faded, patched uniform, his blond hair bleached tow by summer suns, was a different man from the easy-going, drowsy-eyed boy she had loved to desperation before the war. And he was a thousand times more thrilling. He was bronzed and lean now, where he had once been fair and slender, and the long golden moustache drooping about his mouth, cavalry style, was the last touch needed to make him the perfect picture of a soldier.

He stood with military straightness in his old uniform, his pistol in its worn holster, his battered scabbard smartly slapping his high boots, his tarnished spurs dully gleaming – Major Ashley Wilkes, C.S.A. The habit of command sat upon him now, a quiet air of self-reliance and authority, and grim lines were beginning to emerge about his mouth. There was something new and strange about the square set of his shoulders and the cool bright gleam of his eyes. Where he had once been lounging and indolent, he was now as alert as a prowling cat, with the tense alertness of one whose nerves are perpetually drawn as tight as the strings on a violin. In his eyes, there was a fagged, haunted look, and the sunburned skin was tight across the fine bones of his face – her same handsome Ashley, yet so very different.

Scarlett had made her plans to spend Christmas at Tara, but after Ashley's telegram came no power on earth, not even a direct command from the disappointed Ellen, could drag her away from Atlanta. Had Ashley intended going to Twelve Oaks, she would have hastened to Tara to be near him; but he had written his family to join him in Atlanta, and Mr Wilkes and Honey and India were already in town. Go home to Tara and miss seeing him, after two long years? Miss the heart-quickening sound of his voice, miss reading in his eyes that he had not forgotten her? Never! Not for all the mothers in the world.

Ashley came home four days before Christmas, with a group of the County boys also on furlough, a sadly diminished group since Gettysburg. Cade Calvert was among them, a thin, gaunt Cade, who coughed continually, two of the Munroe boys, bubbling with the excitement of their first leave since 1861, and Alex and Tony Fontaine, splendidly drunk, boisterous and quarrelsome. The group had two hours to wait between trains and, as it was taxing the diplomacy of the sober members of the party to keep the Fontaines from fighting each other and perfect strangers in the depot, Ashley brought them all home to Aunt Pittypat's.

'You'd think they'd had enough fighting in Virginia,' said Cade bitterly, as he watched the two bristle like gamecocks over who should be the first to kiss the fluttering and flattered Aunt Pitty. 'But no. They've been drunk and picking fights ever since we got to Richmond. The provost guard took them up there and if it hadn't been for Ashley's slick tongue, they'd have spent Christmas in jail.'

But Scarlett hardly heard a word he said, so enraptured was she at being in the same room with Ashley again. How could she have thought during these two years that other men were nice or handsome or exciting? How could she have even endured hearing them make love to her when Ashley was in the world? He was home again, separated from her only by the width of the parlour rug, and it took all her strength not to dissolve in happy tears every time she looked at him sitting there on the sofa with Melly on one side and India on the other and Honey hanging over his shoulder. If only she had the right to sit there beside him, her arm through his! If only she could pat his sleeve every few minutes to make sure he was really there, hold his hand and use his handkerchief to wipe away her tears of joy. For Melanie was doing all these things, unashamedly. Too happy to be shy and reserved, she hung on her husband's arm and adored him openly with her eyes, with her smiles, her tears. And Scarlett was too happy to resent this, too glad to be jealous. Ashley was home at last!

Now and then she put her hand up to her cheek where he had kissed her and felt again the thrill of his lips and smiled at him. He had not kissed her first, of course. Melly had hurled herself into his arms, crying incoherently, holding him as though she would never let him go. And then, India and Honey had hugged him, fairly tearing him from Melanie's arms. Then he had kissed his father, with a dignified affectionate embrace that showed the strong quiet feeling that lay between them. And then Aunt Pitty, who was jumping up and down on her inadequate little feet with excitement. Finally he turned to her, surrounded by all the boys who were claiming their kisses, and said: 'Oh, Scarlett! You pretty, pretty thing!' and kissed her on the cheek.

With that kiss, everything she had intended to say in welcome took wings. Not until hours later did she recall that he had not kissed her on the lips. Then she wondered feverishly if he would have done it had she met him alone, bending his tall body over hers, pulling her up on tiptoe, holding her for a long, long time. And because it made her happy to think so, she believed that he would. But there would be time for all things, a whole week! Surely she could manoeuvre to get him alone and say: 'Do you remember those rides we used to take down our secret bridle paths?' 'Do you remember how the moon looked that night when we sat on the steps at Tara and you quoted that poem?' (Good Heavens! What was the name of that poem, anyway?) 'Do you remember that afternoon when I sprained my ankle and you carried me home in your arms in the twilight?'

Oh, there were so many things she would preface with 'Do you remember?' So many dear memories that would bring back to him those lovely days when they roamed the County like care-free children, so many things that would call to mind the days before Melanie Hamilton entered on the scene. And while they talked she could perhaps read in his eyes some quickening of emotion, some hint that behind the barrier of husbandly affection for Melanie he still cared, cared as passionately as on that day of the barbecue when he burst forth with the truth. It did not occur to her to plan just what they would do if Ashley should declare his love for her in unmistakable words. It would be enough to know that he did care . . . Yes, she could wait, could let Melanie have her happy hour of squeezing his arm and crying. Her time would come. After all, what did a girl like Melanie know of love?

'Darling, you look like a ragamuffin,' said Melanie when the first excitement of homecoming was over. 'Who did mend your uniform and why did they use blue patches?'

'I thought I looked perfectly dashing,' said Ashley, considering his appearance. 'Just compare me with those rag-tags over there and you'll appreciate me more. Mose mended the uniform and I thought he did very well, considering that he'd never had a needle in his hand before the war. About the blue cloth, when it comes to a choice between having holes in your britches or patching them with pieces of a captured Yankee uniform – well, there just isn't any choice. And as for looking like a ragamuffin, you should thank your stars your husband didn't come home barefooted. Last week my old boots wore completely out, and I would have come home with sacks tied on my feet if we hadn't had the good luck to shoot two Yankee scouts. The boots of one of them fitted me perfectly.'

He stretched out his long legs in their scarred high boots for them to admire.

'And the boots of the other scout didn't fit me,' said Cade. 'They're two sizes too small and they're killing me this minute. But I'm going home in style just the same.'

'And the selfish swine won't give them to either of us,' said Tony. 'And they'd fit our small, aristocratic Fontaine feet perfectly. Hell's afire, I'm ashamed to face Mother in these brogans. Before the war she wouldn't have let one of our darkies wear them.'

'Don't worry,' said Alex, eyeing Cade's boots. 'We'll take them off of him on the train going home. I don't mind facing Mother but I'm da— I mean, I don't intend for Dimity Munroe to see my toes sticking out.'

'Why, they're my boots. I claimed them first,' said Tony, beginning to scowl at his brother; and Melanie, fluttering with fear at the possibility of one of the famous Fontaine quarrels, interposed and made peace.

'I had a full beard to show you girls,' said Ashley, ruefully rubbing his face where half-healed razor nicks still showed. 'It was a beautiful beard and if I do say it myself, neither Jeb Stuart nor Nathan Bedford Forrest had a handsomer one. But when we got to Richmond, those two scoundrels,' indicating the Fontaines, 'decided that as they were shaving their beards, mine should come off too. They got me down and shaved me, and it's a wonder my head didn't come off along with the beard. It was only by the intervention of Evan and Cade that my moustache was saved.'

'Snakes! Mrs Wilkes! You ought to thank us. You'd never have recognized him and wouldn't have let him in the door,' said Alex. 'We did it to show our appreciation of his talking the provost guard out of putting us in jail. If you say the word, we'll take the moustache off for you, right now.'

'Oh, no, thank you!' said Melanie hastily, clutching Ashley in a frightened way, for the two swarthy little men looked capable of any violence. 'I think it's perfectly lovely.'

'That's love,' said the Fontaines, nodding gravely at each other.

When Ashley went out into the cold to see the boys off to the depot in Aunt Pitty's carriage, Melanie caught Scarlett's arm.

'Isn't his uniform dreadful? Won't my coat be a surprise? Oh, if I only had enough cloth for britches too!'

That coat for Ashley was a sore subject with Scarlett, for she wished so ardently that she and not Melanie were bestowing it as a Christmas gift. Grey wool for uniforms was now almost literally more priceless than rubies, and Ashley was wearing the familiar homespun. Even butternut was now none too plentiful, and many of the soldiers were dressed in captured Yankee uniforms which had been turned a dark-brown colour with walnut-shell dye. But Melanie, by rare luck, had come into possession of enough grey broadcloth to make a coat – a rather short coat but a coat just the same. She had nursed a Charleston boy in the hospital and when he died had clipped a lock of his hair and sent it to his mother, along with the scant contents of his pockets and a comforting account of his last hours which made no mention of the torment in which he had died. A correspondence had sprung up between them and, learning that Melanie had a husband at the front, the mother had sent her the length of grey cloth and brass buttons which she had bought for her dead son. It was a beautiful piece of material, thick and warm and with a dull sheen to it, undoubtedly blockade goods and undoubtedly very expensive. It was now in the hands of the tailor and Melanie was hurrying him to have it ready by Christmas morning. Scarlett would have given anything to be able to provide the rest of the uniform, but the necessary materials were simply not to be had in Atlanta.

She had a Christmas present for Ashley, but it paled in insignificance beside the glory of Melanie's grey coat. It was a small 'housewife', made of flannel, containing the whole precious pack of needles Rhett had brought her from Nassau, three of her linen handkerchiefs, obtained from the same source, two spools of thread and a small pair of scissors. But she wanted to give him something more personal, something a wife could give a husband, a shirt, a pair of gauntlets, a hat. Oh, yes, a hat by all means. That little flat-topped forage cap Ashley was wearing looked ridiculous. Scarlett had always hated them. What if Stonewall Jackson had worn one in preference to a slouch felt? That didn't make them any more dignified-looking. But the only hats obtainable in Atlanta were crudely made wool hats, and they were tackier than the monkey-hat forage caps.

When she thought of hats, she thought of Rhett Butler. He had so many hats, wide Panamas for summer, tall beavers for formal occasions, hunting hats, slouch hats of tan and black and blue. What need had he for so many when her darling Ashley rode in the rain with moisture dripping down his collar from the back of his cap?

'I'll make Rhett give me that new black felt of his,' she decided. 'And I'll put a grey ribbon around the brim and sew Ashley's wreath on it and it will look lovely.'

She paused and thought it might be difficult to get the hat without some explanation. She simply could not tell Rhett she wanted it for Ashley. He would raise his brows in that nasty way he always had when she even mentioned Ashley's name and, like as not, would refuse to give her the hat. Well, she'd make up some pitiful story about a soldier in the hospital who needed it and Rhett need never know the truth.

All that afternoon, she manoeuvred to be alone with Ashley, even for a few minutes, but Melanie was beside him constantly, and India and Honey, their pale, lashless eyes glowing, followed him about the house. Even John Wilkes, visibly proud of his son, had no opportunity for quiet conversation with him.

It was the same at supper where they all plied him with questions about the war. The war! Who cared about the war? Scarlett didn't think Ashley cared very much for that subject either. He talked at length, laughed frequently and dominated the conversation more completely than she had ever seen him do before, but he seemed to say very little. He told them jokes and funny stories about friends, talked gaily about makeshifts, making light of hunger and long marches in the rain, and described in detail how General Lee had looked when he rode by on the retreat from Gettysburg and questioned: 'Gentlemen, are you Georgia troops? Well, we can't get along without you Georgians!'

It seemed to Scarlett that he was talking feverishly to keep them from asking questions he did not want to answer. When she saw his eyes falter and drop before the long, troubled gaze of his father, a faint worry and bewilderment rose in her as to what was hidden in Ashley's heart. But it soon passed, for there was no room in her mind for anything except a radiant happiness and a driving desire to be alone with him.

The radiance lasted until everyone in the circle about the open fire began to yawn, and Mr Wilkes and the girls took their departure for the hotel. Then as Ashley and Melanie and Pittypat and Scarlett mounted the stairs, lighted by Uncle Peter, a chill fell on her spirit. Until that moment when they stood in the upstairs hall, Ashley had been hers, only hers, even if she had not had a private word with him that whole afternoon. But now, as she said good night, she saw that Melanie's cheeks were suddenly crimson and she was trembling. Her eyes were on the carpet and, though she seemed overcome with some frightening emotion, she seemed shyly happy. Melanie did not even look up when Ashley opened the bedroom door, but sped inside. Ashley said good night abruptly, and he did not meet Scarlett's eyes either.

The door closed behind them, leaving Scarlett open-mouthed and suddenly desolate. Ashley was no longer hers. He was Melanie's. And as long as Melanie lived, she could go into rooms with Ashley and close the door – and close out the rest of the world.

Now Ashley was going away, back to Virginia, back to the long marches in the sleet, to hungry bivouacs in the snow, to pain and hardship and to the risk of all the bright beauty of his golden head and proud slender body being blotted out in an instant, like an ant beneath a careless heel. The past week with its shimmering, dreamlike beauty, its crowded hours of happiness, was gone.

The week had passed swiftly, like a dream, a dream fragrant with the smell of pine boughs and Christmas trees, bright with little candles and home-made tinsel, a dream where minutes flew as rapidly as heartbeats. Such a breathless week when something within her drove Scarlett with mingled pain and pleasure to pack and cram every minute with incidents to remember after he was gone, happenings which she could examine at leisure in the long months ahead, extracting every morsel of comfort from them – dance, sing, laugh, fetch and carry for Ashley, anticipate his wants, smile when he smiles, be silent when he talks, follow him with your eyes so that each line of his erect body, each lift of his eyebrows, each quirk of his mouth, will be indelibly printed on your mind – for a week goes by so fast and the war goes on forever.

She sat on the divan in the parlour, holding her going-away gift for him in her lap, waiting while he said good-bye to Melanie, praying that when he did come down the stairs he would be alone and she might be granted by Heaven a few moments alone with him. Her ears strained for sounds from upstairs, but the house was oddly still, so still that even the sound of her breathing seemed loud. Aunt Pittypat was crying into her pillows in her room, for Ashley had told her good-bye half an hour before. No sounds of murmuring voices or of tears came from behind the closed door of Melanie's bedroom. It seemed to Scarlett that he had been in that room for hours, and she resented bitterly each moment that he stayed, saying good-bye to his wife, for the moments were slipping by so fast and his time was so short.

She thought of all the things she had intended to say to him during this week. But there had been no opportunity to say them, and she knew now that perhaps she would never have the chance to say them.

Such foolish little things, some of them: 'Ashley, you will be careful, won't you?' 'Please don't get your feet wet. You take cold so easily.' 'Don't forget to put a newspaper across your chest under your shirt. It keeps out the wind so well.' But there were other things, more important things she had wanted to say, much more important things she had wanted to hear him say, things she had wanted to read in his eyes, even if he did not speak them.

So many things to say and now there was no time! Even the few minutes that remained might be snatched away from her if Melanie followed him to the door, to the carriage block. Why hadn't she made the opportunity during this last week? But always, Melanie was at his side, her eyes caressing him adoringly, always friends and neighbours and relatives were in the house and, from morning till night, Ashley was never alone. Then, at night, the door of the bedroom closed and he was alone with Melanie. Never once during these last days had he betrayed to Scarlett by one look, one word, anything but the affection a brother might show a sister or a friend, a lifelong friend. She could not let him go away, perhaps forever, without knowing whether he still loved her. Then, even if he died, she could nurse the warm comfort of his secret love to the end of her days.

After what seemed an eternity of waiting, she heard the sound of his boots in the bedroom above and the door opening and closing. She heard him coming down the steps. Alone! Thank God for that! Melanie must be too overcome by the grief of parting to leave her room. Now she would have him for herself for a few precious minutes.

He came down the steps slowly, his spurs clinking, and she could hear the faint slap-slap of his sabre against his high boots. When he came into the parlour, his eyes were sombre. He was trying to smile but his face was as white and drawn as a man bleeding from an internal wound. She rose as he entered, thinking with proprietary pride that he was the handsomest soldier she had ever seen. His long holster and belt glistened and his silver spurs and scabbard gleamed, from the industrious polishing Uncle Peter had given them. His new coat did not fit very well, for the tailor had been hurried and some of the seams were awry. The bright new sheen of the grey coat was sadly at variance with the worn and patched butternut trousers and the scarred boots, but if he had been clothed in silver armour he could not have looked more the shining knight to her.

'Ashley,' she begged abruptly, 'may I go to the train with you?'

'Please don't. Father and the girls will be there. And anyway, I'd rather remember you saying good-bye to me here than shivering at the depot. There's so much to memories.'

Instantly she abandoned her plan. If India and Honey who disliked her so much were to be present at the leave-taking, she would have no chance for a private word.

'Then I won't go,' she said. 'See, Ashley! I've another present for you.'

A little shy, now that the time had come to give it to him, she unrolled the package. It was a long yellow sash, made of thick China silk and edged with heavy fringe. Rhett Butler had brought her a yellow shawl from Havana several months before, a shawl gaudily embroidered with birds and flowers in magenta and blue. During this last week, she had patiently picked out all the embroidery and cut up the square of silk and stitched it into a sash length.

'Scarlett, it's beautiful! Did you make it yourself? Then I'll value it all the more. Put it on me, my dear. The boys will be green with envy when they see me in the glory of my new coat and sash.'

She wrapped the bright lengths about his slender waist, above his belt, and tied the ends in a lover's knot. Melanie might have given him his new coat but this sash was her gift, her own secret guerdon for him to wear into battle, something that would make him remember her every time he looked at it. She stood back and viewed him with pride, thinking that even Jeb Stuart with his flaunting sash and plume could not look so dashing as her cavalier.

'It's beautiful,' he repeated, fingering the fringe. 'But I know you've cut up a dress or a shawl to make it. You shouldn't have done it, Scarlett. Pretty things are too hard to get these days.'

'Oh, Ashley, I'd—'

She had started to say: 'I'd cut up my heart for you to wear if you wanted it,' but she finished, 'I'd do anything for you!'

'Would you?' he questioned, and some of the sombreness lifted from his face. 'Then, there's something you can do for me, Scarlett, something that will make my mind easier when I'm away.'

'What is it?' she asked joyfully, ready to promise prodigies.

'Scarlett, will you look after Melanie for me?'

'Look after Melly?'

Her heart sank with bitter disappointment. So this was his last request of her, when she so yearned to promise something beautiful, something spectacular! And then anger flared. This moment was her moment with Ashley, hers alone. And yet, though Melanie was absent, her pale shadow lay between them. How could he bring up her name in their moment of farewell? How could he ask such a thing of her?

He did not notice the disappointment on her face. As of old, his eyes were looking through her and beyond her, at something else, not seeing her at all.

'Yes, keep an eye on her, take care of her. She's so frail and she doesn't realize it. She'll wear herself out nursing and sewing. And she's so gentle and timid. Except for Aunt Pitty and Uncle Henry and you, she hasn't a close relative in the world, except the Burrs in Macon and they're third cousins. And Aunt Pitty – Scarlett, you know she's like a child. And Uncle Henry is an old man. Melanie loves you so much, not just because you were Charlie's wife, but because – well, because you're you and she loves you like a sister. Scarlett, I have nightmares when I think what might happen to her if I were killed and she had no one to turn to. Will you promise?'

She did not even hear his last request, so terrified was she by those ill-omened words, 'if I were killed'.

Every day she had read the casualty lists, read them with her heart in her throat, knowing that the world would end if anything should happen to him. But always, always, she had an inner feeling that even if the Confederate Army were entirely wiped out, Ashley would be spared. And now he had spoken the frightful words! Goose-bumps came out all over her and fear swamped her, a superstitious fear she could not combat with reason. She was Irish enough to believe in second sight, especially where death premonitions were concerned, and in his wide grey eyes she saw some deep sadness which she could only interpret as that of a man who has felt the cold finger on his shoulder, has heard the wail of the Banshee.

'You mustn't say it! You mustn't even think it. It's bad luck to speak of death! Oh, say a prayer, quickly!'

'You say it for me and light some candles, too,' he said, smiling at the frightened urgency in her voice.

But she could not answer, so stricken was she by the pictures her mind was drawing, Ashley lying dead in the snows of Virginia, so far away from her. He went on speaking and there was a quality in his voice, a sadness, a resignation, that increased her fear until every vestige of anger and disappointment was blotted out.

'I'm asking you for this reason, Scarlett. I cannot tell what will happen to me or what will happen to any of us. But when the end comes, I shall be far away from here, even if I am alive, too far away to look out for Melanie.

'The – the end?'

'The end of the war – and the end of the world.'

'But, Ashley, surely you can't think the Yankees will beat us? All this week you've talked about how strong General Lee—'

'All this week I've talked lies, like all men talk when they're on furlough. Why should I frighten Melanie and Aunt Pitty before there's any need for them to be frightened? Yes, Scarlett, I think the Yankees have us. Gettysburg was the beginning of the end. The people back home don't know it yet. They can't realize how things stand with us, but— Scarlett, some of my men are barefooted now and the snow is deep in Virginia. And when I see their poor frozen feet, wrapped in rags and old sacks, and see the blood-prints they leave in the snow, and know that I've got a whole pair of boots – well, I feel like I should give mine away and be barefooted too.'

'Oh, Ashley, promise me you won't give them away!'

'When I see things like that and then look at the Yankees – then I see the end of everything. Why, Scarlett, the Yankees are buying soldiers from Europe by the thousands! Most of the prisoners we've taken recently can't even speak English. They're Germans and Poles and wild Irishmen who talk Gaelic. But when we lose a man, he can't be replaced. When our shoes wear out, there are no more shoes. We're bottled up, Scarlett. And we can't fight the whole world.'

She thought wildly: 'Let the whole Confederacy crumble in the dust. Let the world end, but you must not die! I couldn't live if you were dead!'

'I hope you will not repeat what I have said, Scarlett. I do not want to alarm the others. And, my dear, I would not have alarmed you by saying these things, were it not that I had to explain why I ask you to look after Melanie. She's so frail and weak and you're so strong, Scarlett. It will be a comfort to me to know that you two are together if anything happens to me. You will promise, won't you?'

'Oh, yes!' she cried, for at that moment, seeing death at his elbow, she would have promised anything. 'Ashley, Ashley! I can't let you go away! I simply can't be brave about it!'

'You must be brave,' he said, and his voice changed subtly. It was resonant, deeper, and his words fell swiftly as though hurried with some inner urgency. 'You must be brave. For how else can I stand it?'

Her eyes sought his face quickly and with joy, wondering if he meant that leaving her was breaking his heart, even as it was breaking hers. His face was as drawn as when he came down from bidding Melanie good-bye, but she could read nothing in his eyes. He leaned down, took her face in his hands, and kissed her lightly on the forehead.

'Scarlett! Scarlett! You are so fine and strong and good. So beautiful, not just your sweet face, my dear, but all of you, your body and your mind and your soul.'

'Oh, Ashley,' she whispered happily, thrilling at his words and his touch on her face. 'Nobody else but you ever—'

'I like to think that perhaps I know you better than most people and that I can see beautiful things buried deep in you that others are too careless and too hurried to notice.'

He stopped speaking and his hands dropped from her face, but his eyes still clung to her eyes. She waited a moment, breathless for him to continue, a-tiptoe to hear him say the magic three words. But they did not come. She searched his face frantically, her lips quivering, for she saw he had finished speaking.

This second blighting of her hopes was more than heart could bear and she cried 'Oh!' in a childish whisper and sat down, tears stinging her eyes. Then she heard an ominous sound in the driveway, outside the window, a sound that brought home to her even more sharply the imminence of Ashley's departure. A pagan hearing the lapping of the waters around Charon's boat could not have felt more desolate. Uncle Peter, muffled in a quilt, was bringing out the carriage to take Ashley to the train.

Ashley said 'Good-bye,' very softly, caught up from the table the wide felt hat she had inveigled from Rhett and walked into the dark front hall. His hand on the door-knob, he turned and looked at her, a long, desperate look, as if he wanted to carry away with him every detail of her face and figure. Through a blinding mist of tears she saw his face and with a strangling pain in her throat she knew that he was going away, away from her care, away from the safe haven of this house, out of her life, perhaps forever, without having spoken the words she so yearned to hear. Time was going by like a mill-race, and now it was too late. She ran stumbling across the parlour and into the hall and clutched the ends of his sash.

'Kiss me,' she whispered. 'Kiss me good-bye.'

His arms went around her gently, and he bent his head to her face. At the first touch of his lips on hers, her arms were about his neck in a strangling grip. For a fleeting immeasurable instant, he pressed her body close to his. Then she felt a sudden tensing of all his muscles. Swiftly, he dropped the hat to the floor and, reaching up, detached her arms from his neck.

'No, Scarlett, no,' he said in a low voice, holding her crossed wrists in a grip that hurt.

'I love you,' she said, choking. 'I've always loved you. I've never loved anybody else. I just married Charlie to – to try to hurt you. Oh, Ashley, I love you so much I'd walk every step of the way to Virginia just to be near you! And I'd cook for you and polish your boots and groom your horse— Ashley, say you love me! I'll live on it for the rest of my life.'

He bent suddenly to retrieve his hat and she had one glimpse of his face. It was the unhappiest face she was ever to see, a face from which all aloofness had fled. Written on it were his love for her and joy that she loved him, but battling them both were shame and despair.

'Good-bye,' he said hoarsely.

The door clicked open and a gust of cold wind swept the house, fluttering the curtains. Scarlett shivered as she watched him run down the walk to the carriage, his sabre glinting in the feeble winter sunlight, the fringe of his sash dancing jauntily.

Chapter XVI

January and February of 1864 passed, full of cold rains and wild winds, clouded by pervasive gloom and depression. In addition to the defeats at Gettysburg and Vicksburg, the centre of the Southern line had caved. After hard fighting, nearly all of Tennessee was now held by the Union troops. But even with this loss on top of the others, the South's spirit was not broken. True, grim determination had taken the place of high-hearted hopes, but people could still find a silver lining in the cloud. For one thing, the Yankees had been stoutly repulsed in September when they had tried to follow up their victories in Tennessee by an advance into Georgia.

Here in the north-westernmost corner of the state, at Chickamauga, serious fighting had occurred on Georgia soil for the first time since the war began. The Yankees had taken Chattanooga and then had marched through the mountain passes into Georgia, but they had been driven back with heavy losses.

Atlanta and its railroads had played a big part in making Chickamauga a great victory for the South. Over the railroads that led down from Virginia to Atlanta and then northward to Tennessee, General Longstreet's corps had been rushed to the scene of the battle. Along the entire route of several hundred miles, the tracks had been cleared and all the available rolling stock in the South-east had been assembled for the movement.

Atlanta had watched while train after train rolled through the town, hour after hour, passenger coaches, box cars, flat cars, filled with shouting men. They had come without food or sleep, without their horses, ambulances or supply trains and, without waiting for rest, they had leaped from the trains and into the battle. And the Yankees had been driven out of Georgia, back into Tennessee.

It was the greatest feat of the war, and Atlanta took pride and personal satisfaction in the thought that its railroads had made the victory possible.

But the South had needed the cheering news from Chickamauga to strengthen its morale through the winter. No one denied now that the Yankees were good fighters and, at last, they had good generals. Grant was a butcher who did not care how many men he slaughtered for a victory, but victory he would have. Sheridan was a name to bring dread to Southern hearts. And then, there was a man named Sherman who was being mentioned more and more often. He had risen to prominence in the campaigns in Tennessee and the West, and his reputation as a determined and ruthless fighter was growing.

None of them, of course, compared with General Lee. Faith in the General and the army was still strong. Confidence in ultimate victory never wavered. But the war was dragging out so long. There were so many dead, so many wounded and maimed for life, so many widowed, so many orphaned. And there was still a long hard struggle ahead, which meant more dead, more wounded, more widows and orphans.

To make matters worse, a vague distrust of those in high places had begun to creep over the civilian population. Many newspapers were outspoken in their denunciation of President Davis himself and the manner in which he prosecuted the war. There were dissensions within the Confederate cabinet, disagreements between President Davis and his generals. The currency was falling rapidly. Shoes and clothing for the army were scarce, ordnance supplies and drugs were scarcer. The railroads needed new cars to take the place of old ones and new iron rails to replace those torn up by the Yankees. The generals in the field were crying out for fresh troops, and there were fewer and fewer fresh troops to be had. Worst of all, some of the state governors, Governor Brown of Georgia among them, were refusing to send state militia troops and arms out of their borders. There were thousands of able-bodied men in the state troops for whom the army was frantic, but the government pleaded for them in vain.

With the new fall of currency, prices soared again. Beef, pork and butter cost thirty-five dollars a pound, flour fourteen hundred dollars a barrel, soda one hundred dollars a pound, tea five hundred dollars a pound. Warm clothing, when it was obtainable at all, had risen to such prohibitive prices that Atlanta ladies were lining their old dresses with rags and reinforcing them with newspapers to keep out the wind. Shoes cost from two hundred to eight hundred dollars a pair, depending on whether they were made of 'cardboard' or real leather. Ladies now wore gaiters made of their old wool shawls and cut-up carpets. The soles were made of wood.

The truth was that the North was holding the South in a virtual state of siege, though many did not yet realize it. The Yankee gun-boats had tightened the mesh at the ports and very few ships were now able to slip past the blockade.

The South had always lived by selling cotton and buying the things it did not produce, but now it could neither sell nor buy. Gerald O'Hara had three years' crops of cotton stored under the shed near the gin-house at Tara, but little good it did him. In Liverpool it would bring one hundred and fifty thousand dollars, but there was no hope of getting it to Liverpool. Gerald had changed from a wealthy man to a man who was wondering how he would feed his family and his negroes through the winter.

Throughout the South, most of the cotton planters were in the same fix. With the blockade closing tighter and tighter, there was no way to get the South's money crop to its market in England, no way to bring in the necessaries which cotton money had bought in years gone by. And the agricultural South, waging war with the industrial North, was needing so many things now, things it had never thought of buying in times of peace.

It was a situation made to order for speculators and profiteers, and men were not lacking to take advantage of it. As food and clothing grew scarcer and prices rose higher and higher, the public outcry against the speculators grew louder and more venomous. In those early days of 1864, no newspaper could be opened that did not carry scathing editorials denouncing the speculators as vultures and bloodsucking leeches and calling upon the government to put them down with a hard hand. The government did its best, but the efforts came to nothing, for the government was harried by many things.

Against no one was feeling more bitter than against Rhett Butler. He had sold his boats when blockading grew too hazardous, and he was now openly engaged in food speculation. The stories about him that came back to Atlanta from Richmond and Wilmington made those who had received him in other days writhe with shame.

In spite of all these trials and tribulations, Atlanta's ten thousand population had grown to double that number during the war. Even the blockade had added to Atlanta's prestige. From time immemorial, the coast cities had dominated the South, commercially and otherwise. But now with the ports closed and many of the port cities captured or besieged, the South's salvation depended upon itself. The interior section was what counted, if the South was going to win the war, and Atlanta was now the centre of things. The people of the town were suffering hardship, privation, sickness and death as severely as the rest of the Confederacy; but Atlanta, the city, had gained rather than lost as a result of the war. Atlanta, the heart of the Confederacy, was still beating full and strong, the railroads that were its arteries throbbing with the never-ending flow of men, munitions and supplies.

In other days, Scarlett would have been bitter about her shabby dresses and patched shoes but now she did not care, for the one person who mattered was not there to see her. She was happy those two months, happier than she had been in years. Had she not felt the start of Ashley's heart when her arms went round his neck, seen that despairing look on his face which was more open an avowal than any words could be? He loved her. She was sure of that now, and this conviction was so pleasant she could even be kinder to Melanie. She could be sorry for Melanie now, sorry with a faint contempt for her blindness, her stupidity.

'When the war is over!' she thought. 'When it's over – then . . . '

Sometimes she thought with a small dart of fear: 'What then?' But she put the thought from her mind. When the war was over, everything would be settled, somehow. If Ashley loved her, he simply couldn't go on living with Melanie.

But then, divorce was unthinkable; and Ellen and Gerald, staunch Catholics that they were, would never permit her to marry a divorced man. It would mean leaving the Church! Scarlett thought it over and decided that, in a choice between the Church and Ashley, she would choose Ashley. But, oh, it would make such a scandal! Divorced people were under the ban not only of the Church but of society. No divorced person was received. However, she would dare even that for Ashley. She would sacrifice anything for Ashley.

Somehow it would come out all right, when the war was over. If Ashley loved her so much, he'd find a way. She'd make him find a way. And with every day that passed, she became more sure in her own mind of his devotion, more certain he would arrange matters satisfactorily when the Yankees were finally beaten. Of course, he had said the Yankees 'had' them. Scarlett thought that was just foolishness. He had been tired and upset when he said it. But she hardly cared whether the Yankees won or not. The thing that mattered was for the war to finish quickly and for Ashley to come home.

Then, when the sleets of March were keeping everyone indoors, the hideous blow fell. Melanie, her eyes shining with joy, her head ducked with embarrassed pride, told her she was going to have a baby.

'Dr Meade says it will be here in late August or September,' she said. 'I've thought – but I wasn't sure till today. Oh, Scarlett, isn't it wonderful? I've so envied you Wade and so wanted a baby. And I was so afraid that maybe I wasn't ever going to have one and, darling, I want a dozen!'

Scarlett had been combing her hair, preparing for bed, when Melanie spoke and she stopped, the comb in mid-air.

'Dear God!' she said and, for a moment, realization did not come. Then there suddenly leaped to her mind the closed door of Melanie's bedroom and a knifelike pain went through her, a pain as fierce as though Ashley had been her own husband and had been unfaithful to her. A baby. Ashley's baby. Oh, how could he, when he loved her and not Melanie?

'I know you're surprised,' Melanie rattled on, breathlessly. 'And isn't it too wonderful? Oh, Scarlett, I don't know how I shall ever write Ashley! It wouldn't be so embarrassing if I could tell him or – or – well, not say anything and just let him notice gradually, you know—'

'Dear God!' said Scarlett, almost sobbing, as she dropped the comb and caught at the marble top of the dresser for support.

'Darling, don't look like that! You know having a baby isn't so bad. You said so yourself. And you mustn't worry about me, though you are sweet to be so upset. Of course, Dr Meade said I was – was,' Melanie blushed, 'quite narrow but that perhaps I shouldn't have any trouble and – Scarlett, did you write Charlie and tell him when you found out about Wade, or did your mother do it or maybe Mr O'Hara? Oh, dear, if I only had a mother to do it! I just don't see how—'

'Hush!' said Scarlett violently. 'Hush!'

'Oh, Scarlett, I'm so stupid! I'm so sorry. I guess all happy people are selfish. I forgot about Charlie, just for the moment—'

'Hush!' said Scarlett again, fighting to control her face and make her emotions quiet. Never, never must Melanie see or suspect how she felt.

Melanie, the most tactful of women, had tears in her eyes at her own cruelty. How could she have brought back to Scarlett the terrible memories of Wade being born months after poor Charlie was dead? How could she have been so thoughtless?

'Let me help you undress, dearest,' she said humbly. 'And I'll rub your head for you.'

'You leave me alone,' said Scarlett, her face like stone. And Melanie, bursting into tears of self-condemnation, fled from the room, leaving Scarlett to a tearless bed, with wounded pride, disillusionment and jealousy for bedfellows.

She thought that she could not live any longer in the same house with the woman who was carrying Ashley's child, thought that she would go home to Tara, home, where she belonged. She did not see how she could ever look at Melanie again and not have her secret read in her face. And she arose the next morning with the fixed intention of packing her trunk immediately after breakfast. But, as they sat at the table, Scarlett silent and gloomy, Pitty bewildered and Melanie miserable, a telegram came.

It was to Melanie from Ashley's body-servant, Mose.

'I have looked everywhere and I can't find him. Must I come home?'

No one knew what it meant but the eyes of the three women went to one another, wide with terror, and Scarlett forgot all thoughts of going home. Without finishing their breakfasts they drove to town to telegraph Ashley's colonel, but even as they entered the office, there was a telegram from him.

'Regret to inform you Major Wilkes missing since scouting expedition three days ago. Will keep you informed.'

It was a ghastly trip home, with Aunt Pitty crying into her handkerchief, Melanie sitting erect and white and Scarlett slumped, stunned in the corner of the carriage. Once in the house, Scarlett stumbled up the stairs to her bedroom and, clutching her Rosary from the table, dropped to her knees and tried to pray. But the prayers would not come. There only fell on her an abysmal fear, a certain knowledge that God had turned His face from her for her sin. She had loved a married man and tried to take him from his wife, and God had punished her by killing him. She wanted to pray but she could not raise her eyes to Heaven. She wanted to cry but the tears would not come. They seemed to flood her chest, and they were hot tears that burned under her bosom, but they would not flow.

Her door opened and Melanie entered. Her face was like a heart cut from white paper, framed against black hair, and her eyes were wide, like those of a frightened child lost in the dark.

'Scarlett,' she said, putting out her hands. 'You must forgive me for what I said yesterday, for you're – all I've got now. Oh, Scarlett, I know my darling is dead!'

Somehow, she was in Scarlett's arms, her small breasts heaving with sobs, and somehow they were lying on the bed, holding each other close, and Scarlett was crying too, crying with her face pressed close against Melanie's, the tears of one wetting the cheeks of the other. It hurt so terribly to cry, but not so much as not being able to cry. 'Ashley is dead – dead,' she thought, 'and I have killed him by loving him!' Fresh sobs broke from her, and Melanie somehow feeling comfort in her tears tightened her arms about her neck.

'At least,' she whispered, 'at least – I've got his baby.'

'And I,' thought Scarlett, too stricken now for anything so petty as jealousy, 'I've got nothing – nothing – nothing except the look on his face when he told me good-bye.'

The first reports were 'Missing – believed killed' and so they appeared on the casualty list. Melanie telegraphed Colonel Sloan a dozen times and finally a letter arrived, full of sympathy, explaining that Ashley and a squad had ridden out on a scouting expedition and had not returned. There had been reports of a slight skirmish within the Yankee lines and Mose, frantic with grief, had risked his own life to search for Ashley's body but had found nothing. Melanie, strangely calm now, telegraphed him money and instructions to come home.

When 'Missing – believed captured' appeared on the casualty lists, joy and hope reanimated the sad household. Melanie could hardly be dragged away from the telegraph office and she met every train hoping for letters. She was sick now, her pregnancy making itself felt in many unpleasant ways, but she refused to obey Dr Meade's commands and stay in bed. A feverish energy possessed her and would not let her be still; and at night, long after Scarlett had gone to bed, she could hear her walking the floor in the next room.

One afternoon, she came home from town, driven by the frightened Uncle Peter and supported by Rhett Butler. She had fainted at the telegraph office and Rhett, passing by and observing the excitement, had escorted her home. He carried her up the stairs to her bedroom and while the alarmed household fled hither and yon for hot bricks, blankets and whisky, he propped her on the pillows of her bed.

'Mrs Wilkes,' he questioned abruptly, 'you are going to have a baby, are you not?'

Had Melanie not been so faint, so sick, so heartsore, she would have collapsed at his question. Even with women friends she was embarrassed by any mention of her condition, while visits to Dr Meade were agonizing experiences. And for a man, especially Rhett Butler, to ask such a question was unthinkable. But lying weak and forlorn in the bed, she could only nod. After she had nodded, it did not seem so dreadful, for he looked so kind and concerned.

'Then you must take better care of yourself. All this running about and worrying won't help you and may harm the baby. If you will permit me, Mrs Wilkes, I will use what influence I have in Washington to learn about Mr Wilkes' fate. If he is a prisoner, he will be on the Federal lists, and if he isn't – well, there's nothing worse than uncertainty. But I must have your promise. Take care of yourself or, before God, I won't turn a hand.'

'Oh, you are so kind,' cried Melanie. 'How can people say such dreadful things about you?' Then overcome with the knowledge of her tactlessness and also with horror at having discussed her condition with a man, she began to cry weakly. And Scarlett, flying up the stairs with a hot brick wrapped in flannel, found Rhett patting her hand.

He was as good as his word. They never knew what wires he pulled. They feared to ask, knowing it might involve an admission of his too close affiliations with the Yankees. It was a month before he had news, news that raised them to the heights when they first heard it, but later created a gnawing anxiety in their hearts.

Ashley was not dead! He had been wounded and taken prisoner, and the records showed that he was at Rock Island, a prison camp in Illinois. In their first joy, they could think of nothing except that he was alive. But, when calmness began to return, they looked at one another and said 'Rock Island!' in the same voice they would have said 'In Hell!' For even as Andersonville was a name that stank in the North, so was Rock Island one to bring terror to the heart of any Southerner who had relatives imprisoned there.

When Lincoln refused to exchange prisoners, believing it would hasten the end of the war to burden the Confederacy with the feeding and guarding of Union prisoners, there were thousands of bluecoats at Andersonville, Georgia. The Confederates were on scant rations and practically without drugs or bandages for their own sick and wounded. They had little to share with the prisoners. They fed their prisoners on what the soldiers in the field were eating, fat pork and dried peas, and on this diet the Yankees died like flies, sometimes a hundred a day. Inflamed by the reports, the North resorted to harsher treatment of Confederate prisoners and at no place were conditions worse than at Rock Island. Food was scanty, one blanket did for three men, and the ravages of smallpox, pneumonia and typhoid gave the place the name of a pesthouse. Three-fourths of all the men sent there never came out alive.

And Ashley was in that horrible place! Ashley was alive but he was wounded and at Rock Island, and the snow must have been deep in Illinois when he was taken there. Had he died of his wound, since Rhett had learned his news? Had he fallen victim to smallpox? Was he delirious with pneumonia and no blanket to cover him?

'Oh, Captain Butler, isn't there some way— Can't you use your influence and have him exchanged?' cried Melanie.

'Mr Lincoln, the merciful and just, who cried large tears over Mrs Bixby's five boys, hasn't any tears to shed about the thousands of Yankees dying at Andersonville,' said Rhett, his mouth twisting. 'He doesn't care if they all die. The order is out. No exchanges. I – I hadn't told you before, Mrs Wilkes, but your husband had a chance to get out and refused it.'

'Oh, no!' cried Melanie in disbelief.

'Yes, indeed. The Yankees are recruiting men for frontier service to fight the Indians, recruiting them from among Confederate prisoners. Any prisoner who will take the oath of allegiance and enlist for Indian service for two years will be released and sent West. Mr Wilkes refused.'

'Oh, how could he?' cried Scarlett. 'Why didn't he take the oath and then desert and come home as soon as he got out of jail?'

Melanie turned on her like a small fury.

'How can you even suggest that he would do such a thing? Betray his own Confederacy by taking that vile oath and then betray his word to the Yankees! I would rather know he was dead at Rock Island than hear he had taken that oath. I'd be proud of him if he died in prison. But if he did *that*, I would never look on his face again. Never! Of course, he refused.'

When Scarlett was seeing Rhett to the door, she asked indignantly: 'If it were you, wouldn't you enlist with the Yankees to keep from dying in that place and then desert?'

'Of course,' said Rhett, his teeth showing beneath his moustache.

'Then why didn't Ashley do it?'

'He's a gentleman,' said Rhett, and Scarlett wondered how it was possible to convey such cynicism and contempt in that one honourable word.

Part Three

Chapter XVII

May of 1864 came – a hot dry May that wilted the flowers in the buds – and the Yankees under General Sherman were in Georgia again, above Dalton, one hundred miles north-west of Atlanta. Rumour had it that there would be heavy fighting up there near the boundary between Georgia and Tennessee. The Yankees were massing for an attack on the Western and Atlantic Railroad, the line which connected Atlanta with Tennessee and the West, the same line over which the Southern troops had been rushed last fall to win the victory at Chickamauga.

But, for the most part, Atlanta was not disturbed by the prospect of fighting near Dalton. The place where the Yankees were concentrating was only a few miles south-east of the battlefield of Chickamauga. They had been driven back once when they had tried to break through the mountain passes of that region, and they would be driven back again.

Atlanta – and all of Georgia – knew that the state was far too important to the Confederacy for General Joe Johnston to let the Yankees remain inside the state's borders for long. Old Joe and his army would not let even one Yankee get south of Dalton, for too much depended on the undisturbed functioning of Georgia. The unravaged state was a vast granary, machine shop and storehouse for the Confederacy. It manufactured much of the powder and arms used by the army and most of the cotton and woollen goods. Lying between Atlanta and Dalton was the city of Rome with its cannon foundry and its other industries, and Etowah and Allatoona with the largest ironworks south of Richmond. And in Atlanta were not only the factories for making pistols and saddles, tents and ammunition, but also the most extensive rolling mills in the South, the shops of the principal railroads and the enormous hospitals. And in Atlanta was the junction of the four railroads on which the very life of the Confederacy depended.

So no one worried particularly. After all, Dalton was a long way off, up near the Tennessee line. There had been fighting in Tennessee for three years and people were accustomed to the thought of that state as a far-away battlefield, almost as far away as Virginia or the Mississippi River. Moreover, Old Joe and his men were between the Yankees and Atlanta, and everyone knew that, next to General Lee himself, there was no greater general than Johnston, now that Stonewall Jackson was dead.

Dr Meade summed up the civilian point of view on the matter, one warm May evening on the veranda of Aunt Pitty's house, when he said that Atlanta had nothing to fear, for General Johnston was standing in the mountains like an iron rampart. His audience heard him with varying emotions, for all who sat there rocking quietly in the fading twilight, watching the first fireflies of the season moving magically through the dusk, had weighty matters on their minds. Mrs Meade, her hand upon Phil's arm, was hoping that the doctor was right. If the war came closer, she knew that Phil would have to go. He was sixteen now and in the Home Guard. Fanny Elsing, pale and hollow-eyed since Gettysburg, was trying to keep her mind from the torturing picture which had worn a groove in her tired mind these past several months – Lieutenant Dallas McLure dying in a jolting ox-cart in the rain on the long, terrible retreat into Maryland.

Captain Carey Ashburn's useless arm was hurting him again and moreover he was depressed by the thought that his courtship of Scarlett was at a standstill. That had been the situation ever since the news of Ashley Wilkes' capture, though the connection between the two events did not occur to him. Scarlett and Melanie both were thinking of Ashley, as they always did when urgent tasks or the necessity of carrying on a conversation did not divert them. Scarlett was thinking bitterly, sorrowfully: 'He must be dead or else we would have heard.' Melanie, stemming the tide of fear again and again, through endless hours, was telling herself: 'He can't be dead. I'd know it— I'd feel it if he were dead.' Rhett Butler lounged in the shadows, his long legs in their elegant boots crossed negligently, his dark face an unreadable blank. In his arms Wade slept contentedly, a cleanly picked wishbone in his small hand. Scarlett always permitted Wade to sit up late when Rhett called because the shy child was fond of him, and Rhett oddly enough seemed to be fond of Wade. Generally Scarlett was annoyed by the child's presence, but he always behaved nicely in Rhett's arms. As for Aunt Pitty, she was nervously trying to stifle a belch, for the rooster they had had for supper was a tough old bird.

That morning Aunt Pitty had reached the regretful decision that she had better kill the patriarch before he died of old age and pining for his harem which had long since been eaten. For days he had drooped about the empty chicken-run, too dispirited to crow. After Uncle Peter had wrung his neck, Aunt Pitty had been beset by conscience at the thought of enjoying him, en famille, when so many of her friends had not tasted chicken for weeks, so she suggested company for dinner. Melanie, who was now in her fifth month, had not been out in public or received guests for weeks, and she was appalled at the idea. But Aunt Pitty, for once, was firm. It would be selfish to eat the rooster alone, and if Melanie would only move her top hoop a little higher no one would notice anything and she was so flat in the bust anyway.

'Oh, but Auntie, I don't want to see people when Ashley—'

'It isn't as if Ashley were – had passed away,' said Aunt Pitty, her voice quavering, for in her heart she was certain Ashley was dead. 'He's just as much alive as you are and it will do you good to have company. And I'm going to ask Fanny Elsing, too. Mrs Elsing begged me to try to do something to arouse her and make her see people—'

'Oh, but Auntie, it's cruel to force her when poor Dallas has only been dead—'

'Now, Melly, I shall cry with vexation if you argue with me. I guess I'm your auntie and I know what's what. And I want a party.'

So Aunt Pitty had her party, and, at the last minute, a guest she did not expect, or desire, arrived. Just when the smell of roast rooster was filling the house, Rhett Butler, back from one of his mysterious trips, knocked at the door, with a large box of bonbons packed in paper lace under his arm and a mouthful of two-edged compliments for her. There was nothing to do but invite him to stay, although Aunt Pitty knew how the doctor and Mrs Meade felt about him and how bitter Fanny was against any man not in uniform. Neither the Meades nor the Elsings would have spoken to him on the street, but in a friend's home they would, of course, have to be polite to him. Besides, he was now more firmly than ever under the protection of the fragile Melanie. After he had intervened for her to get the news about Ashley, she had announced publicly that her home was open to him as long as he lived and no matter what other people might say about him.

Aunt Pitty's apprehensions quieted when she saw that Rhett was on his best behaviour. He devoted himself to Fanny with such sympathetic deference she even smiled at him, and the meal went well. It was a princely feast. Carey Ashburn had brought a little tea, which he had found in the tobacco-pouch of a captured Yankee en route to Andersonville, and everyone had a cup, faintly flavoured with tobacco. There was a nibble of the tough old bird for each, an adequate amount of dressing made of corn meal and seasoned with onions, a bowl of dried peas, and plenty of rice and gravy, the latter somewhat watery, for there was no flour with which to thicken it. For dessert, there was a sweet potato pie followed by Rhett's bonbons, and when Rhett produced real Havana cigars for the gentlemen to enjoy over their glass of blackberry wine, everyone agreed it was indeed a Lucullan banquet.

When the gentlemen joined the ladies on the front porch, the talk turned to war. Talk always turned to war now, all conversations on any topic led from war or back to war – sometimes sad, often gay, but always war. War romances, war weddings, deaths in hospitals and on the field, incidents of camp and battle and march, gallantry, cowardice, humour, sadness, deprivation and hope. Always, always hope. Hope firm, unshaken despite the defeats of the summer before.

When Captain Ashburn announced he had applied for and been granted transfer from Atlanta to the army at Dalton, the ladies kissed his stiffened arm with their eyes and covered their emotions of pride by declaring he couldn't go, for then who would beau them about?

Young Carey looked confused and pleased at hearing such statements from settled matrons and spinsters like Mrs Meade and Melanie and Aunt Pitty and Fanny, and tried to hope that Scarlett really meant it.

'Why, he'll be back in no time,' said the doctor, throwing an arm over Carey's shoulder. 'There'll be just one brief skirmish and the Yankees will skedaddle back into Tennessee. And when they get there, General Forrest will take care of them. You ladies need have no alarm about the proximity of the Yankees, for General Johnston and his army stands there in the mountains like an iron rampart. Yes, an iron rampart,' he repeated, relishing his phrase. 'Sherman will never pass. He'll never dislodge Old Joe.'

The ladies smiled approvingly, for his lightest utterance was regarded as incontrovertible truth. After all, men understood these matters much better than women, and if he said General Johnston was an iron rampart, he must be one. Only Rhett spoke. He had been silent since supper and had sat in the twilight listening to the war talk with a down-twisted mouth, holding the sleeping child against his shoulder.

'I believe that rumour has it that Sherman has over one hundred thousand men, now that his reinforcements have come up?'

The doctor answered him shortly. He had been under considerable strain ever since he first arrived and found that one of his fellow diners was this man whom he disliked so heartily. Only the respect due Miss Pittypat and his presence under her roof as a guest had restrained him from showing his feelings more obviously.

'Well, sir?' the doctor barked in reply.

'I believe Captain Ashburn said just a while ago that General Johnston had only about forty thousand, counting the deserters who were encouraged to come back to the colours by the last victory.'

'Sir,' said Mrs Meade indignantly. 'There are no deserters in the Confederate army.'

'I beg your pardon,' said Rhett with mock humility. 'I meant those thousands on furlough who forgot to rejoin their regiments and those who have been over their wounds for six months but who remain at home, going about their usual business or doing the spring ploughing.'

His eyes gleamed and Mrs Meade bit her lip in a huff. Scarlett wanted to giggle at her discomfiture, for Rhett had caught her fairly. There were hundreds of men skulking in the swamps and the mountains, defying the provost guard to drag them back to the army. They were the ones who declared it was a 'rich man's war and a poor man's fight', and they had had enough of it. But outnumbering these by far were men who, though carried on company rolls as deserters, had no intention of deserting permanently. They were the ones who had waited three years in vain for furloughs and while they waited received ill-spelled letters from home: 'We air hungry.' 'There won't be no crop this year – there ain't nobody to plough. We air hungry.' 'The commissary took the shoats, and we ain't had no money from you in months. We air livin' on dried peas.'

Always the rising chorus swelled: 'We are hungry, your wife, your babies, your parents. When will it be over? When will you come home? We are hungry, hungry.' When furloughs from the rapidly thinning army were denied, these soldiers went home without them, to plough their land and plant their crops, repair their houses and build up their fences. When regimental officers, understanding the situation, saw a hard fight ahead, they wrote these men, telling them to rejoin their companies and no questions would be asked. Usually the men returned when they saw that hunger at home would be held at bay for a few months longer. 'Plough furloughs' were not looked upon in the same light as desertion in the face of the enemy, but they weakened the army just the same.

Dr Meade hastily bridged over the uncomfortable pause, his voice cold: 'Captain Butler, the numerical difference between our troops and those of the Yankees has never mattered. One Confederate is worth a dozen Yankees.'

The ladies nodded. Everyone knew that.

'That was true at the first of the war,' said Rhett. 'Perhaps it's still true, provided the Confederate soldier has bullets for his gun and shoes on his feet and food in his stomach. Eh, Captain Ashburn?'

His voice was still soft and filled with specious humility. Carey Ashburn looked unhappy, for it was obvious that he, too, disliked Rhett intensely. He gladly would have sided with the doctor but he could not lie. The reason he had applied for transfer to the front, despite his useless arm, was that he realized, as the civilian population did not, the seriousness of the situation. There were many other men, stumping on wooden pegs, blind in one eye, fingers blown away, one arm gone, who were quietly transferring from the commissariat, hospital duties, mail and railroad service back to their old fighting units. They knew Old Joe needed every man.

He did not speak and Dr Meade thundered, losing his temper: 'Our men have fought without shoes before and without food and won victories. And they will fight again and win! I tell you General Johnston cannot be dislodged! The mountain fastnesses have always been the refuge and the strong forts of invaded peoples from ancient times. Think of – think of Thermopylae!'

Scarlett thought hard but Thermopylae meant nothing to her.

'They died to the last man at Thermopylae, didn't they, Doctor?' Rhett asked, and his lips twitched with suppressed laughter.

'Are you being insulting, young man?'

'Doctor! I beg of you! You misunderstand me! I merely asked for information. My memory of ancient history is poor.'

'If need be, our army will die to the last man before they permit the Yankees to advance farther into Georgia,' snapped the doctor. 'But it will not be. They will drive them out of Georgia in one skirmish.'

Aunt Pittypat rose hastily and asked Scarlett to favour them with a piano selection and a song. She saw that the conversation was rapidly getting into deep and stormy water. She had known very well there would be trouble if she invited Rhett to supper. There was always trouble when he was present. Just how he started it, she never exactly understood. Dear! Dear! What did Scarlett see in the man? And how could dear Melly defend him?

As Scarlett went obediently into the parlour, a silence fell on the porch, a silence that pulsed with resentment toward Rhett. How could anyone not believe with heart and soul in the invincibility of General Johnston and his men? Believing was a sacred duty. And those who were so traitorous as not to believe should, at least, have the decency to keep their mouths shut.

Scarlett struck a few chords and her voice floated out to them from the parlour, sweetly, sadly, in the words of a popular song:

> Into a ward of whitewashed walls
> Where the dead and dying lay—
> Wounded with bayonets, shells and balls—
> Somebody's darling was borne one day.
>
> Somebody's darling! so young and so brave!
> Wearing still on his pale, sweet face—
> Soon to be hid by the dust of the grave—
> The lingering light of his boyhood's grace.

'Matted and damp are the curls of gold,' mourned Scarlett's faulty soprano, and Fanny half rose and said in a faint, strangled voice: 'Sing something else!'

The piano was suddenly silent as Scarlett was overtaken with surprise and embarrassment. Then she hastily blundered into the opening bars of 'Jacket of Grey' and stopped with a discord as she remembered how heartrending that selection was too. The piano was silent again for she was utterly at a loss. All the songs had to do with death and parting and sorrow.

Rhett rose swiftly, deposited Wade in Fanny's lap, and went into the parlour.

'Play "My Old Kentucky Home",' he suggested smoothly, and Scarlett gratefully plunged into it. Her voice was joined by Rhett's excellent bass, and as they went into the second verse those on the porch breathed more easily, though Heaven knew it was none too cheery a song, either.

> Just a few more days for to tote the weary load!
> No matter, 'twill never be light!
> Just a few more days, till we totter in the road!
> Then, my old Kentucky home, good night!

Dr Meade's prediction was right – as far as it went. Johnston did stand like an iron rampart in the mountains above Dalton, one hundred miles away. So firmly did he stand and so bitterly did he contest Sherman's desire to pass down the valley toward Atlanta that finally the Yankees drew back and took counsel with themselves. They could not break the grey lines by direct assault and so, under cover of night, they marched through the mountain passes in a semicircle, hoping to come upon Johnston's rear and cut the railroad behind him at Resaca, fifteen miles below Dalton.

With those precious twin lines of iron in danger, the Confederates left their desperately defended rifle-pits and, under the starlight, made a forced march to Resaca by the short, direct road. When the Yankees, swarming out of the hills, came upon them, the Southern troops were waiting for them, entrenched behind breastworks, batteries planted, bayonets gleaming, even as they had been at Dalton.

When the wounded from Dalton brought in garbled accounts of Old Joe's retreat to Resaca, Atlanta was surprised and a little disturbed. It was as though a small, dark cloud had appeared in the north-west, the first cloud of a summer storm. What was the General thinking about, letting the Yankees penetrate eighteen miles farther into Georgia? The mountains were natural fortresses, even as Dr Meade had said. Why hadn't Old Joe held the Yankees there?

Johnston fought desperately at Resaca and repulsed the Yankees again, but Sherman, employing the same flanking movement, swung his vast army in another semicircle, crossed the Oostanaula River and again struck at the railroad in the Confederate rear. Again the grey lines were summoned swiftly from their red ditches to defend the railroad, and, weary for sleep, exhausted from marching and fighting, and hungry, always hungry, they made another rapid march down the valley. They reached the little town of Calhoun, six miles below Resaca, ahead of the Yankees, entrenched and were again ready for the attack when the Yankees came up. The attack came, there was fierce skirmishing and the Yankees were beaten back. Wearily the Confederates lay on their arms and prayed for respite and rest. But there was no rest. Sherman inexorably advanced, step by step, swinging his army about them in a wide curve, forcing another retreat to defend the railroad at their back.

The Confederates marched in their sleep, too tired to think for the most part. But when they did think, they trusted Old Joe. They knew they were retreating but they knew they had not been beaten. They just didn't have enough men to hold their entrenchments and defeat Sherman's flanking movements, too. They could and did lick the Yankees every time the Yankees would stand and fight. What would be the end of this retreat, they did not know. But Old Joe knew what he was doing and that was enough for them. He had conducted the retreat in masterly fashion, for they had lost few men and the Yankee killed and captured ran high. They hadn't lost a single wagon and only four guns. And they hadn't lost the railroad at their back, either. Sherman hadn't laid a finger on it for all his frontal attacks, cavalry dashes and flank movements.

The railroad. It was still theirs, that slender iron line winding through the sunny valley toward Atlanta. Men lay down to sleep where they could see the rails gleaming faintly in the starlight. Men lay down to die, and the last sight that met their puzzled eyes was the rails shining in the merciless sun, heat shimmering along them.

As they fell back down the valley, an army of refugees fell back before them. Planters and Crackers, rich and poor, black and white, women and children, the old, the dying, the crippled, the wounded, the women far gone in pregnancy, crowded the road to Atlanta, on trains, afoot, on horseback, in carriages and wagons piled high with trunks and household goods. Five miles ahead of the retreating army went the refugees, halting at Resaca, at Calhoun, at Kingston, hoping at each stop to hear that the Yankees had been driven back so they could return to their homes. But there was no retracing that sunny road. The grey troops passed by empty mansions, deserted farms, lonely cabins with doors ajar. Here and there some lone woman remained with a few frightened slaves, and they came to the road to cheer the soldiers, to bring buckets of well water for the thirsty men, to bind up the wounds and bury the dead in their own family burying-grounds. But for the most part the sunny valley was abandoned and desolate and the untended crops stood in parching fields.

Flanked again at Calhoun, Johnston fell back to Adairsville, where there was sharp skirmishing, then to Cassville, then south of Cartersville. And the enemy had now advanced fifty-five miles from Dalton. At New Hope Church, fifteen miles farther along the hotly fought way, the grey ranks dug in for a determined stand. On came the blue lines, relentlessly, like a monster serpent, coiling, striking venomously, drawing its injured lengths back, but always striking again. There was desperate fighting at New Hope Church, eleven days of continuous fighting, with every Yankee assault bloodily repulsed. Then Johnston, flanked again, withdrew his thinning lines a few miles farther.

The Confederate dead and wounded at New Hope Church ran high. The wounded flooded Atlanta in trainloads and the town was appalled. Never, even after the battle of Chickamauga, had the town seen so many wounded. The hospitals overflowed and wounded lay on the floors of empty stores and upon cotton bales in the warehouses. Every hotel, boarding-house and private residence was crowded with sufferers. Aunt Pitty had her share, although she protested that it was most unbecoming to have strange men in the house when Melanie was in a delicate condition and when gruesome sights might bring on premature birth. But Melanie reefed up her top hoop a little higher to hide her thickening figure and the wounded invaded the brick house. There was endless cooking and lifting and turning and fanning, endless hours of washing and rerolling bandages and picking lint, and endless warm nights made sleepless by the babbling delirium of men in the next room. Finally the choked town could take care of no more and the overflow of wounded was sent on to the hospitals at Macon and Augusta.

With this backwash of wounded bearing conflicting reports and the increase of frightened refugees crowding into the already crowded town, Atlanta was in an uproar. The small cloud on the horizon had blow up swiftly into a large, sullen storm-cloud and it was as though a faint, chilling wind blew from it.

No one had lost faith in the invincibility of the troops but everyone, the civilians at least, had lost faith in the General. New Hope Church was only thirty-five miles from Atlanta! The General had let the Yankees push him back sixty-five miles in three weeks! Why didn't he hold the Yankees instead of everlastingly retreating? He was a fool and worse than a fool. Greybeards in the Home Guard and members of the state militia, safe in Atlanta, insisted they could have managed the campaign better and drew maps on tablecloths to prove their contentions. As his lines grew thinner and he was forced back farther, the General called desperately on Governor Brown for these very men, but the state troops felt reasonably safe. After all, the Governor had defied Jeff Davis' demand for them. Why should he accede to General Johnston?

Fight and fall back! Fight and fall back! For seventy miles and twenty-five days the Confederates had fought almost daily. New Hope Church was behind the grey troops now, a memory in a mad haze of like memories, heat, dust, hunger, weariness, tramp-tramp on the red rutted roads, slop-slop through the red mud, retreat, entrench, fight – retreat, entrench, fight. New Hope Church was a nightmare of another life and so was Big Shanty, where they turned and fought the Yankees like demons. But, fight the Yankees till the fields were blue with dead, there were always more Yankees, fresh Yankees; there was always that sinister south-east curving of the blue lines toward the Confederate rear, toward the railroad – and toward Atlanta!

From Big Shanty, the weary sleepless lines retreated down the road to Kennesaw Mountain, near the little town of Marietta, and here they spread their lines in a ten-mile curve. On the steep sides of the mountain they dug their rifle-pits and on the towering heights they planted their batteries. Swearing, sweating men hauled the heavy guns up the precipitous slopes, for mules could not climb the hillsides. Couriers and wounded coming into Atlanta gave reassuring reports to the frightened townspeople. The heights of Kennesaw were impregnable. So were Pine Mountain and Lost Mountain near by which were also fortified. The Yankees couldn't dislodge Old Joe's men and they could hardly flank them now for the batteries on the mountain tops commanded all the roads for miles. Atlanta breathed more easily, but—

But Kennesaw Mountain was only twenty-two miles away!

On the day when the first wounded from Kennesaw Mountain were coming in, Mrs Merriwether's carriage was at Aunt Pitty's house at the unheard-of hour of seven in the morning, and black Uncle Levi sent up word that

Scarlett must dress immediately and come to the hospital. Fanny Elsing and the Bonnell girls, roused early from slumber, were yawning on the back seat and the Elsings' mammy sat grumpily on the box, a basket of freshly laundered bandages on her lap. Off Scarlett went, unwillingly, for she had danced till dawn the night before at the Home Guard's party and her feet were tired. She silently cursed the efficient and indefatigable Mrs Merriwether, the wounded and the whole Southern Confederacy, as Prissy buttoned her in her oldest and raggedest calico frock which she used for hospital work. Gulping down the bitter brew of parched corn and dried sweet potatoes that passed for coffee, she went out to join the girls.

She was sick of all this nursing. This very day she would tell Mrs Merriwether that Ellen had written to her to come home for a visit. Much good this did her, for that worthy matron, her sleeves rolled up, her stout figure swathed in a large apron, gave her one sharp look and said: 'Don't let me hear any more such foolishness, Scarlett Hamilton. I'll write your mother today and tell her how much we need you, and I'm sure she'll understand and let you stay. Now, put on your apron and trot over to Dr Meade. He needs someone to help with the dressings.'

'Oh, God,' thought Scarlett drearily, 'that's just the trouble. Mother will make me stay here and I shall die if I have to smell these stinks any longer! I wish I was an old lady so I could bully young ones, instead of getting bullied – and tell old cats like Mrs Merriwether to go to Halifax!'

Yes, she was sick of the hospital, the foul smells, the lice, the aching, unwashed bodies. If there had ever been any novelty and romance about nursing, that had worn off a year ago. Besides, these men wounded in the retreat were not so attractive as the earlier ones had been. They didn't show the slightest interest in her and they had very little to say beyond; 'How's the fightin' goin'? What's Old Joe doin' now? Mighty clever fellow, Old Joe.' She didn't think Old Joe a mighty clever fellow. All he had done was let the Yankees penetrate eighty-eight miles into Georgia. No, they were not an attractive lot. Moreover, many of them were dying, dying swiftly, silently, having little strength left to combat the blood poisoning, gangrene, typhoid and pneumonia which had set in before they could reach Atlanta and a doctor.

The day was hot and the flies came in the open windows in swarms, fat lazy flies that broke the spirits of the men as pain could not. The tide of smells and pain rose and rose about her. Perspiration soaked through her freshly starched dress as she followed Dr Meade about, a basin in her hand.

Oh, the nausea of standing by the doctor, trying not to vomit when his bright knife cut into mortifying flesh! And oh, the horror of hearing the screams from the operating ward where amputations were going on! And the sick, helpless sense of pity at the sight of tense, white faces of mangled men waiting for the doctor to get to them, men whose ears were filled with screams, men waiting for the dreadful words: 'I'm sorry, my boy, but that hand will have to come off. Yes, yes, I know; but look, see those red streaks? It'll have to come off.'

Chloroform was so scarce now it was used only for the worst amputations and opium was a precious thing, used only to ease the dying out of life, not the living out of pain. There was no quinine and no iodine at all. Yes, Scarlett was sick of it all, and that morning she wished that she, like Melanie, had the excuse of pregnancy to offer. That was about the only excuse that was socially acceptable for not nursing these days.

When noon came, she put off her apron and sneaked away from the hospital while Mrs Merriwether was busy writing a letter for a gangling, illiterate mountaineer. Scarlett felt that she could stand it no longer. It was an imposition on her and she knew that when the wounded came in on the noon train there would be enough work to keep her busy until nightfall – and probably without anything to eat.

She went hastily up the two short blocks to Peachtree Street, breathing the unfouled air in as deep gulps as her tightly laced corset would permit. She was standing on the corner, uncertain as to what she would do next, ashamed to go home to Aunt Pitty's but determined not to go back to the hospital, when Rhett Butler drove by.

'You look like the ragpicker's child,' he observed, his eyes taking in the mended lavender calico, streaked with perspiration and splotched here and there with water which had slopped from the basin. Scarlett was furious with embarrassment and indignation. Why did he always notice women's clothing and why was he so rude as to remark upon her present untidiness?

'I don't want to hear a word out of you. You get out and help me in and drive me somewhere where nobody will see me. I won't go back to the hospital if they hang me! My goodness, I didn't start this war and I don't see any reason why I should be worked to death and—'

'A traitor to Our Glorious Cause!'

'The pot's calling the kettle black. You help me in. I don't care where you were going. You're going to take me riding now.'

He swung himself out of the carriage to the ground and she suddenly thought how nice it was to see a man who was whole, who was not minus eyes or limbs, or white with pain or yellow with malaria, and who looked well fed and healthy. He was so well dressed too. His coat and trousers were actually of the same material and they fitted him, instead of hanging in folds or being almost too tight for movement. And they were new, not ragged, with dirty bare flesh and hairy legs showing through. He looked as if he had not a care in the world and that in itself was startling these days, when other men wore such worried, preoccupied, grim looks. His brown face was bland and his mouth, red-lipped, clear-cut as a woman's, frankly sensual, smiled carelessly as he lifted her into the carriage.

The muscles of his big body rippled against his well-tailored clothes as he got in beside her, and, as always, the sense of his great physical power struck her like a blow. She watched the swell of his powerful shoulders against the cloth with a fascination that was disturbing, a little frightening. His body seemed so tough and hard, as tough and hard as his keen mind. His was such an easy, graceful strength, lazy as a panther stretching in the sun, alert as a panther to spring and strike.

'You little fraud,' he said, clucking to the horse. 'You dance all night with the soldiers and give them roses and ribbons and tell them how you'd die for the Cause, and when it comes to bandaging a few wounds and picking off a few lice, you decamp hastily.'

'Can't you talk about something else and drive faster? It would be just my luck for Grandpa Merriwether to come out of his store and see me and tell old lady – I mean, Mrs Merriwether.'

He touched up the mare with the whip and she trotted briskly across Five Points and across the railroad tracks that cut the town in two. The train bearing the wounded had already come in and the litter-bearers were working swiftly in the hot sun, transferring wounded into ambulances and covered ordnance wagons. Scarlett had no qualm of conscience as she watched them but only a feeling of vast relief that she had made her escape.

'I'm just sick and tired of that old hospital,' she said, settling her billowing skirts and tying her bonnet-bow more firmly under her chin. 'And every day more and more wounded come in. It's all General Johnston's fault. If he'd just stood up to the Yankees at Dalton, they'd have—'

'But he did stand up to the Yankees, you ignorant child. And if he'd kept on standing there, Sherman would have flanked him and crushed him between the two wings of his army. And he'd have lost the railroad and the railroad is what Johnston is fighting for.'

'Oh, well,' said Scarlett, on whom military strategy was utterly lost. 'It's his fault anyway. He ought to have done something about it and I think he ought to be removed. Why doesn't he stand and fight instead of retreating?'

'You are like everyone else, screaming "Off with his head" because he can't do the impossible. He was Jesus the Saviour at Dalton, and now he's Judas the Betrayer at Kennesaw Mountain, all in six weeks. Yet, just let him drive the Yankees back twenty miles and he'll be Jesus again. My child, Sherman has twice as many men as Johnston, and he can afford to lose two men for every one of our gallant laddies. And Johnston can't afford to lose a single man. He needs reinforcements badly and what is he getting? "Joe Brown's Pets." What a help they'll be!'

'Is the militia really going to be called out? The Home Guard, too? I hadn't heard. How do you know?'

'There's a rumour floating about to that effect. The rumour arrived on the train from Milledgeville this morning. Both the militia and the Home Guards are going to be sent in to reinforce General Johnston. Yes, Governor Brown's darlings are likely to smell powder at last, and I imagine most of them will be much surprised. Certainly they never expected to see action. The Governor as good as promised them they wouldn't. Well, that's a good joke on them. They thought they had bomb-proofs because the Governor stood up to even Jeff Davis and refused to send them to Virginia. Said they were needed for the defence of their state. Who'd have ever thought the war would come to their own back yard and they'd really have to defend their state?'

'Oh, how can you laugh, you cruel thing! Think of the old gentlemen and the little boys in the Home Guard! Why, little Phil Meade will have to go and Grandpa Merriwether and Uncle Henry Hamilton.'

'I'm not talking about the little boys and the Mexican War veterans. I'm talking about brave young men like Willie Guinan who like to wear pretty uniforms and wave swords—'

'And yourself!'

'My dear, that didn't hurt a bit! I wear no uniform and wave no sword and the fortunes of the Confederacy mean nothing at all to me. Moreover, I wouldn't be caught dead in the Home Guard or in any army, for that matter. I had enough of things military at West Point to do me the rest of my life . . . Well, I wish Old Joe luck. General Lee can't send him any help because the Yankees are keeping him busy in Virginia. So the Georgia state troops are the only reinforcements Johnston can get. He deserves better, for he's a great strategist. He always manages to get places before the Yankees do. But he'll have to keep falling back if he wants to protect the railroad; and mark my words, when they push him out of the mountains and on to the flatter land around here, he's going to be butchered.'

'Around here?' cried Scarlett. 'You know mighty well the Yankees will never get this far!'

'Kennesaw is only twenty-two miles away and I'll wager you—'

'Rhett, look, down the street! That crowd of men! They aren't soldiers. What on earth . . . ? Why, they're darkies!'

There was a great cloud of red dust coming up the street and from the cloud came the sound of the tramping of many feet and a hundred or more negro voices, deep-throated, careless, singing a hymn. Rhett pulled the carriage over to the kerb, and Scarlett looked curiously at the sweating black men, picks and shovels over their shoulders, shepherded along by an officer and a squad of men wearing the insignia of the engineering corps.

'What on earth . . . ?' she began again.

Then her eyes lighted on a singing black buck in the front rank. He stood nearly six and a half feet tall, a giant of a man, ebony black, stepping along with the lithe grace of a powerful animal, his white teeth flashing as he led the gang in 'Go Down, Moses'. Surely there wasn't a negro on earth as tall and loud-voiced as this one except Big Sam, the foreman of Tara. But what was Big Sam doing here, so far away from home, especially now that there was no overseer on the plantation and he was Gerald's right-hand man?

As she half rose from her seat to look closer, the giant caught sight of her and his black face split in a grin of delighted recognition. He halted, dropped his shovel and started toward her, calling to the negroes nearest him: 'Gawdlmighty! It's Miss Scarlett! You, 'Lige! 'Postle! Prophet! Dar's Miss Scarlett!'

There was confusion in the ranks. The crowd halted uncertainly, grinning, and Big Sam, followed by three other large negroes, ran across the road to the carriage, closely followed by the harried, shouting officer.

'Get back in line, you fellows! Get back, I tell you, or I'll— Why, it's Mrs Hamilton. Good morning, Ma'm, and you, too, sir. What are you up to, inciting mutiny and insubordination? God knows, I've had trouble enough with these boys this morning.'

'Oh, Captain Randall, don't scold them! They are our people. This is Big Sam, our foreman, and Elijah and Apostle and Prophet from Tara. Of course, they had to speak to me. How are you, boys?'

She shook hands all around, her small white hand disappearing into their huge black paws, and the four capered with delight at the meeting and with pride at displaying before their comrades what a pretty Young Miss they had.

'What are you boys doing so far from Tara? You've run away, I'll be bound. Don't you know the patterollers will get you sure?'

They bellowed pleasedly at the badinage.

'Runned away?' answered Big Sam. 'No'm, us ain' runned away. Dey done sont an' tuck us, kase us wuz fo' bigges' an' stronges' han's at Tara.' His white teeth showed proudly. 'Dey specially sont fer me, kase Ah could sing so good. Yas'm, Mist' Frank Kennedy, he come by an' tuck us.'

'But why, Big Sam?'

'Lawd, Miss Scarlett! Ain' you heerd? Us is ter dig de ditches fer de w'ite gempmums ter hide in w'en de Yankees comes.'

Captain Randall and the occupants of the carriage smothered smiles at this naïve explanation of rifle-pits.

'Cose, Mist' Gerald might' nigh had a fit w'en dey tuck me, an' he say he kain run de place widout me. But Miss Ellen she say: "Tek him, Mist' Kennedy. De Confedrutsy need Big Sam mo' dan us do." An' she gib me a dollar an' tell me ter do jes' whut de w'ite gempmums tells me. So hyah us is.'

'What does it all mean, Captain Randall?'

'Oh, it's quite simple. We have to strengthen the fortifications of Atlanta with more miles of rifle-pits, and the General can't spare any men from the front to do it. So we've been impressing the strongest bucks in the countryside for the work.'

'But—'

A cold little fear was beginning to throb in Scarlett's breast. More miles of rifle-pits! Why should they need more? Within the last year, a series of huge earth redoubts with battery emplacements had been built all around Atlanta, one mile from the centre of town. These great earthworks were connected with rifle-pits and they ran, mile after mile, completely encircling the city. More rifle-pits!

'But – why should we be fortified any more than we are already fortified? We won't need what we've got. Surely, the General won't let—'

'Our present fortifications are only a mile from town,' said Captain Randall shortly. 'And that's too close for comfort – or safety. These new ones are going to be farther away. You see, another retreat may bring our men into Atlanta.'

Immediately he regretted his last remark, as her eyes widened with fear.

'But, of course, there won't be another retreat,' he added hastily. 'The lines around Kennesaw Mountain are impregnable. The batteries are planted all up the mountain sides and they command the roads, and the Yankees can't possibly get by.'

But Scarlett saw him drop his eyes before the lazy, penetrating look Rhett gave him, and she was frightened. She remembered Rhett's remark: 'When the Yankees push him out of the mountains and on to the flatter land, he'll be butchered.'

'Oh, Captain, do you think—'

'Why, of course not! Don't fret your mind one minute. Old Joe just believes in taking precautions. That's the only reason we're digging more entrenchments . . . But I must be going now. It's been pleasant, talking to you . . . Say good-bye to your mistress, boys, and let's get going.'

'Good-bye, boys. Now, if you get sick or hurt or in trouble, let me know. I live right down Peachtree Street, down there in almost the last house at the end of town. Wait a minute—' She fumbled in her reticule. 'Oh, dear, I haven't a cent. Rhett, give me a few shin-plasters. Here, Big Sam, buy some tobacco for yourself and the boys. And be good and do what Captain Randall tells you.'

The straggling line re-formed, the dust arose again in a red cloud as they moved off and Big Sam started up the singing again.

> *Go do-ow, Mos-es! Waaa-ay, do-own, in Eee-jup laa-an!*
> *An' te-el O-le Faa-ro-o*
> *Ter let mah – peee-pul go!*

'Rhett, Captain Randall was lying to me, just like all the men do – trying to keep the truth from us women for fear we'll faint. Or was he lying? Oh, Rhett, if there's no danger, why are they digging these new breastworks? Is the army so short of men they've got to use darkies?'

Rhett clucked to the mare.

'The army is damned short of men. Why else would the Home Guard be called out? And as for the entrenchments, well, fortifications are supposed to be of some value in case of a siege. The General is preparing to make his final stand here.'

'A siege! Oh, turn the horse around. I'm going home, back home to Tara, right away.'

'What ails you?'

'A siege! Name of God, a siege! I've heard about sieges! Pa was in one or maybe it was his Pa, and Pa told me . . . '

'What siege?'

'The siege at Drogheda when Cromwell had the Irish, and they didn't have anything to eat and Pa said they starved and died in the streets and finally they ate all the cats and rats and even things like cockroaches. And he said they ate each other too, before they surrendered, though I never did know whether to believe that or not. And when Cromwell took the town all the women were— A siege! Mother of God!'

'You are the most barbarously ignorant young person I ever saw. Drogheda was in sixteen hundred and something and Mr O'Hara couldn't possibly have been alive then. Besides, Sherman isn't Cromwell.'

'No, but he's worse! They say—'

'And as for the exotic viands the Irish ate at the siege – personally I'd as soon eat a nice juicy rat as some of the victuals they've been serving me recently at the hotel. I think I shall have to go back to Richmond. They have good food there, if you have the money to pay for it.' His eyes mocked the fear in her face.

Annoyed that she had shown her trepidation, she cried: 'I don't see why you've stayed here this long! All you think about is being comfortable and eating and – and things like that.'

'I know no more pleasant way to pass the time than in eating and – er – things like that,' he said. 'And as for why I stay here – well, I've read a good deal about sieges, beleaguered cities and the like, but I've never seen one. So I think I'll stay here and watch. I won't get hurt because I'm a noncombatant and besides I want the experience. Never pass up new experiences, Scarlett. They enrich the mind.'

'My mind's rich enough.'

'Perhaps you know best about that, but I should say— But that would be ungallant. And perhaps, I'm staying here to rescue you when the siege does come. I've never rescued a maiden in distress. That would be a new experience, too.'

She knew he was teasing her but she sensed a seriousness behind his words. She tossed her head.

'I won't need you to rescue me. I can take care of myself, thank you.'

'Don't say that, Scarlett! Think it, if you like, but never, never say it to a man. That's the trouble with Yankee girls. They'd be most charming if they weren't always telling you that they can take care of themselves, thank you. Generally they are telling the truth, God help them. And so men let them take care of themselves.'

'How you do run on,' she said coldly, for there was no insult worse than being likened to a Yankee girl. 'I believe you're lying about a siege. You know the Yankees will never get to Atlanta.'

'I'll bet you they will be here within the month. I'll bet you a box of bonbons against—' His dark eyes wandered to her lips. 'Against a kiss.'

For a brief moment, fear of a Yankee invasion clutched her heart but at the word 'kiss', she forgot about it. This was familiar ground and far more interesting than military operations. With difficulty she restrained a smile of glee. Since the day when he gave her the green bonnet, Rhett had made no advances which could in any way be construed as those of a lover. He could never be inveigled into personal conversations, try though she might, but now with no angling on her part, he was talking about kissing.

'I don't care for such personal conversation,' she said coolly and managed a frown. 'Besides, I'd just as soon kiss a pig.'

'There's no accounting for tastes and I've always heard the Irish were partial to pigs – kept them under their beds, in fact. But, Scarlett, you need kissing badly. That's what's wrong with you. All your beaux have respected you too much, though God knows why, or they have been too afraid of you to really do right by you. The result is that you are unendurably uppity. You should be kissed and by someone who knows how.'

The conversation was not going the way she wanted it. It never did when she was with him. Always, it was a duel in which she was worsted.

'And I suppose you think you are the proper person?' she asked with sarcasm, holding her temper in check with difficulty.

'Oh, yes, if I cared to take the trouble,' he said carelessly. 'They say I kiss very well.'

'Oh,' she began, indignant at the slight to her charms. 'Why, you . . . ' But her eyes fell in sudden confusion. He was smiling, but in the dark depths of his eyes a tiny light flickered for a brief moment, like a small raw flame.

'Of course, you've probably wondered why I never tried to follow up that chaste peck I gave you, the day I brought you that bonnet—'

'I have never—'

'Then you aren't a nice girl, Scarlett, and I'm sorry to hear it. All really nice girls wonder when men don't try to kiss them. They know they shouldn't want them to and they know they must act insulted if they do, but just the same, they wish the men would try . . . Well, my dear, take heart. Some day, I will kiss you and you will like it. But not now, so I beg you not to be too impatient.'

She knew he was teasing but, as always, his teasing maddened her. There was always too much truth in the things he said. Well, this finished him. If ever, ever he should be so ill-bred as to try to take any liberties with her, she would show him.

'Will you kindly turn the horse around, Captain Butler? I wish to go back to the hospital.'

'Do you indeed, my ministering angel? Then lice and slops are preferable to my conversation? Well, far be it from me to keep a pair of willing hands from labouring for Our Glorious Cause.' He turned the horse's head and they started back toward Five Points.

'As to why I have made no further advances,' he pursued blandly, as though she had not signified that the conversation was at an end, 'I'm waiting for you to grow up a little more. You see, it wouldn't be much fun for me to kiss you now and I'm quite selfish about my pleasures. I never fancied kissing children.'

He smothered a grin, as from the corner of his eyes he saw her bosom heave with silent wrath.

'And then, too,' he continued softly, 'I was waiting for the memory of the estimable Ashley Wilkes to fade.'

At the mention of Ashley's name, sudden pain went through her, sudden hot tears stung her lids. Fade? The memory of Ashley would never fade, not if he were dead a thousand years. She thought of Ashley wounded, dying in a far-off Yankee prison, with no blankets over him, with no one who loved him to hold his hand, and she was filled with hate at the well-fed man who sat beside her, jeers just beneath the surface of his drawling voice.

She was too angry to speak and they rode along in silence for some while.

'I understand practically everything about you and Ashley, now,' Rhett resumed. 'I began with your inelegant scene at Twelve Oaks and, since then, I've picked up many things by keeping my eyes open. What things? Oh, that you still cherish a romantic schoolgirl passion for him which he reciprocates as well as his honourable nature will permit him. And that Mrs Wilkes knows nothing and that, between the two of you, you've done her a pretty trick. I understand practically everything, except one thing and that piques my curiosity. Did the honourable Ashley ever jeopardize his immortal soul by kissing you?'

A stony silence and an averted head were his answers.

'Ah, well, so he did kiss you. I suppose it was when he was here on furlough. And now that's he's probably dead you are cherishing it to your heart. But I'm sure you'll get over it and when you've forgotten his kiss, I'll—'

She turned in fury.

'You go to – Halifax,' she said tensely, her green eyes slits of rage. 'And let me out of this carriage before I jump over the wheels. And I don't ever want to speak to you again.'

He stopped the carriage, but before he could alight and assist her she sprang down. Her hoop caught on the wheel and for a moment the crowd at Five Points had a flashing view of petticoats and pantalets. Then Rhett leaned over and swiftly released it. She flounced off without a word, without even a backward look, and he laughed softly and clicked to the horse.

Chapter XVIII

For the first time since the war began, Atlanta could hear the sound of battle. In the early morning hours before the noises of the town awoke, the cannon at Kennesaw Mountain could be heard faintly, far away, a low dim booming that might have passed for summer thunder. Occasionally it was loud enough to be heard even above the rattle of traffic at noon. People tried not to listen to it, tried to talk, to laugh, to carry on their business, just as though the Yankees were not there, twenty-two miles away, but always ears were strained for the sound. The town wore a preoccupied look, for no matter what occupied their hands, all were listening, listening, their hearts leaping suddenly a hundred times a day. Was the booming louder? Or did they only think it was louder? Would General Johnston hold them this time? Would he?

Panic lay just beneath the surface. Nerves which had been stretched tighter and tighter each day of the retreat began to reach the breaking point. No one spoke of fears. That subject was taboo, but strained nerves found expression in loud criticism of the General. Public feeling was at fever heat. Sherman was at the very doors of Atlanta. Another retreat might bring the Confederates into the town.

Give us a general who won't retreat! Give us a man who will stand and fight!

With the far-off rumbling of cannon in their ears, the state militia, 'Joe Brown's Pets', and the Home Guard marched out of Atlanta, to defend the bridges and ferries of the Chattahoochee River at Johnston's back. It was a grey, overcast day and, as they marched through Five Points and out the Marietta road, a fine rain began to fall. The whole town had turned out to see them off and they stood, close packed, under the wooden awnings of the stores on Peachtree Street and tried to cheer.

Scarlett and Maybelle Merriwether Picard had been given permission to leave the hospital and watch the men go out, because Uncle Henry Hamilton and Grandpa Merriwether were in the Home Guard, and they stood with Mrs Meade, pressed in the crowd, tiptoeing to get a better view. Scarlett, though filled with the universal Southern desire to believe only the pleasantest and most reassuring things about the progress of the fighting, felt cold as she watched the motley ranks go by. Surely, things must be in a desperate pass if this rabble of bomb-proofers, old men and little boys were being called out! To be sure there were young and able-bodied men in the passing lines, tricked out in the bright uniforms of socially select militia units, plumes waving, sashes dancing. But there were so many old men and young boys, and the sight of them made her heart contract with pity and with fear. There were greybeards older than her father trying to step jauntily along in the needle-fine rain to the rhythm of the fife and drum corps. Grandpa Merriwether, with Mrs Merriwether's best plaid shawl laid across his shoulders to keep out the rain, was in the first rank and he saluted the girls with a grin. They waved their handkerchiefs and cried gay good-byes to him; but Maybelle, gripping Scarlett's arm, whispered: 'Oh, the poor old darling! a real good rainstorm will just about finish him! His lumbago—'

Uncle Henry Hamilton marched in the rank behind Grandpa Merriwether, the collar of his long black coat turned up about his ears, two Mexican War pistols in his belt and a small carpet-bag in his hand. Beside him marched his black valet who was nearly as old as Uncle Henry, with an open umbrella held over them both. Shoulder to shoulder with their elders came the young boys, none of them looking over sixteen. Many of them had run away from school to join the army, and here and there were clumps of them in the cadet uniforms of military academies, the black cock feathers on their tight grey caps wet with rain, the clean white canvas straps crossing their chests sodden. Phil Meade was among them, proudly wearing his dead brother's sabre and horse pistols, his hat bravely pinned up on one side. Mrs Meade managed to smile and wave until he had passed and then she leaned her head on the back of Scarlett's shoulder for a moment as though her strength had suddenly left her.

Many of the men were totally unarmed, for the Confederacy had neither rifles nor ammunition to issue to them. These men hoped to equip themselves from killed and captured Yankees. Many carried bowie-knives in their boots and bore in their hands long thick poles with iron-pointed tips known as 'Joe Brown pikes'. The lucky ones had old flintlock muskets slung over their shoulders and powder-horns at their belts.

Johnston had lost around ten thousand men in his retreat. He needed ten thousand more fresh troops. 'And this,' thought Scarlett, frightened, 'is what he is getting!'

As the artillery rumbled by, splashing mud into the watching crowds, a negro on a mule, riding close to a cannon, caught her eye. He was a young, saddle-coloured negro with a serious face, and when Scarlett saw him she cried: 'It's Mose! Ashley's Mose! Whatever is he doing here?' She fought her way through the crowd to the kerb and called: 'Mose! Stop!'

The boy, seeing her, drew rein, smiled delightedly and started to dismount. A soaking sergeant, riding behind him, called: 'Stay on that mule, boy, or I'll light a fire under you! We got to git to the mountain some time.'

Uncertainly, Mose looked from the sergeant to Scarlett and she, splashing through the mud, close to the passing wheels, caught at Mose's stirrup strap.

'Oh, just a minute, Sergeant! Don't get down, Mose. What on earth are you doing here?'

'Ah's off ter de war, agin, Miss Scarlett. Dis time wid Old Mist' John 'stead ob Mist' Ashley.'

'Mr Wilkes!' Scarlett was stunned. Mr Wilkes was nearly seventy. 'Where is he?'

'Back wid de las' cannon, Miss Scarlett. Back dar!'

'Sorry, lady. Move on, boy!'

Scarlett stood for a moment, ankle-deep in mud as the guns lurched by. 'Oh, no!' she thought. 'It can't be. He's too old. And he doesn't like war any more than Ashley did!' She retreated back a few paces toward the kerb and scanned each face that passed. Then, as the last cannon and limber-chest came groaning and splashing up, she saw him, slender, erect, his long silver hair wet upon his neck, riding easily upon a little strawberry mare that picked her way as daintily through the mud-holes as a lady in a satin dress. Why – that mare was Nellie! Mrs Tarleton's Nellie! Beatrice Tarleton's treasured darling!

When he saw her standing in the mud, Mr Wilkes drew rein with a smile of pleasure and, dismounting, came toward her.

'I had hoped to see you, Scarlett. I was charged with so many messages from your people. But there was no time. We just got in this morning and they are rushing us out immediately, as you see.'

'Oh, Mr Wilkes,' she cried desperately, holding his hand. 'Don't go! Why must you go?'

'Ah, so you think I'm too old!' he smiled, and it was Ashley's smile in an older face. 'Perhaps I am too old to march but not to ride and to shoot. And Mrs Tarleton so kindly lent me Nellie, so I am well mounted. I hope nothing happens to Nellie, for if something should happen to her, I could never go home and face Mrs Tarleton. Nellie was the last horse she had left.' He was laughing now, turning away her fears. 'Your mother and father and the girls are well and they sent you their love. Your father nearly came up with us today!'

'Oh, not Pa!' cried Scarlett in terror. 'Not Pa! He isn't going to the war, is he?'

'No, but he was. Of course, he can't walk far with his stiff knee, but he was all for riding away with us. Your mother agreed, providing he was able to jump the pasture fence, for, she said, there would be a lot of rough riding to be done in the army. Your father thought that easy, but – would you believe it? When his horse came to the fence, he stopped dead and over his head went your father! It's a wonder it didn't break his neck! You know how obstinate he is. He got right up and tried it again. Well, Scarlett, he came off three times before Mrs O'Hara and Pork assisted him to bed. He was in a taking about it, swearing that your mother had "spoken a wee word in the beast's ear". He just isn't up to active service, Scarlett. You need have no shame about it. After all, someone must stay home and raise crops for the army.'

Scarlett had no shame at all, only an active feeling of relief.

'I've sent India and Honey to Macon to stay with the Burrs and Mr O'Hara is looking after Twelve Oaks as well as Tara . . . I must go, my dear. Let me kiss your pretty face.'

Scarlett turned up her lips and there was a choking pain in her throat.

She was so fond of Mr Wilkes. Once, long ago, she had hoped to be his daughter-in-law.

'And you must deliver this kiss to Pittypat and this to Melanie,' he said, kissing her lightly two more times. 'And how is Melanie?'

'She is well.'

'Ah!' His eyes looked at her but through her, past her as Ashley's had done, remote grey eyes looking on another world. 'I should have liked to see my first grandchild. Good-bye, my dear.'

He swung on to Nellie and cantered off, his hat in his hand, his silver hair bare to the rain. Scarlett had rejoined Maybelle and Mrs Meade before the import of his last words broke upon her. Then in superstitious terror she crossed herself and tried to say a prayer. He had spoken of death, just as Ashley had done, and now Ashley— No one should ever speak of death! It was tempting Providence to mention death. As the three women started silently back to the hospital in the rain, Scarlett was praying: 'Not him, too, God. Not him and Ashley, too!'

The retreat from Dalton to Kennesaw Mountain had taken from early May to mid-June and as the hot rainy days of June passed and Sherman failed to dislodge the Confederates from the steep slippery slopes, hope again raised its head. Everyone grew more cheerful and spoke more kindly of General Johnston. As wet June days passed into a wetter July and the Confederates, fighting desperately around the entrenched heights, still held Sherman at bay, a wild gaiety took hold of Atlanta. Hope went to their heads like champagne. Hurrah! Hurrah! We're holding them! An epidemic of parties and dances broke out. Whenever groups of men from the fighting were in town for the night, dinners were given for them and afterwards there was dancing and the girls, outnumbering the men ten to one, made much of them and fought to dance with them.

Atlanta was crowded with visitors, refugees, families of wounded men in the hospitals, wives and mothers of soldiers fighting at the mountain who wished to be near them in case of wounds. In addition, bevies of belles from the country districts, where all remaining men were under sixteen or over sixty, descended upon the town. Aunt Pitty disapproved highly of these last, for she felt they had come to Atlanta for no reason at all except to catch husbands, and the shamelessness of it made her wonder what the world was coming to. Scarlett disapproved, too. She did not care for the eager competition furnished by the sixteen-year-olds whose fresh cheeks and bright smiles made one forget their twice-turned frocks and patched shoes. Her own clothes were prettier and newer than most, thanks to the material Rhett Butler had brought her on the last boat he ran in, but, after all, she was nineteen and getting along and men had a way of chasing silly young things.

A widow with a child was at a disadvantage with these pretty minxes, she thought. But in these exciting days her widowhood and her motherhood weighed less heavily upon her than ever before. Between hospital duties in the daytime and parties at night, she hardly ever saw Wade. Sometimes she actually forgot, for long stretches, that she had a child.

In the warm wet summer nights, Atlanta's homes stood open to the soldiers, the town's defenders. The big houses from Washington Street to Peachtree Street blazed with lights, as the muddy fighters in from the rifle-pits were entertained, and the sound of banjo and fiddle and the scrape of dancing feet and light laughter carried far on the night air. Groups hung over pianos and voices sang lustily the sad words of 'Your Letter Came but Came Too Late', while ragged gallants looked meaningly at girls who laughed from behind turkey-tail fans, begging them not to wait until it was too late. None of the girls waited, if they could help it. With the tide of hysterical gaiety and excitement flooding the city, they rushed into matrimony. There were so many marriages that month while Johnston was holding the enemy at Kennesaw Mountain, marriages with the bride turned out in blushing happiness and the hastily borrowed finery of a dozen friends and the groom with sabre banging at patched knees. So much excitement, so many thrills! Hurrah! Johnston is holding the Yanks twenty-two miles away!

Yes, the lines around Kennesaw Mountain were impregnable. After twenty-five days of fighting, even General Sherman was convinced of this, for his losses were enormous. Instead of continuing the direct assault, he swung his army in a wide circle again and tried to come between the Confederates and Atlanta. Again, the strategy worked. Johnston was forced to abandon the heights he had held so well, in order to protect his rear. He had lost a third of his men in that fight and the remainder slogged tiredly through the rain across the country toward the Chattahoochee River. The Confederates could expect no more reinforcements, whereas the railroad, which the Yankees now held from Tennessee south to the battle-line, brought Sherman fresh troops and supplies daily. So the grey lines went back through the muddy fields, back toward Atlanta.

With the loss of the supposedly unconquerable position, a fresh wave of terror swept the town. For twenty-five wild, happy days, everyone had assured everyone else that this could not possibly happen. And now it had happened! But surely the General would hold the Yankees on the opposite bank of the river. Though God knows the river was close enough, only seven miles away!

But Sherman flanked them again, crossing the stream above them, and the weary grey files were forced to hurry across the yellow water and throw themselves again between the invaders and Atlanta. They dug in hastily in shallow pits to the north of the town in the valley of Peachtree Creek. Atlanta was in agony and panic.

Fight and fall back! Fight and fall back! And every retreat was bringing the Yankees closer to the town. Peachtree Creek was only five miles away! What was the General thinking about?

The cries of 'Give us a man who will stand and fight!' penetrated even to Richmond. Richmond knew that if Atlanta was lost, the war was lost, and after the army had crossed the Chattahoochee, General Johnston was removed from command. General Hood, one of his corps commanders, took over the army, and the town breathed a little easier. Hood wouldn't retreat. Not that tall Kentuckian, with his flowing beard and flashing eye! He had the reputation of a bulldog. He'd drive the Yankees back from the creek, yes, back across the river and on up the road every step of the way back to Dalton. But the army cried: 'Give us back Old Joe!' for they had been with Old Joe all the weary miles from Dalton and they knew, as the civilians could not know, the odds that had opposed them.

Sherman did not wait for Hood to get himself in readiness to attack. On the day after the change in command, the Yankee general struck swiftly at the little town of Decatur, six miles beyond Atlanta, captured it and cut the railroad there. This was the railroad connecting Atlanta with Augusta, with Charleston, with Wilmington and with Virginia. Sherman had dealt the Confederacy a crippling blow. The time had come for action! Atlanta screamed for action!

Then, on a July afternoon of steaming heat, Atlanta had its wish. General Hood did more than stand and fight. He assaulted the Yankees fiercely at Peachtree Creek, hurling his men from their rifle-pits against the blue lines where Sherman's men outnumbered him more than two to one.

Frightened, praying that Hood's attack would drive the Yankees back, everyone listened to the sound of booming cannon and the crackling of thousands of rifles which, though five miles away from the centre of town, were so loud as to seem almost in the next block. They could hear the rumblings of the batteries, see the smoke which rolled like low-hanging clouds above the trees, but for hours no one knew how the battle was going.

By late afternoon the first news came, but it was uncertain, contradictory, frightening, brought as it was by men wounded in the early hours of the battle. These men began straggling in, singly and in groups, the less seriously wounded supporting those who limped and staggered. Soon a steady stream of them was established, making their painful way into town toward the hospitals, their faces black as negroes' from powder stains, dust and sweat, their wounds unbandaged, blood drying, flies swarming about them.

Aunt Pitty's was one of the first houses which the wounded reached as they struggled in from the north of the town, and one after another, they tottered to the gate, sank down on the green lawn and croaked:

'Water!'

All that burning afternoon, Aunt Pitty and her family, black and white, stood in the sun with buckets of water and bandages, ladling drinks, binding wounds until the bandages gave out and even the torn sheets and towels were exhausted. Aunt Pitty completely forgot that the sight of blood always made her faint and she worked until her little feet in their too small shoes swelled and would no longer support her. Even Melanie, now great with child, forgot her modesty and worked feverishly side by side with Prissy, Cookie and Scarlett, her face as tense as any of the wounded. When at last she fainted, there was no place to lay her except on the kitchen table, as every bed, chair and sofa in the house was filled with wounded.

Forgotten in the tumult, little Wade crouched behind the banisters on the front porch, peering out on to the lawn like a caged, frightened rabbit, his eyes wide with terror, sucking his thumb and hiccoughing. Once Scarlett saw him and cried sharply: 'Go play in the back yard, Wade Hampton!' but he was too terrified, too fascinated by the mad scene before him to obey.

The lawn was covered with prostrate men, too tired to walk farther, too weak from wounds to move. These Uncle Peter loaded into the carriage and drove to the hospital, making trip after trip until the old horse was lathered. Mrs Meade and Mrs Merriwether sent their carriages and they, too, drove off, springs sagging beneath the weight of wounded.

Later, in the long, hot summer twilight, the ambulances came rumbling down the road from the battlefield and commissary wagons, covered with muddy canvas. Then farm wagons, ox-carts and even private carriages commandeered by the medical corps. They passed Aunt Pitty's house, jolting over the bumpy road, packed with wounded and dying men, dripping blood into the red dust. At the sight of the women with buckets and dippers, the conveyances halted and the chorus went up in cries, in whispers:

'Water!'

Scarlett held wobbling heads that parched lips might drink, poured buckets of water over dusty, feverish bodies and into open wounds that the men might enjoy a brief moment's relief. She tiptoed to hand dippers to ambulance drivers and of each she questioned, her heart in her throat: 'What news? What news?'

From all came back the answer: 'Don't know fer sartin, lady. It's too soon to tell.'

Night came and it was sultry. No air moved and the flaring pine-knots the negroes held made the air hotter. Dust clogged Scarlett's nostrils and dried her lips. Her lavender calico dress, so freshly clean and starched that morning, was streaked with blood, dirt and sweat. This, then, was what Ashley had meant when he wrote that war was not glory but dirt and misery.

Fatigue gave an unreal, nightmarish cast to the whole scene. It couldn't be real – or if it was real, then the world had gone mad. If not, why should she be standing here in Aunt Pitty's peaceful front yard, amid wavering lights, pouring water over dying beaux? For so many of them were her beaux and they tried to smile when they saw her. There were so many men jolting down this dark, dusty road whom she knew so well, so many men dying here before her eyes, mosquitoes and gnats swarming their bloody faces, men with whom she had danced and laughed, for whom she had played music and sung songs, teased, comforted and loved – a little.

She found Carey Ashburn on the bottom layer of wounded in an ox-cart, barely alive from a bullet wound in his head. But she could not extricate him without disturbing six other wounded men, so she let him go on to the hospital. Later, she heard he had died before a doctor ever saw him and was buried somewhere, no one knew exactly. So many men had been buried that month, in shallow, hastily dug graves at Oakland Cemetery. Melanie felt it keenly that they had not been able to get a lock of Carey's hair to send to his mother in Alabama.

As the hot night wore on and their backs were aching and their knees buckling from weariness, Scarlett and Pitty cried to man after man: 'What news? What news?'

And as the long hours dragged past, they had their answer, an answer that made them look whitely into each other's eyes.

'We're falling back.' 'We've got to fall back.' 'They outnumber us by thousands.' 'The Yankees have got Wheeler's cavalry cut off near Decatur. We got to reinforce them.' 'Our boys will all be in town soon.'

Scarlett and Pitty clutched each other's arms for support.

'Are – are the Yankees coming?'

'Yes'm, they're comin' all right but they ain't goin' ter git fer, lady.' 'Don't fret, Miss, they can't take Atlanta.' 'No, Ma'm, we got a million miles of breastworks 'round this town.' 'I heard Old Joe say it myself: "I can hold Atlanta forever." ' 'But we ain't got Old Joe. We got—' 'Shut up, you fool! Do you want to scare the ladies?' 'The Yankees will never take this place, Ma'm.' 'Whyn't you ladies go ter Macon or somewheres that's safer? Ain't you got no kinfolks there?' 'The Yankees ain't goin' ter take Atlanta but still it ain't goin' ter be so healthy for ladies whilst they're tryin' it.' 'There's goin' ter be a powerful lot of shellin'.'

In a warm steaming rain the next day, the defeated army poured through Atlanta by thousands, exhausted by hunger and weariness, depleted by seventy-six days of battle and retreat, their horses starved scarecrows, their cannon and caissons harnessed with odds and ends of rope and strips of rawhide. But they did not come in as a disorderly rabble, in full rout. They marched in good order, jaunty for all their rags, their torn red battle flags flying in the rain. They had learned retreating under Old Joe, who had made it as great a feat of strategy as advancing. The bearded, shabby files swung down Peachtree Street to the tune of 'Maryland! My Maryland!' and all the town turned out to cheer them. In victory or defeat, they were their boys.

The state militia who had gone out so short a time before, resplendent in new uniforms, could hardly be distinguished from the seasoned troops, so dirty and unkempt were they. There was a new look in their eyes. Three years of apologizing, of explaining why they were not at the front, was behind them now. They had traded security behind the lines for the hardships of battle. Many of their number had traded easy living for hard death. They were veterans now, veterans of brief service, but veterans just the same, and they had acquitted themselves well. They searched out the faces of friends in the crowd and stared at them proudly, defiantly. They could hold up their heads now.

The old men and boys of the Home Guard marched by, the greybeards almost too weary to lift their feet, the boys wearing the faces of tired children, confronted too early with adult problems. Scarlett caught sight of Phil Meade and hardly recognized him, so black was his face with powder and grime, so taut with strain and weariness. Uncle Henry went limping by, hatless in the rain, his head stuck through a hole in a piece of old oilcloth. Grandpa Merriwether rode in on a gun-carriage, his bare feet tied in quilt scraps. But search though she might, she saw no sign of John Wilkes.

Johnston's veterans, however, went by with the tireless, careless step which had carried them for three years, and they still had the energy to grin and wave at pretty girls and to call rude gibes to men not in uniform. They were on their way to the entrenchments that ringed the town – no shallow, hastily dug trenches, these, but earthworks, breast high, reinforced with sandbags and tipped with sharpened staves of wood. For mile after mile the trenches encircled the town, red gashes surmounted by red mounds, waiting for the men who would fill them.

The crowd cheered the troops as they would have cheered them in victory. There was fear in every heart but, now that they knew the truth, now that the worst had happened, now that the war was in their front yard, a change came over the town. There was no panic now, no hysteria. Whatever lay in hearts did not show on faces. Everyone looked cheerful even if the cheer was strained. Everyone tried to show brave, confident faces to the troops. Everyone repeated what Old Joe had said, just before he was relieved of command: 'I can hold Atlanta forever.'

Now that Hood had had to retreat, quite a number wished, with the soldiers, that they had Old Joe back, but they forbore saying it and took courage from Old Joe's remark.

'I can hold Atlanta forever!'

Not for Hood the cautious tactics of General Johnston. He assaulted the Yankees on the east, he assaulted them on the west. Sherman was circling the town like a wrestler seeking a fresh hold on an opponent's body, and Hood did not remain behind his rifle-pits waiting for the Yankees to attack. He went out boldly to meet them and savagely fell upon them. Within the space of a few days, the battles of Atlanta and of Ezra Church were fought, and both of them were major engagements which made Peachtree Creek seem like a skirmish.

But the Yankees kept coming back for more. They had suffered heavy losses, but they could afford to lose. And all the while their batteries poured shells into Atlanta, killing people in their homes, ripping roofs off buildings,

·tearing huge craters in the streets. The townsfolk sheltered as best they could in cellars, in holes in the ground and in shallow tunnels dug in railroad cuts. Atlanta was under siege.

Within eleven days after he had taken command, General Hood had lost almost as many men as Johnston had lost in seventy-four days of battle and retreat, and Atlanta was hemmed in on three sides.

The railroad from Atlanta to Tennessee was now in Sherman's hands for its full length. His army was across the railroad to the east and he had cut the railroad running south-west to Alabama. Only the one railroad to the south, to Macon and Savannah, was still open. The town was crowded with soldiers, swamped with wounded, jammed with refugees, and this one line was inadequate for the crying needs of the stricken city. But as long as this railroad could be held, Atlanta could still stand.

Scarlett was terrified when she realized how important this line had become, how fiercely Sherman would fight to take it, how desperately Hood would fight to defend it. For this was the railroad which ran through the County, through Jonesboro. And Tara was only five miles from Jonesboro! Tara seemed like a haven of refuge by comparison with the screaming hell of Atlanta, but Tara was only five miles from Jonesboro!

Scarlett and many other ladies sat on the flat roofs of stores, shaded by their tiny parasols, and watched the fighting on the day of the battle of Atlanta. But when shells began falling in the streets for the first time, they fled to the cellars, and that night the exodus of women, children and old people from the city began. Macon was their destination and many of those who took the train that night had already refugeed five and six times before, as Johnston fell back from Dalton. They were travelling lighter now than when they arrived in Atlanta. Most of them carried only a carpet-bag and a scanty lunch done up in a bandana handkerchief. Here and there, frightened servants carried silver pitchers, knives and forks and a family portrait or two which had been salvaged in the first flight.

Mrs Merriwether and Mrs Elsing refused to leave. They were needed at the hospital and furthermore, they said proudly, they weren't afraid and no Yankees were going to run them out of their homes. But Maybelle and her baby and Fanny Elsing went to Macon. Mrs Meade was disobedient for the first time in her married life and flatly refused to yield to the doctor's command that she take the train to safety. The doctor needed her, she said. Moreover, Phil was somewhere in the trenches and she wanted to be near by in case ...

But Mrs Whiting went and many other ladies of Scarlett's circle. Aunt Pitty, who had been the first to denounce Old Joe for his policy of retreat, was among the first to pack her trunks. Her nerves, she said, were delicate and she could not endure noises. She feared she might faint at an explosion and not be able to reach the cellar. No, she was not afraid. Her baby mouth tried to set in martial lines but failed. She'd go to Macon and stay with her cousin, old Mrs Burr, and the girls should come with her.

Scarlett did not want to go to Macon. Frightened as she was of the shells, she'd rather stay in Atlanta than go to Macon, for she hated old Mrs Burr cordially. Years ago, Mrs Burr had said she was 'fast' after catching her kissing her son Willie at one of the Wilkes house parties. 'No,' she told Aunt Pitty, 'I'll go home to Tara and Melly can go to Macon with you.'

At this Melanie began to cry in a frightened, heartbroken way. When Aunt Pitty fled to get Dr Meade, Melanie caught Scarlett's hand in hers, pleading:

'Dear, don't go to Tara and leave me! I'll be so lonely without you. Oh, Scarlett, I'd just die if you weren't with me when the baby came! Yes – yes, I know I've got Aunt Pitty and she is sweet. But after all, she's never had a baby, and sometimes she makes me so nervous I could scream. Don't desert me, darling. You've been just like a sister to me, and besides,' she smiled wanly, 'you promised Ashley you'd take care of me. He told me he was going to ask you.'

Scarlett stared down at her in wonderment. With her own dislike of this woman so strong she could barely conceal it, how could Melly love her so? How could Melly be so stupid as not to guess the secret of her love of Ashley? She had given herself away a hundred times during these months of torment, waiting for news of him. But Melanie saw nothing, Melanie who could see nothing but good in anyone she loved . . . Yes, she had promised Ashley she would look out for Melanie. 'Oh, Ashley! Ashley! you must be dead, dead these many months! And now your promise reaches out and clutches me!'

'Well,' she said shortly, 'I did promise him that and I don't go back on my promises. But I won't go to Macon and stay with that old Burr cat. I'd claw her eyes out in five minutes. I'm going home to Tara and you can come with me. Mother would love to have you.'

'Oh, I'd like that! Your mother is so sweet. But you know Auntie would just die if she wasn't with me when the baby came, and I know she won't go to Tara. It's too close to the fighting, and Auntie wants to be safe.'

Dr Meade, who had arrived out of breath, expecting to find Melanie in premature labour at least, judging by Aunt Pitty's alarmed summoning, was indignant and said as much. And upon learning the cause of the upset, he settled the matter with words that left no room for argument.

'It's out of the question for you to go to Macon, Miss Melly. I won't answer for you if you move. The trains are crowded and uncertain and the passengers are liable to be put off in the woods at any time, if the trains are needed for the wounded or troops and supplies. In your condition—'

'But if I went to Tara with Scarlett—'

'I tell you I won't have you moved. The train to Tara is the train to Macon and the same conditions prevail. Moreover, no one knows just where the

Yankees are now, but they are all over everywhere. Your train might even be captured. And even if you reached Jonesboro safely, there'd be a five-mile ride over a rough road before you ever reached Tara. It's no trip for a woman in a delicate condition. Besides, there's not a doctor in the County since old Dr Fontaine joined the army.'

'But there are midwives—'

'I said a doctor,' he answered brusquely, and his eyes unconsciously went over her tiny frame. 'I won't have you moved. It might be dangerous. You don't want to have the baby on the train or in a buggy, do you?'

This medical frankness reduced the ladies to embarrassed blushes and silence.

'You've got to stay right here where I can watch you, and you must stay in bed. No running up and down stairs to cellars. No, not even if shells come right in the window. After all, there's not so much danger here. We'll have the Yankees beaten back in no time . . . Now, Miss Pitty, you go right on to Macon and leave the young ladies here.'

'Unchaperoned?' she cried, aghast.

'They are matrons,' said the doctor testily. 'And Mrs Meade is just two houses away. They won't be receiving any male company anyway with Miss Melly in her condition. Good Heavens, Miss Pitty! This is war time. We can't think of the proprieties now. We must think of Miss Melly.'

He stamped out of the room and waited on the front porch until Scarlett joined him.

'I shall talk frankly to you, Miss Scarlett,' he began, jerking at his grey beard. 'You seem to be a young woman of common sense, so spare me your blushes. I do not want to hear any further talk about Miss Melly being moved. I doubt if she could stand the trip. She is going to have a difficult time, even in the best of circumstances – very narrow in the hips, as you know, and probably will need forceps for her delivery, so I don't want any ignorant darky midwife meddling with her. Women like her should never have children, but— Anyway, you pack Miss Pitty's trunk and send her to Macon. She's so scared she'll upset Miss Melly and that won't do any good. And now, Miss,' he fixed her with a piercing glance, 'I don't want to hear about you going home, either. You stay with Miss Melly till the baby comes. Not afraid, are you?'

'Oh, no!' lied Scarlett stoutly.

'That's a brave girl. Mrs Meade will give you whatever chaperonage you need and I'll send over old Betsy to cook for you, if Miss Pitty wants to take her servants with her. It won't be for long. The baby ought to be here in another five weeks, but you never can tell with first babies and all this shelling going on. It may come any day.'

So Aunt Pittypat went to Macon, in floods of tears, taking Uncle Peter and Cookie with her. The carriage and horse she donated to the hospital in a burst of patriotism which she immediately regretted and that brought on more tears. And Scarlett and Melanie were left alone with Wade and Prissy in a house that was much quieter, even though the cannonading continued.

Chapter XIX

In those first days of the siege, when the Yankees crashed here and there against the defences of the city, Scarlett was so frightened by the bursting shells she could only cower helplessly, her hands over her ears, expecting every moment to be blown into eternity. When she heard the whistling screams that heralded their approach, she rushed to Melanie's room and flung herself on the bed beside her, and the two clutched each other, screaming 'Oh! Oh!' as they buried their heads in the pillows. Prissy and Wade scurried for the cellar and crouched in the cobwebbed darkness, Prissy squalling at the top of her voice and Wade sobbing and hiccoughing.

Suffocating under feather pillows while death screamed overhead, Scarlett silently cursed Melanie for keeping her from the safer regions below stairs. But the doctor had forbidden Melanie to walk and Scarlett had to stay with her. Added to her terror of being blown to pieces was her equally active terror that Melanie's baby might arrive at any moment. Sweat broke out on Scarlett with clammy dampness, whenever this thought entered her mind. What would she do if the baby started coming? She knew she'd rather let Melanie die than go out on the streets to hunt for the doctor when the shells were falling like April rain. And she knew Prissy could be beaten to death before she would venture forth. What would she do if the baby came?

These matters she discussed with Prissy in whispers one evening, as they prepared Melanie's supper tray, and Prissy, surprisingly enough, calmed her fears.

'Miss Scarlett, effen we kain git de doctah w'en Miss Melly's time come, doan you bodder. Ah kin manage. Ah knows all 'bout birthin'. Ain' mah ma a midwife? Ain' she raise me ter be a midwife, too? Jes' you leave it ter me.'

Scarlett breathed more easily knowing that experienced hands were near, but she nevertheless yearned to have the ordeal over and done with. Mad to be away from exploding shells, desperate to get home to the quiet of Tara, she prayed every night that the baby would arrive the next day, so she would be released from her promise and could leave Atlanta. Tara seemed so safe, so far away from all this misery.

Scarlett longed for home and her mother as she had never longed for anything in all her life. If she were just near Ellen she wouldn't be afraid, no matter what happened. Every night after a day of screeching, ear-splitting shells, she went to bed determined to tell Melanie the next morning that she could not stand Atlanta another day, that she would have to go home and Melanie would have to go to Mrs Meade's. But, as she lay on her pillow, there always rose the memory of Ashley's face as it had looked when she last saw him, drawn as with an inner pain but with a little smile on his lips: 'You'll take care of Melanie, won't you? You're so strong . . . Promise me.' And she had promised. Somewhere, Ashley lay dead. Wherever he was, he was watching her, holding her to that promise. Living or dead, she could not fail him, no matter what the cost. So she remained day after day.

In response to Ellen's letters, pleading with her to come home, she wrote minimizing the dangers of the siege, explaining Melanie's predicament and promising to come as soon as the baby was born. Ellen, sensitive to the bonds of kin, be they blood or marriage, wrote back reluctantly agreeing that she must stay but demanding that Wade and Prissy be sent home immediately. This suggestion met with the complete approval of Prissy, who was now reduced to teeth-chattering idiocy at every unexpected sound. She spent so much time crouching in the cellar that the girls would have fared badly but for Mrs Meade's solid old Betsy.

Scarlett was as anxious as her mother to have Wade out of Atlanta, not only for the child's safety, but because his constant fear irritated her. Wade was terrified to speechlessness by the shelling, and even when lulls came he clung to Scarlett's skirts, too terrified to cry. He was afraid to go to bed at night, afraid of the dark, afraid to sleep lest the Yankees should come and get him, and the sound of his soft nervous whimpering in the night grated unendurably on her nerves. Secretly she was just as frightened as he was, but it angered her to be reminded of it every minute by his tense, drawn face. Yes, Tara was the place for Wade. Prissy should take him there and return immediately to be present when the baby came.

But before Scarlett could start the two on their homeward journey, news came that the Yankees had swung to the south and were skirmishing along the railroad between Atlanta and Jonesboro. Suppose the Yankees should capture the train on which Wade and Prissy were riding – Scarlett and Melanie turned pale at the thought, for everyone knew that Yankee atrocities on helpless children were even more dreadful than on women. So she feared to send him home and he remained in Atlanta, a frightened, silent little ghost, pattering about desperately after his mother, fearing to have her skirt out of his hand for even a minute.

The siege went on through the hot days of July, thundering days following nights of sullen, ominous stillness, and the town began to adjust itself. It was as though, the worst having happened, they had nothing more to fear. They had feared a siege and now they had a siege and, after all, it wasn't so bad. Life could and did go on almost as usual. They knew they were sitting on a volcano, but until that volcano erupted there was nothing they could do. So why worry now? And probably it wouldn't erupt anyway. Just look how General Hood is holding the Yankees out of the city! And see how the cavalry is holding the railroad to Macon! Sherman will never take it!

But for all their apparent insouciance in the face of falling shells and shorter rations, for all their ignoring the Yankees, barely half a mile away, and for all their boundless confidence in the ragged line of grey men in the rifle-pits, there pulsed, just below the skin of Atlanta, a wild uncertainty over what the next day would bring. Suspense, worry, sorrow, hunger and the torment of rising, falling, rising hope was wearing that skin thin.

Gradually, Scarlett drew courage from the brave faces of her friends and from the merciful adjustment which nature makes when what cannot be cured must be endured. To be sure, she still jumped at the sound of explosions but she did not run screaming to burrow her head under Melanie's pillow. She could now gulp and say weakly: 'That one was close, wasn't it?'

She was less frightened also because life had taken on the quality of a dream, a dream too terrible to be real. It wasn't possible that she, Scarlett O'Hara, should be in such a predicament, with the danger of death about her every hour, every minute. It wasn't possible that the quiet tenor of life could have changed so completely in so short a time.

It was unreal, grotesquely unreal, that morning skies which dawned so tenderly blue could be profaned with cannon smoke that hung over the town like low thunder clouds, that warm noontides filled with the piercing sweetness of massed honeysuckle and climbing roses could be so fearful, as shells screamed into the streets, bursting like the crack of doom, throwing iron splinters hundreds of yards, blowing people and animals to bits.

Quiet, drowsy afternoon siestas had ceased to be, for, though the clamour of battle might lull from time to time, Peachtree Street was alive and noisy at all hours – cannon and ambulances rumbling by, wounded stumbling in from the rifle-pits, regiments hurrying past at double-quick, ordered from the ditches on one side of town to the defence of some hard-pressed earthworks on the other, and couriers dashing headlong down the street toward headquarters as though the fate of the Confederacy hung on them.

The hot nights brought a measure of quiet but it was a sinister quiet. When the night was still, it was too still – as though the tree frogs, katydids and sleepy mocking-birds were too frightened to raise their voices in the usual summer-night chorus. Now and again, the quiet was broken sharply by the crack-cracking of musket fire in the last line of defences.

Often in the late night hours, when the lamps were out and Melanie asleep and deathly silence pressed over the town, Scarlett, lying awake, heard the latch of the front gate click and soft urgent tappings on the front door.

Always, faceless soldiers stood on the dark porch and from the darkness many different voices spoke to her. Sometimes a cultured voice came from the shadows: 'Madam, my abject apologies for disturbing you, but could I have water for myself and my horse?' Sometimes it was the hard burring of a mountain voice, sometimes the odd nasals of the flat Wiregrass country to the far south, occasionally the lulling drawl of the Coast that caught at her heart, reminding her of Ellen's voice.

'Missy, I got a pardner here who I wuz aimin' ter git ter the horsepittle but looks like he ain't goin' ter last that fer. Kin you take him in?'

'Lady, I shore could do with some vittles. I'd shore relish a corn pone if it didn't deprive you none.'

'Madam, forgive my intrusion but – could I spend the night on your porch? I saw the roses and smelled the honeysuckle and it was so much like home that I was emboldened—'

No, these nights were not real! They were a nightmare and the men were part of that nightmare, men without bodies or faces, only tired voices speaking to her from the warm dark. Draw water, serve food, lay pillows on the front porch, bind wounds, hold the dirty heads of the dying. No, this could not be happening to her!

Once, late in July, it was Uncle Henry Hamilton who came tapping in the night. Uncle Henry was minus his umbrella and carpet-bag now, and his fat stomach as well. The skin of his pink fat face hung down in loose folds like the dewlaps of a bulldog and his long white hair was indescribably dirty. He was almost barefoot, crawling with lice, and he was hungry, but his irascible spirit was unimpaired.

Despite his remark, 'It's a foolish war when old fools like me are out toting guns,' the girls received the impression that Uncle Henry was enjoying himself. He was needed, like the young men, and he was doing a young man's work. Moreover, he could keep up with the young men, which was more than Grandpa Merriwether could do, he told them gleefully. Grandpa's lumbago was troubling him greatly and the Captain wanted to discharge him. But Grandpa wouldn't go home. He said frankly that he preferred the Captain's swearing and bullying to his daughter-in-law's coddling, and her incessant demands that he give up chewing tobacco and launder his beard every day.

Uncle Henry's visit was brief, for he had only a four-hour furlough and he needed half of it for the long walk in from the breastworks and back.

'Girls, I'm not going to see you all for a while,' he announced as he sat in Melanie's bedroom, luxuriously wriggling his blistered feet in the tub of cold water Scarlett had set before him. 'Our company is going out in the morning.'

'Where?' questioned Melanie, frightened, clutching his arm.

'Don't put your hand on me,' said Uncle Henry irritably. 'I'm crawling with lice. War would be a picnic if it wasn't for lice and dysentery. Where'm I going? Well, I haven't been told but I've got a good idea. We're marching south, toward Jonesboro, in the morning, unless I'm greatly in error.'

'Oh, why toward Jonesboro?'

'Because there's going to be big fighting there, Missy. The Yankees are going to take that railroad if they possibly can. And if they do take it, it's good-bye, Atlanta!'

'Oh, Uncle Henry, do you think they will?'

'Shucks, girls! No! How can they when I'm there?' Uncle Henry grinned at their frightened faces and then, becoming serious again: 'It's going to be a hard fight, girls. We've got to win it. You know, of course, that the Yankees have got all the railroads except the one to Macon, but that isn't all they've got. Maybe you girls didn't know it, but they've got every road, too, every wagon lane and bridle path, except the McDonough road. Atlanta's in a bag and the strings of the bag are at Jonesboro. And if the Yankees can take the railroad there, they can pull the strings and have us, just like a possum in a poke. So, we don't aim to let them get that railroad ... I may be gone a while, girls. I just came in to tell you all good-bye and to make sure Scarlett was still with you, Melly.'

'Of course, she's with me,' said Melanie fondly. 'Don't you worry about us, Uncle Henry, and do take care of yourself.'

Uncle Henry wiped his wet feet on the rag rug and groaned as he drew on his tattered shoes.

'I got to be going,' he said. 'I've got five miles to walk. Scarlett, you fix me up some kind of lunch to take. Anything you've got.'

After he had kissed Melanie good-bye, he went down to the kitchen where Scarlett was wrapping corn pone and some apples in a napkin.

'Uncle Henry – is it – is it really so serious?'

'Serious? God'lmighty, yes! Don't be a goose. We're in the last ditch.'

'Do you think they'll get to Tara?'

'Why—' began Uncle Henry, irritated at the feminine mind which thought only of personal things when broad issues were involved. Then, seeing her frightened, woebegone face, he softened.

'Of course they won't. Tara's five miles from the railroad and it's the railroad the Yankees want. You've got no more sense than a June bug, Missy.' He broke off abruptly. 'I didn't walk all this way here tonight just to tell you all good-bye. I came to bring Melly some bad news, but when I got up to do it I just couldn't tell her. So I'm going to leave it to you to do.'

'Ashley isn't – you haven't heard anything – that he's – dead?'

'Now, how would I be hearing about Ashley when I've been standing in rifle-pits up to the seat of my pants in mud?' the old gentleman asked testily. 'No. It's about his father. John Wilkes is dead.'

Scarlett sat down suddenly, the half-wrapped lunch in her hand.

'I came to tell Melly – but I couldn't. You must do it. And give her these.'

He hauled from his pockets a heavy gold watch with dangling seals, a small miniature of the long dead Mrs Wilkes and a pair of massive cuff buttons. At the sight of the watch which she had seen in John Wilkes' hands a thousand times, the full realization came over Scarlett that Ashley's father was really dead. And she was too stunned to cry or to speak. Uncle Henry fidgeted, coughed and did not look at her, lest he catch sight of a tear that would upset him.

'He was a brave man, Scarlett. Tell Melly that. Tell her to write it to his girls. And a good soldier for all his years. A shell got him. Came right down on him and his horse. Tore the horse's— I shot the horse myself, poor creature. A fine little mare she was. You'd better write Mrs Tarleton about that, too. She set a store on that mare. Wrap up my lunch, child. I must be going. There, dear, don't take it so hard. What better way can an old man die than doing a young man's work?'

'Oh, he shouldn't have died! He shouldn't have ever gone to the war. He should have lived and seen his grandchild grow up and died peacefully in bed. Oh, why did he go? He didn't believe in secession and he hated the war and—'

'Plenty of us think that way, but what of it?' Uncle Henry blew his nose grumpily. 'Do you think I enjoy letting Yankee riflemen use me for a target at my age? But there's no other choice for a gentleman these days. Kiss me good-bye, child, and don't worry about me. I'll come through this war safely.'

Scarlett kissed him and heard him go down the steps into the dark, heard the latch click on the front gate. She stood for a minute looking at the keepsakes in her hand. And then she went up the stairs to tell Melanie.

At the end of July came the unwelcome news, predicted by Uncle Henry, that the Yankees had swung around again toward Jonesboro. They had cut the railroad four miles below the town, but they had been beaten off by the Confederate cavalry; and the engineering corps, sweating in the broiling sun, had repaired the line.

Scarlett was frantic with anxiety. For three days she waited, fear growing in her heart. Then a reassuring letter came from Gerald. The enemy had not reached Tara. They had heard the sound of the fight but they had seen no Yankees.

Gerald's letter was so full of brag and bluster as to how the Yankees had been driven from the railroad that one would have thought he personally had accomplished the feat, single-handed. He wrote for three pages about the gallantry of the troops and then, at the end of his letter, mentioned briefly that Carreen was ill. The typhoid, Mrs O'Hara said it was. She was not very ill and Scarlett was not to worry about her, but on no condition must she come home now, even if the railroad should become safe. Mrs O'Hara was very glad now that Scarlett and Wade had not come home when the siege began. Mrs O'Hara said Scarlett must go to church and say some Rosaries for Carreen's recovery.

Scarlett's conscience smote her at this last, for it had been months since she had been to church. Once she would have thought this omission a mortal sin but, somehow, staying away from church did not seem so sinful now as it formerly had. But she obeyed her mother and going to her room gabbled a hasty Rosary. When she rose from her knees she did not feel as comforted as she had formerly felt after prayer. For some time she had felt that God was not watching out for her, the Confederates or the South, in spite of the millions of prayers ascending to Him daily.

That night she sat on the front porch with Gerald's letter in her bosom where she could touch it occasionally and bring Tara and Ellen closer to her. The lamp in the parlour window threw odd golden shadows on to the dark vine-shrouded porch, and the matted tangle of yellow climbing roses and honeysuckle made a wall of mingled fragrance about her. The night was utterly still. Not even the crack of a rifle had sounded since sunset and the world seemed far away. Scarlett rocked back and forth, lonely, miserable since reading the news from Tara, wishing that someone, anyone, even Mrs Merriwether, were with her. But Mrs Merriwether was on night duty at the hospital, Mrs Meade was at home making a feast for Phil, who was in from the front lines, and Melanie was asleep. There was not even the hope of a chance caller. Visitors had fallen off to nothing this last week, for every man who could walk was in the rifle-pits or chasing the Yankees about the countryside near Jonesboro.

It was not often that she was alone like this and she did not like it. When she was alone she had to think and, these days, thoughts were not so pleasant. Like everyone else, she had fallen into the habit of thinking of the past, the dead.

Tonight when Atlanta was so quiet, she could close her eyes and imagine she was back in the rural stillness of Tara and that life was unchanged, unchanging. But she knew that life in the County would never be the same again. She thought of the four Tarletons, the red-haired twins and Tom and Boyd, and a passionate sadness caught at her throat. Why, either Stu or Brent might have been her husband. But now, when the war was over and she went back to Tara to live, she would never again hear their wild halloos as they dashed up the avenue of cedars. And Raiford Calvert, who danced so divinely, would never again choose her to be his partner. And the Munroe boys and little Joe Fontaine and—

'Oh, Ashley!' she sobbed, dropping her head into her hands. 'I'll never get used to you being gone!'

She heard the front gate click and she hastily raised her head and dashed her hand across her wet eyes. She rose and saw it was Rhett Butler coming up the walk, carrying his wide Panama hat in his hand. She had not seen him since the day when she had alighted from his carriage so precipitately at Five Points. On that occasion, she had expressed the desire never to lay eyes on him again. But she was so glad now to have someone to talk to, someone to divert her thoughts from Ashley, that she hastily put the memory from her mind. Evidently he had forgotten the contretemps, or pretended to have forgotten it, for he settled himself on the top step at her feet without mention of their late difference.

'So you didn't refugee to Macon! I heard that Miss Pitty had retreated and, of course, I thought you had gone too. So, when I saw your light I came here to investigate. Why did you stay?'

'To keep Melanie company. You see, she – well, she can't refugee just now.'

'Thunderation!' he said, and in the lamplight she saw that he was frowning. 'You don't mean to tell me Mrs Wilkes is still here? I never heard of such idiocy. It's quite dangerous for her in her condition.'

Scarlett was silent, embarrassed, for Melanie's condition was not a subject she could discuss with a man. She was embarrassed, too, that Rhett should know it was dangerous for Melanie. Such knowledge sat ill upon a bachelor.

'It's quite ungallant of you not to think that I might get hurt, too,' she said tartly.

His eyes flickered with amusement.

'I'd back you against the Yankees any day.'

'I'm not sure that that's a compliment,' she said uncertainly.

'It isn't,' he answered. 'When will you stop looking for compliments in men's lightest utterances?'

'When I'm on my deathbed,' she replied and smiled, thinking that there would always be men to compliment her, even if Rhett never did.

'Vanity, vanity,' he said. 'At least, you are frank about it.'

He opened his cigar-case, extracted a black cigar and held it to his nose for a moment. A match flared, he leaned back against a post and, clasping his hands about his knees, smoked a while in silence. Scarlett resumed her rocking and the still darkness of the warm night closed about them. The mocking-bird, which nested in the tangle of roses and honeysuckle, roused from slumber and gave one timid, liquid note. Then, as if thinking better of the matter, it was silent again.

From the shadow of the porch, Rhett suddenly laughed, a low, soft laugh.

'So you stayed with Mrs Wilkes! This is the strangest situation I ever encountered!'

'I see nothing strange about it,' she answered uncomfortably, immediately on the alert.

'No? But then you lack the impersonal viewpoint. My impression has been for some time past that you could hardly endure Mrs Wilkes. You think her silly and stupid and her patriotic notions bore you. You seldom pass by the opportunity to slip in some belittling remark about her, so naturally it seems strange to me that you should elect to do the unselfish thing and stay here with her during this shelling. Now, just why did you do it?'

'Because she's Charlie's sister – and like a sister to me,' answered

Scarlett with as much dignity as possible though her cheeks were growing hot.

'You mean because she's Ashley Wilkes' widow.'

Scarlett rose quickly, struggling with her anger.

'I was almost on the point of forgiving you for your former boorish conduct but now I shan't do it. I wouldn't have ever let you come upon this porch at all, if I hadn't been feeling so blue and—'

'Sit down and smooth your ruffled fur,' he said, and his voice changed. He reached up and taking her hand pulled her back into her chair. 'Why are you blue?'

'Oh, I had a letter from Tara today. The Yankees are close to home and my little sister is ill with typhoid and – and – so now, even if I could go home, like I want to, Mother wouldn't let me for fear I'd catch it too. Oh, dear, and I do so want to go home!'

'Well, don't cry about it,' he said, but his voice was kinder. 'You are much safer here in Atlanta even if the Yankees do come than you'd be at Tara. The Yankees won't hurt you and typhoid would.'

'The Yankees wouldn't hurt me! How can you say such a lie?'

'My dear girl, the Yankees aren't fiends. They haven't horns and hooves, as you seem to think. They are pretty much like Southerners – except with worse manners, of course, and terrible accents.'

'Why, the Yankees would—'

'Rape you? I think not. Though, of course, they'd want to.'

'If you are going to talk vilely I shall go into the house,' she cried, grateful that the shadows hid her crimson face.

'Be frank. Wasn't that what you were thinking?'

'Oh, certainly not!'

'Oh, but it was! No use getting mad at me for reading your thoughts. That's what all our delicately nurtured and pure-minded Southern ladies think. They have it on their minds constantly. I'll wager even dowagers like Mrs Merriwether . . .'

Scarlett gulped in silence, remembering that wherever two or more matrons were gathered together, in these trying days, they whispered of such happenings, always in Virginia or Tennessee or Louisiana, never very close to home. The Yankees raped women and ran bayonets through children's stomachs and burned houses over the heads of old people. Everyone knew these things were true even if they didn't shout them on the street corners. And if Rhett had any decency he would realize they were true. And not talk about them. And it wasn't any laughing matter either.

She could hear him chuckling softly. Sometimes he was odious. In fact, most of the time he was odious. It was awful for a man to know what women really thought about and talked about. It made a girl feel positively undressed. And no man ever learned such things from good women either. She was indignant that he had read her mind. She liked to believe herself a thing of mystery to men, but she knew Rhett thought her as transparent as glass.

'Speaking of such matters,' he continued, 'have you a protector or chaperon in the house? The admirable Mrs Merriwether or Mrs Meade? They always look at me as if they knew I was here for no good purpose.'

'Mrs Meade usually comes over at night,' answered Scarlett, glad to change the subject. 'But she couldn't tonight. Phil, her boy, is home.'

'What luck,' he said softly, 'to find you alone!'

Something in his voice made her heart beat pleasantly faster and she felt her face flush. She had heard that note in men's voices often enough to know that it presaged a declaration of love. Oh, what fun! If he would just say he loved her, how she would torment him and get even with him for all the sarcastic remarks he had flung at her these past three years. She would lead him a chase that would make up for even that awful humiliation of the day he witnessed her slapping Ashley. And then she'd tell him sweetly she could only be a sister to him and retire with the full honours of war. She laughed nervously in pleasant anticipation.

'Don't giggle,' he said, and taking her hand, he turned it over and pressed his lips into the palm. Something vital, electric, leaped from him to her at the touch of his warm mouth, something that caressed her whole body thrillingly. His lips travelled to her wrist and she knew he must feel the leap of her pulse as her heart quickened and she tried to draw back her hand. She had not bargained on this – this treacherous warm tide of feeling that made her want to run her hands through his hair, to feel his lips upon her mouth.

She wasn't in love with him, she told herself confusedly. She was in love with Ashley. But how to explain this feeling that made her hands shake and the pit of her stomach grow cold?

He laughed softly.

'Don't pull away! I won't hurt you!'

'Hurt me? I'm not afraid of you, Rhett Butler, or of any man in shoe leather!' she cried, furious that her voice shook as well as her hands.

'An admirable sentiment, but do lower your voice. Mrs Wilkes might hear you. And pray compose yourself.' He sounded as though delighted at her flurry.

'Scarlett, you do like me, don't you?'

That was more like what she was expecting.

'Well, sometimes,' she answered cautiously. 'When you aren't acting like a varmint.'

He laughed again and held the palm of her hand against his hard cheek.

'I think you like me because I am a varmint. You've known so few dyed-in-the-wool varmints in your sheltered life that my very difference holds a quaint charm for you.'

This was not the turn she had anticipated and she tried again without success to pull her hand free.

'That's not true! I like nice men – men you can depend on to always be gentlemanly.'

'You mean men you can always bully. It's merely a matter of definition. But no matter.'

He kissed her palm again, and again the skin on the back of her neck crawled excitingly.

'But you do like me. Could you ever love me, Scarlett?'

'Ah!' she thought, triumphantly. 'Now I've got him!' and she answered with studied coolness: 'Indeed, no. That is – not unless you mended your manners considerably.'

'And I have no intention of mending them. So you could not love me? That is as I hoped. For while I like you immensely, I do not love you and it would be tragic indeed for you to suffer twice from unrequited love, wouldn't it, dear? May I call you "dear", Mrs Hamilton? I shall call you "dear" whether you like it or not, so no matter, but the proprieties must be observed.'

'You don't love me?'

'No, indeed. Did you hope that I did?'

'Don't be so presumptuous!'

'You hoped! Alas, to blight your hopes! I should love you, for you are charming and talented at many useless accomplishments. But many ladies have charm and accomplishments and are just as useless as you are. No, I don't love you. But I do like you tremendously – for the elasticity of your conscience, for the selfishness which you seldom trouble to hide, and for the shrewd practicality in you which, I fear, you get from some not too remote Irish-peasant ancestor.'

Peasant! Why, he was insulting her! She began to splutter wordlessly.

'Don't interrupt,' he begged, squeezing her hand. 'I like you because I have those same qualities in me and like begets liking. I realize you still cherish the memory of the godlike and wooden-headed Mr Wilkes, who's probably been in his grave these six months. But there must be room in your heart for me too. Scarlett, do stop wriggling! I am making you a declaration. I have wanted you since the first time I laid eyes on you, in the hall at Twelve Oaks, when you were bewitching poor Charlie Hamilton. I want you more than I have ever wanted any woman – and I've waited longer for you than I've ever waited for any woman.'

She was breathless with surprise at his last words. In spite of all his insults, he did love her and he was just so contrary he didn't want to come out frankly and put it into words, for fear she'd laugh. Well, she'd show him and right quickly.

'Are you asking me to marry you?'

He dropped her hand and laughed so loudly she shrank back in her chair.

'Good Lord, no! Didn't I tell you I wasn't a marrying man?'

'But – but – what—'

He rose to his feet and, hand on heart, made her a burlesque bow.

'Dear,' he said quietly, 'I am complimenting your intelligence by asking you to be my mistress without having first seduced you.'

Mistress!

Her mind shouted the word, shouted that she had been vilely insulted. But in that first startled moment she did not feel insulted. She only felt a furious surge of indignation that he should think her such a fool. He must think her a fool if he offered her a proposition like that, instead of the proposal of matrimony she had been expecting. Rage, punctured vanity and disappointment threw her mind into a turmoil and, before she even thought of the high moral grounds on which she should upbraid him, she blurted out the first words which came to her lips:

'Mistress! What would I get out of that except a passel of brats?'

And then her jaw dropped in horror as she realized what she had said. He laughed until he choked, peering at her in the shadows as she sat, stricken dumb, pressing her handkerchief to her mouth.

'That's why I like you! You are the only frank woman I know, the only woman who looks on the practical side of matters without beclouding the issue with mouthings about sin and morality. Any other woman would have swooned first and then shown me the door.'

Scarlett leaped to her feet, her face red with shame. How could she have said such a thing! How could she, Ellen's daughter, with her upbringing, have sat there and listened to such debasing words and then made such a shameless reply? She should have screamed. She should have fainted. She should have turned coldly away in silence and swept from the porch. Too late now!

'I will show you the door,' she shouted, not caring if Melanie or the Meades, down the street, did hear her. 'Get out! How dare you say such things to me! What have I ever done to encourage you – to make you suppose . . . Get out and don't ever come back here. I mean it this time. Don't you ever come back here with any of your piddling papers of pins and ribbons, thinking I'll forgive you. I'll – I'll tell my father and he'll kill you!'

He picked up his hat and bowed, and she saw in the light of the lamp that his teeth were showing in a smile beneath his moustache. He was not ashamed, he was amused at what she had said, and he was watching her with alert interest.

Oh, he was detestable! She swung round on her heel and marched into the house. She grabbed hold of the door to shut it with a bang, but the hook which held it open was too heavy for her. She struggled with it, panting.

'May I help you?' he asked.

Feeling that she would burst a blood-vessel if she stayed another minute, she stormed up the stairs. And as she reached the upper floor, she heard him obligingly slam the door for her.

Chapter XX

As the hot noisy days of August were drawing to a close the bombardment abruptly ceased. The quiet that fell on the town was startling. Neighbours met on the streets and stared at one another, uncertain, uneasy as to what might be impending. The stillness, after the screaming days, brought no surcease to strained nerves but, if possible, made the strain even worse. No one knew why the Yankee batteries were silent; there was no news of the troops except that they had been withdrawn in large numbers from the breastworks about the town and had marched off toward the south to defend the railroad. No one knew where the fighting was, if indeed there was any fighting, or how the battle was going if there was a battle.

Nowadays the only news was that which passed from mouth to mouth. Short of paper, short of ink, short of men, the newspapers had suspended publication after the siege began, and the wildest rumours appeared from nowhere and swept through the town. Now, in the anxious quiet, crowds stormed General Hood's headquarters demanding information, crowds massed about the telegraph office and the depot hoping for tidings, good tidings, for everyone hoped that the silence of Sherman's cannon meant that the Yankees were in full retreat and the Confederates chasing them back up the road to Dalton. But no news came. The telegraph wires were still, no trains came in on the one remaining railroad from the south and the mail service was broken.

Autumn with its dusty, breathless heat was slipping in to choke the suddenly quiet town, adding its dry, panting weight to tired, anxious hearts. To Scarlett, mad to hear from Tara, yet trying to keep up a brave face, it seemed an eternity since the siege began, seemed as though she had always lived with the sound of cannon in her ears until this sinister quiet had fallen. And yet, it was only thirty days since the siege began. Thirty days of siege! The city ringed with red-clay rifle-pits, the monotonous booming of cannon that never rested, the long lines of ambulances and ox-carts dripping blood down the dusty streets toward the hospitals, the overworked burial squads dragging out men when they were hardly cold and dumping them like so many logs in endless rows of shallow ditches. Only thirty days!

And it was only four months since the Yankees moved south from Dalton! Only four months! Scarlett thought, looking back on that far day, that it had occurred in another life. Oh, no! Surely not just four months. It had been a lifetime.

Four months ago! Why, four months ago Dalton, Resaca, Kennesaw Mountain had been to her only names of places on the railroad. Now they were battles – battles desperately, vainly fought as Johnston fell back toward Atlanta. And now, Peachtree Creek, Decatur, Ezra Church and Utoy Creek were no longer pleasant names of pleasant places. Never again could she think of them as quiet villages full of welcoming friends, as green places where she picnicked with handsome officers on the soft banks of slow-moving streams. These names meant battles too, and the soft green grasses where she had sat were cut to bits by heavy cannon wheels, trampled by desperate feet when bayonet met bayonet and flattened where bodies thrashed in agonies . . . And the lazy streams were redder now than ever Georgia clay could make them. Peachtree Creek was crimson, so they said, after the Yankees crossed it. Peachtree Creek, Decatur, Ezra Church, Utoy Creek. Never names of places any more. Names of graves where friends lay buried, names of tangled underbrush and thick woods where bodies rotted unburied, names of the four sides of Atlanta where Sherman had tried to force his army in and Hood's men had doggedly beaten him back.

At last, news came from the south to the strained town and it was alarming news, especially to Scarlett. General Sherman was trying the fourth side of the town again, striking at the railroad at Jonesboro. Yankees in large numbers were on that fourth side of the town now, no skirmishing units or cavalry detachments but the massed Yankee forces. And thousands of Confederate troops had been withdrawn from the lines close about the city to hurl themselves against them. And that explained the sudden silence.

'Why Jonesboro?' thought Scarlett, terror striking at her heart at the thought of Tara's nearness. 'Why must they always hit Jonesboro? Why can't they find some other place to attack the railroad?'

For a week she had not heard from Tara and the last brief note from Gerald had added to her fears. Carreen had taken a turn for the worse and was very, very sick. Now it might be days before the mails came through, days before she heard whether Carreen was alive or dead. Oh, if she had only gone home at the beginning of the siege, Melanie or no Melanie!

There was fighting at Jonesboro — that much Atlanta knew, but how the battle went no one could tell and the most insane rumours tortured the town. Finally a courier came up from Jonesboro with the reassuring news that the Yankees had been beaten back. But they had made a sortie into Jonesboro, burned the depot, cut the telegraph wires and torn up three miles of track before they retreated. The engineering corps was working like mad, repairing the line, but it would take some time because the Yankees had torn up the crossties, made bonfires of them, laid the wrenched-up rails across them until they were red-hot and then twisted them around telegraph poles until they looked like giant corkscrews. These days it was so hard to replace iron rails, to replace anything made of iron.

No, the Yankees hadn't gotten to Tara. The same courier who brought the dispatches to General Hood assured Scarlett of that. He had met Gerald in Jonesboro after the battle, just as he was starting to Atlanta, and Gerald had begged him to bring a letter to her.

But what was Pa doing in Jonesboro? The young courier looked ill at ease as he made answer. Gerald was hunting for an army doctor to go to Tara with him.

As she stood in the sunshine on the front porch, thanking the young man for his trouble, Scarlett felt her knees go weak. Carreen must be dying if she was so far beyond Ellen's medical skill that Gerald was hunting a doctor! As the courier went off in a small whirlwind of red dust, Scarlett tore open Gerald's letter with fingers that trembled. So great was the shortage of paper in the Confederacy now that Gerald's note was written between the lines of her last letter to him and reading it was difficult.

'Dear Daughter, Your mother and both girls have the typhoid. They are very ill but we must hope for the best. When your mother took to her bed she bade me write you that under no condition were you to come home and expose yourself and Wade to the disease. She sends her love and bids you pray for her.'

'Pray for her!' Scarlett flew up the stairs to her room and, dropping on her knees by the bed, prayed as she had never prayed before. No formal Rosaries now but the same words over and over: 'Mother of God, don't let her die! I'll be so good if you don't let her die! Please, don't let her die!'

For the next week Scarlett crept about the house like a stricken animal, waiting for news, starting at every sound of horses' hooves, rushing down the dark stair at night when soldiers came tapping at the door, but no news came from Tara. The width of the continent might have spread between her and home instead of twenty-five miles of dusty road.

The mails were still disrupted, no one knew where the Confederates were or what the Yankees were up to. No one knew anything except that thousands of soldiers, grey and blue, were somewhere between Atlanta and Jonesboro. Not a word from Tara in a week.

Scarlett had seen enough typhoid in the Atlanta hospitals to know what a week meant in that dread disease. Ellen was ill, perhaps dying, and here was Scarlett helpless at Atlanta with a pregnant woman on her hands and two armies between her and home. Ellen was ill – perhaps dying. But Ellen couldn't be ill! She had never been ill. The very thought was incredible and it struck at the very foundations of the security of Scarlett's life. Everyone else got sick, but never Ellen. Ellen looked after sick people and made them well again. She couldn't be sick. Scarlett wanted to be home. She wanted Tara with the desperate desire of a frightened child frantic for the only haven it had ever known.

Home! The sprawling white house with fluttering white curtains at the windows, the thick clover on the lawn with the bees busy on it, the little black boy on the front steps shooing the ducks and turkeys from the flower-beds, the serene red fields and the miles and miles of cotton turning white in the sun! Home!

If she had only gone home at the beginning of the siege, when everyone else was refugeeing! She could have taken Melanie with her in safety with weeks to spare.

'Oh, damn Melanie!' she thought a thousand times. 'Why couldn't she have gone to Macon with Aunt Pitty? That's where she belongs, with her own kinsfolk, not with me. I'm not of her blood. Why does she hang on to me so hard? If she'd only gone to Macon, then I could have gone home to Mother. Even now – even now, I'd take a chance on getting home in spite of the Yankees, if it wasn't for this baby. Maybe General Hood would give me an escort. He's a nice man, General Hood, and I know I could make him give me an escort and a flag of truce to get me through the lines. But I have to wait for this baby! . . . Oh, Mother! Mother! Don't die! . . . Why don't this baby ever come? I'll see Dr Meade today and ask him if there's any way to hurry babies up so I can go home – if I can get an escort. Dr Meade said she'd have a bad time. Dear God! Suppose she should die! Melanie dead. Melanie dead. And Ashley— No, I mustn't think about that, it isn't nice. But Ashley— No, I mustn't think about that because he's probably dead, anyway. But he made me promise I'd take care of her. But – if I didn't take care of her and she died and Ashley is still alive— No, I mustn't think about that. It's sinful. And I promised God I'd be good if He would just not let Mother die. Oh, if the baby would only come. If I could only get away from here – get home – get anywhere but here.'

Scarlett hated the sight of the ominously still town now and once she had loved it. Atlanta was no longer the gay, the desperately gay place she had loved. It was a hideous place like a plague-stricken city, so quiet, so dreadfully quiet after the din of the siege. There had been stimulation in the noise and the danger of the shelling. There was only horror in the quiet that followed. The town seemed haunted, haunted with fear and uncertainty and memories. People's faces looked pinched and the few soldiers Scarlett saw wore the exhausted look of racers forcing themselves on through the last lap of a race already lost.

The last day of August came and with it convincing rumours that the fiercest fighting since the battle of Atlanta was taking place. Somewhere to the south. Atlanta, waiting for news of the turn of battle, stopped even trying to laugh and joke. Everyone knew now what the soldiers had known two weeks before – that Atlanta was in the last ditch, that if the Macon railroad fell, Atlanta would fall too.

On the morning of the first of September, Scarlett awoke with a suffocating sense of dread upon her, a dread she had taken to her pillow the night before. She thought, dulled with sleep: 'What was it I was worrying about when I went to bed last night? Oh, yes, the fighting. There was a battle, somewhere, yesterday! Oh, who won?' She sat up hastily, rubbing her eyes, and her worried heart took up yesterday's load again.

The air was oppressive even in the early morning hour, hot with the scorching promise of a noon of glaring blue sky and pitiless bronze sun. The road outside lay silent. No wagons creaked by. No troops raised the red dust with their tramping feet. There were no sounds of negroes' lazy voices in neighbouring kitchens, no pleasant sounds of breakfasts being prepared, for all the near neighbours except Mrs Meade and Mrs Merriwether had refugeed to Macon. And she could hear nothing from their houses either. Farther down the street the business section was quiet and many of the stores and offices were locked and boarded up, while their occupants were somewhere about the countryside with rifles in their hands.

The stillness that greeted her seemed even more sinister this morning than on any of the mornings of the queer quiet week preceding it. She rose hastily, without her usual preliminary burrowing and stretchings, and went to the window, hoping to see some neighbour's face, some heartening sight. But the road was empty. She noted how the leaves on the trees were still dark green but dry and heavily coated with red dust, and how withered and sad the untended flowers in the front yard looked.

As she stood, looking out of the window, there came to her ears a far-off sound, faint and sullen as the first distant thunder of an approaching storm.

'Rain,' she thought in the first moment, and her country-bred mind added, 'We certainly need it.' But, in a split instant: 'Rain? No! Not rain! Cannon!'

Her heart racing she leaned from the window, her ear cocked to the far-off roaring, trying to discover from which direction it came. But the dim thundering was so distant that, for a moment, she could not tell. 'Make it from Marietta, Lord!' she prayed. 'Or Decatur. Or Peachtree Creek. But not from the south! Not from the south!' She gripped the window-sill tighter and strained her ears and the far-away booming seemed louder. And it was coming from the south.

Cannon to the south! And to the south lay Jonesboro and Tara – and Ellen.

Yankees perhaps at Tara, now, this minute! She listened again but the blood thudding in her ears all but blurred out the sound of far-off firing. No, they couldn't be at Jonesboro yet. If they were that far away, the sound would be fainter, more indistinct. But they must be at least ten miles down the road toward Jonesboro, probably near the little settlement of Rough and Ready. But Jonesboro was scarcely more than ten miles below Rough and Ready.

Cannon to the south, and they might be tolling the knell of Atlanta's fall. But to Scarlett, sick for her mother's safety, fighting to the south only meant fighting near Tara. She walked the floor and wrung her hands and for the first time the thought in all its implications came to her that the grey army might be defeated. It was the thought of Sherman's thousands so close to Tara that brought it all home to her, brought the full horror of the war to her as no sound of siege guns shattering window-panes, no privations of food and clothing and no endless rows of dying men had done. Sherman's army within a few miles of Tara! And even if the Yankees should be defeated, they might fall back down the road to Tara. And Gerald couldn't possibly refugee out of their way with three sick women.

Oh, if she were only there now, Yankees or not. She paced the floor in her bare feet, her nightgown clinging to her legs, and the more she walked the stronger became her foreboding. She wanted to be at home. She wanted to be near Ellen.

From the kitchen below, she heard the rattle of china as Prissy prepared breakfast, but no sound of Mrs Meade's Betsy. The shrill, melancholy minor of Prissy was raised, 'Jes' a few mo' days, ter tote de wee-ry load . . . ' The song grated on Scarlett, its sad implications frightening her, and slipping on a wrapper she pattered out into the hall and to the back stairs and shouted: 'Shut up that singing, Prissy!'

A sullen 'Yas'm' drifted up to her and she drew a deep breath, feeling suddenly ashamed of herself.

'Where's Betsy?'

'Ah doan know. She ain' came.'

Scarlett walked to Melanie's door and opened it a crack, peering into the sunny room. Melanie lay in bed in her nightgown, her eyes closed and circled with black, her heart-shaped face bloated, her slender body hideous and distorted. Scarlett wished viciously that Ashley could see her now. She looked worse than any pregnant woman she had ever seen. As she looked, Melanie's eyes opened and a soft warm smile lit her face.

'Come in,' she invited, turning awkwardly on her side. 'I've been awake since sun-up, thinking, and, Scarlett, there's something I want to ask you.'

She entered the room and sat down on the bed that was glaring with harsh sunshine.

Melanie reached out and took Scarlett's hand in a gentle confiding clasp.

'Dear,' she said, 'I'm sorry about the cannon. It's toward Jonesboro, isn't it?'

Scarlett said 'Um,' her heart beginning to beat faster as the thought recurred.

'I know how worried you are. I know you'd have gone home last week when you heard about your mother, if it hadn't been for me. Wouldn't you?'

'Yes,' said Scarlett ungraciously.

'Scarlett, darling. You've been so good to me. No sister could have been sweeter or braver. And I love you for it. I'm so sorry I'm in the way.'

Scarlett stared. Loved her, did she? The fool!

'And, Scarlett, I've been lying here thinking and I want to ask a very great favour of you.' Her clasp tightened. 'If I should die, will you take my baby?'

Melanie's eyes were wide and bright with soft urgency.

'Will you?'

Scarlett jerked away her hand as fear swamped her. Fear roughened her voice as she spoke.

'Oh, don't be a goose, Melly. You aren't going to die. Every woman thinks she's going to die with her first baby. I know I did.'

'No, you didn't. You've never been afraid of anything. You are just saying that to try to cheer me up. I'm not afraid to die but I'm so afraid to leave the baby, if Ashley is— Scarlett, promise me that you'll take my baby if I should die. Then I won't be afraid. Aunt Pittypat is too old to raise a child and Honey and India are sweet but – I want you to have my baby. Promise me, Scarlett. And if it's a boy, bring him up like Ashley, and if it's a girl – dear, I'd like her to be like you.'

'God's nightgown!' cried Scarlett, leaping from the bed. 'Aren't things bad enough without you talking about dying?'

'I'm sorry, dear. But promise me. I think it'll be today. I'm sure it'll be today. Please promise me.'

'Oh, all right, I promise,' said Scarlett, looking down at her in bewilderment.

Was Melanie such a fool she really didn't know how she cared for Ashley? Or did she know everything and feel that because of that love, Scarlett would take good care of Ashley's child? Scarlett had a wild impulse to cry out questions, but they died on her lips as Melanie took her hand and held it for an instant against her cheek. Tranquillity had come back into her eyes.

'Why do you think it will be today, Melly?'

'I've been having pains since dawn – but not very bad ones.'

'You have? Well, why didn't you call me? I'll send Prissy for Dr Meade.'

'No, don't do that yet, Scarlett. You know how busy he is, how busy they all are. Just send word to him that we'll need him some time today. Send over to Mrs Meade's and tell her and ask her to come over and sit with me. She'll know when to really send for him.'

'Oh, stop being so unselfish. You know you need a doctor as much as anybody in the hospital. I'll send for him right away.'

'No, please don't. Sometimes it takes all day having a baby and I just couldn't let the doctor sit here for hours when all those poor boys need him so much. Just send for Mrs Meade. She'll know.'

'Oh, all right,' said Scarlett.

Chapter XXI

After sending up Melanie's breakfast tray, Scarlett dispatched Prissy for Mrs Meade and sat down with Wade to eat her own breakfast. But for once she had no appetite. Between her nervous apprehension over the thought that Melanie's time was approaching and her unconscious straining to hear the sound of the cannon, she could hardly eat. Her heart acted very queerly, beating regularly for several minutes and then thumping so loudly and swiftly it almost made her sick at her stomach. The heavy hominy stuck in her throat like glue and never before had the mixture of parched corn and ground-up yams that passed for coffee been so repulsive. Without sugar or cream it was bitter as gall, for the sorghum used for 'long sweetening' did little to improve the taste. After one swallow she pushed her cup away. If for no other reason she hated the Yankees because they kept her from having real coffee with sugar and thick cream in it.

Wade was quieter than usual and did not set up his every-morning complaint against the hominy that he so disliked. He ate silently the spoonfuls she pushed into his mouth and washed them down with noisily gulped water. His soft brown eyes followed her every movement, large, round as dollars, a childish bewilderment in them as though her own scarce-hidden fears had been communicated to him. When he had finished she sent him off to the back yard to play and watched him toddle across the straggling grass to his playhouse with great relief.

She arose and stood irresolutely at the foot of the stairs. She should go up and sit with Melanie and distract her mind from her coming ordeal but she did not feel equal to it. Of all days in the world, Melanie had to pick this day to have the baby! And of all days to talk about dying!

She sat down on the bottom step of the stairs and tried to compose herself, wondering again how yesterday's battle had gone, wondering how today's fighting was going. How strange to have a big battle going on just a few miles away and to know nothing of it! How strange the quiet of this deserted end of town in contrast with the day of the fighting at Peachtree Creek! Aunt Pitty's house was one of the last on the north side of Atlanta and with the fighting somewhere to the far south, there were no reinforcements going by at double-quick, no ambulances and staggering lines of walking wounded coming back. She wondered if such scenes were being enacted on the south side of town and thanked God she was not there. If only everyone except the Meades and the Merriwethers had not refugeed from this north end of Peachtree! It made her feel so forsaken and alone. She wished fervently that Uncle Peter were with her so he could go down to headquarters and learn the news. If it wasn't for Melanie she'd go to town this very minute and learn for herself, but she couldn't leave until Mrs Meade arrived. Mrs Meade. Why didn't she come on? And where was Prissy?

She rose and went out on to the front porch and looked for them impatiently, but the Meade house was around a shady bend in the street and she could see no one. After a long while Prissy came into view, alone, idling along as though she had the whole day before her, switching her skirts from side to side and looking over her shoulder to observe the effect.

'You're as slow as molasses in January,' snapped Scarlett as Prissy opened the gate. 'What did Mrs Meade say? How soon will she be over here?'

'She warn't dar,' said Prissy.

'Where is she? When will she be home?'

'Well'm,' answered Prissy, dragging out her words pleasurably to give more weight to her message. 'Dey Cookie say Miss Meade done got wud early dis mawnin' dat young Mist' Phil done been shot an' Miss Meade she tuck de cah'ige an' Ole Talbot an' Betsy an' dey done gone ter fotch him home. Cookie say he bad hurt an' Miss Meade ain' gwine ter be studyin' 'bout comin' up hyah.'

Scarlett stared at her and had an impulse to shake her. Negroes were always so proud of being the bearers of evil tidings.

'Well, don't stand there like a ninny. Go down to Mrs Merriwether's and ask her to come up or send her mammy. Now, hurry.'

'Dey ain' dar, Miss Scarlett. Ah drapped in ter pass time of de day wid Mammy on mah way home. Dey's done gone. House all locked up. Spec dey's at de horsepittle.'

'So that's where you were so long! Whenever I send you somewhere you go where I tell you and don't stop to "pass any time" with anybody. Go—'

She stopped and racked her brain. Who was left in town among their friends who would be helpful? There was Mrs Elsing. Of course, Mrs Elsing didn't like her at all these days but she had always been fond of Melanie.

'Go to Mrs Elsing's, and explain everything very carefully and tell her to please come up here. And, Prissy, listen to me. Miss Melly's baby is due and she may need you any minute now. Now you hurry right straight back.'

'Yas'm,' said Prissy and, turning, sauntered down the walk at snail's gait.

'Hurry, you slow-poke!'

'Yas'm.'

Prissy quickened her gait infinitesimally and Scarlett went back into the house. She hesitated again before going upstairs to Melanie. She would have to explain to her just why Mrs Meade couldn't come and the knowledge that Phil Meade was badly wounded might upset her. Well, she'd tell a lie about it.

She entered Melanie's room and saw that the breakfast tray was untouched. Melanie lay on her side, her face white.

'Mrs Meade's over at the hospital,' said Scarlett. 'But Mrs Elsing is coming. Do you feel bad?'

'Not very,' lied Melanie. 'Scarlett, how long did it take Wade to get born?'

'Less than no time,' answered Scarlett with a cheerfulness she was far from feeling. 'I was out in the yard and I didn't hardly have time to get into the house. Mammy said it was scandalous – just like one of the darkies.'

'I hope I'll be like one of the darkies too,' said Melanie, mustering a smile which suddenly disappeared as pain contorted her face.

Scarlett looked down at Melanie's tiny hips with none too sanguine hopes but said reassuringly: 'Oh, it's not really so bad.'

'Oh, I know it isn't. I'm afraid I'm a little coward. Is – is Mrs Elsing coming right away?'

'Yes, right away,' said Scarlett. 'I'll go down and get some fresh water and sponge you off. It's so hot today.'

She took as long a time as possible in getting the water, running to the front door every two minutes to see if Prissy were coming. There was no sign of Prissy so she went back upstairs, sponged Melanie's perspiring body and combed out her long dark hair.

When an hour had passed she heard scuffing negro feet coming down the street, and looking out of the window, saw Prissy returning slowly, switching herself as before and tossing her head with as many airy affectations as if she had a large and interested audience.

'Some day, I'm going to take a strap to that little wench,' thought Scarlett savagely, hurrying down the stairs to meet her.

'Miss Elsing ober at de horsepittle. Dey Cookie 'lows a whole lot of wounded sojers come in on de early train. Cookie fixin' soup ter tek ober dar. She say—'

'Never mind what she said,' interrupted Scarlett, her heart sinking. 'Put on a clean apron because I want you to go over to the hospital. I'm going to give you a note to Dr Meade, and if he isn't there, give it to Dr Jones or any of the other doctors. And if you don't hurry back this time, I'll skin you alive.'

'Yas'm.'

'And ask any of the gentlemen for news of the fighting. If they don't know, go by the depot and ask the engineers who brought the wounded in. Ask if they are fighting at Jonesboro or near there.'

'Gawdlmighty, Miss Scarlett!' and sudden fright was in Prissy's black face. 'De Yankees ain' at Tara, is dey?'

'I don't know. I'm telling you to ask for news.'

'Gawdlmighty, Miss Scarlett! Whut'll dey do ter Maw?'

Prissy began to bawl suddenly, loudly, the sound adding to Scarlett's own uneasiness.

'Stop bawling! Miss Melanie will hear you. Now go change your apron, quick.'

Spurred to speed, Prissy hurried toward the back of the house while Scarlett scratched a hasty note on the margin of Gerald's last letter to her – the only bit of paper in the house. As she folded it, so that her note was uppermost, she caught Gerald's words, 'Your mother – typhoid – under no condition –

to come home—' She almost sobbed. It it wasn't for Melanie, she'd start home, right this minute, if she had to walk every step of the way.

Prissy went off at a trot, the letter gripped in her hand, and Scarlett went back upstairs, trying to think of some plausible lie to explain Mrs Elsing's failure to appear. But Melanie asked no questions. She lay upon her back, her face tranquil and sweet, and the sight of her quieted Scarlett for a while.

She sat down and tried to talk of inconsequential things, but the thoughts of Tara and a possible defeat by the Yankees prodded cruelly. She thought of Ellen dying and of the Yankees coming into Atlanta, burning everything, killing everybody. Through it all, the dull far-off thundering persisted, rolling into her ears in waves of fear. Finally, she could not talk at all and only stared out of the window at the hot still street and the dusty leaves hanging motionless on the trees. Melanie was silent too, but at intervals her quiet face was wrenched with pain.

She said, after each pain: 'It wasn't very bad, really,' and Scarlett knew she was lying. She would have preferred a loud scream to silent endurance. She knew she should feel sorry for Melanie, but somehow she could not muster a spark of sympathy. Her mind was too torn with her own anguish. Once she looked sharply at the pain-twisted face and wondered why it should be that she, of all people in the world, should be here with Melanie at this particular time – she who had nothing in common with her, who hated her, who would gladly have seen her dead. Well, maybe she'd have her wish, and before the day was over too. A cold superstitious fear swept her at this thought. It was bad luck to wish that someone were dead, almost as bad luck as to curse someone. Curses came home to roost, Mammy said. She hastily prayed that Melanie wouldn't die and broke into feverish small talk, hardly aware of what she said. At last, Melanie put a hot hand on her wrist.

'Don't bother about talking, dear. I know how worried you are. I'm so sorry I'm so much trouble.'

Scarlett relapsed into silence but she could not sit still. What would she do if neither the doctor nor Prissy got here in time? She walked to the window and looked down the street and came back and sat down again. Then she rose and looked out of the window on the other side of the room.

An hour went by and then another. Noon came and the sun was high and hot and not a breath of air stirred the dusty leaves. Melanie's pains were harder now. Her long hair was drenched in sweat and her gown stuck in wet spots to her body. Scarlett sponged her face in silence but fear was gnawing at her. God in Heaven, suppose the baby came before the doctor arrived! What would she do? She knew less than nothing of midwifery. This was exactly the emergency she had been dreading for weeks. She had been counting on Prissy to handle the situation if no doctor should be available. Prissy knew all about midwifery. She'd said so time and again. But where was Prissy? Why didn't she come? Why didn't the doctor come? She went to the window and looked again. She listened hard and suddenly she wondered if it were only her imagination or if the sound of cannon in the distance had died away. If it were farther away it would mean that the fighting was nearer Jonesboro and that would mean—

At last she saw Prissy coming down the street at a quick trot and she leaned out of the window. Prissy, looking up, saw her and her mouth opened to yell. Seeing the panic written on the little black face and fearing she might alarm Melanie by crying out evil tidings, Scarlett hastily put her finger to her lips and left the window.

'I'll get some cooler water,' she said, looking down into Melanie's dark, deep-circled eyes and trying to smile. Then she hastily left the room, closing the door carefully behind her.

Prissy was sitting on the bottom step in the hall, panting.

'Dey's fightin' at Jonesboro, Miss Scarlett! Dey say our gempmums is gittin' beat. Oh, Gawd, Miss Scarlett! Whut'll happen ter Maw an' Poke? Oh, Gawd, Miss Scarlett! Whut'll happen ter us effen de Yankees gits hyah? Oh, Gawd—'

Scarlett clapped a hand over the blubbery mouth.

'For God's sake, hush!'

Yes, what would happen to them if the Yankees came – what would happen to Tara? She pushed the thought firmly back into her mind and grappled with the more pressing emergency. If she thought of these things, she'd begin to scream and bawl like Prissy.

'Where's Dr Meade? When's he coming?'

'Ah ain' nebber seed him, Miss Scarlett.'

'What!'

'No'm, he ain' at de horsepittle. Miss Merriwether an' Miss Elsing ain' dar needer. A man he tole me de doctah down by de car-shed wid the wounded sojers jes' come in frum Jonesboro, but Miss Scarlett, Ah wuz sceered ter go down dar ter de shed – dey's folkses dyin' down dar. Ah's sceered of daid folkses—'

'What about the other doctors?'

'Miss Scarlett, fo' Gawd, Ah couldn' sceercely git one of dem ter read yo' note. Dey wukin' in de horsepittle lak dey all done gone crazy. One doctah he say ter me "Dam yo' hide! Doan you come roun' hyah bodderin' me 'bout babies w'en we got a mess of men dyin' hyah. Git some woman ter he'p you." An' den Ah went aroun' an' about an' ast fer news lak you done tole me an' dey all say "fightin' at Jonesboro" an' Ah—'

'You say Dr Meade's at the depot?'

'Yas'm. He—'

'Now, listen sharp to me. I'm going to get Dr Meade and I want you to sit by Miss Melanie and do anything she says. And if you so much as breathe to her where the fighting is, I'll sell you South as sure as gun's iron. And don't you tell her that the other doctors wouldn't come either. Do you hear?'

'Yas'm.'

'Wipe your eyes and get a fresh pitcher of water and go on up. Sponge her off. Tell her I've gone for Dr Meade.'

'Is her time nigh, Miss Scarlett?'

'I don't know. I'm afraid it is but I don't know. You should know. Go on up.'

Scarlett caught up her wide straw bonnet from the console table and jammed it on her head. She looked in the mirror and automatically pushed up loose strands of hair but she did not see her own reflection. Cold little ripples of fear that started in the pit of her stomach were radiating outward until the fingers that touched her cheeks were cold, though the rest of her body streamed perspiration. She hurried out of the house and into the heat of the sun. It was blindingly, glaringly hot and as she hurried down Peachtree Street her temples began to throb from the heat. From far down the street she could hear the rise and fall and roar of many voices. By the time she caught sight of the Leyden house, she was beginning to pant, for her stays were tightly laced, but she did not slow her gait. The roar of noise grew louder.

From the Leyden house down to Five Points, the street seethed with activity, the activity of an anthill just destroyed. Negroes were running up and down the street, panic in their faces; and on porches, white children sat crying untended. The street was crowded with army wagons and ambulances filled with wounded and carriages piled high with valises and pieces of furniture. Men on horseback dashed out of side streets pell-mell down Peachtree toward Hood's headquarters. In front of the Bonnell house, old Amos stood holding the head of the carriage horse and he greeted Scarlett with rolling eyes.

'Ain' you gone yit, Miss Scarlett? We is goin' now. Old Miss packin' her bag.'

'Going? Where?'

'Gawd knows, Miss. Somewheres. De Yankees is comin'!'

She hurried on, not even saying good-bye. The Yankees were coming! At Wesley Chapel, she paused to catch her breath and wait for her hammering heart to subside. If she did not quiet herself she would certainly faint. As she stood clutching a lamp-post for support, she saw an officer on horseback come charging up the street from Five Points and, on an impulse, she ran out into the street and waved at him.

'Oh, stop! Please, stop!'

He reined in so suddenly the horse went back on its haunches, pawing the air. There were harsh lines of fatigue and urgency in his face but his tattered grey hat was off with a sweep.

'Madam?'

'Tell me, is it true? Are the Yankees coming?'

'I'm afraid so.'

'Do you know so?'

'Yes, Ma'm. I know so. A dispatch came in to headquarters half an hour ago from the fighting at Jonesboro.'

'At Jonesboro? Are you sure?'

'I'm sure. There's no use telling pretty lies, Madam. The message was from General Hardee and it said: "I have lost the battle and am in full retreat." '

'Oh, my God!'

The dark face of the tired man looked down without emotion. He gathered the reins again and put on his hat.

'Oh, sir, please, just a minute. What shall we do?'

'Madam, I can't say. The army is evacuating Atlanta soon.'

'Going off and leaving us to the Yankees?'

'I'm afraid so.'

The spurred horse went off as though on springs and Scarlett was left standing in the middle of the street with the red dust thick upon her ankles.

The Yankees were coming. The army was leaving. The Yankees were coming. What should she do? Where should she run? No, she couldn't run. There was Melanie back there in the bed expecting that baby. Oh, why did women have babies? If it wasn't for Melanie she could take Wade and Prissy and hide in the woods where the Yankees could never find them. But she couldn't take Melanie to the woods. No, not now. Oh, if she'd only had the baby sooner, yesterday even, perhaps they could get an ambulance and take her away and hide her somewhere. But now – she must find Dr Meade and make him come home with her. Perhaps he could hurry the baby.

She gathered up her skirts and ran down the street, and the rhythm of her feet was 'The Yankees are coming! The Yankees are coming!' Five Points was crowded with people who rushed here and there with unseeing eyes, jammed with wagons, ambulances, ox-carts, carriages loaded with wounded. A roaring sound like the breaking of surf rose from the crowd.

Then a strangely incongruous sight struck her eyes. Throngs of women were coming up from the direction of the railroad tracks carrying hams across their shoulders. Little children hurried by their sides, staggering under buckets of streaming molasses. Young boys dragged sacks of corn and potatoes. One old man struggled along with a small barrel of flour on a wheelbarrow. Men, women and children, black and white, hurried, hurried with straining faces, lugging packages and sacks and boxes of food – more food than she had seen in a year. The crowd suddenly gave a lane for a careening carriage and through the lane came the frail and elegant Mrs Elsing, standing up in the front of her victoria, reins in one hand, whip in the other. She was hatless and white-faced and her long grey hair streamed down her back as she lashed the horse like a Fury. Jouncing on the back seat of the carriage was her black mammy, Melissy, clutching a greasy side of bacon to her with one hand, while with the other and both feet she attempted to hold the boxes and bags piled all about her. One bag of dried peas had burst and the peas strewed themselves into the street. Scarlett screamed to her, but the tumult of the crowd drowned her voice and the carriage rocked madly by.

For a moment she could not understand what it all meant and then, remembering that the commissary warehouses were down by the railroad tracks, she realized that the army had thrown them open to the people to salvage what they could before the Yankees came.

She pushed her way swiftly through the crowds, past the packed, hysterical mob surging in the open space of Five Points, and hurried as fast as she could down the short block toward the depot. Through the tangle of ambulances and the clouds of dust, she could see doctors and stretcher-bearers bending, lifting, hurrying. Thank God, she'd find Dr Meade soon. As she rounded the corner of the Atlanta Hotel and came in full view of the depot and the tracks, she halted, appalled.

Lying in the pitiless sun, shoulder to shoulder, head to feet, were hundreds of wounded men, lining the tracks, the sidewalks, stretched out in endless rows under the car-shed. Some lay stiff and still but many writhed under the hot sun, moaning. Everywhere, swarms of flies hovered over the men, crawling and buzzing in their faces, everywhere was blood, dirty bandages, groans, screamed curses of pain as stretcher-bearers lifted men. The smell of sweat, of blood, of unwashed bodies, of excrement rose up in waves of blistering heat until the fetid stench almost nauseated her. The ambulance men hurrying here and there among the prostrate forms frequently stepped on wounded men, so thickly packed were the rows, and those trodden upon stared stolidly up, waiting their turn.

She shrank back, clapping her hand to her mouth, feeling that she was going to vomit. She couldn't go on. She had seen wounded men in the hospitals, wounded men on Aunt Pitty's lawn after the fighting at the creek, but never anything like this. Never anything like these stinking, bleeding bodies broiling under the glaring sun. This was an inferno of pain and smell and noise and hurry – hurry – hurry! The Yankees are coming! The Yankees are coming!

She braced her shoulders and went down among them, straining her eyes among the upright figures to distinguish Dr Meade. But she discovered she could not look for him, for if she did not step carefully she would tread on some poor soldier. She raised her skirts and tried to pick her way among them toward a knot of men who were directing the stretcher-bearers.

As she walked, feverish hands plucked at her skirt and voices croaked: 'Lady – water! Please, lady, water! For Christ's sake, water!'

Perspiration came down her face in streams as she pulled her skirts from clutching hand. If she stepped on one of these men, she'd scream and faint. She stepped over dead men, over men who lay dull-eyed with hands clutched to bellies where dried blood had glued torn uniforms to wounds, over men whose beards were stiff with blood and from whose broken jaws came sounds which must mean:

'Water! Water!'

If she did not find Dr Meade soon, she would begin screaming with hysteria. She looked toward the group of men under the car-shed and cried as loudly as she could: 'Dr Meade! Is Dr Meade there?'

From the group one man detached himself and looked toward her. It was the doctor. He was coatless and his sleeves were rolled up to his shoulders. His shirt and trousers were as red as a butcher's and even the end of his iron-grey beard was matted with blood. His face was the face of a man drunk with fatigue and impotent rage and burning pity. It was grey and dusty, and sweat had streaked long rivulets across his cheeks. But his voice was calm and decisive as he called to her.

'Thank God, you are here. I can use every pair of hands.'

For a moment she stared at him bewildered, dropping her skirts in dismay. They fell over the dirty face of a wounded man who feebly tried to turn his head to escape from their smothering folds. What did the doctor mean? The dust from the ambulances came into her face with choking dryness, and the rotten smells were like a foul liquid in her nostrils.

'Hurry, child! Come here.'

She picked up her skirts and went to him as fast as she could go across the rows of bodies. She put her hand on his arm and felt that it was trembling with weariness but there was no weakness in his face.

'Oh, Doctor!' she cried. 'You must come. Melanie is having her baby.'

He looked at her as if her words did not register on his mind. A man who lay upon the ground at her feet, his head pillowed on his canteen, grinned up companionably at her words.

'They will do it,' he said cheerfully.

She did not even look down but shook the doctor's arm.

'It's Melanie. The baby. Doctor, you must come. She – the—' This was no time for delicacy but it was hard to bring out the words with the ears of hundreds of strange men listening.

'The pains are getting hard. Please, Doctor!'

'A baby? Great God!' thundered the doctor, and his face was suddenly contorted with hate and rage, a rage not directed at her or at anyone except a world wherein such things could happen. 'Are you crazy? I can't leave these men. They are dying, hundreds of them. I can't leave them for a damned baby. Get some woman to help you. Get my wife.'

She opened her mouth to tell him why Mrs Meade could not come and then shut it abruptly. He did not know his own son was wounded! She wondered if he would still be here if he did know, and something told her that even if Phil were dying he would still be standing on this spot, giving aid to the many instead of the one.

'No, you must come, Doctor. You know you said she'd have a hard time—'

Was it really she, Scarlett, standing here saying these dreadful indelicate things at the top of her voice in this hell of heat and groans? 'She'll die if you don't come!'

He shook off her hand roughly and spoke as though he hardly heard her, hardly knew what she said.

'Die? Yes, they'll all die – all these men. No bandages, no salves, no quinine, no chloroform. Oh, God, for some morphia! Just a little morphia for the worst ones. Just a little chloroform. God damn the Yankees! God damn the Yankees!'

'Give um hell, Doctor!' said the man on the ground, his teeth showing in his beard.

Scarlett began to shake and her eyes burned with tears of fright. The doctor wasn't coming with her. Melanie would die and she had wished that she would die. The doctor wasn't coming.

'Name of God, Doctor! Please!'

Dr Meade bit his lip and his jaw hardened as his face went cool again.

'Child, I'll try. I can't promise you. But I'll try. When we get these men tended to. The Yankees are coming and the troops are moving out of town. I don't know what they'll do with the wounded. There aren't any trains. The Macon line has been captured . . . But I'll try. Run along now. Don't bother me. There's nothing much to bringing a baby. Just tie up the cord . . . '

He turned as an orderly touched his arm and began firing directions and pointing to this and that wounded man. The man at her feet looked up at Scarlett compassionately. She turned away, for the doctor had forgotten her.

She picked her way rapidly through the wounded and back to Peachtree Street. The doctor wasn't coming. She would have to see it through herself. Thank God, Prissy knew all about midwifery. Her head ached from the heat and she could feel her basque, soaking wet from perspiration, sticking to her. Her mind felt numb and so did her legs, numb as in a nightmare when she tried to run and could not move them. She thought of the long walk back to the house and it seemed interminable.

Then, 'The Yankees are coming!' began to beat its refrain in her mind again. Her heart began to pound and new life came into her limbs. She hurried into the crowd at Five Points, now so thick there was no room on the narrow sidewalks and she was forced to walk in the street. Long lines of soldiers were passing, dust-covered, sodden with weariness. There seemed thousands of them, bearded, dirty, their guns slung over their shoulders, swiftly passing at route step. Cannon rolled past, the drivers flaying the thin mules with lengths of rawhide. Commissary wagons with torn canvas covers rocked through the ruts. Cavalry raising clouds of choking dust went past endlessly. She had never seen so many soldiers together before. Retreat! Retreat! The army was moving out.

The hurrying lines pushed her back on to the packed sidewalk and she smelled the reek of cheap corn whisky. There were women in the mob near Decatur Street, garishly dressed women whose bright finery and painted faces gave a discordant note of holiday. Most of them were drunk and the soldiers on whose arms they hung were drunker. She caught a fleeting glimpse of a head of red curls and saw that creature, Belle Watling, heard her shrill drunken laughter as she clung for support to a one-armed soldier who reeled and staggered.

When she had shoved and pushed her way through the mob for a block beyond Five Points, the crowd thinned a little and, gathering up her skirts, she began to run again. When she reached Wesley Chapel, she was breathless and dizzy and sick at her stomach. Her stays were cutting her ribs in two. She sank down on the steps of the church and buried her head in her hands until she could breathe more easily. If she could only get one deep breath, way down in her abdomen. If her heart would only stop bumping and drumming and cavorting. If there were only someone in this mad place to whom she could turn.

Why, she had never had to do a thing for herself in all her life. There had always been someone to do things for her, to look after her, shelter and protect her and spoil her. It was incredible that she could be in such a fix. Not a friend, not a neighbour to help her. There had always been friends, neighbours, the competent hands of willing slaves. And now in this hour of greatest need, there was no one. It was incredible that she could be so completely alone, and frightened, and far from home.

Home! If she were only home, Yankees or no Yankees. Home, even if Ellen was sick. She longed for the sight of Ellen's sweet face, for Mammy's strong arms around her.

She rose dizzily to her feet and started walking again. When she came in sight of the house, she saw Wade swinging on the front gate. When he saw her, his face puckered and he began to cry, holding up a grubby bruised finger.

'Hurt!' he sobbed. 'Hurt!'

'Hush! Hush! Hush! Or I'll spank you. Go out in the back yard and make mud pies and don't move from there.'

'Wade hungwy,' he sobbed, and put the hurt finger in his mouth.

'I don't care. Go in the back yard and—'

She looked up and saw Prissy leaning out of the upstairs window, fright and worry written on her face; but in an instant they were wiped away in relief as she saw her mistress. Scarlett beckoned to her to come down and went into the house. How cool it was in the hall! She untied her bonnet and flung it on the table, drawing her forearm across her wet forehead. She heard the upstairs door open and a low wailing moan, wrenched from the depths of agony, came to her ears. Prissy came down the stairs three at a time.

'Is de doctah come?'

'No. He can't come.'

'Gawd, Miss Scarlett! Miss Melly bad off!'

'The doctor can't come. Nobody can come. You've got to bring the baby and I'll help you.'

Prissy's mouth fell open and her tongue wagged wordlessly. She looked at Scarlett sideways and scuffed her feet and twisted her thin body.

'Don't look so simple-minded!' cried Scarlett, infuriated at her silly expression. 'What's the matter?'

Prissy edged back up the stairs.

'Fo' Gawd, Miss Scarlett—' Fright and shame were in her rolling eyes.

'Well?'

'Fo' Gawd, Miss Scarlett! We's got ter have a doctah. Ah – Ah – Miss Scarlett, Ah doan know nuthin' 'bout bringin' babies. Maw wouldn' nebber lemme be 'round folkses whut wuz havin' dem.'

All the breath went out of Scarlett's lungs in one gasp of horror before rage swept her. Prissy made a lunge past her, bent on flight, but Scarlett grabbed her.

'You black liar – what do you mean? You've been saying you knew everything about birthing babies. What is the truth? Tell me!' She shook her until the kinky head rocked drunkenly.

'Ah's lyin', Miss Scarlett! Ah doan know huccome Ah tell sech a lie. Ah jes' see one baby birthed, an' Maw she lak ter wo' me out fer watchin'.'

Scarlett glared at her and Prissy shrank back, trying to pull loose. For a moment her mind refused to accept the truth, but when realization finally came to her that Prissy knew no more about midwifery than she did, anger went over her like a flame. She had never struck a slave in all her life, but now she slapped the black cheek with all the force in her tired arm. Prissy screamed at the top of her voice, more from fright than pain, and began to dance up and down, writhing to break Scarlett's grip.

As she screamed, the moaning from the second floor ceased and a moment later Melanie's voice, weak and trembling, called: 'Scarlett? Is it you? Please come! Please!'

Scarlett dropped Prissy's arm and the wench sank whimpering to the steps. For a moment Scarlett stood still, looking up, listening to the low moaning which had begun again. As she stood there, it seemed as though a yoke descended heavily upon her neck, felt as though a heavy load were harnessed to it, a load she would feel as soon as she took a step.

She tried to think of all the things Mammy and Ellen had done for her when Wade was born but the merciful blurring of the childbirth pains obscured almost everything in mist. She did recall a few things and she spoke to Prissy rapidly, authority in her voice.

'Build a fire in the stove and keep hot water boiling in the kettle. And bring up all the towels you can find and that ball of twine. And get me the scissors. Don't come telling me you can't find them. Get them and get them quick. Now hurry.'

She jerked Prissy to her feet and sent her kitchenwards with a shove.Then she squared her shoulders and started up the stairs. It was going to be difficult, telling Melanie that she and Prissy were to deliver her baby.

Chapter XXII

There would never again be an afternoon as long as this one. Or as hot. Or as full of lazy insolent flies. They swarmed on Melanie despite the fan Scarlett kept in constant motion. Her arms ached from swinging the wide palmetto leaf. All her efforts seemed futile, for while she brushed them from Melanie's moist face, they crawled on her clammy feet and legs and made her jerk them weakly and cry: 'Please! On my feet!'

The room was in semi-gloom, for Scarlett had pulled down the shades to shut out the heat and brightness. Pin-points of sunlight came in through minute holes in the shades and about the edges. The room was an oven and Scarlett's sweat-drenched clothes never dried but became wetter and stickier as the hours went by. Prissy was crouched in a corner, sweating too, and smelled so abominably Scarlett would have sent her from the room had she not feared the girl would take to her heels if once out of sight. Melanie lay on the bed on a sheet dark with perspiration and splotched with dampness where Scarlett had spilled water. She twisted endlessly, to one side, to the other, to left, to right and back again.

Sometimes she tried to sit up and fell back and began twisting again. At first, she had tried to keep from crying out, biting her lips until they were raw, and Scarlett, whose nerves were as raw as the lips, said huskily: 'Melly, for God's sake, don't try to be brave. Yell, if you want to. There's nobody to hear you but us.'

As the afternoon wore on, Melanie moaned whether she wanted to be brave or not, and sometimes she screamed. When she did, Scarlett dropped her head into her hands and covered her ears and twisted her body and wished that she herself were dead. Anything was preferable to being a helpless witness to such pain. Anything was better than being tied here waiting for a baby that took such a long time coming. Waiting, when for all she knew the Yankees were actually at Five Points.

She fervently wished she had paid more attention to the whispered conversations of matrons on the subject of childbirth. If only she had! If only she had been more interested in such matters she'd know whether Melanie was taking a long time or not. She had a vague memory of one of Aunt Pitty's stories of a friend who was in labour for two days and died without ever having the baby. Suppose Melanie should go on like this for two days! But Melanie was so delicate. She couldn't stand two days of this pain. She'd die soon if the baby didn't hurry. And how could she ever face Ashley, if he were still alive, and tell him that Melanie had died – after she had promised to take care of her?

At first, Melanie wanted to hold Scarlett's hand when the pain was bad but she clamped down on it so hard she nearly broke the bones. After an hour of this, Scarlett's hands were so swollen and bruised she could hardly flex them. She knotted two long towels together and tied them to the foot of the bed and put the knotted end in Melanie's hands. Melanie hung on to it as though it were a life-line, straining, pulling it taut, slackening it, tearing at it. Throughout the afternoon, her voice went on like an animal dying in a trap. Occasionally she dropped the towel and rubbed her hands feebly and looked up at Scarlett with eyes enormous with pain.

'Talk to me. Please talk to me,' she whispered, and Scarlett would gabble something until Melanie again gripped the knot and again began writhing.

The dim room swam with heat and pain and droning flies, and time went by on such dragging feet Scarlett could scarcely remember the morning. She felt as if she had been in this steaming, dark, sweating place all her life. She wanted very much to scream every time Melanie did, and only by biting her lips so hard it infuriated her could she restrain herself and drive off hysteria.

Once Wade came tiptoeing up the stairs and stood outside the door, wailing.

'Wade hungwy!' Scarlett started to go to him, but Melanie whispered: 'Don't leave me. Please. I can stand it when you're here.'

So Scarlett sent Prissy down to warm up the breakfast hominy and feed him. For herself, she felt that she could never eat again after this afternoon.

The clock on the mantel had stopped and she had no way of telling the time, but as the heat in the room lessened and the bright pin points of light grew duller, she pulled the shade aside. She saw to her surprise that it was late afternoon and the sun, a ball of crimson, was far down the sky. Somehow, she had imagined it would remain broiling hot noon forever.

She wondered passionately what was going on downtown. Had all the troops moved out yet? Had the Yankees come? Would the Confederates march away without even a fight? Then she remembered with a sick dropping in her stomach how few Confederates there were and how many men Sherman had and how well fed they were. Sherman! The name of Satan himself did not frighten her half so much. But there was no time for thinking now, as Melanie called for water, for a cold towel on her head, to be fanned, to have the flies brushed away from her face.

When twilight came on and Prissy, scurrying like a black wraith, lit a lamp, Melanie became weaker. She began calling for Ashley, over and over, as if in a delirium, until the hideous monotony gave Scarlett a fierce desire to smother her voice with a pillow. Perhaps the doctor would come after all. If he would only come quickly! Hope raising its head, she turned to Prissy and ordered her to run quickly to the Meades' house and see if he were there or Mrs Meade.

'And if he's not there, ask Mrs Meade or Cookie what to do. Beg them to come!'

Prissy was off with a clatter and Scarlett watched her hurrying down the street, going faster than she had ever dreamed the worthless child could move. After a prolonged time she was back, alone.

'De doctah ain' been home all day. Sont wud he mout go off wid de sojers. Miss Scarlett, Mist' Phil's 'ceased.'

'Dead?'

'Yas'm,' said Prissy, expanding with importance. 'Talbot, dey coachman, tole me. He wuz shot—'

'Never mind that.'

'Ah din' see Miss Meade. Cookie say Miss Meade she washin' him an' fixin' ter buhy him fo' de Yankees gits hyah. Cookie say effen de pain git too bad, jes' you put a knife unner Miss Melly's bed an' it cut de pain in two.'

Scarlett wanted to slap her again for this helpful information but Melanie opened wide, dilated eyes and whispered: 'Dear – are the Yankees coming?'

'No,' said Scarlett stoutly. 'Prissy's a liar.'

'Yas'm, Ah sho is,' Prissy agreed fervently.

'They're coming,' whispered Melanie undeceived and buried her face in the pillow. Her voice came out muffled.

'My poor baby. My poor baby.' And, after a long interval: 'Oh, Scarlett, you mustn't stay here. You must go and take Wade.'

What Melanie said was no more than Scarlett had been thinking, but hearing it put into words infuriated her, shamed her as if her secret cowardice was written plainly in her face.

'Don't be a goose. I'm not afraid. You know I won't leave you.'

'You might as well. I'm going to die.' And she began moaning again.

Scarlett came down the dark stairs slowly, like an old woman, feeling her way, clinging to the banisters lest she fall. Her legs were leaden, trembling with fatigue and strain, and she shivered with cold from the clammy sweat that soaked her body. Feebly she made her way on to the front porch and sank down on the top step. She sprawled back against a pillar of the porch and with a shaking hand unbuttoned her basque half-way down her bosom. The night was drenched in warm soft darkness and she lay staring into it, dull as an ox.

It was all over. Melanie was not dead and the small baby boy who made noises like a young kitten was receiving his first bath at Prissy's hands. Melanie was asleep. How could she sleep after that nightmare of screaming pain and ignorant midwifery that hurt more than it helped? Why wasn't she dead? Scarlett knew that she herself would have died under such handling. But, when it was over, Melanie had even whispered, so weakly she had to bend over her to hear: 'Thank you.' And then she had gone to sleep. How could she go to sleep? Scarlett forgot that she too had gone to sleep after Wade was born. She forgot everything. Her mind was a vacuum; the world was a vacuum; there had been no life before this endless day and there would be none hereafter – only a heavily hot night, only the sound of her hoarse tired breathing, only the sweat trickling coldly from armpit to waist, from hip to knee, clammy, sticky, chilling.

She heard her own breath pass from loud evenness to spasmodic sobbing but her eyes were dry and burning as though there would never be tears in them again. Slowly, laboriously, she heaved herself over and pulled her heavy skirts up to her thighs. She was warm and cold and sticky all at the same time and the feel of the night air on her limbs was refreshing. She thought dully what Aunt Pitty would say, if she could see her sprawled here on the front porch with her skirts up and her drawers showing, but she did not care. She did not care about anything. Time had stood still. It might be just after twilight and it might be midnight. She didn't know or care.

She heard sounds of moving feet upstairs and thought, 'May the Lord damn Prissy,' before her eyes closed and something like sleep descended upon her. Then after an indeterminate dark interval, Prissy was beside her, chattering on in a pleased way.

'We done right good, Miss Scarlett. Ah specs Maw couldn' a did no better.'

From the shadows, Scarlett glared at her, too tired to rail, too tired to upbraid, too tired to enumerate Prissy's offences – her boastful assumption of experience she didn't possess, her fright, her blundering awkwardness, her utter inefficiency when the emergency was hot, the misplacing of the scissors, the spilling of the basin of water on the bed, the dropping of the new-born baby. And now she bragged about how good she had been.

And the Yankees wanted to free the negroes! Well, the Yankees were welcome to them.

She lay back against the pillar in silence and Prissy, aware of her mood, tiptoed away into the darkness of the porch. After a long interval in which her breathing finally quieted and her mind steadied, Scarlett heard the sound of faint voices from up the road, the tramping of many feet coming from the north. Soldiers! She sat up slowly, pulling down her skirts, although she knew no one could see her in the darkness. As they came abreast the house, an indeterminate number, passing like shadows, she called to them.

'Oh, please!'

A shadow disengaged itself from the mass and came to the gate.

'Are you going? Are you leaving us?'

The shadow seemed to take off a hat and a quiet voice came from the darkness.

'Yes, Ma'm. That's what we're doing. We're the last of the men from the breastworks, 'bout a mile north of here.'

'Are you – is the army really retreating?'

'Yes, Ma'm. You see, the Yankees are coming.'

The Yankees are coming! She had forgotten that. Her throat suddenly contracted and she could say nothing more. The shadow moved away, merged itself with the other shadows, and the feet tramped off into the darkness. 'The Yankees are coming! The Yankees are coming!' That was what the rhythm of their feet said, that was what her suddenly bumping heart thudded out with each beat. The Yankees are coming!

'Der Yankees is comin'!' bawled Prissy, shrinking close to her. 'Oh, Miss Scarlett, dey'll kill us all! Dey'll run dey baynits in our stummicks! Dey'll—'

'Oh, hush!' It was terrifying enough to think these things without hearing them put into trembling words. Renewed fear swept her. What could she do? How could she escape? Where could she turn for help? Every friend had failed her.

Suddenly she thought of Rhett Butler and calm dispelled her fears. Why hadn't she thought of him this morning when she had been tearing about like a chicken with its head off? She hated him, but he was strong and smart and he wasn't afraid of the Yankees. And he was still in town. Of course, she was mad at him and he had said unforgivable things the last time she'd seen him. But she could overlook such things at a time like this. And he had a horse and carriage, too. Oh, why hadn't she thought of him before! He could take them all away from this doomed place, away from the Yankees, somewhere, anywhere.

She turned to Prissy and spoke with feverish urgency.

'You know where Captain Butler lives – at the Atlanta Hotel?'

'Yas'm, but—'

'Well, go there, now, as quick as you can run and tell him I want him. I want him to come quickly and bring his horse and carriage or an ambulance if he can get one. Tell him about the baby. Tell him I want him to take us out of here. Go, now. Hurry!'

She sat upright and gave Prissy a push to speed her feet.

'Gawdlmighty, Miss Scarlett! Ah's sceered ter go runnin' roun' in de dahk by mahseff! Spose de Yankees gits me?'

'If you run fast you can catch up with those soldiers and they won't let the Yankees get you. Hurry!'

'Ah's sceered! Sposin' Cap'n Butler ain' at de hotel?'

'Then ask where he is. Haven't you any gumption? If he isn't at the hotel, go to the bar-rooms on Decatur Street and ask for him. Go to Belle Watling's house. Hunt for him. You fool, don't you see that if you don't hurry and find him the Yankees will surely get us all?'

'Miss Scarlett, Maw would weah me out wid a cotton stalk, did Ah go in a bahroom or a ho' house.'

Scarlett pulled herself to her feet.

'Well, I'll wear you out if you don't. You can stand outside in the street and yell for him, can't you? Or ask somebody if he's inside. Get going.'

When Prissy still lingered, shuffling her feet and mouthing, Scarlett gave her another push which nearly sent her headlong down the front steps.

'You'll go or I'll sell you down the river. You'll never see your mother again or anybody you know and I'll sell you for a field hand too. Hurry!'

'Gawdlmighty, Miss Scarlett—'

But under the determined pressure of her mistress' hand she started down the steps. The front gate clicked and Scarlett cried: 'Run, you goose!'

She heard the patter of Prissy's feet as she broke into a trot, and then the sound died away on the soft earth.

Chapter XXIII

After Prissy had gone, Scarlett went wearily into the downstairs hall and lit a lamp. The house felt steamingly hot, as though it held in its walls all the heat of the noontide. Some of her dullness was passing now and her stomach was clamouring for food. She remembered she had had nothing to eat since the night before except a spoonful of hominy, and picking up the lamp she went into the kitchen. The fire in the oven had died but the room was stiflingly hot. She found half a pone of hard corn bread in the skillet and gnawed hungrily on it while she looked about for other food. Thee was some hominy left in the pot and she ate it with a big cooking spoon, not waiting to put it on a plate. It needed salt badly but she was too hungry to hunt for it. After four spoonfuls of it, the heat of the room was too much and, taking the lamp in one hand and a fragment of pone in the other, she went out into the hall.

She knew she should go upstairs and sit beside Melanie. If anything went wrong, Melanie would be too weak to call. But the idea of returning to that room where she had spent so many nightmare hours was repulsive to her. Even if Melanie were dying, she couldn't go back up there. She never wanted to see that room again. She set the lamp on the candle-stand by the window and returned to the front porch. It was so much cooler here, even though the night was drowned in soft warmth. She sat down on the steps in the circle of faint light thrown by the lamp and continued gnawing on the corn bread.

When she had finished it, a measure of strength came back to her and with the strength came again the pricking of fear. She could hear a humming of noise far down the street, but what it portended she did not know. She could distinguish nothing but a volume of sound that rose and fell. She strained forward trying to hear and soon she found her muscles aching from the tension. More than anything in the world she yearned to hear the sound of hooves and to see Rhett's careless, self-confident eyes laughing at her fears. Rhett would take them away, somewhere. She didn't know where. She didn't care.

As she sat straining her ears toward town, a faint glow appeared above the trees. It puzzled her. She watched it and saw it grow brighter. The dark sky became pink and then dull red and, suddenly above the trees, she saw a huge tongue of flame leap high to the heavens. She jumped to her feet, her heart beginning again its sickening thudding and bumping.

The Yankees had come! She knew they had come and they were burning the town. The flames seemed to be off to the east of the centre of town. They shot higher and higher and widened rapidly into a broad expanse of red before her terrified eyes. A whole block must be burning. A faint hot breeze that had sprung up bore the smell of smoke to her.

She fled up the stairs to her own room and hung out the window for a better view. The sky was a hideous lurid colour and great swirls of black smoke went twisting up to hang in billowy clouds above the flames. The smell of smoke was stronger now. Her mind rushed incoherently here and there, thinking how soon the flames would spread up Peachtree Street and burn this house, how soon the Yankees would be rushing in upon her, where she would run, what she would do. All the fiends of hell seemed screaming in her ears and her brain swirled with confusion and panic so overpowering she clung to the window-sill for support.

'I must think,' she told herself over and over. 'I must think.'

But thoughts eluded her, darting in and out of her mind like frightened humming-birds. As she stood hanging on to the sill, a deafening explosion burst on her ears, louder than any cannon she had ever heard. The sky was rent with gigantic flame. Then other explosions. The earth shook and the glass in the panes above her head shivered and came down around her.

The world became an inferno of noise and flame and trembling earth as one explosion followed another in ear-splitting succession. Torrents of sparks shot to the sky and descended slowly, lazily, through blood-coloured clouds of smoke. She thought she heard a feeble call from the next room but she paid it no heed. She had no time for Melanie now. No time for anything except a fear that licked through her veins as swiftly as the flames she saw. She was a child and mad with fright and she wanted to bury her head in her mother's lap and shut out this sight. If she were only home! Home with Mother.

Through the nerve-shivering sounds, she heard another sound, that of fear-sped feet coming up the stairs three at a time, heard a voice yelping like a lost hound. Prissy broke into the room and, flying to Scarlett, clutched her arm in a grip that seemed to pinch out pieces of flesh.

'The Yankees—' cried Scarlett.

'No'm, it's our gempmums!' yelled Prissy between breaths, digging her nails deeper into Scarlett's arm. 'Dey's buhnin' de foun'ry an' de ahmy supply depots an' de wa'houses an', fo' Gawd, Miss Scarlett, dey done set off dem sebenty freight cahs of cannon-balls an' gunpowder an', Jesus, we's all gwine ter buhn up!'

She began yelping again shrilly and pinched Scarlett so hard she cried out in pain and fury and shook off her hand.

The Yankees hadn't come yet! There was still time to get away! She rallied her frightened forces together.

'If I don't get a hold on myself,' she thought, 'I'll be squalling like a scalded cat!' and the sight of Prissy's abject terror helped steady her. She took her by the shoulders and shook her.

'Shut up that racket and talk sense. The Yankees haven't come, you fool! Did you see Captain Butler? What did he say? Is he coming?'

Prissy ceased her yelling but her teeth chattered.

'Yas'm, Ah finely foun' him. In a bahroom, lak you tole me. He—'

'Never mind where you found him. Is he coming? Did you tell him to bring his horse?'

'Lawd, Miss Scarlett, he say our gempmums done tuck his hawse an' cah'ige fer a amberlance.'

'Dear God in Heaven!'

'But he comin'—'

'What did he say?'

Prissy had recovered her breath and a small measure of control but her eyes still rolled.

'Well'm, lak you tole me, Ah foun' him in a bahroom. Ah stood outside an' yell fer him an' he come out. An' terreckly he see me an' Ah starts ter tell him, de sojers tech off a sto' house down Decatur Street an' it flame up an' he say Come on an' he grab me an' we runs up ter Fibe Points an' he say den: What now? Talk fas'. An' Ah say you say, Cap'n Butler, come quick an' bring yo' hawse an' cah'ige. Miss Melly done had a chile an' you is bustin' ter git outer town. An' he say: Where all she studyin' 'bout goin'? An' Ah say: Ah doan know, suh, but you is boun' ter go fo' de Yankees gits hyah an' wants him ter go wid you. An' he laugh an' say dey done tuck his hawse.'

Scarlett's heart went leaden as the last hope left her. Fool that she was, why hadn't she thought that the retreating army would naturally take every vehicle and animal left in the city? For a moment she was too stunned to hear what Prissy was saying but she pulled herself together to hear the rest of the story.

'An' den he say, Tell Miss Scarlett ter res' easy. Ah'll steal her a hawse outer de ahmy crall effen dey's ary one lef'. An' he say, Ah done stole hawses befo' dis night. Tell her Ah git her a hawse effen Ah gits shot fer it. Den he laugh agin an' say, Cut an' run home. An' befo' Ah gits started Kerbloom! Off goes a noise an' Ah lak ter drap in mah tracks an' he tell me twarn't nuthin' but de ammernition our gempmums blowin' up so's de Yankees don't git it an'—'

'He is coming? He's going to bring a horse?'

'So he say.'

She drew a long breath of relief. If there was any way of getting a horse, Rhett Butler would get one. A smart man, Rhett. She would forgive him anything if he got them out of this mess. Escape! And with Rhett she would have no fear. Rhett would protect them. Thank God for Rhett! With safety in view she turned practical.

'Wake Wade up and dress him and pack some clothes for all of us. Put them in the small trunk. And don't tell Miss Melanie we're going. Not yet. But wrap the baby in a couple of thick towels and be sure and pack his clothes.'

Prissy still clung to her skirts and hardly anything showed in her eyes except the whites. Scarlett gave her a shove and loosened her grip.

'Hurry,' she cried, and Prissy went off like a rabbit.

Scarlett knew she should go in and quiet Melanie's fear, knew Melanie must be frightened out of her senses by the thunderous noises that continued unabated and the glare that lighted the sky. It looked and sounded like the end of the world.

But she could not bring herself to go back into that room just yet. She ran down the stairs with some idea of packing up Miss Pittypat's china and the little silver she had left when she refugeed to Macon. But when she reached the dining-room, her hands were shaking so badly she dropped three plates and shattered them. She ran out on to the porch to listen and back again to the dining-room and dropped the silver clattering to the floor. Everything she touched she dropped. In her hurry she slipped on the rag rug and fell to the floor with a jolt but leaped up so quickly she was not even aware of the pain. Upstairs she could hear Prissy galloping about like a wild animal and the sound maddened her, for she was galloping just as aimlessly.

For the dozenth time, she ran out on to the porch but this time she did not go back to her futile packing. She sat down. It was just impossible to pack anything. Impossible to do anything but sit with hammering heart and wait for Rhett. It seemed hours before he came. At last, far up the road, she heard the protesting screech of unoiled axles and the slow uncertain plodding of hooves. Why didn't he hurry? Why didn't he make the horse trot?

The sounds came nearer and she leaped to her feet and called Rhett's name. Then she saw him dimly as he climbed down from the seat of a small wagon, heard the clicking of the gate as he came toward her. He came into view and the light of the lamp showed him plainly. His dress was as debonair as if he were going to a ball, well-tailored white linen coat and trousers, embroidered grey watered-silk waistcoat and a hint of ruffle on his shirt bosom. His wide Panama hat was set dashingly on one side of his head and in the belt of his trousers were thrust two ivory-handled, long-barrelled duelling pistols. The pockets of his coat sagged heavily with ammunition.

He came up the walk with the springy stride of a savage and his fine head was carried like a pagan prince. The dangers of the night which had driven Scarlett into panic had affected him like an intoxicant. There was a carefully restrained ferocity in his dark face, a ruthlessness which would have frightened her had she the wits to see it.

His black eyes danced as though amused by the whole affair, as though the earth-splitting sounds and the horrid glare were merely things to frighten children. She swayed toward him as he came up the steps, her face white, her green eyes burning.

'Good evening,' he said, in his drawling voice, as he removed his hat with a sweeping gesture. 'Fine weather we're having. I hear you're going to take a trip.'

'If you make any jokes, I shall never speak to you again,' she said with quivering voice.

'Don't tell me you are frightened!' He pretended to be surprised and smiled in a way that made her long to push him backwards down the steep steps.

'Yes, I am! I'm frightened to death, and if you had the sense God gave a goat, you'd be frightened too. But we haven't got time to talk. We must get out of here.'

'At your service, Madam. But just where were you figuring on going? I made the trip out here for curiosity, just to see where you were intending to go. You can't go north or east or south or west. The Yankees are all around. There's just one road out of town which the Yankees haven't got yet and the army is retreating by that road. And that road won't be open long. General Steve Lee's cavalry is fighting a rearguard action at Rough and Ready to hold it open long enough for the army to get away. If you follow the army down the McDonough road, they'll take the horse away from you and, while it's not much of a horse, I did go to a lot of trouble stealing it. Just where are you going?'

She stood shaking, listening to his words, hardly hearing them. But, at his question, she suddenly knew where she was going, knew that all this miserable day she had known where she was going. The only place.

'I'm going home,' she said.

'Home? You mean to Tara?'

'Yes, yes! To Tara! Oh, Rhett, we must hurry!'

He looked at her as if she had lost her mind.

'Tara? God Almighty, Scarlett! Don't you know they fought all day at Jonesboro? Fought for ten miles up and down the road from Rough and Ready even into the streets of Jonesboro? The Yankees may be all over Tara by now, all over the County. Nobody knows where they are but they're in that neighbourhood. You can't go home! You can't go right through the Yankee army!'

'I will go home!' she cried. 'I will! I will!'

'You little fool,' and his voice was swift and rough. 'You can't go that way. Even if you didn't run into the Yankees, the woods are full of stragglers and deserters from both armies. And lots of our troops are still retreating from Jonesboro. They'd take the horse away from you as quickly as the Yankees would. Your only chance is to follow the troops down the McDonough road and pray that they won't see you in the dark. You can't go to Tara. Even if you got there, you'd probably find it burned down. I won't let you go home. It's insanity.'

'I will go home!' she cried, and her voice broke and rose to a scream. 'I will go home! You can't stop me! I will go home! I want my mother! I'll kill you if you try to stop me! I will go home!'

Tears of fright and hysteria streamed down her face as she finally gave way under the long strain. She beat on his chest with her fists and screamed again: 'I will! I will! If I have to walk every step of the way!'

Suddenly she was in his arms, her wet cheek against the starched ruffle of his shirt, her beating hands stilled against him. His hands caressed her tumbled hair gently, soothingly, and his voice was gentle too. So gentle, so quiet, so devoid of mockery, it did not seem Rhett Butler's voice at all but the voice of some kind strong stranger who smelled of brandy and tobacco and horses, comforting smells because they reminded her of Gerald.

'There, there, darling,' he said softly. 'Don't cry. You shall go home, my brave little girl. You shall go home. Don't cry.'

She felt something brush her hair and wondered vaguely through her tumult if it were his lips. He was so tender, so infinitely soothing, she longed to stay in his arms forever. With such strong arms about her, surely nothing could harm her.

He fumbled in his pocket and produced a handkerchief and wiped her eyes.

'Now, blow your nose like a good child,' he ordered, a glint of a smile in his eyes, 'and tell me what to do. We must work fast.'

She blew her nose obediently, still trembling, but she could not think what to tell him to do. Seeing how her lip quivered and her eyes looked at him helplessly, he took command.

'Mrs Wilkes has had her child? It will be dangerous to move her – dangerous to drive her twenty-five miles in that rickety wagon. We'd better leave her with Mrs Meade.'

'The Meades aren't home. I can't leave her.'

'Very well. Into the wagon she goes. Where is that simple-minded little wench?'

'Upstairs packing the trunk.'

'Trunk? You can't take any trunk in that wagon. It's almost too small to hold all of you and the wheels are ready to come off with no encouragement. Call her and tell her to get the smallest feather bed in the house and put it in the wagon.'

Still Scarlett could not move. He took her arm in a strong grasp and some of the vitality which animated him seemed to flow into her body. If only she could be as cool and casual as he was! He propelled her into the hall but she still stood helplessly looking at him. His lip went down mockingly: 'Can this be the heroic young woman who assured me she feared neither God nor man?'

He suddenly burst into laughter and dropped her arm. Stung, she glared at him, hating him.

'I'm not afraid,' she said.

'Yes, you are. In another moment you'll be in a swoon and I have no smelling salts about me.'

She stamped her foot impotently because she could not think of anything else to do – and without a word picked up the lamp and started up the stairs. He was close behind her and she could hear him laughing softly to himself. That sound stiffened her spine. She went into Wade's nursery and found him sitting clutched in Prissy's arms, half dressed, hiccoughing quietly. Prissy was whimpering. The feather tick on Wade's bed was small and she ordered Prissy to drag it down the stairs and into the wagon. Prissy put down the child and obeyed. Wade followed her down the stairs, his hiccoughs stilled by his interest in the proceedings.

'Come,' said Scarlett, turning to Melanie's door and Rhett followed her, hat in hand.

Melanie lay quietly with the sheet up to her chin. Her face was deathly white but her eyes, sunken and black-circled, were serene. She showed no surprise at the sight of Rhett in her bedroom but seemed to take it as a matter of course. She tried to smile weakly but the smile died before it reached the corners of her mouth.

'We are going home, to Tara,' Scarlett explained rapidly. 'The Yankees are coming. Rhett is going to take us. It's the only way, Melly.'

Melanie tried to nod her head feebly and gestured toward the baby. Scarlett picked up the small baby and wrapped him hastily in a thick towel. Rhett stepped to the bed.

'I'll try not to hurt you,' he said quietly, tucking the sheet about her. 'See if you can put your arms around my neck.'

Melanie tried but they fell back weakly. He bent, slipped an arm under her shoulders and another across her knees and lifted her gently. She did not cry out but Scarlett saw her bite her lip and go even whiter. Scarlett held the lamp high for Rhett to see and started toward the door when Melanie made a feeble gesture toward the wall.

'What is it?' Rhett asked softly.

'Please,' Melanie whispered, trying to point. 'Charles.'

Rhett looked down at her as if he thought her delirious but Scarlett understood and was irritated. She knew Melanie wanted the daguerreotype of Charles which hung on the wall below his sword and pistol.

'Please,' Melanie whispered again, 'the sword.'

'Oh, all right,' said Scarlett, and, after she had lighted Rhett's careful way down the steps, she went back and unhooked the sword and pistol belts. It would be awkward, carrying them as well as the baby and the lamp. That was just like Melanie, not to be at all bothered over nearly dying and having the Yankees at her heels but to worry about Charles' things.

As she took down the daguerreotype, she caught a glimpse of Charles' face. His large brown eyes met hers and she stopped for a moment to look at the picture curiously. This man had been her husband, had lain beside her for a few nights, had given her a child with eyes as soft and brown as his. And she could hardly remember him.

The child in her arms waved small fists and mewed softly and she looked down at him. For the first time, she realized that this was Ashley's baby and suddenly wished with all the strength left in her that he were her baby, hers and Ashley's.

Prissy came bounding up the stairs and Scarlett handed the child to her. They went hastily down, the lamp throwing uncertain shadows on the wall. In the hall, Scarlett saw a bonnet and put it on hurriedly, tying the ribbons under her chin. It was Melanie's black mourning bonnet and it did not fit Scarlett's head but she could not recall where she had put her own bonnet.

She went out of the house and down the front steps, carrying the lamp and trying to keep the sabre from banging against her legs. Melanie lay full length in the back of the wagon, and beside her were Wade and the towel-swathed baby. Prissy climbed in and took the baby in her arms.

The wagon was very small and the boards about the sides very low. The wheels leaned inward as if their first revolution would make them come off. She took one look at the horse and her heart sank. He was a small emaciated animal and he stood with his head dispiritedly low, almost between his forelegs. His back was raw with sores and harness galls and he breathed as no sound horse should.

'Not much of an animal, is it?' grinned Rhett. 'Looks like he'll die in the shafts. But he's the best I could do. Some day I'll tell you with embellishments just where and how I stole him and how narrowly I missed getting shot. Nothing but my devotion to you would make me, at this stage of my career, turn horse thief – and thief of such a horse. Let me help you in.'

He took the lamp from her and set it on the ground. The front seat was only a narrow plank across the sides of the wagon. Rhett picked Scarlett up bodily and swung her to it. How wonderful to be a man and as strong as Rhett, she thought, tucking her wide skirts about her. With Rhett beside her, she did not fear anything, neither the fire nor the noise nor the Yankees.

He climbed on to the seat beside her and picked up the reins.

'Oh, wait!' she cried. 'I forgot to lock the front door.'

He burst into a roar of laughter and flapped the reins upon the horse's back.

'What are you laughing at?'

'At you – locking the Yankees out,' he said, and the horse started off, slowly, reluctantly. The lamp on the sidewalk burned on, making a tiny yellow circle of light which grew smaller and smaller as they moved away.

Rhett turned the horse's slow feet westward from Peachtree and the wobbling wagon jounced into the rutty lane with a violence that wrenched an abruptly stifled moan from Melanie. Dark trees interlaced above their heads, dark silent houses loomed up on either side and the white palings of fences gleamed faintly like a row of tombstones. The narrow street was a dim tunnel, but faintly through the thick leafy ceiling the hideous red glow of the sky penetrated and shadows chased one another down the dark way like mad ghosts. The smell of smoke came stronger and stronger, and on the wings of the hot breeze came a pandemonium of sound from the centre of town – yells, the dull rumbling of heavy army wagons and the steady tramp of marching feet. As Rhett jerked the horse's head and turned him into another street, another deafening explosion tore the air and a monstrous sky-rocket of flame and smoke shot up in the west.

'That must be the last of the ammunition trains,' Rhett said calmly. 'Why didn't they get them out this morning, the fools! There was plenty of time. Well, too bad for us. I thought by circling around the centre of town, we might avoid the fire and that drunken mob on Decatur Street and get through to the south-west part of town without any danger. But we've got to cross Marietta Street somewhere and that explosion was near Marietta Street or I miss my guess.'

'Must – must we go through the fire?' Scarlett quavered.

'Not if we hurry,' said Rhett and, springing from the wagon, he disappeared into the darkness of a yard. When he returned he had a small limb of a tree in his hand and he laid it mercilessly across the horse's back. The animal broke into a shambling trot, his breath panting and laboured, and the wagon swayed forward with a jolt that threw them about like popcorn in a popper. The baby wailed, and Prissy and Wade cried out as they bruised themselves against the sides of the wagon. But from Melanie there was no sound.

As they neared Marietta Street, the trees thinned out and the tall flames roaring up above the buildings threw street and houses into a glare of light brighter than day, casting monstrous shadows that twisted as wildly as torn sails flapping in a gale on a sinking ship.

Scarlett's teeth chattered but so great was her terror she was not even aware of it. She was cold and she shivered, even though the heat of the flames was already hot against their faces. This was hell and she was in it and, if she could only have conquered her shaking knees, she would have leaped from the wagon and run screaming back the dark road they had come, back to the refuge of Miss Pittypat's house. She shrank closer to Rhett, took his arm in fingers that trembled and looked up at him for words, for comfort, for something reassuring. In the unholy crimson glow that bathed them, his dark profile stood out as clearly as the head on an ancient coin, beautiful, cruel and decadent. At her touch he turned to her, his eyes gleaming with a light as frightening as the fire. To Scarlett, he seemed as exhilarated and contemptuous as if he got strong pleasure from the situation, as if he welcomed the inferno they were approaching.

'Here,' he said, laying a hand on one of the long-barrelled pistols in his belt. 'If anyone, black or white, comes up on your side of the wagon and tries to lay hand on the horse, shoot him and we'll ask questions later. But for God's sake, don't shoot the nag in your excitement.'

'I – I have a pistol,' she whispered, clutching the weapon in her lap, perfectly certain that if death stared her in the face, she would be too frightened to pull the trigger.

'You have? Where did you get it?'

'It's Charles'.'

'Charles?'

'Yes, Charles – my husband.'

'Did you ever really have a husband, my dear?' he whispered and laughed softly.

If he would only be serious! If he would only hurry!

'How do you suppose I got my boy?' she cried fiercely.

'Oh, there are other ways than husbands—'

'Will you hush and hurry?'

But he drew rein abruptly, almost at Marietta Street, in the shadow of a warehouse not yet touched by the flames.

'Hurry!' It was the only word in her mind. 'Hurry! Hurry!'

'Soldiers,' he said.

The detachment came down Marietta Street, between the burning buildings, walking at route step, tiredly, rifles held any way, heads down, too weary to hurry, too weary to care if timbers were crashing to right and left and smoke billowing about them. They were all ragged, so ragged that between officers and men there were no distinguishing insignia except here and there a torn hat-brim pinned up with a wreathed 'C.S.A.'. Many were barefooted and here and there a dirty bandage wrapped a head or arm. They went past, looking neither to left nor right, so silent that had it not been for the steady tramp of feet they might all have been ghosts.

'Take a good look at them,' came Rhett's gibing voice, 'so you can tell your grandchildren you saw the rearguard of the Glorious Cause in retreat.'

Suddenly she hated him, hated him with a strength that momentarily overpowered her fear, made it seem petty and small. She knew her safety and that of the others in the back of the wagon depended on him and him alone, but she hated him for his sneering at those ragged ranks. She thought of Charles who was dead and Ashley who might be dead and all the gay and gallant young men who were rotting in shallow graves and she forgot that she, too, had once thought them fools. She could not speak, but hatred and disgust burned in her eyes as she stared at him fiercely.

As the last of the soldiers were passing, a small figure in the rear rank, his rifle-butt dragging the ground, wavered, stopped and stared after the others with a dirty face so dulled by fatigue he looked like a sleepwalker. He was as small as Scarlett, so small his rifle was almost as tall as he was, and his grime-smeared face was unbearded. Sixteen at the most, thought Scarlett irrelevantly, must be one of the Home Guard or a runaway schoolboy.

As she watched, the boy's knees buckled slowly and he went down in the dust. Without a word, two men fell out of the last rank and walked back to him. One, a tall spare man with a black beard that hung to his belt, silently handed his own rifle and that of the boy to the other. Then, stooping, he jerked the boy to his shoulders with an ease that looked like sleight of hand. He started off slowly after the retreating column, his shoulders bowed under the weight, while the boy, weak, infuriated like a child teased by its elders, screamed out: 'Put me down, damn you! Put me down! I can walk!'

The bearded man said nothing and plodded on out of sight around the bend of the road.

Rhett sat still, the reins lax in his hands, looking after them, a curious moody look on his swarthy face. Then there was a crash of falling timbers near by and Scarlett saw a thin tongue of flame lick up over the roof of the warehouse in whose sheltering shadow they sat. Then pennons and battle flags of flame flared triumphantly to the sky above them. Smoke burnt her nostrils and Wade and Prissy began coughing. The baby made soft sneezing sounds.

'Oh, name of God, Rhett! Are you crazy? Hurry! Hurry!'

Rhett made no reply but brought the tree-limb down on the horse's back with a cruel force that made the animal leap forward. With all the speed the horse could summon, they jolted and bounced across Marietta Street. Ahead of them was a tunnel of fire where buildings were blazing on either side of the short, narrow street that led down to the railroad tracks. They plunged into it. A glare brighter than a dozen suns dazzled their eyes, scorching heat seared their skins and the roaring, crackling and crashing beat upon their ears in painful waves. For an eternity, it seemed, they were in the midst of flaming torment and then abruptly they were in semi-darkness again.

As they dashed down the street and bumped over the railroad tracks, Rhett applied the whip automatically. His face looked set and absent, as though he had forgotten where he was. His broad shoulders were hunched forward and his chin jutted out as though the thoughts in his mind were not pleasant. The heat of the fire made sweat stream down his forehead and cheeks but he did not wipe it off.

They pulled into a side street, then another, then turned and twisted from one narrow street to another until Scarlett completely lost her bearings and the roaring of the flames died behind them. Still Rhett did not speak. He only laid on the whip with regularity. The red glow in the sky was fading now and the road became so dark, so frightening, Scarlett would have welcomed words, any words from him, even jeering, insulting words, words that cut. But he did not speak.

Silent or not, she thanked Heaven for the comfort of his presence. It was so good to have a man beside her, to lean close to him and feel the hard swell of his arm and know that he stood between her and unnameable terrors, even though he merely sat there and stared.

'Oh, Rhett,' she whispered, clasping his arm, 'what would we ever have done without you? I'm so glad you aren't in the army!'

He turned his head and gave her one look, a look that made her drop his arm and shrink back. There was no mockery in his eyes now. They were naked and there was anger and something like bewilderment in them. His lip curled down and he turned his head away. For a long time they jounced along in a silence unbroken except for the faint wails of the baby and sniffles from Prissy. When she was able to bear the sniffling noise no longer, Scarlett turned and pinched her viciously, causing Prissy to scream in good earnest before she relapsed into frightened silence.

Finally Rhett turned the horse at right angles and after a while they were on a wider, smoother road. The dim shapes of houses grew farther apart and unbroken woods loomed wall-like on either side.

'We're out of town now,' said Rhett briefly, drawing rein, 'and on the main road to Rough and Ready.'

'Hurry. Don't stop!'

'Let the animal breathe a bit.' Then turning to her, he asked slowly: 'Scarlett, are you still determined to do this crazy thing?'

'Do what?'

'Do you still want to try to get through to Tara? It's suicidal. Steve Lee's cavalry and the Yankee Army are between you and Tara.'

Oh, dear God! Was he going to refuse to take her home, after all she'd gone through this terrible day?

'Oh, yes! Yes! Please, Rhett, let's hurry. The horse isn't tired.'

'Just a minute. You can't go down to Jonesboro on this road. You can't follow the train tracks. They've been fighting up and down there all day from Rough and Ready on south. Do you know any other roads, small wagon roads or lanes that don't go through Rough and Ready or Jonesboro?'

'Oh, yes,' cried Scarlett in relief. 'If we can just get near to Rough and Ready, I know a wagon trace that winds off from the main Jonesboro road and wanders around for miles. Pa and I used to ride it. It comes out right near the MacIntosh place and that's only a mile from Tara.'

'Good. Maybe you can get past Rough and Ready all right. General Steve

Lee was there during the afternoon covering the retreat. Maybe the Yankees aren't there yet. Maybe you can get through there, if Steve Lee's men don't pick up your horse.'

'I – *I* can get through?'

'Yes, *you*.' His voice was rough.

'But, Rhett— You— Aren't you going to take us?'

'No. I'm leaving you here.'

She looked around wildly, at the livid sky behind them, at the dark trees on either hand hemming them in like a prison wall, at the frightened figures in the back of the wagon – and finally at him. Had she gone crazy? Was she not hearing right?

He was grinning now. She could just see his white teeth in the faint light and the old mockery was back in his eyes.

'Leaving us? Where – where are you going?'

'I am going, dear girl, with the army.'

She sighed with relief and irritation. Why did he joke at this time of all times? Rhett in the army! After all he'd said about stupid fools who were enticed into losing their lives by a roll of drums and brave words from orators – fools who killed themselves that wise men might make money!

'Oh, I could choke you for scaring me so! Let's get on.'

'I'm not joking, my dear. And I am hurt, Scarlett, that you do not take my gallant sacrifice with better spirit. Where is your patriotism, your love for Our Glorious Cause? Now is your chance to tell me to return with my shield or on it. But, talk fast, for I want time to make a brave speech before departing for the wars.'

His drawling voice gibed in her ears. He was jeering at her and, somehow, she knew he was jeering at himself too. What was he talking about? Patriotism, shields, brave speeches? It wasn't possible that he meant what he was saying. It just wasn't believable that he could talk so blithely of leaving her here on this dark road with a woman who might be dying, a new-born infant, a foolish black wench and a frightened child, leaving her to pilot them through miles of battlefields and stragglers and Yankees and fire and God knows what.

Once, when she was six years old, she had fallen from a tree, flat on her stomach. She could still recall that sickening interval before breath came back into her body. Now, as she looked at Rhett, she felt the same way she had felt then, breathless, stunned, nauseated.

'Rhett, you are joking!'

She grabbed his arm and felt her tears of fright splash down on her wrist. He raised her hand and kissed it airily.

'Selfish to the end, aren't you, my dear? Thinking only of your own precious hide and not of the gallant Confederacy. Think how our troops will be heartened by my eleventh-hour appearance.' There was a malicious tenderness in his voice.

'Oh, Rhett,' she wailed, 'how can you do this to me? Why are you leaving me?'

'Why?' he laughed jauntily. 'Because, perhaps, of the betraying sentimentality that lurks in all of us Southerners. Perhaps – perhaps because I am ashamed. Who knows?'

'Ashamed? You should die of shame. To desert us here, alone, helpless—'

'Dear Scarlett! You aren't helpless. Anyone as selfish and determined as you are is never helpless. God help the Yankees if they should get you.'

He stepped abruptly down from the wagon and, as she watched him, stunned with bewilderment, he came around to her side of the wagon.

'Get out,' he ordered.

She stared at him. He reached up roughly, caught her under the arms and swung her to the ground beside him. With a tight grip on her he dragged her several paces away from the wagon. She felt the dust and gravel in her slippers hurting her feet. The still hot darkness wrapped her like a dream.

'I'm not asking you to understand or forgive. I don't give a damn whether you do either, for I shall never understand or forgive myself for this idiocy. I am annoyed at myself to find that so much quixoticism still lingers in me. But our fair Southland needs every man. Didn't our brave Governor Brown say just that? No matter. I'm off to the wars.' He laughed suddenly, a ringing, free laugh that startled the echoes in the dark woods.

' "I could not love thee, Dear, so much, loved I not Honour more." That's a pat speech, isn't it? Certainly better than anything I can think up myself, at the present moment. For I do love you, Scarlett, in spite of what I said that night on the porch last month.'

His drawl was caressing and his hands slid up her bare arms, warm strong hands. 'I love you, Scarlett, because we are so much alike, renegades, both of us, dear, and selfish rascals. Neither of us cares a rap if the whole world goes to pot, so long as we are safe and comfortable.'

His voice went on in the darkness and she heard words, but they made no sense to her. Her mind was tiredly trying to take in the harsh truth that he was leaving her here to face the Yankees alone. Her mind said: 'He's leaving me. He's leaving me.' But no emotion stirred.

Then his arms went around her waist and shoulders and she felt the hard muscles of his thighs against her body and the buttons of his coat pressing into her breast. A warm tide of feeling, bewildering, frightening, swept over her, carrying out of her mind the time and place and circumstances. She felt as limp as a rag doll, warm, weak and helpless, and his supporting arms were so pleasant.

'You don't want to change your mind about what I said last month? There's nothing like danger and death to give an added fillip. Be patriotic, Scarlett. Think how you would be sending a soldier to his death with beautiful memories.'

He was kissing her now and his moustache tickled her mouth, kissing her with slow, hot lips that were as leisurely as though he had the whole night before him. Charles had never kissed her like this. Never had the kisses of the Tarleton and Calvert boys made her go hot and cold and shaky like this. He bent her body backward and his lips travelled down her throat to where the cameo fastened her basque.

'Sweet,' he whispered. 'Sweet.'

She saw the wagon dimly in the dark and heard the treble piping of Wade's voice.

'Muvver! Wade fwightened!'

Into her swaying, darkened mind, cold sanity came back with a rush and she remembered what she had forgotten for the moment – that she was frightened too, and Rhett was leaving her, leaving her, the damned cad. And on top of it all, he had the consummate gall to stand here in the road and insult her with his infamous proposals. Rage and hate flowed into her and stiffened her spine and with one wrench she tore herself loose from his arms.

'Oh, you cad!' she cried, and her mind leaped about, trying to think of worse things to call him, things she had heard Gerald call Mr Lincoln, the MacIntoshes and balky mules, but the words would not come. 'You low-down, cowardly, nasty, stinking thing!' And because she could not think of anything crushing enough, she drew back her arm and slapped him across the mouth with all the force she had left. He took a step backward, his hand going to his face.

'Ah,' he said quietly, and for a moment they stood facing each other in the darkness. Scarlett could hear his heavy breathing, and her own breath came in gasps as if she had been running hard.

'They were right! Everybody was right! You aren't a gentleman!'

'My dear girl,' he said, 'how inadequate!'

She knew he was laughing and the thought goaded her.

'Go on! Go on now! I want you to hurry. I don't want to ever see you again. I hope a cannon-ball lands right on you. I hope it blows you to a million pieces. I—'

'Never mind the rest. I follow your general idea. When I'm dead on the altar of my country, I hope your conscience hurts you.'

She heard him laugh as he turned away and walked back toward the wagon. She saw him stand beside it, heard him speak and his voice was changed, courteous and respectful as it always was when he spoke to Melanie.

'Mrs Wilkes?'

Prissy's frightened voice made answer from the wagon.

'Gawdlmighty, Cap'n Butler! Miss Melly done fainted way back yonder.'

'She's not dead? Is she breathing?'

'Yessuh, she breathin'.'

'Then she's probably better off as she is. If she were conscious, I doubt if she could live through all the pain. Take good care of her, Prissy. Here's a shin-plaster for you. Try not to be a bigger fool than you are.'

'Yassuh. Thankee, suh.'

'Good-bye, Scarlett.'

She knew he had turned and was facing her but she did not speak. Hate choked all utterance. His feet ground on the pebbles of the road and for a moment she saw his big shoulders looming up in the dark. Then he was gone. She could hear the sound of his feet for a while and then they died away. She came slowly back to the wagon, her knees shaking.

Why had he gone, stepping off into the dark, into the war, into a Cause that was lost, into a world that was mad? Why had he gone, Rhett who loved the pleasures of women and liquor, the comfort of good food and soft beds, the feel of fine linen and good leather, who hated the South and jeered at the fools who fought for it? Now he had set his varnished boots upon a bitter road where hunger tramped with tireless stride and wounds and weariness and heartbreak ran like yelping wolves. And the end of the road was death. He need not have gone. He was safe, rich, comfortable. But he had gone, leaving her alone in a night as black as blindness, with the Yankee Army between her and home.

Now she remembered all the bad names she had wanted to call him but it was too late. She leaned her head against the bowed neck of the horse and cried.

Chapter XXIV

The bright glare of morning sunlight streaming through the trees overhead awakened Scarlett. For a moment, stiffened by the cramped position in which she had slept, she could not remember where she was. The sun blinded her, the hard boards of the wagon under her were harsh against her body, and a heavy weight lay across her legs. She tried to sit up and discovered that the weight was Wade, who lay sleeping with his head pillowed on her knees. Melanie's bare feet were almost in her face and, under the wagon seat, Prissy was curled up like a black cat with the small baby wedged in between her and Wade.

Then she remembered everything. She popped up to a sitting position and looked hastily all around. Thank God, no Yankees in sight! Their hiding-place had not been discovered in the night. It all came back to her now, the nightmare journey after Rhett's footsteps died away, the endless night, the black road full of ruts and boulders along which they jolted, the deep gullies on either side into which the wagon slipped, the fear-crazed strength with which she and Prissy had pushed the wheels out of the gullies. She recalled with a shudder how often she had driven the unwilling horse into fields and woods when she heard soldiers approaching, not knowing if they were friends or foes – recalled, too, her anguish lest a cough, a sneeze or Wade's hiccoughing might betray them to the marching men.

Oh, that dark road where men went by like ghosts, voices stilled, only the muffled tramping of feet on soft dirt, the faint clicking of bridles and the straining creak of leather! And, oh, that dreadful moment when the sick horse balked and cavalry and light cannon rumbled past in the darkness, past where they sat breathless, so close she could almost reach out and touch them, so close she could smell the stale sweat on the soldiers' bodies!

When, at last, they had neared Rough and Ready, a few camp-fires were gleaming where the last of Steve Lee's rearguard was awaiting orders to fall back. She had circled through a ploughed field for a mile until the light of the fires died out behind her. And then she had lost her way in the darkness and sobbed when she could not find the little wagon path she knew so well. Then finally having found it, the horse sank in the traces and refused to move, refused to rise even when she and Prissy tugged at the bridle.

So she had unharnessed him and crawled, sodden with fatigue, into the back of the wagon and stretched her aching legs. She had a faint memory of Melanie's voice before sleep clamped down her eyelids, a weak voice that apologized even as it begged: 'Scarlett, can I have some water, please?'

She had said: 'There isn't any,' and gone to sleep before the words were out of her mouth.

Now it was morning and the world was still and serene and green and gold with dappled sunshine. And no soldiers in sight anywhere. She was hungry and dry with thirst, aching and cramped and filled with wonder that she, Scarlett O'Hara, who could never rest well except between linen sheets and on the softest of feather beds, had slept like a field hand on hard planks.

Blinking in the sunlight, her eyes fell on Melanie and she gasped, horrified. Melanie lay so still and white Scarlett thought she must be dead. She looked dead. She looked like a dead, old woman with her ravaged face and her dark hair snarled and tangled across it. Then Scarlett saw with relief the faint rise and fall of her shallow breathing and knew that Melanie had survived the night.

Scarlett shaded her eyes with her hand and looked about her. They had evidently spent the night under the trees in someone's front yard, for a sand and gravel driveway stretched out before her, winding away under an avenue of cedars.

'Why, it's the Mallory place!' she thought, her heart leaping with gladness at the thought of friends and help.

But a stillness as of death hung over the plantation. The shrubs and grass of the lawn were cut to pieces where hooves and wheels and feet had torn frantically back and forth until the soil was churned up. She looked toward the house and instead of the old white clapboard place she knew so well, she saw there only a long rectangle of blackened granite foundation stones and two tall chimneys rearing smoke-stained bricks into the charred leaves of still trees.

She drew a deep shuddering breath. Would she find Tara like this, level with the ground, silent as the dead?

'I mustn't think about that now,' she told herself hurriedly. 'I mustn't let myself think about it. I'll get scared again if I think about it.' But, in spite of herself, her heart quickened and each beat seemed to thunder: 'Home! Hurry! Home! Hurry!'

They must be starting on toward home again. But first they must find some food and water, especially water. She prodded Prissy awake. Prissy rolled her eyes as she looked about her.

'Fo' Gawd, Miss Scarlett, Ah din' spec ter wake up agin 'cept in de Promise Lan'.'

'You're a long way from there,' said Scarlett, trying to smooth back her untidy hair. Her face was damp and her body was already wet with sweat. She felt dirty and messy and sticky, almost as if she smelled bad. Her clothes were crushed and wrinkled from sleeping in them and she had never felt more acutely tired and sore in all her life. Muscles she did not know she possessed ached from her unaccustomed exertions of the night before and every movement brought sharp pain.

She looked down at Melanie and saw that her dark eyes were opened. They were sick eyes, fever bright, and dark baggy circles were beneath them. She opened cracking lips and whispered appealingly: 'Water.'

'Get up, Prissy,' ordered Scarlett. 'We'll go to the well and get some water.'

'But, Miss Scarlett! Dey mout be hants up dar. Sposin' somebody daid up dar?'

'I'll make a hant out of you if you don't get out of this wagon,' said Scarlett, who was in no mood for argument, as she climbed lamely down to the ground.

And then she thought of the horse. Name of God! Suppose the horse had died in the night! He had seemed ready to die when she unharnessed him. She ran around the wagon and saw him lying on his side. If he were dead, she would curse God and die too. Somebody in the Bible had done just that thing. Cursed God and died. She knew just how that person felt. But the horse was alive – breathing heavily, sick eyes half closed, but alive. Well, some water would help him too.

Prissy climbed reluctantly from the wagon with many groans and timorously followed Scarlett up the avenue. Behind the ruins the row of whitewashed slave quarters stood silent and deserted under the overhanging trees. Between the quarters and the smoked stone foundations they found the well, and the roof of it still stood with the bucket far down the well. Between them, they wound up the rope, and when the bucket of cool sparkling water appeared out of the dark depths, Scarlett tilted it to her lips and drank with loud sucking noises, spilling the water all over herself.

She drank until Prissy's petulant, 'Well, Ah's thusty, too, Miss Scarlett,' made her recall the needs of the others.

'Untie the knot and take the bucket to the wagon and give them some. And give the rest to the horse. Don't you think Miss Melanie ought to nurse the baby? He'll starve.'

'Law, Miss Scarlett, Miss Melly ain' got no milk – ain' gwine have none.'

'How do you know?'

'Ah's seed too many lak her.'

'Don't go putting on any airs with me. A precious little you knew about babies yesterday. Hurry now. I'm going to try to find something to eat.'

Scarlett's search was futile until in the orchard she found a few apples. Soldiers had been there before her and there were none on the trees. Those she found on the ground were mostly rotten. She filled her skirt with the best of them and came back across the soft earth, collecting small pebbles in her slippers. Why hadn't she thought of putting on stouter shoes last night? Why hadn't she brought her sun-hat? Why hadn't she brought something to eat? She'd acted like a fool. But, of course, she'd thought Rhett would take care of them.

Rhett! She spat on the ground, for the very name tasted bad. How she hated him! How contemptible he had been! And she had stood there in the road and let him kiss her – and almost liked it. She had been crazy last night. How despicable he was!

When she came back, she divided up the apples and threw the rest into the back of the wagon. The horse was on his feet now but the water did not seem to have refreshed him much. He looked far worse in the daylight than he had the night before. His hip-bones stood out like an old cow's, his ribs showed like a washboard and his back was a mass of sores. She shrank from touching him as she harnessed him. When she slipped the bit into his mouth, she saw that he was practically toothless. As old as the hills! While Rhett was stealing a horse, why couldn't he have stolen a good one?

She mounted the seat and brought down the hickory limb on his back. He wheezed and started, but he walked so slowly as she turned him into the road she knew she could walk faster herself with no effort whatever. Oh, if only she didn't have Melanie and Wade and the baby and Prissy to bother with! How swiftly she could walk home! Why, she would run home, run every step of the way that would bring her closer to Tara and to Mother.

They couldn't be more than fifteen miles from home, but at the rate this old nag travelled it would take all day, for she would have to stop frequently to rest him. All day! She looked down the glaring red road, cut in deep ruts where cannon wheels and ambulances had gone over it. It would be hours before she knew if Tara still stood and if Ellen were there. It would be hours before she finished her journey under the broiling September sun.

She looked back at Melanie, who lay with sick eyes closed against the sun, and jerked loose the strings of her bonnet and tossed it to Prissy.

'Put that over her face. It'll keep the sun out of her eyes.' Then as the heat beat down upon her unprotected head, she thought: 'I'll be as freckled as a guinea egg before this day is over.'

She had never in her life been out in the sunshine without a hat or veils, never handled reins without gloves to protect the white skin of her dimpled hands. Yet here she was exposed to the sun in a broken-down wagon with a broken-down horse, dirty, sweaty, hungry, helpless to do anything but plod along at a snail's pace through a deserted land. What a few short weeks it had been since she was safe and secure! What a little while since she and everyone else had thought that Atlanta could never fall, that Georgia could never be invaded. But the small cloud which appeared in the north-west four months ago had blown up into a mighty storm and then into a screaming tornado, sweeping away her world, whirling her out of her sheltered life, and dropping her down in the midst of this still, haunted desolation.

Was Tara still standing? Or was Tara also gone with the wind which had swept through Georgia?

She laid the whip on the tired horse's back and tried to urge him on while the waggling wheels rocked them drunkenly from side to side.

There was death in the air. In the rays of the late afternoon sun, every well-remembered field and forest grove was green and still, with an unearthly quiet that struck terror to Scarlett's heart. Every empty, shell-pitted house they had passed that day, every gaunt chimney standing sentinel over smoke-blackened ruins, had frightened her more. They had not seen a living human being or animal since the night before. Dead men and dead horses, yes, and dead mules, lying by the road, swollen, covered with flies, but nothing alive. No far-off cattle lowed, no birds sang, no wind waved the trees. Only the tired plop-plop of the horse's feet and the weak wailing of Melanie's baby broke the stillness.

The countryside lay as under some dread enchantment. Or worse still, thought Scarlett with a chill, like the familiar and dear face of a mother, beautiful and quiet at last, after death agonies. She felt that the once-familiar woods were full of ghosts. Thousands had died in the fighting near Jonesboro. They were here in these haunted woods where the slanting afternoon sun gleamed eerily through unmoving leaves, friends and foes, peering at her in her rickety wagon, through eyes blinded with blood and red dust – glazed, horrible eyes.

'Mother! Mother!' she whispered. If she could only win through to Ellen! If only, by a miracle of God, Tara were still standing and she could drive up the long avenue of trees and go into the house and see her mother's kind, tender face, could feel once more the soft capable hands that drove out fear, could clutch Ellen's skirts and bury her face in them. Mother would know what to do. She wouldn't let Melanie and her baby die. She would drive away all ghosts and fears with her quiet 'Hush, hush'. But Mother was ill, perhaps dying.

Scarlett laid the whip across the weary rump of the horse. They must go faster! They had crept along this never-ending road all the long hot day. Soon it would be night and they would be alone in this desolation that was death. She gripped the reins tighter with hands that were blistered and slapped them fiercely on the horse's back, her aching arms burning at the movement.

If she could only reach the kind arms of Tara and Ellen and lay down her burdens, far too heavy for her young shoulders – the dying woman, the fading baby, her own hungry little boy, the frightened negro, all looking to her for strength, for guidance, all reading in her straight back courage she did not possess and strength which had long since failed.

The exhausted horse did not respond to the whip or reins but shambled on, dragging his feet, stumbling on small rocks and swaying as if ready to fall to his knees. But, as twilight came, they at last entered the final lap of the long journey. They rounded the bend of the wagon path and turned into the main road. Tara was only a mile away!

Here loomed up the dark bulk of the mock-orange hedge that marked the beginning of the MacIntosh property. A little farther on, Scarlett drew rein in front of the avenue of oaks that led from the road to old Angus MacIntosh's house. She peered through the gathering dusk down the two lines of ancient trees. All was dark. Not a single light showed in the house or in the quarters. Straining her eyes in the darkness, she dimly discerned a sight which had grown familiar through that terrible day – two tall chimneys, like gigantic tombstones towering above the ruined second floor, and broken unlit windows blotching the walls like still, blind eyes.

'Hello!' she shouted, summoning all her strength. 'Hello!'

Prissy clawed at her in a frenzy of fright and Scarlett, turning, saw that her eyes were rolling in her head.

'Doan holler, Miss Scarlett! Please, doan holler agin!' she whispered, her voice shaking. 'Dey ain' no tellin' *whut* mout answer!'

'Dear God!' thought Scarlett, a shiver running through her. 'Dear God! She's right. Anything might come out of there!'

She flapped the reins and urged the horse forward. The sight of the MacIntosh house had pricked the last bubble of hope remaining to her. It was burned, in ruins, deserted, as were all the plantations she had passed that day. Tara lay only half a mile away, on the same road, right in the path of the army. Tara was levelled, too! She would find only the blackened bricks, starlight shining through the roofless walls, Ellen and Gerald gone, the girls gone, Mammy gone, the negroes gone, God knows where, and this hideous stillness over everything.

Why had she come on this fool's errand, against all common sense, dragging Melanie and her child? Better that they had died in Atlanta than, tortured by this day of burning sun and jolting wagon, to die in the silent ruins of Tara.

But Ashley had left Melanie in her care. 'Take care of her.' Oh, that beautiful, heartbreaking day when he had kissed her good-bye before he went away forever! 'You'll take care of her, won't you? Promise!' And she had promised. Why had she ever bound herself with such a promise, doubly binding now that Ashley was gone? Even in her exhaustion she hated Melanie, hated the tiny mewing voice of her child which, fainter and fainter, pierced the stillness. But she had promised and now they belonged to her, even as Wade and Prissy belonged to her, and she must struggle and fight for them as long as she had strength or breath. She could have left them in Atlanta, dumped Melanie into the hospital and deserted her. But had she done that, she could never face Ashley, either on this earth or in the hereafter, and tell him she had left his wife and child to die among strangers.

Oh, Ashley! Where was he tonight while she toiled down this haunted road with his wife and baby? Was he alive and did he think of her as he lay behind the bars at Rock Island? Or was he dead of smallpox months ago, rotting in some long ditch with hundreds of other Confederates?

Scarlett's taut nerves almost cracked as a sudden noise sounded in the underbrush near them. Prissy screamed loudly, throwing herself to the floor of the wagon, the baby beneath her. Melanie stirred feebly, her hands seeking the baby, and Wade covered his eyes and cowered, too frightened to cry. Then the bushes beside them crashed apart under heavy hooves and a low moaning bawl assaulted their ears.

'It's only a cow,' said Scarlett, her voice rough with fright. 'Don't be a fool, Prissy. You've mashed the baby and frightened Miss Melly and Wade.'

'It's a ghos',' moaned Prissy, writhing face down on the wagon boards.

Turning deliberately, Scarlett raised the tree-limb she had been using as a whip and brought it down across Prissy's back. She was too exhausted and weak from fright to tolerate weakness in anyone else.

'Sit up, you fool,' she said, 'before I wear this out on you.'

Yelping, Prissy raised her head and peering over the side of the wagon saw it was, indeed, a cow, a red and white animal which stood looking at them appealingly, with large frightened eyes. Opening its mouth, it lowed again as if in pain.

'Is it hurt? That doesn't sound like an ordinary moo.'

'Soun' ter me lak her bag full an' she need milkin' bad,' said Prissy, regaining some measure of control. 'Spec it one of Mist' MacIntosh's dat de niggers driv in de woods an' de Yankees din' git.'

'We'll take it with us,' Scarlett decided swiftly. 'Then we can have some milk for the baby.'

'How all we gwine tek a cow wid us, Miss Scarlett? We kain tek no cow wid us. Cow ain' no good nohow effen she ain' been milked lately. Dey bags swells up an' busts. Dat's why she hollerin'.'

'Since you know so much about it, take off your petticoat and tear it up and tie her to the back of the wagon.'

'Miss Scarlett, you knows Ah ain' had no petticoat fer a month an' did Ah have one, Ah wouldn' put it on her fer nuthin'. Ah nebber had no truck wid cows. Ah's sceered of cows.'

Scarlett laid down the reins and pulled up her skirt. The lace-trimmed petticoat beneath was the last garment she possessed that was pretty – and whole. She untied the waist tape and slipped it down over her feet, crushing the soft linen folds between her hands. Rhett had brought her that linen and lace from Nassau on the last boat he slipped through the blockade and she had worked a week to make the garment. Resolutely she took it by the hem and jerked, put it in her mouth and gnawed, until finally the material gave with a rip and tore the length. She gnawed furiously, tore with both hands and the petticoat lay in strips in her hands. She knotted the ends with fingers that bled from blisters and shook from fatigue.

'Slip this over her horns,' she directed. But Prissy balked.

'Ah's sceered of cows, Miss Scarlett. Ah ain' nebber had nuthin' ter do wid cows. Ah ain' no yard nigger. Ah's a house nigger.'

'You're a fool nigger, and the worst day's work Pa ever did was to buy you,' said Scarlett slowly, too tired for anger. 'And if I ever get the use of my arm again, I'll wear this whip out on you.'

'There,' she thought, 'I've said "nigger" and Mother wouldn't like that at all.'

Prissy rolled her eyes wildly, peeping first at the set face of her mistress and then at the cow which bawled plaintively. Scarlett seemed the less dangerous of the two, so Prissy clutched at the sides of the wagon and remained where she was.

Stiffly, Scarlett climbed down from the seat, each movement an agony of aching muscles. Prissy was not the only one who was 'sceered' of cows. Scarlett had always feared them, even the mildest cow seemed sinister to her, but this was no time to truckle to small fears when great ones crowded so thick upon her. Fortunately the cow was gentle. In its pain it had sought human companionship and help and it made no threatening gesture as she looped one end of the torn petticoat about its horns. She tied the other end to the back of the wagon as securely as her awkward fingers would permit. Then, as she started back toward the driver's seat, a vast weariness assailed her and she swayed dizzily. She clutched the side of the wagon to keep from falling.

Melanie opened her eyes and, seeing Scarlett standing beside her, whispered: 'Dear – are we home?'

Home! Hot tears came to Scarlett's eyes at the word. Home. Melanie did not know there was no home and that they were alone in a mad and desolate world.

'Not yet,' she said, as gently as the constriction of her throat would permit, 'but we will be, soon. I've just found a cow and soon we'll have some milk for you and the baby.'

'Poor baby,' whispered Melanie, her hand creeping feebly toward her child and falling short.

Climbing back into the wagon required all the strength Scarlett could muster, but at last it was done and she picked up the lines. The horse stood with head drooping dejectedly and refused to start. Scarlett laid on the whip mercilessly. She hoped God would forgive her for hurting a tired animal. If He didn't she was sorry. After all, Tara lay just ahead, and after the next quarter of a mile, the horse could drop in the shafts if he liked.

Finally he started slowly, the wagon creaking and the cow lowing mournfully at every step. The pained animal's voice rasped on Scarlett's nerves until she was tempted to stop and untie the beast. What good would the cow do them anyway if there should be no one at Tara? She couldn't milk her and, even if she could, the animal would probably kick anyone who touched her sore udders. But she had the cow and she might as well keep her. There was little else she had in this world now.

Scarlett's eyes grew misty when, at last, they reached the bottom of a gentle incline, for just over the rise lay Tara! Then her heart sank. The decrepit animal would never pull the hill. The slope had always seemed so slight, so gradual, in days when she galloped up it on her fleet-footed mare. It did not seem possible it could have grown so steep since she saw it last. The horse would never make it with the heavy load.

Wearily she dismounted and took the animal by the bridle.

'Get out, Prissy,' she commanded, 'and take Wade. Either carry him or make him walk. Lay the baby by Miss Melanie.'

Wade broke into sobs and whimperings from which Scarlett could only distinguish: 'Dark – dark— Wade fwightened!'

'Miss Scarlett, Ah kain walk. Mah feets done blistered an' dey's thoo mah shoes, an' Wade an' me doan weigh so much an'—'

'Get out! Get out before I pull you out! And if I do, I'm going to leave you right here, in the dark by yourself. Quick, now!'

Prissy moaned, peering at the dark trees that closed about them on both sides of the road – trees which might reach out and clutch her if she left the shelter of the wagon. But she laid the baby beside Melanie, scrambled to the ground and, reaching up, lifted Wade out. The little boy sobbed, shrinking close to his nurse.

'Make him hush. I can't stand it,' said Scarlett, taking the horse by the bridle and pulling him to a reluctant start. 'Be a little man, Wade, and stop crying or I will come over there and slap you.'

Why had God invented children, she thought savagely as she turned her ankle cruelly on the dark road – useless, crying nuisances they were, always demanding care, always in the way. In her exhaustion, there was no room for compassion for the frightened child, trotting by Prissy's side, dragging at her hand and sniffling – only a weariness that she had borne him, only a tired wonder that she had ever married Charles Hamilton.

'Miss Scarlett,' whispered Prissy, clutching her mistress' arm, 'doan le's go ter Tara. Dey's not dar. Dey's all done gone. Maybe dey daid – Maw an' all'm.'

The echo of her own thoughts infuriated her and Scarlett shook off the pinching fingers.

'Then give me Wade's hand. You can sit right down here and stay.'

'No'm! No'm!'

'Then *hush!*'

How slowly the horse moved! The moisture from his slobbering mouth dripped down upon her hand. Through her mind ran a few words of the song she had once sung with Rhett – she could not recall the rest:

Just a few more days for to tote the weary load—

'Just a few more steps,' hummed her brain, over and over, 'just a few more steps for to tote the weary load.'

Then they topped the rise and before them lay the oaks of Tara, a towering dark mass against the darkening sky. Scarlett looked hastily to see if there was a light anywhere. There was none.

'They are gone!' said her heart, like cold lead in her breast. 'Gone!'

She turned the horse's head into the driveway, and the cedars, meeting over their heads, cast them into midnight blackness. Peering up the long tunnel of darkness, straining her eyes, she saw ahead – or did she see? Were her tired eyes playing her tricks? – the white bricks of Tara blurred and indistinct. Home! Home! The dear white walls, the windows with the fluttering curtains, the wide verandas – were they all there ahead of her, in the gloom? Or did the darkness mercifully conceal such a horror as the MacIntosh house?

The avenue seemed miles long and the horse, pulling stubbornly at her hand, plopped slower and slower. Eagerly her eyes searched the darkness. The roof seemed to be intact. Could it be – could it be—? No, it wasn't possible. War stopped for nothing, not even Tara, built to last five hundred years. It could not have passed over Tara.

Then the shadowy outline did take form. She pulled the horse forward faster. The white walls did show there through the darkness. And untarnished by smoke. Tara had escaped! Home! She dropped the bridle and ran the last few steps, leaped forward with an urge to clutch the walls themselves in her arms. Then she saw a form, shadowy in the dimness, emerging from the blackness of the front veranda and standing at the top of the steps. Tara was not deserted. Someone was home!

A cry of joy rose to her throat and died there. The house was so dark and still and the figure did not move or call to her. What was wrong? What was wrong? Tara stood intact, yet shrouded with the same eerie quiet that hung over the whole stricken countryside. Then the figure moved. Stiffly and slowly, it came down the steps.

'Pa?' she whispered huskily, doubting almost that it was he. 'It's me – Katie Scarlett. I've come home.'

Gerald moved toward her, silent as a sleepwalker, his stiff leg dragging. He came close to her, looking at her in a dazed way as if he believed she was part of a dream. Putting out his hand, he laid it on her shoulder. Scarlett felt it tremble, tremble as if he had been awakened from a nightmare into a half-sense of reality.

'Daughter,' he said with an effort. 'Daughter.'

Then he was silent.

'Why – he's an old man!' thought Scarlett.

Gerald's shoulders sagged. In the face which she could only see dimly, there was none of the virility, the restless vitality of Gerald, and the eyes that looked into hers had almost the same fear-stunned look that lay in little Wade's eyes. He was only a little old man and broken.

And now, fear of unknown things seized her, leaped swiftly out of the darkness at her, and she could only stand and stare at him, all the flood of questioning dammed up at her lips.

From the wagon the faint wailing sounded again and Gerald seemed to rouse himself with an effort.

'It's Melanie and her baby,' whispered Scarlett rapidly. 'She's very ill – I brought her home.'

Gerald dropped his hand from her arm and straightened his shoulders. As he moved slowly to the side of the wagon, there was a ghostly semblance of the old host of Tara welcoming guests, as if Gerald spoke words from out of shadowy memory.

'Cousin Melanie!'

Melanie's voice murmured indistinctly.

'Cousin Melanie, this is your home. Twelve Oaks is burned. You must stay with us.'

Thoughts of Melanie's prolonged suffering spurred Scarlett to action. The present was with her again, the necessity of laying Melanie and her child on a soft bed and doing those small things for her that could be done.

'She must be carried. She can't walk.'

There was a scuffle of feet and a dark figure emerged from the cave of the front hall. Pork ran down the steps.

'Miss Scarlett! Miss Scarlett!' he cried.

Scarlett caught him by the arms. Pork, part and parcel of Tara, as dear as the bricks and the cool corridors! She felt his tears stream down on her hands as he patted her clumsily, crying: 'Sho is glad you back! Sho is—'

Prissy burst into tears and incoherent mumblings: 'Poke! Poke, honey!' And little Wade, encouraged by the weakness of his elders, began sniffling: 'Wade thirsty!'

Scarlett caught them all in hand.

'Miss Melanie is in the wagon and her baby too. Pork, you must carry her upstairs very carefully and put her in the back company room. Prissy, take the baby and Wade and go inside and give Wade a drink of water. Is Mammy here, Pork? Tell her I want her.'

Galvanized by the authority in her voice, Pork approached the wagon and fumbled at the backboard. A moan was wrenched from Melanie as he half-lifted, half-dragged her from the feather tick on which she had lain so many hours. And then she was in Pork's strong arms, her head drooping like a child's across his shoulder. Prissy, holding the baby and dragging Wade by the hand, followed them up the wide steps and disappeared into the blackness of the hall.

Scarlett's bleeding fingers sought her father's hand urgently.

'Did they get well, Pa?'

'The girls are recovering.'

Silence fell and in the silence an idea too monstrous for words took form. She could not, could not force it to her lips. She swallowed and swallowed but a sudden dryness seemed to have stuck the sides of her throat together. Was this the answer to the frightening riddle of Tara's silence? As if answering the question in her mind Gerald spoke.

'Your mother—' he said and stopped.

'And – Mother?'

'Your mother died yesterday.'

Her father's arm held tightly in her own, Scarlett felt her way down the wide dark hall which, even in its blackness, was as familiar as her own mind. She avoided the high-backed chairs, the empty gun-rack, the old sideboard with its protruding claw feet, and she felt herself drawn by instinct to the tiny office at the back of the house where Ellen always sat, keeping her endless accounts. Surely, when she entered that room, Mother would again be sitting there before the secretary and would look up, quill poised, and rise with sweet fragrance and rustling hoops to meet her tired daughter. Ellen could not be dead, not even though Pa had said it, said it over and over like a parrot that knows only one phrase: 'She died yesterday – she died yesterday – she died yesterday.'

Queer that she should feel nothing now, nothing except a weariness that shackled her limbs with heavy iron chains and a hunger that made her knees tremble. She would think of Mother later. She must put her mother out of her mind now, else she would stumble stupidly like Gerald or sob monotonously like Wade.

Pork came down the wide dark steps toward them, hurrying to press close to Scarlett like a cold animal toward a fire.

'Lights?' she questioned. 'Why is the house so dark, Pork? Bring candles.'

'Dey tuck all de candles, Miss Scarlett, all 'cept one we been usin' ter fine things in de dahk wid, an' it's 'bout gone. Mammy been usin' a rag in a dish of hawg fat fer a light fer nussin' Miss Carreen an' Miss Suellen.'

'Bring what's left of the candle,' she ordered. 'Bring it into Mother's – into the office.'

Pork pattered into the dining-room and Scarlett groped her way into the inky small room and sank down on the sofa. Her father's arm still lay in the crook of hers, helpless, appealing, trusting, as only the hands of the very young and the very old can be.

'He's an old man, an old tired man,' she thought again and vaguely wondered why she could not care.

Light wavered into the room as Pork entered carrying high a half-burned candle stuck in a saucer. The dark cave came to life: the sagging old sofa on which they sat, the tall secretary reaching toward the ceiling with Mother's fragile carved chair before it, the racks of pigeonholes, still stuffed with papers written in her fine hand, the worn carpet – all, all were the same, except that Ellen was not there, Ellen with the faint scent of lemon verbena sachet and the sweet look in her tip-tilted eyes. Scarlett felt a small pain in her heart as of nerves numbed by a deep wound, struggling to make themselves felt again. She must not let them come to life now; there was all the rest of her life ahead of her in which they could ache. But, not now! Please, God, not now!

She looked into Gerald's putty-coloured face and, for the first time in her life, she saw him unshaven, his once florid face covered with silvery bristles. Pork placed the candle on the candle-stand and came to her side. Scarlett felt that if he had been a dog he would have laid his muzzle in her lap and whined for a kind hand upon his head.

'Pork, how many darkies are here?'

'Miss Scarlett, dem trashy niggers done runned away an' some of dem went off wid de Yankees an'—'

'How many are left?'

'Dey's me, Miss Scarlett, an' Mammy. She been nussin' de young Misses all day. An' Dilcey, she settin' up wid de young Misses now. Us three, Miss Scarlett.'

'Us three' where there had been a hundred. Scarlett with an effort lifted her head on her aching neck. She knew she must keep her voice steady. To her surprise, words came out as coolly and naturally as if there had never been a war and she could, by waving her hand, call ten house servants to her.

'Pork, I'm starving. Is there anything to eat?'

'No'm. Dey tuck it all.'

'But the garden?'

'Dey tuhned dey hawses loose in it.'

'Even the sweet potato hills?'

Something almost like a pleased smile broke over his thick lips.

'Miss Scarlett, Ah done fergit de yams. Ah specs dey's right dar. Dem Yankee foks ain' never seed no yams an' dey thinks dey's jes' roots an'—'

'The moon will be up soon. You go out and dig us some and roast them. There's no corn meal? No dried peas? No chickens?'

'No'm. No'm. Whut chickens dey din' eat right hyah hey cah'ied off 'cross dey saddles.'

They – They –They – Was there no end to what 'They' had done? Was it not enough to burn and kill? Must they also leave women and children and helpless negroes to starve in a country which they had desolated?

'Miss Scarlett, Ah got some apples Mammy buhied unner de house. We been eatin' on dem today.'

'Bring them before you dig the potatoes. And, Pork – I – I feel so faint. Is there any wine in the cellar, even blackberry?'

'Oh, Miss Scarlett, de cellar wuz de fust place dey went.'

A swimming nausea compounded of hunger, sleeplessness, exhaustion and stunning blows came on suddenly and she gripped the carved roses under her hand.

'No wine,' she said dully, remembering the endless rows of bottles in the cellar. A memory stirred.

'Pork, what of the corn whisky Pa buried in the oak barrel under the scuppernong arbour?'

Another ghost of a smile lit the black face, a smile of pleasure and respect.

'Miss Scarlett, you sho is de beatenes' chile! Ah done plum fergit dat bah'l. But Miss Scarlett, dat whisky ain' no good. Ain' been dar but 'bout a year an' whisky ain' no good fer ladies nohow.'

How stupid negroes were! They never thought of anything unless they were told. And the Yankees wanted to free them.

'It'll be good enough for this lady and for Pa. Hurry, Pork, and dig it up and bring us two glasses and some mint and sugar and I'll mix a julep.'

His face was reproachful.

'Miss Scarlett, you knows dey ain' been no sugar at Tara fer de longes'. An' dey hawses done et up all de mint an' dey done broke all de glasses.'

'If he says "They" once more, I'll scream. I can't help it,' she thought, and then, aloud: 'Well, hurry and get the whisky, quickly. We'll take it neat.' And, as he turned: 'Wait, Pork. There's so many things to do that I can't seem to think . . . Oh, yes, I brought home a horse and a cow and the cow needs milking, badly, and unharness the horse and water him. Go tell Mammy to look after the cow. Tell her she's got to fix the cow up somehow. Miss Melanie's baby will die if he doesn't get something to eat and—'

'Miss Melly ain' – kain—?' Pork paused delicately.

'Miss Melanie has no milk.' Dear God, but Mother would faint at that!

'Well, Miss Scarlett, mah Dilcey ten' ter Miss Melly's chile. Mah Dilcey got a new chile herseff an' she got mo'n nuff fer both.'

'You've got a new baby, Pork?'

Babies, babies, babies. Why did God make so many babies? But no, God didn't make them. Stupid people made them.

'Yas'm, big fat black boy. He—'

'Go tell Dilcey to leave the girls. I'll look after them. Tell her to nurse Miss Melanie's baby and do what she can for Miss Melanie. Tell Mammy to look after the cow and put that poor horse in the stable.'

'Dey ain' no stable, Miss Scarlett. Dey use it fer fiahwood.'

'Don't tell me any more what "They" did. Tell Dilcey to look after them. And you, Pork, go dig up that whisky and then some potatoes.'

'But, Miss Scarlett, Ah ain' got no light ter dig by.'

'You can use a stick of firewood, can't you?'

'Dey ain' no fiahwood— Dey—'

'Do something . . . I don't care what. But dig those things and dig them fast. Now, hurry.'

Pork scurried from the room as her voice roughened and Scarlett was left alone with Gerald. She patted his leg gently. She noted how shrunken were the thighs that once bulged with saddle muscles. She must do something to drag him from his apathy – but she could not ask about Mother. That must come later, when she could stand it.

'Why didn't they burn Tara?'

Gerald stared at her for a moment as if not hearing her and she repeated her question.

'Why—' he fumbled, 'they used the house as a headquarters.'

'Yankees – in this house?'

A feeling that the beloved walls had been defiled rose in her. This house, sacred because Ellen had lived in it, and those – those – in it.

'So they were, Daughter. We saw the smoke from Twelve Oaks, across the river, before they came. But Miss Honey and Miss India and some of their darkies had refugeed to Macon, so we did not worry about them. But we couldn't be going to Macon. The girls were so sick – your mother – we couldn't be going. Our darkies ran – I'm not knowing where. They stole the wagons and the mules. Mammy and Dilcey and Pork – they didn't run. The girls – your mother – we couldn't be moving them.'

'Yes, yes.' He mustn't talk about Mother. Anything else. Even that General Sherman himself had used this room, Mother's office, for his headquarters. Anything else.

'The Yankees were moving on Jonesboro, to cut the railroad. And they came up the road from the river – thousands and thousands – and cannon and horses – thousands. I met them on the front porch.'

'Oh, gallant little Gerald!' thought Scarlett, her heart swelling – Gerald meeting the enemy on the stairs of Tara as if an army stood behind him instead of in front of him.

'They said for me to leave, that they would be burning the place. And I said that they would be burning it over my head. We could not leave – the girls – your mother – were—'

'And then?' Must he revert to Ellen always?

'I told them there was sickness in the house, the typhoid, and it was death to move them. They could burn the roof over us. I did not want to leave anyway – leave Tara—'

His voice trailed off into silence as he looked absently about the walls and Scarlett understood. There were too many Irish ancestors crowding behind Gerald's shoulders, men who had died on scant acres, fighting to the end rather than leave the homes where they had lived, ploughed, loved, begotten sons.

'I said that they would be burning the house over the heads of three dying women. But we would not leave. The young officer was – was a gentleman.'

'A Yankee a gentleman? Why, Pa!'

'A gentleman. He galloped away and soon he was back with a captain, a surgeon, and he looked at the girls – and your mother.'

'You let a damned Yankee into their room?'

'He had opium. We had none. He saved your sisters. Suellen was haemorrhaging. He was as kind as he knew how. And when he reported that they were – ill – they did not burn the house. They moved in, some general, his staff, crowding in. They filled all the rooms except the sick-room. And the soldiers—'

He paused again, as if too tired to go on. His stubbly chin sank heavily in loose folds of flesh on his chest. With an effort he spoke again.

'They camped all round the house, everywhere, in the cotton, in the corn. The pasture was blue with them. That night there were a thousand camp-fires. They tore down the fences and burned them to cook with and the barns and the stables and the smokehouse. They killed the cows and the hogs and the chickens – even my turkeys.' Gerald's precious turkeys. So they were gone. 'They took things, even the pictures – some of the furniture, the china—'

'The silver?'

'Pork and Mammy did something with the silver – put it in the well – but I'm not remembering now.' Gerald's voice was fretful. 'Then they fought the battle from here – from Tara – there was so much noise, people galloping up and stamping about. And later the cannon at Jonesboro – it sounded like thunder – even the girls could hear it, sick as they were, and they kept saying over and over: "Papa, make it stop thundering." '

'And – and Mother? Did she know Yankees were in the house?'

'She – never knew anything.'

'Thank God,' said Scarlett. Mother was spared that. Mother never knew, never heard the enemy in the rooms below, never heard the guns at Jonesboro, never learned that the land which was part of her heart was under Yankee feet.

'I saw few of them for I stayed upstairs with the girls and your mother. I saw the young surgeon mostly. He was kind, so kind, Scarlett. After he'd worked all day with the wounded, he came and sat with them. He even left some medicine. He told me when they moved on that the girls would recover but your mother— She was so frail, he said – too frail to stand it all. He said she had undermined her strength . . . '

In the silence that fell, Scarlett saw her mother as she must have been in those last days, a thin tower of strength in Tara, nursing, working, doing without sleep and food that the others might rest and eat.

'And then, they moved on. Then, they moved on.'

He was silent for a long time and then fumbled at her hand.

'It's glad I am you are home,' he said simply.

There was a scraping noise on the back porch. Poor Pork, trained for forty years to clean his shoes before entering the house, did not forget, even in a time like this. He came in, carefully carrying two gourds, and the strong smell of dripping spirits entered before him.

'Ah spilt a plen'y, Miss Scarlett. It's pow'ful hard ter po' outer a bunghole inter a go'de.'

'That's quite all right, Pork, and thank you.' She took the wet gourd dipper from him, her nostrils wrinkling in distaste at the reek.

'Drink this, Father,' she said, pushing the whisky in its strange receptacle into his hand and taking the second gourd of water from Pork. Gerald raised it, obedient as a child, and gulped noisily. She handed the water to him but he shook his head.

As she took the whisky from him and held it to her mouth, she saw his eyes follow her, a vague stirring of disapproval in them.

'I know no lady drinks spirits,' she said briefly. 'But today I'm no lady, Pa, and there is work to do tonight.'

She tilted the dipper, drew a deep breath and drank swiftly. The hot liquid burned down her throat to her stomach, choking her and bringing tears to her eyes. She drew another breath and raised it again.

'Katie Scarlett,' said Gerald, the first note of authority she had heard in his voice since her return, 'that is enough. You're not knowing spirits and they will be making you tipsy.'

'Tipsy?' She laughed an ugly laugh. 'Tipsy? I hope it makes me drunk. I would like to be drunk and forget all of this.'

She drank again, a slow train of warmth lighting in her veins and stealing through her body until even her finger-tips tingled. What a blessed feeling, this kindly fire! It seemed to penetrate even her ice-locked heart and strength came coursing back into her body. Seeing Gerald's puzzled hurt face, she patted his knee again and managed an imitation of the pert smile he used to love.

'How could it make me tipsy, Pa? I'm your daughter. Haven't I inherited the steadiest head in Clayton County?'

He almost smiled into her tired face. The whisky was bracing him too. She handed it back to him.

'Now you're going to take another drink and then I am going to take you upstairs and put you to bed.'

She caught herself. Why, this was the way she talked to Wade – she should not address her father like this. It was disrespectful. But he hung on her words.

'Yes, put you to bed,' she added lightly, 'and give you another drink – maybe all the dipper and make you go to sleep. You need sleep and Katie Scarlett is here, so you need not worry about anything. Drink.'

He drank again obediently and, slipping her arm through his, she pulled him to his feet.

'Pork . . .'

Pork took the gourd in one hand and Gerald's arm in the other. Scarlett picked up the flaring candle and the three walked slowly into the dark hall and up the winding steps toward Gerald's room.

The room where Suellen and Carreen lay mumbling and tossing on the same bed stank vilely with the smell of the twisted rag burning in a saucer of bacon fat, which provided the only light. When Scarlett first opened the door the thick atmosphere of the room, with all windows closed and the air reeking with sick-room odours, medicine smells and stinking grease, almost made her faint. Doctors might say that fresh air was fatal in a sick-room but if she were to sit here, she must have air or die. She opened the three windows, bringing in the smell of oak leaves and earth, but the fresh air could do little toward dispelling the sickening odours which had accumulated for weeks in this close room.

Carreen and Suellen, emaciated and white, slept brokenly and awoke to mumble with wide, staring eyes in the tall four-poster bed where they had whispered together in better, happier days. In the corner of the room was an empty bed, a narrow French Empire bed with curling head and foot, a bed which Ellen had brought from Savannah. This was where Ellen had lain.

Scarlett sat beside the two girls, staring at them stupidly. The whisky taken on a stomach long empty was playing tricks on her. Sometimes her sisters seemed far away and tiny and their incoherent voices came to her like the buzz of insects. And again, they loomed large, rushing at her with lightning speed. She was tired, tired to the bone. She could lie down and sleep for days.

If she could only lie down and sleep and wake to feel Ellen gently shaking her arm and saying: 'It is late, Scarlett. You must not be so lazy.' But she could not ever do that again. If there were only Ellen, someone older than she, wiser and unweary, to whom she could go! Someone in whose lap she could lay her head, someone on whose shoulders she could rest her burdens!

The door opened softly and Dilcey entered, Melanie's baby held to her breast, the gourd of whisky in her hand. In the smoky, uncertain light, she seemed thinner than when Scarlett last saw her and the Indian blood was more evident in her face. The high cheek-bones were more prominent, the hawk-bridged nose was sharper and her copper skin gleamed with a brighter hue. Her faded calico dress was open to the waist and her large bronze breast exposed. Held close against her, Melanie's baby pressed his pale rosebud mouth greedily to the dark nipple, sucking, gripping tiny fists against the soft flesh like a kitten in the warm fur of its mother's belly.

Scarlett rose unsteadily and put a hand on Dilcey's arm.

'It was good of you to stay, Dilcey.'

'How could I go off wid them trashy niggers, Miss Scarlett, after yo' pa been so good to buy me and my little Prissy and yo' ma been so kine?'

'Sit down, Dilcey. The baby can eat all right, then? And how is Miss Melanie?'

'Nuthin' wrong wid this chile 'cept he hongry, and whut it take to feed a hongry chile I got. No'm, Miss Melanie is all right. She ain' gwine die, Miss Scarlett. Doan you fret yo'seff. I seen too many, white and black, lak her. She mighty tired and nervous like and scared fo' this baby. But I hesh her and give her some of whut was lef' in that go'de and she sleepin'.'

So the corn whisky had been used by the whole family! Scarlett thought hysterically that perhaps she had better give a drink to little Wade and see if it would stop his hiccoughs— And Melanie would not die. And when Ashley came home – if he did come home . . . No, she would think of that later too. So much to think of – later! So many things to unravel – to decide. If only she could put off the hour of reckoning forever! She started suddenly as a creaking noise and a rhythmic 'Ker-bunk – ker-bunk—' broke the stillness of the air outside.

'That's Mammy gettin' the water to sponge off the young Misses. They takes a heap of bathin',' explained Dilcey, propping the gourd on the table between medicine bottles and a glass.

Scarlett laughed suddenly. Her nerves must be shredded if the noise of the well windlass, bound up in her earliest memories, could frighten her. Dilcey looked at her steadily as she laughed, her face immobile in its dignity, but Scarlett felt that Dilcey understood. She sank back in her chair. If she could only be rid of her tight stays, the collar that choked her and the slippers still full of sand and gravel that blistered her feet.

The windlass creaked slowly as the rope wound up, each creak bringing the bucket nearer the top. Soon Mammy would be with her – Ellen's Mammy, her

Mammy. She sat silent, intent on nothing, while the baby, already glutted
with milk, whimpered because he had lost the friendly nipple. Dilcey, silent
too, guided the child's mouth back, quieting him in her arms as Scarlett
listened to the slow scuffing of Mammy's feet across the back yard. How
still the night air was! The slightest sounds roared in her ears.

The upstairs hall seemed to shake as Mammy's ponderous weight came
toward the door. Then Mammy was in the room, Mammy with shoulders
dragged down by two heavy wooden buckets, her kind black face sad with
the uncomprehending sadness of a monkey's face.

Her eyes lighted up at the sight of Scarlett, her white teeth gleamed as she
set down the buckets, and Scarlett ran to her, laying her head on the broad,
sagging breasts which had held so many heads, black and white. Here was
something of stability, thought Scarlett, something of the old life that was
unchanging. But Mammy's first words dispelled this illusion.

'Mammy's chile is home! Oh, Miss Scarlett, now dat Miss Ellen's in de
grabe, whut is we gwine ter do? Oh, Miss Scarlett, effen Ah wuz jes' daid
longside Miss Ellen! Ah kain make out widout Miss Ellen. Ain' nuthin' lef'
now but mizry an' trouble. Jes' weery loads, honey, jes' weery loads.'

As Scarlett lay with her head hugged close to Mammy's breast, two
words caught her attention, 'weery loads'. Those were the words which
had hummed in her brain that afternoon so monotonously they had
sickened her. Now she remembered the rest of the song, remembered
with a sinking heart:

> *Just a few more days for to tote the weary load!*
> *No matter, 'twill never be light!*
> *Just a few more days till we totter in the road—*

'No matter, 'twill never be light' – she took the words to her tired mind.
Would her load never be light? Was coming home to Tara to mean, not
blessed surcease, but only more loads to carry? She slipped from Mammy's
arms and, reaching up, patted the wrinkled black face.

'Honey, yo' han's!' Mammy took the small hands with their blisters and
blood-clots in hers and looked at them with horrified disapproval. 'Miss
Scarlett, Ah done tole you an' tole you dat you kin allus tell a lady by her
han's an' – yo' face sunbuhnt too!'

Poor Mammy, still the martinet about such unimportant things even
though war and death had just passed over her head! In another moment
she would be saying that young Misses with blistered hands and freckles most
generally didn't never catch husbands and Scarlett forestalled the remark.

'Mammy, I want you to tell me about Mother. I couldn't bear to hear
Pa talk about her.'

Tears started from Mammy's eyes as she leaned down to pick up the
buckets. In silence she carried them to the bedside and, turning down the

sheet, began pulling up the night clothes of Suellen and Carreen. Scarlett, peering at her sisters in the dim flaring light, saw that Carreen wore a nightgown, clean but in tatters, and Suellen lay wrapped in an old negligée, a brown linen garment heavy with tagging ends of Irish lace. Mammy cried silently as she sponged the gaunt bodies, using the remnant of an old apron as a cloth.

'Miss Scarlett, it wuz dem Slatterys, dem trashy, no-good, low-down po'-w'ite Slatterys dat kilt Miss Ellen. Ah done tole her an' tole her it doan do no good doin' things fer trashy folks, but Miss Ellen wuz so sot in her ways an' her heart so sof' she couldn' never say no ter nobody whut needed her.'

'Slatterys?' questioned Scarlett, bewildered. 'How do they come in?'

'Dey wuz sick wid disyere thing.' Mammy gestured with her rag to the two naked girls, dripping with water on their damp sheet. 'Ole Miss Slattery's gal, Emmie, come down wid it an' Miss Slattery come hotfootin' it up hyah after Miss Ellen, lak she allus done w'en anything wrong. Why din' she nuss her own? Miss Ellen had mo'n she could tote anyways. But Miss Ellen she went down dar an' she nuss Emmie. An' Miss Ellen wuzn' well a-tall herseff, Miss Scarlett. Yo' ma hadn' been well fer de longes'. Dey ain' been too much ter eat roun' hyah, wid de commissary stealin' eve'y thing us growed. An' Miss Ellen eat lak a bird anyways. An' Ah tole her an' tole her ter let dem w'ite trash alone, but she din' pay me no mine. Well'm, 'bout de time Emmie look lak she gittin' better, Miss Carreen come down wid it. Yas'm, de typhoy fly right up de road an' ketch Miss Carreen, an' den down come Miss Suellen. So Miss Ellen, she tuck an' nuss dem too.

'Wid all de fightin' up de road an' de Yankees 'cross de river an' us not knowin' whut wuz gwine ter happen ter us an' de fe'el han's runnin' off eve'y night, Ah's 'bout crazy. But Miss Ellen jes' as cool as a cucumber. 'Cept she wuz worried ter a ghos' 'bout de young Misses kase we couldn' git no medicines nor nuthin'. An' one night she say ter me affer we done sponge off de young Misses 'bout ten times, she say, "Mammy, effen Ah could sell mah soul, Ah'd sell it fer some ice ter put on mah gals' haids."

'She wouldn' let Mist' Gerald come in hyah, nor Rosa nor Teena, nobody but me, kase Ah done had de typhoy. An' den it tuck her, Miss Scarlett, an' Ah seed right off dat 'twarnt no use.'

Mammy straightened up and, raising her apron, dried her streaming eyes.

'She went fas', Miss Scarlett, an' even dat nice Yankee doctah couldn' do nuthin' fer her. She din' know nuthin' a-tall. Ah call ter her an' talk ter her but she din' even know her own Mammy.'

'Did she – did she ever mention me – call for me?'

'No, honey. She think she a lil gal back in Savannah. She din' call nobody by name.'

Dilcey stirred and laid the sleeping baby across her knees.

'Yes'm, she did. She did call somebody.'

'You hesh yo' mouf, you Injun-nigger!' Mammy turned with threatening violence on Dilcey.

'Hush, Mammy! Who did she call, Dilcey? Pa?'

'No'm. Not yo' pa. It wuz the night the cotton buhnt—'

'Has the cotton gone – tell me quickly!'

'Yes'm, it buhnt up. The sojers rolls it out of the shed into the back yard and hollers, "Here the bigges' bonfiah in Georgia" and tech it off.'

Three years of stored cotton – one hundred and fifty thousand dollars, all in one blaze!

'And the fiah light up the place lak it wuz day – we wuz scared the house would buhn, too, and it wuz so bright in this hyah room that you could mos' pick a needle offen the flo'. And w'en the light shine in the winder, it look lak it wake Miss Ellen up and she set right up in bed and cry out loud, time and agin: "Feeleep! Feeleep!" I ain' never heerd no sech name but it wuz a name and she wuz callin' him.'

Mammy stood as though turned to stone glaring at Dilcey but Scarlett dropped her head into her hands. Philippe – who was he and what had he been to Mother that she had died calling him?

The long road from Atlanta to Tara had ended, ended in a blank wall, the road that was to end in Ellen's arms. Never again could Scarlett lie down, as a child, secure beneath her father's roof with the protection of her mother's love wrapped about her like an eiderdown quilt. There was no security or haven to which she could turn now. No turning or twisting would avoid this dead end to which she had come. There was no one on whose shoulders she could rest her burdens. Her father was old and stunned, her sisters ill, Melanie frail and weak, the children helpless, and the negroes looking up to her with childlike faith, clinging to her skirts, knowing that Ellen's daughter would be the refuge Ellen had always been.

Through the window, in the faint light of the rising moon, Tara stretched before her, negroes gone, acres desolate, barns ruined, like a body bleeding under her eyes, like her own body, slowly bleeding. This was the end of the road, quivering old age, sickness, hungry mouths, helpless hands plucking at her skirts. And at the end of this road there was nothing – nothing but Scarlett O'Hara Hamilton, nineteen years old, a widow with a little child.

What would she do with all of this? Aunt Pitty and the Burrs in Macon could take Melanie and her baby. If the girls recovered, Ellen's family would have to take them, whether they liked it or not. And she and Gerald could turn to Uncle James and Andrew.

She looked at the thin forms tossing before her, the sheets about them moist and dark from dripping water. She did not like Suellen. She saw it now with a sudden clarity. She had never liked her. She did not especially love Carreen – she could not love anyone who was weak. But they were of her blood, part of Tara. No, she could not let them live out their lives in their aunts' homes as poor relations. An O'Hara a poor relation, living on charity bread and sufferance! Oh, never that!

Was there no escape from this dead end? Her tired brain moved so slowly. She raised her hands to her head as wearily as if the air were water against which her arms struggled. She took the gourd from between the glass and the bottle and looked in it. There was some whisky left in the bottom, how much she could not tell in the uncertain light. Strange that the sharp smell did not offend her nostrils now. She drank slowly but this time the liquid did not burn, only a dull warmth followed.

She set down the empty gourd and looked about her. This was all a dream, this smoke-filled dim room, the scrawny girls, Mammy shapeless and huge crouching beside the bed, Dilcey a still bronze image with the sleeping pink morsel against her dark breast – all a dream from which she would awake, to smell bacon frying in the kitchen, hear the throaty laughter of the negroes and the creaking of wagons fieldward bound, and Ellen's gentle insistent hand upon her.

Then she discovered she was in her own room, on her own bed, faint moonlight pricking the darkness, and Mammy and Dilcey were undressing her. The torturing stays no longer pinched her waist and she could breathe deeply and quietly to the bottom of her lungs and her abdomen. She felt her stockings being stripped gently from her and heard Mammy murmuring indistinguishable comforting sounds as she bathed her blistered feet. How cool the water was, how good to lie here in softness, like a child! She sighed and relaxed and after a time which might have been a year or a second, she was alone and the room was brighter as the rays of the moon streamed in across the bed.

She did not know she was drunk, drunk with fatigue and whisky. She only knew she had left her tired body and floated somewhere above it where there was no pain and no weariness and her brain saw things with an inhuman clarity.

She was seeing things with new eyes for, somewhere along the long road to Tara, she had left her girlhood behind her. She was no longer plastic clay, yielding imprint to each new experience. The clay had hardened, some time in this indeterminate day which had lasted a thousand years. Tonight was the last time she would ever be ministered to as a child. She was a woman now and youth was gone.

No, she could not, would not, turn to Gerald's or Ellen's families. The O'Haras did not take charity. The O'Haras looked after their own. Her burdens were her own and burdens were for shoulders strong enough to bear them. She thought without surprise, looking down from her height, that her shoulders were strong enough to bear anything now, having borne the worst that could ever happen to her. She could not desert Tara; she belonged to the red acres far more than they could ever belong to her. Her roots went deep into the blood-coloured soil and sucked up life, as did the cotton. She would stay at Tara and keep it, somehow, keep her father and her sisters, Melanie and Ashley's child, the negroes. Tomorrow – oh, tomorrow! Tomorrow she would fit the yoke about her neck. Tomorrow there would be so many things to do. Go to Twelve Oaks and the MacIntosh place and see if anything was left in the deserted gardens, go to the river swamps and beat them for straying hogs and chickens, go to Jonesboro and Lovejoy with Ellen's jewellery – there must be someone left there who would sell something to eat. Tomorrow – tomorrow – her brain ticked slowly and more slowly, like a clock running down, but the clarity of vision persisted.

Of a sudden, the oft-told family tales to which she had listened since babyhood, listened half-bored, impatient and but partly comprehending, were crystal clear. Gerald, penniless, had raised Tara; Ellen had risen above some mysterious sorrow; Grandfather Robillard, surviving the wreck of Napoleon's throne, had founded his fortunes anew on the fertile Georgia coast; Great-Grandfather Prudhomme had carved a small kingdom out of the dark jungles of Haiti, lost it, and lived to see his name honoured in Savannah. There were the Scarletts who had fought with the Irish Volunteers for a free Ireland and been hanged for their pains, and the O'Haras who died at the Boyne, battling to the end for what was theirs.

All had suffered crushing misfortunes and had not been crushed. They had not been broken by the crash of empires, the machetes of revolting slaves, war, rebellion, proscription, confiscation. Malign fate had broken their necks, perhaps, but never their hearts. They had not whined, they had fought. And when they died, they died spent but unquenched. All of those shadowy folks whose blood flowed in her veins seemed to move quietly in the moonlit room. And Scarlett was not surprised to see them, these kinsmen who had taken the worst that fate could send and hammered it into the best. Tara was her fate, her fight, and she must conquer it.

She turned drowsily on her side, a slow creeping blackness enveloping her mind. Were they really there, whispering wordless encouragement to her, or was this part of her dream?

'Whether you are there or not,' she murmured sleepily, 'good night – and thank you.'

Chapter XXV

The next morning Scarlett's body was so stiff and sore from the long miles of walking and jolting in the wagon that every movement was agony. Her face was crimson with sunburn and her blistered palms raw. Her tongue was furred and her throat parched as if flames had scorched it and no amount of water could assuage her thirst. Her head felt swollen and she winced even when she turned her eyes. A queasiness of the stomach reminiscent of the early days of her pregnancy made the smoking yams on the breakfast table unendurable, even to the smell. Gerald could have told her she was suffering the normal aftermath of her first experience with hard drinking but Gerald noticed nothing. He sat at the head of the table, a grey old man with absent, faded eyes fastened on the door and head cocked slightly to hear the rustle of Ellen's petticoats, to smell the lemon verbena sachet.

As Scarlett sat down, he mumbled: 'We will wait for Mrs O'Hara. She is late.' She raised an aching head, looked at him with startled incredulity and met the pleading eyes of Mammy, who stood behind Gerald's chair. She rose unsteadily, her hand at her throat, and looked down at her father in the morning sunlight. He peered up at her vaguely and she saw that his hands were shaking, that his head trembled a little.

Until this moment she had not realized how much she had counted on Gerald to take command, to tell her what she must do, and now— Why, last night he had seemed almost himself. There had been none of his usual bluster and vitality, but at least he had told a connected story, and now – now, he did not even remember Ellen was dead. The combined shock of the coming of the Yankees and her death had stunned him. She started to speak, but Mammy shook her head vehemently and raising her apron dabbed at her red eyes.

'Oh, can Pa have lost his mind?' thought Scarlett, and her throbbing head felt as if it would crack with this added strain. 'No, no. He's just dazed by it all. It's like he was sick. He'll get over it. He must get over it. What will I do if he doesn't? – I won't think about it now. I won't think of him or Mother or any of these awful things now. No, not till I can stand it. There are too many other things to think about – things that can be helped – without my thinking of those I can't help.'

She left the dining-room without eating, and went out on to the back porch where she found Pork, barefooted and in the ragged remains of his best livery, sitting on the steps cracking peanuts. Her head was hammering and throbbing and the bright sunlight stabbed into her eyes. Merely holding herself erect required an effort of will-power and she talked as briefly as possible, dispensing with the usual forms of courtesy her mother had always taught her to use with negroes.

She began asking questions so brusquely and giving orders so decisively Pork's eyebrows went up in mystification. Miss Ellen didn't never talk so short to nobody, not even when she caught them stealing pullets and water-melons. She asked again about the fields, the gardens, the stock, and her green eyes had a hard bright glaze which Pork had never seen in them before.

'Yas'm, dat hawse daid, layin' dar whar Ah tie him wid his nose in de water-bucket he tuhned over. No'm, de cow ain' daid. Din' you know? She done have a calf las' night. Dat why she beller so.'

'A fine midwife your Prissy will make,' Scarlett remarked caustically. 'She said she was bellowing because she needed milking.'

'Well'm, Prissy ain' fixin' ter be no cow midwife, Miss Scarlett,' Pork said tactfully. 'An' ain' no use quarrellin' wid blessin's, 'cause dat calf gwine ter mean a full cow an' plen'y buttermilk fer de young Misses, lak dat Yankee doctah say dey'd need.'

'All right, go on. Any stock left?'

'No'm. Nuthin' 'cept one ole sow an' her litter. Ah driv dem inter de swamp de day de Yankees come, but de Lawd knows how we gwine git dem. She mean, dat sow.'

'We'll get them all right. You and Prissy can start right now hunting for her.'

Pork was amazed and indignant.

'Miss Scarlett, dat a fe'el han's bizness. Ah's allus been a house nigger.'

A small fiend with a pair of hot tweezers plucked behind Scarlett's eyeballs.

'You two will catch the sow – or get out of here, like the field hands did.'

Tears trembled in Pork's hurt eyes. Oh, if only Miss Ellen were here! She understood such niceties and realized the wide gap between the duties of a field hand and those of a house nigger.

'Git out, Miss Scarlett? Whar'd Ah git out to, Miss Scarlett?'

'I don't know and I don't care. But anyone at Tara who won't work can go hunt up the Yankees. You can tell that to the others too.'

'Yas'm.'

'Now, what about the corn and the cotton, Pork?'

'De cawn? Lawd, Miss Scarlett, dey pasture dey hawses in de cawn an' cah'ied off whut de hawses din' eat or spile. An' dey driv dey cannons an' waggins 'cross de cotton till it plum ruint, 'cept a few acres over on de creek bottom dat dey din' notice. But dat cotton ain' wuth foolin' wid, 'cause ain' but 'bout three bales over dar.'

Three bales. Scarlett thought of the scores of bales Tara usually yielded and her head hurt worse. Three bales. That was little more than the shiftless Slatterys raised. To make matters worse, there was the question of taxes. The Confederate government took cotton for taxes in lieu of money, but three bales wouldn't even cover the taxes. Little did it matter, though, to her or the Confederacy, now that all the field hands had run away and there was no one to pick the cotton.

'Well, I won't think of that either,' she told herself. 'Taxes aren't a woman's job anyway. Pa ought to look after such things, but Pa – I won't think of Pa now. The Confederacy can whistle for its taxes. What we need now is something to eat.'

'Pork, have any of you been to Twelve Oaks or the MacIntosh place to see if there's anything left in the gardens there?'

'No, Ma'm! Us ain' lef' Tara. De Yankees mout git us.'

'I'll send Dilcey over to MacIntosh. Perhaps she'll find something there. And I'll go to Twelve Oaks.'

'Who wid, chile?'

'By myself. Mammy must stay with the girls and Mr Gerald can't—'

Pork set up an outcry which she found infuriating. There might be Yankees or mean niggers at Twelve Oaks. She mustn't go alone.

'That will be enough, Pork. Tell Dilcey to start immediately. And you and Prissy go bring in the sow and her litter,' she said briefly, turning on her heel.

Mammy's old sunbonnet, faded but clean, hung on its peg on the back porch and Scarlett put it on her head, remembering, as from another world, the bonnet with the curling green plume which Rhett had brought her from Paris. She picked up a large split-oak basket and started down the back stairs, each step jouncing her head until her spine seemed to be trying to crash through the top of her skull.

The road down to the river lay red and scorching between the ruined cotton fields. There were no trees to cast a shade and the sun beat down through Mammy's sunbonnet as if it were made of tarlatan instead of heavy quilted calico, while the dust floating upward sifted into her nose and throat until she felt the membranes would crack dryly if she spoke. Deep ruts and furrows were cut into the road where horses had dragged heavy guns along it and the red gullies on either side were deeply gashed by the wheels. The cotton was mangled and trampled where cavalry and infantry, forced off the narrow road by the artillery, had marched through the green bushes, grinding them into the earth. Here and there in road and fields lay buckets and bits of harness leather, canteens flattened by hooves and caisson wheels, buttons, blue caps, worn socks, bits of bloody rags, all the litter left by a marching army.

She passed the clump of cedars and the low brick wall which marked the family burying-ground, trying not to think of the new grave lying by the three short mounds of her little brothers. Oh, Ellen— She trudged on down the dusty hill, passing the heap of ashes and the stumpy chimney where the Slattery house had stood, and she wished savagely that the whole tribe of them had been part of the ashes. If it hadn't been for the Slatterys – if it hadn't been for that nasty Emmie, who'd had a bastard brat by their overseer – Ellen wouldn't have died.

She moaned as a sharp pebble cut into her blistered foot. What was she doing here? Why was Scarlett O'Hara, the belle of the County, the sheltered pride of Tara, tramping down this rough road almost barefoot? Her little feet were made to dance, not to limp, her tiny slippers to peep daringly from under bright silks, not to collect sharp pebbles and dust. She was born to be pampered and waited upon, and here she was, sick and ragged, driven by hunger to hunt for food in the gardens of her neighbours.

At the bottom of the long hill was the river and how cool and still were the tangled trees overhanging the water! She sank down on the low bank and, stripping off the remnants of her slippers and stockings, dabbled her burning feet in the cool water. It would be so good to sit here all day, away from the helpless eyes of Tara, here where only the rustle of leaves and the gurgle of slow water broke the stillness. But reluctantly she replaced her shoes and stockings and trudged down the bank, spongy with moss, under the shady trees. The Yankees had burned the bridge but she knew of a footlog bridge across a narrow point of the stream a hundred yards below. She crossed it cautiously and trudged uphill the hot half-mile to Twelve Oaks.

There towered the twelve oaks, as they had stood since Indian days, but with their leaves brown from fire and the branches burned and scorched. Within their circle lay the ruins of John Wilkes' house, the charred remains of that once stately home which had crowned the hill in white-columned dignity. The deep pit which had been the cellar, the blackened field-stone foundations and two mighty chimneys marked the site. One long column, half-burned, had fallen across the lawn, crushing the cape jessamine bushes.

Scarlett sat down on the column, too sick at the sight to go on. This desolation went to her heart as nothing she had ever experienced. Here was the Wilkes pride in the dust at her feet. Here was the end of the kindly, courteous house which had always welcomed her, the house where in futile dreams she had aspired to be mistress. Here she had danced and dined and flirted, and here she had watched with a jealous, hurting heart how Melanie smiled up at Ashley. Here, too, in the cool shadows of the trees, Charles Hamilton had rapturously pressed her hand when she said she would marry him.

'Oh, Ashley,' she thought, 'I hope you are dead! I could never bear for you to see this.'

Ashley had married his bride here but his son and his son's son would never bring brides to this house. There would be no more matings and births beneath this roof which she had so loved and longed to rule. The house was dead and, to Scarlett, it was as if all the Wilkes, too, were dead in its ashes.

'I won't think of it now. I can't stand it now. I'll think of it later,' she said aloud, turning her eyes away.

Seeking the garden, she limped around the ruins, by the trampled rose-beds the Wilkes girls had tended so zealously, across the back yard and through the ashes of the smokehouse, barns and chicken houses. The split-rail fence around the kitchen garden had been demolished and the once orderly rows of green plants had suffered the same treatment as those at Tara. The soft earth was scarred with hoof-prints and heavy wheels and the vegetables were mashed into the soil. There was nothing for her here.

She walked back across the yard and took the path down toward the silent rows of whitewashed cabins in the quarters, calling 'Hello!' as she went. But no voice answered her. Not even a dog barked. Evidently the Wilkes negroes had taken flight or followed the Yankees. She knew every slave had his own garden patch, and as she reached the quarters she hoped these little patches had been spared.

Her search was rewarded but she was too tired even to feel pleasure at the sight of turnips and cabbages, wilted for want of water but still standing, and straggling butter beans and snap beans, yellowing but edible. She sat down in the furrows and dug into the earth with hands that shook, filling her basket slowly. There would be a good meal at Tara tonight, in spite of the lack of side meat to boil with the vegetables. Perhaps some of the bacon grease Dilcey was using for illumination could be used for seasoning. She must remember to tell Dilcey to use pine-knots and save the grease for cooking.

Close to the back step of one cabin, she found a short row of radishes and hunger assaulted her suddenly. A spicy, sharp-tasting radish was exactly what her stomach craved. Hardly waiting to rub the dirt off on her skirt, she bit off half and swallowed it hastily. It was old and coarse and so peppery that tears started in her eyes. No sooner had the lump gone down than her empty outraged stomach revolted and she lay in the soft dirt and vomited tiredly.

The faint niggery smell which crept from the cabin increased her nausea and, without strength to combat it, she kept on retching miserably while the cabins and the trees revolved swiftly around her.

After a long time, she lay weakly on her face, the earth as soft and comfortable as a feather pillow, and her mind wandered feebly here and there. She, Scarlett O'Hara, was lying behind a negro cabin, in the midst of ruins, too sick and too weak to move, and no one in the world knew or cared. No one would care if they did know, for everyone had too many troubles of their own to worry about her. And all this was happening to her, Scarlett O'Hara, who had never raised her hand even to pick up her discarded stockings from the floor or to tie the laces of her slippers – Scarlett, whose little headaches and tempers had been coddled and catered to all her life.

As she lay prostrate, too weak to fight off memories and worries, they rushed at her, circled about her like buzzards waiting for a death. No longer had she the strength to say: 'I'll think of Mother and Pa and Ashley and all this ruin later— Yes, later when I can stand it.' She could not stand it now, but she was thinking of them whether she willed it or not. The thoughts circled and swooped about her, dived down and drove tearing claws and sharp beaks into her mind. For a timeless time, she lay still, her face in the dirt, the sun beating hotly upon her, remembering things and people who were dead, remembering a way of living that was gone forever – and looking upon the harsh vista of the dark future.

When she arose at last and saw again the black ruins of Twelve Oaks, her head was raised high and something that was youth and beauty and potential tenderness had gone out of her face forever. What was past was past. Those who were dead were dead. The lazy luxury of the old days was gone, never to return. And, as Scarlett settled the heavy basket across her arm, she had settled her own mind and her own life.

There was no going back and she was going forward.

Throughout the South for fifty years there would be bitter-eyed women who looked backward, to dead times, to dead men, evoking memories that hurt and were futile, bearing poverty with bitter pride because they had those memories. But Scarlett was never to look back.

She gazed at the blackened stones and, for the last time, she saw Twelve Oaks rise before her eyes as it had once stood, rich and proud, symbol of a race and a way of living. Then she started down the road toward Tara, the heavy basket cutting into her flesh.

Hunger gnawed at her empty stomach again and she said aloud: 'As God is my witness, as God is my witness, the Yankees aren't going to lick me. I'm going to live through this, and when it's over, I'm never going to be hungry again. No, nor any of my folks. If I have to steal or kill – as God is my witness, I'm never going to be hungry again.'

In the days that followed, Tara might have been Crusoe's desert island, so still it was, so isolated from the rest of the world. The world lay only a few miles away, but a thousand miles of tumbling waves might have stretched between Tara and Jonesboro and Fayetteville and Lovejoy, even between Tara and the neighbours' plantations. With the old horse dead, their one mode of conveyance was gone, and there was neither time nor strength for walking the weary red miles.

Sometimes, in the days of backbreaking work, in the desperate struggle for food and the never-ceasing care of the three sick girls, Scarlett found herself straining her ears for familiar sounds – the shrill laughter of the piccaninnies in the quarters, the creaking of wagons home from the fields, the thunder of Gerald's stallion tearing across the pasture, the crunching of carriage wheels on the drive and the gay voices of neighbours dropping in for an afternoon of gossip. But she listened in vain. The road lay still and deserted and never a cloud of red dust proclaimed the approach of visitors. Tara was an island in a sea of rolling green hills and red fields.

Somewhere was the world and families who ate and slept safely under their own roofs. Somewhere girls in thrice-turned dresses were flirting gaily and singing 'When This Cruel War Is Over', as she had done only a few weeks before. Somewhere there was a war and cannon booming and burning towns and men who rotted in hospitals amid sickening-sweet stinks. Somewhere a barefoot army in dirty homespun was marching, fighting, sleeping, hungry and weary with the weariness that comes when hope is gone. And somewhere the hills of Georgia were blue with Yankees, well-fed Yankees on sleek corn-stuffed horses.

Beyond Tara was the war and the world. But on the plantation the war and the world did not exist except as memories which must be fought back when they rushed to mind in moments of exhaustion. The world outside receded before the demands of empty and half-empty stomachs and life resolved itself into two related thoughts, food and how to get it.

Food! Food! Why did the stomach have a longer memory than the mind? Scarlett could banish heartbreak but not hunger, and each morning as she lay half-asleep, before memory brought back to her mind war and hunger, she curled drowsily expecting the sweet smells of bacon frying and rolls baking. And each morning she sniffed so hard to really smell the food she woke herself up.

There were apples, yams, peanuts and milk on the table at Tara but never enough of even this primitive fare. At the sight of them, three times a day, her memory would rush back to the old days, the meals of the old days, the candle-lit table and the food perfuming the air.

How careless they had been of food then, what prodigal waste! Rolls, corn muffins, biscuit and waffles, dripping butter, all at one meal. Ham at one end of the table and fried chicken at the other, collards swimming richly in pot liquor iridescent with grease, snap beans in mountains on brightly flowered porcelain, fried squash, stewed okra, carrots in cream sauce thick enough to cut. And three desserts, so everyone might have his choice, chocolate layer cake, vanilla blancmange and pound cake topped with sweet whipped cream. The memory of those savoury meals had the power to bring tears to her eyes as death and war had failed to do, had the power to turn her ever-gnawing stomach from rumbling emptiness to nausea. For the appetite Mammy had always deplored, the healthy appetite of a nineteen-year-old girl, now was increased fourfold by the hard and unremitting labour she had never known before.

Hers was not the only troublesome appetite at Tara, for wherever she turned hungry faces, black and white, met her eyes. Soon Carreen and Suellen would have the insatiable hunger of typhoid convalescents. Already little Wade whined monotonously: 'Wade doan like yams. Wade hungwy.'

The others grumbled, too:

'Miss Scarlett, 'ness I gits mo' to eat, I kain nuss neither of these chillun.'

'Miss Scarlett, ef Ah doan have mo' in mah stummick, Ah kain split no wood.'

'Lamb, Ah's perishin' fer real vittles.'

'Daughter, must we always have yams?'

Only Melanie did not complain, Melanie whose face grew thinner and whiter and twitched with pain even in her sleep.

'I'm not hungry, Scarlett. Give my share of the milk to Dilcey. She needs it to nurse the babies. Sick people are never hungry.'

It was her gentle hardihood which irritated Scarlett more than the nagging, whining voices of the others. She could – and did – shout them down with bitter sarcasm but before Melanie's unselfishness she was helpless, helpless and resentful. Gerald, the negroes and Wade clung to Melanie now, because even in her weakness she was kind and sympathetic, and these days Scarlett was neither.

Wade especially haunted Melanie's room. There was something wrong with Wade, but just what it was Scarlett had no time to discover. She took Mammy's word that the little boy had worms and dosed him with the mixture of dried herbs and bark which Ellen always used to worm the piccaninnies. But the vermifuge only made the child look paler. These days Scarlett hardly thought of Wade as a person. He was only another worry, another mouth to feed. Some day when the present emergency was over, she would play with him, tell him stories and teach him his A B C's, but now she did not have the time or the inclination. And, because he always seemed underfoot when she was most weary and worried, she often spoke sharply to him.

It annoyed her that her quick reprimands brought such acute fright to his round eyes, for he looked so simple-minded when he was frightened. She did not realize that the little boy lived shoulder to shoulder with terror too great for an adult to comprehend. Fear lived with Wade, fear that shook his soul and made him wake screaming in the night. Any unexpected noise or sharp word set him to trembling, for in his mind noises and harsh words were inextricably mixed with Yankees and he was more afraid of Yankees than of Prissy's hants.

Until the thunders of the siege began, he had never known anything but a happy, placid, quiet life. Even though his mother paid him little attention, he had known nothing but petting and kind words until the night when he was jerked from slumber to find the sky aflame and the air deafening with explosions. In that night and the day which followed, he had been slapped by his mother for the first time and had heard her voice raised at him in harsh words. Life in the pleasant brick house on Peachtree Street, the only life he knew, had vanished that night and he would never recover from its loss. In the flight from Atlanta, he had understood nothing except that the Yankees were after him, and now he still lived in fear that the Yankees would catch him and cut him to pieces. Whenever Scarlett raised her voice in reproof, he went weak with fright as his vague childish memory brought up the horrors of the first time she had ever done it. Now, Yankees and a cross voice were linked forever in his mind and he was afraid of his mother.

Scarlett could not help noticing that the child was beginning to avoid her and, in the rare moments when her unending duties gave her time to think about it, it bothered her a great deal. It was even worse than having him at her skirts all the time, and she was offended that his refuge was Melanie's bed where he played quietly at games Melanie suggested or listened to stories she told. Wade adored 'Auntee' who had a gentle voice, who always smiled and who never said: 'Hush, Wade! You give me a headache,' or 'Stop fidgeting, Wade, for Heaven's sake!'

Scarlett had neither the time nor the impulse to pet him but it made her jealous to see Melanie do it. When she found him one day standing on his head in Melanie's bed and saw him collapse on her, she slapped him.

'Don't you know better than to jiggle Auntee like that when she's sick? Now, trot right out in the yard and play, and don't come in here again.'

But Melanie reached out a weak arm and drew the wailing child to her.

'There, there, Wade. You didn't mean to jiggle me, did you? He doesn't bother me, Scarlett. Do let him stay with me. Let me take care of him. It's the only thing I can do till I get well, and you've your hands full enough without having to watch him.'

'Don't be a goose, Melly,' said Scarlett shortly. 'You aren't getting well like you should and having Wade fall on your stomach won't help you. Now, Wade, if I ever catch you on Auntee's bed again, I'll wear you out. And stop sniffling. You are always sniffling. Try to be a little man.'

Wade flew sobbing to hide himself under the house. Melanie bit her lip and tears came to her eyes, and Mammy standing in the hall, a witness to the scene, scowled and breathed hard. But no one talked back to Scarlett these days. They were all afraid of her sharp tongue, all afraid of the new person who walked in her body.

Scarlett reigned supreme at Tara now and, like others suddenly elevated to authority, all the bullying instincts in her nature rose to the surface. It was not that she was basically unkind. It was because she was so frightened and unsure of herself she was harsh lest others learn her inadequacies and refuse her authority. Besides, there was some pleasure in shouting at people and knowing they were afraid. Scarlett found that it relieved her overwrought nerves. She was not blind to the fact that her personality was changing. Sometimes when her curt orders made Pork stick out his underlip and Mammy mutter: 'Some folks rides mighty high dese days,' she wondered where her good manners had gone. All the courtesy, all the gentleness Ellen had striven to instil in her had fallen away from her as quickly as leaves fall from trees in the first chill wind of autumn.

Time and again, Ellen had said: 'Be firm but be gentle with inferiors, especially darkies.' But if she was gentle the darkies would sit in the kitchen all day, talking endlessly about the good old days when a house nigger wasn't supposed to do a field hand's work.

'Love and cherish your sisters. Be kind to the afflicted,' said Ellen. 'Show tenderness to those in sorrow and in trouble.'

She couldn't love her sisters now. They were simply a dead weight on her shoulders. And as for cherishing them, wasn't she bathing them, combing their hair and feeding them, even at the expense of walking miles every day to find vegetables? Wasn't she learning to milk the cow, even though her heart was always in her throat when that fearsome animal shook its horns at her? And as for being kind, that was a waste of time. If she was overly kind to them, they'd probably prolong their stay in bed, and she wanted them on their feet again as soon as possible, so there would be four more hands to help her.

They were convalescing slowly and lay scrawny and weak in their bed. While they had been unconscious, the world had changed. The Yankees had come, the darkies had gone and Mother had died. Here were three unbelievable happenings and their minds could not take them in. Sometimes they believed they must still be delirious and these things had not happened at all. Certainly Scarlett was so changed she couldn't be real. When she hung over the foot of their bed and outlined the work she expected them to do when they recovered, they looked at her as if she were a hobgoblin. It was beyond their comprehension that they no longer had a hundred slaves to do the work. It was beyond their comprehension that an O'Hara lady should do manual labour.

'But, Sister,' said Carreen, her sweet childish face black with consternation, 'I couldn't split kindling! It would ruin my hands!'

'Look at mine,' answered Scarlett with a frightening smile as she pushed blistered and calloused palms toward her.

'I think you are hateful to talk to Baby and me like this!' cried Suellen. 'I think you are lying and trying to frighten us. If Mother were only here, she wouldn't let you talk to us like this! Split kindling, indeed!'

Suellen looked with weak loathing at her older sister, feeling sure Scarlett said these things just to be mean. Suellen had nearly died and she had lost her mother and she was lonely and scared and she wanted to be petted and made much of. Instead, Scarlett looked over the foot of the bed each day, appraising their improvement with a hateful new gleam in her slanting green eyes, and talked about making beds, preparing food, carrying water-buckets and splitting kindling. And she looked as if she took a pleasure in saying such awful things.

Scarlett did take pleasure in it. She bullied the negroes and harrowed the feelings of her sisters not only because she was too worried and strained and tired to do otherwise, but because it helped her to forget her own bitterness that everything her mother had told her about life was wrong.

Nothing her mother had taught her was of any value whatsoever now and Scarlett's heart was sore and puzzled. It did not occur to her that Ellen could not have foreseen the collapse of the civilization in which she raised her daughters, could not have anticipated the disappearing of the places in society for which she trained them so well. It did not occur to her that Ellen had looked down a vista of placid future years, all like the uneventful years of her own life, when she had taught her to be gentle and gracious, honourable and kind, modest and truthful. Life treated women well when they had learned those lessons, said Ellen.

Scarlett thought in despair: 'Nothing, no, nothing, she taught me is of any help to me! What good will kindness do me now? What value is gentleness? Better that I'd learned to plough or chop cotton like a darky. Oh, Mother, you were wrong!'

She did not stop to think that Ellen's ordered world was gone and a brutal world had taken its place, a world wherein every standard, every value had changed. She only saw, or thought she saw, that her mother had been wrong, and she changed swiftly to meet this new world for which she was not prepared.

Only her feeling for Tara had not changed. She never came wearily home across the fields and saw the sprawling white house that her heart did not swell with love and the joy of homecoming. She never looked out of her window at green pastures and red fields and tall tangled swamp forest that a sense of beauty did not fill her. Her love for this land with its softly rolling hills of bright-red soil, this beautiful red earth that was blood-coloured, garnet, brick-dust, vermilion, which so miraculously grew green bushes starred with white puffs, was one part of Scarlett which did not change when all else was changing. Nowhere else in the world was there land like this.

When she looked at Tara she could understand, in part, why wars were fought. Rhett was wrong when he said men fought wars for money. No, they fought for swelling acres, softly furrowed by the plough, for pastures green with stubby cropped grass, for lazy yellow rivers and white houses that were cool amid magnolias. These were the only things worth fighting for, the red earth which was theirs and would be their sons', the red earth which would bear cotton for their sons and their sons' sons.

The trampled acres of Tara were all that was left to her, now that Mother and Ashley were gone, now that Gerald was senile from shock, and money and darkies and security and position had vanished overnight. As from another world, she remembered a conversation with her father about the land and wondered how she could have been so young, so ignorant, as not to understand what he meant when he said that the land was the one thing in the world worth fighting for.

'For 'tis the only thing in the world that lasts . . . and to anyone with a drop of Irish blood in them the land they live on is like their mother . . . 'Tis the only thing worth working for, fighting for, dying for.'

Yes, Tara was worth fighting for, and she accepted simply and without question the fight. No one was going to get Tara away from her. No one was going to set her and her people adrift on the charity of relatives. She would hold Tara, if she had to break the back of every person on it.

Chapter XXVI

Scarlett had been at Tara two weeks since her return from Atlanta when the largest blister on her foot began to fester, swelling until it was impossible for her to put on her shoe or do more than hobble about on her heel. Desperation plucked at her when she looked at the angry sore on her toe.

Suppose it should gangrene like the soldiers' wounds and she should die, far away from a doctor? Bitter as life was now, she had no desire to leave it. And who would look after Tara if she should die?

She had hoped when she first came home that Gerald's old spirit would revive and he would take command, but in these two weeks that hope had vanished. She knew now that, whether she liked it or not, she had the plantation and all its people on her two inexperienced hands, for Gerald still sat quietly, like a man in a dream, so frighteningly absent from Tara, so gentle. To her pleas for advice he gave as his only answer: 'Do what you think best, Daughter.' Or worse still, 'Consult with your mother, Puss.'

He would never be any different and now Scarlett realized the truth and accepted it without emotion – that until he died Gerald would always be waiting for Ellen, always listening for her. He was in some dim borderline country where time was standing still and Ellen was always in the next room. The mainspring of his existence was taken away when she died and with it had gone his bounding assurance, his impudence and his restless vitality. Ellen was the audience before which the blustering drama of Gerald O'Hara had been played. Now the curtain had been rung down forever, the footlights dimmed and the audience suddenly vanished, while the stunned old actor remained on his empty stage, waiting for his cues.

That morning the house was still, for everyone except Scarlett, Wade and the three sick girls was in the swamp hunting the sow. Even Gerald had roused a little and stumped off across the furrowed fields, one hand on Pork's arm and a coil of rope in the other. Suellen and Carreen had cried themselves to sleep, as they did at least twice a day when they thought of Ellen, tears of grief and weakness oozing down their sunken cheeks. Melanie, who had been propped up on pillows for the first time that day, lay covered with a mended sheet between two babies, the downy flaxen head of one cuddled in her arm, the kinky black head of Dilcey's child held as gently in the other. Wade sat at the bottom of the bed, listening to a fairy story.

To Scarlett, the stillness at Tara was unbearable, for it reminded her too sharply of the deathlike stillness of the desolate country through which she had passed that long day on her way home from Atlanta. The cow and the calf had made no sound for hours. There were no birds twittering outside her window and even the noisy family of mockers who had lived among the harshly rustling leaves of the magnolia for generations had no song that day. She had drawn a low chair close to the open window of her bedroom, looking out on the front drive, the lawn and the empty green pasture across the road, and she sat with her skirts well above her knees and her chin resting on her arms on the window-sill. There was a bucket of well water on the floor beside her and every now and then she lowered her blistered foot into it, screwing up her face at the stinging sensation.

Fretting, she dug her chin into her arm. Just when she needed her strength most, this toe had to fester. Those fools would never catch the sow. It had taken them a week to capture the pigs, one by one, and now after two weeks the sow was still at liberty. Scarlett knew that if she were just there in the swamp with them, she could tuck up her dress to her knees and take the rope and lasso the sow before you could say Jack Robinson.

But even after the sow was caught – if she were caught? What then, after she and her litter were eaten? Life would go on and so would appetites. Winter was coming and there would be no food, not even the poor remnants of the vegetables from the neighbours' gardens. They must have dried peas and sorghum and meal and rice and – and – oh, so many things. Corn and cotton seed for next spring's planting, and new clothes too. Where was it all to come from and how would she pay for it?

She had privately gone through Gerald's pockets and his cash-box and all she could find was stacks of Confederate bonds and three thousand dollars in Confederate bills. That was about enough to buy one square meal for them all, she thought ironically, now that Confederate money was worth almost less than nothing at all. But if she did have money and could find food, how would she haul it home to Tara? Why had God let the old horse die? Even that sorry animal Rhett had stolen would make all the difference in the world to them. Oh, those fine sleek mules which used to kick up their heels in the pasture across the road, and the handsome carriage horses, her little mare, the girls' ponies and Gerald's big stallion racing about and tearing up the turf— Oh, for one of them, even the balkiest mule!

But, no matter – when her foot healed she would walk to Jonesboro. It would be the longest walk she had ever taken in her life, but walk it she would. Even if the Yankees had burned the town completely, she could certainly find someone in the neighbourhood who could tell her where to get food. Wade's pinched face rose up before her eyes. He didn't like yams, he repeated; wanted a drumstick and some rice and gravy.

The bright sunlight in the front yard suddenly clouded and the trees blurred through tears. Scarlett dropped her head on her arms and struggled not to cry. Crying was so useless now. The only time crying ever did any good was when there was a man around from whom you wished favours. As she crouched there, squeezing her eyes tightly to keep back the tears, she was startled by the sound of trotting hooves. But she did not raise her head. She had imagined that sound too often in the nights and days of these last two weeks, just as she had imagined she heard the rustle of Ellen's skirts. Her heart hammered, as it always did at such moments, before she told herself sternly: 'Don't be a fool.'

But the hooves slowed down in a startlingly natural way to the rhythm of a walk and there was the measured scrunch-scrunch on the gravel. It was a horse – the Tarletons, the Fontaines! She looked up quickly. It was a Yankee cavalryman.

Automatically, she dodged behind the curtain and peered fascinated at him through the dim folds of the cloth, so startled that the breath went out of her lungs with a gasp.

He sat slouched in the saddle, a thick, rough-looking man with an unkempt black beard straggling over his unbuttoned blue jacket. Little close-set eyes, squinting in the sun-glare, calmly surveyed the house from beneath the visor of his tight blue cap. As he slowly dismounted and tossed the bridle reins over the hitching-post, Scarlett's breath came back to her as suddenly and painfully as after a blow in the stomach. A Yankee, a Yankee with a long pistol on his hip! And she was alone in the house with three sick girls and the babies!

As he lounged up the walk, hand on holster, beady little eyes glancing to right and left, a kaleidoscope of jumbled pictures spun in her mind, stories Aunt Pittypat had whispered of attacks on unprotected women, throat-cuttings, houses burned over the heads of dying women, children bayoneted because they cried, all of the unspeakable horrors that lay bound up in the name of 'Yankee'.

Her first terrified impulse was to hide in the closet, crawl under the bed, fly down the back stairs and run screaming to the swamp, anything to escape from him. Then she heard his cautious feet on the front steps and his stealthy tread as he entered the hall and she knew that escape was cut off. Too cold with fear to move, she heard his progress from room to room downstairs, his steps growing louder and bolder as he discovered no one. Now he was in the dining-room and in a moment he would walk out into the kitchen.

At the thought of the kitchen, rage suddenly leaped up in Scarlett's breast, so sharply that it jabbed at her heart like a knife-thrust, and fear fell away before her overpowering fury. The kitchen! There, over the open kitchen fire, were two pots, one filled with apples stewing and the other with a hodge-podge of vegetables brought painfully from Twelve Oaks and the MacIntosh garden – dinner that must serve for nine hungry people and hardly enough for two. Scarlett had been restraining her appetite for hours, waiting for the return of the others, and the thought of the Yankee eating their meagre meal made her shake with anger.

God damn them all! They descended like locusts and left Tara to starve slowly and now they were back again to steal the poor leavings. Her empty stomach writhed within her. By God, this was one Yankee who would do no more stealing!

She slipped off her worn shoe and, barefooted, she pattered swiftly to the bureau, not even feeling her festered toe. She opened the top drawer soundlessly and caught up the heavy pistol she had brought from Atlanta, the weapon Charles had worn but never fired. She fumbled in the leather box that hung on the wall below his sabre and brought out a cap. She slipped it into place with a hand that did not shake. Quickly and noiselessly, she ran into the upper hall and down the stairs, steadying herself on the banisters with one hand and holding the pistol close to her thigh in the folds of her skirt.

'Who's there?' cried a nasal voice, and she stopped on the middle of the stairs, the blood thudding in her ears so loudly she could hardly hear him. 'Halt or I'll shoot!' came the voice.

He stood in the door of the dining-room, crouched tensely, his pistol in one hand and, in the other, the small rosewood sewing-box fitted with gold thimble, gold-handled scissors and tiny gold-topped acorn of emery. Scarlett's legs felt cold to the knees but rage scorched her face. Ellen's sewing-box in his hands. She wanted to cry: 'Put it down! Put it down, you dirty—' but words would not come. She could only stare over the banisters at him and watch his face change from harsh tenseness to a half-contemptuous, half-ingratiating smile.

'So there is somebody ter home,' he said, slipping his pistol back into its holster and moving into the hall until he stood directly below her. 'All alone, little lady?'

Like lightning, she shoved her weapon over the banisters and into the startled bearded face. Before he could even fumble at his belt, she pulled the trigger. The back kick of the pistol made her reel, as the roar of the explosion filled her ears and the acrid smoke stung her nostrils. The man crashed backwards to the floor, sprawling into the dining-room with a violence that shook the furniture. The box clattered from his hand, the contents spilling about him. Hardly aware that she was moving, Scarlett ran down the stairs and stood over him, gazing down into what was left of the face above the beard, a bloody pit where the nose had been, glazing eyes burned with powder. As she looked, two streams of blood crept across the shining floor, one from his face and one from the back of his head.

Yes, he was dead. Undoubtedly. She had killed a man.

The smoke curled slowly to the ceiling and the red streams widened about her feet. For a timeless moment she stood there and in the still hot hush of the summer morning every irrelevant sound and scent seemed magnified, the quick thudding of her heart, like a drumbeat, the slight rough rustling of the magnolia leaves, the far-off plaintive sound of a swamp bird and the sweet smell of the flowers outside the window.

She had killed a man, she who took care never to be in at the kill on a hunt, she who could not bear the squealing of a hog at slaughter or the squeak of a rabbit in a snare. Murder! she thought dully. I've done murder. Oh, this can't be happening to me! Her eyes went to the stubby hairy hand on the floor so close to the sewing-box and suddenly she was vitally alive again, vitally glad with a cool tigerish joy. She could have ground her heel into the gaping wound which had been his nose and taken pleasure in the feel of his warm blood on her bare feet. She had struck a blow of revenge for Tara – and for Ellen.

There were hurried stumbling steps in the upper hall, a pause and then more steps, weak dragging steps now, punctuated by metallic clankings. A sense of time and reality coming back to her, Scarlett looked up and saw Melanie at the top of the stairs, clad only in the ragged chemise which served her as a nightgown, her weak arm weighed down with Charles' sabre. Melanie's eyes took in the scene below in its entirety – the sprawling blue-clad body in the red pool, the sewing-box beside him, Scarlett, barefooted and grey-faced, clutching the long pistol.

In silence her eyes met Scarlett's. There was a glow of grim pride in her usually gentle face, approbation and a fierce joy in her smile that equalled the fiery tumult in Scarlett's own bosom.

'Why – why – she's like me! She understands how I feel!' thought Scarlett in that long moment. 'She'd have done the same thing!'

With a thrill she looked up at the frail swaying girl for whom she had never had any feelings but of dislike and contempt. Now, struggling against hatred for Ashley's wife, there surged a feeling of admiration and comradeship. She saw in a flash of clarity untouched by any petty emotion that beneath the gentle voice and the dovelike eyes of Melanie there was a thin flashing blade of unbreakable steel, felt too that there were banners and bugles of courage in Melanie's quiet blood.

'Scarlett! Scarlett!' shrilled the weak frightened voices of Suellen and Carreen, muffled by their closed door, and Wade's voice screamed, 'Auntee! Auntee!' Swiftly Melanie put her finger to her lips and, laying the sword on the top step, she painfully made her way down the upstairs hall and opened the door of the sick-room.

'Don't be scared, chickens!' came her voice with teasing gaiety. 'Your big sister was trying to clean the rust off Charles' pistol and it went off and nearly scared her to death!' . . . 'Now, Wade Hampton, Mama just shot off your dear Papa's pistol! When you are bigger, she will let you shoot it.'

'What a cool liar!' thought Scarlett with admiration. 'I couldn't have thought that quickly. But why lie? They've got to know I've done it.'

She looked down at the body again and now revulsion came over her as rage and fright melted away, and her knees began to quiver with the reaction. Melanie dragged herself to the top step again and started down, holding on to the banisters, her pale lower lip caught between her teeth.

'Go back to bed, silly, you'll kill yourself!' Scarlett cried, but the half-naked Melanie made her painful way down into the lower hall.

'Scarlett,' she whispered, 'we must get him out of here and bury him. He may not be alone and if they find him here—' She steadied herself on Scarlett's arm.

'He must be alone,' said Scarlett. 'I didn't see anyone else from the upstairs window. He must be a deserter.'

'Even if he is alone, no one must know about it. The negroes might talk and then they'd come and get you. Scarlett, we must get him hidden before the folks come back from the swamp.'

Her mind prodded to action by the feverish urgency of Melanie's voice, Scarlett thought hard.

'I could bury him in the corner of the garden under the arbour – the ground is soft there where Pork dug up the whisky barrel. But how will I get him there?'

'We'll both take a leg and drag him,' said Melanie firmly.

Reluctantly, Scarlett's admiration went still higher.

'You couldn't drag a cat. I'll drag him,' she said roughly. 'You go back to bed. You'll kill yourself. Don't dare try to help me either or I'll carry you back upstairs myself.'

Melanie's white face broke into a sweet understanding smile. 'You are very dear, Scarlett,' she said, and softly brushed her lips against Scarlett's cheek. Before Scarlett could recover from her surprise, Melanie went on: 'If you can drag him out, I'll mop up the – the mess before the folks get home, and Scarlett—'

'Yes?'

'Do you suppose it would be dishonest to go through his knapsack? He might have something to eat.'

'I do not,' said Scarlett, annoyed that she had not thought of this herself. 'You take the knapsack and I'll go through his pockets.'

Stooping over the dead man with distaste, she unbuttoned the remaining buttons of his jacket and systematically began rifling his pockets.

'Dear God,' she whispered, pulling out a bulging wallet, wrapped about with a rag. 'Melanie – Melly, I think it's full of money!'

Melanie said nothing but abruptly sat down on the floor and leaned back against the wall.

'You look,' she said shakily. 'I'm feeling a little weak.'

Scarlett tore off the rag and with trembling hands opened the leather folds.

'Look, Melly – just look!'

Melanie looked and her eyes dilated. Jumbled together was a mass of bills, United States greenbacks mingling with Confederate money and, glinting from between them, were one ten-dollar gold piece and two five-dollar gold pieces.

'Don't stop to count it now,' said Melanie, as Scarlett began fingering the bills. 'We haven't time—'

'Do you realize, Melanie, that this money means that we'll eat?'

'Yes, yes, dear. I know but we haven't time now. You look in his other pockets and I'll take the knapsack.'

Scarlett was loath to put down the wallet. Bright vistas opened before her – real money, the Yankee's horse, food! There was a God after all, and He did provide, even if He did take very odd ways of providing. She sat on her haunches and stared at the wallet, smiling. Food! Melanie plucked it from her hands.

'Hurry!' she said.

The trouser pockets yielded nothing except a candle-end, a jack-knife, a plug of tobacco and a bit of twine. Melanie removed from the knapsack a small package of coffee which she sniffed as if it were the sweetest of perfumes, hardtack and, her face changing, a miniature of a little girl in a gold frame set with seed pearls, a garnet brooch, two broad gold bracelets with tiny dangling gold chains, a gold thimble, a small silver baby's cup, gold embroidery scissors, a diamond solitaire ring and a pair of earrings with pendant pear-shaped diamonds, which even their unpractised eyes could tell were well over a carat each.

'A thief!' whispered Melanie, recoiling from the still body. 'Scarlett, he must have stolen all of this!'

'Of course,' said Scarlett. 'And he came here hoping to steal more from us.'

'I'm glad you killed him,' said Melanie, her gentle eyes hard. 'Now hurry, darling, and get him out of here.'

Scarlett bent over, caught the dead man by his boots and tugged. How heavy he was and how weak she suddenly felt! Suppose she shouldn't be able to move him? Turning so that she backed the corpse, she caught a heavy boot under each arm and threw her weight forward. He moved and she jerked again. Her sore foot, forgotten in the excitement, now gave a tremendous throb that made her grit her teeth and shift her weight to the heel. Tugging and straining, perspiration dripping from her forehead, she dragged him down the hall, a red stain following her path.

'If he bleeds across the yard, we can't hide it.' she gasped. 'Give me your shimmy, Melanie, and I'll wad it around his head.'

Melanie's white face went crimson.

'Don't be silly! I won't look at you,' said Scarlett. 'If I had on a petticoat or pantalets I'd use them.'

Crouching back against the wall, Melanie pulled the ragged linen garment over her head and silently tossed it to Scarlett, shielding herself as best she could with her arms.

'Thank God, I'm not that modest,' thought Scarlett, feeling rather than seeing Melanie's agony of embarrassment, as she wrapped the ragged cloth about the shattered face.

By a series of limping jerks, she pulled the body down the hall toward the back porch and, pausing to wipe her forehead with the back of her hand, glanced back toward Melanie, sitting against the wall hugging her thin knees to her bare breasts. How silly of Melanie to be bothering about modesty at a time like this, Scarlett thought irritably. It was just part of her nicey-nice way of acting which had always made Scarlett despise her. Then shame rose in her. After all – after all, Melanie had dragged herself from bed so soon after having a baby and had come to her aid with a weapon too heavy even for her to lift. That had taken courage, the kind of courage Scarlett honestly knew she herself did not possess, the thin-steel, spun-silk courage which had characterized Melanie on the terrible night Atlanta fell and on the long trip home. It was the same intangible, unspectacular courage that all the Wilkeses possessed, a quality which Scarlett did not understand but to which she gave grudging tribute.

'Go back to bed,' she threw over her shoulder. 'You'll be dead if you don't. I'll clean up the mess after I've buried him.'

'I'll do it with one of the rag rugs,' whispered Melanie, looking at the pool of blood with a sick face.

'Well, kill yourself then and see if I care! And if any of the folks come back before I'm finished, keep them in the house and tell them the horse just walked in from nowhere.'

Melanie sat shivering in the morning sunlight and covered her ears against the sickening series of thuds as the dead man's head bumped down the porch steps.

No one questioned whence the horse had come. It was so obvious he was a stray from the recent battle and they were well pleased to have him. The Yankee lay in the shallow pit Scarlett had scraped out under the scuppernong arbour. The uprights which held the thick vines were rotten, and that night Scarlett hacked at them with the kitchen knife until they fell and the tangled mass ran wild over the grave. The replacing of these posts was one bit of repair work Scarlett did not suggest and, if the negroes knew why, they kept their silence.

No ghost rose from that shallow grave to haunt her in the long nights when she lay awake, too tired to sleep. No feeling of horror or remorse assailed her at the memory. She wondered why, knowing that even a month before she could never have done the deed. Pretty young Mrs Hamilton, with her dimple and her jangling earbobs and her helpless little ways, blowing a man's face to a pulp and then burying him in a hastily scratched-out hole! Scarlett grinned a little grimly, thinking of the consternation such an idea would bring to those who knew her.

'I won't think about it any more,' she decided. 'It's over and done with and I'd have been a ninny not to kill him. I reckon – I reckon I must have changed a little since coming home or else I couldn't have done it.'

She did not think of it consciously but in the back of her mind, whenever she was confronted by an unpleasant and difficult task, the idea lurked, giving her strength: 'I've done murder and so I can surely do this.'

She had changed more than she knew and the shell of hardness which had begun to form about her heart when she lay in the slave garden at Twelve Oaks was slowly thickening.

Now that she had a horse, Scarlett could find out for herself what had happened to their neighbours. Since she came home she had wondered despairingly a thousand times: 'And are we the only folks left in the County? Has everybody else been burned out? Have they all refugeed to Macon?' With the memory of the ruins of Twelve Oaks, the MacIntosh place and the

Slattery shack fresh in her mind, she almost dreaded to discover the truth. But it was better to know the worst than to wonder. She decided to ride to the Fontaines' first, not because they were the nearest neighbours but because old Dr Fontaine might be there. Melanie needed a doctor. She was not recovering as she should and Scarlett was frightened by her white weakness.

So on the first day when her foot had healed enough to stand a slipper, she mounted the Yankee's horse. One foot in the shortened stirrup and the other leg crooked about the pommel in an approximation of a side saddle, she set out across the fields toward Mimosa, steeling herself to find it burned.

To her surprise and pleasure, she saw the faded yellow-stucco house standing amid the mimosa trees, looking as it had always looked. Warm happiness, happiness that almost brought tears, flooded her when the three Fontaine women came out of the house to welcome her with kisses and cries of joy.

But when the first exclamations of affectionate greeting were over and they all had trooped into the dining-room to sit down, Scarlett felt a chill. The Yankees had not reached Mimosa because it was far off the main road. And so the Fontaines still had their stock and their provisions, but Mimosa was held by the same strange silence that hung over Tara, over the whole countryside. All the slaves except four women house servants had run away, frightened by the approach of the Yankees. There was not a man on the place unless Sally's little boy, Joe, hardly out of diapers, could be counted as a man. Alone in the big house were Grandma Fontaine, in her seventies, her daughter-in-law, who would always be known as Young Miss, though she was in her fifties, and Sally, who had barely turned twenty. They were far away from neighbours and unprotected, but if they were afraid it did not show on their faces. Probably, thought Scarlett, because Sally and Young Miss were too afraid of the porcelain-frail but indomitable old Grandma to dare voice any qualms. Scarlett herself was afraid of the old lady, for she had sharp eyes and a sharper tongue and Scarlett had felt them both in the past.

Though unrelated by blood and far apart in age, there was a kinship of spirit and experience binding these women together. All three wore home-dyed mourning, all were worn, sad, worried, all bitter with a bitterness that did not sulk or complain but, nevertheless, peered out from behind their smiles and their words of welcome. For their slaves were gone, their money was worthless, Sally's husband, Joe, had died at Gettysburg and Young Miss was also a widow, for young Dr Fontaine had died of dysentery at Vicksburg. The other two boys, Alex and Tony, were somewhere in Virginia and nobody knew whether they were alive or dead; and old Dr Fontaine was off somewhere with Wheeler's cavalry.

'And the old fool is seventy-three years old though he tries to act younger and he's as full of rheumatism as a hog is of fleas,' said Grandma, proud of her husband, the light in her eyes belying her sharp words.

'Have you all had any news of what's been happening in Atlanta?' asked Scarlett when they were comfortably settled. 'We're completely buried at Tara.'

'Law, child,' said Old Miss, taking charge of the conversation, as was her habit, 'we're in the same fix as you are. We don't know a thing except that Sherman finally got the town.'

'So·he did get it. What's he doing now? Where's the fighting now?'

'And how would three lone women out here in the country know about the war when we haven't seen a letter or a newspaper in weeks?' said the old lady tartly. 'One of our darkies talked to a darky who'd seen a darky who'd been to Jonesboro, and except for that we haven't heard anything. What they said was that the Yankees were just squatting in Atlanta resting up their men and their horses, but whether it's true or not you're as good a judge as I am. Not that they wouldn't need a rest, after the fight we gave them.'

'To think you've been at Tara all this time and we didn't know!' Young Miss broke in. 'Oh, how I blame myself for not riding over to see! But there's been so much to do here with most all the darkies gone that I just couldn't get away. But I should have made time to go. It wasn't neighbourly of me. But, of course, we thought the Yankees had burned Tara like they did Twelve Oaks and the MacIntosh house and that your folks had gone to Macon. And we never dreamed you were home, Scarlett.'

'Well, how were we to know different when Mr O'Hara's darkies came through here so scared they were popeyed and told us the Yankees were going to burn Tara?' Grandma interrupted.

'And we could see—' Sally began.

'I'm telling this, please,' said Old Miss shortly. 'And they said the Yankees were camped all over Tara and you folks were fixing to go to Macon. And then that night we saw the glare of fire over toward Tara and it lasted for hours and it scared our fool darkies so bad they all ran off. What burned?'

'All our cotton – a hundred and fifty thousand dollars' worth,' said Scarlett bitterly.

'Be thankful it wasn't your house,' said Grandma, leaning her chin on her cane. 'You can always grow more cotton and you can't grow a house. By the by, had you all started picking your cotton?'

'No,' said Scarlett, 'and now most of it is ruined. I don't imagine there's more than three bales left standing, in the far field in the creek bottom, and what earthly good will it do? All our field hands are gone and there's nobody to pick it.'

'Mercy me, "all our field hands are gone and there's nobody to pick it"!' mimicked Grandma and bent a satiric glance on Scarlett. 'What's wrong with your own pretty paws, Miss, and those of your sisters?'

'Me? Pick cotton?' cried Scarlett aghast, as if Grandma had been suggesting some repulsive crime. 'Like a field hand? Like white trash? Like the Slattery women?'

'White trash, indeed! Well, isn't this generation soft and ladylike! Let me tell you, Miss, when I was a girl my father lost all his money and I wasn't above doing honest work with my hands and in the fields too, till Pa got enough money to buy some more darkies. I've hoed my row and I've picked cotton and I can do it again if I have to. And it looks like I'll have to. White trash, indeed!'

'Oh, but Mama Fontaine,' cried her daughter-in-law, casting imploring glances at the two girls, urging them to help her smooth the old lady's feathers. 'That was so long ago, a different day entirely, and times have changed.'

'Times never change when there's a need for honest work to be done,' stated the sharp-eyed old lady, refusing to be soothed. 'And I'm ashamed for your mother, Scarlett, to hear you stand there and talk as though honest work made white trash out of nice people. "When Adam delved and Eve span—"'

To change the subject, Scarlett hastily questioned: 'What about the Tarletons and the Calverts? Were they burned out? Have they refugeed to Macon?'

'The Yankees never got to the Tarletons. They're off the main road, like we are, but they did get to the Calverts and they stole all their stock and poultry and got all the darkies to run off with them—' Sally began.

Grandma interrupted.

'Hah! They promised all the black wenches silk dresses and gold earbobs – that's what they did. And Cathleen Calvert said some of the troopers went off with the black fools behind them on their saddles. Well, all they'll get will be yellow babies and I can't say that Yankee blood will improve the stock.'

'Oh, Mama Fontaine!'

'Don't pull such a shocked face, Jane. We're all married, aren't we? And, God knows, we've seen mulatto babies before this.'

'Why didn't they burn the Calverts' house?'

'The house was saved by the combined accents of the second Mrs Calvert and that Yankee overseer of hers, Hilton,' said Old Miss, who always referred to the ex-governess as the 'second Mrs Calvert', although the first Mrs Calvert had been dead twenty years.

' "We are staunch Union sympathizers," ' mimicked the old lady, twanging the words through her long thin nose. 'Cathleen said the two of them swore up hill and down dale that the whole passel of Calverts were Yankees. And Mr Calvert died in the Wilderness! And Raiford at Gettysburg and Cade in Virginia with the army! Cathleen was so mortified she said she'd rather the house had been burned. She said Cade would bust when he came home and heard about it. But then, that's what a man gets for marrying a Yankee woman – no pride, no decency, always thinking about their own skins . . . How come they didn't burn Tara, Scarlett?'

For a moment Scarlett paused before answering. She knew the very next question would be: 'And how are all your folks? And how is your dear mother?' She knew she could not tell them Ellen was dead. She knew that if she spoke those words or even let herself think of them in the presence of these sympathetic women, she would burst into a storm of tears and cry until she was sick. And she could not let herself cry. She had not really cried since she came home and she knew that if she once let down the floodgates, her closely husbanded courage would all be gone. But she knew, too, looking with confusion at the friendly faces about her, that if she withheld the news of Ellen's death, the Fontaines would never forgive her. Grandma in particular was devoted to Ellen and there were very few people in the County for whom the old lady gave a snap of her skinny fingers.

'Well, speak up,' said Grandma, looking sharply at her. 'Don't you know, Miss?'

'Well, you see, I didn't get home till the day after the battle,' she answered hastily. 'The Yankees were all gone then. Pa – Pa told me that – that he got them not to burn the house because Suellen and Carreen were so ill with typhoid they couldn't be moved.'

'That's the first time I ever heard of a Yankee doing a decent thing,' said Grandma, as if she regretted hearing anything good about the invaders. 'And how are the girls now?'

'Oh, they are better, much better, almost well but quite weak,' answered Scarlett. Then, seeing the question she feared hovering on the old lady's lips, she cast hastily about for some other topic of conversation.

'I – I wonder if you could lend us something to eat? The Yankees cleaned us out like a swarm of locusts. But, if you are short on rations, just tell me so plainly and—'

'Send over Pork with a wagon and you shall have half of what we've got, rice, meal, ham, some chickens,' said Old Miss, giving Scarlett a sudden keen look.

'Oh, that's too much! Really, I—'

'Not a word! I won't hear it. What are neighbours for?'

'You are so kind that I can't— But I have to be going now. The folks at home will be worrying about me.'

Grandma rose abruptly and took Scarlett by the arm.

'You two stay here,' she commanded, pushing Scarlett toward the back porch. 'I have a private word for this child. Help me down the steps, Scarlett.'

Young Miss and Sally said good-bye and promised to come calling soon. They were devoured by curiosity as to what Grandma had to say to Scarlett but unless she chose to tell them, they would never know. Old ladies were so difficult, Young Miss whispered to Sally as they went back to their sewing.

Scarlett stood with her hand on the horse's bridle, a dull feeling at her heart.

'Now,' said Grandma, peering into her face, 'what's wrong at Tara? What are you keeping back?'

Scarlett looked up into the keen old eyes and knew she could tell the truth, without tears. No one could cry in the presence of Grandma Fontaine without her express permission.

'Mother is dead,' she said flatly.

The hand on her arm tightened until it pinched and the wrinkled lids over the yellow eyes blinked.

'Did the Yankees kill her?'

'She died of typhoid. Died – the day before I came home.'

'Don't think about it,' said Grandma sternly and Scarlett saw her swallow. 'And your Pa?'

'Pa is – Pa is not himself.'

'What do you mean? Speak up. Is he ill?'

'The shock – he is so strange – he is not—'

'Don't tell me he's not himself. Do you mean his mind is unhinged?'

It was a relief to hear the truth put so baldly. How good the old lady was to offer no sympathy that would make her cry.

'Yes,' she said dully, 'he's lost his mind. He acts dazed and sometimes he can't seem to remember that Mother is dead. Oh, Old Miss, it's more than I can stand to see him sit by the hour, waiting for her and so patiently too, and he used to have no more patience than a child. But it's worse when he does remember that she's gone. Every now and then, after he's sat still with his ear cocked listening for her, he jumps up suddenly and stumps out of the house and down to the burying-ground. And then he comes dragging back with the tears all over his face and he says over and over till I could scream: "Katie Scarlett, Mrs O'Hara is dead. Your mother is dead," and it's just like I was hearing it again for the first time. And sometimes, late at night, I hear him calling her and I get out of bed and go to him and tell him she's down at the quarters with a sick darky. And he fusses because she's always tiring herself out nursing people. And it's so hard to get him back to bed. He's like a child. Oh, I wish Dr Fontaine was here! I know he could do something for Pa! And Melanie needs a doctor too. She isn't getting over her baby like she should—'

'Melly – a baby? And she's with you?'

'Yes.'

'What's Melly doing with you? Why isn't she in Macon with her aunt and her kinfolks? I never thought you liked her any too well, Miss, for all she was Charles' sister. Now, tell me all about it.'

'It's a long story, Old Miss. Don't you want to go back in the house and sit down?'

'I can stand,' said Grandma shortly. 'And if you told your story in front of the others, they'd be bawling and making you feel sorry for yourself. Now, let's have it.'

Scarlett began haltingly with the siege and Melanie's condition, but as her story progressed beneath the sharp old eyes which never faltered in their gaze, she found words, words of power and horror. It all came back to her, the sickeningly hot day of the baby's birth, the agony of fear, the flight and Rhett's desertion. She spoke of the wild darkness of the night, the blazing camp-fires which might be friends or foes, the gaunt chimneys which met her gaze in the morning sun, the dead men and horses along the road, the hunger, the desolation, the fear that Tara had been burned.

'I thought if I could just get home to Mother, she could manage everything and I could lay down the weary load. On the way home I thought the worst had already happened to me, but when I knew she was dead I knew what the worst really was.'

She dropped her eyes to the ground and waited for Grandma to speak. The silence was so prolonged she wondered if Grandma could have failed to comprehend her desperate plight. Finally the old voice spoke and her tones were kind, kinder than Scarlett had ever heard her use in addressing anyone.

'Child, it's a very bad thing for a woman to face the worst that can happen to her, because after she's faced the worst she can't ever really fear anything again. And it's very bad for a woman not to be afraid of something. You think I don't understand what you've told me – what you've been through? Well, I understand very well. When I was about your age I was in the Creek uprising, right after the Fort Mims massacre – yes,' she said in a far-away voice, 'just about your age for that was fifty-odd years ago. And I managed to get into the bushes and hide, and I lay there and saw our house burn and I saw the Indians scalp my brothers and sisters. And I could only lie there and pray that the light of the flames wouldn't show up my hiding-place. And they dragged Mother out and killed her about twenty feet from where I was lying. And scalped her too. And every so often one Indian would go back to her and sink his tommyhawk into her skull again. I – I was my mother's pet and I lay there and saw it all. And in the morning I set out for the nearest settlement and it was thirty miles away. It took me three days to get there, through the swamps and the Indians, and afterward they thought I'd lose my mind . . . That's where I met Dr Fontaine. He looked after me . . . Ah, well, that's been fifty years ago, as I said, and since that time I've never been afraid of anything or anybody because I'd known the worst that could happen to me. And that lack of fear has gotten me into a lot of trouble and cost me a lot of happiness. God intended women to be timid frightened creatures and there's something unnatural about a woman who isn't afraid . . . Scarlett, always save something to fear – even as you save something to love . . .'

Her voice trailed off and she stood silent with eyes looking back over half a century to the day when she had been afraid. Scarlett moved impatiently. She had thought Grandma was going to understand and perhaps show her some way to solve her problems. But like all old people she'd gotten to talking about things that happened before anyone was born, things no one was interested in. Scarlett wished she had not confided in her.

'Well, go home, child, or they'll be worrying about you,' she said suddenly. 'Send Pork with the wagon this afternoon . . . And don't think you can lay down the load, ever. Because you can't. I know.'

Indian summer lingered into November that year and the warm days were bright days for those at Tara. The worst was over. They had a horse now and they could ride instead of walk. They had fried eggs for breakfast and fried ham for supper to vary the monotony of the yams, peanuts and dried apples, and on one festal occasion they even had roast chicken. The old sow had finally been captured and she and her brood rooted and grunted happily under the house where they were penned. Sometimes they squealed so loudly no one in the house could talk but it was a pleasant sound. It meant fresh pork for the white folks and chitterlings for the negroes when cold weather and hog-killing time should arrive, and it meant food for the winter for all.

Scarlett's visit to the Fontaines had heartened her more than she realized. Just the knowledge that she had neighbours, that some of the family friends and old homes had survived, drove out the terrible lost and alone feeling which had oppressed her in her first weeks at Tara. And the Fontaines and Tarletons, whose plantations had not been in the path of the army, were most generous in sharing what little they had. It was the tradition of the County that neighbour helped neighbour and they refused to accept a penny from Scarlett, telling her that she would do the same for them and she could pay them back, in kind, next year when Tara was again producing.

Scarlett now had food for her household, she had a horse, she had the money and jewellery taken from the Yankee straggler, and the greatest need was new clothing. She knew it would be risky business sending Pork south to buy clothes, when the horse might be captured by either Yankees or Confederates. But, at least, she had the money with which to buy the clothes, a horse and wagon for the trip, and perhaps Pork could make the trip without getting caught. Yes, the worst was over.

Every morning when Scarlett arose she thanked God for the pale-blue sky and the warm sun, for each day of good weather put off the inevitable time when warm clothing would be needed. And each warm day saw more and more cotton piling up in the empty slave quarters, the only storage place left on the plantation. There was more cotton in the fields than she or Pork had estimated, probably four bales, and soon the cabins would be full.

Scarlett had not intended to do any cotton picking herself, even after Grandma Fontaine's tart remark. It was unthinkable that she, an O'Hara lady, now the mistress of Tara, should work in the fields. It put her on the same level with the snarly-haired Mrs Slattery and Emmie. She had intended that the negroes should do the field work, while she and the convalescent girls attended to the house, but here she was confronted with a caste feeling even stronger than her own. Pork, Mammy and Prissy set up outcries at the idea of working in the fields. They reiterated that they were house niggers, not field hands. Mammy, in particular, declared vehemently that she had never even been a yard nigger. She had been born in the Robillard great house, not in the quarters, and had been raised in Ole Miss' bedroom, sleeping on a pallet at the foot of the bed. Dilcey alone said nothing and she fixed her Prissy with an unwinking eye that made her squirm.

Scarlett refused to listen to the protests and drove them all into the cotton rows. But Mammy and Pork worked so slowly and with so many lamentations that Scarlett sent Mammy back to the kitchen to cook and Pork to the woods and the river with snares for rabbits and possums and lines for fish. Cotton picking was beneath Pork's dignity but hunting and fishing were not.

Scarlett next had tried her sisters and Melanie in the fields, but that had worked no better. Melanie had picked neatly, quickly and willingly for an hour in the hot sun and then fainted quietly and had to stay in bed for a week. Suellen, sullen and tearful, pretended to faint too, but came back to consciousness spitting like an angry cat when Scarlett poured a gourdful of water in her face. Finally she had refused point-blank.

'I won't work in the fields like a darky! You can't make me. What if any of our friends ever heard of it? What if – if Mr Kennedy ever knew? Oh, if Mother knew about this—'

'You just mention Mother's name once more, Suellen O'Hara, and I'll slap you flat,' cried Scarlett. 'Mother worked harder than any darky on this place and you know it, Miss Fine Airs!'

'She did not! At least, not in the fields. And you can't make me. I'll tell Papa on you and he won't make me work!'

'Don't you dare go bothering Pa with any of our troubles!' cried Scarlett, distracted between indignation at her sister and fear for Gerald.

'I'll help you, Sissy,' interposed Carreen docilely. 'I'll work for Sue and me too. She isn't well yet and she shouldn't be out in the sun.'

Scarlett said gratefully: 'Thank you, Sugarbaby,' but looked worriedly at her younger sister. Carreen, who had always been as delicately pink and white as the orchard blossoms that are scattered by the spring wind, was no longer pink but still conveyed in her sweet thoughtful face a blossomlike quality. She had been silent, a little dazed since she came back to consciousness and found Ellen gone, Scarlett a termagant, the world changed and unceasing labour the order of the new day. It was not in Carreen's delicate nature to adjust herself to change. She simply could not comprehend what had happened and she went about Tara like a sleepwalker, doing exactly what she was told. She looked, and was, frail but she was willing, obedient and obliging. When she was not doing Scarlett's bidding, her rosary beads were always in her hands and her lips moving in prayers for her mother and for Brent Tarleton. It did not occur to Scarlett that Carreen had taken Brent's death so seriously and that her grief was unhealed. To Scarlett,

Carreen was still 'baby sister', far too young to have had a really serious love affair.

Scarlett, standing in the sun in the cotton rows, her back breaking from the eternal bending and her hands roughened by the dry bolls, wished she had a sister who combined Suellen's energy and strength with Carreen's sweet disposition. For Carreen picked diligently and earnestly. But after she had laboured for an hour it was obvious that she, and not Suellen, was the one not yet well enough for such work. So Scarlett sent Carreen back to the house too.

There remained with her now in the long rows only Dilcey and Prissy. Prissy picked lazily, spasmodically, complaining of her feet, her back, her internal miseries, her complete weariness, until her mother took a cotton stalk to her and whipped her until she screamed. After that she worked a little better, taking care to stay far from her mother's reach.

Dilcey worked tirelessly, silently, like a machine, and Scarlett, with her back aching and her shoulder raw from the tugging weight of the cotton-bag she carried, thought that Dilcey was worth her weight in gold.

'Dilcey,' she said, 'when good times come back, I'm not going to forget how you've acted. You've been mighty good.'

The bronze giantess did not grin pleasedly or squirm under praise like the other negroes. She turned an immobile face to Scarlett and said with dignity: 'Thankee, Ma'm. But Mist' Gerald and Miss Ellen been good to me. Mist' Gerald buy my Prissy so I wouldn' grieve and I doan forgit it. I is part Indian and Indians doan forgit them as is good to them. I is sorry 'bout my Prissy. She mighty wuthless. Look lak she all nigger lak her pa. Her pa was mighty flighty.'

In spite of Scarlett's problem of getting help from the others in the picking and in spite of the weariness of doing the labour herself, her spirits lifted as the cotton slowly made its way from the fields to the cabins. There was something about cotton that was reassuring, steadying. Tara had risen to riches on cotton, even as the whole South had risen, and Scarlett was Southerner enough to believe that both Tara and the South would rise again out of the red fields.

Of course, this little cotton she had gathered was not much but it was something. It would bring a little in Confederate money and that little would help her to save the hoarded greenbacks and gold in the Yankee's wallet until they had to be spent. Next spring she would try to make the Confederate government send back Big Sam and the other field hands they had commandeered, and if the government wouldn't release them, she'd use the Yankee's money to hire field hands from the neighbours. Next spring she would plant and plant . . . She straightened her tired back and, looking over the browning autumn fields, she saw next year's crop standing sturdy and green, acre upon acre.

Next spring! Perhaps by next spring the war would be over and good times would be back. And whether the Confederacy won or lost, times would be better. Anything was better than the constant danger of raids from both armies. When the war was over, a plantation could earn an honest living. Oh, if the war were only over! Then people could plant crops with some certainty of reaping them!

There was hope now. The war couldn't last forever. She had her little cotton, she had food, she had a horse, she had her small but treasured hoard of money. Yes, the worst was over!

Chapter XXVII

On a noonday in mid-November, they all sat grouped about the dinner table, eating the last of the dessert concocted by Mammy from corn meal and dried huckleberries, sweetened with sorghum. There was a chill in the air, the first chill of the year, and Pork, standing behind Scarlett's chair, rubbed his hands together in glee and questioned: 'Ain' it 'bout time fer de hawg-killin', Miss Scarlett?'

'You can taste those chitlins already, can't you?' said Scarlett with a grin. 'Well, I can taste fresh pork myself and if the weather holds for a few more days, we'll—'

Melanie interrupted, her spoon at her lips.

'Listen, dear! Somebody's coming!'

'Somebody hollerin',' said Pork uneasily.

On the crisp autumn air came clear the sound of horse's hooves, thudding as swiftly as a frightened heart, and a woman's voice, high pitched, screaming: 'Scarlett! Scarlett!'

Eye met eye for a dreadful second around the table before chairs were pushed back and everyone leaped up. Despite the fear that made it shrill, they recognized the voice of Sally Fontaine who, only an hour before, had stopped at Tara for a brief chat on her way to Jonesboro. Now, as they all rushed pell-mell to crowd the front door, they saw her coming up the drive like the wind on a lathered horse, her hair streaming behind her, her bonnet dangling by its ribbons. She did not draw rein but as she galloped madly toward them, she waved her arm back in the direction from which she had come.

'The Yankees are coming! I saw them! Down the road! The Yankees—'

She sawed savagely at the horse's mouth just in time to swerve him from leaping up the front steps. He swung around sharply, covered the side lawn in three leaps and she put him across the four-foot hedge as if she were on the hunting field. They heard the heavy pounding of his hooves as he went through the back yard and down the narrow lane between the cabins of the quarters and knew she was cutting across the fields to Mimosa.

For a moment they stood paralysed and then Suellen and Carreen began to sob and clutch each other's fingers. Little Wade stood rooted, trembling, unable to cry. What he had feared since the night he left Atlanta had happened. The Yankees were coming to get him.

'Yankees?' said Gerald vaguely. 'But the Yankees have already been here.'

'Mother of God!' cried Scarlett, her eyes meeting Melanie's frightened eyes. For a swift instant there went through her memory again the horrors of her last night in Atlanta, the ruined homes that dotted the countryside, all the stories of rape and torture and murder. She saw again the Yankee soldier standing in the hall with Ellen's sewing-box in his hand. She thought: 'I shall die. I shall die right here. I thought we were through with all that. I shall die. I can't stand any more.'

Then her eyes fell on the horse saddled and hitched and waiting for Pork to ride him to the Tarleton place on an errand. Her horse! Her only horse! The Yankees would take him and the cow and the calf. And the sow and her litter— Oh, how many tiring hours it had taken to catch that sow and her agile young! And they'd take the rooster and the setting hens and the ducks the Fontaines had given her. And the apples and the yams in the pantry bins. And the flour and rice and dried peas. And the money in the Yankee soldier's wallet. They'd take everything and leave them to starve.

'They shan't have them!' she cried aloud, and they all turned startled faces to her, fearful her mind had cracked under the tidings. 'I won't go hungry! They shan't have them!'

'What is it, Scarlett. What is it?'

'The horse! The cow! The pigs! They shan't have them! I won't let them have them!'

She turned swiftly to the four negroes who huddled in the doorway, their black faces a peculiarly ashen shade.

'The swamp,' she said rapidly.

'Whut swamp?'

'The river swamp, you fools! Take the pigs to the swamp. All of you. Quickly. Pork, you and Prissy crawl under the house and get the pigs out. Suellen, you and Carreen fill the baskets with as much food as you can carry and get to the woods. Mammy, put the silver in the well again. And Pork! Pork, listen to me, don't stand there like that! Take Pa with you. Don't ask me where! Anywhere! Go with Pork, Pa. That's a sweet Pa.'

Even in her frenzy she thought what the sight of bluecoats might do to Gerald's wavering mind. She stopped and wrung her hands and the frightened sobbing of little Wade who was clutching Melanie's skirt added to her panic.

'What shall I do, Scarlett?' Melanie's voice was calm amid the wailing and tears and scurrying feet. Though her face was paper white and her whole body trembled, the very quietness of her voice steadied Scarlett, revealing to her that they all looked to her for commands, for guidance.

'The cow and the calf,' she said quickly. 'They're in the old pasture. Take the horse and drive them into the swamp and—'

Before she could finish her sentence, Melanie shook off Wade's clutches and was down the front steps and running toward the horse, pulling up her wide skirts as she ran. Scarlett caught a flashing glimpse of thin legs, a flurry of skirts and underclothing, and Melanie was in the saddle, her feet dangling far above the stirrups. She gathered up the reins and clapped her heels against the animal's sides and then abruptly pulled him in, her face twisting with horror.

'My baby!' she cried. 'Oh, my baby! The Yankees will kill him! Give him to me!'

Her hand was on the pommel and she was preparing to slide off but Scarlett screamed at her.

'Go on! Go on! Get the cow! I'll look after the baby! Go on, I tell you! Do you think I'd let them get Ashley's baby? Go on!'

Melly looked despairingly backward but hammered her heels into the horse and, with a scattering of gravel, was off down the drive toward the pasture.

Scarlett thought: 'I never expected to see Melly Hamilton straddling a horse!' and then she ran into the house. Wade was at her heels, sobbing, trying to catch her flying skirts. As she went up the steps, three at a bound, she saw Suellen and Carreen with split-oak baskets on their arms, running toward the pantry, and Pork tugging none too gently at Gerald's arm, dragging him toward the back porch. Gerald was mumbling querulously and pulling away like a child.

From the back yard she heard Mammy's strident voice: 'You, Priss! You git unner dat house an' han' me dem shoats! You knows mighty well Ah's too big ter crawl thoo dem lattices. Dilcey, comyere an' mek di wuthless chile—'

'And I thought it was such a good idea to keep the pigs under the house, so nobody would steal them,' thought Scarlett, running into her room. 'Why, oh, why didn't I build a pen for them down in the swamp?'

She tore open her top bureau drawer and scratched about in the clothing until the Yankee's wallet was in her hand. Hastily she picked up the solitaire ring and the diamond earbobs from where she had hidden them in her sewing-basket and shoved them into the wallet. But where to hide it? In the mattress? Up the chimney? Throw it in the well? Put it in her bosom? No, never there! The outlines of the wallet might show through her basque and if the Yankees saw it they would strip her naked and search her.

'I shall die if they do!' she thought wildly.

Downstairs there was a pandemonium of racing feet and sobbing voices.

Even in her frenzy, Scarlett wished she had Melanie with her, Melly with her quiet voice, Melly who was so brave the day she shot the Yankee. Melly was worth three of the others. Melly – what had Melly said? Oh, yes, the baby!

Clutching the wallet to her, Scarlett ran across the hall to the room where little Beau was sleeping in the low cradle. She snatched him up into her arms and he awoke, waving small fists and slobbering sleepily.

She heard Suellen crying: 'Come on, Carreen! Come on! We've got enough. Oh, Sister, hurry!' There were wild squealings, indignant gruntings in the back yard and, running to the window, Scarlett saw Mammy waddling hurriedly across the cotton field with a struggling young pig under each arm. Behind her was Pork also carrying two pigs and pushing Gerald before him. Gerald was stumping across the furrows, waving his cane.

Leaning out of the window Scarlett yelled: 'Get the sow, Dilcey! Make Prissy drive her out. You can chase her across the fields.'

Dilcey looked up, her bronzed face harassed. In her apron was a pile of silver tableware. She pointed under the house.

'The sow done bit Prissy and got her penned up unner the house.'

'Good for the sow,' thought Scarlett. She hurried back into her room and hastily gathered from their hiding-place the bracelets, brooch, miniature and cup she had found on the dead Yankee. But where to hide them? It was awkward, carrying little Beau in one arm and the wallet and the trinkets in the other. She started to lay him on the bed.

He set up a wail at leaving her arms and a welcome thought came to her. What better hiding-place could there be than a baby's diaper? She quickly turned him over, pulled up his dress and thrust the wallet down the diaper next to his backside. He yelled louder at this treatment and she hastily tightened the triangular garment about his thrashing legs.

'Now,' she thought, drawing a deep breath, 'now for the swamp!'

Tucking him screaming under one arm and clutching the jewellery to her with the other, she raced into the upstairs hall. Suddenly her rapid steps paused, fright weakening her knees. How silent the house was! How dreadfully still! Had they all gone off and left her? Hadn't anyone waited for her? She hadn't meant for them to leave her here alone. These days anything could happen to a lone woman and with the Yankees coming—

She jumped as a slight noise sounded and, turning quickly, saw crouched by the banisters her forgotten son, his eyes enormous with terror. He tried to speak but his throat only worked silently.

'Get up, Wade Hampton,' she commanded swiftly. 'Get up and walk. Mother can't carry you now.'

He ran to her, like a small frightened animal, and clutching her wide skirt, buried her face in it. She could feel his small hands groping through the folds for her legs. She started down the stairs, each step hampered by Wade's dragging hands, and she said fiercely: 'Turn me loose, Wade! Turn me loose and walk!' But the child only clung the closer.

As she reached the landing, the whole lower floor leaped up at her. All the homely, well-loved articles of furniture seemed to whisper: 'Good-bye! Good-bye!' A sob rose in her throat. There was the open door of the office where Ellen had laboured so diligently and she could glimpse a corner of the old secretary. There was the dining-room, with chairs pushed awry and food still on the plates. There on the floor were the rag rugs Ellen had dyed and woven herself. And there was the old portrait of Grandma Robillard, with bosoms half bared, hair piled high and nostrils cut so deeply as to give her face a perpetual well-bred sneer. Everything which had been part of her earliest memories, everything bound up with the deepest roots in her: 'Good-bye! Good-bye, Scarlett O'Hara!'

The Yankees would burn it all – all!

This was her last view of home, her last view except what she might see from the cover of the woods or the swamp, the tall chimneys wrapped in smoke, the roof crashing in flame.

'I can't leave you,' she thought, and her teeth clattered with fear. 'I can't leave you. Pa wouldn't leave you. He told them they'd have to burn you over his head. Then, they'll burn you over my head for I can't leave you either. You're all I've got left.'

With the decision, some of her fear fell away and there remained only a congealed feeling in her breast, as if all hope and fear had frozen. As she stood there, she heard from the avenue the sound of many horses' feet, the jingle of bridle-bits and sabres rattling in scabbards and a harsh voice crying a command: 'Dismount!' Swiftly she bent to the child beside her and her voice was urgent but oddly gentle.

'Turn me loose, Wade, honey! You run down the stairs quick and through the back yard toward the swamp. Mammy will be there and Aunt Melly. Run quickly, darling, and don't be afraid.'

At the change in her tone, the boy looked up and Scarlett was appalled at the look in his eyes, like a baby rabbit in a trap.

'Oh, Mother of God!' she prayed. 'Don't let him have a convulsion! Not – not before the Yankees. They mustn't know we are afraid.' And, as the child only gripped her skirt the tighter, she said clearly: 'Be a little man, Wade. They're only a passel of damn Yankees!'

And she went down the steps to meet them.

Sherman was marching through Georgia, from Atlanta to the sea. Behind him lay the smoking ruins of Atlanta to which the torch had been set as the blue army tramped out. Before him lay three hundred miles of territory virtually undefended save by a few state militia and the old men and young boys of the Home Guard.

Here lay the fertile state, dotted with plantations, sheltering the women and children, the very old and the negroes. In a swath eighty miles wide the Yankees were looting and burning. There were hundreds of homes in flames, hundreds of homes resounding with their footsteps. But, to Scarlett, watching the bluecoats pour into the front hall, it was not a country-wide affair. It was entirely personal, a malicious action aimed directly at her and hers.

She stood at the foot of the stairs, the baby in her arms, Wade pressed tightly against her, his head hidden in her skirts as the Yankees swarmed through the house, pushing roughly past her up the stairs, dragging furniture on to the front porch, running bayonets and knives into upholstery and digging inside for concealed valuables. Upstairs they were ripping open mattresses and feather beds until the air in the hall was thick with feathers that floated softly down on her head. Impotent rage quelled what little fear was left in her heart as she stood helpless while they plundered and stole and ruined.

The sergeant in charge was a bow-legged, grizzled little man with a large wad of tobacco in his cheek. He reached Scarlett before any of his men and, spitting freely on the floor and her skirts, said briefly:

'Lemme have what you got in yore hand, lady.'

She had forgotten the trinkets she had intended to hide and, with a sneer which she hoped was as eloquent as that pictured on Grandma Robillard's face, she flung the articles to the floor and almost enjoyed the rapacious scramble that ensued.

'I'll trouble you for thet ring and them earbobs.'

Scarlett tucked the baby more securely under her arm so that he hung face downward, crimson and screaming, and removed the garnet earrings which had been Gerald's wedding present to Ellen. Then she stripped off the large sapphire solitaire which Charles had given her as an engagement ring.

'Don't throw um. Hand um to me,' said the sergeant, putting out his hands. 'Them bastards got enough already. What else have you got?' His eyes went over her basque sharply.

For a moment Scarlett went faint, already feeling rough hands thrusting themselves into her bosom, fumbling at her garters.

'That is all, but I suppose it is customary to strip your victims?'

'Oh, I'll take your word,' said the sergeant good-naturedly, spitting again as he turned away. Scarlett righted the baby and tried to soothe him, holding her hand over the place on the diaper where the wallet was hidden, thanking God that Melanie had a baby and that baby had a diaper.

Upstairs she could hear heavy boots trampling, the protesting screech of furniture pulled across the floor, the crashing of china and mirrors, the curses when nothing of value appeared. From the yard came loud cries: 'Head um off! Don't let um get away!' and the despairing squawks of the hens and quacking and honking of the ducks and geese. A pang went through her as she heard an agonized squealing which was suddenly stilled by a pistol shot and she knew that the sow was dead. Damn Prissy! She had run off and left her. If only the shoats were safe! If only the family had gotten safely to the swamp! But there was no way of knowing.

She stood quietly in the hall while the soldiers boiled about her, shouting and cursing. Wade's fingers were in her skirt in a terrified grip. She could feel his body shaking as he pressed against her but she could not bring herself to speak reassuringly to him. She could not bring herself to utter any word to the Yankees, either of pleading, protest or anger. She could only thank God that her knees still had the strength to support her, that her neck was still strong enough to hold her head high. But when a squad of bearded men came lumbering down the steps, laden with an assortment of stolen articles and she saw Charles' sword in the hands of one, she did cry out.

That sword was Wade's. It had been his father's and his grandfather's sword and Scarlett had given it to the little boy on his last birthday. They had made quite a ceremony of it and Melanie had cried, cried with tears of pride and sorrowful memory, and kissed him and said he must grow up to be a brave soldier like his father and his grandfather. Wade was very proud of it and often climbed upon the table beneath where it hung to pat it. Scarlett could endure seeing her own possessions going out of the house in hateful alien hands but not this – not her little boy's pride. Wade, peering from the protection of her skirts at the sound of her cry, found speech and courage in a mighty sob. Stretching out one hand he cried:

'Mine!'

'You can't take that!' said Scarlett swiftly, holding out her hand too.

'I can't, hey?' said the little soldier who held it, grinning impudently at her. 'Well, I can! It's a Rebel sword!'

'It's – it's not. It's a Mexican War sword. You can't take it. It's my little boy's. It was his grandfather's! Oh, Captain,' she cried, turning to the sergeant, 'please make him give it to me!'

The sergeant, pleased at his promotion, stepped forward.

'Lemme see thet sword, Bub,' he said.

Reluctantly, the little trooper handed it to him. 'It's got a solid-gold hilt,' he said.

The sergeant turned it in his hand, held the hilt up to the sunlight to read the engraved inscription.

' "To Colonel William R. Hamilton," ' he deciphered. ' "From His Staff. For Gallantry. Buena Vista. 1847." '

'Ho, lady,' he said, 'I was at Buena Vista myself.'

'Indeed,' said Scarlett icily.

'Was I? Thet was hot fightin', lemme tell you. I ain' seen such hot fightin' in this war as we seen in thet one. So this sword was this little tyke's granddaddy's?'

'Yes.'

'Well, he can have it,' said the sergeant, who was satisfied enough with the jewellery and trinkets tied up in his handkerchief.

'But it's got a solid-gold hilt,' insisted the little trooper.

'We'll leave her thet to remember us by,' grinned the sergeant.

Scarlett took the sword, not even saying 'Thank you'. Why should she thank these thieves for returning her own property to her? She held the sword against her while the little cavalryman argued and wrangled with the sergeant.

'By God, I'll give these damn Rebels something to remember me by,' shouted the private finally when the sergeant, losing his good nature, told him to go to hell and not talk back. The little man went charging toward the back of the house and Scarlett breathed more easily. They had said nothing about burning the house. They hadn't told her to leave so they could fire it. Perhaps – perhaps— The men came rambling into the hall from the upstairs and the out of doors.

'Anything?' questioned the sergeant.

'One hog and a few chickens and ducks.'

'Some corn and a few yams and beans. That wildcat we saw on the horse must have given the alarm, all right.'

'Regular Paul Revere, eh?'

'Well, there ain't much here, Sarge. You got the pickin's. Let's move on before the whole country gets the news we're comin'.'

'Didja dig under the smokehouse? They generally buries things there.'

'Ain't no smokehouse.'

'Didja dig in the nigger cabins?'

'Nothin' but cotton in the cabins. We set fire to it.'

For a brief instant Scarlett saw the long hot days in the cotton field, felt again the terrible ache in her back, the raw bruised flesh of her shoulders. All for nothing. The cotton was gone.

'You ain't got much, for a fac', have you, lady?'

'Your army has been here before,' she said coolly.

'That's a fac'. We were in this neighbourhood in September,' said one of the men, turning something in his hand. 'I'd forgot.'

Scarlett saw it was Ellen's gold thimble that he held. How often she had seen it gleaming in and out of Ellen's fancy work! The sight of it brought back too many hurting memories of the slender hand which had worn it. There it lay in this stranger's calloused dirty palm and soon it would find its way North and on to the finger of some Yankee woman who would be proud to wear stolen things. Ellen's thimble!

Scarlett dropped her head so the enemy could not see her cry and the tears fell slowly down on the baby's head. Through the blur, she saw the men moving toward the doorway, heard the sergeant calling commands in a loud rough voice. They were going and Tara was safe, but with the pain of Ellen's memory on her, she was hardly glad. The sound of the banging sabres and horses' hooves brought little relief and she stood, suddenly weak and nerveless, as they moved off down the avenue, every man laden with stolen goods, clothing, blankets, pictures, hens and ducks, the sow.

Then to her nostrils was borne the smell of smoke and she turned, too weak with lessening strain to care about the cotton. Through the open windows of the dining-room, she saw smoke drifting lazily out of the negro cabins. There went the cotton. There went the tax money and part of the money which was to see them through this bitter winter. There was nothing she could do about it either, except watch. She had seen fires in cotton before and she knew how difficult they were to put out, even with many men labouring at it. Thank God, the quarters were so far from the house! Thank God, there was no wind today to carry sparks to the roof of Tara!

Suddenly she swung about, rigid as a pointer, and stared with horror-struck eyes down the hall, down the covered passageway toward the kitchen. There was smoke coming from the kitchen!

Somewhere between the hall and the kitchen, she laid the baby down. Somewhere she flung off Wade's grip, slinging him against the wall. She burst into the smoke-filled kitchen and reeled back, coughing, her eyes streaming tears from the smoke. Again she plunged in, her skirt held over her nose.

The room was dark, lit as it was by one small window, and so thick with smoke that she was blinded, but she could hear the hiss and crackle of flames. Dashing a hand across her eyes, she peered squinting and saw thin lines of flame creeping across the kitchen floor, toward the walls. Someone had scattered the blazing logs in the open fireplace across the whole room and the tinder-dry pine floor was sucking in the flames and spewing them up like water.

Back she rushed to the dining-room and snatched a rag rug from the floor, spilling two chairs with a crash.

'I'll never beat it out – never, never! Oh, God, if only there was someone to help! Tara is gone – gone! Oh, God! This was what that little wretch meant when he said he'd give me something to remember him by! Oh, if only I'd let him have the sword!'

In the hallway she passed her son lying in the corner with his sword. His eyes were closed and his face had a look of slack, unearthly peace.

'My God! He's dead! They've frightened him to death!' she thought in agony, but she raced by him to the bucket of drinking water which always stood in the passageway by the kitchen door.

She soused the end of the rug into the bucket and drawing a deep breath plunged again into the smoke-filled room, slamming the door behind her. For an eternity she reeled and coughed, beating the rug against the lines of fire that shot swiftly beyond her. Twice her long skirt took fire and she slapped it out with her hands. She could smell the sickening smell of her hair scorching, as it came loose from its pins and swept about her shoulders. The flames raced ever beyond her, toward the walls of the covered runway, fiery snakes that writhed and leaped and, exhaustion sweeping her, she knew that it was hopeless.

Then the door swung open and the sucking draught flung the flames higher. It closed with a bang and, in the swirling smoke, Scarlett, half blind, saw Melanie, stamping her feet on the flames, beating at them with something dark and heavy. She saw her staggering, heard her coughing, caught a lightning-flash glimpse of her set white face and eyes narrowed to slits against the smoke, saw her small body curving back and forth as she swung her rug up and down. For another eternity they fought and swayed, side by side, and Scarlett could see that the lines of fire were shortening. Then suddenly Melaine turned toward her and, with a cry, hit her across the shoulders with all her might. Scarlett went down in a whirlwind of smoke and darkness.

When she opened her eyes she was lying on the back porch, her head pillowed comfortably on Melanie's lap, and the afternoon sunlight was shining on her face. Her hands, face and shoulders smarted intolerably from burns. Smoke was still rolling from the quarters, enveloping the cabins in thick clouds, and the smell of burning cotton was strong. Scarlett saw wisps of smoke drifting from the kitchen and she stirred frantically to rise.

But she was pushed back as Melanie's calm voice said: 'Lie still, dear. The fire's out.'

She lay quiet for a moment, eyes closed, sighing with relief, and heard the slobbery gurgle of the baby near by and the reassuring sound of Wade's hiccoughing. So he wasn't dead, thank God! She opened her eyes and looked up into Melanie's face. Her curls were singed, her face black with smut, but her eyes were sparkling with excitement and she was smiling.

'You look like a nigger,' murmured Scarlett, burrowing her head wearily into its soft pillow.

'And you look like the end man in a minstrel show,' replied Melanie equably.

'Why did you have to hit me?'

'Because, my darling, your back was on fire. I didn't dream you'd faint, though the Lord knows you've had enough today to kill you . . . I came back as soon as I got the stock safe in the woods. I nearly died, thinking about you and the baby alone. Did – the Yankees harm you?'

'If you mean did they rape me, no,' said Scarlett, groaning as she tried to sit up. Though Melanie's lap was soft, the porch on which she was lying was far from comfortable. 'But they've stolen everything, everything. We've lost everything— Well, what is there to look so happy about?'

'We haven't lost each other and our babies are all right and we have a roof over our heads,' said Melanie, and there was a lift in her voice. 'And that's all anyone can hope for now . . . Goodness, but Beau is wet! I suppose the Yankees even stole his extra diapers. He— Scarlett, what on earth is in his diaper?'

She thrust a suddenly frightened hand down the baby's back and brought up the wallet. For a moment she looked at it as if she had never seen it before and then she began to laugh, peal on peal of mirth that had in it no hint of hysteria.

'Nobody but you would ever have thought of it,' she cried, and flinging her arms around Scarlett's neck she kissed her. 'You are the beatenest sister I ever had!'

Scarlett permitted the embrace because she was too tired to struggle, because the words of praise brought balm to her spirit and because, in the dark smoke-filled kitchen, there had been born a greater respect for her sister-in-law, a closer feeling of comradeship.

'I'll say this for her,' she thought grudgingly, 'she's always there when you need her.'

Chapter XXVIII

Cold weather set in abruptly with a killing frost. Chilling winds swept beneath the door-sills and rattled the loose window-panes with a monotonous tinkling sound. The last of the leaves fell from the bare trees and only the pines stood clothed, black and cold against pale skies. The rutted red roads were frozen to flintiness and hunger rode the winds through Georgia.

Scarlett recalled bitterly her conversation with Grandma Fontaine. On that afternoon two months ago, which now seemed years in the past, she had told the old lady she had already known the worst which could possibly happen to her, and she had spoken from the bottom of her heart. Now that remark sounded like schoolgirl hyperbole. Before Sherman's men came through Tara the second time, she had her small riches of food and money, she had neighbours more fortunate than she and she had the cotton which would tide her over until spring. Now the cotton was gone, the food was gone, the money was of no use to her, for there was no food to buy with it, and the neighbours were in a worse plight than she. At least, she had the cow and the calf, a few shoats and the horse, and the neighbours had nothing but the little they had been able to hide in the woods and bury in the ground.

Fairhill, the Tarleton home, was burned to the foundations, and Mrs Tarleton and the four girls were existing in the overseer's house. The Munroe house near Lovejoy was levelled too. The wooden wing of Mimosa had burned and only the thick resistant stucco of the main house and the frenzied work of the Fontaine women and their slaves with wet blankets and quilts had saved it. The Calverts' house had again been spared, due to the intercession of Hilton, the Yankee overseer, but there was not a head of livestock, not a fowl, not an ear of corn left on the place.

At Tara and throughout the County, the problem was food. Most of the families had nothing at all but the remains of their yam crops and their peanuts and such game as they could catch in the woods. What they had, each shared with less fortunate friends, as they had done in more prosperous days. But the time soon came when there was nothing to share.

At Tara, they ate rabbit and possum and catfish, if Pork was lucky. On other days a small amount of milk, hickory nuts, roasted acorns and yams. They were always hungry. To Scarlett it seemed that at every turn she met outstretched hands, pleading eyes. The sight of them drove her almost to madness, for she was as hungry as they.

She ordered the calf killed, because he drank so much of the precious milk, and that night everyone ate so much fresh veal all of them were ill. She knew that she should kill one of the shoats but she put it off from day to day, hoping to raise them to maturity. They were so small. There would be so little of them to eat if they were killed now and so much more if they could be saved a little longer. Nightly she debated with Melanie the advisability of sending Pork abroad on the horse with some greenbacks to try to buy food. But the fear that the horse might be captured and the money taken from Pork deterred them. They did not know where the Yankees were. They might be a thousand miles away or only across the river. Once, Scarlett, in desperation, started to ride out herself to search for food, but the hysterical outbursts of the whole family fearful of the Yankees made her abandon the plan.

Pork foraged far, at times not coming home all night, and Scarlett did not ask him where he went. Sometimes he returned with game, sometimes with a few ears of corn, a bag of dried peas. Once he brought home a rooster which he said he found in the woods. The family ate it with relish but a sense of guilt, knowing very well Pork had stolen it, as he had stolen the peas and corn. One night soon after this, he tapped on Scarlett's door long after the house was asleep and sheepishly exhibited a leg peppered with small shot. As she bandaged it for him, he explained awkwardly that when attempting to get into a hen-coop in Fayetteville, he had been discovered. Scarlett did not ask whose hen-coop but patted Pork's shoulder gently, tears in her eyes. Negroes were provoking sometimes and stupid and lazy, but there was loyalty in them that money couldn't buy, a feeling of oneness with their white folks which made them risk their lives to keep food on the table.

In other days Pork's pilferings would have been a serious matter, probably calling for a whipping. In other days she would have been forced at least to reprimand him severely. 'Always remember, dear,' Ellen had said, 'you are responsible for the moral as well as the physical welfare of the darkies God has entrusted to your care. You must realize that they are like children and must be guarded from themselves like children, and you must always set them a good example.'

But now, Scarlett pushed that admonition into the back of her mind. That she was encouraging theft, and perhaps theft from people worse off than she, was no longer a matter for conscience. In fact the morals of the affair weighed lightly upon her. Instead of punishment or reproof, she only regretted he had been shot.

'You must be more careful, Pork. We don't want to lose you. What should we do without you? You've been mighty good and faithful and when we get some money again, I'm going to buy you a big gold watch and engrave on it something out of the Bible, "Well done, good and faithful servant." '

Pork beamed under the praise and gingerly rubbed his bandaged leg.

'Dat soun' mighty fine, Miss Scarlett. W'en you speckin' ter git dat money?'

'I don't know, Pork, but I'm going to get it some time, somehow.' She bent on him an unseeing glance that was so passionately bitter he stirred uneasily. 'Some day, when this war is over, I'm going to have lots of money, and when I do I'll never be hungry or cold again. None of us will ever be hungry or cold. We'll all wear fine clothes and have fried chicken every day and—'

Then she stopped. The strictest rule at Tara, one which she herself had made and which she rigidly enforced, was that no one should ever talk of the fine meals they had eaten in the past or what they would eat now, if they had the opportunity.

Pork slipped from the room as she remained staring moodily into the distance. In the old days, now dead and gone, life had been so complex, so full of intricate and complicated problems. There had been the problem of trying to win Ashley's love and trying to keep a dozen other beaux dangling and unhappy. There had been small breaches of conduct to be concealed from her elders, jealous girls to be flouted or placated, styles of dresses and materials to be chosen, different coiffures to be tried and, oh, so many, many other matters to be decided! Now life was so amazingly simple. Now all that mattered was food enough to keep off starvation, clothing enough to prevent freezing and a roof overhead which did not leak too much.

It was during these days that Scarlett dreamed and dreamed again the nightmare which was to haunt her for years. It was always the same dream, the details never varied, but the terror of it mounted each time it came to her and the fear of experiencing it again troubled even her waking hours. She remembered so well the incidents of the day when she had first dreamed it.

Cold rain had fallen for days and the house was chill with draughts and dampness. The logs in the fireplace were wet and smoky and gave little heat. There had been nothing to eat except milk since breakfast, for the yams were exhausted and Pork's snares and fishlines had yielded nothing. One of the shoats would have to be killed the next day if they were to eat at all. Strained and hungry faces, black and white, were staring at her, mutely asking her to provide food. She would have to risk losing the horse and send Pork out to buy something. And to make matters worse, Wade was ill with a sore throat and a raging fever and there was neither doctor nor medicine for him.

Hungry, weary with watching her child, Scarlett left him to Melanie's care for a while and lay down on her bed to nap. Her feet icy, she twisted and turned, unable to sleep, weighed down with fear and despair. Again and again, she thought: 'What shall I do? Where shall I turn? Isn't there anybody in the world who can help me?' Where had all the security of the world gone? Why wasn't there someone, some strong and wise person, to take the burdens from her? She wasn't made to carry them. She did not know how to carry them. And then she fell into an uneasy doze.

She was in a wild strange country so thick with swirling mist she could not see her hand before her face. The earth beneath her feet was uneasy. It was a haunted land, still with a terrible stillness, and she was lost in it, lost and terrified as a child in the night. She was bitterly cold and hungry and so fearful of what lurked in the mists about her that she tried to scream and could not. There were things in the fog reaching out fingers to pluck at her skirt, to drag her down into the uneasy quaking earth on which she stood, silent, relentless, spectral hands. Then, she knew that somewhere in the opaque gloom about her there was shelter, help, a haven of refuge and warmth. But where was it? Could she reach it before the hands clutched her and dragged her down into the quicksands?

Suddenly she was running, running through the mist like a mad thing, crying and screaming, throwing out her arms to clutch only empty air and wet mist. Where was the haven? It eluded her but it was there, hidden, somewhere. If she could only reach it! If she could only reach it she would be safe! But terror was weakening her legs, hunger making her faint. She gave one despairing cry and awoke to find Melanie's worried face above her and Melanie's hand shaking her to wakefulness.

The dream returned again and again, whenever she went to sleep with an empty stomach. And that was frequently enough. It so frightened her that she feared to sleep, although she feverishly told herself there was nothing in such a dream to be afraid of. There was nothing in a dream about fog to scare her so. Nothing at all – yet the thought of dropping off into that mist-filled country so terrified her she began sleeping with Melanie, who would wake her up when her moaning and twitching revealed that she was again in the clutch of the dream.

Under the strain she grew white and thin. The pretty roundness left her face, throwing her cheek-bones into prominence, emphasizing her slanting green eyes and giving her the look of a prowling, hungry cat.

'Daytime is enough like a nightmare without my dreaming things,' she thought desperately, and began hoarding her daily ration to eat it just before she went to sleep.

At Christmas time Frank Kennedy and a small troop from the commissary department jogged up to Tara on a futile hunt for grain and animals for the army. They were a ragged and ruffianly-appearing crew, mounted on lame and heaving horses which obviously were in too bad condition to be used for more active service. Like their animals the men had been invalided out of the front-line forces and, except for Frank, all of them had an arm missing or an eye gone or stiffened joints. Most of them wore blue overcoats of captured Yankees and, for a brief instant of horror, those at Tara thought Sherman's men had returned.

They stayed the night on the plantation, sleeping on the floor in the parlour, luxuriating as they stretched themselves on the velvet rug, for it had been weeks since they had slept under a roof or on anything softer than pine needles and hard earth. For all their dirty beards and tatters they were a well-bred crowd, full of pleasant small talk, jokes and compliments, and very glad to be spending Christmas Eve in a big house, surrounded by pretty women, as they had been accustomed to do in days long past. They refused to be serious about the war, told outrageous lies to make the girls laugh and brought to the bare and looted house the first lightness, the first hint of festivity it had known in many a day.

'It's almost like the old days when we had house parties, isn't it?' whispered Suellen happily to Scarlett. Suellen was raised to the skies by having a beau of her own in the house again and she could hardly take her eyes off Frank Kennedy. Scarlett was surprised to see that Suellen could be almost pretty, despite the thinness which had persisted since her illness. Her cheeks were flushed and there was a soft luminous look in her eyes.

'She must really care about him,' thought Scarlett in contempt. 'And I guess she'd be almost human if she ever had a husband of her own, even if her husband was old fuss-budget Frank.'

Carreen had brightened a little too, and some of the sleep-walking look left her eyes that night. She had found that one of the men had known Brent Tarleton and had been with him the day he was killed, and she promised herself a long private talk with him after supper.

At supper Melanie surprised them all by forcing herself out of her timidity and being almost vivacious. She laughed and joked and almost but not quite coquetted with a one-eyed soldier who gladly repaid her efforts with extravagant gallantries. Scarlett knew the effort this involved both mentally and physically, for Melanie suffered torments of shyness in the presence of anything male. Moreover she was far from well. She insisted she was strong and did more work even than Dilcey, but Scarlett knew she was sick. When she lifted things her face went white and she had a way of sitting down suddenly after exertions, as if her legs would no longer support her. But tonight she, like Suellen and Carreen, was doing everything possible to make the soldiers enjoy their Christmas Eve. Scarlett alone took no pleasure in the guests.

The troop had added their ration of parched corn and side meat to the supper of dried peas, stewed dried apples and peanuts which Mammy set before them and they declared it was the best meal they had had in months.

Scarlett watched them eat and she was uneasy. She not only begrudged them every mouthful they ate but she was on tenterhooks lest they discover somehow that Pork had slaughtered one of the shoats the day before. It now hung in the pantry and she had grimly promised her household that she would scratch out the eyes of anyone who mentioned the shoat to their guests or the presence of the dead pig's sisters and brothers, safe in their pen in the swamp. These hungry men could devour the whole shoat at one meal, and if they knew of the live hogs, they could commandeer them for the army. She was alarmed, too, for the cow and the horse and wished they were hidden in the swamp, instead of tied in the woods at the bottom of the pasture. If the commissary took her stock, Tara could not possibly live through the winter. There would be no way of replacing them. As to what the army would eat, she did not care. Let the army feed the army – if it could. It was hard enough for her to feed her own.

The men added as dessert some 'ramrod rolls' from their knapsacks, and this was the first time Scarlett had ever seen this Confederate article of diet about which there were almost as many jokes as about lice. They were charred spirals of what appeared to be wood. The men dared her to take a bite and, when she did, she discovered that beneath the smoke-blackened surface was unsalted corn bread. The soldiers mixed their ration of corn meal with water, and salt too when they could get it, wrapped the thick paste about their ramrods and roasted the mess over camp-fires. It was as hard as rock candy and as tasteless as sawdust, and after one bite Scarlett hastily handed it back amid roars of laughter. She met Melanie's eyes and the same thought was plain in both faces . . . 'How can they go on fighting if they have only this stuff to eat?'

The meal was gay enough and even Gerald, presiding absently at the head of the table, managed to evoke from the back of his dim mind some of the manner of a host and an uncertain smile. The men talked, the women smiled and flattered – but Scarlett, turning suddenly to Frank Kennedy to ask him news of Miss Pittypat, caught an expression on his face which made her forget what she intended to say.

His eyes had left Suellen's and were wandering about the room, to Gerald's childlike puzzled eyes, to the floor, bare of rugs, to the mantelpiece denuded of its ornaments, the sagging springs and torn upholstery into which Yankee bayonets had ripped, the cracked mirror above the sideboard, the unfaded squares on the wall where pictures had hung before the looters came, the scant table service, the decently mended but old dresses of the girls, the flour-sack which had been made into a kilt for Wade.

Frank was remembering the Tara he had known before the war and on his face was a hurt look, a look of tired impotent anger. He loved Suellen, liked her sisters, respected Gerald and had a genuine fondness for the plantation. Since Sherman had swept through Georgia, Frank had seen many appalling sights as he rode about the state trying to collect supplies, but nothing had gone to his heart as Tara did now. He wanted to do something for the O'Haras, especially Suellen, and there was nothing he could do. He was unconsciously wagging his whiskered head in pity and clicking his tongue against his teeth when Scarlett caught his eye. He saw the flame of indignant pride in hers and he dropped his gaze quickly to his plate in embarrassment.

The girls were hungry for news. There had been no mail service since Atlanta fell, now four months past, and they were in complete ignorance as to where the Yankees were, how the Confederate Army was faring, what had happened to Atlanta and to old friends. Frank, whose work took him all over the section, was as good as a newspaper, better even, for he was kin to or knew almost everyone from Macon north to Atlanta, and he could supply bits of interesting personal gossip which the papers always omitted. To cover his embarrassment at being caught by Scarlett, he plunged hastily into a recital of news. The Confederates, he told them, had retaken Atlanta after Sherman marched out, but it was a valueless prize as Sherman had burned it completely.

'But I thought Atlanta burned the night I left,' cried Scarlett, bewildered. 'I thought our boys burned it!'

'Oh, no, Miss Scarlett!' cried Frank, shocked. 'We'd never burn one of our own towns with our own folks in it! What you saw burning was the warehouses and the supplies we didn't want the Yankees to capture and the foundries and the ammunition. But that was all. When Sherman took the town the houses and stores were standing there as pretty as you please. And he quartered his men in them.'

'But what happened to the people? Did he – did he kill them?'

'He killed some – but not with bullets,' said the one-eyed soldier grimly. 'Soon's he marched into Atlanta he told the mayor that all the people in town would have to move out, every living soul. And there were plenty of old folks that couldn't stand the trip and sick folks that ought not to have been moved and ladies who were – well, ladies who hadn't ought to be moved either. And he moved them out in the biggest rainstorm you ever saw, hundreds and hundreds of them, and dumped them in the woods near Rough and Ready and sent word to General Hood to come and get them. And a plenty of the folks died of pneumonia and not being able to stand that sort of treatment.'

'Oh, but why did he do that? They couldn't have done him any harm,' cried Melanie.

'He said he wanted the town to rest his men and horses in,' said Frank. 'And he rested them there till the middle of November and then he lit out. And he set fire to the whole town when he left and burned everything.'

'Oh, surely not everything!' cried the girls in dismay.

It was inconceivable that the bustling town they knew, so full of people, so crowded with soldiers, was gone. All the lovely homes beneath shady trees, all the big stores and the fine hotels – surely they couldn't be gone! Melanie seemed ready to burst into tears, for she had been born there and knew no other home. Scarlett's heart sank because she had come to love the place second only to Tara.

'Well, almost everything,' Frank amended hastily, disturbed by the expressions on their faces. He tried to look cheerful, for he did not believe in upsetting ladies. Upset ladies always upset him and made him feel helpless. He could not bring himself to tell them the worst. Let them find out from someone else.

He could not tell them what the army saw when it marched back into Atlanta: the acres and acres of chimneys standing blackly above ashes, piles of half-burned rubbish and tumbled heaps of bricks clogging the streets, old trees dying from fire, their charred limbs tumbling to the ground in the cold wind. He remembered how the sight had turned him sick, remembered the bitter curses of the Confederates when they saw the remains of the town. He hoped the ladies would never hear of the horrors of the looted cemetery, for they'd never get over that. Charlie Hamilton and Melanie's mother and father were buried there. The sight of that cemetery still gave Frank nightmares. Hoping to find jewellery buried with the dead, the Yankee soldiers had broken open vaults, dug up graves. They had robbed the bodies, stripped from the coffins gold and silver name-plates, silver trimmings and silver handles. The skeletons and corpses, flung helter-skelter among their splintered caskets, lay exposed and so pitiful.

And Frank couldn't tell them about the dogs and the cats. Ladies set such a store by pets. But the thousands of starving animals, left homeless when their masters had been so rudely evacuated, had shocked him almost as much as the cemetery, for Frank loved cats and dogs. The animals had been frightened, cold, ravenous, wild as forest creatures, the strong attacked the weak, the weak waiting for the weaker to die so they could eat them. And, above the ruined town, the buzzards splotched the wintry sky with graceful, sinister bodies.

Frank cast about in his mind for some mitigating information that would make the ladies feel better.

'There's some houses still standing,' he said, 'houses that set on big lots away from other houses and didn't catch fire. And the churches and the Masonic hall are left. And a few stores too. But the business section and all along the railroad tracks and at Five Points – well, ladies, that part of town is flat on the ground.'

'Then,' cried Scarlett bitterly, 'that warehouse Charlie left me, down on the tracks, it's gone too?'

'If it was near the tracks, it's gone, but—' Suddenly he smiled. Why hadn't he thought of it before? 'Cheer up, ladies! Your Aunt Pitty's house is still standing. It's kind of damaged but there it is.'

'Oh, how did it escape?'

'Well, it's made of brick and it's got about the only slate roof in Atlanta and that kept the sparks from setting it afire, I guess. And then it's about the last house on the north end of town and the fire wasn't so bad over that way. Of course, the Yankees quartered there tore it up aplenty. They even burned the baseboard and the mahogany stair-rail for firewood, but shucks! It's in good shape. When I saw Miss Pitty last week in Macon—'

'You saw her? How is she?'

'Just fine. Just fine. When I told her her house was still standing, she made up her mind to come home right away. That is – if that old darky, Peter, will let her come. Lots of the Atlanta people have already come back, because they got nervous about Macon. Sherman didn't take Macon but everybody is afraid Wilson's raiders will get there soon and he's worse than Sherman.'

'But how silly of them to come back if there aren't any houses! Where do they live?'

'Miss Scarlett, they're living in tents and shacks and log cabins and doubling up six and seven families in the few houses still standing. And they're trying to rebuild. Now, Miss Scarlett, don't say they are silly. You know Atlanta folks as well as I do. They are plumb set on that town, most as bad as Charlestonians are about Charleston, and it'll take more than Yankees and a burning to keep them away. Atlanta folks are – begging your pardon, Miss Melly – as stubborn as mules about Atlanta. I don't know why, for I always thought that town a mighty pushy, impudent sort of place. But then, I'm a countryman born and I don't like any town. And let me tell you, the ones who are getting back first are the smart ones. The ones who come back last won't find a stick or stone or brick of their houses, because everyone's out salvaging things all over town to rebuild their houses. Just day before yesterday, I saw Mrs Merriwether and Miss Maybelle and their old darky woman out collecting brick in a wheelbarrow. And Mrs Meade told me she was thinking about building a log cabin when the doctor comes back to help her. She said she lived in a log cabin when she first came to Atlanta, when it was Marthasville, and it wouldn't bother her none to do it again. 'Course, she was only joking, but that shows you how they feel about it.'

'I think they've got a lot of spirit,' said Melanie proudly. 'Don't you, Scarlett?'

Scarlett nodded, a grim pleasure and pride in her adopted town filling her. As Frank said, it was a pushy, impudent place and that was why she liked it. It wasn't hidebound and stick-in-the-muddish like the older towns and it had a brash exuberance that matched her own. 'I'm like Atlanta,' she thought. 'It takes more than Yankees or a burning to keep me down.'

'If Aunt Pitty is going back to Atlanta, we'd better go back and stay with her, Scarlett,' said Melanie, interrupting her train of thought. 'She'll die of fright alone.'

'Now, how can I leave here, Melly?' Scarlett asked crossly. 'If you are so anxious to go, go. I won't stop you.'

'Oh, I didn't mean it that way, darling,' cried Melanie, flushing with distress. 'How thoughtless of me! Of course, you can't leave Tara and – and I guess Uncle Peter and Cookie can take care of Auntie.'

'There's nothing to keep you from going,' Scarlett pointed out shortly.

'You know I wouldn't leave you,' answered Melanie. 'And I – I would be just frightened to death without you.'

'Suit yourself. Besides, you wouldn't catch me going back to Atlanta. Just as soon as they get a few houses up, Sherman will come back and burn it again.'

'He won't be back,' said Frank and, despite his efforts, his face dropped. 'He's gone on through the state to the coast. Savannah was captured this week and they say the Yankees are going on up into South Carolina.'

'Savannah taken!'

'Yes. Why, ladies, Savannah couldn't help but fall. They didn't have enough men to hold it, though they used every man they could get – every man who could drag one foot after another. Do you know that when the Yankees were marching on Milledgeville, they called out all the cadets from the military academies, no matter how young they were, and even opened the state penitentiary to get fresh troops? Yes, sir, they turned loose every convict who was willing to fight and promised him a pardon if he lived through the war. It kind of gave me the creeps to see those little cadets in the ranks with thieves and cut-throats.'

'They turned loose the convicts on us!'

'Now, Miss Scarlett, don't you get upset. They're a long way off from here, and furthermore they're making good soldiers. I guess being a thief don't keep a man from being a good soldier, does it?'

'I think it's wonderful,' said Melanie softly.

'Well, I don't,' said Scarlett flatly. 'There's thieves enough running around the country anyway, what with the Yankees and—' She caught herself in time but the men laughed.

'What with Yankees and our commissary department,' they finished, and she flushed.

'But where's General Hood's army?' interposed Melanie hastily. 'Surely he could have held Savannah.'

'Why, Miss Melanie' – Frank was startled and reproachful – 'General Hood hasn't been down in that section at all. He's been fighting up in Tennessee, trying to draw the Yankees out of Georgia.'

'And didn't his little scheme work well!' cried Scarlett sarcastically. 'He left the damn Yankees to go through us with nothing but schoolboys and convicts and Home Guards to protect us.'

'Daughter,' said Gerald, rousing himself, 'you are profane. Your mother will be grieved.'

'They are damn Yankees!' cried Scarlett passionately. 'And I never expect to call them anything else.'

At the mention of Ellen everyone felt queer and conversation suddenly ceased. Melanie again interposed.

'When you were in Macon did you see India and Honey Wilkes? Did they – had they heard anything of Ashley?'

'Now, Miss Melly, you know if I'd had news of Ashley, I'd have ridden up here from Macon right away to tell you,' said Frank reproachfully. 'No, they didn't have any news but – now, don't you fret about Ashley, Miss Melly. I know it's been a long time since you heard from him, but you can't expect to hear from a fellow when he's in prison, can you? And things aren't as bad in Yankee prisons as they are in ours. After all, the Yankees have plenty to eat and enough medicines and blankets. They aren't like we are – not having enough to feed ourselves, much less our prisoners.'

'Oh, the Yankees have got plenty,' cried Melanie, passionately bitter. 'But they don't give things to the prisoners. You know they don't, Mr Kennedy. You are just saying that to make me feel better. You know that our boys freeze to death up there and starve too and die without doctors and medicine, simply because the Yankees hate us so much! Oh, if we could just wipe every Yankee off the face of the earth! Oh, I know that Ashley is—'

'Don't say it!' cried Scarlett, her heart in her throat. As long as no one said Ashley was dead, there persisted in her heart a faint hope that he lived, but she felt that if she heard the words pronounced, in that moment he would die.

'Now, Mrs Wilkes, don't you bother about your husband,' said the one-eyed man soothingly. 'I was captured after first Manassas and exchanged later, and when I was in prison they fed me off the fat of the land, fried chicken and hot biscuits—'

'I think you are a liar,' said Melanie with a faint smile and the first sign of spirit Scarlett had ever seen her display with a man. 'What do you think?'

'I think so too,' said the one-eyed man and slapped his leg with a laugh.

'If you'll all come into the parlour, I'll sing you some Christmas carols,' said Melanie, glad to change the subject. 'The piano was one thing the Yankees couldn't carry away. Is it terribly out of tune, Suellen?'

'Dreadfully,' answered Suellen, happily beckoning with a smile to Frank.

But as they all passed from the room, Frank hung back, tugging at Scarlett's sleeve.

'May I speak to you alone?'

For an awful moment she feared he was going to ask her about her livestock and she braced herself for a good lie.

When the room was cleared and they stood by the fire, all the false cheerfulness which had coloured Frank's face in front of the others passed and she saw that he looked like an old man. His face was as dried and brown as the leaves that were blowing about the lawn of Tara and his ginger-coloured whiskers were thin and scraggy and streaked with grey. He clawed at them absently and cleared his throat in an annoying way before he spoke.

'I'm mighty sorry about your ma, Miss Scarlett.'

'Please don't talk about it.'

'And your pa— Has he been this way since—?'

'Yes – he's – he's not himself, as you can see.'

'He sure set a store by her.'

'Oh, Mr Kennedy, please don't let's talk—'

'I'm sorry, Miss Scarlett,' and he shuffled his feet nervously. 'The truth is I wanted to take up something with your pa and now I see it won't do any good.'

'Perhaps I can help you, Mr Kennedy. You see – I'm the head of the house now.'

'Well, I—' began Frank and again clawed nervously at his beard. 'The truth is— Well, Miss Scarlett, I was aiming to ask him for Miss Suellen.'

'Do you mean to tell me,' cried Scarlett in amused amazement, 'that you haven't yet asked Pa for Suellen? And you've been courting her for years!'

He flushed and grinned embarrassedly and in general looked like a shy and sheepish boy.

'Well, I – I didn't know if she'd have me. I'm so much older than she is and – there were so many good-looking young bucks hanging around Tara—'

'Hump!' thought Scarlett, 'they were hanging around me, not her!'

'And I don't know yet if she'll have me. I've never asked her but she must know how I feel. I – I thought I'd ask Mr O'Hara's permission and tell him the truth. Miss Scarlett, I haven't got a cent now. I used to have a lot of money, if you'll forgive me mentioning it, but right now all I own is my horse and the clothes I've got on. You see, when I enlisted I sold most of my land and I put all my money in Confederate bonds and you know what they're worth now. Less than the paper they're printed on. And anyway, I haven't got them now, because they burned up when the Yankees burned my sister's house. I know I've got gall asking for Miss Suellen now when I haven't a cent but – well, it's this way. I got to thinking that we don't know how things are going to turn out about this war. It sure looks like the end of the world to me. There's nothing we can be sure of and – and I thought it would be a heap of comfort to me and maybe to her if we were engaged. That would be something sure. I wouldn't ask to marry her till I could take care of her, Miss Scarlett, and I don't know when that will be. But if true love carries any weight with you, you can be certain Miss Suellen will be rich in that if nothing else.'

He spoke the last words with a simple dignity that touched Scarlett, even in her amusement. It was beyond her comprehension that anyone could love Suellen. Her sister seemed to her a monster of selfishness, of complaints and of what she could only describe as pure cussedness.

'Why, Mr Kennedy,' she said kindly, 'it's quite all right. I'm sure I can speak for Pa. He always set a store by you and he always expected Suellen to marry you.'

'Did he now?' cried Frank, happiness in his face.

'Indeed yes,' answered Scarlett, concealing a grin as she remembered how frequently Gerald had rudely bellowed across the supper table to Suellen: 'How now, Missy! Hasn't your ardent beau popped the question yet? Shall I be asking him his intentions?'

'I shall ask her tonight,' he said, his face quivering, and he clutched her hand and shook it. 'You're so kind, Miss Scarlett.'

'I'll send her to you,' smiled Scarlett, starting for the parlour. Melanie was beginning to play. The piano was sadly out of tune but some of the chords were musical, and Melanie was raising her voice to lead the others in 'Hark, the Herald Angels Sing!'

Scarlett paused. It did not seem possible that war had swept over them twice, that they were living in a ravaged country, close to the border of starvation, when this old sweet Christian hymn was being sung. Abruptly she turned to Frank.

'What did you mean when you said it looked like the end of the world to you?'

'I'll talk frankly,' he said slowly, 'but I wouldn't want you to be alarming the other ladies with what I say. The war can't go on much longer. There aren't any fresh men to fill the ranks and the desertions are running high – higher than the army likes to admit. You see, the men can't stand to be away from their families when they know they're starving, so they go home to try to provide for them. I can't blame them but it weakens the army. And the army can't fight without food and there isn't any food. I know because, you see, getting food is my business. I've been all up and down this section since we retook Atlanta and there isn't enough to feed a jaybird. It's the same way for three hundred miles south to Savannah. The folks are starving and the railroads are torn up and there aren't any new rifles and the ammunition is giving out and there's no leather at all for shoes . . . So, you see, the end is almost here.'

But the fading hopes of the Confederacy weighed less heavily on Scarlett than his remark about the scarcity of food. It had been her intention to send Pork out with the horse and wagon, the gold pieces and the United States money to scour the countryside for provisions and material for clothes. But if what Frank said was true—

But Macon hadn't fallen. There must be food in Macon. Just as soon as the commissary department was safely on its way, she'd start Pork for Macon and take the chance of having the precious horse picked up by the army. She'd have to risk it.

'Well, let's don't talk about unpleasant things tonight, Mr Kennedy,' she said. 'You go and sit in Mother's little office and I'll send Suellen to you so you can – well, so you'll have a little privacy.'

Blushing, smiling, Frank slipped out of the room and Scarlett watched him go.

'What a pity he can't marry her now!' she thought. 'That would be one less mouth to feed.'

Chapter XXIX

The following April General Johnston, who had been given back the shattered remnants of his old command, surrendered them in North Carolina and the war was over. But not until two weeks later did the news reach Tara. There was too much to do at Tara for anyone to waste time travelling abroad and hearing gossip and, as the neighbours were just as busy as they, there was little visiting and news spread slowly.

Spring ploughing was at its height and the cotton and garden seed Pork had brought from Macon were being put into the ground. Pork had been almost worthless since the trip, so proud was he of returning safely with his wagonload of dress goods, seed, fowls, hams, side meat and meal. Over and over, he told the story of his many narrow escapes, of the bypaths and country lanes he had taken on his return to Tara, the unfrequented roads, the old trails, the bridle paths. He had been five weeks on the road, agonizing weeks for Scarlett. But she did not upbraid him on his return, for she was happy that he had made the trip successfully and pleased that he brought back so much of the money she had given him. She had a shrewd suspicion that the reason he had so much money left over was that he had not bought the fowls or most of the food. Pork would have taken shame to himself had he spent her money when there were unguarded hen-coops along the road and smokehouses handy.

Now that they had a little food, everyone at Tara was busy trying to restore some semblance of naturalness to life. There was work for every pair of hands, too much work, never-ending work. The withered stalks of last year's cotton had to be removed to make way for this year's seeds and the balky horse, unaccustomed to the plough, dragged unwillingly through the fields. Weeds had to be pulled from the garden and the seeds planted, firewood had to be cut, a beginning had to be made toward replacing the pens and the miles and miles of fences so casually burned by the Yankees. The snares Pork set for rabbits had to be visited twice a day and the fishlines in the river rebaited. There were beds to be made and floors to be swept, food to be cooked and dishes washed, hogs and chickens to be fed and eggs gathered. The cow had to be milked and pastured near the swamp and someone had to watch her all day for fear the Yankees or Frank Kennedy's men would return and take her. Even little Wade had his duties. Every morning he

went out importantly with a basket to pick up twigs and chips to start the
fires with.

It was the Fontaine boys, the first of the County men home from the
war, who brought the news of the surrender. Alex, who still had boots, was
walking and Tony, barefooted, was riding on the bare back of a mule. Tony
always managed to get the best things in that family. They were swarthier
than ever from four years' exposure to sun and storm, thinner, more wiry,
and the wild black beards they brought back from the war made them seem
like strangers.

On their way to Mimosa and eager for home, they only stopped a moment
at Tara to kiss the girls and give them news of the surrender. It was all over,
they said, all finished, and they did not seem to care much or want to talk
about it. All they wanted to know was whether Mimosa had been burned.
On the way south from Atlanta, they had passed chimney after chimney
where the homes of friends had stood and it seemed almost too much to
hope that their own house had been spared. They sighed with relief at the
welcome news and laughed, slapping their thighs when Scarlett told them
of Sally's wild ride and how neatly she had cleared their hedge.

'She's a spunky girl,' said Tony, 'and it's rotten luck for her, Joe getting
killed. You all got any chewing tobacco, Scarlett?'

'Nothing but rabbit tobacco. Pa smokes it in a corn cob.'

'I haven't fallen that low yet,' said Tony, 'but I'll probably come to it.'

'Is Dimity Munroe all right?' asked Alex, eagerly but a little embarrassed,
and Scarlett recalled vaguely that he had been sweet on Sally's younger
sister.

'Oh, yes. She's living with her aunt over in Fayetteville now. You know their
house in Lovejoy was burned. And the rest of her folks are in Macon.'

'What he means is – has Dimity married some brave colonel in the Home
Guard?' jeered Tony, and Alex turned furious eyes upon him.

'Of course, she isn't married,' said Scarlett, amused.

'Maybe it would be better if she had,' said Alex gloomily. 'How the hell
– I beg your pardon, Scarlett. But how can a man ask a girl to marry him
when his darkies are all freed and his stock gone and he hasn't got a cent
in his pockets?'

'You know that wouldn't bother Dimity,' said Scarlett. She could afford
to be loyal to Dimity and say nice things about her, for Alex Fontaine had
never been one of her own beaux.

'Hell's afire— Well, I beg your pardon again. I'll have to quit swearing or
Grandma will sure tan my hide. I'm not asking any girl to marry a pauper.
It mightn't bother her but it would bother me.'

While Scarlett talked to the boys on the front porch, Melanie, Suellen and
Carreen slipped silently into the house as soon as they heard the news of the
surrender. After the boys had gone, cutting across the back fields of Tara
toward home, Scarlett went inside and heard the girls sobbing together on

the sofa in Ellen's little office. It was all over, the bright beautiful dream they had loved and hoped for, the Cause which had taken their friends, lovers, husbands and beggared their families. The Cause they had thought could never fall had fallen forever.

But for Scarlett, there were no tears. In the first moment when she heard the news she thought: 'Thank God! Now the cow won't be stolen. Now the horse is safe. Now we can take the silver out of the well and everybody can have a knife and fork. Now I won't be afraid to drive round the country looking for something to eat.'

What a relief! Never again would she start in fear at the sound of hooves. Never again would she wake in the dark nights, holding her breath to listen, wondering if it were reality or only a dream that she heard in the yard the rattle of bits, the stamping of hooves and the harsh crying of orders by the Yankees. And, best of all, Tara was safe! Now her worst nightmare would never come true. Now she would never have to stand on the lawn and see smoke billowing from the beloved house and hear the roar of flames as the roof fell in.

Yes, the Cause was dead but war had always seemed foolish to her and peace was better. She had never stood starry-eyed when the Stars and Bars ran up a pole or felt cold chills when 'Dixie' sounded. She had not been sustained through privations, the sickening duties of nursing, the fears of the siege and the hunger of the last few months by the fanatic glow which made all these things endurable to others, if only the Cause prospered. It was all over and done with and she was not going to cry about it.

All over! The war which had seemed so endless, the war which, unbidden and unwanted, had cut her life in two, had made so clean a cleavage that it was difficult to remember those other carefree days. She could look back, unmoved, at the pretty Scarlett with her fragile green morocco slippers and her flounces fragrant with lavender, but she wondered if she could be that same girl. Scarlett O'Hara, with the County at her feet, a hundred slaves to do her bidding, the wealth of Tara like a wall behind her and doting parents anxious to grant any desire of her heart. Spoiled, careless Scarlett who had never known an ungratified wish except where Ashley was concerned.

Somewhere, on the long road that wound through those four years, the girl with her sachet and dancing slippers had slipped away and there was left a woman with sharp green eyes, who counted pennies and turned her hands to many menial tasks, a woman to whom nothing was left from the wreckage except the indestructible red earth on which she stood.

As she stood in the hall, listening to the girls sobbing, her mind was busy.

'We'll plant more cotton, lots more. I'll send Pork to Macon tomorrow to buy more seed. Now the Yankees won't burn it and our troops won't need it. Good Lord! Cotton ought to go sky high this fall!'

She went into the little office and, disregarding the weeping girls on the sofa, seated herself at the secretary and picked up a quill to balance the cost of more cotton seed against her remaining cash.

'The war is over,' she thought, and suddenly she dropped the quill as a wild happiness flooded her. The war was over and Ashley – if Ashley was alive he'd be coming home! She wondered if Melanie, in the midst of mourning for the lost Cause, had thought of this.

'Soon we'll get a letter – no, not a letter. We can't get letters. But soon – oh, somehow he'll let us know!'

But the days passed into weeks and there was no news from Ashley. The mail service in the South was uncertain and in the rural districts there was none at all. Occasionally a passing traveller from Atlanta brought a note from Aunt Pitty tearfully begging the girls to come back. But never news of Ashley.

After the surrender, an ever-present feud over the horse smouldered between Scarlett and Suellen. Now that there was no danger of Yankees, Suellen wanted to go calling on the neighbours. Lonely and missing the happy sociability of the old days, Suellen longed to visit friends, if for no other reason than to assure herself that the rest of the County was as bad off as Tara. But Scarlett was adamant. The horse was for work, to drag logs from the woods, to plough and for Pork to ride in search of food. On Sundays he had earned the right to graze in the pasture and rest. If Suellen wanted to go visiting she could go afoot.

Before the last year Suellen had never walked a hundred yards in her life and this prospect was anything but pleasing. So she stayed at home and nagged and cried and said, once too often: 'Oh, if only Mother was here!' At that, Scarlett gave her the long-promised slap, hitting her so hard it knocked her screaming to the bed and caused great consternation throughout the house. Thereafter, Suellen whined the less, at least in Scarlett's presence.

Scarlett spoke truthfully when she said she wanted the horse to rest but that was only half of the truth. The other half was that she had paid one round of calls on the County in the first month after the surrender and the sight of old friends and old plantations had shaken her courage more than she liked to admit.

The Fontaines had fared best of any, thanks to Sally's hard ride, but it was flourishing only by comparison with the desperate situation of the other neighbours. Grandma Fontaine had never completely recovered from the heart attack she had the day she led the others in beating out the flames and saving the house. Old Dr Fontaine was convalescing slowly from an amputated arm. Alex and Tony were turning awkward hands to ploughs and hoe handles. They leaned over the fence rail to shake hands with Scarlett when she called and they laughed at her rickety wagon, their black eyes bitter, for they were laughing at themselves as well as her. She asked to buy seed corn from them and they promised it and fell to discussing farm problems. They had twelve chickens, two cows, five hogs and the mule they brought home from the war. One of the hogs had just died and they were worried about losing the others. At hearing such serious words about hogs from these ex-dandies who had never given life a more serious thought than which cravat was most fashionable, Scarlett laughed and this time her laugh was bitter too.

They had all made her welcome at Mimosa and had insisted on giving, not selling, her the seed corn. The quick Fontaine tempers flared when she put a greenback on the table and they flatly refused payment. Scarlett took the corn and privately slipped a dollar bill into Sally's hand. Sally looked like a different person from the girl who had greeted her eight months before when Scarlett first came home to Tara. Then she had been pale and sad but there had been a buoyancy about her. Now that buoyancy had gone, as if the surrender had taken all hope from her.

'Scarlett,' she whispered as she clutched the bill, 'what was the good of it all? Why did we ever fight? Oh, my poor Joe! Oh, my poor baby!'

'I don't know why we fought and I don't care,' said Scarlett. 'And I'm not interested. I never was interested. War is a man's business, not a woman's. All I'm interested in now is a good cotton crop. Now take this dollar and buy little Joe a dress. God knows, he needs it. I'm not going to rob you of your corn, for all Alex and Tony's politeness.'

The boys followed her to the wagon and assisted her in, courtly for all their rags, gay with the volatile Fontaine gaiety, but with the picture of their destitution in her eyes, she shivered as she drove away from Mimosa. She was so tired of poverty and pinching. What a pleasure it would be to know people who were rich and not worried as to where their next meal was coming from!

Cade Calvert was at home at Pine Bloom and, as Scarlett came up the steps of the old house in which she had danced so often in happier days, she saw that death was in his face. He was emaciated and he coughed as he lay in an easy chair in the sunshine with a shawl across his knees, but his face lit up when he saw her. Just a little cold which had settled on his chest, he said, trying to rise to greet her. Got it from sleeping so much in the rain. But it would be gone soon and then he'd lend a hand in the work.

Cathleen Calvert, who came out of the house at the sound of voices, met Scarlett's eyes above her brother's head and in them Scarlett read knowledge and bitter despair. Cade might not know but Cathleen knew. Pine Bloom looked straggly and overgrown with weeds, seedling pines were beginning to show in the fields and the house was sagging and untidy. Cathleen was thin and taut.

The two of them, with their Yankee stepmother, their four little half-sisters, and Hilton, the Yankee overseer, remained in the silent, oddly echoing house. Scarlett had never liked Hilton any more than she liked their own overseer, Jonas Wilkerson, and she liked him even less now, as he sauntered forward and greeted her like an equal. Formerly he had the same combination of servility and impertinence which Wilkerson possessed but now, with Mr Calvert and Raiford dead in the war and Cade sick, he had dropped all servility. The second Mrs Calvert had never known how to compel respect from negro servants and it was not to be expected that she could get it from a white man.

'Mr Hilton has been so kind about staying with us through these difficult times,' said Mrs Calvert nervously, casting quick glances at her silent stepdaughter. 'Very kind. I suppose you heard how he saved our house twice when Sherman was here. I'm sure I don't know how we could have managed without him, with no money and Cade—'

A flush went over Cade's white face and Cathleen's long lashes veiled her eyes as her mouth hardened. Scarlett knew their souls were writhing in helpless rage at being under obligations to their Yankee overseer. Mrs Calvert seemed ready to weep. She had somehow made a blunder. She was always blundering. She just couldn't understand Southerners, for all that she had lived in Georgia twenty years. She never knew what not to say to her stepchildren and, no matter what she said or did, they were always so exquisitely polite to her. Silently she vowed she would go North to her own people, taking her children with her, and leave these puzzling stiff-necked strangers.

After these visits, Scarlett had no desire to see the Tarletons. Now that the four boys were gone, the house burned and the family cramped in the overseer's cottage, she could not bring herself to go. But Suellen and Carreen begged and Melanie said it would be unneighbourly not to call and welcome Mr Tarleton back from the war, so one Sunday they went.

This was the worst of all.

As they drove up by the ruins of the house, they saw Beatrice Tarleton, dressed in a worn riding habit, a crop under her arm, sitting on the top rail of the fence about the paddock, staring moodily at nothing. Beside her perched the bow-legged little negro who had trained her horses and he looked as glum as his mistress. The paddock, once full of frolicking colts and placid brood mares, was empty now except for one mule, the mule Mr Tarleton had ridden home from the surrender.

'I swear I don't know what to do with myself now that my darlings are gone,' said Mrs Tarleton, climbing down from the fence. A stranger might have thought she spoke of her four dead sons, but the girls from Tara knew her horses were in her mind. 'All my beautiful horses dead. And oh, my poor Nellie! If I just had Nellie! And nothing but a damned mule on the place. A damned mule,' she repeated, looking indignantly at the scrawny beast. 'It's an insult to the memory of my blooded darlings to have a mule in their paddock. Mules are misbegotten, unnatural critters and it ought to be illegal to breed them.'

Jim Tarleton, completely disguised by a bushy beard, came out of the overseer's house to welcome and kiss the girls, and his four red-haired daughters in mended dresses streamed out behind him, tripping over the dozen black and tan hounds which ran barking to the door at the sound of strange voices. There was an air of studied and determined cheerfulness about the whole family which brought a colder chill to Scarlett's bones than the bitterness of Mimosa or the deathly brooding of Pine Bloom.

The Tarletons insisted that the girls stay for dinner, saying they had so few guests these days and wanted to hear all the news. Scarlett did not want to linger, for the atmosphere oppressed her, but Melanie and her two sisters were anxious for a longer visit, so the four stayed for dinner and ate sparingly of the side meat and dried peas which were served them.

There was laughter about the skimpy fare and the Tarleton girls giggled as they told of makeshifts for clothes, as if they were telling the most amusing of jokes. Melanie met them half-way, surprising Scarlett with her unexpected vivacity as she told of trials at Tara, making light of hardships. Scarlett could hardly speak at all. The room seemed so empty without the four great Tarleton boys, lounging and smoking and teasing. And if it seemed empty to her, what must it seem to the Tarletons who were offering a smiling front to their neighbours?

Carreen had said little during the meal but when it was over she slipped over to Mrs Tarleton's side and whispered something. Mrs Tarleton's face changed and the brittle smile left her lips as she put her arm around Carreen's slender waist. They left the room, and Scarlett, who felt she could not endure the house another minute, followed them. They went down the path through the garden and Scarlett saw they were going toward the burying-ground. Well, she couldn't go back to the house now. It would seem too rude. But what on earth did Carreen mean dragging Mrs Tarleton out to the boys' graves when Beatrice was trying so hard to be brave?

There were two new marble markers in the brick-enclosed lot under the funereal cedars – so new that no rain had splashed them with red dust.

'We got them last week,' said Mrs Tarleton proudly. 'Mr Tarleton went to Macon and brought them home in the wagon.'

Tombstones! And what they must have cost! Suddenly Scarlett did not feel as sorry for the Tarletons as she had at first. Anybody who would waste precious money on tombstones when food was so dear, so almost unattainable, didn't deserve sympathy. And there were several lines carved on each of the stones. The more carving, the more money. The whole family must be crazy! And it had cost money, too, to bring the three boys' bodies home. They had never found Boyd or any trace of him.

Between the graves of Brent and Stuart was a stone which read: 'They were lovely and pleasant in their lives, and in their death they were not divided.'

On the other stone were the names of Boyd and Tom with something in Latin which began 'Dulce et—', but it meant nothing to Scarlett who had managed to evade Latin at the Fayetteville Academy.

All that money for tombstones! Why, they were fools! She felt as indignant as if her own money had been squandered.

Carreen's eyes were shining oddly.

'I think it's lovely,' she whispered, pointing to the first stone.

Carreen would think it lovely. Anything sentimental stirred her.

'Yes,' said Mrs Tarleton, and her voice was soft, 'we thought it very fitting – they died almost at the same time, Stuart first and then Brent who caught up the flag he dropped.'

As the girls drove back to Tara, Scarlett was silent for a while, thinking of what she had seen in the various homes, remembering against her will the County in its glory, with visitors at all the big houses and money plentiful, negroes crowding the quarters and the well-tended fields glorious with cotton.

'In another year, there'll be little pines all over these fields,' she thought, and looking toward the encircling forest she shuddered. 'Without the darkies, it will be all we can do to keep body and soul together. Nobody can run a big plantation without the darkies, and lots of the fields won't be cultivated at all and the woods will take over the fields again. Nobody can plant much cotton, and what will we do then? What'll become of country folks? Town folks can manage somehow. They've always managed. But we country folks will go back a hundred years like the pioneers who had little cabins and just scratched a few acres – and barely existed.

'No,' she thought grimly, 'Tara isn't going to be like that. Not even if I have to plough myself. This whole section, this whole state can go back to woods if it wants to, but I won't let Tara go. And I don't intend to waste my money on tombstones or my time crying about the war. We can make out somehow. I know we could make out somehow if the men weren't all dead. Losing the darkies isn't the worst part about this. It's the loss of the men, the young men.' She thought again of the four Tarletons and Joe Fontaine, of Raiford Calvert and the Munroe brothers and all the boys from Fayetteville and Jonesboro whose names she had read on the casualty lists. 'If there were just enough men left, we could manage somehow but—'

Another thought struck her – suppose she wanted to marry again. Of course, she didn't want to marry again. Once was certainly enough. Besides, the only man she'd ever wanted was Ashley and he was married, if he was still living. But suppose she should want to marry. Who would there be to marry her? The thought was appalling.

'Melly,' she said, 'what's going to happen to Southern girls?'

'What do you mean?'

'Just what I say. What's going to happen to them? There's no one to marry them. Why, Melly, with all the boys dead, there'll be thousands of girls all over the South who'll die old maids.'

'And never have any children,' added Melanie, to whom this was the most important thing.

Evidently the thought was not new to Suellen who sat in the back of the wagon, for she suddenly began to cry. She had not heard from Frank Kennedy since Christmas. She did not know if the lack of mail service was the cause, or if he had merely trifled with her affections and then forgotten her. Or maybe he had been killed in the last days of the war! The latter would have been infinitely preferable to his forgetting her, for at least there was some dignity about a dead love, such as Carreen and India Wilkes had, but none about a deserted fiancée.

'Oh, in the name of God, hush!' said Scarlett.

'Oh, you can talk,' sobbed Suellen, 'because you've been married and had a baby and everybody knows some man wanted you. But look at me! And you've got to be mean and throw it up to me that I'm an old maid when I can't help myself. I think you're hateful.'

'Oh, hush! You know how I hate people who bawl all the time. You know perfectly well old Ginger Whiskers isn't dead and that he'll come back and marry you. He hasn't any better sense. But personally, I'd rather be an old maid than marry him.'

There was silence from the back of the wagon for a while and Carreen comforted her sister with absent-minded pats, for her mind was a long way off, riding paths three years old with Brent Tarleton beside her. There was a glow, an exaltation in her eyes.

'Ah,' said Melanie sadly, 'what will the South be like without all our fine boys? What would the South have been if they had lived? We could use their courage and their energy and their brains. Scarlett, all of us with little boys must raise them to take the places of the men who are gone, to be brave men like them.'

'There will never again be men like them,' said Carreen softly. 'No one can take their places.'

They drove home the rest of the way in silence.

One day not long after this, Cathleen Calvert rode up to Tara at sunset. Her sidesaddle was strapped on as sorry a mule as Scarlett had ever seen, a flop-eared lame brute, and Cathleen was almost as sorry-looking as the animal she rode. Her dress was of faded gingham of the type once worn only by house servants, and her sunbonnet was secured under her chin by a piece of twine. She rode up to the front porch but did not dismount, and Scarlett and Melanie, who had been watching the sunset, went down the steps to meet her. Cathleen was as white as Cade had been the day Scarlett called, white and hard and brittle, as if her face would shatter if she spoke. But her back was erect and her head was high as she nodded to them.

Scarlett suddenly remembered the day of the Wilkes barbecue when she and Cathleen had whispered together about Rhett Butler. How pretty and fresh Cathleen had been that day in a swirl of blue organdie with fragrant roses at her sash and little black velvet slippers laced about her small ankles. And now there was not a trace of that girl in the stiff figure sitting on the mule.

'I won't get down, thank you,' she said. 'I just came to tell you that I'm going to be married.'

'What!'

'Who to?'

'Cathy, how grand!'

'When?'

'Tomorrow,' said Cathleen quietly, and there was something in her voice which took the eager smiles from their faces. 'I came to tell you that I'm going to be married tomorrow, in Jonesboro – and I'm not inviting you all to come.'

They digested this in silence, looking up at her, puzzled. Then Melanie spoke.

'Is it someone we know, dear?'

'Yes,' said Cathleen shortly. 'It's Mr Hilton.'

'Mr Hilton?'

'Yes, Mr Hilton, our overseer.'

Scarlett could not even find voice to say 'Oh!' but Cathleen, peering down suddenly at Melanie, said in a low savage voice: 'If you cry, Melly, I can't stand it. I shall die!'

Melanie said nothing, but patted the foot in its awkward home-made shoe which hung from the stirrup. Her head was low.

'And don't pat me! I can't stand that either.'

Melanie dropped her hand but still did not look up.

'Well, I must go. I only came to tell you.' The white brittle mask was back again and she picked up the reins.

'How is Cade?' asked Scarlett, utterly at a loss but fumbling for some words to break the awkward silence.

'He is dying,' said Cathleen shortly. There seemed to be no feeling in her voice. 'And he is going to die in some comfort and peace if I can manage it, without worrying about who will take care of me when he's gone. You see, my stepmother and the children are going North for good, tomorrow. Well, I must be going.'

Melanie looked up and met Cathleen's hard eyes. There were bright tears on Melanie's lashes and understanding in her eyes, and before them, Cathleen's lips curved into the crooked smile of a brave child who tries not to cry. It was all very bewildering to Scarlett, who was still trying to grasp the idea that Cathleen Calvert was going to marry an overseer – Cathleen, daughter of a rich planter, Cathleen who, next to Scarlett, had had more beaux than any girl in the County.

Cathleen bent down and Melanie tiptoed. They kissed. Then Cathleen flapped the bridle reins sharply and the old mule moved off.

Melanie looked after her, the tears streaming down her face. Scarlett stared, still dazed.

'Melly, is she crazy? You know she can't be in love with him.'

'In love? Oh, Scarlett, don't even suggest such a horrid thing! Oh, poor Cathleen! Poor Cade!'

'Fiddle-dee-dee!' cried Scarlett, beginning to be irritated. It was annoying that Melanie always seemed to grasp more of situations than she herself did. Cathleen's plight seemed to her more startling than catastrophic. Of course it was no pleasant thought, marrying Yankee white trash, but after all a girl couldn't live alone on a plantation; she had to have a husband to help her run it.

'Melly, it's like I said the other day. There isn't anybody for girls to marry and they've got to marry someone.'

'Oh, they don't have to marry! There's nothing shameful in being a spinster. Look at Aunt Pitty. Oh, I'd rather see Cathleen dead! I know Cade would rather see her dead. It's the end of the Calverts. Just think what her – what their children will be. Oh, Scarlett, have Pork saddle the horse quickly and you ride after her and tell her to come live with us!'

'Good Lord!' cried Scarlett, shocked at the matter-of-fact way in which Melanie was offering Tara. Scarlett certainly had no intention of feeding another mouth. She started to say this but something in Melanie's stricken face halted the words.

'She wouldn't come, Melly,' she amended. 'You know she wouldn't. She's so proud and she'd think it was charity.'

'That's true, that's true!' said Melanie distractedly, watching the small cloud of red dust disappear down the road.

'You've been with me for months,' thought Scarlett grimly, looking at her sister-in-law, 'and it's never occurred to you that it's charity you're living on. And I guess it never will. You're one of those people the war didn't change and you go right on thinking and acting just like nothing had happened – like we were still rich as Croesus and had more food than we knew what to do with and guests didn't matter. I guess I've got you on my neck for the rest of my life. But I won't have Cathleen too.'

Chapter XXX

In that warm summer after peace came, Tara suddenly lost its isolation. And for months thereafter a stream of scarecrows, bearded, ragged, footsore and always hungry, toiled up the red hill to Tara and came to rest on the shady front steps, wanting food and a night's lodging. They were Confederate soldiers walking home. The railroad had carried the remains of Johnston's army from North Carolina to Atlanta and dumped them there, and from Atlanta they began their pilgrimages afoot. When the wave of Johnston's men had passed, the weary veterans from the Army of Virginia arrived and then men from the Western troops, beating their way south toward homes which might not exist and families which might be scattered or dead. Most of them were walking; a few fortunate ones rode bony horses and mules which the terms of the surrender had permitted them to keep, gaunt animals which even an untrained eye could tell would never reach far-away Florida and south Georgia.

Going home! Going home! That was the only thought in the soldiers' minds. Some were sad and silent, others gay and contemptuous of hardships, but the thought that it was all over and they were going home was the one thing that sustained them. Few of them were bitter. They left bitterness to their women and their old people. They had fought a good fight, had been licked and were willing to settle down peaceably to ploughing beneath the flag they had fought.

Going home! Going home! They could talk of nothing else, neither battles nor wounds, nor imprisonment nor the future. Later, they would refight battles and tell children and grandchildren of pranks and forays and charges, of hunger, forced marches and wounds, but not now. Some of them lacked an arm or a leg or an eye, many had scars which would ache in rainy weather if they lived for seventy years, but these seemed small matters now. Later, it would be different.

Old and young, talkative and taciturn, rich planter and sallow Cracker, they all had two things in common, lice and dysentery. The Confederate soldier was so accustomed to his verminous state he did not give it a thought and scratched unconcernedly even in the presence of ladies. As for dysentery – the 'bloody flux' as the ladies delicately called it – it seemed to have spared no one from private to general. Four years of half-starvation, four years of rations which were coarse or green or half-putrefied, had done its work with them and every soldier who stopped at Tara was either just recovering or was actively suffering from it.

'Dey ain' a soun' set of bowels in de whole Confedrut ahmy,' observed Mammy darkly as she sweated over the fire, brewing a bitter concoction of blackberry roots which had been Ellen's sovereign remedy for such afflictions. 'It's mah notion dat 'twarn't de Yankees whut beat our gempmum. 'Twuz dey own innards. Kain no gempmum fight wid his bowels tuhnin' ter water.'

One and all, Mammy dosed them, never waiting to ask foolish questions about the state of their organs, and, one and all, they drank her doses meekly and with wry faces, remembering, perhaps, other stern black faces in far-off places and other inexorable black hands holding medicine spoons.

In the matter of 'comp'ny' Mammy was equally adamant. No lice-ridden soldier should come into Tara. She marched them behind a clump of thick bushes, relieved them of their uniforms, gave them a basin of water and strong lye soap to wash with and provided them with quilts and blankets to cover their nakedness, while she boiled their clothing in her huge wash-pot. It was useless for the girls to argue hotly that such conduct humiliated the soldiers. Mammy replied that the girls would be a sight more humiliated if they found lice upon themselves.

When the soldiers began arriving almost daily, Mammy protested against their being allowed to use the bedrooms. Always she feared lest some louse had escaped her. Rather than argue the matter, Scarlett turned the parlour with its deep velvet rug into a dormitory. Mammy cried out equally loudly at the sacrilege of soldiers being permitted to sleep on Miss Ellen's rug but Scarlett was firm. They had to sleep somewhere. And, in the months after the surrender, the deep soft nap began to show signs of wear and finally the heavy warp and woof showed through in spots where heels had worn it and spurs dug carelessly.

Of each soldier, they asked eagerly of Ashley. Suellen, bridling, always asked news of Mr Kennedy. But none of the soldiers had ever heard of them nor were they inclined to talk about the missing. It was enough that they themselves were alive, and they did not care to think of the thousands in unmarked graves who would never come home.

The family tried to bolster Melanie's courage after each of these disappointments. Of course, Ashley hadn't died in prison. Some Yankee chaplain would have written if this were true. Of course, he was coming home but his prison was so far away. Why, goodness, it took days riding on a train to make the trip and if Ashley was walking, like these men . . . Why hadn't he written? Well, darling, you know what the mails are now – so uncertain and slipshod even where mail routes are re-established. But suppose – suppose he had died on the way home. Now, Melanie, some Yankee woman would have surely written us about it! . . . Yankee women! Bah! . . . Melly, there *are* some nice Yankee women. Oh, yes, there are! God couldn't make a whole nation without having some nice women in it! Scarlett, you remember we did meet a nice Yankee woman at Saratoga that time – Scarlett, tell Melly about her!

'Nice, my foot!' replied Scarlett. 'She asked me how many bloodhounds we kept to chase our darkies with! I agree with Melly. I never saw a nice Yankee, male or female. But don't cry, Melly! Ashley'll come home. It's a long walk and maybe – maybe he hasn't got any boots.'

Then at the thought of Ashley barefooted, Scarlett could have cried. Let other soldiers limp by in rags with their feet tied up in sacks and strips of carpet, but not Ashley. He should come home on a prancing horse, dressed in fine clothes and shining boots, a plume in his hat. It was the final degradation for her to think of Ashley reduced to the state of these other soldiers.

One afternoon in June when everyone at Tara was assembled on the back porch eagerly watching Pork cut the first half-ripe water-melon of the season, they heard hooves on the gravel of the front drive. Prissy started languidly toward the front door, while those left behind argued hotly as to whether they should hide the melon or keep it for supper, should the caller at the door prove to be a soldier.

Melly and Carreen whispered that the soldier guest should have a share and Scarlett, backed by Suellen and Mammy, hissed to Pork to hide it quickly.

'Don't be a goose, girls! There's not enough for us as it is and if there are two or three famished soldiers out there, none of us will even get a taste,' said Scarlett.

While Pork stood with the little melon clutched to him, uncertain as to the final decision, they heard Prissy cry out.

'Gawdlmighty! Miss Scarlett! Miss Melly! Come quick!'

'Who is it?' cried Scarlett, leaping up from the steps and racing through the hall with Melly at her shoulder and the others streaming after her.

'Ashley!' she thought. 'Oh, perhaps—'

'It's Uncle Peter! Miss Pittypat's Uncle Peter!'

They all ran out to the front porch and saw the tall grizzled old despot of Aunt Pitty's house climbing down from a rat-tailed nag on which a section of quilting had been strapped. On his wide black face, accustomed dignity strove with delight at seeing his old friends, with the result that his brow was furrowed in a frown but his mouth was hanging open like a happy toothless old hound's.

Everyone ran down the steps to greet him, black and white shaking his hand and asking questions, but Melly's voice rose above them all.

'Auntie isn't sick, is she?'

'No'm. She's po'ly, thank God,' answered Peter, fastening a severe look first on Melly and then on Scarlett, so that they suddenly felt guilty but could think of no reason why. 'She's po'ly but she is plum outdone wid you young Misses, an' ef it come right down to it, Ah is too!'

'Why, Uncle Peter! What on earth—'

'Y'all nee'n try ter 'scuse yo'seffs. Ain' Miss Pitty writ you an' writ you ter come back home? Ain' Ah seed her write an' seed her a-cryin' w'en y'all writ her back dat you got too much ter do on disyere ole farm ter come home?'

'But, Uncle Peter—'

'Huccome you leave Miss Pitty by herseff lak dis w'en she so scary lak? You knows well's Ah do Miss Pitty ain' never live by herseff an' she been shakin' in her lil shoes ever since she come back frum Macom. She say fer me ter tell y'all plain as Ah knows how dat she jes' kain unnerstan' y'all desertin' her in her hour of need.'

'Now, hesh!' said Mammy tartly, for it sat ill upon her to hear Tara referred to as an 'ole farm'. Trust an ignorant city-bred darky not to know the difference between a farm and a plantation. 'Ain' us got no hours of need? Ain' us needin' Miss Scarlett an' Miss Melly right hyah an' needin' dem bad? Huccome Miss Pitty doan ast her brudder fer 'sistance, does she need any?'

Uncle Peter gave her a withering look.

'Us ain' had nuthin' ter do wid Mist' Henry fer y'ars, an' us is too ole ter start now.' He turned back to the girls, who were trying to suppress their smiles. 'You young Misses ought ter tek shame, leavin' po' Miss Pitty 'lone, wid half her frens daid an' de other half in Macom, an' 'Lanta full of Yankee sojers an' trashy free issue niggers.'

The two girls had borne the castigation with straight faces as long as they could, but the thought of Aunt Pitty sending Peter to scold them and bring them back bodily to Atlanta was too much for their control. They burst into laughter and hung on each other's shoulders for support. Naturally, Pork and Dilcey and Mammy gave vent to loud guffaws at hearing the detractor of their beloved Tara set at naught. Suellen and Carreen giggled and even Gerald's face wore a vague smile. Everyone laughed except Peter, who shifted from one large splayed foot to the other in mounting indignation.

'Whut's wrong wid you, nigger?' inquired Mammy with a grin. 'Is you gittin' too ole ter perteck yo' own Missus?'

Peter was outraged.

'Too ole! Me too ole? No, Ma'm! Ah kin perteck Miss Pitty lak Ah allus done. Ain' Ah perteck her down ter Macom when us refugeed? Ain' Ah perteck her w'en de Yankees come ter Macom an' she so sceered she faintin' all de time? An' ain' Ah 'quire disyere nag ter bring her back ter 'Lanta an' perteck her an' her pa's silver all de way?' Peter drew himself to his full height as he vindicated himself. 'Ah ain' talkin' about perteckin'. Ah'm talkin' 'bout how it *look*.'

'How who look?'

'Ah'm talkin' 'bout how it look ter folks, seein' Miss Pitty livin' 'lone. Folks talks scan'lous 'bout maiden ladies dat lives by deyseff,' continued Peter, and it was obvious to his listeners that Pittypat, in his mind, was still a plump and charming miss of sixteen who must be sheltered against evil tongues. 'An' Ah ain' figgerin' on havin' folks criticize her. No, Ma'm . . . An' Ah ain' figgerin' on her takin' in no bo'ders, jes' fer comp'ny needer. Ah done tole her dat. "Not w'ile you got yo' flesh an' blood dat belongs wid you," Ah says. An' now her flesh an' blood denyin' her. Miss Pitty ain' nuthin' but a chile an'—'

At this, Scarlett and Melly whooped louder and sank down to the steps. Finally Melly wiped tears of mirth from her eyes.

'Poor Uncle Peter! I'm sorry I laughed. Really and truly. There! Do forgive me. Miss Scarlett and I just can't come home now. Maybe I'll come in September after the cotton is picked. Did Auntie send you all the way down here just to bring us back on that bag of bones?'

At this question, Peter's jaw suddenly dropped and guilt and consternation swept over his wrinkled black face. His protruding underlip retreated to normal as swiftly as a turtle withdraws its head beneath its shell.

'Miss Melly, Ah is gittin' ole, Ah spec', 'cause Ah clean fergit fer de moment whut she sent me fer, an' it's important too. Ah got a letter fer you. Miss Pitty wouldn' trust de mails or nobody but me ter bring it an'—'

'A letter? For me? Who from?'

'Well'm, it's— Miss Pitty, she says ter me, "You, Peter, you brek it gen'ly ter Miss Melly," an' Ah say—'

Melly rose from the steps, her hand at her heart.

'Ashley! Ashley! He's dead!'

'No'm! No'm!' cried Peter, his voice rising to a shrill bawl, as he fumbled in the breast pocket of his ragged coat. 'He's 'live! Disyere a letter frum him. He comin' home. He— Gawdlmighty! Ketch her, Mammy! Lemme—'

'Doan you tech her, you ole fool!' thundered Mammy, struggling to keep Melanie's sagging body from falling to the ground. 'You pious black ape! Brek it gen'ly. You, Poke, tek her feet. Miss Carreen, steady her haid. Lessus lay her on de sofa in de parlour.'

There was a tumult of sound as everyone but Scarlett swarmed about the fainting Melanie, everyone crying out in alarm, scurrying into the house for water and pillows, and in a moment Scarlett and Uncle Peter were left standing alone on the walk. She stood rooted, unable to move from the position to which she had leaped when she heard his words, staring at the old man who stood feebly waving a letter. His old black face was as pitiful as a child's under its mother's disapproval, his dignity collapsed.

For a moment she could not speak or move, and though her mind shouted: 'He isn't dead! He's coming home!' the knowledge brought neither joy nor excitement, only a stunned immobility. Uncle Peter's voice came as from a far distance, plaintive, placating.

'Mist' Willie Burr from Macom whut is kin ter us, he brung it ter Miss Pitty. Mist' Willie he in de same jail house wid Mist' Ashley. Mist' Willie he got a hawse an' he got hyah soon. But Mist' Ashley he a-walkin' an'—'

She snatched the letter from his hand. It was addressed to Melly in Miss Pitty's writing but that did not make her hesitate a moment. She ripped it open and Miss Pitty's enclosed note fell to the ground. Within the envelope there was a piece of folded paper, grimy from the dirty pocket in which it had been carried, creased and ragged about the edges. It bore the inscription in Ashley's hand: 'Mrs George Ashley Wilkes, Care Miss Sarah Jane Hamilton, Atlanta, or Twelve Oaks, Jonesboro, Ga.'

With fingers that shook, she opened it and read:

'Beloved, I am coming home to you—'

Tears began to stream down her face so that she could not read and her heart swelled up until she felt she could not bear the joy of it. Clutching the letter to her, she raced up the porch steps and down the hall, past the parlour where all the inhabitants of Tara were getting in one another's way as they worked over the unconscious Melanie, and into Ellen's office. She shut the door and locked it and flung herself down on the sagging old sofa, crying. laughing, kissing the letter.

'Beloved,' she whispered, 'I am coming home to you.'

Common sense told them that unless Ashley developed wings, it would be weeks or even months before he could travel from Illinois to Georgia, but hearts nevertheless beat wildly whenever a soldier turned into the avenue at Tara. Each bearded scarecrow might be Ashley. And if it were not Ashley, perhaps the soldier would have news of him or a letter from Aunt Pitty about him. Black and white, they rushed to the front porch every time they heard footsteps. The sight of a uniform was enough to bring everyone flying from the woodpile, the pasture and the cotton patch. For a month after the letter came, work was almost at a standstill. No one wanted to be out of the house when he arrived, Scarlett least of all. And she could not insist on the others attending to their duties when she so neglected hers.

But when the weeks crawled by and Ashley did not come or any news of him, Tara settled back into its old routine. Longing hearts could only stand so much of longing. An uneasy fear crept into Scarlett's mind that something had happened to him along the way. Rock Island was so far away and he might have been weak or sick when released from prison. And he had no money and was tramping through a country where Confederates were hated. If only she knew where he was, she would send money to him, send every penny she had and let the family go hungry, so he could come home swiftly on the train.

'Beloved, I am coming home to you.'

In the first rush of joy when her eyes read those words, they had meant only that Ashley was coming home to her. Now, in the light of cooler reason, it was Melanie to whom he was returning, Melanie who went about the house these days singing with joy. Occasionally, Scarlett wondered bitterly why Melanie could not have died in childbirth in Atlanta. That would have made things perfect. Then she could have married Ashley after a decent interval and made little Beau a good stepmother too. When such thoughts came she did not pray hastily to God, telling Him she did not mean it. God did not frighten her any more.

Soldiers came singly and in pairs and dozens and they were always hungry. Scarlett thought despairingly that a plague of locusts would be more welcome. She cursed again the old custom of hospitality which had flowered in an era of plenty, the custom which would not permit any traveller, great or humble, to go on his journey without a night's lodging, food for himself and his horse and the utmost courtesy the house could give. She knew that era had passed forever, but the rest of the household did not, nor did the soldiers, and each soldier was welcomed as if he were a long-awaited guest.

As the never-ending line went by, her heart hardened. They were eating the food meant for the mouths of Tara, vegetables over whose long rows she had wearied her back, food she had driven endless miles to buy. Food was so hard to get and the money in the Yankee's wallet would not last forever. Only a few greenbacks and the two gold pieces were left now. Why should she feed this horde of hungry men? The war was over. They would never again stand between her and danger. So she gave orders to Pork that when the soldiers were in the house, the table should be set sparely. This order prevailed until she noticed that Melanie, who had never been strong since Beau was born, was inducing Pork to put only dabs of food on her plate and giving her share to the soldiers.

'You'll have to stop it, Melanie,' she scolded. 'You're half sick yourself and if you don't eat more, you'll be sick in bed and we'll have to nurse you. Let these men go hungry. They can stand it. They've stood it for four years and it won't hurt them to stand it a little while longer.'

Melanie turned to her and on her face was the first expression of naked emotion Scarlett had ever seen in those serene eyes.

'Oh, Scarlett, don't scold me! Let me do it. You don't know how it helps me. Every time I give some poor man my share I think that maybe, somewhere on the road up north, some woman is giving my Ashley a share of her dinner and it's helping him to get home to me!'

'My Ashley.'

'Beloved, I am coming home to you.'

Scarlett turned away, wordless. After that, Melanie noticed there was more food on the table when guests were present, even though Scarlett might grudge them every mouthful.

When the soldiers were too ill to go on, and there were many such, Scarlett put them to bed with none too good grace. Each sick man meant another mouth to feed. Someone had to nurse him and that meant one less worker at the business of fence building, hoeing, weeding and ploughing. One boy, on whose face a blond fuzz had just begun to sprout, was dumped on the front porch by a mounted soldier bound for Fayetteville. He had found him unconscious by the roadside and had brought him, across his saddle, to Tara, the nearest house. The girls thought he must be one of the little cadets who had been called out of military school when Sherman approached Milledgeville but they never knew, for he died without regaining consciousness and a search of his pockets yielded no information.

A nice-looking boy, obviously a gentleman, and somewhere to the south, some woman was watching the roads, wondering where he was and when he was coming home, just as she and Melanie, with a wild hope in their hearts, watched every bearded figure that came up their walk. They buried the cadet in the family burying-ground, next to the three little O'Hara boys, and Melanie cried sharply as Pork filled in the grave, wondering in her heart if strangers were doing this same thing to the tall body of Ashley.

Will Benteen was another soldier, like the nameless boy, who arrived unconscious across the saddle of a comrade. Will was acutely ill with pneumonia, and when the girls put him to bed, they feared he would soon join the boy in the burying-ground.

He had the sallow malarial face of the south Georgia Cracker, pale pinkish hair and washed-out blue eyes which even in delirium were patient and mild. One of his legs was gone at the knee and to the stump was fitted a roughly whittled wooden peg. He was obviously a Cracker, just as the boy they had buried so short a while ago was obviously a planter's son. Just how the girls knew this they could not say. Certainly Will was no dirtier, no more hairy, no more lice-infested than many fine gentlemen who came to Tara. Certainly the language he used in his delirium was no less grammatical than that of the Tarleton twins. But they knew instinctively, as they knew thoroughbred horses from scrubs, that he was not of their class. But this knowledge did not keep them from labouring to save him.

Emaciated from a year in a Yankee prison, exhausted by his long tramp on his ill-fitting wooden peg, he had little strength to combat pneumonia and for days he lay in the bed moaning, trying to get up, fighting battles over again. Never once did he call for mother, wife, sister or sweetheart and this omission worried Carreen.

'A man ought to have some folks,' she said. 'And he sounds like he didn't have a soul in the world.'

For all his lankiness he was tough, and good nursing pulled him through. The day came when his pale-blue eyes, perfectly cognizant of his surroundings, fell upon Carreen sitting beside him, telling her rosary beads, the morning sun shining through her fair hair.

'Then you warn't a dream, after all,' he said, in his flat toneless voice. 'I hope I ain't troubled you too much, Ma'm.'

His convalescence was a long one and he lay quietly looking out of the window at the magnolias and causing very little trouble to anyone. Carreen liked him because of his placid and unembarrassed silences. She would sit beside him through the long hot afternoons, fanning him and saying nothing.

Carreen had very little to say these days as she moved, delicate and wraithlike, about the tasks which were within her strength. She prayed a good deal, for when Scarlett came into her room without knocking, she always found her on her knees by her bed. The sight never failed to annoy her, for Scarlett felt that the time for prayer had passed. If God had seen fit to punish them so, then God could very well do without prayers. Religion had always been a bargaining process with Scarlett. She promised God good behaviour in exchange for favours. God had broken the bargain time and again, to her way of thinking, and she felt that she owed Him nothing at all now. And whenever she found Carreen on her knees when she should have been taking an afternoon nap or doing the mending, she felt that Carreen was shirking her share of the burdens.

She said as much to Will Benteen one afternoon when he was able to sit up in a chair and was startled when he said in his flat voice: 'Let her be, Miss Scarlett. It comforts her.'

'Comforts her?'

'Yes, she's prayin' for your ma and him.'

'Who is "him"?'

His faded blue eyes looked at her from under sandy lashes without surprise. Nothing seemed to surprise or excite him. Perhaps he had seen too much of the unexpected ever to be startled again. That Scarlett did not know what was in her sister's heart did not seem odd to him. He took it as naturally as he did the fact that Carreen had found comfort in talking to him, a stranger.

'Her beau, that boy Brent something-or-other who was killed at Gettysburg.'

'Her beau?' said Scarlett shortly. 'Her beau, nothing! He and his brother were my beaux.'

'Yes, so she told me. Looks like most of the County was your beaux. But, all the same, he was her beau after you turned him down, because when he come home on his last furlough they got engaged. She said he was the only boy she'd ever cared about and so it kind of comforts her to pray for him.'

'Well, fiddle-dee-dee!' said Scarlett, a very small dart of jealousy entering her.

She looked curiously at this lanky man with his bony stooped shoulders, his pinkish hair and calm unwavering eyes. So he knew things about her own family which she had not troubled to discover. So that was why Carreen mooned about, praying all the time. Well, she'd get over it. Lots of girls got over dead sweethearts, yes, dead husbands, too. She'd certainly gotten over Charles. And she knew one girl in Atlanta who had been widowed three times by the war and was still able to take notice of men. She said as much to Will but he shook his head.

'Not Miss Carreen,' he said with finality.

Will was pleasant to talk to because he had so little to say and yet was so understanding a listener. She told him about her problems of weeding and hoeing and planting, of fattening the hogs and breeding the cow, and he gave good advice for he had owned a small farm in south Georgia and two negroes. He knew his slaves were free now and the farm gone to weeds and seedling pines. His sister, his only relative, had moved to Texas with her husband years ago and he was alone in the world. Yet, none of these things seemed to bother him any more than the leg he had left in Virginia.

Yes, Will was a comfort to Scarlett after hard days when the negroes muttered and Suellen nagged and cried and Gerald asked too frequently where Ellen was. She could tell Will anything. She even told him of killing the Yankee and glowed with pride when he commented briefly: 'Good work!'

Eventually all the family found their way to Will's room to air their troubles – even Mammy, who had at first been distant with him because he was not quality and had owned only two slaves.

When he was able to totter about the house, he turned his hands to weaving baskets of split oak and mending the furniture ruined by the Yankees. He was clever at whittling and Wade was constantly by his side, for he whittled out toys for him, the only toys the little boy had. With Will in the house, everyone felt safe in leaving Wade and the two babies while they went about their tasks, for he could care for them as deftly as Mammy and only Melly surpassed him at soothing the screaming black and white babies.

'You've been mighty good to me, Miss Scarlett,' he said, 'and me a stranger and nothin' to you all. I've caused you a heap of trouble and worry and if it's all the same to you, I'm goin' to stay here and help you all with the work till I've paid you back some for your trouble. I can't ever pay it all, 'cause there ain't no payment a man can give for his life.'

So he stayed and, gradually, unobtrusively, a large part of the burden of Tara shifted from Scarlett's shoulders to the bony shoulders of Will Benteen.

It was September and time to pick the cotton. Will Benteen sat on the front steps at Scarlett's feet in the pleasant sunshine of the early autumn afternoon, and his flat voice went on and on languidly about the exorbitant costs of ginning the cotton at the new gin near Fayetteville. However, he had learned that day in Fayetteville that he could cut this expense a fourth by lending the horse and wagon for two weeks to the gin owner. He had delayed closing the bargain until he discussed it with Scarlett.

She looked at the lank figure leaning against the porch column, chewing a straw. Undoubtedly, as Mammy had frequently declared, Will was something the Lord had provided and Scarlett often wondered how Tara could have lived through the last few months without him. He never had much to say, never displayed any energy, never seemed to take much interest in anything that went on about him, but he knew everything about everybody at Tara. And he did things. He did them silently, patiently and competently. Though he had only one leg, he could work faster than Pork. And he could get work out of Pork, which was, to Scarlett, a marvellous thing. When the cow had the colic and the horse fell ill with a mysterious ailment which threatened to remove him permanently from them, Will sat up nights with them and saved them. That he was a shrewd trader brought him Scarlett's respect, for he could ride out in the mornings with a bushel or two of apples, sweet potatoes and other vegetables and return with seeds, lengths of cloth, flour and other necessities which she knew she could never have acquired, good trader though she was.

He had gradually slipped into the status of a member of the family and slept on a cot in the little dressing-room off Gerald's room. He said nothing of leaving Tara, and Scarlett was careful not to question him, fearful that he might leave them. Sometimes, she thought that if he were anybody and had any gumption he would go home, even if he no longer had a home.

But even with this thought, she would pray fervently that he would remain indefinitely. It was so convenient to have a man about the house.

She thought, too, that if Carreen had the sense of a mouse she would see that Will cared for her. Scarlett would have been eternally grateful to Will, had he asked her for Carreen's hand. Of course, before the war, Will would certainly not have been an eligible suitor. He was not of the planter class at all, though he was not poor white. He was just plain Cracker, a small farmer, half-educated, prone to grammatical errors and ignorant of some of the finer manners the O'Haras were accustomed to in gentlemen. In fact, Scarlett wondered if he could be called a gentleman at all and decided that he couldn't. Melanie hotly defended him, saying that anyone who had Will's kind heart and thoughtfulness of others was of gentle birth. Scarlett knew that Ellen would have fainted at the thought of a daughter of hers marrying such a man, but now Scarlett had been by necessity forced too far away from Ellen's teachings to let that worry her. Men were scarce, girls had to marry someone and Tara had to have a man. But Carreen, deeper and deeper immersed in her prayer-book and every day losing more of her touch with the world of realities, treated Will as gently as a brother and took him as much for granted as she did Pork.

'If Carreen had any sense of gratitude to me for what I've done for her, she'd marry him and not let him get away from here,' Scarlett thought indignantly. 'But no, she must spend her time mooning about a silly boy who probably never gave her a serious thought.'

So Will remained at Tara, for what reason she did not know, and she found his businesslike man-to-man attitude with her both pleasant and helpful. He was gravely deferential to the vague Gerald but it was to Scarlett that he turned as the real head of the house.

She gave her approval to the plan of hiring out the horse even though it meant the family would be without any means of transportation temporarily. Suellen would be especially grieved at this. Her greatest joy lay in going to Jonesboro or Fayetteville with Will when he drove over on business. Adorned in the assembled best of the family, she called on old friends, heard all the gossip of the County and felt herself again Miss O'Hara of Tara. Suellen never missed the opportunity to leave the plantation and give herself airs among people who did not know she weeded the garden and made beds.

'Miss Fine Airs will just have to do without gadding for two weeks,' thought Scarlett, 'and we'll have to put up with her nagging and her bawling.'

Melanie joined them on the veranda, the baby in her arms, and spreading an old blanket on the floor, set little Beau down to crawl. Since Ashley's letter Melanie had divided her time between glowing, singing happiness and anxious longing. But happy or depressed, she was too thin, too white. She did her share of the work uncomplainingly but she was always ailing. Old Dr Fontaine diagnosed her trouble as female complaint and concurred with

Dr Meade in saying she should never have had Beau. And he said frankly that another baby would kill her.

'When I was over to Fayetteville today,' said Will, 'I found somethin' right cute that I thought would interest you ladies and I brought it home.' He fumbled in his back pants pocket and brought out the wallet of calico, stiffened with bark, which Carreen had made him. From it he drew a Confederate bill.

'If you think Confederate money is cute, Will, I certainly don't,' said Scarlett shortly, for the very sight of Confederate money made her mad. 'We've got three thousand dollars of it in Pa's trunk this minute, and Mammy's after me to let her paste it over the holes in the attic walls so the draught won't get her. And I think I'll do it. Then it'll be good for something.'

' "Imperious Caesar, dead and turned to clay," ' said Melanie with a sad smile. 'Don't do that, Scarlett. Keep it for Wade. He'll be proud of it some day.'

'Well, I don't know nothin' about imperious Caesar,' said Will patiently, 'but what I've got is in line with what you've just said about Wade, Miss Melly. It's a poem, pasted on the back of this bill. I know Miss Scarlett ain't much on poems but I thought this might interest her.'

He turned the bill over. On its back was pasted a strip of coarse brown wrapping paper, inscribed in pale home-made ink. Will cleared his throat and read slowly and with difficulty.

'The name is "Lines on the Back of a Confederate Note",' he said.

> *Representing nothing on God's earth now*
> *And naught in the waters below it –*
> *As the pledge of a nation that's passed away*
> *Keep it, dear friend, and show it.*
>
> *Show it to those who will lend an ear*
> *To the tale this trifle will tell*
> *Of Liberty, born of patriots' dream,*
> *Of a storm-cradled nation that fell.*

'Oh, how beautiful! How touching!' cried Melanie. 'Scarlett, you mustn't give the money to Mammy to paste in the attic. It's more than paper – just like this poem said: "The pledge of a nation that's passed away!" '

'Oh, Mellly, don't be sentimental! Paper is paper and we've got little enough of it and I'm tired of hearing Mammy grumble about the cracks in the attic. I hope when Wade grows up I'll have plenty of greenbacks to give him instead of Confederate trash.'

Will, who had been enticing little Beau across the blanket with the bill during this argument, looked up and, shading his eyes, glanced down the driveway.

'More company,' he said, squinting in the sun. 'Another soldier.'

Scarlett followed his gaze and saw a familiar sight, a bearded man coming slowly up the avenue under the cedars, a man clad in a ragged mixture of blue and grey uniforms, head bowed tiredly, feet dragging slowly.

'I thought we were about through with soldiers,' she said. 'I hope this one isn't very hungry.'

'He'll be hungry,' said Will briefly.

Melanie rose.

'I'd better tell Dilcey to set an extra plate,' she said, 'and warn Mammy not to get the poor thing's clothes off his back too abruptly and—'

She stopped so suddenly that Scarlett turned to look at her. Melanie's thin hand was at her throat, clutching it as if it was torn with pain, and Scarlett could see the veins beneath the white skin throbbing swiftly. Her face went whiter and her brown eyes dilated enormously.

'She's going to faint,' thought Scarlett, leaping to her feet and catching her arm.

But, in an instant, Melanie threw off her hand and was down the steps. Down the gravelled path she flew, skimming lightly as a bird, her faded skirts streaming behind her, her arms outstretched. Then Scarlett knew the truth, with the impact of a blow. She reeled back against an upright of the porch as the man lifted a face covered with a dirty blond beard and stopped still, looking toward the house as if he was too weary to take another step. Her heart leaped and stopped and then began racing, as Melly with incoherent cries threw herself into the dirty soldier's arms and his head bent down toward hers. With rapture, Scarlett took two running steps forward but was checked when Will's hand closed upon her skirt.

'Don't spoil it,' he said quietly.

'Turn me loose, you fool! Turn me loose! It's Ashley!'

He did not relax his grip.

'After all, he's *her* husband, ain't he?' Will asked calmly and, looking down at him in a confusion of joy and impotent fury, Scarlett saw in the quiet depth of his eyes understanding and pity.

Part Four

Chapter XXXI

On a cold January afternoon in 1866, Scarlett sat in the office writing a letter to Aunt Pitty, explaining in detail for the tenth time why neither she, Melanie nor Ashley could come back to Atlanta to live with her. She wrote impatiently because she knew Aunt Pitty would read no farther than the opening lines and then write her again, wailing: 'But I'm afraid to live by myself!'

Her hands were chilled and she paused to rub them together and to scuff her feet deeper into the strip of old quilting wrapped about them. The soles of her slippers were practically gone and were reinforced with pieces of carpet. The carpet kept her feet off the floor but did little to keep them warm. That morning Will had taken the horse to Jonesboro to get him shod. Scarlett thought grimly that things were indeed at a pretty pass when horses had shoes and people's feet were as bare as yard dogs'.

She picked up her quill to resume her writing but laid it down when she heard Will coming in at the back door. She heard the thump-thump of his wooden leg in the hall outside the office and then he stopped. She waited for a moment for him to enter and when he made no move she called to him. He came in, his ears red from the cold, his pinkish hair awry, and stood looking down at her, a faintly humorous smile on his lips.

'Miss Scarlett,' he questioned, 'just how much cash money have you got?'

'Are you going to try to marry me for my money, Will?' she asked somewhat crossly.

'No, Ma'm. But I just wanted to know.'

She stared at him inquiringly. Will didn't look serious, but then he never looked serious. However, she felt that something was wrong.

'I've got ten dollars in gold,' she said. 'The last of that Yankee's money.'

'Well, Ma'm, that won't be enough.'

'Enough for what?'

'Enough for the taxes,' he answered and, stumping over to the fireplace, he leaned down and held his red hands to the blaze.

'Taxes?' she repeated. 'Name of God, Will! We've already paid the taxes.'

'Yes'm. But they say you didn't pay enough. I heard about it today over to Jonesboro.'

'But, Will, I can't understand. What do you mean?'

'Miss Scarlett, I sure hate to bother you with more trouble when you've had your share but I've got to tell you. They say you ought to paid lots more taxes than you did. They're runnin' the assessment up on Tara sky high – higher than any in the County, I'll be bound.'

'But they can't make us pay more taxes when we've already paid them once.'

'Miss Scarlett, you don't never go to Jonesboro often and I'm glad you don't. It ain't no place for a lady these days. But if you'd been there much, you'd know there's a mighty rough bunch of Scallawags and Republicans and Carpetbaggers been runnin' things recently. They'd make you mad enough to pop. And then, too, niggers pushin' white folks off the sidewalks, and—'

'But what's that got to do with our taxes?'

'I'm gettin' to it, Miss Scarlett. For some reason the rascals have histed the taxes on Tara till you'd think it was a thousand-bale place. After I heard about it, I sorter oozed around the bar-rooms pickin' up gossip and I found out that somebody wants to buy in Tara cheap at the sheriff's sale, if you can't pay the extra taxes. And everybody knows pretty well that you can't pay them. I don't know yet who it is wants this place. I couldn't find out. But I think that pusillanimous feller, Hilton, that married Miss Cathleen knows, because he laughed kind of nasty when I tried to sound him out.'

Will sat down on the sofa and rubbed the stump of his leg. It ached in cold weather and the wooden peg was neither well padded nor comfortable. Scarlett looked at him wildly. His manner was so casual when he was sounding the death-knell of Tara. Sold out at the sheriff's sale? Where would they all go? And Tara belonging to someone else! No, that was unthinkable!

She had been so engrossed with the job of making Tara produce she had paid little heed to what was going on in the world outside. Now that she had Will and Ashley to attend to whatever business she might have in Jonesboro and Fayetteville, she seldom left the plantation. And even as she had listened with deaf ears to her father's war talk in the days before the war came, so she had paid little heed to Will and Ashley's discussions around the table after supper about the beginnings of Reconstruction.

Oh, of course, she knew about the Scallawags – Southerners who had turned republican very profitably – and the Carpetbaggers, those Yankees who came South like buzzards after the surrender with all their worldly possessions in one carpet-bag. And she had had a few unpleasant experiences with the Freedmen's Bureau. She had gathered, also, that some of the free negroes were getting quite insolent. This last she could hardly believe, for she had never seen an insolent negro in her life.

But there were many things which Will and Ashley had conspired to keep from her. The scourge of war had been followed by the worse scourge of Reconstruction, but the two men had agreed not to mention the more alarming details when they discussed the situation at home. And when Scarlett took the trouble to listen to them at all, most of what they said went in one ear and out the other.

She had heard Ashley say that the South was being treated as a conquered province and that vindictiveness was the dominant policy of the conquerors. But that was the kind of statement which meant less than nothing at all to Scarlett. Politics was men's business. She had heard Will say it looked to him like the North just wasn't aiming to let the South get on its feet again. Well, thought Scarlett, men always had to have something foolish to worry about. As far as she was concerned, the Yankees hadn't whipped her once and they wouldn't do it this time. The thing to do was to work like the devil and stop worrying about the Yankee government. After all, the war was over.

Scarlett did not realize that all the rules of the game had been changed and that honest labour could no longer earn its just reward. Georgia was virtually under martial law now. The Yankee soldiers garrisoned throughout the section and the Freedmen's Bureau were in complete command of everything and they were fixing the rules to suit themselves.

This Bureau, organized by the Federal government to take care of the idle and excited ex-slaves, was drawing them from the plantations into the villages and cities by the thousands. The Bureau fed them while they loafed and poisoned their minds against their former owners. Gerald's old overseer, Jonas Wilkerson, was in charge of the local Bureau and his assistant was Hilton, Cathleen Calvert's husband. These two industriously spread the rumour that the Southerners and Democrats were just waiting for a good chance to put the negroes back into slavery and that the negroes' only hope of escaping this fate was the protection given them by the Bureau and the Republican party.

Wilkerson and Hilton furthermore told the negroes they were as good as the whites in every way and soon white and negro marriages would be permitted, soon the estates of their former owners would be divided and every negro would be given forty acres and a mule for his own. They kept the negroes stirred up with tales of cruelty perpetrated by the whites and, in a section long famed for the affectionate relations between slaves and slave-owners, hate and suspicion began to grow.

The Bureau was backed up by the soldiers and the military had issued many and conflicting orders governing the conduct of the conquered. It was easy to get arrested, even for snubbing the officials of the Bureau. Military orders had been promulgated concerning the schools, sanitation, the kind of buttons one wore on one's suit, the sale of commodities and nearly everything else. Wilkerson and Hilton had the power to interfere in any trade Scarlett might make and to fix their own prices on anything she sold or swapped.

Fortunately Scarlett had come into contact with the two men very little, for Will had persuaded her to let him handle the trading while she managed the plantation. In his mild-tempered way, Will had straightened out several difficulties of this kind and said nothing to her about them. Will could get along with Carpetbaggers and Yankees – if he had to. But now a problem had arisen which was too big for him to handle. The extra tax assessment and the danger of losing Tara were matters Scarlett had to know about – and right away.

She looked at him with flashing eyes.

'Oh, damn the Yankees!' she cried. 'Isn't it enough that they've licked us and beggared us without turning loose scoundrels on us?'

The war was over, peace had been declared, but the Yankees could still rob her, they could still starve her, they could still drive her from her house. And fool that she was, she had thought through weary months that if she could just hold out until spring, everything would be all right. This crushing news brought by Will, coming on top of a year of back-breaking work and hope deferred, was the last straw.

'Oh, Will, and I thought our troubles were all over when the war ended!'

'No'm.' Will raised his lantern-jawed, country-looking face and gave her a long steady look. 'Our troubles are just gettin' started.'

'How much extra taxes do they want us to pay?'

'Three hundred dollars.'

She was struck dumb for a moment. Three hundred dollars! It might just as well be three million dollars.

'Why,' she floundered, 'why – why, then we've got to raise three hundred, somehow.'

'Yes'm – and a rainbow and a moon or two.'

'Oh, but Will! They couldn't sell out Tara. Why—'

His mild pale eyes showed more hate and bitterness than she thought possible.

'Oh, couldn't they? Well, they could and they will and they'll like doin' it! Miss Scarlett, the country's gone plumb to hell, if you'll pardon me. Those Carpetbaggers and Scallawags can vote and most of us Democrats can't. Can't no Democrat in this state vote if he was on the tax books for more than two thousand dollars in 'sixty-five. That lets out folks like your pa and Mr Tarleton and the McRaes and the Fontaine boys. Can't nobody vote who was a colonel and over in the war and, Miss Scarlett, I bet this state's got more colonels than any state in the Confederacy. And can't nobody vote who held office under the Confederate government and that lets out everybody from the notaries to the judges, and the woods are full of folks like that. Fact is, the way the Yankees have framed up that amnesty oath, can't nobody who was somebody before the war vote at all. Not the smart folks nor the quality folks nor the rich folks.

'Huh! I could vote if I took their damned oath. I didn't have any money in 'sixty-five and I certainly warn't a colonel or nothin' remarkable. But I ain't goin' to take their oath. Not by a dinged sight! If the Yankees had acted right, I'd have taken their oath of allegiance but I ain't now. I can be restored to the Union but I can't be reconstructed into it. I ain't going to take their oath even if I don't never vote again— But scum like that Hilton feller, he can vote, and scoundrels like Jonas Wilkerson and pore whites like the Slatterys and no-counts like the MacIntoshes, they can vote. And they're runnin' things now. And if they want to come down on you for extra taxes a dozen times, they can do it. Just like a nigger can kill a white man and not get hung or— ' He paused, embarrassed, and the memory of what had happened to a lone white woman on an isolated farm near Lovejoy was in both their minds . . . 'Those niggers can do anything against us and the Freedmen's Bureau and the soldiers will back them up with guns and we can't vote or do nothin' about it.'

'Vote!' she cried. 'Vote! What on earth has voting got to do with all this, Will? It's taxes we're talking about . . . Will, everybody knows what a good plantation Tara is. We could mortgage it for enough to pay the taxes, if we had to.'

'Miss Scarlett, you ain't any fool but sometimes you talk like one. Who's got any money to lend you on this property? Who except the Carpetbaggers who are tryin' to take Tara away from you? Why, everybody's got land. Everybody's land pore. You can't give away land.'

'I've got those diamond earbobs I got off that Yankee. We could sell them.'

'Miss Scarlett, who 'round here has got money for earbobs? Folks ain't got money to buy side meat, let alone gewgaws. If you've got ten dollars in gold, I take oath that's more than most folks have got.'

They were silent again and Scarlett felt as if she were butting her head against a stone wall. There had been so many stone walls to butt against this last year.

'What are we goin' to do, Miss Scarlett?'

'I don't know,' she said dully and felt that she didn't care. This was one stone wall too many and she suddenly felt so tired that her bones ached. Why should she work and struggle and wear herself out? At the end of every struggle it seemed that defeat was waiting to mock her.

'I don't know,' she said. 'But don't let Pa know. It might worry him.'

'I won't.'

'Have you told anyone?'

'No, I came right to you.'

Yes, she thought, everyone always came right to her with bad news and she was tired of it.

'Where is Mr Wilkes? Perhaps he'll have some suggestion.'

Will turned his mild gaze on her and she felt, as from the first day when Ashley came home, that he knew everything.

'He's down in the orchard splittin' rails. I heard his axe when I was puttin' up the horse. But he ain't got any money any more than we have.'

'If I want to talk to him about it, I can, can't I?' she snapped, rising to her feet and kicking the fragment of quilting from her ankles.

Will did not take offence but continued rubbing his hands before the flame. 'Better get your shawl, Miss Scarlett. It's raw outside.'

But she went without the shawl, for it was upstairs and her need to see Ashley and lay her troubles before him was too urgent to wait.

How lucky for her if she could find him alone! Never once since his return had she had a private word with him. Always the family clustered about him, always Melanie was by his side, touching his sleeve now and again to reassure herself he was really there. The sight of that happy possessive gesture had aroused in Scarlett all the jealous animosity which had slumbered during the months when she thought Ashley probably dead. Now she was determined to see him alone. This time no one was going to prevent her from talking with him alone.

She went through the orchard under the bare boughs and the damp weeds beneath them wet her feet. She could hear the sound of the axe ringing as Ashley split into rails the logs hauled from the swamp. Replacing the fences the Yankees had so blithely burned was a long hard task. Everything was a long hard task, she thought wearily, and she was tired of it, tired and mad and sick of it all. If only Ashley were her husband, instead of Melanie's, how sweet it would be to go to him and lay her head upon his shoulder and cry and shove her burdens on to him to work out as best he might.

She rounded a thicket of pomegranate trees which were shaking bare limbs in the cold wind and saw him leaning on his axe, wiping his forehead with the back of his hand. He was wearing the remains of his butternut trousers and one of Gerald's shirts, a shirt which in better times went only to Court days and barbecues, a ruffled shirt which was far too short for its present owner. He had hung his coat on a tree limb, for the work was hot, and he stood resting as she came up to him.

At the sight of Ashley in rags, with an axe in his hand, her heart went out in a surge of love and of fury at fate. She could not bear to see him in tatters, working, her debonair immaculate Ashley. His hands were not made for work or his body for anything but broadcloth and fine linen. God intended him to sit in a great house, talking with pleasant people, playing the piano and writing things which sounded beautiful and made no sense whatsoever.

She could endure the sight of her own child in aprons made of sacking and the girls in dingy old gingham, could bear it that Will worked harder than any field hand, but not Ashley. He was too fine for all this, too infinitely dear to her. She would rather split logs herself than suffer while he did it.

'They say Abe Lincoln got his start splitting rails,' he said as she came up to him. 'Just think to what heights I may climb!'

She frowned. He was always saying light things like this about their hardships. They were deadly serious matters to her and sometimes she was almost irritated at his remarks.

Abruptly she told him Will's news, tersely and in short words, feeling a sense of relief as she spoke. Surely he'd have something helpful to offer. He said nothing but, seeing her shiver, he took his coat and placed it about her shoulders.

'Well,' she said finally, 'doesn't it occur to you that we'll have to get the money somewhere?'

'Yes,' he said, 'but where?'

'I'm asking you,' she replied, annoyed. The sense of relief at unburdening herself had disappeared. Even if he couldn't help, why didn't he say something comforting, even if it was only, 'Oh, I'm so sorry'?

He smiled.

'In all these months since I've been home I've only heard of one person, Rhett Butler, who actually has money,' he said.

Aunt Pittypat had written Melanie the week before that Rhett was back in Atlanta with a carriage and two fine horses and pocketfuls of greenbacks. She had intimated, however, that he didn't come by them honestly. Aunt Pitty had a theory, largely shared by Atlanta, that Rhett had managed to get away with the mythical millions of the Confederate treasury.

'Don't let's talk about him,' said Scarlett shortly. 'He's a skunk if ever there was one. What's to become of us all?'

Ashley put down the axe and looked away, and his eyes seemed to be journeying to some far-off country where she could not follow.

'I wonder,' he said. 'I wonder not only what will become of us at Tara but what will become of everybody in the South.'

She felt like snapping out abruptly: 'To hell with everybody in the South! What about us?' but she remained silent because the tired feeling was back on her more strongly than ever. Ashley wasn't being any help at all.

'In the end what will happen will be what has happened whenever a civilization breaks up. The people who have brains and courage come through and the ones who haven't are winnowed out. At least, it has been interesting, if not comfortable, to witness a Götterdämmerung.'

'A what?'

'A dusk of the gods. Unfortunately, we Southerners did think we were gods.'

'For Heaven's sake, Ashley Wilkes! Don't stand there and talk nonsense at me when it's us who are going to be winnowed out!'

Something of her exasperated weariness seemed to penetrate his mind, calling it back from its wanderings, for he raised her hands with tenderness and, turning them palm up, looked at the callouses.

'These are the most beautiful hands I know,' he said, and he kissed each palm lightly. 'They are beautiful because they are strong and every callous is a medal, Scarlett, every blister an award for bravery and unselfishness. They've been roughened for all of us, your father, the girls, Melanie, the baby, the negroes and for me. My dear, I know what you are thinking.

You're thinking, "Here stands an impractical fool talking tommyrot about dead gods when living people are in danger." Isn't that true?'

She nodded, wishing he would keep on holding her hands forever but he dropped them.

'And you came to me, hoping I could help you. Well, I can't.'

His eyes were bitter as he looked toward the axe and the pile of logs.

'My home is gone and all the money that I so took for granted I never realized I had it. And I am fitted for nothing in this world, for the world I belonged in has gone. I can't help you, Scarlett, except by learning with as good grace as possible to be a clumsy farmer. And that won't keep Tara for you. Don't you think I realize the bitterness of our situation, living here on your charity— Oh, yes, Scarlett, your charity. I can never repay you what you've done for me and for mine out of the kindness of your heart. I realize it more acutely every day. And every day I see more clearly how helpless I am to cope with what has come on us all— Every day my accursed shrinking from realities makes it harder for me to face the new realities. Do you know what I mean?'

She nodded. She had no very clear idea what he meant but she clung breathlessly on his words. This was the first time he had ever spoken to her of the things he was thinking when he seemed so remote from her. It excited her as if she were on the brink of a discovery.

'It's a curse – this not wanting to look on naked realities. Until the war, life was never more real to me than a shadow show on a curtain. And I preferred it so. I do not like the outlines of things to be too sharp. I like them gently blurred, a little hazy.'

He stopped and smiled faintly, shivering a little as the cold wind went through his thin shirt.

'In other words, Scarlett, I am a coward.'

His talk of shadow shows and hazy outlines conveyed no meaning to her but his last words were in language she could understand. She knew they were untrue. Cowardice was not in him. Every line of his slender body spoke of generations of brave and gallant men and Scarlett knew his war record by heart.

'Why, that's not so! Would a coward have climbed on the cannon at Gettysburg and rallied the men? Would the General himself have written Melanie a letter about a coward? And—'

'That's not courage,' he said tiredly. 'Fighting is like champagne. It goes to the heads of cowards as quickly as of heroes. Any fool can be brave on a battlefield when it's be brave or else be killed. I'm talking of something else. And my kind of cowardice is infinitely worse than if I had run the first time I heard a cannon fired.'

His words came slowly and with difficulty as if it hurt to speak them and he seemed to stand off and look with a sad heart at what he had said. Had any other man spoken so, Scarlett would have dismissed such protestations contemptuously as mock modesty and a bid for praise. But Ashley seemed to mean them and there was a look in his eyes which eluded her – not fear, not apology, but the bracing to a strain which was inevitable and overwhelming. The wintry wind swept her damp ankles and she shivered again, but her shiver was less from the wind than from the dread his words evoked in her heart.

'But, Ashley, what are you afraid of?'

'Oh, nameless things. Things which sound very silly when they are put into words. Mostly of having life suddenly become too real, of being brought into personal, too personal, contact with some of the simple facts of life. It isn't that I mind splitting logs here in the mud, but I do mind what it stands for. I do mind, very much, the loss of the beauty of the old life I loved. Scarlett, before the war, life was beautiful. There was a glamour to it, a perfection and a completeness and a symmetry to it like Grecian art. Maybe it wasn't so to everyone. I know that now. But to me, living at Twelve Oaks, there was a real beauty to living. I belonged in that life. I was a part of it. And now it is gone and I am out of place in this new life, and I am afraid. Now, I know that in the old days it was a shadow show I watched. I avoided everything which was not shadowy, people and situations which were too real, too vital. I resented their intrusion. I tried to avoid you too, Scarlett. You were too full of living and too real and I was cowardly enough to prefer shadows and dreams.'

'But – but – Melly?'

'Melanie is the gentlest of dreams and a part of my dreaming. And if the war had not come I would have lived out my life, happily buried at Twelve Oaks, contentedly watching life go by and never being a part of it. But when the war came, life as it really is thrust itself against me. The first time I went into action – it was at Bull Run, you remember – I saw my boyhood friends blown to bits and heard dying horses scream and learned the sickeningly horrible feeling of seeing men crumple up and spit blood when I shot them. But those weren't the worst things about the war, Scarlett. The worst thing about the war was the people I had to live with.

'I had sheltered myself from people all my life, I had carefully selected my few friends. But the war taught me I had created a world of my own with dream people in it. It taught me what people really are, but it didn't teach me how to live with them. And I'm afraid I'll never learn. Now, I know that in order to support my wife and child, I will have to make my way among a world of people with whom I have nothing in common. You, Scarlett, you are taking life by the horns and twisting it to your will. But where do I fit in in the world any more? I tell you I am afraid.'

While his low resonant voice went on, desolate, with a feeling she could not understand, Scarlett clutched at words here and there, trying to make sense of them. But the words swooped from her hands like wild birds. Something was driving him, driving him with a cruel goad, but she did not understand what it was.

'Scarlett, I don't know just when it was that the bleak realization came over me that my own private shadow show was over. Perhaps in the first five minutes at Bull Run when I saw the first man I killed drop to the ground. But I knew it was over and I could no longer be a spectator. No, I suddenly found myself on the curtain, an actor, posturing and making futile gestures. My little inner world was gone, invaded by people whose thoughts were not my thoughts, whose actions were as alien as a Hottentot's. They'd tramped through my world with slimy feet and there was no place left where I could take refuge when things became too bad to stand. When I was in prison, I thought: "When the war is over, I can go back to the old life and the old dreams and watch the shadow show again." But, Scarlett, there's no going back. And this which is facing all of us now is worse than war and worse than prison – and, to me, worse than death . . . So, you see, Scarlett, I'm being punished for being afraid.'

'But, Ashley,' she began, floundering in a quagmire of bewilderment, 'if you're afraid we'll starve, why – why— Oh, Ashley, we'll manage somehow! I know we will!'

For a moment his eyes came back to her, wide and crystal grey, and there was admiration in them. Then, suddenly, they were remote again and she knew with a sinking heart that he had not been thinking about starving. They were always like two people talking to each other in different languages. But she loved him so much that, when he withdrew as he had now done, it was like the warm sun going down and leaving her in chilly twilight dews. She wanted to catch him by the shoulders and hug him to her, make him realize that she was flesh and blood and not something he had read or dreamed. If she could only feel that sense of oneness with him for which she had yearned since that day, so long ago, when he had come home from Europe and stood on the steps of Tara and smiled up at her.

'Starving's not pleasant,' he said. 'I know for I've starved, but I'm not afraid of that. I am afraid of facing life without the slow beauty of our old world that is gone.'

Scarlett thought despairingly that Melanie would know what he meant. Melly and he were always talking such foolishness, poetry and books and dreams and moonrays and star-dust. He was not fearing the things she feared, not the gnawing of an empty stomach, nor the keenness of the winter wind nor eviction from Tara. He was shrinking before some fear she had never known and could not imagine. For, in God's name, what was there to fear in this wreck of a world but hunger and cold and the loss of home?

And she had thought that if she listened closely she would know the answer to Ashley.

'Oh!' she said, and the disappointment in her voice was that of a child who opens a beautifully wrapped package to find it empty. At her tone, he smiled ruefully as though apologizing.

'Forgive me, Scarlett, for talking so. I can't make you understand because you don't know the meaning of fear. You have the heart of a lion and an utter lack of imagination and I envy you both of those qualities. You'll never mind facing realities and you'll never want to escape from them as I do.'

'Escape!'

It was as if that were the only understandable word he had spoken. Ashley, like her, was tired of the struggle and he wanted to escape. Her breath came fast.

'Oh, Ashley,' she cried, 'you're wrong. I do want to escape, too. I am so very tired of it all!'

His eyebrows went up in disbelief and she laid a hand, feverish and urgent, on his arm.

'Listen to me,' she began swiftly, the words tumbling out one over the other. 'I'm tired of it all, I tell you. Bone tired and I'm not going to stand it any longer. I've struggled for food and for money and I've weeded and hoed and picked cotton and I've even ploughed until I can't stand it another minute. I tell you, Ashley, the South is dead! It's dead! The Yankees and the free niggers and the Carpetbaggers have got it and there's nothing left for us. Ashley, let's run away!'

He peered at her sharply, lowering his head to look into her face, now flaming with colour.

'Yes, let's run away – leave them all! I'm tired of working for the folks. Somebody will take care of them. There's always somebody who takes care of people who can't take care of themselves. Oh, Ashley, let's run away, you and I. We could go to Mexico – they want officers in the Mexican Army and we could be so happy there. I'd work for you, Ashley. I'd do anything for you. You know you don't love Melanie—'

He started to speak, a stricken look on his face, but she stemmed his words with a torrent of her own.

'You told me you loved me better than her that day – oh, you remember that day! And I know you haven't changed! I can tell you haven't changed! And you've just said she was nothing but a dream—Oh, Ashley, let's go away! I could make you so happy. And anyway,' she added venomously, 'Melanie can't – Dr Fontaine said she couldn't ever have any more children and I could give you—'

His hands were on her shoulders so tightly that they hurt and she stopped, breathless.

'We were to forget that day at Twelve Oaks.'

'Do you think I could ever forget it? Have you forgotten it? Can you honestly say you don't love me?'

He drew a deep breath and answered quickly.

'No. I don't love you.'

'That's a lie.'

'Even if it is a lie,' said Ashley, and his voice was deadly quiet, 'it is not something which can be discussed.'

'You mean—'

'Do you think I could go off and leave Melanie and the baby, even if I hated them both? Break Melanie's heart? Leave them both to the charity of friends? Scarlett, are you mad? Isn't there any sense of loyalty in you? You couldn't leave your father and the girls. They're your responsibility, just as Melanie and Beau are mine, and whether you are tired or not, they are here and you've got to bear them.'

'I could leave them – I'm sick of them – tired of them—'

He leaned toward her and, for a moment, she thought with a catch at her heart that he was going to take her in his arms. But instead, he patted her arm and spoke as one comforting a child.

'I know you're sick and tired. That's why you are talking this way. You've carried the load of three men. But I'm going to help you – I won't always be so awkward—'

'There's only one way you can help me,' she said dully, 'and that's to take me away from here and give us a new start somewhere, with a chance for happiness. There's nothing to keep us here.'

'Nothing,' he said quietly, 'nothing – except honour.'

She looked at him with baffled longing and saw, as if for the first time, how the crescents of his lashes were the thick rich gold of ripe wheat, how proudly his head sat upon his bared neck and how the look of grace and dignity persisted in his slim erect body, even through its grotesque rags. Her eyes met his, hers naked with pleading, his remote as mountain lakes under grey skies.

She saw in them defeat of her wild dream, her mad desires.

Heartbreak and weariness sweeping over her, she dropped her head in her hands and cried. He had never seen her cry. He had never thought that women of her strong mettle had tears, and a flood of tenderness and remorse swept him. He came to her swiftly and in a moment had her in his arms, cradling her comfortingly, pressing her black head to his heart, whispering: 'Dear! My brave dear – don't! You mustn't cry!'

At his touch, he felt her change within his grip and there was madness and magic in the slim body he held and a hot soft glow in the green eyes which looked up at him. Of a sudden, it was no longer bleak winter. For Ashley, spring was back again, that half-forgotten balmy spring of green rustlings and murmurings, a spring of ease and indolence, careless days when the desires of youth were warm in his body. The bitter years since then fell away and he saw that the lips turned up to his were red and trembling and he kissed her.

There was a curious low roaring sound in her ears as of sea-shells held against them and through the sound she dimly heard the swift thudding of her heart. Her body seemed to melt into his and, for a timeless time, they stood fused together as his lips took hers hungrily as if he could never have enough.

When he suddenly released her she felt that she could not stand alone and gripped the fence for support. She raised eyes blazing with love and triumph to him.

'You do love me! You do love me! Say it – say it!'

His hands still rested on her shoulders and she felt them tremble and loved their trembling. She leaned toward him ardently but he held her away from him, looking at her with eyes from which all remoteness had fled, eyes tormented with struggle and despair.

'Don't!' he said. 'Don't! If you do, I shall take you now, here.'

She smiled a bright hot smile which was forgetful of time or place or anything but the memory of his mouth on hers.

Suddenly he shook her, shook her until her black hair tumbled down about her shoulders, shook her as if in a mad rage at her – and at himself.

'We won't do this!' he said. 'I tell you we won't do it!'

It seemed as if her neck would snap if he shook her again. She was blinded by her hair and stunned by his action. She wrenched herself away and stared at him. There were small beads of moisture on his forehead and his fists were curled into claws as if in pain. He looked at her directly, his grey eyes piercing.

'It's all my fault – none of yours, and it will never happen again, because I am going to take Melanie and the baby and go.'

'Go?' she cried in anguish. 'Oh, no!'

'Yes, by God! Do you think I'll stay here after this? When this might happen again—'

'But, Ashley, you can't go. Why should you go? You love me—'

'You want me to say it? All right, I'll say it. I love you.'

He leaned over her with a sudden savagery which made her shrink back against the fence.

'I love you, your courage and your stubbornness and your fire and your utter ruthlessness. How much do I love you? So much that a moment ago I would have outraged the hospitality of the house which has sheltered me and my family, forgotten the best wife any man ever had – enough to take you here in the mud like a—'

She struggled with a chaos of thought and there was a cold pain in her heart as if an icicle had pierced it. She said haltingly: 'If you felt like that – and didn't take me – then you don't love me.'

'I can never make you understand.'

They fell silent and looked at each other. Suddenly Scarlett shivered and saw, as if coming back from a long journey, that it was winter and the fields were bare and harsh with stubble and she was very cold. She saw too that the old aloof face of Ashley, the one she knew so well, had come back and it was wintry too, and harsh with hurt and remorse.

She would have turned and left him then, seeking the shelter of the house to hide herself, but she was too tired to move. Even speech was a labour and a weariness.

'There is nothing left,' she said at last. 'Nothing left for me. Nothing to love. Nothing to fight for. You are gone and Tara is going.'

He looked at her for a long space and then, leaning, scooped up a small wad of red clay from the ground.

'Yes, there is something left,' he said, and the ghost of his old smile came back, the smile which mocked himself as well as her. 'Something you love better than me, though you may not know it. You've still got Tara.'

He took her limp hand and pressed the damp clay into it and closed her fingers about it. There was no fever in his hands now, nor in hers. She looked at the red soil for a moment and it meant nothing to her. She looked at him and realized dimly that there was an integrity of spirit in him which was not to be torn apart by her passionate hands, nor by any hands.

If it killed him, he would never leave Melanie. If he burned for Scarlett until the end of his days, he would never take her and he would fight to keep her at a distance. She would never again get through that armour. The words, hospitality and loyalty and honour, meant more to him than she did.

The clay was cold in her hand and she looked at it again.

'Yes,' she said, 'I've still got this.'

At first, the words meant nothing and the clay was only red clay. But unbidden came the thought of the sea of red dirt which surrounded Tara and how very dear it was and how hard she had fought to keep it – how hard she was going to have to fight if she wished to keep it hereafter. She looked at him again and wondered where the hot flood of feeling had gone. She could think but could not feel, not about him nor Tara either, for she was drained of all emotion.

'You need not go,' she said clearly. 'I won't have you all starve, simply because I've thrown myself at your head. It will never happen again.'

She turned away and started back toward the house across the rough fields, twisting her hair into a knot upon her neck. Ashley watched her go and saw her square her small thin shoulders as she went. And that gesture went to his heart, more than any words she had spoken.

CHAPTER XXXII

She was still clutching the ball of red clay when she went up the front steps. She had carefully avoided the back entrance, for Mammy's sharp eyes would certainly have seen that something was greatly amiss. Scarlett did not want to see Mammy or anyone else. She did not feel that she could endure seeing anyone or talking to anyone again. She had no feeling of shame or disappointment or bitterness now, only a weakness of the knees and a great emptiness of heart. She squeezed the clay so tightly it ran out from her clenched fist and she said over and over, parrot-like: 'I've still got this. Yes, I've still got this.'

There was nothing else she did have, nothing but this red land, this land she had been willing to throw away like a torn handkerchief only a few minutes before. Now, it was dear to her again and she wondered dully what madness had possessed her to hold it so lightly. Had Ashley yielded, she could have gone away with him and left family and friends without a backward look but, even in her emptiness, she knew it would have torn her heart to leave these dear red hills and long washed gullies and gaunt black pines. Her thoughts would have turned back to them hungrily until the day she died. Not even Ashley could have filled the empty spaces in her heart where Tara had been uprooted. How wise Ashley was and how well he knew her! He had only to press the damp earth into her hand to bring her to her senses.

She was in the hall preparing to close the door when she heard the sound of horse's hooves and turned to look down the driveway. To have visitors at this of all times was too much. She'd hurry to her room and plead a headache.

But when the carriage came nearer, her flight was checked by her amazement. It was a new carriage, shiny with varnish, and the harness was new too, with bits of polished brass here and there. Strangers, certainly. No one she knew had the money for such a grand new turn-out as this.

She stood in the doorway watching, the cold draught blowing her skirts about her damp ankles. Then the carriage stopped in front of the house and Jonas Wilkerson alighted. Scarlett was so surprised at the sight of their former overseer driving so fine a rig and in so splendid a greatcoat she could not for a moment believe her eyes. Will had told her he looked quite prosperous since he got his new job with the Freedmen's Bureau. Made a lot of money, Will said, swindling the niggers or the government, one or tuther, or confiscating folks' cotton and swearing it was Confederate government cotton. Certainly he never came by all that money honestly in these hard times.

And here he was now, stepping out of an elegant carriage and handing down a woman dressed within an inch of her life. Scarlett saw in a glance that the dress was bright in colour to the point of vulgarity but nevertheless her eyes went over the outfit hungrily. It had been so long since she had even seen stylish new clothes. Well! So hoops aren't so wide this year, she thought, scanning the red plaid gown. And, as she took in the black velvet paletot, how short jackets are! And what a cunning hat! Bonnets must be out of style, for this hat was only an absurd flat red velvet affair, perched on the top of the woman's head like a stiffened pancake. The ribbons did not tie under the chin as bonnet ribbons tied but in the back under the massive bunch of curls which fell from the rear of the hat, curls which Scarlett could not help noticing did not match the woman's hair in either colour or texture.

As the woman stepped to the ground and looked toward the house, Scarlett saw there was something familiar about the rabbity face, caked with white powder.

'Why, it's Emmie Slattery!' she cried, so surprised she spoke the words aloud.

'Yes'm, it's me,' said Emmie, tossing her head with an ingratiating smile and starting toward the steps.

Emmie Slattery! The dirty tow-headed slut whose illegitimate baby Ellen had baptized, Emmie who had given typhoid to Ellen and killed her. This overdressed, common, nasty piece of poor white trash was coming up the steps of Tara, bridling and grinning as if she belonged here. Scarlett thought of Ellen and, in a rush, feeling came back into the emptiness of her mind, a murderous rage so strong it shook her like the ague.

'Get off those steps, you trashy wench!' she cried. 'Get off this land! Get out!'

Emmie's jaw sagged suddenly and she glanced at Jonas who came up with lowering brows. He made an effort at dignity, despite his anger.

'You must not speak that way to my wife,' he said.

'Wife?' said Scarlett, and burst into a laugh that was cutting with contempt. 'High time you made her your wife. Who baptized your other brats after you killed my mother?'

Emmie said 'Oh!' and retreated hastily down the steps, but Jonas stopped her flight toward the carriage with a rough grip on her arm.

'We came out here to pay a call – a friendly call,' he snarled. 'And talk a little business with old friends—'

'Friends?' Scarlett's voice was like a whiplash. 'When were we ever friends with the like of you? The Slatterys lived on our charity and paid it back by killing Mother – and you – you— Pa discharged you about Emmie's brat and you know it. Friends? Get off this place before I call Mr Benteen and Mr Wilkes.'

Under the words, Emmie broke her husband's hold and fled for the carriage, scrambling in with a flash of patent-leather boots with bright-red tops and red tassels.

Now Jonas shook with a fury equal to Scarlett's and his sallow face was as red as an angry turkey gobbler's.

'Still high and mighty, aren't you? Well, I know all about you. I know you haven't got shoes for your feet. I know your father's turned idiot—'

'Get off this place!'

'Oh, you won't sing that way very long. I know you're broke. I know you can't even pay your taxes. I came out here to offer to buy this place from you – to make you a right good offer. Emmie had a hankering to live here. But, by God, I won't give you a cent now! You highflying, bogtrotting Irish will find out who's running things around here when you get sold out for taxes. And I'll buy this place, lock, stock and barrel – furniture and all – and I'll live in it.'

So it was Jonas Wilkerson who wanted Tara – Jonas and Emmie, who in some twisted way thought to even past slights by living in the home where they had been slighted. All her nerves hummed with hate, as they had hummed that day when she shoved the pistol barrel into the Yankee's bearded face and fired. She wished she had that pistol now.

'I'll tear this house down, stone by stone, and burn it and sow every acre with salt before I see either of you put foot over this threshold,' she shouted. 'Get out, I tell you! Get out!'

Jonas glared at her, started to say more and then walked toward the carriage. He climbed in beside his whimpering wife and turned the horse. As they drove off, Scarlett had the impulse to spit at them. She did spit. She knew it was a common, childish gesture but it made her feel better. She wished she had done it while they could see her.

Those damned nigger-lovers daring to come here and taunt her about her poverty! That hound never intended offering her a price for Tara. He just used that as an excuse to come and flaunt himself and Emmie in her face. The dirty Scallawags, the lousy, trashy poor whites, boasting they would live at Tara!

Then sudden terror struck her and her rage melted. God's nightgown! They will come and live here! There was nothing she could do to keep them from buying Tara, nothing to keep them from levying on every mirror and table and bed, on Ellen's shining mahogany and rosewood, and every bit of it precious to her, scarred though it was by the Yankee raiders. And the Robillard silver too. 'I won't let them do it,' thought Scarlett vehemently. 'No, not if I've got to burn the place down! Emmie Slattery will never set her foot on a single bit of flooring Mother ever walked on!'

She closed the door and leaned against it and she was very frightened. More frightened even than she had been that day when Sherman's army was in the house. That day the worst she could fear was that Tara would be burned over her head. But this was worse – these low common creatures living in this house, bragging to their low common friends how they had turned the proud O'Haras out. Perhaps they'd even bring negroes here to dine and sleep. Will had told her Jonas made a great to-do about being equal with the negroes, ate with them, visited in their houses, rode them around with him in his carriage, put his arms around their shoulders.

When she thought of the possibility of this final insult to Tara, her heart pounded so hard she could scarcely breathe. She was trying to get her mind on her problem, trying to figure some way out, but each time she collected her thoughts, fresh gusts of rage and fear shook her. There must be some way out, there must be someone somewhere who had money she could borrow. Money couldn't just dry up and blow away. Somebody had to have money. Then the laughing words of Ashley came back to her:

'Only one person, Rhett Butler . . . who has money.'

Rhett Butler. She walked quickly into the parlour and shut the door behind her. The dim gloom of drawn blinds and winter twilight closed about her. No one would think of hunting for her here and she wanted time to think, undisturbed. The idea which had just occurred to her was so simple she wondered why she had not thought of it before.

'I'll get the money from Rhett. I'll sell him the diamond earbobs. Or I'll borrow the money from him and let him keep the earbobs till I can pay him back.'

For a moment, relief was so great she felt weak. She would pay the taxes and laugh in Jonas Wilkerson's face. But close on this happy thought came relentless knowledge.

'It's not only for this year that I'll need tax money. There's next year and all the years of my life. If I pay up this time, they'll raise the taxes higher next time till they drive me out. If I make a good cotton crop, they'll tax it till I'll get nothing for it or maybe confiscate it outright and say it's Confederate cotton. The Yankees and the scoundrels teamed up with them have got me where they want me. All my life, as long as I live, I'll be afraid they'll get me somehow. All my life I'll be scared and scrambling for money and working myself to death, only to see my work go for nothing and my cotton stolen . . . Just borrowing three hundred dollars for the taxes will be only a stopgap. What I want is to get out of this fix, for good – so I can go to sleep at night without worrying over what's going to happen to me tomorrow, and next month, and next year.'

Her mind ticked on steadily. Coldly and logically an idea grew in her brain. She thought of Rhett, a flash of white teeth against swarthy skin, sardonic black eyes caressing her. She recalled the hot night in Atlanta, close to the end of the siege, when he sat on Aunt Pitty's porch half hidden in the summer darkness, and she felt again the heat of his hand upon her arm as he said: 'I want you more than I have ever wanted any woman – and I've waited longer for you than I've ever waited for any woman.'

'I'll marry him,' she thought coolly. 'And then I'll never have to bother about money again.'

Oh, blessed thought, sweeter than hope of Heaven, never to worry about money again, to know that Tara was safe, that the family was fed and clothed, that she would never again have to bruise herself against stone walls!

She felt very old. The afternoon's events had drained her of all feeling: first the startling news about the taxes, then Ashley and, last, her murderous rage at Jonas Wilkerson. No, there was no emotion left in her. If all her capacity to feel had not been utterly exhausted, something in her would have protested against the plan taking form in her mind, for she hated Rhett as she hated no other person in all the world. But she could not feel. She could only think and her thoughts were very practical.

'I said some terrible things to him that night when he deserted us on the road, but I can make him forget them,' she thought contemptuously, still sure of her power to charm. 'Butter won't melt in my mouth when I'm around him. I'll make him think I always loved him and was just upset and frightened that night. Oh, men are so conceited they'll believe anything that flatters them . . . I must never let him dream what straits we're in, not till I've got him. Oh, he mustn't know! If he even suspected how poor we are, he'd know it was his money I wanted and not himself. After all, there's no way he could know, for even Aunt Pitty doesn't know the worst. And after I've married him, he'll have to help us. He can't let his wife's people starve.'

His wife. Mrs Rhett Butler. Something of repulsion, buried deep beneath her cold thinking, stirred faintly and then was stilled. She remembered the embarrassing and disgusting events of her brief honeymoon with Charles, his fumbling hands, his awkwardness, his incomprehensible emotions – and Wade Hampton.

'I won't think about it now. I'll bother about it after I've married him . . .'

After she had married him. Memory rang a bell. A chill went down her spine. She remembered again that night on Aunt Pitty's porch, remembered how she asked him if he was proposing to her, remembered how hatefully he had laughed and said: 'My dear, I'm not a marrying man.'

Suppose he was still not a marrying man. Suppose, despite all her charms and wiles, he refused to marry her. Suppose – oh, terrible thought! – suppose he had completely forgotten about her and was chasing after some other woman.

'I want you more than I have ever wanted any woman . . .'

Scarlett's nails dug into her palms as she clenched her fists. 'If he's forgotten me, I'll make him remember me. I'll make him want me again.'

And, if he would not marry her but still wanted her, there was a way to get the money. After all, he had once asked her to be his mistress.

In the dim greyness of the parlour she fought a quick decisive battle with the three most binding ties of her soul – the memory of Ellen, the teachings of her religion and her love for Ashley. She knew that what she had in her mind must be hideous to her mother even in that warm far-off Heaven where she surely was. She knew that fornication was a mortal sin. And she knew that, loving Ashley as she did, her plan was doubly prostitution.

But all these things went down before the merciless coldness of her mind and the goad of desperation. Ellen was dead and perhaps death gave an understanding of all things. Religion forbade fornication on pain of hell fire, but if the Church thought she was going to leave one stone unturned in saving Tara and saving the family from starving – well, let the Church bother about that. She wouldn't. At least, not now. And Ashley – Ashley didn't want her. Yes, he did want her. The memory of his warm mouth on hers told her that. But he would never take her away with him. Strange that going away with Ashley did not seem like a sin, but with Rhett—

In the dull twilight of the winter afternoon she came to the end of the long road which had begun the night Atlanta fell. She had set her feet upon that road a spoiled, selfish and untried girl, full of youth, warm of emotion, easily bewildered by life. Now, at the end of the road, there was nothing left of that girl. Hunger and hard labour, fear and constant strain, the terrors of war and the terrors of Reconstruction had taken away all warmth and youth and softness. About the core of her being, a shell of hardness had formed and, little by little, layer by layer, the shell had thickened during the endless months.

But until this very day, two hopes had been left to sustain her. She had hoped that, the war being over, life would gradually resume its old face. She had hoped that Ashley's return would bring back some meaning into life. Now both hopes were gone. The sight of Jonas Wilkerson in the front walk of Tara had made her realize that for her, for the whole South, the war would never end. The bitterest fighting, the most brutal retaliations, were just beginning. And Ashley was imprisoned forever by words which were stronger than any jail.

Peace had failed her and Ashley had failed her, both in the same day, and it was as if the last crevice in the shell had been sealed, the final layer hardened. She had become what Grandma Fontaine had counselled against, a woman who had seen the worst and so had nothing else to fear. Not life nor Mother nor loss of love nor public opinion. Only hunger and her nightmare dream of hunger could make her afraid.

A curious sense of lightness, of freedom, pervaded her now that she had finally hardened her heart against all that bound her to the old days and the old Scarlett. She had made her decision and, thank God, she wasn't afraid. She had nothing to lose and her mind was made up.

If she could only coax Rhett into marrying her, all would be perfect. But if she couldn't – well, she'd get the money just the same. For a brief moment she wondered with impersonal curiosity what would be expected of a mistress. Would Rhett insist on keeping her in Atlanta as people said he kept the Watling woman? If he made her stay in Atlanta, he'd have to pay well – pay enough to balance what her absence from Tara would be worth. Scarlett was very ignorant of the hidden side of men's lives and had no way of knowing just what the arrangement might involve. And she wondered if she would have a baby. That would be distinctly terrible.

'I won't think of that now. I'll think of it later,' and she pushed the unwelcome idea into the back of her mind lest it shake her resolution. She'd tell the family tonight she was going to Atlanta to try to borrow money, to try to mortgage the farm if necessary. That would be all they needed to know until such an evil day when they might find out differently.

With the thought of action, her head went up and her shoulders went back. This affair was not going to be easy, she knew. Formerly, it had been Rhett who asked for her favours and she who held the power. Now she was the beggar and a beggar in no position to dictate terms.

'But I won't go to him like a beggar. I'll go like a queen granting favours. He'll never know.'

She walked to the long pier-glass and looked at herself, her head held high. And she saw framed in the cracking gilt moulding a stranger. It was as if she were really seeing herself for the first time in a year. She had glanced in the mirror every morning to see that her face was clean and her hair tidy but she had always been too pressed by other things to really see herself. But this stranger! Surely this thin hollow-cheeked woman couldn't be Scarlett O'Hara! Scarlett O'Hara had a pretty, coquettish, high-spirited face. This face at which she stared was not pretty at all and had none of the charm she remembered so well. It was white and strained and the black brows above slanting green eyes swooped up startlingly against the white skin like frightened bird's wings. There was a hard and hunted look about this face.

'I'm not pretty enough to get him!' she thought, and desperation came back to her. 'I'm thin – oh, I'm terribly thin!'

She patted her cheeks, felt frantically at her collar-bones, feeling them stand out through her basque. And her breasts were so small, almost as small as Melanie's. She'd have to put ruffles in her bosom to make them look larger and she had always had contempt for girls who resorted to such subterfuges. Ruffles! That brought up another thought. Her clothes. She looked down at her dress, spreading its mended folds wide between her hands. Rhett liked women who were well dressed, fashionably dressed. She remembered with longing the flounced green dress she had worn when she first came out of mourning, the dress she wore with the green plumed bonnet he had brought her, and she recalled the approving compliments he had paid her. She remembered, too, with hate sharpened by envy the red plaid dress, the red-topped boots with tassels and the pancake hat of Emmie Slattery. They were gaudy but they were new and fashionable and certainly they caught the eye. And, oh, how she wanted to catch the eye! Especially the eye of Rhett Butler! If he should see her in her old clothes, he'd know everything was wrong at Tara. And he must not know.

What a fool she had been to think she could go to Atlanta and have him for the asking, she with her scrawny neck and hungry cat eyes and raggedy dress! If she hadn't been able to pry a proposal from him at the height of her beauty, when she had her prettiest clothes, how could she expect to get one now when she was ugly and dressed tackily? If Miss Pitty's story was true, he must have more money than anyone in Atlanta and probably had his pick of all the pretty ladies, good and bad. 'Well,' she thought grimly, 'I've got something that most pretty ladies haven't got – and that's a mind that's made up. And if I had just one nice dress—'

There wasn't a nice dress in Tara or a dress which hadn't been turned twice and mended.

'That's that,' she thought, disconsolately looking down at the floor. She saw Ellen's moss-green velvet carpet, now worn and scuffed and torn and spotted from the numberless men who had slept upon it, and the sight depressed her more, for it made her realize that Tara was just as ragged as she. The whole darkening room depressed her and, going to the window, she raised the sash, unlatched the shutters and let the last light of the wintry sunset into the room. She closed the window and leaned her head against the velvet curtains and looked out across the bleak pasture toward the dark cedars of the burying-ground.

The moss-green velvet curtains felt prickly and soft beneath her cheek and she rubbed her face against them gratefully, like a cat. And then suddenly she looked at them.

A minute later, she was dragging a heavy marble-topped table across the floor, its rusty castors screeching in protest. She rolled the table under the window, gathered up her skirts, climbed on it and tiptoed to reach the heavy curtain-pole. It was almost out of her reach and she jerked at it so impatiently the nails came out of the wood, and the curtains, pole and all, fell to the floor with a clatter.

As if by magic, the door of the parlour opened and the wide black face of Mammy appeared, ardent curiosity and deepest suspicion evident in every wrinkle. She looked disapprovingly at Scarlett, poised on the table top, her skirts above her knees, ready to leap to the floor. There was a look of excitement and triumph on her face which brought sudden distrust to Mammy.

'Whut you up to wid Miss Ellen's po'teers?' she demanded.

'What are you up to listening outside doors?' asked Scarlett, leaping nimbly to the floor and gathering up a length of the heavy dusty velvet.

'Dat ain' needer hyah nor dar,' countered Mammy, girding herself for combat. 'You ain' got no bizness wid Miss Ellen's po'teers, juckin' de poles plum outer de wood, an' drappin' dem on de flo' in de dust. Miss Ellen set gret sto' by dem po'teers an' Ah ain' 'tendin' ter have you muss dem up dat way.'

Scarlett turned green eyes on Mammy, eyes which were feverishly gay, eyes which looked like the bad little girl of the good old days Mammy sighed about.

'Scoot up to the attic and get my box of dress patterns, Mammy,' she cried, giving her a slight shove. 'I'm going to have a new dress.'

Mammy was torn between indignation at the very idea of her two hundred pounds scooting anywhere, much less to the attic, and the dawning of a horrid suspicion. Quickly she snatched the curtain lengths from Scarlett, holding them against her monumental, sagging breasts as if they were holy relics.

'Not outer Miss Ellen's po'teers is you gwine have a new dress, ef dat's whut you figgerin' on. Not w'ile Ah got breaf in mah body.'

For a moment the expression Mammy was wont to describe to herself as 'bullheaded' flitted over her young mistress' face and then it passed into a smile, so difficult for Mammy to resist. But it did not fool the old woman. She knew Miss Scarlett was employing that smile merely to get around her and in this matter she was determined not to be gotten around.

'Mammy, don't be mean. I'm going to Atlanta to borrow some money and I've got to have a new dress.'

'You doan need no new dress. Ain' no other ladies got new dresses. Dey weahs dey ole ones an' dey weahs dem proudfully. Ain' no reason why Miss Ellen's chile kain weah rags ef she wants ter, an' eve'ybody respec' her lak she wo' silk.'

The bullheaded expression began to creep back. Lordy, 'twus right funny how de older Miss Scarlett git de mo' she look lak Mist' Gerald and de less lak Miss Ellen!

'Now, Mammy, you know Aunt Pitty wrote us that Miss Fanny Elsing is getting married this Saturday, and of course I'll go to the wedding. And I'll need a new dress to wear.'

'De dress you got on'll be jes' as nice as Miss Fanny's weddin' dress. Miss Pitty done wrote dat de Elsings mighty po'.'

'But I've got to have a new dress! Mammy, you don't know how we need money. The taxes—'

'Yas'm, Ah knows all 'bout de taxes but—'

'You do?'

'Well'm, Gawd give me ears, din' He, an' ter hear wid? Specially w'en Mist' Will doan never tek trouble ter close de do'.'

Was there nothing Mammy did not overhear? Scarlett wondered how that ponderous body which shook the floors could move with such savage stealth when its owner wished to eavesdrop.

'Well, if you heard all that, I suppose you heard Jonas Wilkerson and that Emmie—'

'Yas'm,' said Mammy with smouldering eyes.

'Well, don't be a mule, Mammy. Don't you see I've got to go to Atlanta and get money for the taxes? I've got to get some money. I've got to do it!' She hammered one small fist into the other. 'Name of God, Mammy, they'll turn us all out into the road and then where'll we go? Are you going to argue with me about a little matter of Mother's curtains when that trash Emmie Slattery who killed Mother is fixing to move into this house and sleep in the bed Mother slept in?'

Mammy shifted from one foot to another like a restive elephant. She had a dim feeling that she was being got around.

'No'm, Ah ain' wantin' ter see trash in Miss Ellen's house or us all in de road but—' She fixed Scarlett with a suddenly accusing eye. 'Who is you fixin' ter git money frum dat you needs a new dress?'

'That,' said Scarlett, taken aback, 'is my own business.'

Mammy looked at her piercingly, just as she had done when Scarlett was small and had tried unsuccessfully to palm off plausible excuses for misdeeds. She seemed to be reading her mind and Scarlett dropped her eyes unwillingly, the first feeling of guilt at her intended conduct creeping over her.

'So you needs a spang new pretty dress ter borry money wid. Dat doan lissen jes' right ter me. An' you ain' sayin' whar de money ter come frum.'

'I'm not saying anything,' said Scarlett indignantly. 'It's my own business. Are you going to give me that curtain and help me make the dress?'

'Yas'm,' said Mammy softly, capitulating with a suddenness which aroused all the suspicion in Scarlett's mind. 'Ah gwine he'p you mek it an' Ah specs we mout git a petticoat outer de satin linin' of de po'teers an' trim a p'ar pantalets wid de lace cuttin's.'

She handed the velvet curtain back to Scarlett and a sly smile spread over her face.

'Miss Melly gwine ter 'Lanta wid you, Miss Scarlett?'

'No,' said Scarlett sharply, beginning to realize what was coming. 'I'm going by myself.'

'Dat's whut you thinks,' said Mammy firmly, 'but Ah is gwine wid you an' dat new dress. Yas, Ma'm, eve'y step of de way.'

For an instant Scarlett envisaged her trip to Atlanta and her conversation with Rhett with Mammy glowering chaperonage like a large black Cerberus in the background. She smiled again and put a hand on Mammy's arm.

'Mammy, darling, you're sweet to want to go with me and help me, but how on earth would the folks here get on without you? You know you just about run Tara.'

'Huh!' said Mammy. 'Doan do no good ter sweet talk me, Miss Scarlett. Ah been knowin' you sence Ah put de fust pa'r of diapers on you. Ah's said Ah's gwine ter 'Lanta wid you an' gwine Ah is. Miss Ellen be tuhnin' in her grabe at you gwine up dar by yo'seff wid dat town full up wid Yankees an' free niggers an' sech like.'

'But I'll be at Aunt Pittypat's,' Scarlett offered frantically.

'Miss Pittypat a fine woman an' she think she see eve'ything but she doan,' said Mammy, and turning with the majestic air of having closed the interview, she went into the hall. The boards trembled as she called:

'Prissy, chile! Fly up de stairs an' fotch Miss Scarlett's pattun box frum de attic an' try an' fine de scissors widout takin' all night 'bout it.'

'This is a fine mess,' thought Scarlett dejectedly. 'I'd as soon have a bloodhound after me.'

After supper had been cleared away, Scarlett and Mammy spread patterns on the dining-room table while Suellen and Carreen busily ripped satin linings from curtains and Melanie brushed the velvet with a clean hairbrush to remove the dust. Gerald, Will and Ashley sat about the room smoking, smiling at the feminine tumult. A feeling of pleasurable excitement which seemed to emanate from Scarlett was on them all, an excitement they could not understand. There was colour in Scarlett's face and a bright hard glitter in her eyes and she laughed a good deal. Her laughter pleased them all, for it had been months since they had heard her really laugh. Especially did it please Gerald. His eyes were less vague than usual as they followed her swishing figure about the room and he patted her approvingly whenever she was within reach. The girls were as excited as if preparing for a ball and they ripped and cut and basted as if making a ball dress of their own.

Scarlett was going to Atlanta to borrow money or to mortgage Tara if necessary. But what was a mortgage, after all? Scarlett said they could easily pay it off out of next year's cotton and have money left over, and she said it with such finality they did not think to question. And when they asked who was going to lend the money she said, 'Layovers catch meddlers,' so archly they all laughed and teased her about her millionaire friend.

'It must be Captain Rhett Butler,' said Melanie slyly, and they exploded with mirth at this absurdity, knowing how Scarlett hated him and never failed to refer to him as 'that skunk, Rhett Butler'.

But Scarlett did not laugh at this and Ashley, who had laughed, stopped abruptly as he saw Mammy shoot a quick, guarded glance at Scarlett.

Suellen, moved to generosity by the party spirit of the occasion, produced her Irish-lace collar, somewhat worn but still pretty, and Carreen insisted that Scarlett wear her slippers to Atlanta, for they were in better condition than any others at Tara. Melanie begged Mammy to leave her enough velvet scraps to re-cover the frame of her battered bonnet and brought shouts of laughter when she said the old rooster was going to part with his gorgeous bronze and green-black tail feathers unless he took to the swamp immediately.

Scarlett, watching the flying fingers, heard the laughter and looked at them all with concealed bitterness and contempt.

'They haven't an idea what is really happening to me or to themselves or to the South. They still think, in spite of everything, that nothing really dreadful can happen to any of them because they are who they are, O'Haras, Wilkeses, Hamiltons. Even the darkies feel that way. Oh, they're all fools! They'll never realize! They'll go right on thinking and living as they always have, and nothing will change them. Melly can dress in rags and pink cotton and even help me murder a man but it doesn't change her. She's still the shy well-bred Mrs Wilkes, the perfect lady! And Ashley can see death and war and be wounded and lie in jail and come home to less than nothing and still be the same gentleman he was when he had all Twelve Oaks behind him. Will is different. He knows how things really are but then Will never had anything much to lose. And as for Suellen and Carreen – they think all this is just a temporary matter. They don't change to meet changed conditions because they think it'll all be over soon. They think God is going to work a miracle especially for their benefit. But He won't. The only miracle that's going to be worked around here is the one I'm going to work on Rhett Butler . . . They won't change. Maybe they can't change. I'm the only one who's changed – and I wouldn't have changed if I could have helped it.'

Mammy finally turned the men out of the dining-room and closed the door, so the fitting could begin. Pork helped Gerald upstairs to bed and

Ashley and Will were left alone in the lamplight in the front hall. They were silent for a while and Will chewed his tobacco like a placid ruminant animal. But his mild face was far from placid.

'This goin' to Atlanta,' he said at last in a slow voice, 'I don't like it. Not one bit.'

Ashley looked at Will quickly and then looked away, saying nothing but wondering if Will had the same awful suspicion which was haunting him. But that was impossible. Will didn't know what had taken place in the orchard that afternoon and how it had driven Scarlett to desperation. Will couldn't have noticed Mammy's face when Rhett Butler's name was mentioned and, besides, Will didn't know about Rhett's money or his foul reputation. At least, Ashley did not think he could know these things, but since coming back to Tara he had realized that Will, like Mammy, seemed to know things without being told, to sense them before they happened. There was something ominous in the air, exactly what Ashley did not know, but he was powerless to save Scarlett from it. She had not met his eyes once that evening and the hard bright gaiety with which she had treated him was frightening. The suspicions which tore at him were too terrible to be put into words. He did not have the right to insult her by asking if they were true. He clenched his fists. He had no rights at all where she was concerned; this afternoon he had forfeited them all, forever. He could not help her. No one could help her. But when he thought of Mammy and the look of grim determination she wore as she cut into the velvet curtains, he was cheered a little. Mammy would take care of Scarlett whether Scarlett wished it or not.

'I have caused all this,' he thought despairingly. 'I have driven her to this.'

He remembered the way she had squared her shoulders when she turned away from him that afternoon, remembered the stubborn lift of her head. His heart went out to her, torn with his own helplessness, wrenched with admiration. He knew she had no such word in her vocabulary as gallantry, knew she would have stared blankly if he had told her she was the most gallant soul he had ever known. He knew she would not understand how many truly fine things he ascribed to her when he thought of her as gallant. He knew that she took life as it came, opposed her tough-fibred mind to whatever obstacles there might be, fought on with a determination that would not recognize defeat and kept on fighting even when she saw defeat was inevitable.

But, for four years, he had seen others who had refused to recognize defeat, men who rode gaily into sure disaster because they were gallant. And they had been defeated, just the same.

He thought as he stared at Will in the shadowy hall that he had never known such gallantry as the gallantry of Scarlett O'Hara going forth to conquer the world in her mother's velvet curtains and the tail feathers of a rooster.

Chapter XXXIII

A cold wind was blowing stiffly and the scudding clouds overhead were the deep grey of slate when Scarlett and Mammy stepped from the train in Atlanta the next afternoon. The depot had not been rebuilt since the burning of the city and they alighted amid cinders and mud a few yards above the blackened ruins which marked the site. Habit strong upon her, Scarlett looked about for Uncle Peter and Pitty's carriage, for she had always been met by them when returning from Tara to Atlanta during the war years. Then she caught herself with a sniff at her own absent-mindedness. Naturally, Peter wasn't there for she had given Aunt Pitty no warning of her coming and, moreover, she remembered that one of the old lady's letters had dealt tearfully with the death of the old nag Peter had ''quired' in Macon to bring her back to Atlanta after the surrender.

She looked about the rutted and cut-up space around the depot for the equipage of some old friend or acquaintance who might drive them to Aunt Pitty's house but she recognized no one, black or white. Probably none of her old friends owned carriages now, if what Pitty had written them was true. Times were so hard it was difficult to feed and lodge humans, much less animals. Most of Pitty's friends, like herself, were afoot these days.

There were a few wagons loading at the freight cars and several mud-splashed buggies with rough-looking strangers at the reins but only two carriages. One was a closed carriage, the other open and occupied by a well-dressed woman and a Yankee officer. Scarlett drew in her breath sharply at the sight of the uniform. Although Pitty had written that Atlanta was garrisoned and the streets full of soldiers, the first sight of the bluecoat startled and frightened her. It was hard to remember that the war was over and that this man would not pursue her, rob her and insult her.

The comparative emptiness around the train took her mind back to that morning in 1862 when she had come to Atlanta as a young widow, swathed in crêpe and wild with boredom. She recalled how crowded this space had been with wagons and carriages and ambulances and how noisy with drivers swearing and yelling and people calling greetings to friends. She sighed for the light-hearted excitement of the war days and sighed again at the thought of walking all the way to Aunt Pitty's house. But she was hopeful that once on Peachtree Street, she might meet someone she knew who would give them a ride.

As she stood looking about her a saddle-coloured negro of middle age drove the closed carriage toward her and, leaning from the box, questioned: 'Cah'ige, lady? Two bits fer any whar in 'Lanta.'

Mammy threw him an annihilating glance.

'A hired hack!' she mumbled. 'Nigger, does you know who we is?'

Mammy was a country negro but she had not always been a country negro and she knew that no chaste woman ever rode in a hired conveyance

– especially a closed carriage – without the escort of some male member of her family. Even the presence of a negro maid would not satisfy the conventions. She gave Scarlett a glare as she saw her look longingly at the hack.

'Come 'way frum dar, Miss Scarlett! A hired hack an' a free issue nigger! Well, dat's a good combination.'

'Ah ain' no free issue nigger,' declared the driver with heat. 'Ah b'longs ter Ole Miss Talbot an' disyere her cah'ige an' Ah drives it ter mek money fer us.'

'Whut Miss Talbot is dat?'

'Miss Suzannah Talbot of Milledgeville. Us done move up hyah affer Ole Marse wuz kilt.'

'Does you know her, Miss Scarlett?'

'No,' said Scarlett, regretfully. 'I know so few Milledgeville folks.'

'Den us'll walk,' said Mammy sternly. 'Drive on, nigger.'

She picked up the carpet-bag which held Scarlett's new velvet frock and bonnet and nightgown and tucked the neat bandana bundle that contained her own belongings under her arm and shepherded Scarlett across the wet expanse of cinders. Scarlett did not argue the matter, much as she preferred to ride, for she wished no disagreement with Mammy. Ever since yesterday afternoon when Mammy had caught her with the velvet curtains, there had been an alert suspicious look in her eyes which Scarlett did not like. It was going to be difficult to escape from her chaperonage and she did not intend to rouse Mammy's fighting blood before it was absolutely necessary.

As they walked along the narrow sidewalk toward Peachtree, Scarlett was dismayed and sorrowful, for Atlanta looked so devastated and different from what she remembered. They passed beside what had been the Atlanta Hotel where Rhett and Uncle Henry had lived and of that elegant hostelry there remained only a shell, a part of the blackened walls. The warehouses which had bordered the train tracks for a quarter of a mile and held tons of military supplies had not been rebuilt and their rectangular foundations looked dreary under the dark sky. Without the wall of buildings on either side and with the car-shed gone, the railroad tracks seemed bare and exposed. Somewhere amid these ruins, indistinguishable from the others, lay what remained of her own warehouse on the property Charles had left her. Uncle Henry had paid last year's taxes on it for her. She'd have to repay that money some time. That was something else to worry about.

As they turned the corner into Peachtree Street and she looked toward Five Points, she cried out with shock. Despite all Frank had told her about the town burning to the ground, she had never really visualized complete destruction. In her mind the town she loved so well still stood full of close-packed buildings and fine houses. But this Peachtree Street she was looking upon was so denuded of landmarks it was as unfamiliar as if she had never seen it before. This muddy street down which she had driven a thousand times during the war, along which she had fled with ducked head and fear-quickened legs when shells burst over her during the siege, this street she had last seen in the heat and hurry and anguish of the day of the retreat, was so strange-looking she felt like crying.

Though many new buildings had sprung up in the year since Sherman marched out of the burning town and the Confederates returned, there were still wide vacant lots around Five Points where heaps of smudged broken bricks lay amid a jumble of rubbish, dead weeds and broomsedge. There were the remains of a few buildings she remembered, roofless brick walls through which the dull daylight shone, glassless windows gaping, chimneys towering lonesomely. Here and there her eyes gladly picked out a familiar store which had partly survived shell and fire and had been repaired, the fresh red of new brick glaring bright against the smut of the old walls. On new store fronts and new office windows she saw the welcome names of men she knew but more often the names were unfamiliar, especially the dozens of shingles of strange doctors and lawyers and cotton merchants. Once she had known practically everyone in Atlanta and the sight of so many strange names depressed her. But she was cheered by the sight of new buildings going up all along the street.

There were dozens of them and several were three stories high! Everywhere building was going on, for as she looked down the street, trying to adjust her mind to the new Atlanta, she heard the blithe sound of hammers and saws, noticed scaffolding rising and saw men climbing ladders with hods of bricks on their shoulders. She looked down the street she loved so well and her eyes misted a little.

'They burned you,' she thought, 'and they laid you flat. But they didn't lick you. They couldn't lick you. You'll grow back just as big and sassy as you used to be!'

As she walked along Peachtree, followed by the waddling Mammy, she found the sidewalks just as crowded as they were at the height of the war and there was the same air of rush and bustle about the resurrecting town which had made her blood sing when she came here, so long ago, on her first visit to Aunt Pitty. There seemed to be just as many vehicles wallowing in the mud-holes as there had been then, except that there were no Confederate ambulances, and just as many horses and mules tethered to hitching-racks in front of the wooden awnings of the stores. Though the sidewalks were jammed, the faces she saw were as unfamiliar as the signs overhead, new people, many rough-looking men and tawdrily dressed women. The streets were black with loafing negroes who leaned against walls or sat on the kerbing watching vehicles go past with the naïve curiosity of children at a circus parade.

'Free issue country niggers,' snorted Mammy. 'Ain' never seed a proper cah'ige in dere lives. An' impident-lookin', too.'

They were impudent-looking, Scarlett agreed, for they stared at her in an insolent manner, but she forgot them in the renewed shock of seeing blue uniforms. The town was full of Yankee soldiers, on horses, afoot, in army wagons, loafing on the street, reeling out of bar-rooms.

'I'll never get used to them,' she thought, clenching her fists. 'Never!' and over her shoulder: 'Hurry, Mammy, let's get out of this crowd.'

'Soon's Ah kick dis black trash outer mah way,' answered Mammy loudly, swinging the carpet-bag at a black buck who loitered tantalizingly in front of her and making him leap aside. 'Ah doan lak disyere town, Miss Scarlett. It's too full of Yankees an' cheap free issue.'

'It's nicer where it isn't so crowded. When we get across Five Points, it won't be so bad.'

They picked their way across the slippery stepping-stones that bridged the mud of Decatur Street and continued up Peachtree, through a thinning crowd. When they reached Wesley Chapel where Scarlett had paused to catch her breath that day in 1864 when she had run for Dr Meade, she looked at it and laughed aloud, shortly and grimly. Mammy's quick old eyes sought hers with suspicion and question but her curiosity went unsatisfied. Scarlett was recalling with contempt the terror which had ridden her that day. She had been crawling with fear, rotten with fear, terrified by the Yankees, terrified by the approaching birth of Beau. Now she wondered how she could have been so frightened, frightened like a child at a loud noise. And what a child she had been to think that Yankees and fire and defeat were the worst things that could happen to her! What trivialities they were beside Ellen's death and Gerald's vagueness, beside hunger and cold and back-breaking work and the living nightmare of insecurity. How easy she would find it now to be brave before an invading army, but how hard to face the danger that threatened Tara! No, she would never again be afraid of anything except poverty.

Up Peachtree came a closed carriage and Scarlett went to the kerb eagerly to see if she knew the occupant, for Aunt Pitty's house was still several blocks away. She and Mammy leaned forward as the carriage came abreast and Scarlett, with a smile arranged, almost called out when a woman's head appeared for a moment at the window – a too bright red head beneath a fine fur hat. Scarlett took a step back as mutual recognition leaped into both faces. It was Belle Watling and Scarlett had a glimpse of nostrils distended with dislike before she disappeared again. Strange that Belle's should be the first familiar face she saw.

'Who dat?' questioned Mammy suspiciously. 'She knowed you but she din' bow. Ah ain' never seed ha'r dat colour in mah life. Not even in de Tarleton fambly. It look – well, it look dyed ter me!'

'It is,' said Scarlett shortly, walking faster.

'Does you know a dyed-ha'rd woman? Ah ast you who she is.'

'She's the town bad woman,' said Scarlett briefly, 'and I give you my word I don't know her, so shut up.'

'Gawdlmighty!' breathed Mammy, her jaw dropping as she looked after the carriage with passionate curiosity. She had not seen a professional bad woman since she left Savannah with Ellen more than twenty years before and she wished ardently that she had observed Belle more closely.

'She sho dressed up fine an' got a fine cah'ige an' coachman,' she muttered. 'Ah doan know whut de Lawd thinkin' bout, lettin' de bad women flurrish lak dat w'en us good folks is hongry an' mos' barefoot.'

'The Lord stopped thinking about us years ago,' said Scarlett savagely. 'And don't go telling me Mother is turning in her grave to hear me say it, either.'

She wanted to feel superior and virtuous about Belle but she could not. If her plans went well, she might be on the same footing with Belle and supported by the same man. While she did not regret her decision one whit, the matter in its true light discomfited her. 'I won't think of it now,' she told herself and hurried her steps.

They passed the lot where the Meade house had stood and there remained of it only a forlorn pair of stone steps and a walk, leading up to nothing. Where the Whitings' home had been was bare ground. Even the foundation stones and the brick chimneys were gone and there were wagon tracks where they had been carted away. The brick house of the Elsings still stood, with a new roof and a new second floor. The Bonnell home, awkwardly patched and roofed with rude boards instead of shingles, managed to look liveable for all its battered appearance. But in neither house was there a face at the window or a figure on the porch, and Scarlett was glad. She did not want to talk to anyone now.

Then the new slate roof of Aunt Pitty's house came in view with its red-brick walls, and Scarlett's heart throbbed. How good of the Lord not to level it beyond repair! Coming out of the front yard was Uncle Peter, a market basket on his arm, and when he saw Scarlett and Mammy trudging along, a wide, incredulous smile split his black face.

'I could kiss the old black fool, I'm so glad to see him,' thought Scarlett joyfully, and she called: 'Run get Auntie's swoon bottle, Peter! It's really me!'

That night the inevitable hominy and dried peas were on Aunt Pitty's supper table and, as Scarlett ate them, she made a vow that these two dishes would never appear on her table when she had money again. And, no matter what price she had to pay, she was going to have money again, more than just enough to pay the taxes on Tara. Somehow, some day she was going to have plenty of money if she had to commit murder to get it.

In the yellow lamplight of the dining-room, she asked Pitty about her finances, hoping against hope that Charles' family might be able to lend her the money she needed. The questions were none too subtle but Pitty, in her pleasure at having a member of the family to talk to, did not even notice the bald way the questions were put. She plunged with tears into the details of her misfortunes. She just didn't know where her farms and town property and money had gone but everything had slipped away. At least, that was what Brother Henry told her. He hadn't been able to pay the taxes on her estate. Everything except the house she was living in was gone and Pitty did not stop to think that the house had never been hers but was the joint property of Melanie and Scarlett. Brother Henry could just barely pay taxes on this house. He gave her a little something every month to live on and, though it was very humiliating to take money from him, she had to do it.

'Brother Henry says he doesn't know how he'll make ends meet with the load he's carrying and the taxes so high, but, of course, he's probably lying and has loads of money and just won't give me much.'

Scarlett knew Uncle Henry wasn't lying. The few letters she had had from him in connection with Charles' property showed that. The old lawyer was battling valiantly to save the house and the one piece of downtown property where the warehouses had been, so Wade and Scarlett would have something left from the wreckage. Scarlett knew he was carrying these taxes for her at a great sacrifice.

'Of course, he hasn't any money,' thought Scarlett grimly. 'Well, check him and Aunt Pitty off my list. There's nobody left but Rhett. I'll have to do it. I must do it. But I mustn't think about it now . . . I must get her to talking about Rhett so I can casually suggest to her to invite him to call tomorrow.'

She smiled and squeezed the plump palms of Aunt Pitty between her own.

'Darling Auntie,' she said, 'don't let's talk about distressing things like money any more. Let's forget about them and talk of pleasanter things. You must tell me all the news about our old friends. How is Mrs Merriwether, and Maybelle? I heard that Maybelle's little Creole came home safely. How are the Elsings and Dr and Mrs Meade?'

Pittypat brightened at the change of subject and her baby face stopped quivering with tears. She gave detailed reports about old neighbours, what they were doing and wearing and eating and thinking. She told with accents of horror how, before René Picard came home from the war, Mrs Merriwether and Maybelle had made ends meet by baking pies and selling them to the Yankee soldiers. Imagine that! Sometimes there were two dozen Yankees standing in the back yard of the Merriwether home, waiting for the baking to be finished. Now that René was home, he drove an old wagon to the Yankee camp every day and sold cakes and pies and beaten biscuits to the soldiers. Mrs Merriwether said that when she made a little more money she was going to open a bake-shop downtown. Pitty did not wish to criticize but after all— As for herself, said Pitty, she would rather starve than have such commerce with Yankees. She made a point of giving a disdainful look to every soldier she met, and crossed to the other side of the street in as insulting a manner as possible, though, she said, this was quite inconvenient in wet weather. Scarlett gathered that no sacrifice, even though it be muddy shoes, was too great to show loyalty to the Confederacy, in so far as Miss Pittypat was concerned.

Mrs Meade and the doctor had lost their home when the Yankees fired the town and they had neither the money nor the heart to rebuild, now that Phil and Darcy were dead. Mrs Meade said she never wanted a home again, for what was a home without children and grandchildren in it? They were very lonely and had gone to live with the Elsings, who had rebuilt the damaged part of their home. Mr and Mrs Whiting had a room there, too, and Mrs Bonnell was talking of moving in, if she was fortunate enough to rent her house to a Yankee officer and his family.

'But how do they all squeeze in?' cried Scarlett. 'There's Mrs Elsing and Fanny and Hugh—'

'Mrs Elsing and Fanny sleep in the parlour and Hugh in the attic,' explained Pitty, who knew the domestic arrangements of all her friends. 'My dear, I do hate to tell you this but – Mrs Elsing calls them "paying guests" but,' Pitty dropped her voice, 'they are really nothing at all except boarders. Mrs Elsing is running a boarding-house! Isn't that dreadful?'

'I think it's wonderful,' said Scarlett shortly. 'I only wish we'd had "paying guests" at Tara for the last year instead of free boarders. Maybe we wouldn't be so poor now.'

'Scarlett, how can you say such things? Your poor mother must be turning in her grave at the very thought of charging money for the hospitality of Tara! Of course, Mrs Elsing was simply forced to it because, while she took in fine sewing and Fanny painted china and Hugh made a little money peddling firewood, they couldn't make ends meet. Imagine darling Hugh forced to peddle wood! And he all set to be a fine lawyer! I could just cry at the things our boys are reduced to!'

Scarlett thought of the rows of cotton beneath the glaring coppery sky at Tara and how her back had ached as she bent over them. She remembered the feel of plough handles between her inexperienced, blistered palms and she felt that Hugh Elsing was deserving of no special sympathy. What an innocent old fool Pitty was and, despite the ruin all around her, how sheltered!

'If he doesn't like peddling, why doesn't he practise law? Or isn't there any law practice left in Atlanta?'

'Oh, dear, yes! There's plenty of law practice. Practically everybody is suing everybody else these days. With everything burned down and boundary lines wiped out, no one knows just where their land begins or ends. But you can't get any pay for suing because nobody has any money. So Hugh sticks to his peddling . . . Oh, I almost forgot! Did I write you? Fanny Elsing is getting married tomorrow night and, of course, you must attend. Mrs Elsing will be only too pleased to have you when she knows you're in town. I do hope you have some other frock besides that one. Not that it isn't a very sweet frock, darling, but – well, it does look a bit worn. Oh, you have a pretty frock? I'm so glad, because it's going to be the first real wedding we've had in Atlanta since before the town fell. Cake and wine and dancing afterward, though I don't know how the Elsings can afford it, they are so poor.'

'Who is Fanny marrying? I thought after Dallas McLure was killed at Gettysburg—'

'Darling, you mustn't criticize Fanny. Everybody isn't as loyal to the dead as you are to poor Charlie. Let me see. What is his name? I can never remember names – Tom somebody. I knew his mother well, we went to LaGrange Female Institute together. She was a Tomlinson from LaGrange and her mother was – let me see . . . Perkins? Parkins? Parkinson! That's it. From Sparta. A very good family but just the same – well, I know I shouldn't say it but I don't see how Fanny can bring herself to marry him!'

'Does he drink or—'

'Dear, no! His character is perfect but, you see, he was wounded low down, by a bursting shell, and it did something to his legs – makes them – makes them, well, I hate to use the word but it makes him spraddle. It gives him a very vulgar appearance when he walks – well, it doesn't look very pretty. I don't see why she's marrying him.'

'Girls have to marry someone.'

'Indeed, they do not,' said Pitty, ruffling. 'I never had to.'

'Now, darling, I didn't mean you! Everybody knows how popular you were and still are! Why, old Judge Carlton used to throw sheep's eyes at you till I—'

'Oh, Scarlett, hush! That old fool!' giggled Pitty, good humour restored. 'But, after all, Fanny was so popular she could have made a better match and I don't believe she loves this Tom what's-his-name. I don't believe she's ever gotten over Dallas McLure getting killed, but she's not like you, darling. You've remained so faithful to dear Charlie, though you could have married dozens of times. Melly and I have often said how loyal you were to his memory when everyone else said you were just a heartless coquette.'

Scarlett passed over this tactless confidence and skilfully led Pitty from one friend to another, but all the while she was in a fever of impatience to bring the conversation around to Rhett. It would never do for her to ask outright about him, so soon after arriving. It might start the old lady's mind to working on channels better left untouched. There would be time enough for Pitty's suspicions to be aroused if Rhett refused to marry her.

Aunt Pitty prattled on happily, pleased as a child at having an audience. Things in Atlanta were in a dreadful pass, she said, due to the vile doings of the Republicans. There was no end to their goings on and the worst thing was the way they were putting ideas in the poor darkies' heads.

'My dear, they want to let the darkies vote! Did you ever hear of anything more silly? Though – I don't know – now that I think about it, Uncle Peter has much more sense than any Republican I ever saw and much better manners but, of course, Uncle Peter is far too well bred to want to vote. But the very notion has upset the darkies till they're right addled. And some of them are so insolent. Your life isn't safe on the streets after dark and even in the broad daylight they push ladies off the sidewalks into the mud. And if any gentleman dares to protest, they arrest him and— My dear, did I tell you that Captain Butler was in jail?'

'Rhett Butler?'

Even with this startling news, Scarlett was grateful that Aunt Pitty had saved her the necessity of bringing his name into the conversation herself.

'Yes, indeed!' Excitement coloured Pitty's cheeks pink and she sat upright. 'He's in jail this very minute for killing a negro and they may hang him! Imagine Captain Butler hanging!'

For a moment, the breath went out of Scarlett's lungs in a sickening gasp, and she could only stare at the fat old lady who was so obviously pleased at the effect of her statement.

'They haven't proved it yet but somebody killed this darky who had insulted a white woman. And the Yankees are very upset because so many uppity darkies have been killed recently. They can't prove it on Captain Butler but they want to make an example of someone, so Dr Meade says. The doctor says that if they do hang him it will be the first good honest job the Yankees ever did, but then, I don't know . . . And to think that Captain Butler was here just a week ago and brought me the loveliest quail you ever saw for a present and he was asking about you and saying he feared he had offended you during the siege and you would never forgive him.'

'How long will he be in jail?'

'Nobody knows. Perhaps till they hang him, but maybe they won't be able to prove the killing on him, after all. However, it doesn't seem to bother the Yankees whether folks are guilty or not, so long as they can hang somebody. They are so upset' – Pitty dropped her voice mysteriously – 'about the Ku Klux Klan. Do you have the Klan down in the County? My dear, I'm sure you must and Ashley just doesn't tell you girls anything about it. Klansmen aren't supposed to tell. They ride around at night dressed up like ghosts and call on Carpetbaggers who steal money and negroes who are uppity. Sometimes they just scare them and warn them to leave Atlanta, but when they don't behave they whip them and' – Pitty whispered – 'sometimes they kill them and leave them where they'll be easily found with the Ku Klux card on them . . . And the Yankees are very angry about it and want to make an example of someone . . . But Hugh Elsing told me he didn't think they'd hang Captain Butler because the Yankees think he does know where the money is and just won't tell. They are trying to make him tell.'

'The money?'

'Didn't you know? Didn't I write you? My dear, you have been buried at Tara, haven't you? The town simply buzzed when Captain Butler came back here with a fine horse and carriage and his pockets full of money, when all the rest of us didn't know where our next meal was coming from. It simply made everybody furious that an old speculator who always said nasty things about the Confederacy should have so much money when we were all so poor. Everybody was bursting to know how he managed to save his money but no one had the courage to ask him – except me, and he just laughed and said: "In no honest way, you may be sure." You know how hard it is to get anything sensible out of him.'

'But, of course, he made his money out of the blockade—'

'Of course he did, honey, some of it. But that's not a drop in the bucket to what that man has really got. Everybody, including the Yankees, believes he's got millions of dollars in gold belonging to the Confederate government hid out somewhere.'

'Millions – in gold?'

'Well, honey, where did all our Confederate gold go to? Somebody got it and Captain Butler must be one of the somebodies. The Yankees thought President Davis had it when he left Richmond but when they captured the poor man he had hardly a cent. There just wasn't any money in the treasury when the war was over and everybody thinks some of the blockade-runners got it and are keeping quiet about it.'

'Millions – in gold! But how—'

'Didn't Captain Butler take thousands of bales of cotton to England and Nassau to sell for the Confederate government?' asked Pitty triumphantly. 'Not only his own cotton but government cotton too? And you know what cotton brought in England during the war! Any price you wanted to ask! He was a free agent acting for the government and he was supposed to sell the cotton and buy guns with the money and run the guns in for us. Well, when the blockade got too tight, he couldn't bring in the guns and he couldn't have spent one one-hundredth of the cotton money on them anyway, so there were simply millions of dollars in English banks put there by Captain Butler and other blockaders, waiting till the blockade loosened. And you can't tell me they banked that money in the name of the Confederacy. They put it in their own names and it's still there . . . Everybody has been talking about it ever since the surrender and criticizing the blockaders severely, and when the Yankees arrested Captain Butler for killing this darky they must have heard the rumour, because they've been at him to tell them where the money is. You see, all of our Confederate funds belong to the Yankees now – at least, the Yankees think so. But Captain Butler says he doesn't know anything . . . Dr Meade says they ought to hang him anyhow, only hanging is too good for a thief and a profiteer—Dear, you look so oddly! Do you feel faint? Have I upset you talking like this? I knew he was once a beau of yours but I thought you'd fallen out long ago. Personally, I never approved of him, for he's such a scamp—'

'He's no friend of mine,' said Scarlett with an effort. 'I had a quarrel with him during the siege, after you went to Macon. Where – where is he?'

'In the firehouse over near the public square!'

'In the firehouse?'

Aunt Pitty crowed with laughter.

'Yes, he's in the firehouse. The Yankees use it for a military jail now. The Yankees are camped in huts all round the city hall in the square and the firehouse is just down the street, so that's where Captain Butler is. And Scarlett, I heard the funniest thing yesterday about Captain Butler. I forget who told me. You know how well groomed he always was – really a dandy – and they've been keeping him in the firehouse and not letting him bathe and every day he's been insisting that he wanted a bath and finally they led him out of his cell on to the square and there was a long horse-trough where the whole regiment had bathed in the same water! And they told him he could bathe there and he said No, that he preferred his own brand of Southern dirt to Yankee dirt and—'

Scarlett heard the cheerful babbling voice going on and on but she did not hear the words. In her mind there were only two ideas, Rhett had more money than she had even hoped and he was in jail. The fact that he was in jail and possibly might be hanged changed the face of matters somewhat, in fact made them look a little brighter. She had very little feeling about Rhett being hanged. Her need of money was too pressing, too desperate, for her to bother about his ultimate fate. Besides, she half shared Dr Meade's opinion that hanging was too good for him. Any man who'd leave a woman stranded between two armies in the middle of the night, just to go off and fight for a Cause already lost, deserved hanging . . . If she could somehow manage to marry him while he was in jail, all those millions would be hers and hers alone should he be executed. And if marriage was not possible, perhaps she could get a loan from him by promising to marry him when he was released or by promising – oh, promising anything! And if they hanged him, her day of settlement would never come.

For a moment her imagination flamed at the thought of being made a widow by the kindly intervention of the Yankee government. Millions in gold! She could repair Tara and hire hands and plant miles and miles of cotton. And she could have pretty clothes and all she wanted to eat and so could Suellen and Carreen. And Wade could have nourishing food to fill out his thin cheeks and warm clothes and a governess and afterward go to the university . . . and not grow up barefooted and ignorant like a Cracker. And a good doctor could look after Pa and as for Ashley – what couldn't she do for Ashley!

Aunt Pittypat's monologue broke off suddenly as she said inquiringly: 'Yes, Mammy?' and Scarlett, coming back from dreams, saw Mammy standing in the doorway, her hands under her apron and in her eyes an alert piercing look. She wondered how long Mammy had been standing there and how much she had heard and observed. Probably everything, to judge by the gleam in her old eyes.

'Miss Scarlett look lak she tared. Ah spec she better go ter bed.'

'I am tired,' said Scarlett, rising and meeting Mammy's eyes with a childlike, helpless look, 'and I'm afraid I'm catching a cold too. Aunt Pitty, would you mind if I stayed in bed tomorrow and didn't go calling with you? I can go calling any time and I'm so anxious to go to Fanny's wedding tomorrow night. And if my cold gets worse I won't be able to go. And a day in bed would be such a lovely treat for me.'

Mammy's look changed to faint worry as she felt Scarlett's hands and looked into her face. She certainly didn't look well. The excitement of her thoughts had abruptly ebbed, leaving her white and shaking.

'Yo' han's lak ice, honey. You come ter bed an' Ah'll brew you some sassfrass tea an' git you a hot brick ter mek you sweat.'

'How thoughtless I've been!' cried the plump old lady, hopping from her chair and patting Scarlett's arm. 'Just chattering on and not thinking of you. Honey, you shall stay in bed all tomorrow and rest up and we can gossip together— Oh, dear, no! I can't be with you. I've promised to sit with Mrs Bonnell tomorrow. She is down with la grippe and so is her cook. Mammy, I'm so glad you are here. You must go over with me in the morning and help me.'

Mammy hurried Scarlett up the dark stairs, muttering fussy remarks about cold hands and thin shoes, and Scarlett looked meek and was well content. If she could only lull Mammy's suspicions further and get her out of the house in the morning, all would be well. Then she could go to the Yankee jail and see Rhett. As she climbed the stairs, the faint rumbling of thunder began and, standing on the well-remembered landing, she thought how like the siege cannon it sounded. She shivered. Forever, thunder would mean cannon and war to her.

Chapter XXXIV

The sun shone intermittently the next morning and the hard wind that drove dark clouds swiftly across its face rattled the window-panes and moaned faintly about the house. Scarlett said a brief prayer of thanksgiving that the rain of the previous night had ceased, for she had lain awake listening to it, knowing that it would mean the ruin of her velvet dress and new bonnet. Now that she could catch fleeting glimpses of the sun, her spirits soared. She could hardly remain in bed and look languid and make croaking noises until Aunt Pitty, Mammy and Uncle Peter were out of the house and on their way to Mrs Bonnell's. When, at last, the front gate banged and she was alone in the house, except for Cookie who was singing in the kitchen, she leaped from the bed and lifted her new clothes from the closet hooks.

Sleep had refreshed her and given her strength and from the cold hard core at the bottom of her heart she drew courage. There was something about the prospect of a struggle of wits with a man – with any man – that put her on her mettle and, after months of battling against countless discouragements, the knowledge that she was at last facing a definite adversary, one whom she might unhorse by her own efforts, gave her a buoyant sensation.

Dressing unaided was difficult but she finally accomplished it and putting on the bonnet with its rakish feathers she ran to Aunt Pitty's room to preen herself in front of the long mirror. How pretty she looked! The cock feathers gave her a dashing air and the dull-green velvet of the bonnet made her eyes startlingly bright, almost emerald-coloured. And the dress was incomparable, so rich and handsome looking and yet so dignified! It was wonderful to have a lovely dress again. It was so nice to know that she looked pretty and provocative, and she impulsively bent forward and kissed her reflection in the mirror and then laughed at her own foolishness. She picked up Ellen's Paisley shawl to wrap about her but the colours of the faded old square clashed with the moss-green dress and made her appear a little shabby. Opening Aunt Pitty's closet she removed a black broadcloth cloak, a thin fall garment which Pitty used only for Sunday wear, and put it on. She slipped into her pierced ears the diamond earrings she had brought from Tara, and tossed her head to observe the effect. They made pleasant clicking noises which were very satisfactory and she thought that she must remember to toss her head frequently when with Rhett. Dancing earrings always attracted a man and gave a girl such a spirited air.

What a shame Aunt Pitty had no other gloves than the ones now on her fat hands! No woman could really feel like a lady without gloves, but Scarlett had not had a pair since she left Atlanta. And the long months of hard work at Tara had roughened her hands until they were far from pretty. Well, it couldn't be helped. She'd take Aunt Pitty's little seal muff and hide her bare hands in it. Scarlett felt that it gave her the final finishing touch of elegance. No one, looking at her now, would suspect that poverty and want were standing at her shoulder.

It was so important that Rhett should not suspect. He must not think that anything but tender feelings were driving her.

She tiptoed down the stairs and out of the house while Cookie bawled on unconcernedly in the kitchen. She hastened down Baker Street to avoid the all-seeing eyes of the neighbours and sat down on a carriage block on Ivy Street in front of a burned house, to wait for some passing carriage or wagon which would give her a ride. The sun dipped in and out from behind hurrying clouds, lighting the street with a false brightness which had no warmth in it, and the wind fluttered the lace of her pantalets. It was colder than she had expected and she wrapped Aunt Pitty's thin cloak about her and shivered impatiently. Just as she was preparing to start walking the long way across town to the Yankee encampment, a battered wagon appeared. In it was an old woman with a lip full of snuff and a weather-beaten face under a drab sunbonnet, driving a dawdling old mule. She was going in the direction of the city hall and she grudgingly gave Scarlett a ride. But it was obvious that the dress, bonnet and muff found no favour with her.

'She thinks I'm a hussy,' thought Scarlett. 'And perhaps she's right at that!'

When at last they reached the town square and the tall white cupola of the city hall loomed up, she made her thanks, climbed down from the wagon and watched the country woman drive off. Looking around carefully to see that she was not observed, she pinched her cheeks to give them colour and bit her lips until they stung to make them red. She adjusted the bonnet and smoothed back her hair and looked about the square. The two-storey red-brick city hall had survived the burning of the city. But it looked forlorn and unkempt under the grey sky. Surrounding the building completely and covering the square of land of which it was the centre were row after row of army huts, dingy and mud-splashed. Yankee soldiers loitered everywhere and Scarlett looked at them uncertainly, some of her courage deserting her. How would she go about finding Rhett in this enemy camp?

She looked down the street toward the firehouse and saw that the wide arched doors were closed and heavily barred and two sentries passed and repassed on each side of the building. Rhett was in there. But what should she say to the Yankee soldiers? And what would they say to her? She squared her shoulders. If she hadn't been afraid to kill one Yankee, she shouldn't fear merely talking to another.

She picked her way precariously across the stepping-stones of the muddy street and walked forward until a sentry, his blue overcoat buttoned high against the wind, stopped her.

'What is it, Ma'm?' His voice had a strange mid-Western twang but it was polite and respectful.

'I want to see a man in there – he is a prisoner.'

'Well, I don't know,' said the sentry, scratching his head. 'They are mighty particular about visitors and—' He stopped and peered into her face sharply. 'Lord, lady! Don't you cry! You go over to post headquarters and ask the officers. They'll let you see him, I bet.'

Scarlett, who had no intention of crying, beamed at him. He turned to another sentry who was slowly pacing his beat: 'Yee-ah, Bill. Come'eer.'

The second sentry, a large man muffled in a blue overcoat from which villainous black whiskers burst, came through the mud toward them.

'You take this lady to headquarters.'

Scarlett thanked him and followed the sentry.

'Mind you don't turn your ankle on those stepping-stones,' said the soldier, taking her arm. 'And you'd better hist up your skirts a little to keep them out of the mud.'

The voice issuing from the whiskers had the same nasal twang but was kind and pleasant and his hand was firm and respectful. Why, Yankees weren't bad at all!

'It's a mighty cold day for a lady to be out in,' said her escort. 'Have you come a fer piece?'

'Oh, yes, from clear across the other side of town,' she said, warming to the kindness in his voice.

'This ain't no weather for a lady to be out in,' said the soldier reprovingly, 'with all this la grippe in the air. Here's Post Command, lady—What's the matter?'

'This house – this house is your headquarters?' Scarlett looked up at the lovely old dwelling facing on the square and could have cried. She had been to so many parties in this house during the war. It had been a gay beautiful place and now – there was a large United States flag floating over it.

'What's the matter?'

'Nothing – only – only – I used to know the people who lived here.'

'Well, that's too bad. I guess they wouldn't know it themselves if they saw it, for it shore is tore up on the inside. Now, you go on in, Ma'm, and ask for the captain.'

She went up the steps, caressing the broken white banisters, and pushed open the front door. The hall was dark and as cold as a vault and a shivering sentry was leaning against the closed folding doors of what had been, in better days, the dining-room.

'I want to see the captain,' she said.

He pulled back the doors and she entered the room, her heart beating rapidly, her face flushing with embarrassment and excitement. There was a close stuffy smell in the room, compounded of the smoking fire, tobacco fumes, leather, damp woollen uniforms and unwashed bodies. She had a confused impression of bare walls with torn wallpaper, rows of blue overcoats and slouch hats hung on nails, a roaring fire, a long table covered with papers and a group of officers in blue uniforms with brass buttons.

She gulped once and found her voice. She mustn't let these Yankees know she was afraid. She must look and be her prettiest and most unconcerned self.

'The captain?'

'I'm one captain,' said a fat man whose tunic was unbuttoned.

'I want to see a prisoner, Captain Rhett Butler.'

'Butler again? He's popular, that man,' laughed the captain, taking a chewed cigar from his mouth. 'You a relative, Ma'm?'

'Yes – his – his sister.'

He laughed again.

'He's got a lot of sisters, one of them here yesterday.'

Scarlett flushed. One of those creatures Rhett consorted with, probably that Watling woman. And these Yankees thought she was another one. It was unendurable. Not even for Tara would she stay here another minute and be insulted. She turned to the door and reached angrily for the knob but another officer was by her side quickly. He was clean-shaven and young and had merry, kind eyes.

'Just a minute, Ma'm. Won't you sit down here by the fire where it's warm? I'll go see what I can do about it. What is your name? He refused to see the – lady who called yesterday.'

She sank into the proffered chair, glaring at the discomfited fat captain, and gave her name. The nice young officer slipped on his overcoat and left the room and the others took themselves off to the far end of the table where they talked in low tones and pawed at the papers. She stretched her feet gratefully toward the fire, realizing for the first time how cold they were and wishing she had thought to put a piece of cardboard over the hole in the sole of one slipper. After a time, voices murmured outside the door and she heard Rhett's laugh. The door opened, a cold draught swept the room and Rhett appeared, hatless, a long cape thrown carelessly across his shoulders. He was dirty and unshaven and without a cravat but somehow jaunty despite his dishabille, and his dark eyes were snapping joyfully at the sight of her.

'Scarlett!'

He had her hands in both of his and, as always, there was something hot and vital and exciting about his grip. Before she quite knew what he was about, he had bent and kissed her cheek, his moustache tickling her. As he felt the startled movement of her body away from him, he hugged her about the shoulders and said: 'My darling little sister!' and grinned down at her as if he relished her helplessness in resisting his caress. She couldn't help laughing back at him for the advantage he had taken. What a rogue he was! Jail had not changed him one bit.

The fat captain was muttering through his cigar to the merry-eyed officer.

'Most irregular. He should be in the firehouse. You know the orders.'

'Oh, for God's sake, Henry! The lady would freeze in that barn.'

'Oh, all right, all right! It's your responsibility.'

'I assure you, gentlemen,' said Rhett, turning to them but still keeping a grip on Scarlett's shoulders, 'my – sister hasn't brought me any saws or files to help me escape.'

They all laughed and, as they did, Scarlett looked quickly about her. Good Heavens, was she going to have to talk to Rhett before six Yankee officers! Was he so dangerous a prisoner they wouldn't let him out of their sight? Seeing her anxious glance, the nice officer pushed open a door and spoke brief low words to two privates who had leaped to their feet at his entrance. They picked up their rifles and went out into the hall, closing the door behind them.

'If you wish, you may sit here in the orderly room,' said the young captain. 'And don't try to bolt through that door. The men are just outside.'

'You see what a desperate character I am, Scarlett,' said Rhett. 'Thank you, Captain. This is most kind of you.'

He bowed carelessly and taking Scarlett's arm pulled her to her feet and propelled her into the dingy orderly room. She was never to remember what the room looked like except that it was small and dim and none too warm and there were hand-written papers tacked on the mutilated walls and chairs which had cowhide seats with the hair still on them.

When he had closed the door behind them, Rhett came to her swiftly and bent over her. Knowing his desire, she turned her head quickly but smiled provocatively at him out of the corners of her eyes.

'Can't I really kiss you now?'

'On the forehead, like a good brother,' she answered demurely.

'Thank you, no. I prefer to wait and hope for better things.' His eyes sought her lips and lingered there a moment. 'But how good of you to come to see me, Scarlett! You are the first respectable citizen who has called on me since my incarceration, and being in jail makes one appreciate friends. When did you come to town?'

'Yesterday afternoon.'

'And you came out this morning? Why, my dear, you are more than good.' He smiled down at her with the first expression of honest pleasure she had ever seen on his face. Scarlett smiled inwardly with excitement and ducked her head as if embarrassed.

'Of course, I came out right away. Aunt Pitty told me about you last night and I – I just couldn't sleep all night for thinking how awful it was. Rhett, I'm so distressed!'

'Why, Scarlett!'

His voice was soft but there was a vibrant note in it, and looking up into his dark face she saw in it none of the scepticism, the jeering humour she knew so well. Before his direct gaze her eyes fell again in real confusion. Things were going even better than she hoped.

'It's worth being in jail to see you again and to hear you say things like that. I really couldn't believe my ears when they brought me your name. You see, I never expected you to forgive me for my patriotic conduct that night on the road near Rough and Ready. But I take it that this call means you have forgiven me?'

She could feel swift anger stir, even at this late date, as she thought of that night but she subdued it and tossed her head until the earrings danced.

'No, I haven't forgiven you,' she said, and pouted.

'Another hope crushed. And after I offered up myself for my country and fought barefooted in the snow at Franklin and got the finest case of dysentery you ever heard of for my pains!'

'I don't want to hear about your – pains,' she said, still pouting but smiling at him from tip-tilted eyes. 'I still think you were hateful that night and I never expect to forgive you. Leaving me alone like that when anything might have happened to me!'

'But nothing did happen to you. So, you see, my confidence in you was justified. I knew you'd get home safely and God help any Yankee who got in your way!'

'Rhett, why on earth did you do such a silly thing – enlisting at the last minute when you knew we were going to get licked? And after all you'd said about idiots who went out and got shot!'

'Scarlett, spare me! I am always overcome with shame when I think about it.'

'Well, I'm glad to learn you are ashamed of the way you treated me.'

'You misunderstand. I regret to say that my conscience has not troubled me at all about deserting you. But as for enlisting – when I think of joining the army in varnished boots and a white linen suit and armed with only a pair of duelling pistols— And those long cold miles in the snow after my boots wore out and I had no overcoat and nothing to eat . . . I cannot understand why I did not desert. It was all the purest insanity. But it's in one's blood. Southerners can never resist a losing cause. But never mind my reasons. It's enough that I'm forgiven.'

'You're not. I think you're a hound.' But she caressed the last word until it might have been 'darling'.

'Don't fib. You've forgiven me. Young ladies don't dare Yankee sentries to see a prisoner, just for charity's sweet sake, and come all dressed up in velvet and feathers and seal muffs too. Scarlett, how pretty you look! Thank God, you aren't in rags or mourning! I get so sick of women in dowdy old clothes and perpetual crêpe. You look like the Rue de la Paix. Turn around, my dear, and let me look at you.'

So he had noticed the dress. Of course, he would notice such things, being Rhett. She laughed in soft excitement and spun about on her toes, her arms extended, her hoops tilting up to show her lace-trimmed pantalets. His black eyes took her in from bonnet to heels in a glance that missed nothing, that old impudent unclothing glance which always gave her goose-bumps.

'You look very prosperous and very, very tidy. And almost good enough to eat. If it wasn't for the Yankees outside – but you are quite safe, my dear. Sit down. I won't take advantage of you as I did the last time I saw you.' He rubbed his cheek with pseudo ruefulness. 'Honestly, Scarlett, don't you think you were a bit selfish that night? Think of all I had done for you, risked my life – stolen a horse – and such a horse! Rushed to the defence of Our Glorious Cause! And what did I get for my pains? Some hard words and a very hard slap in the face.'

She sat down. The conversation was not going in quite the direction she hoped. He had seemed so nice when he first saw her, so genuinely glad she had come. He had almost seemed like a human being and not the perverse wretch she knew so well.

'Must you always get something for your pains?'

'Why, of course! I am a monster of selfishness, as you ought to know. I always expect payment for anything I give.'

That sent a slight chill through her but she rallied and jingled her earbobs again.

'Oh, you really aren't so bad, Rhett. You just like to show off.'

'My word, but you have changed!' he said and laughed. 'What has made a Christian of you? I have kept up with you through Miss Pittypat but she gave me no intimation that you had developed womanly sweetness. Tell me more about yourself, Scarlett. What have you been doing since I last saw you?'

The old irritation and antagonism which he roused in her was hot in her heart and she yearned to speak tart words. But she smiled instead and the dimple crept into her cheek. He had drawn a chair close beside hers and she leaned over and put a gentle hand on his arm, in an unconscious manner.

'Oh, I've been doing nicely, thank you, and everything at Tara is fine now. Of course, we had a dreadful time right after Sherman went through but, after all, he didn't burn the house and the darkies saved most of the livestock by driving it into the swamp. And we cleared a fair crop this last fall, twenty bales. Of course, that's practically nothing compared with what Tara can do but we haven't many field hands. Pa says, of course, we'll do better next year. But, Rhett, it's so dull in the country now! Imagine, there aren't any balls or barbecues and the only thing people talk about is hard times! Goodness, I get sick of it! Finally last week I got too bored to stand it any longer, so Pa said I must take a trip and have a good time. So I came up here to get me some frocks made and then I'm going over to Charleston to visit my aunt. It'll be lovely to go to balls again.'

'There,' she thought with pride, 'I delivered that with just the right airy way! Not too rich but certainly not poor.'

'You look beautiful in ball dresses, my dear, and you know it too, worse luck! I suppose the real reason you are going visiting is that you have run through the County swains and are seeking fresh ones in fields afar.'

Scarlett had a thankful thought that Rhett had spent the last several months abroad and had only recently come back to Atlanta. Otherwise, he would never have made so ridiculous a statement. She thought briefly of the County swains, the ragged embittered little Fontaines, the poverty-stricken Munroe boys, the Jonesboro and Fayetteville beaux who were so busy ploughing, splitting rails and nursing sick old animals that they had forgotten such things as balls and pleasant flirtations ever existed. But she put down this memory and giggled self-consciously as if admitting the truth of this assertion.

'Oh, well,' she said deprecatingly.

'You are a heartless creature, Scarlett, but perhaps that's part of your charm.' He smiled in his old way, one corner of his mouth curving down, but she knew he was complimenting her. 'For, of course, you know you have more charm than the law should permit. Even I have felt it, case-hardened though I am. I've often wondered what it was about you that made me always remember you, for I've known many ladies who were prettier than you and certainly more clever and, I fear, morally more upright and kind.

But, somehow, I always remembered you. Even during the months since the surrender when I was in France and England and hadn't seen you or heard of you and was enjoying the society of many beautiful ladies, I always remembered you and wondered what you were doing.'

For a moment she was indignant that he should say other women were prettier, more clever and kind than she, but that momentary flare was wiped out in her pleasure that he had remembered her and her charm. So he hadn't forgotten! That would make things easier. And he was behaving so nicely, almost like a gentleman would do under the circumstances. Now, all she had to do was bring the subject around to himself, so she could intimate that she had not forgotten him either and then—

She gently squeezed his arm and dimpled again.

'Oh, Rhett, how you do run on, teasing a country girl like me! I know mighty well you never gave me a thought after you left me that night. You can't tell me you ever thought of me with all those pretty French and English girls around you. But I didn't come all the way out here to hear you talk foolishness about me. I came – I came – because— '

'Because?'

'Oh, Rhett, I'm so terribly distressed about you! So frightened for you! When will they let you out of that terrible place?'

He swiftly covered her hand with his and held it hard against his arm.

'Your distress does you credit. There's no telling when I'll be out. Probably when they've stretched the rope a bit more.'

'The rope?'

'Yes, I expect to make my exit from here at the rope's end.'

'They won't really hang you?'

'They will if they can get a little more evidence against me.'

'Oh, Rhett!' she cried, her hand at her heart.

'Would you be sorry? If you are sorry enough, I'll mention you in my will.'

His dark eyes laughed at her recklessly and he squeezed her hand.

His will! She hastily cast down her eyes for fear of betrayal but not swiftly enough, for his eyes gleamed, suddenly curious.

'According to the Yankees, I ought to have a fine will. There seems to be considerable interest in my finances at present. Every day, I am hauled up before another board of inquiry and asked foolish questions. The rumour seems current that I made off with the mythical gold of the Confederacy.'

'Well – did you?'

'What a leading question! You know as well as I do that the Confederacy ran a printing press instead of a mint.'

'Where did you get all your money? Speculating? Aunt Pittypat said— '

'What probing questions you ask!'

Damn him! Of course, he had the money. She was so excited it became difficult to talk sweetly to him.

'Rhett, I'm so upset about your being here. Don't you think there's a chance of your getting out?'

' "Nihil desperandum" is my motto.'

'What does that mean?'

'It means "maybe", my charming ignoramus.'

She fluttered her thick lashes up to look at him and fluttered them down again.

'Oh, you're too smart to let them hang you! I know you'll think of some clever way to beat them and get out! And when you do—'

'And when I do?' he asked softly, leaning closer.

'Well, I—' and she managed a pretty confusion and a blush. The blush was not difficult for she was breathless and her heart was beating like a drum. 'Rhett, I'm so sorry about what I – I said to you that night – you know – at Rough and Ready. I was – oh, so very frightened and upset and you were so – so—' She looked down and saw his brown hand tighten over hers. 'And – I thought then that I'd never, never forgive you! But when Aunt Pitty told me yesterday that you – that they might hang you – it came over me of a sudden and I – I—' She looked up into his eyes with one swift imploring glance and in it she put an agony of heartbreak. 'Oh, Rhett, I'd die if they hanged you! I couldn't bear it! You see, I—' And, because she could no longer sustain the hot leaping light that was in his eyes, her lids fluttered down again.

'In a moment I'll be crying,' she thought in a frenzy of wonder and excitement. 'Shall I let myself cry? Wouldn't that seem more natural?'

He said quickly: 'My God, Scarlett, you can't mean that you—' and his hands closed over hers in so hard a grip that it hurt.

She shut her eyes tightly, trying to squeeze out tears, but remembered to turn her face up slightly so he could kiss her with no difficulty. Now, in an instant his lips would be upon hers, the hard insistent lips which she suddenly remembered with a vividness that left her weak. But he did not kiss her. Disappointment queerly stirring her, she opened her eyes a trifle and ventured a peep at him. His black head was bent over her hands and, as she watched, he lifted one and kissed it and, taking the other, laid it against his cheek for a moment. Expecting violence, this gentle and lover-like gesture startled her. She wondered what expression was on his face but could not tell for his head was bowed.

She quickly lowered her gaze lest he should look up suddenly and see the expression on her face. She knew that the feeling of triumph surging through her was certain to be plain in her eyes. In a moment he would ask her to marry him – or at least say that he loved her and then . . . As she watched him through the veil of her lashes he turned her hand over, palm up, to kiss it too, and suddenly he drew a quick breath. Looking down she saw her own palm, saw it as it really was for the first time in a year, and a cold sinking fear gripped her. This was a stranger's palm, not Scarlett O'Hara's soft, white, dimpled, helpless one. This hand was rough from work, brown with sunburn, splotched with freckles. The nails were broken and irregular, there were heavy callouses on the cushions of the palm, a half-healed blister on the thumb. The red scar which boiling fat had left last month was ugly and glaring. She looked at it in horror and, before she thought, she swiftly clenched her fist.

Still he did not raise his head. Still she could not see his face. He pried her fist open inexorably and stared at it, picked up her other hand and held them both together silently, looking down at them.

'Look at me,' he said, finally raising his head, and his voice was very quiet. 'And drop that demure expression.'

Unwillingly she met his eyes, defiance and perturbation on her face. His black brows were up and his eyes gleamed.

'So you have been doing very nicely at Tara, have you? Cleared so much money on the cotton you can go visiting. What have you been doing with your hands – ploughing?'

She tried to wrench them away but he held them hard, running his thumbs over the callouses.

'These are not the hands of a lady,' he said, and tossed them into her lap.

'Oh, shut up!' she cried, feeling a momentary intense relief at being able to speak her feelings. 'Whose business is it what I do with my hands?'

'What a fool I am,' she thought vehemently. 'I should have borrowed or stolen Aunt Pitty's gloves. But I didn't realize my hands looked so bad. Of course, he would notice them. And now I've lost my temper and probably ruined everything. Oh, to have this happen when he was right at the point of a declaration!'

'Your hands are certainly no business of mine,' said Rhett coolly, and lounged back in his chair indolently, his face a smooth blank.

So he was going to be difficult. Well, she'd have to bear it meekly, much as she disliked it, if she expected to snatch victory from this debacle. Perhaps if she sweet-talked him—

'I think you're real rude to throw off on my poor hands. Just because I went riding last week without my gloves and ruined them—'

'Riding, hell!' he said in the same level voice. 'You've been working with those hands, working like a nigger. What's the answer? Why did you lie to me about everything being nice at Tara?'

'Now, Rhett—'

'Suppose we get down to the truth. What is the real purpose of your visit? Almost, I was persuaded by your coquettish airs that you cared something about me and were sorry for me.'

'Oh, I am sorry! Indeed—'

'No, you aren't. They can hang me higher than Haman for all you care. It's written as plainly on your face as hard work is written on your hands. You wanted something from me and you wanted it badly enough to put on quite a show. Why didn't you come out in the open and tell me what it was? You'd have stood a much better chance of getting it, for if there's one virtue I value in women it's frankness. But no, you had to come jingling your earbobs and pouting and frisking like a prostitute with a prospective client.'

He did not raise his voice at the last words or emphasize them in any way but to Scarlett they cracked like a whiplash, and with despair she saw the end of her hopes of getting him to propose marriage. Had he exploded with rage and injured vanity or upbraided her, as other men would have done, she could have handled him. But the deadly quietness of his voice frightened her, left her utterly at a loss as to her next move. Although he was a prisoner and the Yankees were in the next room, it came to her suddenly that Rhett Butler was a dangerous man to run afoul of.

'I suppose my memory is getting faulty. I should have recalled that you are just like me and that you never do anything without an ulterior motive. Now, let me see. What could you have had up your sleeve, Mrs Hamilton? It isn't possible that you were so misguided as to think I would propose matrimony?'

Her face went crimson and she did not answer.

'But you can't have forgotten my oft-repeated remark that I am not a marrying man?'

When she did not speak, he said with sudden violence:

'You hadn't forgotten? Answer me.'

'I hadn't forgotten,' she said wretchedly.

'What a gambler you are, Scarlett!' he jeered. 'You took a chance that my incarceration away from female companionship would put me in such a state I'd snap at you like a trout at a worm.'

'And that's what you did,' thought Scarlett with inward rage, 'and if it hadn't been for my hands—'

'Now, we have most of the truth, everything except your reason. See if you can tell me the truth about why you wanted to lead me into wedlock.'

There was a suave, almost teasing note in his voice and she took heart. Perhaps everything wasn't lost, after all. Of course, she had ruined any hope of marriage but, even in her despair, she was glad. There was something about this immobile man which frightened her, so that now the thought of marrying him was fearful. But perhaps if she was clever and played on his sympathies and his memories, she could secure a loan. She pulled her face into a placating and childlike expression.

'Oh, Rhett, you can help me so much – if you'll just be sweet.'

'There's nothing I like better than being – sweet.'

'Rhett, for old friendship's sake, I want you to do me a favour.'

'So, at last the horny-handed lady comes to her real mission. I feared that "visiting the sick and the imprisoned" was not your proper rôle. What do you want? Money?'

The bluntness of his question ruined all hopes of leading up to the matter in any circuitous and sentimental way.

'Don't be mean, Rhett,' she coaxed. 'I do want some money. I want you to lend me three hundred dollars.'

'The truth at last. Talking love and thinking money. How truly feminine! Do you need the money badly?'

'Oh, ye— Well, not so terribly, but I could use it.'

'Three hundred dollars. That's a vast amount of money. What do you want it for?'

'To pay taxes on Tara.'

'So you want to borrow some money. Well, since you're so businesslike, I'll be businesslike too. What collateral will you give me?'

'What what?'

'Collateral. Security on my investment. Of course, I don't want to lose all that money.' His voice was deceptively smooth, almost silky, but she did not notice. Maybe everything would turn out nicely after all.

'My earrings.'

'I'm not interested in earrings.'

'I'll give you a mortgage on Tara.'

'Now just what would I do with a farm?'

'Well, you could – you could – it's a good plantation. And you wouldn't lose. I'd pay you back out of next year's cotton.'

'I'm not so sure.' He tilted back in his chair and stuck his hands in his pockets. 'Cotton prices are dropping. Times are so hard and money's so tight.'

'Oh, Rhett, you are teasing me! You know you have millions!'

There was a warm dancing malice in his eyes as he surveyed her.

'So everything is going nicely and you don't need the money very badly. Well, I'm glad to hear that. I like to know that all is well with old friends.'

'Oh, Rhett, for God's sake . . .' she began desperately, her courage and control breaking.

'Do lower your voice. You don't want the Yankees to hear you, I hope. Did anyone ever tell you you had eyes like a cat – a cat in the dark?'

'Rhett, don't! I'll tell you everything. I do need the money so badly. I – I lied about everything being all right. Everything's as wrong as it could be. Father is – is – he's not himself. He's been queer ever since Mother died and he can't help me any. He's just like a child. And we haven't a single field hand to work the cotton and there's so many to feed, thirteen of us. And the taxes – they are so high. Rhett, I'll tell you everything. For over a year we've been just this side of starvation. Oh, you don't know! You can't know! We've never had enough to eat and it's terrible to wake up hungry and go to sleep hungry. And we haven't any warm clothes and the children are always cold and sick and—'

'Where did you get the pretty dress?'

'It's made out of Mother's curtains,' she answered, too desperate to lie about this shame. 'I could stand being hungry and cold but now – now the Carpetbaggers have raised our taxes. And the money's got to be paid right away. And I haven't any money except one five-dollar gold piece. I've got to have money for the taxes! Don't you see? If I don't pay them, I'll – we'll lose Tara and we just can't lose it! I can't let it go!'

'Why didn't you tell me all this at first instead of preying on my susceptible heart – always weak where pretty ladies are concerned? No, Scarlett, don't cry. You've tried every trick except that one and I don't think I could stand it. My feelings are already lacerated with disappointment at discovering it was my money and not my charming self you wanted.'

She remembered that he frequently told bald truths about himself when he spoke mockingly – mocking himself as well as others, and she hastily looked up at him. Were his feelings really hurt? Did he really care about her? Had he been on the verge of a proposal when he saw her palms? Or had he only been leading up to another such odious proposal as he had made twice before? If he really cared about her, perhaps she could smooth him down. But his black eyes raked her in no lover-like way and he was laughing softly.

'I don't like your collateral. I'm no planter. What else have you to offer?'

Well, she had come to it at last. Now for it! She drew a deep breath and met his eyes squarely, all coquetry and airs gone as her spirit rushed out to grapple that which she feared most.

'I – I have myself.'

'Yes?'

Her jaw-line tightened to squareness and her eyes went emerald.

'You remember that night on Aunt Pitty's porch, during the siege? You said – you said then that you wanted me.'

He leaned back carelessly in his chair and looked into her tense face and his own dark face was inscrutable. Something flickered behind his eyes but he said nothing.

'You said – you said you'd never wanted a woman as much as you wanted me. If you still want me, you can have me. Rhett, I'll do anything you say but, for God's sake, write me a draft for the money! My word's good. I swear it. I won't go back on it. I'll put it in writing if you like.'

He looked at her oddly, still inscrutable, and as she hurried on she could not tell if he were amused or repelled. If he would only say something, anything! She felt her cheeks getting hot.

'I have got to have the money soon, Rhett. They'll turn us out in the road and that damned overseer of Father's will own the place and—'

'Just a minute. What makes you think I still want you? What makes you think you are worth three hundred dollars? Most women don't come that high.'

She blushed to her hair-line and her humiliation was complete.

'Why are you doing this? Why not let the farm go and live at Miss Pittypat's. You own half that house.'

'Name of God!' she cried. 'Are you a fool? I can't let Tara go. It's home. I won't let it go. Not while I've got a breath left in me!'

'The Irish,' said he, lowering his chair back to level and removing his hand from his pockets, 'are the damnedest race. They put so much emphasis on so many wrong things. Land, for instance. And every bit of earth is just like every other bit. Now, let me get this straight, Scarlett. You are coming to me with a business proposition. I'll give you three hundred dollars and you'll become my mistress.'

'Yes.'

Now that the repulsive word had been said, she felt somehow easier and hope awoke in her again. He had said 'I'll give you'. There was a diabolic gleam in his eyes as if something amused him greatly.

'And yet, when I had the effrontery to make you this same proposition, you turned me out of the house. And also you called me a number of very hard names and mentioned in passing that you didn't want a "passel of brats". No, my dear, I'm not rubbing it in. I'm only wondering at the peculiarities of your mind. You wouldn't do it for your own pleasure but you will to keep the wolf from the door. It proves my point that all virtue is merely a matter of prices.'

'Oh, Rhett, how you run on! If you want to insult me, go on and do it, but give me the money.'

She was breathing easier now. Being what he was, Rhett would naturally want to torment and insult her as much as possible to pay her back for past slights and for her recent attempted trickery. Well, she could stand it. She could stand anything. Tara was worth it all. For a brief moment it was midsummer and the afternoon skies were blue and she lay drowsily in the thick clover of Tara's lawn, looking up at the billowing cloud castles, the fragrance of white blossoms in her nose and the pleasant busy humming of bees in her ears. Afternoon and hush and the far-off sound of the wagons coming in from the spiralling red fields. Worth it all, worth more.

Her head went up.

'Are you going to give me the money?'

He looked as if he were enjoying himself and when he spoke there was suave brutality in his voice.

'No, I'm not,' he said.

For a moment her mind could not adjust itself to his words.

'I couldn't give it to you, even if I wanted to. I haven't a cent on me. Not a dollar in Atlanta. I have some money, yes, but not here. And I'm not saying where it is or how much. But if I tried to draw a draft on it, the Yankees would be on me like a duck on a June bug and then neither of us would get it. What do you think of that?'

Her face went an ugly green, freckles suddenly standing out across her nose, and her contorted mouth was like Gerald's in a killing rage. She sprang to her feet with an incoherent cry which made the hum of voices in the next room cease suddenly. Swift as a panther, Rhett was beside her, his heavy hand across her mouth, his arm tight about her waist. She struggled against him madly, trying to bite his hand, to kick his legs, to scream her rage, despair, hate, her agony of broken pride. She bent and twisted every way against the iron of his arm, her heart near bursting, her tight stays cutting off her breath. He held her so tightly, so roughly that it hurt and the hand over her mouth pinched into her jaws cruelly. His face was white under its tan, his eyes hard and anxious as he lifted her completely off her feet, swung her up against his chest and sat down in the chair, holding her writhing in his lap.

'Darling, for God's sake! Stop! Hush! Don't yell. They'll be in here in a minute if you do. Do calm yourself. Do you want the Yankees to see you like this?'

She was beyond caring who saw her, beyond anything except a fiery desire to kill him, but dizziness was sweeping her. She could not breathe; he was choking her; her stays were like a swiftly compressing band of iron; his arms about her made her shake with helpless hate and fury. Then his voice became thin and dim and his face above her swirled in a sickening mist which became heavier and heavier until she no longer saw him – or anything else.

When she made feeble swimming motions to come back to consciousness, she was tired to her bones, weak, bewildered. She was lying back in the chair, her bonnet off, Rhett was slapping her wrist, his black eyes searching her face anxiously. The nice young captain was trying to pour a glass of brandy into her mouth and had spilled it down her neck. The other officers hovered helplessly about, whispering and waving their hands.

'I – guess I must have fainted,' she said, and her voice sounded so far away it frightened her.

'Drink this,' said Rhett, taking the glass and pushing it against her lips. Now she remembered and glared feebly at him but she was too tired for anger.

'Please, for my sake.'

She gulped and choked and began coughing but he pushed it to her mouth again. She swallowed deeply and the hot liquid burned suddenly in her throat.

'I think she's better now, gentlemen,' said Rhett, 'and I thank you very much. The realization that I'm to be executed was too much for her.'

The group in blue shuffled their feet and looked embarrassed, and after several clearings of throats they tramped out. The young captain paused in the doorway.

'If there's anything more I can do—'

'No, thank you.'

He went out, closing the door behind him.

'Drink some more,' said Rhett.

'No.'

'Drink it.'

She swallowed another mouthful and the warmth began spreading through her body and strength flowed slowly back into her shaking legs. She pushed away the glass and tried to rise but he pressed her back.

'Take your hands off me. I'm going.'

'Not yet. Wait a minute. You might faint again.'

'I'd rather faint in the road than be here with you.'

'Just the same, I won't have you fainting in the road.'

'Let me go. I hate you.'

A faint smile came back to his face at her words.

'That sounds more like you. You must be feeling better.'

She lay relaxed for a moment, trying to summon anger to her aid, trying to draw on her strength. But she was too tired. She was too tired to hate or to care very much about anything. Defeat lay on her spirit like lead. She had gambled everything and lost everything. Not even pride was left. This was the dead end of her last hope. This was the end of Tara, the end of them all. For a long time she lay back with eyes closed, hearing his heavy breathing near her, and the glow of the brandy crept gradually over her, giving a false strength and warmth. When finally she opened her eyes and looked him in the face, anger had roused again. As her slanting eyebrows rushed down together in a frown Rhett's old smile came back.

'Now you are better. I can tell it by your scowl.'

'Of course, I'm all right. Rhett Butler, you are hateful, a skunk, if ever I saw one! You knew very well what I was going to say as soon as I started talking and you knew you weren't going to give me the money. And yet you let me go right on. You could have spared me—'

'Spared you and missed hearing all that? Not much. I have so few diversions here. I don't know when I've ever heard anything so gratifying.' He laughed his sudden mocking laugh. At the sound she leaped to her feet, snatching up her bonnet.

He suddenly had her by the shoulders.

'Not quite yet. Do you feel well enough to talk sense?'

'Let me go!'

'You are well enough, I see. Then, tell me this. Was I the only iron you had in the fire?' His eyes were keen and alert, watching every change in her face.

'What do you mean?'

'Was I the only man you were going to try this on?'

'Is that any of your business?'

'More than you realize. Are there any other men on your string? Tell me!'

'No.'

'Incredible. I can't imagine you without five or six in reserve. Surely someone will turn up to accept your interesting proposition. I feel so sure of it that I want to give you a little advice.'

'I don't want your advice.'

'Nevertheless I will give it. Advice seems to be the only thing I can give you at present. Listen to it, for it's good advice. When you are trying to get something out of a man, don't blurt it out as you did to me. Do try to be more subtle, more seductive. It gets better results. You used to know how, to perfection. But just now when you offered me your – er – collateral for my money you looked as hard as nails. I've seen eyes like yours above a duelling pistol twenty paces from me and they aren't a pleasant sight. They evoke no ardour in the male breast. That's no way to handle men, my dear. You are forgetting your early training.'

'I don't need you to tell me how to behave,' she said, and wearily put on her bonnet. She wondered how he could jest so blithely with a rope about his neck and her pitiful circumstances before him. She did not even notice that his hands were jammed in his pockets in hard fists as if he were straining at his own impotence.

'Cheer up,' he said, as she tied the bonnet strings. 'You can come to my hanging and it will make you feel lots better. It'll even up all your old scores with me – even this one. And I'll mention you in my will.'

'Thank you, but they may not hang you till it's too late to pay the taxes,' she said with a sudden malice that matched his own, and she meant it.

Chapter XXXV

It was raining when she came out of the building and the sky was a dull putty colour. The soldiers on the square had taken shelter in their huts and the streets were deserted. There was no vehicle in sight and she knew she would have to walk the long way home.

The brandy glow faded as she trudged along. The cold wind made her shiver and the chilly needle-like drops drove hard into her face. The rain quickly penetrated Aunt Pitty's thin cloak until it hung in clammy folds about her. She knew the velvet dress was being ruined and as for the tail feathers on the bonnet, they were as drooping and draggled as when their former owner had worn them about the wet barnyard of Tara. The bricks of the sidewalk were broken and, for long stretches, completely gone. In these spots the mud was ankle deep and her slippers stuck in it as if it were glue, even coming completely off her feet. Every time she bent over to retrieve them, the hem of the dress fell in the mud. She did not even try to avoid puddles but stepped dully into them, dragging her heavy skirts after her. She could feel her wet petticoat and pantalets cold about her ankles, but she was beyond caring about the wreck of the costume on which she had gambled so much. She was chilled and disheartened and desperate.

How could she ever go back to Tara and face them after her brave words? How could she tell them they must all go – somewhere? How could she leave it all, the red fields, the tall pines, the dark swampy bottom lands, the quiet burying-ground where Ellen lay in the cedars' deep shade?

Hatred of Rhett burned in her heart as she plodded along the slippery way. What a blackguard he was! She hoped they did hang him, so she would never have to face him again, with his knowledge of her disgrace and her humiliation. Of course, he could have gotten the money for her if he'd wanted to get it. Oh, hanging was too good for him! Thank God, he couldn't see her now, with her clothes soaking wet and her hair straggling and her teeth chattering. How hideous she must look and how he would laugh!

The negroes she passed turned insolent grins at her and laughed among themselves as she hurried by, slipping and sliding in the mud, stopping, panting, to replace her slippers. How dared they laugh, the black apes! How dared they grin at her, Scarlett O'Hara of Tara! She'd like to have them all whipped until the blood ran down their backs. What devils the Yankees were to set them free, free to jeer at white people!

As she walked down Washington Street, the landscape was as dreary as her own heart. Here there was none of the bustle and cheerfulness which she had noted on Peachtree Street. Here many handsome homes had once stood, but few of them had been rebuilt. Smoked foundations and the lonesome blackened chimneys, now known as 'Sherman's Sentinels', appeared with disheartening frequency. Overgrown paths led to what had been houses – old lawns thick with dead weeds, carriage blocks bearing names she knew so well, hitching-posts which would never again know the knot of reins. Cold wind and rain, mud and bare trees, silence and desolation. How wet her feet were and how long the journey home!

She heard the splash of hooves behind her and moved farther over on the narrow sidewalk to avoid more mud-splotches on Aunt Pittypat's cloak. A horse and buggy came slowly up the road and she turned to watch it, determined to beg a ride if the driver was a white person. The rain obscured her vision as the buggy came abreast, but she saw the driver peer over the tarpaulin that stretched from the dashboard to his chin. There was something familiar about his face and as she stepped out into the road to get a closer view, there was an embarrassed little cough from the man and a well-known voice cried in accents of pleasure and astonishment: 'Surely, it can't be Miss Scarlett!'

'Oh, Mr Kennedy!' she cried, splashing across the road and leaning on the muddy wheel, heedless of further damage to the cloak. 'I was never so glad to see anybody in my life!'

He coloured with pleasure at the obvious sincerity of her words, hastily squirted a stream of tobacco juice from the opposite side of the buggy and leaped spryly to the ground. He shook her hand enthusiastically and holding up the tarpaulin, assisted her into the buggy.

'Miss Scarlett, what are you doing over in this section by yourself? Don't you know it's dangerous these days? And you are soaking wet. Here, wrap the robe around your feet.'

As he fussed over her, clucking like a hen, she gave herself up to the luxury of being taken care of. It was nice to have a man fussing and clucking and scolding, even if it was only that old maid in pants, Frank Kennedy. It was especially soothing after Rhett's brutal treatment. And oh, how good to see a County face when she was so far from home! He was well dressed, she noticed, and the buggy was new too. The horse looked young and well fed, but Frank looked far older than his years, older than on that Christmas Eve when he had been at Tara with his men. He was thin and sallow-faced and his yellow eyes were watery and sunken in creases of loose flesh. His ginger-coloured beard was scantier than ever, streaked with tobacco juice and as ragged as if he clawed at it incessantly. But he looked bright and cheerful, in contrast with the lines of sorrow and worry and weariness which Scarlett saw in faces everywhere.

'It's a pleasure to see you,' said Frank warmly. 'I didn't know you were in town. I saw Miss Pittypat only last week and she didn't tell me you were coming. Did – er – ahem – did anyone else come up from Tara with you?'

He was thinking of Suellen, the silly old fool.

'No,' she said, wrapping the warm lap-robe about her and trying to pull it up around her neck. 'I came alone. I didn't give Aunt Pitty any warning.'

He chirruped to the horse and it plodded off, picking its way carefully down the slick road.

'All the folks at Tara well?'

'Oh, yes, so-so.'

She must think of something to talk about, yet it was so hard to talk. Her mind was leaden with defeat and all she wanted was to lie back in this warm blanket and say to herself: 'I won't think of Tara now. I'll think of it later, when it won't hurt so much.' If she could just get him started talking on some subject which would hold him all the way home, so she would have nothing to do but murmur 'How nice' and 'You certainly are smart' at intervals.

'Mr Kennedy, I'm so surprised to see you. I know I've been a bad girl, not keeping up with old friends, but I didn't know you were here in Atlanta. I thought somebody told me you were in Marietta.'

'I do business in Marietta, a lot of business,' he said. 'Didn't Miss Suellen tell you I had settled in Atlanta? Didn't she tell you about my store?'

Vaguely she had a memory of Suellen chattering about Frank and a store but she never paid much heed to anything Suellen said. It had been sufficient to know that Frank was alive and would some day take Suellen off her hands.

'No, not a word,' she lied. 'Have you a store? How smart you must be!'

He looked a little hurt at hearing that Suellen had not published the news but brightened at the flattery.

'Yes, I've got a store, and a pretty good one, I think. Folks tell me I'm a born merchant.' He laughed pleasedly, the tittery cackling laugh which she always found so annoying.

'Conceited old fool,' she thought.

'Oh, you could be a success at anything you turned your hand to, Mr Kennedy. But how on earth did you ever get started with the store? When I saw you Christmas before last you said you didn't have a cent in the world.'

'Well, it's a long story, Miss Scarlett.'

'Thank the Lord!' she thought. 'Perhaps it will hold him till we get home.' And aloud: 'Do tell!'

'You recall when we came to Tara last, hunting for supplies? Well, not long after that I went into active service. I mean real fighting. No more commissary for me. There wasn't much need for a commissary, Miss Scarlett, because we couldn't hardly pick up a thing for the army, and I thought the place for an able-bodied man was in the fighting line. Well, I fought along with the cavalry for a spell till I got a minie ball through the shoulder.'

He looked very proud and Scarlett said: 'How dreadful!'

'Oh, it wasn't so bad, just a flesh wound,' he said deprecatingly. 'I was sent down south to a hospital and when I was just about well, the Yankee raiders came through. My, my, but that was a hot time! We didn't have much warning and all of us who could walk helped haul out the army stores and the hospital equipment to the train tracks to move it. We'd gotten one train about loaded when the Yankees rode in one end of town and out we went the other end as fast as we could go. My, my, that was a mighty sad sight, sitting on top of that train and seeing the Yankees burn those supplies we had to leave at the depot. Miss Scarlett, they burned about a half-mile of stuff we had piled up there along the tracks. We just did get away ourselves.'

'How dreadful!'

'Yes, that's the word. Dreadful. Our men had come back into Atlanta then and so our train was sent here. Well, Miss Scarlett, it wasn't long before the war was over and – well, there was a lot of china and cots and mattresses and blankets and nobody claiming them. I suppose rightfully they belonged to the Yankees. I think those were the terms of the surrender, weren't they?'

'Um,' said Scarlett absently. She was getting warmer now and a little drowsy.

'I don't know till now if I did right,' he said, a little querulously. 'But the way I figured it, all that stuff wouldn't do the Yankees a bit of good. They'd probably burn it. And our folks had paid good solid money for it, and I thought it still ought to belong to the Confederacy or to the Confederates. Do you see what I mean?'

'Um.'

'I'm glad you agree with me, Miss Scarlett. In a way, it's been on my conscience. Lots of folks have told me: "Oh, forget about it, Frank," but I can't. I couldn't hold up my head if I thought I'd done what wasn't right. Do you think I did right?'

'Of course,' she said, wondering what the old fool had been talking about. Some struggle with his conscience. When a man got as old as Frank Kennedy he ought to have learned not to bother about things that didn't matter. But he always was so nervous and fussy and old-maidish.

'I'm glad to hear you say it. After the surrender I had about ten dollars in silver and nothing else in the world. You know what they did to Jonesboro and my house and store there. I just didn't know what to do. But I used the ten dollars to put a roof on an old store down by Five Points and I moved the hospital equipment in and started selling it. Everybody needed beds and china and mattresses and I sold them cheap, because I figured it was about as much other folks' stuff as it was mine. But I cleared money on it and bought some more stuff and the store just went along fine. I think I'll make a lot of money on it if things pick up.'

At the word 'money', her mind came back to him, crystal clear.

'You say you've made money?'

He visibly expanded under her interest. Few women except Suellen had ever given him more than perfunctory courtesy and it was very flattering to have a former belle like Scarlett hanging on his words. He slowed the horse so they would not reach home before he had finished his story.

'I'm not a millionaire, Miss Scarlett, and considering the money I used to have, what I've got now sounds small. But I made a thousand dollars this year. Of course, five hundred of it went to paying for new stock and repairing the store and paying the rent. But I've made five hundred clear and as things are certainly picking up, I ought to clear two thousand next year. I can sure use it too, for, you see, I've got another iron in the fire.'

Interest had sprung up sharply in her at the talk of money. She veiled her eyes with thick bristly lashes and moved a little closer to him.

'What does that mean, Mr Kennedy?'

He laughed and slapped the reins against the horse's back.

'I guess I'm boring you, talking about business, Miss Scarlett. A pretty little woman like you doesn't need to know anything about business.'

The old fool.

'Oh, I know I'm a goose about business but I'm so interested! Please tell me all about it and you can explain what I don't understand.'

'Well, my other iron is a sawmill.'

'A what?'

'A mill to cut up lumber and plane it. I haven't bought it yet but I'm going to. There's a man named Johnson who has one, way out Peachtree road, and he's anxious to sell it. He needs some cash right away, so he wants to sell and stay and run it for me at a weekly wage. It's one of the few mills in this section, Miss Scarlett. The Yankees destroyed most of them. And anyone who owns a sawmill owns a gold mine, for nowadays you can ask your own price for lumber. The Yankees burned so many houses here and there aren't enough for people to live in and it looks like folks have gone crazy about rebuilding. They can't get enough lumber and they can't get it fast enough. People are just pouring into Atlanta now, all the folks from the country districts who can't make a go of farming without darkies and the Yankees and Carpetbaggers who are swarming in trying to pick our bones a little barer than they already are. I tell you Atlanta's going to be a big town soon. They've got to have lumber for their houses, so I'm going to buy this mill just as soon as – well, as soon as some of the bills owing me are paid. By this time next year, I ought to be breathing easier about money. I – I guess you know why I'm so anxious to make money quickly, don't you?'

He blushed and cackled again. 'He's thinking of Suellen,' Scarlett thought in disgust.

For a moment she considered asking him to lend her three hundred dollars, but wearily she rejected the idea. He would be embarrassed; he would stammer; he would offer excuses, but he wouldn't lend it to her. He had worked hard for it, so he could marry Suellen in the spring, and if he parted with it, his wedding would be postponed indefinitely. Even if she worked on his sympathies and his duty toward his future family and gained his promise of a loan, she knew Suellen would never permit it. Suellen was getting more and more worried over the fact that she was practically an old maid and she would move heaven and earth to prevent anything from delaying her marriage.

What was there in that whining complaining girl to make this old fool so anxious to give her a soft nest? Suellen didn't deserve a loving husband and the profits of a store and a sawmill. The minute Sue got her hands on a little money she'd give herself unendurable airs and never contribute one cent toward the upkeep of Tara. Not Suellen! She'd think herself well out of it and not care if Tara went for taxes or burned to the ground, so long as she had pretty clothes and a 'Mrs' in front of her name.

As Scarlett thought of Suellen's secure future and the precarious one of herself and Tara, anger flamed in her at the unfairness of life. Hastily she looked out of the buggy into the muddy street, lest Frank should see her expression. She was going to lose everything she had, while Sue— Suddenly a determination was born in her.

Suellen should not have Frank and his store and his mill!

Suellen didn't deserve them. She was going to have them herself. She thought of Tara and remembered Jonas Wilkerson, venomous as a rattler, at the foot of the front steps, and she grasped at the last straw floating above the shipwreck of her life. Rhett had failed her but the Lord had provided Frank.

'But can I get him?' Her fingers clenched as she looked unseeingly into the rain. 'Can I make him forget Sue and propose to me real quick? If I could make Rhett almost propose, I know I could get Frank!' Her eyes went over him, her lids flickering. 'Certainly, he's no beauty,' she thought coolly, 'and he's got very bad teeth and his breath smells bad and he's old enough to be my father. Moreover, he's nervous and timid and well-meaning, and I don't know of any more damning qualities a man can have. But at least, he's a gentleman and I believe I could stand living with him better than with Rhett. Certainly I could manage him easier. At any rate, beggars can't be choosers.'

That he was Suellen's fiancé caused her no qualm of conscience. After the complete moral collapse which had sent her to Atlanta and to Rhett, the appropriation of her sister's betrothed seemed a minor affair and not one to be bothered with at this time.

With the rousing of fresh hope, her spine stiffened and she forgot that her feet were wet and cold. She looked at Frank so steadily, her eyes narrowing, that he became somewhat alarmed and she dropped her gaze swiftly, remembering Rhett's words: 'I've seen eyes like yours above a duelling pistol . . . They evoke no ardour in the male breast.'

'What's the matter, Miss Scarlett? You got a chill?'

'Yes,' she answered helplessly. 'Would you mind—' She hesitated timidly. 'Would you mind if I put my hand in your coat pocket? It's so cold and my muff is soaked through.'

'Why – why – of course not! And you haven't any gloves! My, my, what a brute I've been idling along like this, talking my head off when you must be freezing and wanting to get to a fire. Giddap, Sally! By the way, Miss Scarlett, I've been so busy talking about myself I haven't even asked you what you were doing in this section in this weather.'

'I was at the Yankee headquarters,' she answered before she thought.

His sandy brows went up in astonishment.

'But, Miss Scarlett! The soldiers—Why—'

'Mary, Mother of God, let me think of a real good lie,' she prayed hastily. It would never do for Frank to suspect she had seen Rhett. Frank thought Rhett the blackest of blackguards and unsafe for decent women to speak to.

'I went there – I went there to see if – if any of the officers would buy fancy work from me to send home to their wives. I embroider very nicely.'

He sank back against the seat aghast, indignation struggling with bewilderment.

'You went to the Yankees— But, Miss Scarlett! You shouldn't. Why – why . . . Surely your father doesn't know! Surely Miss Pittypat—'

'Oh, I shall die if you tell Aunt Pittypat!' she cried in real anxiety and burst into tears. It was easy to cry, because she was so cold and miserable, but the effect was startling. Frank could not have been more embarrassed or helpless if she had suddenly begun disrobing. He clicked his tongue against his teeth several times, muttering 'My! My!' and made futile gestures at her. A daring thought went through his mind that he should draw her head on to his shoulder and pat her but he had never done this to any woman and hardly knew how to go about it. Scarlett O'Hara, so high-spirited and pretty, crying here in his buggy. Scarlett O'Hara, the proudest of the proud, trying to sell needlework to the Yankees. His heart burned.

She sobbed on, saying a few words now and then, and he gathered that all was not well at Tara. Mr O'Hara was still 'not himself at all', and there wasn't enough food to go around for so many. So she had to come to Atlanta to try to make a little money for herself and her boy. Frank clicked his tongue again and suddenly he found that her head was on his shoulder. He did not quite know how it got there. Surely he had not placed it there, but there her head was and there was Scarlett helplessly sobbing against his thin chest, an exciting and novel sensation for him. He patted her shoulder timidly, gingerly at first, and when she did not rebuff him he became bolder and patted her firmly. What a helpless, sweet, womanly little thing she was. And how brave and silly to try her hand at making money by her needle. But dealing with the Yankees – that was too much.

'I won't tell Miss Pittypat, but you must promise me, Miss Scarlett, that you won't do anything like this again. The idea of your father's daughter—'

Her wet green eyes sought his helplessly.

'But, Mr Kennedy, I must do something. I must take care of my poor little boy and there is no one to look after us now.'

'You are a brave little woman,' he pronounced, 'but I won't have you do this sort of thing. Your family would die of shame.'

'Then what will I do?' The swimming eyes looked up to him as if she knew he knew everything and was hanging on his words.

'Well, I don't know right now. But I'll think of something.'

'Oh, I know you will! You are so smart – Frank.'

She had never called him by his first name before and the sound came to him as a pleasant shock and surprise. The poor girl was probably so upset she didn't even notice her slip. He felt very kindly toward her and very protecting. If there was anything he could do for Suellen O'Hara's sister, he would certainly do it. He pulled out a red bandana handkerchief and handed it to her and she wiped her eyes and began to smile tremulously.

'I'm such a silly little goose,' she said apologetically. 'Please forgive me.'

'You aren't a silly little goose. You're a very brave little woman and you are trying to carry too heavy a load. I'm afraid Miss Pittypat isn't going to be much help to you. I hear she lost most of her property and Mr Henry Hamilton's in bad shape himself. I only wish I had a home to offer you shelter in. But, Miss Scarlett, you just remember this, when Miss Suellen and I are married, there'll always be a place for you under our roof and for Wade Hampton too.'

Now was the time! Surely the saints and angels watched over her to give her such a Heaven-sent opportunity. She managed to look very startled and embarrassed and opened her mouth as if to speak quickly and then shut it with a pop.

'Don't tell me you didn't know I was to be your brother-in-law this spring,' he said with nervous jocularity. And then, seeing her eyes fill up with tears, he questioned in alarm: 'What's the matter? Miss Sue's not ill, is she?'

'Oh, no! No!'

'There is something wrong. You must tell me.'

'Oh, I can't! I didn't know! I thought surely she must have written—Oh, how mean!'

'Miss Scarlett, what is it?'

'Oh, Frank, I didn't mean to let it out but I thought, of course, you knew – that she had written you—'

'Written me what?' He was trembling.

'Oh, to do this to a fine man like you!'

'What's she done?'

'She didn't write you? Oh, I guess she was too ashamed to write you. She should be ashamed! Oh, to have such a mean sister!'

By this time, Frank could not even get questions to his lips. He sat staring at her, grey-faced, the reins slack in his hands.

'She's going to marry Tony Fontaine next month. Oh, I'm so sorry, Frank. So sorry to be the one to tell you. She just got tired of waiting and she was afraid she'd be an old maid.'

Mammy was standing on the front porch when Frank helped Scarlett out of the buggy. She had evidently been standing there for some time, for her head-rag was damp and the old shawl clutched tightly about her showed rain-spots. Her wrinkled black face was a study in anger and apprehension and her lip was pushed out farther than Scarlett could ever remember. She peered quickly at Frank and, when she saw who it was, her face changed – pleasure, bewilderment and something akin to guilt spreading over it. She waddled forward to Frank with pleased greetings and grinned and curtsied when he shook her hand.

'It sho is good ter see home folks,' she said. 'How is you, Mist' Frank? My, ain' you lookin' fine an' gran'! Effen Ah'd knowed Miss Scarlett wuz out wid you, Ah wouldn' worrit so. Ah'd knowed she wuz tekken keer of. Ah come back hyah an' fine she gone an' Ah been as 'stracted as a chicken wid its haid off, thinkin' she runnin' roun' dis town by herseff wid all dese trashy free issue niggers on de street. Huccome you din' tell me you gwine out, honey? An' you wid a cole!'

Scarlett winked slyly at Frank and, for all his distress at the bad news he had just heard, he smiled, knowing she was enjoining silence and making him one in a pleasant conspiracy.

'You run up and fix me some dry clothes, Mammy,' she said. 'And some hot tea.'

'Lawd, yo' new dress is plum ruint,' grumbled Mammy. 'Ah gwine have a time dryin' it an' brushin' it, so it'll be fit ter be wo' ter de weddin' ternight.'

She went into the house and Scarlett leaned close to Frank and whispered: 'Do come to supper tonight. We are so lonesome. And we're going to the wedding afterward. Do be our escort! And, please don't say anything to Aunt Pitty about – about Suellen. It would distress her so much and I can't bear for her to know that my sister—'

'Oh, I won't! I won't!' Frank said hastily, wincing from the very thought.

'You've been so sweet to me today and done me so much good. I feel right brave again.' She squeezed his hand in parting and turned the full battery of her eyes upon him.

Mammy, who was waiting just inside the door, gave her an inscrutable look and followed her, puffing, up the stairs to the bedroom. She was silent while she stripped off the wet clothes and hung them over chairs and tucked Scarlett into bed. When she had brought up a cup of hot tea and a hot brick, rolled in flannel, she looked down at Scarlett and said, with the nearest approach to an apology in her voice Scarlett had ever heard: 'Lamb, huccome you din' tell yo' own Mammy whut you wuz upter? Den Ah wouldn' had ter traipse all dis way up hyah ter 'Lanta. Ah is too ole an' too fat fer sech runnin' roun'.'

'What do you mean?'

'Honey, you kain fool me. Ah knows you. An' Ah seed Mist' Frank's face jes' now an' Ah seed yo' face, an' Ah kin read yo' mine lak a pahson read a Bible. An' Ah heerd dat whisperin' you wuz givin' him 'bout Miss Suellen. Effen Ah'd had a notion 'twiz Mist' Frank you wuz affer, Ah'd stayed home whar Ah b'longs.'

'Well,' said Scarlett shortly, snuggling under the blankets and realizing it was useless to try to throw Mammy off the scent, 'who did you think it was?'

'Chile, Ah din' know but Ah din' lak de look on yo' face yestiddy. An' Ah 'membered Miss Pittypat writin' Miss Melly dat dat rapscallion Butler man had lots of money an' Ah doan fergit whut Ah hears. But Mist' Frank, he a gempmum even ef he ain' so pretty.'

Scarlett gave her a sharp look and Mammy returned the gaze with calm omniscience.

'Well, what are you going to do about it? Tattle to Suellen?'

'Ah is gwine ter he'p you pleasure Mist' Frank eve'y way Ah knows how,' said Mammy, tucking the covers about Scarlett's neck.

Scarlett lay quietly for a while, as Mammy fussed about the room, relief flooding her that there was no need for words between them. No explanations were asked, no reproaches made. Mammy understood and was silent. In Mammy, Scarlett had found a realist more uncompromising than herself. The mottled wise old eyes saw deeply, saw clearly, with the directness of the savage and the child, undeterred by conscience when danger threatened her pet. Scarlett was her baby and what her baby wanted, even though it belonged to another, Mammy was willing to help her obtain. The rights of Suellen and Frank Kennedy did not even enter her mind, save to cause a grim inward chuckle. Scarlett was in trouble and doing the best she could, and Scarlett was Miss Ellen's child. Mammy rallied to her with never a moment's hesitation.

Scarlett felt the silent reinforcement and, as the hot brick at her feet warmed her, the hope which had flickered faintly on the cold ride home grew into a flame. It swept through her, making her heart pump the blood through her veins in pounding surges. Strength was coming back and a reckless excitement which made her want to laugh aloud. Not beaten yet, she thought exultantly.

'Hand me the mirror, Mammy,' she said.

'Keep yo' shoulders unner dat kivver,' ordered Mammy, passing the hand mirror to her, a smile on her thick lips.

Scarlett looked at herself.

'I look white as a hant,' she said, 'and my hair is as wild as a horse's tail.'

'You doan look peart as you mout.'

'Hum . . . Is it raining very hard?'

'You know it's po'in'.'

'Well, just the same, you've got to go downtown for me.'

'Not in dis rain, Ah ain'.'

'Yes, you are or I'll go myself.'

'Whut you got ter do dat woan wait? Look ter me lak you done nuff fer one day.'

'I want,' said Scarlett, surveying herself carefully in the mirror, 'a bottle of cologne water. You can wash my hair and rinse it with cologne. And buy me a jar of quince-seed jelly to make it lie down flat.'

'Ah ain' gwine wash yo' ha'r in dis wedder an' you ain' gwine put no cologne on yo' haid lak a fas' woman needer. Not w'ile Ah got breaf in mah body.'

'Oh, yes, I am. Look in my purse and get that five-dollar gold piece out and go to town. And – er, Mammy, while you are downtown, you might get me a – a pot of rouge.'

'Whut dat?' asked Mammy suspiciously.

Scarlett met her eyes with a coldness she was far from feeling. There was never any way of knowing just how far Mammy could be bullied.

'Never you mind. Just ask for it.'

'Ah ain' buyin' nuthin' dat Ah doan know whut 'tis.'

'Well, it's paint, if you're so curious! Face paint. Don't stand there and swell up like a toad. Go on.'

'Paint!' ejaculated Mammy. 'Face paint! Well, you ain' so big dat Ah kain whup you! Ah ain' never been so scan'lized! You is los' yo' mine! Miss Ellen be tuhnin' in her grabe dis minute! Paintin' yo' face lak a—'

'You know very well Grandma Robillard painted her face and—'

'Yas'm, an' wo' only one petticoat an' it wrang out wid water ter mek it stick an' show the shape of her laigs, but dat ain' sayin' you is gwine do sumpin' lak dat! Times wuz scan'lous w'en Ole Miss wuz young but times changes, dey do an'—'

'Name of God!' cried Scarlett, losing her temper and throwing back the covers. 'You can go straight back to Tara!'

'You kain sen' me ter Tara ness Ah wants ter go. Ah is free,' said Mammy heatedly. 'An' Ah is gwine ter stay right hyah. Git back in dat baid. Does you want ter ketch pneumony jes' now? Put down dem stays! Put dem down, honey. Now, Miss Scarlett, you ain' gwine nowhars in dis wedder. Lawd God! But you sho look lak yo' pa! Git back in baid – Ah kain go buyin' no paint! Ah die of shame, eve'ybody knowin' it wuz fer mah chile! Miss Scarlett, you is so sweet an' pretty lookin' you doan need no paint. Honey, doan nobody but bad womens use dat stuff.'

'Well, they get results, don't they?'

'Jesus, hear her! Lamb, doan say bad things lak dat! Put down dem wet stockin's, honey. Ah kain have you buy dat stuff yo'seff. Miss Ellen would hant me. Git back in baid. Ah'll go. Maybe Ah fine me a sto' whar dey doan know us.'

That night at Mrs Elsing's, when Fanny had been duly married and old Levi and the other musicians were tuning up for the dance, Scarlett looked about her with gladness. It was so exciting to be actually at a party again. She was pleased also with the warm reception she had received. When she entered the house on Frank's arm, everyone had rushed to her with cries of pleasure and welcome, kissed her, shaken her hand, told her they had missed her dreadfully and that she must never go back to Tara. The men seemed gallantly to have forgotten she had tried her best to break their hearts in other days and the girls that she had done everything in her power to entice their beaux away from them. Even Mrs Merriwether, Mrs Whiting, Mrs Meade and the other dowager who had been so cool to her during the last days of the war, forgot her flighty conduct and their disapproval of it and recalled only that she had suffered in their common defeat and that she was Pitty's niece and Charles' widow. They kissed her and spoke gently with tears in their eyes of her dear mother's passing and asked at length about her father and her sisters. Everyone asked about Melanie and Ashley, demanding the reason why they, too, had not come back to Atlanta.

In spite of her pleasure at the welcome, Scarlett felt a slight uneasiness which she tried to conceal, an uneasiness about the appearance of her velvet dress. It was still damp to the knees and still spotted about the hem, despite the frantic efforts of Mammy and Cookie with a steaming kettle, a clean hairbrush and frantic wavings in front of an open fire. Scarlett was afraid someone would notice her bedraggled state and realize that this was her only nice dress. She was a little cheered by the fact that many of the dresses of the other guests looked far worse than hers. They were so old and had such carefully mended and pressed looks. At least, her dress was whole and new, damp though it was – in fact, the only new dress at the gathering with the exception of Fanny's white-satin wedding gown.

Remembering what Aunt Pitty had told her about the Elsing finances, she wondered where the money for the satin dress had been obtained and for the refreshments and decorations and musicians too. It must have cost a pretty penny. Borrowed money probably or else the whole Elsing clan had contributed to give Fanny this expensive wedding. Such a wedding in these hard times seemed to Scarlett an extravagance on a par with the tombstones of the Tarleton boys and she felt the same irritation and lack of sympathy she had felt as she stood in the Tarleton burying-ground. The days when money could be thrown away carelessly had passed. Why did these people persist in making the gestures of the old days when the old days were gone?

But she shrugged off her momentary annoyance. It wasn't her money and she didn't want her evening's pleasure spoiled by irritation at other people's foolishness.

She discovered she knew the groom quite well, for he was Tommy Wellburn from Sparta and she had nursed him in 1863 when he had a wound in his shoulder. He had been a handsome young six-footer then and had given up his medical studies to go in the cavalry. Now he looked like a little old man, so bent was he by the wound in his hip. He walked with some difficulty and, as Aunt Pitty had remarked, spraddled in a very vulgar way. But he seemed totally unaware of his appearance, or unconcerned about it, and had the manner of one who asks no odds from any man. He had given up all hope of continuing his medical studies and was now a contractor, working a labour crew of Irishmen who were building the new hotel. Scarlett wondered how he managed so onerous a job in his condition but asked no questions, realizing wryly that almost anything was possible when necessity drove.

Tommy and Hugh Elsing and the little monkey-like René Picard stood talking with her while the chairs and furniture were pushed back to the wall in preparation for the dancing. Hugh had not changed since Scarlett last saw him in 1862. He was still the thin sensitive boy with the same lock of pale-brown hair hanging over his forehead and the same delicate useless-looking hands she remembered so well. But René had changed since that furlough when he married Maybelle Merriwether. He still had the Gallic twinkle in his black eyes and the Creole zest for living but, for all his easy laughter, there was something hard about his face which had not been there in the early days of the war. And the air of supercilious elegance which had clung about him in his striking Zouave uniform was completely gone.

'Cheeks lak ze rose, eyes lak ze emerald!' he said, kissing Scarlett's hand and paying tribute to the rouge upon her face. 'Pretty lak w'en I first see you at ze bazaar. You remembaire? Nevaire have I forgot how you toss your wedding ring in my basket. Ha, but zat was brave! But I should nevaire have zink you wait so long to get anothaire ring!'

His eyes sparkled wickedly and he dug his elbow into Hugh's ribs.

'And I never thought you'd be driving a pie wagon, Renny Picard,' she said. Instead of being ashamed at having his degrading occupation thrown in his face, he seemed pleased and laughed uproariously, slapping Hugh on the back.

'Touché!' he cried. 'Belle-Mère, Madame Merriwether, she mek me do eet, ze first work I do een all my life, me, René Picard, who was to grow old breezing ze race-horse, playing ze feedle! Now, I drive ze pie wagon and I lak eet! Madame Belle-Mère, she can mek a man do annyzing. She should have been ze general and we win ze war, eh, Tommy?'

'Well!' thought Scarlett. 'The idea of liking to drive a pie wagon when his people used to own ten miles along the Mississippi River and a big house in New Orleans, too!'

'If we'd had our mother-in-laws in the ranks, we'd have beat the Yankees in a week,' agreed Tommy, his eyes straying to the slender, indomitable form of his new mother-in-law. 'The only reason we lasted as long as we did was because of the ladies behind us who wouldn't give up.'

'Who'll *never* give up,' amended Hugh, and his smile was proud but a little wry. 'There's not a lady here tonight who has surrendered, no matter what her men folks did at Appomattox. It's a lot worse on them than it ever was on us. At least, we took it out in fighting.'

'And they in hating,' finished Tommy. 'Eh, Scarlett? It bothers the ladies to see what their men folks have come down to lots more than it bothers us. Hugh was to be a judge, René was to play the fiddle before the crowned heads of Europe—' He ducked as René aimed a blow at him. 'And I was to be a doctor and now—'

'Geeve us ze time!' cried René. 'Zen I become ze Pie Prince of ze South! And my good Hugh ze King of ze Kindling and you, my Tommy, you weel own ze Irish slaves instead of ze darky slaves. What change – what fun! And what eet do for you, Mees Scarlett, and Mees Melly? You meelk ze cow, peek ze cotton?'

'Indeed, no!' said Scarlett coolly, unable to understand René's gay acceptance of hardships. 'Our darkies do that.'

'Mees Melly, I hear she call her boy "Beauregard". You tell her I, René, approve and say that except for "Jesus" there is no bettaire name.'

And though he smiled, his eyes glowed proudly at the name of Louisiana's dashing hero.

'Well, there's "Robert Edward Lee",' observed Tommy. 'And while I'm not trying to lessen Old Beau's reputation, my first son is going to be named "Bob Lee Wellburn".'

René laughed and shrugged.

'I recount to you a joke but eet eez a true story. And you see how Creoles zink of our brave Beauregard and of your General Lee. On ze train near New Orleans a man of Virginia, a man of General Lee, he meet wiz a Creole of ze troops of Beauregard. And ze man of Virginia, he talk, talk, talk how General Lee do zis, General Lee say zat. And ze Creole, he look polite and he wreenkle hees forehead lak he try to remembaire, and zen he smile and say: "General Lee! Ah, oui! Now I know! General Lee! Ze man General Beauregard speak well of!" '

Scarlett tried to join politely in the laughter but she did not see any point to the story except that Creoles were just as stuck-up as Charleston and Savannah people. Moreover, she had always thought Ashley's son should have been named after him.

The musicians after preliminary tunings and whangings broke into 'Old Dan Tucker' and Tommy turned to her.

'Will you dance, Scarlett? I can't favour you but Hugh or René—'

'No, thank you. I'm still mourning my mother,' said Scarlett hastily. 'I will sit them out.'

Her eyes singled out Frank Kennedy and beckoned him from the side of Mrs Elsing.

'I'll sit in that alcove yonder if you'll bring me some refreshments and then we can have a nice chat,' she told Frank as the other three men moved off.

When he had hurried away to bring her a glass of wine and a paper-thin slice of cake, Scarlett sat down in the alcove at the end of the drawing-room and carefully arranged her skirts so that the worst spots would not show. The humiliating events of the morning with Rhett were pushed from her mind by the excitement of seeing so many people and hearing music again. Tomorrow she would think of Rhett's conduct and her shame and they would make her writhe again. Tomorrow she would wonder if she had made any impression on Frank's hurt and bewildered heart. But not tonight. Tonight she was alive to her finger-tips, every sense alert with hope, her eyes sparkling.

She looked from the alcove into the huge drawing-room and watched the dancers, remembering how beautiful this room had been when first she came to Atlanta during the war. Then the hardwood floors had shone like glass, and overhead the chandelier with its hundreds of tiny prisms had caught and reflected every ray of the dozens of candles it bore, flinging them, like gleams from diamonds, flame and sapphire about the room. The old portraits on the walls had been dignified and gracious and had looked down upon guests with an air of mellowed hospitality. The rosewood sofas had been soft and inviting and one of them, the largest, had stood in the place of honour in

this same alcove where she now sat. It had been Scarlett's favourite seat at
parties. From this point stretched the pleasant vista of drawing-room and
dining-room beyond, the oval mahogany table which seated twenty and the
twenty slim-legged chairs demurely against the walls, the massive sideboard
and buffet weighted with heavy silver, with seven-branched candlesticks,
goblets, cruets, decanters and shining little glasses. Scarlett had sat on that
sofa so often in the first years of the war, always with some handsome officer
beside her, and listened to violin and bull fiddle, accordion and banjo, and
heard the exciting swishing noises which dancing feet made on the waxed
and polished floor.

Now the chandelier hung dark. It was twisted askew and most of the prisms
were broken, as if the Yankee occupants had made their beauty a target for
their boots. Now an oil lamp and a few candles lighted the room and the
roaring fire in the wide hearth gave most of the illumination. Its flickering
light showed how irreparably scarred and splintered the dull old floor was.
Squares on the faded paper on the wall gave evidence that once the portraits
had hung there, and wide cracks in the plaster recalled the day during the
siege when a shell had exploded on the house and torn off parts of the roof and
second floor. The heavy old mahogany table, spread with cake and decanters,
still presided in the empty-looking dining-room but it was scratched and the
broken legs showed signs of clumsy repair. The sideboard, the silver and the
spindly chairs were gone. The dull-gold damask draperies which had covered
the arching French windows at the back of the room were missing, and only
the remnants of the lace curtains remained, clean but obviously mended.

In place of the curved sofa she had liked so much was a hard bench that
was none too comfortable. She sat upon it with as good grace as possible,
wishing her skirts were in such condition that she could dance. It would be
so good to dance again. But, of course, she could do more with Frank in this
sequestered alcove than in a breathless reel and she could listen fascinated to
his talk and encourage him to greater flights of foolishness.

But the music certainly was inviting. Her slipper patted longingly in time
with old Levi's large splayed foot as he twanged a strident banjo and
called the figures of the reel. Feet swished and scraped and patted as the
twin lines danced toward each other, retreated, whirled and made arches
of their arms.

> *Ole Dan Tucker he got drunk—*
> *(Swing yo' padners!)*
> *Fell in de fiah an' he kick up a chunk!*
> *(Skip light, ladies!)*

After the dull and exhausting months at Tara it was good to hear music
again and the sound of dancing feet, good to see familiar friendly faces

laughing in the feeble light, calling old jokes and catchwords, bantering, rallying, coquetting. It was like coming to life again after being dead. It almost seemed that the bright days of five years ago had come back again. If she could close her eyes and not see the worn made-over dresses and the patched boots and mended slippers, if her mind did not call up the faces of boys missing from the reel, she might almost think that nothing had changed. But as she looked, watching the old men grouped about the decanter in the dining-room, the matrons lining the walls, talking behind fanless hands, and the swaying, skipping young dancers, it came to her suddenly, coldly, frighteningly that it was all as greatly changed as if these familiar figures were ghosts.

They looked the same but they were different. What was it? Was it only that they were five years older? No, it was something more than the passing of time. Something had gone out of them, out of their world. Five years ago, a feeling of security had wrapped them all around so gently they were not even aware of it. In its shelter they had flowered. Now it was gone and with it had gone the old thrill, the old sense of something delightful and exciting just around the corner, the old glamour of their way of living.

She knew she had changed too, but not as they had changed, and it puzzled her. She sat and watched them and she felt herself an alien among them, as alien and lonely as if she had come from another world, speaking a language they did not understand and she not understanding theirs. Then she knew that this feeling was the same one she felt with Ashley. With him and with people of his kind – and they made up most of her world – she felt outside of something she could not understand.

Their faces were little changed and their manners not at all, but it seemed to her that these two things were all that remained of her old friends. An ageless dignity, a timeless gallantry still clung about them and would cling until they died, but they would carry undying bitterness to their graves, a bitterness too deep for words. They were a soft-spoken, fierce, tired people who were defeated and would not know defeat, broken yet standing determinedly erect. They were crushed and helpless, citizens of conquered provinces. They were looking on the state they loved, seeing it trampled by the enemy, rascals making a mock of the law, their former slaves a menace, their men disfranchised, their women insulted. And they were remembering graves.

Everything in their old world had changed but the old forms. The old usages went on, must go on, for the forms were all that were left to them. They were holding tightly to the things they knew best and loved best in the old days, the leisured manners, the courtesy, the pleasant casualness in human contacts and, most of all, the protecting attitude of the men toward their women. True to the tradition in which they had been reared, the men were courteous and tender and they almost succeeded in creating an atmosphere of sheltering their women from all that was harsh and unfit for feminine eyes. That, thought Scarlett, was the height of absurdity, for there was little, now, which even the most cloistered women had not seen and known in the last five years. They had nursed the wounded, closed dying eyes, suffered war and fire and devastation, known terror and flight and starvation.

But, no matter what sights they had seen, what menial tasks they had done and would have to do, they remained ladies and gentlemen, royalty in exile – bitter, aloof, incurious, kind to one another, diamond hard, as bright and brittle as the crystals of the broken chandelier over their heads. The old days had gone but these people would go their ways as if the old days still existed, charming, leisurely, determined not to rush and scramble for pennies as the Yankees did, determined to part with none of the old ways.

Scarlett knew that she, too, was greatly changed. Otherwise she could not have done the things she had done since she was last in Atlanta; otherwise she would not now be contemplating doing what she desperately hoped to do. But there was a difference in their hardness and hers and just what the difference was, she could not, for the moment, tell. Perhaps it was that there was nothing she would not do, and there were so many things these people would rather die than do. Perhaps it was that they were without hope but still smiling at life, bowing gracefully and passing it by. And this Scarlett could not do.

She could not ignore life. She had to live it and it was too brutal, too hostile, for her even to try to gloss over its harshness with a smile. Of the sweetness and courage and unyielding pride of her friends, Scarlett saw nothing. She saw only a silly stiff-neckedness which observed facts but smiled and refused to look them in the face.

As she stared at the dancers, flushed from the reel, she wondered if things drove them as she was driven, dead lovers, maimed husbands, children who were hungry, acres slipping away, beloved roofs that sheltered strangers. But, of course, they were driven! She knew their circumstances only a little less thoroughly than she knew her own. Their losses had been her losses, their privations her privations, their problems her same problems. Yet they had reacted differently to them. The faces she was seeing in the room were not faces; they were masks, excellent masks which would never drop.

But if they were suffering as acutely from brutal circumstances as she was – and they were – how could they maintain this air of gaiety and lightness of heart? Why, indeed, should they even try to do it? They were beyond her comprehension and vaguely irritating. She couldn't be like them. She couldn't survey the wreck of the world with an air of casual unconcern. She was as hunted as a fox, running with a bursting heart, trying to reach a burrow before the hounds caught up.

Suddenly she hated them all because they were different from her, because they carried their losses with an air that she could never attain, would never wish to attain. She hated them, these smiling, light-footed strangers, these proud fools who took pride in something they had lost, seeming to be proud that they had lost it. The women bore themselves like ladies and she knew they were ladies, though menial tasks were their daily lot and they didn't know where their next dress was coming from. Ladies all! But she could not feel herself a lady, for all her velvet dress and scented hair, for all the pride of birth that stood behind her and the pride of wealth that had once been hers. Harsh contact with the red earth of Tara had stripped gentility from her and she knew she would never feel like a lady again until her table was weighted with silver and crystal and smoking with rich food, until her own horses and carriages stood in her stables, until black hands and not white took the cotton from Tara.

'Ah!' she thought angrily, sucking in her breath. 'That's the difference! Even though they're poor, they still feel like ladies and I don't. The silly fools don't seem to realize that you can't be a lady without money!'

Even in this flash of revelation, she realized vaguely that, foolish though they seemed, theirs was the right attitude. Ellen would have thought so. This disturbed her. She knew she should feel as these people felt, but she could not. She knew she should believe devoutly, as they did, that a born lady remained a lady, even if reduced to poverty, but she could not make herself believe it now.

All her life she had heard sneers hurled at the Yankees because their pretensions to gentility were based on wealth, not breeding. But at this moment, heresy though it was, she could not help thinking the Yankees were right on this one matter, even if wrong in all others. It took money to be a lady. She knew Ellen would have fainted had she ever heard such words from her daughter. No depth of poverty could ever have made Ellen feel ashamed. Ashamed! Yes, that was how Scarlett felt. Ashamed that she was poor and reduced to galling shifts and penury and work that negroes should do.

She shrugged in irritation. Perhaps these people were right and she was wrong but, just the same, these proud fools weren't looking forward as she was doing, straining every nerve, risking even honour and good name to get back what they had lost. It was beneath the dignity of many of them to indulge in a scramble for money. The times were rude and hard. They called for rude and hard struggle if one was to conquer them. Scarlett knew that family tradition would forcibly restrain many of these people from such a struggle – with the making of money admittedly its aim. They all thought that obvious money-making and even talk of money were vulgar in the extreme. Of course, there were exceptions. Mrs Merriwether and her baking and René driving the pie wagon. And Hugh Elsing cutting and peddling firewood and Tommy contracting. And Frank having the gumption to start a store. But what of the rank and file of them? The planters would scratch a few acres and live in poverty. The lawyers and doctors would go back to their professions and wait for clients who might never come. And the rest, those who had lived in leisure on their incomes? What would happen to them?

But she wasn't going to be poor all her life. She wasn't going to sit down and patiently wait for a miracle to help her. She was going to rush into life and wrest from it what she could. Her father had started as a poor immigrant boy and had won the broad acres of Tara. What he had done, his daughter could do. She wasn't like these people who had gambled everything on a Cause that was gone and were content to be proud of having lost that Cause, because it was worth any sacrifice. They drew their courage from the past. She was drawing hers from the future. Frank Kennedy, at present, was her future. At least, he had the store and he had cash money. And if she could only marry him and get her hands on that money, she could make ends meet at Tara for another year. And after that – Frank must buy the sawmill. She could see for herself how quickly the town was rebuilding and anyone who could establish a lumber business now, when there was so little competition, would have a gold mine.

There came to her, from the recesses of her mind, words Rhett had spoken in the early years of the war about the money he made in the blockade. She had not taken the trouble to understand them then, but now they seemed perfectly clear and she wondered if it had been only her youth or plain stupidity which had kept her from appreciating them.

'There's just as much money to be made in the wreck of a civilisation as in the upbuilding of one.'

'This is the wreck he foresaw,' she thought, 'and he was right. There's still plenty of money to be made by anyone who isn't afraid to work – or to grab.'

She saw Frank coming across the floor toward her with a glass of blackberry wine in his hand and a morsel of cake on a saucer and she pulled her face into a smile. It did not occur to her to question whether Tara was worth marrying Frank. She knew it was worth it and she never gave the matter a second thought.

She smiled up at him as she sipped the wine, knowing that her cheeks were more attractively pink than any of the dancers'. She moved her skirts for him to sit by her and waved her handkerchief idly so that the faint sweet smell of the cologne could reach his nose. She was proud of the cologne, for no other woman in the room was wearing any and Frank had noticed it. In a fit of daring he had whispered to her that she was as pink and fragrant as a rose.

If only he were not so shy! He reminded her of a timid old brown field rabbit. If only he had the gallantry and ardour of the Tarleton boys or even the coarse impudence of Rhett Butler. But, if he possessed those qualities, he'd probably have sense enough to feel the desperation that lurked just beneath her demurely fluttering eyelids. As it was, he didn't know enough about women even to suspect what she was up to. That was her good fortune but it did not increase her respect for him.

Chapter XXXVI

She married Frank Kennedy two weeks later after a whirlwind courtship which she blushingly told him left her too breathless to oppose his ardour any longer.

He did not know that during those two weeks she had walked the floor at night, gritting her teeth at the slowness with which he took hints and encouragements, praying that no untimely letter from Suellen would reach him and ruin her plans. She thanked God that her sister was the poorest of correspondents, delighting to receive letters and disliking to write them. But there was always a chance, always a chance, she thought in the long night hours as she padded back and forth across the cold floor of her bedroom, with Ellen's faded shawl clutched about her nightdress. Frank did not know she had received a laconic letter from Will, relating that Jonas Wilkerson had paid another call at Tara and, finding her gone to Atlanta, had stormed about until Will and Ashley threw him bodily off the place. Will's letter hammered into her mind the fact she knew only too well – that time was getting shorter and shorter before the extra taxes must be paid. A fierce desperation drove her as she saw the days slipping by and she wished she might grasp the hour-glass in her hands and keep the sands from running.

But so well did she conceal her feelings, so well did she enact her rôle, Frank suspected nothing, saw no more than what lay on the surface – the pretty and helpless young widow of Charles Hamilton who greeted him every night in Miss Pittypat's parlour and listened, breathless with admiration, as he told of future plans for his store and how much money he expected to make when he was able to buy the sawmill. Her sweet sympathy and her bright-eyed interest in every word he uttered were balm upon the wound left by Suellen's supposed defection. His heart was sore and bewildered at Suellen's conduct, and his vanity, the shy, touchy vanity of a middle-aged bachelor who knows himself to be unattractive to women, was deeply wounded. He could not write Suellen, upbraiding her for her faithlessness; he shrank from the very idea. But he could ease his heart by talking about her to Scarlett. Without saying a disloyal word about Suellen, she could tell him she understood how badly her sister had treated him and what good treatment he merited from a woman who really appreciated him.

Little Mrs Hamilton was such a pretty pink-cheeked person, alternating between melancholy sighs when she thought of her sad plight, and laughter as gay and sweet as the tinkling of tiny silver bells when he made small jokes to cheer her. Her green gown, now neatly cleaned by Mammy, showed off her slender figure with its tiny waist to perfection, and how bewitching was the faint fragrance which always clung about her handkerchief and her hair! It was a shame that such a fine little woman should be alone and helpless in a world so rough that she didn't even understand its harshness. No husband nor brother nor even a father now to protect her. Frank thought the world too rude a place for a lone woman and, in that idea, Scarlett silently and heartily concurred.

He came to call every night, for the atmosphere of Pitty's house was pleasant and soothing. Mammy's smile at the front door was the smile reserved for quality folks, Pitty served him coffee laced with brandy and fluttered about him, and Scarlett hung on his every utterance. Sometimes in the afternoons he took Scarlett riding with him in his buggy when he went out on business. These rides were merry affairs because she asked so many foolish questions – 'just like a woman,' he told himself approvingly. He couldn't help laughing at her ignorance about business matters and she laughed too, saying: 'Well, of course, you can't expect a silly little woman like me to understand men's affairs.'

She made him feel, for the first time in his old-maidish life, that he was a strong upstanding man fashioned by God in a nobler mould than other men, fashioned to protect silly helpless women.

When, at last, they stood together to be married, her confiding little hand in his and her downcast lashes throwing thick black crescents on her pink cheeks, he still did not know how it all came about. He only knew he had done something romantic and exciting for the first time in his life. He, Frank Kennedy, had swept this lovely creature off her feet and into his strong arms. That was a heady feeling.

No friend or relative stood up with them at their marriage. The witnesses were strangers called in from the street. Scarlett had insisted on that and he had given in, though reluctantly, for he would have liked his sister and his brother-in-law from Jonesboro to be with him. And a reception with toasts drunk to the bride in Miss Pitty's parlour amid happy friends would have been a joy to him. But Scarlett would not hear of even Miss Pitty being present.

'Just us two, Frank,' she begged, squeezing his arm. 'Like an elopement. I always did want to run away and be married! Please, sweetheart, just for me!'

It was that endearing term, still so new to his ears, and the bright teardrops which edged her pale-green eyes as she looked up pleadingly at him that won him over. After all, a man had to make some concessions to his bride, especially about the wedding, for women set such a store by sentimental things.

And before he knew it, he was married.

Frank gave her the three hundred dollars, bewildered by her sweet urgency, reluctant at first, because it meant the end of his hope of buying the sawmill immediately. But he could not see her family evicted, and his disappointment soon faded at the sight of her radiant happiness, disappeared entirely at the loving way she 'took on' over his generosity. Frank had never before had a woman 'take on' over him and he came to feel that the money had been well spent, after all.

Scarlett dispatched Mammy to Tara immediately for the triple purpose of giving Will the money, announcing her marriage and bringing Wade to Atlanta. In two days she had a brief note from Will which she carried about with her and read and reread with mounting joy. Will wrote that the taxes had been paid and Jonas Wilkerson 'acted up pretty bad' at the news but had made no other threats so far. Will closed by wishing her happiness, a laconic formal statement which he qualified in no way. She knew Will understood what she had done and why she had done it and neither blamed nor praised. 'But what must Ashley think?' she wondered feverishly. 'What must he think of me now, after what I said to him so short a while ago in the orchard at Tara?'

She also had a letter from Suellen, poorly spelled, violent, abusive, tear-splotched, a letter so full of venom and truthful observations upon her character that she was never to forget it nor forgive the writer. But even Suellen's words could not dim her happiness that Tara was safe, at least from immediate danger.

It was hard to realize that Atlanta and not Tara was her permanent home now. In her desperation to obtain the tax money, no thought save Tara and the fate which threatened it had any place in her mind. Even at the moment of marriage, she had not given a thought to the fact that the price she was paying for the safety of home was permanent exile from it. Now that the deed was done, she realized this with a wave of homesickness hard to dispel. But there it was. She had made her bargain and she intended to stand by it. And she was so grateful to Frank for saving Tara she felt a warm affection for him and an equally warm determination that he should never regret marrying her.

The ladies of Atlanta knew their neighbours' business only slightly less completely than they knew their own and were far more interested in it. They all knew that for years Frank Kennedy had had an 'understanding' with Suellen O'Hara. In fact, he had said, sheepishly, that he expected to get married in the spring. So the tumult of gossip, surmise and deep suspicion which followed the announcement of his quiet wedding to Scarlett was not surprising. Mrs Merriwether, who never let her curiosity go long unsatisfied if she could help it, asked him point-blank just what he meant by marrying one sister when he was betrothed to the other. She reported to Mrs Elsing that all the answer she got for her pains was a silly look. Not even Mrs Merriwether, doughty soul that she was, dared to approach Scarlett on the subject. Scarlett seemed demure and sweet enough these days, but there was a pleased complacency in her eyes which annoyed people and she carried a chip on her shoulder which no one cared to disturb.

She knew Atlanta was talking but she did not care. After all, there wasn't anything immoral in marrying a man. Tara was safe. Let people talk. She had too many other matters to occupy her mind. The most important was how to make Frank realize, in a tactful manner, that his store should bring in more money. After the fright Jonas Wilkerson had given her, she would never rest easy until she and Frank had some money ahead. And even if no emergency developed, Frank would need to make more money, if she was going to save enough for next year's taxes. Moreover, what Frank had said about the sawmill stuck in her mind. Frank could make lots of money out of a mill. Anybody could, with lumber selling at such outrageous prices. She fretted silently because Frank's money had not been enough to pay the taxes on Tara and buy the mill as well. And she made up her mind that he had to make more money on the store somehow, and do it quickly, so he could buy that mill before someone else snapped it up. She could see it was a bargain.

If she were a man she would have that mill, if she had to mortgage the store to raise the money. But, when she intimated this delicately to Frank, the day after they married, he smiled and told her not to bother her sweet pretty little head about business matters. It had come as a surprise to him that she even knew what a mortgage was and, at first, he was amused. But this amusement quickly passed and a sense of shock took its place in the early days of their marriage. Once, incautiously, he had told her that 'people' (he was careful not to mention names) owed him money but could not pay just now and he was, of course, unwilling to press old friends and gentlefolk. Frank regretted ever mentioning it for, thereafter, she had questioned him about it again and again. She had the most charmingly childlike air but she was just curious, she said, to know who owed him and how much they owed. Frank was very evasive about the matter. He coughed nervously and waved his hands and repeated his annoying remark about her sweet pretty little head.

It had begun to dawn on him that this same sweet pretty little head was a 'good head for figures'. In fact, a much better one than his own, and the knowledge was disquieting. He was thunderstruck to discover that she could swiftly add a long column of figures in her head when he needed a pencil and paper for more than three figures. And fractions presented no difficulties to her at all. He felt there was something unbecoming about a woman understanding fractions and business matters and he believed that, should a woman be so unfortunate as to have such unladylike comprehension, she should pretend not to. Now he disliked talking business with her as much as he had enjoyed it before they were married. Then he had thought it all beyond her mental grasp and it had been pleasant to explain things to her. Now he saw that she understood entirely too well and he felt the usual masculine indignation at the duplicity of women. Added to it was the usual masculine disillusionment in discovering that a woman has a brain.

Just how early in his married life Frank learned of the deception Scarlett had used in marrying him, no one ever knew. Perhaps the truth dawned on him when Tony Fontaine, obviously fancy free, came to Atlanta on business. Perhaps it was told him more directly in letters from his sister in Jonesboro who was astounded at his marriage. Certainly he never learned from Suellen herself. She never wrote him and naturally he could not write her and explain.

What good would explanations do anyway, now that he was married? He writhed inwardly at the thought that Suellen would never know the truth and would always think he had senselessly jilted her. Probably everyone else was thinking this too and criticizing him. It certainly put him in an awkward position. And he had no way of clearing himself, for a man couldn't go about saying he had lost his head about a woman – and a gentleman couldn't advertise the fact that his wife had entrapped him with a lie.

Scarlett was his wife and a wife was entitled to the loyalty of her husband. Furthermore, he could not bring himself to believe she had married him coldly and with no affection for him at all. His masculine vanity would not permit such a thought to stay long in his mind. It was more pleasant to think she had fallen so suddenly in love with him she had been willing to lie to get him. But it was all very puzzling. He knew he was no great catch for a woman half his age and pretty and smart to boot, but Frank was a gentleman and he kept his bewilderment to himself. Scarlett was his wife and he could not insult her by asking awkward questions which, after all, would not remedy matters.

Not that Frank especially wanted to remedy matters, for it appeared that his marriage would be a happy one. Scarlett was the most charming and exciting of women and he thought her perfect in all things – except that she was so headstrong. Frank learned early in his marriage that so long as she had her own way, life could be very pleasant, but when she was opposed— Given her own way, she was as gay as a child, laughed a good deal, made foolish little jokes, sat on his knee and tweaked his beard until he vowed he felt twenty years younger. She could be unexpectedly sweet and thoughtful, having his slippers toasting at the fire when he came home at night, fussing affectionately about his wet feet and interminable head colds, remembering that he always liked the gizzard of the chicken and three spoonfuls of sugar in his coffee. Yes, life was very sweet and cosy with Scarlett – as long as she had her own way.

When the marriage was two weeks old, Frank contracted the grippe and Dr Meade put him to bed. In the first year of the war, Frank had spent two months in the hospital with pneumonia and he had lived in dread of another attack since that time, so he was only too glad to lie sweating under three blankets and drink the hot concoctions Mammy and Aunt Pitty brought him every hour.

The illness dragged on and Frank worried more and more about the store as each day passed. The place was in charge of the counter boy, who came to the house every night to report on the day's transactions, but Frank was not satisfied. He fretted until Scarlett, who had been waiting for such an opportunity, laid a cool hand on his forehead and said: 'Now, sweetheart, I shall be vexed if you take on so. I'll go to town and see how things are.'

And she went, smiling as she smothered his feeble protests. During the three weeks of her new marriage, she had been in a fever to see his account-books and find out just how money matters stood. What luck he was bedridden!

The store stood near Five Points, its new roof glaring against the smoked bricks of the old walls. Wooden awnings covered the sidewalk to the edge of the street, and at the long iron bars connecting the uprights horses and mules were hitched, their heads bowed against the cold misty rain, their backs covered with torn blankets and quilts. The inside of the store was almost like Bullard's store in Jonesboro, except that there were no loungers about the roaring red-hot stove, whittling and spitting streams of tobacco juice at the sand-boxes. It was bigger than Bullard's store and much darker. The wooden awnings cut off most of the winter daylight and the interior was dim and dingy, only a trickle of light coming in through the small fly-specked windows high up on the side walls. The floor was covered with muddy sawdust and everywhere was dust and dirt. There was a semblance of order in the front of the store, where tall shelves rose into the gloom stacked with bright bolts of cloth, china, cooking utensils and notions. But in the back, behind the partition, chaos reigned.

Here there was no flooring and the assorted jumble of stock was piled helter-skelter on the hard-packed earth. In the semi-darkness she saw boxes and bales of goods, ploughs and harness and saddles and cheap pine coffins. Second-hand furniture, ranging from cheap gum to mahogany and rosewood, reared up in the gloom, and the rich but worn brocade and horsehair upholstery gleamed incongruously in the dingy surroundings. China chambers and bowl and pitcher sets littered the floor and all around the four walls were deep bins, so dark she had to hold the lamp directly over them to discover they contained seeds, nails, bolts and carpenters' tools.

'I'd think a man as fussy and old-maidish as Frank would keep things tidier,' she thought, scrubbing her grimy hands with her handkerchief. 'This place is a pig-pen. What a way to run a store! If he'd only dust up this stuff and put it out in front where folks could see it, he could sell things much quicker.'

And if his stock was in such condition, what mustn't his accounts be!

'I'll look at his account book now,' she thought and, picking up the lamp, she went into the front of the store. Willie, the counter boy, was reluctant to give her the large dirty-backed ledger. It was obvious that, young as he was, he shared Frank's opinion that women had no place in business. But Scarlett silenced him with a sharp word and sent him out to get his dinner. She felt better when he was gone, for his disapproval annoyed her, and she settled herself in a splint-bottomed chair by the roaring stove, tucked one foot under her and spread the book across her lap. It was dinner-time and the streets were deserted. No customers called and she had the store to herself.

She turned the pages slowly, narrowly scanning the rows of names and figures written in Frank's cramped copperplate hand. It was just as she had expected, and she frowned as she saw this newest evidence of Frank's lack of business sense. At least five hundred dollars in debts, some of them months old, were set down against the names of people she knew well, the Merriwethers and the Elsings among other familiar names. From Frank's deprecatory remarks about the money 'people' owed him, she had imagined the sums to be small. But this!

'If they can't pay, why do they keep on buying?' she thought irritably. 'And if he knows they can't pay, why does he keep on selling them stuff? Lots of them could pay if he'd just make them do it. The Elsings certainly could if they could give Fanny a new satin dress and an expensive wedding. Frank's just too soft-hearted, and people take advantage of him. Why, if he'd collected half this money, he could have bought the sawmill and easily spared me the tax money, too.'

Then she thought: 'Just imagine Frank trying to operate a sawmill! God's nightgown! If he runs this store like a charitable institution, how could he expect to make money on a mill? The sheriff would have it in a month. Why, I could run this store better than he does! And I could run a mill better than he could, even if I don't know anything about the lumber business!'

A startling thought this, that a woman could handle business matters as well or better than a man, a revolutionary thought to Scarlett who had been reared in the tradition that men were omniscient and women none too bright. Of course, she had discovered that this was not altogether true but the pleasant fiction still stuck in her mind. Never before had she put this remarkable idea into words. She sat quite still, with the heavy book across her lap, her mouth a little open with surprise, thinking that during the lean months at Tara she had done a man's work and done it well. She had been brought up to believe that a woman alone could accomplish nothing, yet she had managed the plantation without men to help her until Will came. 'Why, why,' her mind stuttered, 'I believe women could manage everything in the world without men's help – except having babies, and God knows, no woman in her right mind would have babies if she could help it.'

With the idea that she was as capable as a man came a sudden rush of pride and a violent longing to prove it, to make money for herself as men made money. Money which would be her own, which she would neither have to ask for nor account for to any man.

'I wish I had money enough to buy that mill myself,' she said aloud and sighed. 'I'd sure make it hum. And I wouldn't let even one splinter go out on credit.'

She sighed again. There was nowhere she could get any money, so the idea was out of the question. Frank would simply have to collect this money owing him and buy the mill. It was a sure way to make money, and when he got the mill, she would certainly find some way to make him be more businesslike in its operation than he had been with the store.

She pulled a back page out of the ledger and began copying the list of debtors who had made no payments in several months. She'd take the matter up with Frank just as soon as she reached home. She'd make him realize that these people had to pay their bills even if they were old friends, even if it did embarrass him to press them for money. That would probably upset Frank, for he was timid and fond of the approbation of his friends. He was so thin-skinned he'd rather lose the money than be businesslike about collecting it.

And he'd probably tell her that no one had any money with which to pay him. Well, perhaps that was true. Poverty was certainly no news to her. But nearly everybody had saved some silver or jewellery or was hanging on to a little real estate. Frank could take them in lieu of cash.

She could imagine how Frank would moan when she broached such an idea to him. Take the jewellery and property of his friends! 'Well,' she shrugged, 'he can moan all he likes. I'm going to tell him that he may be willing to stay poor for friendship's sake but I'm not. Frank will never get anywhere if he doesn't get up some gumption. And he's got to get somewhere! He's got to make money, even if I've got to wear the pants in the family to make him do it.'

She was writing busily, her face screwed up with the effort, her tongue clamped between her teeth, when the front door opened and a great draught of cold wind swept the store. A tall man came into the dingy room walking with a light Indian-like tread, and looking up she saw Rhett Butler.

He was resplendent in new clothes and a greatcoat with a dashing cape thrown back from his heavy shoulders. His tall hat was off in a deep bow when her eyes met his and his hand went to the bosom of a spotless pleated shirt. His white teeth gleamed startlingly against his brown face and his bold eyes raked her.

'My dear Mrs Kennedy,' he said, walking toward her. 'My very dear Mrs Kennedy!' and he broke into a loud merry laugh.

At first she was as startled as if a ghost had invaded the store and then, hastily removing her foot from beneath her, she stiffened her spine and gave him a cold stare.

'What are you doing here?'

'I called on Miss Pittypat and learned of your marriage and so I hastened here to congratulate you.'

The memory of her humiliation at his hands made her go crimson with shame.

'I don't see how you have the gall to face me!' she cried.

'On the contrary! How have you the gall to face me?'

'Oh, you are the most—'

'Shall we let the bugles sing truce?' He smiled down at her, a wide flashing smile that had impudence in it but no shame for his own actions or condemnation for hers. In spite of herself, she had to smile too, but it was a wry, uncomfortable smile.

'What a pity they didn't hang you!'

'Others share your feeling, I fear. Come, Scarlett, relax. You look like you'd swallowed a ramrod and it isn't becoming. Surely, you've had time to recover from my – er – my little joke.'

'Joke? Ha! I'll never get over it!'

'Oh, yes, you will. You are just putting on this indignant front because you think it's proper and respectable. May I sit down?'

'No.'

He sank into a chair beside her and grinned.

'I hear you couldn't even wait two weeks for me,' he said, and gave a mock sigh. 'How fickle is woman!'

When she did not reply he continued.

'Tell me, Scarlett, just between friends – between very old and very intimate friends – wouldn't it have been wiser to wait until I got out of jail? Or are the charms of wedlock with old Frank Kennedy more alluring than illicit relations with me?'

As always when his mockery aroused wrath within her, wrath fought with laughter at his impudence.

'Don't be absurd.'

'And would you mind satisfying my curiosity on one point which has bothered me for some time? Did you have no womanly repugnance, no delicate shrinking from marrying not just one man but two for whom you had no love or even affection? Or have I been misinformed about the delicacy of our Southern womanhood?'

'Rhett!'

'I have my answer. I always felt that women had a hardness and endurance unknown to men, despite the pretty idea taught me in childhood that women are frail, tender, sensitive creatures. But after all, according to the Continental code of etiquette, it's very bad form for husband and wife to love each other. Very bad taste, indeed. I always felt that the Europeans had the right idea in that matter. Marry for convenience and love for pleasure. A sensible system, don't you think? You are closer to the old country than I thought.'

How pleasant it would be to shout at him: 'I did not marry for convenience!' But unfortunately, Rhett had her there and any protest of injured innocence would only bring more barbed remarks from him.

'How you do run on!' she said coolly. Anxious to change the subject, she asked: 'How did you ever get out of jail?'

'Oh, that!' he answered, making an airy gesture. 'Not much trouble. They let me out this morning. I employed a delicate system of blackmail on a friend in Washington who is quite high in the councils of the Federal government. A splendid fellow – one of the staunch Union patriots from whom I used to buy muskets and hoop skirts for the Confederacy. When my distressing predicament was brought to his attention in the right way, he hastened to use his influence, and so I was released. Influence is everything, Scarlett. Remember that when you get arrested. Influence is everything, and guilt or innocence merely an academic question.'

'I'll take oath you weren't innocent.'

'No, now that I am free of the toils, I'll frankly admit that I'm as guilty as Cain. I did kill the nigger. He was uppity to a lady, and what else could a Southern gentleman do? And while I'm confessing, I must admit that I shot a Yankee cavalryman after some words in a bar-room. I was not charged with that peccadillo, so perhaps some other poor devil has been hanged for it, long since.'

He was so blithe about his murders her blood chilled. Words of moral indignation rose to her lips but suddenly she remembered the Yankee who lay under the tangle of scuppernong vines at Tara. He had not been on her conscience any more than a roach upon which she might have stepped. She could not sit in judgment on Rhett when she was as guilty as he.

'And, as I seem to be making a clean breast of it, I must tell you, in strictest confidence (that means, don't tell Miss Pittypat!) that I did have the money, safe in a bank in Liverpool.'

'The money?'

'Yes, the money the Yankees were so curious about. Scarlett, it wasn't altogether meanness that kept me from giving you the money you wanted. If I'd drawn a draft they could have traced it somehow and I doubt if you'd have gotten a cent. My only hope lay in doing nothing. I knew the money was pretty safe, for if worst came to worst, if they had located it and tried to take it away from me, I would have named every Yankee patriot who sold me bullets and machinery during the war. Then there would have been a stink, for some of them are high up in Washington now. In fact, it was my threat to unbosom my conscience about them that got me out of jail. I—'

'Do you mean you – you actually have the Confederate gold?'

'Not all of it. Good Heavens, no! There must be fifty or more ex-blockaders who have plenty salted away in Nassau and England and Canada. We will be pretty unpopular with the Confederates who weren't as slick as we were. I have got close to half a million. Just think, Scarlett, a half-million dollars, if you'd only restrained your fiery nature and not rushed into wedlock again!'

A half-million dollars. She felt a pang of almost physical sickness at the thought of so much money. His jeering words passed over her head and she did not even hear them. It was hard to believe there was so much money in all this bitter and poverty-stricken world. So much money, so very much money, and someone else had it, someone who took it lightly and didn't need it. And she had only a sick elderly husband and this dirty piddling little store between her and a hostile world. It wasn't fair that a reprobate like Rhett Butler should have so much and she, who carried so heavy a load, should have so little. She hated him, sitting there in his dandified attire, taunting

her. Well, she wouldn't swell his conceit by complimenting him on his cleverness. She longed viciously for sharp words with which to cut him.

'I suppose you think it's honest to keep the Confederate money. Well, it
isn't. It's plain out-and-out stealing and you know it. I wouldn't have that
on my conscience.'

'My! How sour the grapes are today!' he exclaimed, screwing up his face.
'And just who am I stealing from?'

She was silent, trying to think just whom indeed. After all, he had only
done what Frank had done on a small scale.

'Half the money is honestly mine,' he continued, 'honestly made with the
aid of honest Union patriots who were willing to sell out the Union behind
its back – for one hundred per cent profit on their goods. Part I made out
of my little investment in cotton at the beginning of the war, the cotton I
bought cheap and sold for a dollar a pound when the British mills were crying
for it. Part I got from food speculation. Why should I let the Yankees have the
fruits of my labour? But the rest did belong to the Confederacy. It came from
Confederate cotton which I managed to run through the blockade and sell in
Liverpool at sky-high prices. The cotton was given me in good faith to buy
leather and rifles and machinery with. And it was taken by me in good faith
to buy the same. My orders were to leave the gold in English banks, under
my own name, in order that my credit would be good. You remember when
the blockade tightened, I couldn't get a boat out of any Confederate port
or into one, so there the money stayed in England. What should I have
done? Drawn out all that gold from English banks, like a simpleton, and
tried to run it into Wilmington? And let the Yankees capture it? Was it my
fault that the blockade got too tight? Was it my fault that our Cause failed?
The money belonged to the Confederacy. Well, there is no Confederacy
now – though you'd never know it, to hear some people talk. Whom shall
I give the money to? The Yankee government? I should so hate for people
to think me a thief.'

He removed a leather case from his pocket, extracted a long cigar and
smelled it approvingly, meanwhile watching her with pseudo anxiety as if
he hung on her words.

'Plague take him,' she thought, 'he's always one jump ahead of me. There
is always something wrong with his arguments but I never can put my finger
on just what it is.'

'You might,' she said with dignity, 'distribute it to those who are in need.
The Confederacy is gone but there are plenty of Confederates and their
families who are starving.'

He threw back his head and laughed rudely.

'You are never so charming or so absurd as when you are airing some
hypocrisy like that,' he cried in frank enjoyment. 'Always tell the truth,
Scarlett. You can't lie. The Irish are the poorest liars in the world. Come
now, be frank. You never gave a damn about the late lamented Confederacy

and you care less about the starving Confederates. You'd scream in protest if I even suggested giving away all that money unless I started off by giving you the lion's share.'

'I don't want your money,' she began, trying to be coldly dignified.

'Oh, don't you! Your palm is itching to beat the band this very minute. If I showed you a quarter, you'd leap on it.'

'If you have come here to insult me and laugh at my poverty, I will wish you good day,' she retorted, trying to rid her lap of the heavy ledger so she might rise and make her words more impressive. Instantly, he was on his feet bending over her, laughing as he pushed her back into her chair.

'When will you ever get over losing your temper when you hear the truth? You never mind speaking the truth about other people, so why should you mind hearing it about yourself? I'm not insulting you. I think acquisitiveness is a very fine quality.'

She was not sure what acquisitiveness meant but as he praised it she felt slightly mollified.

'I didn't come to gloat over your poverty but to wish you long life and happiness in your marriage. By the way, what did sister Sue think of your larceny?'

'My what?'

'Your stealing Frank from under her nose.'

'I did not—'

'Well, we won't quibble about the word. What did she say?'

'She said nothing,' said Scarlett. His eyes danced as they gave her the lie.

'How unselfish of her! Now, let's hear about your poverty. Surely I have the right to know, after your little trip out to the jail not long ago. Hasn't Frank as much money as you hoped?'

There was no evading his impudence. Either she would have to put up with it or ask him to leave. And now she did not want him to leave. His words were barbed but they were the barbs of truth. He knew what she had done and why she had done it and he did not seem to think the less of her for it. And though his questions were unpleasantly blunt, they seemed actuated by a friendly interest. He was one person to whom she could tell the truth. That would be a relief, for it had been so long since she had told anyone the truth about herself and her motives. Whenever she spoke her mind everyone seemed to be shocked. Talking to Rhett was comparable only to one thing, the feeling of ease and comfort afforded by a pair of old slippers after dancing in a pair too tight.

'Didn't you get the money for the taxes? Don't tell me the wolf is still at the door of Tara.' There was a different tone in his voice.

She looked up to meet his dark eyes and caught an expression which startled and puzzled her at first, and then made her suddenly smile, a sweet and charming smile which was seldom on her face these days. What a perverse wretch he was, but how nice he could be at times! She knew now that the real reason for his call was not to tease her but to make sure she had gotten the money for which she had been so desperate. She knew now that he had hurried to her as soon as he was released, without the slightest appearance of hurry, to lend her the money if she still needed it. And yet he would torment and insult her and deny that such was his intent, should she accuse him. He was quite beyond all comprehension. Did he really care about her, more than he was willing to admit? Or did he have some other motive? Probably the latter, she thought. But who could tell? He did such strange things sometimes.

'No,' she said, 'the wolf isn't at the door any longer. I – I got the money.'

'But not without a struggle, I'll warrant. Did you manage to restrain yourself until you got the wedding ring on your finger?'

She tried not to smile at his accurate summing up of her conduct but she could not help dimpling. He seated himself again, sprawling his long legs comfortably.

'Well, tell me about your poverty. Did Frank, the brute, mislead you about his prospects? He should be soundly thrashed for taking advantage of a helpless female. Come, Scarlett, tell me everything. You should have no secrets from me. Surely, I know the worst about you.'

'Oh, Rhett, you're the worst – well, I don't know what! No, he didn't exactly fool me but—' Suddenly it became a pleasure to unburden herself. 'Rhett, if Frank would just collect the money people owe him, I wouldn't be worried about anything. But, Rhett, fifty people owe him and he won't press them. He's so thin skinned. He says a gentleman can't do that to another gentleman. And it may be months and may be never before we get the money.'

'Well, what of it? Haven't you enough to eat on until he does collect?'

'Yes, but – well, as a matter of fact, I could use a little money right now.' Her eyes brightened as she thought of the mill. Perhaps—

'What for? More taxes?'

'Is that any of your business?'

'Yes, because you are getting ready to touch me for a loan. Oh, I know all the approaches. And I'll lend it to you – without, my dear Mrs Kennedy, that charming collateral you offered me a short while ago. Unless, of course, you insist.'

'You are the coarsest—'

'Not at all. I merely wanted to set your mind at ease. I knew you'd be worried about that point. Not much worried but a little. And I'm willing to lend you the money. But I do want to know how you are going to spend it. I have that right, I believe. If it's to buy you pretty frocks or a carriage, take it with my blessing. But if it's to buy a new pair of breeches for Ashley Wilkes, I fear I must decline to lend it.'

She was hot with sudden rage and she stuttered until words came.

'Ashley Wilkes has never taken a cent from me! I couldn't make him take a cent if he were starving! You don't understand him, how honourable, how proud he is! Of course, you can't understand him, being what you are—'

'Don't let's begin calling names. I could call you a few that would match any you could think of for me. You forget that I have been keeping up with you through Miss Pittypat, and the dear soul tells all she knows to any sympathetic listener. I know that Ashley has been at Tara ever since he came home from Rock Island. I know that you have even put up with having his wife around, which must have been a strain on you.'

'Ashley is—'

'Oh, yes,' he said, waving his hand negligently. 'Ashley is too sublime for my earthy comprehension. But please don't forget I was an interested witness to your tender scene with him at Twelve Oaks and something tells me he hasn't changed since then. And neither have you. He didn't cut so sublime a figure that day, if I remember rightly. And I don't think the figure he cuts now is much better. Why doesn't he take his family and get out and find work? And stop living at Tara? Of course, it's just a whim of mine, but I don't intend to lend you a cent for Tara to help support him. Among men, there's a very unpleasant name for men who permit women to support them.'

'How dare you say such things? He's been working like a field hand!' For all her rage, her heart was wrung by the memory of Ashley splitting fence rails.

'And worth his weight in gold, I dare say. What a hand he must be with the manure and—'

'He's—'

'Oh, yes, I know. Let's grant that he does the best he can but I don't imagine he's much help. You'll never make a farm hand out of a Wilkes – or anything else that's useful. The breed is purely ornamental. Now, quiet your ruffled feathers and overlook my boorish remarks about the proud and honourable Ashley. Strange how these illusions will persist even in women as hard-headed as you are. How much money do you want and what do you want it for?'

When she did not answer he repeated:

'What do you want it for? And see if you can manage to tell me the truth. It will do as well as a lie. In fact, better, for if you lie to me, I'll be sure to find it out, and think how embarrassing that would be. Always remember this, Scarlett, I can stand anything from you but a lie – your dislike for me, your tempers, all your vixenish ways, but not a lie. Now what do you want it for?'

Raging as she was at his attack on Ashley, she would have given anything to spit on him and throw his offer of money proudly into his mocking face. For a moment she almost did, but the cold hand of common sense held her back. She swallowed her anger with poor grace and tried to assume an expression of pleasant dignity. He leaned back in his chair, stretching his legs toward the stove.

'If there's one thing in the world that gives me more amusement than anything else,' he remarked, 'it's the sight of your mental struggles when a matter of principle is laid up against something practical like money. Of course, I know the practical in you will always win, but I keep hanging around to see if your better nature won't triumph some day. And when that day comes I shall pack my bag and leave Atlanta forever. There are too many women whose better natures are always triumphing . . . Well, let's get back to business. How much and what for?'

'I don't know quite how much I'll need,' she said sulkily. 'But I want to buy a sawmill – and I think I can get it cheap. And I'll need two wagons and two mules. I want good mules, too. And a horse and buggy for my own use.'

'A sawmill?'

'Yes, and if you'll lend me the money, I'll give you a half-interest in it.'

'Whatever would I do with a sawmill?'

'Make money! We can make loads of money. Or I'll pay you interest on the loan – let's see, what is good interest?'

'Fifty per cent is considered very fine.'

'Fifty – oh, but you are joking! Stop laughing, you devil. I'm serious.'

'That's why I'm laughing. I wonder if anyone but me realizes what goes on in that head back of your deceptively sweet face.'

'Well, who cares? Listen, Rhett, and see if this doesn't sound like good business to you. Frank told me about this man who has a sawmill, a little one out Peachtree road, and he wants to sell it. He's got to have cash money pretty quick and he'll sell it cheap. There aren't many sawmills around here now, and the way people are rebuilding – why, we could sell lumber sky high. The man will stay and run the mill for a wage. Frank told me about it. Frank would buy the mill himself if he had the money. I guess he was intending buying it with the money he gave me for the taxes.'

'Poor Frank! What is he going to say when you tell him you've bought it yourself right out from under him? And how are you going to explain my lending you the money without compromising your reputation?'

Scarlett had given no thought to this, so intent was she upon the money the mill would bring in.

'Well, I just won't tell him.'

'He'll know you didn't pick it off a bush.'

'I'll tell him – why, yes, I'll tell him I sold you my diamond earbobs. And I will give them to you, too. That'll be my collat – my whatchucallit.'

'I wouldn't take your earbobs.'

'I don't want them. I don't like them. They aren't really mine, anyway.'

'Whose are they?'

Her mind went swiftly back to the still hot noon with the country hush deep about Tara and the dead man in blue sprawled in the hall.

'They were left with me – by someone who's dead. They're mine all right. Take them. I don't want them. I'd rather have the money for them.'

'Good Lord!' he cried impatiently. 'Don't you ever think of anything but money?'

'No,' she replied frankly, turning hard green eyes upon him. 'And if you'd been through what I have, you wouldn't either. I've found out that money is the most important thing in the world and, as God is my witness, I don't ever intend to be without it again.'

She remembered the hot sun, the soft red earth under her sick head, the niggery smell of the cabin behind the ruins of Twelve Oaks, remembered the refrain her heart had beaten: 'I'll never be hungry again. I'll never be hungry again.'

'I'm going to have money some day, lots of it, so I can have anything I want to eat. And then there'll never be any hominy or dried peas on my table. And I'm going to have pretty clothes and all of them are going to be silk—'

'All?'

'All,' she said shortly, not even troubling to blush at his implication. 'I'm going to have money enough so the Yankees can never take Tara away from me. And I'm going to have a new roof for Tara and a new barn and fine mules for ploughing and more cotton than you ever saw. And Wade isn't ever going to know what it means to do without the things he needs. Never! He's going to have everything in the world. And all my family, they aren't ever going to be hungry again. I mean it. Every word. You don't understand, you're such a selfish hound. You've never had the Carpetbaggers trying to drive you out. You've never been cold and ragged and had to break your back to keep from starving!'

He said quietly: 'I was in the Confederate Army for eight months. I don't know any better place for starving.'

'The army! Bah! You've never had to pick cotton and weed corn. You've— Don't you laugh at me!'

His hands were on hers again as her voice rose harshly.

'I wasn't laughing at you. I was laughing at the difference in what you look and what you really are. And I was remembering the first time I ever saw you, at the barbecue at the Wilkes'. You had on a green dress and little green slippers, and you were knee deep in men and quite full of yourself. I'll wager you didn't know then how many pennies were in a dollar. There was only one idea in your whole mind then and that was ensnaring Ash—'

She jerked her hands away from him.

'Rhett, if we are to get on at all, you'll have to stop talking about Ashley Wilkes. We'll always fall out about him, because you can't understand him.'

'I suppose you understand him like a book,' said Rhett maliciously. 'No, Scarlett, if I am to lend you the money I reserve the right to discuss Ashley Wilkes in any terms I care to. I waive the right to collect interest on my loan but not that right. And there are a number of things about that young man I'd like to know.'

'I do not have to discuss him with you,' she answered shortly.

'Oh, but you do! I hold the purse-strings, you see. Some day when you are rich, you can have the power to do the same to others . . . It's obvious that you still care about him—'

'I do not.'

'Oh, it's so obvious from the way you rush to his defence. You—'

'I won't stand having my friends sneered at.'

'Well, we'll let that pass for the moment. Does he still care for you or did Rock Island make him forget? Or perhaps he's learned to appreciate what a jewel of a wife he has?'

At the mention of Melanie, Scarlett began to breathe hard and could scarcely restrain herself from crying out the whole story, that only honour kept Ashley with Melanie. She opened her mouth to speak and then closed it.

'Oh. So he still hasn't enough sense to appreciate Mrs Wilkes? And the rigours of prison didn't dim his ardour for you?'

'I see no need to discuss the subject.'

'I wish to discuss it,' said Rhett. There was a low note in his voice which Scarlett did not understand but did not like to hear. 'And, by God, I will discuss it and I expect you to answer me. So he's still in love with you?'

'Well, what if he is?' cried Scarlett, goaded. 'I don't care to discuss him with you because you can't understand him or his kind of love. The only kind of love you know about is just – well, the kind you carry on with creatures like that Watling woman.'

'Oh,' said Rhett softly. 'So I am only capable of carnal lusts?'

'Well, you know it's true.'

'Now I appreciate your hesitance in discussing the matter with me. My unclean hands and lips besmirch the purity of his love.'

'Well, yes – something like that.'

'I'm interested in this pure love—'

'Don't be so nasty, Rhett Butler. If you are vile enough to think there's ever been anything wrong between us—'

'Oh, the thought never entered my head, really. That's why it all interests me. Just why hasn't there been anything wrong between you?'

'If you think that Ashley would—'

'Ah, so it's Ashley, and not you, who has fought the fight for purity. Really, Scarlett, you should not give yourself away so easily.'

Scarlett looked into his smooth unreadable face in confusion and indignation.

'We won't go any further with this and I don't want your money. So, get out!'

'Oh, yes, you do want my money and, as we've gone this far, why stop? Surely there can be no harm in discussing so chaste an idyll – when there hasn't been anything wrong. So Ashley loves you for your mind, your soul, your nobility of character?'

Scarlett writhed at his words. Of course, Ashley loved her for just these things. It was this knowledge that made life endurable, this knowledge that Ashley, bound by honour, loved her from afar for beautiful things deep buried in her that he alone could see. But they did not seem so beautiful when dragged to the light by Rhett, especially in that deceptively smooth voice that covered sarcasm.

'It gives me back my boyish ideals to know that such a love can exist in this naughty world,' he continued. 'So there's no touch of the flesh in his love for you? It would be the same if you were ugly and didn't have that white skin? And if you didn't have those green eyes which make a man wonder just what you would do if he took you in his arms? And a way of swaying your hips, that's an allurement to any man under ninety? And those lips which are – well, I mustn't let my carnal lusts obtrude. Ashley sees none of these things? Or if he sees them, they move him not at all?'

Unbidden, Scarlett's mind went back to that day in the orchard when Ashley's arms shook as he held her, when his mouth was hot on hers as if he would never let her go. She went crimson at the memory and her blush was not lost on Rhett.

'So,' he said, and there was a vibrant note almost like anger in his voice. 'I see. He loves you for your mind alone.'

How dare he pry with dirty fingers, making the one beautiful sacred thing in her life seem vile? Coolly, determinedly, he was breaking down the last of her reserves and the information he wanted was forthcoming.

'Yes, he does!' she cried, pushing back the memory of Ashley's lips.

'My dear, he doesn't even know you've got a mind. If it was your mind that attracted him, he would not need to struggle against you, as he must have done to keep this love so – shall we say "holy"? He could rest easily for, after all, a man can admire a woman's mind and soul and still be an honourable gentleman and true to his wife. But it must be difficult for him to reconcile the honour of the Wilkeses with coveting your body as he does.'

'You judge everybody's mind by your own vile one!'

'Oh, I've never denied coveting you, if that's what you mean. But, thank God, I'm not bothered about matters of honour. What I want I take if I can get it, and so I wrestle neither with angels nor devils. What a merry hell you must have made for Ashley! Almost I can be sorry for him.'

'I – I make a hell for him?'

'Yes, you! There you are, a constant temptation to him, but like most of his breed he prefers what passes in these parts as honour to any amount of love. And it looks to me as if the poor devil now has neither love nor honour to warm himself!'

'He has love! . . . I mean, he loves me!'

'Does he? Then answer me this and we are through for the day and you can take the money and throw it in the gutter for all I care.'

Rhett rose to his feet and threw his half-smoked cigar into the spittoon. There was about his movements the same pagan freedom and leashed power Scarlett had noted that night Atlanta fell, something sinister and a little frightening. 'If he loved you, then why in hell did he permit you to come to Atlanta to get the tax money? Before I'd let a woman I loved do that, I'd—'

'He didn't know! He had no idea that I—'

'Doesn't it occur to you that he should have known?' There was barely suppressed savagery in his voice. 'Loving you as you say he does, he should have known just what you would do when you were desperate. He should have killed you rather than let you come up here – and to me, of all people! God in Heaven!'

'But he didn't know!'

'If he didn't guess it without being told, he'll never know anything about you and your precious mind.'

How unfair he was! As if Ashley was a mind-reader! As if Ashley could have stopped her, even had he known! But, she knew suddenly, Ashley could have stopped her. The faintest intimation from him, in the orchard, that some day things might be different and she would never have thought of going to Rhett. A word of tenderness, even a parting caress when she was getting on the train, would have held her back. But he had only talked of honour. Yet – was Rhett right? Should Ashley have known her mind? Swiftly she put the disloyal thought from her. Of course, he didn't suspect. Ashley would never suspect that she would even think of doing anything so immoral. Ashley was too fine to have such thoughts. Rhett was just trying to spoil her love. He was trying to tear down what was most precious to her. Some day, she thought viciously, when the store was on its feet and the mill doing nicely and she had money, she would make Rhett Butler pay for the misery and humiliation he was causing her.

He was standing over her, looking down at her, faintly amused. The emotion which had stirred him was gone.

'What does it all matter to you anyway?' she asked. 'It's my business and Ashley's and not yours.'

He shrugged.

'Only this. I have a deep and impersonal admiration for your endurance, Scarlett, and I do not like to see your spirit crushed beneath too many millstones. There's Tara. That's a man-sized job in itself. There's your sick father added on. He'll never be any help to you. And the girls and the darkies. And now you've taken on a husband and probably Miss Pittypat, too. You've enough burdens without Ashley Wilkes and his family on your hands.'

'He's not on my hands. He helps—'

'Oh, for God's sake,' he said impatiently. 'Don't let's have any more of that. He's no help. He's on your hands and he'll be on them, or on somebody's, till he dies. Personally, I'm sick of him as a topic of conversation . . . How much money do you want?'

Vituperative words rushed to her lips. After all his insults, after dragging from her those things which were most precious to her and trampling on them, he still thought she would take his money!

But the words were checked unspoken. How wonderful it would be to scorn his offer and order him out of the store! But only the truly rich and the truly secure could afford this luxury. So long as she was poor, just so long would she have to endure such scenes as this. But when she was rich – oh, what a beautiful warming thought that was! – when she was rich, she wouldn't stand anything she didn't like, do without anything she desired or even be polite to people unless they pleased her.

'I shall tell them all to go to Halifax,' she thought, 'and Rhett Butler will be the first one!'

The pleasure in the thought brought a sparkle into her green eyes and a half-smile to her lips. Rhett smiled too.

'You're a pretty person, Scarlett,' he said. 'Especially when you are meditating devilment. And just for the sight of that dimple I'll buy you a baker's dozen of mules if you want them.'

The front door opened and the counter boy entered, picking his teeth with a quill. Scarlett rose, pulled her shawl about her and tied her bonnet strings firmly under her chin. Her mind was made up.

'Are you busy this afternoon? Can you come with me now?' she asked.

'Where?'

'I want you to drive to the mill with me. I promised Frank I wouldn't drive out of town by myself.'

'To the mill in this rain?'

'Yes, I want to buy that mill now, before you change your mind.'

He laughed so loudly the boy behind the counter started and looked at him curiously.

'Have you forgotten you are married? Mrs Kennedy can't afford to be seen driving out into the country with that Butler reprobate, who isn't received in the best parlours. Have you forgotten your reputation?'

'Reputation, fiddle-dee-dee! I want that mill before you change your mind or Frank finds out that I'm buying it. Don't be a slow-poke, Rhett. What's a little rain? Let's hurry.'

That sawmill! Frank groaned every time he thought of it, cursing himself for ever mentioning it to her. It was bad enough for her to sell her earrings to

Captain Butler (of all people!) and buy the mill without even consulting her own husband about it, but it was worse still that she did not turn it over to him to operate. That looked bad. As if she did not trust him or his judgment.

Frank, in common with all men he knew, felt that a wife should be guided by her husband's superior knowledge, should accept his opinions in full and have none of her own. He would have given most women their own way. Women were such funny little creatures and it never hurt to humour their small whims. Mild and gentle by nature, it was not in him to deny a wife much. He would have enjoyed gratifying the foolish notions of some soft little person and scolding her lovingly for her stupidity and extravagance. But the things Scarlett set her mind on were unthinkable.

That sawmill, for example. It was the shock of his life when she told him with a sweet smile, in answer to his questions, that she intended to run it herself. 'Go into the lumber business myself,' was the way she put it. Frank would never forget the horror of that moment. Go into business for herself! It was unthinkable. There were no women in business in Atlanta. In fact, Frank had never heard of a woman in business anywhere. If women were so unfortunate as to be compelled to make a little money to assist their families in these hard times, they made it in quiet womanly ways – baking as Mrs Merriwether was doing, or painting china and sewing and keeping boarders, like Mrs Elsing and Fanny, or teaching school like Mrs Meade or giving music lessons like Mrs Bonnell. These ladies made money but they kept themselves at home while they did it, as a woman should. But for a woman to leave the protection of her home and venture out into the rough world of men, competing with them in business, rubbing shoulders with them, being exposed to insult and gossip . . . Especially when she wasn't forced to do it, when she had a husband amply able to provide for her!

Frank had hoped she was only teasing or playing a joke on him, a joke of questionable taste, but he soon found she meant what she said. She did operate the sawmill. She rose earlier than he did to drive out Peachtree road and frequently did not come home until long after he had locked up the store and returned to Aunt Pitty's for supper. She drove the long miles to the mill with only the disapproving Uncle Peter to protect her and the woods were full of free niggers and Yankee riffraff. Frank couldn't go with her, the store took all of his time, but when he protested, she said shortly: 'If I don't keep an eye on that slick scamp, Johnson, he'll steal my lumber and sell it and put the money in his pocket. When I can get a good man to run the mill for me, then I won't have to go out there so often. Then I can spend my time in town selling lumber.'

Selling lumber in town! That was worst of all. She frequently did take a day off from the mill and peddle lumber and, on those days, Frank wished he could hide in the dark back room of his store and see no one. His wife selling lumber!

And people were talking terribly about her. Probably about him too, for
permitting her to behave in so unwomanly a fashion. It embarrassed him to
face his customers over the counter and hear them say: 'I saw Mrs Kennedy
a few minutes ago over at . . . ' Everyone took pains to tell him what she
did. Everyone was talking about what happened over where the new hotel
was being built. Scarlett had driven up just as Tommy Wellburn was buying
some lumber from another man and she climbed down out of the buggy
among the rough Irish masons who were laying the foundations, and told
Tommy briefly that he was being cheated. She said her lumber was better
and cheaper too, and to prove it she ran up a long column of figures in her
head and gave him an estimate then and there. It was bad enough that she
had intruded herself among strange rough workmen, but it was still worse
for a woman to show publicly that she could do mathematics like that. When
Tommy accepted her estimate and gave her the order, Scarlett had not taken
her departure speedily and meekly but had idled about, talking to Johnnie
Gallegher, the foreman of the Irish workers, a hard-bitten little gnome of a
man who had a very bad reputation. The town talked about it for weeks.

On top of everything else, she was actually making money out of the mill,
and no man could feel right about a wife who succeeded in so unwomanly
an activity. Nor did she turn over the money or any part of it to him to use
in the store. Most of it went to Tara and she wrote interminable letters to
Will Benteen telling him just how it should be spent. Furthermore, she told
Frank that if the repairs at Tara could ever be completed, she intended to
lend out her money on mortgages.

'My! My!' moaned Frank whenever he thought of this. A woman had no
business even knowing what a mortgage was.

Scarlett was full of plans these days, and each one of them seemed worse
to Frank than the previous one. She even talked of building a saloon on the
property where her warehouse had been until Sherman burned it. Frank was
no teetotaler but he feverishly protested against the idea. Owning saloon
property was a bad business, an unlucky business, almost as bad as renting
to a house of prostitution. Just why it was bad he could not explain to her,
and to his lame arguments she said, 'Fiddle-dee-dee!'

'Saloons are always good tenants. Uncle Henry said so,' she told him.
'They always pay their rent and, look here, Frank, I could put up a cheap
saloon out of poor-grade lumber I can't sell and get good rent for it, and
with the rent money and the money from the mill and what I could get
from mortgages, I could buy some more sawmills.'

'Sugar, you don't need any more sawmills!' cried Frank, appalled. 'What
you ought to do is sell the one you've got. It's wearing you out and you
know what trouble you have keeping free darkies at work there—'

'Free darkies are certainly worthless,' Scarlett agreed, completely ignoring
his hint that she should sell. 'Mr Johnson says he never knows when he
comes to work in the morning whether he'll have a full crew or not. You

just can't depend on the darkies any more. They work a day or two and then lay off till they've spent their wages, and the whole crew is like as not to quit overnight. The more I see of emancipation the more criminal I think it is. It's just ruined the darkies. Thousands of them aren't working at all and the ones we can get to work at the mill are so lazy and shiftless they aren't worth having. And if you so much as swear at them, much less hit them a few licks for the good of their souls, the Freedmen's Bureau is down on you like a duck on a June bug.'

'Sugar, you aren't letting Mr Johnson beat those—'

'Of course not,' she returned impatiently. 'Didn't I just say the Yankees would put me in jail if I did?'

'I'll bet your pa never hit a darky a lick in his life,' said Frank.

'Well, only one. A stable boy who didn't rub down his horse after a day's hunt. But, Frank, it was different then. Free issue niggers are something else, and a good whipping would do some of them a lot of good.'

Frank was not only amazed at his wife's views and her plans but at the change which had come over her in the few months since their marriage. This wasn't the soft, sweet, feminine person he had taken to wife. In the brief period of the courtship, he thought he had never known a woman more attractively feminine in her reactions to life, ignorant, timid and helpless. Now her reactions were all masculine. Despite her pink cheeks and dimples and pretty smiles, she talked and acted like a man. Her voice was brisk and decisive and she made up her mind instantly and with no girlish shilly-shallying. She knew what she wanted and she went after it by the shortest route, like a man, not by the hidden and circuitous routes peculiar to women.

It was not that Frank had never seen commanding women before this. Atlanta, like all Southern towns, had its share of dowagers whom no one cared to cross. No one could be more dominating than stout Mrs Merriwether, more imperious than frail Mrs Elsing, more artful in securing her own ends than the silver-haired, sweet-voiced Mrs Whiting. But no matter what devices these ladies employed in order to get their own way, they were always feminine devices. They made a point of being deferential to men's opinions, whether they were guided by them or not. They had the politeness to appear to be guided by what men said, and that was what mattered. But Scarlett was guided by no one but herself and was conducting her affairs in a masculine way which had the whole town talking about her.

'And,' thought Frank miserably, 'probably talking about me too, for letting her act so unwomanly.'

Then, there was that Butler man. His frequent calls at Aunt Pitty's house were the greatest humiliation of all. Frank had always disliked him, even when he had done business with him before the war. He often cursed the day he had brought Rhett to Twelve Oaks and introduced him to his friends. He despised him for the cold-blooded way he had acted in his speculations during the war and for the fact that he had not been in the army. Rhett's eight months' service with the Confederacy was known only to Scarlett, for Rhett had begged her, with mock fear, not to reveal his 'shame' to anyone. Most of all Frank had contempt for him for holding on to the Confederate gold, when honest men like Admiral Bulloch and others confronted with the same situation had turned back thousands to the Federal treasury. But whether Frank liked it or not, Rhett was a frequent caller.

Ostensibly it was Miss Pitty he came to see and she had no better sense than to believe it and give herself airs over his visits. But Frank had an uncomfortable feeling that Miss Pitty was not the attraction which brought him. Little Wade was very fond of him, though the boy was shy of most people, and even called him 'Uncle Rhett', which annoyed Frank. And Frank could not help remembering that Rhett had squired Scarlett about during the war days and there had been talk about them then. He imagined there might be even worse talk about them now. None of his friends had the courage to mention anything of this sort to Frank, for all their outspoken words on Scarlett's conduct in the matter of the mill. But he could not help noticing that he and Scarlett were less frequently invited to meals and parties and fewer and fewer people came to call on them. Scarlett disliked most of her neighbours and was too busy with her mill to care about seeing the ones she did like, so the lack of calls did not disturb her. But Frank felt it keenly.

All of his life, Frank had been under the domination of the phrase 'What will the neighbours say?' and he was defenceless against the shocks of his wife's repeated disregard of the proprieties. He felt that everyone disapproved of Scarlett and was contemptuous of him for permitting her to 'unsex herself'. She did so many things a husband should not permit, according to his views, but if he ordered her to stop them, argued or even criticized, a storm broke on his head.

'My! My!' he thought helplessly. 'She can get mad quicker and stay mad longer than any woman I ever saw!'

Even at the times when things were most pleasant, it was amazing how completely and how quickly the teasing, affectionate wife who hummed to herself as she went about the house could be transformed into an entirely different person. He had only to say: 'Sugar, if I were you, I wouldn't—' and the tempest would break.

Her black brows rushed together to meet in a sharp angle over her nose and Frank cowered, almost visibly. She had the temper of a Tartar and the rages of a wildcat and, at such times, she did not seem to care what she said or how much it hurt. Clouds of gloom hung over the house on such occasions. Frank went early to the store and stayed late. Pitty scrambled into her bedroom like a rabbit panting for its burrow. Wade and Uncle Peter retired to the carriage-house and Cookie kept to her kitchen and forbore to raise her voice to praise the Lord in song. Only Mammy endured Scarlett's temper with equanimity and Mammy had had many years of training with Gerald O'Hara and his explosions.

Scarlett did not mean to be short-tempered and she really wanted to make Frank a good wife, for she was fond of him and grateful for his help in saving Tara. But he did try her patience to the breaking-point so often and in so many different ways.

She could never respect a man who let her run over him and the timid, hesitant attitude he displayed in any unpleasant situation, with her or with others, irritated her unbearably. But she could have overlooked these things and even been happy, now that some of her money problems were being solved, except for her constantly renewed exasperation growing out of the many incidents which showed that Frank was neither a good business man nor did he want her to be a good business man.

As she expected, he had refused to collect the unpaid bills until she prodded him into it, and then he had done it apologetically and half-heartedly. That experience was the final evidence she needed to show her that the Kennedy family would never have more than a bare living, unless she personally made the money she was determined to have. She knew now that Frank would be contented to dawdle along with his dirty little store for the rest of his life. He didn't seem to realize what a slender fingerhold they had on security and how important it was to make more money in these troublous times when money was the only protection against fresh calamities.

Frank might have been a successful business man in the easy days before the war but he was so annoyingly old-fashioned, she thought, and so stubborn about wanting to do things in the old ways, when the old ways and the old days were gone. He was utterly lacking in the aggressiveness needed in these new bitter times. Well, she had the aggressiveness and she intended to use it, whether Frank liked it or not. They needed money and she was making money and it was hard work. The very least Frank could do, in her opinion, was not to interfere with her plans which were getting results.

With her inexperience, operating the new mill was no easy job and competition was keener now than it had been at first, so she was usually tired and worried and cross when she came home at nights. And when Frank would cough apologetically and say: 'Sugar, I wouldn't do this,' or 'I wouldn't do that, Sugar, if I were you,' it was all she could do to restrain herself from flying into a rage, and frequently she did not restrain herself. If he didn't have the gumption to get out and make some money, why was he always finding fault with her? And the things he nagged her about were so silly! What difference did it make in times like these if she was being unwomanly? Especially when her unwomanly sawmill was bringing in money they needed so badly, she and the family and Tara, and Frank too.

Frank wanted rest and quiet. The war in which he had served so conscientiously had wrecked his health, cost him his fortune and made him an old man. He regretted none of these things, and after four years of war all he asked of life was peace and kindliness, loving faces about him and the approval of friends. He soon found that domestic peace had its price, and that price was letting Scarlett have her own way, no matter what she might wish to do. So, because he was tired, he bought peace at her own terms. Sometimes, he thought it was worth it to have her smiling when she opened the front door in the cold twilights, kissing him on the ear or the nose or some other inappropriate place, to feel her head snuggling drowsily on his shoulder at night under the warm quilts. Home life could be so pleasant when Scarlett was having her own way. But the peace he gained was hollow, only an outward semblance, for he had purchased it at the cost of everything he held to be right in married life.

'A woman ought to pay more attention to her home and her family and not be gadding about like a man,' he thought. 'Now, if she just had a baby—'

He smiled when he thought of a baby, and he thought of a baby very often. Scarlett had been most outspoken about not wanting a child, but then babies seldom waited to be invited. Frank knew that many women said they didn't want babies but that was all foolishness and fear. If Scarlett had a baby, she would love it and be content to stay home and tend it like other women. Then she would be forced to sell the mill and his problems would be ended. All women needed babies to make them completely happy and Frank knew that Scarlett was not happy. Ignorant as he was of women, he was not so blind that he could not see she was unhappy at times.

Sometimes he awoke at night and heard the soft sound of tears muffled in the pillow. The first time he had waked to feel the bed shaking with her sobbing, he had questioned, in alarm: 'Sugar, what is it?' and had been rebuked by a passionate cry: 'Oh, let me alone!'

Yes, a baby would make her happy and would take her mind off things she had no business fooling with. Sometimes Frank sighed, thinking he had caught a tropic bird, all flame and jewel colour, when a wren would have served him just as well. In fact, much better.

Chapter XXXVII

It was on a wild wet night in April that Tony Fontaine rode in from Jonesboro on a lathered horse that was half dead from exhaustion and came knocking at their door, rousing her and Frank from sleep with their hearts in their throats. Then for the second time in four months, Scarlett was made to feel acutely what Reconstruction in all its implications meant, made to understand more completely what was in Will's mind when he said, 'Our troubles have just begun,' to know that the bleak words of Ashley, spoken in the wind-swept orchard of Tara, were true: 'This that's facing all of us is worse than war – worse than prison – worse than death.'

The first time she had come face to face with Reconstruction was when she learned that Jonas Wilkerson with the aid of the Yankees could evict her from Tara. But Tony's advent brought it all home to her in a far more terrifying manner. Tony came in the dark and the lashing rain and in a few minutes he was gone back into the night forever, but in the brief interval between he raised the curtain on a scene of new horror, a curtain that she felt hopelessly would never be lowered again.

That stormy night when the knocker hammered on the door with such hurried urgency, she stood on the landing, clutching her wrapper to her and, looking down into the hall below, had one glimpse of Tony's swarthy saturnine face before he leaned forward and blew out the candle in Frank's hand. She hurried down in the darkness to grasp his cold wet hand and hear him whisper: 'They're after me – going to Texas – my horse is about dead – and I'm about starved. Ashley said you'd— Don't light the candle! Don't wake the darkies . . . I don't want to get you folks in trouble if I can help it.'

With the kitchen blinds drawn and all the shades pulled down to the sills, he permitted a light and he talked to Frank in swift jerky sentences as Scarlett hurried about, trying to scrape together a meal for him.

He was without a greatcoat and soaked to the skin. He was hatless and his black hair was plastered to his little skull. But the merriment of the Fontaine boys, a chilling merriment that night, was in his little dancing eyes as he gulped down the whisky she brought him. Scarlett thanked God that Aunt Pittypat was snoring undisturbed upstairs. She would certainly swoon if she saw this apparition.

'One damned bast— Scallawag less,' said Tony, holding out his glass for another drink. 'I've ridden hard and it'll cost me my skin if I don't get out of here quick, but it was worth it. By God, yes! I'm going to try to get to Texas and lay low there. Ashley was with me in Jonesboro, and he told me to come to you all. Got to have another horse, Frank, and some money. My horse is nearly dead – all the way up here at a dead run – and like a fool I went out of the house today like a bat out of hell without a coat or hat or a cent of money. Not that there's much money in our house.'

He laughed and applied himself hungrily to the cold corn pone and cold turnip greens on which congealed grease was thick in white flakes.

'You can have my horse,' said Frank calmly. 'I've only ten dollars with me but if you can wait till morning—'

'Hell's afire, I can't wait!' said Tony, emphatically but jovially. 'They're probably right behind me. I didn't get much of a start. If it hadn't been for Ashley dragging me out of there and making me get on my horse, I'd have stayed there like a fool and probably had my neck stretched by now. Good fellow, Ashley.'

So Ashley was mixed up in this frightening puzzle. Scarlett went cold, her hand at her throat. Did the Yankees have Ashley now? Why, why didn't Frank ask what it was all about? Why did he take it all so coolly, so much as a matter of course? She struggled to get the question to her lips.

'What—' she began. 'Who—'

'Your father's old overseer – that damned – Jonas Wilkerson.'

'Did you – is he dead?'

'My God, Scarlett O'Hara!' said Tony peevishly. 'When I start out to cut somebody up, you don't think I'd be satisfied with scratching him with the blunt side of my knife, do you? No, by God, I cut him to ribbons.'

'Good,' said Frank casually. 'I never liked the fellow.'

Scarlett looked at him. This was not the meek Frank she knew, the nervous beard-clawer who she had learned could be bullied with such ease. There was an air about him that was crisp and cool and he was meeting the emergency with no unnecessary words. He was a man and Tony was a man and this situation of violence was men's business in which a woman had no part.

'But Ashley— Did he—'

'No. He wanted to kill him but I told him it was my right, because Sally is my sister-in-law, and he saw reason finally. He went into Jonesboro with me, in case Wilkerson got me first. But I don't think old Ash will get in any trouble about it. I hope not. Got any jam for this corn pone? And can you wrap me up something to take with me?'

'I shall scream if you don't tell me everything.'

'Wait till I've gone and then scream if you've got to. I'll tell you about it while Frank saddles the horse. That damned— Wilkerson has caused enough trouble already. You know how he did you about your taxes. That's just one of his meannesses. But the worst thing was the way he kept the darkies stirred up. If anybody had told me I'd ever live to see the day when I'd hate darkies! Damn their black souls, they believe anything those scoundrels tell them and forget every living thing we've done for them. Now the Yankees are talking about letting the darkies vote. And they won't let us vote. Why, there's hardly a handful of Democrats in the whole County who aren't barred from voting, now that they've ruled out every man who fought in the Confederate Army. And if they give the negroes the vote, it's the end of us. Damn it, it's our state! It doesn't belong to the Yankees! By God, Scarlett, it isn't to be borne! And it won't be borne! We'll do something about it if it means another war. Soon we'll be having nigger judges, nigger legislators – black apes out of the jungle—'

'Please – hurry, tell me! What did you do?'

'Give me another mite of that pone before you wrap it up. Well, the word got around that Wilkerson had gone a bit too far with his nigger-equality business. Oh, yes, he talks it to those black fools by the hour. He had the gall – the—' Tony spluttered helplessly, 'to say niggers had a right to – to – white women.'

'Oh, Tony, no!'

'By God, yes! I don't wonder you look sick. But hell's afire, Scarlett, it can't be news to you. They've been telling it to them here in Atlanta.'

'I – I didn't know.'

'Well, Frank would have kept it from you. Anyway, after that, we all sort of thought we'd call on Mr Wilkerson privately by night and tend to him, but before we could— You remember that black buck, Eustis, who used to be our foreman?'

'Yes.'

'Came to the kitchen door today while Sally was fixing dinner and – I don't know what he said to her. I guess I'll never know now. But he said something and I heard her scream and I ran into the kitchen and there he was, drunk as a fiddler's bitch— I beg your pardon, Scarlett, it just slipped out.'

'Go on.'

'I shot him and when Mother ran in to take care of Sally, I got my horse and started to Jonesboro for Wilkerson. He was the one to blame. The damned black fool would never have thought of it but for him. And on the way past Tara, I met Ashley and, of course, he went with me. He said to let him do it because of the way Wilkerson acted about Tara, and I said No, it was my place because Sally was my own dead brother's wife, and he went with me arguing the whole way. And when we got to town, by God, Scarlett, do you know I hadn't even brought my pistol. I'd left it in the stable. So mad I forgot—'

He paused and gnawed the tough pone and Scarlett shivered. The murderous rage of the Fontaines had made County history long before this chapter had opened.

'So I had to take my knife to him. I found him in the bar-room. I got him in a corner with Ashley holding back the others and I told him why before I lit into him. Why, it was over before I knew it,' said Tony, reflecting. 'First thing I knew, Ashley had me on my horse and told me to come to you folks. Ashley's a good man in a pinch. He keeps his head.'

Frank came in, his greatcoat over his arm, and handed it to Tony. It was his only heavy coat but Scarlett made no protest. She seemed so much on the outside of this affair, this purely masculine affair.

'But Tony – they need you at home. Surely, if you went back and explained—'

'Frank, you've married a fool,' said Tony with a grin, struggling into the coat. 'She thinks the Yankees will reward a man for keeping niggers off his women folks. So they will, with a drumhead court and a rope. Give me a kiss, Scarlett. Frank won't mind and I may never see you again. Texas is a long way off. I won't dare write, so let the home folks know I got this far in safety.'

She let him kiss her and the two men went out into the driving rain and stood for a moment, talking on the back porch. Then she heard a sudden splashing of hooves and Tony was gone. She opened the door a crack and saw Frank leading a heaving, stumbling horse into the carriage-house. She shut the door again and sat down, her knees trembling.

Now she knew what Reconstruction meant, knew as well as if the house were ringed about by naked savages, squatting in breech-clouts. Now there came rushing to her mind many things to which she had given little thought recently, conversations she had heard but to which she had not listened, masculine talk which had been checked half finished when she came into rooms, small incidents in which she had seen no significance at the time, Frank's futile warnings to her against driving out to the mill with only the feeble Uncle Peter to protect her. Now they fitted themselves together into one horrifying picture.

The negroes were on top and behind them were the Yankee bayonets. She could be killed, she could be raped and, very probably, nothing would ever be done about it. And anyone who avenged her would be hanged by the Yankees, hanged without benefit of trial by judge and jury. Yankee officers who knew nothing of law and cared less for the circumstances of the crime could go through the motions of holding a trial and put a rope around a Southerner's neck.

'What can we do?' she thought, wringing her hands in an agony of helpless fear. 'What can we do with devils who'd hang a nice boy like Tony just for killing a drunken buck and a scoundrelly Scallawag to protect his women folks?'

'It isn't to be borne!' Tony had cried, and he was right. It couldn't be borne. But what could they do except bear it, helpless as they were? She fell to trembling and, for the first time in her life, she saw people and events as something apart from herself, saw clearly that Scarlett O'Hara, frightened and helpless, was not all that mattered. There were thousands of women like her, all over the South, who were frightened and helpless. And thousands of men, who had laid down their arms at Appomattox, had taken them up again and stood ready to risk their necks on a minute's notice to protect those women.

There had been something in Tony's face which had been mirrored in Frank's, an expression she had seen recently on the faces of other men in Atlanta, a look she had noticed but had not troubled to analyse. It was an expression vastly different from the tired helplessness she had seen in the faces of men coming home from the war after the surrender. Those men had not cared about anything except getting home. Now they were caring about something again, numbed nerves were coming back to life and the old spirit was beginning to burn. They were caring again with a cold ruthless bitterness. And, like Tony, they were thinking: 'It isn't to be borne!'

She had seen Southern men, soft-voiced and dangerous in the days before the war, reckless and hard in the last despairing days of the fighting. But in the faces of the two men who stared at each other across the candle-flame so short a while ago there had been something that was different, something that heartened her but frightened her – fury which could find no words, determination which would stop at nothing.

For the first time, she felt a kinship with the people about her, felt one with them in their fears, their bitterness, their determination. No, it wasn't to be borne! The South was too beautiful a place to be let go without a struggle, too loved to be trampled by Yankees who hated Southerners enough to enjoy grinding them into the dirt, too dear a homeland to be turned over to ignorant negroes drunk with whisky and freedom.

As she thought of Tony's sudden entrance and swift exit, she felt herself akin to him, for she remembered the old story how her father had left Ireland, left hastily and by night, after a murder which was no murder to him or to his family. Gerald's blood was in her, violent blood. She remembered her hot joy in shooting the marauding Yankee. Violent blood was in them all, perilously close to the surface, lurking just beneath the kindly courteous exteriors. All of them, all the men she knew, even the drowsy-eyed Ashley and fidgety old Frank, were like that underneath – murderous, violent if the need arose. Even Rhett, conscienceless scamp that he was, had killed a negro for being 'uppity to a lady'.

When Frank came in dripping with rain and coughing, she leaped to her feet.

'Oh, Frank, how long will it be like this?'

'As long as the Yankees hate us so, Sugar.'

'Is there nothing anybody can do?'

Frank passed a tired hand over his wet beard. 'We are doing things.'

'What?'

'Why talk of them till we have accomplished something? It may take years. Perhaps – perhaps the South will always be like this.'

'Oh, no!'

'Sugar, come to bed. You must be chilled. You are shaking.'

'When will it all end?'

'When we can all vote again, Sugar. When every man who fought for the South can put a ballot in the box for a Southerner and a Democrat.'

'A ballot?' she cried despairingly. 'What good's a ballot when the darkies have lost their minds – when the Yankees have poisoned them against us?'

Frank went on to explain in his patient manner, but the idea that ballots could cure the trouble was too complicated for her to follow. She was thinking gratefully that Jonas Wilkerson would never again be a menace to Tara and she was thinking about Tony.

'Oh, the poor Fontaines!' she exclaimed. 'Only Alex left and so much to do at Mimosa. Why didn't Tony have sense enough to – to do it at night when no one would know who it was? A sight more good he'd do helping with the spring ploughing than in Texas.'

Frank put an arm about her. Usually he was gingerly when he did this, as if he anticipated being impatiently shaken off, but tonight there was a far-off look in his eyes and his arm was firm about her waist.

'There are things more important now than ploughing, Sugar. And scaring the darkies and teaching the Scallawags a lesson is one of them. As long as there are fine boys like Tony left, I guess we won't need to worry about the South too much. Come to bed.'

'But, Frank—'

'If we just stand together and don't give an inch to the Yankees, we'll win, some day. Don't you bother your pretty head about it, Sugar. You let your men folks worry about it. Maybe it won't come in our time, but surely it will come some day. The Yankees will get tired of pestering us when they see they can't even dent us, and then we'll have a decent world to live in and raise our children in.'

She thought of Wade and the secret she had carried silently for some days. No, she didn't want her children raised in this welter of hate and uncertainty, of bitterness and violence lurking just below the surface, of poverty and grinding hardships and insecurity. She never wanted children of hers to know what all this was like. She wanted a secure and well-ordered world in which she could look forward and know there was a safe future ahead for them, a world where her children would know only softness and warmth and good clothes and fine food.

Frank thought this could be accomplished by voting. Voting? What did votes matter? Nice people in the South would never have the vote again. There was only one thing in the world that was a certain bulwark against any calamity which fate could bring, and that was money. She thought feverishly that they must have money, lots of it to keep them safe against disaster.

Abruptly, she told him she was going to have a baby.

For weeks after Tony's escape, Aunt Pitty's house was subjected to repeated searches by parties of Yankee soldiers. They invaded the house at all hours and without warning. They swarmed through the rooms, asking questions, opening closets, prodding clothes hampers, peering under beds. The military authorities had heard that Tony had been advised to go to Miss Pitty's house, and they were certain he was still hiding there or somewhere in the neighbourhood.

As a result, Aunt Pitty was chronically in what Uncle Peter called a 'state', never knowing when her bedroom would be entered by an officer and a squad of men. Neither Frank nor Scarlett had mentioned Tony's brief visit, so the old lady could have revealed nothing, even had she been so inclined. She was entirely honest in her fluttery protestations that she had seen Tony Fontaine only once in her life and that was at Christmas time in 1862.

'And,' she would add breathlessly to the Yankee soldiers, in an effort to be helpful, 'he was quite intoxicated at the time.'

Scarlett, sick and miserable in the early stage of pregnancy, alternated between a passionate hatred of the bluecoats who invaded her privacy, frequently carrying away any little knick-knack that appealed to them, and an equally passionate fear that Tony might prove the undoing of them all. The prisons were full of people who had been arrested for much less reason. She knew that if one iota of the truth were proved against them, not only she and Frank but the innocent Pitty as well would go to jail.

For some time there had been an agitation in Washington to confiscate all 'Rebel property' to pay the United States' war debt and this agitation had kept Scarlett in a state of anguished apprehension. Now, in addition to this, Atlanta was full of wild rumours about the confiscation of property of offenders against military law, and Scarlett quaked lest she and Frank lose not only their freedom but the house, the store and the mill. And even if their property were not appropriated by the military, it would be as good as lost if she and Frank went to jail, for who would look after their business in their absence?

She hated Tony for bringing such trouble upon them. How could he have done such a thing to friends? And how could Ashley have sent Tony to them? Never again would she give aid to anyone if it meant having the Yankees come down on her like a swarm of hornets. No, she would bar the door against anyone needing help. Except, of course, Ashley. For weeks after Tony's brief visit she woke from uneasy dreams at any sound in the road outside, fearing it might be Ashley trying to make his escape, fleeing to Texas because of the aid he had given Tony. She did not know how matters stood with him, for they did not dare write to Tara about Tony's midnight visit. Their letters might be intercepted by the Yankees and bring trouble upon the plantation as well. But, when weeks went by and they heard no bad news, they knew that Ashley had somehow come clear. And finally, the Yankees ceased annoying them.

But even this relief did not free Scarlett from the state of dread which began when Tony came knocking at their door, a dread which was worse than the quaking fear of the siege shells, worse even than the terror of Sherman's men during the last days of the war. It was as if Tony's appearance that wild rainy night had stripped merciful blinders from her eyes and forced her to see the true uncertainty of her life.

Looking about her in that cold spring of 1866, Scarlett realized what was facing her and the whole South. She might plan and scheme, she might work harder than her slaves had ever worked, she might succeed in overcoming all of her hardships, she might through dint of determination solve problems for which her earlier life had provided no training at all. But for all her labour and sacrifice and resourcefulness, her small beginnings purchased at so great a cost might be snatched away from her at any minute. And should this happen, she had no legal rights, no legal redress, except those same drumhead courts of which Tony had spoken so bitterly, those military courts with their arbitrary powers. Only the negroes had rights or redress these days. The Yankees had the South prostrate and they intended to keep it so. The South had been tilted as by a giant malicious hand, and those who had once ruled were now more helpless than their former slaves had ever been.

Georgia was heavily garrisoned with troops and Atlanta had more than its share. The commandants of the Yankee troops in the various cities had complete power, even the power of life and death, over the civilian population, and they used that power. They could and did imprison citizens for any cause, or no cause, seize their property, hang them. They could and did harass and hamstring them with conflicting regulations about the operation of their business, the wages they must pay their servants, what they should say in public and private utterances and what they should write in newspapers. They regulated how, when and where they must dump their garbage and they decided what songs the daughters and wives of ex-Confederates could sing, so that the singing of 'Dixie' or 'Bonnie Blue Flag' became an offence only a little less serious than treason. They ruled that no one could get a letter out of the post office without taking the Iron-Clad oath and, in some instances, they even prohibited the issuance of marriage licences unless the couples had taken the hated oath.

The newspapers were so muzzled that no public protest could be raised against the injustices or depredations of the military, and individual protests were silenced with jail sentences. The jails were full of prominent citizens and there they stayed without hope of early trial. Trial by jury and the law of habeas corpus were practically suspended. The civil courts still functioned after a fashion but they functioned at the pleasure of the military, who could and did interfere with their verdicts, so that citizens so unfortunate as to get arrested were virtually at the mercy of the military authorities. And so many did get arrested. The very suspicion of seditious utterances against the government, suspected complicity in the Ku Klux Klan, or complaint by a negro that a white man had been uppity to him were enough to land a citizen in jail. Proof and evidence were not needed. The accusation was sufficient. And thanks to the incitement of the Freedmen's Bureau, negroes could always be found who were willing to bring accusations.

The negroes had not yet been given the right to vote but the North was determined that they should vote and equally determined that their vote should be friendly to the North. With this in mind, nothing was too good for the negroes. The Yankee soldiers backed them up in anything they chose to do, and the surest way for a white person to get himself into trouble was to bring a complaint of any kind against a negro.

The former slaves were now the lords of creation and, with the aid of the Yankees, the lowest and most ignorant ones were on top. The better class of them, scorning freedom, were suffering as severely as their white masters. Thousands of house servants, the highest caste in the slave population, remained with their white folks, doing manual labour which had been beneath them in the old days. Many loyal field hands also refused to avail themselves of the new freedom, but the hordes of 'trashy free issue niggers', who were causing most of the trouble, were drawn largely from the field-hand class.

In slave days, these lowly blacks had been despised by the house negroes and yard negroes as creatures of small worth. Just as Ellen had done, other plantation mistresses throughout the South had put the piccaninnies through courses of training and elimination to select the best of them for the positions of greater responsibility. Those consigned to the fields were the ones least willing or able to learn, the least energetic, the least honest and trustworthy, the most vicious and brutish. And now this class, the lowest in the black social order, was making life a misery for the South.

Aided by the unscrupulous adventurers who operated the Freedmen's Bureau and urged on by a fervour of Northern hatred almost religious in its fanaticism, the former field hands found themselves suddenly elevated to the seats of the mighty. There they conducted themselves as creatures of small intelligence might naturally be expected to do. Like monkeys or small children turned loose among treasured objects whose value is beyond their comprehension, they ran wild – either from perverse pleasure in destruction or simply because of their ignorance.

To the credit of the negroes, including the least intelligent of them, few were actuated by malice and those few had usually been 'mean niggers' even in slave days. But they were, as a class, childlike in mentality, easily led and from long habit accustomed to taking orders. Formerly their white masters had given the orders. Now they had a new set of masters, the Bureau and the Carpetbaggers, and their orders were: 'You're just as good as any white man, so act that way. Just as soon as you can vote the Republican ticket, you are going to have the white man's property. It's as good as yours now. Take it, if you can get it!'

Dazzled by these tales, freedom became a never-ending picnic, a barbecue every day of the week, a carnival of idleness and theft and insolence. Country negroes flocked into the cities, leaving the rural districts without labour to make the crops. Atlanta was crowded with them and still they came by the hundreds, lazy and dangerous as a result of the new doctrines being taught them. Packed into squalid cabins, smallpox, typhoid and tuberculosis broke out among them. Accustomed to the care of their mistresses when they were ill in slave days, they did not know how to nurse themselves or their sick. Relying upon their masters in the old days to care for their aged and their babies, they now had no sense of responsibility for their helpless. And the Bureau was far too interested in political matters to provide the care the plantation owners had once given.

Abandoned negro children ran like frightened animals about the town until kind-hearted white people took them into their kitchens to raise. Aged country darkies, deserted by their children, bewildered and panic-stricken in the bustling town, sat on the kerbs and cried to the ladies who passed:

'Mistis, please, Ma'm, write mah old Marster down in Fayette County dat Ah's up hyah. He'll come tek dis ole nigger home agin. 'Fo' Gawd, Ah done got nuff of dis freedom!'

The Freedmen's Bureau, overwhelmed by the numbers who poured in upon them, realized too late a part of the mistake and tried to send them back to their former owners. They told the negroes that if they would go back, they would go as free workers, protected by written contracts specifying wages by the day. The old darkies went back to the plantations gladly, making a heavier burden than ever on the poverty-stricken planters who had not the heart to turn them out, but the young ones remained in Atlanta. They did not want to be workers of any kind, anywhere. Why work when the belly is full?

For the first time in their lives the negroes were able to get all the whisky they might want. In slave days, it was something they never tasted except at Christmas, when each one received a 'drap' along with his gift. Now they had not only the Bureau agitators and the Carpetbaggers urging them on, but the incitement of whisky as well, and outrages were inevitable. Neither life nor property was safe from them, and the white people, unprotected by law, were terrorized. Men were insulted on the streets by drunken blacks, houses and barns were burned at night, horses and cattle and chickens stolen in broad daylight, crimes of all varieties were committed and few of the perpetrators were brought to justice.

But these ignominies and dangers were as nothing compared with the peril of white women, many bereft by the war of male protection, who lived alone in the outlying districts and on lonely roads. It was the large number of outrages on women and the ever-present fear for the safety of their wives and daughters that drove Southern men to cold and trembling fury and caused the Ku Klux Klan to spring up overnight. And it was against this nocturnal organization that the newspapers of the North cried out most loudly, never realizing the tragic necessity that brought it into being. The North wanted every member of the Ku Klux Klan hunted down and hanged, because they had dared take the punishment of crime into their own hands at a time when the ordinary processes of law and order had been overthrown by the invaders.

Here was the astonishing spectacle of half a nation attempting, at the point of a bayonet, to force upon the other half the rule of negroes, many of them scarcely one generation out of the African jungles. The vote must be given to them but it must be denied to most of their former owners. The South must be kept down and disfranchisement of the whites was one way to keep the South down. Most of those who had fought for the Confederacy, held office under it or given aid and comfort to it were not allowed to vote, had no choice in the selection of their public officials and were wholly under the power of an alien rule. Many men, thinking soberly of General Lee's words and example, wished to take the oath, become citizens again and forget the past. But they were not permitted to take it. Others who were permitted to take the oath, hotly refused to do so, scorning to swear allegiance to a government which was deliberately subjecting them to cruelty and humiliation.

Scarlett heard over and over until she could have screamed at the repetition: 'I'd have taken their damned oath right after the surrender if they'd acted decent. I can be restored to the Union, but by God, I can't be reconstructed into it!'

Through these anxious days and nights, Scarlett was torn with fear. The ever-present menace of lawless negroes and Yankee soldiers preyed on her mind, the danger of confiscation was constantly with her, even in her dreams, and she dreaded worse terrors to come. Depressed by the helplessness of herself and her friends, of the whole South, it was not strange that she often remembered during these days the words which Tony Fontaine had spoken so passionately:

'By God, Scarlett, it isn't to be borne! And it won't be borne!'

In spite of war, fire and Reconstruction, Atlanta had again become a boom town. In many ways, the place resembled the busy young city of the Confederacy's early days. The only trouble was that the soldiers crowding the streets wore the wrong kind of uniforms, the money was in the hands of the wrong people, and the negroes were living in leisure while their former masters struggled and starved.

Underneath the surface were misery and fear, but all the outward appearances were those of a thriving town that was rapidly rebuilding from its ruins, a bustling, hurrying town. Atlanta, it seemed, must always be hurrying, no matter what its circumstances might be. Savannah, Charleston, Augusta, Richmond, New Orleans would never hurry. It was ill-bred and Yankeefied to hurry. But in this period, Atlanta was more ill-bred and Yankeefied than it had ever been before or would ever be again. With 'new people' thronging in from all directions, the streets were choked and noisy from morning till night. The shiny carriages of Yankee officers' wives and newly rich Carpetbaggers splashed mud on the dilapidated buggies of the townspeople, and gaudy new homes of wealthy strangers crowded in among the sedate dwellings of older citizens.

The war had definitely established the importance of Atlanta in the affairs of the South and the hitherto obscure town was now known far and wide. The railroads for which Sherman had fought an entire summer and killed thousands of men were again stimulating the life of the city they had brought into being. Atlanta was again the centre of activities for a wide region, as it had been before its destruction, and the town was receiving a great influx of new citizens, both welcome and unwelcome.

Invading Carpetbaggers made Atlanta their headquarters and on the streets they jostled against representatives of the oldest families in the South who were likewise newcomers in the town. Families from the country districts who had been burned out during Sherman's march and who could no longer make a living without the slaves to till the cotton had come to Atlanta to live. New settlers were coming in every day from Tennessee and the Carolinas where the hand of Reconstruction lay even heavier than in Georgia. Many Irish and Germans who had been bounty men in the Union Army had settled in Atlanta after their discharge. The wives and families of the Yankee garrison, filled with curiosity about the South after four years of war, came to swell the population. Adventurers of every kind swarmed in, hoping to make their fortunes, and the negroes from the country continued to come by the hundreds.

The town was roaring – wide open like a frontier village, making no effort to cover its vices and sins. Saloons blossomed overnight, two and sometimes three in a block, and after nightfall the streets were full of drunken men, black and white, reeling from wall to kerb and back again. Thugs, pickpockets and prostitutes lurked in the unlit alleys and shadowy streets. Gambling houses ran full blast and hardly a night passed without its shooting or cutting affray. Respectable citizens were scandalized to find that Atlanta had a large and thriving red-light district, larger and more thriving than during the war. All night long pianos jangled from behind drawn shades and rowdy songs and laughter floated out, punctuated by occasional screams and pistol shots. The inmates of these houses were bolder than the prostitutes of the war days and brazenly hung out of their windows and called to passers-by. And on Sunday afternoons, the handsome closed carriages of the madams of the district rolled down the main streets, filled with girls in their best finery, taking the air from behind lowered silk shades.

Belle Watling was the most notorious of the madams. She had opened a new house of her own, a large two-storey building that made neighbouring houses in the district look like shabby rabbit warrens. There was a long bar-room downstairs, elegantly hung with oil paintings, and a negro orchestra played every night. The upstairs, so rumour said, was fitted out with the finest of plush-upholstered furniture, heavy lace curtains and imported mirrors in gilt frames. The dozen young ladies with whom the house was furnished were comely, if brightly painted, and comported themselves more quietly than those of other houses. At least, the police were seldom summoned to Belle's.

This house was something that the matrons of Atlanta whispered about furtively and ministers preached against in guarded terms as a cesspool of iniquity, a hissing and a reproach. Everyone knew that a woman of Belle's type couldn't have made enough money by herself to set up such a luxurious establishment. She had to have a backer and a rich one at that. And Rhett Butler had never had the decency to conceal his relations with her, so it was obvious that he and no other must be that backer. Belle herself presented a prosperous appearance when glimpsed occasionally in her closed carriage driven by an impudent yellow negro. When she drove by, behind a fine pair of bays, all the little boys along the street who could evade their mothers ran to peer at her and whisper excitedly: 'That's her! That's ole Belle! I seen her red hair!'

Shouldering the shell-pitted houses patched with bits of old lumber and smoke-blackened bricks, the fine homes of the Carpetbaggers and war profiteers were rising, with mansard roofs, gables and turrets, stained-glass windows and wide lawns. Night after night, in these newly built homes, the windows were ablaze with gaslight and the sound of music and dancing feet drifted out upon the air. Women in stiff bright-coloured silks strolled about long verandas, squired by men in evening clothes. Champagne corks popped, and on lace tablecloths seven-course dinners were laid. Hams in wine, pressed duck, pâté de foie gras, rare fruits in and out of season, were spread in profusion.

Behind the shabby doors of the old houses, poverty and hunger lived – all the more bitter for the brave gentility with which they were borne, all the more pinching for the outward show of proud indifference to material wants. Dr Meade could tell unlovely stories of those families who had been driven from mansions to boarding-houses and from boarding-houses to dingy rooms on back streets. He had too many lady patients who were suffering from 'weak hearts' and 'declines'. He knew, and they knew he knew, that slow starvation was the trouble. He could tell of consumption making inroads on entire families and of pellagra, once found only among poor whites, which was now appearing in Atlanta's best families. And there were babies with thin rickety legs and mothers who could not nurse them. Once the old doctor had been wont to thank God reverently for each child he brought into the world. Now he did not think life was such a boon. It was a hard world for little babies and so many died in their first few months of life.

Bright lights and wine, fiddles and dancing, brocade and broadcloth in the showy big houses and, just around the corners, slow starvation and cold. Arrogance and callousness for the conquerors, bitter endurance and hatred for the conquered.

Chapter XXXVIII

Scarlett saw it all, lived with it by day, took it to bed with her at night, dreading always what might happen next. She knew that she and Frank were already in the Yankees' black books, because of Tony, and disaster might descend on them at any hour. But, now of all times, she could not afford to be pushed back to her beginnings – not now with a baby coming, the mill just commencing to pay and Tara depending on her for money until the cotton came in in the fall. Oh, suppose she should lose everything!

Suppose she should have to start all over again with only her puny weapons against this mad world! To have to pit her red lips and green eyes and her shrewd shallow brain against the Yankees and everything the Yankees stood for. Weary with dread, she felt that she would rather kill herself than try to make a new beginning.

In the ruin and chaos of that spring of 1866, she single-mindedly turned her energies to making the mill pay. There was money in Atlanta. The wave of rebuilding was giving her the opportunity she wanted and she knew she could make money if only she could stay out of jail. But, she told herself time and again, she would have to walk easily, gingerly, be meek under insults, yielding to injustices, never giving offence to anyone, black or white, who might do her harm. She hated the impudent free negroes as much as anyone and her flesh crawled with fury every time she heard their insulting remarks and high-pitched laughter as she went by. But she never even gave them a glance of contempt. She hated the Carpetbaggers and Scallawags who were getting rich with ease while she struggled, but she said nothing in condemnation of them. No one in Atlanta could have loathed the Yankees more than she, for the very sight of a blue uniform made her sick with rage, but even in the privacy of her family she kept silent about them.

'I won't be a big-mouthed fool,' she thought grimly. Let others break their hearts over the old days and the men who'll never come back. Let others burn with fury over the Yankee rule and losing the ballot. Let others go to jail for speaking their minds and get themselves hanged for being in the Ku Klux Klan. (Oh, what a dreaded name that was, almost as terrifying to Scarlett as to the negroes.) Let other women be proud that their husbands belonged. Thank God, Frank had never been mixed up in it! Let others stew and fume and plot and plan about things they could not help. What did the past matter compared with the tense present and the dubious future? What did the ballot matter when bread, a roof and staying out of jail were the real problems? And, please God, just let me stay out of trouble until June!

Only till June! By that month Scarlett knew she would be forced to retire into Aunt Pitty's house and remain secluded there until after her child was born. Already people were criticizing her for appearing in public when she was in such a condition. No lady ever showed herself when she was pregnant. Already Frank and Pitty were begging her not to expose herself – and them – to embarrassment and she had promised them to stop work in June.

Only till June! By June she must have the mill well enough established for her to leave it. By June she must have money enough to give her at least some little protection against misfortune. So much to do and so little time to do it! She wished for more hours of the day and counted the minutes, as she strained forward feverishly in her pursuit of money and still more money.

Because she nagged the timid Frank, the store was doing better now and he was even collecting some of the old bills. But it was the sawmill on which her hopes were pinned. Atlanta these days was like a giant plant which had been cut to the ground but now was springing up again with sturdier shoots, thicker foliage, more numerous branches. The demand for building materials was far greater than could be supplied. Prices of lumber, brick and stone soared and Scarlett kept the mill running from dawn until lantern-light.

A part of every day she spent at the mill, prying into everything, doing her best to check the thievery she felt sure was going on. But most of the time she was riding about the town, making the rounds of builders, contractors and carpenters, even calling on strangers she had heard might build at future dates, cajoling them into promises of buying from her and her only.

Soon she was a familiar sight on Atlanta's streets, sitting in her buggy beside the dignified, disapproving old darky driver, a lap-robe pulled high about her, her little mittened hands clasped in her lap. Aunt Pitty had made her a pretty green mantelet which hid her figure and a green pancake hat which matched her eyes, and she always wore these becoming garments on her business calls. A faint dab of rouge on her cheeks and a fainter fragrance of cologne made her a charming picture, as long as she did not alight from the buggy and show her figure. And there was seldom any need for this, for she smiled and beckoned and the men came quickly to the buggy and frequently stood bareheaded in the rain to talk business with her.

She was not the only one who had seen the opportunities for making money out of lumber, but she did not fear her competitors. She knew with conscious pride in her own smartness that she was the equal of any of them. She was Gerald's own daughter and the shrewd trading instinct she had inherited was now sharpened by her needs.

At first the other dealers had laughed at her, laughed with good-natured contempt at the very idea of a woman in business. But now they did not laugh. They swore silently as they saw her ride by. The fact that she was a woman frequently worked in her favour, for she could upon occasion look so helpless and appealing that she melted hearts. With no difficulty whatever she could mutely convey the impression of a brave but timid lady, forced by brutal circumstance into a distasteful position, a helpless little lady who would probably starve if customers didn't buy her lumber. But when ladylike airs failed to get results she was coldly businesslike and willingly undersold her competitors at a loss to herself if it would bring her a new customer. She was not above selling a poor grade of lumber for the price of good lumber if she thought she would not be detected, and she had no scruples about blackguarding the other lumber dealers. With every appearance of reluctance at disclosing the unpleasant truth, she would sigh and tell prospective customers that her competitors' lumber was far too high in price, rotten, full of knot-holes and in general of deplorably poor quality.

The first time Scarlett lied in this fashion she felt disconcerted and guilty – disconcerted because the lie sprang so easily and naturally to her lips, guilty because the thought flashed into her mind: What would Mother say?

There was no doubt what Ellen would say to a daughter who told lies and engaged in sharp practices. She would be stunned and incredulous and would speak gentle words that stung despite their gentleness, would talk of honour and honesty and truth and duty to one's neighbour. Momentarily, Scarlett cringed as she pictured the look on her mother's face. And then the picture faded, blotted out by an impulse, hard, unscrupulous and greedy, which had been born in the lean days at Tara and was now strengthened by the present uncertainty of life. So she passed this milestone as she had passed others before it – with a sigh that she was not as Ellen would like her to be, a shrug and the repetition of her unfailing charm: 'I'll think of all this later.'

But she never again thought of Ellen in connection with her business practices, never again regretted any means she used to take trade away from other lumber dealers. She knew she was perfectly safe in lying about them. Southern chivalry protected her. A Southern lady could lie about a gentleman but a Southern gentleman could not lie about a lady or, worse still, call the lady a liar. Other lumbermen could only fume inwardly and state heatedly, in the bosoms of their families, that they wished to God Mrs Kennedy was a man for just about five minutes.

One poor white who operated a mill on the Decatur road did try to fight Scarlett with her own weapons, saying openly that she was a liar and a swindler. But it hurt him rather than helped, for everyone was appalled that even a poor white should say such shocking things about a lady of good family, even when the lady was conducting herself in such an unwomanly way. Scarlett bore his remarks with silent dignity and, as time went by, she turned all her attention to him and his customers. She undersold him so relentlessly and delivered, with secret groans, such an excellent quality of lumber to prove her probity that he was soon bankrupt. Then, to Frank's horror, she triumphantly bought his mill at her own price.

Once in her possession there arose the perplexing problem of finding a trustworthy man to put in charge of it. She did not want another man like Mr Johnson. She knew that despite all her watchfulness he was still selling her lumber behind her back, but she thought it would be easy to find the right sort of man. Wasn't everybody as poor as Job's turkey, and weren't the streets full of men, some of them formerly rich, who were without work? The day never went by that Frank did not give money to some hungry ex-soldier or that Pitty and Cookie did not wrap up food for gaunt beggars.

But Scarlett, for some reason she could not understand, did not want any of these. 'I don't want men who haven't found something to do after a year,' she thought. 'If they haven't adjusted to peace yet, they couldn't adjust to me. And they all look so hangdog and licked. I don't want a man who's licked. I want somebody who's smart and energetic like Renny or Tommy Wellburn or Kells Whiting or one of the Simmons boys or – or any of that tribe. They haven't got that I-don't-care-about-anything look the soldiers had right after the surrender. They look like they cared a heap about a heap of things.'

But to her surprise the Simmons boys, who had started a brick kiln, and Kells Whiting, who was selling a preparation made up in his mother's kitchen that was guaranteed to straighten the kinkiest negro hair in six applications, smiled politely, thanked her and refused. It was the same with the dozen others she approached. In desperation she raised the wage she was offering but she was still refused. One of Mrs Merriwether's nephews observed impertinently that while he didn't especially enjoy driving a dray, it was his own dray and he would rather get somewhere under his own steam than Scarlett's.

One afternoon, Scarlett pulled up her buggy beside René Picard's pie wagon and hailed René and the crippled Tommy Wellburn, who was catching a ride home with his friend.

'Look here, Renny, why don't you come and work for me? Managing a mill is a sight more respectable than driving a pie wagon. I'd think you'd be ashamed.'

'Me, I am dead to shame,' grinned René. 'Who would be respectable? All of my days I was respectable until ze war set me free lak ze darkies. Nevaire again must I be deegneefied and full of ennui. Free lak ze bird! I lak my pie wagon. I lak my mule. I lak ze dear Yankees who so kindly buy ze pie of Madame Belle-Mère. No, my Scarlett, I must be ze King of ze Pies. Eet ees my destiny! Lak Napoleon, I follow my star.' He flourished his whip dramatically.

'But you weren't raised to sell pies any more than Tommy was raised to wrastle with a bunch of wild Irish masons. My kind of work is more—'

'And I suppose you were raised to run a lumber mill,' said Tommy, the corners of his mouth twitching. 'Yes, I can just see little Scarlett at her mother's knee, lisping her lesson, "Never sell good lumber if you can get a better price for bad".'

René roared at this, his small monkey eyes dancing with glee as he whacked Tommy on his twisted back.

'Don't be impudent,' said Scarlett coldly, for she saw little humour in Tommy's remark. 'Of course, I wasn't raised to run a sawmill.'

'I didn't mean to be impudent. But you are running a sawmill, whether you were raised to it or not. And running it very well, too. Well, none of us, as far as I can see, are doing what we intended to do right now, but I think we'll make out just the same. It's a poor person and a poor nation that sits down and cries because life isn't precisely what they expected it to be. Why don't you pick up some enterprising Carpetbagger to work for you, Scarlett? The woods are full of them, God knows.'

'I don't want a Carpetbagger. Carpetbaggers will steal anything that isn't red-hot or nailed down. If they amounted to anything they'd have stayed where they were, instead of coming down here to pick our bones. I want a nice man, from nice folks, who is smart and honest and energetic and—'

'You don't want much. And you won't get it for the wage you're offering. All the men of that description, barring the badly maimed ones, have already got something to do. They may be round pegs in square holes but they've all got something to do. Something of their own that they'd rather do than work for a woman.'

'Men haven't got much sense, have they, when you get down to rock bottom?'

'Maybe not, but they've got a heap of pride,' said Tommy soberly.

'Pride! Pride tastes awfully good, especially when the crust is flaky and you put meringue on it,' said Scarlett tartly.

The two men laughed, a bit unwillingly, and it seemed to Scarlett that they drew together in united masculine disapproval of her. What Tommy said was true, she thought, running over in her mind the men she had approached and the ones she intended to approach. They were all busy, busy at something, working hard, working harder than they would have dreamed possible in the days before the war. They weren't doing what they wanted to do perhaps, or what was easiest to do, or what they had been reared to do, but they were doing something. Times were too hard for men to be choosy. And if they were sorrowing for lost hopes, longing for lost ways of living, no one knew it but them. They were fighting a new war, a harder war than the one before. And they were caring about life again, caring with the same urgency and the same violence that animated them before the war had cut their lives in two.

'Scarlett,' said Tommy awkwardly, 'I do hate to ask a favour of you, after being impudent to you, but I'm going to ask it just the same. Maybe it would help you anyway. My brother-in-law, Hugh Elsing, isn't doing any too well peddling kindling wood. Everybody except the Yankees goes out and collects their own kindling wood. And I know things are mighty hard with the whole Elsing family. I – I do what I can, but you see I've got Fanny to support, and then, too, I've got my mother and two widowed sisters down in Sparta to look after. Hugh is nice, and you wanted a nice man, and he's from nice folks, as you know, and he's honest.'

'But – well, Hugh hasn't got much gumption or else he'd make a success of his kindling.'

Tommy shrugged.

'You've got a hard way of looking at things, Scarlett,' he said. 'But you think Hugh over. You could go far and do worse. I think his honesty and his willingness will outweigh his lack of gumption.'

Scarlett did not answer, for she did not want to be too rude. But to her mind there were few, if any, qualities that outweighed gumption.

After she had unsuccessfully canvassed the town and refused the importuning of many eager Carpetbaggers, she finally decided to take Tommy's suggestion and ask Hugh Elsing. He had been a dashing and resourceful officer during the war, but two severe wounds and four years of fighting seemed to have drained him of all his resourcefulness, leaving him to face the rigours of peace as bewildered as a child. There was a lost-dog look in his eyes these days as he went about peddling his firewood, and he was not at all the kind of man she had hoped to get.

'He's stupid,' she thought. 'He doesn't know a thing about business and I'll bet he can't add two and two. And I doubt if he'll ever learn. But, at least, he's honest and won't swindle me.'

Scarlett had little use these days for honesty in herself, but the less she valued it in herself the more she was beginning to value it in others.

'It's a pity Johnnie Gallegher is tied up with Tommy Wellburn on that construction work,' she thought. 'He's just the kind of man I want. He's hard as nails and slick as a snake, but he'd be honest if it paid him to be honest. I understand him and he understands me and we could do business together very well. Maybe I can get him when the hotel is finished, and till then I'll have to make out on Hugh and Mr Johnson. If I put Hugh in charge of the new mill and leave Mr Johnson at the old one, I can stay in town and see to the selling while they handle the milling and hauling. Until I can get Johnnie I'll have to risk Mr Johnson robbing me if I stay in town all the time. If only he wasn't a thief! I believe I'll build a lumber yard on half that lot Charles left me. If only Frank didn't holler so loud about me building a saloon on the other half! Well, I shall build the saloon just as soon as I get enough money ahead, no matter how he takes on. If only Frank wasn't so thin skinned. Oh, God, if only I wasn't going to have a baby at this of all times! In a little while I'll be so big I can't go out. Oh, God, if only I wasn't going to have a baby! And oh, God, if the damned Yankees will only let me alone! If—'

If! If! If! There were so many ifs in life, never any certainty of anything, never any sense of security, always the dread of losing everything and being cold and hungry again. Of course, Frank was making a little more money now, but Frank was always ailing with colds and frequently forced to stay in bed for days. Suppose he should become an invalid! No, she could not afford to count on Frank for much. She must not count on anything or anybody but herself. And what she could earn seemed so pitiably small. Oh, what would she do if the Yankees came and took it all away from her? If! If! If!

Half of what she made every month went to Will at Tara, part to Rhett to repay his loan and the rest she hoarded. No miser ever counted his gold oftener than she and no miser ever had greater fear of losing it. She would not put the money in the bank, for it might fail or the Yankees might confiscate it. So she carried what she could with her, tucked into her corset, and hid small wads of bills about the house, under loose bricks on the hearth, in her scrap-bag, between the pages of the Bible. And her temper grew shorter and shorter as the weeks went by, for every dollar she saved would be just one more dollar to lose if disaster descended.

Frank, Pitty and the servants bore her outbursts with maddening kindness, attributing her bad disposition to her pregnancy, never realizing the true cause. Frank knew that pregnant women must be humoured, so he put his pride in his pocket and said nothing more about her running the mills and her going about town at such a time, as no lady should do. Her conduct was a constant embarrassment to him but he reckoned he could endure it for a while longer. After the baby came, he knew she would be the same sweet, feminine girl he had courted. But in spite of everything he did to appease her, she continued to have her tantrums and often he thought she acted like one possessed.

No one seemed to realize what really possessed her, what drove her like a mad woman. It was a passion to get her affairs in order before she had to retire behind doors, to have as much money as possible in case the deluge broke upon her again, to have a stout levee of cash against the rising tide of Yankee hate. Money was the obsession dominating her mind these days. When she thought of the baby at all, it was with baffled rage at the untimeliness of it.

'Death and taxes and childbirth! There's never any convenient time for any of them!'

Atlanta had been scandalized enough when Scarlett, a woman, began operating the sawmill but, as time went by, the town decided there was no limit to what she would do. Her sharp trading was shocking, especially when her poor mother had been a Robillard, and it was positively indecent the way she kept on going about the streets when everyone knew she was pregnant. No respectable white woman and few negroes ever went outside their homes from the moment they first suspected they were with child, and Mrs Merriwether declared indignantly that from the way Scarlett was acting she was likely to have the baby on the public streets.

But all the previous criticism of her conduct was as nothing compared with the buzz of gossip that now went through the town. Scarlett was not only trafficking with the Yankees but was giving every appearance of really liking it!

Mrs Merriwether and many other Southerners were also doing business with the newcomers from the North, but the difference was that they did not like it and plainly showed they did not like it. And Scarlett did, or seemed to, which was just as bad. She had actually taken tea with the Yankee officers' wives in their homes! In fact, she had done practically everything short of inviting them into her own home, and the town guessed she would do even that, except for Aunt Pitty and Frank.

Scarlett knew the town was talking but she did not care, could not afford to care. She still hated the Yankees with as fierce a hate as on the day when they tried to burn Tara, but she could dissemble that hate. She knew that if she was going to make money, she would have to make it out of the Yankees, and she had learned that buttering them up with smiles and kind words was the surest way to get their business for her mill.

Some day when she was very rich and her money was hidden away where the Yankees could not find it, then, then she would tell them exactly what she thought of them, tell them how she hated and loathed and despised them. And what a joy that would be! But until that time came, it was just plain common sense to get along with them. And if that was hypocrisy, let Atlanta make the most of it.

She discovered that making friends with the Yankee officers was as easy as shooting birds on the ground. They were lonely exiles in a hostile land, and many of them were starved for polite feminine associations in a town where respectable women drew their skirts aside in passing and looked as if they would like to spit on them. Only the prostitutes and the negro women had kind words for them. But Scarlett was obviously a lady and a lady of family, for all that she worked, and they thrilled to her flashing smile and the pleasant light in her green eyes.

Frequently when Scarlett sat in her buggy talking to them and making her dimples play, her dislike for them rose so strong that it was hard not to curse them to their faces. But she restrained herself and she found that twisting Yankee men around her finger was no more difficult than that same diversion had been with Southern men. Only this was no diversion but a grim business. The rôle she enacted was that of a refined sweet Southern lady in distress. With an air of dignified reserve she was able to keep her victims at their proper distance, but there was nevertheless a graciousness in her manner which left a certain warmth in the Yankee officers' memories of Mrs Kennedy.

This warmth was very profitable – as Scarlett had intended it to be. Many of the officers of the garrison, not knowing how long they would be stationed in Atlanta, had sent for their wives and families. As the hotels and boarding-houses were overflowing, they were building small houses; and they were glad to buy their lumber from the gracious Mrs Kennedy, who treated them more politely than anyone else in town. The Carpetbaggers and Scallawags also, who were building fine homes and stores and hotels with their new wealth, found it more pleasant to do business with her than with the former Confederate soldiers who were courteous but with a courtesy more formal and cold than outspoken hate.

So, because she was pretty and charming and could appear quite helpless and forlorn at times, they gladly patronized her lumber yard and also Frank's store, feeling that they should help a plucky little woman who apparently had only a shiftless husband to support her. And Scarlett, watching the business grow, felt that she was not only safeguarding the present with Yankee money but the future with Yankee friends.

Keeping her relations with the Yankee officers on the plane she desired was easier than she expected, for they all seemed to be in awe of Southern ladies, but Scarlett soon found that their wives presented a problem she had not anticipated. Contacts with the Yankee women were not of her seeking. She would have been glad to avoid them but she could not, for the officers' wives were determined to meet her. They had an avid curiosity about the South and Southern women, and Scarlett gave them their first opportunity to satisfy it. Other Atlanta women would have nothing to do with them and even refused to bow to them in church, so when business brought Scarlett to their homes, she was like an answer to prayer. Often when Scarlett sat in her buggy in front of a Yankee home talking of uprights and shingles with the man of the house, the wife came out to join in the conversation or insist that she come inside for a cup of tea. Scarlett seldom refused, no matter how distasteful the idea might be, for she always hoped to have an opportunity to suggest tactfully that they do their trading at Frank's store. But her self-control was severely tested many times, because of the personal questions they asked and because of the smug and condescending attitude they displayed toward all things Southern.

Accepting *Uncle Tom's Cabin* as revelation second only to the Bible, the Yankee women all wanted to know about the bloodhounds which every Southerner kept to track down runaway slaves. And they never believed her when she told them she had only seen one bloodhound in all her life and it was a small mild dog and not a huge ferocious mastiff. They wanted to know about the dreadful branding-irons which planters used to mark the faces of their slaves and the cat-o'-nine-tails with which they beat them to death, and they evidenced what Scarlett felt was a very nasty and ill-bred interest in slave concubinage. Especially did she resent this in view of the enormous increase in mulatto babies in Atlanta since the Yankee soldiers had settled in the town.

Any other Atlanta woman would have expired in rage at having to listen to such bigoted ignorance but Scarlett managed to control herself. Assisting her in this was the fact that they aroused her contempt more than her anger. After all, they were Yankees and no one expected anything better from Yankees. So their unthinking insults to her state, her people and their morals, glanced off and never struck deep enough to cause her more than a well-concealed sneer until an incident occurred which made her sick with rage and showed her, if she needed any showing, how wide was the gap between North and South and how utterly impossible it was to bridge it.

While driving home with Uncle Peter one afternoon, she passed the house into which were crowded the families of three officers who were building their own homes with Scarlett's lumber. The three wives were standing in the walk as she drove by and they waved to her to stop. Coming out to the carriage block they greeted her in accents that always made her feel that one could forgive Yankees almost anything except their voices.

'You are just the person I want to see, Mrs Kennedy,' said a tall thin woman from Maine. 'I want to get some information about this benighted town.'

Scarlett swallowed the insult to Atlanta with the contempt it deserved and smiled her best.

'And what can I tell you?'

'My nurse, my Bridget, has gone back North. She said she wouldn't stay another day down here among the "naygurs" as she calls them. And the children are just driving me distracted! Do tell me how to go about getting another nurse. I do not know where to apply.'

'That shouldn't be difficult,' said Scarlett and laughed. 'If you can find a darky just in from the country who hasn't been spoiled by the Freedmen's Bureau, you'll have the best kind of servant possible. Just stand at your gate here and ask every darky woman who passes and I'm sure—'

The three women broke into indignant outcries.

'Do you think I'd trust my babies to a black nigger?' cried the Maine woman. 'I want a good Irish girl.'

'I'm afraid you'll find no Irish servants in Atlanta,' answered Scarlett, coolness in her voice. 'Personally, I've never seen a white servant and I shouldn't care to have one in my house. And' – she could not keep a slight note of sarcasm from her words – 'I assure you that darkies aren't cannibals and are quite trustworthy.'

'Goodness, no! I wouldn't have one in my house. The idea!'

'I wouldn't trust them any farther than I could see them and as for letting them handle my babies . . .'

Scarlett thought of the kind, gnarled hands of Mammy worn rough in Ellen's service and hers and Wade's. What did these strangers know of black hands, how dear and comforting they could be, how unerringly they knew how to soothe, to pat, to fondle? She laughed shortly.

'It's strange you should feel that way when it was you all who freed them.'

'Lor'! Not I, dearie,' laughed the Maine woman. 'I never saw a nigger till I came South last month and I don't care if I never see another. They give me the creeps. I wouldn't trust one of them . . .'

For some moments Scarlett had been conscious that Uncle Peter was breathing hard and sitting up very straight as he stared steadily at the horse's ears. Her attention was called to him more forcibly when the Maine woman broke off suddenly with a laugh and pointed him out to her companions.

'Look at that old nigger swell up like a toad,' she giggled. 'I'll bet he's an old pet of yours, isn't he? You Southerners don't know how to treat niggers. You spoil them to death.'

Peter sucked in his breath and his wrinkled brow showed deep furrows but he kept his eyes straight ahead. He had never had the term 'nigger' applied to him by a white person in all his life. By other negroes, yes. But never by a white person. And to be called untrustworthy and an 'old pet', he, Peter, who had been the dignified mainstay of the Hamilton family for years!

Scarlett felt, rather than saw, the black chin begin to shake with hurt pride, and a killing rage swept over her. She had listened with calm contempt while these women had underrated the Confederate Army, blackguarded Jeff Davis and accused Southerners of murder and torture of their slaves. If it were to her advantage she would have endured insults about her own virtue and honesty. But the knowledge that they had hurt the faithful old darky with their stupid remarks fired her like a match in gunpowder. For a moment she looked at the big horse-pistol in Peter's belt and her hands itched for the feel of it. They deserved killing, these insolent, ignorant, arrogant conquerors. But she bit down on her teeth until her jaw muscles stood out, reminding herself that the time had not yet come when she could tell the Yankees just what she thought of them. Some day, yes. My God, yes! But not yet.

'Uncle Peter is one of our family,' she said, her voice shaking. 'Good afternoon. Drive on, Peter.'

Peter laid the whip on the horse so suddenly that the startled animal jumped forward and as the buggy jounced off, Scarlett heard the Maine woman say with puzzled accents: 'Her family? You don't suppose she meant a relative? He's exceedingly black.'

'God damn them! They ought to be wiped off the face of the earth. If ever I get money enough, I'll spit in all their faces! I'll—'

She glanced at Peter and saw that a tear was trickling down his nose. Instantly a passion of tenderness, of grief for his humiliation swamped her, made her eyes sting. It was as though someone had been senselessly brutal to a child. Those women had hurt Uncle Peter – Peter who had been through the Mexican War with old Colonel Hamilton, Peter who had held his master in his arms when he died, who had raised Melly and Charles and looked after the feckless, foolish Pittypat, 'pertecked' her when she refugeed, and ''quired' a horse to bring her back from Macon through a war-torn country after the surrender. And they said they wouldn't trust niggers!

'Peter,' she said, her voice breaking as she put her hand on his thin arm. 'I'm ashamed of you for crying. What do you care? They aren't anything but damned Yankees!'

'Dey talked in front of me lak Ah wuz a mule an' couldn' unnerstan' dem – lak Ah wuz a Affikun an' din' know whut dey wuz talkin' 'bout,' said Peter, giving a tremendous sniff. 'An' dey call me a nigger an' Ah ain' never been call a nigger by no w'ite folks, an' dey call me a ole pet an' say dat niggers ain' ter be trus'ed! Me not ter be trus'ed! Why, w'en de ole Cunnel wuz dyin' he say ter me, "You, Peter! You look affer mah chillun. Tek keer of yo' young Miss Pittypat," he say, "'cause she ain' got no mo' sense dan a hopper-grass." An' Ah done tek keer of her good all dese y'ars—'

'Nobody but the Angel Gabriel could have done better,' said Scarlett soothingly. 'We just couldn't have lived without you.'

'Yas'm, thankee kinely, Ma'm. Ah knows it an' you knows it, but dem Yankee folks doan know it an' dey doan want ter know it. Huccome dey come mixin' in our bizness, Miss Scarlett? Dey doan unnerstan' us Confedruts.'

Scarlett said nothing for she was still burning with the wrath she had not exploded in the Yankee women's faces. The two drove home in silence. Peter's sniffles stopped and his underlip began to protrude gradually until it stuck out alarmingly. His indignation was mounting, now that the initial hurt was subsiding.

Scarlett thought: What damnably queer people Yankees are! Those women seemed to think that because Uncle Peter was black, he had no ears to hear with and no feelings, as tender as their own, to be hurt. They did not know that negroes had to be handled gently, as though they were children, directed, praised, petted, scolded. They didn't understand negroes or the relations between the negroes and their former masters. Yet they had fought a war to free them. And having freed them, they didn't want to have anything to do with them, except to use them to terrorize Southerners. They didn't like them, didn't trust them, didn't understand them, and yet their constant cry was that Southerners didn't know how to get along with them.

Not trust a darky! Scarlett trusted them far more than most white people, certainly more than she trusted any Yankee. There were qualities of loyalty and tirelessness and love in them that no strain could break, no money could buy. She thought of the faithful few who remained at Tara in the face of the Yankee invasion when they could have fled or joined the troops for lives of leisure. But they had stayed. She thought of Dilcey toiling in the cotton fields beside her, of Pork risking his life in neighbouring henhouses that the family might eat, of Mammy coming to Atlanta with her to keep her from doing wrong. She thought of the servants of her neighbours who had stood loyally beside their white owners, protecting their mistresses while the men were at the front, refugeeing with them through the terrors of the war, nursing the wounded, burying the dead, comforting the bereaved, working, begging, stealing to keep food on the tables. And even now, with the Freedmen's Bureau promising all manner of wonders, they still stuck with their white folks and worked much harder than they ever worked in slave times. But the Yankees didn't understand these things and would never understand them.

'Yet they set you free,' she said aloud.

'No, Ma'm! Dey din' sot me free. Ah wouldn' let no sech trash sot me free,' said Peter indignantly. 'Ah still b'longs ter Miss Pitty an' w'en Ah dies she gwine lay me in de Hamilton buhyin'-groun' whar Ah b'longs . . . Mah Miss gwine ter be in a state w'en Ah tells her 'bout how you let dem Yankee women 'sult me.'

'I did no such thing!' cried Scarlett, startled.

'You did so, Miss Scarlett,' said Peter, pushing out his lip even farther. 'De pint is, needer you nor me had no bizness bein' wid Yankees, so dey could 'sult me. Ef you hadn' talked wid dem, dey wouldn' had no chance ter treat me lak a mule or a Affikun. An' you din' tek up fer me, needer.'

'I did, too!' said Scarlett, stung by the criticism. 'Didn't I tell them you were one of the family?'

'Dat ain' tekkin' up. Dat's jes' a fac',' said Peter. 'Miss Scarlett, you ain' got no bizness havin' no truck wid Yankees. Ain' no other ladies doin' it. You wouldn' ketch Miss Pitty wipin' her lil shoes on sech trash. An' she ain' gwine lak it w'en she hear 'bout whut dey said 'bout me.'

Peter's criticism hurt worse than anything Frank or Aunt Pitty or the neighbours had said and it so annoyed her she longed to shake the old darky until his toothless gums clapped together. What Peter said was true but she hated to hear it from a negro and a family negro, too. Not to stand high in the opinion of one's servants was as humiliating a thing as could happen to a Southerner.

'A ole pet!' Peter grumbled. 'Ah specs Miss Pitty ain' gwine want me ter drive you roun' no mo' affer dat. No, Ma'm!'

'Aunt Pitty will want you to drive me as usual,' she said sternly, 'so let's hear no more about it.'

'Ah'll git a mizry in mah back,' warned Peter darkly. 'Mah back huttin' me so bad dis minute Ah kain sceercely set up. Mah Miss ain' gwine want me ter do no drivin' w'en Ah got a mizry . . . Miss Scarlett, it ain' gwine do you no good ter stan' high wid de Yankees an' de w'ite trash, ef yo' own folks doan 'prove of you.'

That was as accurate a summing up of the situation as could be made and Scarlett relapsed into infuriated silence. Yes, the conquerors did approve of her, and her family and her neighbours did not. She knew all the things the town was saying about her. And now even Peter disapproved of her to the point of not caring to be seen in public with her. That was the last straw.

Heretofore she had been careless of public opinion, careless and a little contemptuous. But Peter's words caused fierce resentment to burn in her breast, drove her to a defensive position, made her suddenly dislike her neighbours as much as she disliked the Yankees.

'Why should they care what I do?' she thought. 'They must think I enjoy associating with Yankees and working like a field hand. They're just making a hard job harder for me. But I don't care what they think, I won't let myself care. I can't afford to care now. But some day – some day—'

Oh, some day! When there was security in her world again, then she would sit back and fold her hands and be a great lady as Ellen had been. She would be helpless and sheltered, as a lady should be, and then everyone would approve of her. Oh, how grand she would be when she had money again! Then she could permit herself to be kind and gentle, as Ellen had been, and thoughtful of other people and of the proprieties, too. She would not be driven by fears, day and night, and life would be a placid, unhurried affair. She would have time to play with her children and listen to their lessons.

There would be long warm afternoons when ladies would call and, amid the rustlings of taffeta petticoats and the rhythmic harsh cracklings of palmetto fans, she would serve tea and delicious sandwiches and cakes and leisurely gossip the hours away. And she would be so kind to those who were suffering misfortune, take baskets to the poor and soup and jelly to the sick and 'air' those less fortunate in her fine carriage. She would be a lady in the true Southern manner, as her mother had been. And then, everyone would love her as they had loved Ellen and they would say how unselfish she was and call her 'Lady Bountiful'.

Her pleasure in these thoughts of the future was undimmed by any realization that she had no real desire to be unselfish or charitable or kind. All she wanted was the reputation for possessing these qualities. But the meshes of her brain were too wide, too coarse, to filter such small differences. It was enough that some day, when she had money, everyone would approve of her.

Some day! But not now. Not now, in spite of what anyone might say of her. Now, there was no time to be a great lady.

Peter was as good as his word. Aunt Pitty did get into a state, and Peter's misery developed overnight to such proportions that he never drove the buggy again. Thereafter Scarlett drove alone and the callouses which had begun to leave her palms came back again.

So the spring months went by, the cool rains of April passing into the warm balm of green May weather. The weeks were packed with work and worry and the handicaps of increasing pregnancy, with old friends growing cooler and her family increasingly more kind, more maddeningly solicitous and more completely blind to what was driving her. During those days of anxiety and struggle there was only one dependable, understanding person in her world, and that person was Rhett Butler. It was odd that he of all people should appear in this light, for he was as unstable as quicksilver and as perverse as a demon fresh from the pit. But he gave her sympathy, something she had never had from anyone and never expected from him.

Frequently he was out of town on those mysterious trips to New Orleans which he never explained but which she felt sure, in a faintly jealous way, were connected with a woman – or women. But after Uncle Peter's refusal to drive her, he remained in Atlanta for longer and longer intervals.

While in town, he spent most of his time gambling in the rooms above the Girl of the Period Saloon, or in Belle Watling's bar hobnobbing with the wealthier of the Yankees and Carpetbaggers in money-making schemes which made the townspeople detest him even more than his cronies. He did not call at the house now, probably in deference to the feelings of Frank and Pitty, who would have been outraged at a male caller while Scarlett was in a delicate condition. But she met him by accident almost every day. Time and again, he came riding up to her buggy when she was passing through lonely stretches of Peachtree road and Decatur road where the mills lay. He always drew rein and talked and sometimes he tied his horse to the back of the buggy and drove her on her rounds. She tired more easily these days than she liked to admit and she was always silently grateful when he took the reins. He always left her before they reached the town again but all Atlanta knew about their meetings, and it gave the gossips something new to add to the long list of Scarlett's affronts to the proprieties.

She wondered occasionally if these meetings were not more than accidental. They became more and more numerous as the weeks went by and as the tension in town heightened over negro outrages. But why did he seek her out, now of all times when she looked her worst? Certainly he had no designs upon her if he had ever had any, and she was beginning to doubt even this. It had been months since he made any joking references to their distressing scene at the Yankee jail. He never mentioned Ashley and her love for him or made any coarse and ill-bred remarks about 'coveting her'. She thought it best to let sleeping dogs lie, so she did not ask for an explanation of their frequent meetings. And finally she decided that, because he had little to do besides gamble and had few enough nice friends in Atlanta, he sought her out solely for companionship's sake.

Whatever his reason might be, she found his company most welcome. He listened to her moans about lost customers and bad debts, the swindling ways of Mr Johnson and the incompetency of Hugh. He applauded her triumphs, where Frank merely smiled indulgently and Pitty said 'Dear me!' in a dazed manner. She was sure that he frequently threw business her way, for he knew all the rich Yankees and Carpetbaggers intimately, but he always denied being helpful. She knew him for what he was and she never trusted him, but her spirits always rose with pleasure at the sight of him riding around the curve of a shady road on his big black horse. When he climbed into the buggy and took the reins from her and threw her some impertinent remark, she felt young and gay and attractive again, for all her worries and her increasing bulk. She could talk to him about almost everything, with no care for concealing her motives or her real opinions, and she never ran out of things to say as she did with Frank – or even with Ashley, if she must be honest with herself. But of course, in all her conversations with Ashley there were so many things which could not be said, for honour's sake, that the sheer force of them inhibited other remarks. It was comforting to have a friend like Rhett, now that for some unaccountable reason he had decided to be on good behaviour with her. Very comforting, for she had so few friends these days.

'Rhett,' she asked stormily, shortly after Uncle Peter's ultimatum, 'why do folks in this town treat me so scurvily and talk about me so? It's a toss-up who they talk worst about, me or the Carpetbaggers! I've minded my own business and haven't done anything wrong and—'

'If you haven't done anything wrong, it's because you haven't had the opportunity, and perhaps they dimly realize it.'

'Oh, do be serious! They make me so mad. All I've done is try to make a little money and—'

'All you've done is to be different from other women and you've made a little success of it. As I've told you before, that is the one unforgivable sin in any society. Be different and be damned! Scarlett, the mere fact that you've made a success of your mill is an insult to every man who hasn't succeeded. Remember, a well-bred female's place is in the home and she should know nothing about this busy, brutal world.'

'But if I had stayed in my home, I wouldn't have had any home left to stay in.'

'The inference is that you should have starved genteelly and with pride.'

'Oh, fiddle-dee-dee! But look at Mrs Merriwether. She's selling pies to Yankees and that's worse than running a sawmill, and Mrs Elsing takes in sewing and keeps boarders, and Fanny paints awful-looking china things that nobody wants and everybody buys to help her and—'

'But you miss the point, my pet. They aren't successful and so they aren't affronting the hot Southern pride of their men folks. The men can still say, "Poor sweet sillies, how hard they try! Well, I'll let them think they're helping." And besides, the ladies you mentioned don't enjoy having to work. They let it be known that they are only doing it until some man comes along to relieve them of their unwomanly burdens. And so everybody feels sorry for them. But obviously you do like to work and obviously you aren't going to let any man tend to your business for you, and so no one can feel sorry for you. And Atlanta is never going to forgive you for that. It's so pleasant to feel sorry for people.'

'I wish you'd be serious, sometimes.'

'Did you ever hear the Oriental proverb, "The dogs bark but the caravan passes on"? Let them bark, Scarlett. I fear nothing will stop your caravan.'

'But why should they mind my making a little money?'

'You can't have everything, Scarlett. You can either make money in your present unladylike manner and meet cold shoulders everywhere you go, or you can be poor and genteel and have lots of friends. You've made your choice.'

'I won't be poor,' she said swiftly. 'But – it is the right choice, isn't it?'

'If it's money you want most.'

'Yes, I want money more than anything else in the world.'

'Then you've made the only choice. But there's a penalty attached, as there is to most things you want. It's loneliness.'

That silenced her for a moment. It was true. When she stopped to think about it, she was a little lonely – lonely for feminine companionship. During the war years she had had Ellen to visit when she felt blue. And since Ellen's death, there had always been Melanie, though she and Melanie had nothing in common except the hard work at Tara. Now there was no one, for Aunt Pitty had no conception of life beyond her small round of gossip.

'I think – I think,' she began hesitantly, 'that I've always been lonely where women were concerned. It isn't just my working that makes Atlanta ladies dislike me. They just don't like me anyway. No woman ever really liked me, except Mother. Even my sisters. I don't know why, but even before the war, even before I married Charlie, ladies didn't seem to approve of anything I did—'

'You forget Mrs Wilkes,' said Rhett, and his eyes gleamed maliciously. 'She has always approved of you up to the hilt. I dare say she'd approve of anything you did, short of murder.'

Scarlett thought grimly: 'She's even approved of murder,' and she laughed contemptuously.

'Oh, Melly!' she said, and then, ruefully: 'It's certainly not to my credit that Melly is the only woman who approves of me, for she hasn't the sense of a guinea-hen. If she had any sense—' She stopped in some confusion.

'If she had any sense, she'd realize a few things and she couldn't approve,' Rhett finished. 'Well, you know more about that than I do, of course.'

'Oh, damn your memory and your bad manners!'

'I'll pass over your unjustified rudeness with the silence it deserves and return to our former subject. Make up your mind to this. If you are different, you are isolated, not only from people of your own age but from those of your parents' generation and from your children's generation too. They'll never understand you and they'll be shocked no matter what you do. But your grandparents would probably be proud of you and say: "There's a chip off the old block," and your grandchildren will sigh enviously and say: "What an old rip Grandma must have been!" and they'll try to be like you.'

Scarlett laughed with amusement.

'Sometimes you do hit on the truth! Now there was my Grandma Robillard. Mammy used to hold her over my head whenever I was naughty. Grandma was as cold as an icicle and strict about her manners and everybody else's manners, but she married three times and had any number of duels fought over her and she wore rouge and the most shockingly low-cut dresses and no – well, er – not much under her dresses.'

'And you admired her tremendously, for all that you tried to be like your mother! I had a grandfather on the Butler side who was a pirate.'

'Not really! A walk-the-plank kind?'

'I dare say he made people walk the plank if there was any money to be made that way. At any rate, he made enough money to leave my father quite wealthy. But the family always referred to him carefully as a "sea captain". He was killed in a saloon brawl long before I was born. His death was, needless to say, a great relief to his children, for the old gentleman was drunk most of the time and when in his cups was apt to forget that he was a retired sea captain and give reminiscences that curled his children's hair. However, I admired him and tried to copy him far more than I ever did my father, for

Father is an amiable gentleman full of honourable habits and pious saws – so you see how it goes. I'm sure your children won't approve of you, Scarlett, any more than Mrs Merriwether and Mrs Elsing and their broods approve of you now. Your children will probably be soft, prissy creatures, as the children of hard-bitten characters usually are. And to make them worse, you, like every other mother, are probably determined that they shall never know the hardships you've known. And that's all wrong. Hardships make or break people. So you'll have to wait for approval from your grandchildren.'

'I wonder what our grandchildren will be like!'

'Are you suggesting by that "our" that you and I will have mutual grandchildren? Fie, Mrs Kennedy!'

Scarlett, suddenly conscious of her error of speech, went red. It was more than his joking words that shamed her, for she was suddenly aware again of her thickening body. In no way had either of them ever hinted at her condition and she had always kept the lap-robe high under her armpits when with him, even on warm days, comforting herself in the usual feminine manner with the belief that she did not show at all when thus covered, and she was suddenly sick with quick rage at her own condition and shame that he should know.

'You get out of this buggy, you dirty-minded varmint,' she said, her voice shaking.

'I'll do nothing of the kind,' he returned calmly. 'It'll be dark before you get home and there's a new colony of darkies living in tents and shanties near the next spring, mean niggers I've been told, and I see no reason why you should give the impulsive Ku Klux a cause for putting on their nightshirts and riding abroad this evening.'

'Get out!' she cried, tugging at the reins, and suddenly nausea overwhelmed her. He stopped the horse quickly, passed her two clean handkerchiefs and held her head over the side of the buggy with some skill. The afternoon sun, slanting low through the newly leaved trees, spun sickeningly for a few moments in a swirl of gold and green. When the spell had passed she put her head in her hands and cried from sheer mortification. Not only had she vomited before a man – in itself as horrible a contretemps as could overtake a woman – but by doing so, the humiliating fact of her pregnancy must now be evident. She felt that she could never look him in the face again. To have this happen with him, of all people, with Rhett who had no respect for women! She cried, expecting some coarse and jocular remark from him which she would never be able to forget.

'Don't be a fool,' he said quietly. 'And you are a fool, if you are crying for shame. Come, Scarlett, don't be a child. Surely you must know that, not being blind, I knew you were pregnant.'

She said 'Oh' in a stunned voice and tightened her fingers over her crimson face. The word itself horrified her. Frank always referred to her pregnancy embarrassedly as 'your condition', Gerald had been wont to say delicately 'in the family way', when he had to mention such matters, and ladies genteelly referred to pregnancy as being 'in a fix'.

'You are a child if you thought I didn't know, for all your smothering yourself under that hot lap-robe. Of course, I knew. Why else do you think I've been—'

He stopped suddenly and a silence fell between them. He picked up the reins and clucked to the horse. He went on talking quietly and as his drawl fell pleasantly on her ears, some of the colour faded from her down-tucked face.

'I didn't think you could be so shocked, Scarlett. I thought you were a sensible person and I'm disappointed. Can it be possible that modesty still lingers in your breast? I'm afraid I'm not a gentleman to have mentioned the matter. And I know I'm not a gentleman, in view of the fact that pregnant women do not embarrass me as they should. I find it possible to treat them as normal creatures and not look at the ground or the sky or anywhere else in the universe except their waist-lines, and then cast at them those furtive glances I've always thought the height of indecency. Why should I? It's a perfectly normal state. The Europeans are far more sensible than we are. They compliment expectant mothers upon their expectations. While I wouldn't advise going that far, still it's more sensible than our way of trying to ignore it. It's a normal state and women should be proud of it, instead of hiding behind closed doors as if they'd committed a crime.'

'Proud!' she cried in a strangled voice. 'Proud – ugh!'

'Aren't you proud to be having a child?'

'Oh, dear God, no! I – I hate babies!'

'You mean – Frank's baby?'

'No – anybody's baby.'

For a moment she went sick again at this new error of speech, but his voice went on as easily as though he had not marked it.

'Then we're different. I like babies.'

'You like them?' she cried, looking up, so startled at the statement that she forgot her embarrassment. 'What a liar you are!'

'I like babies and I like little children, till they begin to grow up and acquire adult habits of thought and adult abilities to lie and cheat and be dirty. That can't be news to you. You know I like Wade Hampton a lot, for all that he isn't the boy he ought to be.'

That was true, thought Scarlett, suddenly marvelling. He did seem to enjoy playing with Wade and often brought him presents.

'Now that we've brought this dreadful subject into the light and you admit that you expect a baby some time in the not too distant future, I'll say something I've been wanting to say for weeks – two things. The first is that it's dangerous for you to drive alone. You know it. You've been told it often enough. If you don't care personally whether or not you are raped, you might consider the consequences. Because of your obstinacy, you may get yourself into a situation where your gallant fellow townsmen will be forced to avenge you by stringing up a few darkies. And that will bring the Yankees down on them and someone will probably get hanged. Has it ever occurred to you that perhaps one of the reasons the ladies do not like you is that your conduct may cause the neck-stretching of their sons and husbands? And furthermore, if the Ku Klux handles many more negroes, the Yankees are going to tighten up on Atlanta in a way that will make Sherman's conduct look angelic. I know what I'm talking about, for I'm hand in glove with the Yankees. Shameful to state, they treat me as one of them and I hear them talk openly. They mean to stamp out the Ku Klux if it means burning the whole town again and hanging every male over ten. That would hurt you, Scarlett. You might lose money. And there's no telling where a prairie fire might stop, once it gets started. Confiscation of property, higher taxes, fines for suspected women – I've heard them all suggested. The Ku Klux—'

'Do you know any Ku Klux? Is Tommy Wellburn or Hugh or—'

He shrugged impatiently.

'How should I know? I'm a renegade, a turncoat, a Scallawag. Would I be likely to know? But I do know men who are suspected by the Yankees and one false move from them and they are as good as hanged. While I know you would have no regrets at getting your neighbours on the gallows, I do believe you'd regret losing your mills. I see by the stubborn look on your face that you do not believe me and my words are falling on stony ground. So all I can say is, keep that pistol of yours handy – and when I'm in town, I'll try to be on hand to drive you.'

'Rhett, do you really – is it to protect me that you—'

'Yes, my dear, it is my much advertised chivalry that makes me protect you.' The mocking light began to dance in his black eyes and all signs of earnestness fled from his face. 'And why? Because of my deep love for you, Mrs Kennedy. Yes, I have silently hungered and thirsted for you and worshipped you from afar; but being an honourable man, like Mr Ashley Wilkes, I have concealed it from you. You are, alas, Frank's wife and honour has forbidden my telling this to you. But even as Mr Wilkes' honour cracks occasionally, so mine is cracking now and I reveal my secret passion and my—'

'Oh, for God's sake, hush!' interrupted Scarlett, annoyed as usual when he made her look like a conceited fool, and not caring to have Ashley and his honour become the subject of further conversation. 'What was the other thing you wanted to tell me?'

'What! You change the subject when I am baring a loving but lacerated heart? Well, the other thing is this.' The mocking light died out of his eyes again and his face was dark and quiet.

'I want you to do something about this horse. He's stubborn and he's got a mouth as tough as iron. Tires you to drive him, doesn't it? Well, if he chose to bolt, you couldn't possibly stop him. And if you turned over in a ditch, it might kill your baby and you too. You ought to get the heaviest curb bit you can, or else let me swap him for a gentle horse with a more sensitive mouth.'

She looked up into his blank, smooth face and suddenly her irritation fell away, even as her embarrassment had disappeared after the conversation about her pregnancy. He had been kind, a few moments before, to put her at her ease when she was wishing that she were dead. And he was being kinder now and very thoughtful about the horse. She felt a rush of gratitude to him and she wondered why he could not always be this way.

'The horse is hard to drive,' she agreed meekly. 'Sometimes my arms ache all night from tugging at him. You do what you think best about him, Rhett.'

His eyes sparkled wickedly.

'That sounds very sweet and feminine, Mrs Kennedy. Not in your usual masterful vein at all. Well, it only takes proper handling to make a clinging vine out of you.'

She scowled and her temper came back.

'You will get out of this buggy this time, or I will hit you with the whip. I don't know why I put up with you – why I try to be nice to you. You have no manners. You have no morals. You are nothing but a— Well, get out. I mean it.'

But when he had climbed down and untied his horse from the back of the buggy and stood in the twilight road, grinning tantalizingly at her, she could not smother her own grin as she drove off.

Yes, he was coarse, he was tricky, he was unsafe to have dealings with, and you never could tell when the dull weapon you put into his hands in an unguarded moment might turn into the keenest of blades. But, after all, he was as stimulating as – well, as a surreptitious glass of brandy!

During these months Scarlett had learned the use of brandy. When she came home in the late afternoons, damp from the rain, cramped and aching from long hours in the buggy, nothing sustained her except the thought of the bottle hidden in her top bureau drawer, locked against Mammy's prying eyes. Dr Meade had not thought to warn her that a woman in her condition should not drink, for it never occurred to him that a decent woman would drink anything stronger than scuppernong wine. Except, of course, a glass of champagne at a wedding or a hot toddy when confined to bed with a hard cold. Of course, there were unfortunate women who drank, to the eternal disgrace of their families, just as there were women who were insane or divorced or who believed, with Miss Susan B. Anthony, that women should have the vote. But as much as the doctor disapproved of Scarlett, he never suspected her of drinking.

Scarlett had found that a drink of neat brandy before supper helped immeasurably and she could always chew coffee or gargle with cologne to disguise the smell. Why were people so silly about women drinking, when men could and did get reeling drunk whenever they wanted to? Sometimes when Frank lay snoring beside her and sleep would not come, when she lay tossing, torn with fears of poverty, dreading the Yankees, homesick for Tara and yearning for Ashley, she thought she would go crazy were it not for the brandy bottle. And when the pleasant, familiar warmth stole through her veins, her troubles began to fade. After three drinks, she could always say to herself: 'I'll think of these things tomorrow when I can stand them better.'

But there were some nights when even brandy would not still the ache in her heart, the ache that was even stronger than fear of losing the mills, the ache to see Tara again. Atlanta, with its noises, its new buildings, its strange faces, its narrow streets crowded with horses and wagons and bustling crowds sometimes seemed to stifle her. She loved Atlanta but – oh, for the sweet peace and country quiet of Tara, the red fields and the dark pines about it! Oh, to be back at Tara, no matter how hard the life might be! And to be near Ashley, just to see him, to hear him speak, to be sustained by the knowledge of his love! Each letter from Melanie, saying that they were well, each brief note from Will reporting about the ploughing, the planting, the growing of the cotton made her long anew to be home again.

'I'll go home in June. I can't do anything here after that. I'll go home for a couple of months,' she thought and her heart would rise. She did go home in June but not as she longed to go, for early in that month came a brief message from Will that Gerald was dead.

Chapter XXXIX

The train was very late and the long, deeply blue twilight of June was settling over the countryside when Scarlett alighted in Jonesboro. Yellow gleams of lamplight showed in the stores and houses which remained in the village, but they were few. Here and there were wide gaps between the buildings on the main street where dwellings had been shelled or burned. Ruined houses with shell-holes in their roods and half the walls torn away stared at her, silent and dark. A few saddle horses and mule teams were hitched outside the wooden awning of Bullard's store. The dusty red road was empty and lifeless, and the only sounds in the village were a few whoops and drunken laughs that floated on the still twilight air from a saloon far down the street.

The depot had not been rebuilt since it was burned in the battle and in its place was only a wooden shelter, with no sides to keep out the weather. Scarlett walked under it and sat down on one of the empty kegs that were evidently put there for seats. She peered up and down the street for Will Benteen. Will should have been here to meet her. He should have known she would take the first train possible after receiving his laconic message that Gerald was dead.

She had come so hurriedly that she had in her small carpet-bag only a nightgown and a toothbrush, not even a change of underwear. She was uncomfortable in the tight black dress she had borrowed from Mrs Meade, for she had had no time to get mourning clothes for herself. Mrs Meade was thin now, and Scarlett's pregnancy being advanced, the dress was doubly uncomfortable. Even in her sorrow at Gerald's death, she did not forget the appearance she was making and she looked down at her body with distaste. Her figure was completely gone and her face and ankles were puffy. Heretofore she had not cared very much how she looked but now that she would see Ashley within the hour she cared greatly. Even in her heartbreak, she shrank from the thought of facing him when she was carrying another man's child. She loved him and he loved her, and this unwanted child now seemed to her a proof of infidelity to that love. But much as she disliked having him see her with the slenderness gone from her waist and the lightness from her step, it was something she could not escape now.

She patted her foot impatiently. Will should have met her. Of course, she could go over to Bullard's and inquire after him or ask someone there to drive her over to Tara, should she find he had been unable to come. But she did not want to go to Bullard's. It was Saturday night and probably half the men in the County would be there. She did not want to display her condition in this poorly fitting black dress which accentuated rather than hid her figure. And she did not want to hear the kindly sympathy that would be poured out about Gerald. She did not want sympathy. She was afraid she would cry if anyone even mentioned his name to her. And she wouldn't cry. She knew if she once began it would be like the time she cried into the horse's mane, that dreadful night when Atlanta fell and Rhett had left her on the dark road outside the town, terrible tears that tore her heart and could not be stopped.

No, she wouldn't cry! She felt the lump in her throat rising again, as it had done so often since the news came, but crying wouldn't do any good. It would only confuse and weaken her. Why, oh, why hadn't Will or Melanie or the girls written her that Gerald was ailing? She would have taken the first train to Tara to care for him, brought a doctor from Atlanta if necessary. The fools – all of them! Couldn't they manage anything without her? She couldn't be in two places at once and the good Lord knew she was doing her best for them all in Atlanta.

She twisted about on the keg, becoming nervous and fidgety as Will still did not come. Where was he? Then she heard the scrunching of cinders on the railroad tracks behind her and, twisting her body, she saw Alex Fontaine crossing the tracks toward a wagon, a sack of oats on his shoulder.

'Good Lord! Isn't that you, Scarlett?' he cried, dropping the sack and running to take her hand, pleasure written all over his bitter, swarthy little face. 'I'm so glad to see you. I saw Will over at the blacksmith's shop, getting the horse shod. The train was late and he thought he'd have time. Shall I run fetch him?'

'Yes, please, Alex,' she said, smiling in spite of her sorrow. It was good to see a County face again.

'Oh – er – Scarlett,' he began awkwardly, still holding her hand, 'I'm mighty sorry about your father.'

'Thank you,' she replied, wishing he had not said it. His words brought up Gerald's florid face and bellowing voice so clearly.

'If it's any comfort to you, Scarlett, we're mighty proud of him around here,' Alex continued, dropping her hand. 'He – well, we figure he died like a soldier and in a soldier's cause.'

Now what did he mean by that, she thought confusedly. A soldier? Had someone shot him? Had he gotten into a fight with the Scallawags as Tony had? But she mustn't hear more. She would cry if she talked about him and she mustn't cry, not until she was safely in the wagon with Will and out in the country where no stranger could see her. Will wouldn't matter. He was just like a brother.

'Alex, I don't want to talk about it,' she said shortly.

'I don't blame you one bit, Scarlett,' said Alex, while the dark blood of anger flooded his face. 'If it was my sister, I'd – well, Scarlett, I've never yet said a harsh word about any woman, but personally I think somebody ought to take a rawhide whip to Suellen.'

What foolishness was he talking about now, she wondered. What had Suellen to do with it all?

'Everybody around here feels the same way about her, I'm sorry to say. Will's the only one who takes up for her – and, of course, Miss Melanie, but she's a saint and won't see bad in anyone and—'

'I said I didn't want to talk about it,' she said coldly, but Alex did not seem rebuffed. He looked as though he understood her rudeness and that was annoying. She didn't want to hear bad tidings about her own family from an outsider, didn't want him to know of her ignorance of what had happened. Why hadn't Will sent her the full details?

She wished Alex wouldn't look at her so hard. She felt that he realized her condition and it embarrassed her. But what Alex was thinking as he peered at her in the twilight was that her face had changed so completely he wondered how he had ever recognized her. Perhaps it was because she was going to have a baby. Women did look like the devil at such times. And, of course, she must be feeling badly about old man O'Hara. She had been his pet. But, no, the change was deeper than that. She really looked better than when he had seen her last. At least, she now looked as if she had three square meals a day. And the hunted-animal look had partly gone from her eyes. Now, the eyes which had been fearful and desperate were hard. There was an air of command, assurance and determination about her, even when she smiled. Bet she led old Frank a merry life! Yes, she had changed. She was a handsome woman, to be sure, but all that pretty, sweet softness had gone from her face and that flattering way of looking up at a man, like he knew more than God Almighty, had utterly vanished.

Well, hadn't they all changed? Alex looked down at his rough clothes and his face fell into its usual bitter lines. Sometimes at night when he lay awake, wondering how his mother was going to get that operation and how poor dead Joe's little boy was going to get an education and how he was going to get money for another mule, he wished the war was still going on, wished it had gone on forever. They didn't know their luck then. There was always something to eat in the army, even if it was just corn bread, always somebody to give orders and none of this torturing sense of facing problems that couldn't be solved – nothing to bother about in the army except getting killed. And then there was Dimity Munroe. Alex wanted to marry her and he knew he couldn't when so many were already looking to him for support. He had loved her for so long and now the roses were fading from her cheeks and the joy from her eyes. If only Tony hadn't had to run away to Texas. Another man on the place would make all the difference in the world. His lovable bad-tempered little brother, penniless somewhere in the West. Yes, they had all changed. And why not? He sighed heavily.

'I haven't thanked you for what you and Frank did for Tony,' he said. 'It was you who helped him get away, wasn't it? It was fine of you. I heard in a roundabout way that he was safe in Texas. I was afraid to write and ask you – but did you or Frank lend him any money? I want to repay—'

'Oh, Alex, please hush! Not now!' cried Scarlett. For once, money meant nothing to her.

Alex was silent for a moment.

'I'll get Will for you,' he said, 'and we'll all be over tomorrow for the funeral.'

As he picked up the sack of oats and turned away, a wobbly-wheeled wagon swayed out of a side street and creaked up to them. Will called from the seat: 'I'm sorry I'm late, Scarlett.'

Climbing awkwardly down from the wagon, he stumped toward her and, bending, kissed her cheek. Will had never kissed her before, had never failed to precede her name with 'Miss' and, while it surprised her, it warmed her heart and pleased her very much. He lifted her carefully over the wheel and into the wagon and, looking down, she saw that it was the same old rickety wagon in which she had fled from Atlanta. How had it ever held together so long? Will must have kept it patched up very well. It made her slightly sick to look at it and to remember that night. If it took the shoes off her feet or food from Aunt Pitty's table, she'd see that there was a new wagon at Tara and this one burned.

Will did not speak at first and Scarlett was grateful. He threw his battered straw hat into the back of the wagon, clucked to the horse and they moved off. Will was just the same, lank and gangling, pink of hair, mild of eye, patient as a draught animal.

They left the village behind and turned into the red road to Tara. A faint pink still lingered about the edges of the sky and fat feathery clouds were tinged with gold and palest green. The stillness of the country twilight came down about them as calming as a prayer. How had she ever borne it, she thought, away for all these months, away from the fresh smell of country air, the ploughed earth and the sweetness of summer nights? The moist red earth smelled so good, so familiar, so friendly, she wanted to get out and scoop up a handful. The honeysuckle which draped the gullied red sides of the road in tangled greenery was piercingly fragrant as always after rain, the sweetest perfume in the world. Above their heads a flock of chimney swallows whirled suddenly on swift wings and now and then a rabbit scurried startled across the road, his white tail bobbing like an eiderdown powder-puff. She saw with pleasure that the cotton stood well, as they passed between ploughed fields where the green bushes reared themselves sturdily out of the red earth. How beautiful all this was! The soft grey mist in the swampy bottoms, the red earth and growing cotton, the sloping fields with curving green rows and the black pines rising behind everything like sable walls. How had she ever stayed in Atlanta so long?

'Scarlett, before I tell you about Mr O'Hara – and I want to tell you everything before you get home – I want to ask your opinion on a matter. I figger you're the head of the house now.'

'What is it, Will?'

He turned his mild sober gaze on her for a moment.

'I just wanted your approval to my marryin' Suellen.'

Scarlett clutched the seat, so surprised that she almost fell backwards. Marry Suellen! She'd never thought of anybody marrying Suellen since she had taken Frank Kennedy from her. Who would have Suellen?

'Goodness, Will!'

'Then I take it you don't mind?'

'Mind? No, but— Why, Will, you've taken my breath away! You marry Suellen? Will, I always thought you were sweet on Carreen.'

Will kept his eyes on the horse and flapped the reins. His profile did not change but she thought he sighed slightly.

'Maybe I was,' he said.

'Well, won't she have you?'

'I never asked her.'

'Oh, Will, you're a fool. Ask her. She's worth two of Suellen!'

'Scarlett, you don't know a lot of things that's been going on at Tara. You ain't favoured us with much of your attention these last months.'

'I haven't, haven't I?' she flared. 'What do you suppose I've been doing in Atlanta? Riding around in a coach and four and going to balls? Haven't

I sent you money every month? Haven't I paid the taxes and fixed the roof and bought the new plough and the mules? Haven't—'

'Now, don't fly off the handle and get your Irish up,' he interrupted imperturbably. 'If anybody knows what you've done, I do, and it's been two men's work.'

Slightly mollified, she questioned, 'Well, then, what do you mean?'

'Well, you've kept the roof over us and food in the pantry and I ain't denyin' that, but you ain't given much thought to what's been goin' on in anybody's head here at Tara. I ain't blamin' you, Scarlett. That's just your way. You warn't never very much interested in what was in folks' heads. But what I'm tryin' to tell you is that I didn't never ask Miss Carreen because I knew it wouldn't be no use. She's been like a little sister to me and I guess she talks to me plainer than to anybody in the world. But she never got over that dead boy and she never will. And I might as well tell you now she's aimin' to go in a convent over to Charleston.'

'Are you joking?'

'Well, I knew it would take you back and I just want to ask you, Scarlett, don't you argue with her about it or scold her or laugh at her. Let her go. It's all she wants now. Her heart's broken.'

'But, God's nightgown! Lots of people's hearts have been broken and they didn't run off to convents. Look at me. I lost a husband.'

'But your heart warn't broken,' Will said calmly and, picking up a straw from the bottom of the wagon, he put it in his mouth and chewed slowly. That remark took the wind out of her. As always when she heard the truth spoken, no matter how unpalatable it was, basic honesty forced her to acknowledge it as truth. She was silent a moment, trying to accustom herself to the idea of Carreen as a nun.

'Promise you won't fuss at her.'

'Oh, well, I promise,' and then she looked at him with a new understanding and some amazement. Will had loved Carreen, loved her now enough to take her part and make her retreat easy. And yet he wanted to marry Suellen.

'Well, what's all this about Suellen? You don't care for her, do you?'

'Oh, yes, I do in a way,' he said, removing the straw and surveying it as if it were highly interesting. 'Suellen ain't as bad as you think, Scarlett. I think we'll get along right well. The only trouble with Suellen is that she needs a husband and some children and that's just what every woman needs.'

The wagon jolted over the rutty road and for a few minutes while the two sat silent Scarlett's mind was busy. There must be something more to it than appeared on the surface, something deeper, more important, to make the mild and soft-spoken Will want to marry a complaining nagger like Suellen.

'You haven't told me the real reason, Will. If I'm head of the family, I've got a right to know.'

'That's right,' said Will, 'and I guess you'll understand. I can't leave Tara. It's home to me, Scarlett, the only real home I ever knew and I love every stone of it. I've worked on it like it was mine. And when you put out work on somethin', you come to love it. You know what I mean?'

She knew what he meant and her heart went out in a surge of warm affection for him, hearing him say he, too, loved the thing she loved best.

'And I figger it this way. With your pa gone and Carreen a nun, there'll be just me and Suellen left here and, of course, I couldn't live on at Tara without marryin' Suellen. You know how folks talk.'

'But – but Will, there's Melanie and Ashley—'

At Ashley's name he turned and looked at her, his pale eyes unfathomable. She had the old feeling that Will knew all about her and Ashley, understood all and did not either censure or approve.

'They'll be goin' soon.'

'Going? Where? Tara is their home as well as yours.'

'No, it ain't their home. That's just what's eatin' on Ashley. It ain't his home and he don't feel like he's earnin' his keep. He's a mighty pore farmer and he knows it. God knows he tries his best but he warn't cut out for farmin' and you know it as well as I do. If he splits kindlin', like as not he'll slice off his foot. He can't no more keep a plough straight in a furrow than little Beau can, and what he don't know about makin' things grow would fill a book. It ain't his fault. He just warn't bred for it. And it worries him that he's a man and livin' at Tara on a woman's charity and not givin' much in return.'

'Charity? Has he ever said—'

'No, he's never said a word. You know Ashley. But I can tell. Last night when we were sittin' up with your pa, I told him I had asked Suellen and she'd said yes. And then Ashley said that relieved him because he'd been feelin' like a dog, stayin' on at Tara, and he knew he and Miss Melly would have to keep stayin' on, now that Mr O'Hara was dead, just to keep folks from talkin' about me and Suellen. So then he told me he was aimin' to leave Tara and get work.'

'Work? What kind? Where?'

'I don't know exactly what he'll do but he said he was goin' up North. He's got a Yankee friend in New York who wrote him about workin' in a bank up there.'

'Oh, no!' cried Scarlett from the bottom of her heart and, at the cry, Will gave her the same look as before.

'Maybe 'twould be better all 'round if he did go North.'

'No! No! I don't think so.'

Her mind was working feverishly. Ashley couldn't go North! She might never see him again. Even though she had not seen him in months, had not spoken to him alone since that fateful scene in the orchard, there had not been a day when she had not thought of him, been glad he was sheltered under her roof. She had never sent a dollar to Will that she had not been pleased that it would make Ashley's life easier. Of course, he wasn't any good as a farmer. Ashley was bred for better things, she thought proudly. He was born to rule, to live in a large house, ride fine horses, read books of poetry and tell negroes what to do. That there were no more mansions and horses and negroes and few books did not alter matters. Ashley wasn't bred to plough and split rails. No wonder he wanted to leave Tara.

But she could not let him go away from Georgia. If necessary, she would bully Frank into giving him a job in the store, make Frank turn off the boy he now had behind the counter. But, no – Ashley's place was no more behind a counter than it was behind a plough. A Wilkes a shopkeeper! Oh, never that! There must be something – why, her mill of course! Her relief at the thought was so great that she smiled. But would he accept an offer from her? Would he still think it was charity? She must manage it so he would think he was doing her a favour. She would discharge Mr Johnson and put Ashley in charge of the old mill while Hugh operated the new one. She would explain to Ashley how Frank's ill-health and the pressure of work at the store kept him from helping her, and she would plead her condition as another reason why she needed his help.

She would make him realize somehow that she couldn't do without his aid at this time. And she would give him a half-interest in the mill, if he would only take it over – anything just to have him near her, anything to see that bright smile light up his face, anything for the chance of catching an unguarded look in his eyes that showed he still cared. But, she promised herself, never, never would she again try to prod him into words of love, never again would she try to make him throw away that foolish honour he valued more than love. Somehow, she must delicately convey to him this new resolution of hers. Otherwise he might refuse, fearing another scene such as that last terrible one had been.

'I can get him something to do in Atlanta,' she said.

'Well, that's yours and Ashley's business,' said Will, and put the straw back in his mouth. 'Giddap, Sherman. Now, Scarlett, there's somethin' else I've got to ask you before I tell you about your pa. I won't have you lightin' into Suellen. What she's done, she's done, and you snatchin' her baldheaded won't bring Mr O'Hara back. Besides, she honestly thought she was actin' for the best.'

'I wanted to ask you about that. What is all this about Suellen? Alex talked riddles and said she ought to be whipped. What has she done?'

'Yes, folks are pretty riled up about her. Everybody I run into this afternoon in Jonesboro was promisin' to cut her dead the next time they seen her, but maybe they'll get over it. Now, promise me you won't light into her. I won't be havin' no quarrellin' tonight with Mr O'Hara layin' dead in the parlour.'

'*He* won't be having any quarrelling!' thought Scarlett indignantly. 'He talks like Tara was his already!'

And then she thought of Gerald, dead in the parlour, and suddenly she began to cry, cry in bitter, gulping sobs. Will put his arm around her, drew her comfortably close and said nothing.

As they jolted slowly down the darkening road, her head on his shoulder, her bonnet askew, she had forgotten the Gerald of the last two years, the vague old gentleman who stared at doors waiting for a woman who would never enter. She was remembering the vital, virile old man with his mane of crisp white hair, his bellowing cheerfulness, his stamping boots, his clumsy jokes, his generosity. She remembered how, as a child, he had seemed the most wonderful man in the world, this blustering father who carried her before him on his saddle when he jumped fences, turned her up and paddled her when she was naughty, and then cried when she cried and gave her quarters to get her to hush. She remembered him coming home from Charleston and Atlanta laden with gifts that were never appropriate, remembered too, with a faint smile through tears, how he came home in the wee hours from Court Day at Jonesboro, drunk as seven earls, jumping fences, his rollicking voice raised in 'The Wearin' o' the Green'. And how abashed he was, facing Ellen on the mornings after. Well, he was with Ellen now.

'Why didn't you write me that he was ill? I'd have come so fast—'

'He warn't ill, not a minute. Here, honey, take my handkerchief and I'll tell you all about it.'

She blew her nose on his bandana, for she had come from Atlanta without even a handkerchief, and settled back into the crook of Will's arm. How nice Will was! Nothing ever upset him.

'Well, it was this way, Scarlett. You been sendin' us money right along and Ashley and me, well, we've paid taxes and bought the mule and seeds and what-all and a few hogs and chickens. Miss Melly's done mighty well with the hens, yes, sir, she has. She's a fine woman, Miss Melly is. Well, anyway, after we bought things for Tara, there warn't so much left over for folderols, but none of us warn't complainin'. Except Suellen.

'Miss Melanie and Miss Carreen stay at home and wear their old clothes like they're proud of them, but you know Suellen, Scarlett. She hasn't never got used to doin' without. It used to stick in her craw that she had to wear old dresses every time I took her into Jonesboro or over to Fayetteville. 'Specially as some of those Carpetbaggers' ladi— women was always flouncin' around in fancy trimmin's. The wives of those damn Yankees that run the Freedmen's Bureau, do they dress up! Well, it's kind of been a point of honour with the ladies of the County to wear their worst-lookin' dresses to town, just to show how they didn't care and was proud to wear them. But not Suellen. And she wanted a horse and carriage too. She pointed out that you had one.'

'It's not a carriage, it's an old buggy,' said Scarlett indignantly.

'Well, no matter what. I might as well tell you Suellen never has got over your marryin' Frank Kennedy and I don't know as I blame her. You know that was a kind of scurvy trick to play on a sister.'

Scarlett rose from his shoulder, furious as a rattler ready to strike.

'Scurvy trick, hey? I'll thank you to keep a civil tongue in your head, Will Benteen! Could I help it if he preferred me to her?'

'You're a smart girl, Scarlett, and I figger, yes, you could have helped him preferrin' you. Girls always can. But I guess you kind of coaxed him. You're a mighty takin' person when you want to be, but all the same, he was Suellen's beau. Why, she'd had a letter from him a week before you went to Atlanta and he was sweet as sugar about her and talked about how they'd get married when he got a little more money ahead. I know because she showed me the letter.'

Scarlett was silent because she knew he was telling the truth and she could think of nothing to say. She had never expected Will, of all people, to sit in judgment on her. Moreover, the lie she had told Frank had never weighed heavily upon her conscience. If a girl couldn't keep a beau, she deserved to lose him.

'Now, Will, don't be mean,' she said. 'If Suellen had married him, do you think she'd ever have spent a penny on Tara or any of us?'

'I said you could be right takin' when you wanted to,' said Will, turning to her with a quiet grin. 'No, I don't think we'd ever seen a penny of old Frank's money. But still there's no gettin' 'round it, it was a scurvy trick and if you want to justify the means by the end, it's none of my business and who am I to complain? But just the same Suellen has been like a hornet ever since. I don't think she cared much about old Frank but it kind of teched her vanity, and she's been sayin' as how you had good clothes and a carriage and lived in Atlanta while she was buried here at Tara. She does love to go callin' and to parties, you know, and wear pretty clothes. I ain't blamin' her. Women are like that.

'Well, about a month ago I took her into Jonesboro and left her to go callin' while I tended to business and when I took her home, she was still as a mouse but I could see she was so excited she was ready to bust. I thought she'd found out somebody was goin' to have a – that she'd heard some gossip that was interestin', and I didn't pay her much mind. She went around home for about a week all swelled up and excited and didn't have much to say. She went over to see Miss Cathleen Calvert – Scarlett, you'd cry your eyes out at Miss Cathleen. Pore girl, she'd better be dead than married to that pusillanimous Yankee, Hilton. You knew he'd mortgaged the place and lost it and they're goin' to have to leave?'

'No, I didn't know and I don't want to know. I want to know about Pa.'

'Well, I'm gettin' to that,' said Will patiently. 'When she come back from over there she said we'd all misjudged Hilton. She called him Mr Hilton and she said he was a smart man, but we just laughed at her. Then she took to takin' your pa out to walk in the afternoons and lots of times when I was comin' home from the field, I'd see her sittin' with him on the wall 'round the buryin'-ground, talkin' at him hard and wavin' her hands. And the old gentleman would just look at her sort of puzzled-like and shake his head. You know how he's been, Scarlett. He just got kind of vaguer and vaguer, like he didn't hardly know where he was or who we were. One time, I seen her point to your ma's grave and the old gentleman begun to cry. And when she come in the house all happy and excited-lookin', I gave her a talkin' to, right sharp, too, and I said: "Miss Suellen, why in hell are you devillin' your poor pa and bringin' up your ma to him? Most of the time he don't realize she's dead and here you are rubbin' it in." And she just kind of tossed her head and laughed and said: "Mind your business. Some day you'll all be glad of what I'm doin'." Miss Melanie told me last night that Suellen had told her about her schemes but Miss Melly said she didn't have no notion Suellen was serious. She said she didn't tell none of us because she was so upset at the very idea.'

'What idea? Are you ever going to get to the point? We're half-way home now. I want to know about Pa.'

'I'm tryin' to tell you,' said Will, 'and we're so near home, I guess I'd better stop right here till I've finished.'

He drew rein and the horse stopped and snorted. They had halted by the wild overgrown mock-orange hedge that marked the MacIntosh property. Glancing under the dark trees Scarlett could just discern the tall ghostly chimneys still rearing above the silent ruin. She wished that Will had chosen any other place to stop.

'Well, the long and the short of her idea was to make the Yankees pay for the cotton they burned and the stock they drove off and the fences and the barns they tore down.'

'The Yankees?'

'Haven't you heard about it? The Yankee government's been payin' claims on all destroyed property of Union sympathizers in the South.'

'Of course I've heard about that,' said Scarlett. 'But what's that got to do with us?'

'A heap, in Suellen's opinion. That day I took her to Jonesboro, she run into Mrs MacIntosh and when they were gossipin' along, Suellen couldn't help noticin' what fine-lookin' clothes Mrs MacIntosh had on and she couldn't help askin' about them. Then Mrs MacIntosh gave herself a lot of airs and said as how her husband had put in a claim with the Federal government for destroyin' the property of a loyal Union sympathizer who had never given aid and comfort to the Confederacy in any shape or form.'

'They never gave aid and comfort to anybody,' snapped Scarlett. 'Scotch-Irish!'

'Well, maybe that's true. I don't know them. Anyway, the government gave them, well – I forget how many thousand dollars. A right smart sum it was, though. That started Suellen. She thought about it all week and didn't say nothin' to us because she knew we'd just laugh. But she just had to talk to somebody, so she went over to Miss Cathleen's and that damned white trash, Hilton, gave her a passel of new ideas. He pointed out that your pa warn't even born in this country, that he hadn't fought in the war and hadn't had no sons to fight, and hadn't never held no office under the Confederacy. He said they could strain a point about Mr O'Hara's bein' a loyal Union sympathizer. He filled her up with such truck and she come home and begun workin' on Mr O'Hara. Scarlett, I bet my life your pa didn't even know half the time what she was talkin' about. That was what she was countin' on, that he would take the Iron-Clad oath and not even know it.'

'Pa take the Iron-Clad oath!' cried Scarlett.

'Well, he'd gotten right feeble in his mind these last months and I guess she was countin' on that. Mind you, none of us suspicioned nothin' about it. We knew she was cookin' up somethin', but we didn't know she was usin' your dead ma to reproach him for his daughters bein' in rags when he could get a hundred and fifty thousand dollars out of the Yankees.'

'One hundred and fifty thousand dollars,' murmured Scarlett, her horror at the oath fading.

What a lot of money that was! And to be had for the mere signing of an oath of allegiance to the United States government, an oath stating that the signer had always supported the government and never given aid and comfort to its enemies. One hundred and fifty thousand dollars! That much money for that small lie! Well, she couldn't blame Suellen. Good Heavens! Was that what Alex meant by wanting to rawhide her? What the County meant by intending to cut her? Fools, every one of them. What couldn't she do with that much money! What couldn't any of the folks in the County do with it! And what did so small a lie matter? After all, anything you could get out of the Yankees was fair money, no matter how you got it.

'Yesterday, about noon when Ashley and me were splittin' rails, Suellen got this wagon and got your pa in it and off they went to town without a word to anybody. Miss Melly had a notion what it was all about but she was prayin' somethin' would change Suellen, so she didn't say nothin' to the rest of us. She just didn't see how Suellen could do such a thing.

'Today I heard all about what happened. That pusillanimous fellow, Hilton, had some influence with the other Scallawags and Republicans in town and Suellen had agreed to give them some of the money – I don't know how much – if they'd kind of wink their eye about Mr O'Hara bein' a loyal Union man and play on how he was an Irishman and didn't fight in the army and so on, and sign recommendations. All your pa had to do was take the oath and sign the paper and off it would go to Washington.

'They rattled off the oath real fast and he didn't say nothin' and it went right well till she got him up to the signin' of it. And then the old gentleman kind of come to himself for a minute and shook his head. I don't think he knew what it was all about but he didn't like it and Suellen always did rub him the wrong way. Well, that just about gave her the nervous fits after all the trouble she'd gone to. She took him out of the office and rode him up and down the road and talked to him about your ma cryin' out of her grave at him for lettin' her children suffer when he could provide for them. They tell me your pa sat there in the wagon and cried like a baby, like he always does when he hears her name. Everybody in town saw them and Alex Fontaine went over to see what was the matter, but Suellen gave him the rough side of her tongue and told him to mind his own business, so he went off mad.

'I don't know where she got the notion but some time in the afternoon she got a bottle of brandy and took Mr O'Hara back to the office and begun pourin' it for him. Scarlett, we haven't had no spirits 'round Tara for a year, just a little blackberry wine and scuppernong wine Dilcey makes, and Mr O'Hara warn't used to it. He got real drunk, and after Suellen had argued and nagged a couple of hours he gave in and said yes, he'd sign anything she wanted. They got the oath out again and just as he was about to put pen to paper, Suellen made her mistake. She said: "Well, now, I guess the Slatterys and the MacIntoshes won't be givin' themselves airs over us!" You see, Scarlett, the Slatterys had put in a claim for a big amount for that little shack of theirs that the Yankees burned and Emmie's husband had got it through Washington for them.

'They tell me that when Suellen said those names, your pa kind of straightened up and squared his shoulders and looked at her, sharp-like. He warn't vague no more and he said: "Have the Slatterys and the MacIntoshes signed somethin' like this?" and Suellen got nervous and said yes and no and stuttered, and he shouted right loud: "Tell me, did that God-damned Orangeman and that God-damned poor white sign somethin' like this?" And that feller Hilton spoke up smooth-like and said: "Yes, sir, they did, and they got a pile of money like you'll get."

'And then the old gentleman let out a roar like a bull. Alex Fontaine said he heard him from down the street at the saloon. And he said with a brogue you could cut with a butter-knife: "And were ye after thinkin' an O'Hara of Tara would be follyin' in the dirthy thracks of a God-damned Orangeman and a God-damned poor white?" And he tore the paper in two and threw it in Suellen's face and he bellowed: "Ye're no daughther of mine!" and he was out of the office before you could say Jack Robinson.

'Alex said he saw him come out on the street, chargin' like a bull. He said the old gentleman looked like his old self for the first time since your ma died. Said he was reelin' drunk and cussin' at the top of his lungs. Alex said he never heard such fine cussin'. Alex's horse was standin' there and your pa climbed on it without a by-your-leave and off he went in a cloud of dust so thick it choked you, cussin' every breath he drew.

'Well, about sundown Ashley and me were sittin' on the front step, lookin' down the road and mighty worried. Miss Melly was upstairs cryin' on her bed and wouldn't tell us nothin'. Terrectly, we heard a poundin' down the road and somebody yellin' like they was fox-huntin' and Ashley said:

"That's queer! That sounds like Mr O'Hara when he used to ride over to see us before the war."

'And then we seen him way down at the end of the pasture. He must have jumped the fence right over there. And he come ridin' hell-for-leather up the hill, singin' at the top of his voice like he didn't have a care in the world. I didn't know your pa had such a voice. He was singin' "Peg in a Low-backed Car" and beatin' the horse with his hat and the horse was goin' like mad. He didn't draw rein when he come near the top and we seen he was goin' to jump the pasture fence and we hopped up, scared to death, and then he yelled: "Look, Ellen! Watch me take this one!" But the horse stopped right on his haunches at the fence and wouldn't take the jump and your pa went right over his head. He didn't suffer none. He was dead time we got to him. I guess it broke his neck.'

Will waited a minute for her to speak and when she did not he picked up the reins. 'Giddap, Sherman,' he said, and the horse started on toward home.

Chapter XL

Scarlett slept little that night. When the dawn had come and the sun was creeping over the black pines on the hills to the east, she rose from her tumbled bed and, seating herself on a stool by the window, laid her tired head on her arm and looked out over the barnyard and orchard of Tara toward the cotton fields. Everything was fresh and dewy and silent and green, and the sight of the cotton fields brought a measure of balm and comfort to her sore heart. Tara, at sunrise, looked loved, well tended and at peace, for all that its master lay dead. The squatty log chicken-house was clay-daubed against rats and weasels and clean with whitewash, and so was the log stable. The garden with its rows of corn, bright-yellow squash, butter beans and turnips was well weeded and neatly fenced with split-oak rails. The orchard was cleared of underbrush and only daisies grew beneath the long rows of trees. The sun picked out with faint glistening the apples and the furred pink peaches half hidden in the green leaves. Beyond lay the curving rows of cotton, still and green under the gold of the new sky. The ducks and chickens were waddling and strutting off toward the fields, for under the bushes in the soft ploughed earth were found the choicest worms and slugs.

Scarlett's heart swelled with affection and gratitude to Will who had done all of this. Even her loyalty to Ashley could not make her believe he had been responsible for much of this well-being, for Tara's bloom was not the work of a planter-aristocrat, but of the plodding, tireless 'small farmer' who loved his land. It was a 'two-horse' farm, not the lordly plantation of other days with pastures full of mules and fine horses and cotton and corn stretching as far as eye could see. But what there was of it was good and the acres that were lying fallow could be reclaimed when times grew better, and they would be the more fertile for their rest.

Will had done more than merely farm a few acres. He had kept sternly at bay those two enemies of Georgia planters, the seedling pine and the blackberry brambles. They had not stealthily taken garden and pasture and cotton field and lawn and reared themselves insolently by the porches of Tara, as they were doing on numberless plantations throughout the state.

Scarlett's heart failed a beat when she thought how close Tara had come to going back to wilderness. Between herself and Will, they had done a good job. They had held off the Yankees, the Carpetbaggers and the encroachments of Nature. And, best of all, Will had told her that after the cotton came in in the fall, she need send no more money – unless some other Carpetbagger coveted Tara and skyrocketed the taxes. Scarlett knew Will would have a hard pull without her help but she admired and respected his independence. As long as he was in the position of hired help he would take her money, but now that he was to become her brother-in-law and the man of the house, he intended to stand on his own efforts. Yes, Will was something the Lord had provided.

Pork had dug the grave the night before, close by Ellen's grave, and he stood, spade in hand, behind the moist red clay he was soon to shovel back in place. Scarlett stood behind him in the patchy shade of a gnarled low-limbed cedar, the hot sun of the June morning dappling her, and tried to keep her eyes away from the red trench in front of her. Jim Tarleton, little Hugh Munroe, Alex Fontaine and old man McRae's youngest grandson came slowly and awkwardly down the path from the house bearing Gerald's coffin on two lengths of split oak. Behind them, at a respectful distance, followed a large straggling crowd of neighbours and friends, shabbily dressed, silent. As they came down the sunny path through the garden, Pork bowed his head upon the top of the spade handle and cried; and Scarlett saw with incurious surprise that the kinks on his head, so jettily black when she went to Atlanta a few months before, were now grizzled.

She thanked God tiredly that she had cried all her tears the night before, so now she could stand erect and dry-eyed. The sound of Suellen's tears, just back of her shoulder, irritated her unbearably and she had to clench her fists to keep from turning and slapping the swollen face. Sue had been the cause of her father's death, whether she intended it or not, and she should have the decency to control herself in front of the hostile neighbours. Not a single person had spoken to her that morning or given her one look of sympathy. They had kissed Scarlett quietly, shaken her hand, murmured kind words to Carreen and even to Pork, but had looked through Suellen as if she were not there.

To them she had done worse than murder her father. She had tried to betray him into disloyalty to the South. And to that grim and close-knit community it was as if she had tried to betray the honour of them all. She had broken the solid front the County presented to the world. By her attempt to get money from the Yankee government she had aligned herself with Carpetbaggers and Scallawags, more hated enemies than the Yankee soldiers had ever been. She, a member of an old and staunchly Confederate family, a planter's family, had gone over to the enemy and by so doing had brought shame on every family in the County.

The mourners were seething with indignation and downcast with sorrow, especially three of them – old man McRae, who had been Gerald's crony since he came to the up-country from Savannah so many years before, Grandma Fontaine, who loved him because he was Ellen's husband, and Mrs Tarleton, who had been closer to him than to any of her neighbours because, as she often said, he was the only man in the County who knew a stallion from a gelding.

The sight of the stormy faces of these three in the dim parlour where Gerald lay before the funeral had caused Ashley and Will some uneasiness and they had retired to Ellen's office for a consultation.

'Some of them are goin' to say somethin' about Suellen,' said Will abruptly, biting his straw in half. 'They think they got just cause to say somethin'. Maybe they have. It ain't for me to say. But, Ashley, whether they're right or not, we'll have to resent it, bein' the men of the family, and then there'll be trouble. Can't nobody do nothin' with old man McRae because he's deaf as a post and can't hear folks tryin' to shut him up. And you know there ain't nobody in God's world ever stopped Grandma Fontaine from speakin' her mind. And as for Mrs Tarleton – did you see her roll them russet eyes of hers every time she looked at Sue? She's got her ears laid back and can't hardly wait. If they say somethin', we got to take it up and we got enough trouble at Tara now without bein' at outs with our neighbours.'

Ashley sighed worriedly. He knew the tempers of his neighbours better than Will did and he remembered that fully half of the quarrels and some of the shootings of the days before the war had risen from the County custom of saying a few words over the coffins of departed neighbours. Generally the words were eulogistic in the extreme but occasionally they were not. Sometimes, words meant in the utmost respect were misconstrued by overstrung relatives of the dead and scarcely were the last shovels of earth mounded above the coffin before trouble began.

In the absence of a priest Ashley was to conduct the services with the aid of Carreen's Book of Devotions, the assistance of the Methodist and Baptist preachers of Jonesboro and Fayetteville having been tactfully refused. Carreen, more devoutly Catholic than her sisters, had been very upset that Scarlett had neglected to bring a priest from Atlanta with her and had only been a little eased by the reminder that when the priest came down to marry Will and Suellen, he could read the services over Gerald. It was she who objected to the neighbouring Protestant preachers and gave the matter into Ashley's hands, marking passages in her book for him to read. Ashley, leaning against the old secretary, knew that the responsibility for preventing trouble lay with him and, knowing the hair-trigger tempers of the County, was at a loss as to how to proceed.

'There's no help for it, Will,' he said, rumpling his bright hair. 'I can't knock Grandma Fontaine down or old man McRae either, and I can't hold my hand over Mrs Tarleton's mouth. And the mildest thing they'll say is that Suellen is a murderess and a traitor and but for her Mr O'Hara would still be alive. Damn this custom of speaking over the dead. It's barbarous.'

'Look, Ash,' said Will slowly. 'I ain't aimin' to have nobody say nothin' against Suellen, no matter what they think. You leave it to me. When you've finished with the readin' and the prayin' and you say, "If anyone would like to say a few words," you look right at me, so I can speak first.'

But Scarlett, watching the pall-bearers' difficulty in getting the coffin through the narrow entrance into the burying-ground, had no thought of trouble to come after the funeral. She was thinking with a leaden heart that in burying Gerald she was burying one of the last links that joined her to the old days of happiness and irresponsibility.

Finally the pall-bearers set the coffin down near the grave and stood clenching and unclenching their aching fingers. Ashley, Melanie and Will filed into the enclosure and stood behind the O'Hara girls. All the closer neighbours who could crowd in were behind them and the others stood outside the brick wall. Scarlett, really seeing them for the first time, was surprised and touched by the size of the crowd. With transportation so limited it was kind of so many to come. There were fifty or sixty people there, some of them from so far away she wondered how they had heard in time to come. There were whole families from Jonesboro and Fayetteville and Lovejoy and with them a few negro servants. Many small farmers from far across the river were present and Crackers from the backwoods and a scattering of swamp folk. The swamp men were lean bearded giants in homespun, coon-skin caps on their heads, their rifles easy in the crooks of their arms, their wads of tobacco stilled in their cheeks. Their women were with them, their bare feet sunk in the soft red earth, their lower lips full of snuff. Their faces beneath their sunbonnets were sallow and malarial-looking but shining clean and their freshly ironed calicoes glistened with starch.

The near neighbours were there in full force. Grandma Fontaine, withered, wrinkled and yellow as an old moulted bird, was leaning on her cane, and behind her were Sally Munroe Fontaine and Young Miss Fontaine. They were trying vainly by whispered pleas and jerks at her skirt to make the old lady sit down on the brick wall. Grandma's husband, the Old Doctor, was not there. He had died two months before and much of the bright malicious joy of life had gone from her old eyes. Cathleen Calvert Hilton stood alone as befitted one whose husband had helped bring about the present tragedy, her faded sunbonnet hiding her bowed face. Scarlett saw with amazement that her percale dress had grease-spots on it and her hands were freckled and unclean. There were even black crescents under her finger-nails. There was nothing of quality folks about Cathleen now. She looked Cracker, even worse. She looked poor white, shiftless, slovenly, trifling.

'She'll be dipping snuff soon, if she isn't doing it already,' thought Scarlett in horror. 'Good Lord! What a comedown!'

She shuddered, turning her eyes from Cathleen as she realized how narrow was the chasm between quality folks and poor whites.

'There but for a lot of gumption am I,' she thought, and pride surged through her as she realized that she and Cathleen had started with the same equipment after the surrender – empty hands and what they had in their heads.

'I haven't done so bad,' she thought, lifting her chin and smiling.

But she stopped in mid-smile as she saw the scandalized eyes of Mrs Tarleton upon her. Her eyes were red-rimmed from tears and, after giving Scarlett a reproving look, she turned her gaze back to Suellen, a fierce angry gaze that boded ill for her. Behind her and her husband were the four Tarleton girls, their red locks indecorous notes in the solemn occasion, their russet eyes still looking like the eyes of vital young animals, spirited and dangerous.

Feet were stilled, hats were removed, hands folded and skirts rustled into quietness as Ashley stepped forward with Carreen's worn Book of Devotions in his hand. He stood for a moment looking down, the sun glittering on his golden head. A deep silence fell on the crowd, so deep that the harsh whisper of the wind in the magnolia leaves came clear to their ears and the far-off repetitious note of a mocking-bird sounded unendurably loud and sad. Ashley began to read the prayers and all heads bowed as his resonant, beautifully modulated voice rolled out the brief and dignified words.

'Oh!' thought Scarlett, her throat constricting. 'How beautiful his voice is! If anyone has to do this for Pa, I'm glad it's Ashley. I'd rather have him than a priest. I'd rather have Pa buried by one of his own folks than a stranger.'

When Ashley came to the part of the prayers concerning the souls in Purgatory, which Carreen had marked for him to read, he abruptly closed the book. Only Carreen noticed the omission and looked up puzzled, as he began the Lord's Prayer. Ashley knew that half the people present had never heard of Purgatory and those who had would take it as a personal affront, if he insinuated, even in prayer, that so fine a man as Mr O'Hara had not gone straight to Heaven. So, in deference to public opinion, he skipped all mention of Purgatory. The gathering joined heartily in the Lord's Prayer but their voices trailed off into embarrassed silence when he began the Hail Mary. They had never heard that prayer and they looked furtively at each other as the O'Hara girls, Melanie and the Tara servants gave the response: 'Pray for us, now and at the hour of our death. Amen.'

Then Ashley raised his head and stood for a moment, uncertain. The eyes of the neighbours were expectantly upon him as they settled themselves in easier positions for a long harangue. They were waiting for him to go on with the service, for it did not occur to any of them that he was at the end of the Catholic prayers. County funerals were always long. The Baptist and Methodist ministers who performed them had no set prayers but extemporized as the circumstances demanded and seldom stopped before all mourners were in tears and the bereaved feminine relatives screaming with grief. The neighbours would have been shocked, aggrieved and indignant, had these brief prayers been all the service over the body of their loved friend, and no one knew this better than Ashley. The matter would be discussed at dinner tables for weeks and the opinion of the County would be that the O'Hara girls had not shown proper respect for their father.

So he threw a quick apologetic glance at Carreen and, bowing his head again, began reciting from memory the Episcopal burial service which he had often read over slaves buried at Twelve Oaks.

'I am the Resurrection and the Life ... and whosoever ... believeth in Me shall never die.'

It did not come back to him readily and he spoke slowly, occasionally falling silent for a space as he waited for phrases to rise from his memory. But this measured delivery made his words more impressive, and mourners who had been dry-eyed before began now to reach for handkerchiefs. Sturdy Baptists and Methodists all, they thought it the Catholic ceremony and immediately rearranged their first opinion that the Catholic services were cold and Popish. Scarlett and Suellen were equally ignorant and thought the words comforting and beautiful. Only Melanie and Carreen realized that a devoutly Catholic Irishman was being laid to rest by the Church of England service. And Carreen was too stunned by grief and her hurt at Ashley's treachery to interfere.

When he had finished, Ashley opened wide his sad grey eyes and looked about the crowd. After a pause, his eyes caught those of Will and he said: 'Is there anyone present who would like to say a word?'

Mrs Tarleton twitched nervously but before she could act, Will stumped forward and, standing at the head of the coffin, began to speak.

'Friends,' he began in his flat pale voice, 'maybe you think I'm gettin' above myself, speakin' first – me who never knew Mr O'Hara till 'bout a year ago when you all have known him twenty years or more. But this here is my excuse. If he'd lived a month or so longer, I'd have had the right to call him Pa.'

A startled ripple went over the crowd. They were too well-bred to whisper but they shifted on their feet and stared at Carreen's bowed head. Everyone knew his dumb devotion to her. Seeing the direction in which all eyes were cast, Will went on as if he had taken no note.

'So bein' as how I'm to marry Miss Suellen as soon as the priest comes down from Atlanta, I thought maybe that gives me the right to speak first.'

The last part of his speech was lost in a faint sibilant buzz that went through the gathering, an angry beelike buzz. There were indignation and disappointment in the sound. Everyone liked Will, everyone respected him for what he had done for Tara. Everyone knew his affections lay with Carreen, so the news that he was to marry the neighbourhood pariah instead sat ill upon them. Good old Will marrying that nasty, sneaking little Suellen O'Hara!

For a moment the air was tense. Mrs Tarleton's eyes began to snap and her lips to shape soundless words. In the silence, old man McRae's high voice could be heard imploring his grandson to tell him what had been said. Will faced them all, still mild of face, but there was something in his pale-blue eyes which dared them to say one word about his future wife. For a moment the balance hung between the honest affection everyone had for Will and their contempt for Suellen. And Will won. He continued as if his pause had been a natural one.

'I never knew Mr O'Hara in his prime like you all done. All I knew personally was a fine old gentleman who was a mite addled. But I've heard tell from you all 'bout what he used to be like. And I want to say this. He was a fightin' Irishman and a Southern gentleman and as loyal a Confederate as ever lived. You can't get no better combination than that. And we ain't likely to see many more like him, because the times that bred men like him are as dead as he is. He was born in a furrin country but the man we're buryin' here today was more of a Georgian than any of us mournin' him. He lived our life, he loved our land and, when you come right down to it, he died for our Cause, same as the soldiers did. He was one of us and he had our good points and our bad points and he had our strength and he had our failin's. He had our good points in that couldn't nothin' stop him when his mind was made up and he warn't scared of nothin' that walked in shoe-leather. There warn't nothin' that come to him *from the outside* that could lick him.

'He warn't scared of the English government when they wanted to hang him. He just lit out and left home. And when he come to this country and was pore, that didn't scare him a mite neither. He went to work and he made his money. And he warn't scared to tackle this section when it was part wild and the Injuns had just been run out of it. He made a big plantation out of a wilderness. And when the war come on and his money begun to go, he warn't scared to be pore again. And when the Yankees come through Tara and might of burnt him out or killed him, he warn't fazed a bit and he warn't licked neither. He just planted his front feet and stood his ground. That's why I say he had our good points. There ain't nothin' *from the outside* can lick any of us.

'But he had our failin's too, 'cause he could be licked from the inside. I mean to say that what the whole world couldn't do, his own heart could. When Mrs O'Hara died, his heart died too and he was licked. And what we seen walking 'round here warn't him.'

Will paused and his eyes went quietly around the circle of faces. The crowd stood in the hot sun as if enchanted to the ground and whatever wrath they had felt for Suellen was forgotten. Will's eyes rested for a moment on Scarlett and they crinkled slightly at the corners as if he were inwardly smiling comfort to her. Scarlett, who had been fighting back rising tears, did feel comforted. Will was talking common sense instead of a lot of tootle about reunions in another and better world and submitting her will to God's. And Scarlett had always found strength and comfort in common sense.

'And I don't want none of you to think the less of him for breakin' like he done. All you all and me, too, are like him. We got the same weakness and failin'. There ain't nothin' that walks can lick us, any more than it could lick him, not Yankees nor Carpetbaggers nor hard times nor high taxes nor even downright starvation. But that weakness that's in our hearts can lick us in the time it takes to bat your eye. It ain't always losin' someone you love that does it, like it done Mr O'Hara. Everybody's mainspring is different. And I want to say this – folks whose mainsprings are busted are better dead. There ain't no place for them in the world these days, and they're happier bein' dead . . . That's why I'm sayin' you all ain't got no cause to grieve for Mr O'Hara now. The time to grieve was back when Sherman come through and he lost Mrs O'Hara. Now that his body's gone to join his heart, I don't see that we got reason to mourn, unless we're pretty damned selfish, and I'm sayin' it who loved him like he was my own pa . . . There won't be no more words said, if you folks don't mind. The family is too cut up to listen and it wouldn't be no kindness to them.'

Will stopped and, turning to Mrs Tarleton, he said in a lower voice: 'I wonder couldn't you take Scarlett in the house, Ma'm? It ain't right for her to be standin' in the sun so long. And Grandma Fontaine don't look any too peart neither, meanin' no disrespect.'

Startled at the abrupt switching from the eulogy to herself, Scarlett went red with embarrassment as all eyes turned toward her. Why should Will advertise her already obvious pregnancy? She gave him a shamed indignant look, but Will's placid gaze bore her down.

'Please,' his look said. 'I know what I'm doing.'

Already he was the man of the house and, not wishing to make a scene, Scarlett turned helplessly to Mrs Tarleton. That lady, suddenly diverted, as Will had intended, from thoughts of Suellen to the always fascinating matter of breeding, be it animal or human, took Scarlett's arm.

'Come in the house, honey.'

Her face took on a look of kind, absorbed interest and Scarlett suffered herself to be led through the crowd that gave way and made a narrow path

for her. There was a sympathetic murmuring as she passed and several hands
went out to pat her comfortingly. When she came abreast Grandma Fontaine,
the old lady put out a skinny claw and said: 'Give me your arm, child,' and
added with a fierce glance at Sally and Young Miss: 'No, don't you come.
I don't want you.'

They passed slowly through the crowd which closed behind them and
went up the shady path toward the house, Mrs Tarleton's eager helping
hand so strong under Scarlett's elbow that she was almost lifted from the
ground at each step.

'Now, why did Will do that?' cried Scarlett heatedly, when they were
out of earshot. 'He practically said: "Look at her! She's going to have a
baby!" '

'Well, sakes alive, you are, aren't you?' said Mrs Tarleton. 'Will did right.
It was foolish of you to stand in the hot sun when you might have fainted
and had a miscarriage.'

'Will wasn't bothered about her miscarrying,' said Grandma, a little
breathless as she laboured across the front yard toward the steps. There
was a grim, knowing smile on her face. 'Will's smart. He didn't want either
you or me, Beetrice, at the graveside. He was scared of what we'd say and
he knew this was the only way to get rid of us ... And it was more than
that. He didn't want Scarlett to hear the clods dropping on the coffin. And
he's right. Just remember, Scarlett, as long as you don't hear that sound,
folks aren't actually dead to you. But once you hear it ... Well, it's the most
dreadfully final sound in the world ... Help me up the steps, child, and give
me a hand, Beetrice. Scarlett don't any more need your arm than she needs
crutches and I'm not so peart, as Will observed ... Will knew you were your
father's pet and he didn't want to make it worse for you than it already was.
He figured it wouldn't be so bad for your sisters. Suellen has her shame to
sustain her and Carreen her God. But you've got nothing to sustain you,
have you, child?'

'No,' answered Scarlett, helping the old lady up the steps, faintly surprised
at the truth that sounded in the reedy old voice. 'I've never had anything to
sustain me – except Mother.'

'But when you lost her, you found you could stand alone, didn't you?
Well, some folks can't. Your pa was one. Will's right. Don't you grieve. He
couldn't get along without Ellen and he's happier where he is. Just like I'll
be happier when I join the Old Doctor.'

She spoke without any desire for sympathy and the two gave her none. She
spoke as briskly and naturally as if her husband were alive and in Jonesboro
and a short buggy ride would bring them together. Grandma was too old
and had seen too much to fear death.

'But – you can stand alone too,' said Scarlett.

The old lady gave her a bright birdlike glance.

'Yes, but it's powerful uncomfortable at times.'

'Look here, Grandma,' interrupted Mrs Tarleton, 'you ought not to talk to Scarlett like that. She's upset enough already. What with her trip down here and that tight dress and her grief and the heat, she's got enough to make her miscarry without your adding to it, talking grief and sorrow.'

'God's nightgown!' cried Scarlett in irritation. 'I'm not upset! And I'm not one of those sickly miscarrying fools!'

'You never can tell,' said Mrs Tarleton omnisciently. 'I lost my first when I saw a bull gore one of our darkies and – you remember my red mare, Nellie? Now, there was the healthiest-looking mare you ever saw but she was nervous and high-strung and if I didn't watch her, she'd—'

'Beetrice, hush,' said Grandma. 'Scarlett wouldn't miscarry on a bet. Let's sit here in the hall where it's cool. There's a nice draught through here. Now, you go fetch us a glass of buttermilk, Beetrice, if there's any in the kitchen. Or look in the pantry and see if there's any wine. I could do with a glass. We'll sit here till the folks come up to say goodbye.'

'Scarlett ought to be in bed,' insisted Mrs Tarleton, running her eyes over her with the expert air of one who calculated a pregnancy to the last minute of its length.

'Get going,' said Grandma, giving her a prod with her cane, and Mrs Tarleton went toward the kitchen, throwing her hat carelessly on the sideboard and running her hands through her damp red hair.

Scarlett lay back in her chair and unbuttoned the two top buttons of her tight basque. It was cool and dim in the high-ceilinged hall and the vagrant draught that went from back to front of the house was refreshing after the heat of the sun. She looked across the hall into the parlour where Gerald had lain and, wrenching her thoughts from him, looked up at the portrait of Grandma Robillard hanging above the fireplace. The bayonet-scarred portrait with its high-piled hair, half-exposed breasts and cool insolence had, as always, a tonic effect upon her.

'I don't know which hit Beetrice Tarleton worse, losing her boys or her horses,' said Grandma Fontaine. 'She never did pay much mind to Jim or her girls, you know. She's one of those folks Will was talking about. Her mainspring's busted. Sometimes I wonder if she won't go the way your pa went. She wasn't ever happy unless horses or humans were breeding right in her face and none of her girls are married or got any prospects of catching husbands in this county, so she's got nothing to occupy her mind. If she wasn't such a lady at heart, she'd be downright common . . . Was Will telling the truth about marrying Suellen?'

'Yes,' said Scarlett, looking the old lady full in the eye. Goodness, she could remember the time when she was scared to death of Grandma Fontaine! Well, she'd grown up since then and she'd just as soon as not tell her to go to the devil if she meddled in affairs at Tara.

'He could do better,' said Grandma candidly.

'Indeed?' said Scarlett haughtily.

'Come off your high horse, Miss,' said the old lady tartly. 'I shan't attack your precious sister, though I might have if I'd stayed at the burying-ground. What I mean is with the scarcity of men in the neighbourhood, Will could marry most any of the girls. There's Beetrice's four wildcats and the Munroe girls and the McRae—'

'He's going to marry Sue and that's that.'

'She's lucky to get him.'

'Tara is lucky to get him.'

'You love this place, don't you?'

'Yes.'

'So much that you don't mind your sister marrying out of her class as long as you have a man around to care for Tara?'

'Class?' said Scarlett, startled at the idea. 'Class? What does class matter now, so long as a girl gets a husband who can take care of her?'

'That's a debatable question,' said Old Miss. 'Some folks would say you were talking common sense. Others would say you were letting down bars that ought never be lowered one inch. Will's certainly not quality folks and some of your people were.'

Her sharp old eyes went to the portrait of Grandma Robillard.

Scarlett thought of Will, lank, unimpressive, mild, eternally chewing a straw, his whole appearance deceptively devoid of energy, like that of most Crackers. He did not have behind him a long line of ancestors of wealth, prominence and blood. The first of Will's family to set foot on Georgia soil might even have been one of Oglethorpe's debtors or a bond-servant. Will had not been to college. In fact, four years in a backwoods school was all the education he had ever had. He was honest and he was loyal, he was patient and he was hard-working, but certainly he was not quality. Undoubtedly by Robillard standards, Suellen was coming down in the world.

'So you approve of Will coming into your family?'

'Yes,' answered Scarlett fiercely, ready to pounce upon the old lady at the first words of condemnation.

'You may kiss me,' said Grandma surprisingly, and she smiled in her most approving manner. 'I never liked you much till now, Scarlett. You were always hard as a hickory nut, even as a child, and I don't like hard females, barring myself. But I do like the way you meet things. You don't make a fuss about things that can't be helped, even if they are disagreeable. You take your fences cleanly like a good hunter.'

Scarlett smiled uncertainly and pecked obediently at the withered cheek presented to her. It was pleasant to hear approving words again, even if she had little idea what they meant.

'There's plenty of folks hereabouts who'll have something to say about you letting Sue marry a Cracker – for all that everybody likes Will. They'll say in one breath what a fine man he is and how terrible it is for an O'Hara girl to marry beneath her. But don't you let it bother you.'

'I've never bothered about what people said.'

'So I've heard.' There was a hint of acid in the old voice. 'Well, don't bother about what folks say. It'll probably be a very successful marriage. Of course, Will's always going to look like a Cracker and marriage won't improve his grammar any. And, even if he makes a mint of money, he'll never lend any shine and sparkle to Tara, like your father did. Crackers are short on sparkle. But Will's a gentleman at heart. He's got the right instincts. Nobody but a born gentleman could have put his finger on what is wrong with us accurately as he just did, down there at the burying. The whole world can't lick us but we can lick ourselves by longing too hard for things we haven't got any more – and by remembering too much. Yes, Will will do well by Suellen and by Tara.'

'Then you approve of me letting him marry her?'

'God, no!' The old voice was tired and bitter but vigorous. 'Approve of Crackers marrying into old families? Bah! Would I approve of breeding scrub stock to thoroughbreds? Oh, Crackers are good and solid and honest but—'

'But you said you thought it would be a successful match!' cried Scarlett, bewildered.

'Oh, I think it's good for Suellen to marry Will – to marry anybody, for that matter, because she needs a husband bad. And where else could she get one? And where else could you get as good a manager for Tara? But that doesn't mean I like the situation any better than you do.'

'But I do like it,' thought Scarlett, trying to grasp the old lady's meaning. 'I'm glad Will is going to marry her. Why should she think I minded? She's taking it for granted that I do mind, just like her.'

She felt puzzled and a little ashamed, as always when people attributed to her emotions and motives they possessed and thought she shared.

Grandma fanned herself with her palmetto leaf and went on briskly: 'I don't approve of the match any more than you do but I'm practical and so are you. And when it comes to something that's unpleasant but can't be helped, I don't see any sense in screaming and kicking about it. That's no way to meet the ups and downs of life. I know because my family and the Old Doctor's family have had more than our share of ups and downs. And if we folks have a motto, it's this: "Don't holler – smile and bide your time." We've survived a passel of things that way, smiling and biding our time, and we've gotten to be experts at surviving. We had to be. We've always bet on the wrong horses. Run out of France with the Huguenots, run out of England with the Cavaliers, run out of Scotland with Bonnie Prince Charlie, run out of Haiti by the niggers and now licked by the Yankees. But we always turn up on top in a few years. You know why?'

She cocked her head and Scarlett thought she looked like nothing so much as an old, knowing parrot.

'No, I don't know, I'm sure,' she answered politely. But she was heartily bored, even as she had been the day when Grandma launched on her memories of the Creek uprising.

'Well, this is the reason. We bow to the inevitable. We're not wheat, we're buckwheat! When a storm comes along it flattens ripe wheat because it's dry and can't bend with the wind. But ripe buckwheat's got sap in it and it bends. And when the wind has passed, it springs up almost as straight and strong as before. We aren't a stiff-necked tribe. We're mighty limber when a hard wind's blowing, because we know it pays to be limber. When trouble comes we bow to the inevitable without any mouthing, and we work and we smile and we bide our time. And we play along with lesser folks and we take what we can get from them. And when we're strong enough, we kick the folks whose necks we've climbed over. That, my child, is the secret of the survival.' And after a pause, she added: 'I pass it on to you.'

The old lady cackled, as if she were amused by her words, despite the venom in them. She looked as if she expected some comment from Scarlett but the words had made little sense to her and she could think of nothing to say.

'No, sir,' Old Miss went on, 'our folks get flattened out but they rise up again, and that's more than I can say for plenty of people not so far away from here. Look at Cathleen Calvert. You can see what she's come to. Poor white! And a heap lower than the man she married. Look at the McRae family. Flat to the ground, helpless, don't know what to do, don't know how to do anything. Won't even try. They spend their time whining about the good old days. And look at – well, look at nearly anybody in this County except my Alex and my Sally and you and Jim Tarleton and his girls and some others. The rest have gone under because they didn't have any sap in them, because they didn't have the gumption to rise up again. There never was anything to those folks but money and darkies, and now that the money and darkies are gone, those folks will be Cracker in another generation.'

'You forgot the Wilkes.'

'No, I didn't forget them. I just thought I'd be polite and not mention them, seeing that Ashley's a guest under this roof. But seeing as how you've brought up their names – look at them! There's India, who from all I hear is a dried-up old maid already, giving herself all kinds of widowed airs because Stu Tarleton was killed and not making an effort to forget him and try to catch another man. Of course, she's old but she could catch some widower with a big family if she tried. And poor Honey was always a man-crazy fool with no more sense than a guinea-hen. And as for Ashley, look at him!'

'Ashley is a very fine man,' began Scarlett hotly.

'I never said he wasn't but he's as helpless as a turtle on his back. If the Wilkes family pulls through these hard times, it'll be Melly who pulls them through. Not Ashley.'

'Melly! Lord, Grandma! What are you talking about? I've lived with Melly long enough to know she's sickly and scared and hasn't the gumption to say Boo to a goose.'

'Now why on earth should anyone want to say Boo to a goose? It always sounded like a waste of time to me. She might not say Boo to a goose but she'd say Boo to the world or the Yankee government or anything else that threatened her precious Ashley or her boy or her notions of gentility. Her way isn't your way, Scarlett, or my way. It's the way your mother would have acted if she'd lived. Melly puts me in mind of your mother when she was young ... And maybe she'll pull the Wilkes family through.'

'Oh, Melly's a well-meaning little ninny. But you are very unjust to Ashley. He's—'

'Oh, foot! Ashley was bred to read books and nothing else. That doesn't help a man pull himself out of a tough fix, like we're all in now. From what I hear, he's the worst plough hand in the County! Now you just compare him with my Alex! Before the war, Alex was the most worthless dandy in the world and he never had a thought beyond a new cravat and getting drunk and shooting somebody and chasing girls who were no better than they should be. But look at him now! He learned farming because he had to learn. He'd have starved and so would all of us. Now he raises the best cotton in the County – yes, Miss! It's a heap better than Tara cotton! – and he knows what to do with hogs and chickens. Ha! He's a fine boy for all his bad temper. He knows how to bide his time and change with changing ways and when all this Reconstruction misery is over, you're going to see my Alex as rich a man as his father and his grandfather were. But Ashley—'

Scarlett was smarting at the slight to Ashley.

'It all sounds like tootle to me,' she said coldly.

'Well, it shouldn't,' said Grandma, fastening a sharp eye upon her. 'For it's just exactly the course you've been following since you went to Atlanta. Oh, yes! We hear of your didoes, even if we are buried down here in the country. You've changed with the changing times too. We hear how you suck up to the Yankees and the white trash and the new-rich Carpetbaggers to get money out of them. Butter doesn't melt in your mouth from all I can hear. Well, go to it, I say. And get every cent out of them you can, but when you've got enough money, kick them in the face, because they can't serve you any longer. Be sure you do that and do it properly, for trash hanging on to your coat-tails can ruin you.'

Scarlett looked at her, her brow wrinkling with the effort to digest the words. They still didn't make much sense and she was still angry at Ashley being called a turtle on his back.

'I think you're wrong about Ashley,' she said abruptly.

'Scarlett, you just aren't smart.'

'That's your opinion,' said Scarlett rudely, wishing it were permissible to smack old ladies' jaws.

'Oh, you're smart enough about dollars and cents. That's a man's way of being smart. But you aren't smart at all like a woman. You aren't a speck smart about folks.'

Scarlett's eyes began to snap fire and her hands to clench and unclench.

'I've made you good and mad, haven't I?' asked the old lady, smiling. 'Well, I aimed to do just that.'

'Oh, you did, did you? And why, pray?'

'I had good and plenty reasons.'

Grandma sank back in her chair and Scarlett suddenly realized that she looked very tired and incredibly old. The tiny clawlike hands folded over the fan were yellow and waxy as a dead person's. The anger went out of Scarlett's heart as a thought came to her. She leaned over and took one of the hands in hers.

'You're a mighty sweet old liar,' she said. 'You didn't mean a word of all this rigmarole. You've just been talking to keep my mind off Pa, haven't you?'

'Don't fiddle with me!' said Old Miss grumpily, jerking away her hand. 'Partly for that reason, partly because what I've been telling you is the truth and you're just too stupid to realize it.'

But she smiled a little and took the sting from her words. Scarlett's heart emptied itself of wrath about Ashley. It was nice to know Grandma hadn't meant any of it.

'Thank you, just the same. It was nice of you to talk to me – and I'm glad to know you're with me about Will and Suellen, even if – even if a lot of other people do disapprove.'

Mrs Tarleton came down the hall, carrying two glasses of buttermilk. She did all domestic things badly and the glasses were slopping over.

'I had to go clear to the spring-house to get it,' she said. 'Drink it quick because the folks are coming up from the burying-ground. Scarlett, are you really going to let Suellen marry Will? Not that he isn't a sight too good for her but you know he is a Cracker and—'

Scarlett's eyes met those of Grandma. There was a wicked sparkle in the old eyes that found an answer in her own.

Chapter XLI

When the last goodbye had been said and the last sound of wheels and hooves died away, Scarlett went into Ellen's office and removed a gleaming object from where she had hidden it the night before between the yellowed papers in the pigeon-holes of the secretary. Hearing Pork sniffling in the dining-room as he went about laying the table for dinner she called to him. He came to her, his black face as forlorn as a lost and masterless hound.

'Pork,' she said sternly, 'you cry just once more and I'll – I'll cry, too. You've got to stop.'

'Yas'm. Ah try but eve'y time Ah try Ah thinks of Mist' Gerald an'—'

'Well, don't think. I can stand everybody else's tears but not yours. There,' she broke off gently, 'don't you see? I can't stand yours because I know how you loved him. Blow your nose, Pork. I've got a present for you.'

A little interest flickered in Pork's eyes as he blew his nose loudly but it was more politeness than interest.

'You remember that night you got shot robbing somebody's hen-house?'

'Lawd Gawd, Miss Scarlett! Ah ain' never—'

'Well, you did, so don't lie to me about it at this late date. You remember I said I was going to give you a watch for being so faithful?'

'Yas'm, Ah 'members. Ah figgered you'd done fergot.'

'No, I didn't forget and here it is.'

She held out for him a massive gold watch, heavily embossed, from which dangled a chain with many fobs and seals.

'Fo' Gawd, Miss Scarlett!' cried Pork. 'Dat's Mist' Gerald's watch! Ah done seen him look at dat watch a milyun times!'

'Yes, it's Pa's watch, Pork, and I'm giving it to you. Take it.'

'Oh, no'm!' Pork retreated in horror. 'Dat's a w'ite gempmum's watch an' Mist' Gerald's ter boot. Huccome you talk 'bout givin' it ter me, Miss Scarlett? Dat watch belong by rights ter lil Wade Hampton.'

'It belongs to you. What did Wade Hampton ever do for Pa? Did he look after him when he was sick and feeble? Did he bathe him and dress him and shave him? Did he stick by him when the Yankees came? Did he steal for him? Don't be a fool, Pork. If ever anyone deserved a watch, you do, and I know Pa would approve. Here.'

She picked up the black hand and laid the watch in the palm. Pork gazed at it reverently and slowly delight spread over his face.

'Fer me, truly, Miss Scarlett?'

'Yes, indeed.'

'Well'm – thankee, Ma'm.'

'Would you like for me to take it to Atlanta and have it engraved?'

'Whut's dis engrabed mean?' Pork's voice was suspicious.

'It means to put writing on the back of it, like – like "To Pork from the O'Haras— Well done, good and faithful servant." '

'No'm – thankee, Ma'm. Never mind de engrabin'.' Pork retreated a step, clutching the watch firmly.

A little smile twitched her lips.

'What's the matter, Pork? Don't you trust me to bring it back?'

'Yas'm, Ah trus'es you – only, well'm, you mout change yo' mind.'

'I wouldn't do that.'

'Well'm, you mout sell it. Ah spec it's wuth a heap.'

'Do you think I'd sell Pa's watch?'

'Yas'm – ef you needed de money.'

'You ought to be beat for that, Pork. I've a mind to take the watch back.'

'No'm, you ain'!' The first faint smile of the day showed on Pork's grief-worn face. 'Ah knows you— An', Miss Scarlett—'

'Yes, Pork?'

'Ef you wuz jes' half as nice ter w'ite folks as you is ter niggers, Ah spec de worl' would treat you better.'

'It treats me well enough,' she said. 'Now, go find Mr Ashley and tell him I want to see him here, right away.'

Ashley sat on Ellen's little writing-chair, his long body dwarfing the frail bit of furniture, while Scarlett offered him a half-interest in the mill. Not once did his eyes meet hers and he spoke no word of interruption. He sat looking down at his hands, turning them over slowly, inspecting first palms and then backs, as though he had never seen them before. Despite hard work, they were still slender and sensitive-looking and remarkably well tended for a farmer's hands.

His bowed head and silence disturbed her a little and she redoubled her efforts to make the mill sound attractive. She brought to bear, too, all the charm of smile and glance she possessed but they were wasted, for he did not raise his eyes. If he would only look at her! She made no mention of the information Will had given her of Ashley's determination to go North and spoke with the outward assumption that no obstacle stood in the way of his agreement with her plan. Still he did not speak, and finally her words trailed into silence. There was a determined squareness about his slender shoulders that alarmed her. Surely he wouldn't refuse! What earthly reason could he have for refusing?

'Ashley,' she began again and paused. She had not intended using her pregnancy as an argument, had shrunk from the thought of Ashley even seeing her so bloated and ugly, but as her other persuasions seemed to have made no impression, she decided to use it and her helplessness as a last card.

'You must come to Atlanta. I do need your help so badly now, because I can't look after the mills. It may be months before I can because – you see – well, because . . .'

'Please!' he said roughly. 'Good God, Scarlett!'

He rose and went abruptly to the window and stood with his back to her, watching the solemn file of ducks parade across the barnyard.

'Is that – is that why you won't look at me?' she questioned forlornly. 'I know I look—'

He swung around in a flash and his grey eyes met hers with an intensity that made her hands go to her throat.

'Damn your looks!' he said with a swift violence. 'You know you always look beautiful to me.'

Happiness flooded her until her eyes were liquid with tears.

'How sweet of you to say that! For I was so ashamed to let you see me—'

'You ashamed? Why should you be ashamed? I'm the one to feel shame and I do. If it hadn't been for my stupidity you wouldn't be in this fix. You'd never have married Frank. I should never have let you leave Tara last winter. Oh, fool that I was! I should have known you – known you were desperate, so desperate that you'd—I should have – I should have—' His face went haggard.

Scarlett's heart beat wildly. He was regretting that he had not run away with her!

'The least I could have done was go out and commit highway robbery or murder to get the tax money for you when you had taken us in as beggars. Oh, I messed it up all the way around!'

Her heart contracted with disappointment and some of the happiness went from her, for these were not the words she hoped to hear.

'I would have gone anyway,' she said tiredly. 'I couldn't have let you do anything like that. And anyway, it's done now.'

'Yes, it's done now,' he said with slow bitterness. 'You wouldn't have let me do anything dishonourable but you would sell yourself to a man you didn't love – and bear his child, so that my family and I wouldn't starve. It was kind of you to shelter my helplessness.'

The edge in his voice spoke of a raw, unhealed wound that ached within him and his words brought shame to her eyes. He was swift to see it and his face changed to gentleness.

'You didn't think I was blaming you? Dear God, Scarlett! No. You are the bravest woman I've ever known. It's myself I'm blaming.'

He turned and gazed out of the window again and the shoulders presented to her gaze did not look quite so square. Scarlett waited a long moment in silence, hoping that Ashley would return to the mood in which he spoke of her beauty, hoping he would say more words that she could treasure. It had been so long since she had seen him and she had lived on memories until they were worn thin. She knew he still loved her. That fact was evident, in every line of him, in every bitter, self-condemnatory word, in his resentment at her bearing Frank's child. She so longed to hear him say it in words, longed to speak words herself that would provoke a confession, but she dared not. She remembered her promise given last winter in the orchard, that she would never again throw herself at his head. Sadly she knew that promise must be kept if Ashley were to remain near her. One cry from her of love and longing, one look that pleaded for his arms, and the matter would be settled forever. Ashley would surely go to New York. And he must not go away.

'Oh, Ashley, don't blame yourself! How could it be your fault? You will come to Atlanta and help me, won't you?'

'No.'

'But, Ashley,' her voice was beginning to break with anguish and disappointment, 'but I'd counted on you. I do need you so. Frank can't help me.

He's so busy with the store and if you don't come I don't know where I can get a man! Everybody in Atlanta who is smart is busy with his own affairs and the others are so incompetent and—'

'It's no use, Scarlett.'

'You mean you'd rather go to New York and live among Yankees than come to Atlanta?'

'Who told you that?' He turned and faced her, faint annoyance wrinkling his forehead.

'Will.'

'Yes, I've decided to go North. An old friend who made the Grand Tour with me before the war has offered me a position in his father's bank. It's better so, Scarlett. I'd be no good to you. I know nothing of the lumber business.'

'But you know less about banking and it's much harder! And I know I'd make far more allowances for your inexperience than Yankees would!'

He winced and she knew she had said the wrong thing. He turned and looked out of the window again.

'I don't want allowances made for me. I want to stand on my own feet for what I'm worth. What have I done with my life, up till now? It's time I made something of myself – or went down through my own fault. I've been your pensioner too long already.'

'But I'm offering you a half-interest in the mill, Ashley! You would be standing on your own feet because – you see, it would be your own business.'

'It would amount to the same thing. I'd not be buying the half-interest. I'd be taking it as a gift. And I've taken too many gifts from you already, Scarlett – food and shelter and even clothes for myself and Melanie and the baby. And I've given you nothing in return.'

'Oh, but you have! Will couldn't have—'

'I can split kindling very nicely now.'

'Oh, Ashley!' she cried despairingly, tears in her eyes at the jeering note in his voice. 'What has happened to you since I've been gone? You sound so hard and bitter! You didn't used to be this way.'

'What's happened? A very remarkable thing, Scarlett. I've been thinking. I don't believe I really thought from the time of the surrender until you went away from here. I was in a state of suspended animation and it was enough that I had something to eat and a bed to lie on. But when you went to Atlanta, shouldering a man's burden, I saw myself as much less than a man – much less, indeed, than a woman. Such thoughts aren't pleasant to live with and I do not intend to live with them any longer. Other men came out of the war with less than I had and look at them now. So I'm going to New York.'

'But – I don't understand! If it's work you want, why won't Atlanta do as well as New York? And my mill—'

'No, Scarlett. This is my last chance. I'll go North. If I go to Atlanta and work for you, I'm lost forever.'

The word 'lost – lost – lost' dinged frighteningly in her heart like a death-bell sounding. Her eyes went quickly to his but they were wide and crystal grey and they were looking through her and beyond her at some fate she could not see, could not understand.

'Lost? Do you mean – have you done something the Atlanta Yankees can get you for? I mean, about helping Tony get away or – or— Oh, Ashley, you aren't in the Ku Klux, are you?'

His remote eyes came back to her swiftly and he smiled a brief smile that never reached his eyes.

'I had forgotten you were so literal. No, it's not the Yankees I'm afraid of. I mean if I go to Atlanta and take help from you again, I bury forever any hope of ever standing alone.'

'Oh,' she sighed in quick relief, 'if it's only that!'

'Yes,' and he smiled again, the smile more wintry than before. 'Only that. Only my masculine pride, my self-respect and, if you choose to so call it, my immortal soul.'

'But,' she swung around on another tack, 'you could gradually buy the mill from me and it would be your own and then—'

'Scarlett,' he interrupted fiercely, 'I tell you, no! There are other reasons.'

'What reasons?'

'You know my reasons better than anyone in the world.'

'Oh – that? But – that'll be all right,' she assured swiftly. 'I promised, you know, out in the orchard, last winter, and I'll keep my promise and—'

'Then you are surer of yourself than I am. I could not count on myself to keep such a promise. I should not have said that but I had to make you understand. Scarlett, I will not talk of this any more. It's finished. When Will and Suellen marry, I am going to New York.'

His eyes, wide and stormy, met hers for an instant and then he went swiftly across the room. His hand was on the door-knob. Scarlett stared at him in agony. The interview was ended and she had lost. Suddenly weak from the strain and sorrow of the last day and the present disappointment, her nerves broke abruptly and she screamed: 'Oh, Ashley!' And, flinging herself down on the sagging sofa, she burst into wild crying.

She heard his uncertain footsteps leaving the door and his helpless voice saying her name over and over above her head. There was a swift pattering of feet racing up the hall from the kitchen and Melanie burst into the room, her eyes wide with alarm.

'Scarlett . . . the baby isn't . . . ?'

Scarlett burrowed her head in the dusty upholstery and screamed again.

'Ashley – he's so mean! So doggoned mean – so hateful!'

'Oh, Ashley, what have you done to her?' Melanie threw herself on the floor beside the sofa and gathered Scarlett into her arms. 'What have you said? How could you! You might bring on the baby! There, my darling, put your head on Melanie's shoulder! What is wrong?'

'Ashley – he's so – so bull-headed and hateful!'

'Ashley, I'm surprised at you! Upsetting her so much and in her condition and Mr O'Hara hardly in his grave!'

'Don't you fuss at him!' cried Scarlett illogically, raising her head abruptly from Melanie's shoulder, her coarse black hair tumbling out from its net and her face streaked with tears. 'He's got a right to do as he pleases!'

'Melanie,' said Ashley, his face white, 'let me explain. Scarlett was kind enough to offer me a position in Atlanta as manager of one of her mills— '

'Manager!' cried Scarlett indignantly. 'I offered him a half-interest and he— '

'And I told her I had already made arrangements for us to go North and she— '

'Oh,' cried Scarlett, beginning to sob again, 'I told him and told him how much I needed him – how I couldn't get anybody to manage the mill – how I was going to have this baby – and he refused to come! And now – now, I'll have to sell the mill and I know I can't get anything like a good price for it and I'll lose money and I guess maybe we'll starve, but he won't care. He's so mean!'

She burrowed her head back into Melanie's thin shoulder and some of the real anguish went from her as a flicker of hope woke in her. She could sense that in Melanie's devoted heart she had an ally, feel Melanie's indignation that anyone, even her beloved husband, should make Scarlett cry. Melanie flew at Ashley like a small determined dove and pecked him for the first time in her life.

'Ashley, how could you refuse her? And after all she's done for us! How ungrateful you make us appear! And she so helpless now with the bab— How unchivalrous of you! She helped us when we needed help and now you deny her when she needs you!'

Scarlett peeped slyly at Ashley and saw surprise and uncertainty plain in his face as he looked into Melanie's dark indignant eyes. Scarlett was surprised, too, at the vigour of Melanie's attack, for she knew Melanie considered her husband beyond wifely reproaches and thought his decisions second only to God's.

'Melanie . . .' he began and then threw out his hands helplessly.

'Ashley, how can you hesitate? Think what she's done for us – for me! I'd have died in Atlanta when Beau came if it hadn't been for her! And she – yes, she killed a Yankee, defending us. Did you know that? She killed a man for us. And she worked and slaved before you and Will came home, just to keep food in our mouths. And when I think of her ploughing and picking cotton, I could just— Oh, my darling!' And she swooped her head and kissed Scarlett's tumbled hair in fierce loyalty. 'And now the first time she asks us to do something for her— '

'You don't need to tell me what she has done for us.'

'And Ashley, just think! Besides helping her, just think what it'll mean for us to live in Atlanta among our own people and not have to live with Yankees! There'll be Auntie and Uncle Henry and all our friends, and Beau can have lots of playmates and go to school. If we went North, we couldn't let him go to school and associate with Yankee children and have picca- ninnies in his class! We'd have to have a governess and I don't see how we'd afford—'

'Melanie,' said Ashley, and his voice was deadly quiet, 'do you really want to go to Atlanta so badly? You never said so when we talked about going to New York. You never intimated—'

'Oh, but when we talked about going to New York, I thought there was nothing for you in Atlanta and, besides, it wasn't my place to say anything. It's a wife's duty to go where her husband goes. But now that Scarlett needs us so and has a position that only you can fill we can go home! Home!' Her voice was rapturous as she squeezed Scarlett. 'And I'll see Five Points again and Peachtree road and – and— Oh, how I've missed them all! And maybe we could have a little home of our own! I wouldn't care how little and tacky it was but – a home of our own!'

Her eyes blazed with enthusiasm and happiness and the two stared at her, Ashley with a queer stunned look, Scarlett with surprise mingled with shame. It had never occurred to her that Melanie missed Atlanta so much and longed to be back, longed for a home of her own. She had seemed so contented at Tara it came to Scarlett as a shock that she was homesick.

'Oh, Scarlett, how good of you to plan all this for us! You knew how I longed for home!'

As usual when confronted by Melanie's habit of attributing worthy motives where no worth existed, Scarlett was ashamed and irritated, and suddenly she could not meet either Ashley's or Melanie's eyes.

'We could get a little house of our own. Do you realize that we've been married five years and never had a home?'

'You can stay with us at Aunt Pitty's. That's your home,' mumbled Scarlett, toying with a pillow and keeping her eyes down to hide dawning triumph in them as she felt the tide turning her way.

'No, but thank you just the same, darling. That would crowd us so. We'll get us a house— Oh, Ashley, do say Yes!'

'Scarlett,' said Ashley and his voice was toneless, 'look at me.'

Startled, she looked up and met grey eyes that were bitter and full of tired futility.

'Scarlett, I will come to Atlanta . . . I cannot fight you both.'

He turned and walked out of the room. Some of the triumph in her heart was dulled by a nagging fear. The look in his eyes when he spoke had been the same as when he said he would be lost forever if he came to Atlanta.

*

After Suellen and Will married and Carreen went off to Charleston to the convent, Ashley, Melanie and Beau came to Atlanta, bringing Dilcey with them to cook and nurse. Prissy and Pork were left at Tara until such a time as Will could get other darkies to help him in the fields and then they, too, would come to town.

The little brick house that Ashley took for his family was on Ivy Street directly behind Aunt Pitty's house and the two back yards ran together, divided only by a ragged overgrown privet hedge. Melanie had chosen it especially for this reason. She said, on the first morning of her return to Atlanta as she laughed and cried and embraced Scarlett and Aunt Pitty, she had been separated from her loved ones for so long that she could never be close enough to them again.

The house had originally been two storeys high but the upper floor had been destroyed by shells during the siege and the owner, returning after the surrender, had lacked the money to replace it. He had contented himself with putting a flat roof on the remaining first floor which gave the building the squat, disproportionate look of a child's playhouse built of shoe-boxes. The house was high from the ground, built over a large cellar, and the long sweeping flight of stairs which reached it made it look slightly ridiculous. But the flat, squashed look of the place was partly redeemed by the two fine old oaks which shaded it and a dusty-leaved magnolia, splotched with white blossoms, standing beside the front steps. The lawn was wide and green with thick clover and bordering it was a straggling, unkempt privet hedge, interlaced with sweet-smelling honeysuckle vines. Here and there in the grass, roses threw out sprangles from crushed old stems and pink and white crêpe myrtle bloomed as valiantly as if war had not passed over their heads and Yankee horses gnawed their boughs.

Scarlett thought it quite the ugliest dwelling she had ever seen, but, to Melanie, Twelve Oaks in all its grandeur had not been more beautiful. It was home and she and Ashley and Beau were at last together under their own roof.

India Wilkes came back from Macon, where she and Honey had lived since 1864, and took up her residence with her brother, crowding the occupants of the little house. But Ashley and Melanie welcomed her. Times had changed, money was scarce, but nothing had altered the rule of Southern life that families always made room gladly for indigent or unmarried female relatives.

Honey had married and, so India said, married beneath her, a coarse Westerner from Mississippi who had settled in Macon. He had a red face and a loud voice and jolly ways. India had not approved of the match and, not approving, had not been happy in her brother-in-law's home. She welcomed the news that Ashley now had a home of his own, so she could remove herself from uncongenial surroundings and also from the distressing sight of her sister so fatuously happy with a man unworthy of her.

The rest of the family privately thought that the giggling and simple-minded Honey had done far better than could be expected and they marvelled that she had caught any man. Her husband was a gentleman and a man of some means; but to India, born in Georgia and reared in Virginia traditions, anyone not from the eastern seaboard was a boor and a barbarian. Probably Honey's husband was as happy to be relieved of her company as she was to leave him, for India was not easy to live with these days.

The mantle of spinsterhood was definitely on her shoulders now. She was twenty-five and looked it, and so there was no longer any need for her to try to be attractive. Her pale lashless eyes looked directly and uncompromisingly upon the world and her thin lips were ever set in haughty tightness. There was an air of dignity and pride about her now that, oddly enough, became her better than the determined girlish sweetness of her days at Twelve Oaks. The position she held was almost that of a widow. Everyone knew that Stuart Tarleton would have married her had he not been killed at Gettysburg, and so she was accorded the respect due a woman who had been wanted if not wed.

The six rooms of the little house on Ivy Street were soon scantily furnished with the cheapest pine and oak furniture in Frank's store for, as Ashley was penniless and forced to buy on credit, he refused anything except the least expensive and bought only the barest necessities. This embarrassed Frank who was fond of Ashley and it distressed Scarlett. Both she and Frank would willingly have given, without any charge, the finest mahogany and carved rosewood in the store, but the Wilkeses obstinately refused. Their house was painfully ugly and bare and Scarlett hated to see Ashley living in the uncarpeted, uncurtained rooms. But he did not seem to notice his surroundings and Melanie, having her own home for the first time since her marriage, was so happy she was actually proud of the place. Scarlett would have suffered agonies of humiliation at having friends find her without draperies and carpets and cushions and the proper number of chairs and teacups and spoons. But Melanie did the honours of her house as though plush curtains and brocade sofas were hers.

For all her obvious happiness, Melanie was not well. Little Beau had cost her her health, and the hard work she had done at Tara since his birth had taken further toll of her strength. She was so thin that her small bones seemed ready to come through her white skin. Seen from a distance, romping about the back yard with her child, she looked like a little girl, for her waist was unbelievably tiny and she had practically no figure. She had no bust and her hips were as flat as little Beau's, and as she had neither the pride nor the good sense (so Scarlett thought) to sew ruffles in the bosom of her basque or pads on the back of her corsets, her thinness was very obvious. Like her body, her face was too thin and too pale and her silky brows, arched and delicate as a butterfly's feelers, stood out too blackly against her colourless skin. In her small face, her eyes were too large for beauty, the dark smudges under them making them appear enormous, but the expression in them had not altered since the days of her unworried girlhood. War and constant pain and hard work had been powerless against their sweet tranquillity. They were the eyes of a happy woman, a woman around whom storms might blow without ever ruffling the serene core of her being.

How did she keep her eyes that way, thought Scarlett, looking at her enviously. She knew her own eyes sometimes had the look of a hungry cat. What was it Rhett had said once about Melanie's eyes – some foolishness about them being like candles? Oh, yes, like two good deeds in a naughty world. Yes, they were like candles, candles shielded from every wind, two soft lights glowing with happiness at being home again among her friends.

The little house was always full of company. Melanie had been a favourite even as a child and the town flocked to welcome her home again. Everyone brought presents for the house, bric-à-brac, pictures, a silver spoon or two, linen pillow-cases, napkins, rag rugs, small articles which they had saved from Sherman and treasured but which they now swore were of no earthly use to them.

Old men who had campaigned in Mexico with her father came to see her, bringing visitors to meet 'old Colonel Hamilton's sweet daughter'. Her mother's old friends clustered about her, for Melanie had a respectful deference to her elders that was very soothing to dowagers in these wild days when young people seemed to have forgotten all their manners. Her contemporaries, the young wives, mothers and widows, loved her because she had suffered what they had suffered, had not become embittered and always lent them a sympathetic ear. The young people came, as young people always come, simply because they had a good time at her house and met there the friends they wanted to meet.

Around Melanie's tactful and self-effacing person, there rapidly grew up a clique of young and old who represented what was left of the best of Atlanta's ante-bellum society, all poor in purse, all proud in family, diehards of the stoutest variety. It was as if Atlanta society, scattered and wrecked by war, depleted by death, bewildered by change, had found in her an unyielding nucleus about which it could re-form.

Melanie was young but she had in her all the qualities this embattled remnant prized, poverty and pride in poverty, uncomplaining courage, gaiety, hospitality, kindness and, above all, loyalty to all the old traditions. Melanie refused to change, refused even to admit that there was any reason to change in a changing world. Under her roof the old days seemed to come back again, and people took heart and felt even more contemptuous of the tide of wild life and high living that was sweeping the Carpetbaggers and newly rich Republicans along.

When they looked into her young face and saw there the inflexible loyalty to the old days, they could forget, for a moment, the traitors within their own class who were causing fury, fear and heartbreak. And there were many such. There were men of good family, driven to desperation by poverty, who had gone over to the enemy, become Republicans and accepted positions from the conquerors, so their families would not be on charity. There were young ex-soldiers who lacked the courage to face the long years necessary to build up fortunes. These youngsters, following the lead of Rhett Butler, went hand in hand with the Carpetbaggers in money-making schemes of unsavoury kinds.

Worst of all the traitors were the daughters of some of Atlanta's most prominent families. These girls who had come to maturity since the surrender had only childish memories of the war and lacked the bitterness that animated their elders. They had lost no husbands, no lovers. They had few recollections of past wealth and splendour – and the Yankee officers were so handsome and finely dressed and so carefree. And they gave such splendid balls and drove such fine horses and simply worshipped Southern girls! They treated them like queens and were so careful not to injure their touchy pride and, after all – why not associate with them?

They were so much more attractive than the town swains who dressed so shabbily and were so serious and worked so hard that they had little time for play. So there had been a number of elopements with Yankee officers which broke the hearts of Atlanta families. There were brothers who passed sisters on the streets and did not speak and mothers and fathers who never mentioned daughters' names. Remembering these tragedies, a cold dread ran in the veins of those whose motto was 'No surrender' – a dread which the very sight of Melanie's soft but unyielding face dispelled. She was, as the dowagers said, such an excellent and wholesome example to the young girls of the town. And, because she made no parade of her virtues, the young girls did not resent her.

It never occurred to Melanie that she was becoming the leader of a new society. She only thought the people were nice to come and see her and to want her in their little sewing circles, cotillion clubs and musical societies. Atlanta had always been musical and loved good music, despite the sneering comments of sister cities of the South concerning the town's lack of culture, and there was now an enthusiastic resurrection of interest that grew stronger as the times grew harder and more tense. It was easier to forget the impudent black faces in the streets and the blue uniforms of the garrison while they were listening to music.

Melanie was a little embarrassed to find herself at the head of the newly formed Saturday Night Musical Circle. She could not account for her elevation to this position except by the fact that she could accompany anyone on the piano, even the Misses McLure who were tone-deaf but who would sing duets.

The truth of the matter was that Melanie had diplomatically managed to amalgamate the Lady Harpists, the Gentlemen's Glee Club and the Young Ladies' Mandolin and Guitar Society with the Saturday Night Musical Circle, so that now Atlanta had music worth listening to. In fact, the Circle's rendition of *The Bohemian Girl* was said by many to be far superior to professional performances heard in New York and New Orleans. It was after she had manoeuvred the Lady Harpists into the fold that Mrs Merriwether said to Mrs Meade and Mrs Whiting that they must have Melanie at the head of the Circle. If she could get on with the Harpists, she could get on with anyone, Mrs Merriwether declared. That lady herself played the organ for the choir at the Methodist Church and, as an organist, had scant respect for harps or harpists.

Melanie had also been made secretary for both the Association for the Beautification of the Graves of Our Glorious Dead and the Sewing Circle for the Widows and Orphans of the Confederacy. This new honour came to her after an exciting joint meeting of those societies which threatened to end in violence and the severance of lifelong ties of friendship. The question had arisen at the meeting as to whether or not weeds should be removed from the graves of the Union soldiers near those of Confederate soldiers. The appearance of the scraggly Yankee mounds defeated all the efforts of the Ladies to beautify those of their own dead. Immediately the fires which smouldered beneath tight basques flamed wildly and the two organizations split up and glared hostilely. The Sewing Circle was in favour of the removal of the weeds, the ladies of the Beautification were violently opposed.

Mrs Meade expressed the views of the latter group when she said: 'Dig up the weeds off Yankee graves? For two cents, I'd dig up all the Yankees and throw them in the city dump!'

At these ringing words the two associations arose and every lady spoke her mind and no one listened. The meeting was being held in Mrs Merriwether's parlour and Grandpa Merriwether, who had been banished to the kitchen, reported afterwards that the noise sounded just like the opening guns of the battle of Franklin. And, he added, he guessed it was a dinged sight safer to be present at the battle of Franklin than at the ladies' meeting.

Somehow Melanie made her way to the centre of the excited throng and somehow made her usually soft voice heard above the tumult. Her heart was in her throat with fright at daring to address the indignant gathering and her voice shook but she kept crying: 'Ladies! Please!' till the din died down.

'I want to say – I mean, I've thought for a long time that – that not only should we pull up the weeds but we should plant flowers on—I – I don't care what you think but every time I go to take flowers to dear Charlie's grave, I always put some on the grave of an unknown Yankee which is nearby. It – it looks so forlorn!'

The excitement broke out again in louder words and this time the two organizations merged and spoke as one.

'On Yankee graves! Oh, Melly, how could you!' 'And they killed Charlie!'

'They almost killed you!' 'Why, the Yankees might have killed Beau when he was born!' 'They tried to burn you out of Tara!'

Melanie held on to the back of her chair for support, almost crumpling beneath the weight of a disapproval she had never known before.

'Oh, ladies!' she cried, pleading. 'Please, let me finish! I know I haven't the right to speak on this matter, for none of my loved ones were killed except Charlie, and I know where he lies, thank God! But there are so many among us today who do not know where their sons and husbands and brothers are buried and—'

She choked and there was a dead silence in the room.

Mrs Meade's flaming eyes went sombre. She had made the long trip to Gettysburg after the battle to bring back Darcy's body but no one had been able to tell her where he was buried. Somewhere in some hastily dug trench in the enemy's country. And Mrs Allan's mouth quivered. Her husband and brother had been on that ill-starred raid Morgan made into Ohio and the last information she had of them was that they fell on the banks of the river, just as the Yankee cavalry stormed up. She did not know where they lay. Mrs Allison's son had died in a Northern prison camp and she, the poorest of the poor, was unable to bring his body home. There were others who had read on casualty lists, 'Missing – believed dead', and in those words had learned the last news they were ever to learn of men they had seen march away.

They turned to Melanie with eyes that said: 'Why do you open these wounds again? These are the wounds that never heal – the wounds of not knowing where they lie.'

Melanie's voice gathered strength in the stillness of the room.

'Their graves are somewhere up in the Yankees' country, just like the Yankee graves are here, and oh, how awful it would be to know that some Yankee woman said to dig them up and—'

Mrs Meade made a small, dreadful sound.

'But how nice it would be to know that some good Yankee woman – and there must be *some* good Yankee women. I don't care what people say, they can't all be bad! How nice it would be to know that they pulled weeds off our men's graves and brought flowers to them, even if they were enemies. If Charlie were dead in the North it would comfort me to know that someone—And I don't care what you ladies think of me,' her voice broke again, 'I will withdraw from both clubs and I'll – I'll pull up every weed off every Yankee's grave I can find and I'll plant flowers, too – and – I just dare anyone to stop me!'

With this final defiance Melanie burst into tears and tried to make her stumbling way to the door.

Grandpa Merriwether, safe in the masculine confines of the Girl of the Period Saloon an hour later, reported to Uncle Henry Hamilton that after these words, everybody cried and embraced Melanie and it all ended up in a love feast and Melanie was made secretary of both organizations.

'And they are going to pull up the weeds. The hell of it is Dolly said I'd be only too pleased to help do it, 'cause I didn't have anything much else to do. I got nothing against the Yankees and I think Miss Melly was right and the rest of those lady wild-cats wrong. But the idea of me pulling weeds at my time of life and with my lumbago!'

Melanie was on the board of lady managers of the Orphans' Home and assisted in the collection of books for the newly formed Young Men's Library Association. Even the Thespians who gave amateur plays once a month clamoured for her. She was too timid to appear behind the kerosene-lamp footlights, but she could make costumes out of croker sacks if they were the only material available. It was she who cast the deciding vote at the Shakespeare Reading Circle that the bard's works should be varied with those of Mr Dickens and Mr Bulwer-Lytton and not the poems of Lord Byron, as had been suggested by a young and, Melanie privately feared, very fast bachelor member of the Circle.

In the nights of the late summer her small, feebly lighted house was always full of guests. There were never enough chairs to go around and frequently ladies sat on the steps of the front porch with men grouped about them on the banisters, on packing-boxes or on the lawn below. Sometimes when Scarlett saw guests sitting on the grass, sipping tea, the only refreshment the Wilkeses could afford, she wondered how Melanie could bring herself to expose her poverty so shamelessly. Until Scarlett was able to furnish Aunt Pitty's house as it had been before the war and serve her guests good wine and juleps and baked ham and cold haunches of venison, she had no intention of having guests in her house – especially prominent guests, such as Melanie had.

General John B. Gordon, Georgia's great hero, was frequently there with his family. Father Ryan, the poet-priest of the Confederacy, never failed to call when passing through Atlanta. He charmed gatherings there with his wit and seldom needed much urging to recite his 'Sword of Lee' or his deathless 'Conquered Banner', which never failed to make the ladies cry. Alex Stephens, late Vice-President of the Confederacy, visited whenever in town and, when the word went about that he was at Melanie's, the house was filled and people sat for hours under the spell of the frail invalid with the ringing voice. Usually there were a dozen children present, nodding sleepily in their parents' arms, up hours after their normal bedtime. No family wanted its children to miss being able to say in after years that they had been kissed by the great Vice-President or had shaken the hand that helped to guide the Cause. Every person of importance who came to town found his way to the Wilkes home and often they spent the night there. It crowded the little flat-topped house, forced India to sleep on a pallet in the cubbyhole that was Beau's nursery and sent Dilcey speeding through the back hedge to borrow breakfast eggs from Aunt Pitty's Cookie, but Melanie entertained them as graciously as if hers was a mansion.

No, it did not occur to Melanie that people rallied round her as round a worn and loved standard. And so she was both astounded and embarrassed when Dr Meade, after a pleasant evening at her house where he acquitted himself nobly in reading the part of Macbeth, kissed her hand and made observations in the voice he once used in speaking of Our Glorious Cause.

'My dear Miss Melly, it is always a privilege and a pleasure to be in your home, for you – and ladies like you – are the hearts of all of us, all that we have left. They have taken the flower of our manhood and the laughter of our young women. They have broken our health, uprooted our lives and unsettled our habits. They have ruined our prosperity, set us back fifty years and placed too heavy a burden on the shoulders of our boys who should be in school and our old men who should be sleeping in the sun. But we will build back, because we have hearts like yours to build upon. And as long as we have them, the Yankees can have the rest!'

Until Scarlett's figure reached such proportions that even Aunt Pitty's big black shawl did not conceal her condition, she and Frank frequently slipped through the back hedge to join the summer-night gatherings on Melanie's porch. Scarlett always sat well out of the light, hidden in the protecting shadows where she was not only inconspicuous but could, unobserved, watch Ashley's face to her heart's content.

It was only Ashley who drew her to the house, for the conversations bored and saddened her. They always followed a set pattern – first, hard times; next, the political situation; and then, inevitably, the war. The ladies bewailed the high prices of everything and asked the gentlemen if they thought good times would ever come back. And the omniscient gentlemen always said, indeed they would. Merely a matter of time. Hard times were just temporary. The ladies knew the gentlemen were lying and the gentlemen knew the ladies knew they were lying. But they lied cheerfully just the same and the ladies pretended to believe them. Everyone knew hard times were here to stay.

Once the hard times were disposed of, the ladies spoke of the increasing impudence of the negroes and the outrages of the Carpetbaggers and the humiliation of having the Yankee soldiers loafing on every corner. Did the gentlemen think the Yankees would ever get through with reconstructing Georgia? The reassuring gentlemen thought Reconstruction would be over in no time – that is, just as soon as the Democrats could vote again. The ladies were considerate enough not to ask when this would be. And having finished with politics, the talk about the war began.

Whenever two former Confederates met anywhere, there was never but one topic of conversation, and where a dozen or more gathered together, it was a foregone conclusion that the war would be spiritedly refought. And always the word 'if' had the most prominent part in the talk.

'If England had recognized us—' 'If Jeff Davis had commandeered all the cotton and gotten it to England before the blockade tightened—' 'If Longstreet had obeyed orders at Gettysburg—' 'If Jeb Stuart hadn't been away on that raid when Marse Bob needed him—' 'If we hadn't lost Stonewall Jackson—' 'If Vicksburg hadn't fallen—' 'If we could have held on another year—' And always: 'If they hadn't replaced Johnston with Hood—' or 'If they'd put Hood in command at Dalton instead of Johnston—'

If! If! The soft drawling voices quickened with an old excitement as they talked in the quiet darkness – infantryman, cavalryman, cannoneer, evoking memories of the days when life was ever at high tide, recalling the fierce heat of their midsummer in this forlorn sunset of their winter.

'They don't talk of anything else,' thought Scarlett. 'Nothing but the war. Always the war. And they'll never talk of anything but the war. No, not until they die.'

She looked about, seeing little boys lying in the crooks of their fathers' arms, breath coming fast, eyes glowing, as they heard of midnight sorties and wild cavalry dashes and flags planted on enemy breastworks. They were hearing drums and bugles and the Rebel yell, seeing footsore men going by in the rain with torn flags slanting.

'And these children will never talk of anything else either. They'll think it was wonderful and glorious to fight the Yankees and come home blind and crippled – or not come home at all. They all like to remember the war, to talk about it. But I don't. I don't even like to think about it. I'd forget it all if I could – oh, if I only could!'

She listened with flesh crawling as Melanie told tales of Tara, making Scarlett a heroine as she faced the invaders and saved Charles' sword, bragging how Scarlett had put out the fire. Scarlett took no pleasure or pride in the memory of these things. She did not want to think of them at all.

'Oh, why can't they forget? Why can't they look forward and not back? We were fools to fight that war. And the sooner we forget it, the better we'll be.'

But no one wanted to forget, no one, it seemed, except herself, so Scarlett was glad when she could truthfully tell Melanie that she was embarrassed at appearing, even in the darkness. This explanation was readily understood by Melanie who was hypersensitive about all matters relating to childbirth. Melanie wanted another baby badly, but both Dr Meade and Dr Fontaine had said another child would cost her her life. So, only half resigned to her fate, she spent most of her time with Scarlett, vicariously enjoying a pregnancy not her own. To Scarlett, scarcely wanting her coming child and irritated at its untimeliness, this attitude seemed the height of sentimental stupidity. But she had a guilty sense of pleasure that the doctors' edict had made impossible any real intimacy between Ashley and his wife.

Scarlett saw Ashley frequently now but she never saw him alone. He came by the house every night on his way home from the mill to report on the day's work, but Frank and Pitty were usually present or, worse still, Melanie and India. She could only ask businesslike questions and make suggestions and then say: 'It was nice of you to come by. Good night.'

If only she wasn't having a baby! Here was a God-given opportunity to ride out to the mill with him every morning, through the lonely woods, far from prying eyes, where they could imagine themselves back in the County again in the unhurried days before the war.

No, she wouldn't try to make him say one word of love! She wouldn't refer to love in any way. She'd sworn an oath to herself that she would never do that again. But, perhaps if she were alone with him once more, he might drop that mask of impersonal courtesy he had worn since coming to Atlanta. Perhaps he might be his old self again, be the Ashley she had known before the barbecue, before any word of love had been spoken between them. If they could not be lovers, they could be friends again and she could warm her cold and lonely heart in the glow of his friendship.

'If only I could get this baby over and done with,' she thought impatiently, 'then I could ride with him every day and we could talk—'

It was not only the desire to be with him that made her writhe with helpless impatience at her confinement. The mills needed her. The mills had been losing money ever since she retired from active supervision, leaving Hugh and Ashley in charge.

Hugh was so incompetent, for all that he tried so hard. He was a poor trader and a poorer boss of labour. Anyone could Jew him down on prices. If any slick contractor chose to say that the lumber was of an inferior grade and not worth the price asked, Hugh felt that all a gentleman could do was to apologize and take a lower price. When she heard of the price he received for a thousand feet of flooring, she burst into angry tears. The best grade of flooring the mill had ever turned out and he had practically given it away! And he couldn't manage his labour crews. The negroes insisted on being paid every day and they frequently got drunk on their wages and did not turn up for work the next morning. On these occasions Hugh was forced to hunt up new workmen and the mill was late in starting. With these difficulties Hugh didn't get into town to sell the lumber for days on end.

Seeing the profits slip from Hugh's fingers, Scarlett became frenzied at her impotence and his stupidity. Just as soon as the baby was born and she could go back to work, she would get rid of Hugh and hire someone else. Anyone would do better. And she would never fool with free niggers again. How could anyone get any work done with free niggers quitting all the time?

'Frank,' she said, after a stormy interview with Hugh over his missing workmen, 'I've about made up my mind that I'll lease convicts to work the mills. A while back I was talking to Johnnie Gallegher, Tommy Wellburn's foreman, about the trouble we were having getting any work out of the darkies and he asked me why I didn't get convicts. It sounds like a good idea to me. He said I could sublease them for next to nothing and feed them dirt cheap. And he said I could get work out of them in any way I liked, without having the Freedmen's Bureau swarming down on me like hornets, sticking their bills into things that aren't any of their business. And just as soon as Johnnie Gallegher's contract with Tommy is up, I'm going to hire him to run Hugh's mill. Any man who can get work out of that bunch of wild Irish he bosses can certainly get plenty of work out of convicts.'

Convicts! Frank was speechless. Leasing convicts was the very worst of all the wild schemes Scarlett had ever suggested, worse even than her notion of building a saloon.

At least, it seemed worse to Frank and the conservative circles in which he moved. This new system of leasing convicts had come into being because of the poverty of the state after the war. Unable to support the convicts, the State was hiring them out to those needing large labour crews in the building of railroads, in turpentine forests and lumber camps. While Frank and his quiet church-going friends realized the necessity of the system, they deplored it just the same. Many of them had not even believed in slavery and they thought this was far worse than slavery had ever been.

And Scarlett wanted to lease convicts! Frank knew that if she did he could never hold up his head again. This was far worse than owning and operating the mills herself, or anything else she had done. His past objections had always been coupled with the question: 'What will people say?' But this – this went deeper than fear of public opinion. He felt that it was a traffic in human bodies on a par with prostitution, a sin that would be on his soul if he permitted her to do it.

From this conviction of wrongness, Frank gathered courage to forbid Scarlett to do such a thing, and so strong were his remarks that she, startled, relapsed into silence. Finally, to quiet him, she said meekly she hadn't really meant it. She was just so outdone with Hugh and the free niggers she had lost her temper. Secretly, she still thought about it and with some longing. Convict labour would settle one of her hardest problems, but if Frank was going to take on so about it—

She sighed. If even one of the mills were making money, she could stand it. But Ashley was faring little better with his mill than Hugh.

At first Scarlett was shocked and disappointed that Ashley did not immediately take hold and make the mill pay double what it had paid under her management. He was so smart and he had read so many books and there was no reason at all why he should not make a brilliant success and lots of money. But he was no more successful than Hugh. His inexperience, his errors, his utter lack of business judgment and his scruples about close dealing were the same as Hugh's.

Scarlett's love hastily found excuses for him and she did not consider the two men in the same light. Hugh was just hopelessly stupid, while Ashley was merely new at the business. Still, unbidden, came the thought that Ashley could never make a quick estimate in his head and give a price that was correct, as she could. And she sometimes wondered if he'd ever learn to distinguish between planking and sills. And because he was a gentleman and himself trustworthy, he trusted every scoundrel who came along and several times would have lost money for her if she had not tactfully intervened. And if he liked a person – and he seemed to like so many people! – he sold them lumber on credit without ever thinking to find out if they had money in the bank or property. He was as bad as Frank in that respect.

But surely he would learn! And while he was learning she had a fond and maternal indulgence and patience for his errors. Every evening when he called at her house, weary and discouraged, she was tireless in her tactful, helpful suggestions. But for all her encouragement and cheer, there was a queer dead look in his eyes. She could not understand it and it frightened her. He was different, so different from the man he used to be. If only she could see him alone, perhaps she could discover the reason.

The situation gave her many sleepless nights. She worried about Ashley, both because she knew he was unhappy and because she knew his unhappiness wasn't helping him to become a good lumber dealer. It was a torture to have her mills in the hands of two men with no more business sense than Hugh and Ashley, heartbreaking to see her competitors taking her best customers away when she had worked so hard and planned so carefully for these helpless months. Oh, if she could only get back to work again! She would take Ashley in hand and then he would certainly learn. And Johnnie Gallegher could run the other mill, and she could handle the selling, and then everything would be fine. As for Hugh, he could drive a delivery wagon if he still wanted to work for her. That was all he was good for.

Of course, Gallegher looked like an unscrupulous man, for all of his smartness, but – who else could she get? Why had the other men who were both smart and honest been so perverse about working for her? If she only had one of them working for her now in place of Hugh, she wouldn't have to worry so much, but—

Tommy Wellburn, in spite of his crippled back, was the busiest contractor in town and coining money, so people said. Mrs Merriwether and René were prospering and now had opened a bakery downtown. René was managing it with true French thrift and Grandpa Merriwether, glad to escape from his chimney corner, was driving René's pie wagon. The Simmons boys were so busy they were operating their brick-kiln with three shifts of labour a day. And Kells Whiting was cleaning up money with his hair-straightener, because he told the negroes they wouldn't ever be permitted to vote the Republican ticket if they had kinky hair.

It was the same with all the smart young men she knew, the doctors, the lawyers, the storekeepers. The apathy which had clutched them immediately after the war had completely disappeared and they were too busy building their own fortunes to help her build hers. The ones who were not busy were the men of Hugh's type – or Ashley's.

What a mess it was to try to run a business and have a baby too!

'I'll never have another one,' she decided firmly. 'I'm not going to be like other women and have a baby every year. Good Lord, that would mean six months out of the year when I'd have to be away from the mills! And I see now I can't afford to be away from them even one day. I shall simply tell Frank that I won't have any more children.'

Frank wanted a big family, but she could manage Frank somehow. Her mind was made up. This was her last child. The mills were far more important.

Chapter XLII

Scarlett's child was a girl, a small bald-headed mite, ugly as a hairless monkey and absurdly like Frank. No one except the doting father could see anything beautiful about her, but the neighbours were charitable enough to say that all ugly babies turned out pretty, eventually. She was named Ella Lorena, Ella for her grandmother Ellen, and Lorena because it was the most fashionable name of the day for girls, even as Robert E. Lee and Stonewall Jackson were popular for boys and Abraham Lincoln and Emancipation for negro children.

She was born in the middle of a week when frenzied excitement gripped Atlanta and the air was tense with expectation of disaster. A negro who had boasted of rape had actually been arrested, but before he could be brought to trial the jail had been raided by the Ku Klux Klan and he had been quietly hanged. The Klan had acted to save the as yet unnamed victim from having to testify in open court. Rather than have her appear and advertise her shame, her father and brother would have shot her, so lynching the negro seemed a sensible solution to the townspeople, in fact, the only decent solution possible. But the military authorities were in a fury. They saw no reason why the girl should mind testifying publicly.

The soldiers made arrests right and left, swearing to wipe out the Klan if they had to put every white man in Atlanta in jail. The negroes, frightened and sullen, muttered of retaliatory house burnings. The air was thick with rumours of wholesale hangings by the Yankees should the guilty parties be found and of a concerted uprising against the whites by the negroes. The people of the town stayed at home behind locked doors and shuttered windows, the men fearing to go to their businesses and leave their women and children unprotected.

Scarlett, lying exhausted in bed, feebly and silently thanked God that Ashley had too much sense to belong to the Klan and Frank was too old and poor-spirited. How dreadful it would be to know that the Yankees might swoop down and arrest them at any minute! Why didn't the crack-brained young fools in the Klan leave bad enough alone and not stir up the Yankees like this? Probably the girl hadn't been raped after all. Probably she'd just been frightened silly and, because of her, a lot of men might lose their lives.

In this atmosphere, as nerve-straining as watching a slow fuse burn toward a barrel of gunpowder, Scarlett came rapidly back to strength. The healthy vigour which had carried her through the hard days at Tara stood her in good stead now, and within two weeks of Ella Lorena's birth she was strong enough to sit up and chafe at her inactivity. In three weeks she was up, declaring she had to see to the mills. They were standing idle because both Hugh and Ashley feared to leave their families alone all day.

Then the blow fell.

Frank, full of the pride of new fatherhood, summed up courage enough to forbid Scarlett leaving the house while conditions were so dangerous. His commands would not have worried her at all and she would have gone about her business in spite of them, if he had not put her horse and buggy in the livery stable and ordered that they should not be surrendered to anyone except himself. To make matters worse, he and Mammy had patiently searched the house while she was ill and unearthed her hidden store of money. And Frank had deposited it in the bank in his own name, so now she could not even hire a rig.

Scarlett raged at both Frank and Mammy, then was reduced to begging and finally cried all one morning like a furious thwarted child. But for all her pains she heard only: 'There, Sugar! You're just a sick little girl.' And: 'Miss Scarlett, ef you doan quit cahyin' on so, you gwine sour yo' milk an' de baby have colic, sho as gun's iron.'

In a furious temper, Scarlett charged through her back yard to Melanie's house and there unburdened herself at the top of her voice, declaring she would walk to the mills, she would go about Atlanta telling everyone what a varmint she had married, she would not be treated like a naughty simple-minded child. She would carry a pistol and shoot anyone who threatened her. She had shot one man and she would love, yes, love to shoot another. She would—

Melanie, who feared to venture on to her own front porch, was appalled by such threats.

'Oh, you must not risk yourself! I should die if anything happened to you! Oh, please—'

'I will! I will! I will walk—'

Melanie looked at her and saw that this was not the hysteria of a woman still weak from childbirth. There was the same breakneck, headlong determination in Scarlett's face that Melanie had often seen in Gerald O'Hara's face when his mind was made up. She put her arms around Scarlett's waist and held her tightly.

'It's all my fault for not being brave like you and for keeping Ashley at home with me all this time when he should have been at the mill. Oh, dear! I'm such a ninny! Darling, I'll tell Ashley I'm not a bit frightened and I'll come over and stay with you and Aunt Pitty and he can go back to work and—'

Not even to herself would Scarlett admit that she did not think Ashley could cope with the situation alone and she shouted: 'You'll do nothing of the kind! What earthly good would Ashley do at work if he was worried about you every minute? Everybody is just so hateful! Even Uncle Peter refuses to go out with me! But I don't care! I'll go alone. I'll walk every step of the way and pick up a crew of darkies somewhere—'

'Oh, no! You mustn't do that! Something dreadful might happen to you. They say that Shantytown settlement on the Decatur road is just full of mean darkies and you'd have to pass right by it. Let me think— Darling, promise me you won't do anything today and I'll think of something. Promise me you'll go home and lie down. You look right peaked. Promise me.'

Because she was too exhausted by her anger to do otherwise, Scarlett sulkily promised and went home, haughtily refusing any overtures of peace from her household.

That afternoon a strange figure stumped through Melanie's hedge and across Pitty's back yard. Obviously, he was one of those men whom Mammy and Dilcey referred to as 'de riffraff whut Miss Melly pick up off de streets an' let sleep in her cellar'.

There were three rooms in the basement of Melanie's house which formerly had been servants' quarters and a wine room. Now Dilcey occupied one, and the other two were in constant use by a stream of miserable and ragged transients. No one but Melanie knew whence they came or where they were going and no one but she knew where she collected them. Perhaps the negroes were right and she did pick them up from the streets. But even as the great and the near great gravitated to her small parlour, so unfortunates found their way to her cellar where they were fed, bedded and sent on their way with packages of food. Usually the occupants of the rooms were former Confederate soldiers of the rougher, illiterate type, homeless men, men without families, beating their way about the country in hope of finding work.

Frequently, brown and withered country women with broods of tow-haired silent children spent the night there, women widowed by the war, dispossessed of their farms, seeking relatives who were scattered and lost. Sometimes the neighbourhood was scandalized by the presence of foreigners, speaking little or no English, who had been drawn South by glowing tales of fortunes easily made. Once a Republican had slept there. At least, Mammy insisted he was a Republican, saying she could smell a Republican, same as a horse could smell a rattlesnake; but no one believed Mammy's story, for there must be some limit even to Melanie's charity. At least everyone hoped so.

'Yes,' thought Scarlett, sitting on the side porch in the pale November sunshine with the baby on her lap, 'he is one of Melanie's lame dogs. And he's really lame, at that!'

The man who was making his way across the back yard stumped, like Will Benteen, on a wooden leg. He was a tall, thin old man with a bald head, which shone pinkishly dirty, and a grizzled beard so long he could tuck it in his belt. He was over sixty, to judge by his hard, seamed face, but there was no sag of age to his body. He was lank and ungainly but, even with his wooden peg, he moved as swiftly as a snake.

He mounted the steps and came toward her and, even before he spoke, revealing in his tones a twang and a burring of '*r*'s unusual in the lowlands, Scarlett knew that he was mountain born. For all his dirty, ragged clothes there was about him, as about most mountaineers, an air of fierce silent pride that permitted no liberties and tolerated no foolishness. His beard was stained with tobacco juice and a large wad in his jaw made his face look deformed. His nose was thin and craggy, his eyebrows bushy and twisted into witches' locks and a lush growth of hair sprang from his ears, giving them the tufted look of a lynx's ears. Beneath his brow was one hollow socket from which a scar ran down his cheek, carving a diagonal line through his beard. The other eye was small, pale and cold, an unwinking and remorseless eye. There was a heavy pistol openly in his trouser band and from the top of his tattered boot protruded the hilt of a bowie knife.

He returned Scarlett's stare coldly and spat across the rail of the banister before he spoke. There was contempt in his one eye, not a personal contempt for her, but for her whole sex.

'Miz Wilkes sont me to work for you,' he said shortly. He spoke rustily, as one unaccustomed to speaking, the words coming slowly and almost with difficulty. 'M' name's Archie.'

'I'm sorry but I have no work for you, Mr Archie.'

'Archie's m' fuss name.'

'I beg your pardon. What is your last name?'

He spat again. 'I reckon that's my bizness,' he said. 'Archie'll do.'

'I don't care what your last name is! I have nothing for you to do.'

'I reckon you have. Miz Wilkes was upsot about yore wantin' to run aroun' like a fool by yoreself and she sont me over here to drive aroun' with you.'

'Indeed?' cried Scarlett, indignant both at the man's rudeness and Melly's meddling.

His one eye met hers with an impersonal animosity. 'Yes. A woman's got no bizness botherin' her men folks when they're tryin' to take keer of her. If you're bound to gad about, I'll drive you. I hates niggers – Yankees too.'

He shifted his wad of tobacco to the other cheek and, without waiting for an invitation, sat down on the top step. 'I ain't sayin' I like drivin' women aroun', but Miz Wilkes been good to me, lettin' me sleep in her cellar, and she sont me to drive you.'

'But—' began Scarlett helplessly, and then she stopped and looked at him. After a moment she began to smile. She didn't like the looks of this elderly desperado but his presence would simplify matters. With him beside her, she could go to town, drive to the mills, call on customers. No one could doubt her safety with him and his very appearance was enough to keep from giving rise to scandal.

'It's a bargain,' she said. 'That is, if my husband agrees.'

After a private conversation with Archie, Frank gave his reluctant approval and sent word to the livery stable to release the horse and buggy. He was hurt and disappointed that motherhood had not changed Scarlett as he had hoped it would but, if she was determined to go back to her damnable mills, then Archie was a godsend.

So began the relationship that at first startled Atlanta. Archie and Scarlett were a queerly assorted pair, the truculent dirty old man with his wooden peg sticking stiffly out over the dashboard and the pretty, neatly dressed young woman with forehead puckered in an abstracted frown. They could be seen at all hours and at all places in and near Atlanta, seldom speaking to each other, obviously disliking each other, but bound together by mutual need, he of money, she of protection. At least, said the ladies of the town, it's better than riding around so brazenly with that Butler man. They wondered curiously where Rhett was these days, for he had abruptly left town three months before and no one, not even Scarlett, knew where he was.

Archie was a silent man, never speaking unless spoken to and usually answering with grunts. Every morning he came from Melanie's cellar and sat on the front steps of Pitty's house, chewing and spitting until Scarlett came out and Peter brought the buggy from the stable. Uncle Peter feared him only a little less than the devil or the Ku Klux and even Mammy walked silently and timorously around him. He hated negroes and they knew it and feared him. He reinforced his pistol and knife with another pistol, and his fame spread far among the black population. He never once had to draw a pistol or even lay his hand on his belt. The moral effect was sufficient. No negro dared even laugh while Archie was in hearing.

Once Scarlett asked him curiously why he hated negroes and was surprised when he answered, for generally all questions were answered by 'I reckon that's my bizness.'

'I hates them, like all mountain folks hates them. We never liked them and we never owned none. It was them niggers that started the war. I hates them for that, too.'

'But you fought in the war.'

'I reckon that's a man's privilege. I hates Yankees too, more'n I hates niggers. 'Most as much as I hates talkative women.'

It was such outspoken rudeness as this that threw Scarlett into silent furies and made her long to be rid of him. But how could she do without him? In what other way could she obtain such freedom? He was rude and dirty and, occasionally, very odorous but he served his purpose. He drove her to and from the mills and on her round of customers, spitting and staring off into space while she talked and gave orders. If she climbed down from the buggy, he climbed after her and dogged her footsteps. When she was among rough labourers, negroes or Yankee soldiers, he was seldom more than a pace from her elbow.

Soon Atlanta became accustomed to seeing Scarlett and her bodyguard and, from being accustomed, the ladies grew to envy her her freedom of movement. Since the Ku Klux lynching, the ladies had been practically immured, not even going to town to shop unless there were half a dozen in their group. Naturally social-minded, they became restless and, putting their pride in their pockets, they began to beg the loan of Archie from Scarlett. And whenever she did not need him, she was gracious enough to spare him for the use of other ladies.

Soon Archie became an Atlanta institution and the ladies competed for his free time. There was seldom a morning when a child or a negro servant did not arrive at breakfast-time with a note saying: 'If you aren't using Archie this afternoon, do let me have him. I want to drive to the cemetery with flowers.' 'I must go to the milliner's.' 'I should like Archie to drive Aunt Nelly for an airing.' 'I must go calling on Peters Street and Grandpa is not feeling well enough to take me. Could Archie—'

He drove them all, maids, matrons and widows, and toward all he evidenced the same uncompromising contempt. It was obvious that he did not like women, Melanie excepted, any better than he liked negroes and Yankees. Shocked at first by his rudeness, the ladies finally became accustomed to him and, as he was so silent, except for intermittent explosions of tobacco juice, they took him as much for granted as the horses he drove and forgot his very existence. In fact, Mrs Merriwether related to Mrs Meade the complete details of her niece's confinement before she even remembered Archie's presence on the front seat of the carriage.

At no other time than this could such a situation have been possible. Before the war, he would not have been permitted even in the ladies' kitchens. They would have handed him food through the back door and sent him about his business. But now they welcomed his reassuring presence. Rude, illiterate, dirty, he was a bulwark between the ladies and the terrors of Reconstruction. He was neither friend nor servant. He was a hired bodyguard, protecting the women while their men worked by day or were absent from home at night.

It seemed to Scarlett that after Archie came to work for her Frank was away at night very frequently. He said the books at the store had to be balanced and business was brisk enough now to give him little time to attend to this in working hours. And there were sick friends with whom he had to sit. Then there was the organization of Democrats who foregathered every Wednesday night to devise ways of regaining the ballot and Frank never missed a meeting. Scarlett thought this organization did little else except argue the merits of General John B. Gordon over every other general, except General Lee, and refight the war. Certainly she could observe no progress in the direction of the recovery of the ballot. But

Frank evidently enjoyed the meetings for he stayed out until all hours on those nights.

Ashley also sat up with the sick and he, too, attended the Democratic meetings and he was usually away on the same nights as Frank. On these nights, Archie escorted Pitty, Scarlett, Wade and little Ella through the back yard to Melanie's house and the two families spent the evenings together. The ladies sewed while Archie lay full length on the parlour sofa snoring, his grey whiskers fluttering at each rumble. No one had invited him to dispose himself on the sofa and as it was the finest piece of furniture in the house, the ladies secretly moaned every time he lay down on it, planting his boot on the pretty upholstery. But none of them had the courage to remonstrate with him. Especially after he remarked that it was lucky he went to sleep easy, for otherwise the sound of women clattering like a flock of guinea-hens would certainly drive him crazy.

Scarlett sometimes wondered where Archie had come from and what his life had been before he came to live in Melly's cellar but she asked no questions. There was that about his grim one-eyed face which discouraged curiosity. All she knew was that his voice bespoke the mountains to the north and that he had been in the army and had lost both leg and eye shortly before the surrender. It was words spoken in a fit of anger against Hugh Elsing which brought out the truth of Archie's past.

One morning, the old man had driven her to Hugh's mill and she had found it idle, the negroes gone and Hugh sitting despondently under a tree. His crew had not made their appearance that morning and he was at a loss as to what to do. Scarlett was in a furious temper and did not scruple to expend it on Hugh, for she had just received an order for a large amount of lumber – a rush order at that. She had used energy and charm and bargaining to get that order and now the mill was quiet.

'Drive me out to the other mill,' she directed Archie. 'Yes, I know it'll take a long time and we won't get any dinner, but what am I paying you for? I'll have to make Mr Wilkes stop what he's doing and run me off this lumber. Like as not, his crew won't be working either. Great balls of fire! I never saw such a nincompoop as Hugh Elsing! I'm going to get rid of him just as soon as that Johnnie Gallegher finishes the stores he's building. What do I care if Gallegher was in the Yankee Army? He'll work. I never saw a lazy Irishman yet. And I'm through with free issue darkies. You just can't depend on them. I'm going to get Johnnie Gallegher and lease me some convicts. He'll get work out of them. He'll—'

Archie turned to her, his eye malevolent, and when he spoke there was cold anger in his rusty voice.

'The day you gits convicts is the day I quits you,' he said.

Scarlett was startled. 'Good Heavens! Why?'

'I knows about convict leasin'. I calls it convict murderin'. Buyin' men like they was mules. Treatin' them worse than mules ever was treated. Beatin' them, starvin' them, killin' them. And who cares? The State don't care. It's got the lease money. The folks that gits the convicts, they don't care. All they want is to feed them cheap and git all the work they can out of them. Hell, Ma'm, I never thought much of women and I think less of them now.'

'Is it any of your business?'

'I reckon,' said Archie laconically and, after a pause, 'I was a convict for nigh on to forty years.'

Scarlett gasped and, for a moment, shrank back against the cushions. This then was the answer to the riddle of Archie, his unwillingness to tell his last name or the place of his birth or any scrap of his past life, the answer to the difficulty with which he spoke and his cold hatred of the world. Forty years! He must have gone into prison a young man. Forty years! Why – he must have been a life prisoner and lifers were—

'Was it – murder?'

'Yes,' answered Archie briefly, as he flapped the reins. 'M' wife.'

Scarlett's eyelids batted rapidly with fright.

The mouth beneath the beard seemed to move, as if he were smiling grimly at her fear. 'I ain't goin' to kill you, Ma'm, if that's what's frettin' you. Thar ain't but one reason for killin' a woman.'

'You killed your wife!'

'She was layin' with my brother. He got away. I ain't sorry none that I kilt her. Loose women ought to be kilt. The law ain't got no right to put a man in jail for that but I was sont.'

'But – how did you get out? Did you escape? Were you pardoned?'

'You might call it a pardon.' His thick grey brows writhed together as though the effort of stringing words together was difficult.

''Long in 'sixty-four when Sherman come through, I was at Milledgeville jail, like I been for forty years. And the warden he called all us prisoners together and he says the Yankees are a-comin', a-burnin' and a-killin'. Now if thar's one thing I hates worse than a nigger or a woman, it's a Yankee.'

'Why? Had you—Did you ever know any Yankees?'

'No'm. But I'd hearn tell of them. I'd hearn tell they couldn't never mind their own bizness. I hates folks who can't mind their own bizness. What was they doin' in Georgia, freein' our niggers and burnin' our houses and killin' our stock? Well, the warden he said the army needed more soldiers bad, and any of us who'd jine up would be free at the end of the war – if we come out alive. But us lifers – us murderers, the warden he said the army didn't want us. We was to be sont somewheres else to another jail. But I said to the warden I ain't like most lifers. I'm just in for killin' my wife and she needed killin'. And I wants to fight the Yankees. And the warden he saw my side of it and he slipped me out with the other prisoners.'

He paused and grunted.

'Huh. That was right funny. They put me in jail for killin' and they let me out with a gun in my hand and a free pardon to do more killin'. It shore was good to be a free man with a rifle in my hand again. Us men from Milledgeville did good fightin' and killin' – and a lot of us was kilt. I never knowed one who deserted. And when the surrender come, we was free. I lost this here leg and this here eye. But I ain't sorry.'

'Oh,' said Scarlett weakly.

She tried to remember what she had heard about the releasing of the Milledgeville convicts in that last desperate effort to stem the tide of Sherman's army. Frank had mentioned it that Christmas of 1864. What had he said? But her memories of that time were too chaotic. Again she felt the wild terror of those days, heard the siege guns, saw the line of wagons dripping blood into the red roads, saw the Home Guard marching off, the little cadets and the children like Phil Meade and the old men like Uncle Henry and Grandpa Merriwether. And the convicts had marched out too, to die in the twilight of the Confederacy, to freeze in the snow and sleet of that last campaign in Tennessee.

For a brief moment she thought what a fool this old man was, to fight for a state which had taken forty years from his life. Georgia had taken his youth and his middle years for a crime that was no crime to him, yet he had freely given a leg and an eye to Georgia. The bitter words Rhett had spoken in the early days of the war came back to her, and she remembered him saying he would never fight for a society that had made him an outcast. But when the emergency had arisen, he had gone off to fight for that same society, even as Archie had done. It seemed to her that all Southern men, high or low, were sentimental fools and cared less for their hides than for words which had no meaning.

She looked at Archie's gnarled old hands, his two pistols and his knife, and fear pricked her again. Were there other ex-convicts at large, like Archie, murderers, desperadoes, thieves, pardoned for their crimes, in the name of the Confederacy? Why, any stranger on the street might be a murderer! If Frank ever learned the truth about Archie, there would be the devil to pay. Or if Aunt Pitty – but the shock would kill Pitty. And as for Melanie – Scarlett almost wished she could tell Melanie the truth about Archie. It would serve her right for picking up trash and foisting it off on her friends and relatives.

'I'm – I'm glad you told me, Archie. I – I won't tell anyone. It would be a great shock to Mrs Wilkes and the other ladies if they knew.'

'Huh. Miz Wilkes knows. I told her the night she fuss let me sleep in her cellar. You don't think I'd let a nice lady like her take me into her house not knowin'?'

'Saints preserve us!' cried Scarlett, aghast.

Melanie knew this man was a murderer and a woman-murderer at that and she hadn't ejected him from her house. She had trusted her son with him and her aunt and sister-in-law and all her friends. And she, the most timid of females, had not been frightened to be alone with him in her house.

'Miz Wilkes is right sensible, for a woman. She 'lowed that I was all right. She 'lowed that a liar allus kept on lyin' and a thief kept on stealin' but folks don't do more'n one murder in a lifetime. And she reckoned as how anybody who'd fought for the Confederacy had wiped out anything bad they'd done. Though I don't hold that I done nothin' bad, killin' my wife . . . Yes, Miz Wilkes is right sensible, for a woman . . . And I'm tellin' you, the day you leases convicts is the day I quits you.'

Scarlett made no reply but she thought:

'The sooner you quit me the better it will suit me. A murderer!'

How could Melly have been so – so— Well, there was no word for Melanie's action in taking in this old ruffian and not telling her friends he was a jail-bird. So service in the army wiped out past sins! Melanie had that mixed up with baptism! But then Melly was utterly silly about the Confederacy, its veterans, and anything pertaining to them. Scarlett silently damned the Yankees and added another mark on her score against them. They were responsible for a situation that forced a woman to keep a murderer at her side to protect her.

Driving home with Archie in the chill twilight, Scarlett saw a clutter of saddle horses, buggies and wagons outside the Girl of the Period Saloon. Ashley was sitting on his horse, a strained alert look on his face; the Simmons boys were leaning from their buggy, making emphatic gestures; Hugh Elsing, his lock of brown hair falling in his eyes, was waving his hands. Grandpa Merriwether's pie wagon was in the centre of the tangle and, as she came closer, Scarlett saw that Tommy Wellburn and Uncle Henry Hamilton were crowded on the seat with him.

'I wish,' thought Scarlett irritably, 'that Uncle Henry wouldn't ride home in that contraption. He ought to be ashamed to be seen in it. It isn't as though he didn't have a horse of his own. He just does it so he and Grandpa can go to the saloon together every night.'

As she came abreast the crowd something of their tenseness reached her, insensitive though she was, and made fear clutch at her heart.

'Oh!' she thought. 'I hope no one else has been raped! If the Ku Klux lynch just one more darky the Yankees will wipe us out!' And she spoke to Archie. 'Pull up. Something's wrong.'

'You ain't goin' to stop outside a saloon,' said Archie.

'You heard me. Pull up. Good evening, everybody. Ashley – Uncle Henry – is something wrong? You all look so—'

The crowd turned to her, tipping their hats and smiling, but there was a driving excitement in their eyes.

'Something's right and something's wrong,' barked Uncle Henry. 'Depends on how you look at it. The way I figure is the legislature couldn't have done different.'

The legislature? thought Scarlett in relief. She had little interest in the legislature, feeling that its doings could hardly affect her. It was the prospect of the Yankee soldiers on a rampage again that frightened her.

'What's the legislature been up to now?'

'They've flatly refused to ratify the amendment,' said Grandpa Merriwether, and there was pride in his voice. 'That'll show the Yankees.'

'And there'll be hell to pay for it – I beg your pardon, Scarlett,' said Ashley.

'Oh, the amendment?' questioned Scarlett, trying to look intelligent.

Politics were beyond her and she seldom wasted time thinking about them. There had been a Thirteenth Amendment ratified some time before or maybe it had been the Sixteenth Amendment, but what ratification meant she had no idea. Men were always getting excited about such things. Something of her lack of comprehension showed in her face and Ashley smiled.

'It's the amendment letting the darkies vote, you know,' he explained. 'It was submitted to the legislature and they refused to ratify it.'

'How silly of them! You know the Yankees are going to force it down our throats!'

'That's what I meant by saying there'd be hell to pay,' said Ashley.

'I'm proud of the legislature, proud of their gumption!' shouted Uncle Henry. 'The Yankees can't force it down our throats if we won't have it.'

'They can and they will.' Ashley's voice was calm but there was worry in his eyes. 'And it'll make things just that much harder for us.'

'Oh, Ashley, surely not! Things couldn't be any harder than they are now!'

'Yes, things can get worse, even worse than they are now. Suppose we have a darky legislature? A darky governor? Suppose we have a worse military rule than we now have?'

Scarlett's eyes grew large with fear as some understanding entered her mind.

'I've been trying to think what would be best for Georgia, best for all of us.' Ashley's face was drawn. 'Whether it's wisest to fight this thing like the legislature has done, rouse the North against us and bring the whole Yankee Army on us to cram the darky vote down us, whether we want it or not. Or – swallow our pride as best we can, submit gracefully and get the whole matter over with as easily as possible. It will amount to the same thing in the end. We're helpless. We've got to take the dose they're determined to give us. Maybe it would be better for us to take it without kicking.'

Scarlett hardly heard his words, certainly their full import went over her head. She knew that Ashley, as usual, was seeing both sides of a question. She was seeing only one side – how this slap in the Yankees' faces might affect her.

'Going to turn Radical and vote the Republican ticket, Ashley?' jeered Grandpa Merriwether harshly.

There was a tense silence. Scarlett saw Archie's hand make a swift move toward his pistol and then stop. Archie thought, and frequently said, that Grandpa was an old bag of wind and Archie had no intention of letting him insult Miss Melanie's husband, even if Miss Melanie's husband was talking like a fool.

The perplexity vanished suddenly from Ashley's eyes and hot anger flared. But before he could speak, Uncle Henry charged Grandpa.

'You God–you blast—I beg your pardon, Scarlett—Grandpa, you jackass, don't you say that to Ashley!'

'Ashley can take care of himself without you defending him,' said Grandpa coldly. 'And he is talking like a Scallawag. Submit, hell! I beg your pardon, Scarlett.'

'I didn't believe in secession,' said Ashley, and his voice shook with anger. 'But when Georgia seceded, I went with her. And I didn't believe in war but I fought in the war. And I don't believe in making the Yankees madder than they already are. But if the legislature has decided to do it, I'll stand by the legislature. I—'

'Archie,' said Uncle Henry abruptly, 'drive Miss Scarlett on home. This isn't any place for her. Politics aren't for women folks anyway, and there's going to be cussing in a minute. Go on, Archie. Good night, Scarlett.'

As they drove off down Peachtree Street, Scarlett's heart was beating fast with fear. Would this foolish action of the legislature have any effect on her safety? Would it so enrage the Yankees that she might lose her mills?

'Well, sir,' rumbled Archie, 'I've hearn tell of rabbits spittin' in bulldogs' faces but I ain't never seen it till now. Them legislatures might just as well have hollered "Hurray for Jeff Davis and the Southern Confederacy" for all the good it'll do them – and us. Them nigger-lovin' Yankees have made up their mind to make the niggers our bosses. But you got to admire them legislatures' sperrit!'

'Admire them? Great balls of fire! Admire them? They ought to be shot! It'll bring the Yankees down on us like a duck on a June bug. Why couldn't they have rati– radi– whatever they were supposed to do to it and smoothed the Yankees down instead of stirring them up again? They're going to make us knuckle under and we may as well knuckle now as later.'

Archie fixed her with a cold eye.

'Knuckle under without a fight? Women ain't got no more pride than goats.'

When Scarlett leased ten convicts, five for each of her mills, Archie made good his threat and refused to have anything further to do with her. Not all Melanie's pleading or Frank's promises of higher pay would induce him to take up the reins again. He willingly escorted Melanie and Pitty and India and their friends about the town but not Scarlett. He would not even drive for the other ladies if Scarlett was in the carriage. It was an embarrassing situation, having the old desperado sitting in judgment upon her, and it was still more embarrassing to know that her family and friends agreed with the old man.

Frank pleaded with her against taking the step. Ashley at first refused to work convicts and was persuaded, against his will, only after tears and supplications and promises that when times were better she would hire free darkies. Neighbours were so outspoken in their disapproval that Frank, Pitty and Melanie found it hard to hold up their heads. Even Peter and Mammy declared that it was bad luck to work convicts and no good would come of it. Everyone said it was wrong to take advantage of the miseries and misfortunes of others.

'You didn't have any objections to working slaves!' Scarlett cried indignantly.

Ah, but that was different. Slaves were neither miserable nor unfortunate. The negroes were far better off under slavery than they were now under freedom, and if she didn't believe it, just look about her! But, as usual, opposition had the effect of making Scarlett more determined on her course. She removed Hugh from the management of the mill, put him to driving a lumber wagon and closed the final details of hiring Johnnie Gallegher.

He seemed to be the only person she knew who approved of the convicts. He nodded his bullet head briefly and said it was a smart move. Scarlett, looking at the little ex-jockey, planted firmly on his short bowed legs, his gnomish face hard and businesslike, thought: 'Whoever let him ride their horses didn't care much for horseflesh. I wouldn't let him get within ten feet of any horse of mine.'

But she had no qualms in trusting him with a convict gang.

'And I'm to have a free hand with the gang?' he questioned, his eyes as cold as grey agates.

'A free hand. All I ask is that you keep that mill running and deliver my lumber when I want it and as much as I want.'

'I'm your man,' said Johnnie shortly. 'I'll tell Mr Wellburn I'm leaving him.'

As he rolled off through the crowd of masons and carpenters and hod-carriers Scarlett felt relieved and her spirits rose. Johnnie was indeed her man. He was tough and hard and there was no nonsense about him. 'Shanty Irish on the make,' Frank had contemptuously called him, but for that very reason Scarlett valued him. She knew that an Irishman with a determination to get somewhere was a valuable man to have, regardless of what his personal characteristics might be. And she felt a closer kinship with him than with many men of her own class, for Johnnie knew the value of money.

The first week he took over the mill he justified all her hopes, for he accomplished more with five convicts than Hugh had ever done with his crew of ten free negroes. More than that, he gave Scarlett greater leisure than she had had since she came to Atlanta the year before, because he had no liking for her presence at the mill and said so frankly.

'You tend to your end of selling and let me tend to my end of lumbering,' he said shortly. 'A convict camp ain't any place for a lady and if nobody else'll tell you so, Johnnie Gallegher's telling you now. I'm delivering your lumber, ain't I? Well, I've got no notion to be pestered every day like Mr Wilkes. He needs pestering. I don't.'

So Scarlett reluctantly stayed away from Johnnie's mill, fearing that if she came too often he might quit and that would be ruinous. His remark that Ashley needed pestering stung her, for there was more truth in it than she liked to admit. Ashley was doing little better with convicts than he had done with free labour, although why, he was unable to tell. Moreover, he looked as if he were ashamed to be working convicts and he had little to say to her these days.

Scarlett was worried by the change that was coming over him. There were grey hairs in his bright head now and a tired slump in his shoulder. And he seldom smiled. He no longer looked the debonair Ashley who had caught her fancy so many years before. He looked like a man secretly gnawed by a scarcely endurable pain and there was a grim tight look about his mouth that baffled and hurt her. She wanted to drag his head fiercely down on her shoulder, stroke the greying hair and cry: 'Tell me what's worrying you! I'll fix it! I'll make it right for you!'

But his formal remote air kept her at arm's length.

Chapter XLIII

It was one of those rare December days when the sun was almost as warm as Indian summer. Dry red leaves still clung to the oak in Aunt Pitty's yard and a faint yellow green still persisted in the dying grass. Scarlett, with the baby in her arms, stepped out on to the side porch and sat down in a rocking-chair in a patch of sunshine. She was wearing a new green challis dress trimmed with yards and yards of black rickrack braid and a new lace house-cap which Aunt Pitty had made for her. Both were very becoming to her and she knew it and took great pleasure in them. How good it was to look pretty again after the long months of looking so dreadful!

As she sat rocking the baby and humming to herself, she heard the sound of hooves coming up the side street and, peering curiously through the tangle of dead vines on the porch, she saw Rhett Butler riding toward the house.

He had been away from Atlanta for months, since just after Gerald died, since long before Ella Lorena was born. She had missed him but she now wished ardently that there was some way to avoid seeing him. In fact, the sight of his dark face brought a feeling of guilty panic to her breast. A matter in which Ashley was concerned lay on her conscience and she did not wish to discuss it with Rhett, but she knew he would force the discussion, no matter how disinclined she might be.

He drew up at the gate and swung lightly to the ground and she thought, staring nervously at him, that he looked just like an illustration in a book Wade was always pestering her to read aloud.

'All he needs is earrings and a cutlass between his teeth,' she thought. 'Well, pirate or no, he's not going to cut my throat today if I can help it.'

As he came up the walk she called a greeting to him, summoning her sweetest smile. How lucky that she had on her new dress and the becoming cap and looked so pretty! As his eyes went swiftly over her, she knew he thought her pretty, too.

'A new baby! Why, Scarlett, this is a surprise!' he laughed, leaning down to push the blanket away from Ella Lorena's small ugly face.

'Don't be silly,' she said, blushing. 'How are you, Rhett? You've been away a long time.'

'So I have. Let me hold the baby, Scarlett. Oh, I know how to hold babies. I have many strange accomplishments. Well, he certainly looks like Frank. All except the whiskers, but give him time.'

'I hope not. It's a girl.'

'A girl? That's better still. Boys are such nuisances. Don't ever have any more boys, Scarlett.'

It was on the tip of her tongue to reply tartly that she never intended to have any more babies, boys or girls, but she caught herself in time and smiled, casting about quickly in her mind for some topic of conversation that would put off the bad moment when the subject she feared would come up for discussion.

'Did you have a nice trip, Rhett? Where did you go this time?'

'Oh – Cuba – New Orleans – other places. Here, Scarlett, take the baby. She's beginning to slobber and I can't get to my handkerchief. She's a fine baby, I'm sure, but she's wetting my shirt bosom.'

She took the child back into her lap and Rhett settled himself lazily on the banister and took a cigar from a silver case.

'You are always going to New Orleans,' she said and pouted a little. 'And you never will tell me what you do there.'

'I am a hard-working man, Scarlett, and perhaps my business takes me there.'

'Hard working! You!' she laughed impertinently. 'You never worked in your life. You're too lazy. All you ever do is finance Carpetbaggers in their thieving and take half the profits and bribe Yankee officials to let you in on schemes to rob us taxpayers.'

He threw back his head and laughed.

'And how you would love to have money enough to bribe officials, so you could do likewise!'

'The very idea—' She began to ruffle.

'But perhaps you will make enough money to get into bribery on a large scale one day. Maybe you'll get rich off those convicts you leased.'

'Oh,' she said, a little disconcerted, 'how did you find out about my gang so soon?'

'I arrived last night and spent the evening in the Girl of the Period Saloon, where one hears all the news of the town. It's a clearing-house for gossip. Better than a ladies' sewing circle. Everyone told me that you'd leased a gang and put that little plug-ugly, Gallegher, in charge to work them to death.'

'That's a lie,' she said angrily. 'He won't work them to death. I'll see to that.'

'Will you?'

'Of course I will! How can you even insinuate such things?'

'Oh, I do beg your pardon, Mrs Kennedy! I know your motives are always above reproach. However, Johnnie Gallegher is a cold little bully if I ever saw one. Better watch him or you'll be having trouble when the inspector comes around.'

'You tend to your business and I'll tend to mine,' she said indignantly. 'And I don't want to talk about convicts any more. Everybody's been hateful about them. My gang is my own business—And you haven't told me yet what you do in New Orleans. You go there so often that everybody says—' She paused. She had not intended to say so much.

'What do they say?'

'Well – that you have a sweetheart there. That you are going to get married. Are you, Rhett?'

She had been curious about this for so long that she could not refrain from asking the point-blank question. A queer little pang of jealousy jabbed at her at the thought of Rhett getting married, although why that should be she did not know.

His bland eyes grew suddenly alert and he caught her gaze and held it until a little blush crept up into her cheeks.

'Would it matter much to you?'

'Well, I should hate to lose your friendship,' she said primly and, with an attempt at disinterestedness, bent down to pull the blanket closer about Ella Lorena's head.

He laughed suddenly, shortly, and said: 'Look at me, Scarlett.'

She looked up unwillingly, her blush deepening.

'You can tell your curious friends that when I marry it will be because I couldn't get the woman I wanted in any other way. And I've never yet wanted a woman bad enough to marry her.'

Now she was indeed confused and embarrassed, for she remembered the night on this very porch during the siege when he had said: 'I am not a marrying man' and casually suggested that she become his mistress – remembered, too, the terrible day when he was in jail and was shamed by the memory. A slow malicious smile went over his face as he read her eyes.

'But I will satisfy your vulgar curiosity since you ask such pointed questions. It isn't a sweetheart that takes me to New Orleans. It's a child, a little boy.'

'A little boy!' The shock of this unexpected information wiped out her confusion.

'Yes, he is my legal ward and I am responsible for him. He's in school in New Orleans. I go there frequently to see him.'

'And take him presents?' So, she thought, that's how he always knows what kind of presents Wade likes!

'Yes,' he said shortly, unwillingly.

'Well, I never! Is he handsome?'

'Too handsome for his own good.'

'Is he a nice little boy?'

'No. He's a perfect hellion. I wish he had never been born. Boys are troublesome creatures. Is there anything else you'd like to know?'

He looked suddenly angry and his brow was dark, as though he already regretted speaking of the matter at all.

'Well, not if you don't want to tell me any more,' she said loftily, though she was burning for further information. 'But I just can't see you in the rôle of a guardian,' and she laughed, hoping to disconcert him.

'No, I don't suppose you can. Your vision is pretty limited.'

He said no more and smoked his cigar in silence for a while. She cast about for some remark as rude as his but could think of none.

'I would appreciate it if you'd say nothing of this to anyone,' he said finally. 'Though I suppose that asking a woman to keep her mouth shut is asking the impossible.'

'I can keep a secret,' she said with injured dignity.

'Can you? It's nice to learn unsuspected things about friends. Now, stop pouting, Scarlett. I'm sorry I was rude but you deserved it for prying. Give me a smile and let's be pleasant for a minute or two before I take up an unpleasant subject.'

'Oh, dear!' she thought. 'Now he's going to talk about Ashley and the mill!' and she hastened to smile and show her dimple to divert him. 'Where else did you go, Rhett? You haven't been in New Orleans all this time, have you?'

'No, for the last month I've been in Charleston. My father died.'

'Oh, I'm sorry.'

'Don't be. I'm sure he wasn't sorry to die, and I'm sure I'm not sorry he's dead.'

'Rhett, what a dreadful thing to say!'

'It would be much more dreadful if I pretended to be sorry, when I wasn't, wouldn't it? There was never any love lost between us. I cannot remember when the old gentleman did not disapprove of me. I was too much like his own father and he disapproved heartily of his father. And as I grew older his disapproval of me became downright dislike, which, I admit, I did little to change. All the things Father wanted me to do and be were such boring things. And finally he threw me out into the world without a cent and no training whatsoever to be anything but a Charleston gentleman, a good pistol shot and an excellent poker player. And he seemed to take it as a personal affront that I did not starve but put my poker playing to excellent advantage and supported myself royally by gambling. He was so affronted at a Butler becoming a gambler that when I came home for the first time, he forbade my mother to see me. And all during the war when I was blockading out of Charleston, Mother had to lie and slip off to see me. Naturally that didn't increase my love for him.'

'Oh, I didn't know all that!'

'He was what is pointed out as a fine old gentleman of the old school, which means that he was ignorant, thick-headed, intolerant and incapable of thinking along any lines except what other gentlemen of the old school thought. Everyone admired him tremendously for having cut me off and counted me as dead. "If thy right eye offend thee, pluck it out." I was his right eye, his oldest son, and he plucked me out with a vengeance.'

He smiled a little, his eyes hard with amused memory.

'Well, I could forgive all that but I can't forgive what he's done to Mother and my sister since the war ended. They've been practically destitute. The plantation house was burned and the rice fields have gone back to marsh lands. And the town house went for taxes and they've been living in two rooms that aren't fit for darkies. I've sent money to Mother, but Father has sent it back – tainted money, you see! – and several times I've gone to Charleston and given money, on the sly, to my sister. But Father always found out and raised merry hell with her, till her life wasn't worth living, poor girl. And back the money came to me. I don't know how they've lived . . . Yes, I do know. My brother's given what he could, though he hasn't much to give and he won't take anything from me either – speculator's money is unlucky money, you see! And the charity of their friends. Your Aunt Eulalie, she's been very kind. She's one of Mother's best friends, you know. She's given them clothes and— Good God! My mother on charity!'

It was one of the few times she had ever seen him with his mask off, his face hard with honest hatred for his father and distress for his mother.

'Aunt 'Lalie! But, good Heavens, Rhett, she hasn't got anything much above what I send her!'

'Ah, so that's where it comes from! How ill-bred of you, my dear, to brag of such a thing in the face of my humiliation. You must let me reimburse you!'

'With pleasure,' said Scarlett, her mouth suddenly twisting into a grin, and he smiled back.

'Ah, Scarlett, how the thought of a dollar does make your eyes sparkle! Are you sure you haven't some Scotch or perhaps Jewish blood as well as Irish?'

'Don't be hateful! I didn't mean to throw it in your face about Aunt 'Lalie. But honestly, she thinks I'm made of money. She's always writing me for more and, God knows, I've got enough on my hands without supporting all of Charleston. What did your father die of?'

'Genteel starvation, I think – and hope. It served him right. He was willing to let Mother and Rosemary starve with him. Now that he's dead, I can help them. I've bought them a house on the Battery and they've servants to look after them. But of course, they couldn't let it be known that the money came from me.'

'Why not?'

'My dear, surely you know Charleston! You've visited there. My family may be poor but they have a position to uphold. And they couldn't uphold it if it were known that gambling money and speculator's money and Carpetbag money was behind it. No, they gave it out that Father left an enormous life insurance – that he'd beggared himself and starved himself to death to keep up the payments, so that after he died, they'd be provided for. So he is looked upon as an even greater gentleman of the old school than before . . . In fact, a martyr to his family. I hope he's turning in his grave at the knowledge that Mother and Rosemary are comfortable now, in spite of his efforts . . . In a way, I'm sorry he's dead because he wanted to die – was so glad to die.'

'Why?'

'Oh, he really died when Lee surrendered. You know the type. He never could adjust himself to the new times and spent his time talking about the good old days.'

'Rhett, are all old folks like that?' She was thinking of Gerald and what Will had said about him.

'Heavens, no! Just look at your Uncle Henry and that old wild-cat, Mr Merriwether, just to name two. They took a new lease on life when they marched out with the Home Guard and it seems to me that they've gotten younger and more peppery ever since. I met old man Merriwether this morning driving René's pie wagon and cursing the horse like an army mule-skinner. He told me he felt ten years younger since he escaped from the house and his daughter-in-law's coddling and took to driving the wagon. And your Uncle Henry enjoys fighting the Yankees in court and out and defending the widow and the orphan – free of charge, I fear – against the Carpetbaggers. If there hadn't been a war, he'd have retired long ago and nursed his rheumatism. They're young again because they are of use again and feel that they are needed. And they like this new day that gives old men another chance. But there are plenty of people, young people, who feel like my father and your father. They can't and won't adjust, and that brings me to the unpleasant subject I want to discuss with you, Scarlett.'

His sudden shift so disconcerted her that she stammered: 'What – what—' and inwardly groaned: 'Oh, Lord! Now, it's coming. I wonder if I can butter him down?'

'I shouldn't have expected either truth or honour or fair dealing from you, knowing you as I do. But foolishly, I trusted you.'

'I don't know what you mean.'

'I think you do. At any rate, you look very guilty. As I was riding along Ivy Street a while ago, on my way to call on you, who should hail me from behind a hedge but Mrs Ashley Wilkes! Of course, I stopped and chatted with her.'

'Indeed?'

'Yes, we had an enjoyable talk. She told me she had always wanted to let me know how brave she thought I was to have struck a blow for the Confederacy, even at the eleventh hour.'

'Oh, fiddle-dee-dee! Melly's a fool. She might have died that night because you acted so heroic.'

'I imagine she would have thought her life given in a good cause. And when I asked her what she was doing in Atlanta she looked quite surprised at my ignorance and told me that they were living here now and that you had been kind enough to make Mr Wilkes a partner in your mill.'

'Well, what of it?' questioned Scarlett shortly.

'When I lent you the money to buy that mill I made one stipulation, to which you agreed, and that was that it should not go to the support of Ashley Wilkes.'

'You are being very offensive. I've paid you back your money and I own the mill and what I do with it is my own business.'

'Would you mind telling me how you made the money to pay back my loan?'

'I made it selling lumber, of course.'

'You made it with the money I lent you to give you your start. That's what you mean. My money is being used to support Ashley. You are a woman quite without honour and if you hadn't repaid my loan, I'd take great pleasure in calling it in now and selling you out at public auction if you couldn't pay.'

He spoke lightly but there was anger flickering in his eyes.

Scarlett hastily carried the warfare into the enemy's territory.

'Why do you hate Ashley so much? I believe you're jealous of him.'

After she had spoken she could have bitten her tongue, for he threw back his head and laughed until she went red with mortification.

'Add conceit to dishonour,' he said. 'You'll never get over being the belle of the County, will you? You'll always think you're the cutest little trick in shoe-leather and that every man you meet is expiring for love of you.'

'I don't, either!' she cried hotly. 'But I just can't see why you hate Ashley so much and that's the only explanation I can think of.'

'Well, think something else, pretty charmer, for that's the wrong explanation. And as for hating Ashley—I don't hate him any more than I like him. In fact, my only emotion toward him and his kind is pity.'

'Pity?'

'Yes, and a little contempt. Now, swell up like a gobbler and tell me that he is worth a thousand blackguards like me and that I shouldn't dare be so presumptuous as to feel either pity or contempt for him. And when you have finished swelling, I'll tell you what I mean, if you're interested.'

'Well, I'm not.'

'I shall tell you, just the same, for I can't bear for you to go on nursing your pleasant delusion of my jealousy. I pity him because he ought to be dead and he isn't. And I have a contempt for him because he doesn't know what to do with himself now that his world is gone.'

There was something familiar in the idea he expressed. She had a confused memory of having heard similar words but she could not remember when and where. She did not think very hard about it for her anger was hot.

'If you had your way all the decent men in the South would be dead!'

'And if they had their way, I think Ashley's kind would prefer to be dead. Dead with neat stones above them, saying: "Here lies a soldier of the Confederacy, dead for the Southland" or "Dulce et decorum est—" or any of the other popular epitaphs.'

'I don't see why!'

'You never see anything that isn't written in letters a foot high and then shoved under your nose, do you? If they were dead, their troubles would be over, there'd be no problems to face, problems that have no solutions. Moreover, their families would be proud of them through countless generations. And I've heard the dead are happy. Do you suppose Ashley Wilkes is happy?'

'Why, of course—' she began, and then she remembered the look in Ashley's eyes recently and stopped.

'Is he happy or Hugh Elsing or Dr Meade? Any more than my father and your father were happy?'

'Well, perhaps not as happy as they might be, because they've all lost their money.'

He laughed.

'It isn't losing their money, my pet. I tell you it's losing their world – the world they were raised in. They're like fish out of water or cats with wings. They were raised to be certain persons, to do certain things, to occupy certain niches. And those persons and things and niches disappeared forever when General Lee arrived at Appomattox. Oh, Scarlett, don't look so stupid! What is there for Ashley Wilkes to do, now that his home is gone and his plantation taken up for taxes and fine gentlemen are going twenty for a penny? Can he work with his head or his hands? I'll bet you've lost money hand over fist since he took over that mill.'

'I have not!'

'How nice! May I look over your books some Sunday evening when you are at leisure?'

'You can go to the devil and not at your leisure. You can go now, for all I care.'

'My pet, I've been to the devil and he's a very dull fellow. I won't go there again, even for you . . . You took my money when you needed it desperately and you used it. We had an agreement as to how it should be used and you have broken that agreement. Just remember, my precious little cheat, the time will come when you will want to borrow more money from me. You'll want me to bank you, at some incredibly low interest, so you can buy more mills and more mules and build more saloons. And you can whistle for the money.'

'When I need money I'll borrow it from the bank, thank you,' she said coldly, but her breast was heaving with rage.

'Will you? Try to do it. I own plenty of stock in the bank.'

'You do?'

'Yes, I am interested in some honest enterprises.'

'There are other banks—'

'Plenty of them. And if I can manage it, you'll play hell getting a cent from any of them. You can go to the Carpetbag usurers if you want money.'

'I'll go to them with pleasure.'

'You'll go but with little pleasure when you learn their rates of interest. My pretty, there are penalties in the business world for crooked dealing. You should have played straight with me.'

'You're a fine man, aren't you? So rich and powerful yet picking on people who are down, like Ashley and me!'

'Don't put yourself in his class. You aren't down. Nothing will down you. But he is down and he'll stay there unless there's some energetic person behind him, guiding and protecting him as long as he lives. I'm of no mind to have my money used for the benefit of such a person.'

'You didn't mind helping me and I was down and—'

'You were a good risk, my dear, an interesting risk. Why? Because you didn't plump yourself down on your male relatives and sob for the old days. You got out and hustled and now your fortunes are firmly planted on money stolen from a dead man's wallet and money stolen from the Confederacy. You've got murder to your credit, and husband-stealing, attempted fornication, lying and sharp dealing and any amount of chicanery that won't bear close inspection. Admirable things, all of them. They show you to be a person of energy and determination and a good money risk. It's entertaining, helping people who help themselves. I'd lend ten thousand dollars without even a note to that old Roman matron, Mrs Merriwether. She started with a basket of pies and look at her now! A bakery employing half a dozen people, old Grandpa happy with his delivery wagon and that lazy little Creole, René, working hard and liking it . . . Or that poor devil, Tommy Wellburn, who does two men's work with half a man's body and does it well, or – well, I won't go on and bore you.'

'You do bore me. You bore me to distraction,' said Scarlett coldly, hoping to annoy him and divert him from the ever-unfortunate subject of Ashley. But he only laughed shortly and refused to take up the gauntlet.

'People like them are worth helping. But Ashley Wilkes – bah! His breed is of no use or value in an upside-down world like ours. Whenever the world up-ends, his kind is the first to perish. And why not? They don't deserve to survive because they won't fight – don't know how to fight. This isn't the first time the world's been upside down and it won't be the last. It's happened before and it'll happen again. And when it does happen, everyone loses everything and everyone is equal. And then they all start again at taw, with nothing at all. That is, nothing except the cunning of their brains and the strength of their hands. But some people, like Ashley, have neither cunning nor strength or, having them, scruple to use them. And so they go under and they should go under. It's a natural law and the world is better off without them. But there are always a hardy few who come through and, given time, they are right back where they were before the world turned over.'

'You've been poor! You just said that your father turned you out without a penny!' said Scarlett, furious. 'I should think you'd understand and sympathize with Ashley!'

'I do understand,' said Rhett, 'but I'm damned if I sympathize. After the surrender Ashley had much more than I had when I was thrown out. At least, he had friends who took him in, whereas I was Ishmael. But what has Ashley done with himself?'

'If you are comparing him with yourself, you conceited thing, why— He's not like you, thank God! He wouldn't soil his hands as you do, making money with Carpetbaggers and Scallawags and Yankees. He's scrupulous and honourable!'

'But not too scrupulous and honourable to take aid and money from a woman.'

'What else could he have done?'

'Who am I to say? I only know what I did, both when I was thrown out and nowadays. I only know what other men have done. We saw opportunity in the ruin of a civilization and we made the most of our opportunity, some honestly, some shadily, and we are still making the most of it. But the Ashleys of this world have the same chances and don't take them. They just aren't smart, Scarlett, and only the smart deserve to survive.'

She hardly heard what he was saying, for now there was coming back to her the exact memory which had teased her a few minutes before when he first began speaking. She remembered the cold wind that swept the orchard of Tara and Ashley standing by a pile of rails, his eyes looking beyond her. And he had said – what? Some funny foreign name that sounded like profanity and had talked of the end of the world. She had not known what he meant then but now bewildered comprehension was coming to her and with it a sick, weary feeling.

'Why, Ashley said—'

'Yes?'

'Once at Tara he said something about the – a – dusk of the gods and about the end of the world and some such foolishness.'

'Ah, the Götterdämmerung!' Rhett's eyes were sharp with interest. 'And what else?'

'Oh, I don't remember exactly. I wasn't paying much mind. But – yes – something about the strong coming through and the weak being winnowed out.'

'Ah, so he knows. Then that makes it harder for him. Most of them don't know and will never know. They'll wonder all their lives where the lost enchantment has vanished. They'll simply suffer in proud and incompetent silence. But he understands. He knows he's winnowed out.'

'Oh, he isn't! Not while I've got breath in my body.'

He looked at her quietly and his brown face was smooth.

'Scarlett, how did you manage to get his consent to come to Atlanta and take over the mill? Did he struggle very hard against you?'

She had a quick memory of the scene with Ashley after Gerald's funeral and put it from her.

'Why, of course not,' she replied indignantly. 'When I explained to him that I needed his help because I didn't trust that scamp who was running the mill and Frank was too busy to help me and I was going to – well, there was Ella Lorena, you see. He was very glad to help me out.'

'Sweet are the uses of motherhood! So that's how you got around him. Well, you've got him where you want him now, poor devil, as shackled to you by obligations as any of your convicts are by their chains. And I wish you both joy. But, as I said at the beginning of this discussion, you'll never get another cent out of me for any of your little unladylike schemes, my double-dealing lady.'

She was smarting with anger and with disappointment as well. For some time she had been planning to borrow more money from Rhett to buy a lot downtown and start a lumber yard there.

'I can do without your money,' she cried. 'I'm making money out of Johnnie Gallegher's mill, plenty of it, now that I don't use free darkies, and I have some money out on mortgages and we are coining cash at the store from the darky trade.'

'Yes, so I heard. How clever of you to rook the helpless and the widow and the orphan and the ignorant! But if you must steal, Scarlett, why not steal from the rich and strong instead of the poor and weak? From Robin Hood on down to now, that's been considered highly moral.'

'Because,' said Scarlett shortly, 'it's a sight easier and safer to steal – as you call it – from the poor.'

He laughed silently, his shoulders shaking.

'You're a fine honest rogue, Scarlett!'

A rogue! Queer that that term should hurt. She wasn't a rogue, she told herself vehemently. At least, that wasn't what she wanted to be. She wanted to be a great lady. For a moment her mind went swiftly down the years and she saw her mother, moving with a sweet swish of skirts and a faint fragrance of sachet, her small busy hands tireless in the service of others, loved, respected, cherished. And suddenly her heart was sick.

'If you are trying to devil me,' she said tiredly, 'it's no use. I know I'm not as – scrupulous as I should be these days. Not as kind and as pleasant as I was brought up to be. But I can't help it, Rhett. Truly, I can't. What else could I have done? What would have happened to me, to Wade, to Tara and all of us if I'd been – gentle when that Yankee came to Tara? I should have been – but I don't even want to think of that. And when Jonas Wilkerson was going to take the home place, suppose I'd been – kind and scrupulous? Where would we all be now? And if I'd been sweet and simple-minded and not nagged Frank about bad debts we'd – oh, well. Maybe I am a rogue, but I won't be a rogue forever, Rhett. But during these past years – and even now – what else could I have done? How else could I have acted? I've felt that I was trying to row a heavily loaded boat in a storm. I've had so much trouble just trying to keep afloat that I couldn't be bothered about things that didn't matter, things I could part with easily and not miss, like good manners and – well, things like that. I've been too afraid my boat would be swamped and so I've dumped overboard the things that seemed least important.'

'Pride and honour and truth and virtue and kindliness,' he enumerated silkily. 'You are right, Scarlett. They aren't important when a boat is sinking. But look around you at your friends. Either they are bringing their boats ashore safely with cargoes intact or they are content to go down with all flags flying.'

'They are a passel of fools,' she said shortly. 'There's a time for all things. When I've got plenty of money, I'll be nice as you please, too. Butter won't melt in my mouth. I can afford to be then.'

'You can afford to be – but you won't. It's hard to salvage jettisoned cargo and, if it is retrieved, it's usually irreparably damaged. And I fear that when you can afford to fish up the honour and virtue and kindness you've thrown overboard, you'll find they have suffered a sea change and not, I fear, into something rich and strange . . . '

He rose suddenly and picked up his hat.

'You are going?'

'Yes. Aren't you relieved? I leave you to what remains of your conscience.'

He paused and looked down at the baby, putting out a finger for the child to grip.

'I suppose Frank is bursting with pride?'

'Oh, of course.'

'Has a lot of plans for this baby, I suppose?'

'Oh, well, you know how silly men are about their babies.'

'Then, tell him,' said Rhett, and stopped short, an odd look on his face, 'tell him if he wants to see his plans for his child work out, he'd better stay home at night more often than he's doing.'

'What do you mean?'

'Just what I say. Tell him to stay home.'

'Oh, you vile creature! To insinuate that poor Frank would—'

'Oh, good Lord!' Rhett broke into a roar of laughter. 'I didn't mean he was running around with women! Frank! Oh, good Lord!'

He went down the steps still laughing.

Chapter XLIV

The March afternoon was windy and cold, and Scarlett pulled the lap-robe high under her arms as she drove out the Decatur road toward Johnnie Gallegher's mill. Driving alone was hazardous these days and she knew it, more hazardous than ever before, for now the negroes were completely out of hand. As Ashley had prophesied, there had been hell to pay since the legislature refused to ratify the amendment. The stout refusal had been like a slap in the face of the furious North and retaliation had come swiftly. The North was determined to force the negro vote on the state and, to this end, Georgia had been declared in rebellion and put under the strictest martial law. Georgia's very existence as a state had been wiped out and it had become, with Florida and Alabama, 'Military District Number Three', under the command of a Federal general.

If life had been insecure and frightening before this, it was doubly so now. The military regulations which had seemed so stringent the year before were now mild by comparison with the ones issued by General Pope. Confronted with the prospect of negro rule, the future seemed dark and hopeless, and the embittered state smarted and writhed helplessly. As for the negroes, their new importance went to their heads, and, realizing that they had the Yankee Army behind them, their outrages increased. No one was safe from them.

In this wild and fearful time, Scarlett was frightened – frightened but determined, and she still made her rounds alone, with Frank's pistol tucked in the upholstery of the buggy. She silently cursed the legislature for bringing this worse disaster upon them all. What good had it done, this fine brave stand, this gesture which everyone called gallant? It had just made matters so much worse.

As she drew near the path that led down through the bare trees into the creek bottom where the Shantytown settlement was, she clucked to the horse to quicken his speed. She always felt uneasy driving past this dirty, sordid cluster of discarded army tents and slab cabins. It had the worst reputation of any spot in or near Atlanta, for here lived in filth outcast negroes, black prostitutes and a scattering of poor whites of the lowest order. It was rumoured to be the refuge of negro and white criminals and was the first place the Yankee soldiers searched when they wanted a man. Shootings and cuttings went on here with such regularity that the authorities seldom troubled to investigate and generally left the Shantytowners to settle their own dark affairs. Back in the woods there was a still that manufactured a cheap quality of corn whisky and, by night, the cabins in the creek bottoms resounded with drunken yells and curses.

Even the Yankees admitted that it was a plague-spot and should be wiped out, but they took no steps in this direction. Indignation was loud among the inhabitants of Atlanta and Decatur who were forced to use the road for travel between the two towns. Men went by Shantytown with their pistols loosened in their holsters and nice women never willingly passed it, even under the protection of their men, for usually there were drunken negro slatterns sitting along the road, hurling insults and shouting coarse words.

As long as she had Archie beside her, Scarlett had not given Shantytown a thought, because not even the most impudent negro woman dared laugh in her presence. But since she had been forced to drive alone, there had been any number of annoying, maddening incidents. The negro sluts seemed to try themselves whenever she drove by. There was nothing she could do except ignore them and boil with rage. She could not even take comfort in airing her troubles to her neighbours or family because the neighbours would say triumphantly: 'Well, what else did you expect?' And her family would take on dreadfully again and try to stop her. And she had no intention of stopping her trips.

Thank Heaven, there were no ragged women along the roadside today! As she passed the trail leading down to the settlement she looked with distaste at the group of shacks squatting in the hollow in the dreary slant of the afternoon sun. There was a chill wind blowing, and as she passed there came to her nose the mingled smells of wood smoke, frying pork and untended privies. Averting her nose, she flapped the reins smartly across the horse's back and hurried him past and around the bend of the road.

Just as she was beginning to draw a breath of relief, her heart rose in her throat with sudden fright, for a huge negro slipped silently from behind a large oak tree. She was frightened but not enough to lose her wits and, in an instant, the horse was pulled up and she had Frank's pistol in her hand.

'What do you want?' she cried with all the sternness she could muster. The big negro ducked back behind the oak, and the voice that answered was frightened.

'Lawd, Miss Scarlett, doan shoot Big Sam!'

Big Sam! For a moment she could not take in his words. Big Sam, the foreman of Tara whom she had seen last in the days of the siege. What on earth . . .

'Come out of there and let me see if you are really Sam!'

Reluctantly he slid out of his hiding-place, a giant ragged figure, barefooted, clad in denim breeches and a blue Union uniform jacket that was far too short and tight for his big frame. When she saw it was really Big Sam, she shoved the pistol down into the upholstery and smiled with pleasure.

'Oh, Sam! How nice to see you!'

Sam galloped over to the buggy, his eyes rolling with joy and his white teeth flashing, and clutched her outstretched hand with two black hands as big as hams. His watermelon-pink tongue lapped out, his whole body wiggled and his joyful contortions were as ludicrous as the gambollings of a mastiff.

'Mah Lawd, it sho is good ter see some of de fambly agin!' he cried, scrunching her hand until she felt that the bones would crack. 'Huccome you got so mean lak, totin' a gun, Miss Scarlett?'

'So many mean folks these days, Sam, that I have to tote it. What on earth are you doing in a nasty place like Shantytown, you, a respectable darky? And why haven't you been into town to see me?'

'Law'm, Miss Scarlett, Ah doan lib in Shantytown. Ah jes' bidin' hyah fer a spell. Ah wouldn' lib in dat place fer nuthin'. Ah nebber in mah life seed sech trashy niggers. An' Ah din' know you wuz in 'Lanta. Ah thought you wuz at Tara. Ah wuz aimin' ter come home ter Tara soon as Ah got de chance.'

'Have you been living in Atlanta ever since the siege?'

'No, Ma'm! Ah been trabellin'!' He released her hand and she painfully flexed it to see if the bones were intact. ''Member w'en you seed me las'?'

Scarlett remembered the hot day before the siege when she and Rhett had sat in the carriage and the gang of negroes with Big Sam at their head had marched down the dusty street toward the entrenchments singing 'Go Down, Moses'. She nodded.

'Well, Ah wuked lak a dawg diggin' bresswuks an' fillin' san'-bags, tell de Confedruts lef' 'Lanta. De cap'n gempmum whut had me in charge, he wuz kilt an' dar warn't nobody ter tell Big Sam whut ter do, so Ah jes' lay low in de bushes. Ah thought Ah'd try ter git home ter Tara, but den Ah hear dat all de country roun' Tara done buhnt up. 'Sides, Ah din' hab no way ter git back an' Ah wuz sceered de patterollers pick me up, kase Ah din' hab no pass. Den de Yankees come in an' a Yankee gempmum, he wuz a cunnel, he tek a shine ter me an' he keep me ter ten' ter his hawse an' his boots.

'Yas, Ma'm! Ah sho did feel biggity, bein' a body serbant lak Poke, w'en Ah ain' nuthin' but a fe'el han'. Ah ain' tell de Cunnel Ah wuz a fe'el han' an' he— Well, Miss Scarlett, Yankees is iggerunt folks! He din' know de diffunce! So Ah stayed wid him an' Ah went ter Sabannah wid him w'en Gin'ul Sherman went dar, an' fo' Gawd, Miss Scarlett, Ah nebber seed sech awful goin'-ons as Ah seed on de way ter Sabannah! A-stealin' an' a-buhnin' – did dey buhn Tara, Miss Scarlett?'

'They set fire to it, but we put it out.'

'Well'm, Ah sho glad ter hear dat. Tara mah home an' Ah is aimin' ter go back dar. An' w'en de wah ober, de Cunnel he say ter me: "You, Sam! You come on back Nawth wid me. Ah pay you good wages." Well'm, lak all de niggers, Ah wuz honin' ter try disyere freedom fo' Ah went home, so Ah goes Nawth wid de Cunnel. Yas'm, us went ter Washin'ton an' Noo Yawk an' den ter Bawston whar de Cunnel lib. Yas, Ma'm, Ah's a trabelled nigger! Miss Scarlett, dar's mo' hawses and cah'iges on dem Yankee streets dan you kin shake a stick at! Ah wuz sceered all de time Ah wuz gwine git runned ober!'

'Did you like it up North, Sam?'

Sam scratched his woolly head.

'Ah did – an' Ah din't. De Cunnel, he a mighty fine man an' he unnerstan' niggers. But his wife, she sumpin' else. His wife, she call me "Mister" fust time she seed me. Yas'm, she do dat an' Ah lak ter drap in mah tracks w'en she do it. De Cunnel, he tell her ter call me "Sam" an' den she do it. But all dem Yankee folks, fust time dey meet me, dey call me "Mist' O'Hara". An' dey ast me ter set down wid dem, lak Ah wuz jes' as good as dey wuz. Well, Ah ain' nebber set down wid w'ite folks an' Ah is too ole ter learn. Dey treat me lak Ah jes' as good as dey wuz, Miss Scarlett, but in dere hearts, dey din' like me – dey din' lak no niggers. An' dey wuz sceered of me, kase Ah's so big. An' dey wuz allus astin' me 'bout de bloodhoun's dat chase me an' de beatin's Ah got. An', Lawd, Miss Scarlett, Ah ain' nebber got no beatin's! You know Mist' Gerald ain' gwine let nobody beat a 'spensive nigger lak me!

'W'en Ah tell dem dat an' tell dem how good Miss Ellen ter de niggers, an' how she set up a whole week wid me w'en Ah had de pneumony, dey doan b'lieve me. An', Miss Scarlett, Ah got ter honin' fer Miss Ellen an' Tara, tell it look lak Ah kain stan' it no longer, an' one night Ah lit out fer home, an' Ah rid de freight cahs all de way down ter 'Lanta. Ef you buy me a ticket ter Tara, Ah sho be glad ter git home. Ah sho be glad ter see Miss Ellen and Mist' Gerald agin. Ah done had nuff freedom. Ah wants somebody ter feed me good vittles reg'lar, and tell me whut ter do an' whut not ter do, an' look affer me w'en Ah gits sick. S'pose Ah gits de pneumony agin? Is dat Yankee lady gwine tek keer of me? No, Ma'm! She gwine call me "Mist' O'Hara" but she ain' gwine nuss me. But Miss Ellen, she gwine nuss me, do Ah git sick an' – whut's de mattuh, Miss Scarlett?'

'Pa and Mother are both dead, Sam.'

'Daid? Is you funnin' wid me, Miss Scarlett? Dat ain' no way ter treat me!'

'I'm not funning. It's true. Mother died when Sherman's men came through Tara and Pa – he went last June. Oh, Sam, don't cry. Please don't! If you do, I'll cry too. Sam, don't! I just can't stand it. Let's don't talk about it now. I'll tell you all about it some other time . . . Miss Suellen is at Tara and she's married to a mighty fine man, Mr Will Benteen. And Miss Carreen, she's in a—' Scarlett paused. She could never make plain to the weeping giant what a convent was. 'She's living in Charleston now. But Pork and Prissy are at Tara . . . There, Sam, wipe your nose. Do you really want to go home?'

'Yas'm, but it ain' gwine be lak Ah thought wid Miss Ellen an'—'

'Sam, how'd you like to stay here in Atlanta and work for me? I need a driver and I need one bad with so many mean folks around these days.'

'Yas'm. You sho do. Ah been aimin' ter say you ain' got no bizness drivin' 'round by yo'seff, Miss Scarlett. You ain' got no notion how mean some niggers is dese days, specially dem whut live hyah in Shantytown. It ain' safe fer you. Ah ain' been in Shantytown but two days, but Ah hear dem talk 'bout you. An' yestiddy w'en you druv by an' dem trashy black wenches holler at you, Ah recernize you but you went by so fas' Ah couldn' ketch you. But Ah sho tan de hides of dem niggers! Ah sho did. Ain' you notice dar ain' none of dem roun' hyah terday?'

'I did notice and I certainly thank you, Sam. Well, how would you like to be my carriage man?'

'Miss Scarlett, thankee, Ma'm, but Ah specs Ah better go ter Tara.'

Big Sam looked down and his bare toe traced aimless marks in the road. There was a furtive uneasiness about him.

'Now, why? I'll pay you good wages. You must stay with me.'

The big black face, stupid and as easily read as a child's, looked up at her and there was fear in it. He came closer and, leaning over the side of the buggy, whispered: 'Miss Scarlett, Ah got ter git outer 'Lanta. Ah got ter git ter Tara whar dey woan fine me. Ah – Ah done kilt a man.'

'A darky?'

'No'm. A w'ite man. A Yankee sojer and dey's lookin' fer me. Dat de reason Ah'm hyah at Shantytown.'

'How did it happen?'

'He wuz drunk an' he said sumpin' Ah couldn' tek noways an' Ah got mah han's on his neck – an' Ah din' mean ter kill him, Miss Scarlett, but mah han's is pow'ful strong, an' fo' Ah knowed it, he wuz kilt. An' Ah wuz so sceered Ah din' know whut ter do! So Ah come out hyah ter hide an' w'en Ah seed you go by yestiddy, Ah says, "Bress Gawd! Dar Miss Scarlett! She tek keer of me. She ain' gwine let de Yankees git me. She sen' me back ter Tara.'

'You say they're after you? They know you did it?'

'Yas'm, Ah's so big dar ain' no mistakin' me. Ah spec Ah's de bigges' nigger in 'Lanta. Dey done been out hyah already affer me las' night but a nigger gal, she hid me in a cabe ober in de woods, tell dey wuz gone.'

Scarlett sat frowning for a moment. She was not in the least alarmed or distressed that Sam had committed murder, but she was disappointed that she could not have him as a driver. A big negro like Sam would be as good a bodyguard as Archie. Well, she must get him safe to Tara somehow, for of course the authorities must not get him. He was too valuable a darky to be hanged. Why, he was the best foreman Tara had ever had! It did not enter Scarlett's mind that he was free. He still belonged to her, like Pork and Mammy and Peter and Cookie and Prissy. He was still 'one of our family' and, as such, must be protected.

'I'll send you to Tara tonight,' she said finally. 'Now, Sam, I've got to drive out the road a piece, but I ought to be back here before sundown. You be waiting here for me when I come back. Don't tell anyone where you are going and if you've got a hat, bring it along to hide your face.'

'Ah ain' got no hat.'

'Well, here's a quarter. You buy a hat from one of those shanty darkies and meet me here.'

'Yas'm.' His face glowed with relief at once more having someone to tell him what to do.

Scarlett drove on thoughtfully. Will would certainly welcome a good field hand at Tara. Pork had never been any good in the fields and never would be any good. With Sam on the place, Pork could come to Atlanta and join Dilcey as she had promised him when Gerald died.

When she reached the mill the sun was setting and it was later than she cared to be out. Johnnie Gallegher was standing in the doorway of the miserable shack that served as cook-room for the little lumber camp. Sitting on a log in front of the slab-sided shack that was their sleeping quarters were four of the five convicts Scarlett had apportioned to Johnnie's mill. Their convict uniforms were dirty and foul with sweat, shackles clanked between their ankles when they moved tiredly, and there was an air of apathy and despair about them. They were a thin, unwholesome lot, Scarlett thought, peering sharply at them, and when she had leased them, so short a time before, they were an upstanding crew. They did not even raise their eyes as she dismounted from the buggy but Johnnie turned toward her, carelessly dragging off his hat. His little brown face was as hard as a nut as he greeted her.

'I don't like the look of the men,' she said abruptly. 'They don't look well. Where's the other one?'

'Says he's sick,' said Johnnie laconically. 'He's in the bunk-house.'

'What ails him?'

'Laziness, mostly.'

'I'll go see him.'

'Don't do that. He's probably nekkid. I'll tend to him. He'll be back at work tomorrow.'

Scarlett hesitated and saw one of the convicts raise a weary head and give Johnnie a stare of intense hatred before he looked at the ground again.

'Have you been whipping these men?'

'Now, Mrs Kennedy, begging your pardon, who's running this mill? You put me in charge and told me to run it. You said I'd have a free hand. You ain't got no complaints to make of me, have you? Ain't I making twice as much for you as Mr Elsing did?'

'Yes, you are,' said Scarlett, but a shiver went over her, like a goose walking across her grave.

There was something sinister about this camp with its ugly shacks, something which had not been here when Hugh Elsing had it. There was a loneliness, an isolation about it that chilled her. These convicts were so far away from everything, so completely at the mercy of Johnnie Gallegher, and if he chose to whip them or otherwise mistreat them, she would probably never know about it. The convicts would be afraid to complain to her for fear of worse punishment after she was gone.

'The men look thin. Are you giving them enough to eat? God knows, I spend enough money on their food to make them fat as hogs. The flour and pork alone cost thirty dollars last month. What are you giving them for supper?'

She stepped over to the cook shack and looked in. A fat mulatto woman, who was leaning over a rusty old stove, dropped a half curtsy as she saw Scarlett and went on stirring a pot in which black-eyed peas were cooking. Scarlett knew Johnnie Gallegher lived with her but thought it best to ignore the fact. She saw that except for the peas and a pan of corn pone there was no other food being prepared.

'Haven't you got anything else for these men?'

'No'm.'

'Haven't you got any side meat in these peas?'

'No'm.'

'No boiling bacon in the peas? But black-eyed peas are no good without bacon. There's no strength to them. Why isn't there any bacon?'

'Mist' Johnnie, he say dar ain' no use puttin' in no side meat.'

'You'll put bacon in. Where do you keep your supplies?'

The negro woman rolled frightened eyes toward the small closet that served as a pantry and Scarlett threw the door open. There was an open barrel of cornmeal on the floor, a small sack of flour, a pound of coffee, a little sugar, a gallon jug of sorghum and two hams. One of the hams sitting on the shelf had been recently cooked and only one or two slices had been cut from it. Scarlett turned in a fury on Johnnie Gallegher and met his coldly angry gaze.

'Where are the five sacks of white flour I sent out last week? And the sugar sack and the coffee? And I had five hams sent and ten pounds of side meat and God knows how many bushels of yams and Irish potatoes. Well, where are they? You can't have used them all in a week if you fed the men five meals a day. You've sold them! That's what you've done, you thief! Sold my good supplies and put the money in your pocket and fed these men on dried peas and corn pone. No wonder they look so thin. Get out of the way.'

She stormed past him to the doorway.

'You, man, there on the end – yes, you! Come here!'

The man rose and walked awkwardly toward her, his shackles clanking, and she saw that his bare ankles were red and raw from the chafing of the iron.

'When did you last have ham?'

The man looked down at the ground.

'Speak up!'

Still the man stood silent and abject. Finally he raised his eyes, looked Scarlett in the face imploringly and dropped his gaze again.

'Scared to talk, eh? Well, go in that pantry and get that ham off the shelf. Rebecca, give him your knife. Take it out to those men and divide it up. Rebecca, make some biscuits and coffee for the men. And serve plenty of sorghum. Start now, so I can see you do it.'

'Dat's Mist' Johnnie's privut flour an' coffee,' Rebecca muttered frightenedly.

'Mr Johnnie's, my foot! I suppose it's his private ham too. You do what I say. Get busy. Johnnie Gallegher, come out to the buggy with me.'

She stalked across the littered yard and climbed into the buggy, noticing with grim satisfaction that the men were tearing at the ham and cramming bits into their mouths voraciously. They looked as if they feared it would be taken from them at any minute.

'You are a rare scoundrel!' she cried furiously to Johnnie as he stood at the wheel, his hat pushed back from his lowering brow. 'And you can just hand over to me the price of my supplies. In the future, I'll bring you provisions every day instead of ordering them by the month. Then you can't cheat me.'

'In the future I won't be here,' said Johnnie Gallegher.

'You mean you are quitting!'

For a moment it was on Scarlett's hot tongue to cry: 'Go and good riddance!' but the cool hand of caution stopped her. If Johnnie should quit, what would she do? He had been doubling the amount of lumber Hugh turned out. And just now she had a big order, the biggest she had ever had and a rush order at that. She had to get that lumber into Atlanta. If Johnnie quit, whom would she get to take over the mill?

'Yes, I'm quitting. You put me in complete charge here and you told me that all you expected of me was as much lumber as I could possibly get out. You didn't tell me how to run my business then and I'm not aiming to have you start now. How I get the lumber out is no affair of yours. You can't complain that I've fallen down on my bargain. I've made money for you and I've earned my salary – and what I could pick up on the side, too. And here you come out here, interfering, asking questions and breaking my authority in front of the men. How can you expect me to keep discipline after this? What if the men do get an occasional lick? The lazy scum deserve worse. What if they ain't fed up and pampered? They don't deserve nothing better. Either you tend to your business and let me tend to mine or I quit tonight.'

His hard little face looked flintier than ever and Scarlett was in a quandary. If he quit tonight, what would she do? She couldn't stay here all night guarding the convicts!

Something of her dilemma showed in her eyes for Johnnie's expression changed subtly and some of the hardness went out of his face. There was an easy agreeable note in his voice when he spoke.

'It's getting late, Mrs Kennedy, and you'd better be getting on home. We ain't going to fall out over a little thing like this, are we? S'pose you take ten dollars out of my next month's wages and let's call it square.'

Scarlett's eyes went unwillingly to the miserable group gnawing on the ham and she thought of the sick man lying in the windy shack. She ought to get rid of Johnnie Gallegher. He was a thief and a brutal man. There was no telling what he did to the convicts when she wasn't there. But, on the other hand, he was smart and, God knows, she needed a smart man. Well, she couldn't part with him now. He was making money for her. She'd just have to see to it that the convicts got their proper rations in the future.

'I'll take twenty dollars out of your wages,' she said shortly, 'and I'll be back and discuss the matter further in the morning.'

She picked up the reins. But she knew there would be no further discussion. She knew that the matter had ended there and she knew Johnnie knew it.

As she drove off down the path to the Decatur road her conscience battled with her desire for money. She knew she had no business exposing human lives to the hard little man's mercies. If he should cause the death of one of them she would be as guilty as he was, for she had kept him in charge after learning of his brutalities. But, on the other hand – well, on the other hand, men had no business getting to be convicts. If they broke laws and got caught, then they deserved what they got. This partly salved her conscience but as she drove down the road the dull thin faces of the convicts would keep coming back into her mind.

'Oh, I'll think of them later,' she decided, and pushed the thought into the lumber-room of her mind and shut the door upon it.

The sun had completely gone when she reached the bend in the road above Shantytown and the woods about her were dark. With the disappearance of the sun, a bitter chill had fallen on the twilight world and a cold wind blew through the dark woods, making the bare boughs crack and the dead leaves rustle. She had never been out this late by herself and she was uneasy and wished herself home.

Big Sam was nowhere to be seen and, as she drew rein to wait for him, she worried about his absence, fearing the Yankees might have already picked him up. Then she heard footsteps coming up the path from the settlement and a sigh of relief went through her lips. She'd certainly dress Sam down for keeping her waiting.

But it wasn't Sam who came round the bend.

It was a big ragged white man and a squat black negro with shoulders and chest like a gorilla. Swiftly she flapped the reins on the horse's back and clutched the pistol. The horse started to trot and suddenly shied as the white man threw up his hand.

'Lady,' he said, 'can you give me a quarter? I'm sure hungry.'

'Get out of the way,' she answered, keeping her voice as steady as she could. 'I haven't got any money. Giddap.'

With a sudden swift movement the man's hand was on the horse's bridle.

'Grab her!' he shouted to the negro. 'She's probably got her money in her bosom!'

What happened next was like a nightmare to Scarlett, and it all happened so quickly. She brought up her pistol swiftly and some instinct told her not to fire at the white man for fear of shooting the horse. As the negro came running to the buggy, his black face twisted in a leering grin, she fired point-blank at him. Whether or not she hit him, she never knew, but the next minute the pistol was wrenched from her hand by a grasp that almost broke her wrist. The negro was beside her, so close that she could smell the rank odour of him as he tried to drag her over the buggy side. With her one free hand she fought madly, clawing at his face, and then she felt his big hand at her throat and, with a ripping noise, her basque was torn open from neck to waist. Then the black hand fumbled between her breasts, and terror and revulsion such as she had never known came over her and she screamed like an insane woman.

'Shut her up! Drag her out!' cried the white man, and the black hand fumbled across Scarlett's face to her mouth. She bit as savagely as she could and then screamed again, and through her screaming she heard the white man swear and realized that there was a third man in the dark road. The black hand dropped from her mouth and the negro leaped away as Big Sam charged at him.

'Run, Miss Scarlett!' yelled Sam, grappling with the negro; and Scarlett, shaking and screaming, clutched up the reins and whip and laid them both over the horse. It went off at a jump and she felt the wheels pass over something soft, something resistant. It was the white man who lay in the road where Sam had knocked him down.

Maddened by terror, she lashed the horse again and again and it struck a gait that made the buggy rock and sway. Through her terror she was conscious of the sound of feet running behind her and she screamed at the horse to go faster. If that black ape got her again, she would die before he even got his hands upon her.

A voice yelled behind her: 'Miss Scarlett! Stop!'

Without slacking, she looked trembling over her shoulder and saw Big Sam racing down the road behind her, his long legs working like hard-driven pistons. She drew rein as he came up and he flung himself into the buggy, his big body crowding her to one side. Sweat and blood were streaming down his face as he panted:

'Is you hu't? Did dey hu't you?'

She could not speak, but seeing the direction of his eyes and their quick averting, she realized that her basque was open to the waist and her bare bosom and corset-cover were showing. With a shaking hand she clutched the two edges together and bowing her head began to cry in terrified sobs.

'Gimme dem lines,' said Sam, snatching the reins from her. 'Hawse, mek tracks!'

The whip cracked and the startled horse went off at a wild gallop that threatened to throw the buggy into the ditch.

'Ah hope Ah done kill dat black baboon. But ah din' wait ter fine out,' he panted. 'But ef he hahmed you, Miss Scarlett, Ah'll go back an' mek sho of it.'

'No – no – drive on quickly,' she sobbed.

Chapter XLV

That night, when Frank deposited her and Aunt Pitty and the children at Melanie's and rode off down the street with Ashley, Scarlett could have burst with rage and hurt. How could he go off to a political meeting on this of all nights in the world? A political meeting! And on the same night when she had been attacked, when anything might have happened to her! It was unfeeling and selfish of him. But then, he had taken the whole affair with maddening calm, ever since Sam had carried her sobbing into the house, her basque gaping to the waist. He hadn't clawed his beard even once when she cried out her story. He had just questioned gently: 'Sugar, are you hurt – or just scared?'

Wrath mingling with her tears she had been unable to answer, and Sam had volunteered that she was just scared.

'Ah got dar fo' dey done mo'n t'ar her dress.'

'You're a good boy, Sam, and I won't forget what you've done. If there's anything I can do for you—'

'Yassah, you kin sen' me ter Tara, quick as you kin. De Yankees is affer me.'

Frank had listened to this statement calmly too, and had asked no questions. He had looked very much as he did the night Tony came beating on their door, as though this was an exclusively masculine affair and one to be handled with a minimum of words and emotions.

'You go get in the buggy. I'll have Peter drive you as far as Rough and Ready tonight and you can hide in the woods till morning and then catch the train to Jonesboro. It'll be safer . . . Now, Sugar, stop crying. It's all over now and you aren't really hurt. Miss Pitty, could I have your smelling salts? And, Mammy, fetch Miss Scarlett a glass of wine.'

Scarlett had burst into renewed tears, this time tears of rage. She wanted comforting, indignation, threats of vengeance. She would even have preferred him storming at her, saying that this was just what he had warned her would happen – anything rather than have him take it all so casually and treat her danger as a matter of small moment. He was nice and gentle, of course, but in an absent way as if he had something far more important on his mind.

And that important thing had turned out to be a small political meeting.

She could hardly believe her ears when he told her to change her dress and get ready for him to escort her over to Melanie's for the evening. He must know how harrowing her experience had been, must know she did not want to spend an evening at Melanie's when her tired body and jangled nerves cried out for the warm relaxation of bed and blankets – with a hot brick to make her toes tingle and a hot toddy to soothe her fears. If he really loved her, nothing could have forced him from her side on this of all nights. He would have stayed home and held her hand and told her over and over that he would have died if anything had happened to her. And when he came home tonight and she had him alone, she would certainly tell him so.

Melanie's small parlour looked as serene as it usually did on nights when Frank and Ashley were away and the women gathered together to sew. The room was warm and cheerful in the firelight. The lamp on the table shed a quiet yellow glow on the four smooth heads bent to their needlework. Four skirts billowed modestly, eight small feet were daintily placed on low hassocks. The quiet breathing of Wade, Ella and Beau came through the open door of the nursery. Archie sat on a stool by the hearth, his back against the fireplace, his cheek distended with tobacco, whittling industriously on a bit of wood. The contrast between the dirty, hairy old man and the four neat, fastidious ladies was as great as though he were a grizzled, vicious old watchdog and they four small kittens.

Melanie's soft voice, tinged with indignation, went on and on as she told of the recent outburst of temperament on the part of the Lady Harpists. Unable to agree with the Gentlemen's Glee Club as to the programme for their next recital, the ladies had waited on Melanie that afternoon and announced their intention of withdrawing completely from the Musical Circle. It had taken all of Melanie's diplomacy to persuade them to defer their decision.

Scarlett, overwrought, could have screamed: 'Oh, damn the Lady Harpists!' She wanted to talk about her dreadful experience. She was bursting to relate it in detail, so she could ease her own fright by frightening the others. She wanted to tell how brave she had been, just to assure herself by the sound of her own words that she had, indeed, been brave. But every time she brought up the subject, Melanie deftly steered the conversation into other and innocuous channels. This irritated Scarlett almost beyond endurance. They were as mean as Frank.

How could they be so calm and placid when she had just escaped so terrible a fate? They weren't even displaying common courtesy in denying her the relief of talking about it.

The events of the afternoon had shaken her more than she cared to admit, even to herself. Every time she thought of that malignant black face peering at her from the shadows of the twilight forest road, she fell to trembling. When she thought of the black hand at her bosom and what would have happened if Big Sam had not appeared, she bent her head lower and squeezed her eyes tightly shut. The longer she sat silent in the peaceful room, trying to sew, listening to Melanie's voice, the tighter her nerves stretched. She felt that at any moment she would actually hear them break with the same pinging sound a banjo string makes when it snaps.

Archie's whittling annoyed her and she frowned at him. Suddenly it seemed odd that he should be sitting there occupying himself with a piece of wood. Usually he lay flat on the sofa, during the evenings when he was on guard, and slept and snored so violently that his long beard leaped into the air with each rumbling breath. It was odder still that neither Melanie nor India hinted to him that he should spread a paper on the floor to catch his litter of shavings. He had already made a perfect mess on the hearth-rug but they did not seem to have noticed it.

While she watched him, Archie turned suddenly toward the fire and spat a stream of tobacco juice on it with such vehemence that India, Melanie and Pitty leaped as though a bomb had exploded.

'*Need* you expectorate so loudly?' cried India in a voice that cracked with nervous annoyance. Scarlett looked at her in surprise for India was always so self-contained.

Archie gave her look for look.

'I reckon I do,' he answered coldly and spat again. Melanie gave a little frowning glance at India.

'I was always so glad dear Papa didn't chew,' began Pitty, and Melanie, her frown creasing deeper, swung on her and spoke sharper words than Scarlett had ever heard her speak.

'Oh, do hush, Auntie! You're so tactless.'

'Oh, dear!' Pitty dropped her sewing in her lap and her mouth pursed up in hurt. 'I declare, I don't know what ails you all tonight. You and India are just as jumpy and cross as two old sticks.'

No one answered her. Melanie did not even apologize for her crossness but went back to her sewing with small violence.

'You're taking stitches an inch long,' declared Pitty with some satisfaction. 'You'll have to take every one of them out. What's the matter with you?'

But Melanie still did not answer.

Was there anything the matter with them? Scarlett wondered. Had she been too absorbed with her own fears to notice? Yes, despite Melanie's attempts to make the evening appear like any one of fifty they had all spent together, there was a difference in the atmosphere, a nervousness that could not be altogether due to their alarm and shock at what happened that afternoon. Scarlett stole glances at her companions and intercepted a look from India. It discomfited her because it was a long, measuring glance that carried in its cold depths something stronger than hate, something more insulting than contempt.

'As though she thought I was to blame for what happened,' Scarlett thought indignantly.

India turned from her to Archie and, all annoyance at him gone from her face, gave him a look of veiled anxious inquiry. But he did not meet her eyes. He did, however, look at Scarlett, staring at her in the same cold hard way India had done.

Silence fell dully in the room as Melanie did not take up the conversation again and, in the silence, Scarlett heard the rising wind outside. It suddenly began to be a most unpleasant evening. Now she began to feel the tension in the air and she wondered if it had been present all during the evening – and she too upset to notice it. About Archie's face there was an alert waiting look and his tufted, hairy old ears seemed pricked up like a lynx's. There was a severely repressed uneasiness about Melanie and India that made them raise their heads from their sewing at each sound of hooves in the road, at each groan of bare branches under the wailing wind, at each scuffing sound of dry leaves tumbling across the lawn. They started at each soft snap of burning logs on the hearth as if they were stealthy footsteps.

Something was wrong and Scarlett wondered what it was. Something was afoot and she did not know about it. A glance at Aunt Pitty's plump guileless face, screwed up in a pout, told her that the old lady was as ignorant as she. But Archie and Melanie and India knew. In the silence she could almost feel the thoughts of India and Melanie whirling as madly as squirrels in a cage. They knew something, were waiting for something, despite their efforts to make things appear as usual. And their inner unease communicated itself to Scarlett, making her more nervous than before. Handling her needle awkwardly, she jabbed it into her thumb and with a little scream of pain and annoyance that made them all jump, she squeezed it until a bright red drop appeared.

'I'm just too nervous to sew,' she declared, throwing her mending to the floor. 'I'm nervous enough to scream. I want to go home and go to bed. And Frank knew it and he oughtn't to have gone out. He talks, talks, talks about protecting women against darkies and Carpetbaggers and when the time comes for him to do some protecting, where is he? At home, taking care of me? No, indeed, he's gallivanting around with a lot of other men who don't do anything but talk and—'

Her snapping eyes came to rest on India's face and she paused. India was breathing fast and her pale lashless eyes were fastened on Scarlett's face with a deadly coldness.

'If it won't pain you too much, India,' she broke off sarcastically, 'I'd be much obliged if you'd tell me why you've been staring at me all evening. Has my face turned green or something?'

'It won't pain me to tell you. I'll do it with pleasure,' said India, and her eyes glittered. 'I hate to see you underrate a fine man like Mr Kennedy when, if you knew—'

'India!' said Melanie warningly, her hands clenching on her sewing.

'I think I know my husband better than you do,' said Scarlett, the prospect of a quarrel, the first open quarrel she had ever had with India, making her spirits rise and her nervousness depart. Melanie's eyes caught India's and reluctantly India closed her lips. But almost instantly she spoke again and her voice was cold with hate.

'You make me sick, Scarlett O'Hara, talking about being protected! You don't care about being protected! If you did you'd never have exposed yourself as you have done all these months, prissing yourself about this town, showing yourself off to strange men, hoping they'll admire you! What happened to you this afternoon was just what you deserved and if there was any justice you'd have gotten worse.'

'Oh, India, hush!' cried Melanie.

'Let her talk,' cried Scarlett. 'I'm enjoying it. I always knew she hated me and she was too much of a hypocrite to admit it. If she thought anyone would admire her, she'd be walking the streets naked from dawn till dark.'

India was on her feet, her lean body quivering with insult.

'I do hate you,' she said in a clear but trembling voice. 'But it hasn't been hypocrisy that's kept me quiet. It's something you can't understand, not possessing any – any common courtesy, common good breeding. It's the realization that if all of us don't hang together and submerge our own small hates, we can't expect to beat the Yankees. But you – you – you've done all you could to lower the prestige of decent people – working and bringing shame on a good husband, giving Yankees and riffraff the right to laugh at us and make insulting remarks about our lack of gentility. Yankees don't know that you aren't one of us and have never been. Yankees haven't sense enough to know that you haven't any gentility. And when you've ridden about the woods exposing yourself to attack, you've exposed every well-behaved woman in town to attack by putting temptation in the ways of darkies and mean white trash. And you've put our men folks' lives in danger because they've got to—'

'My God, India!' cried Melanie, and even in her wrath, Scarlett was stunned to hear Melanie take the Lord's name in vain. 'You must hush! She doesn't know and she – you must hush! You promised—'

'Oh, girls!' pleaded Miss Pittypat, her lips trembling.

'What don't I know?' Scarlett was on her feet, furious, facing the coldly blazing India and the imploring Melanie.

'Guinea-hens,' said Archie suddenly and his voice was contemptuous. Before anyone could rebuke him, his grizzled head went up sharply and he rose swiftly. 'Somebody comin' up the walk. 'Tain't Mr Wilkes neither. Cease your cackle.'

There was male authority in his voice and the women stood suddenly silent, anger fading swiftly from their faces as he stumped across the room to the door.

'Who's thar?' he questioned before the caller even knocked.

'Captain Butler. Let me in.'

Melanie was across the floor so swiftly that her hoops swayed up violently, revealing her pantalets to the knees, and before Archie could put his hand on the knob she flung the door open. Rhett Butler stood in the doorway, his black slouch hat low over his eyes, the wild wind whipping his cape about him in snapping folds. For once his good manners had deserted him. He neither took off his hat nor spoke to the others in the room. He had eyes for no one but Melanie and he spoke abruptly without greeting.

'Where have they gone? Tell me quickly. It's life or death.'

Scarlett and Pitty, startled and bewildered, looked at each other in wonderment and, like a lean old cat, India streaked across the room to Melanie's side.

'Don't tell him anything,' she cried swiftly. 'He's a spy, a Scallawag!'

Rhett did not even favour her with a glance.

'Quickly, Mrs Wilkes! There may still be time.'

Melanie seemed in a paralysis of terror and only stared into his face.

'What on earth—' began Scarlett.

'Shet yore mouth,' directed Archie briefly. 'You too, Miss Melly. Git the hell out of here, you damned Scallawag.'

'No, Archie, no!' cried Melanie, and she put a shaking hand on Rhett's arm as though to protect him from Archie. 'What has happened? How did – how did you know?'

On Rhett's dark face impatience fought with courtesy.

'Good God, Mrs Wilkes, they've all been under suspicion since the beginning – only they've been too clever – until tonight! How do I know? I was playing poker tonight with two drunken Yankee captains and they let it out. The Yankees knew there'd be trouble tonight and they've prepared for it. The fools have walked into a trap.'

For a moment it was as though Melanie swayed under the impact of a heavy blow and Rhett's arm went around her waist to steady her.

'Don't tell him! He's trying to trap you!' cried India, glaring at Rhett. 'Didn't you hear him say he'd been with Yankee officers tonight?'

Still Rhett did not look at her. His eyes were bent insistently on Melanie's white face.

'Tell me. Where did they go? Have they a meeting-place?'

Despite her fear and incomprehension, Scarlett thought she had never seen a blanker, more expressionless face than Rhett's, but evidently Melanie saw something else, something that made her give her trust. She straightened her small body away from the steadying arm and said quietly but with a voice that shook: 'Out the Decatur road near Shantytown. They meet in the cellar of the old Sullivan plantation – the one that's half burned.'

'Thank you. I'll ride fast. When the Yankees come here, none of you know anything.'

He was gone so swiftly, his black cape melting into the night, that they could hardly realize he had been there at all until they heard the spattering of gravel and the mad pounding of a horse going off at full gallop.

'The Yankees coming here?' cried Pitty and, her small feet turning under her, she collapsed on the sofa, too frightened for tears.

'What's it all about? What did he mean? If you don't tell me I'll go crazy!' Scarlett laid hands on Melanie and shook her violently as if by force she could shake an answer from her.

'Mean? It means you've probably been the cause of Ashley's and Mr Kennedy's death!' In spite of the agony of fear there was a note of triumph in India's voice. 'Stop shaking Melly. She's going to faint.'

'No, I'm not,' whispered Melanie, clutching the back of a chair.

'My God, my God! I don't understand! Kill Ashley? Please, somebody tell me—'

Archie's voice, like a rusty hinge, cut through Scarlett's words.

'Set down,' he ordered briefly. 'Pick up yore sewin'. Sew like nothin' had happened. For all we know, the Yankees might have been spyin' on this house since sundown. Set down, I say, and sew.'

Trembling they obeyed, even Pitty picking up a sock and holding it in shaking fingers while her eyes, wide as a frightened child's, went around the circle for an explanation.

'Where is Ashley? What has happened to him, Melly?' cried Scarlett.

'Where's your husband? Aren't you interested in him?' India's pale eyes blazed with insane malice as she crumpled and straightened the torn towel she had been mending.

'India, please!' Melanie had mastered her voice but her white, shaken face and tortured eyes showed the strain under which she was labouring. 'Scarlett, perhaps we should have told you but – but – you had been through so much this afternoon that we – that Frank didn't think – and you were always so outspoken against the Klan—'

'The Klan—'

At first, Scarlett spoke the word as if she had never heard it before and had no comprehension of its meaning, and then: 'The Klan!' she almost screamed it. 'Ashley isn't in the Klan! Frank can't be! Oh, he promised me!'

'Of course Mr Kennedy is in the Klan and Ashley, too, and all the men we know,' cried India. 'They are men, aren't they? And white men and Southerners. You should have been proud of him instead of making him sneak out as though it were something shameful and—'

'You all have known all along and I didn't—'

'We were afraid it would upset you,' said Melanie sorrowfully.

'Then that's where they go when they're supposed to be at the political meetings? Oh, he promised me! Now, the Yankees will come and take my mills and the store and put him in jail – oh, what did Rhett Butler mean?'

India's eyes met Melanie's in wild fear. Scarlett rose, flinging her sewing down.

'If you don't tell me, I'm going downtown and find out. I'll ask everybody I see until I find—'

'Set,' said Archie, fixing her with his eye. 'I'll tell you. Because you went gallivantin' this afternoon and got yoreself into trouble through yore own fault, Mr Wilkes and Mr Kennedy and the other men are out tonight to kill that thar nigger and that thar white man, if they can catch them, and wipe out that whole Shantytown settlement. And if what that Scallawag said is true, the Yankees suspected sumpin' or got wind somehow and they've sont out troops to lay for them. And our men have walked into a trap. And if what Butler said warn't true, then he's a spy and he is goin' to turn them up to the Yankees and they'll git kilt just the same. And if he does turn them up, then I'll kill him, if it's the last deed of m' life. And if they ain't kilt, then they'll all have to light out of here for Texas and lay low and maybe never come back. It's all yore fault and thar's blood on yore hands.'

Anger wiped out the fear from Melanie's face as she saw comprehension come slowly across Scarlett's face and then horror follow swiftly. She rose and put her hand on Scarlett's shoulder.

'Another such word and you go out of this house, Archie,' she said sternly. 'It's not her fault. She only did – did what she felt she had to do. And your men did what they felt they had to do. People must do what they must do. We don't all think alike or act alike and it's wrong to – to judge others by ourselves. How can you and India say such cruel things when her husband as well as mine may be – may be—'

'Hark!' interrupted Archie softly. 'Set, Ma'm. Thar's horses.'

Melanie sank into a chair, picked up one of Ashley's shirts and, bowing her head over it, unconsciously began to tear the frills into small ribbons.

The sound of hooves grew louder as horses trotted up to the house. There was the jangling of bits and the strain of leather and the sound of voices. As the hooves stopped in front of the house, one voice rose above the others in a command and the listeners heard feet going through the side yard toward the back porch. They felt that a thousand inimical eyes looked at them through the unshaded front window and the four women, with fear in their hearts, bent their heads and plied their needles. Scarlett's heart screamed in her breast: 'I've killed Ashley! I've killed him!' And in that wild moment she did not even think that she might have killed Frank too. She had no room in her mind for any picture save that of Ashley, lying at the feet of Yankee cavalrymen, his fair hair dappled with blood.

As the harsh rapid knocking sounded at the door, she looked at Melanie and saw come over the small, strained face a new expression, an expression as blank as she had just seen on Rhett Butler's face, the bland blank look of a poker player bluffing a game with only two deuces.

'Archie, open the door,' she said quietly.

Slipping his knife into his boot-top and loosening the pistol in his trouser-band, Archie stumped over to the door and flung it open. Pitty gave a little squeak, like a mouse who feels the trap snap down, as she saw massed in the doorway, a Yankee captain and a squad of bluecoats. But the others said nothing. Scarlett saw with the faintest feeling of relief that she knew this officer. He was Captain Tom Jaffery, one of Rhett's friends. She had sold him lumber to build his house. She knew him to be a gentleman. Perhaps, as he was a gentleman, he wouldn't drag them away to prison. He recognized her instantly and, taking off his hat, bowed, somewhat embarrassed.

'Good evening, Mrs Kennedy. And which of you ladies is Mrs Wilkes?'

'I am Mrs Wilkes,' answered Melanie, rising, and for all her smallness, dignity flowed from her. 'And to what do I owe this intrusion?'

The eyes of the captain flickered quickly about the room, resting for an instant on each face, passing quickly from their faces to the table and the hat-rack as though looking for signs of male occupancy.

'I should like to speak to Mr Wilkes and Mr Kennedy, if you please.'

'They are not here,' said Melanie, a chill in her soft voice.

'Are you sure?'

'Don't you question Miz Wilkes' word,' said Archie, his beard bristling.

'I beg your pardon, Mrs Wilkes. I meant no disrespect. If you give me your word, I will not search the house.'

'You have my word. But search if you like. They are at a meeting downtown at Mr Kennedy's store.'

'They are not at the store. There was no meeting tonight,' answered the captain grimly. 'We will wait outside until they return.'

He bowed briefly and went out, closing the door behind him. Those in the house heard a sharp order, muffled by the wind: 'Surround the house. A man at each window and door.' There was a tramping of feet. Scarlett checked a start of terror as she dimly saw bearded faces peering in the windows at them. Melanie sat down and with a hand that did not tremble reached for a book on the table. It was a ragged copy of *Les Misérables*, that book which caught the fancy of the Confederate soldiers. They had read it by camp-fire light and took some grim pleasure in calling it 'Lee's Miserables'. She opened it at the middle and began to read in a clear monotonous voice.

'Sew,' commanded Archie in a hoarse whisper, and the three women, nerved by Melanie's cool voice, picked up their sewing and bowed their heads.

How long Melanie read beneath that circle of watching eyes, Scarlett never knew but it seemed hours. She did not even hear a word that Melanie read. Now she was beginning to think of Frank as well as Ashley. So this was the explanation of his apparent calm this evening! He had promised her he would have nothing to do with the Klan. Oh, this was just the kind of trouble she had feared would come upon them! All the work of this last year would go for nothing. All her struggles and fears and labours in rain and cold had been wasted. And who would have thought that spiritless old Frank would get himself mixed up in the hot-headed doings of the Klan? Even at this minute, he might be dead. And if he wasn't dead and the Yankees caught him, he'd be hanged. And Ashley, too!

Her nails dug into her palms until four bright-red crescents showed. How could Melanie read on and on so calmly when Ashley was in danger of being hanged? When he might be dead? But something in the cool soft voice reading the sorrows of Jean Valjean steadied her, kept her from leaping to her feet and screaming.

Her mind fled back to the night Tony Fontaine had come to them, hunted, exhausted, without money. If he had not reached their house and received money and a fresh horse, he would have been hanged long since. If Frank and Ashley were not dead at this very minute, they were in Tony's position, only worse. With the house surrounded by soldiers they couldn't come home and get money and clothes without being captured. And probably every house up and down the street had a similar guard of Yankees, so they could not apply to friends for aid. Even now they might be riding wildly through the night, bound for Texas.

But Rhett – perhaps Rhett had reached them in time. Rhett always had plenty of cash in his pocket. Perhaps he would lend them enough to see them through. But that was queer. Why should Rhett bother himself about Ashley's safety? Certainly he disliked him, certainly he professed a contempt for him. Then why – but this riddle was swallowed up in a renewed fear for the safety of Ashley and Frank.

'Oh, it's all my fault!' she wailed to herself. 'India and Archie spoke the truth. It's all my fault. But I never thought either of them was foolish enough to join the Klan! And I never thought anything would really happen to me! But I couldn't have done otherwise. Melly spoke the truth. People have to do what they have to do. And I had to keep the mills going! I had to have money! And now I'll probably lose it all and somehow it's all my fault!'

After a long time Melanie's voice faltered, trailed off and was silent. She turned her head toward the window and stared as though no Yankee soldier stared back from behind the glass. The others raised their heads, caught by her listening pose, and they too listened.

There was a sound of horses' feet and of singing, deadened by the closed windows and doors, borne away by the wind but still recognizable. It was the most hated and hateful of all songs, the song about Sherman's men – 'Marching through Georgia' – and Rhett Butler was singing it.

Hardly had he finished the first lines when two other voices, drunken voices, assailed him, enraged foolish voices that stumbled over words and blurred them together. There was a quick command from Captain Jaffery on the front porch and the rapid tramp of feet. But even before these sounds arose, the ladies looked at one another stunned. For the drunken voices expostulating with Rhett were those of Ashley and Hugh Elsing.

Voices rose louder on the front walk, Captain Jaffery's curt and questioning, Hugh's shrill with foolish laughter, Rhett's deep and reckless and Ashley's queer, unreal, shouting: 'What the hell! What the hell!'

'That can't be Ashley!' thought Scarlett wildly. 'He never gets drunk! And Rhett – why, when Rhett's drunk he gets quieter and quieter – never loud like that!'

Melanie rose and, with her, Archie rose. They heard the captain's sharp voice: 'These two men are under arrest.' And Archie's hand closed over his pistol-butt.

'No,' whispered Melanie firmly. 'No. Leave it to me.'

There was in her face the same look Scarlett had seen that day at Tara when Melanie had stood at the top of the steps, looking down at the dead Yankee, her weak wrist weighed down by the heavy sabre – a gentle and timid soul nerved by circumstances to the caution and fury of a tigress. She threw the front door open.

'Bring him in, Captain Butler,' she called in a clear tone that bit with venom. 'I suppose you've gotten him intoxicated again. Bring him in.'

From the dark windy walk, the Yankee captain spoke: 'I'm sorry, Mrs Wilkes, but your husband and Mr Elsing are under arrest.'

'Arrest? For what? For drunkenness? If everyone in Atlanta was arrested for drunkenness, the whole Yankee garrison would be in jail continually. Well, bring him in, Captain Butler – that is, if you can walk yourself.'

Scarlett's mind was not working quickly and for a brief moment nothing made sense. She knew neither Rhett nor Ashley was drunk and she knew Melanie knew they were not drunk. Yet here was Melanie, usually so gentle and refined, screaming like a shrew and in front of Yankees too, that both of them were too drunk to walk.

There was a short mumbled argument, punctuated with curses, and uncertain feet ascended the stairs. In the doorway appeared Ashley, white-faced, his head lolling, his bright hair tousled, his long body wrapped from neck to knees in Rhett's black cape. Hugh Elsing and Rhett, none too steady on their feet, supported him on either side and it was obvious he would have fallen to the floor but for their aid. Behind them came the Yankee captain, his face a study of mingled suspicion and amusement. He stood in the open doorway with his men peering curiously over his shoulders and the cold wind swept the house.

Scarlett, frightened, puzzled, glanced at Melanie and back to the sagging Ashley and then half-comprehension came to her. She started to cry out, 'But he can't be drunk!' and bit back the words. She realized she was witnessing a play, a desperate play on which lives hinged. She knew she was not part of it nor was Aunt Pitty but the others were and they were tossing cues to one another like actors in an oft-rehearsed drama. She understood only half but she understood enough to keep silent.

'Put him in the chair,' cried Melanie indignantly. 'And you, Captain Butler, leave this house immediately! How dare you show your face here after getting him in this condition again!'

The two men eased Ashley into a rocker and Rhett, swaying, caught hold of the back of the chair to steady himself and addressed the captain with pain in his voice.

'That's fine thanks I get, isn't it? For keeping the police from getting him and bringing him home and him yelling and trying to claw me!'

'And you, Hugh Elsing, I'm ashamed of you! What will your poor mother say? Drunk and out with a – a Yankee-loving Scallawag like Captain Butler! And, oh, Mr Wilkes, how could you do such a thing?'

'Melly, I ain't so very drunk,' mumbled Ashley, and with the words fell forward and lay face down on the table, his head buried in his arms.

'Archie, take him to his room and put him to bed – as usual,' ordered Melanie. 'Aunt Pitty, please run and fix the bed and oo-oh,' she suddenly burst into tears. 'Oh, how could he? After he promised!'

Archie already had his arm under Ashley's shoulder and Pitty, frightened and uncertain, was on her feet when the captain interposed.

'Don't touch him. He's under arrest. Sergeant!'

As the sergeant stepped into the room, his rifle at trail, Rhett, evidently trying to steady himself, put a hand on the captain's arm and, with difficulty, focused his eyes.

'Tom, what you arresting him for? He ain't so very drunk. I've seen him drunker.'

'Drunk be damned,' cried the captain. 'He can lie in the gutter for all I care. I'm no policeman. He and Mr Elsing are under arrest for complicity in a Klan raid at Shantytown tonight. A nigger and a white man were killed. Mr Wilkes was the ringleader in it.'

'Tonight?' Rhett began to laugh. He laughed so hard that he sat down on the sofa and put his head in his hands. 'Not tonight, Tom,' he said when he could speak. 'These two have been with me tonight – ever since eight o'clock when they were supposed to be at the meeting.'

'With you, Rhett? But—' A frown came over the captain's forehead and he looked uncertainly at the snoring Ashley and his weeping wife. 'But – where were you?'

'I don't like to say,' and Rhett shot a look of drunken cunning at Melanie.

'You'd better say!'

'Let's go out on the porch and I'll tell you where we were.'

'You'll tell me now.'

'Hate to say it in front of ladies. If you ladies'll step out of the room—'

'I won't go,' cried Melanie, dabbing angrily at her eyes with her handkerchief. 'I have a right to know. Where was my husband?'

'At Belle Watling's sporting house,' said Rhett, looking abashed. 'He was there and Hugh and Frank Kennedy and Dr Meade and – and a whole lot of them. Had a party. Big party. Champagne. Girls—'

'At – at Belle Watling's?'

Melanie's voice rose until it cracked with such pain that all eyes turned frightenedly to her. Her hand went clutching at her bosom and, before Archie could catch her, she had fainted. Then a hubbub ensued, Archie picking her up, India running to the kitchen for water, Pitty and Scarlett fanning her and slapping her wrists, while Hugh Elsing shouted over and over: 'Now you've done it! Now you've done it!'

'Now it'll be all over town,' said Rhett savagely. 'I hope you're satisfied, Tom. There won't be a wife in Atlanta who'll speak to her husband tomorrow.'

'Rhett, I had no idea—' Though the chill wind was blowing through the open door on his back, the captain was perspiring. 'Look here! You take oath they were at – er – at Belle's?'

'Hell, yes,' growled Rhett. 'Go ask Belle herself if you don't believe me. Now, let me carry Mrs Wilkes to her room. Give her to me, Archie. Yes, I can carry her. Miss Pitty, go ahead with a lamp.'

He took Melanie's limp body from Archie's arms with ease.

'You get Mr Wilkes to bed, Archie. I don't want to ever lay eyes or hands on him again after this night.'

Pitty's hand trembled so that the lamp was a menace to the safety of the house, but she held it and trotted ahead toward the dark bedroom. Archie, with a grunt, got an arm under Ashley and raised him.

'But – I've got to arrest these men!'

Rhett turned in the dim hallway.

'Arrest them in the morning then. They can't run away in this condition – and I never knew before that it was illegal to get drunk in a sporting house. Good God, Tom, there are fifty witnesses to prove they were at Belle's.'

'There are always fifty witnesses to prove a Southerner was somewhere where he wasn't,' said the captain morosely. 'You come with me, Mr Elsing. I'll parole Mr Wilkes on the word of—'

'I am Mr Wilkes' sister. I will answer for his appearance,' said India coldly. 'Now, will you please go? You've caused enough trouble for one night.'

'I regret it exceedingly.' The captain bowed awkwardly. 'I only hope they can prove their presence at the – er – Miss – Mrs Watling's house. Will you tell your brother that he must appear before the provost marshal tomorrow morning for questioning?'

India bowed coldly and, putting her hand upon the door-knob, intimated silently that his speedy retirement would be welcome. The captain and the sergeant backed out, Hugh Elsing with them, and she slammed the door behind them. Without even looking at Scarlett, she went swiftly to each window and drew down the shade. Scarlett, her knees shaking, caught hold of the chair in which Ashley had been sitting to steady herself. Looking down at it, she saw that there was a dark moist spot, larger than her hand, on the cushion in the back of the chair. Puzzled, her hand went over it and, to her horror, a sticky red wetness appeared on her palm.

'India,' she whispered, 'India, Ashley's – he's hurt.'

'You fool! Did you think he was really drunk?'

India snapped down the last shade and started on flying feet for the bedroom, with Scarlett close behind her, her heart in her throat. Rhett's big body barred the doorway, but, past his shoulder, Scarlett saw Ashley lying white and still on the bed. Melanie, strangely quick for one so recently in a faint, was rapidly cutting off his blood-soaked shirt with embroidery scissors. Archie held the lamp low over the bed to give light and one of his gnarled fingers was on Ashley's wrist.

'Is he dead?' cried both girls together.

'No, just fainted from loss of blood. It's through his shoulder,' said Rhett.

'Why did you bring him here, you fool?' cried India. 'Let me get to him! Let me pass! Why did you bring him here to be arrested?'

'He was too weak to travel. There was nowhere else to bring him, Miss Wilkes. Besides – do you want him to be an exile like Tony Fontaine? Do you want a dozen of your neighbours to live in Texas under assumed names for the rest of their lives? There's a chance that we may get them all off if Belle—'

'Let me pass!'

'No, Miss Wilkes. There's work for you. You must go for a doctor – not Dr Meade. He's implicated in this and is probably explaining to the Yankees at this very minute. Get some other doctor. Are you afraid to go out alone at night?'

'No,' said India, her pale eyes glittering. 'I'm not afraid.' She caught up Melanie's hooded cape which was hanging on a hook in the hall. 'I'll go for old Dr Dean.' The excitement went out of her voice as, with an effort, she forced calmness. 'I'm sorry I called you a spy and a fool. I did not understand. I'm deeply grateful for what you've done for Ashley – but I despise you just the same.'

'I appreciate frankness – and I thank you for it.' Rhett bowed and his lip curled down in an amused smile. 'Now, go quickly and by back ways and when you return do not come in this house if you see signs of soldiers about.'

India shot one more quick anguished look at Ashley, and, wrapping her cape about her, ran lightly down the hall to the back door and let herself out quietly into the night.

Scarlett, straining her eyes past Rhett, felt her heart beat again as she saw Ashley's eyes open. Melanie snatched a folded towel from the washstand rack and pressed it against his streaming shoulder and he smiled up weakly, reassuringly into her face. Scarlett felt Rhett's hard penetrating eyes upon her, knew that her heart was plain upon her face, but she did not care. Ashley was bleeding, perhaps dying, and she who loved him had torn that hole through his shoulder. She wanted to run to the bed, sink down beside it and clasp him to her but her knees trembled so that she could not enter the room. Hand at her mouth, she stared while Melanie packed a fresh towel against his shoulder, pressing it hard as though she could force back the blood into his body. But the towel reddened as though by magic.

How could a man bleed so much and still live? But, thank God, there was no bubble of blood at his lips – oh, those frothy red bubbles, forerunners of death that she knew so well from the dreadful day of the battle at Peachtree Creek when the wounded had died on Aunt Pitty's lawn with bloody mouths.

'Brace up,' said Rhett, and there was a hard, faintly jeering note in his voice. 'He won't die. Now, go take the lamp and hold it for Mrs Wilkes. I need Archie to run errands.'

Archie looked across the lamp at Rhett.

'I ain't takin' no orders from you,' he said briefly, shifting his wad of tobacco to the other cheek.

'You do what he says,' said Melanie sternly, 'and do it quickly. Do everything Captain Butler says. Scarlett, take the lamp.'

Scarlett went forward and took the lamp, holding it in both hands to keep from dropping it. Ashley's eyes had closed again. His bare chest heaved up slowly and sank quickly and the red stream seeped from between Melanie's small frantic fingers. Dimly she heard Archie stump across the room to Rhett and heard Rhett's low rapid words. Her mind was so fixed upon Ashley that of the first half-whispered words of Rhett, she only heard: 'Take my horse . . . tied outside . . . ride like hell.'

Archie mumbled some question and Scarlett heard Rhett reply: 'The old Sullivan plantation. You'll find the robes pushed up the biggest chimney. Burn them.'

'Um,' grunted Archie.

'And there's two – men in the cellar. Pack them over the horse as best you can and take them to that vacant lot behind Belle's – the one between her house and the railroad tracks. Be careful. If anyone sees you, you'll hang as well as the rest of us. Put them in that lot and put pistols near them – in their hands. Here – take mine.'

Scarlett, looking across the room, saw Rhett reach under his coat-tails and produce two revolvers which Archie took and shoved into his waistband.

'Fire one shot from each. It's got to appear like a plain case of shooting. You understand?'

Archie nodded as if he understood perfectly and an unwilling gleam of respect shone in his cold eye. But understanding was far from Scarlett. The last half-hour had been so nightmarish that she felt nothing would ever be plain and clear again. However, Rhett seemed in perfect command of the bewildering situation and that was a small comfort.

Archie turned to go and then swung about and his one eye went questioningly to Rhett's face.

'Him?'

'Yes.'

Archie grunted and spat on the floor.

'Hell to pay,' he said as he stumped down the hall to the back door.

Something in the last low interchange of words made a new fear and suspicion rise up in Scarlett's breast like a chill ever-swelling bubble. When that bubble broke—

'Where's Frank?' she cried.

Rhett came swiftly across the room to the bed, his big body swinging as lightly and noiselessly as a cat's.

'All in good time,' he said and smiled briefly. 'Steady that lamp, Scarlett. You don't want to burn Mr Wilkes up. Miss Melly—'

Melanie looked up like a good little soldier awaiting a command and so tense was the situation it did not occur to her that for the first time Rhett was calling her familiarly by the name which only family and old friends used.

'I beg your pardon, I mean, Mrs Wilkes . . .'

'Oh, Captain Butler, do not ask my pardon! I should feel honoured if you called me "Melly" without the Miss! I feel as though you were my – my brother or – or my cousin. How kind you are and how clever! How can I ever thank you enough?'

'Thank you,' said Rhett and for a moment he looked almost embarrassed. 'I should never presume so far, but Miss Melly,' and his voice was apologetic, 'I'm sorry I had to say that Mr Wilkes was in Belle Watling's house. I'm sorry to have involved him and the others in such a – a— But I had to think fast when I rode away from here and that was the only plan that occurred to me. I knew my word would be accepted because I have so many friends among the Yankee officers. They do me the dubious honour of thinking me almost one of them because they know my – shall we call it my "unpopularity"? – among my townsmen. And you see, I was playing poker in Belle's bar earlier in the evening. There are a dozen Yankee soldiers who can testify to that. And Belle and her girls will gladly lie themselves black in the face and say Mr Wilkes and the others were – upstairs all evening. And the Yankees will believe them. Yankees are queer that way. It won't occur to them that women of – their profession are capable of intense loyalty or patriotism. The Yankees wouldn't take the word of a single nice Atlanta lady as to the whereabouts of the men who were supposed to be at the meeting tonight but they will take the word of – fancy ladies. And I think that between the word of honour of a Scallawag and a dozen fancy ladies, we may have a chance of getting the men off.'

There was a sardonic grin on his face at the last words but it faded as Melanie turned up to him a face that blazed with gratitude.

'Captain Butler, you are so smart! I wouldn't have cared if you'd said they were in hell itself tonight, if it saves them! For I know and everyone else who matters knows that my husband was never in a dreadful place like that!'

'Well—' began Rhett awkwardly, 'as a matter of fact, he was at Belle's tonight.'

Melanie drew herself up coldly.

'You can never make me believe such a lie!'

'Please, Miss Melly! Let me explain! When I got out to the old Sullivan place tonight, I found Mr Wilkes wounded and with him were Hugh Elsing and Dr Meade and old man Merriwether—'

'Not the old gentleman!' cried Scarlett.

'Men are never too old to be fools. And your Uncle Henry—'

'Oh, mercy!' cried Aunt Pitty.

'The others had scattered after the brush with the troops and the crowd that stuck together had come to the Sullivan place to hide their robes in the chimney and to see how badly Mr Wilkes was hurt. But for his wound, they'd be headed for Texas by now – all of them – but he couldn't ride far and they wouldn't leave him. It was necessary to prove that they had been somewhere instead of where they had been, and so I took them by back ways to Belle Watling's.'

'Oh – I see. I do beg your pardon for my rudeness, Captain Butler. I see now it was necessary to take them there but— Oh, Captain Butler, people must have seen you going in!'

'No one saw us. We went in through a private back entrance that opens on the railroad tracks. It's always dark and locked.'

'Then how—?'

'I have a key,' said Rhett laconically, and his eyes met Melanie's evenly.

As the full impact of the meaning smote her, Melanie became so embarrassed that she fumbled with the bandage until it slid off the wound entirely.

'I did not mean to pry—' she said in a muffled voice, her white face reddening, as she hastily pressed the towel back into place.

'I regret having to tell a lady such a thing.'

'Then it's true!' thought Scarlett with an odd pang. 'Then he does live with that dreadful Watling creature! He does own her house!'

'I saw Belle and explained to her. We gave her a list of the men who were out tonight and she and her girls will testify that they were all in her house tonight. Then to make our exit more conspicuous, she called the two desperadoes who keep order at her place and had us dragged downstairs, fighting, and through the bar-room and thrown out into the street as brawling drunks who were disturbing the place.'

He grinned reminiscently. 'Dr Meade did not make a very convincing drunk. It hurt his dignity to even be in such a place. But your Uncle Henry and old man Merriwether were excellent. The stage lost two great actors when they did not take up the drama. They seemed to enjoy the affair. I'm afraid your Uncle Henry has a black eye due to Mr Merriwether's zeal for his part. He—'

The back door swung open and India entered, followed by old Dr Dean, his long white hair tumbled, his worn leather bag bulging under his cape. He nodded briefly but without words to those present and quickly lifted the bandage from Ashley's shoulder.

'Too high for the lung,' he said. 'If it hasn't splintered his collarbone it's not so serious. Get me plenty of towels, ladies, and cotton if you have it, and some brandy.'

Rhett took the lamp from Scarlett and set it on the table as Melanie and India sped about, obeying the doctor's orders.

'You can't do anything here. Come into the parlour by the fire.' He took her arm and propelled her from the room. There was a gentleness foreign to him in both hand and voice. 'You've had a rotten day, haven't you?'

She allowed herself to be led into the front room and though she stood on the hearth-rug in front of the fire she began to shiver. The bubble of suspicion in her breast was swelling larger now. It was more than a suspicion. It was almost a certainty and a terrible certainty. She looked up into Rhett's immobile face and for a moment she could not speak. Then:

'Was Frank at – Belle Watling's?'

'No.'

Rhett's voice was blunt.

'Archie's carrying him to the vacant lot near Belle's. He's dead. Shot through the head.'

Chapter XLVI

Few families in the north end of town slept that night, for the news of the disaster to the Klan, and Rhett's stratagem, spread swiftly on silent feet as the shadowy form of India Wilkes slipped through back yards, whispered urgently through kitchen doors and slipped away into the windy darkness. And in her path, she left fear and desperate hope.

From without, houses looked black and silent and wrapped in sleep but, within, voices whispered vehemently into the dawn. Not only those involved in the night's raid but every member of the Klan was ready for flight, and in almost every stable along Peachtree Street horses stood saddled in the darkness, pistols in holsters and food in saddlebags. All that prevented a wholesale exodus was India's whispered message: 'Captain Butler says not to run. The roads will be watched. He has arranged with that Watling creature—' In dark rooms men whispered: 'But why should I trust that damned Scallawag Butler? It may be a trap!' And women's voices implored: 'Don't go! If he saved Ashley and Hugh, he may save everybody. If India and Melanie trust him—' And they half trusted and stayed because there was no other course open to them.

Earlier in the night, the soldiers had knocked at a dozen doors and those who could not or would not tell where they had been that night were marched off under arrest. René Picard and one of Mrs Merriwether's nephews and the Simmons boys and Andy Bonnell were among those who spent the night in jail. They had been in the ill-starred foray but had separated from the others after the shooting. Riding hard for home they were arrested before they learned of Rhett's plan. Fortunately they all replied, to questions, that where they had been that night was their own business and not that of any damned Yankees. They had been locked up for further questioning in the morning. Old man Merriwether and Uncle Henry Hamilton declared shamelessly that they had spent the evening at Belle Watling's sporting house, and when Captain Jaffery remarked irritably that they were too old for such goings-on, they wanted to fight him.

Belle Watling herself answered Captain Jaffery's summons, and before he could make known his mission she shouted that the house was closed for the night. A passel of quarrelsome drunks had called in the early part of the evening and had fought one another, torn the place up, broken her finest mirrors and so alarmed the young ladies that all business had been suspended for the night. But if Captain Jaffery wanted a drink, the bar was still open—

Captain Jaffery, acutely conscious of the grins of his men and feeling helplessly that he was fighting a mist, declared angrily that he wanted neither the young ladies nor a drink and demanded if Belle knew the names of her destructive customers. Oh, yes, Belle knew them. They were her regulars. They came every Wednesday night and called themselves the

Wednesday Democrats, though what they meant by that she neither knew nor cared. And if they didn't pay for the damage to the mirrors in the upper hall, she was going to have the law on them. She kept a respectable house and—Oh, their names? Belle unhesitatingly reeled off the names of twelve under suspicion. Captain Jaffery smiled sourly.

'These damned Rebels are as efficiently organized as our Secret Service,' he said. 'You and your girls will have to appear before the provost marshal tomorrow.'

'Will the provost make them pay for my mirrors?'

'To hell with your mirrors! Make Rhett Butler pay for them. He owns the place, doesn't he?'

Before dawn, every ex-Confederate family in town knew everything. And their negroes, who had been told nothing, knew everything too, by that black grapevine telegraph system which defies white understanding. Everyone knew the details of the raid, the killing of Frank Kennedy and crippled Tommy Wellburn and how Ashley was wounded in carrying Frank's body away.

Some of the feeling of bitter hatred the women bore Scarlett for her share in the tragedy was mitigated by the knowledge that her husband was dead and she knew it and could not admit it and have the poor comfort of claiming his body. Until morning light disclosed the bodies and the authorities notified her, she must know nothing. Frank and Tommy, pistols in cold hands, lay stiffening among the dead weeds in a vacant lot. And the Yankees would say they killed each other in a common drunken brawl over a girl in Belle's house. Sympathy ran high for Fanny, Tommy's wife, who had just had a baby, but no one could slip through the darkness to see her and comfort her because a squad of Yankees surrounded the house, waiting for Tommy to return. And there was another squad about Aunt Pitty's house, waiting for Frank.

Before dawn the news had trickled about that the military inquiry would take place that day. The townspeople, heavy-eyed from sleeplessness and anxious waiting, knew that the safety of some of their most prominent citizens rested on three things – the ability of Ashley Wilkes to stand on his feet and appear before the military board, as though he suffered nothing more serious than a morning-after headache, the word of Belle Watling that these men had been in her house all evening and the word of Rhett Butler that he had been with them.

The town writhed at these last two! Belle Watling! To owe their men's lives to her! It was intolerable! Women who had ostentatiously crossed the street when they saw Belle coming, wondered if she remembered and trembled for fear she did. The men felt less humiliation at taking their lives from Belle than the women did, for many of them thought her a good sort. But they were stung that they must owe lives and freedom to Rhett Butler, a speculator and a Scallawag. Belle and Rhett, the town's best-known fancy woman and the town's most hated man. And they must be under obligation to them.

Another thought that stung them to impotent wrath was the knowledge that the Yankees and Carpetbaggers would laugh. Oh, how they would laugh! Twelve of the town's most prominent citizens revealed as habitual frequenters of Belle Watling's sporting house! Two of them killed in a fight over a cheap little girl, others ejected from the place as too drunk to be tolerated even by Belle, and some under arrest, refusing to admit they were there when everyone knew they were there!

Atlanta was right in fearing that the Yankees would laugh. They had squirmed too long beneath Southern coldness and contempt and now they exploded with hilarity. Officers woke comrades and retailed the news. Husbands roused wives at dawn and told them as much as could be decently told to women. And the women, dressing hastily, knocked on their neighbours' doors and spread the story. The Yankee ladies were charmed with it all and laughed until the tears ran down their faces. This was Southern chivalry and gallantry for you! Maybe those women who carried their heads so high and snubbed all attempts at friendliness wouldn't be so uppity, now that everyone knew where their husbands spent their time when they were supposed to be at political meetings. Political meetings! Well, that was funny!

But even as they laughed, they expressed regret for Scarlett and her tragedy. After all, Scarlett was a lady and one of the few ladies in Atlanta who were nice to Yankees. She had already won their sympathy by the fact that she had to work because her husband couldn't or wouldn't support her properly. Even though her husband was a sorry one, it was dreadful that the poor thing should discover he had been untrue to her. And it was doubly dreadful that his death should occur simultaneously with the discovery of his infidelity. After all, a poor husband was better than no husband at all, and the Yankee ladies decided they'd be extra nice to Scarlett. But the others, Mrs Meade, Mrs Merriwether, Mrs Elsing, Tommy Wellburn's widow and most of all, Mrs Ashley Wilkes, they'd laugh in their faces every time they saw them. That would teach them a little courtesy.

Much of the whispering that went on in the dark rooms on the north side of town that night was on this same subject. Atlanta ladies vehemently told their husbands that they did not care a rap what the Yankees thought. But inwardly they felt that running an Indian gauntlet would be infinitely preferable to suffering the ordeal of Yankee grins and not being able to tell the truth about their husbands.

Dr Meade, beside himself with outraged dignity at the position into which Rhett had jockeyed him and the others, told Mrs Meade that, but for the fact that it would implicate the others, he would rather confess and be hanged than say he had been at Belle's house.

'It is an insult to you, Mrs Meade,' he fumed.

'But everyone will know you weren't there for – for—'

'The Yankees won't know. They'll have to believe it if we save our necks.

And they'll laugh. The very thought that anyone will believe it and laugh infuriates me. And it insults you because – my dear, I have always been faithful to you.'

'I know that,' and in the darkness Mrs Meade smiled and slipped a thin hand into the doctor's. 'But I'd rather it were really true than have one hair of your head in danger.'

'Mrs Meade, do you know what you are saying?' cried the doctor, aghast at the unsuspected realism of his wife.

'Yes, I know. I've lost Darcy and I've lost Phil and you are all I have and, rather than lose you, I'd have you take up your permanent abode at that place.'

'You are distrait! You cannot know what you are saying.'

'You old fool,' said Mrs Meade tenderly and laid her head against his sleeve.

Dr Meade fumed into silence and stroked her cheek and then exploded again. 'And to be under obligation to that Butler man! Hanging would be easy compared with that. No, not even if I owe him my life, can I be polite to him. His insolence is monumental and his shamelessness about his profiteering makes me boil. To owe my life to a man who never went in the army—'

'Melly said he enlisted after Atlanta fell.'

'It's a lie. Miss Melly will believe any plausible scoundrel. And what I can't understand is why he is doing all this – going to all this trouble. I hate to say it but – well, there's always been talk about him and Mrs Kennedy. I've seen them coming in from rides together too often this last year. He must have done it because of her.'

'If it was because of Scarlett, he wouldn't have lifted his hand. He'd have been glad to see Frank Kennedy hanged. I think it's because of Melly—'

'Mrs Meade, you can't be insinuating that there's ever been anything between those two!'

'Oh, don't be silly! But she's always been unaccountably fond of him ever since he tried to get Ashley exchanged during the war. And I must say this for him, he never smiles in that nasty-nice way when he's with her. He's just as pleasant and thoughtful as can be – really a different man. You can tell by the way he acts with Melly that he could be decent if he wanted to. Now, my idea of why he's doing all this is . . . ' She paused. 'Doctor, you won't like my idea.'

'I don't like anything about this whole affair!'

'Well, I think he did it partly for Melly's sake but mostly because he thought it would be a huge joke on us all. We've hated him so much and showed it so plainly and now he's got us in a fix where all of you have your choice of saying you were at that Watling woman's house and shaming yourselves and wives before the Yankees – or telling the truth and getting hanged. And he knows we'll all be under obligation to him and his – mistress and that we'd almost rather be hanged than be obliged to them. Oh, I'll wager he's enjoying it.'

The doctor groaned. 'He did look amused when he took us upstairs in that place.'

'Doctor,' Mrs Meade hesitated, 'what did it look like?'

'What are you saying, Mrs Meade?'

'Her house. What did it look like? Are there cut-glass chandeliers? And red plush curtains and dozens of full-length gilt mirrors? And were the girls – were they unclothed?'

'Good God!' cried the doctor, thunderstruck, for it had never occurred to him that the curiosity of a chaste woman concerning her unchaste sisters was so devouring. 'How can you ask such immodest questions? You are not yourself. I will mix you a sedative.'

'I don't want a sedative. I want to know. Oh, dear, this is my only chance to know what a bad house looks like and now you are mean enough not to tell me!'

'I noticed nothing. I assure you I was too embarrassed at finding myself in such a place to take note of my surroundings,' said the doctor formally, more upset at this unsuspected revelation of his wife's character than he had been by all the previous events of the evening. 'If you will excuse me now, I will try to get some sleep.'

'Well, go to sleep then,' she answered, disappointment in her tones. Then as the doctor leaned over to remove his boots, her voice spoke from the darkness with renewed cheerfulness. 'I imagine Dolly has gotten it all out of old man Merriwether and she can tell me about it.'

'Good Heavens, Mrs Meade! Do you mean to tell me that nice women talk about such things among them—'

'Oh, go to bed,' said Mrs Meade.

It sleeted the next day, but as the wintry twilight drew on the icy particles stopped falling and a cold wind blew. Wrapped in her cloak, Melanie went bewilderedly down her front walk behind a strange negro coachman who had summoned her mysteriously to a closed carriage waiting in front of the house. As she came up to the carriage the door was opened and she saw a woman in the dim interior.

Leaning closer, peering inside, Melanie questioned: 'Who is it? Won't you come in the house? It's so cold—'

'Please come in here and set with me a minute, Miz Wilkes,' came a faintly familiar voice, an embarrassed voice from the depths of the carriage.

'Oh, you're Miss – Mrs – Watling!' cried Melanie. 'I did so want to see you! You must come in the house.'

'I can't do that, Miz Wilkes.' Belle Watling's voice sounded scandalized. 'You come in here and set a minute with me.'

Melanie entered the carriage and the coachman closed the door behind her. She sat down beside Belle and reached for her hand.

'How can I ever thank you enough for what you did today! How can any of us thank you enough!'

'Miz Wilkes, you hadn't ought of sent me that note this mornin'. Not that I wasn't proud to have a note from you but the Yankees might of got it. And as for sayin' you was goin' to call on me to thank me – why, Miz Wilkes, you must of lost your mind! The very idea! I come up here as soon as 'twas dark to tell you you mustn't think of any sech thing. Why, I – why, you – it wouldn't be fittin' at all.'

'It wouldn't be fitting for me to call and thank a kind woman who saved my husband's life?'

'Oh, shucks, Miz Wilkes! You know what I mean!'

Melanie was silent for a moment, embarrassed by the implication. Somehow this handsome, sedately dressed woman sitting in the darkness of the carriage didn't look and talk as she imagined a bad woman, the Madam of a House, should look and talk. She sounded like – well, a little common and countrified but nice and warm-hearted.

'You were wonderful before the provost marshal today, Mrs Watling! You and the other – your – the young ladies certainly saved our men's lives.'

'Mr Wilkes was the wonderful one. I don't know how he even stood up and told his story, much less look as cool as he done. He was sure bleedin' like a pig when I seen him last night. Is he goin' to be all right, Miz Wilkes?'

'Yes, thank you. The doctor says it's just a flesh wound, though he did lose a tremendous lot of blood. This morning he was – well, he was pretty well laced with brandy or he'd never have had the strength to go through with it all so well. But it was you, Mrs Watling, who saved them. When you got mad and talked about the broken mirrors you sounded so – so convincing.'

'Thank you, Ma'm. But I – I thought Captain Butler done mighty fine too,' said Belle, shy pride in her voice.

'Oh, he was wonderful!' cried Melanie warmly. 'The Yankees couldn't help but believe his testimony. He was so smart about the whole affair. I can never thank him enough – or you either! How good and kind you are!'

'Thank you kindly, Miz Wilkes. It was a pleasure to do it. I – I hope it ain't goin' to embarrass you none, me sayin' Mr Wilkes come regular to my place. He never, you know—'

'Yes, I know. No, it doesn't embarrass me at all. I'm just so grateful to you.'

'I'll bet the other ladies ain't grateful to me,' said Belle with sudden venom. 'And I'll bet they ain't grateful to Captain Butler neither. I'll bet they'll hate him just this much more. I'll bet you'll be the only lady who even says thanks to me. I'll bet they won't even look me in the eye when they see me on the street. But I don't care. I wouldn't of minded if all their husbands got hung. But I did mind about Mr Wilkes. You see, I ain't forgot how nice you was to me durin' the war, about the money for the hospital. There ain't never been a lady in this town nice to me like you was and I don't forget a kindness.

And I thought about you bein' left a widder with a little boy if Mr Wilkes got hung and – he's a nice little boy, your boy is, Miz Wilkes. I got a boy myself and so I—'

'Oh, you have? Does he live – er—'

'Oh, no'm! He ain't here in Atlanta. He ain't never been here. He's off at school. I ain't seen him since he was little. I – well, anyway, when Captain Butler wanted me to lie for those men I wanted to know who the men was and when I heard Mr Wilkes was one I never hesitated. I said to my girls, I said, "I'll whale the livin' daylights out of you all if you don't make a special point of sayin' you was with Mr Wilkes all evenin'." '

'Oh!' said Melanie, still more embarrassed by Belle's off-hand reference to her 'girls'. 'Oh, that was – er – kind of you and – of them, too.'

'No more'n you deserve,' said Belle warmly. 'But I wouldn't of did it for just anybody. If it had been that Miz Kennedy's husband by hisself, I wouldn't of lifted a finger, no matter what Captain Butler said.'

'Why?'

'Well, Miz Wilkes, people in my business knows a heap of things. It'd surprise and shock a heap of fine ladies if they had any notion how much we knows about them. And she ain't no good, Miz Wilkes. She kilt her husband and that nice Wellburn boy, same as if she shot them. She caused it all, prancin' about Atlanta by herself, enticin' niggers and trash. Why, not one of my girls—'

'You must not say unkind things about my sister-in-law.' Melanie stiffened coldly.

Belle put an eager placating hand on Melanie's arm and then hastily withdrew it.

'Don't freeze me, please, Miz Wilkes. I couldn't stand it after you been so kind and sweet to me. I forgot how you liked her and I'm sorry for what I said. I'm sorry about poor Mr Kennedy bein' dead too. He was a nice man. I used to buy some of the stuff for my house from him and he always treated me pleasant. But Miz Kennedy – well, she just ain't in the same class with you, Miz Wilkes. She's a mighty cold woman and I can't help it if I think so . . . When are they goin' to bury Mr Kennedy?'

'Tomorrow morning. And you are wrong about Mrs Kennedy. Why, this very minute she's prostrated with grief.'

'Maybe so,' said Belle with evident disbelief. 'Well, I got to be goin'. I'm afraid somebody might recognize this carriage if I stayed here longer and that wouldn't do you no good. And, Miz Wilkes, if you ever see me on the street, you – you don't have to speak to me. I'll understand.'

'I shall be proud to speak to you. Proud to be under obligation to you. I hope – I hope we meet again.'

'No,' said Belle. 'That wouldn't be fittin'. Good night.'

Chapter XLVII

Scarlett sat in her bedroom, picking at the supper tray Mammy had brought her, listening to the wind hurling itself out of the night. The house was frighteningly still, quieter even than when Frank had lain in the parlour just a few hours before. Then there had been tiptoeing feet and hushed voices, muffled knocks on the front door, neighbours rustling in to whisper sympathy, and occasional sobs from Frank's sister who had come up from Jonesboro for the funeral.

But now the house was cloaked in silence. Although her door was open she could near no sounds from below stairs. Wade and the baby had been at Melanie's since Frank's body was brought home and she missed the sound of the boy's feet and Ella's gurgling. There was a truce in the kitchen and no sound of quarrelling from Peter, Mammy and Cookie floated up to her. Even Aunt Pitty, downstairs in the library, was not rocking her creaking chair in deference to Scarlett's sorrow.

No one intruded upon her, believing that she wished to be left alone with her grief, but to be left alone was the last thing Scarlett desired. Had it only been grief that companioned her, she could have borne it as she had borne other griefs. But, added to her stunned sense of loss at Frank's death, were fear and remorse and the torment of a suddenly awakened conscience. For the first time in her life she was regretting things she had done, regretting them with a sweeping superstitious fear that made her cast sidelong glances at the bed upon which she had lain with Frank.

She had killed Frank. She had killed him just as surely as if it had been her finger that pulled the trigger. He had begged her not to go about alone but she had not listened to him. And now he was dead because of her obstinacy. God would punish her for that. But there lay upon her conscience another matter that was heavier and more frightening even than causing his death – a matter which had never troubled her until she looked upon his coffined face. There had been something helpless and pathetic in that still face which had accused her. God would punish her for marrying him when he really loved Suellen. She would have to cower at the seat of judgment and answer for that lie she told him coming back from the Yankee camp in his buggy.

Useless for her to argue now that the end justified the means, that she was driven into trapping him, that the fate of too many people hung on her for her to consider either his or Suellen's rights and happiness. The truth stood out boldly and she cowered away from it. She had married him coldly and used him coldly. And she had made him unhappy during the last six months when she could have made him very happy. God would punish her for not being nicer to him – punish her for all her bullyings and proddings and storms of temper and cutting remarks, for alienating his friends and shaming him by operating the mills and building the saloon and leasing convicts.

She had made him very unhappy and she knew it, but he had borne it all like a gentleman. The only thing she had ever done that gave him any real happiness was to present him with Ella. And she knew if she could have kept from having Ella, Ella would never have been born.

She shivered, frightened, wishing Frank were alive, so she could be nice to him, so very nice to him to make up for it all. Oh, if only God did not seem so furious and vengeful! Oh, if only the minutes did not go by so slowly and the house were not so still! If only she were not so alone!

If only Melanie were with her, Melanie could calm her fears. But Melanie was at home, nursing Ashley. For a moment Scarlett thought of summoning Pittypat to stand between her and her conscience but she hesitated. Pitty would probably make matters worse, for she honestly mourned Frank. He had been more her contemporary than Scarlett's and she had been devoted to him. He had filled to perfection Pitty's need for 'a man in the house', for he brought her little presents and harmless gossip, jokes and stories, read the paper to her at night and explained topics of the day to her while she mended his socks. She had fussed over him and planned special dishes for him and coddled him during his innumerable colds. Now she missed him acutely and repeated over and over as she dabbed at her red swollen eyes: 'If only he hadn't gone out with the Klan!'

If there were only someone who could comfort her, quiet her fears, explain to her just what were these confused fears which made her heart sink with such cold sickness! If only Ashley – but she shrank from the thought. She had almost killed Ashley, just as she had killed Frank. And if Ashley ever knew the real truth about how she lied to Frank to get him, knew how mean she had been to Frank, he could never love her any more. Ashley was so honourable, so truthful, so kind and he saw so straightly, so clearly. If he knew the whole truth, he would understand. Oh, yes, he would understand only too well! But he would never love her any more. So he must never know the truth because he must keep on loving her. How could she live if that secret source of her strength, his love, were taken from her? But what a relief it would be to put her head on his shoulder and cry and unburden her guilty heart!

The still house with the sense of death heavy upon it pressed about her loneliness until she felt she could not bear it unaided any longer. She arose cautiously, pushed her door half-closed and then dug about in the bottom bureau drawer beneath her underwear. She produced Aunt Pitty's 'swoon bottle' of brandy which she had hidden there and held it up to the lamp. It was nearly half-empty. Surely she hadn't drunk that much since last night! She poured a generous amount into her water glass and gulped it down. She would have to put the bottle back in the cellaret before morning, filled to the top with water. Mammy had hunted for it, just before the funeral when the pall-bearers wanted a drink, and already the air in the kitchen was electric with suspicion between Mammy, Cookie and Peter.

The brandy burned with fiery pleasantness. There was nothing like it when you needed it. In fact, brandy was good almost any time, so much better than insipid wine. Why on earth should it be proper for a woman to drink wine and not spirits? Mrs Merriwether and Mrs Meade had sniffed her breath most obviously at the funeral and she had seen the triumphant look they had exchanged. The old cats!

She poured another drink. It wouldn't matter if she did get a little tipsy tonight for she was going to bed soon and she could gargle cologne before Mammy came up to unlace her. She wished she could get as completely and thoughtlessly drunk as Gerald used to get on Court Day. Then perhaps she could forget Frank's sunken face accusing her of ruining his life and then killing him.

She wondered if everyone in town thought she had killed him. Certainly the people at the funeral had been cold to her. The only people who had put any warmth into their expressions of sympathy were the wives of the Yankee officers with whom she did business. Well, she didn't care what the town said about her. How unimportant that seemed beside what she would have to answer for to God!

She took another drink at the thought, shuddering as the hot brandy went down her throat. She felt very warm now but still she couldn't get the thought of Frank out of her mind. What fools men were when they said liquor made people forget! Unless she drank herself into insensibility, she'd still see Frank's face as it had looked the last time he begged her not to drive alone, timid, reproachful, apologetic.

The knocker on the front door hammered with a dull sound that made the still house echo and she heard Aunt Pitty's waddling steps crossing the hall and the door opening. There was the sound of greeting and an indistinguishable murmur. Some neighbour calling to discuss the funeral or to bring a blancmange. Pitty would like that. She had taken an important and melancholy pleasure in talking to the condolence callers.

She wondered incuriously who it was and, when a man's voice, resonant and drawling, rose above Pitty's funereal whispering, she knew. Gladness and relief flooded her. It was Rhett. She had not seen him since he broke the news of Frank's death to her, and now she knew, deep in her heart, that he was the one person who could help her tonight.

'I think she'll see me,' Rhett's voice floated up to her.

'But she is lying down now, Captain Butler, and won't see anyone. Poor child, she is quite prostrated. She—'

'I think she will see me. Please tell her I am going away tomorrow and may be gone some time. It's very important.'

'But—' fluttered Aunt Pittypat.

Scarlett ran out into the hall, observing with some astonishment that her knees were a little unsteady, and leaned over the banisters.

'I'll be down terrectly, Rhett,' she called.

She had a glimpse of Aunt Pittypat's plump upturned face, her eyes owlish with surprise and disapproval. 'Now it'll be all over town that I conducted myself most improperly on the day of my husband's funeral,' thought Scarlett, as she hurried back to her room and began smoothing her hair. She buttoned her black basque up to the chin and pinned down the collar with Pittypat's mourning brooch. 'I don't look very pretty,' she thought, leaning toward the mirror, 'too white and scared.' For a moment her hand went toward the lock box where she kept her rouge hidden but she decided against it. Poor Pittypat would be upset in earnest if she came downstairs pink and blooming. She picked up the cologne bottle and took a large mouthful, carefully rinsed her mouth and then spat into the slop-jar.

She rustled down the stairs toward the two who still stood in the hall, for Pittypat had been too upset by Scarlett's action to ask Rhett to sit down. He was decorously clad in black, his linen frilly and starched, and his manner was all that custom demanded from an old friend paying a call of sympathy on one bereaved. In fact, it was so perfect that it verged on the burlesque, though Pittypat did not see it. He was properly apologetic for disturbing Scarlett and regretted that in his rush of closing up business before leaving town he had been unable to be present at the funeral.

'Whatever possessed him to come?' wondered Scarlett. 'He doesn't mean a word he's saying.'

'I hate to intrude on you at this time but I have a matter of business to discuss that will not wait. Something that Mr Kennedy and I were planning—'

'I didn't know you and Mr Kennedy had business dealings,' said Aunt Pittypat, almost indignant that some of Frank's activities were unknown to her.

'Mr Kennedy was a man of wide interests,' said Rhett respectfully. 'Shall we go into the parlour?'

'No!' cried Scarlett, glancing at the closed folding doors. She could still see the coffin in that room. She hoped she never had to enter it again. Pitty, for once, took a hint, although with none too good grace.

'Do use the library. I must – I must go upstairs and get out the mending. Dear me, I've neglected it so this last week. I declare—'

She went up the stairs with a backward look of reproach which was noticed by neither Scarlett nor Rhett. He stood aside to let her pass before him into the library.

'What business did you and Frank have?' she questioned abruptly.

He came closer and whispered: 'None at all. I just wanted to get Miss Pitty out of the way.' He paused as he leaned over her. 'It's no good, Scarlett.'

'What?'

'The cologne.'

'I'm sure I don't know what you mean.'

'I'm sure you do. You've been drinking pretty heavily.'

'Well, what if I have? Is it any of your business?'

'The soul of courtesy, even in the depths of sorrow. Don't drink alone,

Scarlett. People always find it out and it ruins the reputation. And besides, it's a bad business, this drinking alone. What's the matter, honey?'

He led her to the rosewood sofa and she sat down in silence.

'May I close the doors?'

She knew if Mammy saw the closed doors she would be scandalized and would lecture and grumble about it for days, but it would be still worse if Mammy should overhear this discussion of drinking, especially in light of the missing brandy bottle. She nodded and Rhett drew the sliding doors together. When he came back and sat down beside her, his dark eyes alertly searching her face, the pall of death receded before the vitality he radiated and the room seemed pleasant and homelike again, the lamps rosy and warm.

'What's the matter, honey?'

No one in the world could say that foolish word of endearment as caressingly as Rhett, even when he was joking, but he did not look as if he were joking now. She raised tormented eyes to his face and somehow found comfort in the blank inscrutability she saw there. She did not know why this should be, for he was such an unpredictable, callous person. Perhaps it was because, as he often said, they were so much alike. Sometimes she thought that all the people she had ever known were strangers except Rhett.

'Can't you tell me?' He took her hand, oddly gentle. 'It's more than just old Frank leaving you? Do you need money?'

'Money? God, no! Oh, Rhett, I'm so afraid.'

'Don't be a goose, Scarlett, you've never been afraid in your life.'

'Oh, Rhett, I am afraid.'

The words bubbled up faster than she could speak them. She could tell him. She could tell Rhett anything. He'd been so bad himself that he wouldn't sit in judgment on her. How wonderful to know someone who was bad and dishonourable and a cheat and a liar, when all the world was filled with people who would not lie to save their souls and who would rather starve than do a dishonourable deed!

'I'm afraid I'll die and go to hell.'

If he laughed at her she would die, right then. But he did not laugh.

'You are pretty healthy – and maybe there isn't any hell after all.'

'Oh, but there is, Rhett! You know there is!'

'I know there is but it's right here on earth. Not after we die. There's nothing after we die, Scarlett. You are having your hell now.'

'Oh, Rhett, that's blasphemous!'

'But singularly comforting. Tell me, why are you going to hell?'

He was teasing now, she could see the glint in his eyes but she did not mind. His hands felt so warm and strong, so comforting to cling to.

'Rhett, I oughtn't to have married Frank. It was wrong. He was Suellen's beau and he loved her, not me. But I lied to him and told him she was going to marry Tony Fontaine. Oh, how could I have done it?'

'Ah, so that was how it came about! I always wondered.'

'And then I made him so miserable. I made him do all sorts of things he didn't want to do, like making people pay their bills when they really couldn't afford to pay them. And it hurt him so when I ran the mills and built the saloon and leased convicts. He could hardly hold up his head for shame. And, Rhett, I killed him. Yes, I did! I didn't know he was in the Klan. I never dreamed he had that much gumption. But I ought to have known. And I killed him.'

' "Will all great Neptune's ocean wash this blood clean from my hands?" '

'What?'

'No matter. Go on.'

'Go on? That's all. Isn't it enough? I married him, I made him unhappy and I killed him. Oh, my God! I don't see how I could have done it! I lied to him and I married him. It all seemed so right when I did it but now I see how wrong it was. Rhett, it doesn't seem like it was me who did all these things. I was so mean to him but I'm not really mean. I wasn't raised that way. Mother—' She stopped and swallowed. She had avoided thinking of Ellen all day but she could no longer blot out her image.

'I often wondered what she was like. You seemed to me so like your father.'

'Mother was— Oh, Rhett, for the first time I'm glad she's dead, so she can't see me. She didn't raise me to be mean. She was so kind to everybody, so good. She'd rather I'd have starved than done this. And I so wanted to be just like her in every way and I'm not like her one bit. I hadn't thought of that – there's been so much else to think about – but I wanted to be like her. I didn't want to be like Pa. I loved him but he was – so – so thoughtless. Rhett, sometimes I did try so hard to be nice to people and kind to Frank, but then the nightmare would come back and scare me so bad I'd want to rush out and just grab money away from people, whether it was mine or not.'

Tears were streaming unheeded down her face and she clutched his hand so hard that her nails dug into his flesh.

'What nightmare?' His voice was calm and soothing.

'Oh – I forgot you didn't know. Well, just when I would try to be nice to folks and tell myself that money wasn't everything, I'd go to bed and dream that I was back at Tara right after Mother died, right after the Yankees went through. Rhett, you can't imagine—I get cold when I think about it. I can see how everything is burned and so still and there's nothing to eat. Oh, Rhett, in my dream I'm hungry again.'

'Go on.'

'I'm hungry and everybody, Pa and the girls and the darkies, are starving and they keep saying over and over, "We're hungry," and I'm so empty it hurts, and so frightened. My mind keeps saying, "If I ever get out of this, I'll never, never be hungry again," and then the dream goes off into a grey mist and I'm running, running in the mist, running so hard my heart's about to burst and something is chasing me, and I can't breathe but I keep thinking that if I can just get there, I'll be safe. But I don't know where I'm trying to get to. And then I'd wake up and I'd be cold with fright and so afraid that I'd be hungry again. When I wake up from that dream, it seems like there's not enough money in the world to keep me from being afraid of being hungry again. And then Frank would be so mealy-mouthed and slow-poky that he would make me mad and I'd lose my temper. He didn't understand, I guess, and I couldn't make him understand. I kept thinking that I'd make it up to him some day when we had money and I wasn't so afraid of being hungry. And now he's dead and it's too late. Oh, it seemed so right when I did it but it was all so wrong. If I had it to do over again, I'd do it so differently.'

'Hush,' he said, disentangling her frantic grip and pulling a clean handkerchief from his pocket. 'Wipe your face. There is no sense in your tearing yourself to pieces this way.'

She took the handkerchief and wiped her damp cheeks, a little relief stealing over her as if she had shifted some of her burden to his broad shoulders. He looked so capable and calm and even the slight twist of his mouth was comforting as though it proved her agony and confusion unwarranted.

'Feel better now? Then let's get to the bottom of this. You say if you had it to do over again, you'd do it differently. But would you? Think, now. Would you?'

'Well—'

'No, you'd do the same things again. Did you have any other choice?'

'No.'

'Then what are you sorry about?'

'I was so mean and now he's dead.'

'And if he wasn't dead, you'd still be mean. As I understand it, you are not really sorry for marrying Frank and bullying him and inadvertently causing his death. You are only sorry because you are afraid of going to hell. Is that right?'

'Well – that sounds so mixed up.'

'Your ethics are considerably mixed up too. You are in the exact position of a thief who's been caught red-handed and isn't sorry he stole but is terribly, terribly sorry he's going to jail.'

'A thief—'

'Oh, don't be so literal! In other words, if you didn't have this silly idea that you were damned to hell-fire eternal, you'd think you were well rid of Frank.'

'Oh, Rhett!'

'Oh, come! You are confessing and you might as well confess the truth as a decorous lie. Did your – er – conscience bother you much when you offered to – shall we say – part with that jewel which is dearer than life for three hundred dollars?'

The brandy was spinning in her head now and she felt giddy and a little reckless. What was the use in lying to him? He always seemed to read her mind.

'I really didn't think about God much then – or hell. And when I did think – well, I just reckoned God would understand.'

'But you don't credit God with understanding why you married Frank?'

'Rhett, how can you talk so about God when you know you don't believe there is one?'

'But you believe in a God of Wrath and that's what's important at present. Why shouldn't the Lord understand? Are you sorry you still own Tara and there aren't Carpetbaggers living there? Are you sorry you aren't hungry and ragged?'

'Oh, no!'

'Well, did you have any alternative except marrying Frank?'

'No.'

'He didn't have to marry you, did he? Men are free agents. And he didn't have to let you bully him into doing things he didn't want to, did he?'

'Well—'

'Scarlett, why worry about it? If you had it to do over again you would be driven to the lie and he to marrying you. You would still have run yourself into danger and he would have had to avenge you. If he had married Sister Sue, she might not have caused his death but she'd probably have made him twice as unhappy as you did. It couldn't have happened differently.'

'But I could have been nicer to him.'

'You could have been – if you'd been somebody else. But you were born to bully anyone who'll let you do it. The strong were made to bully and the weak to knuckle under. It's all Frank's fault for not beating you with a buggy-whip . . . I'm surprised at you, Scarlett, for sprouting a conscience this late in life. Opportunists like you shouldn't have them.'

'What is an oppor— what did you call it?'

'A person who takes advantage of opportunities.'

'Is that wrong?'

'It has always been held in disrepute – especially by those who had the same opportunities and didn't take them.'

'Oh, Rhett, you are joking and I thought you were going to be nice!'

'I am being nice – for me. Scarlett, darling, you are tipsy. That's what's the matter with you.'

'You dare—'

'Yes, I dare. You are on the verge of what is vulgarly called a "crying jag" and so I shall change the subject and cheer you up by telling you some news that will amuse you. In fact, that's why I came here this evening, to tell you my news before I went away.'

'Where are you going?'

'To England and I may be gone for months. Forget your conscience, Scarlett. I have no intention of discussing your soul's welfare any further. Don't you want to hear my news?'

'But—' she began feebly and paused. Between the brandy which was smoothing out the harsh contours of remorse and Rhett's mocking but comforting words, the pale spectre of Frank was receding into shadows. Perhaps Rhett was right. Perhaps God did understand. She recovered enough to push the idea from the top of her mind and decide: 'I'll think about it all tomorrow.'

'What's your news?' she said with an effort, blowing her nose on his handkerchief and pushing back the hair that had begun to straggle.

'My news is this,' he answered, grinning down at her. 'I still want you more than any woman I've ever seen and now that Frank is gone, I thought you'd be interested to know it.'

Scarlett jerked her hands away from his grasp and sprang to her feet.

'I – you are the most ill-bred man in the world, coming here at this time of all times with your filthy – I should have known you'd never change. And Frank hardly cold! If you had any decency— Will you leave this—'

'Do be quiet or you'll have Miss Pittypat down here in a minute,' he said, not rising but reaching up and taking both her fists. 'I'm afraid you miss my point.'

'Miss your point? I don't miss anything.' She pulled against his grip. 'Turn me loose and get out of here. I never heard of such bad taste. I—'

'Hush,' he said. 'I am asking you to marry me. Would you be convinced if I knelt down?'

She said, 'Oh,' breathlessly and sat down hard on the sofa.

She stared at him, her mouth open, wondering if the brandy were playing tricks on her mind, remembering senselessly his jibing: 'My dear, I'm not a marrying man.' She was drunk or he was crazy. But he did not look crazy. He looked as calm as though he were discussing the weather, and his smooth drawl fell on her ears with no particular emphasis.

'I always intended having you, Scarlett, since that first day I saw you at Twelve Oaks when you threw that vase and swore and proved that you weren't a lady. I always intended having you, one way or another. But as you and Frank have made a little money, I know you'll never be driven to me again with any interesting propositions of loans and collaterals. So I see I'll have to marry you.'

'Rhett Butler, is this one of your vile jokes?'

'I bare my soul and you are suspicious! No, Scarlett, this is a bona fide honourable declaration. I admit that it's not in the best of taste, coming at this time, but I have a very good excuse for my lack of breeding. I'm going away tomorrow for a long time and I fear that if I wait till I return you'll have married someone else with a little money. So I thought, why not me and my money? Really, Scarlett, I can't go all my life, waiting to catch you between husbands.'

He meant it. There was no doubt about it. Her mouth was dry as she assimilated this knowledge and she swallowed and looked into his eyes, trying to find some clue. They were full of laughter but there was something else, deep in them, which she had never seen before, a gleam that defied analysis. He sat easily, carelessly, but she felt that he was watching her as alertly as a cat watches a mouse-hole. There was a sense of leashed power straining beneath his calm that made her draw back, a little frightened.

He was actually asking her to marry him; he was committing the incredible. Once she had planned how she would torment him should he ever propose. Once she had thought that if he ever spoke those words she would humble him and make him feel her power and take a malicious pleasure in doing it. Now, he had spoken and the plans did not even occur to her, for he was no more in her power than he had ever been. In fact, he held the whip hand of the situation so completely that she was as flustered as a girl at her first proposal and she could only blush and stammer.

'I – I shall never marry again.'

'Oh, yes, you will. You were born to be married. Why not me?'

'But Rhett, I – I don't love you.'

'That should be no drawback. I don't recall that love was prominent in your other two ventures.'

'Oh, how can you? You know I was fond of Frank!'

He said nothing.

'I was! I was!'

'Well, we won't argue that. Will you think over my proposition while I'm gone?'

'Rhett, I don't like for things to drag on. I'd rather tell you now. I'm going home to Tara soon and India Wilkes will stay with Aunt Pittypat. I want to go home for a long spell and – I – I don't ever want to get married again.'

'Nonsense. Why?'

'Oh, well – never mind why. I just don't like being married.'

'But, my poor child, you've never really been married. How can you know? I'll admit you've had bad luck – once for spite and once for money. Did you ever think of marrying just for the fun of it?'

'Fun! Don't talk like a fool. There's no fun being married.'

'No? Why not?'

A measure of calm had returned and with it all the natural bluntness which brandy brought to the surface.

'It's fun for men – though God knows why. I never could understand it. But all a woman gets out of it is something to eat and a lot of work and having to put up with a man's foolishness – and a baby every year.'

He laughed so loudly that the sound echoed in the stillness and Scarlett heard the kitchen door open.

'Hush! Mammy has ears like a lynx and it isn't decent to laugh so soon after— Hush laughing. You know it's true. Fun! Fiddle-dee-dee!'

'I said you'd had bad luck and what you've just said proves it. You've been married to a boy and to an old man. And into the bargain I'll bet your mother told you that women must bear "these things" because of the compensating joys of motherhood. Well, that's all wrong. Why not try marrying a fine young man who has a bad reputation and a way with women? It'll be fun.'

'You are coarse and conceited and I think this conversation has gone far enough. It's – it's quite vulgar.'

'And quite enjoyable too, isn't it? I'll wager you never discussed the marital relation with a man before, even Charles or Frank.'

She scowled at him. Rhett knew too much. She wondered where he had learned all he knew about women. It wasn't decent.

'Don't frown. Name the day, Scarlett. I'm not urging instant matrimony because of your reputation. We'll wait the decent interval. By the way, just how long is a "decent interval"?'

'I haven't said I'd marry you. It isn't decent to even talk of such things at such a time.'

'I've told you why I'm talking of them. I'm going away tomorrow and I'm too ardent a lover to restrain my passion any longer. But perhaps I've been too precipitate in my wooing.'

With a suddenness that startled her, he slid off the sofa on to his knees and with one hand placed delicately over his heart, he recited rapidly: 'Forgive me for startling you with the impetuosity of my sentiments, my dear Scarlett – I mean, my dear Mrs Kennedy. It cannot have escaped your notice that for some time past the friendship I have had in my heart for you has ripened into a deeper feeling, a feeling more beautiful, more pure, more sacred. Dare I name it you? Ah! It is love which makes me so bold!'

'Do get up,' she entreated. 'You look such a fool and suppose Mammy should come in and see you?'

'She would be stunned and incredulous at the first signs of my gentility,' said Rhett, arising lightly. 'Come, Scarlett, you are no child, no schoolgirl to put me off with foolish excuses about decency and so forth. Say you'll marry me when I come back or, before God, I won't go. I'll stay around here and play a guitar under your window every night and sing at the top of my voice and compromise you, so you'll have to marry me to save your reputation.'

'Rhett, do be sensible. I don't want to marry anybody.'

'No? You aren't telling me the real reason. It can't be girlish timidity. What is it?'

Suddenly she thought of Ashley, saw him as vividly as though he stood beside her, sunny-haired, drowsy-eyed, full of dignity, so utterly different from Rhett. He was the real reason she did not want to marry again, although she had no objections to Rhett and at times was genuinely fond of him. She belonged to Ashley, for ever and ever. She had never belonged to Charles or Frank, could never really belong to Rhett. Every part of her, almost everything she had ever done, striven after, attained, belonged to Ashley, were done because she loved him. Ashley and Tara, she belonged to them. The smiles, the laughter, the kisses she had given Charles and Frank were Ashley's, even though he had never claimed them, would never claim them. Somewhere deep in her was the desire to keep herself for him, although she knew he would never take her.

She did not know that her face had changed, that reverie had brought a softness to her face which Rhett had never seen before. He looked at the slanting green eyes, wide and misty, and the tender curve of her lips, and for a moment his breath stopped. Then his mouth went down violently at one corner and he swore with passionate impatience.

'Scarlett O'Hara, you're a fool!'

Before she could withdraw her mind from its far places, his arms were around her, as sure and hard as on the dark road to Tara, so long ago. She felt again the rush of helplessness, the sinking yielding, the surging tide of warmth that left her limp. And the quiet face of Ashley Wilkes was blurred and drowned to nothingness. He bent back her head across his arm and kissed her, softly at first, and then with a swift gradation of intensity that made her cling to him as the only solid thing in a dizzy swaying world. His insistent mouth was parting her shaking lips, sending wild tremors along her nerves, evoking from her sensations she had never known she was capable of feeling. And before a swimming giddiness spun her round and round, she knew that she was kissing him back.

'Stop – please, I'm faint!' she whispered, trying to turn her head weakly from him. He pressed her head back hard against his shoulder and she had a dizzy glimpse of his face. His eyes were wide and blazing queerly and the tremor in his arms frightened her.

'I want to make you faint. I will make you faint. You've had this coming to you for years. None of the fools you've known have kissed you like this – have they? Your precious Charles or Frank or your stupid Ashley—'

'Please—'

'I said your stupid Ashley. Gentlemen all – what do they know about women? What did they know about you? I know you.'

His mouth was on hers again and she surrendered without a struggle, too weak even to turn her head, without even the desire to turn it, her heart shaking her with its poundings, fear of his strength and her nerveless weakness sweeping her. What was he going to do? She would faint if he did not stop. If he would only stop – if he would never stop.

'Say yes!' His mouth was poised above hers and his eyes were so close that they seemed enormous, filling the world. 'Say Yes, damn you, or—'

She whispered 'Yes,' before she even thought. It was almost as if he had willed the word and she had spoken it without her own volition. But even as she spoke it, a sudden calm fell on her spirit, her head began to stop spinning and even the giddiness of the brandy was lessened. She had promised to marry him when she had had no intention of promising. She hardly knew how it had all come about but she was not sorry. It now seemed very natural that she had said Yes – almost as if, by divine intervention, a hand stronger than hers was about her affairs, settling her problems for her.

He drew a quick breath as she spoke and bent as if to kiss her again and her eyes closed and her head fell back. But he drew back and she was faintly disappointed. It made her feel so strange to be kissed like this and yet there was something exciting about it.

He sat very still for a while holding her head against his shoulder and, as if by effort, the trembling of his arms ceased. He moved away from her a little and looked down at her. She opened her eyes and saw that the frightening glow had gone from his face. But somehow she could not meet his gaze and dropped her eyes in a rush of tingling confusion.

When he spoke his voice was very calm.

'You meant it? You don't want to take it back?'

'No.'

'It's not just because I've – what is the phrase? – "swept you off your feet" by my – er – ardour?'

She could not answer for she did not know what to say, nor could she meet his eyes. He put a hand under her chin and lifted her face.

'I told you once that I could stand anything from you except a lie. And now I want the truth. Just why did you say Yes?'

Still the words would not come, but a measure of poise returning, she kept her eyes demurely down and tucked the corners of her mouth into a little smile.

'Look at me. Is it my money?'

'Why, Rhett! What a question!'

'Look up and don't try to sweet-talk me. I'm not Charles or Frank or any of the County boys to be taken in by your fluttering lids. Is it my money?'

'Well – yes, a part.'

'A part?'

He did not seem annoyed. He drew a swift breath and with an effort wiped from his eyes the eagerness her words had brought, an eagerness which she was too confused to see.

'Well,' she floundered helplessly, 'money does help, you know, Rhett, and God knows Frank didn't leave any too much. But then – well, Rhett, we do get on, you know. And you are the only man I ever saw who could stand the truth from a woman, and it would be nice having a husband who didn't think me a silly fool and expect me to tell lies – and – well, I am fond of you.'

'Fond of me?'

'Well,' she said fretfully, 'if I said I was madly in love with you, I'd be lying and what's more, you'd know it.'

'Sometimes I think you carry your truth-telling too far, my pet. Don't you think, even if it was a lie, that it would be appropriate for you to say, "I love you, Rhett," even if you didn't mean it?'

What was he driving at, she wondered, becoming more confused. He looked so queer, eager, hurt, mocking. He took his hands from her and shoved them deep in his trouser pockets and she saw him ball his fists.

'If it costs me a husband, I'll tell the truth,' she thought grimly, her blood up as always when he baited her.

'Rhett, it would be a lie, and why should we go through all that foolishness? I'm fond of you, like I said. You know how it is. You told me once that you didn't love me but that we had a lot in common. Both rascals, was the way you—'

'Oh, God!' he whispered rapidly, turning his head away. 'To be taken in my own trap!'

'What did you say?'

'Nothing,' and he looked at her and laughed, but it was not a pleasant laugh. 'Name the day, my dear,' and he laughed again and bent and kissed her hands. She was relieved to see his mood pass and good humour apparently return, so she smiled too.

He played with her hand for a moment and grinned up at her.

'Did you ever in your novel-reading come across the old situation of the disinterested wife falling in love with her own husband?'

'You know I don't read novels,' she said and, trying to equal his jesting mood, went on: 'Besides, you once said it was the height of bad form for husbands and wives to love each other.'

'I once said too God damn many things,' he retorted abruptly and rose to his feet.

'Don't swear.'

'You'll have to get used to it and learn to swear too. You'll have to get used to all my bad habits. That'll be part of the price of being – fond of me and getting your pretty paws on my money.'

'Well, don't fly off the handle so, because I didn't lie and make you feel conceited. You aren't in love with me, are you? Why should I be in love with you?'

'No, my dear, I'm not in love with you, no more than you are with me, and if I were, you would be the last person I'd ever tell. God help the man who ever really loves you. You'd break his heart, my darling, cruel, destructive little cat who is so careless and confident she doesn't even trouble to sheath her claws.'

He jerked her to her feet and kissed her again, but this time his lips were different for he seemed not to care if he hurt her – seemed to want to hurt her, to insult her. His lips slid down to her throat and finally he pressed them against the taffeta over her breast, so hard and so long that his breath burnt to her skin. Her hands struggled up, pushing him away in outraged modesty.

'You mustn't! How dare you!'

'Your heart's going like a rabbit's,' he said mockingly. 'All too fast for mere fondness I would think, if I were conceited. Smooth your ruffled feathers. You are just putting on these virginal airs. Tell me what I shall bring you from England. A ring? What kind would you like?'

She wavered momentarily between interest in his last words and a feminine desire to prolong the scene with anger and indignation.

'Oh – a diamond ring – and Rhett, do buy a great big one.'

'So you can flaunt it before your poverty-stricken friends and say, "See what I caught!" Very well, you shall have a big one, one so big that your less-fortunate friends can comfort themselves by whispering that it's really vulgar to wear such large stones.'

He abruptly started off across the room and she followed him, bewildered, to the closed doors.

'What is the matter? Where are you going?'

'To my rooms to finish packing.'

'Oh, but—'

'But, what?'

'Nothing. I hope you have a nice trip.'

'Thank you.'

He opened the door and walked into the hall. Scarlett trailed after him, somewhat at a loss, a trifle disappointed as at an unexpected anticlimax. He slipped on his coat and picked up his gloves and hat.

'I'll write you. Let me know if you change your mind.'

'Aren't you—'

'Well?' He seemed impatient to be off.

'Aren't you going to kiss me goodbye?' she whispered, mindful of the ears of the house.

'Don't you think you've had enough kissing for one evening?' he retorted and grinned down at her. 'To think of a modest, well-brought-up young woman—Well, I told you it would be fun, didn't I?'

'Oh, you are impossible!' she cried in wrath, not caring if Mammy did hear. 'And I don't care if you never come back.'

She turned and flounced toward the stairs, expecting to feel his warm hand on her arm, stopping her. But he only pulled open the front door and a cold draught swept in.

'But I will come back,' he said and went out, leaving her on the bottom step looking at the closed door.

The ring Rhett brought back from England was large indeed, so large it embarrassed Scarlett to wear it. She loved gaudy and expensive jewellery but she had an uneasy feeling that everyone was saying, with perfect truth, that this ring was vulgar. The central stone was a four-carat diamond and, surrounding it, were a number of emeralds. It reached to the knuckle of her finger and gave her hand the appearance of being weighted down. Scarlett had a suspicion that Rhett had gone to great pains to have the ring made up and, for pure meanness, had ordered it made as ostentatious as possible.

Until Rhett was back in Atlanta and the ring on her finger she told no one, not even her family, of her intentions, and when she did announce her engagement a storm of bitter gossip broke out. Since the Klan affair Rhett and Scarlett had been, with the exception of the Yankees and Carpetbaggers, the town's most unpopular citizens. Everyone had disapproved of Scarlett since the far-away day when she abandoned the weeds worn for Charlie Hamilton. Their disapproval had grown stronger because of her unwomanly conduct in the matter of the mills, her immodesty in showing herself when she was pregnant and so many other things. But when she brought about the death of Frank and Tommy and jeopardized the lives of a dozen other men, their dislike flamed into public condemnation.

As for Rhett, he had enjoyed the town's hatred since his speculations during the war and he had not further endeared himself to his fellow citizens by his alliances with the Republicans since then. But, oddly enough, the fact that he had saved the lives of some of Atlanta's most prominent men was what aroused the hottest hate of Atlanta's ladies.

It was not that they regretted their men were still alive. It was that they bitterly resented owing the men's lives to such a man as Rhett and to such an embarrassing trick. For months they had writhed under Yankee laughter and scorn, and the ladies felt and said that if Rhett really had the good of the Klan at heart he would have managed the affair in a more seemly fashion. They said he had deliberately dragged in Belle Watling to put the nice people of the town in a disgraceful position. And so he deserved neither thanks for rescuing the men nor forgiveness for his past sins.

These women, so swift to kindness, so tender to the sorrowing, so untiring in times of stress, could be as implacable as furies to any renegade who broke one small law of their unwritten code. This code was simple. Reverence for the Confederacy, honour to the veterans, loyalty to old forms, pride in poverty, open hands to friends and undying hatred to Yankees. Between them, Scarlett and Rhett had outraged every tenet of this code.

The men whose lives Rhett had saved attempted, out of decency and a sense of gratitude, to keep their women silent but they had little success. Before the announcement of their coming marriage, the two had been unpopular enough but people could still be polite to them in a formal way. Now even that cold courtesy was no longer possible. The news of their engagement came like an explosion, unexpected and shattering, rocking the town, and even the mildest-mannered women spoke their minds heatedly. Marrying barely a year after Frank's death and she had killed him! And marrying that Butler man who owned a brothel and who was in with the Yankees and Carpetbaggers in all kinds of thieving schemes! Separately, the two of them could be endured, but the brazen combination of Scarlett and Rhett was too much to be borne. Common and vile, both of them! They ought to be run out of town!

Atlanta might perhaps have been more tolerant toward the two if the news of their engagement had not come at a time when Rhett's Carpetbagger and Scallawag cronies were more odious in the sight of respectable citizens than they had ever been before. Public feeling against the Yankees and all their allies was at fever heat at the very time when the town learned of the engagement, for the last citadel of Georgia's resistance to Yankee rule had just fallen. The long campaign which had begun when Sherman moved southward from above Dalton, four years before, had finally reached its climax, and the state's humiliation was complete.

Three years of Reconstruction had passed and they had been three years of terrorism. Everyone had thought that conditions were already as bad as they could ever be. But now Georgia was discovering that Reconstruction at its worst had just begun.

For three years the Federal government had been trying to impose alien ideas and an alien rule upon Georgia and, with an army to enforce its commands, it had largely succeeded. But only the power of the military upheld the new régime. The state was under the Yankee rule but not by the state's consent. Georgia's leaders had kept on battling for the state's right to govern itself according to its own ideas. They had continued resisting all efforts to force them to bow down and accept the dictates of Washington as their own state law.

Officially, Georgia's government had never capitulated but it had been a futile fight, an ever-losing fight. It was a fight that could not win but it had, at least, postponed the inevitable. Already many other Southern states had illiterate negroes in high public office and legislatures dominated by negroes and Carpetbaggers. But Georgia, by its stubborn resistance, had so far escaped this final degradation. For the greater part of three years, the state's capitol had remained in the control of white men and Democrats. With Yankee soldiers everywhere, the state officials could do little but protest and resist. Their power was nominal but they had at least been able to keep the state government in the hands of native Georgians. Now even that last stronghold had fallen.

Just as Johnston and his men had been driven back step by step from Dalton to Atlanta, four years before, so had the Georgia Democrats been driven back little by little, from 1865 on. The power of the Federal government over the state's affairs and the lives of its citizens had been steadily made greater and greater. Force had been piled on top of force and military edicts in increasing numbers had rendered the civil authority more and more impotent. Finally, with Georgia in the status of a military province, the polls had been ordered thrown open to the negroes, whether the state's laws permitted it or not.

A week before Scarlett and Rhett announced their engagement, an election for governor had been held. The Southern Democrats had General John B. Gordon, one of Georgia's best-loved and most honoured citizens, as their candidate. Opposing him was a Republican named Bullock. The election had lasted three days instead of one. Trainloads of negroes had been rushed from town to town, voting at every precinct along the way. Of course, Bullock had won.

If the capture of Georgia by Sherman had caused bitterness, the final capture of the state's capitol by the Carpetbaggers, Yankees and negroes caused an intensity of bitterness such as the state had never known before. Atlanta and Georgia seethed and raged.

And Rhett Butler was a friend of the hated Bullock!

Scarlett, with her usual disregard for all matters not directly under her nose, had scarcely known an election was being held. Rhett had taken no part in the election and his relations with the Yankees were no different from what they had always been. But the fact remained that Rhett was a Scallawag and a friend of Bullock. And, if the marriage went through, Scarlett also would be turning Scallawag. Atlanta was in no mood to be tolerant or charitable toward anyone in the enemy camp and, the news of the engagement coming when it did, the town remembered all of the evil things about the pair and none of the good.

Scarlett knew the town was rocking but she did not realize the extent of public feeling until Mrs Merriwether, urged on by her church circle, took it upon herself to speak to her for her own good.

'Because your own dear mother is dead and Miss Pitty, not being a matron, is not qualified to – er – well, to talk to you upon such a subject, I feel that I must warn you, Scarlett. Captain Butler is not the kind of a man for any woman of good family to marry. He is a—'

'He managed to save Grandpa Merriwether's neck and your nephew's, too.'

Mrs Merriwether swelled. Hardly an hour before she had had an irritating talk with Grandpa. The old man had remarked that she must not value his hide very much if she did not feel some gratitude to Rhett Butler, even if the man was a Scallawag and a scoundrel.

'He only did that as a dirty trick on us all, Scarlett, to embarrass us in front of the Yankees,' Mrs Merriwether continued. 'You know as well as I do that the man is a rogue. He always has been and now he's unspeakable. He is simply not the kind of man decent people receive.'

'No? That's strange, Mrs Merriwether. He was in your parlour often enough during the war. And he gave Maybelle her white satin wedding dress, didn't he? Or is my memory wrong?'

'Things were so different during the war and nice people associated with many men who were not quite— It was all for the Cause and very proper, too. Surely you can't be thinking of marrying a man who wasn't in the army, who jeered at men who did enlist?'

'He was, too, in the army. He was in the army eight months. He was in the last campaign and fought at Franklin and was with General Johnston when he surrendered.'

'I had not heard that,' said Mrs Merriwether, and she looked as if she did not believe it either. 'But he wasn't wounded,' she added, triumphantly.

'Lots of men weren't.'

'Everybody who was anybody got wounded. I know no one who wasn't wounded.'

Scarlett was goaded.

'Then I guess all the men you knew were such fools they didn't know when to come in out of a shower of rain – or of minie balls. Now, let me tell you this, Mrs Merriwether, and you can take it back to your busybody friends. I'm going to marry Captain Butler and I wouldn't care if he'd fought on the Yankee side.'

When that worthy matron went out of the house with her bonnet jerking with rage, Scarlett knew she had an open enemy now instead of a disapproving friend. But she did not care. Nothing Mrs Merriwether could say or do could hurt her. She did not care what anyone said – anyone except Mammy.

Scarlett had borne with Pitty's swooning at the news and had steeled herself to see Ashley look suddenly old and avoid her eyes as he wished her happiness. She had been amused and irritated at the letters from Aunt Pauline and Aunt Eulalie in Charleston, horror-struck at the news, forbidding the marriage, telling her it would not only ruin her social position but endanger theirs. She had even laughed when Melanie with a worried pucker in her brows said loyally: 'Of course, Captain Butler is much nicer than most people realize and he was so kind and clever, the way he saved Ashley. And after all, he did fight for the Confederacy. But, Scarlett, don't you think you'd better not decide so hastily?'

No, she didn't mind what anybody said, except Mammy. Mammy's words were the ones that made her most angry and brought the greatest hurt.

'Ah has seed you do a heap of things dat would hu't Miss Ellen, did she know. An' it has done sorrered me a plen'y. But disyere is de wust yit. Mahyin' trash! Yas'm, Ah said trash! Doan go tellin' me he come frum fine folkses. Dat doan mek no diffunce. Trash come outer de high places, same as de low, and he trash! Yas'm, Miss Scarlett, Ah's seed you tek Mist' Charles 'way frum Miss Honey w'en you din' keer nuthin' 'bout him. An' Ah's seed you rob yo' own sister of Mist' Frank. An' Ah's heshed mah mouf 'bout a heap of things you is done, lak sellin' po' lumber fer good, an' lyin' 'bout de other lumber gempmums, an' ridin' roun' by yo'seff, exposin' yo'seff ter free issue niggers an' gittin' Mist' Frank shot, an' not feedin' dem po' convicts nuff ter keep dey souls in dey bodies. Ah's done heshed mah mouf, even ef Miss Ellen in de Promise Lan' wuz sayin', "Mammy, Mammy! You ain' look affer mah chile right!" Yas'm, Ah's stood fer all dat but Ah ain' gwine stand fer dis, Miss Scarlett. You kain mahy wid trash. Not w'ile Ah got breaf in mah body.'

'I shall marry whom I please,' said Scarlett coldly. 'I think you are forgetting your place, Mammy.'

'An' high time, too! Ef Ah doan say dese wuds ter you, who gwine ter do it?'

'I've been thinking the matter over, Mammy, and I've decided that the best thing for you to do is to go back to Tara. I'll give you some money and—'

Mammy drew herself up with all her dignity.

'Ah is free, Miss Scarlett. You kain sen' me nowhar Ah doan wanter go. An' w'en Ah goes back ter Tara, it's gwine be w'en you goes wid me. Ah ain' gwine leave Miss Ellen's chile, an' dar ain' no way in de worl' ter mek me go. An' Ah ain' gwine leave Miss Ellen's gran'chillun fer no trashy step-pa ter bring up, needer. Hyah Ah is and hyah Ah stays!'

'I will not have you staying in my house and being rude to Captain Butler. I am going to marry him and there's no more to be said.'

'Dar is plen'y mo' ter be said,' retorted Mammy slowly, and into her blurred old eyes there came the light of battle.

'But Ah ain' never thought ter say it ter none of Miss Ellen's blood. But, Miss Scarlett, lissen ter me. You ain' nuthin' but a mule in hawse harness. You kin polish a mule's feets an' shine his hide an' put brass all over his harness an' hitch him ter a fine cah'ige. But he a mule jes' de same. He doan fool nobody. An' you is jes' de same. You got silk dresses an' de mills an' de sto' an' de money, an' you give yo'seff airs lak a fine hawse, but you a mule jes' de same. An' you ain' foolin' nobody, needer. An' dat Butler man, he come of good stock and he all slicked up lak a race-hawse, but he a mule in hawse harness, jes' lak you.'

Mammy bent a piercing look on her mistress. Scarlett was speechless and quivering with insult.

'Ef you say you gwine mahy him, you gwine do it, 'cause you is bull-haided lak yo' pa. But 'member dis, Miss Scarlett, Ah ain' leavin' you. Ah gwine stay right hyah an see dis thing thoo.'

Without waiting for a reply, Mammy turned and left Scarlett and if she had said, 'Thou shalt see me at Philippi!' her tones could not have been more ominous.

While they were honeymooning in New Orleans Scarlett told Rhett of Mammy's words. To her surprise and indignation he laughed at Mammy's statement about mules in horse harness.

'I have never heard a profound truth expressed so succinctly,' he said. 'Mammy's a smart old soul and one of the few people I know whose respect and goodwill I'd like to have. But, being a mule, I suppose I'll never get either from her. She even refused the ten-dollar gold piece which I, in my groomlike fervour, wished to present her after the wedding. I've seen so few people who did not melt at the sight of cash. But she looked me in the eye and thanked me and said she wasn't a free issue nigger and didn't need my money.'

'Why should she take on so? Why should everybody gabble about me like a bunch of guinea-hens? It's my own affair whom I marry and how often I marry. I've always minded my own business. Why don't other people mind theirs?'

'My pet, the world can forgive practically anything except people who mind their own business. But why should you squall like a scalded cat? You've said often enough that you didn't mind what people said about you. Why not prove it? You know you've laid yourself open to criticism so often in small matters, you can't expect to escape gossip in this large matter. You knew there'd be talk if you married a villain like me. If I were a low-bred, poverty-stricken villain, people wouldn't be so mad. But a rich, flourishing villain – of course, that's unforgivable.'

'I wish you'd be serious sometimes!'

'I am serious. It's always annoying to the godly when the ungodly flourish like the green bay tree. Cheer up, Scarlett, didn't you tell me once that the main reason you wanted a lot of money was so you could tell everybody to go to hell? Now's your chance.'

'But you were the main one I wanted to tell to go to hell,' said Scarlett, and laughed.

'Do you still want to tell me to go to hell?'

'Well, not as often as I used to.'

'Do it whenever you like, if it makes you happy.'

'It doesn't make me especially happy,' said Scarlett and, bending, she kissed him carelessly. His dark eyes flickered quickly over her face, hunting for something in her eyes which he did not find, and he laughed shortly.

'Forget about Atlanta. Forget about the old cats. I brought you to New Orleans to have fun and I intend that you shall have it.'

Part Five

Chapter XLVIII

She did have fun, more fun than she had had since the spring before the war. New Orleans was such a strange, glamorous place and Scarlett enjoyed it with the headlong pleasure of a pardoned life prisoner. The Carpetbaggers were looting the town, many honest folk were driven from their homes and did not know where to look for their next meal, and a negro sat in the lieutenant-governor's chair. But the New Orleans Rhett showed her was the gayest place she had ever seen. The people she met seemed to have all the money they wanted and no cares at all. Rhett introduced her to dozens of women, pretty women in bright gowns, women who had soft hands that showed no signs of hard work, women who laughed at everything and never talked of stupid serious things or hard times. And the men she met – how thrilling they were! And how different from Atlanta men – and how they fought to dance with her, and paid her the most extravagant compliments as though she were a young belle.

These men had the same hard reckless look Rhett wore. Their eyes were always alert, like men who have lived too long with danger to be ever quite careless. They seemed to have no pasts or futures, and they politely discouraged Scarlett when, to make conversation, she asked what or where they were before they came to New Orleans. That, in itself, was strange, for in Atlanta every respectable newcomer hastened to present his credentials, to tell proudly of his home and family, to trace the tortuous mazes of relationship that stretched over the entire South.

But these men were a taciturn lot, picking their words carefully. Sometimes when Rhett was alone with them and Scarlett in the next room, she heard laughter and caught fragments of conversation that meant nothing to her, scraps of words, puzzling names – Cuba and Nassau in the blockade days, the gold rush and claim-jumping, gun-running and filibustering, Nicaragua and William Walker and how he died against a wall at Truxillo. Once her sudden entrance abruptly terminated a conversation about what had happened to the members of Quantrill's band of guerrillas, and she caught the names of Frank and Jesse James.

But they were all well mannered, beautifully tailored, and they evidently admired her, so it mattered little to Scarlett that they chose to live utterly in the present. What really mattered was that they were Rhett's friends and had large houses and fine carriages, and they took her and Rhett driving, invited them to suppers, gave parties in their honour. And Scarlett liked them very well. Rhett was amused when she told him so.

'I thought you would,' he said and laughed.

'Why not?' her suspicions aroused as always by his laughter.

'They're all second-raters, black sheep, rascals. They're all adventurers or Carpetbag aristocrats. They all made their money speculating in food like your loving husband or out of dubious government contracts or in shady ways that won't bear investigation.'

'I don't believe it. You're teasing. They're the nicest people . . .'

'The nicest people in town are starving,' said Rhett. 'And living politely in hovels, and I doubt if I'd be received in those hovels. You see, my dear, I was engaged in some of my nefarious schemes here during the war and these people have devilish long memories! Scarlett, you are a constant joy to me. You unerringly manage to pick the wrong people and the wrong things.'

'But they are your friends!'

'Oh, but I like rascals. My early youth was spent as a gambler on a river boat and I can understand people like that. But I'm not blind to what they are. Whereas you' – he laughed again – 'you have no instinct about people, no discrimination between the cheap and the great. Sometimes I think that the only great ladies you've ever associated with were your mother and Miss Melly and neither seems to have made any impression on you.'

'Melly! Why, she's as plain as an old shoe and her clothes always look tacky and she never has two words to say for herself!'

'Spare me your jealousy, Madam. Beauty doesn't make a lady, nor clothes a great lady.'

'Oh, don't they! Just you wait, Rhett Butler, and I'll show you. Now that I've – we've got money, I'm going to be the greatest lady you ever saw!'

'I shall wait with interest,' he said.

More exciting than the people she met were the frocks Rhett bought her, superintending the choice of colours, materials and designs himself. Hoops were out now, and the new styles were charming with the skirts pulled back from the front and draped over bustles, and on the bustles were wreaths of flowers and bows and cascades of lace. She thought of the modest hoops of the war years and she felt a little embarrassed at these new skirts which undeniably outlined her abdomen. And the darling little bonnets that were not really bonnets at all, but flat little affairs worn over one eye and laden with fruits and flowers, dancing plumes and fluttering ribbons! (If only Rhett had not been so silly and burned the false curls she bought to augment her knot of Indian-straight hair that peeked from the rear of these little hats!) And the delicate convent-made underwear! How lovely it was and how many sets she had! Chemises and nightgowns and petticoats of the finest linen trimmed with dainty embroidery and infinitesimal tucks. And the satin slippers Rhett bought her! They had heels three inches high and huge glittering paste buckles on them. And silk stockings, a dozen pairs and not a one had cotton tops! What riches!

She recklessly bought gifts for the family. A furry St Bernard puppy for Wade, who had always longed for one, a Persian kitten for Beau, a coral bracelet for little Ella, a heavy necklace with moonstone pendants for Aunt Pitty, a complete set of Shakespeare for Melanie and Ashley, an elaborate livery for Uncle Peter, including a high silk coachman's hat with a brush upon it, dress-lengths for Dilcey and Cookie, expensive gifts for everyone at Tara.

'But what have you bought for Mammy?' questioned Rhett, looking over the pile of gifts spread out on the bed in their hotel room, and removing the puppy and kitten to the dressing-room.

'Not a thing. She was hateful. Why should I bring her a present when she called us mules?'

'Why should you so resent hearing the truth, my pet? You must bring Mammy a present. It would break her heart if you didn't – and hearts like hers are too valuable to be broken.'

'I won't take her a thing. She doesn't deserve it.'

'Then I'll buy her one. I remember my mammy always said that when she went to Heaven she wanted a taffeta petticoat so stiff that it would stand by itself and so rustly that the Lord God would think it was made of angels' wings. I'll buy Mammy some red taffeta and have an elegant petticoat made.'

'She won't take it from you. She'd die rather than wear it.'

'I don't doubt it. But I'll make the gesture just the same.'

The shops of New Orleans were so rich and exciting and shopping with Rhett was an adventure. Dining with him was an adventure too, and one more thrilling than shopping, for he knew what to order and how it should be cooked. The wines and liqueurs and champagnes of New Orleans were new and exhilarating to her, acquainted with only home-made blackberry and scuppernong vintages and Aunt Pitty's 'swoon' brandy; but oh, the food Rhett ordered! Best of all things in New Orleans was the food. Remembering the bitter hungry days at Tara and her more recent penury, Scarlett felt that she could never eat enough of these rich dishes. Gumboes and shrimp Creole, doves in wine and oysters in crumbly patties full of creamy sauce, mushrooms and sweetbreads and turkey livers, fish baked cunningly in oiled paper and limes. Her appetite never dulled, for whenever she remembered the everlasting goobers and dried peas and sweet potatoes at Tara, she felt an urge to gorge herself anew on Creole dishes.

'You eat as though each meal were your last,' said Rhett. 'Don't scrape the plate, Scarlett. I'm sure there's more in the kitchen. You have only to ask the waiter. If you don't stop being such a glutton, you'll be as fat as the Cuban ladies and then I shall divorce you.'

But she only put out her tongue at him and ordered another pastry, thick with chocolate and stuffed with meringue.

What fun it was to be able to spend as much money as you liked and not count pennies and feel you should save them to pay taxes or buy mules. What fun to be with people who were gay and rich and not genteelly poor like Atlanta people. What fun to wear rustling brocade dresses that showed your waist and all your neck and arms and more than a little of your breast and know that men were admiring you. And what fun to eat all you wanted without having censorious people say you weren't ladylike. And what fun to drink all the champagne you pleased. The first time she drank too much, she was embarrassed when she awoke the next morning with a splitting headache and an awful memory of singing 'Bonnie Blue Flag' all the way back to the hotel, through the streets of New Orleans, in an open carriage. She had never seen a lady even tipsy, and the only drunken woman she had ever seen had been that Watling creature on the day when Atlanta fell. She hardly knew how to face Rhett, so great was her humiliation, but the affair seemed only to amuse him. Everything she did seemed to amuse him, as though she were a gambolling kitten.

It was exciting to go out with him for he was so handsome. Somehow she had never given his looks a thought before, and in Atlanta everyone had been too preoccupied with his shortcomings ever to talk about his appearance. But here in New Orleans she could see how the eyes of other women followed him and how they fluttered when he bent over their hands. The realization that other women were attracted by her husband, and perhaps envied her, made her suddenly proud to be seen by his side.

'Why, we're a handsome couple,' thought Scarlett with pleasure.

Yes, as Rhett had prophesied, marriage could be a lot of fun. Not only was it fun but she was learning many things. That was odd in itself, because Scarlett had thought life could teach her no more. Now she felt like a child, every day on the brink of a new discovery.

First, she learned that marriage with Rhett was a far different matter from marriage with either Charles or Frank. They had respected her and been afraid of her temper. They had begged for favours and if it pleased her, she had bestowed them. Rhett did not fear her and, she often thought, did not respect her very much either. What he wanted to do, he did, and if she did not like it, he laughed at her. She did not love him but he was undoubtedly an exciting person to live with. The most exciting thing about him was that even in his outbursts of passion, which were flavoured sometimes with cruelty, sometimes with irritating amusement, he seemed always to be holding himself under restraint, always riding his emotions with a curb bit.

'I guess that's because he isn't really in love with me,' she thought and was content enough with the state of affairs. 'I should hate for him to ever turn completely loose in any way.' But still the thought of the possibility teased her curiosity in an exciting way.

Living with Rhett, she learned many new things about him, and she had thought she knew him so well. She learned that his voice could be silky as cat's fur one moment and crisp and crackling with oaths the next. He could tell, with apparent sincerity and approval, stories of courage and honour and virtue and love in the odd places he had been, and follow them with ribald stories of coldest cynicism. She knew no man should tell such stories to his wife but they were entertaining and they appealed to something coarse and earthy in her. He could be an ardent, almost a tender, lover for a brief while, and almost immediately a mocking devil who ripped the lid from her gunpowder temper, fired it and enjoyed the explosion. She learned that his compliments were always two-edged and his tenderest expressions open to suspicion. In fact, in those two weeks in New Orleans, she learned everything about him except what he really was.

Some mornings he dismissed the maid and brought her the breakfast tray himself and fed her as though she were a child, took the hairbrush from her hand and brushed her long dark hair until it snapped and crackled. Yet other mornings she was torn rudely out of deep slumber when he snatched all the bed-covers from her and tickled her bare feet. Sometimes he listened with dignified interest to details of her businesses, nodding approval at her sagacity, and at other times he called her somewhat dubious tradings scavenging, highway robbery and extortion. He took her to plays and annoyed her by whispering that God probably didn't approve of such amusements, and to churches and, sotto voce, retailed funny obscenities and then reproved her for laughing. He encouraged her to speak her mind, to be flippant and daring. She picked up from him the gift of stinging words and sardonic phrases and learned to relish using them for the power they gave her over other people. But she did not possess his sense of humour which tempered his malice, nor his smile that jeered at himself even while he was jeering at others.

He made her play and she had almost forgotten how. Life had been so serious and so bitter. He knew how to play and swept her along with him. But he never played like a boy; he was a man and no matter what he did, she could never forget it. She could not look down on him from the heights of womanly superiority, smiling as women have always smiled at the antics of men who are boys at heart.

This annoyed her a little, whenever she thought of it. It would be pleasant to feel superior to Rhett. All the other men she had known she could dismiss with a half-contemptuous, 'What a child!' Her father, the Tarleton twins with their love of teasing and their elaborate practical jokes, the hairy little Fontaines with their childish rages, Charles, Frank, all the men who had paid court to her during the war – everyone, in fact, except Ashley. Only Ashley and Rhett eluded her understanding and her control for they were both adults, and the elements of boyishness were lacking in them.

She did not understand Rhett, nor did she trouble to understand him, though there were things about him which occasionally puzzled her. There was the way he looked at her sometimes, when he thought she was unaware. Turning quickly she frequently caught him watching her, an alert, eager, waiting look in his eyes.

'Why do you look at me like that?' she once asked irritably. 'Like a cat at a mouse-hole!'

But his face had changed swiftly and he only laughed. Soon she forgot it and did not puzzle her head about it any more, or about anything concerning Rhett. He was too unpredictable to bother about and life was very pleasant – except when she thought of Ashley.

Rhett kept her too busy to think of Ashley often. Ashley was hardly ever in her thoughts during the day, but at night when she was tired from dancing or her head was spinning from too much champagne – then she thought of Ashley. Frequently when she lay drowsily in Rhett's arms with the moonlight streaming over the bed, she thought how perfect life would be if it were only Ashley's arms which held her so closely, if it were only Ashley who drew her black hair across his face and wrapped it about his throat.

Once when she was thinking this, she sighed and turned her head toward the window, and after a moment she felt the heavy arm beneath her neck become like iron, and Rhett's voice spoke in the stillness: 'May God damn your cheating little soul to hell for all eternity!'

And, getting up, he put on his clothes and left the room despite her startled protests and questions. He reappeared the next morning as she was breakfasting in her room, dishevelled, quite drunk and in his worst sarcastic mood, and neither made excuses nor gave an account of his absence.

Scarlett asked no questions and was quite cool to him, as became an injured wife, and when she had finished the meal, she dressed under his bloodshot gaze and went shopping. He was gone when she returned and did not appear again until time for supper.

It was a silent meal and Scarlett's temper was straining because it was her last supper in New Orleans and she wanted to do justice to the crawfish. And she could not enjoy it under his gaze. Nevertheless she ate a large one, and drank a quantity of champagne. Perhaps it was this combination that brought back her old nightmare that evening, for she awoke, cold with sweat, sobbing brokenly. She was back at Tara again and Tara was desolate. Mother was dead and with her all the strength and wisdom of the world. Nowhere in the world was there anyone to turn to, anyone to rely upon. And something terrifying was pursuing her and she was running, running till her heart was bursting, running in a thick swimming fog, crying out, blindly seeking that nameless, unknown haven of safety that was somewhere in the mist about her.

Rhett was leaning over her when she woke, and without a word he picked her up in his arms like a child and held her close, his hard muscles comforting, his wordless murmuring soothing, until her sobbing ceased.

'Oh, Rhett, I was so cold and so hungry and so tired and I couldn't find it. I ran through the mist and I ran but I couldn't find it.'

'Find what, honey?'

'I don't know. I wish I did know.'

'Is it your old dream?'

'Oh, yes!'

He gently placed her on the bed, fumbled in the darkness and lit a candle. In the light his face with bloodshot eyes and harsh lines was as unreadable as stone. His shirt, opened to the waist, showed a brown chest covered with thick black hair. Scarlett, still shaking with fright, thought how strong and unyielding that chest was, and she whispered: 'Hold me, Rhett.'

'Darling!' he said swiftly, and picking her up he sat down in a large chair, cradling her body against him.

'Oh, Rhett, it's awful to be hungry.'

'It must be awful to dream of starvation after a seven-course dinner including that enormous crawfish.' He smiled but his eyes were kind.

'Oh, Rhett, I just run and run and hunt and I can't ever find what it is I'm hunting for. It's always hidden in the mist. I know if I could find it, I'd be safe for ever and ever and never be cold or hungry again.'

'Is it a person or a thing you're hunting?'

'I don't know. I never thought about it. Rhett, do you think I'll ever dream that I get there to safety?'

'No,' he said, smoothing her tumbled hair, 'I don't. Dreams aren't like that. But I do think that if you get used to being safe and warm and well-fed in your everyday life, you'll stop dreaming that dream. And, Scarlett, I'm going to see that you are safe.'

'Rhett, you are so nice.'

'Thanks for the crumbs from your table, Mrs Dives. Scarlett, I want you to say to yourself every morning when you wake up: "I can't ever be hungry again and nothing can ever touch me so long as Rhett is here and the United States government holds out." '

'The United States government?' she questioned, sitting up, startled, tears still on her cheeks.

'The ex-Confederate money has now become an honest woman. I invested most of it in government bonds.'

'God's nightgown!' cried Scarlett, sitting up in his lap, forgetful of her recent terror. 'Do you mean to tell me you've loaned your money to the Yankees?'

'At a fair per cent.'

'I don't care if it's a hundred per cent! You must sell them immediately. The idea of letting the Yankees have the use of your money!'

'And what must I do with it?' he questioned with a smile, noting that her eyes were no longer wide with fright.

'Why – why, buy property at Five Points. I'll bet you could buy all of Five Points with the money you have.'

'Thank you, but I wouldn't have Five Points. Now that the Carpetbagger government has really gotten control of Georgia, there's no telling what may happen. I wouldn't put anything beyond the swarm of buzzards that's swooping down on Georgia now from north, east, south and west. I'm playing along with them, you understand, as a good Scallawag should do, but I don't trust them. And I'm not putting my money in real estate. I prefer bonds. You can hide them. You can't hide real estate very easily.'

'Do you think—' she began, paling as she thought of the mills and the store.

'I don't know. But don't look so frightened, Scarlett. Our charming new governor is a good friend of mine. It's just that times are too uncertain now and I don't want much of my money tied up in real estate.'

He shifted her to one knee and, leaning back, reached for a cigar and lit it. She sat with her bare feet dangling, watching the play of muscles on his brown chest, her terrors forgotten.

'And while we are on the subject of real estate, Scarlett,' he said, 'I am going to build a house. You might have bullied Frank into living in Miss Pitty's house, but not me. I don't believe I could bear her vapourings three times a day and, moreover, I believe Uncle Peter would assassinate me before he would let me live under the sacred Hamilton roof. Miss Pitty can get Miss India Wilkes to stay with her and keep the bogyman away. When we get back to Atlanta we are going to stay in the bridal suite of the National Hotel until our house is finished. Before we left Atlanta I was dickering for that big lot on Peachtree, the one near the Leyden house. You know the one I mean?'

'Oh, Rhett, how lovely! I do so want a house of my own. A great big one.'

'Then at last we are agreed on something. What about a white stucco with wrought-iron work like these Creole houses here?'

'Oh, no, Rhett. Not anything old-fashioned like these New Orleans houses. I know just what I want. It's the newest thing because I saw a picture of it in – let me see – it was in that *Harper's Weekly* I was looking at. It was modelled after a Swiss chalet.'

'A Swiss what?'

'A chalet.'

'Spell it.'

She complied.

'Oh,' he said and stroked his moustache.

'It was lovely. It had a high mansard roof with a picket fence on the top and a tower made of fancy shingles at each end. And the towers had windows with red and blue glass in them. It was so stylish looking.'

'I suppose it had jigsaw work on the porch banisters?'

'Yes.'

'And a fringe of wooden scrollwork hanging from the roof of the porch?'

'Yes. You must have seen one like it.'

'I have – but not in Switzerland. The Swiss are a very intelligent race and keenly alive to architectural beauty. Do you really want a house like that?'

'Oh, yes!'

'I had hoped that association with me might improve your taste. Why not a Creole house or a Colonial with six white columns?'

'I tell you I don't want anything tacky and old-fashioned looking. And inside let's have red wallpaper and red velvet portières over all the folding doors and – oh, Rhett, everybody will be pea-green when they see our house!'

'Is it very necessary that everyone shall be envious? Well, if you like they shall be green. But, Scarlett, has it occurred to you that it's hardly in good taste to furnish the house on so lavish a scale when everyone is so poor?'

'I want it that way,' she said obstinately. 'I want to make everybody who's been mean to me feel bad. And we'll give big receptions that'll make the whole town wish they hadn't said such nasty things.'

'But who will come to our receptions?'

'Why, everybody, of course.'

'I doubt it. The Old Guard dies but it never surrenders.'

'Oh, Rhett, how you run on! If you've got money, people always like you.'

'Not Southerners. It's harder for speculators' money to get into the best parlours than for the camel to go through the needle's eye. And as for Scallawags – that's you and me, my pet – we'll be lucky if we aren't spit upon. But if you'd like to try, I'll back you, my dear, and I'm sure I shall enjoy your campaign intensely. And while we are on the subject of money, let me make this clear to you. You can have all the cash you want for the house and all you want for your fal-lals. And if you like jewellery, you can have it but I'm going to pick it out. You have such execrable taste, my pet. And anything you want for Wade or Ella. And if Will Benteen can't make a go of the cotton, I'm willing to chip in and help out on that white elephant in Clayton County that you love so much. That's fair enough, isn't it?'

'Of course. You're very generous.'

'But listen closely. Not one cent for the store and not one cent for that kindling factory of yours.'

'Oh,' said Scarlett, her face falling. All during the honeymoon she had been thinking how she could bring up the subject of the thousand dollars she needed to buy fifty feet more of land to enlarge her lumber yard.

'I thought you always bragged about being broad-minded and not caring what people said about my running a business, and you're just like every other man – so afraid people will say I wear the pants in the family.'

'There's never going to be any doubt in anybody's mind about who wears the pants in the Butler family,' drawled Rhett. 'I don't care what fools say. In fact, I'm ill-bred enough to be proud of having a smart wife. I want you to keep on running the store and the mills. They are your children's. When Wade grows up he won't feel right about being supported by his stepfather, and then he can take over the management. But not one cent of mine goes into either business.'

'Why?'

'Because I don't care to contribute to the support of Ashley Wilkes.'

'Are you going to begin that again?'

'No. But you asked my reasons and I have given them. And another thing. Don't think you can juggle books on me and lie about how much your clothes cost and how much it takes to run the house, so that you can use the money to buy more mules or another mill for Ashley. I intend to look over and carefully check your expenditures and I know what things cost. Oh, don't get insulted. You'd do it. I wouldn't put it beyond you. In fact, I wouldn't put anything beyond you where either Tara or Ashley is concerned. I don't mind Tara. But I must draw the line at Ashley. I'm riding you with a slack rein, my pet, but don't forget that I'm riding with curb and spurs just the same.'

Chapter XLIX

Mrs Elsing cocked her ear toward the hall. Hearing Melanie's steps die away into the kitchen where rattling dishes and clinking silverware gave promise of refreshments, she turned and spoke softly to the ladies who sat in a circle in the parlour, their sewing-baskets in their laps.

'Personally, I do not intend to call on Scarlett now or ever,' she said, the chill elegance of her face colder than usual.

The other members of the Ladies' Sewing Circle for the Widows and Orphans of the Confederacy eagerly laid down their needles and edged their rocking-chairs closer. All the ladies had been bursting to discuss Scarlett and Rhett but Melanie's presence prevented it. Just the day before, the couple had returned from New Orleans and they were occupying the bridal suite at the National Hotel.

'Hugh says that I must call out of courtesy for the way Captain Butler saved his life,' Mrs Elsing continued. 'And poor Fanny sides with him and says she will call too. I said to her, "Fanny," I said, "if it wasn't for Scarlett, Tommy would be alive this minute. It is an insult to his memory to call." And Fanny had no better sense than to say, "Mother, I'm not calling on Scarlett. I'm calling on Captain Butler. He tried his best to save Tommy and it wasn't his fault if he failed." '

'How silly young people are!' said Mrs Merriwether. 'Call, indeed!' Her stout bosom swelled indignantly as she remembered Scarlett's rude reception of her advice on marrying Rhett. 'My Maybelle is just as silly as your Fanny. She says she and René will call, because Captain Butler kept René from getting hanged. And I said if it hadn't been for Scarlett exposing herself, René would never have been in any danger. And Father Merriwether intends to call and he talks like he was in his dotage and says he's grateful to that scoundrel, even if I'm not. I vow, since Father Merriwether was in that Watling creature's house he has acted in a disgraceful way. Call, indeed! I certainly shan't call. Scarlett has outlawed herself by marrying such a man. He was bad enough when he was a speculator during the war and making money out of our hunger, but now that he is hand in glove with the Carpetbaggers and Scallawags and a friend – actually a friend – of that odious wretch, Governor Bullock— Call, indeed!'

Mrs Bonnell sighed. She was a plump brown wren of a woman with a cheerful face.

'They'll only call once, for courtesy, Dolly. I don't know that I blame them. I've heard that all the men who were out that night intend to call, and I think they should. Somehow, it's hard for me to think that Scarlett is her mother's child. I went to school with Ellen Robillard in Savannah and there was never a lovelier girl than she was and she was very dear to me. If only her father had not opposed her match with her cousin, Philippe Robillard! There was nothing really wrong with the boy – boys must sow their wild oats. But Ellen must run off and marry old man O'Hara and have a daughter like Scarlett. But really, I feel that I must call once out of memory to Ellen.'

'Sentimental nonsense!' snorted Mrs Merriwether with vigour. 'Kitty Bonnell, are you going to call on a woman who married a bare year after her husband's death? A woman—'

'And she really killed Mr Kennedy,' interrupted India. Her voice was cool but acid. Whenever she thought of Scarlett it was hard for her even to be polite, remembering, always remembering Stuart Tarleton. 'And I have always thought there was more between her and that Butler man before Mr Kennedy was killed than most people suspected.'

Before the ladies could recover from their shocked astonishment at her statement and at a spinster mentioning such a matter, Melanie was standing in the doorway. So engrossed had they been in their gossip that they had not heard her light tread and now, confronted by their hostess, they looked like whispering schoolgirls caught by a teacher. Alarm was added to consternation at the change in Melanie's face. She was pink with righteous anger, her gentle eyes snapping fire, her nostrils quivering. No one had ever seen Melanie angry before. Not a lady present thought her capable of wrath. They all loved her but they thought her the sweetest, most pliable of young women, deferential to her elders and without any opinions of her own.

'How dare you, India?' she questioned in a low voice that shook. 'Where will your jealousy lead you? For shame!'

India's face went white but her head was high.

'I retract nothing,' she said briefly. But her mind was seething.

'Jealous, am I?' she thought. With the memory of Stuart Tarleton and of Honey and Charles, didn't she have good reason to be jealous of Scarlett?

Didn't she have good reason to hate her, especially now that she had a suspicion that Scarlett had somehow entangled Ashley in her web? She thought: 'There's plenty I could tell you about Ashley and your precious Scarlett.' India was torn between the desire to shield Ashley by her silence and to extricate him by telling all her suspicions to Melanie and the whole world. That would force Scarlett to release whatever hold she had on Ashley. But this was not the time. She had nothing definite, only suspicions.

'I retract nothing,' she repeated.

'Then it is fortunate that you are no longer living under my roof,' said Melanie, and her words were cold.

India leapt to her feet, red flooding her sallow face.

'Melanie, you – my sister-in-law – you aren't going to quarrel with me over that fast piece—'

'Scarlett is my sister-in-law too,' said Melanie, meeting India's eyes squarely as though they were strangers. 'And dearer to me than any blood sister could ever be. If you are so forgetful of my favours at her hands, I am not. She stayed with me through the whole siege when she could have gone home, when even Aunt Pitty had run away to Macon. She brought my baby for me when the Yankees were almost in Atlanta and she burdened herself with me and Beau all that dreadful trip to Tara when she could have left me here in a hospital for the Yankees to get me. And she nursed and fed me, even if she was tired and even if she went hungry. Because I was sick and weak, I had the best mattress at Tara. When I could walk, I had the only whole pair of shoes. You can forget those things she did for me, India, but I cannot. And when Ashley came home, sick, discouraged, without a home, without a cent in his pockets, she took him in like a sister. And when we thought we would have to go North and it was breaking our hearts to leave Georgia, Scarlett stepped in and gave him the mill to run. And Captain Butler saved Ashley's life out of the kindness of his heart. Certainly Ashley had no claim on him! And I am grateful, grateful to Scarlett and to Captain Butler. But you, India! How can you forget the favours Scarlett has done me and Ashley? How can you hold your brother's life so cheap as to cast slurs on the man who saved him? If you went down on your knees to Captain Butler and Scarlett, it would not be enough.'

'Now, Melly,' began Mrs Merriwether briskly, for she had recovered her composure, 'that's no way to talk to India.'

'I heard what you said about Scarlett too,' cried Melanie, swinging on the stout old lady with the air of a duellist who, having withdrawn a blade from one prostrate opponent, turns hungrily toward another. 'And you too, Mrs Elsing. What you think of her in your own petty minds, I do not care, for that is your business. But what you say about her in my own house or in my own hearing, ever, is my business. But how can you even think such dreadful things, much less say them? Are your men so cheap to you that you would rather see them dead than alive? Have you no gratitude to the man who saved them and saved them at risk of his own life? The Yankees might easily have thought him a member of the Klan if the whole truth had come out! They might have hanged him. But he risked himself for your men. For your father-in-law, Mrs Merriwether, and your son-in-law and your two nephews, too. And your brother, Mrs Bonnell, and your son and son-in-law, Mrs Elsing. Ingrates, that's what you are! I ask an apology from all of you.'

Mrs Elsing was on her feet, cramming her sewing into her box, her mouth set.

'If anyone had ever told me that you could be so ill-bred, Melly— No, I will not apologize. India is right. Scarlett is a flighty, fast bit of baggage. I can't forget how she acted during the war. And I can't forget how poor white trashy she's acted since she got a little money—'

'What you can't forget,' cut in Melanie, clenching her small fists against her sides, 'is that she demoted Hugh because he wasn't smart enough to run her mill.'

'Melly!' moaned a chorus of voices.

Mrs Elsing's head jerked up and she started toward the door. With her hand on the knob of the front door, she stopped and turned.

'Melly,' she said and her voice softened, 'honey, this breaks my heart. I was your mother's best friend and I helped Dr Meade bring you into this world and I've loved you like you were mine. If it were something that mattered it wouldn't be so hard to hear you talk like this. But about a woman like Scarlett O'Hara who'd just as soon do you a dirty turn as the next of us—'

Tears had started in Melanie's eyes at the first words Mrs Elsing spoke, but her face hardened when the old lady had finished.

'I want it understood,' she said, 'that any of you who do not call on Scarlett need never, never call on me.'

There was a loud murmur of voices, confusion as the ladies got to their feet. Mrs Elsing dropped her sewing-box on the floor and came back into the room, her false fringe jerking awry.

'I won't have it!' she cried. 'I won't have it! You are beside yourself, Melly, and I don't hold you responsible. You shall be my friend and I shall be yours. I refuse to let this come between us.'

She was crying, and somehow Melanie was in her arms, crying too, but declaring between sobs that she meant every word she said. Several of the other ladies burst into tears and Mrs Merriwether, trumpeting loudly into her handkerchief, embraced both Mrs Elsing and Melanie. Aunt Pitty, who had been a petrified witness to the whole scene, suddenly slid to the floor in what was one of the few real fainting spells she had ever had. Amid the tears and confusion and kissing and scurrying for smelling-salts and brandy, there was only one calm face, one dry pair of eyes. India Wilkes took her departure unnoticed by anyone.

Grandpa Merriwether, meeting Uncle Henry Hamilton in the Girl of the Period Saloon several hours later, related the happenings of the morning which he had heard from Mrs Merriwether. He told it with relish, for he was delighted that someone had the courage to face down his redoubtable daughter-in-law. Certainly, he had never had such courage.

'Well, what did the pack of silly fools finally decide to do?' asked Uncle Henry irritably.

'I dunno for sure,' said Grandpa, 'but it looks to me like Melly won hands down on this go-round. I'll bet they'll all call, at least once. Folks set a store by that niece of yours, Henry.'

'Melly's a fool and the ladies are right. Scarlett is a slick piece of baggage and I don't see why Charlie ever married her,' said Uncle Henry gloomily. 'But Melly was right too, in a way. It's only decent that the families of the men Captain Butler saved should call. When you come right down to it, I haven't got so much against Butler. He showed himself a fine man that night he saved our hides. It's Scarlett who sticks under my tail like a cocklebur. She's a sight too smart for her own good. Well, I've got to call. Scallawag or not, Scarlett is my niece by marriage, after all. I was aiming to call this afternoon.'

'I'll go with you, Henry. Dolly will be fit to be tied when she hears I've gone. Wait till I get one more drink.'

'No, we'll get a drink off Captain Butler. I'll say this for him, he always has good licker.'

Rhett had said that the Old Guard would never surrender and he was right. He knew how little significance there was to the few calls made upon them, and he knew why the calls were made. The families of the men who had been in the ill-starred Klan foray did call at first, but called with obvious infrequency thereafter. And they did not invite the Rhett Butlers to their homes.

Rhett said they would not have come at all, except for fear of violence at the hands of Melanie. Where he got this idea Scarlett did not know, but she dismissed it with the contempt it deserved. For what possible influence could Melanie have on people like Mrs Elsing and Mrs Merriwether? That they did not call again worried her very little; in fact, their absence was hardly noticed, for her suite was crowded with guests of another type. 'New people', established Atlantians called them, when they were not calling them something less polite.

There were many 'new people' staying at the National Hotel who, like Rhett and Scarlett, were waiting for their houses to be completed. They were gay, wealthy people, very much like Rhett's New Orleans friends, elegant of dress, free with their money, vague as to their antecedents. All the men were Republicans and were 'in Atlanta on business connected with the state government'. Just what the business was, Scarlett did not know and did not trouble to learn.

Rhett could have told her exactly what it was – the same business that buzzards have with dying animals. They smelled death from afar and were drawn unerringly to it, to gorge themselves. Government of Georgia by its own citizens was dead, the state was helpless and the adventurers were swarming in.

The wives of Rhett's Scallawag and Carpetbagger friends called in droves and so did the 'new people' she had met when she sold lumber for their homes. Rhett said that, having done business with them, she should receive them and, having received them, she found them pleasant company. They wore lovely clothes and never talked about the war or hard times, but confined their conversation to fashions, scandals and whist. Scarlett had never played cards before and she took to whist with joy, becoming a good player in a short time.

Whenever she was at the hotel there was a crowd of whist players in her suite. But she was not often in her suite these days, for she was too busy with the building of her new house to be bothered with callers. These days she did not much care whether she had callers or not. She wanted to delay her social activities until the day when the house was finished and she could emerge as the mistress of Atlanta's largest mansion, the hostess of the town's most elaborate entertainments.

Through the long warm days she watched her red stone and grey shingle house rise grandly, to tower above any other house on Peachtree Street. Forgetful of the store and the mills, she spent her time on the lot, arguing with carpenters, bickering with masons, harrying the contractor. As the walls went swiftly up she thought with satisfaction that, when finished, it would be larger and finer-looking than any other house in town. It would be even more imposing than the nearby James residence which had just been purchased for the official mansion of Governor Bullock.

The governor's mansion was brave with jigsaw work on banisters and eaves, but the intricate scrollwork on Scarlett's house put the mansion to shame. The mansion had a ballroom, but it looked like a billiard table compared with the enormous room that covered the entire third floor of Scarlett's house. In fact, her house had more of everything than the mansion, or any other house in town for that matter, more cupolas and turrets and towers and balconies and lightning rods and far more windows with coloured panes.

A veranda encircled the entire house, and four flights of steps on the four sides of the building led up to it. The yard was wide and green and scattered about it were rustic iron benches, an iron summer-house, fashionably called a 'gazebo', which, Scarlett had been assured, was of pure Gothic design, and two large iron statues, one a stag and the other a mastiff as large as a Shetland pony. To Wade and Ella, a little dazzled by the size, splendour and fashionable dark gloom of their new home, these two metal animals were the only cheerful notes.

Within, the house was furnished as Scarlett had desired, with thick red carpeting which ran from wall to wall, red velvet portières and the newest of highly varnished black-walnut furniture, carved wherever there was an inch for carving and upholstered in such slick horsehair that ladies had to deposit themselves thereon with great care for fear of sliding off. Everywhere on the walls were gilt-framed mirrors and long pier-glasses – as many, Rhett said idly, as there were in Belle Watling's establishment. Interspersed were steel engravings in heavy frames, some of them eight feet long, which Scarlett had ordered especially from New York. The walls were covered with rich dark paper, the ceilings were high and the house was always dim, for the windows were overdraped with plum-coloured plush hangings that shut out most of the sunlight.

All in all it was an establishment to take one's breath away and Scarlett, stepping on the soft carpets and sinking into the embrace of the deep feather beds, remembered the cold floors and the straw-stuffed bedticks of Tara and was satisfied. She thought it the most beautiful and most elegantly furnished house she had ever seen, but Rhett said it was a nightmare. However, if it made her happy, she was welcome to it.

'A stranger without being told a word about us would know this house was built with ill-gotten gains,' he said. 'You know, Scarlett, money ill come by never comes to good and this house is proof of the axiom. It's just the kind of house a profiteer would build.'

But Scarlett, abrim with pride and happiness and full of plans for the entertainments she would give when they were thoroughly settled in the house, only pinched his ear playfully and said: 'Fiddle-dee-dee! How you do run on!'

She knew, by now, that Rhett loved to take her down a peg, and would spoil her fun whenever he could, if she lent an attentive ear to his jibes. Should she take him seriously, she would be forced to quarrel with him and she did not care to match swords, for she always came off second best. So she hardly ever listened to anything he said, and what she was forced to hear she tried to turn off as a joke. At least, she tried for a while.

During their honeymoon and for the greater part of their stay at the National Hotel, they had lived together with amiability. But scarcely had they moved into the new house and Scarlett gathered her new friends about her, when sudden sharp quarrels sprang up between them. They were brief quarrels, short-lived because it was impossible to keep a quarrel going with Rhett, who remained coolly indifferent to her hot words and waited his chance to pink her in an unguarded spot. She quarrelled; Rhett did not. He only stated his unequivocal opinion of herself, her actions, her house and her new friends. And some of his opinions were of such a nature that she could no longer ignore them and treat them as jokes.

For instance, when she decided to change the name of 'Kennedy's General Store' to something more edifying, she asked him to think of a title that would include the word 'emporium'. Rhett suggested 'Caveat Emptorium', assuring her that it would be a title most in keeping with the type of goods sold in the store. She thought it had an imposing sound and even went so far as to have the sign painted, when Ashley Wilkes, embarrassed, translated the real meaning. And Rhett had roared at her rage.

And there was the way he treated Mammy. Mammy had never yielded an inch from her stand that Rhett was a mule in horse harness. She was polite but cold to Rhett. She always called him 'Cap'n Butler', never 'Mist' Rhett'. She never even dropped a curtsy when Rhett presented her with the red petticoat and she never wore it either. She kept Ella and Wade out of Rhett's way whenever she could, despite the fact that Wade adored Uncle Rhett and Rhett was obviously fond of the boy. But instead of discharging Mammy or being short and stern with her, Rhett treated her with the utmost deference, with far more courtesy than he treated any of the ladies of Scarlett's recent acquaintance. In fact, with more courtesy than he treated Scarlett herself. He always asked Mammy's permission to take Wade riding and consulted with her before he bought Ella dolls. And Mammy was hardly polite to him.

Scarlett felt that Rhett should be firm with Mammy, as became the head of the house, but Rhett only laughed and said that Mammy was the real head of the house.

He infuriated Scarlett by saying coolly that he was preparing to be very sorry for her some years hence, when the Republican rule was gone from Georgia and the Democrats back in power.

'When the Democrats get a governor and a legislature of their own, all your new vulgar Republican friends will be wiped off the chessboard and sent back to minding bars and emptying slops where they belong. And you'll be left out on the end of a limb, with never a Democratic friend or a Republican either. Well, take no thought of the morrow.'

Scarlett laughed, and with some justice, for at that time Bullock was safe in the governor's chair, twenty-seven negroes were in the legislature and thousands of the Democratic voters of Georgia were disfranchised.

'The Democrats will never get back. All they do is make the Yankees madder and put off the day when they could get back. All they do is talk big and run around at night Ku Kluxing.'

'They will get back. I know Southerners. I know Georgians. They are a tough and a bullheaded lot. If they've got to fight another war to get back, they'll fight another war. If they've got to buy black votes like the Yankees have done, then they will buy black votes. If they've got to vote ten thousand dead men like the Yankees did, every corpse in every cemetery in Georgia will be at the polls. Things are going to get so bad under the benign rule of our good friend Rufus Bullock that Georgia is going to vomit him up.'

'Rhett, don't use such vulgar words!' cried Scarlett. 'You talk like I wouldn't be glad to see the Democrats come back! And you know that isn't so! I'd be very glad to see them back. Do you think I like to see these soldiers hanging around, reminding me of – do you think I like – why, I'm a Georgian too! I'd like to see the Democrats get back. But they won't. Not ever. And even if they did, how would that affect my friends? They'd still have their money, wouldn't they?'

'If they kept their money. But I doubt the ability of any of them to keep money more than five years at the rate they're spending. Easy come, easy go. Their money won't do them any good. Any more than my money has done you any good. It certainly hasn't made a horse out of you yet, has it, my pretty mule?'

The quarrel which sprang from this last remark lasted for days. After the fourth day of Scarlett's sulks and obvious silent demands for an apology, Rhett went to New Orleans, taking Wade with him, over Mammy's protests, and he stayed away until Scarlett's tantrum had passed. But the sting of not humbling him remained with her.

When he came back from New Orleans, cool and bland, she swallowed her anger as best she could, pushing it into the back of her mind to be thought of at some later date. She did not want to bother with anything unpleasant now. She wanted to be happy, for her mind was full of the first party she would give in the new house. It was to be an enormous night reception with palms and an orchestra and all the porches shrouded in canvas, and a collation that made her mouth water in anticipation. To it she intended to invite everyone she had ever known in Atlanta, all the old friends and all the new and charming ones she had met since returning from her honeymoon. The excitement of the party banished, for the most part, the memory of Rhett's barbs and she was happy, happier than she had been in years as she planned her reception.

Oh, what fun it was to be rich! To give parties and never count the cost! To buy the most expensive furniture and dresses and food and never think about the bills! How marvellous to be able to send tidy cheques to Aunt Pauline and Aunt Eulalie in Charleston, and to Will at Tara! Oh, the jealous fools who said money wasn't everything! How perverse of Rhett to say that it had done nothing for her!

Scarlett issued cards of invitation to all her friends and acquaintances, old and new, even those she did not like. She did not except even Mrs Merriwether who had been almost rude when she called on her at the National Hotel, or Mrs Elsing who had been cool to frigidness. She invited Mrs Meade and Mrs Whiting who she knew disliked her and who she knew would be embarrassed because they did not have the proper clothes to wear to so elegant a function. For Scarlett's housewarming, or 'crush' as it was fashionable to call such evening parties, half reception, half ball, was by far the most elaborate affair Atlanta had ever seen.

That night the house and canvas-covered veranda were filled with guests who drank her champagne punch and ate her patties and creamed oysters and danced to the music of the orchestra that was carefully screened by a wall of palms and rubber plants. But none of those whom Rhett had termed the 'Old Guard' were present except Melanie and Ashley, Aunt Pitty and Uncle Henry, Dr and Mrs Meade and Grandpa Merriwether.

Many of the Old Guard had reluctantly decided to attend the 'crush'. Some had accepted because of Melanie's attitude, others because they felt they owed Rhett a debt for saving their lives and those of their relatives. But, two days before the function, a rumour went about Atlanta that Governor Bullock had been invited. The Old Guard signified their disapproval by a sheaf of cards, regretting their inability to accept Scarlett's kind invitation. And the small group of old friends who did attend took their departure, embarrassed but firm, as soon as the governor entered Scarlett's house.

Scarlett was so bewildered and infuriated at these slights that the party was utterly ruined for her. Her elegant 'crush'! She had planned it so lovingly and so few old friends and no old enemies had been there to see how wonderful it was! After the last guest had gone home at dawn, she would have cried and stormed had she not been afraid that Rhett would roar with laughter, afraid that she would read 'I told you so' in his dancing black eyes, even if he did not speak the words. So she swallowed her wrath with poor grace and pretended indifference.

Only to Melanie, the next morning, did she permit herself the luxury of exploding.

'You insulted me, Melly Wilkes, and you made Ashley and the others insult me! You know they'd have never gone home so soon if you hadn't dragged them. Oh, I saw you! Just when I started to bring Governor Bullock over to present him to you, you ran like a rabbit!'

'I did not believe – I could not believe that he would really be present,' answered Melanie unhappily. 'Even though everybody said—'

'Everybody? So everybody's been clacking and blabbing about me, have they?' cried Scarlett furiously. 'Do you mean to tell me that if you'd known the governor was going to be present, you wouldn't have come either?'

'No,' said Melanie in a low voice, her eyes on the floor. 'Darling, I just couldn't have come.'

'Great balls of fire! So you'd have insulted me like everybody else did!'

'Oh, mercy!' cried Melly, in real distress. 'I didn't mean to hurt you. You're my own sister, darling, my own Charlie's widow, and I—'

She put a timid hand on Scarlett's arm. But Scarlett flung it off, wishing fervently that she could roar as loudly as Gerald used to roar when in a temper. But Melanie faced her wrath. And as she looked into Scarlett's stormy green eyes, her slight shoulders straightened and a mantle of dignity, strangely at variance with her childish face and figure, fell upon her.

'I'm sorry you're hurt, my dear, but I cannot meet Governor Bullock or any Republican or any Scallawag. I will not meet them, in your house or any other house. No, not even if I have to – if I have to' – Melanie cast about her for the worst thing she could think of – 'not even if I have to be rude.'

'Are you criticizing my friends?'

'No, dear. But they are your friends and not mine.'

'Are you criticizing me for having the governor at my house?'

Cornered, Melanie still met Scarlett's eyes unwaveringly.

'Darling, what you do, you always do for a good reason and I love you and trust you and it is not for me to criticize. And I will not permit anyone to criticize you in my hearing. But, oh, Scarlett!' Suddenly words began to bubble out, swift hot words, and there was inflexible hate in the low voice. 'Can you forget what these people did to us? Can you forget darling Charlie dead and Ashley's health ruined and Twelve Oaks burned? Oh, Scarlett, you can't forget that terrible man you shot with your mother's sewing-box in his hands! You can't forget Sherman's men at Tara and how they even stole our underwear! And tried to burn the place down and actually handled my father's sword! Oh, Scarlett, it was these same people who robbed us and tortured us and left us to starve that you invited to your party! The same people who have set the darkies up to lord it over us, who are robbing us and keeping our men from voting! I can't forget. I won't forget. I won't let my Beau forget and I'll teach my grandchildren to hate these people – and my grandchildren's grandchildren if God lets me live that long! Scarlett, how can you forget?'

Melanie paused for breath and Scarlett stared at her, startled out of her own anger by the quivering note of violence in Melanie's voice.

'Do you think I'm a fool?' she questioned impatiently. 'Of course, I remember! But all that's past, Melly. It's up to us to make the best of things and I'm trying to do it. Governor Bullock and some of the nicer Republicans can help us a lot if we handle them right.'

'There are no nice Republicans,' said Melanie flatly. 'And I don't want their help. And I don't intend to make the best of things – if they are Yankee things.'

'Good Heaven, Melly, why get in such a pet?'

'Oh!' cried Melanie, looking conscience-stricken. 'How I have run on! Scarlett, I didn't mean to hurt your feelings or to criticize. Everybody thinks differently and everybody's got a right to their own opinion. Now, dear, I love you and you know I love you and nothing you could ever do would make me change. And you still love me, don't you? I haven't made you hate me, have I? Scarlett, I couldn't stand it if anything ever came between us – after all we've been through together! Say it's all right.'

'Fiddle-dee-dee, Melly, what a tempest you make in a teapot,' said Scarlett grudgingly, but she did not throw off the hand that stole around her waist.

'Now, we're all right again,' said Melanie pleasedly, but she added softly, 'I want us to visit each other just like we always did, darling. Just you let me know what days Republicans and Scallawags are coming to see you and I'll stay at home on those days.'

'It's a matter of supreme indifference to me whether you come or not,' said

Scarlett, putting on her bonnet and going home in a huff. There was some satisfaction to her wounded vanity in the hurt look on Melanie's face.

In the weeks that followed her first party, Scarlett was hard put to keep up her pretence of supreme indifference to public opinion. When she did not receive calls from old friends, except Melanie and Pitty and Uncle Henry and Ashley, and did not get cards to their modest entertainments, she was genuinely puzzled and hurt. Had she not gone out of her way to bury old hatchets and to show these people that she bore them no ill-will for their gossiping and back-biting? Surely they must know that she didn't like Governor Bullock any more than they did but that it was expedient to be nice to him. The idiots! If everybody would be nice to the Republicans, Georgia would get out of the fix she was in very quickly.

She did not realize then that with one stroke she had cut forever any fragile tie that still bound her to the old days, to old friends. Not even Melanie's influence could repair the break of that gossamer thread. And Melanie, bewildered, broken-hearted but still loyal, did not try to repair it. Even had Scarlett wanted to turn back to old ways, old friends, there was no turning back possible now. The face of the town was set against her as stonily as granite. The hate that enveloped the Bullock régime enveloped her too, a hate that had little fire and fury in it but much cold implacability. Scarlett had cast her lot with the enemy and, whatever her birth and family connections, she was now in the category of a turncoat, a nigger-lover, a traitor, a Republican – and a Scallawag.

After a miserable while, Scarlett's pretended indifference gave way to the real thing. She had never been one to worry long over the vagaries of human conduct or to be cast down for long if one line of action failed. Soon she did not care what the Merriwethers, the Elsings, the Whitings, the Bonnells, the Meades and the others thought of her. At least, Melanie called, bringing Ashley, and Ashley was the one who mattered the most. And there were other people in Atlanta who would come to her parties, other people far more congenial than those hidebound old hens. Any time she wanted to fill her house with guests, she could do so and these guests would be far more entertaining, far more handsomely dressed than those prissy, strait-laced old fools who disapproved of her.

These people were newcomers to Atlanta. Some of them were acquaintances of Rhett, some associated with him in those mysterious affairs which he referred to as 'mere business, my pet'. Some were couples Scarlett had met when she was living at the National Hotel and some were Governor Bullock's appointees.

The set with which she was now moving was a motley crew. Among them were the Gelerts who had lived in a dozen different states and who apparently had left each one hastily upon detection of their swindling schemes; the Conningtons whose connection with the Freedmen's Bureau in a distant state had been highly lucrative at the expense of the ignorant blacks they were supposed to protect; the Deals who had sold 'cardboard' shoes to the Confederate government until it became necessary for them to spend the last year of the war in Europe; the Hundons who had police records in many cities but nevertheless were often successful bidders on state contracts; the Carahans who had gotten their start in a gambling house and now were gambling for bigger stakes in the building of non-existent railroads with the state's money; the Flahertys who had bought salt at one cent a pound in 1861 and made a fortune when salt went to fifty cents in 1863, and the Barts who had owned the largest brothel in a Northern metropolis during the war and now were moving in the best circles of Carpetbagger society.

Such people were Scarlett's intimates now, but those who attended her larger receptions included others of some culture and refinement, many of excellent families. In addition to the Carpetbag gentry, substantial people from the North were moving into Atlanta, attracted by the never-ceasing business activity of the town in this period of rebuilding and expansion. Yankee families of wealth sent young sons to the South to pioneer on the new frontier, and Yankee officers after their discharge took up permanent residence in the town they had fought so hard to capture. At first, strangers in a strange town, they were glad to accept invitations to the lavish entertainments of the wealthy and hospitable Mrs Butler, but they soon drifted out of her set. They were good people and they needed only a short acquaintance with Carpetbaggers and Carpetbag rule to become as resentful of them as the native Georgians were. Many became Democrats and more Southern than the Southerners.

Other misfits in Scarlett's circle remained there only because they were not welcome elsewhere. They would have much preferred the quiet parlours of the Old Guard, but the Old Guard would have none of them. Among these were the Yankee schoolmarms who had come South imbued with the desire to uplift the Negro, and the Scallawags who had been born good Democrats but had turned Republican after the surrender.

It was hard to say which class was more cordially hated by the settled citizenry, the impractical Yankee schoolmarms or the Scallawags, but the balance probably fell with the latter. The schoolmarms could be dismissed with, 'Well, what can you expect of nigger-loving Yankees? Of course they think the nigger is just as good as they are!' But for those Georgians who had turned Republican for personal gain, there was no excuse.

'Starving is good enough for us. It ought to be good enough for you,' was the way the Old Guard felt. Many ex-Confederate soldiers, knowing the frantic fear of men who saw their families in want, were more tolerant of former comrades who had changed political colours in order that their families might eat. But not the women of the Old Guard, and the women were the implacable and inflexible power behind the social throne. The Lost Cause was stronger, dearer now in their hearts than it had ever been at the height of its glory. It was a fetish now. Everything about it was sacred: the graves of the men who had died for it, the battlefields, the torn flags, the crossed sabres in their halls, the fading letters from the front, the veterans. These women gave no aid, comfort or quarter to the late enemy, and now Scarlett was numbered among the enemy.

In this mongrel society thrown together by the exigencies of the political situation, there was but one thing in common. That was money. As most of them had never had twenty-five dollars at one time in their whole lives, previous to the war, they were now embarked on an orgy of spending such as Atlanta had never seen before.

With the Republicans in the political saddle the town entered into an era of waste and ostentation, with the trappings of refinement thinly veneering the vice and vulgarity beneath. Never before had the cleavage of the very rich and the very poor been so marked. Those on top took no thought for those less fortunate. Except for the negroes, of course. They must have the very best. The best of schools and lodgings and clothes and amusements, for they were the power in politics and every negro vote counted. But as for the recently impoverished Atlanta people, they could starve and drop in the streets for all the newly rich Republicans cared.

On the crest of this wave of vulgarity, Scarlett rode triumphantly, newly a bride, dashingly pretty in her fine clothes, with Rhett's money solidly behind her. It was an era that suited her, crude, garish, showy, full of overdressed women, overfurnished houses, too many jewels, too many horses, too much food, too much whisky. When Scarlett infrequently stopped to think about the matter she knew that none of her new associates could be called ladies by Ellen's strict standards. But she had broken with Ellen's standards too many times since that far-away day when she stood in the parlour at Tara and decided to be Rhett's mistress, and she did not often feel the bite of conscience now.

Perhaps these new friends were not, strictly speaking, ladies and gentlemen, but like Rhett's New Orleans friends, they were so much fun! So very much more fun than the subdued, church-going, Shakespeare-reading friends of her earlier Atlanta days. And, except for her brief honeymoon interlude, she had not had fun in so long. Nor had she had any sense of security. Now secure, she wanted to dance, to play, to riot, to gorge on foods and fine wine, to deck herself in silks and satins, to wallow on soft feather beds and fine upholstery. And she did all these things. Encouraged by Rhett's amused tolerance, freed now from the restraints of her childhood, freed even from that last fear of poverty, she was permitting herself the luxury she had often dreamed – of doing exactly what she pleased and telling people who didn't like it to go to hell.

To her had come that pleasant intoxication peculiar to those whose lives are a deliberate slap in the face of organized society – the gambler, the confidence man, the polite adventuress, all those who succeed by their wits.

She said and did exactly what she pleased and, in practically no time, her insolence knew no bounds.

She did not hesitate to display arrogance to her new Republican and Scallawag friends but to no class was she ruder or more insolent than the Yankee officers of the garrison and their families. Of all the heterogeneous mass of people who had poured into Atlanta, the army people alone she refused to receive or tolerate. She even went out of her way to be bad-mannered to them. Melanie was not alone in being unable to forget what a blue uniform meant. To Scarlett, that uniform and those gold buttons would always mean the fears of the siege, the terror of flight, the looting and burning, the desperate poverty and the grinding work at Tara. Now that she was rich and secure in the friendship of the governor and many prominent Republicans, she could be insulting to every blue uniform she saw. And she was insulting.

Rhett once lazily pointed out to her that most of the male guests who assembled under their roof had worn that same blue uniform not so long ago, but she retorted that a Yankee didn't seem like a Yankee unless he had on a blue uniform. To which Rhett replied: 'Consistency, thou art a jewel,' and shrugged.

Scarlett, hating the bright hard blue they wore, enjoyed snubbing them all the more because it so bewildered them. The garrison families had a right to be bewildered for most of them were quiet, well-bred folk, lonely in a hostile land, anxious to go home to the North, a little ashamed of the riffraff whose rule they were forced to uphold – an infinitely better class than that of Scarlett's associates. Naturally, the officers' wives were puzzled that the dashing Mrs Butler took to her bosom such women as the common red-haired Bridget Flaherty and went out of her way to slight them.

But even the ladies whom Scarlett took to her bosom had to endure much from her. However, they did it gladly. To them, she not only represented wealth and elegance but the old régime, with its old names, old families, old traditions with which they wished ardently to identify themselves. The old families they yearned after might have cast Scarlett out but the ladies of the new aristocracy did not know it. They only knew that Scarlett's father had been a great slave-owner, her mother a Robillard of Savannah and her husband was Rhett Butler of Charleston. And this was enough for them. She was their opening wedge into the old society they wished to enter, the society which scorned them, would not return calls and bowed frigidly in churches. In fact, she was more than their wedge into society. To them, fresh from obscure beginnings, she *was* society. Pinchbeck ladies themselves, they no more saw through Scarlett's pinchbeck pretensions than she herself did. They took her at her own valuation and endured much at her hands, her airs, her graces, her tempers, her arrogance, her downright rudeness and her frankness about their shortcomings.

They were so lately come from nothing and so uncertain of themselves they were doubly anxious to appear refined and feared to show their temper or make retorts in kind, lest they be considered unladylike. At all costs they must be ladies. They pretended to great delicacy, modesty and innocence. To hear them talk one would have thought they had no legs, natural functions or knowledge of the wicked world. No one would have thought that red-haired Bridget Flaherty, who had a sun-defying white skin and a brogue that could be cut with a butter-knife, had stolen her father's hidden hoard to come to America to be chambermaid in a New York hotel. And to observe the delicate vapours of Sylvia (formerly Sadie Belle) Connington and Mamie Bart, no one would have suspected that the first grew up above her father's saloon in the Bowery and waited on the bar at rush times, and that the latter, so it was said, had come out of one of her husband's own brothels. No, they were delicate sheltered creatures now.

The men, though they had made money, learned new ways less easily or were, perhaps, less patient with the demands of the new gentility. They drank heavily at Scarlett's parties, far too heavily, and usually after a reception there were one or more unexpected guests who stayed the night. They did not drink like the men of Scarlett's girlhood. They became sodden, stupid, ugly or obscene. Moreover, no matter how many spittoons she might put out in plain view, the rugs always showed signs of tobacco juice on the mornings after.

She had a contempt for these people but she enjoyed them. Because she enjoyed them, she filled the house with them. And because of her contempt, she told them to go to hell as often as they annoyed her. But they stood it.

They even stood for Rhett, a more difficult matter, for Rhett saw through them and they knew it. He had no hesitation about stripping them verbally, even under his own roof, always in a manner that left them no reply. Unashamed of how he came by his fortune, he pretended that they, too, were unashamed of their beginnings and he seldom missed an opportunity to remark upon matters which, by common consent, everyone felt were better left in polite obscurity.

There was never any knowing when he would remark affably, over a punch cup: 'Ralph, if I'd had any sense I'd have made my money selling gold-mine stocks to widows and orphans, like you, instead of blockading. It's so much safer.' 'Well, Bill, I see you have a new span of horses. Been selling a few thousand more bonds for non-existent railroads? Good work, boy!' 'Congratulations, Amos, on landing that state contract. Too bad you had to grease so many palms to get it.'

The ladies felt that he was odiously, unendurably vulgar. The men said, behind his back, that he was a swine and a bastard. New Atlanta liked Rhett no better than old Atlanta had done and he made as little attempt to conciliate the one as he had the other. He went his way, amused, contemptuous, impervious to the opinions of those about him, so courteous that his courtesy was an affront in itself. To Scarlett, he was still an enigma but an enigma about which she no longer bothered her head. She was convinced that nothing ever pleased him or ever would please him; that he either wanted something badly and didn't have it, or never had wanted anything and so didn't care about anything. He laughed at everything she did, encouraged her extravagances and insolences, jeered at her pretences – and paid the bills.

Chapter L

Rhett never deviated from his smooth, imperturbable manners, even in their most intimate moments. But Scarlett never lost the old feeling that he was watching her covertly, knew that if she turned her head suddenly she would surprise in his eyes that speculative, waiting look, that look of almost terrible patience that she did not understand.

Sometimes, he was a very comfortable person to live with, for all his unfortunate habit of not permitting anyone in his presence to act a lie, palm off a pretence or indulge in bombast. He listened to her talk of the store and the mills and the saloon, the convicts and the cost of feeding them, and gave shrewd hard-headed advice. He had untiring energy for the dancing and parties she loved and an unending supply of coarse stories with which he regaled her on their infrequent evenings alone when the table was cleared and brandy and coffee before them. She found that he would give her anything she desired, answer any question she asked as long as she was forthright, and refuse her anything she attempted to gain by indirection, hints and feminine angling. He had a disconcerting habit of seeing through her and laughing rudely.

Contemplating the suave indifference with which he generally treated her, Scarlett frequently wondered, but with no real curiosity, why he had married her. Men married for love or a home and children or money, but she knew he had married her for none of these things. He certainly did not love her. He referred to her lovely house as an architectural horror and said he would rather live in a well-regulated hotel than a home. And he never once hinted about children as Charles and Frank had done. Once when trying to coquet with him she asked him why he married her and was infuriated when he replied with an amused gleam in his eyes: 'I married you to keep you for a pet, my dear.'

No, he hadn't married her for any of the usual reasons men marry women. He had married her solely because he wanted her and couldn't get her any other way. He had admitted as much the night he proposed to her. He had wanted her, just as he had wanted Belle Watling. This was not a pleasant thought. In fact, it was a barefaced insult. But she shrugged it off as she had learned to shrug off all unpleasant facts. They had made a bargain and she was quite pleased with her side of the bargain. She hoped he was equally pleased but she did not care very much whether he was or not.

But one afternoon when she was consulting Dr Meade about a digestive upset, she learned an unpleasant fact which she could not shrug off. It was with real hate in her eyes that she stormed into her bedroom at twilight and told Rhett that she was going to have a baby.

He was lounging in a silk dressing-gown in a cloud of smoke and his eyes went sharply to her face as she spoke. But he said nothing. He watched her in silence but there was a tenseness about his pose, as he waited for her next words, that was lost on her. Indignation and despair had claimed her to the exclusion of all other thoughts.

'You know I don't want any more children! I never wanted any at all. Every time things are going right with me I have to have a baby. Oh, don't sit there and laugh! You don't want it either. Oh, Mother of God!'

If he was waiting for words from her, these were not the words he wanted. His face hardened slightly and his eyes became blank.

'Well, why not give it to Miss Melly? Didn't you tell me she was so misguided as to want another baby?'

'Oh, I could kill you! I won't have it, I tell you, I won't!'

'No? Pray continue.'

'Oh, there are things to do. I'm not the stupid country fool I used to be. Now, I know that a woman doesn't have to have children if she doesn't want them! There are things—'

He was on his feet and had her by the wrist and there was a hard, driving fear in his face.

'Scarlett, you fool, tell me the truth! You haven't done anything?'

'No, I haven't, but I'm going to. Do you think I'm going to have my figure ruined all over again, just when I've gotten my waistline down and am having a good time and—'

'Where did you get this idea? Who's been telling you things?'

'Mamie Bart – she—'

'The madam of a whore-house would know such tricks. That woman never puts foot in this house again, do you understand? After all, it is my house and I'm the master of it. I do not even want you to speak to her again.'

'I'll do as I please. Turn me loose. Why should you care?'

'I don't care whether you have one child or twenty, but I do care if you die.'

'Die? Me?'

'Yes, die. I don't suppose Mamie Bart told you the chances a woman takes when she does a thing like that?'

'No,' said Scarlett reluctantly. 'She just said it would fix things up fine.'

'By God, I will kill her!' cried Rhett and his face was black with rage. He looked down into Scarlett's tear-stained face and some of the wrath faded but it was still hard and set. Suddenly he picked her up in his arms and sat down in the chair, holding her close to him, tightly, as if he feared she would get away from him.

'Listen, my baby, I won't have you take your life in your hands. Do you hear? Good God, I don't want children any more than you do, but I can support them. I don't want to hear any more foolishness out of you, and if you dare try to— Scarlett, I saw a girl die that way once. She was only a – well, but she was a pretty good sort at that. It's not an easy way to die. I—'

'Why, Rhett!' she cried, startled out of her misery at the emotion in his voice. She had never seen him so moved. 'Where – who—'

'In New Orleans – oh, years ago. I was young and impressionable.' He bent his head suddenly and buried his lips in her hair. 'You'll have your baby, Scarlett, if I have to handcuff you to my wrist for the next nine months.'

She sat up in his lap and stared into his face with frank curiosity. Under her gaze it was suddenly smooth and bland as though wiped clear by magic. His eyebrows were up and the corner of his mouth was down.

'Do I mean so much to you?' she questioned, dropping her eyelids.

He gave her a level look as though estimating how much coquetry was behind the question. Reading the true meaning of her demeanour, he made casual answer.

'Well, yes. You see, I've invested a good deal of money in you, and I'd hate to lose it.'

Melanie came out of Scarlett's room, weary from the strain but happy to tears at the birth of Scarlett's daughter. Rhett stood tensely in the hall, surrounded by cigar butts which had burned holes in the fine carpet.

'You can go in now, Captain Butler,' she said shyly.

Rhett went swiftly past her into the room and Melanie had a brief glimpse of him bending over the small naked baby in Mammy's lap before Dr Meade shut the door. Melanie sank into a chair, her face pinkening with embarrassment that she had unintentionally witnessed so intimate a scene.

'Ah!' she thought. 'How sweet! How worried poor Captain Butler has been! And he did not take a single drink all this time! How nice of him! So many gentlemen are so intoxicated by the time their babies are born. I fear he needs a drink badly. Dare I suggest it? No, that would be very forward of me.'

She sank gratefully into a chair, her back, which always ached these days, feeling as though it would break in two at the waistline. Oh, how fortunate Scarlett was to have Captain Butler just outside her door while the baby was being born! If only she had had Ashley with her that dreadful day Beau came she would not have suffered half so much. If only that small girl behind those closed doors were hers and not Scarlett's! 'Oh, how wicked I am,' she thought guiltily. 'I am coveting her baby and Scarlett has been so good to me. Forgive me, Lord. I wouldn't really want Scarlett's baby but – but I would so like a baby of my own!'

She pushed a small cushion behind her aching back and thought hungrily of a daughter of her own. But Dr Meade had never changed his opinion on that subject. And though she was quite willing to risk her life for another child, Ashley would not hear of it. A daughter. How Ashley would love a daughter!

A daughter! Mercy! She sat up in alarm. 'I never told Captain Butler it was a girl! And of course he was expecting a boy. Oh, how dreadful!'

Melanie knew that to a woman a child of either sex was equally welcome, but to a man, and especially such a self-willed man as Captain Butler, a girl would be a blow, a reflection upon his manhood. Oh, how thankful she was that God had permitted her only child to be a boy! She knew that, had she been the wife of the fearsome Captain Butler, she would have thankfully died in childbirth rather than present him with a daughter as his first-born.

But Mammy, waddling grinning from the room, set her mind at ease – and at the same time made her wonder just what kind of a man Captain Butler really was.

'W'en Ah wuz bathin' dat chile jes' now,' said Mammy, 'Ah kinder 'pologized ter Mist' Rhett 'bout it not bein' a boy. But, Lawd, Miss Melly, you know whut he say? He say, "Hesh yo' mouf, Mammy! Who want a boy? Boys ain' no fun. Dey's jes' a passel of trouble. Gals is whut is fun. Ah wouldn' swap disyere gal fer a baker's dozen of boys." Den he try ter snatch de chile from me, buck nekked as she wuz, an' Ah slap his wrist an' say, "B'have yo'seff, Mist' Rhett! Ah'll jes' bide mah time tell you gits a boy, an' den Ah'll laff out loud to hear you holler fer joy." He grin an' shake his haid an' say, "Mammy, you is a fool. Boys ain' no use ter nobody. Ain' Ah a proof of dat?" Yas'm, Miss Melly, he ack lak a gempmum 'bout it,' finished Mammy graciously. It was not lost on Melanie that Rhett's conduct had gone far toward redeeming him in Mammy's eyes. 'Maybe Ah done been a mite wrong 'bout Mist' Rhett. Dis sho is a happy day ter me, Miss Melly. Ah done diapered three ginrations of Robillard gals, an' it sho is a happy day.'

'Oh, yes, it is a happy day, Mammy! The happiest days are the days when babies come!'

To one person in the house it was not a happy day. Scolded and for the most part ignored, Wade Hampton idled miserably about the dining-room. Early that morning, Mammy had waked him abruptly, dressed him hurriedly and sent him with Ella to Aunt Pitty's house for breakfast. The only explanation he received was that his mother was sick and the noise of his playing might upset her. Aunt Pitty's house was in an uproar, for the news of Scarlett's sickness had sent the old lady to bed in a state with Cookie in attendance, and breakfast was a scant meal that Peter concocted for the children. As the morning wore on fear began to possess Wade's soul. Suppose Mother died? Other boys' mothers had died. He had seen the hearses move away from the houses and heard his small friends sobbing. Suppose Mother should die? Wade loved his mother very much, almost as much as he feared her, and the thought of her being carried away in a black hearse behind black horses with plumes on their bridles made his small chest ache so that he could hardly breathe.

When noon came and Peter was busy in the kitchen, Wade slipped out the front door and hurried home as fast as his short legs could carry him, fear speeding him. Uncle Rhett or Aunt Melly or Mammy surely would tell him the truth. But Uncle Rhett and Aunt Melly were not to be seen and Mammy and Dilcey sped up and down the back stairs with towels and basins of hot water and did not notice him in the front hall. From upstairs he could hear occasionally the curt tones of Dr Meade whenever a door opened. Once he heard his mother groan and he burst into sobbing hiccoughs. He knew she was going to die. For comfort, he made overtures to the honey-coloured cat which lay on the sunny window-sill in the front hall. But Tom, full of years and irritable at disturbances, switched his tail and spat softly.

Finally Mammy, coming down the front stairs, her apron rumpled and spotted, her head-rag awry, saw him and scowled. Mammy had always been Wade's mainstay and her frown made him tremble.

'You is de wustes' boy Ah ever seed,' she said. 'Ain' Ah done sont you ter Miss Pitty's? Gwan back dar!'

'Is Mother going to – will she die?'

'You is de troublesomes' chile Ah ever seed! Die? Gawdlmighty, no! Lawd, boys is a tawment. Ah doan see why de Lawd sen's boys ter folks. Now, gwan way from here.'

But Wade did not go. He retreated behind the portières in the hall, only half convinced by her words. The remark about the troublesomeness of boys stung, for he had always tried his best to be good. Aunt Melly hurried down the stairs half an hour later, pale and tired but smiling to herself. She looked thunderstruck when she saw his woebegone face in the shadows of the drapery. Usually Aunt Melly had all the time in the world to give him. She never said, as Mother so often did: 'Don't bother me now. I'm in a hurry,' or 'Run away, Wade. I am busy.'

But this morning she said: 'Wade, you've been very naughty. Why didn't you stay at Aunt Pitty's?'

'Is Mother going to die?'

'Gracious, no, Wade! Don't be a silly child,' and then, relenting: 'Dr Meade has just brought her a nice little baby, a sweet little sister for you to play with, and if you are real good you can see her tonight. Now, run out and play and don't make any noise.'

Wade slipped into the quiet dining-room, his small and insecure world tottering. Was there no place for a worried little seven-year-old boy on this sunshiny day when the grown-ups acted so curiously? He sat down on the window-sill in the alcove and nibbled a bit of the elephant's-ear which grew in a box in the sun. It was so peppery that it stung his eyes to tears and he began to cry. Mother was probably dying, nobody paid him any heed and, one and all, they rushed about because of a new baby – a girl baby. Wade had little interest in babies, still less in girls. The only little girl he knew intimately was Ella and, so far, she had done nothing to command his respect or liking.

After a long interval Dr Meade and Uncle Rhett came down the stairs and stood talking in the hall in low voices. After the door shut behind the doctor, Uncle Rhett came swiftly into the dining-room and poured himself a large drink from the decanter before he saw Wade. Wade shrank back, expecting to be told again that he was naughty and must return to Aunt Pitty's, but instead, Uncle Rhett smiled. Wade had never seen him smile like that or look so happy and, encouraged, he leaped from the sill and ran to him.

'You've got a sister,' said Rhett, squeezing him. 'By God, the most beautiful baby you ever saw! Now, why are you crying?'

'Mother—'

'Your mother's eating a great big dinner, chicken and rice and gravy and coffee, and we're going to make her some ice-cream in a little while and you can have two plates if you want them. And I'll show you your sister too.'

Weak with relief, Wade tried to be polite about his new sister but failed. Everyone was interested in this girl. No one cared anything about him any more, not even Aunt Melly or Uncle Rhett.

'Uncle Rhett,' he began, 'do people like girls better than boys?'

Rhett set down his glass and looked sharply into the small face and instant comprehension came into his eyes.

'No, I can't say they do,' he answered seriously, as though giving the matter due thought. 'It's just that girls are more trouble than boys and people are apt to worry more about troublesome people than those who aren't.'

'Mammy just said boys were troublesome.'

'Well, Mammy was upset. She didn't mean it.'

'Uncle Rhett, wouldn't you rather have had a little boy than a little girl?' questioned Wade hopefully.

'No,' answered Rhett swiftly and, seeing the boy's face fall, he continued: 'Now, why should I want a boy when I've already got one?'

'You have?' cried Wade, his mouth falling open at this information. 'Where is he?'

'Right here,' answered Rhett and, picking the child up, drew him to his knee. 'You are boy enough for me, son.'

For a moment, the security and happiness of being wanted was so great that Wade almost cried again. His throat worked and he ducked his head against Rhett's waistcoat.

'You are my boy, aren't you?'

'Can you be – well, two men's boy?' questioned Wade, loyalty to the father he had never known struggling with love for the man who held him so understandingly.

'Yes,' said Rhett firmly. 'Just like you can be your mother's boy and Aunt Melly's, too.'

Wade digested this statement. It made sense to him and he smiled and wriggled against Rhett's arm shyly.

'You understand little boys, don't you, Uncle Rhett?'

Rhett's dark face fell into its old harsh lines and his lip twisted.

'Yes,' he said bitterly, 'I understand little boys.'

For a moment, fear came back to Wade, fear and a sudden sense of jealousy. Uncle Rhett was not thinking of him but of someone else.

'You haven't got any other little boys, have you?'

Rhett set him on his feet.

'I'm going to have a drink and so are you, Wade, your first drink, a toast to your new sister.'

'You haven't got any other—' began Wade, and then, seeing Rhett reach for the decanter of claret, the excitement at being included in this grown-up ceremony diverted him.

'Oh, I can't, Uncle Rhett! I promised Aunt Melly I wouldn't drink till I graduated from the university and she's going to give me a watch if I don't.'

'And I'll give you a chain for it – this one I'm wearing now, if you want it,' said Rhett, and he was smiling again. 'Aunt Melly's quite right. But she was talking about spirits, not wine. You must learn to drink wine like a gentleman, son, and there's no time like the present to learn.'

Skilfully, he diluted the claret with water from the carafe until the liquid was barely pink and handed the glass to Wade. At that moment, Mammy entered the dining-room. She had changed to her best Sunday black and her apron and head-rag were fresh and crisp. As she waddled, she switched herself and from her skirts came the whisper and rustle of silk. The worried look had gone from her face and her almost toothless gums showed in a wide smile.

'Burfday gif', Mist' Rhett!' she said.

Wade stopped with his glass to his lips. He knew Mammy had never liked his stepfather. He had never heard her call him anything except 'Cap'n Butler', and her conduct toward him had been dignified but cold. And here she was beaming and sidling and calling him 'Mist' Rhett'! What a topsy-turvy day!

'You'd rather have rum than claret, I suppose,' said Rhett, reaching into the cellaret and producing a squat bottle. 'She is a beautiful baby, isn't she, Mammy?'

'She sho is,' answered Mammy, smacking her lips as she took the glass.

'Did you ever see a prettier one?'

'Well, suh, Miss Scarlett wuz mout nigh as pretty w'en she come but not quite.'

'Have another glass, Mammy. And, Mammy,' his tone was stern but his eyes twinkled, 'what's that rustling noise I hear?'

'Lawd, Mist' Rhett, dat ain' nuthin' but mah red silk petticoat!' Mammy giggled and switched till her huge bulk shook.

'Nothing but your petticoat! I don't believe it. You sound like a peck of dried leaves rubbing together. Let me see. Pull up your skirt.'

'Mist' Rhett, you is bad! Yeah-O, Lawd!'

Mammy gave a little shriek and retreated and, from a distance of a yard, modestly elevated her dress a few inches and showed the ruffle of a red taffeta petticoat.

'You took long enough about wearing it,' grumbled Rhett, but his black eyes laughed and danced.

'Yassuh, too long.'

Then Rhett said something that Wade did not understand.

'No more mule in horse harness?'

'Mist' Rhett, Miss Scarlett wuz bad ter tell you dat! You ain' holin' dat agin dis ole nigger?'

'No. I'm not holding it. I just wanted to know. Have another drink, Mammy. Have the whole bottle. Drink up, Wade! Give us a toast.'

'To Sissy,' cried Wade, and gulped the liquid down. Choking, he began to cough and hiccough and the other two laughed and beat him on the back.

From the moment his daughter was born, Rhett's conduct was puzzling to all observers and he upset many settled notions about himself, notions which both the town and Scarlett were loath to surrender. Whoever would have thought that he of all people would be so shamelessly, so openly proud of fatherhood? Especially in view of the embarrassing circumstance that his first-born was a girl and not a boy.

The novelty of fatherhood did not wear off. This caused some secret envy among women whose husbands took offspring for granted, long before the children were christened. He buttonholed people on the street and related details of his child's miraculous progress without even prefacing his remarks with the hypocritical but polite: 'I know everyone thinks their own child is smart but—' He thought his daughter marvellous, not to be compared with lesser brats, and he did not care who knew it. When the new nurse permitted the baby to suck a bit of fat pork, thereby bringing on the first attack of colic, Rhett's conduct sent seasoned fathers and mothers into gales of laughter. He hurriedly summoned Dr Meade and two other doctors, and with difficulty he was restrained from beating the unfortunate nurse with his crop. The nurse was discharged and thereafter followed a series of nurses who remained, at the most, a week. None of them was good enough to satisfy the exacting requirements Rhett laid down.

Mammy likewise viewed with displeasure the nurses that came and went, for she was jealous of any strange negro and saw no reason why she could not care for the baby and Wade and Ella, too. But Mammy was showing her age and rheumatism was slowing her lumbering tread. Rhett lacked the courage to cite these reasons for employing another nurse. He told her instead that a man of his position could not afford to have only one nurse. It did not look well. He would hire two others to do the drudgery and leave her as Mammy-in-chief. This Mammy understood very well. More servants were a credit to her position as well as Rhett's. But she would not, she told him firmly, have any trashy free issue niggers in her nursery. So Rhett sent to Tara for Prissy. He knew her shortcomings but, after all, she was a family darky. And Uncle Peter produced a great-niece named Lou who had belonged to one of Miss Pitty's Burr cousins.

Even before Scarlett was able to be about again, she noticed Rhett's preoccupation with the baby and was somewhat nettled and embarrassed at his pride in her in front of callers. It was all very well for a man to love his child but she felt there was something unmanly in the display of such love. He should be offhand and careless, as other men were.

'You are making a fool of yourself,' she said irritably, 'and I don't see why.'

'No? Well, you wouldn't. The reason is that she's the first person who's ever belonged utterly to me.'

'She belongs to me, too!'

'No, you have two other children. She's mine.'

'Great balls of fire!' said Scarlett. 'I had the baby, didn't I? Besides, honey, I belong to you.'

Rhett looked at her over the black head of the child and smiled oddly.

'Do you, my dear?'

Only the entrance of Melanie stopped one of those swift hot quarrels which seemed to spring up so easily between them these days. Scarlett swallowed her wrath and watched Melanie take the baby. The name agreed upon for the child was Eugenie Victoria, but that afternoon Melanie unwittingly bestowed a name that clung, even as 'Pittypat' had blotted out all memory of Sarah Jane.

Rhett leaning over the child had said: 'Her eyes are going to be pea-green.'

'Indeed they are not,' cried Melanie indignantly, forgetting that Scarlett's eyes were almost that shade. 'They are going to be blue, like Mr O'Hara's eyes, as blue as – as blue as the bonnie blue flag.'

'Bonnie Blue Butler,' laughed Rhett, taking the child from her and peering more closely into the small eyes. And Bonnie she became until even her parents did not recall that she had been named for two queens.

Chapter LI

When she was finally able to go out again, Scarlett had Lou lace her into her stays as tightly as the strings would pull. Then she passed the tape-measure about her waist. Twenty inches! She groaned aloud. That was what having babies did to your figure! Her waist was as large as Aunt Pitty's, as large as Mammy's.

'Pull them tighter, Lou. See if you can't make it eighteen and a half inches or I can't get into any of my dresses.'

'It'll bust de strings,' said Lou. 'Yo' wais' jes' done got bigger, Miss Scarlett, an' dar ain' nuthin' ter do 'bout it.'

'There is something to do about it,' thought Scarlett as she ripped savagely at the seams of her dress to let out the necessary inches. 'I just won't have any more babies.'

Of course, Bonnie was pretty and a credit to her, and Rhett adored the child, but she would not have another baby. Just how she would manage this she did not know, for she couldn't handle Rhett as she had Frank. Rhett wasn't afraid of her. It would probably be difficult with Rhett acting so foolishly about Bonnie and probably wanting a son next year, for all that he said he'd drown any boy she gave him. Well, she wouldn't give him a boy or girl either. Three children were enough for any woman to have.

When Lou had stitched up the ripped seams, pressed them smooth and buttoned Scarlett into the dress, she called the carriage and Scarlett set out for the lumber yard. Her spirits rose as she went and she forgot about her waistline, for she was going to meet Ashley at the yard to go over the books with him. And, if she was lucky, she might see him alone. She hadn't seen him since long before Bonnie was born. She hadn't wanted to see him at all when she was so obviously pregnant. And she had so missed the daily contact with him, even if there was always someone around. She had missed the importance and activity of her lumber business while she was immured. Of course, she did not have to work now. She could easily sell the mills and invest the money for Wade and Ella. But that would mean she would hardly ever see Ashley, except in a formal social way with crowds of people around. And working by Ashley's side was her greatest pleasure.

When she drove up to the yard she saw with interest how high the piles of lumber were and how many customers were standing among them, talking to Hugh Elsing. And there were six mule teams and wagons being loaded by the negro drivers. 'Six teams,' she thought, with pride. 'And I did all this by myself!'

Ashley came to the door of the little office, his eyes joyful with the pleasure of seeing her again, and he handed her out of her carriage and into the office as if she were a queen.

But some of her pleasure was dimmed when she went over the books of his mill and compared them with Johnnie Gallegher's books. Ashley had barely made expenses and Johnnie had a remarkable sum to his credit. She forbore to say anything as she looked at the two sheets but Ashley read her face.

'Scarlett, I'm sorry. All I can say is that I wish you'd let me hire free darkies instead of using convicts. I believe I could do better.'

'Darkies! Why, their pay would break us. Convicts are dirt cheap. If Johnnie can make this much with them—'

Ashley's eyes went over her shoulder, looking at something she could not see, and the glad light went out of his eyes.

'I can't work convicts like Johnnie Gallegher. I can't drive men.'

'God's nightgown! Johnnie's a wonder at it. Ashley, you are just too soft-hearted. You ought to get more work out of them. Johnnie told me that any time a malingerer wanted to get out of work he told you he was sick and you gave him a day off. Good Lord, Ashley! That's no way to make money. A couple of licks will cure most any sickness short of a broken leg—'

'Scarlett! Scarlett! Stop! I can't bear to hear you talk that way,' cried Ashley, his eyes coming back to her with a fierceness that stopped her short. 'Don't you realize that they are men – some of them sick, underfed, miserable and—Oh, my dear, I can't bear to see the way he has brutalized you, you who were always so sweet—'

'Who has whatted me?'

'I've got to say it and I haven't any right. But I've got to say it. Your – Rhett Butler. Everything he touches he poisons. And he has taken you who were so sweet and generous and gentle, for all your spirited ways, and he has done this to you – hardened you, brutalized you by his contact.'

'Oh,' breathed Scarlett, guilt struggling with joy that Ashley should feel so deeply about her, should still think her sweet. Thank God, he thought Rhett to blame for her penny-pinching ways. Of course, Rhett had nothing to do with it and the guilt was hers but, after all, another black mark on Rhett could do him no harm.

'If it were any other man in the world, I wouldn't care so much – but Rhett Butler! I've seen what he's done to you. Without your realizing it, he's twisted your thoughts into the same hard path his own run in. Oh, yes, I know I shouldn't say this—He saved my life and I am grateful but I wish to God it had been any man but him! And I haven't the right to talk to you like—'

'Oh, Ashley, you have the right – no one else has!'

'I tell you I can't bear it, seeing your fineness coarsened by him, knowing that your beauty and your charm are in the keeping of a man who—When I think of him touching you, I—'

'He's going to kiss me!' thought Scarlett ecstatically. 'And it won't be my fault!' She swayed toward him. But he drew back suddenly, as if realizing he had said too much – said things he never intended to say.

'I apologize most humbly, Scarlett. I – I've been insinuating that your husband is not a gentleman and my own words have proved that I'm not one. No one has a right to criticize a husband to a wife. I haven't any excuse except – except—' he faltered and his face twisted. She waited breathless.

'I haven't any excuse at all.'

All the way home in the carriage Scarlett's mind raced No excuse at all except – except that he loved her! And the thought of her lying in Rhett's arms roused a fury in him that she did not think possible. Well, she could understand that. If it wasn't for the knowledge that his relations with Melanie were, necessarily, those of brother and sister, her own life would be a torment. And Rhett's embraces coarsened her, brutalized her! Well, if Ashley thought that, she could do very well without those embraces. She thought how sweet and romantic it would be for them both to be physically true to each other, even though married to other people. The idea possessed her imagination and she took pleasure in it. And then, too, there was the practical side of it. It would mean that she would not have to have any more children.

When she reached home and dismissed the carriage, some of the exaltation which had filled her at Ashley's words began to fade as she faced the prospect of telling Rhett that she wanted separate bedrooms and all which that implied. It would be difficult. Moreover, how could she tell Ashley that she had denied herself to Rhett, because of his wishes? What earthly good was a sacrifice if no one knew about it? What a burden modesty and delicacy were! If she could only talk to Ashley as frankly as she could to Rhett! Well, no matter. She'd insinuate the truth to Ashley somehow.

She went up the stairs and, opening the nursery door, found Rhett sitting beside Bonnie's crib with Ella upon his lap and Wade displaying the contents of his pocket to him. What a blessing Rhett liked children and made much of them! Some stepfathers were so bitter about children of former marriages.

'I want to talk to you,' she said and passed on into their bedroom. Better have this over now while her determination not to have any more children was hot within her and while Ashley's love was giving her strength.

'Rhett,' she said abruptly when he had closed the bedroom door behind him, 'I've decided that I don't want any more children.'

If he was startled at her unexpected statement he did not show it. He lounged to a chair and, sitting down, tilted it back.

'My pet, as I told you before Bonnie was born, it is immaterial to me whether you have one child or twenty.'

How perverse of him to evade the issue so neatly, as if not caring whether children came had anything to do with their actual arrival.

'I think three are enough. I don't intend to have one every year.'

'Three seems an adequate number.'

'You know very well—' she began, embarrassment making her cheeks red. 'You know what I mean?'

'I do. Do you realize that I can divorce you for refusing me my marital rights?'

'You are just low enough to think of something like that,' she cried, annoyed that nothing was going as she planned it. 'If you had any chivalry you'd – you'd be nice like— Well, look at Ashley Wilkes. Melanie can't have any children and he—'

'Quite the little gentleman, Ashley,' said Rhett, and his eyes began to gleam oddly. 'Pray go on with your discourse.'

Scarlett choked, for her discourse was at its end and she had nothing more to say. Now she saw how foolish had been her hope of amicably settling so important a matter, especially with a selfish swine like Rhett.

'You've been to the lumber office this afternoon, haven't you?'

'What has that to do with it?'

'You like dogs, don't you, Scarlett? Do you prefer them in kennels or mangers?'

The allusion was lost on her as the tide of her anger and disappointment rose.

He got lightly to his feet and coming to her put his hand under her chin and jerked her face up to his.

'What a child you are! You have lived with three men and still know nothing of men's natures. You seem to think they are like old ladies past the change of life.'

He pinched her chin playfully and his hand dropped away from her. One black eyebrow went up as he bent a cool long look on her.

'Scarlett, understand this. If you and your bed still held any charms for me, no locks and no entreaties could keep me away. And I would have no sense of shame for anything I did, for I made a bargain with you – a bargain which I have kept and you are now breaking. Keep your chaste bed, my dear.'

'Do you mean to tell me,' cried Scarlett indignantly, 'that you don't care—'

'You have tired of me, haven't you? Well, men tire more easily than women. Keep your sanctity, Scarlett. It will work no hardship on me. It doesn't matter.' He shrugged and grinned. 'Fortunately the world is full of beds – and most of the beds are full of women.'

'You mean you'd actually be so—'

'My dear innocent! But, of course. It's a wonder I haven't strayed long ere this. I never held fidelity to be a virtue.'

'I shall lock my door every night!'

'Why bother? If I wanted you, no lock would keep me out.'

He turned, as though the subject were closed and left the room. Scarlett heard him going back to the nursery where he was welcomed by the children. She sat down abruptly. She had had her way. This was what she wanted and Ashley wanted. But it was not making her happy. Her vanity was sore and she was mortified at the thought that Rhett had taken it all so lightly, that he didn't want her, that he put her on the level of other women in other beds.

She wished she could think of some delicate way to tell Ashley that she and Rhett were no longer actually man and wife. But she knew now she could not. It all seemed a terrible mess and she half heartedly wished she had said nothing about it. She would miss the long amusing conversations in bed with Rhett when the ember of his cigar glowed in the dark. She would miss the comfort of his arms when she woke terrified from dreams that she was running through cold mist.

Suddenly she felt very unhappy and, leaning her head on the arm of the chair, she cried.

Chapter LII

One rainy afternoon when Bonnie was barely past her first birthday, Wade moped about the sitting-room, occasionally going to the window and flattening his nose on the dripping pane. He was a slender, weedy boy, small for his eight years, quiet almost to shyness, never speaking unless spoken to. He was bored and obviously at loss for entertainment, for Ella was busy in the corner with her dolls, Scarlett was at her secretary muttering to herself as she added a long column of figures, and Rhett was lying on the floor swinging his watch by its chain, just out of Bonnie's reach.

After Wade had picked up several books and let them drop with bangs and sighed deeply, Scarlett turned to him in irritation.

'Heavens, Wade! Run out and play.'

'I can't. It's raining.'

'Is it? I hadn't noticed. Well, do something. You make me nervous, fidgeting about. Go tell Pork to hitch up the carriage and take you over to play with Beau.'

'He isn't home,' sighed Wade. 'He's at Raoul Picard's birthday party.'

Raoul was the small son of Maybelle and René Picard – a detestable little brat, Scarlett thought, more like an ape than a child.

'Well, you can go to see anyone you want to. Run tell Pork.'

'Nobody's at home,' answered Wade. 'Everybody's at the party.'

The unspoken words 'everybody – but me' hung in the air; but Scarlett, her mind on her account-books, paid no heed.

Rhett raised himself to a sitting posture and said: 'Why aren't you at the party too, son?'

Wade edged closer to him, scuffing one foot and looking unhappy.

'I wasn't invited, sir.'

Rhett handed his watch into Bonnie's destructive grasp and rose lightly to his feet.

'Leave those damned figures alone, Scarlett. Why wasn't Wade invited to this party?'

'For Heaven's sake, Rhett! Don't bother me now. Ashley has gotten these accounts in an awful snarl— Oh, that party? Well, I think it's nothing unusual that Wade wasn't invited and I wouldn't let him go if he had been. Don't forget that Raoul is Mrs Merriwether's grandchild and Mrs Merriwether would as soon have a free issue nigger in her sacred parlour as one of us.'

Rhett, watching Wade's face with meditative eyes, saw the boy flinch.

'Come here, son,' he said, drawing the boy to him. 'Would you like to be at that party?'

'No, sir,' said Wade bravely, but his eyes fell.

'Hum. Tell me, Wade, do you go to little Joe Whiting's parties or Frank Bonnell's or – well, any of your playmates?'

'No, sir. I don't get invited to many parties.'

'Wade, you are lying!' cried Scarlett, turning. 'You went to three last week, the Bart children's party and the Gelerts' and the Huntingdons'.'

'As choice a collection of mules in horse harness as you could group together,' said Rhett, his voice going into a soft drawl. 'Did you have a good time at those parties? Speak up.'

'No, sir.'

'Why not?'

'I – I dunno, sir. Mammy – Mammy says they're white trash.'

'I'll skin Mammy this minute!' cried Scarlett, leaping to her feet. 'And as for you, Wade, talking so about Mother's friends—'

'The boy's telling the truth and so is Mammy,' said Rhett. 'But, of course, you've never been able to know the truth if you met it in the road . . . Don't bother, son. You don't have to go to any more parties you don't want to go to. Here,' he pulled a bill from his pocket, 'tell Pork to harness the carriage and take you downtown. Buy yourself some candy – a lot, enough to give you a wonderful stomach-ache.'

Wade, beaming, pocketed the bill and looked anxiously toward his mother for confirmation. But she, with a pucker in her brows, was watching Rhett. He had picked Bonnie from the floor and was cradling her to him, her small face against his cheek. She could not read his face but there was something in his eyes almost like fear – fear and self-accusation.

Wade, encouraged by his stepfather's generosity, came shyly toward him.

'Uncle Rhett, can I ask you sumpin'?'

'Of course.' Rhett's look was anxious, absent, as he held Bonnie's head closer. 'What is it, Wade?'

'Uncle Rhett, were you – did you fight in the war?'

Rhett's eyes came alertly back and they were sharp, but his voice was casual.

'Why do you ask, son?'

'Well, Joe Whiting said you didn't and so did Frankie Bonnell.'

'Ah,' said Rhett, 'and what did you tell them?'

Wade looked unhappy.

'I – I said – I told them I didn't know.' And with a rush, 'But I didn't care and I hit them. Were you in the war, Uncle Rhett?'

'Yes,' said Rhett, suddenly violent. 'I was in the war. I was in the army for eight months. I fought all the way from Lovejoy up to Franklin, Tennessee. And I was with Johnston when he surrendered.'

Wade wriggled with pride but Scarlett laughed.

'I thought you were ashamed of your war record,' she said. 'Didn't you tell me to keep it quiet?'

'Hush,' he said briefly. 'Does that satisfy you, Wade?'

'Oh, yes, sir! I knew you were in the war. I knew you weren't scared like they said. But – why weren't you with the other little boys' fathers?'

'Because the other little boys' fathers were such fools they had to put them in the infantry. I was a West Pointer and so I was in the artillery. In the regular artillery, Wade, not the Home Guard. It takes a pile of sense to be in the artillery, Wade.'

'I bet,' said Wade, his face shining. 'Did you get wounded, Uncle Rhett?'

Rhett hesitated.

'Tell him about your dysentery,' jeered Scarlett.

Rhett carefully set the baby on the floor and pulled his shirt and undershirt out of his trouser-band.

'Come here, Wade, and I'll show you where I was wounded.'

Wade advanced, excited, and gazed where Rhett's finger pointed. A long raised scar ran across his brown chest and down into his heavily muscled abdomen. It was the souvenir of a knife fight in the California gold-fields but Wade did not know it. He breathed heavily and happily.

'I guess you're 'bout as brave as my father, Uncle Rhett.'

'Almost but not quite,' said Rhett, stuffing his shirt into his trousers. 'Now, go on and spend your dollar and whale hell out of any boy who says I wasn't in the army.'

Wade went dancing out happily, calling to Pork, and Rhett picked up the baby again.

'Now why all these lies, my gallant soldier laddie?' asked Scarlett.

'A boy has to be proud of his father – or his stepfather. I can't let him be ashamed before the other little brutes. Cruel creatures, children.'

'Oh, fiddle-dee-dee!'

'I never thought about what it meant to Wade,' said Rhett slowly. 'I never thought how he's suffered. And it's not going to be that way for Bonnie.'

'What way?'

'Do you think I'm going to have my Bonnie ashamed of her father? Have her left out of parties when she's nine or ten? Do you think I'm going to have her humiliated like Wade for things that aren't her fault but yours and mine?'

'Oh, children's parties!'

'Out of children's parties grow young girls' début parties. Do you think I'm going to let my daughter grow up outside of everything decent in Atlanta? I'm not going to send her North to school and to visit because she won't be accepted here or in Charleston or Savannah or New Orleans. And I'm not going to see her forced to marry a Yankee or a foreigner because no decent Southern family will have her – because her mother was a fool and her father a blackguard.'

Wade, who had come back to the door, was an interested but puzzled listener.

'Bonnie can marry Beau, Uncle Rhett.'

The anger went from Rhett's face as he turned to the little boy, and he considered his words with apparent seriousness as he always did when dealing with the children.

'That's true, Wade. Bonnie can marry Beau Wilkes, but who will you marry?'

'Oh, I shan't marry anyone,' said Wade confidently, luxuriating in a man-to-man talk with the one person, except Aunt Melly, who never reproved and always encouraged him. 'I'm going to go to Harvard and be a lawyer, like my father, and then I'm going to be a brave soldier just like him.'

'I wish Melly would keep her mouth shut,' cried Scarlett. 'Wade, you are not going to Harvard. It's a Yankee school and I won't have you going to a Yankee school. You are going to the University of Georgia and after you graduate you are going to manage the store for me. And as for your father being a brave soldier—'

'Hush,' said Rhett curtly, not missing the shining light in Wade's eyes when he spoke of the father he had never known. 'You grow up and be a brave man like your father, Wade. Try to be just like him, for he was a hero and don't let anyone tell you differently. He married your mother, didn't he? Well, that's proof enough of heroism. And I'll see that you go to Harvard and become a lawyer. Now, run along and tell Pork to take you to town.'

'I'll thank you to let me manage my children,' cried Scarlett as Wade obediently trotted from the room.

'You're a damned poor manager. You've wrecked whatever chances Ella and Wade had, but I won't permit you to do Bonnie that way. Bonnie's going to be a little princess and everyone in the world is going to want her. There's not going to be any place she can't go. Good God, do you think I'm going to let her grow up and associate with the riffraff that fills this house?'

'They are good enough for you—'

'And a damned sight too good for you, my pet. But not for Bonnie. Do you think I'd let her marry any of this runagate gang you spend your time with? Irishmen on the make, Yankees, white trash, Carpetbag parvenus— My Bonnie with her Butler blood and her Robillard strain—'

'The O'Haras—'

'The O'Haras might have been kings of Ireland once but your father was nothing but a smart Mick on the make. And you are no better— But then, I'm at fault too. I've gone through life like a bat out of hell, never caring what I did, because nothing ever mattered to me. But Bonnie matters. God, what a fool I've been! Bonnie wouldn't be received in Charleston, no matter what my mother or your Aunt Eulalie or Aunt Pauline did – and it's obvious that she won't be received here unless we do something quickly—'

'Oh, Rhett, you take it so seriously you're funny. With our money—'

'Damn our money! All our money can't buy what I want for her. I'd rather Bonnie was invited to eat dry bread in the Picards' miserable house or Mrs Elsing's rickety barn than to be the belle of a Republican inaugural ball. Scarlett, you've been a fool. You should have ensured a place for your children in the social scheme years ago – but you didn't. You didn't even bother to keep what position you had. And it's too much to hope that you'll mend your ways at this late date. You're too anxious to make money and too fond of bullying people.'

'I consider this whole affair a tempest in a teapot,' said Scarlett coldly, rattling her papers to indicate that as far as she was concerned the discussion was finished.

'We have only Mrs Wilkes to help us and you do your best to alienate and insult her. Oh, spare me your remarks about her poverty and her tacky clothes. She's the soul and the centre of everything in Atlanta that's sterling. Thank God for her. She'll help me do something about it.'

'And what are you going to do?'

'Do? I'm going to cultivate every female dragon of the Old Guard in this town, especially Mrs Merriwether, Mrs Elsing, Mrs Whiting and Mrs Meade. If I have to crawl on my belly to every fat old cat who hates me, I'll do it. I'll be meek under their coldness and repentant of my evil ways. I'll contribute to their damned charities and I'll go to their damned churches. I'll admit and brag about my services to the Confederacy and, if worst comes to worst, I'll join their damned Klan – though a merciful God could hardly lay so heavy a penance on my shoulders as that. And I shall not hesitate to remind the fools whose necks I saved that they owe me a debt. And you, Madam, will kindly refrain from undoing my work behind my back by foreclosing mortgages on any of the people I'm courting or selling them rotten lumber or in other ways insulting them. And Governor Bullock never sets foot in this house again. Do you hear? And none of this gang of elegant thieves you've been associating with, either. If you do invite them, over my request, you will find yourself in the embarrassing position of having no host in your home. If they come in this house, I will spend the time in Belle Watling's bar telling anyone who cares to hear that I won't stay under the same roof with them.'

Scarlett, who had been smarting under his words, laughed shortly.

'So the river-boat gambler and the speculator is going to be respectable! Well, your first move toward respectability had better be the sale of Belle Watling's house.'

That was a shot in the dark. She had never been absolutely certain that Rhett owned the house. He laughed suddenly, as though he read her mind.

'Thanks for the suggestion.'

Had he tried, Rhett could not have chosen a more difficult time to beat his way back to respectability. Never before or after did the names Republican and Scallawag carry such odium, for now the corruption of the Carpetbag régime was at its height. And, since the surrender, Rhett's name had been inextricably linked with Yankees, Republicans and Scallawags.

Atlanta people had thought, with helpless fury, in 1866, that nothing could be worse than the harsh military rule they had then, but now, under Bullock, they were learning the worst. Thanks to the negro vote, the Republicans and their allies were firmly entrenched and they were riding rough-shod over the powerless but still protesting minority.

Word had been spread among the negroes that there were only two political parties mentioned in the Bible, the Publicans and the Sinners. No negro wanted to join a party made up entirely of sinners, so they hastened to join the Republicans. Their new masters voted them over and over again, electing poor whites and Scallawags to high places, electing even some negroes. These negroes sat in the legislature where they spent most of their time eating goobers and easing their unaccustomed feet into and out of new shoes. Few of them could read or write. They were fresh from cotton patch and canebrake, but it was within their power to vote taxes and bonds as well as enormous expense accounts to themselves and their Republican friends. And they voted them. The state staggered under taxes which were paid in fury, for the taxpayers knew that much of the money voted for public purposes was finding its way into private pockets.

Completely surrounding the state capitol was a host of promoters, speculators, seekers after contracts and others hoping to profit from the orgy of spending, and many were growing shamelessly rich. They had no difficulty at all in obtaining the state's money for building railroads that were never built, for buying cars and engines that were never bought, for erecting public buildings that never existed except in the minds of their promoters.

Bonds were issued running into the millions. Most of them were illegal and fraudulent but they were issued just the same. The state treasurer, a Republican but an honest man, protested against the illegal issues and refused to sign them, but he and others who sought to check the abuses could do nothing against the tide that was running.

The state-owned railroad had once been an asset to the state but now it was a liability and its debts had piled up to the million mark. It was no longer a railroad. It was an enormous bottomless trough in which the hogs could swill and wallow. Many of its officials were appointed for political reasons, regardless of their knowledge of the operation of railroads, there were three times as many people employed as were necessary, Republicans rode free on passes, carloads of negroes rode free on their happy jaunts about the state to vote and revote in the same elections.

The mismanagement of the state road especially infuriated the taxpayers, for out of the earnings of the road was to come the money for free schools. But there were no earnings, there were only debts, and so there were no free schools. Few had money to send their children to pay schools and there was a generation of children growing up in ignorance who would spread the seeds of illiteracy down the years.

But far and above their anger at the waste and mismanagement and graft was the resentment of the people at the bad light in which the governor represented them in the North. When Georgia howled against corruption, the governor hastily went North, appeared before congress and told of white outrages against negroes, of Georgia's preparation for another rebellion and the need for a stern military rule in the state. No Georgian wanted trouble with the negroes and they tried to avoid trouble. No one wanted another war, no one wanted or needed bayonet rule. All Georgia wanted was to be let alone so the state could recuperate. But with the operation of what came to be known as the governor's 'slander mill', the North saw only a rebellious state that needed a heavy hand, and a heavy hand was laid upon it.

It was a glorious spree for the gang which had Georgia by the throat. There was an orgy of grabbing and over all there was a cold cynicism about open theft in high places that was chilling to contemplate. Protests and efforts to resist accomplished nothing, for the state government was being upheld and supported by the power of the United States Army.

Atlanta cursed the name of Bullock and his Scallawags and Republicans and they cursed the name of anyone connected with them. And Rhett was connected with them. He had been in with them, so everyone said, in all their schemes. But now, he turned against the stream in which he had drifted so short a while before, and began swimming arduously back against the current.

He went about his campaign slowly, subtly, not arousing the suspicions of Atlanta by the spectacle of a leopard trying to change his spots overnight. He avoided his dubious cronies and was seen no more in the company of Yankee officers, Scallawags and Republicans. He attended Democratic rallies and he ostentatiously voted the Democratic ticket. He gave up high-stake card games and stayed comparatively sober. If he went to Belle Watling's house at all, he went by night and by stealth as did more respectable townsmen, instead of leaving his horse hitched in front of her door in the afternoons as an advertisement of his presence within.

And the congregation of the Episcopal Church almost fell out of their pews when he tiptoed in, late for services, with Wade's hand held in his. The congregation was as much stunned by Wade's appearance as by Rhett's, for the little boy was supposed to be a Catholic. At least, Scarlett was one. Or she was supposed to be one. But she had not put foot in the church in years, for religion had gone from her as many of Ellen's other teachings had gone. Everyone thought she had neglected her boy's religious education and thought more of Rhett for trying to rectify the matter, even if he did take the boy to the Episcopal Church instead of the Catholic.

Rhett could be grave of manner and charming when he chose to restrain his tongue and keep his black eyes from dancing maliciously. It had been years since he had chosen to do this but he did it now, putting on gravity and charm, even as he put on waistcoats of more sober hues. It was not difficult to gain a foothold of friendliness with the men who owed their necks to him. They would have showed their appreciation long ago, had Rhett not acted as if their appreciation were a matter of small moment. Now, Hugh Elsing, René, the Simmons boys, Andy Bonnell and the others found him pleasant, diffident about putting himself forward and embarrassed when they spoke of the obligation they owed him.

'It was nothing,' he would protest. 'In my place you'd have all done the same thing.'

He subscribed handsomely to the fund for the repairs of the Episcopal Church and he gave a large, but not vulgarly large, contribution to the Association for the Beautification of the Graves of Our Glorious Dead. He sought out Mrs Elsing to make this donation and embarrassedly begged that she keep his gift a secret, knowing very well that this would spur her to spreading the news. Mrs Elsing hated to take his money – 'speculator money' – but the Association needed money badly.

'I don't see why you of all people should be subscribing,' she said acidly.

When Rhett told her with the proper sober mien that he was moved to contribute by the memories of former comrades in arms, braver than he but less fortunate, who now lay in unmarked graves, Mrs Elsing's aristocratic jaw dropped. Dolly Merriwether had told her Scarlett had said Captain Butler was in the army but, of course, she hadn't believed it. Nobody had believed it.

'You in the army? What was your company – your regiment?'

Rhett gave them.

'Oh, the artillery! Everyone I knew was either in the cavalry or the infantry. Then, that explains—' She broke off, disconcerted, expecting to see his eyes snap with malice. But he only looked down and toyed with his watch-chain.

'I would have liked the infantry,' he said, passing completely over her insinuation, 'but when they found that I was a West Pointer – though I did not graduate, Mrs Elsing, due to a boyish prank – they put me in the artillery, the regular artillery, not the militia. They needed men with specialized knowledge in that last campaign. You know how heavy the losses had been, so many artillerymen killed. It was pretty lonely in the artillery. I didn't see a soul I knew. I don't believe I saw a single man from Atlanta during my whole service.'

'Well!' said Mrs Elsing, confused. If he had been in the army then she was in the wrong. She had made many sharp remarks about his cowardice and the memory of them made her feel guilty. 'Well! And why haven't you ever told anybody about your service? You act as though you were ashamed of it.'

Rhett looked her squarely in the eyes, his face blank.

'Mrs Elsing,' he said earnestly, 'believe me when I say that I am prouder of my services to the Confederacy than of anything I have ever done or will do. I feel – I feel—'

'Well, why did you keep it hidden?'

'I was ashamed to speak of it, in the light of – of some of my former actions.'

Mrs Elsing reported the contribution and the conversation in detail to Mrs Merriwether.

'And, Dolly, I give you my word that when he said that about being ashamed, tears came into his eyes! Yes, tears! I nearly cried myself.'

'Stuff and nonsense!' cried Mrs Merriwether in disbelief. 'I don't believe tears came into his eyes any more than I believe he was in the army. And I can find out mighty quick. If he was in that artillery outfit, I can get at the truth, for Colonel Carleton who commanded it married the daughter of one of my grandfather's sisters and I'll write him.'

She wrote Colonel Carleton and to her consternation received a reply praising Rhett's services in no uncertain terms. A born artilleryman, a brave soldier and an uncomplaining gentleman, a modest man who wouldn't even take a commission when it was offered him.

'Well!' said Mrs Merriwether, showing the letter to Mrs Elsing. 'You can knock me down with a feather! Maybe we did misjudge the scamp about not being a soldier. Maybe we should have believed what Scarlett and Melanie said about him enlisting the day the town fell. But, just the same, he's a Scallawag and a rascal and I don't like him!'

'Somehow,' said Mrs Elsing uncertainly, 'somehow, I don't think he's so bad. A man who fought for the Confederacy can't be all bad. It's Scarlett who is the bad one. Do you know, Dolly, I really believe that he – well, that he's ashamed of Scarlett but is too much of a gentleman to let on.'

'Ashamed! Pooh! They're both cut out of the same piece of cloth. Where did you ever get such a silly notion?'

'It isn't silly,' said Mrs Elsing indignantly. 'Yesterday, in the pouring rain, he had those three children, even the baby, mind you, out in his carriage riding them up and down Peachtree Street and he gave me a lift home. And then I said: "Captain Butler, have you lost your mind keeping these children out in the damp? Why don't you take them home?" And he didn't say a word but just looked embarrassed. But Mammy spoke up and said: "De house full of w'ite trash an' it healthier fer de chillun in de rain dan at home!" '

'What did he say?'

'What could he say? He just scowled at Mammy and passed it over. You know Scarlett was giving a big whist party yesterday afternoon with all those common ordinary women there. I guess he didn't want them kissing his baby.'

'Well!' said Mrs Merriwether, wavering but still obstinate. But the next week she, too, capitulated.

Rhett now had a desk in the bank. What he did at this desk the bewildered officials of the bank did not know, but he owned too large a block of the stock for them to protest his presence there. After a while they forgot that they had objected to him, for he was quiet and well-mannered and actually knew something about banking and investments. At any rate he sat at his desk all day, giving every appearance of industry, for he wished to be on equal terms with his respectable fellow townsmen who worked and worked hard.

Mrs Merriwether, wishing to expand her growing bakery, had tried to borrow two thousand dollars from the bank with her house as security. She had been refused because there were already two mortgages on the house. The stout old lady was storming out of the bank when Rhett stopped her, learned the trouble and said, worriedly: 'But there must be some mistake, Mrs Merriwether. Some dreadful mistake. You of all people shouldn't have to bother about collateral. Why, I'd lend you money just on your word! Any lady who could build up the business you've built up is the best risk in the world. The bank wants to lend money to people like you. Now, do sit down right here in my chair and I will attend to it for you.'

When he came back he was smiling blandly, saying that there had been a mistake, just as he had thought. The two thousand dollars was right there waiting for her whenever she cared to draw against it. Now, about her house – would she just sign right here?

Mrs Merriwether, torn with indignation and insult, furious that she had to take this favour from a man she disliked and distrusted, was hardly gracious in her thanks.

But he failed to notice it. As he escorted her to the door, he said: 'Mrs Merriwether, I have always had a great regard for your knowledge and I wonder if you could tell me something?'

The plumes on her bonnet barely moved as she nodded.

'What did you do when your Maybelle was little and she sucked her thumb?

'What?

'My Bonnie sucks her thumb. I can't make her stop it.'

'You should make her stop it,' said Mrs Merriwether vigorously. 'It will ruin the shape of her mouth.'

'I know! I know! And she has a beautiful mouth. But I don't know what to do.'

'Well, Scarlett ought to know,' said Mrs Merriwether shortly. 'She's had two other children.'

Rhett looked down at his shoes and sighed.

'I've tried putting soap under her finger-nails,' he said, passing over her remark about Scarlett.

'Soap! Bah! Soap is no good at all. I put quinine on Maybelle's thumb and let me tell you, Captain Butler, she stopped sucking that thumb mighty quick.'

'Quinine! I would never have thought of it! I can't thank you enough, Mrs Merriwether. It was worrying me.'

He gave her a smile, so pleasant, so grateful that Mrs Merriwether stood uncertainly for a moment. But as she told him goodbye she was smiling too. She hated to admit to Mrs Elsing that she had misjudged the man but she was an honest person and she said there had to be something good about a man who loved his child. What a pity Scarlett took no interest in so pretty a creature as Bonnie! There was something pathetic about a man trying to raise a little girl all by himself! Rhett knew very well the pathos of the spectacle, and if it blackened Scarlett's reputation he did not care.

From the time the child could walk he took her about with him constantly, in the carriage or in front of his saddle. When he came home from the bank in the afternoon, he took her walking down Peachtree Street, holding her hand, slowing his long strides to her toddling steps, patiently answering her thousand questions. People were always in their front yards or on their porches at sunset and, as Bonnie was such a friendly, pretty child, with her tangle of black curls and her bright blue eyes, few could resist talking to her. Rhett never presumed on these conversations but stood by, exuding fatherly pride and gratification at the notice taken of his daughter.

Atlanta had a long memory and was suspicious and slow to change. Times were hard and feeling was bitter against anyone who had had anything to do with Bullock and his crowd. But Bonnie had the combined charm of Scarlett and Rhett at their best and she was the small opening wedge Rhett drove into the wall of Atlanta's coldness.

Bonnie grew rapidly and every day it became more evident that Gerald O'Hara had been her grandfather. She had short sturdy legs and wide eyes of Irish blue and a small square jaw that went with a determination to have her own way. She had Gerald's sudden temper to which she gave vent in screaming tantrums that were forgotten as soon as her wishes were gratified. And as long as her father was near her, they were always gratified hastily. He spoiled her despite all the efforts of Mammy and Scarlett, for in all things she pleased him, except one. And that was her fear of the dark.

Until she was two years old she went to sleep readily in the nursery she shared with Wade and Ella. Then, for no apparent reason, she began to sob whenever Mammy waddled out of the room, carrying the lamp. From this she progressed to wakening in the late night hours, screaming with terror, frightening the other two children and alarming the house. Once Dr Meade had to be called and Rhett was short with him when he diagnosed only bad dreams. All anyone could get from her was one word, 'Dark.'

Scarlett was inclined to be irritated with the child and favoured a spanking. She would not humour her by leaving a lamp burning in the nursery, for then Wade and Ella would be unable to sleep. Rhett, worried but gentle, attempting to extract further information from his daughter, said coldly that if any spanking were done, he would do it personally and to Scarlett.

The upshot of the situation was that Bonnie was removed from the nursery to the room Rhett now occupied alone. Her small bed was placed beside his large one and a shaded lamp burned on the table all night long. The town buzzed when this story got about. Somehow, there was something indelicate about a girl child sleeping in her father's room, even though the girl was only two years old. Scarlett suffered from this gossip in two ways. First, it proved indubitably that she and her husband occupied separate rooms, in itself a shocking enough state of affairs. Second, everyone thought that if the child was afraid to sleep alone, her place was with her mother. And Scarlett did not feel equal to explaining that she could not sleep in a lighted room nor would Rhett permit the child to sleep with her.

'You'd never wake up unless she screamed and then you'd probably slap her,' he said shortly.

Scarlett was annoyed at the weight he attached to Bonnie's night terrors but she thought she could eventually remedy the state of affairs and transfer the child back to the nursery. All children were afraid of the dark and the only cure was firmness. Rhett was just being perverse in the matter, making her appear a poor mother, just to pay her back for banishing him from her room.

He had never put foot in her room or even rattled the door-knob since the night she told him she did not want any more children. Thereafter and until he began staying at home on account of Bonnie's fears, he had been absent from the supper table more often than he had been present. Sometimes he had stayed out all night and Scarlett, lying awake behind her locked door, hearing the clock count off the early morning hours, wondered where he was. She remembered: 'There are other beds, my dear!' Though the thought made her writhe, there was nothing she could do about it. There was nothing she could say that would not precipitate a scene in which he would be sure to remark upon her locked door and the probable connection Ashley had with it. Yes, his foolishness about Bonnie sleeping in a lighted room – in his lighted room – was just a mean way of paying her back.

She did not realize the importance he attached to Bonnie's foolishness nor the completeness of his devotion to the child until one dreadful night. The family never forgot that night.

That day Rhett had met an ex-blockade-runner and they had had much to say to each other. Where they had gone to talk and drink, Scarlett did not know but she suspected, of course, Belle Watling's house. He did not come home in the afternoon to take Bonnie walking nor did he come home to supper. Bonnie, who had watched from the window impatiently all afternoon, anxious to display a mangled collection of beetles and roaches to her father, had finally been put to bed by Lou, amid wails and protests.

Either Lou had forgotten to light the lamp or it had burned out. No one ever knew exactly what happened but when Rhett finally came home, somewhat the worse for drink, the house was in an uproar and Bonnie's screams reached him even in the stables. She had waked in darkness and called for him and he had not been there. All the nameless horrors that peopled her small imagination clutched her. All the soothing and bright lights brought by Scarlett and the servants could not quiet her, and Rhett, coming up the stairs three at a jump, looked like a man who has seen Death.

When he finally had her in his arms and from her sobbing gasps had recognized only one word, 'Dark,' he turned on Scarlett and the negroes in fury.

'Who put out the light? Who left her alone in the dark? Prissy, I'll skin you for this, you—'

'Gawdlmighty, Mist' Rhett! 'Twarn't me! 'Twuz Lou!'

'Fo' Gawd, Mist' Rhett, Ah—'

'Shut up. You know my orders. By God, I'll – Get out. Don't come back. Scarlett, give her some money and see that she's gone before I come downstairs. Now, everybody get out, everybody!'

The negroes fled, the luckless Lou wailing into her apron. But Scarlett remained. It was hard to see her favourite child quieting in Rhett's arms when she had screamed so pitifully in her own. It was hard to see the small arms going around his neck and hear the choking voice relate what had frightened her, when she, Scarlett, had gotten nothing coherent out of her.

'So it sat on your chest,' said Rhett softly. 'Was it a big one?'

'Oh, yes! Dretful big. And claws.'

'Ah, claws too. Well, now. I shall certainly sit up all night and shoot him if he comes back.' Rhett's voice was interested and soothing and Bonnie's sobs died away. Her voice became less choked as she went into detailed description of her monster guest in a language which only he could understand. Irritation stirred in Scarlett as Rhett discussed the matter as if it had been something real.

'For Heaven's sake, Rhett—'

But he made a sign for silence. When Bonnie was at last asleep, he laid her in her bed and pulled up the sheet.

'I'm going to skin that nigger alive,' he said quietly. 'It's your fault too. Why didn't you come up here to see if the light was burning?'

'Don't be a fool, Rhett,' she whispered. 'She gets this way because you humour her. Lots of children are afraid of the dark but they get over it. Wade was afraid but I didn't pamper him. If you'd just let her scream for a night or two—'

'Let her scream!' For a moment Scarlett thought he would hit her. 'Either you are a fool or the most inhuman woman I've ever seen.'

'I don't want her to grow up nervous and cowardly.'

'Cowardly? Hell's afire! There isn't a cowardly bone in her body! But you haven't any imagination and, of course, you can't appreciate the tortures of people who have one – especially a child. If something with claws and horns came and sat on your chest, you'd tell it to get the hell off you, wouldn't you? Like hell you would! Kindly remember, Madam, that I've seen you wake up squalling like a scalded cat simply because you dreamed of running in a fog. And that's not been so long ago either!'

Scarlett was taken aback, for she never liked to think of that dream. Moreover, it embarrassed her to remember that Rhett had comforted her in much the same manner he comforted Bonnie. So she swung rapidly to a different attack.

'You are just humouring her and—'

'And I intend to keep on humouring her. If I do, she'll outgrow it and forget about it.'

'Then,' said Scarlett acidly, 'if you intend to play nursemaid, you might try coming home at nights and sober too, for a change.'

'I shall come home early but drunk as a fiddler's bitch if I please.'

He did come home early thereafter, arriving long before time for Bonnie to be put to bed. He sat beside her, holding her hand until sleep loosened her grasp. Only then did he tiptoe downstairs, leaving the lamp burning brightly and the door ajar so he might hear her should she awake and become frightened. Never again did he intend her to have a recurrence of fear of the dark. The whole household was acutely conscious of the burning light, Scarlett, Mammy, Prissy and Pork frequently tiptoeing upstairs to make sure that it still burned.

He came home sober too, but that was none of Scarlett's doing. For months he had been drinking heavily, though he was never actually drunk, and one evening the smell of whisky was especially strong upon his breath. He picked up Bonnie, swung her to his shoulder and asked her: 'Have you a kiss for your sweetheart?'

She wrinkled her small upturned nose and wriggled to get down from his arms.

'No,' she said frankly. 'Nasty.'

'I'm what?'

'Smell nasty. Uncle Ashley don't smell nasty.'

'Well, I'll be damned,' he said ruefully, putting her on the floor. 'I never expected to find a temperance advocate in my own home, of all places!'

But, thereafter, he limited his drinking to a glass of wine after supper.

Bonnie, who was always permitted to have the last drops in the glass, did not think the smell of wine nasty at all. As a result, the puffiness which had begun to obscure the hard lines of his cheeks slowly disappeared and the circles beneath his black eyes were not so dark or so harshly cut. Because Bonnie liked to ride on the front of his saddle, he stayed out of doors more and the sunburn began to creep across his dark face, making him swarthier than ever. He looked healthier and laughed more and was again like the dashing young blockader who had excited Atlanta early in the war.

People who had never liked him came to smile as he went by with the small figure perched before him on his saddle. Women who had heretofore believed that no woman was safe with him, began to stop and talk with him on the streets, to admire Bonnie. Even the strictest old ladies felt that a man who could discuss the ailments and problems of childhood as well as he did could not be altogether bad.

Chapter LIII

It was Ashley's birthday and Melanie was giving him a surprise reception that night. Everyone knew about the reception, except Ashley. Even Wade and little Beau knew and were sworn to a secrecy that puffed them up with pride. Everyone in Atlanta who was nice had been invited and was coming. General Gordon and his family had graciously accepted, Alexander Stephens would be present if his ever-uncertain health permitted, and even Bob Toombs, the stormy petrel of the Confederacy, was expected.

All that morning, Scarlett, with Melanie, India and Aunt Pitty, flew about the little house, directing the negroes as they hung freshly laundered curtains, polished silver, waxed the floor and cooked, stirred and tasted the refreshments. Scarlett had never seen Melanie so excited or so happy.

'You see, dear, Ashley hasn't had a birthday party since – since, you remember the barbecue at Twelve Oaks? The day we heard about Mr Lincoln's call for volunteers? Well, he hasn't had a birthday party since then. And he works so hard and he's so tired when he gets home at night that he really hasn't thought about today being his birthday. And won't he be surprised after supper when everybody troops in!'

'How you goin' to manage them lanterns on the lawn without Mr Wilkes seein' them when he comes home to supper?' demanded Archie grumpily.

He had sat all morning watching the preparations, interested but unwilling to admit it. He had never been behind the scenes at a large town folks' party and it was a new experience. He made frank remarks about women running around like the house was afire, just because they were having company, but wild horses could not have dragged him from the scene. The coloured-paper

lanterns which Mrs Elsing and Fanny had made and painted for the occasion
held a special interest for him, as he had never seen 'sech contraptions' before.
They had been hidden in his room in the cellar and he had examined them
minutely.

'Mercy! I hadn't thought of that!' cried Melanie. 'Archie, how fortunate
that you mentioned it. Dear, dear! What shall I do? They've got to be strung
on the bushes and trees and little candles put in them and lighted just at the
proper time when the guests are arriving. Scarlett, can you send Pork down
to do it while we're eating supper?'

'Miz Wilkes, you got more sense than most women but you gits flurried
right easy,' said Archie. 'And as for that fool nigger, Pork, he ain't got no
bizness with them thar contraptions. He'd set them afire in no time. They
are – right pretty,' he conceded. 'I'll hang them for you, whilst you and
Mr Wilkes are eatin'.'

'Oh, Archie, how kind of you!' Melanie turned childlike eyes of gratitude
and dependence upon him. 'I don't know what I should do without you.
Do you suppose you could go put the candles in them now, so we'd have
that much out of the way?'

'Well, I could, p'raps,' said Archie ungraciously and stumped off toward
the cellar stairs.

'There's more ways of killing a cat than choking him to death with butter,'
giggled Melanie when the whiskered old man had thumped down the stairs.
'I had intended all along for Archie to put up those lanterns but you know
how he is. He won't do a thing if you ask him to. And now we've got him
out from underfoot for a while. The darkies are so scared of him they just
won't do any work when he's around, breathing down their necks.'

'Melly, I wouldn't have that old desperado in my house,' said Scarlett
crossly. She hated Archie as much as he hated her and they barely spoke.
Melanie's was the only house in which he would remain if she were present.
And even in Melanie's house, he stared at her with suspicion and cold
contempt. 'He'll cause you trouble, mark my words.'

'Oh, he's harmless if you flatter him and act like you depend on him,' said
Melanie. 'And he's so devoted to Ashley and Beau that I always feel safe
having him around.'

'You mean he's so devoted to you, Melly,' said India, her cold face relaxing
into a faintly warm smile as her gaze rested fondly on her sister-in-law. 'I
believe you're the first person that old ruffian has loved since his wife – er
– since his wife. I think he'd really like for somebody to insult you, so he
could kill them to show his respect for you.'

'Mercy! How you run on, India!' said Melanie, blushing. 'He thinks I'm
a terrible goose and you know it.'

'Well, I don't see that what that smelly old hillbilly thinks is of any
importance,' said Scarlett abruptly. The very thought of how Archie had
sat in judgment upon her about the convicts always enraged her. 'I have to

go now. I've got to go get dinner and then go by the store and pay off the clerks and go by the lumber yard and pay the drivers and Hugh Elsing.'

'Oh, are you going to the lumber yard?' asked Melanie. 'Ashley is coming into the yard in the late afternoon to see Hugh. Can you possibly hold him there till five o'clock? If he comes home earlier he'll be sure to catch us finishing up a cake or something and then he won't be surprised at all.'

Scarlett smiled inwardly, good temper restored.

'Yes, I'll hold him,' she said.

As she spoke, India's pale lashless eyes met hers piercingly. 'She always looks at me so oddly when I speak of Ashley,' thought Scarlett.

'Well, hold him there as long as you can after five o'clock,' said Melanie. 'And then India will drive down and pick him up . . . Scarlett, do come early tonight. I don't want you to miss a minute of the reception.'

As Scarlett rode home she thought sullenly: 'She doesn't want me to miss a minute of the reception, eh? Well, then, why didn't she invite me to receive with her and India and Aunt Pitty?'

Generally, Scarlett would not have cared whether she received at Melly's piddling parties or not. But this was the largest party Melanie had ever given and Ashley's birthday party too, and Scarlett longed to stand by Ashley's side and receive with him. But she knew why she had not been invited to receive. Even had she not known it, Rhett's comment on the subject had been frank enough.

'A Scallawag receive when all the prominent ex-Confederates and Democrats are going to be there? Your notions are as enchanting as they are muddle-headed. It's only because of Miss Melly's loyalty that you are invited at all.'

Scarlett dressed with more than usual care that afternoon for her trip to the store and the lumber yard, wearing the new dull-green changeable taffeta frock that looked lilac in some lights and the new pale-green bonnet, circled about with dark-green plumes. If only Rhett would let her cut bangs and frizzle them on her forehead, how much better this bonnet would look! But he had declared that he would shave her whole head if she banged her forelocks. And these days he acted so atrociously he really might do it.

It was a lovely afternoon, sunny but not too hot, bright but not glaring, and the warm breeze that rustled the trees along Peachtree Street made the plumes on Scarlett's bonnet dance. Her heart danced too, as always when she was going to see Ashley. Perhaps, if she paid off the team drivers and Hugh early, they would go home and leave her and Ashley alone in the square little office in the middle of the lumber yard. Chances to see Ashley alone were all too infrequent these days. And to think that Melanie had asked her to hold him! That was funny!

Her heart was merry when she reached the store, and she paid off Willie and the other counter boys without even asking what the day's business had been. It was Saturday, the biggest day of the week for the store, for all the farmers came to town to shop that day, but she asked no questions.

Along the way to the lumber yard she stopped a dozen times to speak with Carpetbagger ladies in splendid equipages – not so splendid as her own, she thought with pleasure – and with many men who came through the red dust of the street to stand hat in hand and compliment her. It was a beautiful afternoon, she was happy, she looked pretty and her progress was a royal one. Because of these delays she arrived at the lumber yard later than she intended and found Hugh and the team drivers sitting on a low pile of lumber waiting for her.

'Is Ashley here?'

'Yes, he's in the office,' said Hugh, the habitually worried expression leaving his face at the sight of her happy, dancing eyes. 'He's trying to – I mean, he's going over the books.'

'Oh, he needn't bother about that today,' she said, and then lowering her voice: 'Melly sent me down to keep him here till they get the house straight for the reception tonight.'

Hugh smiled for he was going to the reception. He liked parties and he guessed Scarlett did too from the way she looked this afternoon. She paid off the teamsters and Hugh and, abruptly leaving them, walked toward the office, showing plainly by her manner that she did not care to be accompanied. Ashley met her at the door and stood in the afternoon sunshine, his hair bright and on his lips a little smile that was almost a grin.

'Why, Scarlett, what are you doing downtown this time of the day? Why aren't you out at my house helping Melly get ready for the surprise party?'

'Why, Ashley Wilkes!' she cried indignantly. 'You weren't supposed to know a thing about it. Melly will be so disappointed if you aren't surprised.'

'Oh, I won't let on. I'll be the most surprised man in Atlanta,' said Ashley, his eyes laughing.

'Now, who was mean enough to tell you?'

'Practically every man Melly invited. General Gordon was the first. He said it had been his experience that when women gave surprise parties they usually gave them on the very nights men had decided to polish and clean all the guns in the house. And then Grandpa Merriwether warned me. He said Mrs Merriwether gave him a surprise party once and she was the most surprised person there, because Grandpa had been treating his rheumatism, on the sly, with a bottle of whisky and he was too drunk to get out of bed and – oh, every man who's ever had a surprise party given him told me.'

'The mean things!' cried Scarlett, but she had to smile.

He looked like the old Ashley she knew at Twelve Oaks when he smiled like this. And he smiled so seldom these days. The air was so soft, the sun so gentle, Ashley's face so gay, his talk so unconstrained that her heart leaped with happiness. It swelled in her bosom until it positively ached with pleasure, ached as with a burden of joyful, hot, unshed tears. Suddenly she felt sixteen again and happy, a little breathless and excited. She had a mad impulse to snatch off her bonnet and toss it into the air and cry 'Hurray!' Then she thought how startled Ashley would be if she did this, and she suddenly laughed, laughed until tears came to her eyes. He laughed, too, throwing back his head as though he enjoyed laughter, thinking her mirth came from the friendly treachery of the men who had given Melly's secret away.

'Come in, Scarlett. I'm going over the books.'

She passed into the small room, blazing with the afternoon sun, and sat down in the chair before the roll-topped desk. Ashley, following her, seated himself on the corner of the rough table, his long legs dangling easily.

'Oh, don't let's fool with any books this afternoon, Ashley! I just can't be bothered. When I'm wearing a new bonnet, it seems like all the figures I know leave my head.'

'Figures are well lost when the bonnet's as pretty as that one,' he said. 'Scarlett, you get prettier all the time!'

He slipped from the table and, laughing, took her hands, spreading them wide so he could see her dress. 'You are so pretty! I don't believe you'll ever get old!'

At his touch she realized that, without being conscious of it, she had hoped that just this thing would happen. All this happy afternoon, she had hoped for the warmth of his hands, the tenderness of his eyes, a word that would show he cared. This was the first time they had been utterly alone since the cold day in the orchard at Tara, the first time their hands had met in any but formal gestures, and through the long months she had hungered for closer contact. But now—

How odd that the touch of his hands did not excite her! Once his very nearness would have set her a-tremble. Now she felt only a curious warm friendliness and content. No fever leaped from his hands to hers and in his hands her heart hushed to happy quietness. This puzzled her, made her a little disconcerted. He was still her Ashley, still her bright, shining darling, and she loved him better than life. Then why—

But she pushed the thought from her mind. It was enough that she was with him and he was holding her hands and smiling, completely friendly, without strain or fever. It seemed miraculous that this could be when she thought of all the unsaid things that lay between them. His eyes looked into hers, clear and shining, smiling in the old way she loved, smiling as though there had never been anything between them but happiness. There was no barrier between his eyes and hers now, no baffling remoteness. She laughed.

'Oh, Ashley, I'm getting old and decrepit.'

'Ah, that's very apparent! No, Scarlett, when you are sixty, you'll look the same to me. I'll always remember you as you were that day of our last barbecue, sitting under an oak with a dozen boys around you. I can even tell you just how you were dressed, in a white dress covered with tiny green flowers and a white lace shawl about your shoulders. You had on little green slippers with black lacings and an enormous leghorn hat with long green streamers. I know that dress by heart because when I was in prison and things got too bad, I'd take out my memories and thumb them over like pictures, recalling every little detail—'

He stopped abruptly and the eager light faded from his face. He dropped her hands gently and she sat waiting, waiting for his next words.

'We've come a long way, both of us, since that day, haven't we, Scarlett? We've travelled roads we never expected to travel. You've come swiftly, directly, and I, slowly and reluctantly.'

He sat down on the table again and looked at her and a small smile crept back into his face. But it was not the smile that had made her so happy so short a while before. It was a bleak smile.

'Yes, you came swiftly, dragging me at your chariot wheels. Scarlett, sometimes I have an impersonal curiosity as to what would have happened to me without you.'

Scarlett went quickly to defend him from himself, more quickly because treacherously there rose to her mind Rhett's words on this same subject.

'But I've never done anything for you, Ashley. Without me, you'd have been just the same. Some day, you'd have been a rich man, a great man like you are going to be.'

'No, Scarlett, the seeds of greatness were never in me. I think that if it hadn't been for you, I'd have gone down into oblivion – like poor Cathleen Calvert and so many other people who once had great names, old names.'

'Oh, Ashley, don't talk like that. You sound so sad.'

'No, I'm not sad. Not any longer. Once – once I was sad. Now, I'm only—'

He stopped and suddenly she knew what he was thinking. It was the first time she had ever known what Ashley was thinking when his eyes went past her, crystal clear, absent. When the fury of love had beaten in her heart, his mind had been closed to her. Now, in the quiet friendliness that lay between them, she could walk a little way into his mind, understand a little. He was not sad any longer. He had been sad after the surrender, sad when she begged him to come to Atlanta. Now, he was only resigned.

'I hate to hear you talk like that, Ashley,' she said vehemently. 'You sound just like Rhett. He's always harping on things like that and something he calls the survival of the fitting till I'm so bored I could scream.'

Ashley smiled.

'Did you ever stop to think, Scarlett, that Rhett and I are fundamentally alike?'

'Oh, no! You are so fine, so honourable, and he—' She broke off, confused.

'But we are. We came of the same kind of people, we were raised in the same pattern, brought up to think the same things. And somewhere along the road we took different turnings. We still think alike but we react differently. As, for instance, neither of us believed in war but I enlisted and fought and he stayed out till nearly the end. We both knew the war was all wrong. We both knew it was a losing fight. I was willing to fight a losing fight. He wasn't. Sometimes I think he was right and then, again—'

'Oh, Ashley, when will you stop seeing both sides of questions?' she asked. But she did not speak impatiently as she once would have done. 'No one ever gets anywhere seeing both sides.'

'That's true but – Scarlett, just where do you want to get? I've often wondered. You see, I never wanted to get anywhere at all. I've only wanted to be myself.'

Where did she want to get? That was a silly question. Money and security, of course. And yet— Her mind fumbled. She had money and as much security as one could hope for in an insecure world. But, now that she thought about it, they weren't quite enough. Now that she thought about it, they hadn't made her particularly happy, though they had made her less harried, less fearful of the morrow. 'If I'd had money and security and you, that would have been where I wanted to get,' she thought, looking at him yearningly. But she did not speak the words, fearful of breaking the spell that lay between them, fearful that his mind would close against her.

'You only want to be yourself?' she laughed, a little ruefully. 'Not being myself has always been my hardest trouble! As to where I want to get, well, I guess I've gotten there. I wanted to be rich and safe and—'

'But, Scarlett, did it ever occur to you that I don't care whether I'm rich or not?'

No, it had never occurred to her that anyone would not want to be rich.

'Then, what do you want?'

'I don't know, now. I knew once but I've half forgotten. Mostly to be left alone, not to be harried by people I don't like, driven to do things I don't want to do. Perhaps – I want the old days back again and they'll never come back, and I am haunted by the memory of them and of the world falling about my ears.'

Scarlett set her mouth obstinately. It was not that she did not know what he meant. The very tones of his voice called up other days as nothing else could, made her heart hurt suddenly, as she too remembered. But since the day she had lain sick and desolate in the garden at Twelve Oaks and said, 'I won't look back,' she had set her face against the past.

'I like these days better,' she said. But she did not meet his eyes as she spoke. 'There's always something exciting happening now, parties and so on. Everything's got a glitter to it. The old days were so dull.' (Oh, lazy days and warm still country twilights! The high soft laughter from the quarters!

The golden warmth life had then and the comforting knowledge of what all tomorrows would bring! How can I deny you?)

'I like these days better,' she said but her voice was tremulous.

He slipped from the table, laughing softly in unbelief. Putting his hand under her chin, he turned her face up to his.

'Ah, Scarlett, what a poor liar you are! Yes, life has a glitter now – of a sort. That's what's wrong with it. The old days had no glitter but they had a charm, a beauty, a slow-paced glamour.'

Her mind pulled two ways, she dropped her eyes. The sound of his voice, the touch of his hand were softly unlocking doors that she had locked forever. Behind those doors lay the beauty of the old days, and a sad hunger for them welled up within her. But she knew that no matter what beauty lay behind, it must remain there. No one could go forward with a load of aching memories.

His hand dropped from her chin and he took one of her hands between his two and held it gently.

'Do you remember,' he said – and a warning bell in her mind rang: Don't look back! Don't look back!

But she swiftly disregarded it, swept forward on a tide of happiness. At last she was understanding him, at last their minds had met. This moment was too precious to be lost, no matter what pain came after.

'Do you remember,' he said, and under the spell of his voice the bare walls of the little office faded and the years rolled aside and they were riding country bridle paths together in a long-gone spring. As he spoke, his light grip tightened on her hand and in his voice was the sad magic of old half-forgotten songs. She could hear the gay jingle of bridle bits as they rode under the dogwood trees to the Tarletons' picnic, hear her own careless laughter, see the sun glinting on his silver-gilt hair and note the proud easy grace with which he sat his horse. There was music in his voice, the music of fiddles and banjoes to which they had danced in the white house that was no more. There was the far-off yelping of possum dogs in the dark swamp under cool autumn moons and the smell of eggnog bowls, wreathed with holly at Christmas time, and smiles on black and white faces. And old friends came trooping back, laughing as though they had not been dead these many years: Stuart and Brent with their long legs and their red hair and their practical jokes, Tom and Boyd as wild as young horses, Joe Fontaine with his hot black eyes, and Cade and Raiford Calvert who moved with such languid grace. There was John Wilkes, too; and Gerald, red with brandy; and a whisper and a fragrance that was Ellen. Over it all rested a sense of security, a knowledge that tomorrow could only bring the same happiness today had brought.

His voice stopped and they looked for a long quiet moment into each other's eyes and between them lay the sunny lost youth that they had so unthinkingly shared.

'Now I know why you can't be happy,' she thought sadly. 'I never understood before. I never understood before why I wasn't altogether happy either. But – why, we are talking like old people talk!' she thought with dreary surprise. 'Old people looking back fifty years. And we're not old! It's just that so much has happened in between. Everything's changed so much that it seems fifty years ago. But we're not old!'

But when she looked at Ashley he was no longer young and shining. His head was bowed as he looked down absently at her hand which he still held and she saw that his once bright hair was very grey, silver grey as moonlight on still water. Somehow the bright beauty had gone from the April afternoon and from her heart as well and the sad sweetness of remembering was as bitter as gall.

'I shouldn't have let him make me look back,' she thought despairingly. 'I was right when I said I'd never look back. It hurts too much, it drags at your heart till you can't ever do anything else except look back. That's what's wrong with Ashley. He can't look forward any more. He can't see the present, he fears the future, and so he looks back. I never understood it before. I never understood Ashley before. Oh, Ashley, my darling, you shouldn't look back! What good will it do? I shouldn't have let you tempt me into talking of the old days. This is what happens when you look back to happiness, this pain, this heartbreak, this discontent.'

She rose to her feet, her hand still in his. She must go. She could not stay and think of the old days and see his face, tired and sad and bleak as it now was.

'We've come a long way since those days, Ashley,' she said, trying to steady her voice, trying to fight the constriction in her throat. 'We had fine notions then, didn't we?' And then, with a rush, 'Oh, Ashley, nothing has turned out as we expected!'

'It never does,' he said. 'Life's under no obligation to give us what we expect. We take what we get and are thankful it's no worse than it is.'

Her heart was suddenly dull with pain, with weariness, as she thought of the long road she had come since those days. There rose up in her mind the memory of Scarlett O'Hara who loved beaux and pretty dresses and who intended, some day, when she had the time, to be a great lady like Ellen.

Without warning, tears started in her eyes and rolled slowly down her cheeks and she stood looking at him dumbly, like a hurt bewildered child. He said no word but took her gently in his arms, pressed her head against his shoulder and, leaning down, laid his cheek against hers. She relaxed against him and her arms went round his body. The comfort of his arms helped dry her sudden tears. Ah, it was good to be in his arms, without passion, without tenseness, to be there as a loved friend. Only Ashley who shared her memories and her youth, who knew her beginnings and her present could understand.

She heard the sound of feet outside but paid little heed, thinking it was the teamsters going home. She stood for a moment, listening to the slow beat of Ashley's heart. Then suddenly he wrenched himself from her, confusing her by his violence. She looked up into his face in surprise but he was not looking at her. He was looking over her shoulder at the door.

She turned and there stood India, white-faced, her pale eyes blazing, and Archie, malevolent as a one-eyed parrot. Behind them stood Mrs Elsing.

How she got out of the office she never remembered. But she went instantly, swiftly, by Ashley's order, leaving Ashley and Archie in grim converse in the little room and India and Mrs Elsing outside with their backs to her. Shame and fear sped her homeward and, in her mind, Archie with his patriarch's beard assumed the proportions of an avenging angel straight from the pages of the Old Testament.

The house was empty and still in the April sunset. All the servants had gone to a funeral and the children were playing in Melanie's back yard. Melanie—

Melanie! Scarlett went cold at the thought of her as she climbed the stairs to her room. Melanie would hear of this. India had said she would tell her. Oh, India would glory in telling her, not caring if she blackened Ashley's name, not caring if she hurt Melanie, if by so doing she could injure Scarlett! And Mrs Elsing would talk too, even though she had really seen nothing, because she was behind India and Archie in the door of the lumber office. But she would talk, just the same. The news would be all over town by supper-time. Everyone, even the negroes, would know by tomorrow's breakfast. At the party tonight, women would gather in corners and whisper discreetly and with malicious pleasure. Scarlett Butler tumbled from her high and mighty place! And the story would grow and grow. There was no way of stopping it. It wouldn't stop at the bare facts, that Ashley was holding her in his arms while she cried. Before nightfall people would be saying she had been taken in adultery. And it had been so innocent, so sweet! Scarlett thought wildly: 'If we had been caught that Christmas of his furlough when I kissed him goodbye – if we had been caught in the orchard at Tara when I begged him to run away with me – oh, if we'd been caught any of the times when we were really guilty, it wouldn't be so bad! But now! Now! When I went to his arms as a friend—'

But no one would believe that. She wouldn't have a single friend to take her part, not a single voice would be raised to say: 'I don't believe she was doing anything wrong.' She had outraged old friends too long to find a champion among them now. Her new friends, suffering in silence under her insolences, would welcome a chance to blackguard her. No, everybody would believe anything about her, though they might regret that so fine a man as Ashley Wilkes was mixed up in so dirty an affair. As usual they would cast the blame upon the woman and shrug at the man's guilt. And in this case they would be right. She had gone into his arms.

Oh, she could stand the cuts, the slights, the covert smiles, anything the town might say, if she had to stand them – but not Melanie! Oh, not Melanie! She did not know why she should mind Melanie knowing, more than anyone else. She was too frightened and weighed down by a sense of past guilt to try to understand it. But she burst into tears at the thought of what would be in Melanie's eyes when India told her that she had caught Ashley fondling Scarlett. And what would Melanie do when she knew? Leave Ashley? What else could she do, with any dignity? 'And what will Ashley and I do then?' she thought frenziedly, the tears streaming down her face. 'Oh, Ashley will die of shame and hate me for bringing this on him.' Suddenly her tears stopped short as a deadly fear went through her heart. What of Rhett? What would he do?

Perhaps he'd never know. What was that old saying, that cynical saying? 'The husband is always the last to find out.' Perhaps no one would tell him. It would take a brave man to break such news to Rhett, for Rhett had the reputation for shooting first and asking questions afterwards. Please, God, don't let anybody be brave enough to tell him! But she remembered the face of Archie in the lumber office, the cold, pale eye, remorseless, full of hate for her and all women. Archie feared neither God nor man and he hated loose women. He had hated them enough to kill one. And he had said he would tell Rhett. And he'd tell him in spite of all Ashley could do to dissuade him. Unless Ashley killed him, Archie would tell Rhett, feeling it his Christian duty.

She pulled off her clothes and lay down on the bed, her mind whirling round and round. If she could only lock her door and stay in this safe place for ever and ever and never see anyone again. Perhaps Rhett wouldn't find out tonight. She'd say she had a headache and didn't feel like going to the reception. By morning she would have thought up some excuse to offer, some defence that might hold water.

'I won't think of it now,' she said desperately, burying her face in the pillow. 'I won't think of it now. I'll think of it later when I can stand it.'

She heard the servants come back as night fell and it seemed to her that they were very silent as they moved about preparing supper. Or was it her guilty conscience? Mammy came to the door and knocked but Scarlett sent her away, saying she did not want any supper. Time passed and finally she heard Rhett coming up the steps. She held herself tensely as he reached the upper hall, gathered all her strength for a meeting, but he passed into his room. She breathed easier. He hadn't heard. Thank God, he still respected her icy request that he never put foot in her bedroom again, for if he saw her now, her face would give her away. She must gather herself together enough to tell him that she felt too ill to go to the reception. Well, there was time enough for her to calm herself. Or was there time? Since the awful moment that afternoon, life had seemed timeless. She heard Rhett moving about in his room for a long time, speaking occasionally to Pork. Still she could not find courage to call to him. She lay still on the bed in the darkness, shaking.

After a long time, he knocked on the door and she said, trying to control her voice: 'Come in.'

'Am I actually being invited into the sanctuary?' he questioned, opening the door. It was dark and she could not see his face. Nor could she make anything of his voice. He entered and closed the door.

'Are you ready for the reception?'

'I'm so sorry but I have a headache.' How odd that her voice sounded natural! Thank God for the dark! 'I don't believe I'll go. You go, Rhett, and give Melanie my regrets.'

There was a long pause and he spoke drawlingly, bitingly in the dark.

'What a white-livered, cowardly little bitch you are.'

He knew! She lay shaking, unable to speak. She heard him fumble in the dark, strike a match and the room sprang into light. He walked over to the bed and looked down at her. She saw that he was in evening clothes.

'Get up,' he said and there was nothing in his voice. 'We are going to the reception. You will have to hurry.'

'Oh, Rhett, I can't. You see—'

'I can see. Get up.'

'Rhett, did Archie dare—'

'Archie dared. A very brave man, Archie.'

'You should have killed him for telling lies—'

'I have a strange way of not killing people who tell the truth. There's no time to argue now. Get up.'

She sat up, hugging her wrapper close to her, her eyes searching his face. It was dark and impassive.

'I won't go, Rhett. I can't until this – misunderstanding is cleared up.'

'If you don't show your face tonight, you'll never be able to show it in this town as long as you live. And while I may endure a trollop for a wife, I won't endure a coward. You are going tonight, even if everyone, from Alex Stephens down, cuts you and Mrs Wilkes asks us to leave the house.'

'Rhett, let me explain.'

'I don't want to hear. There isn't time. Get on your clothes.'

'They misunderstood – India and Mrs Elsing and Archie. And they hate me so. India hates me so much that she'd even tell lies about her own brother to make me appear in a bad light. If you'll only let me explain—'

'Oh, Mother of God,' she thought in agony, 'suppose he says: "Pray do explain!" What can I say? How can I explain?'

'They'll have told everybody lies. I can't go tonight.'

'You will go,' he said, 'if I have to drag you by the neck and plant my boot on your ever so charming bottom every step of the way.'

There was a cold glitter in his eyes as he jerked her to her feet. He picked up her stays and threw them at her.

'Put them on. I'll lace you. Oh, yes, I know all about lacing. No, I won't call Mammy to help you and have you lock the door and skulk here like the coward you are.'

'I'm not a coward,' she cried, stung out of her fear. 'I—'

'Oh, spare me your saga about shooting Yankees and facing Sherman's army. You're a coward – among other things. If not for your own sake, you are going tonight for Bonnie's sake. How could you further ruin her chances? Put on your stays, quick.'

Hastily she slipped off her wrapper and stood clad only in her chemise. If only he would look at her and see how nice she looked in her chemise, perhaps that frightening look would leave his face. After all, he hadn't seen her in her chemise for ever and ever so long. But he did not look. He was in her closet, going through her dresses swiftly. He fumbled and drew out her new jade-green watered-silk dress. It was cut low over the bosom and the skirt was draped back over an enormous bustle and on the bustle was a huge bunch of pink velvet roses.

'Wear that,' he said, tossing it on the bed and coming toward her. 'No modest, matronly dove greys and lilacs tonight. Your flag must be nailed to the mast, for obviously you'd run it down if it wasn't. And plenty of rouge. I'm sure the woman the Pharisees took in adultery didn't look half so pale. Turn around.'

He took the strings of the stays in his hands and jerked them so hard that she cried out, frightened, humiliated, embarrassed at such an untoward performance.

'Hurts, does it?' He laughed shortly and she could not see his face. 'Pity it isn't around your neck.'

Melanie's house blazed lights from every room and they could hear the music far up the street. As they drew up in front, the pleasant exciting sounds of many people enjoying themselves floated out. The house was packed with guests. They overflowed on verandas and many were sitting on the benches in the dim lantern-hung yard.

'I can't go in – I can't,' thought Scarlett, sitting in the carriage, gripping her balled-up handkerchief. 'I can't. I won't. I will jump out and run away, somewhere, back home to Tara. Why did Rhett force me to come here? What will people do? What will Melanie do? What will she look like? Oh, I can't face her. I will run away.'

As though he read her mind, Rhett's hand closed upon her arm in a grip that would leave a bruise, the rough grip of a careless stranger.

'I've never known an Irishman to be a coward. Where's your much-vaunted courage?'

'Rhett, do, please, let me go home and explain.'

'You have eternity in which to explain and only one night to be a martyr in the amphitheatre. Get out, darling, and let me see the lions eat you. Get out.'

She went up the walk somehow, the arm she was holding as hard and steady as granite, communicating to her some courage. By God, she could face them and she would. What were they but a bunch of howling, clawing cats who were jealous of her? She'd show them. She didn't care what they thought. Only Melanie – only Melanie.

They were on the porch and Rhett was bowing right and left, his hat in his hand, his voice cool and soft. The music stopped as they entered and the crowd of people seemed to her confused mind to surge up to her like the roar of the sea and then ebb away, with lessening, ever-lessening sound. Was everyone going to cut her? Well, God's nightgown, let them do it! Her chin went up and she smiled, the corners of her eyes crinkling.

Before she could turn to speak to those nearest to the door, someone came through the press of people. There was an odd hush that caught at Scarlett's heart. Then through the lane came Melanie on small feet that hurried, hurried to meet Scarlett at the door, to speak to her before anyone else could speak. Her narrow shoulders were squared and her small jaw set indignantly and, for all her notice, she might have had no other guest but Scarlett. She went to her side and slipped an arm about her waist.

'What a lovely dress, darling,' she said in her small, clear voice. 'Will you be an angel? India was unable to come tonight and assist me. Will you receive with me?'

Chapter LIV

Safe in her room again, Scarlett fell on the bed, careless of her moiré dress, bustle and roses. For a time she could only lie still and think of standing between Melanie and Ashley, greeting guests. What a horror! She would face Sherman's army again rather than repeat that performance! After a time, she rose from the bed and nervously paced the floor, shedding garments as she walked.

Reaction from strain set in and she began to shake. Hairpins slipped out of her fingers and tinkled to the floor, and when she tried to give her hair its customary hundred strokes, she banged the back of the brush hurtingly against her temple. A dozen times she tiptoed to the door to listen for noises downstairs but the hall below lay like a black silent pit.

Rhett had sent her home alone in the carriage when the party was over and she had thanked God for the reprieve. He had not come in yet. Thank God, he had not come in. She could not face him tonight, shamed, frightened, shaking. But where was he? Probably at that creature's place. For the first time, Scarlett was glad there was such a person as Belle Watling. Glad there was some other place than this house to shelter Rhett until his glittering, murderous mood had passed. That was wrong, being glad a husband was at the house of a prostitute, but she could not help it. She would be almost glad if he were dead, if it meant she would not have to see him tonight.

Tomorrow – well, tomorrow was another day. Tomorrow she would think of some excuse, some counter-accusations, some way of putting Rhett in the wrong. Tomorrow the memory of this hideous night would not be driving her so fiercely that she shook. Tomorrow she would not be so haunted by the memory of Ashley's face, his broken pride and his shame – shame that she had caused, shame in which he had so little part. Would he hate her now, her darling honourable Ashley, because she had shamed him? Of course he would hate her now – now that they had both been saved by the indignant squaring of Melanie's thin shoulders and the love and outspoken trust which had been in her voice as she crossed the glassy floor to slip her arm through Scarlett's and face the curious, malicious, covertly hostile crowd. How neatly Melanie had scotched the scandal, keeping Scarlett at her side all through the dreadful evening! People had been a bit cool, somewhat bewildered, but they had been polite.

Oh, the ignominy of it all, to be sheltered behind Melanie's skirts from those who hated her, who would have torn her to bits with their whispers! To be sheltered by Melanie's blind trust, Melanie of all people!

Scarlett shook as with a chill at the thought. She must have a drink, a number of drinks before she could lie down and hope to sleep. She threw a wrapper about her gown and went hastily out into the dark hall, her backless slippers making a great clatter in the stillness. She was half-way down the stairs before she looked toward the closed door of the dining-room and saw a narrow line of light streaming from under it. Her heart stopped for a moment. Had that light been burning when she came home and had she been too upset to notice it? Or was Rhett home after all? He could have come in quietly through the kitchen door. If Rhett were home, she would tiptoe back to bed without her brandy, much as she needed it. Then she wouldn't have to face him. Once in her room she would be safe, for she could lock the door.

She was leaning over to pluck off her slippers, so she might hurry back in silence, when the dining-room door swung open abruptly and Rhett stood silhouetted against the dim candle-light behind him. He looked huge, larger than she had ever seen him, a terrifying faceless black bulk that swayed slightly on its feet.

'Pray join me, Mrs Butler,' he said, and his voice was a little thick.

He was drunk and showing it and she had never before seen him show his liquor, no matter how much he drank. She paused irresolutely, saying nothing, and his arm went up in a gesture of command.

'Come here, damn you!' he said roughly.

'He must be very drunk,' she thought with a fluttering heart. Usually, the more he drank, the more polished became his manners. He sneered more, his words were apt to be more biting, but the manner that accompanied them was always punctilious – too punctilious.

'I must never let him know I'm afraid to face him,' she thought, and, clutching the wrapper closer to her throat, she went down the stairs with her head up and her heels clacking noisily.

He stood aside and bowed her through the door with a mockery that made her wince. She saw that he was coatless and his cravat hung down on either side of his open collar. His shirt was open down to the thick mat of black hair on his chest. His hair was rumpled and his eyes bloodshot and narrow. One candle burned on the table, a tiny spark of light that threw monstrous shadows about the high-ceilinged room and made the massive sideboards and buffet look like still, crouching beasts. On the table on the silver tray stood the decanter with cut-glass stopper out, surrounded by glasses.

'Sit down,' he said curtly, following her into the room.

Now a new kind of fear crept into her, a fear that made her alarm at facing him seem very small. He looked and talked and acted like a stranger. This was an ill-mannered Rhett she had never seen before. Never at any time, even in most intimate moments, had he been other than nonchalant. Even in anger, he was suave and satirical, and whisky usually served to intensify these qualities. At first it had annoyed her and she had tried to break down that nonchalance but soon she had come to accept it as a very convenient thing. For years she had thought that nothing mattered very much to him, that he thought everything in life, including her, an ironic joke. But as she faced him across the table, she knew with a sinking feeling in her stomach that at last something was mattering to him, mattering very much.

'There is no reason why you should not have your nightcap, even if I am ill-bred enough to be at home,' he said. 'Shall I pour it for you?'

'I did not want a drink,' she said stiffly. 'I heard a noise and came—'

'You heard nothing. You wouldn't have come down if you'd thought I was home. I've sat here and listened to you racing up and down the floor upstairs. You must need a drink badly. Take it.'

'I do not—'

He picked up the decanter and sloshed a glassful, untidily.

'Take it,' he said, shoving it into her hand. 'You are shaking all over. Oh, don't give yourself airs. I know you drink on the quiet and I know how much you drink. For some time I've been intending to tell you to stop your elaborate pretences and drink openly if you want to. Do you think I give a damn if you like your brandy?'

She took the wet glass, silently cursing him. He read her like a book. He had always read her and he was the one man in the world from whom she would like to hide her real thoughts.

'Drink it, I say.'

She raised the glass and bolted the contents with one abrupt motion of her arm, wrist stiff, just as Gerald had always taken his neat whisky, bolted it before she thought how practised and unbecoming it looked. He did not miss the gesture and his mouth went down at the corner.

'Sit down and we will have a pleasant domestic discussion of the elegant reception we have just attended.'

'You are drunk,' she said coldly, 'and I am going to bed.'

'I am very drunk and I intend to get still drunker before the evening's over. But you aren't going to bed – not yet. Sit down.'

His voice still held a remnant of its wonted cool drawl but beneath the words she could feel violence fighting its way to the surface, violence as cruel as the crack of a whip. She wavered irresolutely and he was at her side, his hand on her arm in a grip that hurt. He gave it a slight wrench and she hastily sat down with a little cry of pain. Now, she was afraid, more afraid than she had ever been in her life. As he leaned over her, she saw that his face was dark and flushed and his eyes still held their frightening glitter. There was something in their depths she did not recognize, could not understand, something deeper than anger, stronger than pain, something driving him until his eyes glowed redly like twin coals. He looked down at her for a long time, so long that her defiant gaze wavered and fell, and then he slumped into a chair opposite her and poured himself another drink. She thought rapidly, trying to lay a line of defences. But until he spoke, she would not know what to say for she did not know exactly what accusation he intended to make.

He drank slowly, watching her over the glass, and she tightened her nerves, trying to keep from trembling. For a time his face did not change its expression but finally he laughed, still keeping his eyes on her, and at the sound she could not still her shaking.

'It was an amusing comedy, this evening, wasn't it?'

She said nothing, curling her toes in the loose slippers in an effort at controlling her quivering.

'A pleasant comedy with no character missing. The village assembled to stone the erring woman, the wronged husband supporting his wife as a gentleman should, the wronged wife stepping in with Christian spirit and casting the garments of her spotless reputation over it all. And the lover—'

'Please.'

'I don't please. Not tonight. It's too amusing. And the lover looking like a damned fool and wishing he were dead. How does it feel, my dear, to have the woman you hate stand by you and cloak your sins for you? Sit down.'

She sat down.

'You don't like her any the better for it, I imagine. You are wondering if she knows all about you and Ashley – wondering why she did this if she does know – if she just did it to save her own face. And you are thinking she's a fool for doing it, even if it did save your hide, but—'

'I will not listen—'

'Yes, you will listen. And I'll tell you this to ease your worry. Miss Melly is a fool but not the kind you think. It was obvious that someone had told her but she didn't believe it. Even if she saw, she wouldn't believe. There's too much honour in her to conceive of dishonour in anyone she loves. I don't know what lie Ashley Wilkes told her – but any clumsy one would do, for she loves Ashley and she loves you. I'm sure I can't see why she loves you but she does. Let that be one of your crosses.'

'If you were not so drunk and insulting, I would explain everything,' said Scarlett, recovering some dignity. 'But now—'

'I am not interested in your explanations. I know the truth better than you do. By God, if you get up out of that chair just once more—

'And what I find more amusing than even tonight's comedy is the fact that while you have been so virtuously denying me the pleasures of your bed because of my many sins, you have been lusting in your heart after Ashley Wilkes. "Lusting in your heart." That's a good phrase, isn't it? There are a number of good phrases in that Book, aren't there?'

'What book? What book?' her mind ran on, foolishly, irrelevantly, as she cast frantic eyes about the room, noting how dully the massive silver gleamed in the dim light, how frighteningly dark the corners were.

'And I was cast out because my coarse ardours were too much for your refinement – because you didn't want any more children. How bad that made me feel, dear heart! How it cut me! So I went out and found pleasant consolation and left you to your refinements. And you spent that time tracking the long-suffering Mr Wilkes. God damn him, what ails him? He can't be faithful to his wife with his mind or unfaithful with his body. Why doesn't he make up his mind? You wouldn't object to having his children, would you – and passing them off as mine?'

She sprang to her feet with a cry and he lunged from his seat, laughing that soft laugh that made her blood cold. He pressed her back into her chair with large brown hands and leaned over her.

'Observe my hands, my dear,' he said, flexing them before her eyes. 'I could tear you to pieces with them with no trouble whatsoever and I would do it if it would take Ashley out of your mind. But it wouldn't. So I think I'll remove him from your mind forever, this way. I'll put my hands, so, on each side of your head and I'll smash your skull between them like a walnut and that will blot him out.'

His hands were on her head, under her flowing hair, caressing, hard, turning her face up to his. She was looking into the face of a stranger, a drunken drawling-voiced stranger. She had never lacked animal courage and in the face of danger it flooded back hotly into her veins, stiffening her spine, narrowing her eyes.

'You drunken fool,' she said. 'Take your hands off me.'

To her surprise, he did so and seating himself on the edge of the table he poured himself another drink.

'I have always admired your spirit, my dear. Never more than now, when you are cornered.'

She drew her wrapper close about her body. Oh, if she could only reach her room and turn the key in the stout door and be alone. Somehow, she must stand him off, bully him into submission, this Rhett she had never seen before. She rose without haste, though her knees shook, tightened the wrapper across her hips and threw back her hair from her face.

'I'm not cornered,' she said cuttingly. 'You'll never corner me, Rhett Butler, or frighten me. You are nothing but a drunken beast who's been with bad women so long that you can't understand anything else but badness. You can't understand Ashley or me. You've lived in dirt too long to know anything else. You are jealous of something you can't understand. Good night.'

She turned casually and started toward the door and a burst of laughter stopped her. She turned and he swayed across the room toward her. Name of God, if he would only stop that terrible laugh! What was there to laugh about in all of this? As he came toward her, she backed toward the door and found herself against the wall. He put his hands heavily upon her and pinned her shoulders to the wall.

'Stop laughing.'

'I am laughing because I am so sorry for you.'

'Sorry – for me? Be sorry for yourself.'

'Yes, by God, I'm sorry for you, my dear, my pretty little fool. That hurts, doesn't it? You can't stand either laughter or pity, can you?'

He stopped laughing, leaning so heavily against her shoulders that they ached. His face changed and he leaned so close to her that the heavy whisky smell of his breath made her turn her head.

'Jealous, am I?' he said. 'And why not? Oh, yes, I'm jealous of Ashley Wilkes. Why not? Oh, don't try to talk and explain. I know you've been physically faithful to me. Was that what you were trying to say? Oh, I've known that all along. All these years. How do I know? Oh, well, I know Ashley Wilkes and his breed. I know he is honourable and a gentleman. And that, my dear, is more than I can say for you – or for me, for that matter. We are not gentlemen and we have no honour, have we? That's why we flourish like green bay trees.'

'Let me go. I won't stand here and be insulted.'

'I'm not insulting you. I'm praising your physical virtue. And it hasn't fooled me one bit. You think men are such fools, Scarlett. It never pays to underestimate your opponent's strength and intelligence. And I'm not a fool. Don't you suppose I know that you've lain in my arms and pretended I was Ashley Wilkes?'

Her jaw dropped and fear and astonishment were written plainly in her face.

'Pleasant thing, that. Rather ghostly, in fact. Like having three in a bed where there ought to be just two.' He shook her shoulders, ever so slightly, hiccoughed and smiled mockingly.

'Oh, yes, you've been faithful to me because Ashley wouldn't have you. But, hell, I wouldn't have grudged him your body. I know how little bodies mean – especially women's bodies. But I do grudge him your heart and your dear, hard, unscrupulous, stubborn mind. He doesn't want your mind, the fool, and I don't want your body. I can buy women cheap. But I do want your mind and your heart, and I'll never have them, any more than you'll ever have Ashley's mind. And that's why I'm sorry for you.'

Even through her fear and bewilderment, his sneer stung.

'Sorry – for me?'

'Yes, sorry because you're such a child, Scarlett. A child crying for the moon. What would a child do with the moon if it got it? And what would you do with Ashley? Yes, I'm sorry for you – sorry to see you throwing away happiness with both hands and reaching out for something that would never make you happy. I'm sorry because you are such a fool you don't know there can't ever be happiness except when like mates like. If I were dead, if Miss Melly were dead and you had your precious honourable lover, do you think you'd be happy with him? Hell, no! You would never know him, never know what he was thinking about, never understand him any more than you understand music and poetry and books or anything that isn't dollars and cents. Whereas, we, dear wife of my bosom, could have been perfectly happy if you had ever given us half a chance, for we are so much alike. We are both scoundrels, Scarlett, and nothing is beyond us when we want something. We could have been happy, for I loved you and I know you, Scarlett, down to your bones, in a way that Ashley could never know you. And he would despise you if he did know . . . But no, you must go mooning all your life after a man you cannot understand. And I, my darling, will continue to moon after whores. And, I dare say, we'll do better than most couples.'

He released her abruptly and made a weaving way back toward the decanter. For a moment, Scarlett stood rooted, thoughts tearing in and out of her mind so swiftly that she could seize none of them long enough to examine them. Rhett had said he loved her. Did he mean it? Or was he merely drunk? Or was this one of his horrible jokes? And Ashley – the moon – crying for the moon. She ran swiftly into the dark hall, fleeing as though demons were upon her. Oh, if she could only reach her room! She turned her ankle and the slipper fell half off. As she stopped to kick it loose frantically, Rhett, running lightly as an Indian, was beside her in the dark. His breath was hot on her face and his hands went round her roughly, under the wrapper, against her bare skin.

'You turned me out on the town while you chased him. By God, this is one night when there are only going to be two in my bed.'

He swung her off her feet into his arms and started up the stairs. Her head was crushed against his chest and she heard the hard hammering of his heart beneath her ears. He hurt her and she cried out, muffled, frightened. Up the stairs he went in the utter darkness, up, up, and she was wild with fear. He was a mad stranger and this was a black darkness she did not know, darker than death. He was like death, carrying her away in arms that hurt. She screamed, stifled against him, and he stopped suddenly on the landing and, turning her swiftly in his arms, bent over her and kissed her with a savagery and a completeness that wiped out everything from her mind but the dark into which she was sinking and the lips on hers. He was shaking, as though he stood in a strong wind, and his lips, travelling from her mouth downward to where the wrapper had fallen from her body, fell on her soft flesh. He was muttering things she did not hear, his lips were evoking feelings never felt before. She was darkness and he was darkness and there had never been anything before this time, only darkness and his lips upon her. She tried to speak and his mouth was over hers again. Suddenly she had a wild thrill such as she had never known: joy, fear, madness, excitement, surrender to arms that were too strong, lips too bruising, fate that moved too fast. For the first time in her life she had met someone, something stronger than she, someone she could neither bully nor break, someone who was bullying and breaking her. Somehow, her arms were around his neck and her lips trembling beneath his and they were going up, up into the darkness again, a darkness that was soft and swirling and all-enveloping.

When she awoke the next morning, he was gone and had it not been for the rumpled pillow beside her, she would have thought the happenings of the night before a wild preposterous dream. She went crimson at the memory and, pulling the bed-covers up about her neck, lay bathed in sunlight, trying to sort out the jumbled impressions in her mind.

Two things stood to the fore. She had lived for years with Rhett, slept with him, eaten with him, quarrelled with him and borne his child – and yet, she did not know him. The man who had carried her up the dark stairs was a stranger of whose existence she had not dreamed. And now, though she tried to make herself hate him, tried to be indignant, she could not. He had humbled her, hurt her, used her brutally through a wild mad night and she had gloried in it.

Oh, she should be ashamed, should shrink from the very memory of the hot swirling darkness! A lady, a real lady, could never hold up her head after such a night. But, stronger than shame, was the memory of rapture, of the ecstasy of surrender. For the first time in her life she had felt alive, felt passion as sweeping and primitive as the fear she had known the night she fled Atlanta, as dizzy sweet as the cold hate when she had shot the Yankee.

Rhett loved her! At least, he said he loved her, and how could she doubt it now? How odd and bewildering and how incredible that he loved her, this savage stranger with whom she had lived in such coolness. She was not altogether certain how she felt about this revelation but as an idea came to her she suddenly laughed aloud. He loved her and so she had him at last. She had almost forgotten her early desire to entrap him into loving her, so she could hold the whip over his insolent black head. Now, it came back and it gave her great satisfaction. For one night, he had had her at his mercy but now she knew the weakness of his armour. From now on she had him where she wanted him. She had smarted under his jeers for a long time, but now she had him where she could make him jump through any hoops she cared to hold.

When she thought of meeting him again, face to face in the sober light of day, a nervous tingling embarrassment that carried with it an exciting pleasure enveloped her.

'I'm nervous as a bride,' she thought. 'And about Rhett!' And at the idea she fell to giggling foolishly.

But Rhett did not appear for dinner, nor was he at his place at the supper table. The night passed, a long night during which she lay awake until dawn, her ears strained to hear his key in the latch. But he did not come. When the second day passed with no word from him, she was frantic with disappointment and fear. She went by the bank but he was not there. She went to the store and was very sharp with everyone, for every time the door opened to admit a customer she looked up with a flutter, hoping it was Rhett. She went to the lumber yard and bullied Hugh until he hid himself behind a pile of lumber. But Rhett did not seek her there.

She could not humble herself to ask friends if they had seen him. She could not make inquiries among the servants for news of him. But she felt they knew something she did not know. Negroes always knew everything. Mammy was unusually silent those two days. She watched Scarlett out of the corner of her eye and said nothing. When the second night had passed Scarlett made up her mind to go to the police. Perhaps he had had an accident, perhaps his horse had thrown him and he was lying helpless in some ditch. Perhaps – oh, horrible thought – perhaps he was dead.

The next morning when she had finished her breakfast and was in her room putting on her bonnet, she heard swift feet on the stairs. As she sank to the bed in weak thankfulness, Rhett entered the room. He was freshly barbered, shaved and massaged and he was sober, but his eyes were bloodshot and his face puffy from drink. He waved an airy hand at her and said: 'Oh, hello.'

How could a man say 'Oh, hello' after being gone without explanation for two days? How could he be so nonchalant with the memory of such a night as they had spent? He couldn't unless – unless—The terrible thought leaped into her mind. Unless such nights were the usual thing to him. For a moment she could not speak and all the pretty gestures and smiles she had thought to use upon him were forgotten. He did not even come to her to give her his usual offhand kiss but stood looking at her, with a grin, a smoking cigar in his hand.

'Where – where have you been?'

'Don't tell me you don't know! I thought surely the whole town knew by now. Perhaps they all do, except you. You know the old adage: "The wife is always the last one to find out." '

'What do you mean?'

'I thought that after the police called at Belle's night before last—'

'Belle's – that – that woman! You have been with—'

'Of course. Where else would I be? I hope you haven't worried about me.'

'You went from me to – oh!'

'Come, come, Scarlett! Don't play the deceived wife. You must have known about Belle long ago.'

'You went to her from me, after – after—'

'Oh, that.' He made a careless gesture. 'I will forget my manners. My apologies for my conduct at our last meeting. I was very drunk, as you doubtless know, and quite swept off my feet by your charms – need I enumerate them?'

Suddenly she wanted to cry, to lie down on the bed and sob endlessly. He hadn't changed, nothing had changed, and she had been a fool, a stupid, conceited, silly fool, thinking he loved her. It had all been one of his repulsive drunken jests. He had taken her and used her when he was drunk, just as he would use any woman in Belle's house. And now he was back, insulting, sardonic, out of reach. She swallowed her tears and rallied. He must never, never know what she had thought. How he would laugh if he knew! Well, he'd never know. She looked up quickly at him and caught that old, puzzling, watchful glint in his eyes – keen, eager as though he hung on her next words, hoping they would be – what was he hoping? That she'd make a fool out of herself and bawl and give him something to laugh about? Not she! Her slanting brows rushed together in a cold frown.

'I had naturally suspected what your relations with that creature were.'

'Only suspected? Why didn't you ask me and satisfy your curiosity? I'd have told you. I've been living with her ever since the day you and Ashley Wilkes decided that we should have separate bedrooms.'

'You have the gall to stand there and boast to me, your wife, that—'

'Oh, spare me your moral indignation. You never gave a damn what I did as long as I paid the bills. And you know I've been no angel recently. And as for you being my wife – you haven't been much of a wife since Bonnie came, have you? You've been a poor investment, Scarlett. Belle's been a better one.'

'Investment? You mean you gave her—?'

' "Set her up in business" is the correct term, I believe. Belle's a smart woman. I wanted to see her get ahead and all she needed was money to start a house of her own. You ought to know what miracles a woman can perform when she has a bit of cash. Look at yourself.'

'You compare me—'

'Well, you are both hard-headed business women and both successful. Belle's got the edge on you, of course, because she's a kind-hearted, good-natured soul—'

'Will you get out of this room?'

He lounged toward the door, one eyebrow raised quizzically. How could he insult her so, she thought in rage and pain. He was going out of his way to hurt and humiliate her and she writhed as she thought how she had longed for his homecoming, while all the time he was drunk and brawling with police in a bawdy house.

'Get out of this room and don't ever come back in it. I told you that once before and you weren't enough of a gentleman to understand. Hereafter I will lock my door.'

'Don't bother.'

'I will lock it. After the way you acted the other night – so drunk, so disgusting—'

'Come now, darling! Not disgusting, surely!'

'Get out.'

'Don't worry. I'm going. And I promise I'll never bother you again. That's final. And I just thought I'd tell you that if my infamous conduct was too much for you to bear, I'll let you have a divorce. Just give me Bonnie and I won't contest it.'

'I would not think of disgracing the family with a divorce.'

'You'd disgrace it quick enough if Miss Melly was dead, wouldn't you? It makes my head spin to think how quickly you'd divorce me.'

'Will you go?'

'Yes, I'm going. That's what I came home to tell you. I'm going to Charleston and New Orleans and – oh, well, a very extended trip. I'm leaving today.'

'Oh!'

'And I'm taking Bonnie with me. Get that foolish Prissy to pack her little duds. I'll take Prissy too.'

'You'll never take my child out of this house.'

'My child too, Mrs Butler. Surely you do not mind me taking her to Charleston to see her grandmother?'

'Her grandmother, my foot! Do you think I'll let you take that baby out of here when you'll be drunk every night and most likely taking her to houses like that Belle's—'

He threw down the cigar violently and it smoked acridly on the carpet, the smell of scorching wool rising to their nostrils. In an instant he was across the floor and by her side, his face black with fury.

'If you were a man, I would break your neck for that. As it is, all I can say is for you to shut your God-damn mouth. Do you think I do not love Bonnie, that I would take her where – my daughter! Good God, you fool! And as for you, giving yourself pious airs about your motherhood, why, a cat's a better mother than you! What have you ever done for the children? Wade and Ella are frightened to death of you and if it wasn't for Melanie Wilkes, they'd never know what love and affection are. But Bonnie, my Bonnie! Do you think I can't take better care of her than you? Do you think I'll ever let you bully her and break her spirit, as you've broken Wade's and Ella's? Hell, no! Have her packed up and ready for me in an hour or I warn you what happened the other night will be mild beside what will happen. I've always thought a good lashing with a buggy-whip would benefit you immensely.'

He turned on his heel before she could speak and went out of the room on swift feet. She heard him cross the floor of the hall to the children's play-room and open the door. There was a glad, quick treble of childish voices and she heard Bonnie's tones rise over Ella's.

'Daddy, where you been?'

'Hunting for a rabbit's skin to wrap my little Bonnie in. Give your best sweetheart a kiss, Bonnie – and you too, Ella.'

Chapter LV

'Darling, I don't want any explanation from you and I won't listen to one,' said Melanie firmly, as she gently laid a small hand across Scarlett's tortured lips and stilled her words. 'You insult yourself and Ashley and me by even thinking there could be need of explanations between us. Why, we three have been – have been like soldiers fighting the world together for so many years that I'm ashamed of you for thinking idle gossip could come between us. Do you think I'd believe that you and my Ashley—Why, the idea! Don't you realize I know you better than anyone in the world knows you? Do you think I've forgotten all the wonderful, unselfish things you've done for Ashley and Beau and me – everything from saving my life to keeping us from starving! Do you think I could remember you walking in a furrow behind that Yankee's horse almost barefooted and with your hands blistered – just so the baby and I could have something to eat – and then believe such dreadful things about you? I don't want to hear a word out of you, Scarlett O'Hara. Not a word.'

'But—' Scarlett fumbled and stopped.

Rhett had left town the hour before with Bonnie and Prissy, and desolation was added to Scarlett's shame and anger. The additional burden of her guilt with Ashley and Melanie's defence was more than she could bear. Had Melanie believed India and Archie, cut her at the reception or even greeted her frigidly, then she could have held her head high and fought back with every weapon in her armoury. But now, with the memory of Melanie standing between her and social ruin, standing like a thin, shining blade, with trust and a fighting light in her eyes, there seemed nothing honest to do but confess. Yes, blurt out everything from that far-off beginning on the sunny porch at Tara.

She was driven by a conscience which, though long suppressed, could still rise up, an active Catholic conscience. 'Confess your sins and do penance for them in sorrow and contrition,' Ellen had told her a hundred times and, in this crisis, Ellen's religious training came back and gripped her. She would confess – yes, everything, every look and word, those few caresses – and then God would ease her pain and give her peace. And, for her penance, there would be the dreadful sight of Melanie's face changing from fond love and trust to incredulous horror and repulsion. Oh, that was too hard a penance, she thought in anguish, to have to live out her life remembering Melanie's face, knowing that Melanie knew all the pettiness, the meanness, the two-faced disloyalty and the hypocrisy that were in her.

Once, the thought of flinging the truth tauntingly in Melanie's face and seeing the collapse of her fool's paradise had been an intoxicating one, a gesture worth everything she might lose thereby. But now, all that had changed overnight and there was nothing she desired less. Why this should be she did not know. There was too great a tumult of conflicting ideas in her mind for her to sort them out. She only knew that as she had once desired to keep her mother thinking her modest, kind, pure of heart, so she now passionately desired to keep Melanie's high opinion. She only knew that she did not care what the world thought of her or what Ashley or Rhett thought of her, but Melanie must not think her other than she had always thought her.

She dreaded to tell Melanie the truth but one of her rare honest instincts arose, an instinct that would not let her masquerade in false colours before the woman who had fought her battles for her. So she had hurried to Melanie that morning, as soon as Rhett and Bonnie had left the house.

But at her first tumbled-out words: 'Melly, I must explain about the other day—' Melanie had imperiously stopped her. Scarlett, looking shamefaced into the dark eyes that were flashing with love and anger, knew with a sinking heart that the peace and calm following confession could never be hers. Melanie had forever cut off that line of action by her first words. With one of the few adult emotions Scarlett had ever had, she realized that to unburden her own tortured heart would be the purest selfishness. She would be ridding herself of her burden and laying it on the heart of an innocent and trusting person. She owed Melanie a debt for her championship and that debt could only be paid with silence. What cruel payment it would be to wreck Melanie's life with the unwelcome knowledge that her husband was unfaithful to her, and her beloved friend a party to it!

'I can't tell her,' she thought miserably. 'Never, not even if my conscience kills me.' She remembered irrelevantly Rhett's drunken remark:

'She can't conceive of dishonour in anyone she loves . . . let that be your cross.'

Yes, it would be her cross, until she died, to keep this torment silent within her, to wear the hair shirt of shame, to feel it chafing her at every tender look and gesture Melanie would make throughout the years, to subdue forever the impulse to cry: 'Don't be so kind! Don't fight for me! I'm not worth it!'

'If you only weren't such a fool, such a sweet, trusting, simple-minded fool, it wouldn't be so hard,' she thought desperately. 'I've toted lots of weary loads but this is going to be the heaviest and most galling load I've ever toted.'

Melanie sat facing her, in a low chair, her feet firmly planted on an ottoman so high that her knees stuck up like a child's, a posture she would never have assumed had not rage possessed her to the point of forgetting proprieties. She held a line of tatting in her hands and she was driving the shining needle back and forth as furiously as though handling a rapier in a duel.

Had Scarlett been possessed of such an anger, she would have been stamping both feet and roaring like Gerald in his finest days, calling on God to witness the accursed duplicity and knavishness of mankind and uttering blood-curdling threats of retaliation. But only by the flashing needle and the delicate brows drawn down toward her nose did Melanie indicate that she was inwardly seething. Her voice was cool and her words more close clipped than usual. But the forceful words she uttered were foreign to Melanie, who seldom voiced an opinion at all and never an unkind word. Scarlett realized suddenly that the Wilkeses and the Hamiltons were capable of furies equal to and surpassing those of the O'Haras.

'I've gotten mighty tired of hearing people criticize you, darling,' Melanie said, 'and this is the last straw and I'm going to do something about it. All this has happened because people are jealous of you, because you are so smart and successful. You've succeeded where lots of men, even, have failed. Now, don't be vexed with me, dear, for saying that. I don't mean you've ever been unwomanly or unsexed yourself, as lots of folks have said. Because you haven't. People just don't understand you and people can't bear for women to be smart. But your smartness and your success don't give people the right to say that you and Ashley— Stars above!'

The soft vehemence of this last ejaculation would have been, upon a man's lips, profanity of no uncertain meaning. Scarlett stared at her, alarmed by so unprecedented an outburst.

'And for them to come to me with the filthy lies they'd concocted – Archie, India, Mrs Elsing! How did they dare? Of course, Mrs Elsing didn't come here. No, indeed, she didn't have the courage. But she's always hated you, darling, because you were more popular than Fanny. And she was so incensed at your demoting Hugh from the management of the mill. But you were quite right in demoting him. He's just a piddling, do-less, good-for-nothing!' Swiftly Melanie dismissed the playmate of her childhood and the beau of her teen years. 'I blame myself about Archie. I shouldn't have given the old scoundrel shelter. Everyone told me so but I wouldn't listen. He didn't like you, dear, because of the convicts, but who is he to criticize you? A murderer, and the murderer of a woman too! And after all I've done for him, he comes to me and tells me—I shouldn't have been a bit sorry if Ashley had shot him. Well, I packed him off with a large flea in his ear, I can tell you! And he's left town.

'And as for India, the vile thing! Darling, I couldn't help noticing from the first time I saw you two together that she was jealous of you and hated you, because you were so much prettier and had so many beaux. And she hated you especially about Stuart Tarleton. And she's brooded about Stuart so much that – well, I hate to say it about Ashley's sister but I think her mind has broken with thinking so much! There's no other explanation for her action . . . I told her never to put foot in this house again and that if I heard her breathe so vile an insinuation I would – I would call her a liar in public!'

Melanie stopped speaking and abruptly the anger left her face and sorrow swamped it. Melanie had all that passionate clan loyalty peculiar to Georgians and the thought of a family quarrel tore her heart. She faltered for a moment. But Scarlett was dearest, Scarlett came first in her heart, and she went on loyally:

'She's always been jealous because I loved you best, dear. She'll never come in this house again and I'll never put foot under any roof that receives her. Ashley agrees with me, but it's just about broken his heart that his own sister should tell such a—'

At the mention of Ashley's name, Scarlett's overwrought nerves gave way and she burst into tears. Would she never stop stabbing him to the heart? Her only thought had been to make him happy and safe but at every turn she seemed to hurt him. She had wrecked his life, broken his pride and self-respect, shattered that inner peace, that calm based on integrity. And now she had alienated him from the sister he loved so dearly. To save her own reputation and his wife's happiness, India had to be sacrificed, forced into the light of a lying, half-crazed, jealous old maid – India who was absolutely justified in every suspicion she had ever harboured and every accusing word she had uttered. Whenever Ashley looked into India's eyes, he would see the truth shining there, truth and reproach and the cold contempt of which the Wilkes were masters.

Knowing how Ashley valued honour above his life, Scarlett knew he must be writhing. He, like Scarlett, was forced to shelter behind Melanie's skirts. While Scarlett realized the necessity for this and knew that the blame for his false position lay mostly at her own door, still – still—Womanlike she would have respected Ashley more, had he shot Archie and admitted everything to Melanie and the world. She knew she was being unfair but she was too miserable to care for such fine points. Some of Rhett's taunting words of contempt came back to her and she wondered if indeed Ashley had played the manly part in this mess. And, for the first time, some of the bright glow which had enveloped him since the first day she fell in love with him began to fade imperceptibly. The tarnish of shame and guilt that enveloped her spread to him as well. Resolutely she tried to fight off this thought but it only made her cry harder.

'Don't! Don't!' cried Melanie, dropping her tatting and flinging herself on to the sofa and drawing Scarlett's head down on to her shoulder. 'I shouldn't have talked about it all and distressed you so. I know how dreadfully you must feel and we'll never mention it again. No, not to each other or to anybody. It'll be as though it never happened. But,' she added with quiet venom, 'I'm going to show India and Mrs Elsing what's what. They needn't think they can spread lies about my husband and my sister-in-law. I'm going to fix it so neither of them can hold up their heads in Atlanta. And anybody who believes them or receives them is my enemy.'

Scarlett, looking sorrowfully down the long vista of years to come, knew that she was the cause of a feud that would split the town and the family for generations.

Melanie was as good as her word. She never again mentioned the subject to Scarlett or to Ashley. Nor, for that matter, would she discuss it with anyone. She maintained an air of cool indifference that could speedily change to icy formality if anyone even dared hint about the matter. During the weeks that followed her surprise party, while Rhett was mysteriously absent and the town in a frenzied state of gossip, excitement and partisanship, she gave no quarter to Scarlett's detractors, whether they were her old friends or her blood kin. She did not speak, she acted.

She stuck by Scarlett's side like a cocklebur. She made Scarlett go to the store and the lumber yard, as usual, every morning and she went with her. She insisted that Scarlett go driving in the afternoons, little though Scarlett wished to expose herself to the eager curious gaze of her fellow townspeople. And Melanie sat in the carriage beside her. Melanie took her calling on formal afternoons, gently forcing her into parlours in which Scarlett had not sat for more than two years. And Melanie, with a fierce 'love-me-love-my-dog' look on her face, made converse with astounded hostesses.

She made Scarlett arrive early on these afternoons and remain until the last callers had gone, thereby depriving the ladies of the opportunity for enjoyable group discussion and speculation, a matter which caused some mild indignation. These calls were an especial torment to Scarlett but she dared not refuse to go with Melanie. She hated to sit amid crowds of women who were secretly wondering if she had been actually taken in adultery. She hated the knowledge that these women would not have spoken to her, had it not been that they loved Melanie and did not want to lose her friendship. But Scarlett knew that, having once received her, they could not cut her thereafter.

It was characteristic of the regard in which Scarlett was held that few people based their defence or their criticism of her on her personal integrity. 'I wouldn't put much beyond her,' was the universal attitude. Scarlett had made too many enemies to have many champions now. Her words and her actions rankled in too many hearts for many people to care whether this scandal hurt her or not. But everyone cared violently about hurting Melanie or India and the storm revolved around them, rather than Scarlett, centring upon the one question – 'Did India lie?'

Those who espoused Melanie's side pointed triumphantly to the fact that Melanie was constantly with Scarlett these days. Would a woman of Melanie's high principles champion the cause of a guilty woman, especially a woman guilty with her own husband? No, indeed! India was just a cracked old maid who hated Scarlett and lied about her and induced Archie and Mrs Elsing to believe her lies.

But, questioned India's adherents, if Scarlett isn't guilty, where is Captain Butler? Why isn't he here at his wife's side, lending her the strength of his countenance? That was an unanswerable question and, as the weeks went by and the rumour spread that Scarlett was pregnant, the pro-India group nodded with satisfaction. It couldn't be Captain Butler's baby, they said. For too long the fact of their estrangement had been public property. For too long the town had been scandalized by the separate bedrooms.

So the gossip ran, tearing the town apart, tearing apart, too, the close-knit clan of Hamiltons, Wilkes, Burrs, Whitmans and Winfields. Everyone in the family connection was forced to take sides. There was no neutral ground. Melanie with cool dignity and India with acid bitterness saw to that. But no matter which side the relatives took, they all were resentful that Scarlett should have been the cause of the family breach. None of them thought her worth it. And no matter which side they took, the relatives heartily deplored the fact that India had taken it upon herself to wash the family dirty linen so publicly and involve Ashley in so degrading a scandal. But now that she had spoken, many rushed to her defence and took her side against Scarlett, even as others, loving Melanie, stood by her and Scarlett.

Half of Atlanta was kin to or claimed kin with Melanie and India. The ramifications of cousins, double cousins, cousins-in-law and kissing cousins were so intricate and involved that no one but a born Georgian could ever unravel them. They had always been a clannish tribe, presenting an unbroken phalanx of overlapping shields to the world in time of stress, no matter what their private opinions of the conduct of individual kinsmen might be. With the exception of the guerrilla warfare carried on by Aunt Pitty against Uncle Henry, which had been a matter for hilarious laughter within the family for years, there had never been an open breach in the pleasant relations. They were gentle, quiet-spoken, reserved people and not given to even the amiable bickering that characterized most Atlanta families.

But now they were split in twain and the town was privileged to witness cousins of the fifth and sixth degree taking sides in the most shattering scandal Atlanta had ever seen. This worked great hardship and strained the tact and forbearance of the unrelated half of the town, for the India-Melanie feud made a rupture in practically every social organization. The Thalians, the Sewing Circle for the Widows and Orphans of the Confederacy, the Association for the Beautification of the Graves of Our Glorious Dead, the Saturday Night Musical Circle, the Ladies' Evening Cotillion Society, the Young Men's Library were all involved. So were four churches with their Ladies' Aid and Missionary societies. Great care had to be taken to avoid putting members of warring factions on the same committees.

On their regular afternoons at home, Atlanta matrons were in anguish from four to six o'cock for fear Melanie and Scarlett would call at the same time India and her loyal kin were in their parlours.

Of all the family, poor Aunt Pitty suffered the most. Pitty, who desired nothing except to live comfortably amid the love of her relatives, would have been very pleased, in this matter, to run with the hares and hunt with the hounds. But neither the hares nor the hounds would permit this.

India lived with Aunt Pitty and, if Pitty sided with Melanie, as she wished to do, India would leave. And if India left her, what would poor Pitty do then? She could not live alone. She would have to get a stranger to live with her or she would have to close up her house and go and live with Scarlett. Aunt Pitty felt vaguely that Captain Butler would not care for this. Or she would have to go and live with Melanie and sleep in the little cubbyhole that was Beau's nursery.

Pitty was not overly fond of India, for India intimidated her with her dry, stiff-necked ways and her passionate convictions. But she made it possible for Pitty to keep her own comfortable establishment and Pitty was always swayed more by considerations of personal comfort than by moral issues. And so India remained.

But her presence in the house made Aunt Pitty a storm centre, for both Scarlett and Melanie took that to mean that she sided with India. Scarlett curtly refused to contribute more money to Pitty's establishment as long as India was under the same roof. Ashley sent India money every week and every week India proudly and silently returned it, much to the old lady's alarm and regret. Finances at the red-brick house would have been in a deplorable state, but for Uncle Henry's intervention, and it humiliated Pitty to take money from him.

Pitty loved Melanie better than anyone in the world, except herself, and now Melly acted like a cool, polite stranger. Though she practically lived in Pitty's back yard, she never once came through the hedge and she used to run in and out a dozen times a day. Pitty called on her and wept and protested her love and devotion, but Melanie always refused to discuss matters and never returned the calls.

Pitty knew very well what she owed Scarlett – almost her very existence.

Certainly in those black days after the war when Pitty was faced with the alternative of Brother Henry or starvation, Scarlett had kept her home for her, fed her, clothed her and enabled her to hold up her head in Atlanta society. And since Scarlett had married and moved into her own home, she had been generosity itself. And that frightening, fascinating Captain Butler – frequently after he called with Scarlett, Pitty found brand-new purses stuffed with bills on her console table or lace handkerchiefs knotted about gold pieces which had been slyly slipped into her sewing-box. Rhett always vowed he knew nothing about them and accused her, in a very unrefined way, of having a secret admirer, usually the bewhiskered Grandpa Merriwether.

Yes, Pitty owed love to Melanie, security to Scarlett, and what did she owe India? Nothing, except that India's presence kept her from having to break up her pleasant life and make decisions for herself. It was all most distressing and too, too vulgar, and Pitty, who had never made a decision for herself in her whole life, simply let matters go on as they were and as a result spent much time in uncomforted tears.

In the end, some people believed whole-heartedly in Scarlett's innocence, not because of her own personal virtue but because Melanie believed in it. Some had mental reservations but they were courteous to Scarlett and called on her because they loved Melanie and wished to keep her love. India's adherents bowed coldly and some few cut her openly. These last were embarrassing, infuriating, but Scarlett realized that, except for Melanie's championship and her quick action, the face of the whole town would have been set against her and she would have been an outcast.

Chapter LVI

Rhett was gone for three months and during that time Scarlett had no word from him. She did not know where he was or how long he would be gone. Indeed, she had no idea if he would ever return. During this time, she went about her business with her head high and her heart sick. She did not feel well physically but, forced by Melanie, she went to the store every day and tried to keep up a superficial interest in the mills. But the store palled on her for the first time and, although the business was treble what it had been the year before and the money rolling in, she could take no interest in it and was sharp and cross with the clerks. Johnnie Gallegher's mill was thriving and the lumber yard selling all his supply easily, but nothing Johnnie did or said pleased her. Johnnie, as Irish as she, finally erupted into rage at her naggings and threatened to quit, after a long tirade which ended with 'and the back of both me hands to you, Ma'm, and the curse of Cromwell on you.' She had to appease him with the most abject of apologies.

She never went to Ashley's mill. Nor did she go to the lumber-yard office when she thought he would be there. She knew he was avoiding her, knew that her constant presence in his house, at Melanie's inescapable invitations, was a torment to him. They never spoke alone and she was desperate to question him. She wanted to know whether he now hated her and exactly what he had told Melanie, but he held her at arm's length and silently pleaded with her not to speak. The sight of his face, old, haggard with remorse, added to her load, and the fact that his mill lost money every week was an extra irritant which she could not voice.

His helplessness in the face of the present situation irked her. She did not know what he could do to better matters but she felt that he should do something. Rhett would have done something. Rhett always did something, even if it was the wrong thing, and she unwillingly respected him for it.

Now that her first rage at Rhett and his insults had passed, she began to miss him and she missed him more and more as days went by without news of him. Out of the welter of rapture and anger and heartbreak and hurt pride that he had left, depression emerged to sit upon her shoulder like a carrion crow. She missed him, missed his light flippant touch in anecdotes that made her shout with laughter, his sardonic grin that reduced troubles to their proper proportions, missed even his jeers that stung her to angry retort. Most of all she missed having him to tell things to. Rhett was so satisfactory in that respect. She could recount shamelessly and with pride how she had skinned people out of their eyeteeth and he would applaud. And if she even mentioned such things to other people they were shocked.

She was lonely without him and Bonnie. She missed the child more than she had thought possible. Remembering the last harsh words Rhett had hurled at her about Wade and Ella, she tried to fill in some of her empty hours with them. But it was no use. Rhett's words and the children's reactions opened her eyes to a startling, a galling truth. During the babyhood of each child she had been too busy, too worried with money matters, too sharp and easily vexed, to win either their confidence or affection. And now, it was either too late or she did not have the patience or the wisdom to penetrate their small secretive hearts.

Ella! It annoyed Scarlett to realize that Ella was a silly child but she undoubtedly was. She couldn't keep her little mind on one subject any longer than a bird could stay on one twig, and even when Scarlett tried to tell her stories, Ella went off at childish tangents, interrupting with questions about matters that had nothing to do with the story and forgetting what she had asked long before Scarlett could get the explanation out of her mouth. And as for Wade – perhaps Rhett was right. Perhaps he was afraid of her. That was odd and it hurt her. Why should her own boy, her only boy, be afraid of her? When she tried to draw him out in talk, he looked at her with Charles' soft brown eyes and squirmed and twisted his feet in embarrassment. But with Melanie, he bubbled over with talk and brought from his pocket everything from fishing worms to old strings to show her.

Melanie had a way with brats. There was no getting around it. Her own little Beau was the best-behaved and most lovable child in Atlanta. Scarlett got on better with him than she did with her own son because little Beau had no self-consciousness where grown people were concerned and climbed on her knee, uninvited, whenever he saw her. What a beautiful blond boy he was, just like Ashley! Now if only Wade were like Beau— Of course, the reason Melanie could do so much with him was that she had only one child and she hadn't had to worry and work as Scarlett had. At least, Scarlett tried to excuse herself that way but honesty forced her to admit that Melanie loved children and would have welcomed a dozen. And the over-brimming affection she had was poured out on Wade and the neighbours' broods.

Scarlett would never forget the shock of the day she drove by Melanie's house to pick up Wade and heard, as she came up the front walk, the sound of her son's voice raised in a very fair imitation of the Rebel yell – Wade who was always as still as a mouse at home. And manfully seconding Wade's yell was the shrill piping of Beau. When she had walked into the sitting-room she had found the two charging at the sofa with wooden swords. They had hushed abashed as she entered and Melanie had arisen, laughing and clutching at hairpins and flying curls, from where she was crouching behind the sofa.

'It's Gettysburg,' she explained. 'And I'm the Yankees and I've certainly gotten the worst of it. This is General Lee,' pointing to Beau, 'and this is General Pickett,' putting an arm about Wade's shoulder.

Yes, Melanie had a way with children that Scarlett could never fathom.

'At least,' she thought, 'Bonnie loves me and likes to play with me.' But honesty forced her to admit that Bonnie infinitely preferred Rhett to her. And perhaps she would never see Bonnie again. For all she knew, Rhett might be in Persia or Egypt and intending to stay there forever.

When Dr Meade told her she was pregnant, she was astounded, for she had been expecting a diagnosis of biliousness and overwrought nerves. Then her mind fled back to that wild night and her face went crimson at the memory. So a child was coming from those moments of high rapture – even if the memory of the rapture was dimmed by what followed. And for the first time she was glad that she was going to have a child. If it were only a boy! A fine boy, not a spiritless little creature like Wade. How she would care for him! Now that she had the leisure to devote to a baby and the money to smooth his path, how happy she would be! She had an impulse to write to Rhett in care of his mother in Charleston and tell him. Good Heavens, he must come home now! Suppose he stayed away till after the baby was born! She could never explain that! But if she wrote him he'd think she wanted him to come home and he would be amused. And he mustn't ever think she wanted him or needed him.

She was very glad she had stifled this impulse when her first news of Rhett came in a letter from Aunt Pauline in Charleston where, it seemed, Rhett was visiting his mother. What a relief to know he was still in the United States, even if Aunt Pauline's letter was infuriating. Rhett had brought Bonnie to see her and Aunt Eulalie and the letter was full of praise.

'Such a little beauty! When she grows up she will certainly be a belle. But I suppose you know that any man who courts her will have a tussle with Captain Butler, for I never saw such a devoted father. Now, my dear, I wish to confess something. Until I met Captain Butler, I felt that your marriage with him had been a dreadful mésalliance for, of course, no one in Charleston hears anything good about him and everyone is so sorry for his family. In fact, Eulalie and I were uncertain as to whether or not we should receive him – but, after all, the dear child is our great-niece. When he came, we were pleasantly surprised, most pleasantly, and realized how un-Christian it is to credit idle gossip. For he is most charming. Quite handsome, too, we thought, and so very grave and courteous. And so devoted to you and the child.

'And now, my dear, I must write you of something that has come to our ears – something Eulalie and I were loath to believe at first. We had heard, of course, that you sometimes did about at the store that Mr Kennedy had left you. We had heard rumours but, of course, we denied them. We realized that in those first dreadful days after the war, it was perhaps necessary, conditions being what they were. But there is no necessity now for such conduct on your part, as I know Captain Butler is in quite comfortable circumstances and is, moreover, fully capable of managing for you any business and property you may own. We had to know the truth of these rumours and were forced to ask Captain Butler point-blank questions which was most distressing to all of us.

'With reluctance he told us that you spent your mornings at the store and would permit no one else to do the book-keeping. He also admitted that you had some interest in a mill or mills (we did not press him on this, being most upset at this information which was news to us) that necessitated your riding about alone, or attended by a ruffian who, Captain Butler assures us, is a murderer. We could see how this wrung his heart and think he must be a most indulgent – in fact, a far too indulgent husband. Scarlett, this must stop. Your mother is not here to command you and I must do it in her place. Think how your little children will feel when they grow older and realize that you were in trade! How mortified they will be to know that you exposed yourself to the insults of rude men and the dangers of careless gossip in attending to mills. Such unwomanly—'

Scarlett flung down the letter unfinished, with an oath. She could just see Aunt Pauline and Aunt Eulalie sitting in judgment on her in the crumbling house on the Battery with little between them and starvation except what she, Scarlett, sent them every month. Unwomanly? By God, if she hadn't been unwomanly Aunt Pauline and Aunt Eulalie probably wouldn't have a roof over their heads this very moment. And damn Rhett for telling them about the store and the book-keeping and the mills! Reluctant, was he? She knew very well the joy he took in palming himself off on the old ladies as grave, courteous and charming, the devoted husband and father. How he must have loved harrowing them with descriptions of her activities with the store, the mills, the saloon. What a devil he was! Why did such perverse things give him such pleasure?

But soon, even this rage passed into apathy. So much of the keen zest had gone out of life recently. If only she could recapture the thrill and the glow of Ashley – if only Rhett would come home and make her laugh.

They were home again, without warning. The first intimation of their return was the sound of luggage being thumped on the front-hall floor and Bonnie's voice crying, 'Mother!'

Scarlett hurried from her room to the top of the stairs and saw her daughter stretching her short plump legs in an effort to climb the steps. A resigned striped kitten was clutched to her breast.

'Gran'ma gave him to me,' she cried excitedly, holding the kitten out by the scruff.

Scarlett swept her up into her arms and kissed her, thankful that the child's presence spared her her first meeting alone with Rhett. Looking over Bonnie's head, she saw him in the hall below, paying the cab-driver. He looked up, saw her and swept off his hat in a wide gesture, bowing as he did. When she met his dark eyes, her heart leaped. No matter what he was, no matter what he had done, he was home and she was glad.

'Where's Mammy?' asked Bonnie, wriggling in Scarlett's grasp, and she reluctantly set the child on her feet.

It was going to be more difficult than she anticipated, greeting Rhett with just the proper degree of casualness, and as for telling him about the new baby! She looked at his face as he came up the steps, that dark nonchalant face, so impervious, so blank. No, she'd wait to tell him. She couldn't tell him right away. And yet, such tidings as these belonged first to a husband, for a husband was always happy to hear them. But she did not think he would be happy about it.

She stood on the landing, leaning against the banisters, and wondered if he would kiss her. But he did not. He only said: 'You are looking pale, Mrs Butler. Is there a rouge shortage?'

No word of missing her, even if he didn't mean it. And he might have at least kissed her in front of Mammy who, after bobbing a curtsy, was leading Bonnie away down the hall to the nursery. He stood beside her on the landing, his eyes appraising her carelessly.

'Can this wanness mean that you've been missing me?' he questioned, and though his lips smiled, his eyes did not.

So that was going to be his attitude. He was going to be as hateful as ever. Suddenly the child she was carrying became a nauseating burden instead of something she had gladly carried, and this man before her, standing carelessly with his wide Panama hat upon his hip, her bitterest foe, the cause of all her troubles. There was venom in her eyes as she answered, venom that was too unmistakable to be missed, and the smile went from his face.

'If I'm pale it's your fault and not because I've missed you, you conceited thing. It's because—' Oh, she hadn't intended to tell him like this but the hot words rushed to her lips and she flung them at him, careless of the servants who might hear. 'It's because I'm going to have a baby!'

He sucked in his breath suddenly and his eyes went rapidly over her. He took a quick step toward her as though to put a hand on her arm, but she twisted away from him, and before the hate in her eyes his face hardened.

'Indeed!' he said coolly. 'Well, who's the happy father? Ashley?'

She clutched the newel-post until the ears of the carved lion dug with sudden pain into her palm. Even she who knew him so well had not anticipated this insult. Of course, he was joking but there were some jokes too monstrous to be borne. She wanted to rake her sharp nails across his eyes and blot out that queer light in them.

'Damn you!' she began, her voice shaking with sick rage. 'You – you know it's yours. And I don't want it any more than you do. No – no woman would want the children of a cad like you. I wish – oh, God, I wish it was anybody's baby but yours!'

She saw his swarthy face change suddenly, anger and something she could not analyse making it twitch as though stung.

'There!' she thought in a hot rage of pleasure. 'There! I've hurt him now!'

But the old impassive mask was back across his face and he stroked one side of his moustache.

'Cheer up,' he said, turning from her and starting up the stairs, 'maybe you'll have a miscarriage.'

For a dizzy moment she thought what child-bearing meant: the nausea that tore her, the tedious waiting, the thickening of her figure, the hours of pain. Things no man could ever realize. And he dared to joke. She would claw him. Nothing but the sight of blood upon his dark face would ease this pain in her heart. She lunged for him, swift as a cat, but with a light startled movement, he sidestepped, throwing up his arm to ward her off. She was standing on the edge of the freshly waxed top step, and as her arm, with the whole weight of her body behind it, struck his out-thrust arm, she lost her balance. She made a wild clutch for the newel-post and missed it. She went down the stairs backwards, feeling a sickening dart of pain in her ribs as she landed. And, too dazed to catch herself, she rolled over and over to the bottom of the flight.

*

It was the first time Scarlett had ever been ill, except when she had her babies, and somehow those times did not count. She had not been forlorn and frightened then, as she was now, weak and pain-racked and bewildered. She knew she was sicker than they dared tell her, feebly realized that she might die. The broken rib stabbed when she breathed, her bruised face and head ached and her whole body was given over to demons who plucked at her with hot pincers and sawed on her with dull knives and left her, for short intervals, so drained of strength that she could not regain grip on herself before they returned. No, childbirth had not been like this. She had been able to eat hearty meals two hours after Wade and Ella and Bonnie had been born, but now the thought of anything but cool water brought on feeble nausea.

How easy it was to have a child and how painful not to have one! Strange, what a pang it had been even in her pain, to know that she would not have this child. Stranger still that it should have been the first child she really wanted. She tried to think why she wanted it but her mind was too tired. Her mind was too tired to think of anything except fear of death. Death was in the room and she had no strength to confront it, to fight it back, and she was frightened. She wanted someone strong to stand by her and hold her hand and fight off death until enough strength came back for her to do her own fighting.

Rage had been swallowed up in pain and she wanted Rhett. But he was not there and she could not bring herself to ask for him.

Her last memory of him was how he looked as he picked her up in the dark hall at the bottom of the steps, his face white and wiped clean of all save hideous fear, his voice hoarsely calling for Mammy. And then there was a faint memory of being carried upstairs, before darkness came over her mind. And then pain and more pain and the room full of buzzing voices and Aunt Pittypat's sobs and Dr Meade's brusque orders and feet that hurried on the stairs and tiptoed in the upper hall. And then like a blinding ray of lightning the knowledge of death and fear that suddenly made her try to scream a name and the scream was only a whisper.

But that forlorn whisper brought instant response from somewhere in the darkness beside the bed and the soft voice of the one she called made answer in lullaby tones: 'I'm here, dear. I've been right here all the time.'

Death and fear receded gently as Melanie took her hand and laid it quietly against her cool cheek. Scarlett tried to turn to see her face and could not. Melly was having a baby and the Yankees were coming. The town was afire and she must hurry, hurry. But Melly was having a baby and she couldn't hurry. She must stay with her till the baby came and be strong because Melly needed her strength. Melly was hurting so bad – there were hot pincers at her and dull knives and recurrent waves of pain. She must hold Melly's hand.

But Dr Meade was there after all, he had come, even if the soldiers at the depot did need him, for she heard him say: 'Delirious. Where's Captain Butler?'

That night was dark and then light and sometimes she was having a baby and sometimes it was Melanie who cried out, but through it all Melly was there and her hands were cool and she did not make futile anxious gestures or sob like Aunt Pitty. Whenever Scarlett opened her eyes, she said, 'Melly?' and the voice answered. And usually she started to whisper: 'Rhett – I want Rhett,' and remembered, as from a dream, that Rhett didn't want her, that Rhett's face was dark as an Indian's and his teeth were white in a jeer. She wanted him and he didn't want her.

Once she said 'Melly?' and Mammy's voice said: ''S me, chile,' and Mammy put a cold rag on her forehead, and she cried fretfully, 'Melly – Melanie' over and over but for a long time Melanie did not come. For Melanie was sitting on the edge of Rhett's bed and Rhett, drunk and sobbing, was sprawled on the floor, crying, his head in her lap.

Every time she had come out of Scarlett's room she had seen him, sitting on his bed, his door wide, watching the door across the hall. The room was untidy, littered with cigar-butts and dishes of untouched food. The bed was tumbled and unmade and he sat on it, unshaven and suddenly gaunt, endlessly smoking. He never asked questions when he saw her. She always stood in the doorway for a minute, giving the news: 'I'm sorry, she's worse,' or 'No, she hasn't asked for you yet. You see, she's delirious,' or 'You mustn't give up hope, Captain Butler. Let me fix you some hot coffee and something to eat. You'll make yourself ill.'

Her heart always ached with pity for him, although she was almost too tired and sleepy to feel anything. How could people say such mean things about him – say he was heartless and wicked and unfaithful to Scarlett, when she could see him getting thin before her eyes, see the torment in his face? Tired as she was, she always tried to be kinder than usual when she gave bulletins from the sick-room. He looked so like a damned soul waiting judgment – so like a child in a suddenly hostile world. But everyone was like a child to Melanie.

But when, at last, she went joyfully to his door to tell him that Scarlett was better, she was unprepared for what she found. There was a half-empty bottle of whisky on the table by the bed and the room reeked with the odour. He looked up at her with bright glazed eyes and his jaw muscles trembled despite his efforts to set his teeth.

'She's dead?'

'Oh, no. She's much better.'

He said: 'Oh, my God,' and put his head in his hands. She saw his wide shoulders shake as with a nervous chill and, as she watched him pityingly, her pity changed to horror for she saw that he was crying. Melanie had never seen a man cry and of all men, Rhett, so suave, so mocking, so eternally sure of himself.

It frightened her, the desperate choking sound he made. She had a terrified thought that he was drunk and Melanie was afraid of drunkenness. But when he raised his head and she caught one glimpse of his eyes, she stepped swiftly into the room, closed the door softly behind her and went to him. She had never seen a man cry but she had comforted the tears of many children. When she put a soft hand on his shoulder, his arms went suddenly around her skirts. Before she knew how it happened she was sitting on the bed and he was on the floor, his head in her lap and his arms and hands clutching her in a frantic clasp that hurt her.

She stroked the black head gently and said: 'There! There!' soothingly. 'There! She's going to get well.'

At her words, his grip tightened and he began speaking rapidly, hoarsely, babbling as though to a grave which would never give up its secrets, babbling the truth for the first time in his life, baring himself mercilessly to Melanie who was, at first, utterly uncomprehending, utterly maternal. He talked brokenly, burrowing his head in her lap, tugging at the folds of her skirt. Sometimes his words were blurred, muffled, sometimes they came far too clearly to her ears, harsh, bitter words of confession and abasement, speaking of things she had never heard even a woman mention, secret things that brought the hot blood of modesty to her cheeks and made her grateful for his bowed head.

She patted his head as she did little Beau's and said: 'Hush! Captain Butler! You must not tell me these things! You are not yourself. Hush!' But his voice went on in a wild torrent of outpouring and he held on to her dress as though it were his hope of life.

He accused himself of deeds she did not understand; he mumbled the name of Belle Watling and then he shook her with his violence as he cried: 'I've killed Scarlett, I've killed her. You don't understand. She didn't want this baby and—'

'You must hush! You are beside yourself! Not want a baby? Why, every woman wants—'

'No! No! You want babies. But she doesn't. Not my babies—'

'You must stop!'

'You don't understand. She didn't want a baby and I made her. This – this baby – it's all my damned fault. We hadn't been sleeping together—'

'Hush, Captain Butler! It is not fit—'

'And I was drunk and insane and I wanted to hurt her – because she had hurt me. I wanted to – and I did – but she didn't want me. She's never wanted me. She never has and I tried – I tried so hard and—'

'Oh, please!'

'And I didn't know about this baby till the other day – when she fell. She didn't know where I was to write to me and tell me – but she wouldn't have written me if she had known. I tell you – I tell you I'd have come straight home – if I'd only known – whether she wanted me home or not . . .'

'Oh, yes, I know you would!'

'God, I've been crazy these weeks, crazy and drunk! And when she told me, there on the steps – what did I do? What did I say? I laughed and said: "Cheer up. Maybe you'll have a miscarriage." And she—'

Melanie suddenly went white and her eyes widened with horror as she looked down at the black tormented head writhing in her lap. The afternoon sun streamed in through the open window and suddenly she saw, as for the first time, how large and brown and strong his hands were and how thickly the black hairs grew along the backs of them. Involuntarily, she recoiled from them. They seemed so predatory, so ruthless and yet, twined in her skirt, so broken, so helpless.

Could it be possible that he had heard and believed the preposterous lie about Scarlett and Ashley and become jealous? True, he had left town immediately after the scandal broke but—No, it couldn't be that. Captain Butler was always going off abruptly on journeys. He couldn't have believed the gossip. He was too sensible. If that had been the cause of the trouble, wouldn't he have tried to shoot Ashley? Or at least demanded an explanation?

No, it couldn't be that. It was only that he was drunk and sick from strain and his mind was running wild, like a man delirious, babbling wild fantasies. Men couldn't stand strains as well as women. Something had upset him, perhaps he had had a small quarrel with Scarlett and magnified it. Perhaps some of the awful things he had said were true. But all of them could not be true. Oh, not that last, certainly! No man could say such a thing to a woman he loved as passionately as this man loved Scarlett. Melanie had never seen evil, never seen cruelty, and now that she looked on them for the first time she found them too inconceivable to believe. He was drunk and sick. And sick children must be humoured.

'There! There!' she said crooningly. 'Hush, now. I understand.'

He raised his head violently and looked up at her with bloodshot eyes, fiercely throwing off her hands.

'No, by God, you don't understand. You can't understand! You're – you're too good to understand. You don't believe me but it's all true and I'm a dog. Do you know why I did it? I was mad, crazy with jealousy. She never cared for me and I thought I could make her care. But she never cared. She doesn't love me. She never has. She loves—'

His passionate, drunken gaze met hers and he stopped, mouth open, as though for the first time he realized to whom he was speaking. Her face was white and strained but her eyes were steady and sweet and full of pity and unbelief. There was a luminous serenity in them and the innocence in the soft brown depths struck him like a blow in the face, clearing some of the alcohol out of his brain, halting his mad, careering words in mid-flight. He trailed off into a mumble, his eyes dropping away from hers, his lids batting rapidly as he fought back to sanity.

'I'm a cad,' he muttered, dropping his head tiredly back into her lap. 'But not that big a cad. And if I did tell you, you wouldn't believe me, would you? You're too good to believe me. I never before knew anybody who was really good. You wouldn't believe me, would you?'

'No, I wouldn't believe you,' said Melanie soothingly, beginning to stroke his hair again. 'She's going to get well. There, Captain Butler! Don't cry! She's going to get well.'

Chapter LVII

It was a pale, thin woman that Rhett put on the Jonesboro train a month later. Wade and Ella, who were to make the trip with her, were silent and uneasy at their mother's still, white face. They clung close to Prissy, for even to their childish minds there was something frightening in the cold, impersonal atmosphere between their mother and their stepfather.

Weak as she was, Scarlett was going home to Tara. She felt that she would stifle if she stayed in Atlanta another day, with her tired mind forcing itself round and round the deeply worn circle of futile thoughts about the mess she was in. She was sick in body and weary in mind and she was standing like a lost child in a nightmare country in which there was no familiar landmark to guide her.

As she had once fled Atlanta before an invading army, so she was fleeing it again, pressing her worries into the back of her mind with her old defence against the world: 'I won't think of it now. I can't stand it if I do. I'll think of it tomorrow at Tara. Tomorrow's another day.' It seemed that if she could only get back to the stillness and the green cotton fields of home, all her troubles would fall away and she would somehow be able to mould her shattered thoughts into something she could live by.

Rhett watched the train until it was out of sight and on his face there was a look of speculative bitterness that was not pleasant. He sighed, dismissed the carriage and, mounting his horse, rode down Ivy Street toward Melanie's house.

It was a warm morning and Melanie sat on the vine-shaded porch, her mending basket piled high with socks. Confusion and dismay filled her when she saw Rhett alight from his horse and toss the reins over the arm of the cast-iron negro boy who stood at the sidewalk. She had not seen him alone since that too dreadful day when Scarlett had been so ill and he had been so – well – so drunk. Melanie hated even to think the word. She had spoken to him only casually during Scarlett's convalescence and, on those occasions, she had found it difficult to meet his eyes. However, he had been his usual bland self at those times, and never by look or word showed that such a scene had taken place between them. Ashley had told her once that men frequently did not remember things said and done in drink, and Melanie prayed heartily that Captain Butler's memory had failed him on that occasion. She felt she would rather die than learn that he remembered his outpourings. Timidity and embarrassment swept over her and waves of colour mounted her cheeks as he came up the walk. But perhaps he had only come to ask if Beau could spend the day with Bonnie. Surely he wouldn't have the bad taste to come and thank her for what she had done that day!

She rose to meet him, noting with surprise, as always, how lightly he walked for a big man.

'Scarlett has gone?'

'Yes. Tara will do her good,' he said, smiling. 'Sometimes I think she's like the giant Antaeus who became stronger each time he touched Mother Earth. It doesn't do for Scarlett to stay away too long from that patch of red mud she loves. The sight of cotton growing will do her more good than all Dr Meade's tonics.'

'Won't you sit down?' said Melanie, her hands fluttering. He was so very large and male, and excessively male creatures always discomposed her. They seemed to radiate a force and vitality that made her feel smaller and weaker even than she was. He looked so swarthy and formidable and the heavy muscles in his shoulders swelled against his white linen coat in a way that frightened her. It seemed impossible that she had seen all this strength and insolence brought low. And she had held that black head in her lap!

'Oh, dear!' she thought in distress and blushed again.

'Miss Melly,' he said gently, 'does my presence annoy you? Would you rather I went away? Pray be frank.'

'Oh!' she thought. 'He does remember! And he knows how upset I am!'

She looked up at him, imploringly, and suddenly her embarrassment and confusion faded. His eyes were so quiet, so kind, so understanding that she wondered how she could ever have been silly enough to be flurried. His face looked tired and, she thought with surprise, more than a little sad. How could she have even thought he'd be ill-bred enough to bring up subjects both would rather forget?

'Poor thing, he's been so worried about Scarlett,' she thought, and managing a smile, she said: 'Do sit down, Captain Butler.'

He sat down heavily and watched her as she picked up her darning.

'Miss Melly, I've come to ask a very great favour of you and,' he smiled and his mouth twisted down, 'to enlist your aid in a deception from which I know you will shrink.'

'A – deception?'

'Yes. Really, I've come to talk business to you.'

'Oh, dear. Then it's Mr Wilkes you'd better see. I'm such a goose about business. I'm not smart like Scarlett.'

'I'm afraid Scarlett is too smart for her own good,' he said, 'and that is exactly what I want to talk to you about. You know how – ill she's been. When she gets back from Tara she will start again hammer and tongs with the store and those mills which I wish devoutly would explode some night. I fear for her health, Miss Melly.'

'Yes, she does far too much. You must make her stop and take care of herself.'

He laughed.

'You know how headstrong she is. I never even try to argue with her. She's just like a wilful child. She won't let me help her – she won't let anyone help her. I've tried to get her to sell her share in the mills but she won't. And now, Miss Melly, I come to the business matter. I know Scarlett would sell the remainder of her interest in the mills to Mr Wilkes but to no one else, and I want Mr Wilkes to buy her out.'

'Oh, dear me! That would be nice but—' Melanie stopped and bit her lip. She could not mention money matters to an outsider. Somehow, despite what he made from the mill, she and Ashley never seemed to have enough money. It worried her that they saved so little. She did not know where the money went. Ashley gave her enough to run the house on, but when it came to extra expenses they were often pinched. Of course, her doctors' bills were so much, and then the books and furniture Ashley ordered from New York did run into money. And they had fed and clothed any number of waifs who slept in their cellar. And Ashley never felt like refusing a loan to any man who'd been in the Confederate Army. And—

'Miss Melly, I want to lend you the money,' said Rhett.

'That's so kind of you, but we might never repay it.'

'I don't want it repaid. Don't be angry with me, Miss Melly! Please hear me through. It will repay me enough to know that Scarlett will not be exhausting herself driving miles to the mills every day. The store will be enough to keep her busy and happy . . . Don't you see?'

'Well – yes—' said Melanie uncertainly.

'You want your boy to have a pony, don't you? And want him to go to the university and to Harvard and to Europe on a Grand Tour?'

'Oh, of course,' cried Melanie, her face lighting up, as always, at the mention of Beau. 'I want him to have everything, but – well, everyone is so poor these days that—'

'Mr Wilkes could make a pile of money out of the mills some day,' said Rhett. 'And I'd like to see Beau have all the advantages he deserves.'

'Oh, Captain Butler, what a crafty wretch you are!' she cried, smiling. 'Appealing to a mother's pride! I can read you like a book.'

'I hope not,' said Rhett, and for the first time there was a gleam in his eye. 'Now will you let me lend you the money?'

'But where does the deception come in?'

'We must be conspirators and deceive both Scarlett and Mr Wilkes.'

'Oh, dear! I couldn't!'

'If Scarlett knew I had plotted behind her back, even for her own good – well, you know her temper. And I'm afraid Mr Wilkes would refuse any loan I offered him. So neither of them must know where the money comes from.'

'Oh, but I'm sure Mr Wilkes wouldn't refuse, if he understood the matter. He is so fond of Scarlett.'

'Yes, I'm sure he is,' said Rhett smoothly. 'But just the same he would refuse. You know how proud all the Wilkes are.'

'Oh, dear!' cried Melanie miserably. 'I wish— Really, Captain Butler, I couldn't deceive my husband.'

'Not even to help Scarlett?' Rhett looked very hurt. 'And she so fond of you!'

Tears trembled on Melanie's eyelids.

'You know I'd do anything in the world for her. I can never, never half repay her for what she's done for me. You know.'

'Yes,' he said shortly, 'I know what she's done for you. Couldn't you tell Mr Wilkes that the money was left you in the will of some relative?'

'Oh, Captain Butler, I haven't a relative with a penny to bless him!'

'Then, if I sent the money through the mail to Mr Wilkes without his knowing who sent it, would you see that it was used to buy the mills and not – well, given away to destitute ex-Confederates?'

At first she looked hurt at his last words, as though they implied criticism of Ashley, but he smiled so understandingly she smiled back.

'Of course I will.'

'So it's settled? It's to be our secret?'

'But I have never kept anything secret from my husband!'

'I'm sure of that, Miss Melly.'

As she looked at him she thought how right she had always been about him and how wrong so many other people were. People had said he was brutal and sneering and bad-mannered and even dishonest. Though many of the nicest people were now admitting they had been wrong. Well! She had known from the very beginning that he was a fine man. She had never received from him anything but the kindest treatment, thoughtfulness, utter respect and what understanding! And then, how he loved Scarlett! How sweet of him to take this roundabout way of sparing Scarlett one of the loads she carried!

In an impulsive rush of feeling, she said: 'Scarlett's lucky to have a husband who's so nice to her!'

'You think so? I'm afraid she wouldn't agree with you, if she could hear you. Besides, I want to be nice to you too, Miss Melly. I'm giving you more than I'm giving Scarlett.'

'Me?' she questioned, puzzled. 'Oh, you mean for Beau.'

He picked up his hat and rose. He stood for a moment looking down at the plain, heart-shaped face with its long widow's peak and serious dark eyes. Such an unworldly face, a face with no defences against life.

'No, not Beau. I'm trying to give you something more than Beau, if you can imagine that.'

'No, I can't,' she said, bewildered again. 'There's nothing in the world— more precious to me than Beau except Ash– except Mr Wilkes.'

Rhett said nothing and looked down at her, his dark face still.

'You're mighty nice to want to do things for me, Captain Butler, but really, I'm so lucky. I have everything in the world any woman could want.'

'That's fine,' said Rhett, suddenly grim. 'And I intend to see that you keep them.'

When Scarlett came back from Tara, the unhealthy pallor had gone from her face and her cheeks were rounded and faintly pink. Her green eyes were alert and sparkling again, and she laughed aloud for the first time in weeks when Rhett and Bonnie met her and Wade and Ella at the depot – laughed in annoyance and amusement. Rhett had two straggling turkey feathers in the brim of his hat, and Bonnie, dressed in a sadly torn dress that was her Sunday frock, had diagonal lines of indigo blue on her cheeks and a peacock feather half as long as she was in her curls. Evidently a game of Indian had been in progress when the time came to meet the train, and it was obvious from the look of quizzical helplessness on Rhett's face and the lowering indignation of Mammy that Bonnie had refused to have her toilet remedied, even to meet her mother.

Scarlett said: 'What a ragamuffin!' as she kissed the child and turned a cheek for Rhett's lips. There were crowds of people in the depot or she would never have invited this caress. She could not help noticing, for all her embarrassment at Bonnie's appearance, that everyone in the crowd was smiling at the figure father and daughter cut, smiling not in derision but in genuine amusement and kindness. Everyone knew that Scarlett's youngest had her father under her thumb and Atlanta was amused and approving. Rhett's great love for his child had gone far toward reinstating him in public opinion.

On the way home, Scarlett was full of County news. The hot, dry weather was making the cotton grow so fast you could almost hear it, but Will said cotton prices were going to be low this fall. Suellen was going to have another baby – she spelled this out so the children would not comprehend – and Ella had shown unwonted spirit in biting Suellen's oldest girl. Though, observed Scarlett, it was no more than little Susie deserved, she being her mother all over again. But Suellen had become infuriated and they had had an invigorating quarrel that was just like old times. Wade had killed a water moccasin, all by himself. 'Randa and Camilla Tarleton were teaching school, and wasn't that a joke? Not a one of the Tarletons had ever been able to spell cat! Betsy Tarleton had married a fat one-armed man from Lovejoy and they and Hetty and Jim Tarleton were raising a good cotton crop at Fairhill. Mrs Tarleton had a brood mare and a colt and was as happy as though she had a million dollars. And there were negroes living in the old Calvert house! Swarms of them and they actually owned it! They'd bought it in at the sheriff's sale. The place was dilapidated and it made you cry to look at it. No one knew where Cathleen and her no-good husband had gone. And Alex was to marry Sally, his brother's widow! Imagine that, after them living in the same house for so many years! Everybody said it was a marriage of convenience because people were beginning to gossip about them living there alone, since both Old Miss and Young Miss had died. And it had about broken Dimity Munroe's heart. But it served her right. If she'd had any gumption she'd have caught her another man long ago, instead of waiting for Alex to get money enough to marry her.

Scarlett chattered on cheerfully but there were many things about the County which she suppressed, things that hurt to think about. She had driven over the County with Will, trying not to remember when these thousands of fertile acres had stood green with cotton. Now, plantation after plantation was going back to the forest, and dismal fields of broomsedge, scrub oak and runty pines had grown stealthily about silent ruins and over old cotton fields. Only one acre was being farmed now where once a hundred had been under the plough. It was like moving through a dead land.

'This section won't come back for fifty years – if it ever comes back,' Will had said. 'Tara's the best farm in the County, thanks to you and me, Scarlett, but it's a farm, a two-mule farm, not a plantation. And the Fontaine place, it comes next to Tara and then the Tarletons'. They ain't makin' much money but they're gettin' along and they got gumption. But most of the rest of the folks, the rest of the farms . . .'

No, Scarlett did not like to remember the way the deserted County looked. It seemed even sadder, in retrospect, beside the bustle and prosperity of Atlanta.

'Has anything happened here?' she asked when they were finally home and were seated on the front porch. She had talked rapidly and continuously all the way home, fearing that a silence would fall. She had not had a word alone with Rhett since that day when she fell down the steps and she was none too anxious to be alone with him now. She did not know how he felt toward her. He had been kindness itself during her miserable convalescence, but it was the kindness of an impersonal stranger. He had anticipated her wants, kept the children from bothering her and supervised the store and the mills. But he had never said: 'I'm sorry.' Well, perhaps he wasn't sorry. Perhaps he still thought that child that was never born was not his child. How could she tell what went on in the mind behind the bland dark face? But he had showed a disposition to be courteous, for the first time in their married life, and a desire to let life go on as though there had never been anything unpleasant between them – as though, thought Scarlett, cheerlessly, as though there had never been anything at all between them. Well, if that was what he wanted, she could act her part too.

'Is everything all right?' she repeated. 'Did you get the new shingles for the store? Did you swap the mules? For Heaven's sake, Rhett, take those feathers out of your hat. You look a fool and you'll be likely to wear them downtown without remembering to take them out.'

'No,' said Bonnie, picking up her father's hat, defensively.

'Everything has gone very well, here,' replied Rhett. 'Bonnie and I have had a nice time and I don't believe her hair has been combed since you left. Don't suck the feathers, darling, they may be nasty. Yes, the shingles are fixed and I got a good trade on the mules. No, there's really no news. Everything has been quite dull.'

Then, as an afterthought, he added: 'The honourable Ashley was over here last night. He wanted to know if I thought you would sell him your mill and the part interest you have in his.'

Scarlett, who had been rocking and fanning herself with a turkey-tail fan, stopped abruptly.

'Sell? Where on earth did Ashley get the money? You know they never have a cent. Melanie spends it as fast as he makes it.'

Rhett shrugged. 'I always thought her a frugal little person, but then I'm not as well informed about the intimate details of the Wilkes family as you seem to be.'

That jab seemed in something of Rhett's old style and Scarlett grew annoyed.

'Run away, dear,' she said to Bonnie. 'Mother wants to talk to Father.'

'No,' said Bonnie positively and climbed upon Rhett's lap.

Scarlett frowned at her child and Bonnie scowled back in so complete a resemblance to Gerald O'Hara that Scarlett almost laughed.

'Let her stay,' said Rhett comfortably. 'As to where he got the money, it seems it was sent him by someone he nursed through a case of smallpox at Rock Island. It renews my faith in human nature to know that gratitude still exists.'

'Who was it? Anyone we know?'

'The letter was unsigned and came from Washington. Ashley was at a loss to know who could have sent it. But then, one of Ashley's unselfish temperament goes about the world doing so many good deeds that you can't expect him to remember all of them.'

Had she not been so surprised at Ashley's windfall, Scarlett would have taken up this gauntlet, although while at Tara she had decided that never again would she permit herself to be involved in any quarrel with Rhett about Ashley. The ground on which she stood in this matter was entirely too uncertain and, until she knew exactly where she stood with both men, she did not care to be drawn out.

'He wants to buy me out?'

'Yes. But, of course, I told him you wouldn't sell.'

'I wish you'd let me mind my own business.'

'Well, you know you wouldn't part with the mills. I told him that he knew as well as I did that you couldn't bear not to have your finger in everybody's pie, and if you sold out to him, then you wouldn't be able to tell him how to mind his own business.'

'You dared say that to him about me?'

'Why not? It's true, isn't it? I believe he heartily agreed with me but, of course, he was too much of a gentleman to come right out and say so.'

'It's a lie! I will sell them to him!' cried Scarlett angrily.

Until that moment, she had had no idea of parting with the mills. She had several reasons for wanting to keep them and their monetary value was the least reason. She could have sold them for large sums any time in the last few years, but she had refused all offers. The mills were the tangible evidence of what she had done, unaided and against great odds, and she was proud of them and of herself. Most of all, she did not want to sell them because they were the only path that lay open to Ashley. If the mills went from her control it would mean that she would seldom see Ashley and probably never see him alone. And she had to see him alone. She could not go on this way any longer, wondering what his feelings toward her were now, wondering if all his love had died in shame since the dreadful night of Melanie's party. In the course of business she could find many opportune times for conversations without it appearing to anyone that she was seeking him out. And, given time, she knew she could gain back whatever ground she had lost in his heart. But if she sold the mills—

No, she did not want to sell but, goaded by the thought that Rhett had exposed her to Ashley in so truthful and so unflattering a light, she had made up her mind instantly. Ashley should have the mills and at a price so low he could not help realizing how generous she was.

'I will sell!' she cried furiously. 'Now, what do you think of that?'

There was the faintest gleam of triumph in Rhett's eyes as he bent to tie Bonnie's shoestring.

'I think you'll regret it,' he said.

Already she was regretting the hasty words. Had they been spoken to anyone save Rhett she would have shamelessly retracted them. Why had she burst out like that? She looked at Rhett with an angry frown and saw that he was watching her with his old keen, cat-at-a-mouse-hole look. When he saw her frown, he laughed suddenly, his white teeth flashing. Scarlett had an uncertain feeling that he had jockeyed her into this position.

'Did you have anything to do with this?' she snapped.

'I?' His brows went up in mock surprise. 'You should know me better. I never go about the world doing good deeds if I can avoid it.'

*

That night she sold the mills and all her interest in them to Ashley. She did not lose thereby for Ashley refused to take advantage of her first low offer and met the highest bid that she had ever had for them. When she had signed the papers and the mills were irrevocably gone and Melanie was passing small glasses of wine to Ashley and Rhett to celebrate the transaction, Scarlett felt bereft, as though she had sold one of her children.

The mills had been her darlings, her pride, the fruit of her small grasping hands. She had started with one little mill in those black days when Atlanta was barely struggling up from ruin and ashes and want was staring her in the face. She had fought and schemed and nursed them through the dark times when Yankee confiscation loomed, when money was tight and smart men going to the wall. And now, when Atlanta was covering its scars and buildings were going up everywhere and newcomers flocking to the town every day, she had two fine mills, two lumber yards, a dozen mule teams and convict labour to operate the business at low cost. Bidding farewell to them was like closing a door forever on a part of her life, a bitter, harsh part but one which she recalled with a nostalgic satisfaction.

She had built up this business and now she had sold it and she was oppressed with the certainty that, without her at the helm, Ashley would lose it all – everything that she had worked to build. Ashley trusted everyone and still hardly knew a two-by-four from a six-by-eight. And now she would never be able to give him the benefit of her advice – all because Rhett had told him that she liked to boss everything.

'Oh, damn Rhett!' she thought, and as she watched him the conviction grew that he was at the bottom of all this. Just how and why she did not know. He was talking to Ashley and his words brought her up sharply.

'I suppose you'll turn the convicts back right away,' he said.

Turn the convicts back? Why should there be any idea of turning them back? Rhett knew perfectly well that the large profits from the mills grew out of the cheap convict labour. And why did Rhett speak with such certainty about what Ashley's future actions would be? What did he know of him?

'Yes, they'll go back immediately,' replied Ashley, and he avoided Scarlett's dumbfounded gaze.

'Have you lost your mind?' she cried. 'You'll lose all the money on the lease and what kind of labour can you get, anyway?'

'I'll use free darkies,' said Ashley.

'Free darkies! Fiddle-dee-dee! You know what their wages will cost, and besides you'll have the Yankees on your neck every minute to see if you're giving them chicken three times a day and tucking them to sleep under eiderdown quilts. And if you give a lazy darky a couple of licks to speed him up, you'll hear the Yankees scream from here to Dalton and you'll end up in jail. Why, convicts are the only—'

Melanie looked down into her lap at her twisted hands. Ashley looked unhappy but obdurate. For a moment he was silent. Then his gaze crossed Rhett's and it was as if he found understanding and encouragement in Rhett's eyes – a glance that was not lost on Scarlett.

'I won't work convicts, Scarlett,' he said quietly.

'Well, sir!' Her breath was taken away. 'And why not? Are you afraid people will talk about you like they do about me?'

Ashley raised his head.

'I'm not afraid of what people say as long as I am right. And I have never felt that convict labour was right.'

'But why—'

'I can't make money from the enforced labour and misery of others.'

'But you owned slaves!'

'They weren't miserable. And besides, I'd have freed them all when Father died if the war hadn't already freed them. But this is different, Scarlett. The system is open to too many abuses. Perhaps you don't know it but I do. I know very well that Johnnie Gallegher has killed at least one man at his camp. Maybe more – who cares about one convict, more or less? He said the man was killed trying to escape, but that's not what I've heard elsewhere. And I know he works men who are too sick to work. Call it superstition, but I do not believe that happiness can come from money made from the sufferings of others.'

'God's nightgown! You mean – goodness, Ashley, you didn't swallow all the Reverend Wallace's bellowings about tainted money?'

'I didn't have to swallow it. I believed it long before he preached on it.'

'Then, you must think all my money is tainted,' cried Scarlett, beginning to be angry. 'Because I worked convicts and own saloon property and—' She stopped short. Both the Wilkes looked embarrassed and Rhett was grinning broadly. 'Damn him,' thought Scarlett vehemently. 'He's thinking that I'm sticking my finger in other people's pies again and so is Ashley. I'd like to crack their heads together!' She swallowed her wrath and tried to assume an aloof air of dignity but with little success.

'Of course, it's immaterial to me,' she said.

'Scarlett, don't think I'm criticizing you! I'm not. It's just that we look at things in different ways and what is good for you might not be good for me.'

She suddenly wished that they were alone, wished ardently that Rhett and Melanie were at the end of the earth, so she could cry out: 'But I want to look at things the way you look at them! Tell me just what you mean, so I can understand and be like you!'

But with Melanie present, trembling with the distress of the scene, and Rhett lounging, grinning at her, she could only say with as much coolness and offended virtue as she could muster: 'I'm sure it's your own business, Ashley, and far be it from me to tell you how to run it. But, I must say, I do not understand your attitude or your remarks.'

Oh, if they were only alone, so she would not be forced to say these cool things to him, these words that were making him unhappy!

'I've offended you, Scarlett, and I did not mean to. You must believe me and forgive me. There is nothing enigmatic in what I said. It is only that I believe that money which comes in certain ways seldom brings happiness.'

'But you're wrong!' she cried, unable to restrain herself any longer. 'Look at me! You know how my money came. You know how things were before I made my money! You remember that winter at Tara when it was so cold and we were cutting up the carpets for shoes and there wasn't enough to eat and we used to wonder how we were going to give Beau and Wade an education. You remem—'

'I remember,' said Ashley tiredly, 'but I'd rather forget.'

'Well, you can't say any of us were happy then, can you? And look at us now! You've a nice home and a good future. And has anyone a prettier house than mine or nicer clothes or finer horses? Nobody sets as fine a table as me or gives nicer receptions and my children have everything they want. Well, how did I get the money to make it possible? Off trees? No, sir! Convicts and saloon rentals and—'

'And don't forget murdering that Yankee,' said Rhett softly. 'He really gave you your start.'

Scarlett swung on him, furious words on her lips.

'And the money has made you very, very happy, hasn't it, darling?' he asked, poisonously sweet.

Scarlett stopped short, her mouth open, and her eyes went swiftly to the eyes of the other three. Melanie was almost crying with embarrassment, Ashley was suddenly bleak and withdrawn and Rhett was watching her over his cigar with impersonal amusement. She started to cry out: 'But of course, it's made me happy!'

But somehow, she could not speak.

Chapter LVIII

In the time that followed her illness Scarlett noticed a change in Rhett and she was not altogether certain that she liked it. He was sober and quiet and preoccupied. He was at home more often for supper now and he was kinder to the servants and more affectionate to Wade and Ella. He never referred to anything in their past, pleasant or otherwise, and silently seemed to dare her to bring up such subjects. Scarlett held her peace, for it was easier to let well enough alone, and life went on smoothly enough, on the surface. His impersonal courtesy toward her that had begun during her convalescence continued and he did not fling softly drawled barbs at her or sting her with sarcasm. She realized now that though he had infuriated her with his malicious comments and roused her to heated rejoinders, he had done it because he cared what she did and said. Now she wondered if he cared about anything she did. He was polite and disinterested and she missed his interest, perverse though it had been, missed the old days of bickering and retort.

He was pleasant to her now, almost as though she were a stranger; but, as his eyes had once followed her, they now followed Bonnie. It was as though the swift flood of his life had been diverted into one narrow channel. Sometimes Scarlett thought that if Rhett had given her one-half the attention and tenderness he lavished on Bonnie, life would have been different. Sometimes it was hard to smile when people said: 'How Captain Butler idolizes that child!' But, if she did not smile, people would think it strange and Scarlett hated to acknowledge, even to herself, that she was jealous of a little girl, especially when that little girl was her favourite child. Scarlett always wanted to be first in the hearts of those around her and it was obvious now that Rhett and Bonnie would always be first with each other.

Rhett was out late many nights but he came home sober on these nights. Often she heard him whistling softly to himself as he went down the hall past her closed door. Sometimes men came home with him in the late hours and sat talking in the dining-room around the brandy decanter. They were not the same men with whom he had drunk the first year they were married. No rich Carpetbaggers, no Scallawags, no Republicans came to the house now at his invitation. Scarlett, creeping on tiptoe to the banister of the upstairs hall, listened and, to her amazement, frequently heard the voices of René Picard, Hugh Elsing, the Simmons boys and Andy Bonnell. And always Grandpa Merriwether and Uncle Henry were there. Once, to her astonishment, she heard the tones of Dr Meade. And these men had once thought hanging too good for Rhett!

This group was always linked in her mind with Frank's death, and the late hours Rhett kept these days reminded her still more of the times preceding the Klan foray when Frank lost his life. She remembered with dread Rhett's remark that he would even join their damned Klan to be respectable, though he hoped God would not lay so heavy a penance on his shoulders. Suppose Rhett, like Frank—

One night when he was out later than usual she could stand the strain no longer. When she heard the rasp of his key in the lock, she threw on a wrapper and, going into the gas-lit upper hall, met him at the top of the stairs. His expression, absent, thoughtful, changed to surprise when he saw her standing there.

'Rhett, I've got to know! I've got to know if you – if it's the Klan – is that why you stay out so late? Do you belong—'

In the flaring gas-light he looked at her incuriously and then he smiled.

'You are way behind the times,' he said. 'There is no Klan in Atlanta now.

Probably not in Georgia. You've been listening to the Klan outrage stories of your Scallawag and Carpetbagger friends.'

'No Klan? Are you lying to try to soothe me?'

'My dear, when did I ever try to soothe you? No, there is no Klan now. We decided that it did more harm than good because it just kept the Yankees stirred up and furnished more grist for the slander-mill of his excellency, Governor Bullock. He knows he can stay in power just so long as he can convince the Federal government and the Yankee newspapers that Georgia is seething with rebellion and there's a Klansman hiding behind every bush. To keep in power he's been desperately manufacturing Klan outrage stories where none exist, telling of loyal Republicans being hung up by the thumbs and honest darkies lynched for rape. But he's shooting at a non-existent target and he knows it. Thank you for your apprehensions, but there hasn't been an active Klan since shortly after I stopped being a Scallawag and became an humble Democrat.'

Most of what he said about Governor Bullock went in one ear and out the other for her mind was mainly occupied with relief that there was no Klan any longer. Rhett would not be killed as Frank was killed; she wouldn't lose her store or his money. But one word of his conversation swam to the top of her mind. He had said 'we', linking himself naturally with those he had once called the 'Old Guard'.

'Rhett,' she asked suddenly, 'did you have anything to do with the breaking up of the Klan?'

He gave her a long look and his eyes began to dance.

'My love, I did. Ashley Wilkes and I are mainly responsible.'

'Ashley – and you?'

'Yes, platitudinously but truly, politics make strange bedfellows. Neither Ashley nor I care much for each other as bedfellows but— Ashley never believed in the Klan because he's against violence of any sort. And I never believed in it because it's damned foolishness and not the way to get what we want. It's the one way to keep the Yankees on our necks till Kingdom Come. And between Ashley and me, we convinced the hotheads that watching, waiting and working would get us further than nightshirts and fiery crosses.'

'You don't mean the boys actually took your advice when you—'

'When I was a speculator? A Scallawag? A consorter with Yankees? You forget, Mrs Butler, that I am now a Democrat in good standing, devoted to my last drop of blood to recovering our beloved state from the hands of her ravishers! My advice was good advice and they took it. My advice in other political matters is equally good. We have a Democratic majority in the legislature now, haven't we? And soon, my love, we will have some of our good Republican friends behind the bars. They are a bit too rapacious these days, a bit too open.'

'You'd help put them in jail? Why, they were your friends! They let you in on that railroad-bond business that you made thousands out of!'

Rhett grinned suddenly, his old mocking grin.

'Oh, I bear them no ill will. But I'm on the other side now and if I can assist in any way in putting them where they belong, I'll do it. And how that will redound to my credit! I know just enough about the inside of some of these deals to be very valuable when the legislature starts digging into them – and that won't be far off, from the way things look now. They're going to investigate the governor, too, and they'll put him in jail if they can. Better tell your good friends the Gelerts and the Hundons to be ready to leave town on a minute's notice, because if they can nab the governor, they'll nab them too.'

For too many years Scarlett had seen the Republicans, backed up by the force of the Yankee Army, in power in Georgia to believe Rhett's light words. The governor was too strongly entrenched for any legislature to do anything to him, much less put him in jail.

'How you do run on,' she observed.

'If he isn't put in jail, at least he won't be re-elected. We're going to have a Democratic governor next time, for a change.'

'And I suppose you'll have something to do with it?' she questioned sarcastically.

'My pet, I will. I am having something to do with it now. That's why I stay out so late at nights. I'm working harder than I ever worked with a shovel in the gold rush, trying to help get the election organized. And – I know this will hurt you, Mrs Butler, but I am contributing plenty of money to the organization, too. Do you remember telling me, years ago, in Frank's store, that it was dishonest for me to keep the Confederate gold? At last I've come to agree with you and the Confederate gold is being spent to get the Confederates back into power.'

'You're pouring money down a rat-hole!'

'What! You call the Democratic party a rat-hole?' His eyes mocked her and then were quiet, expressionless. 'It doesn't matter a damn to me who wins this election. What does matter is that everyone knows I've worked for it and that I've spent money on it. And that'll be remembered in Bonnie's favour in years to come.'

'I was almost afraid from your pious talk that you'd had a change of heart, but I see you've got no more sincerity about the Democrats than about anything else.'

'Not a change of heart at all. Merely a change of hide. You might possibly sponge the spots off a leopard but he'd remain a leopard, just the same.'

Bonnie, awakened by the sound of voices in the hall, called sleepily but imperiously: 'Daddy!' and Rhett started past Scarlett.

'Rhett, wait a minute. There's something else I want to tell you. You must stop taking Bonnie around with you in the afternoons to political meetings. It just doesn't look well. The idea of a little girl at such places! And it makes you look so silly. I never dreamed that you took her until Uncle Henry mentioned it, as though he thought I knew and—'

He swung round on her and his face was hard.

'How can you read wrong in a little girl sitting on her father's lap while he talks to friends? You may think it looks silly but it isn't silly. People will remember for years that Bonnie sat on my lap while I helped run the Republicans out of this state. People will remember for years—' The hardness went out of his face and a malicious light danced in his eyes. 'Did you know that when people ask her who she loves best, she says "Daddy and the Demiquats", and who she hates most, she says "The Scallywags"? People, thank God, remember things like that.'

Scarlett's voice rose furiously. 'And I suppose you tell her I'm a Scallawag!'

'Daddy!' said the small voice, indignant now, and Rhett, still laughing, went down the hall to his daughter.

That October Governor Bullock resigned his office and fled from Georgia. Misuse of public funds, waste and corruption had reached such proportions during his administration that the edifice was toppling of its own weight. Even his own party was split, so great had public indignation become. The Democrats had a majority in the legislature now, and that meant just one thing. Knowing that he was going to be investigated and fearing impeachment, Bullock did not wait. He hastily and secretly decamped, arranging that his resignation would not become public until he was safely in the North.

When it was announced, a week after his flight, Atlanta was wild with excitement and joy. People thronged the streets, men laughing and shaking hands in congratulation, ladies kissing each other and crying. Everybody gave parties in celebration and the fire department was kept busy fighting the flames that spread from the bonfires of jubilant small boys.

Almost out of the woods! Reconstruction's almost over! To be sure, the acting governor was a Republican too, but the election was coming up in December and there was no doubt in anyone's mind as to what the result would be. And when the election came, despite the frantic efforts of the Republicans, Georgia once more had a Democratic governor.

There was joy then, excitement too, but of a different sort from that which seized the town when Bullock took to his heels. This was a more sober heartfelt joy, a deep-souled feeling of thanksgiving, and the churches were filled as ministers reverently thanked God for the deliverance of the state. There was pride too, mingled with the elation and joy, pride that Georgia was back in the hands of her own people again, in spite of all the administration in Washington could do, in spite of the army, the Carpetbaggers, the Scallawags and the native Republicans.

Seven times Congress had passed crushing acts against the state to keep it a conquered province, three times the army had set aside civil law. The negroes had frolicked through the legislature, grasping aliens had mismanaged the government, private individuals had enriched themselves from public funds. Georgia had been helpless, tormented abused, hammered down. But now, in spite of them all, Georgia belonged to herself again and through the efforts of her own people.

The sudden overturn of the Republicans did not bring joy to everyone. There was consternation in the ranks of the Scallawags, the Carpetbaggers and the Republicans. The Gelerts and Hundons, evidently apprised of Bullock's departure before his resignation became public, left town abruptly, disappearing into that oblivion from which they had come. The other Carpetbaggers and Scallawags who remained were uncertain, frightened, and they hovered together for comfort, wondering what the legislative investigation would bring to light concerning their own private affairs. They were not insolent now. They were stunned, bewildered, afraid. And the ladies who called on Scarlett said over and over: 'But who would have thought it would turn out this way? We thought the governor was too powerful. We thought he was here to stay. We thought—'

Scarlett was equally bewildered by the turn of events, despite Rhett's warning as to the direction it would take. It was not that she was sorry Bullock had gone and the Democrats were back again. Though no one would have believed it she, too, felt a grim happiness that the Yankee rule was at last thrown off. She remembered all too vividly her struggles during those first days of Reconstruction, her fears that the soldiers and the Carpetbaggers would confiscate her money and her property. She remembered her helplessness and her panic at her helplessness and her hatred of the Yankees who had imposed this galling system upon the South. And she had never stopped hating them. But, in trying to make the best of things, in trying to obtain complete security, she had gone with the conquerors. No matter how much she disliked them, she had surrounded herself with them, cut herself off from her old friends and her old way of living. And now the power of the conquerors was at an end. She had gambled on the continuance of the Bullock régime and she had lost.

As she looked about her, that Christmas of 1871, the happiest Christmas the state had known in over ten years, she was disquieted. She could not help seeing that Rhett, once the most execrated man in Atlanta, was now one of the most popular, for he had humbly recanted his Republican heresies and given his time and money and labour and thought to helping Georgia fight her way back. When he rode down the streets, smiling, tipping his hat, the small blue bundle that was Bonnie perched before him on his saddle, everyone smiled back, spoke with enthusiasm and looked with affection on the little girl. Whereas, she, Scarlett—

Chapter LIX

There was no doubt in anyone's mind that Bonnie Butler was running wild and needed a firm hand, but she was so general a favourite that no one had the heart to attempt the necessary firmness. She had first gotten out of control during the months when she travelled with her father. When she had been with Rhett in New Orleans and Charleston she had been permitted to sit up as late as she pleased and had gone to sleep in his arms in theatres, restaurants and at card-tables. Thereafter, nothing short of force would make her go to bed at the same time as the obedient Ella. While she had been away with him, Rhett had let her wear any dress she chose and, since that time, she had gone into tantrums when Mammy tried to dress her in dimity frocks and pinafores instead of blue taffeta and lace collars.

There seemed no way to regain the ground which had been lost when the child was away from home and later when Scarlett had been ill and at Tara. As Bonnie grew older Scarlett tried to discipline her, tried to keep her from becoming too headstrong and spoiled, but with little success. Rhett always sided with the child, no matter how foolish her desires or how outrageous her behaviour. He encouraged her to talk and treated her as an adult, listening to her opinions with apparent seriousness and pretending to be guided by them. As a result, Bonnie interrupted her elders whenever she pleased and contradicted her father and put him in his place. He only laughed and would not permit Scarlett even to slap the little girl's hand by way of reprimand.

'If she wasn't such a sweet, darling thing, she'd be impossible,' thought Scarlett ruefully, realizing that she had a child with a will equal to her own. 'She adores Rhett and he could make her behave better if he wanted to.'

But Rhett showed no inclination to make Bonnie behave. Whatever she did was right and if she wanted the moon she could have it, if he could reach it for her. His pride in her beauty, her curls, her dimples, her graceful little gestures was boundless. He loved her pertness, her high spirits and the quaint sweet manner she had of showing her love for him. For all her spoiled and wilful ways she was such a lovable child that he lacked the heart to try to curb her. He was her god, the centre of her small world, and that was too precious for him to risk losing by reprimands.

She clung to him like a shadow. She woke him earlier than he cared to wake, sat beside him at the table, eating alternately from his plate and her own, rode in front of him on his horse and permitted no one but Rhett to undress her and put her to sleep in the small bed beside his.

It amused and touched Scarlett to see the iron hand with which the small child ruled her father. Who would have thought that Rhett, of all people, would take fatherhood so seriously? But sometimes a dart of jealousy went through Scarlett because Bonnie, at the age of four, understood Rhett better than she had ever understood him and could manage him better than she had ever managed him.

When Bonnie was four years old, Mammy began to grumble about the impropriety of a girl child riding 'a-straddle in front of her pa wid her dress flyin' up'. Rhett lent an attentive ear to this remark, as he did to all Mammy's remarks about the proper raising of little girls. The result was a small brown and white Shetland pony with a long silky mane and tail and a tiny side-saddle with silver trimmings. Ostensibly the pony was for all three children and Rhett bought a saddle for Wade too. But Wade infinitely preferred his St Bernard dog and Ella was afraid of all animals. So the pony became Bonnie's own and was named 'Mr Butler'. The only flaw in Bonnie's possessive joy was that she could not still ride astride like her father, but after he had explained how much more difficult it was to ride on a side-saddle, she was content and learned rapidly. Rhett's pride in her good seat and her good hands was enormous.

'Wait till she's old enough to hunt,' he boasted. 'There'll be no one like her on any field. I'll take her to Virginia then. That's where the real hunting is. And Kentucky where they appreciate good riders.'

When it came to making her riding habit, as usual she had her choice of colours and as usual chose blue.

'But, my darling! Not that blue velvet! The blue velvet is for a party dress for me,' laughed Scarlett. 'A nice black broadcoth is what little girls wear.' Seeing the small black brows coming together: 'For Heaven's sake, Rhett, tell her how unsuitable it would be and how dirty it will get.'

'Oh, let her have the blue velvet. If it gets dirty, we'll make her another one,' said Rhett easily.

So Bonnie had her blue velvet habit with a skirt that trailed down the pony's side and a black hat with a red plume in it, because Aunt Melly's stories of Jeb Stuart's plume had appealed to her imagination. On days that were bright and clear the two could be seen riding down Peachtree Street, Rhett reining in his big black horse to keep pace with the fat pony's gait. Sometimes they went tearing down the quiet roads about the town, scattering chickens and dogs and children, Bonnie beating Mr Butler with her crop, her tangled curls flying, Rhett holding in his horse with a firm hand that she might think Mr Butler was winning the race.

When he had assured himself of her seat, her hands, her utter fearlessness, Rhett decided that the time had come for her to learn to make the low jumps that were within the reach of Mr Butler's short legs. To this end, he built a hurdle in the back yard and paid Wash, one of Uncle Peter's small nephews, twenty-five cents a day to teach Mr Butler to jump. He began with a bar two inches from the ground and gradually worked up to the height of a foot.

This arrangement met with the disapproval of the three parties most concerned, Wash, Mr Butler and Bonnie. Wash was afraid of horses and only the princely sum offered induced him to take the stubborn pony over the bar dozens of times a day; Mr Butler, who bore with equanimity having his tail pulled by his small mistress and his hooves examined constantly, felt that the Creator of ponies had not intended him to put his fat body over the bar; Bonnie, who could not bear to see anyone else upon her pony, danced with impatience while Mr Butler was learning his lessons.

When Rhett finally decided that the pony knew his business well enough to trust Bonnie upon him, the child's excitement was boundless. She made her first jump with flying colours and, thereafter, riding abroad with her father held no charms for her. Scarlett could not help laughing at the pride and enthusiasm of father and daughter. She thought, however, that once the novelty had passed, Bonnie would turn to other things and the neighbourhood would have some peace. But this sport did not pall. There was a bare track worn from the arbour at the far end of the back yard to the hurdle, and all morning long the yard resounded with excited yells. Grandpa Merriwether, who had made the overland trip in 1849, said that the yells sounded just like an Apache after a successful scalping.

After the first week, Bonnie begged for a higher bar, a bar that was a foot and a half from the ground

'When you are six years old,' said Rhett. 'Then you'll be big enough for a higher jump and I'll buy you a bigger horse. Mr Butler's legs aren't long enough.'

'They are, too. I jumped Aunt Melly's rose bushes and they are 'normously high!'

'No, you must wait,' said Rhett, firm for once. But the firmness gradually faded away before her incessant importunings and tantrums.

'Oh, all right,' he said with a laugh one morning and moved the narrow white cross-bar higher. 'If you fall off, don't cry and blame me!'

'Mother!' screamed Bonnie, turning her head up toward Scarlett's bedroom. 'Mother! Watch me! Daddy says I can!'

Scarlett, who was combing her hair, came to the window and smiled down at the tiny excited figure, so absurd in the soiled blue habit.

'I really must get her another habit,' she thought. 'Though Heaven only knows how I'll make her give up that dirty one.'

'Mother, watch!'

'I'm watching, dear,' said Scarlett, smiling.

As Rhett lifted the child and set her on the pony, Scarlett called with a swift rush of pride at the straight back and the proud set of the head: 'You're mighty pretty, precious!'

'So are you,' said Bonnie generously and, hammering a heel into Mr Butler's ribs, she galloped down the yard toward the arbour.

'Mother, watch me take this one!' she cried, laying on the crop.

Watch me take this one!

Memory rang a bell far back in Scarlett's mind. There was something ominous about those words. What was it? Why couldn't she remember? She looked down at her small daughter, so lightly poised on the galloping pony, and her brow wrinkled as a chill swept swiftly through her breast.

Bonnie came on with a rush, her crisp black curls jerking, her blue eyes blazing.

'They are like Pa's eyes,' thought Scarlett, 'Irish blue eyes, and she's just like him in every way.'

And, as she thought of Gerald, the memory for which she had been fumbling came to her swiftly, came with the heart-stopping clarity of summer lightning, throwing, for an instant, a whole countryside into unnatural brightness. She could hear an Irish voice singing, hear the hard rapid pounding of hooves coming up the pasture hill at Tara, hear a reckless voice, so like the voice of her child: 'Ellen! Watch me take this one!'

'No!' she cried. 'No! Oh, Bonnie, stop!'

Even as she leaned from the window there was a fearful sound of splintering wood, a hoarse cry from Rhett, a mêlée of blue velvet and flying hooves on the ground. Then Mr Butler scrambled to his feet and trotted off with an empty saddle.

On the third night after Bonnie's death, Mammy waddled slowly up the kitchen steps of Melanie's house. She was dressed in black from her huge men's shoes, slashed to permit freedom for her toes, to her black head-rag. Her blurred old eyes were bloodshot and red-rimmed, and misery cried out in every line of her mountainous figure. Her face was puckered in the sad bewilderment of an old ape but there was determination in her jaw.

She spoke a few soft words to Dilcey who nodded kindly, as though an unspoken armistice existed in their old feud. Dilcey put down the supper dishes she was holding and went quietly through the pantry toward the dining-room. In a minute Melanie was in the kitchen, her table-napkin in her hand, anxiety in her face.

'Miss Scarlett isn't—'

'Miss Scarlett bearin' up, same as allus,' said Mammy heavily. 'Ah din' ten' ter 'sturb yo' supper, Miss Melly. Ah kin wait tell you thoo ter tell you whut Ah got on mah mine.'

'Supper can wait,' said Melanie. 'Dilcey, serve the rest of the supper. Mammy, come with me.'

Mammy waddled after her, down the hall past the dining-room where Ashley sat at the head of the table, his own little Beau beside him and Scarlett's two children opposite, making a great clatter with their soup-spoons. The happy voices of Wade and Ella filled the room. It was like a picnic for them to spend so long a visit with Aunt Melly. Aunt Melly was always so kind and she was especially so now. The death of their younger sister had affected them very little. Bonnie had fallen off her pony and Mother had cried a long time and Aunt Melly had taken them home with her to play in the back yard with Beau and have tea-cakes whenever they wanted them.

Melanie led the way to the small book-lined room, shut the door and motioned Mammy to the sofa.

'I was going over right after supper,' she said. 'Now that Captain Butler's mother has come, I suppose the funeral will be tomorrow morning.'

'De fune'l. Dat's jes' it,' said Mammy. 'Miss Melly, we's all in deep trouble an' Ah's come ter you fer he'p. Ain' nuthin' but weery load, honey, nuthin' but weery load.'

'Has Miss Scarlett collapsed?' questioned Melanie worriedly. 'I've hardly seen her since Bonnie—She has been in her room and Captain Butler has been out of the house and—'

Suddenly tears began to flow down Mammy's black face. Melanie sat down beside her and patted her arm and, after a moment, Mammy lifted the hem of her black skirt and dried her eyes.

'You got ter come he'p us, Miss Melly. Ah done de bes' Ah kin but it doan do no good.'

'Miss Scarlett—'

Mammy straightened.

'Miss Melly, you knows Miss Scarlett well's Ah does. Whut dat chile got ter stan', de good Lawd give her strent ter stan'. Disyere done broke her heart but she kin stan' it. It's Mist' Rhett Ah come 'bout.'

'I have so wanted to see him but whenever I've been there, he has either been downtown or locked in his room with—And Scarlett has looked like a ghost and wouldn't speak—Tell me quickly, Mammy. You know I'll help if I can.'

Mammy wiped her nose on the back of her hand.

'Ah say Miss Scarlett kin stan' whut de Lawd sen', kase she done had ter stan' a-plen'y, but Mist' Rhett— Miss Melly, he ain' never had ter stan' nuthin' he din' wanter stan', not nuthin'. It's him Ah come ter see you 'bout.'

'But—'

'Miss Melly, you got ter come home wid me, dis evenin'.' There was urgency in Mammy's voice. 'Maybe Mist' Rhett lissen ter you. He allus did think a heap of yo' 'pinion.'

'Oh, Mammy, what is it? What do you mean?'

Mammy squared her shoulders.

'Miss Melly, Mist' Rhett done – done los' his mine. He woan let us put Lil Miss away.'

'Lost his mind? Oh, Mammy, no!'

'Ah ain' lyin'. It's de Gawd's truff. He ain' gwine let us buhy dat chile. He done tole me so hisseff, not mo'n an hour ago.'

'But he can't – he isn't—'

'Dat's huccome Ah say he los' his mine.'

'But why—'

'Miss Melly, Ah tell you eve'ything. Ah oughtn' tell nobody, but you is our fambly an' you is de onlies' one Ah kin tell. Ah tell you eve'thing. You knows whut a sto' he set by dat chile. Ah ain' never seed no man, black or w'ite, set sech a sto' by any chile. Look lak he go plumb crazy w'en Doctah Meade say her neck broke. He grab his gun an' he run right out an' shoot dat po' pony an', fo' Gawd, Ah think he gwine shoot hisseff. Ah wuz plumb 'stracted whut wid Miss Scarlett in a swoon an' all de neighbours in an' outer de house an' Mist' Rhett cahyin' on an' jes' holin' dat chile an' not even lettin' me wash her lil face whar de grabble cut it. An' w'en Miss Scarlett come to, Ah think, bress Gawd! Now dey kin comfo't each other.'

Again the tears began to fall but this time Mammy did not even wipe them away.

'But w'en she come to, she go inter de room whar he settin', holin' Miss Bonnie, an' she say: "Gimme mah baby whut you kilt." '

'Oh, no! She couldn't!'

'Yas'm. Dat whut she say. She say: "You kilt her." An' Ah felt so sorry fer Mist' Rhett Ah bust out cryin', kase he look lak a whup houn'. An' Ah say: "Give dat chile ter its mammy. Ah ain' gwine have no sech goin's-on over mah Lil Miss." An' Ah tek de chile away frum him an' tek her inter her room an' wash her face. An' Ah hear dem talkin' an' it lak ter tuhn mah blood cole, whut dey say. Miss Scarlett wuz callin' him a mudderer for lettin' her try ter jump dat high, an' him sayin' Miss Scarlett hadn' never keered nuthin' 'bout Miss Bonnie nor none of her chillun . . .'

'Stop, Mammy! Don't tell me any more. It isn't right for you to tell me this!' cried Melanie, her mind shrinking away from the picture Mammy's words evoked.

'Ah knows Ah got no bizness tellin' you, but mah heart too full ter know jes' whut not ter say. Den he tuck her ter de unnertaker's hisseff an' he bring her back an' he put her in her baid in his room. An' w'en Miss Scarlett say she b'long in de pahlour in de coffin, Ah thought Mist' Rhett gwine hit her. An' he say, right cole lak: "She b'long in mah room." An' he tuhn ter me an' he say: "Mammy, you see dat she stay right hyah tell Ah gits back." Den he light outer de house on de hawse an' he wuz gone tell 'bout sundown. W'en he come t'arin' home, Ah seed dat he'd been drinkin' an' drinkin' heavy, but he wuz cahyin' it well's usual. He fling inter de house an' not even speak ter Miss Scarlett or Miss Pitty or any of de ladies as wuz callin', but he fly up de steps an' th'ow open de do' of his room an' den he yell fer me. W'en Ah comes runnin' as fas' as Ah kin, he wuz stan'in' by de baid an' it wuz so dahk in de room Ah couldn' sceercely see him, kase de shutters wuz done drawed.

'An' he say ter me, right fierce lak: "Open dem shutters. It's dahk in hyah." An' Ah fling dem open an' he look at me an', fo' Gawd, Miss Melly, mah knees 'bout give way, kase he look so strange. Den he say: "Bring lights. Bring lots of lights. An' keep dem buhnin'. An' doan draw no shades an' no shutters. Doan you know Miss Bonnie's 'fraid of de dahk?" '

Melanie's horror-struck eyes met Mammy's and Mammy nodded ominously.

'Dat's whut he say. "Miss Bonnie's 'fraid of de dahk." '

Mammy shivered.

'W'en Ah gits him a dozen candles, he say "Git!" An' den he lock de do' an' dar he set wid Lil Miss, an' he din' open de do' fer Miss Scarlett even w'en she beat an' hollered ter him. An' dat's de way it been fer two days. He woan say nuthin' 'bout de fune'l, an' in de mawnin' he lock de do' an' git on his hawse an' go off ter town. An' he come back at sundown drunk an' lock hisseff in agin, an' he ain' et nuthin' or slept none. An' now his ma, Ole Miss Butler, she come frum Cha'ston fer de fune'l an' Miss Suellen an' Mist' Will, dey come frum Tara, but Mist' Rhett woan talk ter none of dem. Oh, Miss Melly, it been awful! An' it's gwine be wuss, an' folks gwine talk sumpin' scan'lous.

'An' den, dis evenin'.' Mammy paused and again wiped her nose on her hand. 'Dis evenin' Miss Scarlett ketch him in de upstairs hall w'en he come in, an' she go in de room wid him an' she say: "De fune'l set fer termorrer mawnin'." An' he say: "Do dat an' Ah kills you termorrer." '

'Oh, he must have lost his mind!'

'Yas'm. An' den dey talks kinder low an' Ah doan hear all whut dey say, 'cept he say agin 'bout Miss Bonnie bein' sceered of de dahk an' de grabe pow'ful dahk. An' affer a w'ile, Miss Scarlett say: "You is a fine one ter tek on so, affer killin' her ter please yo' pride." An' he say: "Ain' you got no mercy?" An' she say: "No. An' Ah ain' got no chile, needer. An' Ah'm wo' out wid de way you been ackin' sence Bonnie wuz kilt. You is a scan'al ter de town. You been drunk all de time an' ef you doan think Ah knows whar you been spendin' yo' days, you is a fool. Ah knows you been down ter dat creeter's house, dat Belle Watling." '

'Oh, Mammy, no!'

'Yas'm. Dat whut she said. An', Miss Melly, it's de truff. Niggers knows a heap of things quicker dan w'ite folks, an' Ah knowed dat's whar he been but Ah ain' said nuthin' 'bout it. An' he doan deny it. He say: "Yas'm, dat's whar Ah been an' you neen tek on, kase you doan give a damn. A bawdy-house is a haben of refuge affer dis house of hell. An' Belle is got one of de worl's kin'es' hearts. She doan th'ow it up ter me dat Ah done kilt mah chile." '

'Oh,' cried Melanie, stricken to the heart.

Her own life was so pleasant, so sheltered, so wrapped about with people who loved her, so full of kindness that what Mammy told her was almost beyond comprehension or belief. Yet there crawled into her mind a memory, a picture which she hastily put from her, as she would put from her the thought of another's nudity. Rhett had spoken of Belle Watling the day he cried with his head on her knees. But he loved Scarlett. She could not have been mistaken that day. And, of course, Scarlett loved him. What had come between them? How could a husband and wife cut each other to pieces with such sharp knives?

Mammy took up her story heavily.

'Affer a w'ile, Miss Scarlett come outer de room, w'ite as a sheet but her jaw set, an' she see me stan'in' dar an' she say: "De fune'l be termorrer, Mammy." An' she pass me by lak a ghos'. Den mah heart tuhn over, kase whut Miss Scarlett say, she mean. An' whut Mist' Rhett say, he mean too. An' he say he kill her ef she do dat. Ah wuz plumb 'stracted, Miss Melly, kase Ah done had sumpin' on mah conscience all de time an' it weighin' me down. Miss Melly, it wuz me as sceered Lil Miss of de dahk.'

'Oh, but Mammy, it doesn't matter – not now.'

'Yas'm, it do. Dat whut de whole trouble. An' it come ter me Ah better tell Mist' Rhett even ef he kill me, kase it on mah conscience. So Ah slip in de do' real quick, fo' he kin lock it, an' Ah say: "Mist' Rhett, Ah's come ter confess." An' he swing roun' on me lak a crazy man an' say: "Git!" An', fo' Gawd, Ah ain' never been so sceered! But Ah say: "Please, suh, Mist' Rhett, let me tell you. It's 'bout ter kill me. It wuz me as sceered Lil Miss of de dahk." An' den, Miss Melly, Ah put mah haid down an' waited fer him ter hit me. But he din' say nuthin'. An' Ah say: "Ah din' mean no hahm. But, Mist' Rhett, dat chile din' have no caution an' she wuzn' sceered of nuthin'. An' she wuz allus gittin' outer baid affer eve'ybody sleep an' runnin' roun' de house barefoot. An' it worrit me, kase Ah 'fraid she hu't herseff. So Ah tells her dar's ghos'es an' buggerboos in de dahk."

'An' den – Miss Melly, you know whut he done? His face got right gentle lak an' he come ter me an' put his han' on mah arm. Dat's de fust time he ever done dat. An' he say: "She wuz so brave, wuzn' she? 'Cept fer de dahk, she wuzn' sceered of nuthin'." An' w'en Ah bust out cryin' he say: "Now, Mammy," an' he pat me. "Now, Mammy, doan you cahy on so. Ah's glad you tole me. Ah knows you love Miss Bonnie an' kase you love her, it doan matter. It's whut de heart is dat matter." Well'm, dat kinder cheered me up, so Ah ventu' ter say: "Mist' Rhett, suh, whut 'bout de fune'l?" Den he tuhn on me lak a wile man an' his eyes glitter an' he say: "Good Gawd, Ah thought you'd unnerstan' even ef nobody else din'! Does you think Ah'm gwine ter put mah chile away in de dahk w'en she so sceered of it? Right now Ah kin hear de way she useter scream w'en she wake up in de dahk. Ah ain' gwine have her sceered." Miss Melly, den Ah know he los' his mine. He drunk an' he need sleep an' sumpin' ter eat but dat ain' all. He plumb crazy. He jes' push me outer de do' an' say: "Git de hell outer hyah!"

'Ah goes downstairs an' Ah gits ter thinkin' dat he say dar ain' gwine be no fune'l an' Miss Scarlett say it be termorrer mawnin' an' he say dar be shootin'. An' all de kinfolks in de house an' all de neighbours already gabblin' 'bout it lak a flock of guinea-hens, an' Ah thought of you, Miss Melly. You got ter come he'p us.'

'Oh, Mammy, I couldn't intrude!'

'Ef you kain, who kin?'

'But what could I do, Mammy?'

'Miss Melly, Ah doan know. But you kin do sumpin'. You kin talk ter

Mist' Rhett an' maybe he lissen ter you. He set a gret sto' by you, Miss Melly. Maybe you doan know it, but he do. Ah done hear him say time an' agin, you is de onlies' gret lady he knows.'

'But—'

Melanie rose to her feet, confused, her heart quailing at the thought of confronting Rhett. The thought of arguing with a man as grief-crazed as the one Mammy depicted made her go cold. The thought of entering that brightly lighted room where lay the little girl she loved so much wrung her heart. What could she do? What could she say to Rhett that would ease his grief and bring him back to reason? For a moment she stood irresolute and through the closed door came the sound of her boy's treble laughter. Like a cold knife in her heart came the thought of him dead. Suppose her Beau were lying upstairs, his little body cold and still, his merry laughter hushed.

'Oh,' she cried aloud, in fright, and in her mind she clutched him close to her heart. She knew how Rhett felt. If Beau were dead, how could she put him away, alone with the wind and the rain and the darkness?

'Oh! Poor, poor Captain Butler!' she cried. 'I'll go to him now, right away.'

She sped back to the dining-room, said a few soft words to Ashley and surprised her little boy by hugging him close to her and kissing his blond curls passionately.

She left the house without a hat, her dinner-napkin still clutched in her hand, and the pace she set was hard for Mammy's old legs. Once in Scarlett's front hall, she bowed briefly to the gathering in the library, to the frightened Miss Pittypat, the stately old Mrs Butler, Will and Suellen. She went up the stairs swiftly, with Mammy panting behind her. For a moment, she paused before Scarlett's closed door but Mammy hissed, 'No'm, doan do dat.'

Down the hall Melly went, more slowly now, and stopped in front of Rhett's room. She stood irresolutely for a moment as though she longed to take flight. Then, bracing herself, like a small soldier going into battle, she knocked on the door and called softly: 'Please let me in, Captain Butler. It's Mrs Wilkes. I want to see Bonnie.'

The door opened quickly and Mammy, shrinking back into the shadows of the hall, saw Rhett huge and dark against the blazing background of candles. He was swaying on his feet and Mammy could smell the whisky on his breath. He looked down at Melly for a moment and then, taking her by the arm, he pulled her into the room and shut the door.

Mammy edged herself stealthily to a chair beside the door and sank into it wearily, her shapeless body overflowing it. She sat still, weeping silently and praying. Now and then she lifted the hem of her dress and wiped her eyes. Strain her ears as hard as she might, she could hear no words from the room, only a low broken humming sound.

After an interminable period, the door cracked open and Melly's face, white and strained, appeared.

'Bring me a pot of coffee, quickly, and some sandwiches.'

When the devil drove, Mammy could be as swift as a lithe black sixteen-year-old and her curiosity to get into Rhett's room made her work faster. But her hope turned to disappointment when Melly merely opened the door a crack and took the tray. For a long time Mammy strained her sharp ears but she could distinguish nothing except the clatter of silver on china, and the muffled soft tones of Melanie's voice. Then she heard the creaking of the bed as a heavy body fell upon it and, soon after, the sound of boots dropping to the floor. After an interval, Melanie appeared in the doorway but, strive though she might, Mammy could not see past her into the room. Melanie looked tired and there were tears glistening on her lashes but her face was serene again.

'Go tell Miss Scarlett that Captain Butler is quite willing for the funeral to take place tomorrow morning,' she whispered.

'Bress Gawd!' ejaculated Mammy. 'How on uth—'

'Don't talk so loud. He's going to sleep. And, Mammy, tell Miss Scarlett, too, that I'll be here all night and you bring me some coffee. Bring it here.'

'Ter disyere room?'

'Yes, I promised Captain Butler that if he would go to sleep I would sit up by her all night. Now go tell Miss Scarlett, so she won't worry any more.'

Mammy started off down the hall, her weight shaking the floor, her relieved heart singing, 'Hallelujah! Hallelujah!' She paused thoughtfully outside of Scarlett's door, her mind in a ferment of thankfulness and curiosity.

'How Miss Melly done it beyon' me. De angels fight on her side, Ah specs. Ah'll tell Miss Scarlett de fune'l termorrer but Ah specs Ah better keep hid dat Miss Melly settin' up wid Lil Miss. Miss Scarlett ain' gwine lak dat a-tall.'

Chapter LX

Something was wrong with the world, a sombre, frightening wrongness that pervaded everything like a dark impenetrable mist, stealthily closing around Scarlett. This wrongness went even deeper than Bonnie's death, for now the first unbearable anguish was fading into resigned acceptance of her loss. Yet this eerie sense of disaster to come persisted, as though something black and hooded stood just at her shoulder, as though the ground beneath her feet might turn to quicksand as she trod upon it.

She had never before known this type of fear. All her life her feet had been firmly planted in common sense and the only things she had ever feared had been the things she could see, injury, hunger, poverty, loss of Ashley's love. Unanalytical, she was trying to analyse now and with no success. She had lost her dearest child but she could stand that, somehow, as she had stood other crushing losses. She had her health, she had as much money as she could wish and she still had Ashley, though she saw less and less of him these days. Even the constraint which had been between them since the day of Melanie's ill-starred surprise party did not worry her, for she knew it would pass. No, her fear was not of pain or hunger or loss of love. Those fears had never weighed her down as this feeling of wrongness was doing – this blighting fear that was oddly like that which she knew in her old nightmare, a thick, swimming mist through which she ran with bursting heart, a lost child seeking a haven that was hidden from her.

She remembered how Rhett had always been able to laugh her out of her fears. She remembered the comfort of his broad brown chest and his strong arms. And so she turned to him with eyes that really saw him for the first time in weeks. And the change she saw shocked her. This man was not going to laugh, nor was he going to comfort her.

For some time after Bonnie's death she had been too angry with him, too preoccupied with her own grief to do more than speak politely in front of the servants. She had been too busy remembering the swift running patter of Bonnie's feet and her bubbling laugh to think that he, too, might be remembering and with pain even greater than her own. Throughout these weeks they had met and spoken as courteously as strangers meeting in the impersonal walls of a hotel, sharing the same roof, the same table, but never sharing the thoughts of each other.

Now that she was frightened and lonely, she would have broken through this barrier if she could, but she found that he was holding her at arm's length, as though he wished to have no words with her that went beneath the surface. Now that her anger was fading she wanted to tell him that she held him guiltless of Bonnie's death. She wanted to cry in his arms and say that she, too, had been overly proud of the child's horsemanship, overly indulgent to her wheedlings. Now she would willingly have humbled herself and admitted that she had only hurled that accusation at him out of her misery, hoping by hurting him to alleviate her own hurt. But there never seemed an opportune moment. He looked at her out of black blank eyes that made no opportunity for her to speak. And apologies, once postponed, become harder and harder to make, and finally impossible.

She wondered why this should be. Rhett was her husband and between them there was the unbreakable bond of two people who have shared the same bed, begotten and borne a loved child and seen that child, too soon, laid away in the dark. Only in the arms of the father of that child could she find comfort, in the exchange of memories and grief that might hurt at first but would help to heal. But, now, as matters stood between them, she would as soon go to the arms of a complete stranger.

He was seldom at home. When they did sit down to supper together, he was usually drunk. He was not drinking as he had formerly, becoming increasingly more polished and biting as the liquor took hold of him, saying amusing, malicious things that made her laugh in spite of herself. Now he was silently, morosely drunk and, as the evenings progressed, soddenly drunk. Sometimes, in the early hours of the dawn, she heard him ride into the back yard and beat on the door of the servants' house so that Pork might help him up the back stairs and put him to bed. Put him to bed! Rhett who had always drunk others under the table without turning a hair and then put them to bed.

He was untidy now, where once he had been well groomed, and it took all Pork's scandalized arguing even to make him change his linen before supper. Whisky was showing in his face and the hard line of his long jaw was being obscured under an unhealthy bloat and puffs rising under his bloodshot eyes. His big body with its hard swelling muscles looked soft and slack and his waistline began to thicken.

Often he did not come home at all or even send word that he would be away overnight. Of course, he might be snoring drunkenly in some room above a saloon, but Scarlett always believed that he was at Belle Watling's house on these occasions. Once she had seen Belle in a store, a coarse overblown woman now, with most of her good looks gone. But, for all her paint and flashy clothes, she was buxom and almost motherly-looking. Instead of dropping her eyes or glaring defiantly, as did other light women when confronted by ladies, Belle gave her stare for stare, searching her face with an intent, almost pitying look that brought a flush to Scarlett's cheek.

But she could not accuse him now, could not rage at him, demand fidelity or try to shame him, any more than she could bring herself to apologize for accusing him of Bonnie's death. She was clutched by a bewildered apathy, an unhappiness that she could not understand, an unhappiness that went deeper than anything she had ever known. She was lonely and she could never remember being so lonely before. Perhaps she had never had the time to be very lonely until now. She was lonely and afraid and there was no one to whom she could turn, no one except Melanie. For now, even Mammy, her mainstay, had gone back to Tara. Gone permanently.

Mammy gave no explanation for her departure. Her tired old eyes looked sadly at Scarlett when she asked for the train fare home. To Scarlett's tears and pleading that she stay, Mammy only answered: 'Look ter me lak Miss Ellen say ter me: "Mammy, come home. Yo' wuk done finish." So Ah's gwine home.'

Rhett, who had listened to the talk, gave Mammy the money and patted her arm.

'You're right, Mammy. Miss Ellen is right. Your work here is done. Go home. Let me know if you ever need anything.' And as Scarlett broke into renewed indignant commands: 'Hush, you fool! Let her go! Why should anyone want to stay in this house – now?'

There was such a savage bright glitter in his eyes when he spoke that Scarlett shrank from him, frightened.

'Dr Meade, do you think he can – can have lost his mind?' she questioned afterwards, driven to the doctor by her own sense of helplessness.

'No,' said the doctor, 'but he's drinking like a fish and will kill himself if he keeps it up. He loved the child, Scarlett, and I guess he drinks to forget about her. Now, my advice to you, Miss, is to give him another baby just as quickly as you can.'

'Hah!' thought Scarlett bitterly, as she left his office. That was easier said than done. She would gladly have another child, several children, if they would take that look out of Rhett's eyes and fill up the aching spaces in her own heart. A boy who had Rhett's dark handsomeness and another little girl. Oh, for another girl, pretty and gay and wilful and full of laughter, not like the giddy-brained Ella. Why, oh, why couldn't God have taken Ella if He had to take one of her children? Ella was no comfort to her, now that Bonnie was gone. But Rhett did not seem to want any other children. At least he never came to her bedroom, though now the door was never locked and usually invitingly ajar. He did not seem to care. He did not seem to care for anything now except whisky and that blowzy red-haired woman.

He was bitter now, where he had been pleasantly jeering, brutal where his thrusts had once been tempered with humour. After Bonnie died, many of the good ladies of the neighbourhood who had been won over to him by his charming manners with his daughter were anxious to show him kindness. They stopped him on the street to give him their sympathy and spoke to him from over their hedges, saying that they understood. But now that Bonnie, the reason for his good manners, was gone the manners went too. He cut the ladies and their well-meant condolences off shortly, rudely.

But, oddly enough, the ladies were not offended. They understood, or thought they understood. When he rode home in the twilight almost too drunk to stay in the saddle, scowling at those who spoke to him, the ladies said 'Poor thing!' and redoubled their efforts to be kind and gentle. They felt very sorry for him, broken-hearted and riding home to no better comfort than Scarlett.

Everybody knew how cold and heartless she was. Everybody was appalled at the seeming ease with which she had recovered from Bonnie's death, never realizing or caring to realize the effort that lay behind that seeming recovery. Rhett had the town's tenderest sympathy and he neither knew nor cared. Scarlett had the town's dislike and, for once, she would have welcomed the sympathy of old friends.

Now, none of her old friends came to the house, except Aunt Pitty, Melanie and Ashley. Only the new friends came calling in their shining carriages, anxious to tell her of their sympathy, eager to divert her with gossip about other new friends in whom she was not at all interested. All these 'new people', strangers, every one! They didn't know her. They would never know her. They had no realization of what her life had been before she reached her present safe eminence in her mansion on Peachtree Street. They didn't care to talk about what their lives had been before they attained stiff brocades and victorias with fine teams of horses. They didn't know of her struggles, her privations, all the things that made this great house and pretty clothes and silver and receptions worth having. They didn't know. They didn't care, these people from God-knows-where who seemed to live always on the surface of things, who had no common memories of war and hunger and fighting, who had no common roots going down into the same red earth.

Now, in her loneliness, she would have liked to while away the afternoons with Maybelle or Fanny or Mrs Elsing or Mrs Whiting or even that redoubtable old warrior, Mrs Merriwether. Or Mrs Bonnell or – or any of her old friends and neighbours. For they knew. They had known war and terror and fire, had seen dear ones dead before their time; they had hungered and been ragged, had lived with the wolf at the door. And they had rebuilt fortune from ruin.

It would be a comfort to sit with Maybelle, remembering that Maybelle had buried a baby, dead in the mad flight before Sherman. There would be solace in Fanny's presence, knowing that she and Fanny both had lost husbands in the black days of martial law. It would be grim fun to laugh with Mrs Elsing, recalling the old lady's face as she flogged her horse through Five Points the day Atlanta fell, her loot from the commissary jouncing from her carriage. It would be pleasant to match stories with Mrs Merriwether, now secure on the proceeds of her bakery, pleasant to say: 'Do you remember how bad things were right after the surrender? Do you remember when we didn't know where our next pair of shoes was coming from? And look at us now!'

Yes, it would be pleasant. Now she understood why when two ex-Confederates met, they talked of the war with so much relish, with pride, with nostalgia. Those had been days that tried their hearts but they had come through them. They were veterans. She was a veteran too, but she had no cronies with whom she could refight old battles. Oh, to be with her own kind of people again, those people who had been through the same things and knew how they hurt – and yet how great a part of you they were!

But, somehow, these people had slipped away. She realized that it was her own fault. She had never cared until now – now that Bonnie was dead and she was lonely and afraid and she saw across her shining dinner table a swarthy sodden stranger disintegrating under her eyes.

Chapter LXI

Scarlett was in Marietta when Rhett's urgent telegram came. There was a train leaving for Atlanta in ten minutes and she caught it, carrying no baggage except her reticule and leaving Wade and Ella at the hotel with Prissy.

Atlanta was only twenty miles away but the train crawled interminably through the wet early autumn afternoon, stopping at every bypath for passengers. Panic-stricken at Rhett's message, mad for speed, Scarlett almost screamed at every halt. Down the road lumbered the train through forests faintly, tiredly gold, past red hillsides still scarred with serpentine breastworks, past old battery emplacements and weed-grown craters, down the road over which Johnston's men had retreated so bitterly, fighting every step of the way. Each station, each crossroad the conductor called was the name of a battle, the site of a skirmish. Once they would have stirred Scarlett to memories of terror but now she had no thought for them.

Rhett's message had been:

'Mrs Wilkes ill. Come home immediately.'

Twilight had fallen when the train pulled into Atlanta and a light misting rain obscured the town. The gas street-lamps glowed dully, blobs of yellow in the fog. Rhett was waiting for her at the depot with the carriage. The very sight of his face frightened her more than his telegram. She had never seen it so expressionless before.

'She isn't—' she cried.

'No. She's still alive.' Rhett assisted her into the carriage. 'To Mrs Wilkes' house and as fast as you can go,' he ordered the coachman.

'What's the matter with her? I didn't know she was ill. She looked all right last week. Did she have an accident? Oh, Rhett, it isn't really as serious as you—'

'She's dying,' said Rhett, and his voice had no more expression than his face. 'She wants to see you.'

'Not Melly! Oh, not Melly! What's happened to her?'

'She's had a miscarriage.'

'A – a – mis— But, Rhett, she—' Scarlett floundered. This information on top of the horror of his announcement took her breath away.

'You did not know she was going to have a baby?'

She could not even shake her head.

'Ah, well. I suppose not. I don't think she told anyone. She wanted it to be a surprise. But I knew.'

'You knew? But surely she didn't tell you!'

'She didn't have to tell me. I knew. She's been so – happy these last two months I knew it couldn't mean anything else.'

'But, Rhett, the doctor said it would kill her to have another baby!'

'It has killed her,' said Rhett. And to the coachman: 'For God's sake, can't you drive faster?'

'But, Rhett, she can't be dying! I – I didn't and I—'

'She hasn't your strength. She's never had any strength. She's never had anything but heart.'

The carriage rocked to a standstill in front of the flat little house and Rhett handed her out. Trembling, frightened, a sudden feeling of loneliness upon her, she clasped his arm.

'You're coming in, Rhett?'

'No,' he said and got back into the carriage.

She flew up the front steps, across the porch and threw open the door. There, in the yellow lamplight, were Ashley, Aunt Pitty and India. Scarlett thought: 'What's India doing here? Melanie told her never to set foot in this house again.' The three rose at the sight of her, Aunt Pitty biting her trembling lips to still them, India staring at her, grief-stricken and without hate. Ashley looked dull as a sleepwalker and, as he came to her and put his hand upon her arm, he spoke like a sleepwalker.

'She asked for you,' he said. 'She asked for you.'

'Can I see her now?' She turned toward the closed door of Melanie's room.

'No. Dr Meade is in there now. I'm glad you've come, Scarlett.'

'I came as quickly as I could.' Scarlett shed her bonnet and her cloak. 'The train—She isn't really—Tell me, she's better, isn't she, Ashley? Speak to me! Don't look like that! She isn't really—'

'She kept asking for you,' said Ashley and looked her in the eyes. And in his eyes she saw the answer to her question. For a moment her heart stood still, and then a queer fear, stronger than anxiety, stronger than grief, began to beat in her breast. 'It can't be true,' she thought vehemently, trying to push back the fear. 'Doctors make mistakes. I won't think it's true. I can't let myself think it's true. I'll scream if I do. I must think of something else.'

'I don't believe it!' she cried stormily, looking into the three drawn faces as though defying them to contradict her. 'And why didn't Melanie tell me? I'd never have gone to Marietta if I'd known!'

Ashley's eyes awoke and were tormented.

'She didn't tell anyone, Scarlett, especially not you. She was afraid you'd scold her if you knew. She wanted to wait three – till she thought it safe and sure and then surprise you all and laugh and say how wrong the doctors had been. And she was so happy. You know how she was about babies – how much she's wanted a little girl. And everything went so well until – and then for no reason at all—'

The door of Melanie's room opened quietly and Dr Meade came out into the hall, shutting the door behind him. He stood for a moment, his grey beard sunk on his chest, and looked at the suddenly frozen four. His gaze fell last on Scarlett. As he came toward her, she saw that there was grief in his eyes and also dislike and contempt that flooded her frightened heart with guilt.

'So you finally got here,' he said.

Before she could answer, Ashley started toward the closed door.

'Not you, yet,' said the doctor. 'She wants to speak to Scarlett.'

'Doctor,' said India, putting a hand on his sleeve. Though her voice was toneless, it pleaded more loudly than words. 'Let me see her for a moment. I've been here since this morning, waiting, but she— Let me see her for a moment. I want to tell her – must tell her – that I was wrong about – something.'

She did not look at Ashley or Scarlett as she spoke, but Dr Meade allowed his cold glance to fall on Scarlett.

'I'll see, Miss India,' he said briefly. 'But only if you'll give me your word not to use up her strength telling her you were wrong. She knows you were wrong and it will only worry her to hear you apologize.'

Pitty began, timidly: 'Please, Dr Meade—'

'Miss Pitty, you know you'd scream and faint.'

Pitty drew up her stout little body and gave the doctor glance for glance. Her eyes were dry and there was dignity in every curve.

'Well, all right, honey, a little later,' said the doctor, more kindly. 'Come, Scarlett.'

They tiptoed down the hall to the closed door and the doctor put his hand on Scarlett's shoulder in a hard grip.

'Now, Miss,' he whispered briefly, 'no hysterics and no deathbed confessions from you or, before God, I will wring your neck! Don't give me any of your innocent stares. You know what I mean. Miss Melly is going to die easily and you aren't going to ease your own conscience by telling her anything about Ashley. I've never harmed a woman yet, but if you say anything now – you'll answer to me.'

He opened the door before she could answer, pushed her into the room and closed the door behind her. The little room, cheaply furnished in black walnut, was in semi-darkness, the lamp shaded with a newspaper. It was as small and prim a room as a schoolgirl's, the narrow little low-backed bed, the plain net curtains looped back, the clean faded rag rugs on the floor, were so different from the lavishness of Scarlett's own bedroom with its towering carved furniture, pink brocade draperies and rose-strewn carpet.

Melanie lay in the bed, her figure under the counterpane shrunken and flat like a little girl's. Two black braids fell on either side of her face and her closed eyes were sunken in twin purple circles. At the sight of her Scarlett stood transfixed, leaning against the door. Despite the gloom of the room, she could see that Melanie's face was of a waxy yellow colour. It was drained of life's blood and there was a pinched look about the nose. Until that moment, Scarlett had hoped Dr Meade was mistaken. But now she knew. In the hospitals during the war she had seen too many faces wearing this pinched look not to know what it inevitably presaged.

Melanie was dying, but for a moment Scarlett's mind refused to take it in. Melanie could not die. It was impossible for her to die. God wouldn't let her die when she, Scarlett, needed her so much. Never before had it occurred to her that she needed Melanie. But now, the truth surged in, down to the deepest recesses of her soul. She had relied on Melanie, even as she had relied upon herself, and she had never known it. Now, Melanie was dying and Scarlett knew she could not get along without her. Now, as she tiptoed across the room toward the quiet figure, panic clutching at her heart, she knew that Melanie had been her sword and her shield, her comfort and her strength.

'I must hold her! I can't let her get away!' she thought, and sank beside the bed with a rustle of skirts. Hastily she grasped the limp hand lying on the coverlet and was frightened anew by its chill.

'It's me, Melly,' she said.

Melanie's eyes opened a slit and then, as if having satisfied herself that it was really Scarlett, she closed them again. After a pause she drew a breath and whispered: 'Promise me?'

'Oh, anything!'

'Beau – look after him.'

Scarlett could only nod, a strangled feeling in her throat, and she gently pressed the hand she held by way of assent.

'I give him to you.' There was the faintest trace of a smile. 'I gave him to you, once before – 'member? – before he was born.'

Did she remember? Could she ever forget that time? Almost as clearly as if that dreadful day had returned, she could feel the stifling heat of the September noon, remember her terror of the Yankees, hear the tramp of the retreating troops, recall Melanie's voice begging her to take the baby should she die – remember, too, how she had hated Melanie that day and hoped that she would die.

'I've killed her,' she thought, in superstitious agony. 'I wished so often she would die and God heard me and is punishing me.'

'Oh, Melly, don't talk like that! You know you'll pull through this—'

'No. Promise.'

Scarlett gulped.

'You know I promise. I'll treat him like he was my own boy.'

'College?' asked Melanie's faint flat voice.

'Oh, yes! The university and Harvard and Europe and anything he wants – and – and – a pony – and music lessons—Oh, please, Melly, do try! Do make an effort!'

The silence fell again and in Melanie's face there were signs of a struggle to gather strength to speak again.

'Ashley,' she said. 'Ashley and you—' Her voice faltered into stillness.

At the mention of Ashley's name, Scarlett's heart stood still, cold as granite within her. Melanie had known all the time. Scarlett dropped her head on the coverlet and a sob that would not rise caught her throat with a cruel hand. Melanie knew. Scarlett was beyond shame now, beyond any feeling save a wild remorse that she had hurt this gentle creature throughout the long years. Melanie had known – and yet, she had remained her loyal friend. Oh, if she could only live those years over again! She would never even let her eyes meet those of Ashley.

'Oh, God,' she prayed rapidly, 'do, please, let her live! I'll make it up to her. I'll be so good to her. I'll never even speak to Ashley again as long as I live, if You'll only let her get well!'

'Ashley,' said Melanie feebly and her fingers reached out to touch Scarlett's bowed head. Her thumb and forefinger tugged with no more strength than that of a baby at Scarlett's hair. Scarlett knew what that meant, knew Melanie wanted her to look up. But she could not, could not meet Melanie's eyes and read that knowledge in them.

'Ashley,' Melanie whispered again, and Scarlett gripped herself. When she looked God in the face on the Day of Judgment and read her sentence in His eyes, it would not be as bad as this. Her soul cringed but she raised her head.

She saw only the same dark loving eyes, sunken and drowsy with death, the same tender mouth tiredly fighting pain for breath. No reproach was there, no accusation and no fear – only an anxiety that she might not find strength for words.

For a moment Scarlett was too stunned to even feel relief. Then, as she held Melanie's hand more closely, a flood of warm gratitude to God swept over her and, for the first time since her childhood, she said a humble unselfish prayer.

'Thank you, God. I know I'm not worth it, but thank you for not letting her know.'

'What about Ashley, Melly?'

'You'll – look after him?'

'Oh, yes.'

'He catches cold – so easily.'

There was a pause.

'Look after – his business – you understand?'

'Yes, I understand. I will.'

She made a great effort.

'Ashley isn't – practical.'

Only death could have forced that disloyalty from Melanie.

'Look after him, Scarlett – but – don't ever let him know.'

'I'll look after him and the business too, and I'll never let him know. I'll just kind of suggest things to him.'

Melanie managed a small smile but it was a triumphant one as her eyes met Scarlett's again. Their glance sealed the bargain that the protection of Ashley Wilkes from a too harsh world was passing from one woman to another and that Ashley's masculine pride should never be humbled by this knowledge.

Now the struggle went out of the tired face as though, with Scarlett's promise, ease had come to her.

'You're so smart – so brave – always been so good to me—'

At these words, the sob came freely to Scarlett's throat and she clapped her hand over her mouth. Now she was going to bawl like a child and cry out: 'I've been a devil! I've wronged you so! I never did anything for you! It was all for Ashley.'

She rose to her feet abruptly, sinking her teeth into her thumb to regain her control. Rhett's words came back to her again. 'She loves you. Let that be your cross.' Well, the cross was heavier now. It was bad enough that she had tried by every art to take Ashley from her. But now it was worse that Melanie, who had trusted her blindly through life, was laying the same love and trust on her in death. No, she could not speak. She could not even say again: 'Make an effort to live.' She must let her go easily, without a struggle, without tears, without sorrow.

The door opened slightly and Dr Meade stood on the threshold, beckoning imperiously. Scarlett bent over the bed, choking back her tears and taking Melanie's hand, laid it against her cheek.

'Good night,' she said, and her voice was steadier than she thought it possibly could be.

'Promise me—' came the whisper, very softly now.

'Anything, darling.'

'Captain Butler – be kind to him. He – loves you so.'

'Rhett?' thought Scarlett, bewildered, and the words meant nothing to her.

'Yes, indeed,' she said automatically and, pressing a light kiss on the hand, laid it back on the bed.

'Tell the ladies to come in immediately,' whispered the doctor as she passed through the door.

Through blurred eyes she saw India and Pitty follow the doctor into the room, holding their skirts close to their sides to keep them from rustling. The door closed behind them and the house was still. Ashley was nowhere to be seen. Scarlett leaned her head against the wall, like a naughty child in a corner, and rubbed her aching throat.

Behind that door, Melanie was going and, with her, the strength upon which she had relied unknowingly for so many years. Why, oh, why had she not realized before this how much she loved and needed Melanie? But who would have thought of small plain Melanie as a tower of strength? Melanie who was shy to tears before strangers, timid about raising her voice in an opinion of her own, fearful of the disapproval of old ladies, Melanie who lacked the courage to say Boo to a goose? And yet—

Scarlett's mind went back through the years to the still hot noon at Tara when grey smoke curled above a blue-clad body and Melanie stood at the top of the stairs with Charles' sabre in her hand. Scarlett remembered that she had thought at the time: 'How silly! Melly couldn't even heft that sword!' But now she knew that had the necessity arisen, Melanie would have charged down those stairs and killed the Yankee – or been killed herself.

Yes, Melanie had been there that day with a sword in her small hand, ready to do battle for her. And now, as Scarlett looked sadly back, she realized that Melanie had always been there beside her with a sword in her hand, unobtrusive as her own shadow, loving her, fighting for her with blind passionate loyalty, fighting Yankees, fire, hunger, poverty, public opinion and even her beloved blood kin.

Scarlett felt her courage and self-confidence ooze from her as she realized that the sword which had flashed between her and the world was sheathed forever.

'Melly is the only woman friend I ever had,' she thought forlornly, 'the only woman except Mother who really loved me. She's like Mother, too. Everyone who knew her has clung to her skirts.'

Suddenly it was as if Ellen were lying behind that closed door, leaving the world for a second time. Suddenly she was standing at Tara again with the world about her ears, desolate with the knowledge that she could not face life without the terrible strength of the weak, the gentle, the tender-hearted.

She stood in the hall, irresolute, frightened, and the flaring light of the fire in the sitting-room threw tall dim shadows on the walls about her. The house was utterly still and the stillness soaked into her like a fine chill rain. Ashley! Where was Ashley?

She went toward the sitting-room seeking him like a cold animal seeking the fire, but he was not there. She must find him. She had discovered Melanie's strength and her dependence on it only to lose it in the moment of discovery, but there was still Ashley left. There was Ashley who was strong and wise and comforting. In Ashley and his love lay strength upon which to lay her weakness, courage to bolster her fear, ease for her sorrow.

'He must be in his room,' she thought, and tiptoeing down the hall, she knocked softly. There was no answer, so she pushed the door open. Ashley was standing in front of the dresser, looking at a pair of Melanie's mended gloves. First he picked up one and looked at it, as though he had never seen it before. Then he laid it down gently, as though it were made of glass, and picked up the other one.

She said, 'Ashley!' in a trembling voice and he turned slowly and looked at her. The drowsy aloofness had gone from his grey eyes and they were wide and unmasked. In them she saw fear that matched her own fear, helplessness weaker than her own, bewilderment more profound than she would ever know. The feeling of dread which had possessed her in the hall deepened as she saw his face. She went toward him.

'I'm frightened,' she said. 'Oh, Ashley, hold me. I'm so frightened!'

He made no move to her but stared, gripping the glove tightly in both hands. She put a hand on his arm and whispered: 'What is it?'

His eyes searched her intently, hunting, hunting desperately for something he did not find. Finally he spoke and his voice was not his own.

'I was wanting you,' he said. 'I was going to run and find you – run like a child wanting comfort – and I find a child, more frightened, running to me.'

'Not you – you can't be frightened,' she cried. 'Nothing has ever frightened you. But I— You've always been so strong—'

'If I've ever been strong, it was because she was behind me,' he said, his voice breaking, and he looked down at the glove and smoothed the fingers. 'And – and – all the strength I ever had is going with her.'

There was such a note of wild despair in his low voice that she dropped her hand from his arm and stepped back. And in the heavy silence that fell between them, she felt that she really understood him for the first time in her life.

'Why— ' she said slowly, 'why, Ashley, you love her, don't you?'

She spoke as with an effort.

'She is the only dream I ever had that lived and breathed and did not die in the face of reality.'

'Dreams!' she thought, an old irritation stirring. 'Always dreams with him! Never common sense!'

With a heart that was heavy and a little bitter, she said: 'You've been such a fool, Ashley. Why couldn't you see that she was worth a million of me?'

'Scarlett, please! If you only knew what I've gone through since the doctor—'

'What you've gone through! Don't you think that I— Oh, Ashley, you should have known, years ago, that you loved her and not me! Why didn't you? Everything would have been so different, so— Oh, you should have realized and not kept me dangling with all your talk about honour and sacrifice! If you'd told me, years ago, I'd have— It would have killed me but I could have stood it somehow. But you wait till now, till Melly's dying, to find it out and now it's too late to do anything. Oh, Ashley, men are supposed to know such things – not women! You should have seen so clearly that you loved her all the time and only wanted me like – like Rhett wants that Watling woman!'

He winced at her words but his eyes still met hers, imploring silence, comfort. Every line of his face admitted the truth of her words. The very droop of his shoulders showed that his own self-castigation was more cruel than any she could give. He stood silent before her, clutching the glove as though it were an understanding hand, and, in the stillness that followed her words, her indignation fell away and pity, tinged with contempt, took its place. Her conscience smote her. She was kicking a beaten and defenceless man – and she had promised Melanie that she would look after him.

'And just as soon as I promised her, I said mean, hurting things to him and there's no need for me to say them or for anyone to say them. He knows the truth and it's killing him,' she thought desolately. 'He's not grown up. He's a child, like me, and he's sick with fear at losing her. Melly knew how it would be – Melly knew him far better than I do. That's why she said look after him and Beau, in the same breath. How can Ashley ever stand this? I can stand it. I can stand anything. I've had to stand so much. But he can't – he can't stand anything without her.'

'Forgive me, darling,' she said gently, putting out her arms. 'I know what you must be suffering. But remember, she doesn't know anything – she never even suspected – God was that good to us.'

He came to her quickly and his arms went round her blindly. She tiptoed to bring her warm cheek comfortingly against his and with one hand she smoothed the back of his hair.

'Don't cry, sweet. She'd want you to be brave. She'll want to see you in a moment and you must be brave. She mustn't see that you've been crying. It would worry her.'

He held her in a grip that made breathing difficult and his choking voice was in her ear.

'What will I do? I can't – I can't live without her!'

'I can't either,' she thought, shuddering away from the picture of the long years to come, without Melanie. But she caught herself in a strong grasp. Ashley was depending on her, Melanie was depending on her. As once before, in the moonlight at Tara, drunk, exhausted, she had thought: 'Burdens are for shoulders strong enough to carry them.' Well, her shoulders were strong and Ashley's were not. She squared her shoulders for the load and, with a calmness she was far from feeling, kissed his wet cheek without fever or longing or passion, only with cool gentleness.

'We shall manage – somehow,' she said.

A door opened with sudden violence into the hall and Dr Meade called with sharp urgency: 'Ashley! Quick!'

'My God! She's gone!' thought Scarlett. 'And Ashley didn't get to tell her goodbye! But maybe—'

'Hurry!' she cried aloud, giving him a push, for he stood staring like one stunned. 'Hurry!'

She pulled open the door and motioned him through. Galvanized by her words, he ran into the hall, the glove still clasped closely in his hand. She heard his rapid steps for a moment and then the closing of a door.

She said 'My God!' again, and walking slowly to the bed sat down upon it and dropped her head in her hands. She was suddenly tired, more tired than she had ever been in all her life. With the sound of the closing door, the strain under which she had been labouring, the strain which had given her strength, suddenly snapped. She felt exhausted in body and drained of emotions. Now she felt no sorrow or remorse, no fear or amazement. She was tired and her mind ticked away dully, mechanically, as the clock on the mantel.

Out of the dullness, one thought arose. Ashley did not love her and had never really loved her and the knowledge did not hurt. It should hurt. She should be desolate, broken-hearted, ready to scream at fate. She had relied upon his love for so long. It had upheld her through so many dark places. Yet, there the truth was. He did not love her and she did not care. She did not care because she did not love him. She did not love him and so nothing he could do or say could hurt her.

She lay down on the bed and put her head on the pillow tiredly. Useless to try to combat the idea, useless to say to herself: 'But I do love him. I've loved him for years. Love can't change to apathy in a minute.'

But it could change and it had changed.

'He never really existed at all, except in my imagination,' she thought wearily. 'I loved something I made up, something that's just as dead as Melly is. I made a pretty suit of clothes and fell in love with it. And when Ashley came riding along, so handsome, so different, I put that suit on him and made him wear it whether it fitted him or not. And I wouldn't see what he really was. I kept on loving the pretty clothes – and not him at all.'

Now she could look back down the long years and see herself in green flowered dimity, standing in the sunshine at Tara, thrilled by the young horseman with his blond hair shining like a silver helmet. She could see so clearly now that he was only a childish fancy, no more important really than her spoiled desire for the aquamarine earbobs she had coaxed out of Gerald. For, once she owned the earbobs, they had lost their value, as everything except money lost its value once it was hers. And so he, too, would have become cheap if, in those first far-away days, she had ever had the satisfaction of refusing to marry him. If she had ever had him at her mercy, seen him grow passionate, importunate, jealous, sulky, pleading, like the other boys, the wild infatuation which had possessed her would have passed, blowing away as lightly as mist before sunshine and light wind when she met a new man.

'What a fool I've been,' she thought bitterly. 'And now I've got to pay for it. What I've wished for so often has happened. I've wished Melly was dead so I could have him. And now she's dead and I've got him and I don't want him. His damned honour will make him ask me if I want to divorce Rhett and marry him. Marry him? I wouldn't have him on a silver platter! But, just the same, I've got him round my neck for the rest of my life. As long as I live I'll have to look after him and see that he doesn't starve and that people don't hurt his feelings. He'll be just another child, clinging to my skirts. I've lost my lover and I've got another child. And if I hadn't promised Melly, I'd – I wouldn't care if I never saw him again.'

Chapter LXII

She heard whispering voices outside, and going to the door she saw the frightened negroes standing in the back hall, Dilcey with her arms sagging under the heavy weight of the sleeping Beau, Uncle Peter crying, and Cookie wiping her wide wet face on her apron. All three looked at her, dumbly asking what they were to do now. She looked up the hall toward the sitting-room and saw India and Aunt Pitty standing speechless, holding each other's hands, and for once India had lost her stiff-necked look. Like the negroes, they looked imploringly at her, expecting her to give instructions. She walked into the sitting-room and the two women closed about her.

'Oh, Scarlett, what—' began Aunt Pitty, her fat, child's mouth shaking.

'Don't speak to me or I'll scream,' said Scarlett. Overwrought nerves brought sharpness to her voice and her hands clenched at her sides. The thought of speaking of Melanie now, of making the inevitable arrangements that follow a death made her throat tighten again. 'I don't want a word out of either of you.'

At the authoritative note in her voice, they fell back, helpless hurt looks on their faces. 'I mustn't cry in front of them,' she thought. 'I mustn't break now or they'll begin crying too, and then the darkies will begin screaming and we'll all go mad. I must pull myself together. There's so much I'll have to do. See the undertaker and arrange the funeral and see that the house is clean and be here to talk to people who'll cry on my neck. Ashley can't do those things, Pitty and India can't do them. I've got to do them. Oh, what a weary load! It's always been a weary load and always someone else's load!'

She looked at the dazed hurt faces of India and Pitty and contrition swept her. Melanie would not like her to be sharp with those who loved her.

'I'm sorry I was cross,' she said, speaking with difficulty. 'It's just that I – I'm sorry I was cross, Auntie. I'm going out on the porch for a minute. I've got to be alone. Then I'll come back and we'll—'

She patted Aunt Pitty and went swiftly by her to the front door, knowing if she stayed in this room another minute her control would crack. She had to be alone. And she had to cry or her heart would break.

She stepped on to the dark porch and closed the door behind her and the moist night air was cool upon her face. The rain had ceased and there was no sound except for the occasional drip of water from the eaves. The world was wrapped in a thick mist, a faintly chill mist that bore on its breath the smell of the dying year. All the houses across the street were dark except one, and the light from a lamp in the window, falling into the street, struggled feebly with the fog, golden particles floating in its rays. It was as if the whole world were enveloped in an unmoving blanket of grey smoke. And the whole world was still.

She leaned her head against one of the uprights of the porch and prepared to cry but no tears came. This was a calamity too deep for tears. Her body shook. There still reverberated in her mind the crashes of the two impregnable citadels of her life, thundering to dust about her ears. She stood for a while, trying to summon up her old charm: 'I'll think of all this tomorrow when I can stand it better.' But the charm had lost its potency. She had to think of two things, now – Melanie and how much she loved and needed her; Ashley and the obstinate blindness that had made her refuse to see him as he really was. And she knew that thoughts of them would hurt just as much tomorrow and all the tomorrows of her life.

'I can't go back in there and talk to them now,' she thought. 'I can't face Ashley tonight and comfort him. Not tonight! Tomorrow morning I'll come early and do the things I must do, say the comforting things I must say. But not tonight. I can't. I'm going home.'

Home was only five blocks away. She would not wait for the sobbing Peter to harnesss the buggy, would not wait for Dr Meade to drive her home. She could not endure the tears of the one, the silent condemnation of the other. She went swiftly down the dark front steps without her coat or bonnet and into the misty night. She rounded the corner and started up the long hill toward Peachtree Street, walking in a still wet world, and even her footsteps were as noiseless as a dream.

As she went up the hill, her chest tight with tears that would not come, there crept over her an unreal feeling, a feeling that she had been in this same dim chill place before, under a like set of circumstances – not once but many times before. 'How silly,' she thought uneasily, quickening her steps. Her nerves were playing her tricks. But the feeling persisted, stealthily pervading her mind. She peered about her uncertainly and the feeling grew, eerie but familiar, and her head went up sharply like an animal scenting danger. 'It's just that I'm worn out,' she tried to soothe herself. 'And the night's so queer, so misty. I never saw such thick mist before except – except!'

And then she knew and fear squeezed her heart. She knew now. In a hundred nightmares, she had fled through fog like this, through a haunted country without landmarks, thick with cold cloaking mist, peopled with clutching ghosts and shadows. Was she dreaming again or was this her dream come true?

For an instant, reality went out of her and she was lost. The old nightmare feeling was sweeping her, stronger than ever, and her heart began to race. She was standing again amid death and stillness, even as she had once stood at Tara. All that mattered in the world had gone out of it, life was in ruins and panic howled through her heart like a cold wind. The horror that was in the mist and was the mist laid hands upon her. And she began to run. As she had run a hundred times in dreams, she ran now, flying blindly she knew not where, driven by a nameless dread, seeking in the grey mist for the safety that lay somewhere.

Up the dim street she fled, her head down, her heart hammering, the night air wet on her lips, the trees overhead menacing. Somewhere, somewhere in this wild land of moist stillness, there was a refuge! She sped gasping up the long hill, her wet skirts wrapping coldly about her ankles, her lungs bursting, the tight-laced stays pressing her ribs into her heart.

Then before her eyes there loomed a light, a row of lights, dim and flickering but none the less real. In her nightmare, there had never been any lights, only grey fog. Her mind seized on those lights. Lights meant safety, people, reality. Suddenly she stopped running, her hands clenching, struggling to pull herself out of her panic, staring intently at the row of gas-lamps which had signalled to her brain that this was Peachtree Street, Atlanta, and not the grey world of sleep and ghosts.

She sank down panting on a carriage-block, clutching at her nerves as though they were ropes slipping swiftly through her hands.

'I was running – running like a crazy person!' she thought, her body shaking with lessening fear, her thudding heart making her sick. 'But where was I running?'

Her breath came more easily now and she sat with her hand pressed to her side and looked up Peachtree Street. There, at the top of the hill, was her own house. It looked as though every window bore lights, lights defying the mist to dim their brilliance. Home! It was real! She looked at the dim far-off bulk of the house thankfully, longingly, and something like calm fell on her spirit.

Home! That was where she wanted to go. That was where she was running. Home to Rhett!

At this realization it was as though chains fell away from her and with them the fear which had haunted her dreams since the night she stumbled to Tara to find the world ended. At the end of the road to Tara she had found security gone, all strength, all wisdom, all loving tenderness, all understanding gone – all those things which, embodied in Ellen, had been the bulwark of her girlhood. And, though she had won material safety since that night, in her dreams she was still a frightened child, searching for the lost security of that lost world.

Now she knew the haven she had sought in dreams, the place of warm safety which had always been hidden from her in the mist. It was not Ashley – oh, never Ashley! There was no more warmth in him than in a marsh-light, no more security than in quicksand. It was Rhett – Rhett who had strong arms to hold her, a broad chest to pillow her tired head, jeering laughter to pull her affairs into proper perspective. And complete understanding, because he, like her, saw truth as truth, unobstructed by impractical notions of honour, sacrifice, or high belief in human nature. He loved her! Why hadn't she realized that he loved her, for all his taunting remarks to the contrary? Melanie had seen it and with her last breath had said, 'Be kind to him.'

'Oh,' she thought, 'Ashley's not the only stupidly blind person. I should have seen.'

For years she had had her back against the stone wall of Rhett's love and had taken it as much for granted as she had taken Melanie's love, flattering herself that she drew her strength from herself alone. And even as she had realized earlier in the evening that Melanie had been beside her in her bitter campaigns against life, now she knew that, silent in the background, Rhett had stood, loving her, understanding her, ready to help. Rhett at the bazaar, reading her impatience in her eyes and leading her out in the reel, Rhett helping her out of the bondage of mourning, Rhett convoying her through the fire and explosions the night Atlanta fell, Rhett lending her the money that gave her her start, Rhett who comforted her when she woke in the nights crying with fright from her dreams – why, no man did such things without loving a woman to distraction!

The trees dripped dampness upon her but she did not feel it. The mist swirled about her and she paid it no heed. For when she thought of Rhett, with his swarthy face, flashing teeth and dark alert eyes, a trembling came over her.

'I love him,' she thought and, as always, she accepted the truth with little wonder, as a child accepting a gift. 'I don't know how long I've loved him but it's true. And if it hadn't been for Ashley, I'd have realized it long ago. I've never been able to see the world at all, because Ashley stood in the way.'

She loved him, scamp, blackguard, without scruple or honour – at least, honour as Ashley saw it. 'Damn Ashley's honour!' she thought. 'Ashley's honour has always let me down. Yes, from the very beginning when he kept on coming to see me, even though he knew his family expected him to marry Melanie. Rhett has never let me down, even that dreadful night of Melly's reception when he ought to have wrung my neck. Even when he left me on the road the night Atlanta fell, he knew I'd be safe. He knew I'd get through somehow. Even when he acted like he was going to make me pay to get that money from him at the Yankee camp. He wouldn't have taken me. He was just testing me. He's loved me all along and I've been so mean to him. Time and again, I've hurt him and he was too proud to show it. And when Bonnie died—Oh, how could I?'

She stood up straight and looked at the house on the hill. She had thought, half an hour ago, that she had lost everything in the world, except money, everything that made life desirable – Ellen, Gerald, Bonnie, Mammy, Melanie and Ashley. She had to lose them all to realize that she loved Rhett – loved him because he was strong and unscrupulous, passionate and earthy, like herself.

'I'll tell him everything,' she thought. 'He'll understand. He's always understood. I'll tell him what a fool I've been and how much I love him and I'll make it all up to him.'

Suddenly she felt strong and happy. She was not afraid of the darkness or the fog and she knew with a singing in her heart that she would never fear them again. No matter what mists might curl around her in the future, she knew her refuge. She started briskly up the street toward home and the blocks seemed very long. Far, far too long. She caught up her skirts to her knees and began to run lightly. But this time she was not running from fear. She was running because Rhett's arms were at the end of the street.

Chapter LXIII

The front door was slightly ajar and she trotted, breathless, into the hall and paused for a moment under the rainbow prisms of the chandelier. For all its brightness the house was very still, not with the serene stillness of sleep but with a watchful, tired silence that was faintly ominous. She saw at a glance that Rhett was not in the parlour or the library and her heart sank. Suppose he should be out – out with Belle or wherever it was he spent the many evenings when he did not appear at the supper table? She had not bargained on this.

She had started up the steps in search of him when she saw that the door of the dining-room was closed. Her heart contracted a little with shame at the sight of that closed door, remembering the many nights of this last summer when Rhett had sat there alone, drinking until he was sodden and Pork came to urge him to bed. That had been her fault but she'd change it all. Everything was going to be different from now on – but, please God, don't let him be too drunk tonight. If he's too drunk he won't believe me and he'll laugh at me and that will break my heart.

She quietly opened the dining-room door a crack and peered in. He was seated before the table, slumped in his chair, and a full decanter stood before him with the stopper in place, the glass unused. Thank God, he was sober! She pulled open the door, holding herself back from running to him. But when he looked up at her, something in his gaze stopped her dead on the threshold, stilled the words on her lips.

He looked at her steadily with dark eyes that were heavy with fatigue and there was no leaping light in them. Though her hair was tumbling about her shoulders, her bosom heaving breathlessly and her skirts mud-splattered to the knees, his face did not change with surprise or question or his lips twist with mockery. He was sunken in his chair, his suit wrinkling untidily against his thickening waist, every line of him proclaiming the ruin of a fine body and the coarsening of a strong face. Drink and dissipation had done their work on the coin-clear profile and now it was no longer the head of a young pagan prince on new-minted gold but a decadent, tired Caesar on copper debased by long usage. He looked up at her as she stood there, hand on heart, looked quietly, almost in a kindly way, and that frightened her.

'Come and sit down,' he said. 'She is dead?'

She nodded and advanced hesitantly toward him, uncertainty taking form in her mind at this new expression on his face. Without rising, he pushed back a chair with his foot and she sank into it. She wished he had not spoken of Melanie so soon. She did not want to talk of her now, to relive the agony of the last hour. There was all the rest of her life in which to speak of Melanie. But it seemed to her now, driven by a fierce desire to cry, 'I love you,' that there was only this night, this hour, in which to tell Rhett what was in her mind. But there was something in his face that stopped her and she was suddenly ashamed to speak of love when Melanie was hardly cold.

'Well, God rest her,' he said heavily. 'She was the only completely kind person I ever knew.'

'Oh, Rhett!' she cried miserably, for his words brought up too vividly all the kind things Melanie had ever done for her. 'Why didn't you come in with me? It was dreadful – and I needed you so!'

'I couldn't have borne it,' he said simply and for a moment he was silent. Then he spoke with an effort and said, softly: 'A very great lady.'

His sombre gaze went past her and in his eyes was the same look she had seen in the light of the flames the night Atlanta fell, when he told her he was going off with the retreating army – the surprise of a man who knows himself utterly, yet discovers in himself unexpected loyalties and emotions and feels a faint self-ridicule at the discovery.

His moody eyes went over her shoulder as though he saw Melanie silently passing through the room to the door. In the look of farewell on his face there was no sorrow, no pain, only a speculative wonder at himself, only a poignant stirring of emotions dead since boyhood, as he said again: 'A very great lady.'

Scarlett shivered and the glow went from her heart, the fine warmth, the splendour which had sent her home on winged feet. She half grasped what was in Rhett's mind as he said farewell to the only person in the world he respected and she was desolate again with a terrible sense of loss that was no longer personal. She could not wholly understand or analyse what he was feeling, but it seemed almost as if she too had been brushed by whispering skirts, touching her softly in a last caress. She was seeing through Rhett's eyes the passing, not of a woman but a legend – the gentle, self-effacing but steel-spined women on whom the South had builded its house in war and to whose proud and loving arms it had returned in defeat.

His eyes came back to her and his voice changed. Now it was light and cool.

'So she's dead. That makes it nice for you, doesn't it?'

'Oh, how can you say such things?' she cried, stung, the quick tears coming to her eyes. 'You know how I loved her!'

'No, I can't say I did. Most unexpected, and it's to your credit, considering your passion for white trash, that you could appreciate her at last.'

'How can you talk so? Of course I appreciated her! You didn't. You didn't know her like I did! It isn't in you to understand her – how good she was—'

'Indeed? Perhaps not.'

'She thought of everybody except herself – why, her last words were about you.'

There was a flash of genuine feeling in his eyes as he turned to her.

'What did she say?'

'Oh, not now, Rhett.'

'Tell me.'

His voice was cool but the hand he put on her wrist hurt. She did not want to tell, this was not the way she had intended to lead up to the subject of her love but his hand was urgent.

'She said – she said – "Be kind to Captain Butler. He loves you so much." '

He stared at her and dropped her wrist. His eyelids went down, leaving his face a dark blank. Suddenly he rose and, going to the window, he drew the curtains and looked out intently as if there were something to see outside except blinding mist.

'Did she say anything else?' he questioned, not turning his head.

'She asked me to take care of little Beau and I said I would, like he was my own boy.'

'What else?'

'She said – Ashley – she asked me to look after Ashley, too.'

He was silent for a moment and then he laughed softly.

'It's convenient to have the first wife's permission, isn't it?'

'What do you mean?'

He turned and even in her confusion she was surprised that there was no mockery in his face. Nor was there any more interest in it than in the face of a man watching the last act of a none-too-amusing comedy.

'I think my meaning's plain enough. Miss Melly is dead. You certainly have all the evidence you want to divorce me and you haven't enough reputation left for a divorce to hurt you. And you haven't any religion left, so the Church won't matter. Then – Ashley and dreams come true with the blessings of Miss Melly.'

'Divorce?' she cried. 'No! No!' Incoherent for a moment she leaped to her feet and running to him caught his arm. 'Oh, you're all wrong! Terribly wrong. I don't want a divorce – I—' She stopped for she could find no other words.

He put his hand under her chin, quietly turned her face up to the light and looked for an intent moment into her eyes. She looked up at him, her heart in her eyes, her lips quivering as she tried to speak. But she could marshal no words because she was trying to find in his face some answering emotions, some leaping light of hope, of joy. Surely he must know, now! But the smooth dark blankness which had baffled her so often was all that her frantic, searching eyes could find. He dropped her chin and, turning, walked back to his chair and sprawled tiredly again, his chin on his breast, his eyes looking up at her from under black brows in an impersonal speculative way.

She followed him back to his chair, her hands twisting, and stood before him.

'You are wrong,' she began again, finding words. 'Rhett, tonight, when I knew, I ran every step of the way home to tell you. Oh, darling, I—'

'You are tired,' he said, still watching her. 'You'd better go to bed.'

'But I must tell you!'

'Scarlett,' he said heavily, 'I don't want to hear – anything.'

'But you don't know what I'm going to say!'

'My pet, it's written plainly on your face. Something, someone has made you realize that the unfortunate Mr Wilkes is too large a mouthful of Dead Sea fruit for even you to chew. And that same something has suddenly set my charms before you in a new and attractive light.' He sighed slightly. 'And it's no use to talk about it.'

She drew a sharp surprised breath. Of course, he had always read her easily. Heretofore she had resented it but now, after the first shock at her own transparency, her heart rose with gladness and relief. He knew, he understood, and her task was miraculously made easy. No use to talk about it! Of course he was bitter at her long neglect, of course he was mistrustful of her sudden turnabout. She would have to woo him with kindness, convince him with a rich outpouring of love, and what a pleasure it would be to do it!

'Darling, I'm going to tell you everything,' she said, putting her hands on the arm of his chair and leaning down to him. 'I've been so wrong, such a stupid fool—'

'Scarlett, don't go on with this. Don't be humble before me. I can't bear it. Leave us some dignity, some reticence to remember out of our marriage. Spare us this last.'

She straightened up abruptly. Spare us this last? What did he mean by 'this last'? Last? This was their first, their beginning.

'But I will tell you,' she began rapidly, as if fearing his hand upon her mouth, silencing her. 'Oh, Rhett, I love you so, darling! I must have loved you for years and I was such a fool I didn't know it. Rhett, you must believe me!'

He looked at her, standing before him, for a moment, a long look that went to the back of her mind. She saw there was belief in his eyes but little interest. Oh, was he going to be mean, at this of all times? To torment her, pay her back in her own coin?

'Oh, I believe you,' he said at last. 'But what of Ashley Wilkes?'

'Ashley!' she said, and made an impatient gesture. 'I – I don't believe I've cared anything about him for ages. It was – well, a sort of habit I hung on to from when I was a little girl. Rhett, I'd never even thought I cared about him if I'd ever known what he was really like. He's such a helpless, poor-spirited creature, for all his prattle about truth and honour and—'

'No,' said Rhett. 'If you must see him as he really is, see him straight. He's only a gentleman caught in a world he doesn't belong in, trying to make a poor best of it by the rules of the world that's gone.'

'Oh, Rhett, don't let's talk of him! What does he matter now? Aren't you glad to know—I mean, now that I—'

As his tired eyes met hers, she broke off in embarrassment, shy as a girl with her first beau. If he'd only make it easier for her! If only he would hold out his arms, so she could crawl thankfully into his lap and lay her head on his chest. Her lips on his could tell him better than all her stumbling words. But as she looked at him, she realized that he was not holding her off just to be mean. He looked drained and as though nothing she had said was of any moment.

'Glad?' he said. 'Once I would have thanked God, fasting, to hear you say all of this. But, now, it doesn't matter.'

'Doesn't matter? What are you talking about? Of course it matters! Rhett, you do care, don't you? You must care. Melly said you did.'

'Well, she was right, as far as she knew. But, Scarlett, did it ever occur to you that even the most deathless love could wear out?'

She looked at him speechless, her mouth a round *O*.

'Mine wore out,' he went on, 'against Ashley Wilkes and your insane obstinacy that makes you hold on like a bulldog to anything you think you want . . . Mine wore out.'

'But love can't wear out!'

'Yours for Ashley did.'

'But I never really loved Ashley!'

'Then, you certainly gave a good imitation of it – up till tonight. Scarlett, I'm not upbraiding you, accusing you, reproaching you. That time has passed. So spare me your defences and your explanations. If you can manage to listen to me for a few minutes without interrupting, I can explain what I mean. Though, God knows, I see no need for explanations. The truth's so plain.'

She sat down, the harsh gas-light falling on her white bewildered face. She looked into the eyes she knew so well – and knew so little – listened to his quiet voice saying words which at first meant nothing. This was the first time he had ever talked to her in this manner, as one human being to another, talked as other people talked, without flippancy, mockery or riddles.

'Did it ever occur to you that I loved you as much as a man can love a woman? Loved you for years before I finally got you? During the war I'd go away and try to forget you, but I couldn't and I always had to come back. After the war I risked arrest, just to come back and find you. I cared so much I believe I would have killed Frank Kennedy if he hadn't died when he did. I loved you but I couldn't let you know it. You're so brutal to those who love you, Scarlett. You take their love and hold it over their heads like a whip.'

Out of it all only the fact that he loved her meant anything. At the faint echo of passion in his voice, pleasure and excitement crept back into her. She sat, hardly breathing, listening, waiting.

'I knew you didn't love me when I married you. I knew about Ashley, you see. But, fool that I was, I thought I could make you care. Laugh, if you like, but I wanted to take care of you, to pet you, to give you everything you wanted. I wanted to marry you and protect you and give you a free rein in anything that would make you happy – just as I did Bonnie. You'd had such a struggle, Scarlett. No one knew better than I what you'd gone through and I wanted you to stop fighting and let me fight for you. I wanted you to play, like a child – for you were a child, a brave, frightened, bullheaded child. I think you are still a child. No one but a child could be so headstrong and so insensitive.'

His voice was calm and tired but there was something in the quality of it that raised a ghost of memory in Scarlett. She had heard a voice like this once before and at some other crisis of her life. Where had it been? The voice of a man facing himself and his world without feeling, without flinching, without hope.

Why – why – it had been Ashley in the wintry, windswept orchard at Tara, talking of life and shadow-shows with a tired calmness that had more finality in its timbre that any desperate bitterness could have revealed. Even as Ashley's voice then had turned her cold with dread of things she could not understand, so now Rhett's voice made her heart sink. His voice, his manner, more than the content of his words, disturbed her, made her realize that her pleasurable excitement of a few moments ago had been untimely. Something was wrong, badly wrong. What it was she did not know but she listened desperately, her eyes on his brown face, hoping to hear words that would dissipate her fears.

'It was so obvious that we were meant for each other. So obvious that I was the only man of your acquaintance who could love you after knowing you as you really are – hard and greedy and unscrupulous, like me. I loved you and I took the chance. I thought Ashley would fade out of your mind. But,' he shrugged, 'I tried everything I knew and nothing worked. And I loved you so, Scarlett. If you had only let me, I could have loved you as gently and as tenderly as ever a man loved a woman. But I couldn't let you know, for I knew you'd think me weak and try to use my love against me. And always – always there was Ashley. It drove me crazy. I couldn't sit across the table from you every night, knowing you wished Ashley was sitting there in my place. And I couldn't hold you in my arms at night and know that – well, it doesn't matter now. I wonder, now, why it hurt. That's what drove me to Belle. There is a certain swinish comfort in being with a woman who loves you utterly and respects you for being a fine gentleman – even if she is an illiterate whore. It soothed my vanity. You've never been very soothing, my dear.'

'Oh, Rhett . . . ' she began, miserable at the very mention of Belle's name, but he waved her to silence and went on.

'And then, that night when I carried you upstairs – I thought – I hoped – I hoped so much I was afraid to face you the next morning, for fear I'd been mistaken and you didn't love me. I was so afraid you'd laugh at me I went off and got drunk. And when I came back, I was shaking in my boots and if you had come even half-way to meet me, had given me some sign, I think I'd have kissed your feet. But you didn't.'

'Oh, but Rhett, I did want you then but you were so nasty! I did want you! I think – yes, that must have been when I first knew I cared about you. Ashley – I never was happy about Ashley after that, but you were so nasty that I—'

'Oh, well,' he said. 'It seems we've been at cross purposes, doesn't it? But it doesn't matter now. I'm only telling you, so you won't ever wonder about it all. When you were sick and it was all my fault, I stood outside your door, hoping you'd call for me, but you didn't, and then I knew what a fool I'd been and that it was all over.'

He stopped and looked through her and beyond her, even as Ashley had often done, seeing something she could not see. And she could only stare speechless at his brooding face.

'But then, there was Bonnie and I saw that everything wasn't over, after all. I liked to think that Bonnie was you, a little girl again, before the war and poverty had done things to you. She was so like you, so wilful, so brave and gay and full of high spirits, and I could pet her and spoil her – just as I wanted to pet you. But she wasn't like you – she loved me. It was a blessing that I could take the love you didn't want and give it to her . . . When she went, she took everything.'

Suddenly she was sorry for him, sorry with a completeness that wiped out her own grief and her fear of what his words might mean. It was the first time in her life she had ever been sorry for anyone without feeling contemptuous as well, because it was the first time she had ever approached understanding any other human being. And she could understand his shrewd caginess, so like her own, his obstinate pride that kept him from admitting his love for fear of a rebuff.

'Ah, darling,' she said, coming forward, hoping he would put out his arms and draw her to his knees. 'Darling, I am so sorry but I'll make it all up to you! We can be so happy, now that we know the truth, and – Rhett – look at me, Rhett! There – there can be other babies – not like Bonnie but—'

'Thank you, no,' said Rhett, as if he were refusing a piece of bread. 'I'll not risk my heart a third time.'

'Rhett, don't say such things! Oh, what can I say to make you understand? I've told you how sorry I am—'

'My darling, you're such a child. You think that by saying, "I'm sorry," all the errors and hurts of years past can be remedied, obliterated from the mind, all the poison drawn from old wounds . . . Take my handkerchief, Scarlett. Never, at any crisis of your life, have I known you to have a handkerchief.'

She took the handkerchief, blew her nose and sat down. It was obvious that he was not going to take her in his arms. It was beginning to be obvious that all his talk about loving her meant nothing. It was a tale of a time long past, and he was looking at it as though it had never happened to him. And that was frightening. He looked at her in an almost kindly way, speculation in his eyes.

'How old are you, my dear? You never would tell me.'

'Twenty-eight,' she answered dully, muffled in the handkerchief.

'That's not a vast age. It's a young age to have gained the whole world and lost your own soul, isn't it? Don't look frightened. I'm not referring to hell-fire to come for your affair with Ashley. I'm merely speaking metaphorically. Ever since I've known you, you've wanted two things. Ashley and to be rich enough to tell the world to go to hell. Well, you are rich enough and you've spoken sharply to the world and you've got Ashley, if you want him. But all that doesn't seem to be enough now.'

She was frightened but not at the thought of hell-fire. She was thinking: 'But Rhett is my soul and I'm losing him. And if I lose him, nothing else matters! No, not friends or money or – or anything. If only I had him I wouldn't even mind being poor again. No, I wouldn't mind being cold again or even hungry. But he can't mean— Oh, he can't!'

She wiped her eyes and said desperately: 'Rhett, if you once loved me so much, there must be something left for me!'

'Out of it all I find only two things that remain and they are the two things you hate the most – pity and an odd feeling of kindness.'

Pity! Kindness! 'Oh, my God!' she thought despairingly. Anything but pity and kindness. Whenever she felt these two emotions for anyone, they went hand in hand with contempt. Was he contemptuous of her too? Anything would be preferable to that. Even the cynical coolness of the war days, the drunken madness that drove him the night he carried her up the stairs, his hard fingers bruising her body, or the barbed drawling words that she now realized had covered a bitter love. Anything except this impersonal kindness that was written so plainly in his face.

'Then – then you mean I've ruined it all – that you don't love me any more?'

'That's right.'

'But—' she said stubbornly, like a child who still feels that to state a desire is to gain that desire, 'but I love you!'

'That's your misfortune.'

She looked up quickly to see if there was a jeer behind those words but there was none. He was simply stating a fact. But it was a fact she still would not believe – could not believe. She looked at him with slanting eyes that burned with a desperate obstinacy, and the sudden hard line of jaw that sprang out through her soft cheek was Gerald's jaw.

'Don't be a fool, Rhett! I can make—'

He flung up a hand in mock horror and his black brows went up in the old sardonic crescents.

'Don't look so determined, Scarlett! You frighten me. I see you are contemplating the transfer of your tempestuous affections from Ashley to me and I fear for my liberty and my peace of mind. No, Scarlett, I will not be pursued as the luckless Ashley was pursued. Besides, I am going away.'

Her jaw trembled before she clenched her teeth to steady it. Go away? No, anything but that! How could life go on without him? Everyone had gone from her, everyone who mattered except Rhett. He couldn't go. But how could she stop him? She was powerless against his cool mind, his disinterested words.

'I am going away. I intended to tell you when you came home from Marietta.'

'You are deserting me?'

'Don't be the neglected, dramatic wife, Scarlett. The rôle isn't becoming. I take it, then, you do not want a divorce or even a separation? Well, then, I'll come back often enough to keep gossip down.'

'Damn gossip!' she said fiercely. 'It's you I want. Take me with you!'

'No,' he said, and there was finality in his voice. For a moment she was on the verge of an outburst of childish wild tears. She could have thrown herself on the floor, cursed and screamed and drummed her heels. But some remnant of pride, of common sense stiffened her. She thought, 'If I did, he'd only laugh, or just look at me. I mustn't bawl; I mustn't beg. I mustn't do anything to risk his contempt. He must respect me even – even if he doesn't love me.'

She lifted her chin and managed to ask quietly:

'Where will you go?'

There was a faint gleam of admiration in his eyes as he answered: 'Perhaps to England – or to Paris. Perhaps to Charleston to try to make peace with my people.'

'But you hate them! I've heard you laugh at them so often and—'

He shrugged.

'I still laugh – but I've reached the end of roaming, Scarlett. I'm forty-five – the age when a man begins to value some of the things he's thrown away so lightly in youth, the clannishness of families, honour and security, roots that go deep—Oh, no! I'm not recanting, I'm not regretting anything I've ever done. I've had a hell of a good time – such a hell of a good time that it's begun to pall and now I want something different. No, I never intend to change more than my spots. But I want the outer semblance of the things I used to know, the utter boredom of respectability – other people's respectability, my pet, not my own – the calm dignity life can have when it's lived by gentle folks, the genial grace of days that are gone. When I lived those days I didn't realize the slow charm of them—'

Again Scarlett was back in the windy orchard of Tara and there was the same look in Rhett's eyes that had been in Ashley's eyes that day. Ashley's words were as clear in her ears as though he and not Rhett were speaking. Fragments of words came back to her and she quoted, parrot-like: 'A glamour to it – a perfection, a symmetry like Grecian art.'

Rhett said sharply: 'Why did you say that? That's what I meant.'

'It was something that – that Ashley said once, about the old days.'

He shrugged and the light went out of his eyes.

'Always Ashley,' he said and was silent for a moment.

'Scarlett, when you are forty-five, perhaps you will know what I'm talking about and then perhaps you, too, will be tired of imitation gentry and shoddy manners and cheap emotions. But I doubt it. I think you'll always be more attracted by glister than by gold. Anyway, I can't wait that long to see. And I have no desire to wait. It just doesn't interest me. I'm going to hunt in old towns and old countries where some of the old times must still linger. I'm that sentimental. Atlanta's too raw for me, too new.'

'Stop,' she said suddenly. She had hardly heard anything he had said. Certainly her mind had not taken it in. But she knew she could no longer endure with any fortitude the sound of his voice when there was no love in it.

He paused and looked at her quizzically.

'Well, you get my meaning, don't you?' he questioned, rising to his feet.

She threw out her hands to him, palms up, in the age-old gesture of appeal and her heart, again, was in her face.

'No,' she cried. 'All I know is that you do not love me and you are going away! Oh, my darling, if you go, what shall I do?'

For a moment he hesitated as if debating whether a kind lie were kinder in the long run than the truth. Then he shrugged.

'Scarlett, I was never one to patiently pick up broken fragments and glue them together and tell myself that the mended whole was as good as new. What is broken is broken – and I'd rather remember it as it was at its best than mend it and see the broken places as long as I lived. Perhaps, if I were younger—' He sighed. 'But I'm too old to believe in such sentimentalities as clean slates and starting all over. I'm too old to shoulder the burden of constant lies that go with living in polite disillusionment. I couldn't live with you and lie to you and I certainly couldn't lie to myself. I can't even lie to you now. I wish I could care what you do or where you go, but I can't.'

He drew a short breath and said lightly but softly:

'My dear, I don't give a damn.'

*

She silently watched him go up the stairs, feeling that she would strangle at the pain in her throat. With the sound of his feet dying away in the upper hall was dying the last thing in the world that mattered. She knew now that there was no appeal of emotion or reason which would turn that cool brain from its verdict. She knew now that he had meant every word he said, lightly though some of them had been spoken. She knew because she sensed in him something strong, unyielding, implacable – all the qualities she had looked for in Ashley and never found.

She had never understood either of the men she had loved and so she had lost them both. Now, she had a fumbling knowledge that, had she ever understood Ashley, she would never have loved him; had she ever understood Rhett, she would never have lost him. She wondered forlornly if she had ever really understood anyone in the world.

There was a merciful dullness in her mind now, a dullness that she knew from long experience would soon give way to sharp pain, even as severed tissues, shocked by the surgeon's knife, have a brief instant of insensibility before their agony begins.

'I won't think of it now,' she thought grimly, summoning up her old charm. 'I'll go crazy if I think about losing him now. I'll think of it tomorrow.'

'But,' cried her heart, casting aside the charm and beginning to ache, 'I can't let him go! There must be some way!'

'I won't think of it now,' she said again, aloud, trying to push her misery to the back of her mind, trying to find some bulwark against the rising tide of pain. 'I'll – why, I'll go home to Tara tomorrow,' and her spirits lifted faintly.

She had gone back to Tara once in fear and defeat and she had emerged from its sheltering walls strong and armed for victory. What she had done once, somehow – please God, she could do again! How, she did not know. She did not want to think of that now. All she wanted was a breathing-space in which to hurt, a quiet place to lick her wounds, a haven in which to plan her campaign. She thought of Tara and it was as if a gentle cool hand were stealing over her heart. She could see the white house gleaming welcome to her through the reddening autumn leaves, feel the quiet hush of the country twilight coming down over her like a benediction, feel the dews falling on the acres of green bushes starred with fleecy white, see the raw colour of the red earth and the dismal dark beauty of the pines on the rolling hills.

She felt vaguely comforted, strengthened by the picture, and some of her hurt and frantic regret was pushed from the top of her mind. She stood for a moment remembering small things – the avenue of dark cedars leading to Tara, the banks of cape jessamine bushes, vivid green against the white walls, the fluttering white curtains. And Mammy would be there. Suddenly she wanted Mammy desperately, as she had wanted her when she was a little girl, wanted the broad bosom on which to lay her head, the gnarled black hand on her hair. Mammy, the last link with the old days.

With the spirit of her people who would not know defeat, even when it stared them in the face, she raised her chin. She could get Rhett back. She knew she could. There had never been a man she couldn't get, once she set her mind upon him.

'I'll think of it all tomorrow, at Tara. I can stand it then. Tomorrow, I'll think of some way to get him back. After all, tomorrow is another day.'